The Longwood Introduction to Fiction

The Longwood Introduction to Fiction

SVEN BIRKERTS
HARVARD UNIVERSITY
Department of Expository Writing

ALLYN AND BACON
Boston London Toronto Sydney Tokyo Singapore

Executive Editor: Joseph Opiela
Series Editorial Assistant: Amy Capute
Editorial-Production Administrator: Rowena Dores
Editorial-Production Service: Editorial Inc.
Cover Administrator: Linda Dickinson
Text Designer: Deborah Schneck
Manufacturing Buyer: Megan Cochran

A Division of Simon & Schuster, Inc.
160 Gould Street
Needham Heights, Massachusetts 02194

Library of Congress Cataloging-in-Publication Data

Birkerts, Sven.
The Longwood introduction to fiction / Sven Birkerts.
p. cm.
ISBN 0-205-13335-5 (acid-free paper)
1. Short stories. I. Title.
PN6014.B57 1992
808.83′1—dc20 91-31547
CIP
AC

Credits

Anonymous, "The Lady Who Loved Insects," translated by Arthur Waley in *Anthology of Japanese Literature from the Earliest Era to the Mid-Nineteenth Century* edited by Donald Keene. Copyright © 1955 by Grove Press, Inc. Used by permission of Grove Press, Inc.

Credits continued on page 883, which constitutes a continuation of the copyright page.

Printed in the United States of America
10 9 8 7 6 5 4 3 2 1 96 95 94 93 92 91

Dedication

To my wife Lynn
and to my friends Askold and Tom

CONTENTS

Part 2

Appendices

PREFACE

In recent years a strong debate has raged in U.S. academia about whether the literary canon (that distillation of great Western literary works which has been set forth as the classic model for students to appreciate and emulate) needs revision. Excoriated as the choice of a ruling clique of old white males, the traditional literary canon, it is argued, must be expanded (or perhaps overthrown) to include multicultural and international literatures.

In a way, it is the American founding struggle played out all over again. Voices clamor for representation, and pressure builds. And institutions adapt curricula—some more willingly, some less so. A survey of current U.S. literature textbooks reveals how the maps are being redrawn. The only question is which text will be the most inclusive and exhibit the greatest sensitivity to previously marginalized groups.

Every such sign of progress is welcome, of course. But there is a danger, too, that the multicultural agenda will swamp all others and that the new perspective will overlook no less vital considerations. There are other issues that might be deemed as important. One of these is internationalism. Every day we come closer to realizing Marshall McLuhan's prediction that the world will become—via information and electronic media—a "global village." The United States is being reshaped by diverse cultural forces from within, but it is also fast becoming one of the prime energy centers of an emerging world culture. The students who will use this text, or others of its kind, are stepping into a world very different from the one in which their teachers grew up. Who will prepare them? What will that preparation require?

In putting this anthology together I have tried to keep the needs of these students in mind. I have tried to implement a perspective that might help rather than hinder the inevitable processes of adaptation to a rapidly changing world.

The Longwood Introduction to Fiction reflects the new cosmopolitanism. I have sought to assemble a true diversity of readings—a diversity that not only recognizes the reality of a multicultural society but also the inevitable emergence of internationalism. Students and instructors will find here a balance between the pertinent claims of the Western tradition and new literatures in the United States and the rest of the world. Choosing the selections has been less a question of making compromises than of finding a natural accommodation for an abundance of riches. Readers will find some of the classic masterpieces of short fiction—works by Gogol, Twain, Woolf, James, Chopin, Joyce, and others—as well as vital, if less familiar, stories by writers like Bessie Head (Botswana), Junichiro Tanizaki (Japan), Patrick White (Australia), Luisa Valenzuela (Argentina), Lars Gustafsson (Sweden), and others. The selections have been made, in many instances, on the strength of their teachability—they are stories that have withstood the tests of class discussion and writing assignments.

It is not enough, of course, to arrange a group of familiar and unfamiliar texts from different parts of the world. Students clearly need a context, a way of understanding the major historical developments that underlie the changing complexion of world literature. I have tried to address this need. As I make clear in the Introduction, literature, like any art, is best understood where there is some grasp of the historical forces involved in its making. In terms of the short story, the line of development has been significantly determined by changes in the dominant modes of communication. Most world literatures have reflected the shift from oral to print-based cultures; the dissemination of the printed word has been bound up with a whole array of societal changes and hence with changes in the art.

I have approached the arrangement of the anthology accordingly, beginning with a generous selection—chronologically arranged—of narratives drawn from the oral tradition, and continuing with works from the First Golden Age of the short story. The development that reaches its culmination in the modernism of Woolf, Joyce, and Hemingway is discussed in historical as well as artistic terms. The introduction sets out a comprehensive contextual framework. In addition, short section introductions as well as study questions devised for this purpose enforce the awareness of context.

The section of Additional Readings assembles a collection of works by men and women of diverse ethnic groups from all parts of the world. There is strong representation from Latin America, Asia, Africa, and the Middle East as well as from Continental Europe. I have also included stories that take up significant thematic concerns—stories like Susan Sontag's "The Way We Live Now," which deals with moral survival in an age of AIDS; Tim O'Brien's Vietnam narrative, "The Things They Carried"; and Nadine Gordimer's "Town and Country Lovers," which probes issues of race and class in South Africa.

Recognizing that students and instructors may wish to compare works by a single author, I have provided two extra stories by each of three authors: Frank O'Connor, Joyce Carol Oates, and Raymond Carver. Every author is introduced with a biographical note, so that a specific sense of context can supplement the more general materials given in the introductory sections. Essays on Elements of Fiction and Writing about Literature offer specific guidance on approaches to literature. The Writing about Literature section includes two versions of a representative student essay. A glossary of terms rounds out the book.

I would like to acknowledge assistance from the following, all of whom gave generously of time, materials, and advice: my editor, Joseph Opiela, and his resourceful assistant, Amy Capute; Carolyn Woznick; my colleagues in the Expository Writing Department at Harvard, in particular Askold Melnyczuk, George Packer, Alex Johnson, Linda Simon, Jodi Daynard, Judith Grossman, Myra McLarey, Jerome Doolittle, Douglas Bauer, Carl Nagin, Victor Burg, Christopher Catchick, Alfred Alcorn, Gordon Harvey, Lynn Geltman, Michele Souda, Joseph Finder, Pat C. Hoy, Nancy Sommer, Richard Marius, Norm Katz, William Corbett, and John de Cuevas. I also thank my colleagues at Emerson College, especially DeWitt Henry, Jonathan Aaron, and Jenifer Shute. Loyal and helpfully bookish friends include Thomas Frick, Thomas Sleigh, Stuart Dischell, Stratis Haviaras, George Scialabba, Sue Standing, Seamus Heaney, and the booksellers at the Harvard Book Store.

I am grateful also to the reviewers who offered helpful advice along the way:

> Kenneth Boyer, *St. Louis Community College at Florissant Valley;* Paula Buck, *Tyler Junior College;* John Clifford, *University of North Carolina at Wilmington;* Robert Creed, *University of Massachusetts at Amherst;* Larry Danielson, *University of Illinois;* Michael Dean, *University of Mississippi;* C. R. Embry, *Truckee Meadows Community College;* James Evans, *University of North Carolina at Greensboro;* Carol Fairbanks, *University of Wisconsin, Eau Claire;* Jay Funston, *James Madison University;* David Hamilton, *University of Iowa;* Patricia Harkin, *University of Akron;* David Himber, *St. Petersburg Junior College;* Clayton Hudnall, *University of Hartford;* Maurice Hunt, *Baylor University;* Lee Jacobus, *University of Connecticut;* Michael Joyce, *Jackson Community College;* Joseph LaBriola, *Sinclair Community College;* Joseph Lostracco, *Austin Community College;* Barry Maid, *University of Arkansas at Little Rock;* Thomas Martinez, *Villanova University;* George Searles, *Mohawk Valley Community College;* Barbara Weaver, *Ball State University;* and Steven Weisenberger, *University of Kentucky.*

Finally, I must honor the good humor, tolerance, and expert counsel of my wife, Lynn Marie Focht; the spirited support of my parents, brother, and sister; and the human alarm clock services of my daughter, Mara Sophia.

The Longwood Introduction to Fiction

Introduction

There has never been a time quite as rich as the present for the student or devotee of the short story. The sheer quantity of outstanding prose that is available staggers the imagination. A well-intentioned and energetic reader could start at one end of this literary wealth and never get to the other side. Writers keep writing, presses keep printing, and there is no sign that the flood will soon abate.

In one sense, of course, such *never before in history* statements are always true. For every period both inherits the legacy of the past and adds to it. But our period, I would argue, is doubly blessed. Not only are we at every moment discovering and translating hitherto unknown works from the past (or rediscovering and retranslating neglected authors), thereby adding to our sense of history but we are also living in the midst of what many have called a renaissance of the short story. Whatever else may be said about the present state of literature, there is a general consensus that the art of the short story is thriving.

What's more, this activity is not confined to the English-speaking world. Its scope is international, so much so, in fact, that we might label the whole development the internationalization of the short story.

The reasons for this are many. To begin with, the global spread of literacy continues. More and more countries are joining the global culture of modernity; their artists and writers are giving expression to their people's struggles. Important new literatures are springing up in African, Asian, and Latin American countries; formerly isolated traditions are being reinvigorated and changed by the impact of global modernism.

But this profusion of literatures would not have nearly so great an effect were it not for the work of translators. Here we see a linked development, the emergence in recent years of the professional translator, the individual trained in the art of carrying a work of literature from one language to another (*translation*, Latin, "carried over"). This new professionalism marks a great departure from earlier periods, when translators were often poorly paid amateurs (often themselves writers) who worked more for the love of literature than for financial reward.

But translation represents only part of the picture. The reasons for the international literary boom include transformations of another kind. New developments in technology—especially electronic media—are rapidly creating what the philosopher Marshall McLuhan once called "the global village." Geographical distances (and cultural differences) are being steadily bridged—some would say eradicated—by technology, just as once-isolated national economies are becoming ever more integrated into the network of a single global economy. To take just one example, consider how a single invention, the fax machine, has changed the way we do business. I could relay these words to the other side of the world in minutes. And this is just another step in the process that began when Samuel Morse invented the telegraph in the early nineteenth century. The definition of "elsewhere" keeps changing; the world is shrinking before our tools of access. It is natural, therefore, that we as readers take a greater interest in cultures, histories, and artistic productions of other countries.

These transformations bring with them a redefinition of the possibilities of the writing art. Writers are influenced not only by their neighbors and predecessors but by fellow craftsmen from all parts of the world. Canadians read Czechoslovakians, and vice versa; an American story writer picks up a new image or a stylistic trick from a newly translated Japanese writer. The barriers posed by unfamiliar languages and national boundaries are steadily dissolving. The possibilities for cross-fertilization increase.

Here we might pause to consider a related matter of great importance—the liberation of voices that were formerly silenced or repressed. The period of the 1960s in the United States and elsewhere saw the beginning of a revolutionary impulse toward societal change. The feminist movement, the struggle for racial equality, collective action on the part of Native Americans, Hispanics, gays, and other previously marginalized groups—have affected cultural life no less than political life. New, energized—but also angry and bitter—voices announced themselves in all the arts. Nowadays many bookstores have whole sections devoted to these diverse literatures. As the reader of this anthology (especially of its section "Additional Readings") will discover, the short story is no longer the property predominantly of the white, English-speaking male. The new cultural infusions are fresh and bracing. They allow us to see the world from previously unsuspected points of vantage.

BACKGROUNDS

Before we begin to sample some of the pleasures of the traditional and the contemporary short story, we must take time to explore the origins of the form and trace the main stages of its evolution. For it is only with a clear sense of the background history that we can hope to discern some order in what might otherwise seem just a dazzling chaos.

This history, as I hope to make clear, involves more than a simple recitation of names and historical periods like Romanticism and Modernism. We must go a bit deeper in order to find some guiding principle, some structure or explanation, that can impart meaning to the chronicle of the evolution of the form. This is obviously a risky business, for history is always more complex than after-the-fact reasoning can accommodate. Histories are forced to leave out most of the facts and to generalize.

The reader should realize that the explanations I offer are approximations, hand-drawn maps of impossibly intricate landscapes. They emphasize trends over the exceptions, and they move in leaps and bounds where life can always be said to go on foot.

Further, the writer of history, be it of a country, a culture, or some specific phenomenon, does so from a certain viewpoint. We all have our assumptions, beliefs, and biases, and they determine our ways of seeing things. The historian should articulate these insofar as is possible so that the reader knows that the account is an interpretation, not the gospel truth. There *is* no gospel truth in these matters. Here, then, are what I understand to be my own guiding assumptions about the history of the short story.

First, I believe that the development of the short story over the centuries represents something more than just a set of random responses to varying historical conditions. I think it is an evolution—a steady movement toward a more complete and accurate picture of the human condition. I also assume that the underlying impulse of storytelling is something more than providing amusement. The story, even in its earliest incarnations, has been a way of giving shape to the sufferings, joys, and perplexities of being alive.

Second, one should not infer from this evolution that literature is always getting better and better. Rather, it seems there is some universal law that balances gains against losses in every art. Contemporary fiction is a great deal more subtle and complicated than the storytelling of the ancients, but it has surely sacrificed some elements of vigor and directness. When we speak in terms of evolution, then, we should be careful to curb any urges toward condescension.

Third—and here I would signal special emphasis—I am convinced that the short story did not spring into existence suddenly in the mid-eighteenth century, as some anthologists suggest, but that it has flourished in various guises since the first piece of gossip was exchanged by our distant ancestors. The short story as we know it is a natural outgrowth of the most fundamental human inclination: to impart interest to what one is saying and to give sensible shape to the chaos of experience.

Fourth, I would argue that the basic pattern of growth and change of the short story has been similar from place to place and culture to culture. Of course, there are deviations, but the main path is clear. The first stories belong to the realm of myth and legend, telling of origins and extraordinary events. As cultures begin to assume their modern configurations, and as social life becomes more organized and complex, stories tend toward realism (that is, they strive to represent actual circumstances). The third great shift, which comes with the modern age, is toward a greater concern with inner states and questions of psychological motivation. This is not to say that the realistic stories ignored human psychology or that modern stories turn away from external depictions—neither is true—it is just a matter of emphasis.

I have been careful with my use of the word *evolution*, for it carries the implication that the latest is the best. This is a tricky business. For if one looks at the worldwide history of the short story form, one must acknowledge that many areas lagged behind Europe and the United States and followed their lead. What the scholar Ivan Morris has written about Japanese literature has general bearing: "The modern Japanese novel and story are essentially Western forms; insofar as literary influence has played a part, most Japanese prose writers are indebted to Western literature far more than to their own country's classical tradition." The point is not that the other cultures are delayed or deficient—clearly they are not—but that the direction of change has been largely dictated by the West. There are reasons for this, the key one being that changes in art have been tied to societal changes, specifically industrialization, social revolution, and the growth of a literate middle class. These developments often assumed their earliest forms in the West. The international boom of our time has much to do with the fact that many of the so-called developing nations are going through accelerated versions of the same processes. Their literature will naturally reflect their historical conditions. But while the art may tend to follow a roughly marked out path, this does not mean that we should view the process as a race between cultures. Every work, no matter where the writer is from, shows a different and essential picture of the present.

My fifth, and final, article of faith is closely bound to this idea of cultural change. I believe that the *what* of human expression is significantly determined by the *how*, that our modes of communication influence the content we are communicating. The communication modes of human societies have, by and large, developed from being strictly oral; (word-of-mouth) to oral and written; to oral, written, and print-based; to oral, written, print-based, and electronics-based. Each stage retains previous modes but changes their function. Each new expansion also brings transformations—in how we think, behave, and structure information. The stories told in an oral culture (like some that survive from the early Greeks or Hebrews) were *made* differently than the stories we write today, even if their underlying messages—about love, or friendship, or fear—are similar. The discussion that follows will try to make clear how these various technological changes have affected the storyteller's art.

STORYTELLING AND ORAL CULTURES

As long as philosophers have existed, they have sought to establish how human beings—*homo sapiens*—differ from other members of the animal kingdom. They have said that we are the only creatures that laugh, or wear clothes, or use language. These are a few of the more obvious distinctions, and we might consider adding another: we are the only creatures that tell stories to others of our kind. And this telling is something more than simply a by-product of our having language. It is deeply rooted and reflects a need at the core of our being. For we are also, so far as we know, the only creatures that seek to experience our lives as meaningful. We organize the elements of our existence into shapes and patterns; we find ways to link our lives to the lives of those who come before and after us; we test our understanding, comparing the patterns we find with those found by others. And we do this mainly by way of language, by talking and telling.

Our days are filled with *narratives*,[1] events ordered into some coherent linguistic sequence. We tell our seat-mate on the bus how we lost our keys or couldn't start the car; we tell our friends about a great or terrible party we went to. We also talk to ourselves constantly, often giving account of what we have done, are doing, or plan: "When I finish raking the leaves, I'm going to take a shower." "I'll call Gary to see if he still wants to go out." A story this is not, but it *is* a rudimentary narrative. And narrative is the engine that drives the story.

We can only imagine what the earliest narratives were like or what needs they fulfilled. Most likely they emerged as families and clans gathered by a fire at night and told what events had befallen them, what animals they had seen, and so on. It is also likely that the narratives tried to make some sense of the more mysterious features of the world—thunder, the movement of the stars, fire, changes in weather, and so on.

In any event, the telling impulse has been with us from the first. With the different kinds of telling there emerged the basic elements—or tools—of narrative. The tribal speaker no doubt made some effort to organize the material. Instead of presenting experiences in haphazard order, the teller looked for a meaningful sequence: "First I went to the river, down by the trees. Then I saw the bear. The bear moved toward me, and I threw the stone." An ordering such as I imagine here is the basis of what we now identify as *plot*, the sequence of events in a narrative. It also reveals the rudiments of *point of view* (the situation is presented strictly from the perspective of the first-person "I") and *setting* (the action is placed so that the listener can better picture what occurred).

We can imagine further that when a speaker was relating events to a group of listeners certain parts of the sequence were given greater prominence and that, in time, details were added to heighten the effect. "At first I saw nothing. Then I heard a noise, leaves shaking. Then the bushes opened and a very large creature came rushing toward me." It cannot have been long before the element of *suspense* was incorporated as a natural part of narrative. We can think of suspense as the teller's deliberate withholding of certain information, a tactic for keeping the audience in a state of expectation. We might go so far as to say that the first story was told when

1. A more complete discussion of *narrative, plot,* and other terms is given in the Appendices.

the speaker arranged information with some thought to its effect upon the audience.

This part of my account may seem obvious or too basic, but in truth we often forget that most of what we take for granted—including language and rules of communication—had to be invented and that the process was no doubt slow and painstaking, a fumbling by way of trial-and-error. I think we need such a recapitulation in order to emphasize the vital bond that exists between teller and listener (and later, writer and reader). The speaker feels the need to express some experience and takes pleasure in the ordering of unruly materials; the listener is drawn to hear and takes pleasure in reliving the experience of another. Some part of the enjoyment derives from the suspense and its eventual resolution. The formula has not changed all that much over millenia. When a friend says, "You'll never believe what happened to me last night," we are all ears. We are curious to learn something new, and we want to experience the inner quickening that suspense invariably creates.

If we take the panoramic view of human evolution, we would have to say that writing—the preservation of spoken words in signs and symbols—was a relatively late development. Strictly oral cultures flourished around the world for many centuries before the first modes of transcription were invented. And though we can't know precisely what these oral cultures were like, we can make some guesses about what needs their narratives fulfilled. For when written languages did appear, in Greece ca. 700 B.C., the materials put into writing eventually included the epics, legends, and fables that had been circulating by word-of-mouth for centuries. In these earliest pieces of documentary evidence we can trace out the basic forms of the narrative impulse. In Greece alone we find the fables of Aesop, the philosophy of Socrates, the histories of Herodotus, and the epics of Homer as well as lyrics and plays. We know that cultural forms of the Orient and Middle East were similarly profuse.

Naturally it is difficult to speak in terms of isolated, clearly defined kinds of storytelling. Often one mode—an epic poem like the *Iliad* or the *Odyssey*, for instance—served multiple functions: recording episodes from history, telling of the gods and their ways, imparting useful information about navigation, and so on. Making a meaningful record of the past—telling the stories of the culture in a way that explained and ennobled—was obviously of great importance. This record can include the kind of genealogical information that we find in the Hebrew Bible, the Old Testament, with its lengthy lists of who begat whom. It can also include tales of wars, conquests, and journeys of exploration, as we find in Herodotus, known as the "father of history."

Nor can we ignore those narratives that set out the myths of origin, explaining how things and places came to be, and generally attributing deeds and motives to God or a pantheon of gods. After all, Genesis, the first book of the Bible, recounts the most astonishing of stories, complete with *protagonists* (Adam and Eve), a *conflict* (whether to disobey God's command that they not taste the fruit from the Tree of Life), an *antagonist* (the snake), a *climax* (when Adam and Eve give in to temptation), and a *resolution*, or *denouement* (when Adam and Eve are banished from Eden). It could be said that we are living out now the denouement of one of the oldest and most compelling of origin stories.

HOMER AND THE EPIC

One of the most gifted storytellers of all time was the poet Homer, who lived (or is said to have lived) in Greece about 700 B.C. His two epics, the *Iliad* and the *Odyssey*, are a storehouse of narrative riches. They unfold episodes from the bloody history of Greek tribal warfare and are packed with subplots, anecdotes, and passages celebrating the rituals of feasting and the diverse beauties of nature. There is some debate in scholarly circles about whether one man should be credited with composing these two monumental works, but their overall unity and uniformly high quality suggest a single intelligence.

However, this does not mean that the writer invented both works solely out of his imagination. Far more likely, the poet gathered up the legends about the Trojan War that had passed orally from generation to generation and put them together in memorable form. His genius was not so much for inventing as for weaving together diverse materials and presenting them vividly.

Homer the Bard, the "singer of tales" (the phrase is from Albert Lord, noted scholar of oral narratives), would have recited his epics from memory—writing had not yet been invented in Greece. He would have declaimed hundreds of lines at a time, a feat that seems miraculous in our day. But we should remember that oral cultures functioned differently than print-based or electronics-based cultures do. Human abilities change as needs change. Indeed, the very nature of a society limited strictly to the spoken word determined many things about the form and content of the epic. If we look more closely at the *Iliad* and the *Odyssey*, we can isolate some of the distinctive features of storytelling in its earliest phase. Later we will see how these features have been modified to become elements in the stories being written today.

Homer's great art, as I have said, was to bring together the tales and legends that had been told in different places for generations. He did so in a powerful and memorable way. His long lines of hexameter verse (lines of six "feet") were organized into sections, now known as "books." Some scholars contend that the stories were presented in verse form—verse characterized by strong rhythms and repeated phrases—primarily to assist memory. The poet would chant the highly patterned lines, using their structure to help recall the order of the material. He had a large fund of stock phrases and descriptions readily available—"wine-dark sea," "rosy fingers of dawn," "cunning Odysseus"; these, too, were aids to memory.

The means of communication further dictated the shape of the telling. Characters were generally typed by attribute and were easily recalled by means of identifying tags—a help to listeners in keeping track of the story. In addition, the narrative was broken up into episodes, each one having its own dramatic focus. The spoken format would not allow for too many subtleties or digressions. The actions were depicted in stark dramatic form, and descriptions were action-oriented and concrete. A short excerpt (in a prose translation) from the Cyclops episode of the *Odyssey* (see Homer, page 35) will illustrate what I mean:

> No sooner had the tender Dawn shown her roses in the East, than the Cyclops lit up the fire and milked his splendid ewes, all in their proper order, putting her young to each. This business over and his morning labors done, he once more snatched up a couple of my men and prepared his meal. When he had eaten, he turned his fatted sheep out of the cave, removing the great doorstone without an effort. But he replaced it immediately, as easily as though he were putting the lid on a quiver. Then, with many a whistle, he drove his rich flocks off towards the high pasture, while I was left, with murder in my heart, beating about for some scheme by which I might pay him back if only Athene would grant me my prayer.
>
> *Translated by E. V. Rieu*

That the epic can be made to read so naturally in straightforward prose demonstrates how central the storytelling element really was.

The elements of oral storytelling are the basis for all later narrative modes. These tales, and the public functions they fulfilled—providing entertainment and allowing for communal audience participation—lived on for centuries. After all, even after writing had been invented, it remained a skill possessed by few. Most of the transactions of society—in Greece, Rome, Arabia, and China—were carried on by word-of-mouth, not in writing.

FROM ORAL CULTURES TO THE FIRST PRINTED BOOK

Once the technology of writing had been invented, however, as educated scribes began to record the words of poets, historians, and philosophers, the basic form of the story began to change. A writer like Apuleius (who was born in the African part of the Roman Empire in about 123 A.D.) set down his often fantastical tales primarily for the pleasure of educated people like himself. The episodes of his *The Golden Ass*, while drawing heavily on popular lore about gods and demons, nonetheless have a verbal complexity and subtlety not found in Homer. Apuleius is, like Homer, a storyteller, but he directs his words to an audience that does not have to rely strictly on its memory of the spoken tale. His readers can pause over a turn of phrase and are free to go back to verify an impression. The difference between hearing and reading cannot be stressed sufficiently. Spoken art depends upon the attention of listeners. Written art can take greater liberties. Events can be set out in more varied ways; characters need not be so flat and simple; and the expression can reflect greater nuances. The style of presentation becomes more important.

Western literature—and Western culture in general—might have developed very differently under other historical circumstances. But enormous shifts and upheavals aborted all possibility of orderly growth. With the rise of Christianity and the decline of the great imperial empire of the Romans, Europe entered upon a centuries-long period often referred to as the Dark Ages. Cities and towns learned the terrors of sudden barbarian invasion; a series of devastating plagues swept over the continent, killing millions. Cultural life changed. Monastaries became the major centers of learning; the arts of reading and writing (indeed, the preservation of past writing) belonged mainly to educated monks. And much of what was written was either religious or philosophical in character. Yet the profane, or nonsacred, arts survived. In the Mediterranean lands, and to some extent in Germany, the tradition of wandering storytellers, or troubadours, flourished. These travelers criss-crossed Europe, exchanging stories, songs, and news for lodging and food. They entertained members of isolated courts with legends of love and loss. Some historians claim that our romantic idea of love was an invention of these troubadours.

Throughout this period, from the eighth to the thirteenth century, people did not stop inventing and telling stories. But because the vast majority were unlettered—lacking in reading and writing skills—many of these stories disappeared. Others, probably the better ones, survived, surfacing in the works of Boccaccio, Chaucer, and Rabelais. Others would turn up in collections like those made by the Brothers Grimm in nineteenth-century Germany.

With the Italian, and later Northern, Renaissance, we witness a tremendous rebirth of culture and learning. Writings from an earlier day (mainly Greek and Roman) were rediscovered, translated, and circulated. Works like the *Iliad* and the *Odyssey* could make their influence felt anew. Education and literacy began to spread among the new merchant classes, and wealthy nobles, particularly in Italy, sponsored the arts as a public duty. In this period we find Giovanni Boccaccio (1313–1375) writing the many books of the *Decameron*, a cycle of profane, often bawdy stories supposedly exchanged by a group of travelers waiting out the Black Death, or plague. These stories took their inspiration from the popular folk tales that had circulated by word-of-mouth for many years. They are rowdy and irreverent, poking fun at the self-important officials of the Church, but they also express the idealized conception of love that was part of the troubadour ethos.

The English poet Geoffrey Chaucer (ca. 1342–1400) was greatly inspired by Boccaccio in his writing of *The Canterbury Tales*. Here, as in Homer, we see a powerful storytelling impulse expressing itself in poetic form. The *Tales*, which make use of a full range of narrative modes, are told by a group of pilgrims on their way to the town of Canterbury, in England. Although the purpose of the journey is devotional, the stories they relate reflect the pleasures and tragedies of everyday life. The episodic structure of the narratives as well as the direct and energetic presentation owe much to the oral tradition.

Elsewhere, in the Middle East and the Far East, we find different societal formations. Persia and Arabia were ruled by powerful princes, or sheikhs; reading and writing were the prerogative of the few. But, as in the West, there was a rich tradition of storytelling, as the vast compendium of *The Arabian Nights* tales testifies. (Many of the tales are believed to have originated in Egypt and the Caliphate of Baghdad (present-day Iraq) during the eighth to the tenth century). China and Japan, meanwhile, were under dynastic rule. Their written works, too, were produced by and for a small élite. Much of the literature reflected the concerns of courtly life. And just as Middle Eastern lore was saturated with the spirit of Islam, so did Eastern literature express the powerful influence of Buddhism.

THE PRINTED WORD

In the middle of the fifteenth century the German printer Johannes Gutenberg (ca. 1390–1468) invented a system of printing from blocks of movable type. He had no notion that this breakthrough would alter the world as much as any invention had before or since. The first printed book, an edition of the Bible, was printed before 1456, but it was to be many years before the impact of the new technology would penetrate European society. Once the diffusion began, as printers everywhere began to publish broadsides, pamphlets, and books, there was no turning back. The ramifications of print are too many and various to be treated here. We must be content to note some of the effects on what would become the short story form.

With the spread of printing presses and the growing availability of printed matter, new needs and possibilities arose. Literacy, formerly confined to the small class serving the nobility, began making inroads among the other layers of society. It is fitting that the first book, the Bible, was vital in paving the way. Bibles were printed in great numbers, and formerly unlettered folk began to master the rudiments of reading. For many decades, the most popular stories were those in the books of the Old and New Testaments. But other uses for literacy were quickly discovered. Tradespeople, for instance, found it very useful to be able to read bills and documents. And in the growing urban centers, printed sheets of information, the first newspapers, became popular. In short, an audience developed for the printed word—an audience that sought not only religious instruction and information but entertainment as well.

The late seventeenth and early eighteenth centuries in Europe saw the dawn of printed literature; with it would come the emergence of the short story as a distinct genre. It was in this period, too, that the first novels appeared, by writers like Daniel Defoe (1660–1731), Jonathan Swift (1667–1745), Samuel Richardson (1689–1761), Henry Fielding (1707–1754), and Laurence Sterne (1713–1768). Their works were directed mainly toward more educated audiences, but the contents might interest the self-taught commoner as well. Similarly, when the essayists Richard Steele (1672–1729) and Joseph Addison (1672–1719) founded their enormously influential journal, *The Tatler*, it was with a sharp eye toward winning a popular readership. *The Tatler* mixed topical and witty writings with its more serious, often literary, columns and articles.

A look at the literary prose of the time reveals what a change had befallen the formerly simple and straightforward art of storytelling. Here is a passage from the opening of Henry Fielding's novel *Tom Jones*, which takes many hundreds of pages to relate the various adventures of its hero:

> In that part of the western division of this kingdom which is commonly called Somersetshire, there lately lived and perhaps lives still, a gentleman whose name was Allworthy, and who might well be called the favorite of both Nature and Fortune; for both of these seem to have contended which should bless and enrich him most. In this contention Nature may seem to some to have come off victorious, as she bestowed on him many gifts, while Fortune had only one gift in her power; but in pouring forth this, she was so very profuse, that others perhaps may think this single endowment to have been more than equivalent to all the various blessings which he enjoyed from Nature.

We are immediately struck by several things: the casual, leisurely pace of the prose, and the relative complexity of the expression. *Tom Jones*, like most of the writings of this time, was meant to be read from the printed page. The pace and complexity are directly related to the changes wrought by print technology. The author assumes a reader who is willing to follow along at his or her own pace, who will pause over witticisms and involved figures of expression, and who is under no pressure to remember everything. The same could be said for a written manuscript, but print emphasized the fixity and standardization. The eye moved easily over lines of regular type; the bound pages held the material like a perfect memory. Homer's listeners had no such option available.

Still, we must not forget that these early novels also depended to a great degree upon storytelling conventions as they had developed over millenia of oral transmission. Characters like Fielding's Tom Jones and Defoe's Moll Flanders were followed from episode to episode, misadventure to misadventure, and the connecting links from one part to another were often casual. The plots were marked by comic misunderstandings, mistaken identities, lucky escapes—all elements familiar from Boccaccio, Chaucer, or *The Arabian Nights*. Characters still tended to be broadly drawn, or *stereotyped;* the kind of psychological complexity that we take for granted nowadays was not yet central to the writer's art.

THE FIRST SHORT STORIES

The first short stories appeared in Europe in the later decades of the eighteenth century. This emergence of this new literary form was in part the result of various social and historical forces, and some general background observations are necessary here.

This was a period of industrial and commercial awakening, with burgeoning trade, newly discovered markets, and factories (the Industrial Revolution was well under way). Before the newly empowered merchant and manufacturing classes, the traditional authority of the aristocracy came under vigorous attack. The American colonists waged war to free themselves from the oppressive control of the British monarchy. Thirteen years later, in 1789, the French Revolution erupted, ending the rule of the nobility. Change and disturbance were in the air—and great excitement. Throughout Europe in the late 1700s a cultural and intellectual movement arose that we designate as Romanticism.

Romanticism was a complex phenomenon that took many forms. It found expression as a drive toward social revolution, and it celebrated individuality and imagination in opposition to the forces of industrial standardization. Poet William Blake (1757–1827) raised a cry against the "dark satanic mills." Elsewhere, the romantic impulse emerged as a highly charged other-worldliness and brought forth works of fancy and supernaturalism. In Germany, where a young writer named Johann Wolfgang von Goethe (1749–1832) wrote a short novel entitled *The Sorrows of Young Werther*—about a sensitive man driven to suicide by an uncomprehending society—a rash of imitative suicides resulted.

The short story had its first genuine flowering, then, in a climate of turbulence and excess. And just as Romanticism took on different forms from place to place, so did the story. In France, where the tradition of rational skepticism was strongest (some have called this the main component of the French national character), Voltaire (1694–1778) published his ironic masterpiece *Candide* and a collection of short *Philosophical Tales*. In Germany writers like Heinrich von Kleist (1777–1811) and E.T.W. Hoffmann (1776–1822) conjured up strangely fanciful works of imagination. The Russian genius of Nikolai Gogol (1809–1852), produced eccentric satires about the conditions of life under a tyrannical czar. His comic tales, like "The Overcoat" and "The Nose," were prized for their absurdist touches.

The circumstances in America were somewhat different. For one thing, the society was new, without its own traditions. Writers faced the overwhelming presence and challenge of what they took to be an undomesticated wilderness. Strains of the romantic impulse did carry over from Europe, but the literary works that surfaced were distinctive, altogether unlike anything seen on the Continent. Washington Irving (1783–1859), who can be considered America's first short story writer, brought forth dreamy imaginings of rural life in his "Rip Van Winkle" and "The Legend of Sleepy Hollow." Shortly thereafter, Nathaniel Hawthorne (1804–1864) and Edgar Allan Poe (1809–1849) reflected, respectively, the more religious and fantastical facets of the imagination. Hawthorne, in books like *The Scarlet Letter* and stories like "Young Goodman Brown" and "The Minister's Black Veil," explored the often frightening roots of Puritan fanaticism. Poe, driven by his own inner turmoil, explored madness and the collapse of normal modes of behavior. He is also credited with writing the first detective story, "The Murders in the Rue Morgue," which was published in 1841.

THE RISE OF REALISM

The mid-nineteenth century brought yet another development in literature and the arts—Realism. Some scholars contend that the great swerve toward Realism—the faithful representation of ordinary life—came with the rise to power of a newly educated and enfranchised middle class, or bourgeoisie. Quite suddenly, at least in long-range historical terms, a large population was avid to rise in society and to acquire the trappings of culture. A population with money and leisure time—here was the perfect audience for the periodicals and newspapers that were springing up in urban centers and provincial towns. What this audience most desired, interestingly, were not fanciful works that would take them away from their daily concerns. As a newly awakened, increasingly powerful social force, they wanted to study themselves. Art became, for a time, a kind of looking-glass held up to the world.

There is, it must be said, a great irony at work here. Many of the writers who set about to document this world had a profound contempt for the materialistic ambitions and often trivial interests of this new class. In their works—in stories and novels by Gustave Flaubert (1821–1880) and Guy de Maupassant (1850–1893) in France, Anton Chekhov (1860–1904) and

Leo Tolstoy (1828–1910) in Russia, for example—we often see the middle classes portrayed as narrow-minded and greedy, utterly lacking in civilized refinements.

With the writings of these mid-nineteenth century Europeans and Americans, we are in the midst of the first great golden age of the short story. Culturally speaking, this was a fortunate moment: historical circumstances quickened individual talent, much as they had in Athens in the time of Plato and in Italy during the Renaissance. It was, for Western literature, a period of great ferment directly bound to societal conditions. Similar bursts would come in other cultures, but later—often *much* later.

The triumph of the realist mode stamped the short story with a new set of features. No longer was the writer's primary goal to shock, amuse, or sweep the reader into the grip of some extraordinary adventure. The realist was after something different: to show the world as it is experienced by ordinary people. Characters were presented, in these stories, in real-life situations—loving, but also dealing with loss; worrying about money and status; coming to terms with failure. When Frank O'Connor, in his important study of the short story, *The Lonely Voice*, defined the genre as the arena of the underdog—the outsider—he was referring to a development that began with these mid-nineteenth century writers.

In these short stories the plot is often lacking in suspense, as if the writers felt that suspense would falsify the illusion of reality they were after. Instead, they implement more complex and nondramatic—some might say deliberately boring—devices (Chekhov, a master of the nondramatic approach, even titled one of his works "A Boring Story"). The subject matter chosen was often of a somewhat dreary, even grim, nature.

One way to look upon the short story, then, is as a vehicle for examining the world around us. As we make history, so do we change our conditions and our modes of relating to our surroundings. The stories of Homer's day, gathered in his epics, express the passions, terrors, and aggressions of a war-ridden, deity worshipping culture. The episodes were often fantastic because humankind itself was, in the words of the poet Shelley, "in its infancy." No one knew where the world ended, or what held the heavens up. Outlandish tales and legends were, to a degree, attempts at explanation and understanding.

Later, in the period of the Renaissance in the West, cycles of profane, often bawdy stories of love and misadventure gave voice to the needs that the dominant religious institutions did not acknowledge. Romanticism obviously expressed the energy and turbulence of cultures in the throes of intense transformation. And now, with Realism, the more sober and purposeful order of the emerging societies found reflection. Different styles of portraiture, then, manifested different stages of human self-awareness.

MODERNISM

With the beginning of the twentieth century, another watershed in the art is reached. Realism had been and continues to be (in the work of certain stylists) tremendously influential. But the approach had limits. Writers mainly confined themselves to documenting the features of the exterior world—presenting characters, events, and descriptions while asking the reader to supply the inner psychology. Certain changes and departures were inevitable. For writers, like all artists, are forever pressing at the boundaries of their art, looking for new things to say, and new ways of saying them. Even in the mid-nineteenth century, there were those, like Fyodor Dostoevsky (1821–1881), who were searching for a language that could dramatize the thoughts, longings, and spiritual struggles of the individual. Dostoevsky's *Notes from the Underground* was one pioneering attempt to bring those neglected elements into literature. Then, only decades later, in turn-of-the-century Vienna, psychologist Sigmund Freud ventured the first sustained scientific understanding of what would come to be known as the subconscious mind. Inwardness came into view like a new continent to be explored and colonized.

But the beginning of our century was also a period of cataclysmic social change. The great colonial empires were starting to come apart, and bitter conflicts loomed among rival powers. Moreover, manufacture was bringing more and more people into urban centers, rapidly eradicating ancient patterns of rural life. And in 1914, Europe went to war, with unprecedented brutality. The feeling that the world had gone mad was widespread; many people believed that the familiar ways of life were lost forever.

Out of this crucible came the powerful and many-faceted artistic response known as Modernism. Fiction, like art, music, and drama, was destined to reflect the tensions and transformations. The calm mirror of Realism, with its subtle reflections of ordinary scenes was shattered. Writers ventured inward. James Joyce (1882–1941), D. H. Lawrence (1885–1930), Marcel Proust (1871–1922), Virginia Woolf (1882–1941), and others looked for ways to record the troubled life of the psyche. Joyce moved from presenting subtle inward revelations (epiphanies) in his early stories to charting the fluid momentum of consciousness in his grandly experimental novel, *Ulysses*. Others, like Ernest Hemingway (1899–1961) deliberately simplified and roughened the surface of their prose in order to suggest the deforming power of war and the inner deadness that came in its wake. Hemingway's characters carry themselves with a numb reserve; behind their words and movements we sense a great pressure of pain and disappointment.

The period from the turn of the century to the beginning of World War II saw a bright profusion of stylistic strategies, from the stream-of-consciousness experiments of Joyce and Woolf, who attempted to convey the actual sensations of inner life in the complex flow of their sentences; to the understated surfaces of Hemingway's work; to the florid, often clotted prose of William Faulkner (1897–1962), who used the idea of the decaying South as a kind of emblem for the state of civilization at large and who made innovative use of shifting narrators and perspectives.

From this period on, we can say without fear of contradiction that the short story has become a many-headed creature. Writers are free to draw from a large arsenal of different techniques. Indeed, since the early postwar period a number of options, many of them experimental, have been introduced. In the 1950s and 1960s, especially, writers from every part of the world approached the short story form in a spirit of cosmopolitan innovation. New techniques included multiple narrators, fractured or scrambled story lines, and complex time frames. Others introduced elements of nonsense and absurdity, or repackaged formulas from fairy tales. Almost everything has been attempted: stories that unfold in reverse, stories that give contradictory versions of the same event, even stories that the reader must assemble like a jigsaw puzzle. The innovators are as apt to be Japanese, Latin American, or Czechoslovakian as German, French, or American. With speedy communications networks and legions of skilled translators, the formerly isolated literary communities are all becoming part of a single world network.

In recent years, in the 1970s and 1980s, a mode popularly known as Minimalism has achieved great influence. Minimalism presents what is often a bare, simplified snapshot of some event, insisting that the reader imagine the rest of the circumstances and guess about their impact. The approach reflects, in part, what is perceived as the growing complexity of the world (how is the writer to present a reality that is awash in gadgets and running on obscure electronic impulses?) But there is also an awareness that modern life has become too bland and standardized to support a strongly dramatic art. Another explanation for the arrival of Minimalism might be the huge change wrought in our lives by yet another new communications technology—the electronic media. Many of these stories, by Ann Beattie, Amy Hempel, and others, remind us of nothing so much as the quick-cut superficiality of television dramas. Consider this short excerpt from Amy Hempel's story "The Cemetery Where Al Jolson Is Buried":

> She introduces me to a nurse as the Best Friend. The impersonal article is more intimate. It tells me that *they* are intimate, the nurse and my friend.
>
> "I was telling her we used to drink Canada Dry ginger ale and pretend we were in Canada."
>
> "That's how dumb we were," I say.
>
> "You could be sisters," the nurse says.

The scene continues in this vein, choppy, barbed, its pace and presentation resembling a situation-comedy routine. But should we be surprised? Communication modes have all along, as we have seen, shaped the form of story narrative—there is no reason to think that the new media will not exert every bit as much influence as writing or print did in their time.

Unlike citizens of other historical epochs, however, we are living globally, in a condition of simultaneity. What happens in Tokyo, Moscow or Tel Aviv, is on our news monitors instantly. We orient ourselves—*try* to orient ourselves—within an overwhelming rush of imagery and information. The slow formation of distinctive cultural styles is a thing of the past. Everything seems to happen at once, and the range of possible responses is enormous. This pluralism is one of the dominant features of the so-called Postmodern era. What this means for the short story—indeed, for the arts in general—is an open question. The one certainty is that given the enormous quantity and diversity of materials, readers will have many more paths of exploration open to them.

I realize that I have been concentrating largely upon the Western literary tradition, even though this anthology claims to represent an international range in its selections. There are several reasons for my procedure, and I have tried to give explanatory reminders from time to time. Basically, the Western tradition is, so far as the short story is concerned, the most conspicuous and influential, and other literatures—many of them coming into their own only in the last century—would be difficult to understand without some reference to it. This may be unfortunate, especially as the root causes have everything to do with the tangled legacy of colonialism. Most of the non-European world has been directly or indirectly implicated in the unfolding of European history. That is the bad news. The good news is that our present era is witnessing a great reaction worldwide to centuries of imperial domination. Nations and cultures are battling to regain sovereignty, and the energy—manifested in the arts no less than the politics—is astonishing. The stories assembled here can only give a whisper of this.

A last word is necessary—about the arrangement of the contents. The first part of the anthology is designed to give a historical picture of the basic development of the story form. It presents the story from its oral beginnings (I include examples of literature that are not, strictly speaking, prose fiction) through its emergence in Romanticism and Realism as well as modern variations that probe the interior realm and begin to experiment with structure. The section of additional readings tries to account for the grand profusion of short fiction the world over, a profusion that warrants this being called the new golden age of the short story.

Reading Literature

The reading of literature is at once simpler and more demanding than many other kinds of reading. This may sound like a self-canceling statement, but actually it points toward the complexity of the act itself. Reading literature is often simpler because the work in question has a natural appeal; involvement in the subject brings absorption. Literature—for our purposes, short fiction—is rooted in the teller's or writer's deep desire to seduce, compel, or enchant the audience. The story's natural terrain is human nature, a subject in which we are all interested, and its aim is to shed new light upon some aspect of our shared experience. James Joyce, in "The Dead," tells a story about failure, regret, and the need to salvage meaning from experience. Eudora Welty's "Powerhouse" shows how the ache of loss is transformed into musical expression. And so on.

When we read a story, we are not, as we might be if we had to read a lengthy nonfiction article, forced against the grain. If we can open ourselves up, strike a receptive posture, the work will very likely do the rest. We will read on because we want to know what happens next or because we sense that we are learning something that might be useful to us in our living.

But reading literature can also be more challenging, and require more concentration, than other kinds of reading. The language is often used differently; it asks more of us. We have to pay heed not only to the *what* but also the *how*. Most of the time—when we race through a newspaper, or work through a chapter in a textbook—we turn pages for the sake of information. We read the words for their *denotative* value—what might be called their immediate dictionary meaning—stripping off the facts, the ideas, and moving on. We do not expect that an article in *Time* magazine will use ambiguous language or that its sentences will be structured with high regard for rhythm.

But as soon as we enter into the literary realm, a new set of requirements is introduced. We must learn to understand language in both its denotative and *connotative*, or suggestive, usages. And reading becomes necessarily more complex. Suddenly we must pay attention not only to the meanings of words but also to their associations. Moreover, we have to read the author's tone, looking for clues about how to interpret the actions of the characters. We watch out for images that might signal deeper thematic meanings. We listen to the sentences themselves, hearing cues in rhythms and changes of rhythm. To put it simply, we can make sense of the newspaper while wearing headphones, but to read a short story—or a novel, a poem, or a play—we need to concentrate in silence.

Any work of literature worth reading at all is probably worth reading twice. Indeed, any work that you hope to be able to discuss or write about *should* be read twice (see Appendix B, "Writing about Literature"). Of course, you don't always find yourself in ideal circumstances. You probably find that in the course of a busy semester it is all you can do to keep up with required reading for classes, never mind the luxury of rereading. Still, there is some explanatory value to be derived from speaking in terms of the ideal, considering the first and second approaches and different vantages. These are here treated as separate processes, although in fact most practiced readers combine the two in a single concentrated act.

Reading fiction, as you no doubt know, can be a taxing business. You are plunged into an alien world, a place with characters, situations, and assumptions that need to be figured out. As often as not, the language itself requires maximum attention—the writer is trying to tell and suggest as much as possible in a condensed form. Sometimes you will feel your head start to reel, you will have to step away and take a break.

It might be useful to think of the work—the story or the novel—as an unknown terrain. As the reader, you walk forward slowly, not knowing what to expect, following whatever path has been set down. In time, of course, your patience and attentiveness will bring rewards. The characters will start to come alive, the situations will sort themselves out, and your desire to find out what happens next will win out over your natural uncertainty. By the end of the reading you will generally have the scenario clear in your mind; you will be able to say with some confidence, "I've read the story."

But what a revealing experience it is to then read the work a second time. The element of surprise is missing, but your mind is suddenly free to observe and explore. As a traveler you no longer expend most of your energy in following the path and looking for direction markers; you are free to study and enjoy your surroundings. The energy that in the first reading went into fleshing out and tracking the characters and holding the turns of plot in mind can now be directed elsewhere. Now that you know that the romance between X and Y will fizzle out, you can monitor their actions and interchanges to get further clues about the failure. No less important, you can begin to enjoy the language for its own sake, lingering over images, descriptions, and subtle turns of phrase.

Sometimes, however, you don't have the luxury of the second look and can only get through a work of fiction once. In this case, you have no choice but to double up, to play the part of the busy traveler who hustles to stay on the path but who also pauses here and there to sweep a glance over the particulars of the surroundings.

Strangely, this complex operation is seldom mentioned in discussions of reading. The process is all too often assumed to be continuous, as if when reading you start with the first word and don't stop until you reach the final period. A more accurate depiction would show discontinuous motion. Short forward jerks, pauses, countless backtrackings, sudden rushes, more pauses. You are not only working to comprehend or pausing to savor, but you are also constantly fending off the thoughts, memories, and associations that the words on the page evoke. How many times have you finished reading a page only to realize that you looked at all the words without absorbing a bit of the sense? Reading is a constant struggle to keep your mind from being elsewhere.

This brings up another essential point about reading literature. Namely, just as painters love color, writers love language; and they use its sounds and rhythms as visual artists use shape and pigment. The prose of newspapers and advertising brochures may be written for rapid visual consumption, but most literary fiction is written to be *heard*. This does not mean that you need to read the stories out loud to get their full effect, but it does mean that you should try to hear the words and sentences clearly in your auditory imagination (one of our linguistic abilities is to hear words in our thoughts almost as if they had been spoken). The operation is a natural one. As you read this sentence you are most likely sounding it out silently to yourself. You do the same thing when you read a work of literature, but you probably exercise more care, making sure that you hear the words clearly and completely. This takes time and energy, but there is no way around it—not if you want the full reading experience. If you speed-read, you create the effect of a sound-blur. You may get through the story more quickly, but you will have little sense about what transpired. No less important, you thereby insult the artist. It is just as if you went racing along the walls of an art gallery, glancing quickly at works that the painter struggled with for months. True appreciation ought to begin with a simple gesture of respect.

CLOSE READING

There is nothing mysterious about that operation required of all serious students of literature—close reading. It is merely a heightened attentiveness, a way of slowing down the reading process in order to focus upon the contribution that diction (word choice), sentence construction, and rhythm make to the meaning of the work or passage in question. To read closely is to treat every element of the prose as significant; the scrutiny is as intense as that given to poetry. Of course, not every writer stands up under the pressure. A close reading of a passage from a dime-store romance will not yield up many wonders. But among serious practitioners of fiction, there are a number of stylists who reveal their finest insights only when closely interpreted.

Close reading requires patience and stamina. It is essentially the same process as *explication* (see Appendix B, "Writing about Literature") except that explication presents the fruits of attentive reading in written form. Unless you are writing a doctoral dissertation on a given work, you are not likely to bring such scrutiny to bear upon an entire story or novel. But even the examination of a passage from a work of fiction generally brings insights that can be useful in understanding the whole.

Let me give an instance of what such attentiveness in reading involves. Here is the opening paragraph from John Updike's story "Separating":

> The day was fair. Brilliant. All that June the weather had mocked the Maples' internal misery with solid sunlight—golden shafts and cascades of green in which their conversations had wormed unseeing, their sad murmuring selves the only stain in Nature. Usually by this time of the year they had acquired tans; but when they met their elder daughter's plane on her return from a year in England they were almost as pale as she, though Judith was too dazzled by the sunny opulent jumble of her native land to notice. They did not spoil her homecoming by telling her immediately. Wait a few days, let her recover from jet lag, had been one of their formulations, in that string of gray dialogues—over coffee, over cocktails, over Cointreau—that had shaped the strategy of their dissolution, while the earth performed its annual stunt of dissolution unnoticed beyond their closed windows. Richard had thought to leave at Easter; Joan had insisted they wait until the four children were at last assembled, with all exams passed and ceremonies attended, and the bauble of summer to console them. So he had drudged away, in love, in dread, repairing screens, getting the mowers sharpened, rolling and patching their new tennis court.

Updike is renowned for his stylistic skills, his ability to put the full resources of language to work. There is much to be gained from a careful inspection of his opening. The title, "Separating," tells you what to expect, and a preliminary reading of the paragraph provides the basic information: Richard and Joan, the parents of four children, have decided to separate. They have done so with some planning and intend to wait until all their children have finished their school obligations before breaking the news. In the meantime, life must go on with some appearance of normalcy.

If you were reading quickly, you would absorb this information and move along. But by close reading, by going back and working through the paragraph slowly, heeding the language and drawing inferences from the details provided, you can learn a good deal more. You can deduce, for instance, that the Maples are probably quite well-off, certainly well-off enough to send their daughter to England for a year and to have a tennis court. You can also get the impression that they follow the rituals of the upper-middle class, drinking cocktails and Cointreau, acquiring tans, and so on. The fact that their "formulations" had been made gradually, "over coffee, over cocktails, over Cointreau," suggests that they are, at least in most obvious respects, reasonable people—you don't hear of drunken fights or sudden desertions. Indeed, the fact that they can wait for the right moment, carrying on as always, tells a good deal about their marriage. Appearances and codes of behavior are all-important in this world.

But if you now listen to the diction and monitor Updike's use of images, the other part of the story emerges. Right from the start he opposes the outer and inner, appearances with realities. The sunny weather, as he describes it, "had mocked the Maples' internal misery." Exteriors and interiors are set into opposition, as are darkness and light. Conversations "had wormed," and their "sad murmuring selves" are seen as "the only stain in Nature," as if they alone were going against some universal system of laws. Against the bright sunlight, he tells of their "gray dialogues."

Updike then finds a very subtle way to accentuate the growing seriousness of the situation. He achieves his desired effect by suddenly trivializing Nature, by describing the coming of Spring as an "annual stunt" that passes "unnoticed." The Maples are so absorbed in their private melodrama that they disregard the changing of seasons: they disregard it because in view of their situation, the renewal is unwelcome—it would make the deterioration of the family even more unbearable.

One could continue in this vein, questioning the significance of Richard's desire to leave at Easter, the day of the resurrection, commenting upon the condescension implied by the parents thinking of summer as a "bauble" that might "console" the children, focusing upon the ambivalence of Richard drudging away, "in love, in dread," but the point is probably clear. Artistic prose not only repays close reading; it demands it.

A reading like this raises the interesting and vexing question of interpretation. Basically, no two individuals reading a work will discover the same significance or supply the same explanations. These are one reader's comments on Updike's opening paragraph, and another reader may very well have different reactions. Indeed, Updike himself, if he made himself available for an interview, might assert that he had an entirely different set of stylistic intentions. Which interpretation is best? Who should we listen to?

These questions have been taken up in great detail by literary theoreticians, and their responses span a considerable gamut. Some would argue, for example, that the meaning of a literary work is absolute, conforming exactly to the author's intention, and that any other stance opens the door to the chaotic forces of relativism. Others, including some believers in chaotic relativism, insist that there is no right reading, not even the author's, and that there are only different readings. In other words, if a reader chooses to understand *King Lear* not as a tragedy but as a satire, she is entitled to do so. Who is to judge otherwise?

Most readers and critics, however, incline to a commonsensical compromise. Language is, after all, a public medium; the meanings and associations of words can be established with at least approximate accuracy.

Interpretations can be compared and tested; they can, like any idea or opinion, be measured against consensus. This is not to say that the consensus view is always the best, but we cannot deny the implications of the fact that it exists. The reader who would declare *King Lear* a satiric work is entitled to her view, but she must be willing to reply to the generations of readers who have deemed the play a tragedy. Interpretation is not constrained, except by a certain responsibility to the considered views of other readers.

When you approach a literary work, then, you should be willing to read attentively, to respond openly, and to explore possible interpretations independently. One of the great values of a course in literature is that it allows for discussion; you can test your ideas and intuitions in a public context and then refine your insights in written work. What you need to keep in mind—for it is too easy to forget in an academic setting—is that every work, every *word*, was originally composed by an individual who sat in a room, alone, bent upon passing along some vision of human experience. If you keep that in mind, you will realize that the final goal of any interpretation is not to produce an impressive paper but to add to the store of your understanding of life itself.

1

ORAL TRADITIONS

While the emergence of the short story as a distinct literary genre may be traced back only to the late eighteenth century, storytelling itself is surely as old as spoken language. The selections in this part—which range from an episode from Homer's Odyssey (ca. 700 B.C.) to a version of the well-known Cinderella story, transcribed from popular lore by Wilhelm and Jacob Grimm in the early 1800s—are presented to remind the reader that the short story form has ancient and intricate roots, not just in Europe but the world over. (I have included representative tales from the Japanese and Arabian traditions.)

The reader will be surprised time and again to note the similarities that exist among works of diverse cultures and from one era to another. Of course, this is not to suggest that some blandly uniform universality applies to all cultural products. The narratives are quite distinct in their particularities of tone, character, and incident. But running beneath these varied surfaces are commonalities shared by all people. After all, we love, hate, fear, and rejoice in similar ways, no matter what our cultural affiliation. Thus, whether we are reading a comically grotesque tale by the Roman Apuleius or an Arabic legend ascribed to Scheherazade, we get caught up in a process—that of a storyteller seeking to bewitch listeners'—that does not differ much from one place or time to another.

To understand this process more fully, it might help if we put ourselves through a kind of cleansing process. We will be better able to grasp the power of these early stories—and share some of the amazement they brought to their audiences—if we make an effort to recreate the context of the telling. We should try to imagine, then, what the world must have been like before the transformations brought on by technology and instant communications.

Living as we do now in a world where instant access to information is the rule, we may find it difficult to picture the pre-electronic past. But consider: At least until the middle of the nineteenth century (and to this day in certain places), most people grew up, lived, labored, and died within a few miles of their birthplace; practically everyone lived in harsh rural surroundings. Few had the knowledge or leisure for reading or learning. Information about the world—discoveries, battles, natural disasters—came in stray fragments, largely by word-of-mouth. Whereas we might watch a talk show or the nightly news, or read a book or a newspaper, earlier audiences most likely gathered in groups near a fire or stove to hear stories or reports from the mouth of a teller, be it a traveler passing through or a member of the community possessed of narrative skills.

The selections in this section can best be appreciated if we keep in mind the circumstances of their original telling. This is not to say that they cannot bring pleasure and instruction in their printed form (they were selected because they *could*), but the reader is likely to gain a deeper appreciation for the origins and history of the storytelling art if the effort to understand the original context is made. Just as we cannot grasp the full magic of movies without sitting before a big screen in a crowded theater, so we cannot get the full effect of the stories emerging out of the oral tradition without transporting ourselves in imagination to the circumstances in which they were told.

Let's stay with this notion just a moment longer. Here, on the one hand, is a student in the late twentieth century reading a selection from Homer that has been translated from the ancient Greek into English; edited, simplified, and arranged into lines of paragraphed prose; and sandwiched among a dozen other excerpts of diverse origins. Picture, on the other hand, the original circumstances of teller and listeners before the world was known to be a sphere, before giants, heroes, and gods had been reduced in status to "interesting myths." As a bard wove the incidents and descriptions into a rhythmic chant, the listeners were fascinated, amused, horrified, uplifted. Can we say that the two audiences experience *anything* in common? What is for us a collection of obscure places and people was for the ancient Greeks a body of meaningful lore. We labor to keep the plot outlines clear, perhaps even consult a reference book. The first listeners, however, followed the twists and turns of the story as readily as we follow gossip that concerns us.

And yet, with a patient effort to suspend disbelief, we can recover at least some of the force and interest felt by the original audiences. For the story form is itself a time-tested device—it works. We are lifted up from our daily lives into the atmosphere of the extraordinary. If we allow ourselves to identify with the hero Odysseus and accept the terms of his situation—he is journeying homeward with his men after the long years of battle at Troy—the forward momentum of the narrative will do the rest. For Homer knew how to pull his audiences along from scene to scene by using suspense.

The reader of the Cyclops episode will see how Odysseus and his men first approach the one-eyed giant in a spirit of trust, only to have their expectations completely reversed. The creature is suspicious, then cruel. He captures the hero and his men and imprisons them in his cave. Then, without so much as a blink of his enormous eye, he begins his cannibal feast. Odysseus is, of course, terrified. But he is also the responsible leader and a man of rare cunning. So he devises a plan. . . . Homer hooks us, playing on our fears but also gratifying our intelligence; his descriptions set the scene, but they never get in the way of the pace. When Odysseus finally drives the sharpened stake into the giant's eye, we feel relief and exaltation.

The other tales will, naturally, elicit different responses. The cultural and historical circumstances vary tremendously. Homer's Greece, twelfth-century Japan, medieval Arabia, fourteenth-century Italy are very different settings. And certainly the kinds of stories told, and the specifics of the telling—Apuleius' grisly fancies, Rabelais' lusty catalogs of exaggeration—have little in common, at least at first glance. But we should remember that each of these tales (even those originally *written*: by Rabelais, Boccaccio, and Apuleius) has its roots in the age-old oral tradition. At the core of each, without exception, we find some of the dynamism that arises whenever teller and listeners come together.

There are other similarities as well, similarities that will seem more striking once we have had a chance to compare these early narratives with those of more recent vintage:

1) The tales are seldom realistic. The psychology of the characters may be credible, but the situations themselves—the plot premises—are very often uncanny: Coincidences abound; prophecies are made and fulfilled; gods and goddesses come down from Olympus to interfere in the lives of humans. In Homer we read about a one-eyed giant; Apuleius asks us to believe that the spirit of a dead man can be made to return to the corpse in order to give testimony; the selection from *The Arabian Nights* turns upon the fulfillment of the strangest of prophecies.

2) To a modern reader, the characters may seem flat, psychologically one-dimensional. In part, this is because the story focuses on deeds, not motives. The oral tradition was based on a teller-listener compact—people wanted to know of miraculous doings and enchanted places. One could almost think of character as a device necessary for plot development. Simple

outlines sufficed: a brave and resourceful Odysseus; passionate and noble-hearted lovers in Boccaccio; a lusty Pantagruel in Rabelais.

3) Much of the action, or plot, depends upon vivid confrontations and acts of violence. A character is insulted or attacked and seeks retribution. In the tale from Boccaccio, the watchful father seeks to thwart his daughter and her lover and ends up cutting the young man's heart out. Cinderella's stepsisters mock and belittle the heroine, only to have their eyes pecked out by birds at the end.

4) Most of these narratives unfold in no specific place or time. Although several of the tales give some attention to geography—the Cyclops needs to be on an island with high crags and with caves for the drama to progress, for instance—this mainly serves the action. Places are often fantastical (as in the tale from *The Arabian Nights*) or unimportant (as in "Cinderella"). In the same way, the *when* of the story is all but irrelevant. A great many of these stories were passed along from person to person and place to place over generations. The specifics of time and place, if they ever existed, would have been worn away or changed by repeated telling. More important, these narratives functioned as windows upon the marvelous—their purpose was to carry listeners away from real space and time.

5) Finally, the tales tend to unfold in fairly formulaic patterns. Scholars like the Russian folklorist Vladimir Propp, who devoted years to studying and cataloging tales, especially those gathered from oral tradition, have found that the majority conform to one of a very few basic patterns. This is partly a function of subject matter. (There are only so many good ways to tell a story.) Also, one might argue, these simple patterns are archetypes that have proved to elicit certain reactions from listeners, like the laws of musical harmony or color values in paintings. On a simpler level, one might note that because oral tradition depended upon memory and repetition, stories were bound to be structured in terms of the most readily recollected patterns.

These five characteristics of early narrative make perfect sense—indeed, appear inevitable—if we pay heed to the circumstances of oral transmission. The act of telling naturally imposes a whole set of constraints upon the teller, constraints that will change once words become fixed on the printed page.

The writings preserved as the Old and New Testaments, which together form the Christian Bible, are cornerstones of Western sacred and cultural tradition. Of the thirty-nine books of the Old Testament (the Jewish Bible), "Genesis" is perhaps the best known. It tells of the creation of the universe, of Adam and Eve, and of the first human generations. The enormous authority of the biblical texts went unquestioned for many centuries. Only with the ascendancy of the scientific world view in the eighteenth and nineteenth centuries was the factual truth of the creation story questioned. Even now some religious groups maintain that the biblical account of creation is factual.

Whatever the factual status of Old Testament texts, their central place in Western art and literature is beyond dispute. The story of Adam and Eve, included here, can be seen as one of the earliest attempts to account for human origins. It is, at the same time, a powerfully suggestive depiction of human moral and sexual awakening. Short though the narrative is, it exhibits many of the features that are now seen as central to the storytelling tradition.

The origins of the Old Testament texts will probably never be exactly established. Certainly, many of the tales, genealogies, and laws were passed along for generations by word-of-mouth before they were set down in classical Hebrew. Scholars cite a period of ten centuries—from the twelfth to the second centuries B.C.—as the probable period of composition. They speculate that one strong motive for making a written record of the materials may have been the capture of Jerusalem by the Babylonians in 587 B.C.

The earliest surviving manuscripts that contain any portions of the Old Testament (called the Dead Sea Scrolls) date from 100 B.C. to A.D. 135; they were discovered in caves near the Dead Sea in 1947. The full text of the Old Testament is thought to have been assembled from many source manuscripts, a number of which contain mistakes made by copyists. For all of this, the work looms massively over centuries of secular and spiritual life.

GENESIS

from the Old Testament

In the beginning of creation, when God made heaven and earth,[a] the earth was without form and void, with darkness over the face of the abyss, and a mighty wind that swept[b] over the surface of the waters. God said, 'Let there be light', and there was light;

[a]*Or* In the beginning God created heaven and earth.
[b]*Or* and the spirit of God hovering.

and God saw that the light was good, and he separated light from darkness. He called the light day, and the darkness night. So evening came, and morning came, the first day.

God said, 'Let there be a vault between the waters, to separate water from water.' So God made the vault, and separated the water under the vault from the water above it, and so it was; and God called the vault heaven. Evening came, and morning came, a second day.

God said, 'Let the waters under heaven be gathered into one place, so that dry land may appear'; and so it was. God called the dry land earth, and the gathering of the waters he called seas; and God saw that it was good. Then God said, 'Let the earth produce fresh growth, let there be on the earth plants bearing seed, fruit-trees bearing fruit each with seed according to its kind.' So it was; the earth yielded fresh growth, plants bearing seed according to their kind and trees bearing fruit each with seed according to its kind; and God saw that it was good. Evening came, and morning came, a third day.

God said, 'Let there be lights in the vault of heaven to separate day from night, and let them serve as signs both for festivals and for seasons and years. Let them also shine in the vault of heaven to give light on earth.' So it was; God made the two great lights, the greater to govern the day and the lesser to govern the night; and with them he made the stars. God put these lights in the vault of heaven to give light on earth, to govern day and night, and to separate light from darkness; and God saw that it was good. Evening came, and morning came, a fourth day.

God said, 'Let the waters teem with countless living creatures, and let birds fly above the earth across the *vault* of heaven.' God then created the great sea-monsters and all living creatures that move and swarm in the waters, according to their kind, and every kind of bird; and God saw that it was good. So he blessed them and said, 'Be fruitful and increase, fill the waters of the seas; and let the birds increase on land.' Evening came, and morning came, a fifth day.

God said, 'Let the earth bring forth living creatures, according to their kind: cattle, reptiles, and wild animals, all according to their kind.' So it was; God made wild animals, cattle, and all reptiles, each according to its kind; and he saw that it was good. Then God said, 'Let us make man in our image and likeness to rule the fish in the sea, the birds of heaven, the cattle, all wild animals on earth, and all reptiles that crawl upon the earth.' So God created man in his own image; in the image of God he created him; male and female he created them. God blessed them and said to them, 'Be fruitful and increase, fill the earth and subdue it, rule over the fish in the sea, the birds of heaven, and every living thing that moves upon the earth.' God also said, 'I give you all plants that bear seed everywhere on earth, and every tree bearing fruit which yields seed: they shall be yours for food. All green plants I give for food to the wild animals, to all the birds of heaven, and to all reptiles on earth, every living creature.' So it was; and God saw all that he had made, and it was very good. Evening came, and morning came, a sixth day.

Thus heaven and earth were completed with all their mighty throng. On the sixth day God completed all the work he had been doing, and on the seventh day he ceased from all his work. God blessed the seventh day and made it holy, because on that day he ceased from all the work he had set himself to do.

This is the story of the making of heaven and earth when they were created.

WHEN THE LORD GOD MADE EARTH AND HEAVEN, there was neither shrub nor plant growing wild upon the earth, because the LORD God had sent no rain on the earth; nor was there any man to till the ground. A flood[a] used to rise out of the earth and water all the surface of the ground. Then the LORD God formed a man[b] from the dust of the ground[c] and breathed into his nostrils the breath of life. Thus the man became a living creature. Then the LORD God planted a garden in Eden away to the east, and there he put the man whom he had formed. The LORD God made trees spring from the ground, all trees pleasant to look at and good for food; and in the middle of the garden he set the tree of life and the tree of the knowledge of good and evil.

There was a river flowing from Eden to water the garden, and when it left the garden it branched into four streams. The name of the first is Pishon; that is the river which encircles all the land of Havilah, where the gold[d] is. The gold[d] of that land is good; bdellium[e] and cornelians are also to be found there. The name of the second river is Gihon; this is the one which encircles all the land of Cush. The name of the third is Tigris; this is the river which runs east of Asshur. The fourth river is the Euphrates.

The LORD God took the man and put him in the garden of Eden to till it and care for it. He told the man, 'You may eat from every tree in the garden, but not from the tree of the knowledge of good and evil; for on the day that you eat from it, you will certainly die.' Then the LORD God said, 'It is not good for the man to be alone. I will provide a partner for him.' So God formed out of the ground all the wild animals and all the birds of heaven. He brought them to the man to see what he would call them, and whatever the man called each living creature, that was its name. Thus the man gave names to all cattle, to the birds of heaven, and to every wild animal; but for the man himself no partner had yet been found. And so the LORD God put the man into a trance, and while he slept, he took one of his ribs and closed the flesh over the place. The LORD God then built up the rib, which he had taken out of the man, into a woman. He brought her to the man, and the man said:

[a] *Or* mist. [b] *Heb.* adam. [c] *Heb.* adamah. [d] *Or* frankincense. [e] *Or* gum resin.

Now this, at last—
bone from my bones,
flesh from my flesh!—
this shall be called woman,[a]
for from man[b] was this taken.

That is why a man leaves his father and mother and is united to his wife, and the two become one flesh. Now they were both naked, the man and his wife, but they had no feeling of shame towards one another.

THE SERPENT WAS MORE CRAFTY than any wild creature that the LORD God had made. He said to the woman, 'Is it true that God has forbidden you to eat from any tree in the garden?' The woman answered the serpent, 'We may eat the fruit of any tree in the garden, except for the tree in the middle of the garden; God has forbidden us either to eat or to touch the fruit of that; if we do, we shall die.' The serpent said, 'Of course you will not die. God knows that as soon as you eat it, your eyes will be opened and you will be like gods[c] knowing both good and evil.' When the woman saw that the fruit of the tree was good to eat, and that it was pleasing to the eye and tempting to contemplate, she took some and ate it. She also gave her husband some and he ate it. Then the eyes of both of them were opened and they discovered that they were naked; so they stitched fig-leaves together and made themselves loincloths.

The man and his wife heard the sound of the LORD God walking in the garden at the time of the evening breeze and hid from the LORD God among the trees of the garden. But the LORD God called to the man and said to him, 'Where are you?' He replied, 'I heard the sound as you were walking in the garden, and I was afraid because I was naked, and I hid myself.' God answered, 'Who told you that you were naked? Have you eaten from the tree which I forbade you?' The man said, 'The woman you gave me for a companion, she gave me fruit from the tree and I ate it.' Then the LORD God said to the woman, 'What is this that you have done?' The woman said, 'The serpent tricked me, and I ate.' Then the LORD God said to the serpent:

Because you have done this you are accursed
more than all cattle and all wild creatures.
On your belly you shall crawl, and dust you shall eat
all the days of your life.
I will put enmity between you and the woman,
between your brood and hers.
They shall strike at your head,
and you shall strike at their heel.

[a] *Heb.* ishshah. [b] *Heb.* ish. [c] *Or* God.

To the woman he said:

I will increase your labour and your groaning,
and in labour you shall bear children.
You shall be eager[a] for your husband,
and he shall be your master.

And to the man he said:

Because you have listened to your wife
and have eaten from the tree which I forbade you,
accursed shall be the ground on your account.
With labour you shall win your food from it
all the days of your life.
It will grow thorns and thistles for you,
none but wild plants for you to eat.
You shall gain your bread by the sweat of your
brow until you return to the ground;
for from it you were taken.
Dust you are, to dust you shall return.

The man called his wife Eve[b] because she was the mother of all who live. The LORD God made tunics of skins for Adam and his wife and clothed them. He said, 'The man has become like one of us, knowing good and evil; what if he now reaches out his hand and takes fruit from the tree of life also, eats it and lives for ever?' So the LORD God drove him out of the garden of Eden to till the ground from which he had been taken. He cast him out, and to the east of the garden of Eden he stationed the cherubim and a sword whirling and flashing to guard the way to the tree of life.

QUESTIONS

The Biblical creation story, passed along for untold centuries in the Hebrew oral tradition, can be considered one of the earliest structured narratives.

1. Identify and discuss some of the conventional storytelling elements (protagonist, antagonist, symbol, suspense, climax, resolution). While keeping in mind that this sacred text was not composed to be a story, evaluate its success and failure from an objective standpoint.

2. Is the simplicity essential? If so, why? Would the impact be different if the story were told more fully, with more suspense and character development? How so?

3. How much do we learn about Adam and Eve? Can they be said to have personalities, or are they meant to be representative types? If so, what does their portrayal suggest about the nature of man and woman?

[a]*Or* feel an urge. [b]*That* is Life.

4. Comment upon the roles of Adam and Eve in this story. Are we to see them as wrongdoers or as victims?

5. Does the punishment fit the crime? What values and beliefs of the early Hebrews are apparent in this biblical text?

Homer

Scholars have been wrangling for centuries as to whether Homer, the blind Greek poet of legend, really lived. And they dispute to this day whether the celebrated books the *Iliad* and the *Odyssey* bear the stamp of a single author or might have been pieced together from a variety of sources in the Greek oral tradition. As Homer, if he existed, would have lived in the eighth or ninth century B.C. and the Greeks did not implement writing until the fifth century B.C., the question may never be resolved.

The popular image of Homer is an attractive one: a wise, bearded, blind bard who composed, remembered, and recited the vivid stories of the Trojan War and of the homeward wanderings of the hero Odysseus and his men. In the absence of definitive contradictory evidence, we may wish to regard this image as true.

The *Odyssey*, from which the episode of the Cyclops is drawn, begins ten years after the sack of Troy by the Greek king Agamemnon and his warriors. It traces, with many a flashback, Odysseus' journey to his ancestral home at Ithaca. When the narrative begins, the hero has been detained against his will on a remote island by the nymph Calypso. At a council of the Olympian gods, Zeus rules that Odysseus be allowed to continue his voyage. But the Greek seas are dotted with alluring and dangerous islands, and Odysseus will not rejoin his wife, Penelope, and son, Telemachus, until he has suffered through an elaborate series of ordeals. The visit to the island of Polyphemus, the Cyclops ("one-eyed monster"), is just one of many tests of his courage and resourcefulness.

THE CYCLOPS

from the *Odyssey*

For nine days I was chased by those accursed winds across the fish-infested seas. But on the tenth we made the country of the Lotus-eaters, a race that live on vegetable foods. We disembarked to draw water, and my crews quickly set to on their midday meal by the ships. But as soon as we had a mouthful and a drink, I sent some of my followers inland to find out what sort of human beings might be there, detailing two men for the duty with a third as messenger. Off they went, and it was not long before they were in touch with the Lotus-eaters. Now it never entered the heads of these natives to kill my friends; what they did was to give them some lotus to taste, and as soon as each had eaten the honeyed fruit of the plant, all thoughts of reporting to us or escaping were banished from his mind. All they now wished for was to stay where they were with the Lotus-eaters, to browse on the lotus, and to forget that they had a home to return to. I had to use force to bring them back to the ships, and they wept on the way, but once on board I dragged them under the benches and left them in irons. I then commanded the rest of my loyal band to embark with all speed on their fast ships, for fear that others of them might eat the lotus and think no more of home. They came on board at once, went to the benches, sat down in their proper places, and struck the white surf with their oars.

So we left that country and sailed on sick at heart. And we came to the land of the Cyclopes, a fierce, uncivilized people who never lift a hand to plant or plough but put their trust in Providence. All the crops they require spring up unsown and untilled, wheat and barley and the vines whose generous clusters give them wine when ripened for them by the timely rains. The Cyclopes have no assemblies for the making of laws, nor any settled customs, but live in hollow caverns in the mountain heights, where each man is lawgiver to his children and his wives, and nobody cares a jot for his neighbours.

Not very far from the harbour on their coast, and not so near either, there lies a luxuriant island, covered with woods, which is the home of innumerable goats. The goats are wild, for man has made no pathways that might frighten them off, nor do hunters visit the island with their hounds to rough it in the forests and to range the mountain-tops. Used neither for grazing nor for ploughing, it lies for ever unsown and untilled; and this land where no man goes makes a happy pasture for the bleating goats. I must explain that the Cyclopes have nothing like our ships with their crimson prows; nor have they any shipwrights to build merchantmen that could serve their needs by plying to foreign ports in the course of that overseas traffic which ships have established between the nations. Such craftsmen would have turned the island into a fine colony for the Cyclopes. For it is by no means a poor country, but capable of yielding any crop in due season. Along the shore of the grey sea there are soft water-meadows where the vine would never wither; and there is plenty of land level enough for the plough, where they could count on cutting a deep crop at every harvesttime, for the soil below the surface is exceedingly rich. Also it has a safe harbour, in which there is no occasion to tie up at all. You need neither cast anchor nor make fast with hawsers: all your crew have to do is to beach their boat and wait till the spirit moves them and the right wind blows. Finally, at the head of the harbour there is a stream of fresh water, running out of a cave in a grove of poplar-trees.

This is where we came to land. Some god must have guided us through the murky night, for it was impossible to see ahead. The ships were in a thick fog, and overhead not a gleam of light came through from the moon, which was obscured by clouds. In these circumstances not a man among us caught sight of the island nor did we even see the long rollers beating up to the coast, before our good ships ran aground. It was not till they were beached that we lowered sail. We then jumped out on the shore, fell asleep where we were and so waited for the blessed light of day.

When the fresh Dawn came and with her crimson streamers lit the sky, we were delighted with what we saw of the island and set out to explore it. Presently, in order that my company might have something to eat, the Nymphs, those Children of Zeus, set the mountain goats on the move. Directly we saw them we fetched our curved bows and our long spears from the ships, separated into three parties, and let fly at the game; and in a short time Providence had sent us a satisfactory bag. There were twelve ships in my squadron: nine goats fell to each, while to me they made a special allotment of ten. So the whole day long till the sun set we sat and enjoyed this rich supply of meat, which we washed down by mellow wine, since the ships had not yet run dry of our red vintage. There was still some in the holds, for when we took the sacred citadel of the Cicones, every member of the company had drawn off a generous supply in jars. There we sat, and as we looked across at the neighbouring land of the Cyclopes, we could not only see the smoke from their fires but hear their voices and the bleating of their sheep and goats. The sun went down, night fell, and we slept on the sea-shore.

With the first rosy light of Dawn, I assembled my company and gave them their orders. "My good friends," I said, "for the time being I want you to stay here, while I go in my own ship with my own crew to find out what kind of men are over there, and whether they are brutal and lawless savages or hospitable and god-fearing people."

Then I climbed into my ship and told my men to follow me and loose the hawsers. They came on board at once, went to the benches, sat down in their places and churned the grey water with their oars. It was no great distance to the mainland coast. As we approached its nearest point, we made out a cave there, close to the sea, was a high entrance overhung by laurels. Here large flocks of sheep and goats were penned at night, and round the mouth a yard had been built with a great wall of stones bedded deep between tall pines and high-branched oaks. It was the den of a giant, the lonely shepherd of sequestered flocks, who had no truck with others of his kind but lived aloof in his own lawless way. And what a formidable monster he was! No one would have taken him for a man who ate bread like ourselves; he reminded one rather of some wooded peak in the high hills, lifting itself in solitary state.

At this point, I told the rest of my loyal following to stay there on guard by the ship while I myself picked out the twelve best men in the company and advanced. I took with me in a goatskin some dark and mellow wine which had been given to me by Maron son of Euanthes, the priest of Apollo (who was patron-deity of Ismarus), because we had protected him and his child and wife out of respect for his office, when we came upon his home in a grove of trees sacred to Phoebus Apollo. This man made me some fine presents: he gave me seven talents of wrought gold, with a mixing-bowl of solid silver, and he drew off for me as well a full dozen jars of mellow unmixed wine. And a wonderful drink it was. It had been kept secret from all his serving-men and maids, in fact from everyone in the house but himself, his good wife, and a single stewardess. When they drank this red and honeyed vintage, he used to pour one cupful of wine into twenty of water, and the sweet fumes that came up from the bowl were irresistible—those were occasions when abstinence could have no charms.

Well, I filled a big bottle with this wine and took some food in a wallet along with me also; for I had an instant foreboding, though I am no coward, that we were going to find ourselves face to face with some being of colossal strength and ferocity, to whom the law of man and god meant nothing. It took us very little time to reach the cave, but we did not find its owner at home: he was tending his fat sheep in the pastures. So we went inside and had a good look round. There were baskets laden with cheeses, and the folds were thronged with lambs and kids, each class, the firstlings, the summer lambs, and the little ones, being separately penned. All his well-made vessels, the pails and bowls he used for milking, were swimming with whey.

Now my men's idea was first to make off with some of the cheeses, then come back, drive the kids and lambs quickly out of of the pens down to the good ship, and so set sail across the salt water. They pleaded with me; but though it would have been far better so, I was not to be persuaded. I wished to see the owner of the cave and had hopes of some friendly gifts from my host. As things fell out, my company were to have an unpleasant surprise when he did put in an appearance.

We lit a fire, killed a beast and made offerings, took some cheeses just for ourselves, and when we had eaten, sat down in the cave to await his arrival. At last he came up, shepherding his flocks and carrying a huge bundle of dry wood to burn at supper-time. With a great din he cast this down inside the cavern, giving us such a fright that we hastily retreated to an inner recess. Meanwhile he drove his fat sheep into the wider part of the cave—I mean all the ewes that he milked: the rams and he-goats he left out of doors in the walled yard. He then picked up a huge stone, with which he closed the entrance. It was a mighty slab, such as you couldn't have budged from the ground, not with a score of heavy four-wheeled waggons to help you. That will give you some idea of the monstrous size of the rock with which he closed the cave. Next he sat down to milk his ewes and bleating goats, which he did methodically, putting her young to each mother as he finished. He then curdled half the white milk, gathered it all up, and stored it in wicker baskets; the remainder he left standing in pails, so that it would be handy at supper-time and when he wanted a drink. When he had done with his business and finished all his jobs, he lit up the fire, spied us, and began asking questions.

"Strangers!" he said. "And who may you be? Where do you hail from over the highways of the sea? Is yours a trading venture; or are you cruising the main on chance, like roving pirates, who risk their lives to ruin other people?"

Our hearts sank within us. The booming voice and the very sight of the monster filled us with panic. Still, I managed to find words to answer him.

"We are Achaeans," I said, "on our way back from Troy, driven astray by contrary winds across a vast expanse of sea. Far from planning to come here, we meant to sail straight home; but we lost our bearings, as Zeus, I suppose, intended that we should. We are proud to belong to the forces of Agamemnon, Atreus' son, who by sacking the great city of Ilium and destroying all its armies has made himself the most famous man in the world today. We, less fortunate, are visiting you here as suppliants, in the hope that you may give us friendly entertainment or even go further in your generosity. You know the laws of hospitality: I beseech you, good sir, to remember your duty to the gods. For we throw ourselves on your mercy; and Zeus is there to avenge the suppliant and the guest. He is the travellers' god: he guards their steps and he invites them with their rights."

So said I, and promptly he answered me out of his pitiless heart: "Stranger, you must be a fool, or must have come from very far afield, to preach to me of fear or reverence for the gods. We Cyclopes care not a jot for Zeus with his aegis, nor for the rest of the blessed gods, since we are much stronger than they. It would never occur to me to spare you or your men against my will for fear of trouble from Zeus. But tell me where you moored your good ship when you came. Was it somewhere up the coast, or near by? I should like to see her."

He was trying to get the better of me, but I knew enough of the world to see through him and I met him with deceit.

"As for my ship," I answered, "it was wrecked by the Earthshaker Poseidon on the confines of your land. The wind had carried us onto a lee shore. He drove the ship up to a headland and hurtled it on the rocks. But I and my friends here managed to escape with our lives."

To this the cruel brute made no reply. Instead, he jumped up, and reaching out towards my men, seized a couple and dashed their heads against the floor as though they had been puppies. Their brains ran out on the ground and soaked the earth. Limb by limb he tore them to pieces to make his meal, which he devoured like a mountain lion, never pausing till entrails and flesh, marrow and bones, were all consumed, while we could do nothing but weep and lift up our hands to Zeus in horror at the ghastly sight, paralysed by our sense of utter helplessness. When the Cyclops had filled his great belly with this meal of human flesh, which he washed down with unwatered milk, he stretched himself out for sleep among his flocks inside the cave. And now my manhood prompted me to action: I thought I would draw my sharp sword from the scabbard at my side, creep up to him, feel for the right place with my hand and stab him in the breast where the liver is supported by the midriff. But on second thoughts I refrained, realizing that we should have perished there as surely as the Cyclops, for we should have found it impossible with our unaided hands to push aside the huge rock with which he had closed the great mouth of the cave. So for the time being we just sat groaning there and waited for the blessed light of day.

No sooner had the tender Dawn shown her roses in the East, than the Cyclops lit up the fire and milked his splendid ewes, all in their proper order, putting her young to each. This business over and his morning labours done, he once more snatched up a couple of my men and prepared his meal. When he had eaten, he turned his fatted sheep out of the cave, removing the great doorstone without an effort. But he replaced it immediately, as easily as though he were putting the lid on a quiver. Then, with many a whistle, he drove his rich flocks off towards the high pasture, while I was left, with murder in my heart, beating about for some scheme by which I might pay him back if only Athene would grant me my prayer. The best plan I could think of was this. Lying by the pen, the Cyclops had a huge staff of green olive-wood, which he had cut to carry in his hand when it was seasoned. To us it looked more like the mast of some black ship of twenty oars, a broad-bottomed freighter such as they use for long sea voyages. That was the impression which its length and thickness made on us. On this piece of timber I set to work and cut off a fathom's length, which I handed over to my men and told them to smooth down. When they had dressed it, I took a hand and sharpened it to a point. Then I poked it into the blazing fire to make it hard, and finally I laid it carefully by, hiding it under the dung, of which there were heaps scattered in profusion throughout the cave. I then told my company to cast lots among themselves for the dangerous task of helping me to lift the pole and twist it in the Cyclops' eye when he was sound asleep. The lot fell on the very men that I myself should have chosen, four of them, so that counting myself we made a party of five.

Evening came, and with it the Cyclops, shepherding his woolly sheep, every one of which he herded into the broad part of the cave, leaving none out in the walled yard, either because he suspected something or because a god had warned him. He raised the great doorstone, set it in its place, and then sat down to milk his ewes and bleating goats, which he did in an orderly way, giving each mother its young one in due course. When this business was over and his work finished, he once more seized upon two of us and prepared his supper. Then came my chance. With an ivy-wood bowl of my dark wine in my hands, I went up to him and said: "Here, Cyclops, have some wine to wash down that meal of human flesh, and find out for yourself what kind of vintage was stored away in our ship's hold. I brought it for you by way of an offering in the hope that you would be charitable and help me on my homeward way. But your savagery is more than we can bear. Cruel monster, how can you expect ever to have a visitor again from the world of men, after such deeds as you have done?"

The Cyclops took the wine and drank it up. And the delicious draught gave him such exquisite pleasure that he asked me for another bowlful.

"Be good enough," he said, "to let me have some more; and tell me your name, here and now, so that I may make you a gift that you will value. We Cyclopes have wine of our own made from the grapes that our rich soil and timely rains produce. But this vintage of yours is nectar and ambrosia distilled."

So said the Cyclops, and I handed him another bowlful of the ruddy wine. Three times I filled up for him; and three times the fool drained the bowl to the dregs. At last, when the wine had fuddled his wits, I addressed him with disarming suavity.

"Cyclops," I said, "you wish to know the name I bear. I'll tell it to you; and in return I should like to have the gift you promised me. My name is Nobody. That is what I am called by my mother and father and by all my friends."

The Cyclops answered me with a cruel jest. "Of all his company I will eat Nobody last, and the rest before him. That shall be your gift."

He had hardly spoken before he toppled over and fell face upwards on the floor, where he lay with his great neck twisted to one side, conquered, as all men are, by sleep. His drunkenness made him vomit, and a stream of wine mixed with morsels of men's flesh poured from his throat. I went at once and thrust our pole deep under the ashes of the fire to make it hot, and meanwhile gave a word of encouragement to all my men, to make sure that no one should play the coward and leave me in the lurch. When the fierce glow from the olive stake warned me that it was about to catch alight in the flames, green as it was, I withdrew it from the fire and brought it over to the spot where my men were standing ready. Heaven now inspired them with a reckless courage. Seizing the olive pole, they drove its sharpened end into the Cyclops' eye, while I used my weight from above to twist it home, like a man boring a ship's timber with a drill which his mates below him twirl with a strap they hold at either end, so that it spins continuously. In much the same way we handled our pole with its red-hot point and twisted it in his eye till the blood boiled up round the burning wood. The fiery smoke from the blazing eyeball singed his lids and brow all round, and the very roots of his eye crackled in the heat. I was reminded of the loud hiss that comes from a great axe or adze when a smith plunges it into cold water—to temper it and give strength to the iron. That is how the Cyclops' eye hissed round the olive stake. He gave a dreadful shriek, which echoed round the rocky walls, and we backed away from him in terror, while he pulled the stake from his eye, streaming with blood. Then he hurled it away from him with frenzied hands and raised a great shout for the other Cyclopes who lived in neighbouring caves along the windy heights.

These, hearing his screams, came up from every quarter, and gathering outside the cave asked him what ailed him:

"What on earth is wrong with you, Polyphemus? Why must you disturb the peaceful night and spoil our sleep with all this shouting? Is a robber driving off your sheep, or is somebody trying by treachery or violence to kill you?"

Out of the cave came Polyphemus' great voice in reply: "O my friends, it's Nobody's treachery, no violence, that is doing me to death."

"Well, then," they answered, in a way that settled the matter, "if nobody is assaulting you in your solitude, you must be sick. Sickness comes from almighty Zeus and cannot be helped. All you can do is to pray to your father, the Lord Poseidon."

And off they went, while I chuckled to myself at the way in which my happy *notion* of a false name had taken them in. The Cyclops, still moaning in agonies of pain, groped about with his hands and pushed the rock away from the mouth of the cave. But then he sat himself down in the doorway and stretched out both arms in the hope of catching us in the act of slipping out among the sheep. What a fool he must have thought me! Meanwhile I was cudgelling my brains for the best possible course, trying to hit on some way of saving my friends as well as my own skin. Plan after plan, dodge after dodge, passed through my mind. It was a matter of life or death: we were in mortal peril. And this was the scheme I eventually chose. There were in the flock some well-bred, thick-fleeced rams, fine, big animals in their coats of black wool. These I quietly lashed together with the plaited withes which the savage monster used for his bed. I took them in threes. The middle one in each case was to carry one of my followers, while its fellows went on either side to protect him. Each of my men thus had three sheep to bear him. But for myself I chose a full-grown ram who was the pick of the whole flock. Seizing him by the back, I curled myself up under his shaggy belly and lay there upside down, with a firm grip on his wonderful fleece and with patience in my heart. Thus in fear and trembling we waited for the blessed Dawn.

As soon as she arrived and flecked the East with red, the rams of the flock began to scramble out and make for the pastures, but the ewes, unmilked as they were and with udders full to bursting, stood bleating by the pens. Their master, though he was worn out by the agonies he had gone through, passed his hands along the backs of all the animals as they came to a stand before him; but the idiot never noticed that my men were tied up under the breasts of his own woolly sheep. The last of the flock to come up to the doorway was the big ram, burdened by his own fleece and by me with my teeming brain. As he felt him with his hands the great Polyphemus broke into speech:

"Sweet ram," he said, "what does this mean? Why are you the last of the flock to pass out of the cave, you who have never lagged behind the sheep, you who always step so proudly out and are the first of them to crop the lush shoots of the grass, first to make your way to the flowing stream, and first to turn your head homewards to the sheepfold when the evening falls? Yet today you are the last of all. Are you grieved for your master's eye, blinded by wicked man and his accursed friends, when he had robbed me of my wits with wine? Nobody was his name; and I swear that he has not yet saved his skin! Ah, if only you could feel as I do and find a voice to tell me where he's hiding from my fury! Wouldn't I hammer him and splash his brains all over the floor of the cave, till that miserable Nobody had eased my heart of the suffering I owe to him!"

So he passed the ram out; and when we had put a little distance between ourselves and the courtyard of the cave, I first freed myself from under my ram and next untied my men from theirs. Then, quickly, though with many a backward look, we drove our long-legged sheep right down to the ship—and a rich, fat flock they made. My dear companions were overjoyed when they caught sight of us survivors, though their relief soon changed to lamentation for their slaughtered friends. I would have none of this weeping, however, and with a nod made clear my will to each, bidding them make haste instead to tumble all the fleecy sheep on board and put to sea. So in they jumped, ran to the benches, sorted themselves out, and plied the grey water with their oars.

But before we were out of earshot, I let Polyphemus have a piece of my mind. "Cyclops!" I called. "So he was not such a weakling after all, the man whose friends you meant to overpower and eat in that snug cave of yours! And your crimes came home to roost, you brute, who have not even the decency to refrain from devouring your own guests. Now Zeus and all his fellow-gods have paid you out."

My taunts so exasperated the angry Cyclops that he tore the top off a great pinnacle of rock and hurled it at us. The rock fell just ahead of our blue-painted bows. As it plunged in, the water rose and the backwash, like a swell from the open sea, swept us landward and nearly drove us on the beach. Seizing a long pole, I succeeded in punting her off, at the same time rousing my crew with urgent nods to dash in with their oars and save us from disaster. They buckled to and rowed with a will; but when they had brought us across the water to twice our previous distance I was for giving the Cyclops some more of my talk, though from all parts of the ship my men's voices were raised in gentle remonstrance.

"Aren't you rash, sir," they said, "to provoke this savage? The rock he threw into the sea just now drove the ship back to the land, and we thought we were done for then and there. Had he heard a cry, or so much as a word, from a single man, he'd have smashed in our heads and the ship's timbers with another jagged boulder from his hand. You have seen how he can throw!"

But all this went for nothing with me. My spirit was up, and in my rage I called to him once more:

"Cyclops, if anyone ever asks you how you came by your unsightly blindness, tell him your eye was put out by Odysseus, Sacker of Cities, the son of Laertes, who lives in Ithaca."

The Cyclops gave a groan. "Alas!" he cried. "So the old prophecy has come home to me with a vengeance! We had a prophet with us once, a fine, upstanding man, Telemus son of Eurymus, who was an excellent seer and grew old among us in the practice of his art. All that has now happened he foretold, when he warned me that a man called Odysseus would rob me of my sight. But I always expected some big and handsome fellow of tremendous strength to come along. And now, a puny, good for nothing, little runt fuddles me with wine and then puts out my eye! But come here, Odysseus, so that I may make you some friendly gifts and prevail on the great Earthshaker to see you safely home. For I am his son, and he is not ashamed to call himself my father. He is the one who will heal me if he's willing—a thing no other blessed god nor any man on earth could do."

To which I shouted in reply: "I only wish I could make as sure of robbing you of life and breath and sending you to Hell, as I am certain that not even the Earthshaker will ever heal your eye."

At this the Cyclops lifted up his hands to the heavens that hold the stars and prayed to the Lord Poseidon: "Hear me, Poseidon, Girdler of Earth, god of the sable locks. If I am yours indeed and you accept me as your son, grant that Odysseus, who styles himself Sacker of Cities and son of Laertes, may never reach his home in Ithaca. But if he is destined to reach his native land, to come once more to his own house and see his friends again, let him come late, in evil plight, with all his comrades dead, and when he is landed, by a foreign ship, let him find trouble in his home."

So Polyphemus prayed; and the god of the sable locks heard his prayer. Then once again the Cyclops picked a boulder up—bigger by far, this time—and hurled it with a swing, putting such boundless force into his throw that the rock fell only just astern of our blue-painted ship, missing the end of the steering-oar by inches. The water heaved up as it plunged into the sea; but the wave that it raised carried us on toward the farther shore. And so we reached our island, where the rest of our good ships were awaiting us in a body, while their crews sat round disconsolate and kept a constant watch for our return. Once there, we beached our ship, jumped out on the shore, and unloaded the Cyclops' sheep from the hold. We then divided our spoil so that no one, as far as I could help it, should go short of his proper share. But my comrades-in-arms did me the special honor, when the sheep were distributed, of presenting me with the big ram in addition. Him I sacrificed on the beach, burning slices from his thighs as an offering to Zeus of the Black Clouds, the Son of Cronos, who is lord of us all. But Zeus took no notice of my sacrifice; his mind must already have been full of plans for the destruction of all my gallant ships and of my trusty band.

So the whole day long till sundown we sat and feasted on our rich supply of meat washed down by mellow wine. When the sun set and darkness fell, we lay down to sleep on the sea-shore. But as soon as Dawn first showed her rosy fingers in the East, I roused my men and ordered them to get on board and let the hawsers go. Climbing in at once, they went to the benches, sorted themselves out, and struck the grey water with their oars. Thus we left the island and sailed on with heavy hearts, for the joy we felt at our escape from death was tempered by grief for the dear friends we had lost.

Translated by E. V. Rieu

QUESTIONS

Keeping in mind that this selection is but one self-contained episode from a longer work and that it is a prose translation of a verse epic, answer the following questions:

1. What evidence can you find that this tale is rooted in the oral tradition? Consider the structure, the presentation of characters and action, and the use of formulas and repetitions.
2. If you had only this short selection to go by, what could you guess about the culture it emerged from—the beliefs, codes of behavior, and values of that culture?
3. Odysseus is regarded as one of the first epic heroes. What qualities distinguish him? How does he behave toward his men, and how does his behavior change in time of danger? How does he establish his leadership? Give an example of Odysseus' wisdom, his cunning.
4. In which one instance do we see that Odysseus is fallible? Does this change our view of his character? How?
5. How does Homer use physical description to establish the terrifying presence of Polyphemus? How does he suggest the giant's size?
6. How does Homer achieve and maintain suspense? What specific developments might have made his listeners pay particular attention?
7. Find the places where the gods are mentioned or invoked. Speculate upon their role in the epic and in the Greek culture that spawned it.
8. What is the role of ritual (sacrifice, feasting, and so on) in this episode? What are the codes of expected behavior shared by Odysseus and his men? How does Polyphemus violate these codes?

Apuleius

Apuleius was born about A.D. 123 in the African city of Madaurus, which was then part of the Roman Empire. His schooling took him from Carthage to Athens to Rome. Advised by a friend to marry a wealthy widow, Apuleius was accused of having secured her love by means of witchcraft. He defended himself at the trial (his speech, *Apologia*, was later celebrated for its skillful rhetoric) and was acquitted. Some time later he surfaced again in Carthage, where he achieved renown as a poet and speechmaker. The date of his death is not known.

Apuleius' *The Golden Ass* (known as *Metamorphoses* in Latin) is the only full-length story cycle in Latin to have survived in its entirety. Apuleius recounts the wanderings and adventures of a certain Lucius who, after dabbling too carelessly in the arts of black magic, is turned into an ass. The goddess Isis later restores him to human form.

But the metamorphosis is largely a pretext. In his four-footed condition, Lucius wanders far and wide and encounters a great variety of people. He also hears a good number of stories, which the book recounts with gusto. More than a few, "The Story of Thelyphron" among them, incorporate magic and mystical doctrine, suggesting that Apuleius' accuser may have had some basis for his declaration.

Apuleius' style was greatly influenced by the practice of rhetoric—it is elaborate and studded with strange turns of phrase and archaic words. Robert Graves, who translated *The Golden Ass*, admits to having streamlined and simplified the diction. This may be fortunate, for the plot of this tale is itself full of strange turns.

THE STORY OF THELYPHRON

from The Golden Ass

One day Byrrhaena sent me a pressing invitation to a supper party, and though I made various excuses she refused to accept any of them. There was nothing for it but to go to Fotis, as one might approach the priestess of an oracular shrine, and ask her advice. She now resented my straying a yard from her company, but I was generously excused my military duties that evening and granted a short pass. However, she warned me: 'Listen, darling! Don't stay too long at the party. Come back as soon as you can, for in the early hours Hypata is terrorized by a gang of Mohocks who think it amusing to murder whoever happens to be passing by and to leave the streets strewn with corpses. They are members of the first families in the town, and the nearest Roman barracks are some miles away, so nothing can be done to end the nuisance. You are in particular danger of being attacked, because these Mohocks have no respect for foreigners. And they'll be all the keener to practise their swordmanship on you when they see that you're dressed as a nobleman.'

'You needn't worry, dearest Fotis,' I told her. 'That supper party has far less attraction for me than our love-banquets here; so I promise to shorten your anxiety by coming home as soon as I can. Besides, I shall wear this sword, which I know very well how to handle in self-defence, and take one of my slaves along with me, too.'

The supper party proved to be a regular banquet. Byrrhaena was the leading hostess of Hypata and everybody was there who was anybody. The tables were made of polished citrus wood richly inlaid with ivory; the couches were upholstered in cloth of gold; each of the large wine-cups, though all were of different workmanship, was a masterpiece of its kind—whether of glass encrusted with fine cameos, or cut rock-crystal, or highly polished silver, or gold, or beautifully carved amber, or whether hollowed from some semi-precious stone. In short, think of anything impossible in the way of cups, and there you had it.

A swarm of liveried waiters darting deftly about kept the tables well supplied with food, while pretty curly-headed pages in handsome clothes ran up and down replenishing those jewels of cups with vintage wines of great age.

It was growing dark, so the lights were brought in, and the conversation began to get lively. Byrrhaena turned to me and asked: 'Well, cousin, what do you think of our beloved Thessaly? So far as I know we are a long way in advance of all other countries in the world, if you judge by temples, baths and other public buildings, and our private houses are incomparably better furnished. Besides, anyone who visits our town is at perfect liberty to choose what sort of time he will have: if he is on business he can enjoy all the bustle of Rome at our Exchanges, and if he wants a thorough rest there are houses here as peaceful as any country manor. Hypata, in fact, has come to be the chief holiday centre of the province.'

I agreed with her warmly. 'Nowhere in all my travels have I ever felt more at home than I do here—though I suppose I ought to qualify this by admitting my terror of the mysterious arts of your local witches, against which there seems to be no known means of protecting oneself. I am told that not even the dead are respected by them—that they rifle graves and funeral pyres in search of bones, and cut pieces of flesh from unburned corpses to use for blasting their neighbours' lives. And that some of these old sorceresses, the moment they smell death anywhere about, run off at top speed and mutilate the corpse before the mourners arrive.'

'There's no doubt at all about that,' said a man at my table, 'and, what's more, they don't even spare the living. Not long ago a fellow whose name I needn't mention got dreadfully bitten about the face by that hell pack.'

An uncontrolled burst of laughter greeted this remark, and everyone turned round to look at a guest reclining inconspicuously at a corner table. The laughter went on and on, and the man, thoroughly embarrassed and muttering angrily to himself, was on the point of walking out when Byrrhaena signalled to him to remain where he was.

'No, no, my dear Thelyphron,' she protested. 'You mustn't rush off like that. Show your usual good humour and tell us that adventure of yours once again; I am anxious that my cousin Lucius, who is as dear to me as a son, should have the pleasure of hearing it from your own lips. It is a wonderful story.'

He answered, still very angry: 'My lady Byrrhaena, you are always the perfect hostess and your goodness of heart never fails; but the insolence of my fellow-guests is past endurance.'

Byrrhaena told him firmly that he would be doing her a great disservice if he went against her wishes, however disagreeable he might find the task that she had set him. So he made a little heap of the coverings of his couch and propped himself up on it with his left elbow: then with his right hand he signalled for attention in oratorical style, protruding the forefinger and middle finger, pointing the thumb upward and folding down the two remaining fingers for good luck.

This was the story he told:

'While I was still a University student at Miletus I came over to attend the Olympian Games. Afterwards, feeling a strong desire to visit northern Greece, I travelled through most of Thessaly. One unlucky day I arrived at Larissa, having run through nearly all the money I had brought with me, and while I was wandering up and down the streets, wondering how to refill my purse, I saw a tall old man standing on a stone block in the middle of the market place. He was making a public announcement at the top of his voice, offering a large reward to anyone who would stand guard over a corpse that night.

'I asked a bystander: "What is the meaning of this? Are the corpses of Larissa in the habit of running away?"

"Hush, my lad," he answered. "I can see that you are very much of a stranger here, else you would realize that you are in Thessaly where witches are in the habit of gnawing bits of flesh off dead men's faces for use in their magical concoctions."

"Oh, I see! And would you mind telling me what this guardianship of the dead involves?"

' "Not at all. It means watching attentively the whole night, one's eyes fixed on the corpse without a single sideways glance. You see, these abominable women have the power of changing their shape at pleasure: they turn into birds or dogs or mice, or even flies—disguises that would pass scrutiny even in a Court of Law, and by daylight too—and then charm the guardians asleep. I won't try to tell you all the extraordinarily ingenious tricks that they use when they want to indulge their beastly appetites; at any rate, the usual reward of from a hundred to a hundred and fifty drachmae for the night's job is hardly worth the risk. Oh—I was almost forgetting to tell you that if next morning the guardian fails to hand over the corpse to the undertakers in exactly the same condition as he found it, he is obliged by Law to have bits cut from his own face to supply whatever is missing."

'That did not frighten me. I boldly told the crier that he need not repeat the announcement. "I'm ready to undertake the job," I said. "What fee do they offer?"

' "A thousand drachmae, because this is a job that calls for more than usual alertness against those terrible harpies: the deceased was the son of one of our first citizens."

' "All this nonsense leaves me unmoved," I said. "I am a man of iron, I never trouble to go to sleep, and I have sharper eyesight than Lynceus, the *Argo's* look-out man. In fact, I may say that I am all eyes, like the giant Argus whom Jupiter once put in charge of the nymph Io."

'I had hardly finished recommending myself for the job before the old man hurried me along to a big house with its gates locked and barred. He took me through a small side door and along corridors until I reached a bedroom with closed shutters, where a woman in deep black sat wailing loudly in the half-light.

'The crier went up to her and said: "This man undertakes to guard your husband's body to-night; and he agrees to the fee."

'She pushed back the hair that shaded her beautiful griefstricken face, and implored me to be vigilant at my post.

' "You need have no anxiety, Madam, if you make it worth my while afterwards."

'Nodding absently, she got up and led me into an adjoining room, where she showed me the corpse lying on a slab and wrapped in a pure white linen shroud. After another fit of weeping, she called in seven mourners as witnesses, also her secretary who had his writing materials with him. Then she said: "Gentlemen, I call you to witness that the nose is undamaged, so are both ears, the eyes are still in their sockets, the lips are whole, the chin the same." She touched each feature as she mentioned it, and the secretary wrote out the inventory, which the witnesses signed and sealed.

'I asked her as she was going away: "Will you be good enough, Madam, to see that I have everything I need for my vigil tonight?"

' "What sort of things?"

' "A good large lamp with enough oil in it to last until daybreak; pots of wine; warm water for tempering; a cup; and a plateful of cold meat and vegetables left over from your supper."

'She shook her head angrily: "What an absurd request! Cooked meat and vegetables indeed in this house of mourning, where no fire has been lighted for days! Do you imagine that you have come here for a jolly supper party? You are expected to mourn and weep like the rest of us." Then, turning to her maid: "Myrrhina, fill the lamp, bring it back at once, shut the door and leave the guardian to his task."

'All alone with the corpse, I fortified my eyes for their vigil by rubbing them hard and kept up my spirits by singing. Twilight shaded into night, and night grew deeper and deeper, blacker and blacker, until my usual bed-time had passed and it was close on midnight. I had been only a little uncomfortable at first, but now I was beginning to feel thoroughly frightened when all of a sudden a weasel squeezed in through a hole in the door, stopped close by me and fixed her eyes intently on mine. The boldness of the creature was most disconcerting, but I managed to shout out: "Get away from here, you filthy little beast, or I'll break your neck. Run off and play hide and seek with your friends the mice. Do you hear me? I mean it."

'She turned tail and skipped out of the room, but as she did so, a sudden deep sleep stole over me and dragged me down with it into bottomless gulfs of dream. I fell on the floor and lay there so dead asleep that not even Delphic Apollo could have readily decided which of us two was the corpse; the body on the slab or the body on the floor. It was almost as though I had actually died and my corpse had been left without a guardian.

'At last the darkness began to fade and

"The sentries of the Crested Watch 'gan shout"

—crowing so loud that I eventually awoke, picked up the lamp and ran in terror to the slab. I pulled back the shroud and examined the corpse's face closely; to my huge relief I found it unmutilated. Almost at once the poor widow came running in, still weeping, with the seven witnesses behind her. She threw herself on the corpse and after kissing it again and again had the lamp brought close to make sure that all was well. Then she turned and called: "Philodespotus, come here!"

'Her steward appeared. "Philodespotus, pay this young man his fee at once. He has kept watch very well."

'As he counted me out the money she said: "Many thanks, young man, for your loyal services; they have earned you the freedom of this house."

'Delighted with my unexpected good luck, I gently tossed the bright gold coins up and down in my hand and answered: "I am much obliged to you, Madam. I shall be only too pleased to help you out again, whenever you may need my services."

'These words were scarcely out of my mouth when the whole household rushed at me with blows and curses, in an attempt to cancel their dreadful ominousness. One punched me in the face with his fists, another dug his elbows into my shoulder, someone else kicked me; my ribs were pummelled, my hair pulled, my clothes torn and before they finally threw me out of the house I felt like Adonis mauled by the wild boar, or Orpheus torn in pieces by the Thracian women.

'When I paused in the next street to collect my senses, and realized what I had said—it had certainly been a most tactless remark—I decided that I had got off lightly enough, all considered.

'By and by, after the customary 'last summons,' the agonized calling of his name by the relatives in case he might be only in a coma, the dead man was brought out of the house; and since he had been a man of such importance he was honoured with a public procession. As the cortège turned into the market place, an old man came running up, the tears streaming down his face. In a frenzy of grief he tore out tufts of his fine white hair, grabbed hold of the open coffin with both hands and screamed for vengeance.

' "Gentlemen of Hypata!" he cried, his voice choking with sobs, "I appeal to your honour, I appeal to your sense of justice and public duty! Stand by your fellow-citizen, this poor nephew of mine; see that his death is avenged in full on that evil woman, his widow. She, and she alone, is the murderess. To cover up a secret love-affair and to get possession of her husband's estate she killed him—she killed him with a slow poison." He continued to sob and scream, until the crowd was stirred to indignant sympathy, thinking that he probably had good ground for his accusations. Some shouted: "Burn her! Burn her!" and some: "Stone her to death!" and a gang of young hooligans was encouraged to lynch her.

'However, she denied her guilt with oaths and tears (though these carried little conviction), and devout appeals to all the gods and goddesses in Heaven to witness that she was utterly incapable of doing anything so wicked.

' "So be it then," said the old man, "I am willing to refer the case to divine arbitration. And here is Zatchlas the Egyptian, one of the leading necromancers of his country, who has undertaken, for a large fee, to recall my nephew's soul from the Underworld and persuade it to reanimate the corpse for a few brief moments."

'The person whom he introduced to the crowd was dressed in white linen, with palm-leaf sandals on his feet and a tonsured head. The old man kissed his hands and clasped his knees in a formal act of supplication. "Your reverence," he cried, "take pity on me. I implore you by the stars of Heaven, by the gods of the Underworld, by the five elements of nature, by the silence of night, by the dams that the swallows of Isis build about the Coptic island, by the flooding of the Nile, by the mysteries of Memphis, and by the sacred rattle of Pharos—I implore you by these holy things to grant my nephew's soul a brief return to the warmth of the sun, and so re-illumine his eyes that they may open and momentarily regain the sight that he has forfeited by his descent to the Land of the Dead. I do not argue with fate, I do not deny the grave what is her due; my plea is only for a brief leave of absence, during which the dead man may assist me in avenging his own murder—the only possible consolation I can have in my overwhelming grief."

'The necromancer, yielding to his entreaties, touched the corpse's mouth three times with a certain small herb and laid another on its breast. Then he turned to the east, with a silent prayer to the sacred disk of the rising sun. The whole market place gasped expectantly at the sight of these solemn preparations, and stood prepared for a miracle. I pushed in among the crowd and climbed up on a stone just behind the coffin, from which I watched the whole scene with rising curiosity.

'Presently the breast of the corpse began to heave, blood began to pour again through its veins, breath returned to its nostrils. He sat up and spoke in a querulous voice: "Why do you call me back to the troubles of this transitory life, when I have already drunk of the stream of Lethe and floated on the marshy waters of the Styx? Leave me alone, I say, leave me alone! Let me sleep undisturbed."

'The necromancer raised his voice excitedly: "What? You refuse to address your fellow-citizens here and clear up the mystery of your death? Don't you realize that if you hold back a single detail, I am prepared to call up the dreadful Furies and have your weary limbs tortured on the rack?"

'At this the dead man roused himself again and groaned out to the crowd: "The bed in which I lay only yesterday is no longer empty; my rival sleeps in it. My newly-married wife has bewitched and poisoned me."

'The widow showed remarkable courage in the circumstance. She denied everything with oaths, and began contradicting and arguing with her late husband as though there were no such thing as respect for the dead. The crowd took different sides. Some were for burying the wicked woman alive in the same grave as her victim: but others refused to admit the evidence of a senseless corpse—it was quite untrustworthy, they said.

'The corpse soon settled the dispute. With another hollow groan it said: "I will give you incontrovertible proof that what I say is true, by disclosing something that is known to nobody but myself." Then he pointed up at me and said: "While that learned young student was keeping careful watch over my corpse, the ghoulish witches who were hovering near, waiting for a chance to rob it, did their best to deceive him by changing shape, but he saw through all their tricks. Though the bedroom doors were carefully bolted, they had slipped in through a knot-hole disguised as weasels and mice. But they threw a fog of sleep over him, so that he fell insensible, and then they called me by name, over and over again, trying to make me obey their magical commands. My weakened joints and cold limbs, despite convulsive struggles, could not respond immediately, but this student who had been cast into a trance that was a sort of death, happened to have the same name as I. So when they called: 'Thelyphron, Thelyphron, come!' he answered mechanically. Rising up like a senseless ghost he offered his face for the mutilation that they intended for mine; and they nibbled off first his nose and then his ears. But to divert attention from what they had done, they cleverly fitted him with a wax nose exactly like his own, and a pair of wax ears. The poor fellow remains under the illusion that he has been well rewarded for his vigilance, not meanly compensated for a frightful injury."

'Terrified by this story, I clapped my hand to my face to see if there were any truth in it, and my nose fell off; then I touched my ears, and they fell off too. A hundred fingers pointed at me from the crowd and a great roar of laughter went up. I burst into a cold sweat, leaped down from the stone, and slipped away between their legs like a frightened dog. Mutilated and ridiculous, I have never since cared to return to Miletus; and now I disguise the loss of my ears by growing my hair long and glue this canvas nose on my face for decency's sake.'

The drunken diners laughed as heartily as before when Thelyphron reached the climax of his story, and called for the usual toast to the God of Laughter. Byrrhaena explained. 'At Hypata, ever since the city was founded, we have celebrated a unique festival: the happy celebration of Laughter Day. I do trust you will be present at the ceremony tomorrow, and especially that you will be able to think out some joke of your own as a contribution to the proceedings; you see, Laughter is a god whom we hold in the very greatest esteem.'

'Certainly I'll be there,' I answered cheerfully. 'And I only hope that I'll be able to invent something really good, something so funny that I should not be ashamed to tie it around the neck of your great local deity himself.'

By this time I had drunk as much as I wanted, and when my slave came up to my table and told me that it was now midnight, I took a hasty leave of Byrrhaena and went unsteadily out into the darkness. The slave was carrying a lantern, but a sudden gust of wind extinguished it half way down the first street and we had a difficult time groping our way from door to door, continually catching our toes in the cobbles and falling over. And when at last I reached our lane, I came suddenly on three strapping great men heaving with all their strength at Milo's gate, trying to force their way in. They seemed not in the least alarmed by our arrival, but began using greater violence than before, aiming kicks at the gate as if to burst it off its hinges. I had no doubt that they were house-breakers, desperate ones too, and neither had the slave. Drawing my sword from under my cloak where I was holding it ready for just such an emergency as this, I rushed straight at them, and as they turned to close with me I lunged at each in turn and drove the blade into his body up to the hilt. They fell, and I thrust at them repeatedly as they attempted to rise, until all three gasped out their lives at my feet.

The disturbance woke Fotis, who ran up and opened the gate for me. I crawled into the house, panting for breath and dripping with sweat, and flung myself on my bed. There I fell asleep in a moment, as exhausted by my fight as if I had been battling, like Hercules, with Geryon, the King of Red Island, who had three bodies in one.

Translated by Robert Graves

QUESTIONS

1. How does Apuleius first engage our interest in the story?
2. What is our very first impression of Thelyphron, and how does *he* secure the reader's involvement? Does his behavior to his hostess and the guests have any connection with the story that he tells?
3. How does Thelyphron build up the atmosphere and create suspense? Once Thelyphron falls asleep, what do we assume will happen? How are we fooled?
4. How does Thelyphron give offense to the woman? What is the implication of his words? And does that implication have any bearing upon the episodes that follow?
5. Do we believe the story of the woman or that of the returned ghost? Why?
6. Does the coincidence of names—the fact that corpse was also called Thelyphron—enhance or undermine your response to the story?
7. What role is played in this tale by superstition and religious ritual?
8. What does Thelyphron's tale—as well as the narrative that encloses it—have to tell about conditions in Greece in Apuleius' time?

Anonymous*

The author of this bewitching little tale is not known. The work dates from the late Heian period of Japanese history (794–1185). Of the literature of this period, scholar and translator Donald Keene has written that much of it reveals the strong influence of the Buddhist religion. "When in the novels—and indeed in real life—a situation was reached for which no other solution was immediately apparent, the person involved would usually "abandon the world," an act accompanied by the ritual gesture of shaving the head or at least trimming the hair. . . ." The protagonist of this short narrative does not go quite that far, but she does take refuge in a distinctively Buddhist attitude.

THE LADY WHO LOVED INSECTS

from *The Tales of Tsutsumi Chūnagon*

Next door to the lady who loved butterflies was the house of a certain provincial inspector. He had an only daughter, to whose upbringing he and his wife devoted endless care. She was a strange girl, and used to say: "Why do people make so much fuss about butterflies and never give a thought to the creatures out of which butterflies grow? It is the natural form of things that is always the most important." She collected all kinds of reptiles and insects such as most people are frightened to touch, and watched them day by day to see what they would turn into, keeping them in various sorts of little boxes and cages. Among all these creatures her favorite was the common caterpillar. Hour after hour, her hair pushed back from her eyes, she would sit gazing at the furry black form that nestled in the palm of her hand. She found that other girls were frightened of these pets, and her only companions were a number of rather rough little boys, who were not in the least afraid. She got them to carry about the insect-boxes, find out the names of the insects or, if this could not be done, help her to give them new names. She hated anything that was not natural. Consequently she would not pluck a single hair from her eyebrows nor would she blacken her teeth, saying it was a dirty and disagreeable custom. So morning, noon, and night she

*Twelfth century

tended her insects, bending over them with a strange, white gleaming smile.[1] People on the whole were frightened of her and kept away; the few who ventured to approach her came back with the strangest reports. If anyone showed the slightest distaste for her pets, she would ask him indignantly how he could give way to so silly and vulgar a prejudice, and as she said this she would stare at the visitor under her black, bushy eyebrows in a way that made him feel extremely uncomfortable.

Her parents thought all this very peculiar and would much rather she had been more like other children; but they saw it was no use arguing with her. She for her part took immense trouble in explaining her ideas, but this only resulted in making them feel that she was much cleverer than they. "No doubt," they would say, "all you tell us is quite true, and so far as we are concerned you may do as you please. But people as a rule only make pets of charming and pretty things. If it gets about that you keep hairy caterpillars you will be thought a disgusting girl and no one will want to know you." "I do not mind what they think," she answered. "I want to inquire into everything that exists and find out how it began. Nothing else interests me. And it is very silly of them to dislike caterpillars, all of which will soon turn into lovely butterflies." Then she again explained to them carefully how the cocoon, which is like the thick winter clothes that human beings wear, wraps up the caterpillar till its wings have grown and it is ready to be a butterfly. Then it suddenly waves its white sleeves and flits away. . . .

This was no doubt quite accurate, and they could think of nothing to say in reply; but all the same her views on such matters made them feel very uncomfortable. She would never sit in the same room with her elders, quoting in self-defense the proverb, "Ghosts and girls are best unseen"; and the above attempt to bring her parents to reason was made through a chink in the half-raised blinds of the living room. Hearing of such conversations as this, the young people of the district were amazed at the profundity of her researches. "But what things for a girl to play with!" they said. "She must be an oddity indeed. Let us go and call upon the girl who loves butterflies."

Hearing some of the unflattering comparisons that were being made between herself and the butterfly lady, she rejoined: "I do not see anything very admirable in making a fuss over butterflies. Even those young men must know by now that the prettiest butterflies are but the sheddings of creatures like my hairy caterpillars, who discard them as a snake drops its skin. And caterpillars are much friendlier playthings. For it you catch hold of a butterfly it frees itself as soon as it can, leaving its golden powder on your hand, and this powder is very dangerous, often causing fevers and agues. Fancy trying to make pets of butterflies! It is horrible to think of."

To the little boys who formed her retinue she would give pretty things

1. Because of her unblackened teeth.

such as she knew they wanted, and in return they would give her all kinds of terrifying insects. She said the caterpillars would be unhappy if there were no creatures with them to admire their glossy coats, and she therefore collected a number of snails, and also of grass-crickets whose ferocious and incessant cries seemed to suggest that they were at war with one another, thus recalling to her mind the line, "For the ground between a snail's horns what use to fight?"[2] She said she was tired of ordinary boys' names and called her servitors by insect-names, such as Kerao (mole-cricket boy), Inagomaro (locust-man), Amabiko (centipede), and the like. All this was thought very queer and stupid.

Among those who had heard gossip about the girl and her odd pets was a certain young man of good family who vowed that, fond of strange creatures though she might be, he would undertake to give her a fright. So saying he made a marvelously lifelike snake with joints that moved and putting it into a scaly bag sent it to her with the poem: "Creeping and crawling I shall sneak my way to your side, for my persistence[3] is tireless as my body is long." The servant who brought the bag had no idea what it contained. "I wonder what can be in it," he said, as he untied the string. "Certainly something remarkably heavy!" The bag was opened, and to the horror of everyone present a snake protruded its head. But the lady was not at all put out, and having repeated several times the prayer *Namu Amida Butsu* she said, "Do not be frightened! Remember that any one of you may have been a snake in his former existence. Look at the kindly expression of his face and how he is making himself tremble all down his back. Could anything be clearer than that he is signaling to you not to be afraid? I am amazed that anyone should not understand him." So she muttered to herself, and drew the bag toward her. But all the same it seemed as though even she were a little bit afraid, for now she hovered near the creature and now fluttered away again, like a moth at the candle, crooning to it all the while in a low insect voice.

Seeing several of the servants rush out of her room tumbling over one another and screaming with laughter the lady's father asked them what had happened, and at the mention of a snake exclaimed in great consternation, "A nice trick to play upon a young woman! I cannot understand anyone doing such a dastardly thing. A fine pack of rascals you are, to run off like this and leave her with a dangerous viper in the room." So saying, he seized his sword and brandishing it over his head rushed to his daughter's side. But the moment he saw the snake a doubt crossed his mind and examining it attentively he discovered it was only an extremely well-made toy. Picking it up he said, "I remember now that I have heard people say how clever the fellow is at making things of this sort. You must be sure to write at once and thank him for his kindness." When it was known that

2. From one of five drinking songs written by the Chinese poet Po Chü-i about 829.
3. "Persistence" is "length of heart" *(kokoro-nagasa)* in Japanese.

the snake was only a toy the people who had run away from it declared the joke to be a very silly one. But the lady agreed that it would be rude not to reply and taking a stout, sensible-looking sheet of paper she wrote the following poem, not in *hiragana*, which she never used, but in *katakana*:[4] "If indeed we are fated to meet, not here will it be, but in Paradise, thou crafty image of a snake." And at the side was written: "In the Garden of Blessings you must plant your seed."[5]

It happened that a certain Captain of Horse saw this letter and being much struck with it he determined to obtain an interview with the writer. Choosing a time when he knew her father to be busy elsewhere, he posted himself at a wattled gate on the woman's side of the house and peeped in. Several little boys were poking about among some very dull-looking bushes and shrubs. Presently one of them called out, "Just look at these bushes! They're simply covered with creatures. It's the best place we have ever found." And going to the window he pulled the blind. "Do look at them," he said again. "You can see them from the window. Aren't they the loveliest caterpillars you ever saw?" "Yes, they're not at all bad," said a voice from within. "You may bring them in here if you like." "I've nothing to put them in," said the boy. "You must look at them where they are." Presently the blind was pulled right aside and a girl appeared at the window, craning out toward the nearest boughs of the shrubbery. She had pulled her mantle over her head, but her hair hung loose beneath it, and very lovely hair it was too, but rather untidy-looking, and the Captain thought it must be a long time since she had combed it. Her thick, very dark eyebrows gave her face a rather forbidding air. Her other features were by no means bad. But when she smiled her white teeth gleamed and flashed in a manner that rather disgusted him, for there was something wild and barbaric about it.

"What a sad case!" thought the Captain. "If only she took an ordinary amount of trouble with herself she really would not be bad-looking." Even as she was he did not find her altogether unattractive; for there was about her a strange kind of vehemence, a liveliness of expression, a brilliance of complexion and coloring that could not fail to make some impression on him. With her clothes in themselves there was nothing wrong. She wore a robe of soft, glossy silk, with a spinner's jacket, and white trousers. In order to get a good view of the caterpillars she leaned right out of the window, crying, "Aren't they clever! They've come here in order to be out of the sun. Boy, you might just bring me that one there. I should like to have a better look at him. Be sure not to let him fall." Upon which the boy at once bumped into something and the caterpillar fell with a thud upon the ground.

4. A square, inelegant, but eminently "sensible" form of syllabary, now used for telegrams, etc.

5. The snake must by good behavior get itself reborn in some more dignified incarnation.

She then handed him a white fan with some Chinese characters written upon it in black ink, saying, "Pick him up quickly and carry him in on this."

It was only now that she caught sight of the Captain, who was still loitering at the wicker gate. To see anyone there was a considerable surprise, for the young men of the neighborhood had long ago decided that she was what they called "a disastrous character," and it was seldom indeed that anyone came that way. The little boy, too, had become aware of the visitor's presence and cried out in astonishment, "Look, there's a gentleman standing at the wicker gate. I can't make out what he is doing. He seems to be staring at us." One of the maids now came along and began to scold her. "Fie upon you," she said, "I shall go straight to your father and tell him you're busy with your nasty insects again, and leaning right out of the window where anyone can see you." But the girl continued to fiddle about with the hairy caterpillars on the bushes near the window. The maid, who had a horror of such creatures, was far too frightened to come any closer, but called again, "Madam, go in this instant. You can be seen!" "Well, what if I can be seen? I am not doing anything to be ashamed of." "I'm not joking, I assure you," said the maid indignantly. "There's a fine gentleman standing right there at the gate. Go away from the window at once!" "Kerao," said the girl at last, "just go to the gate and see if there is still someone there." He ran a little distance toward the gate and presently called out, "It's quite true, there is somebody." Upon which she gathered several caterpillars in her sleeve and stepped back into the interior of the house.

For a moment he saw her at full length. She was rather tall. Her hair floated out behind her as she moved. It was very thick, but the ends were somewhat wispy, no doubt through lack of trimming. But with a little more looking after it would have made (he thought) a fine crop of hair. Certainly she was no great beauty, but if she dressed and behaved like other people she would, he was sure, be capable of cutting quite a decent figure in society. What a pity it was! Where had she picked up the distressing opinions that forced her to make such a melancholy spectacle of herself?

He felt that he must at any rate let her know that he had seen her; and using the juice of a flower stem as ink he wrote the following poem on a piece of thickly folded paper: "Forgive me that at your wicker gate so long I stand. But from the caterpillar's bushy brows I cannot take my eyes." He tapped with his fan, and at once one of the little boys ran out to ask what he wanted. "Take this to your mistress," he said. But it was intercepted by the maid, to whom the little boy explained that the poem came from the fine gentleman who had been standing about near the gate. "Woe upon us all," cried the maid, "this is the handwriting of Captain So-and-So, that is in the Horse Guard. And to think that he has been watching you mess about with your nauseous worms!" And she went on for some time lamenting over the girl's deplorable oddity. At last the insect-lover could bear it no longer and said, "If you looked a little more below the surface of things you would not mind so much what other people thought about you. The world in which we live has no reality, it is a mirage, a dream. Suppose someone is offended by what we do or, for the matter of that, is pleased by it, does his opinion make any difference to us in the end? Before long both he and we shall no longer even appear to exist."

Several of the younger servants had by now gathered round. They found her argument hard to answer, but secretly felt that this was a very dismal view of life. It was not thought likely that she would send an answer, but the Captain was still waiting at the gate and the little boys, who had now all been called back into the house, said the gentleman was looking very unhappy; upon which everyone urged her to write something, and very reluctantly she sent the poem, "By this you may know the strangeness of my mood. Had you not called me *kawamushi*,[6] I would not have replied." To which he answered, "In all the world, I fear, exists no man so delicate that to the hairtips of a caterpillar's brow he could attune his life." Then he went back laughing to his home.

What happened next will be found in the second chapter![7]

Translated by Arthur Waley

6. Hairy caterpillar.
7. No second chapter exists.

QUESTIONS

1. What do our first impressions lead us to assume about the character of the girl? What is the effect of the suggested contrast with her neighbor?
2. Knowing as we do that "ugly" caterpillars turn into beautiful butterflies, what are our expectations about how the story will end? Do these change in any way once the Captain appears?
3. Do the caterpillars and insects play a symbolic role for the girl or the reader? Discuss.
4. Does the incident with the toy snake add anything to the story? If so, what? Does it in any way prepare us for the Captain?
5. What is the Captain's character? Is he serious, or just amusing himself? Do we have any indication that he might be a desirable match?
6. What is the role in the story of verses and notes? How is their language different from the language of the narrative? Does this difference have an effect?
7. "The world in which we live has no reality," says the girl. What does she mean? Do we believe her words, or believe that *she* believes them?
8. How are we to understand the meaning of the Captain's final words?
9. The story is not continued, but based on the narrative we have, what outcome could you imagine? Whose character would have to change?

Giovanni Boccaccio

Giovanni Boccaccio was born in 1313, most probably in Florence, to the family of a well-to-do banker. He was sent to Naples to study, with the expectation that he would take his place in the family profession. Boccaccio rebelled, however, and devoted his energies to the study of literature as well as to the high life of the Neapolitan nobility. Upon his return to Florence in 1341, he took up writing in earnest.

While Boccaccio wrote voluminously in both Latin and the vernacular Italian, he is remembered chiefly for his enormous story cycle the *Decameron*. The work, divided into ten sections, each representing a day (each day being further divided into ten stories), collects the diverse tales told by a group of nobles who have taken refuge from the plague in a villa outside Florence. Boccaccio himself had been in Florence during the plague years of 1347–1349 and began work on his masterpiece shortly thereafter. The idiom, like that of Dante's celebrated *Divine Comedy*, is the vernacular Italian.

There has been some controversy as to whether Boccaccio is more properly a representative of the spirit of the Middle Ages or a herald of the Renaissance. Scholars have argued both sides of the matter, some citing his idealized portrayal of women as evidence of the medieval, others pointing to his free views in religious matters as revealing a Renaissance sensibility. The stories can be seen as a magnificent fusion of effects. They are passionate and earthy but also manifest a vision of the purity of love; they feature episodes of corruption and craftiness but hold out the possibility of human betterment. Boccaccio drew heavily on the oral tradition of the Middle Ages, shaping the tales and legends to reveal new facets. The Renaissance can be said to have reached England when Geoffrey Chaucer incorporated Boccaccio's influence to produce *The Canterbury Tales*.

THE FIRST STORY OF THE FOURTH DAY

from the *Decameron*

Tancredi, Prince of Salerno, kills his daughter's lover and sends her his heart in a golden chalice; she besprinkles the heart with a poisonous liquid, which she then drinks, and so dies.

Cruel indeed is the topic for discussion assigned to us today by our king, especially when you consider that, having come here to fortify our spirits, we are obliged to recount people's woes, the telling of which cannot fail to arouse compassion in speaker and listener alike. Perhaps he has done it in order to temper in some degree the gaiety of the previous days; but whatever his motive, it is not for me to alter his decree, and I shall therefore relate an occurrence that was not only pitiful, but calamitous, and fully worthy of our tears.

Tancredi, Prince of Salerno, was a most benevolent ruler, and kindly of disposition, except for the fact that in his old age he sullied his hands with the blood of passion. In all his life he had but a single child, a daughter, and it would have been better for him if he had never had any at all.

He was as passionately fond of this daughter as any father who has ever lived, and being unable to bring himself to part with her, he refused to marry her off, even when she was several years older than the usual age for taking a husband. Eventually, he gave her to a son of the Duke of Capua, but shortly after her marriage she was left a widow and returned to her father. In physique and facial appearance, she was as beautiful a creature as there ever was; she was youthful and vivacious, and she possessed rather more intelligence than a woman needs. In the house of her doting father she led the life of a great lady, surrounded by comforts of every description. But realizing that her father was so devoted to her that he was in no hurry to make her a second marriage, and feeling that it would be shameless to approach him on the subject, she decided to see whether she could find herself a secret lover who was worthy of her affections.

In her father's court, she encountered many people of the kind to be found in any princely household, of whom some were nobly bred and others not. Having studied the conduct and manners of several of these, she was attracted to one above all the rest—a young valet of her father's called Guiscardo, who was a man of exceedingly humble birth but noble in character and bearing. By dint of seeing him often, before very long she fell madly and secretly in love with him, and her admiration of his ways grew steadily more profound. As for the young man himself, not being slow to take a hint, from the moment he perceived her interest in him he lost his heart to her so completely that he could think of virtually nothing else.

And so they were secretly in love with each other. The young woman was longing to be with him, and being unwilling to confide in anyone on the subject of her love, she thought of a novel idea for informing him how they could meet. Having written him a letter, explaining what he was to do in order to be with her on the following day, she inserted it into a length of reed, which later on she handed to Guiscardo, saying as though for the fun of it:

"Turn it into a bellows-pipe for your serving-wench, so that she can use it to kindle the fire this evening."

Guiscardo took it and went about his business, reflecting that she could hardly have given it to him or spoken as she had without some special motive. As soon as he returned home, he examined the reed, saw that it was split, opened it, and found her letter inside. And when he had read it and taken careful note of what he was to do, he was the happiest man that ever lived, and set about making his preparations for going to see her in the way she had suggested.

Inside the mountain on which the Prince's palace stood, there was a cavern, formed at some remote period of the past, which was partially lit from above through a shaft driven into the hillside. But since the cavern was no longer used, the mouth of the shaft was almost entirely covered over by weeds and brambles. There was a secret staircase leading to the cavern from a room occupied by the lady, on the ground-floor of the palace, but the way was barred by a massive door. So many years had passed since the staircase had last been used, that hardly anybody remembered it was still there; but Love, to whose eyes nothing remains concealed, had reminded the enamoured lady of its existence.

For several days, she had been struggling to open this door by herself, using certain implements of her own as picklocks so that no one should perceive what was afoot. Having finally got it open, she had descended alone into the cavern, seen the shaft, and written to Guiscardo, giving him a rough idea of the distance between the top of the shaft and the floor of the cavern, and telling him to try and use the shaft as his means of access. With this object in view, Guiscardo promptly got hold of a suitable length of rope, tied various knots and loops in it to allow him to climb up and down, and the following night, without breathing a word to anyone, he made his way to the shaft, wearing a suit of leather to protect himself from the brambles. Firmly tying one end of the rope to a stout bush that had taken root at the mouth of the opening, he lowered himself into the cavern and waited for the lady to come.

In the course of the following day, the princess dismissed her ladies-in-waiting on the pretext of wanting to sleep, and having locked herself in her chamber, she opened the door and descended into the cavern, where she found Guiscardo waiting. After giving each other a rapturous greeting, they made their way into her chamber, where they spent a goodly portion of the day in transports of bliss. Before parting, they agreed on the wisest way of pursuing their lovemaking in future so that it should remain a secret, and then Guiscardo returned to the cavern, whilst the princess, having bolted the door behind him, came forth to rejoin her ladies-in-waiting.

During the night, Guiscardo climbed back up the rope, made his way out through the aperture by which he had entered, and returned home. And now that he was conversant with the route, he began to make regular use of it.

But their pleasure, being so immense and so continuous, attracted the envy of Fortune, who brought about a calamity, turning the joy of the two lovers into tears and sorrow.

From time to time, Prince Tancredi was in the habit of going alone to visit his daughter, with whom he would stay and converse for a while in her chamber and then go away. And one day, after breakfast, he came down to see her, entering her room without anyone hearing or noticing, only to discover that the princess (whose name was Ghismonda) had gone into her garden with all her ladies-in-waiting. Not wishing to disturb her whilst she was enjoying her walk in the garden, he sat down to wait for her on a low stool at a corner of her bed. The windows of the room were closed, and the bed-curtains had been drawn aside, and Tancredi rested his head against the side of the bed, drew the curtain round his body as though to conceal himself there on purpose, and fell asleep.

Whilst he was asleep, Ghismonda, who unfortunately had made an appointment with Guiscardo for that very day, left her attendants in the garden and stole quietly into the room, locking herself in without perceiving that anyone was there. Having opened the door for Guiscardo, who was waiting for her, they then went to bed in the usual way; but whilst they were playing and cavorting together, Tancredi chanced to wake up, and heard and saw what Guiscardo and his daughter were doing. The sight filled him with dismay, and at first he wanted to cry out to them, but then he decided to hold his peace and, if possible, remain hidden, so that he could carry out, with greater prudence and less detriment to his honour, the plan of action that had already taken shape in his mind.

The two lovers remained together for a considerable time, as was their custom, without noticing Tancredi; and when they felt it was time for them to part, they got up from the bed and Guiscardo returned to the cavern. She too left the room, and Tancredi, though he was getting on in years, clambered through a window and lowered himself into the garden without being seen, returning thence in deep distress to his own apartment.

On Tancredi's orders, Guiscardo was taken prisoner by two guards soon after dark that very night, just as he was emerging, hindered by the suit of leather he was wearing, from the hole in the ground. He was then conducted in secret to Tancredi, who almost burst into tears on seeing him, and said:

"Guiscardo, my benevolence towards you deserved a better reward than the shameful deed I saw you committing today, with my own eyes, against that which belongs to me."

By way of reply, all that Guiscardo said was:

"Neither you nor I can resist the power of Love."

Tancredi then ordered him to be placed under secret guard in one of the inner rooms, and this was done.

Ghismonda knew nothing of this, and after breakfast on the next day, Tancredi, who had been thinking all manner of strange and terrible thoughts, paid his usual call upon his daughter in her chamber. And having locked the door behind him, his eyes filled with tears, and he said to her:

"Never having doubted your virtue and honesty, Ghismonda, it would never have occurred to me, whatever people might have said, that you would ever so much as think of yielding to a man who was not your husband. But now I have actually seen you doing it with my own eyes, and the memory of it will always torment me during what little remains of my old age.

"Moreover, since you felt bound to bring so much dishonour upon yourself, in God's name you might at least have chosen someone whose rank was suited to your own. But of all the people who frequent my court, you have to choose Guiscardo, a youth of exceedingly base condition, whom we took into our court and raised from early childhood mainly out of charity. Your conduct has faced me with an appalling dilemma, inasmuch as I have no idea how I am to deal with you. I have already come to a decision about Guiscardo, who is under lock and key, having been arrested last night on my orders as he was emerging from the cavern; but God knows what I am to do with you. I am drawn in one direction by the love I have always borne you, deeper by far than that of any other father for a daughter; but on the other hand I seethe with all the indignation that the folly of your actions demands. My love prompts me to forgive you; my indignation demands that I should punish you without mercy, though it would be against my nature to do so. But before I reach any decision, I should like to hear what you have to say for yourself on the subject." And so saying, he lowered his gaze and began to wail as though he were a child who had been soundly beaten.

Realizing, from what her father had said, that not only had her secret been discovered but Guiscardo was captured, Ghismonda was utterly overcome with sorrow, and needed all the self-control she possessed to prevent herself from screaming and sobbing as most other women would have done. But her proudness of heart more than made up for her shattered spirits, and by a miraculous effort of will, she remained impassive, and rather than make excuses for herself, she resolved to live no longer, being convinced that her Guiscardo was already dead.

She therefore allowed no trace of contrition or womanly distress to cloud her features, but addressed her father in a firm, unworried voice, staring him straight in the face without a single tear in her eyes.

"Tancredi," she said, "I am resolved neither to contradict you nor to implore your forgiveness, because denial would be pointless and I want none of your clemency. Nor do I have the slightest intention of appealing either to your better nature or to your affection. On the contrary, I propose to tell you the whole truth, setting forth convincing arguments in defence of my good name, and afterwards I shall act unflinchingly in accordance with the promptings of my noble heart. It is true that I loved Guiscardo, and that I love him still. I shall continue to love him until I die, which I expect to do very soon. And if people love each other beyond the grave, I shall never cease to love him. I was prompted to act as I did, not so much by my womanly frailty as by your lack of concern to marry me, together with his own outstanding worth. You are made of flesh and blood, Tancredi, and it should have been obvious to you that the daughter you fathered was also made of flesh and blood, and not of stone or iron. Although you are now an old man, you should have remembered, indeed you should still remember, the nature and power of the laws of youth. And although much of your own youth was spent in pursuit of military glory, you should nonetheless have realized how the old and the young are alike affected by living in comfort and idleness.

"As I have said, since you were the person who fathered me, I am made of flesh and blood like yourself. Moreover, I am still a young woman. And for both of these reasons, I am full of amorous longings, intensified beyond belief by my marriage, which enabled me to discover the marvellous joy that comes from their fulfillment. As I was incapable of resisting these forces, I made up my mind, being a woman in the prime of life, to follow the path along which they were leading, and I fell in love. But though I was prepared to commit a natural sin, I was determined to spare no effort to ensure that neither your good name nor mine should suffer any harm. To this end, I was assisted by compassionate Love and benign Fortune, who taught me the means whereby I could secretly achieve the fulfilment of my desires. No matter who told you about my secret, no matter how you came to discover it, I do not deny that the thing has happened.

"I did not take a lover at random, as many women do, but deliberately chose Guiscardo in preference to any other, only conceding my love to him after careful reflection; and through the patience and good judgement of us both, I have long been enjoying the gratification of my desires. It seems, however, that you prefer to accept a common fallacy rather than the truth, for you reproach me more bitterly, not for committing the crime of loving a man, but for consorting with a person of lowly rank, thus implying that if I had selected a nobleman for the purpose, you would not have had anything to worry about. You clearly fail to realize that in this respect, your strictures should be aimed, not at me, but at Fortune, who frequently raises the unworthy to positions of eminence and leaves the worthiest in low estate.

"But leaving this aside, consider for a moment the principles of things, and you will see that we are all of one flesh and that our souls were created by a single Maker, who gave the same capacities and powers and faculties to each. We were all born equal, and still are, but merit first set us apart, and those who had more of it, and used it the most, acquired the name of nobles to distinguish them from the rest. Since then, this law has been obscured by a contrary practice, but nature and good manners ensure that its force still remains unimpaired; hence any man whose conduct is virtuous proclaims himself a noble, and those who call him by any other name are in error.

"Consider each of your nobles in turn, compare their lives, their customs and manners with those of Guiscardo, and if you judge the matter impartially, you will conclude that he alone is a patrician whilst all these nobles of yours are plebeians. Besides, it was not through hearsay that Guiscardo's merit and virtues came to my notice, but through your good opinion of him, together with the evidence of my own eyes. For was it not you yourself who sang his praises more loudly than any, claiming for him all the qualities by which one measures a man's excellence? Nor were you mistaken by any means, for unless my eyes have played me false, I have seen him practise the very virtues for which you commended him, in a manner more wonderful than your words could express. So that if I was deceived in my estimate of Guiscardo, it was you alone who deceived me.

"If, then, you maintain that I gave myself to a man of base condition, you are wrong. If, on the other hand, you were to describe him as poor, then perhaps you would be right, and you should hang your head in shame for the paltry rewards you bestowed on so excellent a servant. But in any case, a man's nobility is not affected by poverty, as it is by riches. Many kings, many great princes, were once poor; many a ploughman or shepherd, not only in the past but in the present, was once exceedingly wealthy.

"As for the last of your dilemmas, concerning how you are to deal with me, you can dismiss it from your thoughts entirely. If you are intent, in your extreme old age, upon behaving as you never behaved in your youth, and resorting to cruelty, then let your cruelty be aimed at me, for it was I who caused this so-called sin to be committed. I am resolved not to plead for clemency, and I swear that unless you do the same to me as you have already done, or intend to do, to Guiscardo, these hands of mine will do it for you.

"Now get you hence to shed your tears among the women, and if you think we have earned your cruelty, see that you slaughter us both at one and the same time."

Although Tancredi knew that his daughter had a will of iron, he doubted her resolve to translate her words into action. So he went away and decided that whilst he would dismiss all thought of venting his rage on Ghismonda, he would cool her ardent passion by taking revenge on her paramour. He therefore ordered the two men who were guarding Guiscardo to strangle him noiselessly that same night, after which they were to take out his heart and bring it to him; and they carried out his orders to the letter.

Early next day, the Prince called for a fine, big chalice made of gold, and having placed Guiscardo's heart inside it, he ordered one of his most trusted servants to take it to his daughter, bidding him utter these words as he handed it over: "Your father sends you this to comfort you in the loss of your dearest possession, just as you have comforted him in the loss of his."

After her father had left, Ghismonda, unflinching in her harsh resolve, had called for poisonous herbs and roots, which she then distilled and converted into a potion, so that, if things turned out as she feared, she would have it ready to hand. And when the servant came to her with her father's gift and recited the message, she accepted it with great composure and removed the lid, no sooner seeing the heart and hearing the servant's words than she knew for certain that this was the heart of Guiscardo.

So she looked up at the servant, and said to him:

"Nothing less splendid than a golden sepulchre would have suited so noble a heart; in this respect, my father has acted wisely."

Having spoken these words, she raised it to her lips and kissed it, then continued:

"Throughout my life, which is now approaching its end, I have had constant reminders of my father's devoted love, but never so patent a token as this. And in thanking him for the last time, I bid you tell him how grateful I was for so priceless a gift."

Then she turned to the chalice, which she was holding firmly in her two hands, and gazing down upon Guiscardo's heart, she said:

"Ah! dear, sweet vessel of all my joys, cursed be the cruelty of him who has compelled me to see you with the eyes of my body, when it was enough that I should keep you constantly in the eyes of my mind! Your life has run the brief course allotted to it by Fortune, you have reached the end to which all men hasten, and in leaving behind the trials and tribulations of our mortal life, you have received at the hands of your enemy a burial worthy of your excellence. Your funeral rites lacked nothing but the tears of the woman you loved so dearly; but so that you should not be without them, God impelled my pitiless father to send you to me, and I shall cry for you even though I had resolved to die with tearless eyes and features unclouded by fear. And the instant my tears are finished I shall see that my soul is united with that other soul which you kept in your loving care. How could I wish for a better or surer companion as I set forth towards the unknown? I feel certain that his soul still lingers here within you, waiting for mine and surveying the scenes of our mutual happiness, and that our love for one another is as deep and enduring as ever."

She said no more, but leaned over the chalice, suppressing all sound of womanly grief, and began to cry in a fashion wondrous to behold, her tears gushing forth like water from a fountain; and she implanted countless kisses upon the lifeless heart.

Her ladies-in-waiting, by whom she was surrounded, were at a loss to know what heart this was, nor were they able to make any sense of her words, but they too began to cry in unison, being filled with compassion for their mistress. They pleaded with her to explain why she was weeping, but to no avail; and for all their strenuous efforts, they were unable to console her.

But when she had cried as much as she deemed sufficient, she raised her head from the chalice, and after drying her eyes, she said:

"Oh, heart that I love so dearly, now that I have fully discharged my duties towards you, all that remains to be done is to bring my soul and unite it with yours."

Having pronounced these words, she called for the phial containing the potion she had prepared on the previous day, and, pouring it into the chalice, where the heart lay bathed in her own abundant tears, she raised the mixture to her lips without any show of fear and drank it. After which, still holding on to the chalice, she climbed on to her bed, arranged herself as decorously as she could, and placing the heart of her dead lover close to her own, she silently waited for death.

Her ladies-in-waiting had no idea what potion it was that she had drunk, but her speech and actions were so strange that they had sent to inform Tancredi of all that was happening, and he, fearing the worst, had hurried down at once to his daughter's chamber, arriving there just as she had settled herself upon the bed. On seeing the state she was in, he tried to console her with honeyed words, and burst into floods of tears, but the time for pity was past, and Ghismonda said to him:

"Save those tears of yours for a less coveted fate than this of mine, Tancredi, and shed them not for me, for I do not want them. Who ever heard of anyone, other than yourself, who wept on achieving his wishes? But if you still retain some tiny spark of your former love for me, grant me one final gift, and since it displeased you that I should live quietly with Guiscardo in secret, see that my body is publicly laid to rest beside his in whatever spot you chose to cast his remains."

The vehemence of his sobbing prevented the Prince from offering any reply, and the young woman, sensing that she was about to breathe her last, clasped the dead heart tightly to her bosom, saying:

"God be with you all, for I now take my leave of you."

Then her vision grew blurred, she lost the use of her senses, and she left this life of sorrow behind her.

Thus the love of Guiscardo and Ghismonda came to its sad conclusion, as you have now heard. And as for Tancredi, after shedding countless tears and making tardy repentance for his cruelty, he saw that they were honorably interred together in a single grave, amid the general mourning of all the people of Salerno.

Translated by G. H. McWilliam

QUESTIONS

1. Isolate the elements suggesting that this story derives from the oral tradition. Describe the basic structure of the plot, the characters (are they merely types?), the resolution.
2. What role does coincidence play in this story?

3. Consider Boccaccio's presentation of his principal characters. How much are we simply asked to assume? How would the story change if the characters and their actions were made psychologically complex in the modern sense?

4. In what ways are social position and nobility of soul at odds in this story? What does Boccaccio have to tell us about nobility of soul?

5. What is the function of Ghismonda's speech to her father?

6. Does Boccaccio ask us to take sides? How does he present the events to heighten our involvement in the story? Does the fact that he presents crucial scenes "off-stage" direct our focus? Explain.

7. Does love indeed conquer all? What is Boccaccio's view of love? Is there a sense in which Guiscardo and Ghismonda can be said to triumph? Explain.

8. Is Tancredi evil, foolish, or admirable? Discuss briefly how each case could be argued.

9. Imagine a version of this story in which all the characters came from humble backgrounds. Is social position an indispensable ingredient to the unfolding drama? How so?

François Rabelais

François Rabelais was born sometime between 1490 and 1494 at Chinon, France. Little is known about his early years apart from the fact that he studied for the priesthood, first in the Benedictine orders and later with the Franciscans. Soon enough, however, there was evidence of his inquisitive, exuberant, and contrary temperament. While studying with the Franciscans, Rabelais determined to learn Greek in order to read the New Testament in the original. As it happens, the officials of the church had outlawed the study of Greek in France—they were alarmed by the progressive commentaries that the philosopher and humanist Erasmus had written on the Greek gospels. But Rabelais was not to be deterred. He accepted the patronage of a free-thinking Benedictine abbot and under his protection pursued his inquires; during this time he also tried his hand at literature, writing verses.

In 1528 Rabelais traveled to Paris, where he experienced at first hand the intellectual warfare between representatives of the old learning and champions of the more liberal humanist philosophy. While never fully abandoning his affiliations with the Benedictines, Rabelais took up the study of medicine, and by 1532 he was practicing in Lyon. At the same time he became ever more deeply immersed in writing. In short order he published the first installments of what would become the mammoth saga of two giants, *Gargantua and Pantagruel.* The Pantagruel episodes were, interestingly, written first; the Gargantua sections were published in 1534.

Rabelais had little interest in plot or character. He borrowed freely from tales and legends already in circulation. What made his works unique—and enormously popular—was his extravagant verbal art, not to mention his gift for satirizing the hypocrisies of the Church and the stodgy self-importance of conservative schoolmen. He was unabashed in his celebration of the bodily appetites and functions.

Rabelais' writings, needless to say, were not appreciated by the high officials of the Church. From the first publication of the Pantagruel story until his death in 1553, the outspoken monk–doctor–free-thinking satirist was hounded and forced to move from place to place. His works were banned, and their further publication and circulation were prohibited. But even the sternest edicts could not stop the more adventurous printers from disseminating his writings. As the spirit of humanism spread through Europe, the popularity of Rabelais' robust farce could only grow. He is now revered as one of the great liberating spirits of literature.

Reading Rabelais, one might note in his work the convergence of what might be called oral and print-based tendencies. (Gutenberg had invented his system of movable type only a few decades before Rabelais' birth.) The energetic momentum of the narrative and its anecdotal tendency emerge straight from the oral storytelling tradition of unlettered peasants. But also present as a kind of overlay is Rabelais' fascination with the possibilities of print: he often reproduces complex scholastic arguments (if only to mock them) and indulges in what may be seen as one of his many contributions to the literature of excess—the list. Rabelais' narrative includes hilarious lists of all manner of things, some of them running for pages.

The episode included here, which tells of the birth of Pantagruel and the death of his mother, is one of the tamer parts of this book.

THE BIRTH AND CHILDHOOD OF PANTAGRUEL

from *Gargantua and Pantagruel*

CHAPTER 2: *Of the Nativity of the Most Redoubted Pantagruel*

Gargantua at the age of four hundred, four score, and forty-four years begat his son Pantagruel upon his wife Badebec, daughter of the king of the Amaurots in Utopia, who died in childbirth; for he was so amazingly large and so heavy that he could not come into the world without suffocating his mother.

But in order fully to understand the cause and reason of the name which was given to him at baptism, you will note that in that year there was so great a drought throughout all the land of Africa, that thirty-six months, three weeks, four days, thirteen hours, and somewhat more passed without rain, and with the sun's heat so torrid that the whole earth was parched by it. Indeed the heat was no more violent in the days of Elijah than it was then. For there was not a tree in the land that had either leaf or flower. The grass lost its green; the rivers drained away; the springs ran dry; the poor fish, abandoned by their own element, strayed and cried on the ground most horribly; the birds fell from the air through lack of dew; the wolves, foxes, stags, boars, deer, hares, rabbits, weasels, martens, badgers, and other animals were to be found dead in the fields, with their throats gaping. As for men, their case was most piteous. You would have seen them lolling out their tongues like greyhounds that have run for six hours; many threw themselves into wells; others crept into a cow's belly, to be in the shade, and these Homer calls *Alibantes*. The whole country was at a standstill. It was pitiable to see the pains that mortals took to save themselves from this dreadful plight. It was hard work to keep the holy water in the churches from being exhausted. But they so organized it, by the advice of My Lords the Cardinals and the Holy Father, that no one dared to take more than one dip. Yet when anyone entered the church you might have seen scores of poor thirsty souls coming up behind him, and him distributing it to anyone who had his mouth wide open to catch a drop of it, like the wicked rich man,[1] in order that nothing should be lost. Oh, how fortunate in that year was the man who had a cool and well furnished cellar!

The Philosopher relates, in debating the question why the waters of the sea are salt, that at the time when Phoebus handed over the driving of his light-giving chariot to his son Phaeton, the said Phaeton unskilled in the art and not knowing how to follow the ecliptic line between the two tropics of the sun's orbit, strayed from his track and approached so near to the earth that he dried up all the lands beneath him, scorching a large portion of the sky which the philosophers call *Via lactea*,[2] and simpletons call St James's Path, although the more highfalutin' poets say that it is the region where Juno's milk fell when she suckled Hercules. That was the time when the earth was so heated that it burst into a great sweat, which caused it to sweat out the whole sea, which for that reason is salt, for all sweat is salt; which you will admit to be true if you taste your own, or that of pox-patients when they make them sweat. It is all one to me.

An almost similar case occurred in that year. For one Friday, when everyone was at devotions, and they were making a fine procession with all manner of litanies and grand sermons, calling on God Almighty to deign with his eye of mercy to look down on them in their great distress, great drops of water were plainly seen to break out of the earth, as when someone bursts into a copious sweat. And the poor people began to rejoice, as if this had been something to their profit. For some said that there was not a drop of moisture in the air from which they could expect rain, and that the earth was making up for this lack. Other learned people said that it was rain from the Antipodes, about which Seneca tells in the fourth book of his *Questiones naturales*, in speaking of the origin and source of the River Nile. But they were mistaken. For after the procession, when each one wanted to gather up some of this dew and drink it by the bowlful, they found that it was only brine, saltier and far nastier than sea-water.

And because Pantagruel was born on that very day, his father gave him the name he did: for *Panta* in Greek is equivalent to *all*, and *Gruel*, in the Hagarene language, is as much as to say *thirsty*; by this meaning to infer that at the hour of the child's nativity the world was all thirsty, and also seeing, in a spirit of prophecy, that one day his son would be ruler over the thirsty, as was demonstrated to him at that very hour by another sign even more convincing. For when the child's mother Badebec was being delivered of him and the midwives were waiting to receive him, there came first out of her womb sixty-eight muleteers, each pulling by the collar a mule heavily laden with salt; after which came out nine dromedaries loaded with hams and smoked ox-tongues, seven camels loaded with salted eels;

1. A reference to the story of Dives, the rich man (Luke 16, 19–25).
2. The Milky Way.

and then twenty-four cartloads of leeks, garlics, and onions: all of which greatly alarmed the said midwives.

But some of them said: "Here is fine fare. We were only drinking slackly, not like Saxons. This is bound to be a good sign. These are spurs to wine." And whilst they were gossiping amongst themselves about such little matters, out came Pantagruel, as shaggy as a bear. Whereupon one of them said in a spirit of prophecy: "He is born with all his hair. He will perform wonders; and if he lives he'll reach a ripe age."

CHAPTER 3: *Of the Mourning Gargantua Made for the Death of his Wife Badebec*

When Pantagruel was born no one could have been more astonished and perplexed than his father Gargantua. For, seeing on the one side his wife Badebec newly dead, and on the other his son Pantagruel newly born, and so big and handsome, he did not know what to say or do. His mind was troubled with the doubt whether he ought to weep in mourning for his wife, or laugh out of delight at his son. On either side he found sophistical arguments which took his breath away. For he framed them very well *in modo et figura*,[3] but he could not resolve them. And consequently he remained trapped, like a mouse caught in pitch, or a kite taken in a noose.

'Shall I weep?' said he. 'Yes. Why then? Because my wife who was so good is dead. She was the most this, and the most that, that ever was in the world. I shall never see her again, and I shall never find one like her. This is a loss beyond all calculation! O my God, what have I done to thee that thou shouldst punish me so? Why didst Thou not send death to me before sending it to her? For to live without her is no more than a lingering death. Ah, Badebec, my sweet, my darling, my little coney—hers was a good three acres and two roods in size for all that—my tenderling, my codpiece, my shoe, my slipper, never shall I see you again. Oh, poor Pantagruel, you have lost your good mother, your sweet nurse, your beloved lady. Ah, false death, how unkind you are to me, how cruel you are to me, to wrench from me her whose rightful due was immortality!'

And as he spoke he bellowed like a cow. But when Pantagruel came into his mind, he suddenly began laughing like a calf. "Ho, my little son," he cried, "my ballocklet, my footkin, how pretty you are! How grateful I am to God for having given me such a fine son, such a jolly little fellow, so smiling and gay! Ho, ho, ho, ho! How glad I am. Let's drink, ho, and banish all melancholy! Bring some of the best. Rinse the glasses. Lay the cloth. Drive out those dogs. Blow up that fire. Light that candle. Shut that door. Cut up this toast for soup. Send these poor people away, and give

3. By the method and figure of the syllogism.

them that they want. Take my gown, and let me strip to my doublet the better to entertain my company."

As he said this he heard the litanies and dirges of the priests who were carrying his wife to the grave. So he broke off his talk, and was suddenly carried off in another direction, saying: "Lord God, must I turn sad again? It grieves me. I am no longer young. I am growing old. The weather is dangerous. I might catch some fever, and then I should be done for. By my faith as a nobleman, it's better to weep less and drink more. My wife is dead. Well, in God's name—*da jurandi*[4]—I shan't bring her back to life by my tears. She is well off. She is in Paradise at least, if in no better place. She's praying to God for us, she's very happy, she's not worrying any more about our miseries and calamities. The same fate hangs over our heads! God care for those who remain alive! I must think of finding another."

"But this is what you must do," said he to the midwives, the wise women. "But where are they? Good creatures, I cannot see you anywhere—Go to her burial, and in the meantime I'll rock my son here. For I feel very unwell, and might be in danger of falling sick. But drink a good draught beforehand. You'll find yourselves the better for it, believe me, on my honour."

In obedience to his orders, they went to the funeral service and burial, and poor Gargantua remained at home, during which time he composed an epitaph to be engraved as follows:

Dead is the noble Badebec
Who had a face like a Rebec;
A Spanish body and a belly
Like a Swiss frau; she died, I tell ye
In child-bed. Pray to God that her
He pardon wherein she did err.
Here lies her body, which did live
Free from all vice, as I believe,
And did decease, poor simple bride,
The year and day on which she died.

CHAPTER 4: *Of Pantagruel's Childhood*

I find from the old historiographers and poets that many were born into this world in very strange manners, which would take too long to recount. Read the seventh book of Pliny, if you have the leisure. Yet never did you hear of so marvellous a birth as Pantagruel's, for it was almost beyond belief how he grew in body and strength in so short a time. What Hercules did was as nothing, when in his cradle he killed two serpents, for those serpents

4. *Da jurandi [veniam].* Pardon my swearing.

were only small and weak. But Pantagruel, while still in the cradle, did quite astounding things. I will omit to relate here how, at each of his meals, he swigged off the milk of four thousand six hundred cows; and how all the saucepan makers of Saumur in Anjou, of Villedieu in Normandy, and of Bramont in Lorraine were employed in making him a saucepan to boil his soup in; and how they gave him this soup in a great drinking-trough, which is to this day at Bourges, near the palace. But his teeth were already so well grown and strong that he broke a great piece out of this trough, as can well be seen.

One day, in the early morning, when they wanted him to suck one of his cows—for he never had any other wet-nurses, so the history tells us—he got one of his arms free from the bands that held him in the cradle, and he ups with the cow, gripping her under the ham. Then he ate her two udders and half of her paunch, together with the liver and kidneys, and would have devoured her entire, had she not bellowed horribly, as if the wolves had caught her by the legs. At this noise people rushed up, and got her out of Pantagruel's grasp. But they could not prevent the ham's remaining in his hands; and this he ate right off, as if it were a sausage. Indeed when they tried to get the bone from him, he bolted it down as a cormorant would a little fish, and afterwards began to say: "Good, good, good." For he was not able to speak well yet, but wished them to understand that he had found it very good, and would like nothing better than the same again. When they saw this his attendants tied him down with stout cables, like those that are made at Tain for the salt traffic to Lyons; or like those of the great ship *Françoise* which lies at Havre-de-Grace in Normandy.

But at a certain time when a great bear which his father kept escaped and came to lick his face—for his nurses had not properly wiped his mouth—he freed himself from those cables as easily as did Samson from the Philistines and, seizing Master Bear, tore him to pieces like a chicken. He made a nice tit-bit of him for that meal. Whereupon, for fear that he might hurt himself, Gargantua had four great iron chains made to bind him, and buttresses firmly fixed to his cradle. Of these chains you have one at La Rochelle, which is drawn up at night between the two great towers of the harbour; another is at Lyons; another at Angers and the fourth was carried off by the devils to bind Lucifer, who was breaking loose at the time because of a colic that tormented him horribly, as a result of his eating the fricasseed soul of a sergeant for his breakfast. So you can well believe Nicolas de Lyra's comment on that passage in the Psalms, where it is written: *Et Og regem Basan*, to the effect that the same Og, while still small, was so strong and vigorous that he had to be bound to his cradle with iron chains. So Pantagruel remained quiet and peaceable; for he could not break those chains so easily, especially as he had no room in his cradle to swing his arms.

But this is what happened on one great festival day, when his father Gargantua was giving a grand banquet to all the princes of his court. I believe that all his court officers were so busily occupied with the preparation of this banquet that no one bothered about poor Pantagruel, and he was left neglected. What did he do? Listen, my good people, to what he did. He tried to break the chains of his cradle with his arms; but they were too strong and he could not. Then he banged so hard with his feet that he broke the end of his cradle, even though it was made of a beam five foot square; and as soon as he had got his feet outside he slid down as well as he could until his feet touched the ground. Then with great strength he raised himself up, carrying his cradle thus tied on his back, just like a tortoise climbing up a wall; and to look at him, he seemed like a great five-hundred-ton carrack on its end. In this condition he went into the hall where they were banqueting, so boldly that he greatly alarmed the company. Since he had his arms bound inside, however, he could not take anything to eat, but with a great effort bent down to pick up a snack with his tongue. When his father saw this he realized that they had left him without anything to eat, and ordered that he should be loosed from those chains. This was the advice of the princes and lords assembled; and in addition, Gargantua's physicians observed that if he were kept in his cradle like this, he would be subject to gravel all his life. When he was released they made him sit up, and he ate very heartily. Then he broke that cradle of his into more than five hundred thousand pieces with a blow of his fist, which he struck at the middle of it in his rage, swearing that he would never go back into it.

Translated by J. M. Cohen

QUESTIONS

1. How does Rabelais use classical references to satirize the learned schoolmen and philosophers of his day? Give two examples.
2. We see Gargantua alternating between sorrowful mourning and celebration. Why is the effect of this ridiculous?
3. Rabelais has been said to express an all-embracing and life-loving philosophy in his work. Find a passage that exemplifies this, and examine how the author achieves his effects.
4. How does Rabelais use our expectations about size and proportion to achieve comic effect?
5. Based upon the events narrated about Pantagruel's infancy, what expectations do we have about his adult character?
6. How does Rabelais create such a persuasive sense of human physicality? Find two passages that illustrate this, and comment.

Very little is known about the origins of the tales collected in *The Arabian Nights.* They were certainly handed along for many generations in the oral traditions of the Arabs, Persians, and Egyptians. The bulk of the stories appear to have their roots in the culture of medieval Cairo and in the Caliphate of Baghdad (present-day Iraq) in the eighth to tenth centuries. Scholars believe that the organizing framework evolved later: a jealous king named Shahriyar, who took a new wife every evening and had her put to death in the morning; a resourceful young beauty named Scheherazade, who was determined to stall off her fate by telling her husband the most bewitching stories, breaking off every morning and promising to finish the following night.

The Arabian Nights was most likely not recorded in manuscript (in Arabic) until the fifteenth century. The work was discovered several hundred years later by the French Orientalist Galland, and it has not lacked for Western readers since.

As this selection will suggest, the tales are passionate and violent, full of sudden encounters, abrupt turns of fate, and mysterious destinies. Presiding over all is God, whom Muslims call Allah. The flavor of this story, as the reader will quickly discover, is strikingly different from anything in the Western tradition.

THE PORTER AND THE LADIES OF BAGHDAD

from The *Arabian Nights*

O illustrious lady, my story is not like those of my two companions, but more wonderful: the course of fate and destiny brought upon them events against which they could not guard; but as to myself, the shaving of my beard and the loss of my eye were occasioned by my provoking fate and misfortune; and the cause was this:—

I was a King, and the son of a King; and when my father died, I succeeded to his throne, and governed my subjects with justice and beneficence. I took pleasure in sea-voyages; and my capital was on the shore of an extensive sea, interspersed with fortified and garrisoned islands, which I desired, for my amusement, to visit; I therefore embarked with a fleet of ten ships, and took with me provisions sufficient for a whole month. I proceeded twenty days, after which there arose against us a contrary wind; but at daybreak it ceased, and the sea became calm, and we arrived at an island, where we landed, and cooked some provisions and ate; after which we remained there two days. We then continued our voyage; and when twenty days more had passed, we found ourselves in strange waters, unknown to the captain, and desired the watch to look out from the mast-head: so he went aloft, and when he had come down he said to the captain, I saw, on my right hand, fish floating upon the surface of the water; and looking towards the midst of the sea, I perceived something looming in the distance, sometimes black, and sometimes white.

When the captain heard this report of the watch, he threw his turban on the deck, and plucked his beard, and said to those who were with him, Receive warning of our destruction, which will befall all of us: not one will escape! So saying, he began to weep; and all of us in like manner bewailed our lot. I desired him to inform us of that which the watch had seen. O my lord, he replied, know that we have wandered from our course since the commencement of the contrary wind that was followed in the morning by a calm, in consequence of which we remained stationary two days: from that period we have deviated from our course for twenty-one days, and we have no wind to carry us back from the fate which awaits us after this day: to-morrow we shall arrive at a mountain of black stone, called loadstone: the current is now bearing us violently towards it, and the ships will fall in pieces, and every nail in them will fly to the mountain, and adhere to it; for God hath given to the loadstone a secret property by virtue of which everything of iron is attracted towards it.

On that mountain is such a quantity of iron as no one knoweth but God, whose name be exalted; for from times of old great numbers of ships have been destroyed by the influence of that mountain.[1] There is, upon the summit of the mountain, a cupola of brass supported by ten columns, and upon the top of this cupola is a horseman upon a horse of brass, having in his hand a brazen spear, and upon his breast suspended a tablet of lead, upon which are engraved mysterious names and talismans: and as long, O King, as this horseman remains upon the horse, so long will every ship that approaches be destroyed, with every person on board, and all the iron contained in it will cleave to the mountain: no one will be safe until the horseman shall have fallen from the horse.—The captain then wept bitterly; and we felt assured that our destruction was inevitable, and every one of us bade adieu to his friend.

On the following morning we drew near to the mountain; the current carried us towards it with violence, and when the ships were almost close to it, they fell asunder, and all the nails, and everything else that was of iron, flew from them towards the loadstone. It was near the close of day when the ships fell in pieces. Some of us were drowned, and some escaped; but the greater number were drowned, and of those who saved their lives none knew what became of the others, so stupefied were they by the waves and the boisterous wind.

As for myself, O my mistress, God, whose name be exalted, spared me

1. Legendary mountain on the shore of the Indian Ocean, said to have special magnetic powers.

on account of the trouble and torment and affliction that He had predestined to befall me. I placed myself upon a plank, and the wind and waves cast it upon the mountain; and when I had landed, I found a practicable way to the summit, resembling steps cut in the rock: so I exclaimed, In the name of God!—and offered up a prayer, and attempted the ascent, holding fast by the notches; and presently God stilled the wind and assisted me in my endeavours, so that I arrived in safety at the summit. Rejoicing greatly in my escape, I immediately entered the cupola, and performed the prayers of two rek'ahs[2] in gratitude to God for my preservation; after which I slept beneath the cupola, and heard a voice saying to me, O son of Khaseeb,[3] when thou awakest from thy sleep, dig beneath thy feet, and thou wilt find a bow of brass, and three arrows of lead, whereon are engraved talismans: then take the bow and arrows and shoot at the horseman that is upon the top of the cupola, and relieve mankind from this great affliction; for when thou hast shot at the horseman he will fall into the sea; the bow will also fall, and do thou bury it in its place; and as soon as thou hast done this, the sea will swell and rise until it attains the summit of the mountain; and there will appear upon it a boat bearing a man, different from him whom thou shalt have cast down, and he will come to thee, having an oar in his hand: then do thou embark with him; but utter not the name of God; and he will convey thee in ten days to a safe sea, where, on thy arrival, thou wilt find one who will take thee to thy city. All this shall be done if thou utter not the name of God.

Awakening from my sleep, I sprang up, and did as the voice had directed. I shot at the horseman, and he fell into the sea; and the bow having fallen from my hand, I buried it: the sea then became troubled, and rose to the summit of the mountain, and when I had stood waiting there a little while, I beheld a boat in the midst of the sea, approaching me. I praised God, whose name be exalted, and when the boat came to me, I found in it a man of brass, with a tablet of lead upon his breast, engraven with names and talismans. Without uttering a word, I embarked in the boat, and the man rowed me ten successive days, after which I beheld the islands of security, whereupon, in the excess of my joy, I exclaimed, In the name of God! There is no deity but God! God is most great!—and as soon as I had done this, he cast me out of the boat, and sank in the sea.

Being able to swim, I swam until night, when my arms and shoulders were tired, and, in this perilous situation, I repeated the profession of the faith, and gave myself up as lost; but the sea rose with the violence of the wind, and a wave like a vast castle threw me upon the land, in order to the accomplishment of the purpose of God. I ascended the shore, and after I had wrung out my clothes, and spread them upon the ground to

2. The repetition of a set number of words, chiefly from the Koran, the holy book of Islam.

3. Khaseeb means "endowed with plenty."

dry, I slept; and in the morning I put on my clothes again, looking about to see which way I should go, I found a tract covered with trees, to which I advanced; and when I had walked round it, I found that I was upon a small island in the midst of the sea; upon which I said within myself, Every time that I escape from one calamity I fall into another that is worse:—but while I was reflecting upon my unfortunate case, and wishing for death, I beheld a vessel bearing a number of men. I arose immediately, and climbed into a tree; and lo, the vessel came to the shore, and there landed from it ten black slaves bearing axes.

They proceeded to the middle of the island, and, digging up the earth, uncovered and lifted up a trap-door, after which they returned to the vessel, and brought from it bread and flour and clarified butter and honey and sheep and everything that the wants of an inhabitant would require, continuing to pass backwards and forwards between the vessel and the trap-door, bringing loads from the former, and entering the latter, until they had removed all the stores from the ship. They then came out of the vessel with various clothes of the most beautiful description, and in the midst of them was an old sheykh, enfeebled and wasted by extreme age, leading by the hand a young man cast in the mould of graceful symmetry, and invested with such perfect beauty as deserved to be a subject for proverbs. He was like a fresh and slender twig, enchanting and captivating every heart by his elegant form. The party proceeded to the trap-door, and, entering it, became concealed from my eyes.

They remained beneath about two hours, or more; after which, the sheykh and the slaves came out; but the youth came not with them; and they replaced the earth, and embarked and set sail. Soon after, I descended from the tree, and went to the excavation. I removed the earth, and, entering the aperture, saw a flight of wooden steps, which I descended; and, at the bottom, I beheld a handsome dwelling-place, furnished with a variety of silken carpets; and there was the youth, sitting upon a high mattress, with sweet-smelling flowers and fruits placed before him. On seeing me, his countenance became pale; but I saluted him, and said, Let thy mind be composed, O my master: thou hast nothing to fear, O delight of my eye; for I am a man, and the son of a King, like thyself: fate hath impelled me to thee, that I may cheer thee in thy solitude. The youth, when he heard me thus address him, and was convinced that I was one of his own species, rejoiced exceedingly at my arrival, his colour returned, and, desiring me to approach him, he said, O my brother, my story is wonderful: my father is a jeweller; he had slaves who made voyages by his orders, for the purposes of commerce, and he had dealings with Kings; but he had never been blest with a son; and he dreamt that he was soon to have a son, but one whose life would be short; and he awoke sorrowful.[4]

Shortly after, in accordance with the decrees of God, my mother con-

4. Dreams are believed by Muslims to fortell the future.

ceived me, and when her time was complete, she gave birth to me; and my father was greatly rejoiced: the astrologers, however, came to him, and said, Thy son will live fifteen years: his fate is intimated by the fact that there is, in the sea, a mountain called the Mountain of Loadstone, whereon is a horseman on a horse of brass, on the former of which is a tablet of lead suspended to his neck; and when the horseman shall be thrown down from his horse, thy son will be slain: the person who is to slay him is he who will throw down the horseman, and his name is King 'Ajeeb,[5] the son of King Khaseeb. My father was greatly afflicted at this announcement; and when he had reared me until I had nearly attained the age of fifteen years, the astrologers came again, and informed him that the horseman had fallen into the sea, and that it had been thrown down by King 'Ajeeb, the son of King Khaseeb; on hearing which, he prepared for me this dwelling, and here left me to remain until the completion of the term, of which there now remain ten days. All this he did from fear lest King 'Ajeeb should kill me.

When I heard this, I was filled with wonder, and said within myself, I am King 'Ajeeb, the son of King Khaseeb, and it was I who threw down the horseman; but, by Allah, I will neither kill him nor do him any injury. Then said I to the youth, Far from thee be both destruction and harm if it be the will of God, whose name be exalted: thou hast nothing to fear: I will remain with thee to serve thee, and will go forth with thee to thy father, and beg of him to send me back to my country, for which he will obtain a reward. The youth rejoiced at my words, and I sat and conversed with him until night, when I spread his bed for him, and covered him, and slept near to his side. And in the morning I brought him water, and he washed his face, and said to me, May God requite thee for me with every blessing. If I escape from King 'Ajeeb, I will make my father reward thee with abundant favours.—Never, I replied, may the day arrive that would bring thee misfortune. I then placed before him some refreshments, and after we had eaten together, we passed the day conversing with the utmost cheerfulness.

I continued to serve him for nine days; and on the tenth day the youth rejoiced at finding himself in safety, and said to me, O my brother, I wish that thou wouldst in thy kindness warm for me some water, that I may wash myself and change my clothes; for I have smelt the odour of escape from death, in consequence of thy assistance.—With pleasure, I replied:—and I arose, and warmed the water; after which, he entered a place concealed from my view, and, having washed himself and changed his clothes, laid himself upon the mattress to rest after his bath. He then said to me, Cut up for me, O my brother, a watermelon, and mix its juice with some sugar:—so I arose, and, taking a melon, brought it upon a plate, and said to him, Knowest thou, O my master, where is the knife?—See, here it is,

5. 'Ajeeb' means "A wonder."

he answered, upon the shelf over my head. I sprang up hastily, and took it from its sheath, and as I was drawing back, my foot slipped, as God had decreed, and I fell upon the youth, grasping in my hand the knife, which entered his body, and he died instantly. When I perceived that he was dead, and that I had killed him, I uttered a loud shriek, and beat my face and rent my clothes, saying, This is, indeed, a calamity! O what a calamity! O my Lord, I implore thy pardon, and declare to Thee my innocence of his death! Would that I had died before him! How long shall I devour trouble after trouble!

With these reflections I ascended the steps, and, having replaced the trap-door, returned to my first station, and looked over the sea, where I saw the vessel that had come before, approaching, and cleaving the waves in its rapid course. Upon this I said within myself, Now will the men come forth from the vessel, and find the youth slain, and they will slay me also:—so I climbed into a tree, and concealed myself among its leaves, and sat there till the vessel arrived and cast anchor, when the slaves landed with the old sheykh, the father of the youth, and went to the place, and removed the earth. They were surprised at finding it moist, and, when they had descended the steps, they discovered the youth lying on his back, exhibiting a face beaming with beauty, though dead, and clad in white and clean clothing, with the knife remaining in his body. They all wept at the sight, and the father fell down in a swoon, which lasted so long that the slaves thought he was dead. At length, however, he recovered, and came out with the slaves, who had wrapped the body of the youth in his clothes. They then took back all that was in the subterranean dwelling to the vessel, and departed.

I remained, O my mistress, by day hiding myself in a tree, and at night walking about the open part of the island. Thus I continued for the space of two months; and I perceived that, on the western side of the island, the water of the sea every day retired, until, after three months, the land that had been beneath it became dry. Rejoicing at this, and feeling confident now in my escape, I traversed this dry tract, and arrived at an expanse of sand; whereupon I emboldened myself, and crossed it. I then saw in the distance an appearance of fire, and, advancing towards it, found it to be a palace, overlaid with plates of copper, which, reflecting the rays of the sun, seemed from a distance to be fire: and when I drew near to it, reflecting upon this sight, there approached me an old sheykh, accompanied by ten young men who were all blind of one eye, at which I was extremely surprised. As soon as they saw me, they saluted me, and asked me my story, which I related to them from first to last: and they were filled with wonder. They then conducted me into the palace, where I saw ten benches, upon each of which was a mattress covered with a blue stuff;[6] and each of the young men seated himself upon one of these benches, while the sheykh

6. Blue is the color of mourning.

took his place upon a smaller one; after which they said to me, Sit down, O young man, and ask no question respecting our condition, nor respecting our being blind of one eye. Then the sheykh arose, and brought to each of them some food, and the same to me also; and next he brought to each of us some wine: and after we had eaten, we sat drinking together until the time for sleep, when the young men said to the sheykh, Bring to us our accustomed supply:—upon which the sheykh arose, and entered a closet, from which he brought, upon his head, ten covered trays. Placing these upon the floor, he lighted ten candles, and stuck one of them upon each tray; and, having done this, he removed the covers, and there appeared beneath them ashes mixed with pounded charcoal. The young men then tucked up their sleeves above the elbow, and blackened their faces, and slapped their cheeks,[7] exclaiming, We were reposing at our ease, and our impertinent curiosity suffered us not to remain so! Thus they did until the morning, when the sheykh brought them some hot water, and they washed their faces, and put on other clothes.

On witnessing this conduct, my reason was confounded, my heart was so troubled that I forgot my own misfortunes, and I asked them the cause of their strange behaviour; upon which they looked towards me, and said, O young man, ask not respecting that which doth not concern thee; but be silent; for in silence is security from error.—I remained with them a whole month, during which, every night they did the same; and at length I said to them, I conjure you by Allah to remove this disquiet from my mind, and to inform me of the cause of your acting in this manner, and of your exclaiming, We were reposing at our ease, and our impertinent curiosity suffered us not to remain so!—if ye inform me not, I will leave you, and go my way; for the proverb saith, When the eye seeth not, the heart doth not grieve.—On hearing these words, they replied, We have not concealed this affair from thee but in our concern for thy welfare, lest thou shouldst become like us, and the same affliction that hath fallen us happen also to thee. I said, however, Ye must positively inform me of this matter.—We give thee good advice, said they, and do thou receive it, and ask us not respecting our case; otherwise thou wilt become blind of one eye, like us:—but I still persisted in my request; whereupon they said, O young man, if this befall thee, know that thou wilt be banished from our company.

They then all arose, and, taking a ram, slaughtered and skinned it, and said to me, Take this knife with thee, and introduce thyself into the skin of the ram, and we will sew thee up in it, and go away; whereupon a bird called the rukh[8] will come to thee, and, taking thee up by its talons, will fly away with thee, and set thee down upon a mountain: then cut open the skin with this knife, and get out, and the bird will fly away. Thou must

7. Common practices of mourning in Islam.
8. Fabulous bird, said to be able to carry a rhinocerous.

arise, as soon as it hath gone, and journey for half a day, and thou wilt see before thee a lofty palace, encased with red gold, set with various precious stones, such as emeralds and rubies, &c.; and if thou enter it thy case will be as ours; for our entrance into that palace was the cause of our being blind of one eye; and if one of us would relate to thee all that hath befallen him, his story would be too long for thee to hear.

They then sewed me up in the skin, and entered their palace; and soon after, there came an enormous white bird, which seized me, and flew away with me, and set me down upon the mountain; whereupon I cut open the skin, and got out; and the bird, as soon as it saw me, flew away. I rose up quickly, and proceeded towards the palace, which I found to be as they had described it to me; and when I had entered it, I beheld, at the upper end of a saloon, forty young damsels, beautiful as so many moons, and magnificently attired, who, as soon as they saw me, exclaimed, Welcome! Welcome! O our master and our lord! We have been for a month expecting thee. Praise be to God who hath blessed us with one who is worthy of us, and one of whom we are worthy!—After having thus greeted me, they seated me upon a mattress, and said, Thou art from this day our master and prince, and we are thy handmaids, and entirely under thy authority. They then brought to me some refreshments, and, when I had eaten and drunk, they sat and conversed with me, full of joy and happiness. So lovely were these ladies, that even a devotee, if he saw them, would gladly consent to be their servant, and to comply with all that they would desire. At the approach of night they all assembled around me, and placed before me a table of fresh and dried fruits, with other delicacies that the tongue cannot describe, and wine; and one began to sing, while another played upon the lute. The wine-cups circulated among us, and joy overcame me to such a degree as to obliterate from my mind every earthly care, and make me exclaim, This is indeed a delightful life! I passed a night of such enjoyment as I had never before experienced; and on the morrow I entered the bath; and, after I had washed myself, they brought me a suit of the richest clothing, and we again sat down to a repast.

In this manner I lived with them a whole year: but on the first day of the new year, they seated themselves around me, and began to weep, and bade me farewell, clinging to my skirts.—What calamity hath befallen you? said I. Ye have broken my heart.—They answered, Would that we had never known thee; for we have associated with many men, but have seen none like thee. May God, therefore, not deprive us of thy company.—And they wept afresh. I said to them, I wish that you would acquaint me with the cause of this weeping.—Thou, they replied, art the cause; yet now, if thou wilt attend to what we tell thee, we shall never be parted; but if thou act contrary to it, we are separated from this time; and our hearts whisper to us that thou wilt not regard our warning.—Inform me, said I, and I will attend to your directions:—and they replied, If then thou wouldst inquire respecting our history, know that we are the daughters of Kings:

for many years it hath been our custom to assemble here, and every year we absent ourselves during a period of forty days; then returning, we indulge ourselves for a year in feasting and drinking.

This is our usual practice; and now we fear that thou wilt disregard our directions when we are absent from thee. We deliver to thee the keys of the palace, which are a hundred in number, belonging to a hundred closets. Open each of these, and amuse thyself, and eat and drink, and refresh thyself, excepting the closet that hath a door of red gold; for if you open this, the consequence will be a separation between us and thee. We conjure thee, therefore, to observe our direction, and to be patient during this period.—Upon hearing this, I swore to them that I would never open the closet to which they alluded; and they departed, urging me to be faithful to my promise.

I remained alone in the palace, and at the approach of evening I opened the first closet, and, entering it, found a mansion like paradise, with a garden containing green trees loaded with ripe fruits, abounding with singing birds; and watered by copious streams. My heart was soothed by the sight, and I wandered among the trees, scenting the fragrance of the flowers, and listening to the warbling of the birds as they sang the praises of the One, the Almighty.[9] After admiring the mingled colours of the apple resembling the hue upon the cheek of a beloved mistress and the sallow countenance of the perplexed and timid lover, the sweet-smelling quince diffusing an odour like musk and ambergris, and the plum shining as the ruby, I retired from this place, and, having locked the door, opened that of the next closet, within which I beheld a spacious tract planted with numerous palm-trees and watered by a river flowing among rose-trees, and jasmine, and marjoram, and eglantine, and narcissus and gilliflower, the odours of which, diffused in every direction by the wind, inspired me with the utmost delight. I locked again the door of the second closet, and opened that of the third. Within this I found a large saloon, paved with marbles of various colours, and with costly minerals and precious gems, and containing cages constructed of sandal and aloes-wood with singing birds within them, and others upon the branches of trees which were planted there. My heart was charmed, my trouble was dissipated, and I slept there until the morning. I then opened the door of the fourth closet, and within this door I found a great building in which were forty closets with open doors; and, entering these, I beheld pearls, and rubies, and chrysolites, and emeralds, and other precious jewels such as the tongue cannot describe. I was astonished at the sight, and said, Such things as these, I imagine, are not found in the treasury of any King. I am now the King of my age, and all these treasures, through the goodness of God, are mine, together with forty damsels under my authority who have no man to share them with me.

9. Birds are believed to have their own language.

Thus I continued to amuse myself, passing from one place to another, until thirty-nine days had elapsed, and I had opened the doors of all the closets excepting that which they had forbidden me to open. My heart was then disturbed by curiosity respecting this hundredth closet, and the Devil, in order to plunge me into misery, induced me to open it. I had not patience to abstain, though there remained of the appointed period only one day: so I approached the closet, and opened the door; and when I had entered, I perceived a fragrant odour, such as I had never before smelt, which intoxicated me so that I fell down insensible, and remained some time in this state: but at length recovering, I fortified my heart, and proceeded. I found the floor overspread with saffron, and the place illuminated by golden lamps and by candles, which diffused the odours of musk and ambergris; and two large perfuming-vessels filled with aloes-wood and ambergris, and a perfume compounded with honey, spread fragrance through the whole place.

I saw also a black horse, of the hue of the darkest night, before which was a manger of white crystal filled with cleansed sesame, and another, similar to it, containing rose-water infused with musk: he was saddled and bridled, and his saddle was of red gold. Wondering at the sight of him, I said within myself, This must be an animal of extraordinary qualities;—and, seduced by the Devil, I led him out, and mounted him; but he moved not from his place: I kicked him with my heel; but still he moved not: so I took a mikra'ah and struck him with it; and as soon as he felt the blow he uttered a sound like thunder, and, expanding a pair of wings, soared with me to an immense height through the air, and then alighted upon the roof of another palace, where he threw me from his back, and, by a violent blow with his tail upon my face, as I sat on the roof, struck out my eye, and left me.

In this state I descended from the roof, and below I found the one-eyed young men before mentioned, who, as soon as they beheld me, exclaimed, No welcome to thee!—Receive me, said I, into your company:—but they replied, By Allah, thou shalt not remain with us:—so I departed from them, with mournful heart and weeping eye, and, God having decreed me a safe journey hither, I arrived at Baghdád after I had shaved my beard, and become a mendicant.

Translated by Edward William Lore

QUESTIONS

1. This is one of the stories supposedly told by Scheherezade in order to keep the sultan in suspense. How is suspense achieved? How does the teller capture and keep the interest of the listener?
2. What parts of this tale suggest that its origins were in the oral tradition?

3. The narrator explains in the opening passage that he was guilty of provoking fate. Explain what he means with reference to the story.

4. Discuss the role of prophecies in the story. Would the final effect be different if the prophecies were different?

5. What are the elements of the various prophecies? Do they have anything in common?

6. This is, in a sense, the story of how a king became a mendicant, or beggar. What is its message, or moral? What lessons does it teach about human nature? Can you think of any similar tales?

7. How does the teller create an atmosphere of unreality and enchantment?

8. Speculate upon the significance of numbers and numerical precision in this story.

9. Find out the basic tenets of the Islamic faith. In what ways does this story derive from that culture?

Jacob and Wilhelm Grimm

The Brothers Grimm, Jacob (1785–1863) and Wilhelm (1786–1859), were not, strictly speaking, the authors of the tales that have been gathered under their name. They were, in fact, scholars of myths, legends, and linguistic origins. Their interest in word origins, along with their belief that ancient folktales preserved something of the childhood of the human race, led them to undertake the enormous task of searching out storytellers and transcribing their words. The result was a large collection of stories and anecdotes, a cross-section of the European folk imagination. Some of the better-known fruits of their work include "Little Red Riding Hood," "Snow White," "Rumpelstiltskin," "The Frog King," and, of course, "Cinderella."

Jacob Grimm wrote of these tales that they were "the common possession of the common people . . . whose origin mortal eyes cannot see and which therefore is full of mystery like all living things." Behind the simple plot and flat characterizations of "Cinderella," the reader may catch a glimmer of the mystery to which Grimm alludes.

CINDERELLA

from *Grimm's Fairy Tales*

The wife of a rich man fell sick, and as she felt that her end was drawing near, she called her only daughter to her bedside and said: "Dear child, be good and pious, and then the good God will always protect you, and I will look down on you from heaven and be near you." Thereupon she closed her eyes and departed. Every day the maiden went out to her mother's grave and wept, and she remained pious and good. When winter came the snow spread a white sheet over the grave, and by the time the spring sun had drawn it off again, the man had taken another wife.

The woman had brought with her into the house two daughters, who were beautiful and fair of face, but vile and black of heart. Now began a bad time for the poor step-child. "Is the stupid goose to sit in the parlor with us?" they said. "He who wants to eat bread must earn it; out with the kitchen-wench." They took her pretty clothes away from her, put an old grey bedgown on her, and gave her wooden shoes. "Just look at the proud princess, how decked out she is!" they cried, and laughed, and led her into the kitchen. There she had to do hard work from morning till night, get up before daybreak, carry water, light fires, cook and wash. Besides this, the sisters did her every imaginable injury—they mocked her and emptied her peas and lentils into the ashes, so that she was forced to sit and pick them out again. In the evening when she had worked till she was weary she had no bed to go to, but had to sleep by the hearth in the cinders. And as on that account she always looked dusty and dirty, they called her Cinderella.

It happened that the father was once going to the fair, and he asked his two step-daughters what he should bring back for them. "Beautiful dresses," said one, "pearls and jewels," said the second. "And you, Cinderella," said he, "what will you have?" "Father, break off for me the first branch which knocks against your hat on your way home." So he bought beautiful dresses, pearls and jewels for his two step-daughters, and on his way home, as he was riding through a green thicket, a hazel twig brushed against him and knocked off his hat. Then he broke off the branch and took it with him. When he reached home he gave his step-daughters the things which they had wished for, and to Cinderella he gave the branch from the hazel-bush. Cinderella thanked him, went to her mother's grave and planted the branch on it, and wept so much that the tears fell down on it and watered it. And it grew and became a handsome tree. Thrice a day Cinderella went and sat beneath it, and wept and prayed, and a little white bird always came on the tree, and if Cinderella expressed a wish, the bird threw down to her what she had wished for.

It happened, however, that the King gave orders for a festival which was to last three days, and to which all the beautiful young girls in the country were invited, in order that his son might choose himself a bride. When the two step-sisters heard that they too were to appear among the number, they were delighted, called Cinderella and said: "Comb our hair for us, brush our shoes and fasten our buckles, for we are going to the wedding at the King's palace." Cinderella obeyed, but wept, because she too would have liked to go with them to the dance, and begged her step-mother to allow her to do so. "You go, Cinderella!" said she; "covered in dust and dirt as you are, and would go to the festival? You have no clothes and shoes, and yet would dance!" As, however, Cinderella went on asking, the step-mother said at last: "I have emptied a dish of lentils into the ashes for you, if you have picked them out again in two hours, you shall go with us." The maiden went through the back-door into the garden, and called: "You tame pigeons, you turtle-doves, and all you birds beneath the sky, come and help me to pick

The good into the pot,
The bad into the crop."

Then two white pigeons came in by the kitchen-window, and afterwards the turtle-doves, and at last all the birds beneath the sky, came whirring and crowding in, and alighted amongst the ashes. And the pigeons nodded with their heads and began pick, pick, pick, pick, and the rest began also pick, pick, pick, pick, and gathered all the good grains into the dish. Hardly had one hour passed before they had finished, and all flew out again. Then the girl took the dish to her step-mother, and was glad, and believed that now she would be allowed to go with them to the festival. But the step-mother said: "No, Cinderella, you have no clothes and you can not dance; you would only be laughed at." And as Cinderella wept at this, the step-mother said: "If you can pick two dishes of lentils out of the ashes for me in one hour, you shall go with us." And she thought to herself: "That she most certainly cannot do again." When the step-mother had emptied the two dishes of lentils amongst the ashes, the maiden went through the back-door into the garden and cried: "You tame pigeons, you turtle-doves, and all you birds beneath the sky, come and help me to pick

The good into the pot,
The bad into the crop."

Then two white pigeons came in by the kitchen-window, and afterwards the turtle-doves, and at length all the birds beneath the sky, came whirring and crowding in, and alighted amongst the ashes. And the doves nodded with their heads and began pick, pick, pick, pick, and the others began also pick, pick, pick, pick, and gathered all the good seeds into the dishes, and before half an hour was over they had already finished, and all flew out again. Then the maiden carried the dishes to the step-mother and was delighted, and believed that she might now go with them to the wedding. But the step-mother said: "All this will not help; you cannot go with us, for you have no clothes and can not dance; we should be ashamed of you!" On this she turned her back on Cinderella, and hurried away with her two proud daughters.

As no one was now at home, Cinderella went to her mother's grave beneath the hazel-tree, and cried:

Shiver and quiver, little tree.
Silver and gold throw down over me.

Then the bird threw a gold and silver dress down to her, and slippers embroidered with silk and silver. She put on the dress with all speed, and went to the wedding. Her step-sisters and the step-mother however did not know her, and thought she must be a foreign princess, for she looked so beautiful in the golden dress. They never once thought of Cinderella, and believed that she was sitting at home in the dirt, picking lentils out of the ashes. The prince approached her, took her by the hand and danced with her. He would dance with no other maiden, and never let loose of her hand, and if any one else came to invite her, he said: "This is my partner."

She danced till it was evening, and then she wanted to go home. But the King's son said: "I will go with you and bear you company," for he wished to see to whom the beautiful maiden belonged. She escaped from him, however, and sprang into the pigeon-house. The King's son waited until her father came, and then he told him that the unknown maiden had leapt into the pigeon-house. The old man thought: "Can it be Cinderella?" and they had to bring him an axe and a pickaxe that he might hew the pigeon-house to pieces, but no one was inside it. And when they got home Cinderella lay in her dirty clothes among the ashes, and a dim little oil-lamp was burning on the mantle-piece, for Cinderella had jumped quickly down from the back of the pigeon-house and had run to the little hazel-tree, and there she had taken off her beautiful clothes and laid them on the grave, and the bird had taken them away again, and then she had seated herself in the kitchen amongst the ashes in her grey gown.

Next day when the festival began afresh, and her parents and the step-sisters had gone once more, Cinderella went to the hazel-tree and said:

Shiver and quiver, my little tree,
Silver and gold throw down over me.

Then the bird threw down a much more beautiful dress than on the preceding day. And when Cinderella appeared at the wedding in this dress, every one was astonished at her beauty. The King's son had waited until she came, and instantly took her by the hand and danced with no one but her. When others came and invited her, he said: "This is my partner." When evening came she wished to leave, and the King's son followed her and wanted to see into which house she went. But she sprang away from him, and into the garden behind the house. Therein stood a beautiful tall tree on which hung the most magnificent pears. She clambered so nimbly between the branches like a squirrel that the King's son did not know where she was gone. He waited until her father came, and said to him: "The unknown maiden has escaped from me, and I believe she has climbed up the pear-tree." The father thought: "Can it be Cinderella?" and had an axe brought and cut the tree down, but no one was on it. And when they got into the kitchen, Cinderella lay there among the ashes, as usual, for she had jumped down on the other side of the tree, had taken the beautiful dress to the bird on the little hazel-tree, and put on her grey gown.

On the third day, when the parents and sisters had gone away, Cinderella went once more to her mother's grave and said to the little tree:

Shiver and quiver, my little tree,
Silver and gold throw down over me.

And now the bird threw down to her a dress which was more splendid and magnificent than any she had yet had, and the slippers were golden.

And when she went to the festival in the dress, no one knew how to speak for astonishment. The King's son danced with her only, and if any one invited her to dance, he said: "This is my partner."

When evening came, Cinderella wished to leave, and the King's son was anxious to go with her, but she escaped from him so quickly that he could not follow her. The King's son, however, had employed a ruse, and had caused the whole staircase to be smeared with pitch, and there, when she ran down, had the maiden's left slipper remained stuck. The King's son picked it up, and it was small and dainty, and all golden. Next morning, he went with it to the father, and said to him: "No one shall be my wife but she whose foot this golden slipper fits." Then were the two sisters glad, for they had pretty feet. The eldest went with the shoe into her room and wanted to try it on, and her mother stood by. But she could not get her big toe into it, and the shoe was too small for her. Then her mother gave her a knife and said: "Cut the toe off; when you are Queen you will have no more need to go on foot." The maiden cut the toe off, forced the foot into the shoe, swallowed the pain, and went out to the King's son. Then he took her on his horse as his bride and rode away with her. They were obliged, however, to pass the grave, and there, on the hazel-tree, sat the two pigeons and cried:

Turn and peep, turn and peep,
There's blood within the shoe,
The shoe it is too small for her,
The true bride waits for you.

Then he looked at her foot and saw how the blood was trickling from it. He turned his horse round and took the false bride home again, and said she was not the true one, and that the other sister was to put the shoe on. Then this one went into her chamber and got her toes safely into the shoe, but her heel was too large. So her mother gave her a knife and said: "Cut a bit off your heel; when you are Queen you will have no more need to go on foot." The maiden cut a bit off her heel, forced her foot into the shoe, swallowed the pain, and went out to the King's son. He took her on his horse as his bride, and rode away with her, but when they passed by the hazel-tree, the two little pigeons sat on it and cried:

Turn and peep, turn and peep,
There's blood within the shoe,
The shoe it is too small for her,
The true bride waits for you.

He looked down at her foot and saw how the blood was running out of her shoe, and how it had stained her white stocking quite red. Then he turned his horse and took the false bride home again. "This also is not the right one," said he, "have you no other daughter?" "No," said the man, "there is still a little stunted kitchen-wench which my late wife left behind her, but she cannot possibly be the bride." The King's son said he was to send her up to him; but the mother answered: "Oh no, she is much too dirty, she cannot show herself!" But he absolutely insisted on it, and Cinderella had to be called. She first washed her hands and face clean, and then went and bowed down before the King's son, who gave her the golden shoe. Then she seated herself on a stool, drew her foot out of the heavy wooden shoe, and put it into the slipper, which fitted like a glove. And when she rose up and the King's son looked at her face he recognized the beautiful maiden who had danced with him and cried: "That is the true bride!" The step-mother and the two sisters were horrified and became pale with rage; he, however, took Cinderella on his horse and rode away with her. As they passed by the hazel-tree, the two white doves cried:

Turn and peep, turn and peep,
No blood is in the shoe,
The shoe is not too small for her,
The true bride rides with you,

and when they had cried that, the two came flying down and placed themselves on Cinderella's shoulders, one on the right, the other on the left, and remained sitting there.

When the wedding with the King's son was to be celebrated, the two false sisters came and wanted to get into favor with Cinderella and share her good fortune. When the betrothed couple went to church, the elder was at the right side and the younger at the left, and the pigeons pecked out one eye from each of them. Afterwards as they came back, the elder was at the left, and the younger at the right, and then the pigeons pecked out the other eye from each. And thus, for their wickedness and falsehood, they were punished with blindness all their days.

QUESTIONS

1. This narrative is built around repetitions. Find three instances, and comment upon the effect created. How would the story be different without repetitions?
2. What are our first indications about Cinderella's character? Does she change or remain constant over the course of the story?
3. Cinderella is the only person in the story who can invoke the supernatural. Does this have any connection with her character? Comment. How does she come to possess this magical touch?
4. Are the stepmother and her daughters to be seen as evil or simply as foolish? Do the sisters deserve the punishments inflicted upon them at the end of the tale?
5. Psychologist Bruno Bettelheim once theorized that grisly children's stories fulfill the important social function of teaching children about the harsh truths of the real world. What would a child learn about the world, and the place in it of good and evil, from "Cinderella"?

2

THE FIRST GOLDEN AGE OF THE SHORT STORY

As noted in the Introduction, the first appearance of the written short story coincided with certain historical developments, at least, in Europe and North America. (Africa, Asia, and South America were governed by different historical circumstances and generally followed the lead of Western nations.) The period of the late eighteenth and early nineteenth centuries was one of intensive, often convulsive, social change. The growth of manufacture and trade had created an increasingly powerful middle class, which used its power to question and challenge the rule of the aristocrats. The American Revolution, which was on one level a revolt carried out against sanctions imposed by the British monarchy, was followed by the bloody class revolution in France. Both ultimately empowered commoners and expanded the influence of the mercantile class.

This massive reordering of society (reform movements flourished throughout Europe) brought with it a steady improvement in public education programs; literacy increased dramatically throughout the West. Along with a newly educated readership, improved technological resources and an increase of leisure time among the middle class ensured that newspapers and journals would grow in number and influence. Conditions were ripe for the appearance of the short story—the self-contained work of the imagination that could be read in a single sitting.

The first stories, as I have emphasized, did not spring forth from a vacuum. Writers were able to draw upon a long tradition of diverse narrative works, those directly transcribed from the oral tradition as well as the episode-based novels that had been in circulation for a century or so.

But what is at first glance striking about these early short stories is how different they are in their essentials from the tales and legends that had been passed along for centuries. While the structuring of episodes, the building of suspense, and so on, owe a great deal to the traditions of storytelling, the subject matter, approaches to character, and even the underlying assumptions about the world were new. These came out of changed societal circumstances.

One of these changes, which I have discussed at greater length in the Introduction, was the invention and spread of print technology. A writer tells things differently to readers of the printed page than does a speaker standing before a group of listeners. On the printed page the writer can follow up subtleties and complexities that the teller of oral stories must avoid.

But as important as it was, this shift from oral modes to written ones cannot account for the full spectrum of changes that we discover. Many of these have to do with the appearance of new needs and desires in the audience and of new kinds of audiences. Illiterate villagers want one sort of narrative, educated merchants quite another.

The most evident change in the short story is that it has become (with certain important exceptions) realistic. Gone for the most part are gods and witches, sudden transformations from man to beast, and astonishing coincidences. Instead, we find a familiar world governed by known patterns and laws. (This is *not* the case with Gogol's satire "The Nose," in which a man wakes up to find his nose missing, or with Poe's "The Masque of the Red Death," which features a ghoulish personification of death.) Most of the stories are set in identifiable locales—the Hudson Valley countryside in Washington Irving's "The Legend of Sleepy Hollow," a Maine farmstead in Jewett's "A White Heron"—and make use of careful naturalistic description to set the scene.

The time periods, too, are specified; most of the authors set their stories either in the recent past or in the fictional present. We are not asked, as with literature of earlier periods, to suspend disbelief. Rather, the author tries to compel our engagement by establishing the believability of the scenarios.

The greatest difference, however, between the short stories of the first Golden Age and the narratives that preceded them has to do with the presentation of character. The earlier narratives presented protagonists with simplified, stereotyped characteristics (the wily Odysseus, the pure and humble Cinderella); the later stories give more attention to distinct and idiosyncratic details of character. True, Irving's Ichabod Crane may appear to be a caricature of the gangly bookworm, and Maupassant's peasant may be a somewhat stereotyped provincial, but even in these cases the portrayals keep faith with the complexities of human character. Ichabod is shy and bumbling, but he also raps his pupils with a yardstick; Maupassant's Hauchecorne, while not developed to great depth, is complicated enough that we can see him as both ludicrous and tragic.

Not only are the characters in these stories rendered with great particularity, they are also strikingly nonheroic, even antiheroic. Nearly every one is drawn from the ranks of ordinary people. This is not mere chance. It is far more likely that these individuals have been created to prove a point—to give a face and a name to the once invisible commoner. The rise of realism goes hand-in-hand with the overthrow of peacock aristocrats and the emergence of ordinary people from obscurity. The message is simple: there is life, joy, sorrow, complication, and importance everywhere. This is the true manifestation of the democratic impulse in the arts. Simple people are no more simple than the rest; this assumption, which abetted their oppression, was false.

As with characters, so with incidents. The sharply drawn, dramatic plots that dominated the tales of earlier storytellers give way to actions and encounters that seem drab by comparison. Maupassant's Hauchecorne stoops to pick up a piece of string and finds, in time, that the deed has changed his life. Chekhov's lovers live through the unspectacular stages of their adulterous passion. Twain spins a whole story around the reputed jumping ability of a frog. Together, these various writers demonstrate that nothing is too small or trivial to warrant attention and that the whole point is in the looking.

By and large, these stories confine themselves to the scrupulous presentation of actions and interchanges, with occasional transcriptions of a character's more salient thoughts. They achieve remarkable insight, but they do so essentially through external means. That is, we are asked to supply much of the psychological background ourselves, to infer motives and feelings from behavior. More explicit exploration of the interior life will be carried out later by the Modernists. Even so, these pre-twentieth-century stories—Olive Schreiner's "The Woman's Rose," Chekhov's "Lady with Lapdog," James's "Brooksmith"—are not lacking in delicate and sophisticated suggestions of the psychological processes underlying behavior. Freud had not yet named the unconscious, but the most perceptive writers were already anticipating him.

The flowering of realism in the short story was part of more general artistic developments in the nineteenth century. Artists were holding up a looking glass to the face of society. Remember, photography was still in the early stages of its development; television and radio were nonexistent. People needed to see themselves—individually and collectively. The short story helped to answer that need. It became less a means of lifting audiences out of daily life to the magical and more a way of helping them perceive social and personal actualities.

Jippensha Ikku

The *Hizakurige* (which means "a journey on foot") of Jippensha Ikku (1766–1831) is a comically anecdotal work much beloved by the Japanese. The book, which was issued in serial form beginning in the early 1800s, belongs to the Tokugawa period (1600–1868) of Japanese history. In Japan, as in Europe at this time, an educated merchant class gained ascendancy. Not only did many of the writers emerge from the mercantile ranks, but they wrote, as did their European peers, for the members of the new constituency. The serialized adventures of Yaji and Kita drew great acclaim for their earthy humor and irrepressible spirits. The appeal clearly derived from the fact that these travelers had no trace of the uprightness and sobriety expected of the merchant class.

HIZAKURIGE

They went down the hill till they reached Nissaka, the rain coming down harder and harder till it was impossible to go on, as everything was blotted out. Finally they took refuge under the eaves of an inn.

"How annoying!" said Yaji, "Such terrible rain!"

"Well, we're not willow trees, to be planted by the roadside," said Kita. "We can't stand under the eaves of people's houses forever. What do you think, Yaji? We've crossed the River Ōi. Don't you think we might stop here for the night?"

"What?" said Yaji. "Don't talk nonsense! It can't be two o'clock yet. It would be absurd to stop now."

Then the old landlady came out of the inn.

"You can't go on in this rain," she said. "Please stop here."

"I think we ought to," said Kita. "I say, Yaji, look! There are some women stopping in the back room there."

"Eh?" said Yaji. "Where? That's interesting."

"Won't your honors stop here?" repeated the old woman.

"Well, suppose we do," said Yaji.

They went in and washed their feet, and were soon conducted to a room at the back next to the one where they had seen the women. . . .

Then the supper trays were brought in and they set to work to eat, uttering all sorts of jokes.

"By the way," said Yaji to the maid, "the guests in the back room are women, aren't they? Who are they?"

"They're witches," said the maid.

"What, witches?" said Kita. "That's interesting. Let's call up somebody."

"It's too late, isn't it?" said Yaji. "They won't come after four o'clock."

"It's only a little past two," said the maid.

"Well, just ask them," said Yaji. "I'd like to have a talk with my dead wife."

"Fancy wanting to do that!" said Kita.

"I'll ask them afterward," said the maid.

So when the meal was finished she went into the next room to ask the witches. They agreed, and Yaji and Kita were conducted into their room. There the witches produced the usual box and arranged it, while the maid, who knew what was wanted, drew some water and brought it.

Yaji, with his mind fixed on his departed wife, poured some water over the anise leaves and the younger witch began to invoke the gods.

"First of all," she chanted, "I reverently call upon Bonten and Taishaku and the four gods of Heaven, and in the underworld the great Emma and the five attendants who wait on him. Of our country's gods I invoke the seven gods of Heaven and the five gods of Earth, and of the gods of Ise, Amaterasu Ōmikami, and the forty descendants of the Outer Shrine and the eight descendants of the Inner Shrine. I invoke the God of Rain, the God of Wind, the God of the Moon and the God of the Sun, the God of the North Shrine of the Benku Mirror, and the spirit of the great Sun Goddess of Ama no iwato, and Kokuzō, the God of Ten Thousand Good Fortunes of Asama ga dake, and the others in the sixty provinces of Japan, and also in the country of the gods, at the Great Shrine of Izumo. By the ninety-eight thousand gods of the country and the thirteen thousand Buddhas of the holy places, through the fearful road of the underworld I come. Ah, horror! The spirits of his ancestors crowd upon me, each couple as inseparable as the bow and the arrow. The skies may change and the waters may change, but the bow is unchangeable. One shot from it sends an echo through all the holy places of the temples. Ah! Ah! Oh, joyful sight! Well have you summoned me. I had for a bedfellow a warrior famous with the bow, but alas! averse to a pure diet, in life he devoured fish even to the bones, and now, in punishment, is changed into a devil in the shape of an ox, his duty being to keep the gates of Hell, from which he has no release. Thus have I come alone."

"Who are you?" asked Yaji. "I don't understand what it's all about!"

"I have come for the sake of him who offered me water, the mirror of my body, my child-treasure."

"Mirror of the body?" said Kita. "I'll tell you what, Yaji, it's your mother."

"My mother, eh?" said Yaji. "I don't have anything to say to her."

"Has the mirror of my body nothing to say to me?" continued the witch. "To me, your bedfellow, whom you have thus without shame summoned from the depths? Ah, what agony I went through when I was married to you—time and again suffering the pangs of hunger and shivering with cold in the winter. Ah, hateful! Hateful!"

"Forgive me," said Yaji. "At that time my fortunes were low. How pitiful your lot that you should have been brought to the grave with care and hardships."

"Halloa, Yaji," said Kita. "Are you crying? Ha, ha, ha! Even devils have tears."

"I shall never forget it," the witch went on. "When you were ill you gave your sickness to me. Our only child, who had to carry on our name, grew weak and thin because there was no rice to fill his empty stomach. Every day the bill collectors were knocking at the door and the rent remained unpaid. Yet I did not complain—not even when I slipped in the dogs' dirt in the lane."

"Don't talk of it," said Yaji. "You'll break my heart."

"And then, when through my labors I had saved enough money to buy a kimono, I had to pawn it for your sake and never saw it again. Never again did it come back to me from the pawnbroker's."

"At the same time you must remember what a pleasant place you are in now," said Yaji, "while I have to worry along down here."

"What? What is there pleasant about it? It is true that by the help of your friends you erected a stone over my grave, but you never go near it, and you never contribute to the temple to get the priests to say prayers for my soul. I am nothing to you. The stone over my grave has been taken away and put into the wall, where all the dogs come and make water against it. Not a drop of water is ever placed on my grave. Truly in death we suffer all sorts of troubles."

"True, true," said Yaji.

"But while you thus treat me with neglect," the witch went on, "lying in my grave I think of nobody but you and long for the time when you will join me in the underworld. Shall I come to meet you?"

"No, no, don't do that," said Yaji. "It's really too far for you."

"Well then, I have one request to make."

"Yes, yes. What is it?"

"Give this witch plenty of money."

"Of course, of course."

"How sad the parting!" cried the witch. "I have yet much to tell you, countless questions to ask you, but the messenger of Hell recalls me!"

Then, recovering from her trance, the witch twanged her bow.

"Thank you very much," said Yaji. He took out some money and wrapped it in paper and gave it to her.

"Ha, ha!" laughed Kita. "Now all your hidden shames are revealed to the world. Ha, ha, ha! But I say, Yaji, you look very downcast. What do you say to a drink?"

Yaji agreed and clapping his hands ordered the maid to bring some saké.

"How far have you come today?" asked the witch.

"We came from Okabe," answered Yaji.

"How quick you are," said the witch.

"Oh, that's nothing," said Yaji. "We can walk as fast as Idaten.[1] If we're put to it we can walk thirty-five miles a day."

"But then we shouldn't be fit for anything for ten days after," put in Kita.

While they were talking the saké was brought in.

"Won't you have a little?" said Yaji to the young witch.

"I never touch a drop," she answered.

"Will your companion have any?" asked Yaji.

"Mother, Mother! Come here," called the young witch.

"Oh, it's your mother, is it?" said Kita. "I must take care what I say in front of her. But come, do have some."

Soon they began to drink and enjoy themselves, the cup passing from hand to hand very quickly. Yet strangely enough, the witches, however much they drank, never seemed to be any the worse for it, while Yaji and Kita got so drunk they could not speak plainly. After making all sorts of jokes which it would be too tedious to repeat, Kita at last in a drunken voice said, "I say, Mother, won't you lend me your daughter for the night?"

"No, no, she's going to lend her to me," said Yaji.

"What an idea!" cried Kita. "You'd better try and be good tonight. Haven't you any pity for your dead wife who spends her time in thinking of you and hoping you will join her quickly? Didn't she say she'd come and meet you after a bit?"

"Here, don't talk about that," said Yaji. "What should I do if she did come to meet me?"

"Then you had better be good," said Kita. "Now, old lady, what do you think?"

Kita here gave the young witch a loving caress, but she pushed him off and ran away, saying "Be quiet."

"If my daughter doesn't want to," said the mother, "what about me?"

"Well, if it comes to that I don't care who it is," said Kita, who was lost in a drunken dream.

While they were talking the supper was brought in and there was a good deal of joking too tedious to repeat, and finally Yaji and Kita, the effects of the saké having already passed off, went back into their own

1. A Buddhist protecting god, known for his swiftness.

room where, as soon as it was dark, they went to bed. In the next room also the witches were apparently going to bed, worn out by their travels.

"That young witch is sleeping on this side, I know," said Kita in a low voice. "I'll creep in to her after a bit. Yaji, you'd better go to sleep."

"Get out," said Yaji. "I'm going to be the one to get her."

"Isn't he bold?" said Kita. "It would make a cat laugh."

Thus talking they crept into bed and fell asleep. It was already about nine o'clock, and the night watchman's rattle, as he went round the inn, echoed through the pillows of the travelers. In the kitchen the sound of the preparations for the next morning's meal had died away, and all that could be heard was the barking of the dogs. It was just when night was at its darkest and eeriest that Kitahachi decided the time was right to creep out of bed and peep into the next room. The night light had gone out, and he felt his way in very softly and crept into the bed where he thought the young witch was sleeping. To his surprise the witch, without saying anything, caught hold of his hand and pulled him in. Delighted with his reception, Kitahachi sank down under the coverlet with her arm for a pillow and soon realized his desire, after which they both fell asleep quite unconscious of their surroundings.

Yajirobei, who was thus left sleeping alone, soon opened his eyes. "I wonder what time it is," he muttered. "I must go to the toilet. It's so dark I can't see the way."

Thus pretending that he was going to the toilet he crept into the next room, quite unaware of the fact that Kitahachi was already in there. Feeling about, he came to the side of the bed where Kita was lying, and thinking in the darkness that it was the young witch's lips from which moans were coming, he put his lips to those of Kitahachi and took a bite.

"Oh! Oh!" yelled Kitahachi.

"Halloa! Is that you, Kitahachi?" said Yaji.

"Oh, it's Yaji, is it?" said Kita. "Ugh! Ugh! How beastly!" and he began spitting.

At the sound of their voices the witch into whose bed Kita had crept woke up.

"What are you doing?" she said. "Don't make such a noise. You'll wake my daughter up."

This was another surprise for Kita, for it was the old witch's voice. Cursing himself for his stupidity he got out of the bed and crept away softly into the next room. Yaji was going to do the same when the old witch caught hold of him.

"You mustn't make a fool of an old woman by running away," she said.

"No, no," stuttered Yaji. "You've made a mistake. It wasn't me."

"You mustn't try to deceive me," said the old woman. "I don't make a regular business of this, but when I meet a traveler on the road and sleep with him I like to get a little just to help me along. It's a shame to make a fool of me by running away. There, just go to sleep in my bosom till dawn."

"What a nuisance you are," said Yaji. "Here, Kitahachi, Kitahachi."

"Take care," said the old woman. "You mustn't call so loud."

"But I don't know anything about it," said Yaji. "It's that Kitahachi that's got me into all this mess."

Thus saying Yaji struggled out of her grasp, only to be caught again and thrown down. But at last, after a good deal of kicking, he managed to get away into the next room, where he repeated to himself.

By stealth I entered, witch's love to earn,
But which was witch I could not well discern.

Translated by Thomas Satchell

QUESTIONS

1. *Hizakurige* is one of the most popular story cycles in the Japanese tradition. Judging from this episode, what is the source of its appeal? How does it generate its comic effect?
2. Discuss the characters of Yaji and Kita. How do we first pick up on the nature of their relationship? Who is presented as the wiser, who as the fool?
3. Do we believe that the two women at the inn are really witches? At what point are we most inclined to doubt this?
4. What can we determine about Yaji's marriage from his actions and statements? What do we learn about his character in general? How is it that a character can have so many faults and still be portrayed as likable?
5. Does Ikku supply any foreshadowing? Do we have any reason to suspect the outcome? Discuss.
6. Who proves to be the bigger fool, Yaji or Kita?
7. Applying a feminist perspective, discuss the presentation of gender roles in this story. What are the assumptions about men and women?

Washington Irving

It is fitting that Washington Irving (1783–1859) was named for the first president of the United States, for he is this country's first great man of letters. Born and raised in Manhattan, Irving received most of his education through his own voluminous reading. Though he studied law as a young man, frail health threw him off the track of a legal career. When his family sent him to Europe early in 1804, he was already trying his hand at literary ventures. Two years after his return, in 1808, he published *Knickerbocker's History of New York.*

Irving quickly perceived the difficulty that a writer would have in making a living strictly with his pen. The young nation, he wrote, was too busy building itself to care for the more meditative enterprises of literature. Consequently, in 1815, Irving set sail for England, ostensibly to work in the family import-export business. But after the family company went bankrupt in 1818, he stayed on to pursue his artistic career. He did not return to New York until 1832. In the interval he published his celebrated *The Sketch Book* (1819), *Bracebridge Hall* (1822), and a number of other works. Following his return, Irving took up the immense task of a five-volume life of George Washington. He died shortly after the final volume was published.

In one sense, Irving set a precedent for American writers. More than a few of our finest talents have felt the need to travel away from their native country in order to fulfill their artistic destinies. Other well-known expatriates include Cooper, Hawthorne, Melville, James, Wharton, Eliot, Pound, and Hemingway. Irving, for his part, gave vivid expression to the longings such self-distancing can inspire. In a letter to his friend Henry Brevoort he wrote:

> Do not let yourself be persuaded . . . that time or distance has estranged me in thought or feeling from my native country, my native place, or the friends of my youth. The fact is, that the longer I remain from home the greater charm it has in my eyes, and all the coloring that the imagination once gave to distant Europe now gathers about the scenes of my native country.

That coloring is nowhere more feelingly captured than in "The Legend of Sleepy Hollow." Indeed, the evocations of place go hand-in-hand with Irving's fond comedy—the work stands as one of the first, and best, American short stories.

NOTE: *Irving's shyness, as well as his desire to add a resonance of the legendary to his work, often made use of invented personae. That "The Legend of Sleepy Hollow" is supposedly found among the papers of one Diedrich Knickerbocker is part of the fiction.*

THE LEGEND OF SLEEPY HOLLOW

A pleasing land of drowsy head it was,
Of dreams that wave before the half-shut eye,
And of gay castles in the clouds that pass,
For ever flushing round a summer sky.

CASTLE OF INDOLENCE

In the bosom of one of those spacious coves which indent the eastern shore of the Hudson, at that broad expansion of the river denominated by the ancient Dutch navigators the Tappan Zee, and where they always prudently shortened sail, and implored the protection of St. Nicholas when they crossed, there lies a small market-town or rural port, which by some is called Greensburgh, but which is more generally and properly known by the name of Tarry Town. This name was given, we are told, in former days, by the good housewives of the adjacent country, from the inveterate propensity of their husbands to linger about the village tavern on market-days. Be that as it may, I do not vouch for the fact, but merely advert to it for the sake of being precise and authentic. Not far from this village, perhaps about two miles, there is a little valley, or rather lap of land, among high hills, which is one of the quietest places in the whole world. A small brook glides through it, with just murmur enough to lull one to repose; and the occasional whistle of a quail, or tapping of a woodpecker, is almost the only sound that ever breaks in upon the uniform tranquillity.

I recollect that, when a stripling, my first exploit in squirrel-shooting was in a grove of tall walnut-trees that shades one side of the valley. I had wandered into it at noon-time, when all nature is particularly quiet, and was startled by the roar of my own gun, as it broke the Sabbath stillness around, and was prolonged and reverberated by the angry echoes. If ever I should wish for a retreat, whither I might steal from the world and its distractions, and dream quietly away the remnant of a troubled life, I know of none more promising than this little valley.

From the listless repose of the place, and the peculiar character of its inhabitants, who are descendants from the original Dutch settlers, this sequestered glen has long been known by the name of SLEEPY HOLLOW, and its rustic lads are called the Sleepy Hollow Boys throughout all the neighboring country. A drowsy, dreamy influence seems to hang over the land, and to pervade the very atmosphere. Some say that the place was bewitched by a high German doctor, during the early days of the settlement; others, that an old Indian chief, the prophet or wizard of his tribe, held his pow-wows there before the country was discovered by Master Hendrick

Hudson. Certain it is, the place still continues under the sway of some bewitching power, that holds a spell over the minds of the good people, causing them to walk in a continual reverie. They are given to all kinds of marvellous beliefs; are subject to trances and visions; and frequently see strange sights, and hear music and voices in the air. The whole neighborhood abounds with local tales, haunted spots, and twilight superstitions; stars shoot and meteors glare oftener across the valley than in any other part of the country, and the nightmare, with her whole ninefold, seems to make it the favorite scene of her gambols.

The dominant spirit, however, that haunts this enchanted region, and seems to be commander-in-chief of all the powers of the air, is the apparition of a figure on horseback without a head. It is said by some to be the ghost of a Hessian trooper, whose head had been carried away by a cannon-ball, in some nameless battle during the Revolutionary War, and who is ever and anon seen by the country folk, hurrying along in the gloom of night, as if on the wings of the wind. His haunts are not confined to the valley, but extend at times to the adjacent roads, and especially to the vicinity of a church at no great distance. Indeed, certain of the most authentic historians of those parts, who have been careful in collecting and collating the floating facts concerning this spectre, allege that the body of the trooper, having been buried in the churchyard, the ghost rides forth to the scene of battle in nightly quest of his head; and that the rushing speed with which he sometimes passes along the Hollow, like a midnight blast, is owing to his being belated, and in a hurry to get back to the churchyard before daybreak.

Such is the general purport of this legendary superstition, which has furnished materials for many a wild story in that region of shadows; and the spectre is known, at all the country firesides, by the name of the Headless Horseman of Sleepy Hollow.

It is remarkable that the visionary propensity I have mentioned is not confined to the native inhabitants of the valley, but is unconsciously imbibed by every one who resides there for a time. However wide awake they may have been before they entered that sleepy region, they are sure, in a little time, to inhale the witching influence of the air, and begin to grow imaginative, to dream dreams, and see apparitions.

I mention this peaceful spot with all possible laud; for it is in such little retired Dutch valleys, found here and there embosomed in the great State of New York, that population, manners, and customs remain fixed; while the great torrent of migration and improvement, which is making such incessant changes in other parts of this restless country, sweeps by them unobserved. They are like those little nooks of still water which border a rapid stream; where we may see the straw and bubble riding quietly at anchor, or slowly revolving in their mimic harbor, undisturbed by the rush of the passing current. Though many years have elapsed since I trod the drowsy shades of Sleepy Hollow, yet I question whether I should not still find the same trees and the same families vegetating in its sheltered bosom.

In this by-place of nature, there abode, in a remote period of American history, that is to say, some thirty years since, a worthy wight of the name of Ichabod Crane; who sojourned, or, as he expressed it, "tarried," in Sleepy Hollow, for the purpose of instructing the children of the vicinity. He was a native of Connecticut, a State which supplies the Union with pioneers for the mind as well as for the forest, and sends forth yearly its legions of frontier woodsmen and country schoolmasters. The cognomen of Crane was not inapplicable to his person. He was tall, but exceedingly lank, with narrow shoulders, long arms and legs, hands that dangled a mile out of his sleeves, feet that might have served for shovels, and his whole frame most loosely hung together. His head was small, and flat at top, with huge ears, large green glassy eyes, and a long snipe nose, so that it looked like a weathercock perched upon his spindle neck, to tell which way the wind blew. To see him striding along the profile of a hill on a windy day, with his clothes bagging and fluttering about him, one might have mistaken him for the genius of famine descending upon the earth, or some scarecrow eloped from a corn-field.

His school-house was a low building of one large room, rudely constructed of logs; the windows partly glazed, and partly patched with leaves of old copy-books. It was most ingeniously secured at vacant hours by a withe twisted in the handle of the door, and stakes set against the window-shutters; so that, though a thief might get in with perfect ease, he would find some embarrassment in getting out: an idea most probably borrowed by the architect, Yost Van Houten, from the mystery of an eel-pot. The school-house stood in a rather lonely but pleasant situation, just at the foot of a woody hill, with a brook running close by, and a formidable birch-tree growing at one end of it. From hence the low murmur of his pupils' voices, conning over their lessons, might be heard on a drowsy summer's day, like the hum of a bee-hive; interrupted now and then by the authoritative voice of the master, in the tone of menace or command; or, peradventure, by the appalling sound of the birch, as he urged some tardy loiterer along the flowery path of knowledge. Truth to say, he was a conscientious man, and ever bore in mind the golden maxim, "Spare the rod and spoil the child."—Ichabod Crane's scholars certainly were not spoiled.

I would not have it imagined, however, that he was one of those cruel potentates of the school, who joy in the smart of their subjects; on the contrary, he administered justice with discrimination rather than severity, taking the burden off the backs of the weak, and laying it on those of the strong. Your mere puny stripling, that winced at the least flourish of the rod, was passed by with indulgence; but the claims of justice were satisfied by inflicting a double portion on some little, tough, wrong-headed, broad-skirted Dutch urchin, who sulked and swelled and grew dogged and sullen beneath the birch. All this he called "doing his duty" by their parents; and he never inflicted a chastisement without following it by the assurance, so consolatory to the smarting urchin, that "he would remember it, and thank him for it the longest day he had to live."

When school-hours were over, he was even the companion and playmate of the larger boys; and on holiday afternoons would convoy some of the smaller ones home, who happened to have pretty sisters, or good housewives for mothers, noted for the comforts of the cupboard. Indeed it behooved him to keep on good terms with his pupils. The revenue arising from his school was small, and would have been scarcely sufficient to furnish him with daily bread, for he was a huge feeder, and, though lank, had the dilating powers of an anaconda; but to help out his maintenance, he was, according to country custom in those parts, boarded and lodged at the houses of the farmers, whose children he instructed. With these he lived successively a week at a time; thus going the rounds of the neighborhood, with all his worldly effects tied up in a cotton handkerchief.

That all this might not be too onerous on the purses of his rustic patrons, who are apt to consider the costs of schooling a grievious burden, and schoolmasters as mere drones, he had various ways of rendering himself both useful and agreeable. He assisted the farmers occasionally in the lighter labors of their farms; helped to make hay; mended the fences; took the horses to water; drove the cows from pasture; and cut wood for the winter fire. He laid aside, too, all the dominant dignity and absolute sway with which he lorded it in his little empire, the school, and became wonderfully gentle and ingratiating. He found favor in the eyes of the mothers, by petting the children, particularly the youngest; and like the lion bold, which whilom so magnanimously the lamb did hold, he would sit with a child on one knee, and rock a cradle with his foot for whole hours together.

In addition to his other vocations, he was the singing-master of the neighborhood, and picked up many bright shillings by instructing the young folks in psalmody. It was a matter of no little vanity to him, on Sundays, to take his station in front of the church-gallery, with a band of chosen singers; where, in his own mind, he completely carried away the palm from the parson. Certain it is, his voice resounded far above all the rest of the congregation; and there are peculiar quavers still to be heard in that church, and which may even be heard half a mile off, quite to the opposite side of the mill-pond, on a still Sunday morning, which are said to be legitimately descended from the nose of Ichabod Crane. Thus, by divers little makeshifts in that ingenious way which is commonly denominated "by hook and by crook," the worthy pedagogue got on tolerably enough, and was thought, by all who understood nothing of the labor of headwork, to have a wonderfully easy life of it.

The schoolmaster is generally a man of some importance in the female circle of a rural neighborhood; being considered a kind of idle, gentlemanlike personage, of vastly superior taste and accomplishments to the rough country swains, and, indeed, inferior in learning only to the parson. His appearance, therefore, is apt to occasion some little stir at the tea-table of a farm-house, and the addition of a supernumerary dish of cakes or sweet-meats, or, peradventure, the parade of a silver tea-pot. Our man of letters, therefore, was peculiarly happy in the smiles of all the country damsels. How he would figure among them in the churchyard, between services on Sundays! gathering grapes for them from the wild vines that overrun the surrounding trees; reciting for their amusement all the epitaphs on the tombstones; or sauntering, with a whole bevy of them, along the banks of the adjacent mill-pond; while the more bashful country bumpkins hung sheepishly back, envying his superior elegance and address.

From his half itinerant life, also, he was a kind of travelling gazette, carrying the whole budget of local gossip from house to house: so that his appearance was always greeted with satisfaction. He was, moreover, esteemed by the women as a man of great erudition, for he had read several books quite through, and was a perfect master of Cotton Mather's *History of New England Witchcraft,* in which, by the way, he most firmly and potently believed.

He was, in fact, an odd mixture of small shrewdness and simple credulity. His appetite for the marvellous, and his powers of digesting it, were equally extraordinary; and both had been increased by his residence in this spellbound region. No tale was too gross or monstrous for his capacious swallow. It was often his delight, after his school was dismissed in the afternoon, to stretch himself on the rich bed of clover bordering the little brook that whimpered by his school-house, and there con over old Mather's direful tales, until the gathering dusk of the evening made the printed page a mere mist before his eyes. Then, as he wended his way, by swamp and stream, and awful woodland, to the farm-house where he happened to be quartered, every sound of nature, at that witching hour, fluttered his excited imagination; the moan of the whippoorwill[1] from the hill-side, the boding cry of the tree-toad, that harbinger of storm; the dreary hooting of the screech-owl, or the sudden rustling in the thicket of birds frightened from their roost. The fire-flies, too, which sparkled most vividly in the darkest places, now and then startled him, as one of uncommon brightness would stream across his path; and if, by chance, a huge blockhead of a beetle came winging his blundering flight against him, the poor varlet was ready to give up the ghost, with the idea that he was struck with a witch's token. His only resource on such occasions, either to drown thought or drive away evil spirits, was to sing psalm-tunes; and the good people of Sleepy Hollow, as they sat by their doors of an evening, were often filled with awe, at hearing his nasal melody, "in linked sweetness long drawn out," floating from the distant hill, or along the dusky road.

1. The whippoorwill is a bird which is only heard at night. It receives its name from its note, which is thought to resemble those words.

Another of his sources of fearful pleasure was, to pass long winter evenings with the old Dutch wives, as they sat spinning by the fire, with a row of apples roasting and spluttering along the hearth, and listen to their marvellous tales of ghosts and goblins, and haunted fields, and haunted brooks, and haunted bridges, and haunted houses, and particularly of the headless horseman, or Galloping Hessian of the Hollow, as they sometimes called him. He would delight them equally by his anecdotes of witchcraft, and the direful omens and portentous sights and sounds in the air, which prevailed in the earlier times of Connecticut; and would frighten them wofully with speculations upon comets and shooting-stars, and with the alarming fact that the world did absolutely turn round, and that they were half the time topsy-turvy!

But if there was a pleasure in all this, while snugly cuddling in the chimney-corner of a chamber that was all of a ruddy glow from the crackling wood-fire, and where, of course, no spectre dared to show his face, it was dearly purchased by the terrors of his subsequent walk homewards. What fearful shapes and shadows beset his path amidst the dim and ghastly glare of a snowy night!—With what wistful look did he eye every trembling ray of light streaming across the waste fields from some distant window!—How often was he appalled by some shrub covered with snow, which, like a sheeted spectre, beset his very path!—How often did he shrink with curdling awe at the sound of his own steps on a frosty crust beneath his feet; and dread to look over his shoulder, lest he should behold some uncouth being tramping close behind him!—and how often was he thrown into complete dismay by some rushing blast, howling among the trees, in the idea that it was the Galloping Hessian on one of his nightly scourings!

All these, however, were mere terrors of the night, phantoms of the mind that walk in darkness; and though he had seen many spectres in his time, and been more than once beset by Satan in divers shapes, in his lonely perambulations, yet daylight put an end to all these evils; and he would have passed a pleasant life of it, in despite of the devil and all his works, if his path had not been crossed by a being that causes more perplexity to mortal man than ghosts, goblins, and the whole race of witches put together, and that was—a woman.

Among the musical disciples who assembled, one evening in each week, to receive his instructions in psalmody, was Katrina Van Tassel, the daughter and only child of a substantial Dutch farmer. She was a blooming lass of fresh eighteen; plump as a partridge; ripe and melting and rosy-cheeked as one of her father's peaches, and universally famed, not merely for her beauty, but her vast expectations. She was withal a little of a coquette, as might be perceived even in her dress, which was a mixture of ancient and modern fashions, as most suited to set off her charms. She wore the ornaments of pure yellow gold, which her great-great-grandmother had brought over from Saardam; the tempting stomacher of the olden time;

and withal a provokingly short petticoat, to display the prettiest foot and ankle in the country round.

Ichabod Crane had a soft and foolish heart towards the sex; and it is not to be wondered at that so tempting a morsel soon found favor in his eyes; more especially after he had visited her in her paternal mansion. Old Baltus Van Tassel was a perfect picture of a thriving, contented, liberal-hearted farmer. He seldom, it is true, sent either his eyes or his thoughts beyond the boundaries of his own farm; but within those everything was snug, happy, and well-conditioned. He was satisfied with his wealth, but not proud of it; and piqued himself upon the hearty abundance rather than the style in which he lived. His stronghold was situated on the banks of the Hudson, in one of those green, sheltered, fertile nooks in which the Dutch farmers are so fond of nestling. A great elm-tree spread its broad branches over it; at the foot of which bubbled up a spring of the softest and sweetest water, in a little well, formed of a barrel; and then stole sparkling away through the grass, to a neighboring brook, that bubbled along among alders and dwarf willows. Hard by the farm-house was a vast barn, that might have served for a church; every window and crevice of which seemed bursting forth with the treasures of the farm; the flail was busily resounding within it from morning till night; swallows and martins skimmed twittering about the eaves; and rows of pigeons, some with one eye turned up, as if watching the weather, some with their heads under their wings, or buried in their bosoms, and others swelling, and cooing, and bowing about their dames, were enjoying the sunshine on the roof. Sleek unwieldly porkers were grunting in the repose and abundance of their pens; whence sallied forth, now and then, troops of sucking pigs, as if to snuff the air. A stately squadron of snowy geese were riding in an adjoining pond, convoying whole fleets of ducks; regiments of turkeys were gobbling through the farm-yard, and guinea fowls fretting about it, like ill-tempered housewives, with their peevish discontented cry. Before the barn-door strutted the gallant cock, that pattern of a husband, a warrior, and a fine gentleman, clapping his burnished wings, and crowing in the pride and gladness of his heart—sometimes tearing up the earth with his feet, and then generously calling his ever-hungry family of wives and children to enjoy the rich morsel which he had discovered.

The pedagogue's mouth watered, as he looked upon this sumptuous promise of luxurious winter fare. In his devouring mind's eye he pictured to himself every roasting-pig running about with a pudding in his belly, and an apple in his mouth; the pigeons were snugly put to bed in a comfortable pie, and tucked in with a coverlet of crust; the geese were swimming in their own gravy; and the ducks pairing cosily in dishes, like snug married couples, with a decent competency of onion-sauce. In the porkers he saw carved out the future sleek side of bacon, and juicy relishing ham; not a turkey but he beheld daintily trussed up, with its gizzard under its wing, and, peradventure, a necklace of savory sausages; and even bright chanticleer himself lay sprawling on his back, in a side-dish, with uplifted claws, as if craving that quarter which his chivalrous spirit disdained to ask while living.

As the enraptured Ichabod fancied all this, and as he rolled his great green eyes over the fat meadow-lands, the rich fields of wheat, of rye, of buckwheat, and Indian corn, and the orchard burdened with ruddy fruit, which surrounded the warm tenement of Van Tassel, his heart yearned after the damsel who was to inherit these domains, and his imagination expanded with the idea how they might be readily turned into cash, and the money invested in immense tracts of wild land, and shingle palaces in the wilderness. Nay, his busy fancy already realized his hopes, and presented to him the blooming Katrina, with a whole family of children, mounted on the top of a wagon loaded with household trumpery, with pots and kettles dangling beneath; and he beheld himself bestriding a pacing mare, with a colt at her heels, setting out for Kentucky, Tennessee, or the Lord knows where.

When he entered the house, the conquest of his heart was complete. It was one of those spacious farm-houses, with high-ridged, but lowly-sloping roofs, built in the style handed down from the first Dutch settlers; the low projecting eaves forming a piazza along the front, capable of being closed up in bad weather. Under this were hung flails, harness, various utensils of husbandry, and nets for fishing in the neighboring river. Benches were built along the sides for summer use; and a great spinning-wheel at one end, and a churn at the other, showed the various uses to which this important porch might be devoted. From this piazza the wandering Ichabod entered the hall, which formed the centre of the mansion and the place of usual residence. Here, rows of resplendent pewter, ranged on a long dresser, dazzled his eyes. In one corner stood a huge bag of wool ready to be spun; in another a quantity of linsey-woolsey just from the loom; ears of Indian corn, and strings of dried apples and peaches, hung in gay festoons along the walls, mingled with the gaud of red peppers; and a door left ajar gave him a peep into the best parlor, where the claw-footed chairs and dark mahogany tables shone like mirrors; and irons, with their accompanying shovel and tongs, glistened from their covert of asparagus tops; mock-oranges and conch-shells decorated the mantel-piece; strings of various colored birds' eggs were suspended above it, a great ostrich egg was hung from the centre of the room, and a corner-cupboard, knowingly left open, displayed immense treasures of old silver and well-mended china.

From the moment Ichabod laid his eyes upon these regions of delight, the peace of his mind was at an end, and his only study was how to gain the affections of the peerless daughter of Van Tassel. In this enterprise, however, he had more real difficulties than generally fell to the lot of a knight-errant of yore, who seldom had anything but giants, enchanters, fiery dragons, and such like easily conquered adversaries, to contend with;

and had to make his way merely through gates of iron and brass, and walls of adamant, to the castle-keep, where the lady of his heart was confined; all which he achieved as easily as a man would carve his way to the centre of a Christmas pie; and then the lady gave him her hand as a matter of course. Ichabod, on the contrary, had to win his way to the heart of a country coquette, beset with a labyrinth of whims and caprices, which were forever presenting new difficulties and impediments; and he had to encounter a host of fearful adversaries of real flesh and blood, the numerous rustic admirers, who beset every portal to her heart; keeping a watchful and angry eye upon each other, but ready to fly out in the common cause against any new competitor.

Among these the most formidable was a burly, roaring, roistering blade, of the name of Abraham, or, according to the Dutch abbreviation, Brom Van Brunt, the hero of the country round, which rang with his feats of strength and hardihood. He was broad-shouldered and double-jointed, with short, curly black hair, and a bluff but not unpleasant countenance, having a mingled air of fun and arrogance. From his Herculean frame and great powers of limb, he had received the nickname of BROM BONES, by which he was universally known. He was famed for great knowledge and skill in horsemanship, being as dexterous on horseback as a Tartar. He was foremost at all races and cockfights; and, with the ascendency which bodily strength acquires in rustic life, was the umpire in all disputes, setting his hat on one side, and giving his decisions with an air and tone admitting of no gainsay or appeal. He was always ready for either a fight or a frolic; but had more mischief than ill-will in his composition; and, with all his overbearing roughness, there was a strong dash of waggish good-humor at the bottom. He had three or four boon companions, who regarded him as their model, and at the head of whom he scoured the country, attending every scene of feud or merriment for miles round. In cold weather he was distinguished by a fur cap, surmounted with a flaunting fox's tail; and when the folks at a country gathering descried this well-known crest at a distance, whisking about among a squad of hard riders, they always stood by for a squall. Sometimes his crew would be heard dashing along past the farm-houses at midnight, with whoop and halloo, like a troop of Don Cossacks; and the old dames, startled out of their sleep, would listen for a moment till the hurry-scurry had clattered by, and then exclaim, "Ay, there goes Brom Bones and his gang!" The neighbors looked upon him with a mixture of awe, admiration, and good-will; and when any madcap prank, or rustic brawl, occurred in the vicinity, always shook their heads, and warranted Brom Bones was at the bottom of it.

This rantipole hero had for some time singled out the blooming Katrina for the object of his uncouth gallantries; and though his amorous toyings were something like the gentle caresses and endearments of a bear, yet it was whispered that she did not altogether discourage his hopes. Certain it is, his advances were signals for rival candidates to retire, who felt no inclination to cross a line in his amours; insomuch, that, when his horse was seen tied to Van Tassel's paling on a Sunday night, a sure sign that his master was courting, or, as it is termed, "sparking," within, all other suitors passed by in despair, and carried the war into other quarters.

Such was the formidable rival with whom Ichabod Crane had to contend, and, considering all things, a stouter man than he would have shrunk from the competition, and a wiser man would have despaired. He had, however, a happy mixture of pliability and perseverance in his nature; he was in form and spirit like a supple-jack—yielding, but tough; though he bent, he never broke; and though he bowed beneath the slightest pressure yet, the moment it was away—jerk! he was as erect, and carried his head as high as ever.

To have taken the field openly against his rival would have been madness; for he was not a man to be thwarted in his amours, any more than that stormy lover, Achilles. Ichabod, therefore, made his advances in a quiet and gently insinuating manner. Under cover of his character of singing-master, he had made frequent visits at the farm-house; not that he had anything to apprehend from the meddlesome interference of parents, which is so often a stumbling-block in the path of lovers. Balt Van Tassel was an easy, indulgent soul; he loved his daughter better even than his pipe, and, like a reasonable man and an excellent father, let her have her way in everything. His notable little wife, too, had enough to do to attend to her housekeeping and manage her poultry; for, as she sagely observed, ducks and geese are foolish things, and must be looked after, but girls can take care of themselves. Thus while the busy dame bustled about the house, or plied her spinning-wheel at one end of the piazza, honest Balt would sit smoking his evening pipe at the other, watching the achievements of a little wooden warrior, who, armed with a sword in each hand, was most valiantly fighting the wind on the pinnacle of the barn. In the meantime, Ichabod would carry on his suit with the daughter by the side of the spring under the great elm, or sauntering along in the twilight,—that hour so favorable to the lover's eloquence.

I profess not to know how women's hearts are wooed and won. To me they have always been matters of riddle and admiration. Some seem to have but one vulnerable point or door of access, while others have a thousand avenues, and may be captured in a thousand different ways. It is a great triumph of skill to gain the former, but a still greater proof of generalship to maintain possession of the latter, for the man must battle for his fortress at every door and window. He who wins a thousand common hearts is therefore entitled to some renown; but he who keeps undisputed sway over the heart of a coquette, is indeed a hero. Certain it is, this was not the case with the redoubtable Brom Bones; and from the moment Ichabod Crane made his advances, the interests of the former evidently declined; his horse was no longer seen tied at the palings on Sunday nights, and a deadly feud gradually arose between him and the preceptor of Sleepy Hollow.

Brom, who had a degree of rough chivalry in his nature, would fain have carried matters to open warfare, and have settled their pretensions to the lady according to the mode of those most concise and simple reasoners, the knights-errant of yore—by single combat; but Ichabod was too conscious of the superior might of his adversary to enter the lists against him: he had overheard a boast of Bones, that he would "double the schoolmaster up, and lay him on a shelf of his own school-house;" and he was too wary to give him an opportunity. There was something extremely provoking in this obstinately pacific system; it left Brom no alternative but to draw upon the funds of rustic waggery in his disposition, and to play off boorish practical jokes upon his rival. Ichabod became the object of whimsical persecution to Bones and his gang of rough riders. They harried his hitherto peaceful domains; smoked out his singing-school, by stopping up the chimney; broke into the school-house at night, in spite of its formidable fastenings of withe and window-stakes, and turned everything topsy-turvy: so that the poor schoolmaster began to think all the witches in the country held their meetings there. But what was still more annoying, Brom took opportunities of turning him into ridicule in presence of his mistress, and had a scoundrel dog whom he taught to whine in the most ludicrous manner, and introduced as a rival of Ichabod's to instruct her in psalmody.

In this way matters went on for some time, without producing any material effect on the relative situation of the contending powers. On a fine autumnal afternoon, Ichabod, in pensive mood, sat enthroned on the lofty stool whence he usually watched all the concerns of his little literary realm. In his hand he swayed a ferule, that sceptre of despotic power; the birch of justice reposed on three nails, behind the throne, a constant terror to evil-doers; while on the desk before him might be seen sundry contraband articles and prohibited weapons, detected upon the persons of idle urchins; such as half-munched apples, pop-guns, whirligigs, fly-cages, and whole legions of rampant little paper game-cocks. Apparently there had been some appalling act of justice recently inflicted, for his scholars were all busily intent upon their books, or slyly whispering behind them with one eye kept upon the master; and a kind of buzzing stillness reigned throughout the school-room. It was suddenly interrupted by the appearance of a negro, in tow-cloth jacket and trousers, a round-crowned fragment of a hat, like the cap of Mercury, and mounted on the back of a ragged, wild, half-broken colt, which he managed with a rope by way of halter. He came clattering up to the school-door with an invitation to Ichabod to attend a merry-making or "quilting frolic," to be held that evening at Mynheer Van Tassel's; and having delivered his message with that air of importance, and effort at fine language, which a negro is apt to display on petty embassies of the kind, he dashed over the brook, and was seen scampering away up the Hollow, full of the importance and hurry of his mission.

All was now bustle and hubbub in the late quiet school-room. The scholars were hurried through their lessons, without stopping at trifles; those who were nimble skipped over half with impunity, and those who were tardy had a smart application now and then in the rear, to quicken their speed, or help them over a tall word. Books were flung aside without being put away on the shelves, inkstands were overturned, benches thrown down, and the whole school was turned loose an hour before the usual time, bursting forth like a legion of young imps, yelping and racketing about the green, in joy at their early emancipation.

The gallant Ichabod now spent at least an extra half-hour at his toilet, brushing and furbishing up his best and indeed only suit of rusty black, and arranging his locks by a bit of broken looking-glass, that hung up in the school-house. That he might make his appearance before his mistress in the true style of a cavalier, he borrowed a horse from the farmer with whom he was domiciliated, a choleric old Dutchman, of the name of Hans Van Ripper, and, thus gallantly mounted, issued forth, like a knight-errant in quest of adventures. But it is meet I should, in the true spirit of romantic story, give some account of the looks and equipments of my hero and his steed. The animal he bestrode was a broken-down plough-horse, that had outlived almost everything but his viciousness. He was gaunt and shagged, with a ewe neck and a head like a hammer; his rusty mane and tail were tangled and knotted with burrs; one eye had lost its pupil, and was glaring and spectral; but the other had the gleam of a genuine devil in it. Still he must have had fire and mettle in his day, if we may judge from the name he bore of Gunpowder. He had, in fact, been a favorite steed of his master's, the choleric Van Ripper, who was a furious rider, and had infused, very probably, some of his own spirit into the animal; for, old and broken-down as he looked, there was more of the lurking devil in him than in any young filly in the country.

Ichabod was a suitable figure for such a steed. He rode with short stirrups, which brought his knees nearly up to the pommel of the saddle; his sharp elbows stuck out like grasshoppers'; he carried his whip perpendicularly in his hand, like a sceptre, and, as his horse jogged on, the motion of his arms was not unlike the flapping of a pair of wings. A small wool hat rested on the top of his nose, for so his scanty strip of forehead might be called; and the skirts of his black coat fluttered out almost to the horse's tail. Such was the appearance of Ichabod and his steed, as they shambled out of the gate of Hans Van Ripper, and it was altogether such an apparition as is seldom to be met with in broad daylight.

It was, as I have said, a fine autumnal day, the sky was clear and nature wore that rich and golden livery which we always associate with the idea of abundance. The forests had put on their sober brown and yellow, while some trees of the tenderer kind had been nipped by the frosts into brilliant dyes of orange, purple, and scarlet. Streaming files of wild ducks began to make their appearance high in the air; the bark of the squirrel might be heard from the groves of beech and hickory nuts, and the pensive whistle of the quail at intervals from the neighboring stubble-field.

The small birds were taking their farewell banquets. In the fulness of their revelry, they fluttered, chirping and frolicking, from bush to bush, and tree to tree, capricious from the very profusion and variety around them. There was the honest cockrobin, the favorite game of stripling sportsmen, with its loud querulous notes; and the twittering blackbirds flying in sable clouds; and the golden-winged woodpecker, with his crimson crest, his broad black gorget, and splendid plumage; and the cedar-bird, with its red-tipt wings and yellow-tipt tail, and its little monteiro cap of feathers; and the blue jay, that noisy coxcomb, in his gay light-blue coat and white under-clothes, screaming and chattering, nodding and bobbing and bowing, and pretending to be on good terms with every songster of the grove.

As Ichabod jogged slowly on his way, his eye, ever open to every symptom of culinary abundance, ranged with delight over the treasures of jolly autumn. On all sides he beheld vast store of apples; some hanging in oppressive opulence on the trees; some gathered into baskets and barrels for the market; others heaped up in rich piles for the cider-press. Farther on he beheld great fields of Indian corn, with its golden ears peeping from their leafy coverts, and holding out the promise of cakes and hasty-pudding; and the yellow pumpkins lying beneath them, turning up their fair round bellies to the sun, and giving ample prospects of the most luxurious of pies; and anon he passed the fragrant buckwheat fields, breathing the odor of the bee-hive, and as he beheld them, soft anticipations stole over his mind of dainty slapjacks, well buttered, and garnished with honey or treacle, by the delicate little dimpled hand of Katrina Van Tassel.

Thus feeding his mind with many sweet thoughts and "sugared suppositions," he journeyed along the sides of a range of hills which look out upon some of the goodliest scenes of the mighty Hudson. The sun gradually wheeled his broad disk down into the west. The wide bosom of the Tappan Zee lay motionless and glossy, excepting that here and there a gentle undulation waved and prolonged the blue shadow of the distant mountain. A few amber clouds floated in the sky, without a breath of air to move them. The horizon was of a fine golden tint, changing gradually into a pure apple-green, and from that into the deep blue of the mid-heaven. A slanting ray lingered on the woody crests of the precipices that overhung some parts of the river, giving greater depth to the dark-gray and purple of their rocky sides. A sloop was loitering in the distance, dropping slowly down with the tide, her sail hanging uselessly against the mast; and as the reflection of the sky gleamed along the still water, it seemed as if the vessel was suspended in the air.

It was toward evening that Ichabod arrived at the castle of the Heer Van Tassel, which he found thronged with the pride and flower of the adjacent country. Old farmers, a spare leathern-faced race, in homespun coats and breeches, blue stockings, huge shoes, and magnificent pewter buckles. Their brisk withered little dames, in close crimped caps, long-waisted shortgowns, homespun petticoats, with scissors and pin-cushions, and gay calico pockets hanging on the outside. Buxom lasses, almost as antiquated as their mothers, excepting where a straw hat, a fine ribbon, or perhaps a white frock, gave symptoms of city innovation. The sons, in short square-skirted coats with rows of stupendous brass buttons, and their hair generally queued in the fashion of the times, especially if they could procure an eel-skin for the purpose, it being esteemed, throughout the country, as a potent nourisher and strengthener of the hair.

Brom Bones, however, was the hero of the scene, having come to the gathering on his favorite steed, Daredevil, a creature, like himself, full of mettle and mischief, and which no one but himself could manage. He was, in fact, noted for preferring vicious animals, given to all kinds of tricks, which kept the rider in constant risk of his neck, for he held a tractable well-broken horse as unworthy of a lad of spirit.

Fain would I pause to dwell upon the world of charms that burst upon the enraptured gaze of my hero, as he entered the state parlor of Van Tassel's mansion. Not those of the bevy of buxom lasses, with their luxurious display of red and white; but the ample charms of a genuine Dutch country tea-table, in the sumptuous time of autumn. Such heaped-up platters of cakes of various and almost indescribable kinds, known only to experienced Dutch housewives! There was the doughty doughnut, the tenderer oly koek, and the crisp and crumbling cruller; sweet cakes and short cakes, ginger-cakes and honey-cakes, and the whole family of cakes. And then there were apple-pies and peach-pies and pumpkin-pies; besides slices of ham and smoked beef; and moreover delectable dishes of preserved plums, and peaches, and pears, and quinces; not to mention broiled shad and roasted chickens; together with bowls of milk and cream, all mingled higgledy-piggledy, pretty much as I have enumerated them, with the motherly tea-pot sending up its clouds of vapor from the midst—Heaven bless the mark! I want breath and time to discuss this banquet as it deserves, and am too eager to get on with my story. Happily, Ichabod Crane was not in so great a hurry as his historian, but did ample justice to every dainty.

He was a kind and thankful creature, whose heart dilated in proportion as his skin was filled with good cheer; and whose spirits rose with eating as some men's do with drink. He could not help, too, rolling his large eyes round him as he ate, and chuckling with the possibility that he might one day be lord of all this scene of almost unimaginable luxury and splendor. Then, he thought, how soon he'd turn his back upon the old school-house; snap his fingers in the face of Hans Van Ripper, and every other niggardly patron, and kick any itinerant pedagogue out-of-doors that should dare to call him comrade!

Old Baltus Van Tassel moved about among his guests with a face dilated with content and good-humor, round and jolly as the harvest-moon. His hospitable attentions were brief, but expressive, being confined to a shake of the hand, a slap on the shoulder, a loud laugh, and a pressing invitation to "fall to, and help themselves."

And now the sound of the music from the common room, or hall, summoned to the dance. The musician was an old gray-headed negro, who had been the itinerant orchestra of the neighborhood for more than half a century. His instrument was as old and battered as himself. The greater part of the time he scraped on two or three strings, accompanying every movement of the bow with a motion of the head; bowing almost to the ground, and stamping with his foot whenever a fresh couple were to start.

Ichabod prided himself upon his dancing as much as upon his vocal powers. Not a limb, not a fibre about him was idle; and to have seen his loosely hung frame in full motion, and clattering about the room, you would have thought Saint Vitus himself, that blessed patron of the dance, was figuring before you in person. He was the admiration of all the negroes; who, having gathered, of all ages and sizes, from the farm and the neighborhood, stood forming a pyramid of shining black faces at every door and window, gazing with delight at the scene, rolling their white eyeballs, and showing grinning rows of ivory from ear to ear. How could the flogger of urchins be otherwise than animated and joyous? The lady of his heart was his partner in the dance, and smiling graciously in reply to all his amorous oglings; while Brom Bones, sorely smitten with love and jealousy, sat brooding by himself in one corner.

When the dance was at an end, Ichabod was attracted to a knot of the sager folks, who, with old Van Tassel, sat smoking at one end of the piazza, gossiping over former times, and drawing out long stories about the war.

This neighborhood, at the time of which I am speaking, was one of those highly favored places which abound with chronicle and great men. The British and American line had run near it during the war; it had, therefore, been the scene of marauding, and infested with refugees, cowboys, and all kinds of border chivalry. Just sufficient time has elapsed to enable each story-teller to dress up his tale with a little becoming fiction, and, in the indistinctness of his recollection, to make himself the hero of every exploit.

There was the story of Doffue Martling, a large blue-bearded Dutchman, who had nearly taken a British frigate with an old iron nine-pounder from a mud breastwork, only that his gun burst at the sixth discharge. And there was an old gentleman who shall be nameless, being too rich a mynheer to be lightly mentioned, who, in the battle of White Plains, being an excellent master of defence, parried a musketball with a small sword, insomuch that he absolutely felt it whiz round the blade, and glance off at the hilt; in proof of which he was ready at any time to show the sword, with the hilt a little bent. There were several more that had been equally great in the field, not one of whom but was persuaded that he had a considerable hand in bringing the war to a happy termination.

But all these were nothing to the tales of ghosts and apparitions that succeeded. The neighborhood is rich in legendary treasures of the kind. Local tales and superstitions thrive best in these sheltered long-settled retreats; but are trampled underfoot by the shifting throng that forms the population of most of our country places. Besides, there is no encouragement for ghosts in most of our villages, for they have scarcely had time to finish their first nap, and turn themselves in their graves before their surviving friends have travelled away from the neighborhood; so that when they turn out at night to walk their rounds, they have no acquaintance left to call upon. This is perhaps the reason why we so seldom hear of ghosts, except in our long-established Dutch communities.

The immediate cause, however, of the prevalence of supernatural stories in these parts was doubtless owing to the vicinity of Sleepy Hollow. There was a contagion in the very air that blew from the haunted region; it breathed forth an atmosphere of dreams and fancies infecting all the land. Several of the Sleepy Hollow people were present at Van Tassel's and, as usual, were doling out their wild and wonderful legends. Many dismal tales were told about funeral trains, and mourning cries and wailings heard and seen about the great tree where the unfortunate Major André was taken, and which stood in the neighborhood. Some mention was made also of the woman in white, that haunted the dark glen at Raven Rock, and was often heard to shriek on winter nights before a storm, having perished there in the snow. The chief part of the stories, however, turned upon the favorite spectre of Sleepy Hollow, the headless horseman, who had been heard several times of late, patrolling the country; and, it was said, tethered his horse nightly among the graves in the churchyard.

The sequestered situation of this church seems always to have made it a favorite haunt of troubled spirits. It stands on a knoll, surrounded by locust-trees and lofty elms, from among which its decent white-washed walls shine modestly forth, like Christian purity beaming through the shades of retirement. A gentle slope descends from it to a silver sheet of water, bordered by high trees, between which, peeps may be caught at the blue hills of the Hudson. To look upon its grass-grown yard, where the sunbeams seem to sleep so quietly, one would think that there at least the dead might rest in peace. On one side of the church extends a wide woody dell, along which raves a large brook among broken rocks and trunks of fallen trees. Over a deep black part of the stream, not far from the church, was formerly thrown a wooden bridge; the road that led to it, and the bridge itself, were thickly shaded by overhanging trees, which cast a gloom about it, even in the daytime, but occasioned a fearful darkness at night. This was one of the favorite haunts of the headless horseman; and the place where he was most frequently encountered. The tale was told of old Brouwer, a most heretical disbeliever in ghosts, how he met the horseman returning from his foray into Sleepy Hollow, and was obliged to get up behind him; how they galloped over bush and brake, over hill and swamp, until they reached the bridge; when the horseman suddenly turned into a skeleton, threw old Brouwer into the brook, and sprang away over the tree-tops with a clap of thunder.

This story was immediately matched by a thrice marvellous adventure of Brom Bones, who made light of the galloping Hessian as an arrant jockey. He affirmed that, on returning one night from the neighboring village of Sing Sing, he had been overtaken by this midnight trooper; that he had offered to race with him for a bowl of punch, and should have won it too, for Daredevil beat the goblin horse all hollow, but, just as they came to the church bridge, the Hessian bolted, and vanished in a flash of fire.

All these tales, told in that drowsy undertone with which men talk in the dark, the countenances of the listeners only now and then receiving a casual gleam from the glare of a pipe, sank deep in the mind of Ichabod. He repaid them in kind with large extracts from his invaluable author, Cotton Mather, and added many marvellous events that had taken place in his native State of Connecticut, and fearful sights which he had seen in his nightly walks about the Sleepy Hollow.

The revel now gradually broke up. The old farmers gathered together their families in their wagons, and were heard for some time rattling along the hollow roads, and over the distant hills. Some of the damsels mounted on pillions behind their favorite swains, and their light-hearted laughter, mingling with the clatter of hoofs, echoed along the silent woodlands, sounding fainter and fainter until they gradually died away—and the late scene of noise and frolic was all silent and deserted. Ichabod only lingered behind, according to the custom of country lovers, to have a *tête-à-tête* with the heiress, fully convinced that he was now on the high road to success. What passed at this interview I will not pretend to say, for in fact I do not know. Something, however, I fear me, must have gone wrong, for he certainly sallied forth, after no very great interval, with an air quite desolate and chop-fallen.—Oh, these women! these women! Could that girl have been playing off any of her coquettish tricks?—Was her encouragement of the poor pedagogue all a mere sham to secure her conquest of his rival?—Heaven only knows, not I!—Let it suffice to say, Ichabod stole forth with the air of one who had been sacking a hen-roost, rather than a fair lady's heart. Without looking to the right or left to notice the scene of rural wealth on which he had so often gloated, he went straight to the stable, and with several hearty cuffs and kicks, roused his steed most uncourteously from the comfortable quarters in which he was soundly sleeping, dreaming of mountains of corn and oats, and whole valleys of timothy and clover.

It was the very witching time of night that Ichabod, heavy-hearted and crestfallen, pursued his travel homewards, along the sides of the lofty hills which rise above Tarry Town, and which he had traversed so cheerily in the afternoon. The hour was as dismal as himself. Far below him, the Tappan Zee spread its dusky and indistinct waste of waters, with here and there the tall mast of a sloop riding quietly at anchor under the land. In the dead hush of midnight he could even hear the barking of the watch-dog from the opposite shore of the Hudson; but it was so vague and faint as only to give an idea of his distance from this faithful companion of man. Now and then, too, the long-drawn crowing of a cock, accidentally awakened, would sound far, far off, from some farm-house away among the hills—but it was like a dreaming sound in his ear. No signs of life occurred near him, but occasionally the melancholy chirp of a cricket, or perhaps the gutteral twang of a bull-frog, from a neighboring marsh, as if sleeping uncomfortably, and turning suddenly in his bed.

All the stories of ghosts and goblins that he had heard in the afternoon, now came crowding upon his recollection. The night grew darker and darker; the stars seemed to sink deeper in the sky, and driving clouds occasionally hid them from his sight. He had never felt so lonely and dismal. He was, moreover, approaching the very place where many of the scenes of the ghost-stories had been laid. In the centre of the road stood an enormous tulip-tree, which towered like a giant above all the other trees of the neighborhood, and formed a kind of landmark. Its limbs were gnarled, and fantastic, large enough to form trunks for ordinary trees, twisting down almost to the earth, and rising again into the air. It was connected with the tragical story of the unfortunate André, who had been taken prisoner hard by; and was universally known by the name of Major André's tree. The common people regarded it with a mixture of respect and superstition, partly out of sympathy for the fate of its ill-starred name-sake, and partly from the tales of strange sights and doleful lamentations told concerning it.

As Ichabod approached this fearful tree, he began to whistle: he thought his whistle was answered,—it was but a blast sweeping sharply through the dry branches. As he approached a little nearer, he thought he saw something white, hanging in the midst of the tree,—he paused and ceased whistling; but on looking more narrowly, perceived that it was a place where the tree had been scathed by lightning, and the white wood laid bare. Suddenly he heard a groan,—his teeth chattered and his knees smote against the saddle: it was but the rubbing of one huge bough upon another, as they were swayed about by the breeze. He passed the tree in safety; but new perils lay before him.

About two hundred yards from the tree a small brook crossed the road, and ran into a marshy and thickly wooded glen, known by the name of Wiley's swamp. A few rough logs, laid side by side, served for a bridge over this stream. On that side of the road where the brook entered the wood, a group of oaks and chestnuts, matted thick with wild grape-vines, threw a cavernous gloom over it. To pass this bridge was the severest trial. It was at this identical spot that the unfortunate André was captured, and under the covert of those chestnuts and vines were the sturdy yeomen concealed who surprised him. This has ever since been considered a haunted stream, and fearful are the feelings of the school boy who has to pass it alone after dark.

As he approached the stream, his heart began to thump; he summoned up, however, all his resolution, gave his horse half a score of kicks in the ribs, and attempted to dash briskly across the bridge; but instead of starting forward, the perverse old animal made a lateral movement, and ran broadside against the fence. Ichabod, whose fears increased with the delay, jerked the reins on the other side, and kicked lustily with the contrary foot: it was all in vain; his steed started, it is true, but it was only to plunge to the opposite side of the road into a thicket of brambles and alder bushes. The schoolmaster now bestowed both whip and heel upon the starveling ribs of old Gunpowder, who dashed forward, snuffling and snorting, but came to a stand just by the bridge, with a suddenness that had nearly sent his rider sprawling over his head. Just at this moment a plashy tramp by the side of the bridge caught the sensitive ear of Ichabod. In the dark shadow of the grove, on the margin of the brook, he beheld something huge, misshapen, black, and towering. It stirred not, but seemed gathered up in the gloom, like some gigantic monster ready to spring upon the traveller.

The hair of the affrighted pedagogue rose upon his head with terror. What was to be done? To turn and fly was now too late; and besides, what chance was there of escaping ghost or goblin, if such it was, which could ride upon the wings of the wind? Summoning up, therefore, a show of courage, he demanded in stammering accents—"Who are you?" He received no reply. He repeated his demand in a still more agitated voice. Still there was no answer. Once more he cudgelled the sides of the inflexible Gunpowder, and, shutting his eyes, broke forth with involuntary fervor into a psalm-tune. Just then the shadowy object of alarm put itself in motion, and, with a scramble and a bound, stood at once in the middle of the road. Though the night was dark and dismal, yet the form of the unknown might now in some degree be ascertained. He appeared to be a horseman of large dimensions, and mounted on a black horse of powerful frame. He made no offer of molestation or sociability, but kept aloof on one side of the road, jogging along on the blind side of old Gunpowder, who had now got over his fright and waywardness.

Ichabod, who had no relish for this strange midnight companion, and bethought himself of the adventure of Brom Bones with the Galloping Hessian, now quickened his steed, in hopes of leaving him behind. The stranger, however, quickened his horse to an equal pace. Ichabod pulled up, and fell into a walk, thinking to lag behind,—the other did the same. His heart began to sink within him; he endeavored to resume his psalm-tune, but his parched tongue clove to the roof of his mouth, and he could not utter a stave. There was something in the moody and dogged silence of this pertinacious companion, that was mysterious and appalling. It was soon fearfully accounted for. On mounting a rising ground, which brought the figure of his fellow-traveller in relief against the sky, gigantic in height, and muffled in a cloak, Ichabod was horror-struck, on perceiving that he was headless!—but his horror was still more increased, on observing that the head, which should have rested on his shoulders, was carried before him on the pommel of the saddle: his terror rose to desperation; he rained a shower of kicks and blows upon Gunpowder, hoping, by a sudden movement, to give his companion the the slip,—but the spectre started full jump with him. Away then they dashed, through thick and thin; stones flying, and sparks flashing at every bound. Ichabod's flimsy garments fluttered in the air, as he stretched his long lank body away over his horse's head, in the eagerness of his flight.

They had now reached the road which turns off to Sleepy Hollow; but Gunpowder, who seemed possessed with a demon, instead of keeping up it, made an opposite turn, and plunged headlong downhill to the left. This road leads through a sandy hollow, shaded by trees for about a quarter of a mile, where it crosses the bridge famous in goblin story, and just beyond swells the green knoll on which stands the white-washed church.

As yet the panic of the steed had given his unskilful rider an apparent advantage in the chase; but just as he had got half-way through the hollow, the girths of the saddle gave way, and he felt it slipping from under him. He seized it by the pommel, and endeavored to hold it firm, but in vain; and had just time to save himself by clasping old Gunpowder round the neck, when the saddle fell to the earth, and he heard it trampled underfoot by his pursuer. For a moment, the terror of Hans Van Ripper's wrath passed across his mind—for it was his Sunday saddle; but this was no time for petty fears; the goblin was hard on his haunches; and (unskilful rider that he was!) he had much ado to maintain his seat; sometimes slipping on one side, sometimes on another, and sometimes jolted on the high ridge of his horse's backbone, with a violence that he verily feared would cleave him asunder.

An opening in the trees now cheered him with the hopes that the church-bridge was at hand. The wavering reflection of a silver star in the bosom of the brook told him that he was not mistaken. He saw the walls of the church dimly glaring under the trees beyond. He recollected the place where Brom Bones' ghostly competitor had disappeared. "If I can but reach that bridge," thought Ichabod, "I am safe." Just then he heard the black steed panting and blowing close behind him; he even fancied that he felt his hot breath. Another convulsive kick in the ribs, and old Gunpowder sprang upon the bridge; he thundered over the resounding planks; he gained the opposite side; and now Ichabod cast a look behind to see if his pursuer should vanish, according to rule, in a flash of fire and brimstone. Just then he saw the goblin rising in his stirrups, and in the very act of hurling his head at him. Ichabod endeavored to dodge the horrible missile, but too late. It encountered his cranium with a tremendous crash,—he was tumbled headlong into the dust, and Gunpowder, the black steed, and the goblin rider, passed by like a whirlwind.

The next morning the old horse was found without his saddle, and with the bridle under his feet, soberly cropping the grass at his master's gate. Ichabod did not make his appearance at breakfast;—dinner-hour came, but no Ichabod. The boys assembled at the school-house, and strolled idly about the banks of the brook; but no schoolmaster. Hans Van Ripper now began to feel some uneasiness about the fate of poor Ichabod, and his saddle. An inquiry was set on foot, and after diligent investigation they came upon his traces. In one part of the road leading to the church was found the saddle trampled in the dirt; the tracks of horses' hoofs deeply dented in the road, and evidently at furious speed, were traced to the bridge, beyond which, on the bank of a broad part of the brook, where the water ran deep and black, was found the hat of the unfortunate Ichabod, and close beside it a shattered pumpkin.

The brook was searched, but the body of the schoolmaster was not to be discovered. Hans Van Ripper, as executor of his estate, examined the bundle which contained all his worldly effects. They consisted of two shirts and a half; two stocks for the neck; a pair or two of worsted stockings, an old pair of corduroy small-clothes; a rusty razor; a book of psalm-tunes, full of dogs' ears; and a broken pitch-pipe. As to the books and furniture of the school-house, they belonged to the community, excepting Cotton Mather's *History of Witchcraft,* a *New England Almanac,* and a book of dreams and fortune-telling; in which last was a sheet of foolscap much scribbled and blotted in several fruitless attempts to make a copy of verses in honor of the heiress of Van Tassel. These magic books and the poetic scrawl were forthwith consigned to the flames by Hans Van Ripper; who from that time forward determined to send his children no more to school; observing, that he never knew any good come of this same reading and writing. Whatever money the schoolmaster possessed, and he had received his quarter's pay but a day or two before, he must have had about his person at the time of his disappearance.

The mysterious event caused much speculation at the church on the following Sunday. Knots of gazers and gossips were collected in the churchyard, at the bridge, and at the spot where the hat and pumpkin had been found. The stories of Brouwer, of Bones, and a whole budget of others, were called to mind; and when they had diligently considered them all, and compared them with the symptoms of the present case, they shook their heads, and came to the conclusion that Ichabod had been carried off by the Galloping Hessian. As he was a bachelor, and in nobody's debt, nobody troubled his head any more about him. The school was removed to a different quarter of the Hollow, and another pedagogue reigned in his stead.

It is true, an old farmer, who had been down to New York on a visit several years after, and from whom this account of the ghastly adventure was received, brought home the intelligence that Ichabod Crane was still alive; that he had left the neighborhood, partly through fear of the goblin and Hans Van Ripper, and partly in mortification at having been suddenly dismissed by the heiress; that he had changed his quarters to a distant part of the country; had kept school and studied law at the same time, had been admitted to the bar, turned politician, electioneered, written for the newspapers, and finally had been made a justice of the Ten Pound Court. Brom Bones too, who shortly after his rival's disappearance conducted the blooming Katrina in triumph to the altar, was observed to look exceedingly knowing whenever the story of Ichabod was related, and always burst into a hearty laugh at the mention of the pumpkin; which led some to suspect that he knew more about the matter than he chose to tell.

The old country wives, however, who are the best judges of these matters, maintain to this day that Ichabod was spirited away by supernatural means; and it is a favorite story often told about the neighborhood round the winter evening fire. The bridge became more than ever an object of superstitious awe, and that may be the reason why the road has been altered of late years, so as to approach the church by the border of the millpond. The school-house, being deserted, soon fell to decay, and was reported to be haunted by the ghost of the unfortunate pedagogue; and the ploughboy, loitering homeward of a still summer evening, has often fancied his voice at a distance, chanting a melancholy psalm-tune, among the tranquil solitudes of Sleepy Hollow.

POSTSCRIPT, *found in the handwriting of Mr. Knickerbocker.*

The preceding Tale is given, almost in the precise words in which I heard it related at a Corporation meeting of the ancient city of Manhattoes, at which were present many of its sagest and most illustrious burghers. The narrator was a pleasant, shabby, gentlemanly old fellow, in pepper-and-salt clothes, with a sadly humorous face; and one whom I strongly suspected of being poor,—he made such efforts to be entertaining. When his story was concluded, there was much laughter and approbation, particularly from two or three deputy aldermen, who had been asleep the greater part of the time. There was, however, one tall, dry-looking old gentleman, with beetling eyebrows, who maintained a grave and rather severe face throughout; now and then folding his arms, inclining his head, and looking down upon the floor, as if turning a doubt over in his mind. He was one of your wary men, who never laugh, but on good grounds—when they have reason and the law on their side. When the mirth of the rest of the company had subsided and silence was restored, he leaned one arm on the elbow of his chair, and sticking the other akimbo, demanded, with a slight but exceedingly sage motion of the head, and contraction of the brow, what was the moral of the story, and what it went to prove?

The story-teller, who was just putting a glass of wine to his lips, as a refreshment after his toils, paused for a moment, looked at his inquirer with an air of infinite deference, and, lowering the glass slowly to the table, observed, that the story was intended most logically to prove:

"There is no situation in life but has its advantages and pleasures—provided we will but take a joke as we find it;

"That, therefore, he that runs races with goblin troopers is likely to have rough riding of it.

"*Ergo,* for a country schoolmaster to be refused the hand of a Dutch heiress, is a certain step to high preferment in the state."

The cautious old gentleman knit his brows tenfold closer after this explanation, being sorely puzzled by ratiocination of the syllogism; while, methought, the one in pepper-and-salt eyed him with something of a triumphant leer. At length he observed, that all this was very well, but still he thought the story a little on the extravagant—there were one or two points on which he had his doubts.

"Faith, sir," replied the story-teller, "as to that matter, I don't believe one half of it myself."

QUESTIONS

1. Discuss the role of the narrator, the "I" of the story. Is his perspective essential to the story? What does it contribute?
2. How does the teller establish atmosphere, and what kind? Comment upon the importance of setting. How do descriptions contribute to the development of the narrative?
3. How does Irving describe Ichabod's appearance? Are we meant to take him seriously? In what ways is he a complex character rather than a caricature?
4. Is Ichabod in love with Katrina, or with her expectations? How does Irving depict his growing interest?
5. What effect do Irving's comparisons with knights and mythic heroes have on the story?
6. Discuss the role of women in the story. What stereotypes does Irving employ in order to characterize the difference between the sexes?
7. How does Irving use characterizations of Ichabod's and Brom's horses to intensify the narration? Does our perception of Brom change as the story develops? Explain.
8. What role is played by tales, legends, and rumors?
9. How does Irving build tension before the final encounter of Ichabod and the Headless Horseman?
10. What is the prevailing attitude toward teachers and schooling? Does Irving expect us to share that attitude?
11. How does the postscript function? Is it essential? How would the story change if it were to be eliminated?

Nathaniel Hawthorne

Nathaniel Hawthorne (1804–1864) might be considered the conscience of American literature. The passions and phantasmagoric imaginings that ran riot in the works of Poe, his near-contemporary, are in Hawthorne bridled by the stern hand of the moralist. His family background, one might argue, had some part to play in the shaping of his disposition. His Salem, Massachusetts, forebears included a great-grandfather who had persecuted Quakers from the judicial bench; his grandfather, another judge, had been one of the presiding figures at the Salem witch trials.

Hawthorne decided early upon the writer's vocation. He attended Bowdoin College in Maine for four years, then returned to Salem to work at his craft. He began selling his darkly allegorical writings (of which "The Minister's Black Veil" is a prime example) to periodicals, publishing his first collection, *Twice-Told Tales,* in 1837. He lived for a while at Brook Farm, a communal experiment in West Roxbury, Massachusetts; his novel *The Blithedale Romance* (1852) draws some of its background from that period. Hawthorne similarly made use of his experience of working at the Boston Customs House, incorporating it into the introduction of *The Scarlet Letter.* This novel, published in 1850, is regarded as his masterpiece.

In 1853 President Franklin Pierce, whom Hawthorne had befriended at Bowdoin, appointed the writer to the post of Consul to Liverpool. Hawthorne lived in England and later traveled in Italy, returning to the United States only four years before his death.

Hawthorne wrote voluminously. His writings include the novels *The House of the Seven Gables* (1851) and *The Marble Faun* (1860) and the stories of *Mosses from an Old Manse* (1846).

Hawthorne's thematic interests—sin, punishment, absolution, belief, and the human moral reflex—were well suited to his artistic gifts. His way with allegory and symbolic suggestion is unrivaled in American literature. Indeed, we have to look to Franz Kafka (who was born in Prague nearly twenty years after Hawthorne's death) to find a possible heir. The difference, however, is enormous. Kafka wrote allegories for a world abandoned by God, Hawthorne for a world trembling before God's judgments.

THE MINISTER'S BLACK VEIL

The sexton stood in the porch of Milford meeting-house, pulling busily at the bell-rope. The old people of the village came stooping along the street. Children, with bright faces, tripped merrily beside their parents, or mimicked a graver gait, in the conscious dignity of their Sunday clothes. Spruce bachelors looked sidelong at the pretty maidens, and fancied that the Sabbath sunshine made them prettier than on week days. When the throng had mostly streamed into the porch, the sexton began to toll the bell, keeping his eye on the Reverend Mr. Hooper's door. The first glimpse of the clergyman's figure was the signal for the bell to cease its summons.

"But what has good Parson Hooper got upon his face?" cried the sexton in astonishment.

All within hearing immediately turned about, and beheld the semblance of Mr. Hooper, pacing slowly his meditative way towards the meeting-house. With one accord they started, expressing more wonder than if some strange minister were coming to dust the cushions of Mr. Hooper's pulpit.

"Are you sure it is our parson?" inquired Goodman Gray of the sexton.

"Of a certainty it is good Mr. Hooper," replied the sexton. "He was to have exchanged pulpits with Parson Shute, of Westbury; but Parson Shute sent to excuse himself yesterday, being to preach a funeral sermon."

The cause of so much amazement may appear sufficiently slight. Mr. Hooper, a gentlemanly person, of about thirty, though still a bachelor, was dressed with due clerical neatness, as if a careful wife had starched his band, and brushed the weekly dust from his Sunday's garb. There was but one thing remarkable in his appearance. Swathed about his forehead, and hanging down over his face, so low as to be shaken by his breath, Mr. Hooper had on a black veil. On a nearer view it seemed to consist of two folds of crepe, which entirely concealed his features, except the mouth and chin, but probably did not intercept his sight, further than to give a darkened aspect to all living and inanimate things. With this gloomy shade before him, good Mr. Hooper walked onward, at a slow and quiet pace, stooping somewhat, and looking on the ground, as is customary with abstracted men, yet nodding kindly to those of his parishioners who still waited on the meeting-house steps. But so wonderstruck were they that his greeting hardly met with a return.

"I can't really feel as if good Mr. Hooper's face was behind that piece of crape," said the sexton.

"I don't like it," muttered an old woman, as she hobbled into the meeting-house. "He has changed himself into something awful, only by hiding his face."

"Our parson has gone mad!" cried Goodman Gray, following him across the threshold.

A rumor of some unaccountable phenomenon had preceded Mr. Hooper into the meeting-house, and set all the congregation astir. Few could refrain from twisting their heads towards the door; many stood upright, and turned directly about; while several little boys clambered upon the seats, and came down again with a terrible racket. There was a general bustle, a rustling of the women's gowns and shuffling of the men's feet, greatly at variance with that hushed repose which should attend the entrance of the minister. But Mr. Hooper appeared not to notice the perturbation of his people. He entered with an almost noiseless step, bent his head mildly to the pews on each side, and bowed as he passed his oldest parishioner, a white-haired great-grandsire, who occupied an arm-chair in the centre of the aisle. It was strange to observe how slowly this venerable man became conscious of something singular in the appearance of his pastor. He seemed not fully to partake of the prevailing wonder, till Mr. Hooper had ascended the stairs, and showed himself in the pulpit, face to face with his congregation, except for the black veil. That mysterious emblem was never once withdrawn. It shook with his measured breath, as he gave out the psalm; it threw its obscurity between him and the holy page, as he read the Scriptures; and while he prayed, the veil lay heavily on his uplifted countenance. Did he seek to hide it from the dread Being whom he was addressing?

Such was the effect of this simple piece of crape, that more than one woman of delicate nerves was forced to leave the meeting-house. Yet perhaps the pale-faced congregation was almost as fearful a sight to the minister, as his black veil to them.

Mr. Hooper had the reputation of a good preacher, but not an energetic one: he strove to win his people heavenward by mild, persuasive influences, rather than to drive them thither by the thunders of the Word. The sermon which he now delivered was marked by the same characteristics of style and manner as the general series of his pulpit oratory. But there was something, either in the sentiment of the discourse itself, or in the imagination of the auditors, which made it greatly the most powerful effort that they had ever heard from their pastor's lips. It was tinged, rather more darkly than usual, with the gentle gloom of Mr. Hooper's temperament. The subject had reference to secret sin, and those sad mysteries which we hide from our nearest and dearest, and would fain conceal from our own consciousness, even forgetting that the Omniscient can detect them. A subtle power was breathed into his words. Each member of the congregation, the most innocent girl, and the man of hardened breast, felt as if the preacher had crept upon them, behind his awful veil, and discovered their hoarded iniquity of deed or thought. Many spread their clasped hands on their bosoms. There was nothing terrible in what Mr. Hooper said, at least, no violence; and yet, with every tremor of his melancholy voice, the hearers quaked. An unsought pathos came hand in hand with awe. So sensible were the audience of some unwonted attribute in their minister, that they longed for a breath of wind to blow aside the veil, almost believing that a stranger's visage would be discovered, though the form, gesture, and voice were those of Mr. Hooper.

At the close of the services, the people hurried out with indecorous confusion, eager to communicate their pent-up amazement, and conscious of lighter spirits the moment they lost sight of the black veil. Some gathered in little circles, huddled closely together, with their mouths all whispering in the centre; some went homeward alone, wrapt in silent meditation; some talked loudly, and profaned the Sabbath day with ostentatious laughter. A few shook their sagacious heads, intimating that they could penetrate the mystery; while one or two affirmed that there was no mystery at all, but only that Mr. Hooper's eyes were so weakened by the midnight lamp, as to require a shade. After a brief interval, forth came good Mr. Hooper also, in the rear of his flock. Turning his veiled face from one group to another, he paid due reverence to the hoary heads, saluted the middle aged with kind dignity as their friend and spiritual guide, greeted the young with mingled authority and love, and laid his hands on the little children's heads to bless them. Such was always his custom on the Sabbath day. Strange and bewildered looks repaid him for his courtesy. None, as on former occasions, aspired to the honor of walking by their pastor's side. Old Squire Saunders, doubtless by an accidental lapse of memory, neglected to invite Mr. Hooper to his table, where the good clergyman had been wont to bless the food, almost every Sunday since his settlement. He returned, therefore, to the parsonage, and, at the moment of closing the door, was observed to look back upon the people, all of whom had their eyes fixed upon the minister. A sad smile gleamed faintly from beneath the black veil, and flickered about his mouth, glimmering as he disappeared.

"How strange," said a lady, "that a simple black veil, such as any woman might wear on her bonnet should become such a terrible thing on Mr. Hooper's face!"

"Something must surely be amiss with Mr. Hooper's intellects," observed her husband, the physician of the village. "But the strangest part of the affair is the effect of this vagary, even on a sober-minded man like myself. The black veil, though it covers only our pastor's face, throws its influence over his whole person, and makes him ghostlike from head to foot. Do you not feel it so?"

"Truly do I," replied the lady; "and I would not be alone with him for the world. I wonder he is not afraid to be alone with himself!"

"Men sometimes are so," said her husband.

The afternoon service was attended with similar circumstances. At its conclusion, the bell tolled for the funeral of a young lady. The relatives and friends were assembled in the house, and the more distant acquaintances stood about the door, speaking of the good qualities of the deceased, when their talk was interrupted by the appearance of Mr. Hooper, still covered with his black veil. It was now an appropriate emblem. The clergyman stepped into the room where the corpse was laid, and bent over the coffin, to take a last farewell of his deceased parishioner. As he stooped, the veil hung straight down from his forehead, so that, if her eyelids had not been closed forever, the dead maiden might have seen his face. Could Mr. Hooper be fearful of her glance, that he so hastily caught back the black veil? A person who watched the interview between the dead and living, scrupled not to affirm, that, at the instant when the clergyman's features were disclosed, the corpse had slightly shuddered, rustling the shroud and muslin cap, though the countenance retained the composure of death. A superstitious old woman was the only witness of this prodigy. From the coffin Mr. Hooper passed into the chamber of the mourners, and thence to the head of the staircase, to make the funeral prayer. It was a tender and heart-dissolving prayer, full of sorrow, yet so imbued with celestial hopes, that the music of a heavenly harp, swept by the fingers of the dead, seemed faintly to be heard among the saddest accents of the minister. The people trembled, though they but darkly understood him when he prayed that they, and himself, and all of mortal race, might be ready, as he trusted this young maiden had been, for the dreadful hour that should snatch the veil from their faces. The bearers went heavily forth, and the mourners followed, saddening all the street, with the dead before them, and Mr. Hooper in his black veil behind.

"Why do you look back?" said one in the procession to his partner.

"I had a fancy," replied she, "that the minister and the maiden's spirit were walking hand in hand."

"And so had I, at the same moment," said the other.

That night, the handsomest couple in Milford village were to be joined in wedlock. Though reckoned a melancholy man, Mr. Hooper had a placid cheerfulness for such occasions, which often excited a sympathetic smile where livelier merriment would have been thrown away. There was no quality of his disposition which made him more beloved than this. The company at the wedding awaited his arrival with impatience, trusting that the strange awe, which had gathered over him throughout the day, would now be dispelled. But such was not the result. When Mr. Hooper came, the first thing that their eyes rested on was the same horrible black veil, which had added deeper gloom to the funeral, and could portend nothing but evil to the wedding. Such was its immediate effect on the guests that a cloud seemed to have rolled duskily from beneath the black crape, and dimmed the light of the candles. The bridal pair stood up before the minister. But the bride's cold fingers quivered in the tremulous hand of the bridegroom, and her deathlike paleness caused a whisper that the maiden who had been buried a few hours before was come from her grave to be married. If ever another wedding were so dismal, it was that famous one where they tolled the wedding knell. After performing the ceremony, Mr. Hooper raised a glass of wine to his lips, wishing happiness to the new-married couple in a strain of mild pleasantry that ought to have brightened the features of the guests, like a cheerful gleam from the hearth. At that instant, catching a glimpse of his figure in the looking-glass, the black veil involved his own spirit in the horror with which it overwhelmed all others. His frame shuddered, his lips grew white, he spilt the untasted wine upon the carpet, and rushed forth into the darkness. For the Earth, too, had on her Black Veil.

The next day, the whole village of Milford talked of little else than Parson Hooper's black veil. That, and the mystery concealed behind it, supplied a topic for discussion between acquaintances meeting in the street, and good women gossiping at their open windows. It was the first item of news that the tavern-keeper told to his guests. The children babbled of it on their way to school. One imitative little imp covered his face with an old black handkerchief, thereby so affrighting his playmates that the panic seized himself, and he well-nigh lost his wits by his own waggery.

It was remarkable that of all the busybodies and impertinent people in the parish, not one ventured to put the plain question to Mr. Hooper, wherefore he did this thing. Hitherto, whenever there appeared the slightest call for such interference, he had never lacked advisers, nor shown himself averse to be guided by their judgment. If he erred at all, it was by so painful a degree of self-distrust, that even the mildest censure would lead him to consider an indifferent action as a crime. Yet, though so well acquainted with this amiable weakness, no individual among his parishioners chose to make the black-veil a subject of friendly remonstrance. There was a feeling of dread, neither plainly confessed nor carefully concealed, which caused each to shift the responsibility upon another, till at length it was found expedient to send a deputation of the church, in order to deal with Mr. Hooper about the mystery, before it should grow into a scandal. Never did an embassy so ill discharge its duties. The minister received them with friendly courtesy, but became silent, after they were seated, leaving to his visitors the whole burden of introducing their important business. The topic, it might be supposed, was obvious enough. There was the black veil swathed round Mr. Hooper's forehead, and concealing every feature above his placid mouth, on which, at times, they could perceive the glimmering of a melancholy smile. But that piece of crape, to their imagination, seemed to hang down before his heart, the symbol of a fearful secret between him and them. Were the veil but cast aside, they might speak freely of it, but not till then. Thus they sat a considerable time, speechless, confused, and shrinking uneasily from Mr. Hooper's eye, which they felt to be fixed upon them with an invisible glance. Finally, the deputies returned abashed to their constituents, pronouncing the matter too weighty to be handled, except by a council of the churches, if, indeed, it might not require a general synod.

But there was one person in the village unappalled by the awe with which the black veil had impressed all beside herself. When the deputies returned without an explanation, or even venturing to demand one, she, with the calm energy of her character, determined to chase away the strange cloud that appeared to be settling round Mr. Hooper, every moment more darkly than before. As his plighted wife, it should be her privilege to know what the black veil concealed. At the minister's first visit, therefore, she entered upon the subject with a direct simplicity, which made the task easier both for him and her. After he had seated himself, she fixed her eyes steadfastly upon the veil, but could discern nothing of the dreadful gloom that had so overawed the multitude: it was but a double fold of crape, hanging down from his forehead to his mouth, and slightly stirring with his breath.

"No," said she aloud, and smiling, "there is nothing terrible in this piece of crape, except that it hides a face which I am always glad to look upon. Come, good sir, let the sun shine from behind the cloud. First lay aside your black veil: then tell me why you put it on."

Mr. Hooper's smile glimmered faintly.

"There is an hour to come," said he, "when all of us shall cast aside our veils. Take it not amiss, beloved friend, if I wear this piece of crape till then."

"Your words are a mystery, too," returned the young lady. "Take away the veil from them, at least."

"Elizabeth, I will," said he, "so far as my vow may suffer me. Know, then, this veil is a type and a symbol, and I am bound to wear it ever, both in light and darkness, in solitude and before the gaze of multitudes, and as with strangers, so with my familiar friends. No mortal eye will see it withdrawn. This dismal shade must separate me from the world: even you, Elizabeth, can never come behind it!"

"What grievous affliction hath befallen you," she earnestly inquired, "that you should thus darken your eyes forever?"

"If it be a sign of mourning," replied Mr. Hooper, "I, perhaps, like most other mortals, have sorrows dark enough to be typified by a black veil."

"But what if the world will not believe that it is the type of an innocent sorrow?" urged Elizabeth. "Beloved and respected as you are, there may be whispers that you hide your face under the consciousness of secret sin. For the sake of your holy office, do away this scandal!"

The color rose into her cheeks as she intimated the nature of the rumors that were already abroad in the village. But Mr. Hooper's mildness did not forsake him. He even smiled again—that same sad smile, which always appeared like a faint glimmering of light, proceeding from the obscurity beneath the veil.

"If I hide my face for sorrow, there is cause enough," he merely replied; "and if I cover it for secret sin, what mortal might not do the same?"

And with this gentle, but unconquerable obstinacy did he resist all her entreaties. At length Elizabeth sat silent. For a few moments she appeared lost in thought, considering, probably, what new methods might be tried to withdraw her lover from so dark a fantasy, which, if it had no other meaning, was perhaps a symptom of mental disease. Though of a firmer character than his own, the tears rolled down her cheeks. But, in an instant, as it were, a new feeling took the place of sorrow: her eyes were fixed insensibly on the black veil, when, like a sudden twilight in the air, its terrors fell around her. She arose, and stood trembling before him.

"And do you feel it then, at last?" said he mournfully.

She made no reply, but covered her eyes with her hand, and turned to leave the room. He rushed forward and caught her arm.

"Have patience with me, Elizabeth!" cried he, passionately. "Do not desert me, though this veil must be between us here on earth. Be mine, and hereafter there shall be no veil over my face, no darkness between our souls! It is but a mortal veil—it is not for eternity! O! you know not how lonely I am, and how frightened, to be alone behind my black veil. Do not leave me in this miserable obscurity forever!"

"Lift the veil but once, and look me in the face," said she.

"Never! It cannot be!" replied Mr. Hooper.

"Then farewell!" said Elizabeth.

She withdrew her arm from his grasp, and slowly departed, pausing at the door, to give one long shuddering gaze, that seemed almost to penetrate the mystery of the black veil. But, even amid his grief, Mr. Hooper smiled to think that only a material emblem had separated him from happiness, though the horrors, which it shadowed forth, must be drawn darkly between the fondest of lovers.

From that time no attempts were made to remove Mr. Hooper's black veil, or, by a direct appeal, to discover the secret which it was supposed to hide. By persons who claimed a superiority to popular prejudice, it was reckoned merely an eccentric whim, such as often mingles with the sober actions of men otherwise rational, and tinges them all with its own semblance of insanity. But with the multitude, good Mr. Hooper was irreparably a bugbear. He could not walk the street with any peace of mind, so conscious was he that the gentle and timid would turn aside to avoid him, and that others would make it a point of hardihood to throw themselves in his way. The impertinence of the latter class compelled him to give up his customary walk at sunset to the burial ground; for when he leaned pensively over the gate, there would always be faces behind the gravestones, peeping at his black veil. A fable went the rounds that the stare of the dead people drove him thence. It grieved him, to the very depth of his kind heart, to observe how the children fled from his approach, breaking up their merriest sports, while his melancholy figure was yet afar off. Their instinctive dread caused him to feel more strongly than aught else, that a preternatural horror was interwoven with the threads of the black crape. In truth, his own antipathy to the veil was known to be so great, that he never willingly passed before a mirror, nor stooped to drink at a still fountain, lest, in its peaceful bosom, he should be affrighted by himself. This was what gave plausibility to the whispers, that Mr. Hooper's conscience tortured him for some great crime too horrible to be entirely concealed, or otherwise than so obscurely intimated. Thus, from beneath the black veil, there rolled a cloud into the sunshine, an ambiguity of sin or sorrow, which enveloped the poor minister, so that love or sympathy could never reach him. It was said that ghost and fiend consorted with him there. With self-shudderings and outward terrors, he walked continually in its shadow, groping darkly within his own soul, or gazing through a medium that saddened the whole world. Even the lawless wind, it was believed, respected his dreadful secret, and never blew aside the veil. But still good Mr. Hooper sadly smiled at the pale visages of the worldly throng as he passed by.

Among all its bad influences, the black veil had the one desirable effect, of making its wearer a very efficient clergyman. By the aid of his mysterious emblem—for there was no other apparent cause—he became a man of awful power over souls that were in agony for sin. His converts always regarded him with a dread peculiar to themselves, affirming, though but figuratively, that, before he brought them to celestial light, they had been with him behind the black veil. Its gloom, indeed, enabled him to sympathize with all dark affections. Dying sinners cried aloud for Mr. Hooper, and would not yield their breath till he appeared; though ever, as he stooped to whisper consolation, they shuddered at the veiled face so near their own. Such were the terrors of the black veil, even when Death had bared his visage! Strangers came long distances to attend service at his church, with the mere idle purpose of gazing at his figure, because it was forbidden them to behold his face. But many were made to quake ere they departed! Once, during Governor Belcher's administration, Mr. Hooper was appointed to preach the election sermon. Covered with his black veil, he stood before the chief magistrate, the council, and the representatives, and wrought so deep an impression, that the legislative measures of that year were characterized by all the gloom and piety of our earliest ancestral sway.

In this manner Mr. Hooper spent a long life, irreproachable in outward act, yet shrouded in dismal suspicions; kind and loving, though unloved, and dimly feared; a man apart from men, shunned in their health and joy, but ever summoned to their aid in mortal anguish. As years wore on, shedding their snows above his sable veil, he acquired a name throughout the New England churches, and they called him Father Hooper. Nearly all his parishioners, who were of mature age when he was settled, had been borne away by many a funeral: he had one congregation in the church, and a more crowded one in the churchyard; and having wrought so late into the evening, and done his work so well, it was now good Father Hooper's turn to rest.

Several persons were visible by the shaded candlelight, in the death chamber of the old clergyman. Natural connections he had none. But there was the decorously grave, though unmoved physician, seeking only to mitigate the last pangs of the patient whom he could not save. There were the deacons, and other eminently pious members of his church. There, also, was the Reverend Mr. Clark, of Westbury, a young and zealous divine, who had ridden in haste to pray by the bedside of the expiring minister. There was the nurse, no hired hand-maiden of death, but one whose calm affection had endured thus long in secrecy, in solitude, amid the chill of age, and would not perish, even at the dying hour. Who, but Elizabeth! And there lay the hoary head of good Father Hooper upon the death pillow, with the black veil still swathed about his brow, and reaching down over his face, so that each more difficult gasp of his faint breath caused it to stir. All through life that piece of crape had hung between him and the world: it had separated him from cheerful brotherhood and woman's love, and kept him in that saddest of all prisons, his own heart; and still it lay upon his face, as if to deepen the gloom of his darksome chamber, and shade him from the sunshine of eternity.

For some time previous, his mind had been confused, wavering doubtfully between the past and the present, and hovering forward, as it were, at intervals, into the indistinctness of the world to come. There had been feverish turns, which tossed him from side to side, and wore away what little strength he had. But in his most convulsive struggles, and in the wildest vagaries of his intellect, when no other thought retained its sober influence, he still showed an awful solicitude lest the black veil should slip aside. Even if his bewildered soul could have forgotten, there was a faithful woman at his pillow, who, with averted eyes, would have covered that aged face, which she had last beheld in the comeliness of manhood. At length the death-stricken old man lay quietly in the torpor of mental and bodily exhaustion, with an imperceptible pulse, and breath that grew fainter and fainter, except when a long, deep, and irregular inspiration seemed to prelude the flight of his spirit.

The minister of Westbury approached the bedside.

"Venerable Father Hooper," said he, "the moment of your release is at hand. Are you ready for the lifting of the veil that shuts in time from eternity?"

Father Hooper at first replied merely by a feeble motion of his head; then, apprehensive, perhaps, that his meaning might be doubtful, he exerted himself to speak.

"Yea," said he, in faint accents, "my soul hath a patient weariness until that veil be lifted."

"And is it fitting," resumed the Reverend Mr. Clark, "that a man so given to prayer, of such a blameless example, holy in deed and thought, so far as mortal judgment may pronounce; is it fitting that a father in the church should leave a shadow on his memory, that may seem to blacken a life so pure? I pray you, my venerable brother, let not this thing be! Suffer us to be gladdened by your triumphant aspect as you go to your reward. Before the veil of eternity be lifted, let me cast aside this black veil from your face!"

And thus speaking, the Reverend Mr. Clark bent forward to reveal the mystery of so many years. But, exerting a sudden energy, that made all the beholders stand aghast, Father Hooper snatched both his hands from beneath the bedclothes, and pressed them strongly on the black veil, resolute to struggle, if the minister of Westbury would contend with a dying man.

"Never!" cried the veiled clergyman. "On earth, never!"

"Dark old man!" exclaimed the affrighted minister, "with what horrible crime upon your soul are you now passing to the judgment?"

Father Hooper's breath heaved; it rattled in his throat; but, with a mighty effort, grasping forward with his hands, he caught hold of life, and held it back till he should speak. He even raised himself in bed; and there he sat, shivering with the arms of death around him, while the black veil hung down, awful, at that last moment, in the gathered terrors of a lifetime. And yet the faint, sad smile, so often there, now seemed to glimmer from its obscurity, and linger on Father Hooper's lips.

"Why do you tremble at me alone?" cried he, turning his veiled face round the circle of pale spectators. "Tremble also at each other! Have men avoided me, and women shown no pity, and children screamed and fled, only for my black veil? What, but the mystery which it obscurely typifies, has made this piece of crape so awful? When the friend shows his inmost heart to his friend; the lover to his best beloved; when man does not vainly shrink from the eye of his Creator, loathsomely treasuring up the secret of his sin; then deem me a monster, for the symbol beneath which I have lived, and die! I look around me, and, lo! on every visage a Black Veil!"

While his auditors shrank from one another, in mutual affright, Father Hooper fell back upon his pillow, a veiled corpse, with a faint smile lingering on the lips. Still veiled, they laid him in his coffin, and a veiled corpse they bore him to the grave. The grass of many years has sprung up and withered on that grave, the burial stone is moss-grown, and good Mr. Hooper's face is dust; but awful is still the thought that it mouldered beneath the Black Veil!

QUESTIONS

1. How does Hawthorne use the actions and reactions of the townspeople to build a mood of ominousness? Find examples of different responses.

2. What fears and suspicions does the Rev. Mr. Hooper's veil inspire in the members of his congregation? How does it make him in some ways a better minister?

3. Comment upon the interplay between the literal and the symbolic levels of the veil's significance.

4. How much do we learn about the minister's personality? How is his wife-to-be (whom he never marries) portrayed? What part does she play in the story?

5. What is Mr. Hooper's reaction to seeing his own reflection? Why should he try to avoid it?

6. How does our understanding of Mr. Hooper and his "act" change and deepen with the passage of time?

7. What does the veil suggest or symbolize? Find the different suggestions offered by the story.

8. What moral is Hawthorne trying to communicate by way of this story?

Edgar Allan Poe

Edgar Allan Poe (1809–1849) has the reputation—not unjustified—of being one of the "damned." An older view might have it that some agent of providence had simultaneously cursed and kissed him, decreeing that he should live and die an unredeemed drunkard and gambler but that he should nonetheless be gifted with a sublime imagination and writing talent. A more modern explanation might be that the miseries of his circumstances drove him to seek compensation in art. Certainly, the subject matter of most of his writing supports this contention—it is dark and demon-haunted.

Poe was born in Boston. His parents were both traveling actors, and when his mother died (before he was three) the boy was adopted by a merchant living in Virginia. Poe was sent to the military academy at West Point, but his taste for alcohol and carousing got him expelled after a year; his father disowned him soon after. His marriage in 1836 to his thirteen-year-old cousin, Virginia Clemm, did nothing to enhance his public image. (Virginia died twelve years later of tuberculosis.)

Like so many writers of his day, Poe struggled to make a living with his pen. He wrote journalism and reviews for hire and had some success selling his stories to magazines. The stories captured the attention of readers, and for a period Poe was selling work as fast as he could produce it. And he was remarkably prolific. But Poe squandered his earnings in gambling dens and drinking establishments. He was only forty when he was found unconscious on a street in Baltimore; he died several days later.

Poe's temperament was marked by a sharp split, which is conspicuously manifested in his literary output. On the one hand, he was gripped by a profound fascination with the demonic/romantic, by anything that smacked of passionate excess or morbid desire. On the other, he possessed a keen—indeed, rigorously keen—rational intellect. The one side of his sensibility led him to write unforgettable tales like "The Cask of Amontillado," "The Masque of Red Death," "The Black Cat," and "The Fall of the House of Usher"; the other bore fruit in stories like "Murders in the Rue Morgue" and "The Purloined Letter." These latter writings, marvels of criminal ratiocination, secure his reputation as the father of the modern detective story.

THE MASQUE OF THE RED DEATH

The "Red Death" had long devastated the country. No pestilence had ever been so fatal, or so hideous. Blood was its Avatar and its seal—the redness and the horror of blood. There were sharp pains, and sudden dizziness, and then profuse bleeding at the pores, with dissolution. The scarlet stains upon the body and especially upon the face of the victim, were the pest ban which shut him out from the aid and from the sympathy of his fellow-men. And the whole seizure, progress, and termination of the disease, were the incidents of half an hour.

But the Prince Prospero was happy and dauntless and sagacious. When his dominions were half depopulated, he summoned to his presence a thousand hale and light-hearted friends from among the knights and dames of his court, and with these retired to the deep seclusion of one of his castellated abbeys. This was an extensive and magnificent structure, the creation of the prince's own eccentric yet august taste. A strong and lofty wall girdled it in. This wall had gates of iron. The courtiers, having entered, brought furnaces and massy hammers and welded the bolts. They resolved to leave means neither of ingress nor egress to the sudden impulses of despair or of frenzy from within. The abbey was amply provisioned. With such precautions the courtiers might bid defiance to contagion. The external world could take care of itself. In the meantime it was folly to grieve, or to think. The prince had provided all the appliances of pleasure. There were buffoons, there were improvisatori, there were ballet-dancers, there were musicians, there was Beauty, there was wine. All these and security were within. Without was the "Red Death."

It was toward the close of the fifth or sixth month of his seclusion, and while the pestilence raged most furiously abroad, that the Prince Prospero entertained his thousand friends at a masked ball of the most unusual magnificence.

It was a voluptuous scene, that masquerade. But first let me tell of the rooms in which it was held. There were seven—an imperial suite. In many palaces, however, such suites form a long and straight vista, while the folding doors slide back nearly to the walls on either hand, so that the view of the whole extent is scarcely impeded. Here the case was very different; as might have been expected from the duke's love of the *bizarre*. The apartments were so irregularly disposed that the vision embraced but little more than one at a time. There was a sharp turn at every twenty or thirty yards, and at each turn a novel effect. To the right and left, in the middle of each wall, a tall and narrow Gothic window looked out upon a closed corridor which pursued the windings of the suite. These windows were of stained glass whose color varied in accordance with the prevailing hue of the decorations of the chamber into which it opened. That at the eastern extremity was hung, for example in blue—and vividly blue were its windows. The second chamber was purple in its ornaments and tapestries, and here the panes were purple. The third was green throughout, and so were the casements. The fourth was furnished and lighted with orange—the fifth with white—the sixth with violet. The seventh apartment was closely shrouded in black velvet tapestries that hung all over the ceiling and down the walls, falling in heavy folds upon a carpet of the same material and hue. But in this chamber only, the color of the windows failed to correspond with the decorations. The panes here were scarlet—a deep blood color. Now in no one of the seven apartments was there any lamp or candelabrum, amid the profusion of golden ornaments that lay scattered to and fro or depended from the roof. There was no light of any kind emanating from lamp or candle within the suite of chambers. But in the corridors that followed the suite, there stood, opposite to each window, a heavy tripod, bearing a brazier of fire, that projected its rays through the tinted glass and so glaringly illumined the room. And thus were produced a multitude of gaudy and fantastic appearances. But in the western or black chamber the effect of the firelight that streamed upon the dark hangings through the blood-tinted panes was ghastly in the extreme, and produced so wild a look upon the countenances of those who entered, that there were few of the company bold enough to set foot within its precincts at all.

It was in this apartment, also, that there stood against the western wall, a gigantic clock of ebony. Its pendulum swung to and fro with a dull, heavy, monotonous clang; and when the minute-hand made the circuit of the face and the hour was to be stricken, there came from the brazen lungs of the clock a sound which was clear and loud and deep and exceedingly musical, but of so peculiar a note and emphasis that, at each lapse of an hour, the musicians of the orchestra were constrained to pause momentarily, in their performance, to hearken to the sound; and thus the waltzers perforce ceased their evolutions; and there was a brief disconcert of the whole gay company; and, while the chimes of the clock yet rang, it was observed that the giddiest grew pale, and the more aged and sedate passed their hands over their brows as if in confused revery or meditation. But when the echoes had fully ceased, a light laughter at once pervaded the assembly; the musicians looked at each other and smiled as if at their own nervousness and folly, and made whispering vows, each to the other, that the next chiming of the clock should produce in them no similar emotion; and then, after the lapse of sixty minutes (which embrace three thousand and six hundred seconds of the Time that flies), there came yet another chiming of the clock, and then were the same disconcert and tremulousness and meditation as before.

But, in spite of these things, it was a gay and magnificent revel. The tastes of the duke were peculiar. He had a fine eye for colors and effects. He disregarded the *decora* of mere fashion. His plans were bold and fiery, and his conceptions glowed with barbaric lustre. There are some who would have thought him mad. His followers felt that he was not. It was necessary to hear and see and touch him to be *sure* that he was not.

He had directed, in great part, the movable embellishments of the seven chambers, upon occasion of this great *fête*: and it was his own guiding taste which had given character to the masqueraders. Be sure they were grotesque. There were much glare and glitter and piquancy and phantasm—much of what has been since seen in "Hernani." There were arabesque figures with unsuited limbs and appointments. There were delirious fancies such as the mad-man fashions. There were much of the beautiful, much of the wanton, much of the *bizarre*, something of the terrible, and not a little of that which might have excited disgust. To and fro in the seven chambers there stalked, in fact, a multitude of dreams. And these—the dreams—writhed in and about, taking hue from the rooms, and causing the wild music of the orchestra to seem as the echo of their steps. And, anon, there strikes the ebony clock which stands in the hall of the velvet. And then, for a moment, all is still, and all is silent save the voice of the clock. The dreams are stiff-frozen as they stand. But the echoes of the chime die away—they have endured but an instant—and a light, half-subdued laughter floats after them as they depart. And now again the music swells, and the dreams live, and writhe to and fro more merrily than ever, taking hue from the many-tinted windows through which stream the rays from the tripods. But to the chamber which lies most westwardly of the seven there are now none of the maskers who venture; for the night is waning away; and there flows a ruddier light through the blood-colored panes; and the blackness of the sable drapery appals; and to him whose foot falls upon the sable carpet, there comes from the near clock of ebony a muffled peal more solemnly emphatic than any which reaches *their* ears who indulge in the more remote gaieties of the other apartments.

But these other apartments were densely crowded, and in them beat feverishly the heart of life. And the revel went whirlingly on, until at length there commenced the sounding of midnight upon the clock. And then the music ceased, as I have told; and the evolutions of the waltzers were quieted; and there was an uneasy cessation of all things as before. But now there were twelve strokes to be sounded by the bell of the clock; and thus it happened, perhaps that more of thought crept, with more of time, into the meditations of the thoughtful among those who revelled. And thus too, it happened, perhaps, that before the last echoes of the last chime had utterly sunk into silence, there were many individuals in the crowd who had found leisure to become aware of the presence of a masked figure which had arrested the attention of no single individual before. And the rumor of this new presence having spread itself whisperingly around, there arose at length from the whole company a buzz, or murmur, expressive of disapprobation and surprise—then, finally, of terror, of horror, and of disgust.

In an assembly of phantasms such as I have painted, it may well be supposed that no ordinary appearance could have excited such sensation. In truth the masquerade license of the night was nearly unlimited; but the figure in question had out-Heroded Herod, and gone beyond the bounds of even the prince's indefinite decorum. There are chords in the hearts of the most reckless which cannot be touched without emotion. Even with the utterly lost, to whom life and death are equally jests, there are matters of which no jest can be made. The whole company, indeed, seemed now deeply to feel that in the costume and bearing of the stranger neither wit nor propriety existed. The figure was tall and gaunt, and shrouded from head to foot in the habiliments of the grave. The mask which concealed the visage was made so nearly to resemble the countenance of a stiffened corpse that the closest scrutiny must have had difficulty in detecting the cheat. And yet all this might have been endured, if not approved, by the mad revellers around. But the mummer had gone so far as to assume the type of the Red Death. His vesture was dabbled in *blood*—and his broad brow, with all the features of the face, was besprinkled with the scarlet horror.

When the eyes of Prince Prospero fell upon this spectral image (which, with a slow and solemn movement, as if more fully to sustain its *rôle*, stalked to and fro among the waltzers) he was seen to be convulsed, in the first moment with a strong shudder either of terror or distaste; but, in the next, his brow reddened with rage.

"Who dares"—he demanded hoarsely of the courtiers who stood near him—"who dares insult us with this blasphemous mockery? Seize him and unmask him—that we may know whom we have to hang, at sunrise, from the battlements!"

It was in the eastern or blue chamber in which stood the Prince Prospero as he uttered these words. They rang throughout the seven rooms loudly and clearly, for the prince was a bold and robust man, and the music had become hushed at the waving of his hand.

It was in the blue room where stood the prince, with a group of pale courtiers by his side. At first, as he spoke, there was a slight rushing movement of this group in the direction of the intruder, who, at the moment was also near at hand, and now, with deliberate and stately step, made closer approach to the speaker. But from a certain nameless awe with which the mad assumptions of the mummer had inspired the whole party, there were found none who put forth hand to seize him; so that, unimpeded, he passed within a yard of the prince's person; and, while the vast assembly, as if with one impulse, shrank from the centres of the rooms to the walls, he made his way uninterruptedly, but with the same solemn and measured step which had distinguished him from the first, through the blue chamber to the purple—through the purple to the green—through the green to the orange—through this again to the white—and even thence to the violet, ere a decided movement had been made to arrest him. It was then, however, that the Prince Prospero, maddening with rage and the shame of his own momentary cowardice, rushed hurriedly through the six chambers, while none followed him on account of a deadly terror that had seized upon all. He bore aloft a drawn dagger, and had approached, in rapid impetuosity, to within three or four feet of the retreating figure, when the latter, having attained the extremity of the velvet apartment, turned suddenly and confronted his pursuer. There was a sharp cry—and the dagger dropped gleaming upon the sable carpet, upon which, instantly afterward, fell prostrate in death the Prince Prospero. Then, summoning the wild courage of despair, a throng of the revellers at once threw themselves into the black apartment, and, seizing the mummer, whose tall figure stood erect and motionless within the shadow of the ebony clock, gasped in unutterable horror at finding the grave cerements and corpse-like mask, which they handled with so violent a rudeness, untenanted by any tangible form.

And now was acknowledged the presence of the Red Death. He had come like a thief in the night. And one by one dropped the revellers in the blood-bedewed halls of their revel, and died each in the despairing posture of his fall. And the life of the ebony clock went out with that of the last of the gay. And the flames of the tripods expired. And Darkness and Decay and the Red Death held illimitable dominion over all.

QUESTIONS

1. How does Poe first indicate Prince Prospero's character? What is our response to his defiant decision to outwait the plague?
2. How does Poe build up the atmosphere essential for his final effect? What makes his description of the various rooms so ominous? Discuss his use of different colors. Do they have distinct symbolic value, or are they merely suggestive?
3. Poe is celebrated for his way of using the musical sounds of words. Can you find several examples in this story?
4. How does Poe build to the moment of revelation? What are his tricks for achieving suspense?
5. Is Poe expressing a moral in this story? Is he punishing Prince Prospero? If so, for what?
6. Discuss the relevance to this story of the old proverb "Pride cometh before the fall."
7. Poe is deliberately nonspecific about the time and place of the story. How does this affect our reading? Would we react differently if he had set the story in fourteenth-century Italy?

Nikolai Gogol

Nikolai Gogol (1809–1852), like Edgar Allan Poe, suffered through a short, mainly unhappy life but left a literary legacy of astonishing richness. Born in the Russian Ukraine, Gogol moved to St. Petersburg when he was nineteen. He passed his civil service exams and held several low-level government posts. But as any reader of Gogol knows, his was not a temperament suited to those drab and often senseless employments. He threw himself with increasing fervor into literary projects, and in 1831 and 1832 he published the two-volume collection of stories, *Evenings on a Farm near Dikanka,* which made his reputation. Four years later Gogol wrote *The Inspector General,* a satiric play. His vicious ridicule of government officials promptly made him *persona non grata* in the Russian Empire, and he exiled himself to Rome. There he remained for the last decade of his life, returning only briefly to Russia. In the face of deteriorating mental health—he would die insane—Gogol wrote his best-known book, *Dead Souls* (1842). The novel ridiculed the institution of serfdom ("soul" was the name for a serf), which was the backbone of the Russian system of agricultural economy. The writer did not live to see the abolition of serfdom in the 1860s (which came shortly before the abolition of slavery in the United States).

Gogol's story "The Nose" dates from 1835. It reflects his preoccupation with the drab, unvalorous "little man" and makes abundant use of the humorous absurdity that became his writing trademark. Like other writers of his era—Flaubert, Poe, Hawthorne—Gogol practiced the art of the airless enclosure. The settings, often urban, are constricted, without open vistas or gusts of fresh air; the action takes place among narrow streets and confining walls. Where space feels cramped, the twistings of the human soul must appear magnified.

Vladimir Nabokov has written brilliantly about his countryman. Of his idiosyncratic approach he once observed:

> Imagine a trap-door that opens under your feet with absurd suddenness, and a lyrical gust that sweeps you up and then lets you fall with a bump into the next traphole. The absurd was Gogol's favorite muse—but when I say "the absurd," I do not mean the quaint or the comic. The absurd has as many shades and degrees as the tragic has, and moreover, in Gogol's case, it borders upon the latter. It would be wrong to assert that Gogol placed his characters in absurd situations. You cannot place a man in an absurd situation if the whole world he lives in is absurd.

THE NOSE

I

A most extraordinary thing happened in Petersburg on the twenty-fifth of March. The barber, Ivan Yakovlevich, who lives on the Voznessensky Avenue (his surname is lost, and even on his signboard, depicting a gentleman with a lathered face and bearing the inscription: "Also lets blood," no surname appears)—the barber Ivan Yakovlevich woke up rather early and inhaled the smell of hot bread. Raising himself a little in bed, he saw that his wife, a highly respectable lady who was very fond of a cup of coffee, was taking out of the oven some freshly baked bread.

"I won't have coffee today, my dear," said Ivan Yakovlevich. "Instead I'd like some hot bread with onions."

(That is to say, Ivan Yakovlevich would have liked both, but he knew that it was absolutely impossible to ask for two things at once; for his wife disliked such absurd whims.)

"Let the fool eat bread," his wife thought to herself. "All the better for me: there'll be an extra cup of coffee left." And she flung a loaf on the table.

After putting on, for propriety's sake, his frock coat over his shirt, Ivan Yakovlevich sat down at the table, sprinkled some salt, peeled two onions, picked up a knife, and, assuming a solemn expression, began cutting the bread. Having cut it in two, he had a look into the middle of one of the halves and, to his astonishment, noticed some white object there. Ivan Yakovlevich prodded it carefully with the knife and felt it with a finger. "It's solid," he said to himself. "What on earth can it be?"

He dug his fingers into the bread and pulled out—a nose! Ivan Yakovlevich's heart sank: he rubbed his eyes and felt it again: a nose! There could be no doubt about it: it was a nose! And a familiar nose, too, apparently. Ivan Yakovlevich looked horrified. But his horror was nothing compared to the indignation with which his wife was overcome.

"Where have you cut off that nose, you monster?" she screamed angrily. "Blackguard! Drunkard! I shall inform the police against you myself. What a cutthroat! Three gentlemen have told me already that when you are shaving them you pull so violently at their noses that it is a wonder they still remain on their faces!"

But Ivan Yakovlevich was more dead than alive. He recognised the nose as belonging to no other person than the Collegiate Assessor Kovalyov, whom he shaved every Wednesday and every Sunday.

"Wait, my dear, I'll wrap it in a rag and put it in a corner: let it stay there for a bit and then I'll take it out."

"I won't hear of it! What do you take me for? Keep a cutoff nose in my room? You heartless villain, you! All you know is to strop your razor. Soon you won't be fit to carry out your duties at all, you whoremonger, you scoundrel, you! You don't expect me to answer to the police for you, do you? Oh, you filthy wretch, you blockhead, you! Out with it! Out! Take it where you like, only don't let me see it here again!"

Ivan Yakovlevich stood there looking utterly crushed. He thought and thought and did not know what to think.

"Damned if I know how it happened," he said at last, scratching behind his ear. "Did I come home drunk last night? I'm sure I don't know. And yet the whole thing is quite impossible—it can't be true however you look at it: for bread is something you bake, and a nose is something quite different. Can't make head or tail of it!"

Ivan Yakovlevich fell silent. The thought that the police might find the nose at his place and charge him with having cut it off made him feel utterly dejected. He could already see the scarlet collar, beautifully embroidered with silver, the sabre—and he trembled all over. At last he got his trousers and boots, pulled on these sorry objects, and, accompanied by his wife's execrations, wrapped the nose in a rag and went out into the street.

He wanted to shove it under something, either under the seat by the gates or drop it, as it were, by accident and then turn off into a side street. But as ill luck would have it, he kept coming across people he knew, who at once addressed him with the question: "Where are you off to?" or "Who are you going to shave so early in the morning?"—so that he could not find a right moment for getting rid of it. On one occasion he did succeed in dropping it, but a policeman shouted to him from the distance, pointing to it with his halberd: "Hey, you, pick it up! You've dropped something!" And Ivan Yakovlevich had to pick up the nose and put it in his pocket. He was overcome by despair, particularly as the number of people in the streets was continually increasing with the opening of the stores and the small shops.

He decided to go to the Issakiyevsky Bridge, for it occurred to him that he might be able to throw it into the Neva. But I'm afraid I am perhaps a little to blame for not having so far said something more about Ivan Yakovlevich, an estimable man in many respects.

Ivan Yakovlevich, like every other Russian working man, was a terrible drunkard. And though every day he shaved other people's chins, he never bothered to shave his own. Ivan Yakovlevich's frock coat (he never wore an ordinary coat) was piebald; that is to say, it was black, but covered all over with large brown, yellow, and grey spots; his collar was shiny; and instead of three buttons only bits of thread dangled from his coat. Ivan Yakovlevich was a great cynic, and every time the Collegiate Assessor Kovalyov said to him: "Your hands always stink, Ivan Yakovlevich," he would reply with the question: "Why should they stink, sir?" "I don't know why, my dear fellow," the Collegiate Assessor would say, "only they do stink." And after taking a pinch of snuff, Ivan Yakovlevich would lather him for that all over his cheeks, under the nose, behind his ears, and under his beard, in short, wherever he fancied.

This worthy citizen had in the meantime reached Issakiyevsky Bridge. First of all he looked round cautiously, then he leaned over the parapet, as though anxious to see whether there were a great many fishes swimming by, and as he did so he stealthily threw the rag with the nose into the river. He felt as though a heavy weight had been lifted from his shoulders: Ivan Yakovlevich even grinned. Instead of going to shave the chins of civil servants, he set off towards an establishment which bore the inscription: "Tea and Victuals," intending to ask for a glass of punch, when he suddenly noticed at the end of the bridge a police inspector of noble exterior, with large whiskers, with a three-cornered hat, and with a sabre. He stood rooted to the spot; meanwhile the police officer beckoned to him and said: "Come here, my man!"

Knowing the rules, Ivan Yakovlevich took off his cap some way off and, coming up promptly, said: "I hope your honour is well."

"No, no, my good man, not 'your honour.' Tell me, what were you doing there on the bridge?"

"Why, sir, I was going to shave one of my customers and I just stopped to have a look how fast the current was running."

"You're lying, sir, you're lying! You won't get off with that. Answer my question, please!"

"I'm ready to shave you two or even three times a week, sir, with no conditions attached," replied Ivan Yakovlevich.

"No, my dear sir, that's nothing! I have three barbers who shave me and they consider it a great honour, too. You'd better tell me what you were doing there!"

Ivan Yakovlevich turned pale. . . . But here the incident is completely shrouded in a fog and absolutely nothing is known of what happened next.

II

Collegiate Assessor Kovalyov woke up fairly early and muttered, "Brrr . . ." with his lips, which he always did when he woke up, though he could not say himself why he did so. Kovalyov stretched and asked for the little looking glass standing on the table. He wanted to look at the pimple which had appeared on his nose the previous evening, but to his great astonishment, instead of his nose, he saw a completely empty, flat place! Frightened, Kovalyov asked for some water and rubbed his eyes with a towel: there was no nose! He began feeling with his hand and pinched himself to see whether he was still asleep: no, he did not appear to be asleep. The Collegiate Assessor Kovalyov jumped out of bed and shook himself: he had no nose! He immediately told his servant to help him dress and rushed off straight to the Commissioner of Police.

Meanwhile we had better say something about Kovalyov so that the reader may see what sort of a person this Collegiate Assessor was. Collegiate Assessors who receive that title in consequence of their learned diplomas cannot be compared with those Collegiate Assessors who obtain this rank in the Caucasus. They are two quite different species. Learned Collegiate Assessors . . . But Russia is such a wonderful country that if you say something about one Collegiate Assessor, all the Collegiate Assessors, from Riga to Kamchatka, will most certainly think that you are referring to them. The same, of course, applies to all other callings and ranks. Kovalyov was a Caucasian Collegiate Assessor. He had obtained that rank only two years earlier and that was why he could not forget it for a moment; and to add to his own importance and dignity, he never described himself as a Collegiate Assessor, that is to say, a civil servant of the eighth rank, but always as a major, that is to say, by the corresponding rank in the army. "Look here, my good woman," he used to say when he met a peasant woman selling shirt fronts in the street, "you go to my house—I live on Sadovaya Street—and just ask: Does Major Kovalyov live here? Anyone will show you." But if he met some pretty little minx, he'd give her besides a secret instruction, adding: "You just ask for Major Kovalyov's apartment, darling." And that is why we, too, will in future refer to this Collegiate Assessor as Major Kovalyov.

Major Kovalyov was in the habit of taking a stroll on Nevsky Avenue every day. The collar of his shirt front was always extremely clean and well starched. His whiskers were such as one can still see nowadays on provincial district surveyors, architects, and army doctors, as well as on police officers performing various duties and, in general, on all gallant gentlemen who have full, ruddy cheeks and are very good at a game of boston: these whiskers go right across the middle of the cheek and straight up to the nose. Major Kovalyov wore a great number of cornelian seals, some with crests and others which had engraved on them: Wednesday, Thursday, Monday, and so on. Major Kovalyov came to Petersburg on business, to wit, to look for a post befitting his rank: if he were lucky, the post of a vice-governor, if not, one of an administrative clerk in some important department. Major Kovalyov was not averse to matrimony, either, but only if he could find a girl with a fortune of two hundred thousand. The reader can, therefore, judge for himself the state in which the major was when he saw, instead of a fairly handsome nose of moderate size, a most idiotic, flat, smooth place.

As misfortune would have it, there was not a single cab to be seen in the street and he had to walk, wrapping himself in his cloak and covering his face with a handkerchief, as though his nose were bleeding. "But perhaps I imagined it all," he thought. "It's impossible that I could have lost my nose without noticing it!" He went into a pastry cook's for the sole purpose of having a look at himself in a mirror. Fortunately, there was no one in the shop: the boys were sweeping the rooms and arranging the chairs; some of them, sleepy-eyed, were bringing in hot cream puffs on trays; yesterday's papers, stained with coffee, were lying about on tables and chairs. "Well, thank God, there's nobody here," he said. "Now I can have a look." He went timidly up to the mirror and looked. "Damn it," he said, disgusted, "the whole thing is too ridiculous for words! If only there'd be something instead of a nose, but there's just nothing!"

Biting his lips with vexation, Kovalyov went out of the pastry cook's and made up his mind, contrary to his usual practice, not to look or smile at anyone. Suddenly he stopped dead in his tracks at the front doors of a house; a most inexplicable thing happened before his very eyes: a carriage drew up before the entrance, the carriage door opened, and a gentleman in uniform jumped out and, stooping, rushed up the steps. Imagine the horror and, at the same time, amazement of Kovalyov when he recognised that this was his own nose! At this extraordinary sight everything went swimming before his eyes. He felt that he could hardly stand on his feet; but he made up his mind that, come what may, he would wait for the gentleman's return to the carriage. He was trembling all over as though in a fever. Two minutes later the nose really did come out. He wore a gold-embroidered uniform with a large stand-up collar, chamois-leather breeches, and a sword at his side. From his plumed hat it could be inferred that he was a State Councillor, a civil servant of the fifth rank. Everything showed that he was going somewhere to pay a visit. He looked round to the right and to the left, shouted to his driver, who had driven off a short distance, to come back, got into the carriage, and drove off.

Poor Kovalyov nearly went out of his mind. He did not know what to think of such a strange occurrence. And, indeed, how was it possible for a nose which had only the day before been on his face and which could neither walk nor drive—to be in a uniform! He ran after the carriage which, luckily, did not go far, stopping before the Kazan Cathedral.

He hastened into the cathedral, pushing his way through the crowd of beggarwomen with bandaged faces and only two slits for the eyes, at whom he used to laugh so much before, and went into the church. There were only a few worshippers inside the church; they were all standing near the entrance. Kovalyov felt so distraught that he was unable to pray and he kept searching with his eyes for the gentleman in the State Councillor's uniform. At last he saw him standing apart from the other worshippers. The nose was hiding his face completely in his large stand-up collar and was saying his prayers with the expression of the utmost piety.

"How am I to approach him?" thought Kovalyov. "It is clear from everything, from his uniform, from his hat, that he is a State Councillor. I'm damned if I know how to do it!"

He went up to him and began clearing his throat; but the nose did not change his devout attitude for a moment and carried on with his genuflections.

"Sir," said Kovalyov, inwardly forcing himself to take courage, "Sir—"

"What do you want?" answered the nose, turning round.

"I find it strange, sir, I—I believe you ought to know your proper place. And all of a sudden I find you in church of all places! You—you must admit that—"

"How sorry but I can't understand what you are talking about. . . . Explain yourself."

"How can I explain it to him?" thought Kovalyov and, plucking up courage, began: "Of course—er—you see—I—I am a major and—and you must admit that it isn't right for—er—a man of my rank to walk about without a nose. I mean—er—a tradeswoman selling peeled oranges on Voskressensky Bridge can sit there without a nose; but for a man like me who expects to obtain the post of a governor, which without a doubt he will obtain and—er—besides, being received in many houses by ladies of good position, such as Mrs. Chekhtaryov, the widow of a State Councillor, sir, and many others—er—Judge for yourself, sir, I mean, I—I don't know"—Major Kovalyov shrugged his shoulders—"I am sorry but if one were to look upon it according to the rules of honour and duty—er—you can understand yourself, sir—"

"I don't understand anything, sir," replied the nose. "Please explain yourself more clearly."

"Sir," said Kovalyov with a consciousness of his own dignity, "I don't know how to understand your words. It seems to me the whole thing is perfectly obvious. Or do you wish—I mean, you are my own nose, sir!"

The nose looked at the major and frowned slightly.

"You are mistaken, sir. I am *myself*. Besides, there can be no question of any intimate relationship between us. I see, sir, from the buttons of your uniform that you are serving in a different department."

Having said this, the nose turned away and went on praying.

Kovalyov was utterly confounded, not knowing what to do or even what to think. At that moment he heard the agreeable rustle of a lady's dress; an elderly lady, her dress richly trimmed with lace, walked up to them, accompanied by a slim girl in a white dress, which looked very charming on her slender figure, and in a straw-coloured hat, as light as a pastry puff. Behind them, opening a snuffbox, stood a tall flunkey with enormous whiskers and quite a dozen collars on his Cossack coat.

Kovalyov came nearer, pulled out the cambric collar of his shirt front, straightened the seals hanging on his gold watch chain and, turning his head this way and that and smiling, turned his attention to the ethereal young lady who, like a spring flower, bent forward a little, as she prayed, and put her little white hand with its semi-transparent fingers to her forehead to cross herself. The smile on Kovalyov's face distended a little more when he caught sight under her pretty hat of a chin of dazzling whiteness and part of her cheek, suffused with the colour of the first spring rose. But suddenly he sprang back as though he had burnt himself. He recollected that, instead of a nose, he had absolutely nothing on his face, and tears started to his eyes. He turned round, intending to tell the gentleman in uniform plainly that he was merely pretending to be a State Councillor, that he was a rogue and an impostor and nothing else than his own nose. . . . But the nose was no longer there: he had managed to gallop off, no doubt to pay another visit. . . .

That plunged Kovalyov into despair. He left the church and stopped for a moment under the colonnade, carefully looking in all directions to see whether he could catch sight of the nose anywhere. He remembered very well that he wore a hat with a plume and a gold-embroidered uniform; but he had not noticed his cloak, nor the colour of his carriage, nor his horses, nor even whether he had a footman behind him and, if so, in what livery. Besides, there were so many carriages careering backwards and forwards that it was difficult to distinguish one from another. But even if he had been able to distinguish any of them, there was no way of stopping it. It was a lovely, sunny day. There were hundreds of people on Nevsky Avenue. A whole flowery cascade of ladies was pouring all over the pavement from the Police Bridge to the Anichkin Bridge. There he saw coming a good acquaintance of his, a civil servant of the seventh rank, whom he always addressed as lieutenant colonel, especially in the presence of strangers. And there was Yaryzhkin, the head clerk in the Senate, a great friend of his, who always lost points when he went eight at boston. And here was another major, who had received the eighth rank of Collegiate Assessor in the Caucasus, waving to him to come up. . . .

"Oh, hell!" said Kovalyov. "Hey, cabby, take me straight to the Commissioner of Police!"

Kovalyov got into the cab and kept shouting to the driver: "Faster! Faster!"

"Is the Police Commissioner at home?" he asked, entering the hall.

"No, sir," replied the janitor. "He's just gone out."

"Well, of all things!"

"Yes, sir," the janitor added, "he's not been gone so long, but he's gone all right. If you'd come a minute earlier, you'd probably have found him at home."

Without taking his handkerchief off his face, Kovalyov got into the cab and shouted in an anguished voice:

"Drive on!"

"Where to, sir?" asked the cabman.

"Straight ahead!"

"Straight ahead, sir? But there's a turning here: to right or to left?"

This question stumped Kovalyov and made him think again. A man in his position ought first of all apply to the City Police Headquarters, not because they dealt with matters of this kind there, but because instructions coming from there might be complied with much more quickly than those coming from any other place; to seek satisfaction from the authorities of the department in which the nose claimed to be serving would have been unreasonable, for from the nose's replies he perceived that nothing was sacred to that individual and that he was quite capable of telling a lie just as he had lied in denying that he had ever seen him. Kovalyov was, therefore, about to tell the cabman to drive him to Police Headquarters, when it again occurred to him that this rogue and impostor, who had treated him in such a contumelious way, might take advantage of the first favourable opportunity and slip out of town, and then all his searches would be in vain or, which God forbid, might go on for a whole month. At last it seemed that Heaven itself had suggested a plan of action to him. He decided to go straight to a newspaper office and, while there was still time, put in an advertisement with a circumstantial description of the nose so that anyone meeting it might bring it to him at once or, at any rate, let him know where it was. And so, having made up his mind, he told the cabman to drive him to the nearest newspaper office and all the way there he kept hitting the cabman on the back with his fist, repeating, "Faster, you rogue! Faster, you scoundrel!" "Good Lord, sir, what are you hitting me for?" said the cabman, shaking his head and flicking with the rein at the horse, whose coat was as long as a lap dog's. At last the cab came to a stop and Kovalyov ran panting into a small reception room where a grey-haired clerk, in an old frock coat and wearing spectacles, sat at a table, with a pen between his teeth, counting some coppers.

"Who receives advertisements here?" cried Kovalyov. "Oh, good morning!"

"How do you do?" said the clerk, raising his eyes for a moment and dropping them again on the carefully laid out heaps of coppers before him.

"I should like to insert—"

"One moment, sir, I must ask you to wait a little," said the clerk, writing down a figure on a piece of paper with one hand and moving two beads on his abacus with the other.

A footman with galloons on his livery and a personal appearance which showed that he came from an aristocratic house, was standing beside the clerk with a note in his hand. He thought it an opportune moment for displaying his knowledge of the world.

"Would you believe it, sir," he said, "the little bitch isn't worth eighty copecks, and indeed I shouldn't give even eight copecks for her, but the countess dotes on her, sir, she simply dotes on her, and that's why she's offering a hundred roubles to anyone who finds her! Now, to put it politely, sir, just as you and me are speaking now, you can never tell what people's tastes may be. What I mean is that if you are a sportsman, then keep a pointer or a poodle, don't mind spending five hundred or even a thousand roubles, so long as your dog is a good one."

The worthy clerk listened to this with a grave air and at the same time kept counting the number of letters in the advertisement the footman had brought. The room was full of old women, shop assistants, and house porters—all with bits of paper in their hands. In one a coachman of sober habits was advertised as being let out on hire; in another an almost new, secondhand carriage, brought from Paris in 1814, was offered for sale; in still others were offered for sale: a serf girl of nineteen, experienced in laundry work and suitable for other work, a well-built open carriage with only one spring broken, a young, dappled-grey, mettlesome horse of seventeen years of age, a new consignment of turnip and radish seed from London, a summer residence with all the conveniences, including two boxes for horses and a piece of land on which an excellent birchwood or pinewood could be planted; there was also an advertisement containing a challenge to those who wished to purchase old boot soles with an invitation to come to the auction rooms every day from eight o'clock in the morning to three o'clock in the afternoon. The room, in which all these people were crowded, was very small and the air extremely thick; but the Collegiate Assessor Kovalyov did not notice the bad smell because he kept the handkerchief over his face and also because his nose was at the time goodness knows where.

"Excuse me, sir," he said at last with impatience, "it's very urgent. . . ."

"Presently, presently," said the grey-haired gentleman, flinging their notes back to the old women and the house porters. "Two roubles forty copecks! One moment, sir! One rouble sixty-four copecks! What can I do for you?" he said at last, turning to Kovalyov.

"Thank you, sir," said Kovalyov. "You see, I've been robbed or swindled, I can't so far say which, but I should like you to put in an advertisement that anyone who brings the scoundrel to me will receive a handsome reward."

"What is your name, sir?"

"What do you want my name for? I'm sorry I can't give it to you. I have a large circle of friends: Mrs. Chekhtaryov, the widow of a State Councillor, Pelageya Grigoryevna Podtochin, the widow of a first lieutenant. . . . God forbid that they should suddenly find out! You can simply say: a Collegiate Assessor or, better still, a gentleman of the rank of major."

"And is the runaway your house serf?"

"My house serf? Good Lord, no! That wouldn't have been so bad! You see, it's my—er—nose that has run away from me. . . ."

"Dear me, what a strange name! And has this Mr. Nosov robbed you of a large sum of money?"

"I said nose, sir, nose! You're thinking of something else! It is my nose, my own nose that has disappeared I don't know where. The devil himself must have played a joke on me!"

"But how did it disappear? I'm afraid I don't quite understand it."

"I can't tell you how it happened. The worst of it is that now it is driving about all over the town under the guise of a State Councillor. That's why

I should like you to insert an advertisement that anyone who catches him should bring him at once to me. You can see for yourself, sir, that I cannot possibly carry on without such a conspicuous part of myself. It's not like some little toe which no one can see whether it is missing or not once I'm wearing my boots. I call on Thursdays on Mrs. Chekhtaryov, the widow of a State Councillor. Mrs. Podtochin, the widow of a first lieutenant, and her pretty daughter are also good friends of mine, and you can judge for yourself the position I am in now. I can't go and see them now, can I?"

The clerk pursed his lips tightly which meant that he was thinking hard.

"I'm sorry, sir," he said at last, after a long pause, "but I can't possibly insert such an advertisement in the papers."

"What? Why not?"

"Well, you see, sir, the paper might lose its reputation. If everyone were to write that his nose had run away, why—As it is, people are already saying that we are publishing a lot of absurd stories and false rumours."

"But why is it so absurd? I don't see anything absurd in it."

"It only seems so to you. Last week, for instance, a similar thing happened. A civil servant came to see me just as you have now. He brought an advertisement, it came to two roubles and seventy-three copecks, but all it was about was that a poodle with a black coat had run away. You wouldn't think there was anything in that, would you? And yet it turned out to be a libellous statement. You see, the poodle was the treasurer of some institution or other. I don't remember which."

"But I am not asking you to publish an advertisement about a poodle, but about my own nose, which is the same as about myself."

"No, sir, I cannot possibly insert such an advertisement."

"Not even if my own nose really has disappeared?"

"If it's lost, then it's a matter for a doctor. I'm told there are people who can fit you with a nose of any shape you like. But I can't help observing, sir, that you are a gentleman of a merry disposition and are fond of pulling a person's leg."

"I swear to you by all that is holy! Why, if it has come to that, I don't mind showing you."

"Don't bother, sir," said the clerk, taking a pinch of snuff. "Still," he added, unable to suppress his curiosity, "if it's no bother, I'd like to have a look."

The Collegiate Assessor removed the handkerchief from his face.

"It is very strange, indeed!" said the clerk. "The place is perfectly flat, just like a pancake from a frying pan. Yes, quite incredibly flat."

"Well, you won't dispute it now, will you? You can see for yourself that you simply must insert it. I shall be infinitely grateful to you and very glad this incident has given me the pleasure of making your acquaintance. . . ."

It may be seen from that that the major decided to lay it on a bit thick this time.

"Well, of course, it's easy enough to insert an advertisement," said the clerk, "but I don't see that it will do you any good. If you really want to publish a thing like that, you'd better put it in the hands of someone skilful with his pen and let him describe it as a rare natural phenomenon and publish it in *The Northern Bee*"—here he took another pinch of snuff—"for the benefit of youth"—here he wiped his nose—"or just as a matter of general interest."

The Collegiate Assessor was utterly discouraged. He dropped his eyes and glanced at the bottom of the newspaper where the theatrical announcements were published; his face was ready to break into a smile as he read the name of a very pretty actress, and his hand went automatically to his pocket to feel whether he had a five-rouble note there, for, in Kovalyov's opinion, officers of the higher ranks ought to have a seat in the stalls—but the thought of his nose spoilt it all!

The clerk himself appeared to be touched by Kovalyov's embarrassing position. Wishing to relieve his distress a little, he thought it proper to express his sympathy in a few words.

"I'm very sorry indeed, sir," he said, "that such a thing should have happened to you. Would you like a pinch of snuff? It relieves headaches, dispels melancholy moods, and it is even a good remedy against haemorrhoids."

Saying this, the clerk offered his snuffbox to Kovalyov, very deftly opening the lid with the portrait of a lady in a hat on it.

This unintentional action made Kovalyov lose his patience.

"I can't understand, sir," he said angrily, "how you can joke in a matter like this! Don't you see I haven't got the thing with which to take a pinch of snuff? To hell with your snuff! I can't bear the sight of it now, and not only your rotten beresina brand, but even if you were to offer me rappee itself!"

Having said this, he walked out of the newspaper office, greatly vexed, and went to see the police inspector of his district, a man who had a great liking for sugar. At his home, the entire hall, which was also the dining room, was stacked with sugar loaves with which local tradesmen had presented him out of friendship. When Kovalyov arrived, the police inspector's cook was helping him off with his regulation top boots; his sabre and the rest of his martial armour were already hung peaceably in the corners of the room, and his three-year-old son was playing with his awe-inspiring three-cornered hat. He himself was getting ready to partake of the pleasures of peace after his gallant, warlike exploits.

Kovalyov walked in at the time when he stretched, cleared his throat, and said: "Oh, for a couple of hours of sleep!" It could, therefore, be foreseen that the Collegiate Assessor could have hardly chosen a worse time to arrive; indeed, I am not sure whether he would have got a more cordial reception even if he had brought the police inspector several pounds of sugar or a piece of cloth. The inspector was a great patron of the arts and manufactures, but he preferred a bank note to everything else. "This is something," he used to say. "There is nothing better than that: it doesn't ask for food, it doesn't take up a lot of space, there's always room for it in the pocket, and when you drop it, it doesn't break."

The inspector received Kovalyov rather coldly and said that after dinner was not the time to carry out investigations and that nature herself had fixed it so that after a good meal a man had to take a nap (from which the Collegiate Assessor could deduce that the inspector was not unfamiliar with the sayings of the ancient sages), and that a respectable man would not have his nose pulled off.

A bull's eye! . . . It must be observed that Kovalyov was extremely quick to take offence. He could forgive anything people said about himself, but he could never forgive an insult to his rank or his calling. He was even of the opinion that any reference in plays to army officers or civil servants of low rank was admissible, but that the censorship ought not to pass any attack on persons of higher rank. The reception given him by the police inspector disconcerted him so much that he tossed his head and said with an air of dignity, with his hands slightly parted in a gesture of surprise: "I must say that after such offensive remarks, I have nothing more to say. . . ." and went out.

He arrived home hardly able to stand on his feet. By now it was dusk. After all these unsuccessful quests his rooms looked melancholy or rather extremely disgusting to him. On entering the hall, he saw his valet Ivan lying on his back on the dirty leather sofa and spitting on the ceiling and rather successfully aiming at the same spot. Such an indifference on the part of his servant maddened him; he hit him on the forehead with his hat, saying: "You pig, you're always doing something stupid!"

Ivan jumped up and rushed to help him off with his cloak.

On entering his room, the major, tired and dejected, threw himself into an armchair and, at last, after several sighs, said:

"Lord, oh Lord, why should I have such bad luck? If I had lost an arm or a leg, it would not be so bad; if I had lost my ears, it would be bad enough, but still bearable; but without a nose a man is goodness knows what, neither fish, nor flesh, nor good red herring—he isn't a respectable citizen at all! He is simply something to take and chuck out of the window! If I had had it cut off in battle or in a duel or had been the cause of its loss myself, but to lose it without any reason whatever, for nothing, for absolutely nothing! . . . But no," he added after a brief reflection, "it can't be. It's inconceivable that a nose should be lost, absolutely inconceivable. I must be simply dreaming or just imagining it all. Perhaps by some mistake I drank, instead of water, the spirits which I rub on my face after shaving.

Ivan, the blithering fool, did not take it away and I must have swallowed it by mistake."

To convince himself that he was not drunk, the major pinched himself so painfully that he cried out. The pain completely convinced him that he was fully awake and that everything had actually happened to him. He went up slowly to the looking glass and at first screwed up his eyes with the idea that perhaps he would see his nose in its proper place; but almost at the same moment he jumped back, saying: "What a horrible sight!"

And, indeed, the whole thing was quite inexplicable. If he had lost a button, a silver spoon, his watch, or something of the kind, but to lose—and in his own apartment, too! Taking all the circumstances into consideration, Major Kovalyov decided that he would not be far wrong in assuming that the whole thing was the fault of no other person than Mrs. Podtochin, who wanted him to marry her daughter. He was not himself averse to flirting with her, but he avoided a final decision. But when Mrs. Podtochin told him plainly that she would like her daughter to marry him, he quietly hung back with his compliments, declaring that he was still too young, that he had to serve another five years, as he had decided not to marry till he was exactly forty-two. That was why Mrs. Podtochin, out of revenge no doubt, had made up her mind to disfigure him and engaged some old witch to do the foul deed, for he simply refused to believe that his nose had been cut off: no one had entered his room, and his barber, Ivan Yakovlevich, had shaved him on Wednesday, and during the whole of that day and even on Thursday his nose was intact—he remembered that, he knew that for certain; besides, he would have felt pain and the wound could not possibly have healed so quickly and become as smooth as a pancake. He made all sorts of plans in his head: to issue a court summons against her or to go to see her and confront her with the undeniable proof of her crime. His thoughts were interrupted by a gleam of light through all the cracks of the door, which let him know that Ivan had lighted a candle in the hall. Soon Ivan himself appeared, carrying the candle in front of him and lighting the whole room brightly. Kovalyov instinctively seized his handkerchief and covered the place where his nose had been only the day before so that the stupid fellow should not stand there gaping, seeing his master so strangely transformed.

Ivan had scarcely had time to go back to his cubbyhole when an unfamiliar voice was heard in the hall, saying:

"Does the Collegiate Assessor Kovalyov live here?"

"Come in," said Kovalyov, jumping up quickly and opening the door. "Major Kovalyov is here."

A police officer of a handsome appearance, with whiskers that were neither too dark nor too light and with fairly full cheeks, came in. It was, in fact, the same police officer who, at the beginning of this story, had been standing at the end of Issakiyevsky Bridge.

"Did you lose your nose, sir?"

"That's right."

"It's been found now."

"What are you saying?" cried Major Kovalyov.

He was bereft of speech with joy. He stared fixedly at the police officer who was standing before him and whose full lips and cheeks reflected the flickering light of the candle.

"How was it found?"

"By a most extraordinary piece of luck, sir. It was intercepted just before he was leaving town. It was about to get into the stagecoach and leave for Riga. He even had a passport made out in the name of a certain civil servant. And the funny thing is that at first I was myself inclined to take him for a gentleman. But luckily I was wearing my glasses at the time and I saw at once that it was a nose. You see, sir, I am shortsighted, and if you were to stand in front of me I would just see that you have a face, but would not be able to make out either your nose or your beard or anything else for that matter. My mother-in-law, that is to say, my wife's mother, can't see anything, either."

Kovalyov was beside himself with excitement.

"Where is it? Where? I'll go at once!"

"Don't trouble, sir. Realising how much you must want it, I brought it with me. And the funny part about it is that the chief accomplice in this affair is the scoundrel of a barber on Voznessensky Avenue, who is now locked up in a cell at the police station. I've suspected him for a long time of theft and drunkenness and, as a matter of fact, he stole a dozen buttons from a shop only the other day. Your nose, sir, is just as it was."

At these words, the police officer put his hand in his pocket and pulled out the nose wrapped in a piece of paper.

"Yes, yes, it's my nose!" cried Kovalyov. "It's my nose all right! Won't you have a cup of tea with me, sir?"

"I'd be very glad to, sir, but I'm afraid I'm rather in a hurry. I have to go to the House of Correction from here. Food prices have risen a great deal, sir. . . . I have my mother-in-law, that is to say, my wife's mother, living with me and, of course, there are the children. My eldest, in particular, is a very promising lad, sir. A very clever boy he is, sir, but I haven't the means to provide a good education for him—none at all. . . ."

Kovalyov took the hint and, snatching up a ten-rouble note from the table, thrust it into the hand of the police officer, who bowed and left the room, and almost at the same moment Kovalyov heard his voice raised in the street, where he was boxing the ears of a foolish peasant who had happened to drive with his cart on to the boulevard.

After the departure of the police officer, the Collegiate Assessor remained for a time in a sort of daze, and it was only after several minutes that he was able to recover his senses, so overwhelmed was he by his joy at the unexpected recovery of his nose. He took the newly found nose very carefully in both his cupped hands and examined it attentively once more.

"Yes, it's my nose all right!" said Major Kovalyov. "There's the pimple on the left side which I only got the other day."

The major almost laughed with joy. But nothing lasts very long in the world, and that is why even joy is not so poignant after the first moment. A moment later it grows weaker still and at last it merges imperceptibly into one's ordinary mood, just as a circle made in the water by a pebble at last merges into its smooth surface. Kovalyov began to ponder and he realised that the matter was not at an end: the nose had been found, but it had still to be affixed, to be put back in its place.

"And what it if doesn't stick?"

At this question that he had put to himself the major turned pale.

With a feeling of indescribable panic he rushed up to the table and drew the looking glass closer to make sure that he did not stick his nose on crookedly. His hands trembled. Carefully and with the utmost circumspection he put it back on its former place. Oh horror! The nose did not stick! . . . He put it to his mouth, breathed on it to warm it a little, and once more put it back on the smooth place between his two cheeks; but, try as he might, the nose refused to stick.

"Come on, come on! Stick, you idiot!" he kept saying to it.

But the nose, as though made of wood, kept falling down on the table with so strange a sound that it might have been cork. The major's face contorted spasmodically. "Won't it adhere?" he asked himself in a panic. But though he kept putting it back on its own place a great many times, his efforts were as unavailing as ever.

He called Ivan and sent him for the doctor, who occupied the best flat on the ground floor of the same house. The doctor was a fine figure of a man; he had wonderful pitch-black whiskers, a fresh, healthy wife, he ate fresh apples in the morning and kept his mouth quite extraordinarily clean, rinsing it every morning for nearly three quarters of an hour and brushing his teeth with five different kinds of toothbrushes. The doctor came at once. After asking how long it was since the accident, he lifted up Major Kovalyov's face by the chin and gave a fillip with his thumb, on the spot where the nose had been, with such force that the major threw back his head so violently that he hit the wall. The doctor said that it was nothing and, after advising him to move away from the wall a little, told him to bend his head to the right. After feeling the place where the nose had been, he said: "H'm!" Then he told him to bend his head to the left, and again said: "H'm!" In conclusion he gave him another fillip with the thumb so that the major tossed his head like a horse whose teeth are being examined. Having carried out this experiment, the doctor shook his head and said:

"No, I'm afraid it can't be done! You'd better remain like this, for it might be much worse. It is, of course, quite possible to affix your nose. In fact, I could do it right now. But I assure you that it might be the worse for you."

"How do you like that! How am I to remain without a nose?" said Kovalyov. "It can't possibly be worse than now. It's—it's goodness only knows what! How can I show myself with such a horrible face? I know lots of people of good social position. Why, today I have been invited to two parties. I have a large circle of friends: Mrs. Chekhtaryov, the widow of a State Councillor, Mrs. Podtochin, the widow of an army officer—though after what she did to me now I shall have no further dealings with her except through the police. Do me a favour, Doctor," said Kovalyov in an imploring voice. "Is there no way at all? Stick it on somehow. It may not be quite satisfactory, but so long as it sticks I don't mind. I could even support it with a hand in an emergency. Besides, I don't dance, so that I could hardly do any harm to it by some inadvertent movement. As for my gratitude for your visits, you may be sure that I will recompense you as much as I can. . . ."

"Believe me, sir," said the doctor neither in too loud nor in too soft a voice, but in a very persuasive and magnetic one, "I never allow any selfish motives to interfere with the treatment of my patients. This is against my principles and my art. It is true I charge for my visits, but that is only because I hate to offend by my refusal. Of course, I could put your nose back, but I assure you on my honour, if you won't believe my words, that it will be much worse. You'd better leave it to nature. Wash it often with cold water, and I assure you that without a nose you will be as healthy as with one. As for your nose, I'd advise you to put it in a bottle of spirits or, better still, pour two spoonfuls of aqua fortis and warmed-up vinegar into the bottle, and you'd be able to get a lot of money for it. I might take it myself even, if you won't ask too much for it."

"No, no," cried the desperate Major Kovalyov, "I'd rather it rotted away!"

"I'm sorry," said the doctor, taking his leave, "I wish I could be of some help to you, but there's nothing I can do! At least you saw how anxious I was to help you."

Having said this, the doctor left the room with a dignified air. Kovalyov did not even notice his face, and in his profound impassivity only caught sight of the cuffs of his spotlessly clean white shirt peeping out of his black frock coat.

On the following day he decided, before lodging his complaint, to write to Mrs. Podtochin a letter with a request to return to him without a fight what she had taken away from him. The letter was as follows:

> Dear Mrs. Podtochin,
>
> I cannot understand your strange treatment of me. I assure you that, by acting like this, you will gain nothing and will certainly not force me

to marry your daughter. Believe me, I know perfectly well what happened to my nose and that you, and no one else, are the chief instigator of this affair. Its sudden detachment from its place, its flight, and its disguise, first in the shape of a civil servant and then in its own shape, is nothing more than the result of witchcraft employed by you or by those who engage in the same honourable occupations as yourself. For my part, I deem it my duty to warn you that if the aforementioned nose is not back in its usual place today, I shall be forced to have recourse to the protection and the safeguard of the law.

However, I have the honour of remaining, madam, with the utmost respect

Your obedient servant,

Platon Kovalyov

Dear Platon Kuzmich,

Your letter has greatly surprised me. To be quite frank, I never expected it, particularly as regards your unjust reproaches. I wish to inform you that I have never received the civil servant you mention, neither in disguise nor in his own shape. It is true, Filipp Ivanovich Potachkin used to come to see me. And though he did ask me for my daughter's hand and is a man of good and sober habits and of great learning, I have never held out any hopes to him. You also mention your nose. If you mean by that that I wished to put your nose out of joint, that is, to give you a formal refusal, I am surprised that you should speak of such a thing when, as you know perfectly well, I was quite of the contrary opinion and if you should now make a formal proposal to my daughter, I should be ready to satisfy you immediately, for that has always been my dearest wish, in the hope of which

I remain always at your service,

Pelageya Podtochin

"No," said Kovalyov, after he had read the letter, "she had certainly nothing to do with it. It's impossible! The letter is not written as a guilty person would have written it." The Collegiate Assessor was an expert on such things, for, while serving in the Caucasus, he had several times been under judicial examination. "How then, in what way, did it happen? The devil alone can sort it out!" he said at last, utterly discouraged.

Meanwhile the rumours about this extraordinary affair spread all over the town and, as usually happens, not without all sorts of embellishments. At that time people's minds were particularly susceptible to anything of an extraordinary nature: only a short time before everybody had shown a great interest in the experiments of magnetism. Besides, the story of the dancing chairs in Konyushennaya Street was still fresh in people's minds, and it is therefore not surprising that people soon began talking about the Collegiate Assessor Kovalyov's nose which, it was alleged, was taking a walk on Nevsky Avenue at precisely three o'clock in the afternoon. Thousands of curious people thronged Nevsky Avenue every day. Someone said that the nose was in Junker's Stores, and such a crowd of people collected at the stores that the police had to be called to restore order. One enterprising, bewhiskered businessman of respectable appearance, who was selling all sorts of dry pasties at the entrance to the theatre, had purposely made beautiful wooden benches on which it was perfectly safe to stand and invited people to use them for eighty copecks each. One highly estimable colonel, who had left his home earlier than usual so that he could see the nose, pushed his way through the crowd with great difficulty; but, to his great indignation, he saw in the window of the stores, instead of the nose, an ordinary woollen sweater and a lithograph of a girl pulling up her stocking and a dandy, with a small beard and an open waistcoat, peeping at her from behind a tree—a picture that had hung in the same place for over ten years. On stepping back from the window, he said with vexation: "One should not be allowed to create a disturbance among the common people by such stupid and improbable stories."

Then the rumour spread that Major Kovalyov's nose was not taking a walk on Nevsky Avenue but in Tavrichesky Gardens and that he had been there for a long time; in fact, that when the Persian Prince Khozrev Mirza had lived there he had greatly marvelled at that curious freak of nature. A few students of the Surgical Academy set off there. One highly aristocratic lady wrote a letter to the head keeper of the gardens specially to ask him to show that rare phenomenon to her children and, if possible, with instructive and edifying explanations for young boys.

All men about town, without whom no important social gathering is complete, who liked to amuse the ladies and whose stock of amusing stories had been entirely used up at the time, were extremely glad of all this affair. A small section of respectable and well-meaning people were highly dissatisfied. One gentleman declared indignantly that he failed to understand how in our enlightened age such absurd stories could be spread abroad and that he was surprised the government paid no attention to it. This gentleman evidently was one of those gentlemen who would like to involve the government in everything, even in his daily tiffs with his wife. After that—but here again a thick fog descends on the whole incident, and what happened afterwards is completely unknown.

III

The world is full of all sorts of absurdities. Sometimes there is not even a semblance of truth: suddenly the very same nose, which had been driving about disguised as a State Councillor and had created such an uproar in town, found itself, as if nothing had happened, on its accustomed place again, namely, between the two cheeks of Major Kovalyov. This happened on the seventh of April. Waking up and looking quite accidentally into the mirror, he saw—his nose! He grabbed it with his hand—it was his nose all right! . . . "Aha!" said Kovalyov, and nearly went leaping barefoot all over the room in a roisterous dance in his joy. But Ivan, who entered just then, prevented him. He told Ivan to bring in some water for washing at once and, while washing, glanced once again into the mirror: he had a nose! While wiping himself with a towel, he again glanced into the mirror: he had a nose!

"Have a look, Ivan, there seems to be a pimple on my nose," he said, thinking to himself: "Won't it be awful if Ivan were to say, No, sir, there's no pimple and no nose, either!"

But Ivan said: "There's nothing, sir. I can't see no pimple. Nothing at all on your nose, sir."

"That's good, damn it!" said the major to himself, snapping his fingers.

At that moment the barber Ivan Yakovlevich poked his head through the door, but as timidly as a cat which had just been thrashed for the theft of suet.

"Tell me first of all—are your hands clean?" Kovalyov shouted to him from the other end of the room.

"They are clean, sir."

"You're lying!"

"I swear they are clean, sir!"

"Very well, they'd better be!"

Kovalyov sat down. Ivan Yakovlevich put a napkin round him and in a twinkling, with the aid of his brush alone, transformed his whole beard and part of his cheek into the sort of cream that is served in a merchant's home at a name-day party.

"Well, I never!" said Ivan Yakovlevich to himself as he glanced at the nose. Then he bent his head to the other side and looked at the nose sideways. "Well, I'm damned," he went on, looking at the nose for some considerable time.

"Dear, oh dear, just think of it!" At last, gently and as cautiously as can only be imagined, he raised two fingers to grasp it by its end. Such was Ivan Yakovlevich's system.

"Mind, mind what you're doing!" cried Kovalyov.

Ivan Yakovlevich was utterly discouraged, perplexed, and confused as he had never been confused before. At last he began carefully titillating him with the razor under the beard, and though he found it difficult and not at all convenient to shave without holding on to the olfactory organ, he did at last overcome all the obstacles by pressing his rough thumb against the cheek and the lower jaw and finished shaving him.

When everything was ready, Kovalyov hastened to dress at once, took a cab, and drove straight to the nearest pastry cook's. On entering, he at once shouted to the boy at the other end of the shop: "Boy, a cup of chocolate!" and immediately went up to the looking glass: he had a nose all right! He turned round gaily and glanced ironically, screwing up one eye a little, at two military gentlemen, one of whom had a nose no bigger than a waistcoat button. After that he set off for the office of the department where he was trying to obtain the post of vice-governor or, if unsuccessful, of an administrative clerk. On passing through the reception room, he glanced into the looking glass: he had a nose all right! Then he went to see another Collegiate Assessor, a man who was very fond of sneering at people, to whom he often used to say in reply to his biting remarks: "Oh, away with you! I know you, Mr. Pinprick!" On the way he thought: "If the major does not split his sides with laughter when he sees me, it's a sure sign that everything is in its proper place." But the Collegiate Assessor showed no signs of merriment. "It's perfect, perfect, damn it!" thought Kovalyov to himself. On the way back he met Mrs. Podtochin and her daughter, greeted them, and was met with joyful exclamations, which again proved to him that there was nothing wrong with him. He talked a long time with them and, taking out his snuffbox deliberately, kept stuffing his nose with snuff at both entrances for a great while, saying to himself: "There, I'm putting on this show specially for you, stupid females! And I won't marry your daughter all the same. Flirt with her—by all means, but nothing more!" And Major Kovalyov took his walks after that as if nothing had happened. He was to be seen on Nevsky Avenue, in the theatres—everywhere. And his nose, too, just as if nothing had happened, remained on his face, without as much as a hint that he had been playing truant. And after that Major Kovalyov was always seen in the best of humour, smiling, running after all the pretty ladies, and once even stopping before a little shop in the Arcade and buying himself a ribbon of some order for some mysterious reason, for he had never been a member of any order.

So that is the sort of thing that happened in the northern capital of our far-flung Empire. Only now, on thinking it all over, we can see that there is a great deal that is improbable in it. Quite apart from the really strange fact of the supernatural displacement of the nose and its appearance in various parts of the town in the guise of a State Councillor, how did Kovalyov fail to realise that he could not advertise about his nose in a newspaper? I am not saying that because I think that advertisement rates are too high—that's nonsense, and I am not at all a mercenary person. But it's improper, awkward, not nice! And again—how did the nose come to be in a loaf of bread and what about Ivan Yakovlevich? No, that I cannot understand, I simply cannot understand it! But what is even stranger and more incomprehensible than anything is that authors should choose such subjects. I confess that is entirely beyond my comprehension. It's like—no, I simply don't understand it. In the first place it's of no benefit whatever to our country, and in the second place—but even in the second place there's no benefit whatever. I simply don't know what to make of it. . . .

And yet, in spite of it all, though, of course, we may take for granted this and that and the other—may even—— But then where do you not find all sorts of absurdities? All the same, on second thoughts, there really is something in it. Say what you like, but such things do happen—not often, but they do happen.

Translated by David Magarshack

QUESTIONS

1. What is our first indication of the farcical nature of the story?
2. What do the first interactions involving the barber suggest about Gogol's view of human nature? Are these confirmed or contradicted by later developments?
3. What does Kovalyov's reaction to the disappearance of his nose tell us about his character?
4. What kind of picture does Gogol draw of life in the St. Petersburg of his day? How does he convey the obsession with rank and position of Kovalyov and others?
5. What kind of atmosphere do his physical descriptions evoke? Give examples.
6. Comment on the effect of Gogol's unusual storytelling device of suddenly shrouding events in a fog.
7. What does this story suggest about Gogol's vision of love, of the relations between men and women?
8. Is there any way in which we come to care about Kovalyov as a person or about his plight? What is our reaction when his nose is returned to him? And, later, when it is restored to his face?
9. What was Gogol's probable purpose in writing this tale? Is it meant to change our estimate of human nature? How so?

Mark Twain

Mark Twain, born Samuel Langhorne Clemens (1835–1910) in Missouri, hardly needs an introduction. As author of *The Adventures of Tom Sawyer* (1876), *The Prince and the Pauper* (1882), *A Connecticut Yankee in King Arthur's Court* (1889), *The Adventures of Huckleberry Finn* (1884), and innumerable other works, he is one of the towering figures of American literature. In his day, he worked as a newspaperman, editor, printer, steamboat pilot, stand-up humorist, and gold prospector—jobs that all added grist to the tirelessly inventive mill of his writing. Twain, as do very few other writers, conveys the flavor of a crucial epoch in American life—the opening of the great frontier. His novels, tales, and sketches are studded with rough and rowdy characters. They are set on the page in all of their outlandishness, humor, and pathos—Twain was extraordinarily gifted at rendering gestures and turns of speech—but over their heads and behind their backs blows the wind of freedom. The land is still big. There are pockets, whole territories, where an unruly character might hunker down to be himself. The rules and proprieties belong to the schoolteachers and church ladies—everything else is up for grabs.

"The Notorious Jumping Frog of Calaveras County" is one of Twain's best-loved short stories. Written in 1865, it preserves, folded up in its easy rambling humor, a glimmer of life in the American West in the days of the Gold Rush. Twain's shrewd exaggerations summon up something of the irresistible gambler's itch that sent so many thousands into the dusty hills to hunt for gold.

THE NOTORIOUS JUMPING FROG OF CALAVERAS COUNTY

In compliance with the request of a friend of mine who wrote me from the East, I called on good-natured, garrulous old Simon Wheeler and inquired after my friend's friend, Leonidas W. Smiley, as requested to do, and I hereunto append the result. I have a lurking suspicion that *Leonidas W.* Smiley is a myth, that my friend never knew such a personage, and that he only conjectured that if I asked old Wheeler about him, it would remind him of his infamous *Jim* Smiley and he would go to work and bore me to death with some exasperating reminiscence of him as long and as tedious as it should be useless to me. If that was the design, it succeeded.

I found Simon Wheeler dozing comfortably by the barroom stove of the dilapidated tavern in the decayed mining camp of Angel's, and I noticed that he was fat and bald-headed and had an expression of winning gentleness and simplicity upon his tranquil countenance. He roused up and gave me good day. I told him that a friend of mine had commissioned me to make some inquiries about a cherished companion of his boyhood named *Leonidas* W. Smiley—*Rev. Leonidas* W. Smiley, a young minister of the Gospel, who he had heard was at one time a resident of Angel's Camp. I added that if Mr. Wheeler could tell me anything about this Rev. Leonidas W. Smiley, I would feel under many obligations to him.

Simon Wheeler backed me into a corner and blockaded me there with his chair, and then sat down and reeled off the monotonous narrative which follows this paragraph. He never smiled, he never frowned, he never changed his voice from the gentle-flowing key to which he tuned his initial sentence, he never betrayed the slightest suspicion of enthusiasm, but all through the interminable narrative there ran a vein of impressive earnestness and sincerity which showed me plainly that, so far from his imagining that there was anything ridiculous or funny about his story, he regarded it as a really important matter and admired its two heroes as men of transcendent genius in *finesse.* I let him go on in his own way and never interrupted him once.

"Rev. Leonidas W. H'm, Reverend Le—— Well, there was a feller here once by the name of *Jim* Smiley, in the winter of '49—or maybe it was the spring of '50—I don't recollect exactly, somehow, though what makes me think it was one or the other is because I remember the big flume warn't finished when he first come to the camp; but anyway, he was the curiousest man about always betting on anything that turned up you ever see, if he could get anybody to bet on the other side, and if he couldn't he'd change sides. Any way that suited the other man would suit *him*—any way just so's he got a bet, *he* was satisfied. But still he was lucky, uncommon lucky; he most always come out winner. He was always ready and laying for a chance; there couldn't be no solit'ry thing mentioned but that feller'd offer to bet on it and take ary side you please, as I was just telling you. If there was a horse-race, you'd find him flush or you'd find him busted at the end of it; if there was a dog-fight, he'd bet on it; if there was a cat-fight, he'd bet on it; if there was a chicken-fight, he'd bet on it; why, if there was two birds setting on a fence, he would bet you which one would fly first; or if there was a camp-meeting, he would be there reg'lar to bet on Parson Walker, which he judged to be the best exhorter about here, and so he was too, and a good man. If he even see a straddle-bug start to go anywheres, he would bet you how long it would take him to get to—to wherever he was going to, and if you took him up, he would foller that straddle-bug to Mexico but what he would find out where he was bound for and how long he was on the road. Lots of the boys here has seen that Smiley and can tell you about him. Why, it never made no difference to *him*—he'd bet on *any* thing—the dangdest feller. Parson Walker's wife laid very sick once for a good while, and it seemed as if they warn't going to save her; but one morning he come in and Smiley up and asked him how she was, and he said she was considerable better—thank the Lord for his inf'nite mercy—and coming on so smart that with the blessing of Prov'dence she'd get well yet; and Smiley, before he thought, says, 'Well, I'll resk two-and-a-half she don't anyway.'

"Thish-yer Smiley had a mare—the boys called her the fifteen-minute nag but that was only in fun, you know, because of course she was faster than that—and he used to win money on that horse, for all she was so slow and always had the asthma, or the distemper, or the consumption, or something of that kind. They used to give her two or three hundred yards' start and then pass her under way, but always at the fag end of the race she'd get excited and desperate like, and come cavorting and straddling up and scattering her legs around limber, sometimes in the air and sometimes out to one side among the fences, and kicking up m-o-r-e dust and raising m-o-r-e racket with her coughing and sneezing and blowing her nose—and *always* fetch up at the stand just about a neck ahead, as near as you could cipher it down.

"And he had a little small bull-pup, that to look at him you'd think he warn't worth a cent but to set around and look ornery and lay for a chance to steal something. But as soon as money was up on him he was a different dog; his under-jaw'd begin to stick out like the fo'castle of a steamboat and his teeth would uncover and shine like the furnaces. And a dog might tackle him and bully-rag him, and bite him and the throw him over his shoulder two or three times, and Andrew Jackson—which was the name of the pup—Andrew Jackson would never let on but what *he* was satisfied and hadn't expected nothing else—and the bets being doubled and doubled on the other side all the time, till the money was all up; and then all of a sudden he would grab that other dog jest by the j'int of his hind leg and freeze to it—not chaw, you understand, but only just grip and hang on till they throwed up the sponge, if it was a year. Smiley always come out winner on that pup till he harnessed a dog once that didn't have no hind legs, because they'd been sawed off in a circular saw, and when the thing had gone along far enough and the money was all up and he come to make a snatch for his pet holt, he see in a minute how he'd been imposed on and how the other dog had him in the door, so to speak, and he 'peared surprised, and then he looked sorter discouraged-like and didn't try no more to win the fight, and so he got shucked out bad. He give Smiley a look, as much as to say his heart was broke, and it was *his* fault for putting up a dog that hadn't no hind legs for him to take holt of, which was his main dependence in a fight, and then he limped off a piece and laid down and died. It was a good pup, was that Andrew Jackson, and would have made a name for hisself if he'd lived, for the stuff was in him and he had genius—I know it, because he hadn't no opportunities to speak of, and it don't stand to reason that a dog could make such a fight as he could under them circumstances if he hadn't no talent. It always makes me feel sorry when I think of that last fight of his'n and the way it turned out.

"Well, thish-yer Smiley had rat-tarriers, and chicken cocks, and tomcats and all them kind of things till you couldn't rest, and you couldn't fetch nothing for him to bet on but he'd match you. He ketched a frog one day and took him home, and said he cal'lated to educate him; and so he never done nothing for three months but set in his back yard and learn that frog to jump. And you bet you he *did* learn him, too. He'd give him a little punch behind, and the next minute you'd see that frog whirling in the air like a doughnut—see him turn one summerset, or maybe a couple if he got a good start, and come down flat-footed and all right, like a cat. He got him up so in the matter of ketching flies, and kep' him in practice so constant, that he'd nail a fly every time as fur as he could see him. Smiley said all a frog wanted was education and he could do 'most anything—and I believe him. Why, I've seen him set Dan'l Webster down here on this floor—Dan'l Webster was the name of the frog—and sing out, 'Flies, Dan'l, flies!' and quicker'n you could wink he'd spring straight up and snake a fly off'n the counter there, and flop down on the floor ag'in as solid as a gob of mud, and fall to scratching the side of his head with his hind foot as indifferent as if he hadn't no idea he'd been doin' any more'n any frog might do. You never see a frog so modest and straight-for'ard as he was, for all he was so gifted. And when it come to fair and square jumping on a dead level, he could get over more ground at one straddle than any animal of his breed you ever see. Jumping on a dead level was his strong suit, you understand; and when it come to that, Smiley would ante up money on him as long as he had a red. Smiley was monstrous proud of his frog, and well he might be for fellers that had traveled and been everywheres all said he laid over any frog that ever *they* see.

"Well, Smiley kep' the beast in a little lattice box, and he used to fetch him down-town sometimes and lay for a bet. One day a feller—a stranger in the camp, he was—come acrost him with his box and says:

" 'What might it be that you've got in the box?'

"And Smiley says, sorter indifferent-like, 'It might be a parrot, or it might be a canary, maybe, but it ain't—it's only just a frog.'

"And the feller took it and looked at it careful, and turned it round this way and that, and says, 'H'm—so 'tis. Well, what's *he* good for?'

" 'Well,' Smiley says, easy and careless, 'he's good enough for *one* thing, I should judge—he can outjump any frog in Calaveras County.'

"The feller took the box again and took another long, particular look, and give it back to Smiley and says, very deliberate, 'Well,' he says, 'I don't see no p'ints about that frog that's any better'n any other frog.'

" 'Maybe you don't,' Smiley says. 'Maybe you understand frogs and maybe you don't understand 'em; maybe you've had experience and maybe you ain't only a amature, as it were. Anyways, I've got *my* opinion, and I'll resk forty dollars that he can outjump any frog in Calaveras County.'

"And the feller studied a minute and then says, kinder sad-like, 'Well, I'm only a stranger here and I ain't got no frog; but if I had a frog, I'd bet you.'

"And then Smiley says, 'That's all right—that's all right—if you'll hold my box a minute, I'll go and get you a frog.' And so the feller took the box and put up his forty dollars along with Smiley's, and set down to wait.

"So he set there a good while thinking and thinking to himself, and then he got the frog out and prized his mouth open and took a teaspoon and filled him full of quail-shot—filled him pretty near up to his chin—and set him on the floor. Smiley he went to the swamp and slopped around in the mud for a long time, and finally he ketched a frog and fetched him in and give him to this feller, and says:

" 'Now, if you're ready, set him alongside of Dan'l, with his forepaws just even with Dan'l's, and I'll give the word.' Then he says, 'One—two—three—*git!*' and him and the feller touched up the frogs from behind, and the new frog hopped off lively, but Dan'l give a heave and hysted up his shoulders—so—like a Frenchman, but it warn't no use—he couldn't budge; he was planted as solid as a church, and he couldn't no more stir than if he was anchored out. Smiley was a good deal surprised, and he was disgusted too, but he didn't have no idea what the matter was, of course.

"The feller took the money and started away, and when he was going out at the door, he sorter jerked his thumb over his shoulder—so—at Dan'l and says again, very deliberate, 'Well,' he says, '*I* don't see no p'ints about that frog that's any better'n any other frog.'

"Smiley he stood scratching his head and looking down at Dan'l a long time, and at last he says, 'I do wonder what in the nation that frog throw'd off for—I wonder if there ain't something the matter with him—he 'pears to look mighty baggy, somehow.' And he ketched Dan'l by the nap of the neck and hefted him, and says, 'Why, blame my cats if he don't weigh five pound!' and turned him upside down and he belched out a double handful of shot. And then he see how it was, and he was the maddest man—he set the frog down and took out after that feller, but he never ketched him. And—"

[Here Simon Wheeler heard his name called from the front yard and got up to see what was wanted.] And turning to me as he moved away, he said: "Just set where you are, stranger, and rest easy—I ain't going to be gone a second."

But, by your leave, I did not think that a continuation of the history of the enterprising vagabond *Jim* Smiley would be likely to afford me much information concerning the Rev. *Leonidas* W. Smiley and so I started away.

At the door I met the sociable Wheeler returning, and he buttonholed me and recommenced:

"Well, thish-yer Smiley had a yaller one-eyed cow that didn't have no tail, only just a short stump like a bannanner, and—"

However, lacking both time and inclination, I did not wait to hear about the afflicted cow but took my leave.

QUESTIONS

1. How do the first sentences alert us to the kind of story we will be reading?
2. How does Twain's presentation of the circumstances of finding Simon Wheeler undermine the credibility of his telling?
3. Why should a storyteller *want* to undermine that credibility? Or: if we don't believe the story, why are we reading it?
4. Why does Twain make use of the story-within-a-story device? Compare with Apuleius' use of the same device in "The Story of Thelyphron."
5. Describe the sequence of the kinds of bets that Jim Smiley is said to have made. Is there a pattern, or logic, to the presentation? How does the background information pave the way to the story of the jumping frog?
6. How does Twain use colloquialisms and dialect to convey humor? Cite several examples of colorful figures of speech.
7. How do we respond to the abrupt ending? Do we feel that Twain is just having fun with us? Does the ending heighten our response or detract from it? Explain.

Henry James

Henry James (1843–1916) had the good fortune to be born into a prominent intellectual family in New York City. His father was a religious thinker, his brother William was one of the foremost philosophers of his era, and his sister, Alice, has achieved an important posthumous reputation as a diarist and feminist thinker. Like Flaubert, whom he befriended (along with Maupassant and Turgenev), James can best be described in terms of his prolific career as a writer. He never married; he all but disappeared into his craft.

But what a craft it was! Even to list James's major works would require a lengthy paragraph. The best-known are probably *The Portrait of a Lady* (1881), *The Bostonians* (1886), *The Wings of the Dove* (1902), *The Ambassadors* (1903), and *The Golden Bowl* (1904), all novels. But James also wrote short novels, stories, criticism, and sketches of various descriptions—all with great success. The only literary realm in which he failed was drama—it seems that the subtle webbing that was his perception of human affairs did not lend itself to stage presentation.

James's great theme, worked through in every conceivable variation, was the encounter of American innocence with European experience. Youth went up against age, purity and naiveté against cunning and corruption. That James could build up such an edifice of prose upon a single idea is a testimony to the enormous resourcefulness of his verbal art. He showed, more than any writer before or since, that the social encounter was an inexhaustible object of study. With the passing of years, his treatment of action and the motives that must underlie it attained a near-impenetrable density. Jamesian sentences, stuffed with turns and counter turns, clauses and qualifications, often wander on for pages. But those scholars who have mastered his late works argue that they are unrivaled in the subtlety of their disclosures.

"Brooksmith," written in 1891, conveys many of the pleasures of James without exacting the penalties imposed by his late prose. It is a portrait of the waning days of a once-proud butler, and it may be regarded as one of James's more accessible works of fiction.

BROOKSMITH

We are scattered now, the friends of the late Mr. Oliver Offord; but whenever we chance to meet I think we are conscious of a certain esoteric respect for each other. "Yes, you too have been in Arcadia," we seem not too grumpily to allow. When I pass the house in Mansfield Street I remember that Arcadia was there. I don't know who has it now, and don't want to know; it's enough to be so sure that if I should ring the bell there would be no such luck for me as that Brooksmith should open the door. Mr. Offord, the most agreeable, the most attaching of bachelors, was a retired diplomatist, living on his pension and on something of his own over and above; a good deal confined, by his infirmities, to his fireside and delighted to be found there any afternoon in the year, from five o'clock on, by such visitors as Brooksmith allowed to come up. Brooksmith was his butler and his most intimate friend, to whom we all stood, or I should say sat, in the same relation in which the subject of the sovereign finds himself to the prime minister. By having been for years, in foreign lands, the most delightful Englishman any one had ever known, Mr. Offord had in my opinion rendered signal service to his country. But I suppose he had been too much liked—liked even by those who didn't like *it*—so that as people of that sort never get titles or dotations for the horrid things they've *not* done, his principal reward was simply that we went to see him.

Oh we went perpetually, and it was not our fault if he was not overwhelmed with this particular honour. Any visitor who came once came again; to come merely once was a slight nobody, I'm sure, had ever put upon him. His circle therefore was essentially composed of habitués, who were habitués for each other as well as for him, as those of a happy salon should be. I remember vividly every element of the place, down to the intensely Londonish look of the grey opposite houses, in the gap of the white curtains of the high windows, and the exact spot where, on a particular afternoon, I put down my tea-cup for Brooksmith, lingering an instant, to gather it up as if he were plucking a flower. Mr. Offord's drawing-room was indeed Brooksmith's garden, his pruned and tended human parterre, and if we all flourished there and grew well in our places it was largely owing to his supervision.

Many persons have heard much, though most have doubtless seen little, of the famous institution of the salon, and many are born to the depression of knowing that this finest flower of social life refuses to bloom where the English tongue is spoken. The explanation is usually that our women have not the skill to cultivate it—the art to direct through a smiling land, between suggestive shores, a sinuous stream of talk. My affectionate, my pious memory of Mr. Offord contradicts this induction only, I fear, more insidiously to confirm it. The sallow and slightly smoked drawing-room in which he spent so large a portion of the last years of his life certainly deserved the distinguished name; but on the other hand it couldn't be said at all to owe its stamp to any intervention throwing into relief the fact that there was no Mrs. Offord. The dear man had indeed, at the most, been capable of one of those sacrifices to which women are deemed peculiarly apt: he had recognised—under the influence, in some degree, it is true, of physical infirmity—that if you wish people to find you at home you must manage not to be out. He had in short accepted the truth which many dabblers in the social art are slow to learn, that you must really, as they say, take a line, and that the only way as yet discovered of being at home is to stay at home. Finally his own fireside had become a summary of his habits. Why should he ever have left it?—since this would have been leaving what was notoriously pleasantest in London, the compact charmed cluster (thinning away indeed into casual couples) round the fine old last-century chimney-piece which, with the exception of the remarkable collection of miniatures, was the best thing the place contained. Mr. Offord wasn't rich; he had nothing but his pension and the use for life of the somewhat superannuated house.

When I'm reminded by some opposed discomfort of the present hour how perfectly we were all handled there, I ask myself once more what had been the secret of such perfection. One had taken it for granted at the time, for anything that is supremely good produces more acceptance than surprise. I felt we were all happy, but I didn't consider how our happiness was managed. And yet there were questions to be asked, questions that strike me as singularly obvious now that there's nobody to answer them. Mr. Offord had solved the insoluble; he had, without feminine help—save in the sense that ladies were dying to come to him and that he saved the lives of several—established a salon; but I might have guessed that there was a method in his madness, a law in his success. He hadn't hit it off by a mere fluke. There was an art in it all, and how was the art so hidden? Who indeed if it came to that was the occult artist? Launching this enquiry the other day I had already got hold of the tail of my reply. I was helped by the very wonder of some of the conditions that came back to me—those that used to seem as natural as sunshine in a fine climate.

How was it for instance that we never were a crowd, never either too many or too few, always the right people *with* the right people—there must really have been no wrong people at all—always coming and going, never sticking fast nor overstaying, yet never popping in or out with an indecorous familiarity? How was it that we all sat where we wanted and moved when we wanted and met whom we wanted and escaped whom we wanted; joining, according to the accident of inclination, the general circle or falling in with a single talker on a convenient sofa? Why were all the sofas so convenient, the accidents so happy, the talkers so ready, the listeners so willing, the subjects presented to you in a rotation as quickly foreordained as the courses at dinner? A dearth of topics would have been as unheard of as a lapse in the service. These speculations couldn't fail to lead me to the fundamental truth that Brooksmith had been somehow at the bottom of the mystery. If he hadn't established the salon at least he had carried it on. Brooksmith in short was the artist!

We felt this covertly at the time, without formulating it, and were conscious, as an ordered and prosperous community, of his evenhanded justice, all untainted with flunkeyism. He had none of that vulgarity—his touch was infinitely fine. The delicacy of it was clear to me on the first occasion my eyes rested, as they were so often to rest again, on the domestic revealed, in the turbid light of the street, by the opening of the house-door. I saw on the spot that though he had plenty of school he carried it without arrogance—he had remained articulate and human. *L'Ecole Anglaise* Mr. Offord used laughingly to call him when, later on, it happened more than once that we had some conversation about him. But I remember accusing Mr. Offord of not doing him quite ideal justice. That he wasn't one of the giants of the school, however, was admitted by my old friend, who really understood him perfectly and was devoted to him, as I shall show; which doubtless poor Brooksmith had himself felt, to his cost, when his value in the market was originally determined. The utility of his class in general is estimated by the foot and the inch, and poor Brooksmith had only about five feet three to put into circulation. He acknowledged the inadequacy of this provision, and I'm sure was penetrated with the ever-lasting fitness of the relation between service and stature. If *he* had been Mr. Offord he certainly would have found Brooksmith wanting, and indeed the laxity of his employer on this score was one of many things he had had to condone and to which he had at last indulgently adapted himself.

I remember the old man's saying to me: "Oh my servants, if they can live with me a fortnight they can live with me for ever. But it's the first fortnight that tries 'em." It was in the first fortnight for instance that Brooksmith had had to learn that he was exposed to being addressed as "my dear fellow" and "my poor child." Strange and deep must such a probation have been to him, and he doubtless emerged from it tempered and purified. This was written to a certain extent in his appearance; in his spare brisk little person, in his cloistered white face and extraordinarily polished hair, which told of responsibility, looked as if it were kept up to the same high standard as the plate; in his small clear anxious eyes, even in the permitted, though not exactly encouraged, tuft on his chin. "He thinks me rather mad, but I've broken him in, and now he likes the place, he likes the company," said the old man. I embraced this fully after I had become aware that Brooksmith's main characteristic was a deep and and shy refinement, though I remember I was rather puzzled when, on another occasion, Mr. Offord remarked: "What he likes is the talk-mingling in the conversation." I was conscious I had never seen Brooksmith permit himself this freedom, but I guessed in a moment that what Mr. Offord alluded to was a participation more intense than any speech could have represented—that of being perpetually present on a hundred legitimate pretexts, errands, necessities, and breathing the very atmosphere of criticism, the famous criticism of life. "Quite an education, sir, isn't it, sir?" he said to me one day at the foot of the stairs when he was letting me out; and I've always remembered the words and the tone as the first sign of the quickening drama of poor Brooksmith's fate. It was indeed an education, but to what was this sensitive young man of thirty-five, of the servile class, being educated?

Practically and inevitably, for the time, to companionship, to the perpetual, the even exaggerated reference and appeal of a person brought to dependence by his time of life and his infirmities and always addicted moreover—this was the exaggeration—to the art of giving you pleasure by letting you do things for him. There were certain things Mr. Offord was capable of pretending he liked you to do even when he didn't—this, I mean, if he thought *you* liked them. If it happened that you didn't either—which was rare, yet might be—of course there were cross-purposes; but Brooksmith was there to prevent their going very far. This was precisely the way he acted as moderator; he averted misunderstandings or cleared them up. He had been capable, strange as it may appear, of acquiring for this purpose an insight into the French tongue, which was often used at Mr. Offord's; for besides being habitual to most of the foreigners, and they were many, who haunted the place or arrived with letters—letters often requiring a little worried consideration, of which Brooksmith always had cognisance—it had really become the primary language of the master of the house. I don't know if all the *malentendus* were in French, but almost all the explanations were, and this didn't a bit prevent Brooksmith's following them. I know Mr. Offord used to read passages to him from Montaigne and Saint-Simon, for he read perpetually when alone—when *they* were alone, that is—and Brooksmith was always about. Perhaps you'll say no wonder Mr. Offord's butler regarded him as "rather mad." However, if I'm not sure what he thought about Montaigne I'm convinced he admired Saint-Simon. A certain feeling for letters must have rubbed off on him from the mere handling of his master's books, which he was always carrying to and fro and putting back in their places.

I often noticed that if an anecdote or a quotation, much more a lively discussion, was going forward, he would, if busy with the fire or the curtains, the lamp or the tea, find a pretext for remaining in the room till the point should be reached. If his purpose was to catch it you weren't discreet, you were in fact scarce human, to call him off, and I shall never forget a look, a hard stony stare—I caught it in its passage—which, one day when there were a good many people in the room, he fastened upon the footman who was helping him in the service and who, in an undertone, had asked him some irrelevant question. It was the only manifestation of harshness I ever observed on Brooksmith's part, and I at first wondered what was the matter. Then I became conscious that Mr. Offord was relating a very curious anecdote, never before perhaps made so public, and imparted to the narrator by an eye-witness of the fact, bearing on Lord Byron's life in Italy. Nothing would induce me to reproduce it here, but Brooksmith had been in danger of losing it. If I ever should venture to reproduce it I shall feel how much I lose in not having my fellow auditor to refer to.

The first day Mr. Offord's door was closed was therefore a dark date in contemporary history. It was raining hard and my umbrella was wet, but Brooksmith received it from me exactly as if this were a preliminary for going upstairs. I observed however that instead of putting it away he held it poised and trickling over the rug, and I then became aware that he was looking at me with deep acknowledging eyes—his air of universal responsibility. I immediately understood—there was scarce need of question and answer as they passed between us. When I took in that our good friend had given up as never before, though only for the occasion, I exclaimed dolefully: "What a difference it will make—and to how many people!"

"I shall be one of them, sir!" said Brooksmith; and that was the beginning of the end.

Mr. Offord came down again, but the spell was broken, the great sign being that the conversation was for the first time not directed. It wandered and stumbled, a little frightened, like a lost child—it had let go the nurse's hand. "The worst of it is that now we shall talk about my health—*c'est la fin de tout,*" Mr. Offord said when he reappeared; and then I recognised what a note of change that would be—for he had never tolerated anything so provincial. We "ran" to each other's health as little as to the daily weather. The talk became ours, in a word—not his; and as ours, even when *he* talked, it could only be inferior. In this form it was a distress to Brooksmith, whose attention now wandered from it altogether: he had so much closer a vision of his master's intimate conditions than our superficialities represented. There were better hours, and he was more in and out of the room, but I could see he was conscious of the decline, almost of the collapse, of our great institution. He seemed to wish to take counsel with me about it, to feel responsible for its going on in some form or other. When for the second period—the first had lasted several days—he had to tell me that his employer didn't receive, I half-expected to hear him say after a moment "Do you think I ought to, sir, in his place?"—as he might have asked me, with the return of autumn, if I thought he had better light the drawing-room fire.

He had a resigned philosophic sense of what his guests—our guests, as I came to regard them in our colloquies—would expect. His feeling was that he wouldn't absolutely have approved of himself as a substitute for Mr. Offord; but he was so saturated with the religion of habit that he would have made, for our friends, the necessary sacrifice to the divinity. He would take them on a little further and till they could look about them. I think I saw him also mentally confronted with the opportunity to deal—for once in his life—with some of his own dumb preferences, his limitations of sympathy, *weeding* a little in prospect and returning to a purer tradition. It was not unknown to me that he considered that toward the end of our host's career a certain laxity of selection had crept in.

At last it came to be the case that we all found the closed door more often than the open one; but even when it was closed Brooksmith managed a crack for me to squeeze through; so that practically I never turned away without having paid a visit. The difference simply came to be that the visit was to Brooksmith. It took place in the hall, at the familiar foot of the stairs, and we didn't sit down, at least Brooksmith didn't; moreover it was devoted wholly to one topic and always had the air of being already over—beginning, so to say, at the end. But it was always interesting—it always gave me something to think about. It's true that the subject of my meditation was ever the same—ever "It's all very well, but what *will* become of Brooksmith?" Even my private answer to this question left me still unsatisfied. No doubt Mr. Offord would provide for him, but *what* would he provide?—that was the great point. He couldn't provide society; and society had become a necessity of Brooksmith's nature. I must add that he never showed a symptom of what I may call sordid solicitude—anxiety on his own account. He was rather livid and intensely grave, as befitted a man before whose eyes the "shade of that which once was great" was passing away. He had the solemnity of a person winding up, under depressing circumstances, a long-established and celebrated business; he was a kind of social executor or liquidator. But his manner seemed to testify exclusively to the uncertainty of *our* future. I couldn't in those days have afforded it—I lived in two rooms in Jermyn Street and didn't "keep a man"; but even if my income had permitted I shouldn't have ventured to say to Brooksmith (emulating Mr. Offord) "My dear fellow, I'll take you on." The whole tone of our intercourse was so much more an implication that it was *I* who should now want a lift. Indeed there was a tacit assurance in Brooksmith's whole attitude that he should have me on his mind.

One of the most assiduous members of our circle had been Lady Kenyon, and I remember his telling me one day that her ladyship had in spite of her own infirmities, lately much aggravated, been in person to inquire. In answer to this I remarked that she would feel it more than any one. Brooksmith had a pause before saying in a certain tone—there's no reproducing some of his tones—"I'll go and see her." I went to see her myself and learned he had waited on her; but when I said to her, in the form of a joke but with a core of earnest, that when all was over some of us ought to combine, to club together, and set Brooksmith up on his own account, she replied a trifle disappointingly: "Do you mean in a public-house?" I looked at her in a way that I think Brooksmith himself would have approved, and then I answered: "Yes, the Offord Arms." What I had meant of course was that for the love of art itself we ought to look to it that such a peculiar faculty and so much acquired experience shouldn't be wasted. I really think that if we had caused a few black-edged cards to be struck off and circulated—"Mr. Brooksmith will continue to receive on the old premises from four to seven; business carried on as usual during the alterations"—the greater number of us would have rallied.

Several times he took me upstairs—always by his own proposal—and our dear old friend, in bed (in a curious flowered and brocaded casaque which made him, especially as his head was tied up in a handkerchief to match, look, to my imagination, like the dying Voltaire) held for ten minutes a sadly shrunken little salon. I felt indeed each time as if I were attending the last *coucher* of some social sovereign. He was royally whimsical about his sufferings and not at all concerned—quite as if the Constitution provided for the case—about his successor. He glided over *our* sufferings charmingly, and none of his jokes—it was a gallant abstention, some of them would have been so easy—were at our expense. Now and again, I confess, there was one at Brooksmith's, but so pathetically sociable as to make the excellent man look at me in a way that seemed to say: "Do exchange a glance with me, or I shan't be able to stand it." What he wasn't able to stand was not what Mr. Offord said about him, but what he wasn't able to say in return. His idea of conversation for himself was giving you the convenience of speaking to him; and when he went to "see" Lady Kenyon for instance it was to carry her the tribute of his receptive silence. Where would the speech of his betters have been if proper service had been a manifestation of sound? In that case the fundamental difference would have had to be shown by *their* dumbness, and many of them, poor things, were dumb enough without that provision. Brooksmith took an unfailing interest in the preservation of the fundamental difference; it was the thing he had most on his conscience.

What had become of it however when Mr. Offord passed away like any inferior person—was relegated to eternal stillness after the manner of a butler above-stairs. His aspect on the event—for the several successive days—may be imagined, and the multiplication by funereal observance of the things he didn't say. When everything was over—it was late the same day—I knocked at the door of the house of mourning as I so often had done before. I could never call on Mr. Offord again, but I had come literally to call on Brooksmith. I wanted to ask him if there was anything I could do for him, tainted with vagueness as this enquiry could only be. My presumptuous dream of taking him into my own service had died away: my service wasn't worth his being taken into. My offer could only be to help him to find another place, and yet there was an indelicacy, as it were, in taking for granted that his thoughts would immediately be fixed on another. I had a hope that he would be able to give his life a different form—though certainly not the form, the frequent result of such bereavements, of his setting up a little shop. That would have been dreadful; for I should have wished to forward any enterprise he might embark in, yet how could I have brought myself to go and pay him shillings and take back coppers over a counter? My visit then was simply an intended compliment. He took it as such, gratefully and with all the tact in the world. He knew I really couldn't help him and that I knew he knew I couldn't; but we discussed the situation—with a good deal of elegant generality—at the foot of the stairs, in the hall already dismantled, where I had so often discussed other situations with him. The executors were in possession, as was still more apparent when he made me pass for a few minutes into the dining-room, where various objects were muffled up for removal.

Two definite facts, however, he had to communicate; one being that he was to leave the house for ever that night (servants, for some mysterious reason, seem always to depart by night), and the other—he mentioned it only at the last and with hesitation—that he was already aware his late master had left him a legacy of eighty pounds. "I'm very glad," I said, and Brooksmith was of the same mind: "It was so like him to think of me." This was all that passed between us on the subject, and I know nothing of his judgement of Mr. Offord's memento. Eighty pounds are always eighty pounds, and no one has ever left *me* an equal sum; but, all the same, for Brooksmith, I was disappointed. I don't know what I had expected, but it was almost a shock. Eighty pounds might stock a small shop—a *very* small shop; but, I repeat, I couldn't bear to think of that. I asked my friend if he had been able to save a little, and he replied: "No, sir; I've had to do things." I didn't enquire what things they might have been; they were his own affair, and I took his word for them as assentingly as if he had had the greatness of an ancient house to keep up; especially as there was something in his manner that seemed to convey a prospect of further sacrifice.

"I shall have to turn round a bit, sir—I shall have to look about me," he said; and then he added indulgently, magnanimously: "If you should happen to hear of anything for me—"

I couldn't let him finish; this was, in its essence, too much in the really grand manner. It would be a help to my getting him off my mind to be able to pretend I *could* find the right place, and that help he wished to give me, for it was doubtless painful to him to see me in so false a position. I interposed with a few words to the effect of how well aware I was that wherever he should go, whatever he should do, he would miss our old friend terribly—miss him even more than I should, having been with him so much more. This led him to make the speech that has remained with me as the very text of the whole episode.

"Oh sir, it's sad for *you,* very sad indeed, and for a great many gentlemen and ladies; that it is, sir. But for me, sir, it is, if I may say so, still graver even than that: it's just the loss of something that was everything. For me, sir," he went on with rising tears, "he was just *all,* if you know what I mean, sir. You have others, sir, I dare say—not that I would have you understand me to speak of them as in any way tantamount. But you have the pleasures of society, sir; if it's only in talking about him, sir, as I dare say you do freely—for all his blest memory has to fear from it—with gentlemen and ladies who have had the same honour. That's not for me, sir, and I've to keep my associations to myself. Mr. Offord was *my* society, and now, you see, I just haven't any. You go back to conversation, sir, after all, and I go back to my place," Brooksmith stammered, without exaggerated irony or dramatic bitterness, but with a flat unstudied veracity and his hand on the knob of the street-door. He turned it to let me out and then he added: "I just go downstairs, sir, again, and I stay there."

"My poor child," I replied in my emotion, quite as Mr. Offord used to speak, "my dear fellow, leave it to me: *we'll* look after you, we'll all do something for you."

"Ah if you could give me some one *like* him! But there ain't two such in the world," Brooksmith said as we parted.

He had given me his address—the place where he would be to be heard of. For a long time I had no occasion to make use of the information: he proved on trial so very difficult a case. The people who knew him and had known Mr. Offord didn't want to take him, and yet I couldn't bear to try to thrust him among strangers—strangers to his past when not to his present. I spoke to many of our old friends about him and found them all governed by the odd mixture of feelings of which I myself was conscious—as well as disposed, further, to entertain a suspicion that he was "spoiled," with which I then would have nothing to do. In plain terms a certain embarrassment, a sensible awkwardness when they thought of it, attached to the idea of using him as a menial: they had met him so often in society. Many of them would have asked him, and did ask him, or rather did ask me to ask him, to come and see them; but a mere visiting-list was not what I wanted for him. He was too short for people who were very particular; nevertheless I heard of an opening in a diplomatic household which led me to write him a note, though I was looking much less for something grand than for something human. Five days later I heard from him. The secretary's wife had decided, after keeping him waiting till then, that she couldn't take a servant out of a house in which there hadn't been a lady. The note had a P.S.: "It's a good job there wasn't, sir, such a lady as some."

A week later he came to see me and told me he was "suited," committed to some highly respectable people—they were something quite immense in the City—who lived on the Bayswater side of the Park. "I dare say it will be rather poor, sir," he admitted; "but I've seen the fireworks, haven't I, sir?—it can't be fireworks *every* night. After Mansfield Street there ain't much choice." There was a certain amount, however, it seemed; for the following year, calling one day on a country cousin, a lady of a certain age who was spending a fortnight in town with some friends of her own, a family unknown to me and resident in Chester Square, the door of the house was opened, to my surprise and gratification, by Brooksmith in person. When I came out I had some conversation with him from which I gathered that he had found the large City people too dull for endurance, and I guessed, though he didn't say it, that he had found them vulgar as well. I don't know what judgement he would have passed on his actual patrons if my relative hadn't been their friend; but in view of that connexion he abstained from comment.

None was necessary, however, for before the lady in question brought her visit to a close they honoured me with an invitation to dinner, which

I accepted. There was a largeish party on the occasion, but I confess I thought of Brooksmith rather more than of the seated company. They required no depth of attention—they were all referable to usual irredeemable inevitable types. It was the world of cheerful commonplace and conscious gentility and prosperous density, a full-fed material insular world, a world of hideous florid plate and ponderous order and thin conversation. There wasn't a word said about Byron, or even about a minor bard then much in view. Nothing would have induced me to look at Brooksmith in the course of the repast, and I felt sure that not even my overturning the wine would have induced him to meet my eye. We were in intellectual sympathy—we felt, as regards each other, a degree of social responsibility. In short we had been in Arcadia together, and we had both come to *this!* No wonder we were ashamed to be confronted. When he had helped on my overcoat, as I was going away, we parted, for the first time since the earliest days of Mansfield Street, in silence. I thought he looked lean and wasted, and I guessed that his new place wasn't more "human" than his previous one. There was plenty of beef and beer, but there was no reciprocity. The question for him to have asked before accepting the position wouldn't have been "How many footmen are kept?" but "How much imagination?"

The next time I went to the house—I confess it wasn't very soon—I encountered his successor, a personage who evidently enjoyed the good fortune of never having quitted his natural level. Could any be higher? he seemed to ask—over the heads of three footmen and even of some visitors. He made me feel as if Brooksmith were dead; but I didn't dare to enquire—I couldn't have borne his "I haven't the least idea, sir." I dispatched a note to the address that worthy had given me after Mr. Offord's death, but I received no answer. Six months later however I was favoured with a visit from an elderly dreary dingy person who introduced herself to me as Mr. Brooksmith's aunt and from whom I learned that he was out of place and out of health and had allowed her to come and say to me that if I could spare half an hour to look in at him he would take it as a rare honour.

I went the next day—his messenger had given me a new address—and found my friend lodged in a short sordid street in Marylebone, one of those corners of London that wear the last expression of sickly meanness. The room into which I was shown was above the small establishment of a dyer and cleaner who had inflated kid gloves and discoloured shawls in his shop-front. There was a great deal of grimy infant life up and down the place, and there was a hot moist smell within, as of the "boiling" of dirty linen. Brooksmith sat with a blanket over his legs at a clean little window where, from behind stiff bluish-white curtains, he could look across at a huckster's and a tinsmith's and a small greasy public-house. He had passed through an illness and was convalescent, and his mother, as well as his aunt, was in attendance on him. I liked the nearer relative, who was bland and intensely humble, but I had my doubts of the remoter, whom

I connected perhaps unjustly with the opposite public-house—she seemed somehow greasy with the same grease—and whose furtive eye followed every movement of my hand as if to see if it weren't going into my pocket. It didn't take this direction—I couldn't, unsolicited, put myself at that sort of ease with Brooksmith. Several times the door of the room opened and mysterious old women peeped in and shuffled back again. I don't know who they were; poor Brooksmith seemed encompassed with vague prying beery females.

He was vague himself, and evidently weak, and much embarrassed, and not an allusion was made between us to Mansfield Street. The vision of the salon of which he had been an ornament hovered before me however, by contrast, sufficiently. He assured me he was really getting better, and his mother remarked that he would come round if he could only get his spirits up. The aunt echoed this opinion, and I became more sure that in her own case she knew where to go for such a purpose. I'm afraid I was rather weak with my old friend, for I neglected the opportunity, so exceptionally good, to rebuke the levity which had led him to throw up honourable positions—fine stiff steady berths in Bayswater and Belgravia, with morning prayers, as I knew, attached to one of them. Very likely his reasons had been profane and sentimental; he didn't want morning prayers, he wanted to be somebody's dear fellow; but I couldn't be the person to rebuke him. He shuffled these episodes out of sight—I saw he had no wish to discuss them. I noted further, strangely enough, that it would probably be a questionable pleasure for him to see me again: he doubted now even of my power to condone his aberrations. He didn't wish to have to explain; and his behaviour was likely in future to need explanation. When I bade him farewell he looked at me a moment with eyes that said everything: "How can I talk about those exquisite years in this place, before these people, with the old women poking their heads in? It was very good of you to come to see me; it wasn't my idea—*she* brought you. We've said everything; it's over; you'll lose all patience with me, and I'd rather you shouldn't see the rest." I sent him some money in a letter the next day, but I saw the rest only in the light of a barren sequel.

A whole year after my visit to him I became aware once, in dining out, that Brooksmith was one of the several servants who hovered behind our chairs. He hadn't opened the door of the house to me, nor had I recognised him in the array of retainers in the hall. This time I tried to catch his eye, but he never gave me a chance, and when he handed me a dish I could only be careful to thank him audibly. Indeed I partook of two *entrées* of which I had my doubts, subsequently converted into certainties, in order not to snub him. He looked well enough in health, but much older, and wore in an exceptionally marked degree the glazed and expressionless mask of the British domestic *de race*. I saw with dismay that if I hadn't known him I should have taken him, on the showing of his countenance, for an extravagant illustration of irresponsive servile gloom. I said to myself that he had become a reactionary, gone over to the Philistines, thrown himself into religion, the religion of his "place," like a foreign lady *sur le retour*. I divined moreover that he was only engaged for the evening—he had become a mere waiter, had joined the band of the white-waistcoated who "go out." There was something pathetic in this fact—it was a terrible vulgarisation of Brooksmith. It was the mercenary prose of butlerhood; he had given up the struggle for the poetry. If reciprocity was what he had missed where was the reciprocity now? Only in the bottoms of the wine-glasses and the five shillings—or whatever they get—clapped into his hand by the permanent man. However, I supposed he had taken up a precarious branch of his profession because it after all sent him less downstairs. His relations with London society were more superficial, but they were of course more various. As I went away on this occasion I looked out for him eagerly among the four or five attendants whose perpendicular persons, fluting the walls of London passages, are supposed to lubricate the process of departure; but he was not on duty. I asked one of the others if he were not in the house, and received the prompt answer: "Just left, sir. Anything I can do for you, sir?" I wanted to say "Please give him my kind regards"; but I abstained—I didn't want to compromise him; and I never came across him again.

Often and often, in dining out, I looked for him, sometimes accepting invitations on purpose to multiply the chances of my meeting him. But always in vain; so that as I met many other members of the casual class over and over again I at last adopted the theory that he always procured a list of expected guests beforehand and kept away from the banquets which he thus learned I was to grace. At last I gave up hope, and one day at the end of three years I received another visit from his aunt. She was drearier and dingier, almost squalid, and she was in great tribulation and want. Her sister, Mrs. Brooksmith, had been dead a year, and three months later her nephew had disappeared. He had always looked after her a bit—since her troubles; I never knew what her troubles had been—and now she hadn't so much as a petticoat to pawn. She had also a niece, to whom she had been everything before her troubles, but the niece had treated her most shameful. These were details; the great and romantic fact was Brooksmith's final evasion of his fate. He had gone out to wait one evening as usual, in a white waistcoat she had done up for him with her own hands—being due at a large party up Kensington way. But he had never come home again and had never arrived at the large party, nor at any party that any one could make out. No trace of him had come to light—no gleam of the white waistcoat had pierced the obscurity of his doom. This news was a sharp shock to me, for I had my ideas about his real destination. His aged relative had promptly, as she said, guessed the worst. Somehow and somewhere he had got out of the way altogether, and now I trust that, with characteristic deliberation, he is changing the plates of the immortal gods. As my depressing visitant also said, he never *had* got his spirits up. I was fortunately able to dismiss her with her own somewhat improved. But the dim ghost of poor Brooksmith is one of those that I see. He had indeed been spoiled.

QUESTIONS

1. Can you characterize the telling voice? What kind of person is speaking? What is his class, and what are his attitudes?

2. Describe the stages whereby the character of Brooksmith takes shape. At what moment does he begin to dominate the story?

3. What is a salon? What purpose does it serve in a society like the one James describes?

4. In what way is the managing of relationships an art? How does Brooksmith demonstrate his mastery of this art?

5. What impressions do we gather about Brooksmith's physical appearance? Why is it important that we know about his height?

6. What qualities go to make up the ideal servant?

7. How do we become aware that Brooksmith possesses a rare complexity of character?

8. How does the ritual of the salon end? What happens? How does James communicate the change? Comment upon the effectiveness of indirectness in this story.

9. What is this story finally *about*? Does James have a message about human nature?

10. Comment on how the shifting backgrounds of Brooksmith's employment mirror his decline? How do the narrator's responses to Brooksmith change? Why?

11. What is the role of the unstated in this story? How does James keep our interest despite the fact that there is so little action?

12. When Brooksmith says, "I've seen the fireworks," what does he mean?

13. What is the narrator's last view of Brooksmith? its importance?

14. What finally happens to Brooksmith? What can we conclude about his character from this?

Guy de Maupassant

In his story "Guy de Maupassant," the Russian writer Isaac Babel tells of a young man with some literary ambitions who undertakes to translate the works of the great French storyteller. Babel, himself one of the masters, writes:

> I took the manuscript with me, and in Kazantsev's attic, among my sleeping friends, spent the night cutting my way through the tangled undergrowth of her [his co-translator's] prose. It was not such dull work as it might seem. A phrase is born into the world both good and bad at the same time. The secret lies in a slight, an almost invisible twist. The lever should rest in your hand, getting warm, and you can only turn it once, not twice.

The passage is as much about Maupassant as it is about the act of translation. The effect of his stories—he wrote hundreds—depends as much on this twist of the handle, this timing, as it does upon his skill at capturing a dazzle of impressions in a single telling detail.

But then Maupassant (1850–1893) was fortunate enough to have as his teacher the greatest prose writer of his age, Gustave Flaubert. Flaubert taught his young apprentice to go in quest of the unrepeatable, defining detail: "You must make me see, with a single word, in what way one cab-horse is totally unlike fifty others that go before and after it."

The instruction bore abundant fruit. Beginning with the publication of his story "Boule de Suif" ("Ball of Fat") in 1880, Maupassant built a career as one of the shrewdest and most readable writers ever to have worked in the genre. His clear gaze, his keen sense of human motivation and action, and his unencumbered style continue to exert an influence on practitioners of the short story form.

Maupassant's life was, like those of so many other gifted writers (Poe, Gogol), short and—at least at the end—wretched. He had contracted syphilis while a young man, most likely while serving in the French army. The disease erupted again when he was at the height of his productivity, driving him into total insanity before his death of paresis. If he left a monument to himself, it was an image of the full range of the life of his times refracted through hundreds of imagined destinies.

THE STRING

Along all the roads around Goderville the peasants and their wives were coming toward the little town, for it was market-day. The men walked with slow steps, their whole bodies bent forward at each movement of their long twisted legs, deformed by their hard work, by the weight on the plough which, at the same time, raises the left shoulder and distorts the figure, by the reaping of the wheat which forces the knees apart to get a firm stand, by all the slow and painful labors of the country. Their blouses, blue, starched, shining as if varnished, ornamented with a little design in white at the neck and wrists, puffed about their bony bodies, seemed like balloons ready to carry them off. From each of them a head, two arms, and two feet protruded.

Some led a cow or a calf at the end of a rope, and their wives, walking behind the animal, whipped its haunches with a leafy branch to hasten its progress. They carried on their arms large wicker-baskets, out of which a chicken here, a duck there, thrust out its head. And they walked with a quicker, livelier step than their husbands. Their spare, straight figures were wrapped in a scanty little shawl, pinned over their flat bosoms, and their heads were enveloped in a piece of white linen tightly pressed on the hair and surmounted by a cap.

Then a wagon passed, its nag's jerky trot shaking up and down two men seated side by side and a woman in the bottom of the vehicle, the latter holding on to the sides to lessen the hard jolts.

In the square of Goderville there was a crowd, a throng of human beings and animals mixed together. The horns of the cattle, the rough-napped top-hats of the rich peasants, and the head-gear of the peasant women rose above the surface of the crowd. And the clamorous, shrill, screaming voices made a continuous and savage din which sometimes was dominated by the robust lungs of some countryman's laugh, of the long lowing of a cow tied to the wall of a house.

It all smacked of the stable, the dairy, and the dung-heap, of hay and sweat, giving forth that sharp, unpleasant odor, human and animal, peculiar to the people of the fields.

Maître Hauchecorne, of Bréauté, had just arrived at Goderville, and was directing his steps toward the square, when he perceived upon the ground a little piece of string. Maître Hauchecorne, economical like a true Norman, thought that everything useful ought to be picked up, and he stooped painfully, for he suffered from rheumatism. He took the bit of thin cord from the ground and was beginning to roll it carefully when he noticed Maître Malandain, the harness-maker, on the threshold of his door, looking at him. They had once had a quarrel together on the subject of a halter, and they had remained on bad terms, being both good haters. Maître Hauchecorne was seized with a sort of shame to be seen thus by his enemy, picking a bit of string out of the dirt. He concealed his find quickly under his blouse, then in his trousers pocket; then he pretended to be still looking on the ground for something which he did not find, and he went towards the market, his head thrust forward, bent double by his pains.

He was soon lost in the noisy and slowly moving crowd, which was busy with interminable bargainings. The peasants looked at cows, went away, came back, perplexed, always in fear of being cheated, not daring to decide, watching the vendor's eye, ever trying to find the trick in the man and the flaw in the beast.

The women, having placed their great baskets at their feet, had taken out the poultry, which lay upon the ground, tied together by the feet, with terrified eyes and scarlet crests.

They heard offers, stated their prices with a dry air and impassive face, or perhaps, suddenly deciding on some proposed reduction, shouted to the customer who was slowly going away: "All right, Maître Anthime, I'll give it to you for that."

Then little by little the square was deserted, the Angelus rang for noon, and those who lived too far away went to the different inns.

At Jourdain's the great room was full of people eating, as the big yard was full of vehicles of all kinds, carts, gigs, wagons, nondescript carts, yellow with dirt, mended and patched, raising their shafts to the sky like two arms, or perhaps with their shafts on the ground and their backs in the air.

Right against the diners seated at the table, the immense fireplace, filled with bright flames, cast a lively heat on the backs of the row on the right. Three spits were turning on which were chickens, pigeons, and legs of mutton; and an appetizing odor of roast meat and gravy dripping over the nicely browned skin rose from the hearth, lightened hearts, and made mouths water.

All the aristocracy of the plough ate there, at Maître Jourdain's, tavern keeper and horse dealer, a clever fellow who had money.

The dishes were passed and emptied, as were the jugs of yellow cider. Everyone told his affairs, his purchases, and sales. They discussed the crops. The weather was favorable for the greens but rather damp for the wheat.

Suddenly the drum began to beat in the yard, before the house. Everybody rose, except a few indifferent persons, and ran to the door, or to the windows, their mouths still full, their napkins in their hands.

After the public crier had stopped beating his drum, he called out in a jerky voice, speaking his phrases irregularly:

"It is hereby made known to the inhabitants of Goderville, and in general to all persons present at the market, that there was lost this morning, on the road to Benzeville, between nine and ten o'clock, a black leather pocket-book containing five hundred francs and some business papers.

The finder is requested to return same to the Mayor's office or to Maître Fortuné Houlbrèque of Manneville. There will be twenty francs reward."

Then the man went away. The heavy roll of the drum and the crier's voice were again heard at a distance.

Then they began to talk of this event discussing the chances that Maître Houlbrèque had of finding or not finding his pocket-book.

And the meal concluded. They were finishing their coffee when the chief of the gendarmes appeared upon the threshold.

He inquired:

"Is Maître Hauchecorne, of Bréauté, here?"

Maître Hauchecorne, seated at the other end of the table, replied:

"Here I am."

And the officer resumed:

"Maître Hauchecorne, will you have the goodness to accompany me to the Mayor's office? The Mayor would like to talk to you."

The peasant, surprised and disturbed, swallowed at a draught his tiny glass of brandy, rose, even more bent than in the morning, for the first steps after each rest were specially difficult, and set out, repeating: "Here I am, here I am."

The Mayor was awaiting him, seated in an armchair. He was the local lawyer, a stout, serious man, fond of pompous phrases.

"Maître Hauchecorne," said he, "you were seen this morning picking up, on the road to Benzeville, the pocket-book lost by Maître Houlbrèque, of Manneville."

The countryman looked at the Mayor in astonishment, already terrified by this suspicion resting on him without his knowing why.

"Me? Me? I picked up the pocket-book?"

"Yes, you, yourself."

"On my word of honor, I never heard of it."

"But you were seen."

"I was seen, me? Who says he saw me?"

"Monsieur Malandain, the harness-maker."

The old man remembered, understood, and flushed with anger.

"Ah, he saw me, the clodhopper, he saw me pick up this string, here, Mayor." And rummaging in his pocket he drew out the little piece of string.

But the Mayor, incredulous, shook his head.

"You will not make me believe, Maître Hauchecorne, that Monsieur Malandain, who is a man we can believe, mistook this cord for a pocket-book."

The peasant, furious, lifted his hand, spat at one side to attest his honor, repeating:

"It is nevertheless God's own truth, the sacred truth. I repeat it on my soul and my salvation."

The Mayor resumed:

"After picking up the object, you stood like a stilt, looking a long while in the mud to see if any piece of money had fallen out."

The old fellow choked with indignation and fear.

"How anyone can tell—how anyone can tell—such lies to take away an honest man's reputation! How can anyone———"

There was no use in his protesting, nobody believed him. He was confronted with Monsieur Malandain, who repeated and maintained his affirmation. They abused each other for an hour. At his own request, Maître Hauchecorne was searched. Nothing was found on him.

Finally the Mayor, very much perplexed, discharged him with the warning that he would consult the Public Prosecutor and ask for further orders.

The news had spread. As he left the Mayor's office, the old man was surrounded and questioned with a serious or bantering curiosity, in which there was no indignation. He began to tell the story of the string. No one believed him. They laughed at him.

He went along, stopping his friends, beginning endlessly his statement and his protestations showing his pockets turned inside out, to prove that he had nothing.

They said:

"Ah, you old devil!"

And he grew angry, becoming exasperated, hot, and distressed at not being believed, not knowing what to do and always repeating himself.

Night came. He had to leave. He started on his way with three neighbors to whom he pointed out the place where he had picked up the bit of string; and all along the road he spoke of his adventure.

In the evening he took a turn in the village of Bréauté, in order to tell it to everybody. He only met with incredulity.

It made him ill all night.

The next day about one o'clock in the afternoon, Marius Paumelle, a hired man in the employ of Maître Breton, husbandman at Ymauville, returned the pocket-book and its contents to Maître Houlbrèque of Manneville.

This man claimed to have found the object in the road; but not knowing how to read, he had carried it to the house and given it to his employer.

The news spread through the neighborhood. Maître Hauchecorne was informed of it. He immediately went the circuit and began to recount his story completed by the happy climax. He triumphed.

"What grieved me so much was not the thing itself, as the lying. There is nothing so shameful as to be placed under a cloud on account of a lie."

He talked of his adventure all day long, he told it on the highway to people who were passing by, in the inn to people who were drinking there, and to persons coming out of church the following Sunday. He stopped strangers to tell them about it. He was calm now, and yet something disturbed him without his knowing exactly what it was. People had the air of joking while they listened. They did not seem convinced. He seemed to feel that remarks were being made behind his back.

On Tuesday of the next week he went to the market at Goderville, urged solely by the necessity he felt of discussing the case.

Malandain, standing at his door, began to laugh on seeing him pass. Why?

He approached a farmer from Criquetot, who did not let him finish, and giving him a thump in the stomach said to his face:

"You clever rogue."

Then he turned his back on him.

Maître Hauchecorne was confused, why was he called a clever rogue?

When he was seated at the table, in Jourdain's tavern he commenced to explain "the affair."

A horse dealer from Monvilliers called to him:

"Come, come, old sharper, that's an old trick; I know all about your piece of string!"

Hauchecorne stammered:

"But the pocket-book was found."

But the other man replied:

"Shut up, papa, there is one that finds, and there is one that brings back. No one is any the wiser, so you get out of it."

The peasant stood choking. He understood. They accused him of having had the pocket-book returned by a confederate, by an accomplice.

He tried to protest. All the table began to laugh.

He could not finish his dinner and went away, in the midst of jeers.

He went home ashamed and indignant, choking with anger and confusion, the more dejected that he was capable with his Norman cunning of doing what they had accused him of, and even of boasting of it as a good trick. His innocence seemed to him, in a confused way, impossible to prove, as his sharpness was known. And he was stricken to the heart by the injustice of the suspicion.

Then he began to recount the adventure again, enlarging his story every day, adding each time new reasons, more energetic protestations, more solemn oaths which he imagined and prepared in his hours of solitude, his whole mind given up to the story of the string. He was believed so much the less as his defense was more complicated and his arguing more subtle.

"Those are lying excuses," they said behind his back.

He felt it, consumed his heart over it, and wore himself out with useless efforts. He was visibly wasting away.

The wags now made him tell about the string to amuse them, as they make a soldier who has been on a campaign tell about his battles. His mind, seriously affected, began to weaken.

Towards the end of December he took to his bed.

He died in the first days of January, and in the delirium of his death struggles he kept claiming his innocence, reiterating:

"A piece of string, a piece of string—look—here it is."

Translated by Ernest Boyd

QUESTIONS

1. Discuss the opening description and Maupassant's use of images. What mood is created, and what expectations?
2. What general assumptions does the story make about the character of the French peasant? How does Maupassant communicate these?
3. Why does Hauchecorne have the feeling that nobody believes him? To what extent are our self-images determined by the way we perceive others relating to us? Try to think of an example from your own experience.
4. What is the central irony of the story?
5. Does Maupassant show contempt or compassion for Hauchecorne? Explain.
6. How does Maupassant use details to fix character types? Give examples.
7. Does this story impart a useful moral lesson? If so, what is it?
8. Can you imagine an updated version of this story? Sketch out a few possibilities. Is the underlying character psychology still valid?

Olive Schreiner

Olive Schreiner (1855–1920) was born on the Eastern Cape frontier of Southern Africa, daughter of a German missionary and an English mother. She received little in the way of formal education but taught herself out of books while serving as a governess on various remote farmsteads. Her novel *The Story of an African Farm* (1883) won wide acclaim—it is one of the first works in English by a colonial to have broken through to a larger readership. During the 1890s Schreiner wrote a large number of short stories, many of them a kind of impressionistic play with her own memories. ("The Woman's Rose" dates from this period.)

Schreiner was one of a great many women writers rediscovered after the advent of the women's movement. Her own feminist manifesto, *Woman and Labour* (1911), found new readers in the 1970s and 1980s. *From Man to Man,* a novel treating of feminist and racial issues, was published posthumously in 1926.

THE WOMAN'S ROSE

I have an old, brown, carved box; the lid is broken and tied with a string. In it I keep little squares of paper, with hair inside, and a little picture which hung over my brother's bed when we were children, and other things as small. I have in it a rose. Other women also have such boxes where they keep such trifles, but no one has my rose.

When my eye is dim, and my heart grows faint, and my faith in woman flickers, and her present is an agony to me, and her future a despair, the scent of that dead rose, withered for twelve years, comes back to me. I know there will be spring; as surely as the birds know it when they see above the snow two tiny, quivering green leaves. Spring cannot fail us.

There were other flowers in the box once: a bunch of white acacia flowers, gathered by the strong hand of a man, as we passed down a village street on a sultry afternoon, when it had rained, and the drops fell on us from the leaves of the acacia trees. The flowers were damp; they made mildew marks on the paper I folded them in. After many years I threw them away. There is nothing of them left in the box now, but a faint, strong smell of dried acacia, that recalls that sultry summer afternoon; but the rose is in the box still.

It is many years ago now; I was a girl of fifteen, and I went to visit in a small up-country town. It was young in those days, and two days' journey from the nearest village; the population consisted mainly of men. A few were married, and had their wives and children, but most were single. There was only one young girl there when I came. She was about seventeen, fair, and rather fully-fleshed; she had large dreamy blue eyes, and wavy light hair; full, rather heavy lips, until she smiled; then her face broke into dimples, and all her white teeth shone. The hotel-keeper may have had a daughter, and the farmer in the outskirts had two, but we never saw them. She reigned alone. All the men worshipped her. She was the only woman they had to think of. They talked of her on the 'stoep,' at the market, at the hotel; they watched for her at street corners; they hated the man she bowed to or walked with down the street. They brought flowers to the front door; they offered her their horses; they begged her to marry them when they dared. Partly, there was something noble and heroic in this devotion of men to the best woman they knew; partly there was something natural in it, that these men, shut off from the world, should pour at the feet of one woman the worship that otherwise would have been given to twenty; and partly there was something mean in their envy of one another. If she had raised her little finger, I suppose, she might have married any one out of twenty of them.

Then I came. I do not think I was prettier; I do not think I was so pretty as she was. I was certainly not as handsome. But I was vital, and I was new, and she was old—they all forsook her and followed me. They worshipped me. It was to my door that the flowers came; it was I had twenty horses offered me when I could only ride one; it was for me they waited at street corners; it was what I said and did that they talked of. Partly I liked it. I had lived alone all my life; no one ever had told me I was beautiful and a woman. I believed them. I did not know it was simply a fashion, which one man had set and the rest followed unreasoningly. I liked them to ask me to marry them, and to say, No. I despised them. The mother heart had not swelled in me yet; I did not know all men were my children, as the large woman knows when her heart is grown. I was too small to be tender. I liked my power. I was like a child with a new whip, which it goes about cracking everywhere, not caring against what. I could not wind it up and put it away. Men were curious creatures, who liked me, I could never tell why. Only one thing took from my pleasure; I could not bear that they had deserted her for me. I liked her great dreamy blue eyes, I liked her slow walk and drawl; when I saw her sitting among men, she seemed to me much too good to be among them; I would have given all their compliments if she would once have smiled at me as she smiled at them, with all her face breaking into radiance, with her dimples and flashing teeth. But I knew it never could be; I felt sure she hated me; that she wished I was dead; that she wished I had never come to the village. She did not know, when we went out riding, and a man who had always ridden beside her came to ride beside me, that I sent him away; that once when a man thought to win my favour by ridiculing her slow drawl before me I turned on him so fiercely that he never dared come before me again. I knew she knew that at the hotel men had made a bet as to which was the prettier, she or I, and had asked each man who came in, and that the one who had staked on me won. I hated them for it, but I would not let her see that I cared about what she felt towards me.

She and I never spoke to each other.

If we met in the village street we bowed and passed on; when we shook hands we did so silently, and did not look at each other. But I thought she felt my presence in a room just as I felt hers.

At last the time for my going came. I was to leave the next day. Someone I knew gave a party in my honour, to which all the village was invited.

It was midwinter. There was nothing in the gardens but a few dahlias and chrysanthemums, and I suppose that for two hundred miles round there was not a rose to be bought for love or money. Only in the garden of a friend of mine, in a sunny corner between the oven and the brick wall, there was a rose tree growing which had on it one bud. It was white, and it had been promised to the fair-haired girl to wear at the party.

The evening came; when I arrived and went to the waiting-room, to take off my mantle, I found the girl there already. She was dressed in pure white, with her great white arms and shoulders showing, and her bright hair glittering in the candlelight, and the white rose fastened at her breast. She looked like a queen. I said 'Good-evening,' and turned away quickly to the glass to arrange my old black scarf across my old black dress.

Then I felt a hand touch my hair.

'Stand still,' she said.

I looked in the glass. She had taken the white rose from her breast, and was fastening it in my hair.

'How nice dark hair is; it sets off flowers so.' She stepped back and looked at me. 'It looks much better there!'

I turned round.

'You are so beautiful to me,' I said.

'Y-e-s,' she said, with her slow Colonial drawl; 'I'm so glad.'

We stood looking at each other.

Then they came in and swept us away to dance. All the evening we did not come near to each other. Only once, as she passed, she smiled at me.

The next morning I left the town.

I never saw her again.

Years afterwards I heard she had married and gone to America; it may or may not be so—but the rose—the rose is in the box still! When my faith in woman grows dim, and it seems that for want of love and magnanimity she can play no part in any future heaven; then the scent of that small withered thing comes back—spring cannot fail us.

QUESTIONS

1. Schreiner tells the woman's story as a memory. How would the story be different if the central episode were told in the present?

2. The woman had preserved both acacia flowers and a rose in her box—what does each signify to her? How is it significant that only the rose remains?

3. What is the view of male-female relations expressed in this story?

4. What is the feeling or recognition that passes between the two women? Why is it so important to the protagonist?

5. Compare this story with Kate Chopin's "The Story of an Hour" and discuss how both can be said to reflect feminist perspectives.

Sarah Orne Jewett

Sarah Orne Jewett (1849–1909) was born in South Berwick, in southern Maine, the daughter of a country doctor. For sixty years she kept her attentive eye fastened upon the lives of her fellow New Englanders. Under the influence first of Harriet Beecher Stowe, later of Flaubert, Tolstoy, and James, she forged a serene naturalistic style that was wonderfully suited for capturing the rural and small-town lives that so intrigued her. Jewett published her first collection of stories, *Deerhaven,* in 1877. *A White Heron and Other Stories* followed nine years later. And in 1896 Jewett published her best-known work, *The Country of the Pointed Firs,* a series of linked sketches detailing the entwined lives in a Maine seacoast village.

But Jewett, as the reader will see, is more than just a dispassionate observer and recorder of simple lives. Her work is also haunted by intense dreams and longings. The private passions of her characters flash like heat lightning. At moments, as in "A White Heron," Jewett can almost sound like D. H. Lawrence.

A WHITE HERON

I

The woods were already filled with shadows one June evening, just before eight o'clock, though a bright sunset still glimmered faintly among the trunks of the trees. A little girl was driving home her cow, a plodding, dilatory, provoking creature in her behavior, but a valued companion for all that. They were going away from the western light, and striking deep into the dark woods, but their feet were familiar with the path, and it was no matter whether their eyes could see it or not.

There was hardly a night the summer through when the old cow could be found waiting at the pasture bars; on the contrary, it was her greatest pleasure to hide herself away among the high huckleberry bushes, and though she wore a loud bell she had made the discovery that if one stood perfectly still it would not ring. So Sylvia had to hunt for her until she found her, and call Co'! Co'! with never an answering Moo, until her childish patience was quite spent. If the creature had not given good milk and plenty of it, the case would have seemed very different to her owners. Besides, Sylvia had all the time there was, and very little use to make of it. Sometimes in pleasant weather it was a consolation to look upon the cow's pranks as an intelligent attempt to play hide and seek, and as the child had no playmates she lent herself to this amusement with a good deal of zest. Though this chase had been so long that the wary animal herself had given an unusual signal of her whereabouts, Sylvia had only laughed when she came upon Mistress Moolly at the swamp-side, and urged her affectionately homeward with a twig of birch leaves. The old cow was not inclined to wander farther, she even turned in the right direction for once as they left the pasture, and stepped along the road at a good pace. She was quite ready to be milked now, and seldom stopped to browse. Sylvia wondered what her grandmother would say because they were so late. It was a great while since she had left home at half past five o'clock, but everybody knew the difficulty of making this errand a short one. Mrs. Tilley had chased the horned torment too many summer evenings herself to blame any one else for lingering, and was only thankful as she waited that she had Sylvia, nowadays, to give such valuable assistance. The good woman suspected that Sylvia loitered occasionally on her own account; there never was such a child for straying about out-of-doors since the world was made! Everybody said that it was a good change for a little maid who had tried to grow for eight years in a crowded manufacturing town, but, as for Sylvia herself, it seemed as if she never had been alive at all before she came to live at the farm. She thought often with wistful compassion of a wretched dry geranium that belonged to a town neighbor.

" 'Afraid of folks,' " old Mrs. Tilley said to herself, with a smile, after she had made the unlikely choice of Sylvia from her daughter's houseful of children, and was returning to the farm. " 'Afraid of folks,' they said! I guess she won't be troubled no great with 'em up to the old place!" When they reached the door of the lonely house and stopped to unlock it, and the cat came to purr loudly, and rub against them, a deserted pussy, indeed, but fat with young robins, Sylvia whispered that this was a beautiful place to live in, and she never should wish to go home.

The companions followed the shady wood-road, the cow taking slow steps, and the child very fast ones. The cow stopped long at the brook to drink, as if the pasture were not half a swamp, and Sylvia stood still and waited, letting her bare feet cool themselves in the shoal water, while the great twilight moths struck softly against her. She waded on through the brook as the cow moved away, and listened to the thrushes with a heart that beat fast with pleasure. There was a stirring in the great boughs overhead. They were full of little birds and beasts that seemed to be wide-awake, and going about their world, or else saying good-night to each other in sleepy twitters. Sylvia herself felt sleepy as she walked along. However, it was not much farther to the house, and the air was soft and sweet. She was not often in the woods so late as this, and it made her feel as if she were a part of the gray shadows and the moving leaves. She was just thinking how long it seemed since she first came to the farm a year ago, and wondering if everything went on in the noisy town just the same as when she was there; the thought of the great red-faced boy who used to chase and frighten her made her hurry along the path to escape from the shadow of the trees.

Suddenly this little woods-girl is horror-stricken to hear a clear whistle not very far away. Not a bird's whistle, which would have a sort of friendliness, but a boy's whistle, determined, and somewhat aggressive. Sylvia left the cow to whatever sad fate might await her, and stepped discreetly aside into the bushes, but she was just too late. The enemy had discovered her, and called out in a very cheerful and persuasive tone, "Halloa, little girl, how far is it to the road?" and trembling Sylvia answered almost inaudibly, "A good ways."

She did not dare to look boldly at the tall young man, who carried a gun over his shoulder, but she came out of her bush and again followed the cow, while he walked alongside.

"I have been hunting for some birds," the stranger said kindly, "and I have lost my way, and need a friend very much. Don't be afraid," he added gallantly. "Speak up and tell me what your name is, and whether you think I can spend the night at your house, and go out gunning early in the morning."

Sylvia was more alarmed than before. Would not her grandmother consider her much to blame? But who could have foreseen such an accident as this? It did not appear to be her fault, and she hung her head as if the stem of it were broken, but managed to answer, "Sylvy," with much effort when her companion again asked her name.

Mrs. Tilley was standing in the doorway when the trio came into view. The cow gave a loud moo by way of explanation.

"Yes, you'd better speak up for yourself, you old trial! Where'd she tucked herself away this time, Sylvy?" Sylvia kept an awed silence; she knew by instinct that her grandmother did not comprehend the gravity of the situation. She must be mistaking the stranger for one of the farmer-lads of the region.

The young man stood his gun beside the door, and dropped a heavy game-bag beside it; then he bade Mrs. Tilley good-evening, and repeated his wayfarer's story, and asked if he could have a night's lodging.

"Put me anywhere you like," he said. "I must be off early in the morning, before day; but I am very hungry, indeed. You can give me some milk at any rate, that's plain."

"Dear sakes, yes," responded the hostess, whose long slumbering hospitality seemed to be easily awakened. "You might fare better if you went out on the main road a mile or so, but you're welcome to what we've got. I'll milk right off, and you make yourself at home. You can sleep on husks or feathers," she proffered graciously. "I raised them all myself. There's good pasturing for geese just below here towards the ma'sh. Now step round and set a plate for the gentleman, Sylvy!" And Sylvia promptly stepped. She was glad to have something to do, and she was hungry herself.

It was a surprise to find so clean and comfortable a little dwelling in this New England wilderness. The young man had known the horrors of its most primitive housekeeping, and the dreary squalor of that level of society which does not rebel at the companionship of hens. This was the best thrift of an old-fashioned farmstead, though on such a small scale that it seemed like a hermitage. He listened eagerly to the old woman's quaint talk, he watched Sylvia's pale face and shining gray eyes with ever growing enthusiasm, and insisted that this was the best supper he had eaten for a month; then, afterward, the new-made friends sat down in the doorway together while the moon came up.

Soon it would be berry-time, and Sylvia was a great help at picking. The cow was a good milker, though a plaguy thing to keep track of, the hostess gossiped frankly, adding presently that she had buried four children, so that Sylvia's mother, and a son (who might be dead) in California were all the children she had left. "Dan, my boy, was a great hand to go gunning," she explained sadly. "I never wanted for pa'tridges or gray squer'ls while he was to home. He's been a great wand'rer, I expect, and he's no hand to write letters. There, I don't blame him, I'd ha' seen the world myself if it had been so I could.

"Sylvia takes after him," the grandmother continued affectionately, after a minute's pause. "There ain't a foot o' ground she don't know her way over, and the wild creatur's counts her one o' themselves. Squer'ls she'll tame to come an' feed right out o' her hands, and all sorts o' birds. Last winter she got the jay-birds to bangeing here, and I believe she'd 'a' scanted herself of her own meals to have plenty to throw out amongst 'em, if I hadn't kep' watch. Anything but crows, I tell her, I'm willin' to help support,—though Dan he went an' tamed one o' them that did seem to have reason same as folks. It was round here a good spell after he went away. Dan an' his father they didn't hitch,—but he never held up his head ag'in after Dan had dared him an' gone off."

The guest did not notice this hint of family sorrows in his eager interest in something else.

"So Sylvy knows all about birds, does she?" he exclaimed, as he looked round at the little girl who sat, very demure but increasingly sleepy, in the moonlight. "I am making a collection of birds myself. I have been at it ever since I was a boy." (Mrs. Tilley smiled.) "There are two or three very rare ones I have been hunting for these five years. I mean to get them on my own ground if they can be found."

"Do you cage 'em up?" asked Mrs. Tilley doubtfully, in response to this enthusiastic announcement.

"Oh, no, they're stuffed and preserved, dozens and dozens of them," said the ornithologist, "and I have shot or snared every one myself. I caught a glimpse of a white heron three miles from here on Saturday, and I have followed it in this direction. They have never been found in this district at all. The little white heron, it is," and he turned again to look at Sylvia with the hope of discovering that the rare bird was one of her acquaintances.

But Sylvia was watching a hop-toad in the narrow footpath.

"You would know the heron if you saw it," the stranger continued eagerly. "A queer tall white bird with soft feathers and long thin legs. And it would have a nest perhaps in the top of a high tree, made of sticks, something like a hawk's nest."

Sylvia's heart gave a wild beat; she knew that strange white bird, and had once stolen softly near where it stood in some bright green swamp grass away over at the other side of the woods. There was an open place where the sunshine always seemed strangely yellow and hot, where tall, nodding rushes grew, and her grandmother had warned her that she might sink in the soft black mud underneath and never be heard of more. Not far beyond were the salt marshes and beyond those was the sea, the sea which Sylvia wondered and dreamed about, but never had looked upon, though its great voice could often be heard above the noise of the woods on stormy nights.

"I can't think of anything I should like so much as to find that heron's nest," the handsome stranger was saying. "I would give ten dollars to anybody who could show it to me," he added desperately, "and I mean to spend my whole vacation hunting for it if need be. Perhaps it was only migrating, or had been chased out of its own region by some bird of prey."

Mrs. Tilley gave amazed attention to all this, but Sylvia still watched the toad, not divining, as she might have done at some calmer time, that the creature wished to get to its hole under the doorstep, and was much hindered by the unusual spectators at that hour of the evening. No amount of thought, that night, could decide how many wished-for treasures the ten dollars, so lightly spoken of, would buy.

The next day the young sportsman hovered about the woods, and Sylvia kept him company, having lost her first fear of the friendly lad, who proved to be most kind and sympathetic. He told her many things about the birds and what they knew and where they lived and what they did with themselves. And he gave her a jack-knife, which she thought as great a treasure as if she were a desert-islander. All day long he did not once make her troubled or afraid except when he brought down some unsuspecting singing creature from its bough. Sylvia would have liked him vastly better without his gun; she could not understand why he killed the very birds he seemed to like so much. But as the day waned, Sylvia still watched the young man with loving admiration. She had never seen anybody so charming and delightful; the woman's heart, asleep in the child, was vaguely thrilled by a dream of love. Some premonition of that great power stirred and swayed these young foresters who traversed the solemn woodlands with soft-footed silent care. They stopped to listen to a bird's song; they pressed forward again eagerly, parting the branches—speaking to each other rarely and in whispers; the young man going first and Sylvia following, fascinated, a few steps behind, with her gray eyes dark with excitement.

She grieved because the longed-for white heron was elusive, but she did not lead the guest, she only followed, and there was no such thing as speaking first. The sound of her own unquestioned voice would have terrified her—it was hard enough to answer yes or no when there was need of that. At last evening began to fall, and they drove the cow home together, and Sylvia smiled with pleasure when they came to the place where she heard the whistle and was afraid only the night before.

II

Half a mile from home, at the farther edge of the woods, where the land was highest, a great pine-tree stood, the last of its generation. Whether it was left for a boundary mark, or for what reason, no one could say; the woodchoppers who had felled its mates were dead and gone long ago, and a whole forest of sturdy trees, pines and oaks and maples, had grown again. But the stately head of this old pine towered above them all and made a landmark for sea and shore miles and miles away. Sylvia knew it well. She had always believed that whoever climbed to the top of it could see the ocean; and the little girl had often laid her hand on the great rough trunk and looked up wistfully at those dark boughs that the wind always stirred, no matter how hot and still the air might be below. Now she thought of the tree with a new excitement, for why, if one climbed it at break of day, could not one see all the world, and easily discover whence the white heron flew, and mark the place, and find the hidden nest?

What a spirit of adventure, what wild ambition! What fancied triumph and delight and glory for the later morning when she could make known the secret! It was almost too real and too great for the childish heart to bear.

All night the door of the little house stood open, and the whippoorwills came and sang upon the very step. The young sportsman and his old hostess were sound asleep, but Sylvia's great design kept her broad awake and watching. She forgot to think of sleep. The short summer night seemed as long as the winter darkness, and at last when the whippoorwills ceased, and she was afraid the morning would after all come too soon, she stole out of the house and followed the pasture path through the woods, hastening toward the open ground beyond, listening with a sense of comfort and companionship to the drowsy twitter of a half-awakened bird, whose perch she had jarred in passing. Alas, if the great wave of human interest which flooded for the first time this dull little life should sweep away the satisfactions of an existence heart to heart with nature and the dumb life of the forest!

There was the huge tree asleep yet in the paling moonlight, and small and hopeful Sylvia began with utmost bravery to mount to the top of it, with tingling, eager blood coursing the channels of her whole frame, with her bare feet and fingers, that pinched and held like bird's claws to the monstrous ladder reaching up, up, almost to the sky itself. First she must mount the white oak tree that grew alongside, where she was almost lost among the dark branches and the green leaves heavy and wet with dew; a bird fluttered off its nest, and a red squirrel ran to and fro and scolded pettishly at the harmless housebreaker. Sylvia felt her way easily. She had often climbed there, and knew that higher still one of the oak's upper branches chafed against the pine trunk, just where its lower boughs were set close together. There, when she made the dangerous pass from one tree to the other, the great enterprise would really begin.

She crept out along the swaying oak limb at last, and took the daring step across into the old pine-tree. The way was harder than she thought; she must reach far and hold fast, the sharp dry twigs caught and held her and scratched her like angry talons, the pitch made her thin little fingers clumsy and stiff as she went round and round the tree's great stem, higher and higher upward. The sparrows and robins in the woods below were beginning to wake and twitter to the dawn, yet it seemed much lighter there aloft in the pine-tree, and the child knew that she must hurry if her project were to be of any use.

The tree seemed to lengthen itself out as she went up, and to reach farther and farther upward. It was like a great main-mast to the voyaging earth; it must truly have been amazed that morning through all its ponderous frame as it felt this determined spark of human spirit creeping and climbing from higher branch to branch. Who knows how steadily the least twigs held themselves to advantage this light, weak creature on her way! The old pine must have loved his new dependent. More than all the hawks, and bats, and moths, and even the sweet-voiced thrushes, was the brave, beating heart of the solitary gray-eyed child. And the tree stood still and held away the winds that June morning while the dawn grew bright in the east.

Sylvia's face was like a pale star, if one had seen it from the ground, when the last thorny bough was past, and she stood trembling and tired but wholly triumphant, high in the tree-top. Yes, there was the sea with the dawning sun making a golden dazzle over it, and toward that glorious east flew two hawks with slow-moving pinions. How low they looked in the air from that height when before one had only seen them far up, and dark against the blue sky. Their gray feathers were as soft as moths; they seemed only a little way from the tree, and Sylvia felt as if she too could go flying away among the clouds. Westward, the woodlands and farms reached miles and miles into the distance; here and there were church steeples, and white villages; truly it was a vast and awesome world.

The birds sang louder and louder. At last the sun came up bewilderingly bright. Sylvia could see the white sails of ships out at sea, and the clouds that were purple and rose-colored and yellow at first began to fade away. Where was the white heron's nest in the sea of green branches, and was this wonderful sight and pageant of the world the only reward for having climbed to such a giddy height? Now look down again, Sylvia, where the green marsh is set among the shining birches and dark hemlocks; there where you saw the white heron once you will see him again; look, look! a white spot of him like a single floating feather comes up from the dead hemlock and grows larger, and rises, and comes close at last, and goes by the landmark pine with steady sweep of wing and outstretched slender neck and crested head. And wait! wait! do not move a foot or a finger, little girl, do not send an arrow of light and consciousness from your two eager eyes, for the heron has perched on a pine bough not far beyond yours, and cries back to his mate on the nest, and plumes his feathers for the new day!

The child gives a long sigh a minute later when a company of shouting cat-birds comes also to the tree, and vexed by their fluttering and lawlessness the solemn heron goes away. She knows his secret now, the wild, light, slender bird that floats and wavers, and goes back like an arrow presently to his home in the green world beneath. Then Sylvia, well satisfied, makes her perilous way down again, not daring to look far below the branch she stands on, ready to cry sometimes because her fingers ache and her lamed feet slip. Wondering over and over again what the stranger would say to her, and what he would think when she told him how to find his way straight to the heron's nest.

"Sylvy, Sylvy!" called the busy old grandmother again and again, but nobody answered, and the small husk bed was empty, and Sylvia had disappeared.

The guest waked from a dream, and remembering his day's pleasure hurried to dress himself that it might sooner begin. He was sure from the way the shy little girl looked once or twice yesterday that she had at least seen the white heron, and now she must really be persuaded to tell. Here she comes now, paler than ever, and her worn old frock is torn and tattered, and smeared with pine pitch. The grandmother and the sportsman stand in the door together and question her, and the splendid moment has come to speak of the dead hemlock-tree by the green marsh.

But Sylvia does not speak after all, though the old grandmother fretfully rebukes her, and the young man's kind appealing eyes are looking straight in her own. He can make them rich with money; he has promised it, and they are poor now. He is so well worth making happy, and he waits to hear the story she can tell.

No, she must keep silence! What is it that suddenly forbids her and makes her dumb? Has she been nine years growing, and now, when the great world for the first time puts out a hand to her, must she thrust it aside for a bird's sake? The murmur of the pine's green branches is in her ears, she remembers how the white heron came flying through the golden air and how they watched the sea and the morning together, and Sylvia cannot speak; she cannot tell the heron's secret and give its life away.

Dear loyalty, that suffered a sharp pang as the guest went away disappointed later in the day, that could have served and followed him and loved him as a dog loves! Many a night Sylvia heard the echo of his whistle haunting the pasture path as she came home with the loitering cow. She forgot even her sorrow at the sharp report of his gun and the piteous sight of thrushes and sparrows dropping silent to the ground, their songs hushed and their pretty feathers stained and wet with blood. Were the birds better friends than their hunter might have been,—who can tell? Whatever treasures were lost to her, woodlands and summer-time, remember! Bring your gifts and graces and tell your secrets to this lonely country child!

QUESTIONS

1. What impression of Sylvia's character do we get from the first scene of the story? How does this impression change or deepen later? What makes the change?
2. How does Jewett use natural description to set a mood, and how does the mood enhance the effect of the story? Comment on her evocation of twilight and dawn. Are these atmospheric considerations important to the story?
3. How are we asked to view the young man—the hunter? What is the symbolic significance of his hobby of stuffing birds?
4. What hints does Jewett give of Sylvia's confusion?
5. How does Jewett build tension through the second half of the story? Discuss her presentation of the tree-climbing scene and its significance. How does Sylvia's emotional view of things change along with her literal change of vantage?
6. What do we expect Sylvia to do once she has returned to her home?
7. Is the white heron meant to be a symbol? If so, of what? What are its symbolic virtues, and how are they contrasted with the aims of the hunter?
8. What is Sylvia finally struggling to choose between?
9. Does Jewett have a message about differences between men and women? Explain.

KATE CHOPIN

Kate Chopin (1851–1904) has come to be revered in recent years as an important early champion of feminist consciousness. While her avowed master was Maupassant, whose work she translated, she was able to inflect his more neutral clear-sightedness with a decidedly critical slant. As "The Story of an Hour" demonstrates with such economy, Chopin's primary interest was in tracing a woman's emotional life. Her best-known work, the novel *The Awakening* (1899), was seen as shocking in its day. Few writers—certainly no women—had treated the theme of adultery with such candor. Chopin's other works include *Bayou Folk* (1894) and *A Night in Arcadie* (1897), both story collections.

Though born in St. Louis, Chopin spent many years in Louisiana. After her husband, a cotton broker, died in 1882, she moved back to St. Louis with her six children. The public outcry surrounding *The Awakening* embittered her and all but silenced her writing for the last years of her life.

THE STORY OF AN HOUR

Knowing that Mrs. Mallard was afflicted with a heart trouble, great care was taken to break to her as gently as possible the news of her husband's death.

It was her sister Josephine who told her, in broken sentences; veiled hints that revealed in half concealing. Her husband's friend Richards was there, too, near her. It was he who had been in the newspaper office when intelligence of the railroad disaster was received, with Brently Mallard's name leading the list of "killed." He had only taken the time to assure himself of its truth by a second telegram, and had hastened to forestall any less careful, less tender friend in bearing the sad message.

She did not hear the story as many women have heard the same, with a paralyzed inability to accept its significance. She wept at once, with sudden, wild abandonment, in her sister's arms. When the storm of grief had spent itself she went away to her room alone. She would have no one follow her.

There stood, facing the open window, a comfortable, roomy armchair. Into this she sank, pressed down by a physical exhaustion that haunted her body and seemed to reach into her soul.

She could see in the open square before her house the tops of trees that were all aquiver with the new spring life. The delicious breath of rain was in the air. In the street below a peddler was crying his wares. The notes of a distant song which some one was singing reached her faintly, and countless sparrows were twittering in the eaves.

There were patches of blue sky showing here and there through the clouds that had met and piled one above the other in the west facing her window.

She sat with her head thrown back upon the cushion of the chair, quite motionless, except when a sob came up into her throat and shook her, as a child who had cried itself to sleep continues to sob in its dreams.

She was young, with a fair, calm face, whose lines bespoke repression and even a certain strength. But now there was a dull stare in her eyes, whose gaze was fixed away off yonder on one of those patches of blue sky. It was not a glance of reflection, but rather indicated a suspension of intelligent thought.

There was something coming to her and she was waiting for it, fearfully. What was it? She did not know; it was too subtle and elusive to name. But she felt it, creeping out of the sky, reaching toward her through the sounds, the scents, the color that filled the air.

Now her bosom rose and fell tumultuously. She was beginning to recognize this thing that was approaching to possess her, and she was striving to beat it back with her will—as powerless as her two white slender hands would have been.

When she abandoned herself a little whispered word escaped her slightly parted lips. She said it over and over under her breath: "free, free, free!" The vacant stare and the look of terror that had followed it went from her eyes. They stayed keen and bright. Her pulses beat fast, and the coursing blood warmed and relaxed every inch of her body.

She did not stop to ask if it were or were not a monstrous joy that held her. A clear and exalted perception enabled her to dismiss the suggestion as trivial.

She knew that she would weep again when she saw the kind, tender hands folded in death; the face that had never looked save with love upon her, fixed and gray and dead. But she saw beyond that bitter moment a long procession of years to come that would belong to her absolutely. And she opened and spread her arms out to them in welcome.

There would be no one to live for her during those coming years: she would live for herself. There would be no powerful will bending hers in that blind persistence with which men and women believe they have a right to impose a private will upon a fellow-creature. A kind intention or a cruel intention made the act seem no less a crime as she looked upon it in that brief moment of illumination.

And yet she had loved him—sometimes. Often she had not. What did it matter! What could love, the unsolved mystery, count for in face of this possession of self-assertion which she suddenly recognized as the strongest impulse of her being!

"Free! Body and soul free!" she kept whispering.

Josephine was kneeling before the closed door with her lips to the keyhole, imploring for admission. "Louise, open the door! I beg; open the door—you will make yourself ill. What are you doing, Louise? For heaven's sake open the door."

"Go away. I am not making myself ill." No; she was drinking in a very elixir of life through that open window.

Her fancy was running riot along those days ahead of her. Spring days, and summer days, and all sorts of days that would be her own. She breathed a quick prayer that life might be long. It was only yesterday she had thought with a shudder that life might be long.

She arose at length and opened the door to her sister's importunities. There was a feverish triumph in her eyes, and she carried herself unwittingly like a goddess of Victory. She clasped her sister's waist, and together they descended the stairs. Richards stood waiting for them at the bottom.

Some one was opening the front door with a latchkey. It was Brently Mallard who entered, a little travel-stained, composedly carrying his grip-sack and umbrella. He had been far from the scene of accident, and did not even know there had been one. He stood amazed at Josephine's piercing cry; at Richards' quick motion to screen him from the view of his wife.

But Richards was too late.

When the doctors came they said she had died of heart disease—of joy that kills.

QUESTIONS

1. How does Chopin set up an expectation in the reader, and how does she reverse it? How does our view of the woman change—and deepen—from this single revelation?

2. What does the story have to say about freedom and love? Do we believe that freedom *is* more important, or do we suppose that the woman has simply never known true love?

3. What is Chopin's attitude toward the woman? the man? Does she want us to admire the woman or pity her? What is the reader's response when the husband suddenly appears?

4. How does Chopin orchestrate the story around fundamental misunderstandings?

5. Comment upon the kinds of images used to suggest freedom. Are these matched, or counterpointed, by opposite suggestions elsewhere in the story?

6. Is there a sense in which the woman's sudden death is a blessing? Explain.

Anton Chekhov

Writers, like all craftsmen, have their own pantheon of cherished heroes, and their lists of masters are not always in accord with the judgments of scholars and critics. Anton Chekhov (1860–1904), the great favorite among generations of writers, is a case in point. His continuing popularity is almost solely the consequence of the passion he has inspired in writers and lay readers. The critics, while willing to regard him seriously, have never quite known what to make of his genius—it is fresh and distinct, and it defies every effort to place it in a critical category.

Chekhov, still another in the ranks of the short-lived, was the son of a failed grocer. He studied medicine at Moscow University but at a very young age began to write stories and sketches for newspapers in order to support his family. His gift for imbuing the slightest cluster of impressions with life was immediately obvious, and he never lacked for markets for his work.

Chekhov published two collections of stories in rapid succession—in 1886 and 1887—and their reception encouraged him to put his medical practice to the side. (But while he gave up the profession, he never stopped ministering to the sick; for years he treated peasants who lived near his estate outside Moscow.)

In 1890, determined to face for himself the extremities of human suffering, Chekhov journeyed overland to the distant penal island of Sakhalin. At the time of the trip he was already suffering from the tuberculosis that would finally kill him, but he bore the arduous miles cheerfully—one might even say with a masochistic cheerfulness.

By the time of his thirties, Chekhov had already achieved renown throughout Russia. He befriended Tolstoy and exerted great influence on the literary life of his times. He also turned his hand to play writing, in a few years writing some of the great plays of the world stage. (*The Seagull, Uncle Vanya, The Cherry Orchard,* and *The Three Sisters* were all penned between 1896 and 1904.) In 1901, in failing health, he married the celebrated actress Olga Knipper. He died three years later in Yalta from tuberculosis.

The Chekhov magic is very hard to describe but almost impossible to miss. He had the gift, to put the matter simply, of making words seem like life. Drawn to portray simple people, odd encounters, and seemingly insignificant events, Chekhov found that these were the cracks where life leaked through in its purest form. Like Flaubert, he knew the power of the detail. Unlike Flaubert, however, he was free of any impulse to despise. In Chekhov's stories we see a sad world, but it remains iridescent with beauty.

LADY WITH LAPDOG

I

The appearance on the front of a new arrival—a lady with a lapdog—became the topic of general conversation. Dmitry Dmitrich Gurov, who had been a fortnight in Yalta and got used to its ways, was also interested in new arrivals. One day, sitting on the terrace of Vernet's restaurant, he saw a young woman walking along the promenade; she was fair, not very tall, and wore a toque; behind her trotted a white pomeranian.

Later he came across her in the park and in the square several times a day. She was always alone, always wearing the same toque, followed by the white pomeranian. No one knew who she was, and she became known simply as the lady with the lapdog.

'If she's here without her husband and without any friends,' thought Gurov, 'it wouldn't be a bad idea to strike up an acquaintance with her.'

He was not yet forty, but he had a twelve-year-old daughter and two schoolboy sons. He had been married off when he was still in his second year at the university, and his wife seemed to him now to be almost twice his age. She was a tall, black-browed woman, erect, dignified, austere, and, as she liked to describe herself, a 'thinking person'. She was a great reader, preferred the new 'advanced' spelling, called her husband by the more formal 'Dimitry' and not the familiar 'Dmitry'; and though he secretly considered her not particularly intelligent, narrow-minded, and inelegant, he was afraid of her and disliked being at home. He had been unfaithful to her for a long time, he was often unfaithful to her, and that was why, perhaps, he almost always spoke ill of women, and when men discussed women in his presence, he described them as *the lower breed.*

He could not help feeling that he had had enough bitter experience to have the right to call them as he pleased, but all the same without *the lower breed* he could not have existed a couple of days. He was bored and ill at ease among men, with whom he was reticent and cold, but when he was among women he felt at ease, he knew what to talk about with them and how to behave; even when he was silent in their company he experienced no feeling of constraint. There was something attractive, something elusive in his appearance, in his character and his whole person, that women found interesting and irresistible; he was aware of it, and was himself drawn to them by some irresistible force.

Long and indeed bitter experience had taught him that every new affair, which at first relieved the monotony of life so pleasantly and appeared to be such a charming and light adventure, among decent people and especially among Muscovites, who are so irresolute and so hard to rouse, inevitably developed into an extremely complicated problem and finally the whole situation became rather cumbersome. But at every new meeting with an attractive woman he forgot all about this experience, he wanted to enjoy life so badly and it all seemed so simple and amusing.

And so one afternoon, while he was having dinner at a restaurant in the park, the woman in the toque walked in unhurriedly and took a seat at the table next to him. The way she looked, walked, and dressed, wore her hair, told him that she was of good social standing, that she was married, that she was in Yalta for the first time, that she was alone and bored. . . . There was a great deal of exaggeration in the stories about the laxity of morals among the Yalta visitors, and he dismissed them with contempt, for he knew that such stories were mostly made up by people who would gladly have sinned themselves if they had had any idea how to go about it; but when the women sat down at the table three yards away from him he remembered these stories of easy conquests and excursions to the mountains and the tempting thought of a quick and fleeting affair, an affair with a strange woman whose very name he did not know, suddenly took possession of him.

He tried to attract the attention of the dog by calling softly to it, and when the pomeranian came up to him he shook a finger at it. The pomeranian growled. Gurov again shook a finger at it.

The woman looked up at him and immediately lowered her eyes.

'He doesn't bite,' she said and blushed.

'May I give him a bone?' he asked, and when she nodded, he said amiably: 'Have you been long in Yalta?'

'About five days.'

'And I am just finishing my second week here.'

They said nothing for the next few minutes.

'Time flies,' she said without looking at him, 'and yet it's so boring here.'

'That's what one usually hears people saying here. A man may be living in Belev and Zhizdra or some other God-forsaken hole and he isn't bored, but the moment he comes here all you hear from him is "Oh, it's so boring! Oh, the dust!" You'd think he'd come from Granada!'

She laughed. Then both went on eating in silence, like complete strangers; but after dinner they strolled off together, and they embarked on the light playful conversation of free and contented people who do not care where they go or what they talk about. They walked, and talked about the strange light that fell on the sea; the water was of such a soft and warm lilac, and the moon threw a shaft of gold across it. They talked about how close it was after a hot day. Gurov told her that he lived in Moscow, that he was a graduate in philology but worked in a bank, that he had at one time thought of singing in a private opera company but had given up the idea, that he owned two houses in Moscow. . . . From her he learnt that she had grown up in Petersburg, but had got married in the town of S——, where she had been living for the past two years, that she would stay another month in Yalta, and that her husband, who also needed a rest, might join her. She was quite unable to tell him what her husband's job was, whether he served in the offices of the provincial governor or the rural council, and she found this rather amusing herself. Gurov also found out that her name and patronymic were Anna Sergeyevna.

Later, in his hotel room, he thought about her and felt sure that he would meet her again the next day. It had to be. As he went to bed he remembered that she had only recently left her boarding school, that she had been a schoolgirl like his own daughter; he recalled how much diffidence and angularity there was in her laughter and her conversation with a stranger—it was probably the first time in her life she had found herself alone, in a situation when men followed her, looked at her, and spoke to her with only one secret intention, an intention she could hardly fail to guess. He remembered her slender, weak neck, her beautiful grey eyes.

'There's something pathetic about her, all the same,' he thought as he fell asleep.

II

A week had passed since their first meeting. It was a holiday. It was close indoors, while in the streets a strong wind raised clouds of dust and tore off people's hats. All day long one felt thirsty, and Gurov kept going to the terrace of the restaurant, offering Anna Sergeyevna fruit drinks and ices. There was nowhere to go.

In the evening, when the wind had dropped a little, they went to the pier to watch the arrival of the steamer. There were a great many people taking a walk on the landing pier; some were meeting friends, they had bunches of flowers in their hands. It was there that two peculiarities of the Yalta smart set at once arrested attention: the middle-aged women dressed as if they were still young girls and there was a great number of generals.

Because of the rough sea the steamer arrived late, after the sun had set, and she had to swing backwards and forwards several times before getting alongside the pier. Anna Sergeyevna looked at the steamer and the passengers through her lorgnette, as though trying to make out some friends, and when she turned to Gurov her eyes were sparkling. She talked a lot, asked many abrupt questions, and immediately forgot what it was she had wanted to know; then she lost her lorgnette in the crowd of people.

The smartly dressed crowd dispersed; soon they were all gone, the wind had dropped completely, but Gurov and Anna were still standing there as though waiting to see if someone else would come off the boat. Anna Sergeyevna was no longer talking. She was smelling her flowers without looking at Gurov.

'It's a nice evening,' he said. 'Where shall we go now? Shall we go for a drive?'

She made no answer.

Then he looked keenly at her and suddenly put his arms round her and kissed her on the mouth. He felt the fragrance and dampness of the flowers and immediately looked round him fearfully: had anyone seen them?

'Let's go to your room,' he said softly.

And both walked off quickly.

It was very close in her hotel room, which was full of the smell of the scents she had bought in a Japanese shop. Looking at her now, Gurov thought: 'Life is full of strange encounters!' From his past he preserved the memory of carefree, good-natured women, whom love had made gay and who were grateful to him for the happiness he gave them, however short-lived; and of women like his wife, who made love without sincerity, with unnecessary talk, affectedly, hysterically, with such an expression, as though it were not love or passion, but something much more significant; and of two or three very beautiful, frigid women, whose faces suddenly lit up with a predatory expression, an obstinate desire to take, to snatch from life more than it could give; these were women no longer in their first youth, capricious, unreasoning, despotic, unintelligent women, and when Gurov lost interest in them, their beauty merely aroused hatred in him and the lace trimmings on their négligés looked to him then like the scales of a snake.

But here there was still the same diffidence and angularity of inexperienced youth—an awkward feeling; and there was also the impression of embarrassment, as if someone had just knocked at the door. Anna Sergeyevna, this lady with the lapdog, apparently regarded what had happened in a peculiar sort of way, very seriously, as though she had become a fallen women—so it seemed to him, and he found it odd and disconcerting. Her features lengthened and drooped, and her long hair hung mournfully on either side of her face; she sank into thought in a despondent pose, like a woman taken in adultery in an old painting.

'It's wrong,' she said. 'You'll be the first not to respect me now.'

There was a water-melon on the table. Gurov cut himself a slice and began to eat it slowly. At least half an hour passed in silence.

Anna Sergeyevna was very touching; there was an air of a pure, decent, naïve woman about her, a woman who had very little experience of life; the solitary candle burning on the table scarcely lighted up her face, but it was obvious that she was unhappy.

'But, darling, why should I stop respecting you?' Gurov asked. 'You don't know yourself what you're saying.'

'May God forgive me,' she said, and her eyes filled with tears. 'It's terrible.'

'You seem to wish to justify yourself.'

'How can I justify myself? I am a bad, despicable creature. I despise myself and have no thought of justifying myself. I haven't deceived my husband, I've deceived myself. And not only now. I've been deceiving myself for a long time. My husband is, I'm sure, a good and honest man, but, you see, he is a flunkey. I don't know what he does at his office, all I know is that he is a flunkey. I was only twenty when I married him, I was eaten up by curiosity, I wanted something better. There surely must be a different kind of life, I said to myself. I wanted to live. To live, to live! I was burning with curiosity. I don't think you know what I am talking about, but I swear I could no longer control myself, something was happening to me, I could not be held back, I told my husband I was ill, and I came here. . . . Here too I was going about as though in a daze, as though I was mad, and now I've become a vulgar worthless woman whom everyone has a right to despise.'

Gurov could not help feeling bored as he listened to her; he was irritated by her naïve tone of voice and her repentance, which was so unexpected and so out of place; but for the tears in her eyes, he might have thought that she was joking or play-acting.

'I don't understand,' he said gently, 'what it is you want.'

She buried her face on his chest and clung close to him.

'Please, please believe me,' she said. 'I love a pure, honest life. I hate immorality. I don't know myself what I am doing. The common people say "the devil led her astray." I too can now say about myself that the devil has led me astray.'

'There, there . . .' he murmured.

He gazed into her staring, frightened eyes, kissed her, spoke gently and affectionately to her, and gradually she calmed down and her cheerfulness returned; both of them were soon laughing.

Later, when they went out, there was not a soul on the promenade, the town with its cypresses looked quite dead, but the sea was still roaring and dashing itself against the shore; a single launch tossed on the waves, its lamp flickering sleepily.

They hailed a cab and drove to Oreanda.

'I've just found out your surname, downstairs in the lobby,' said Gurov. 'Von Diederitz. Is your husband a German?'

'No. I believe his grandfather was German. He is of the Orthodox faith himself.'

In Oreanda they sat on a bench not far from the church, looked down on the sea, and were silent. Yalta could scarcely be seen through the morning mist. White clouds lay motionless on the mountain tops. Not a leaf stirred on the trees, the cicadas chirped, and the monotonous, hollow roar of the sea, coming up from below, spoke of rest, of eternal sleep awaiting us all. The sea had roared like that down below when there was no Yalta or Oreanda, it was roaring now, and it would go on roaring as indifferently and hollowly when we were here no more. And in this constancy, in this complete indifference to the life and death of each one of us, there is perhaps hidden the guarantee of our eternal salvation, the never-ceasing movement of life on earth, the never-ceasing movement towards perfection. Sitting beside a young woman who looked so beautiful at the break of day, soothed and enchanted by the sight of all that fairy-land scenery—the sea, the mountains, the clouds, the wide sky—Gurov reflected that, when you came to think of it, everything in the world was really beautiful, everything but our own thoughts and actions when we lose sight of the higher aims of existence and our dignity as human beings.

Someone walked up to them, a watchman probably, looked at them, and went away. And there seemed to be something mysterious and also beautiful in this fact, too. They could see the Theodosia boat coming towards the pier, lit up by the sunrise, and with no lights.

'There's dew on the grass,' said Anna Sergeyevna, breaking the silence.

'Yes. Time to go home.'

They went back to the town.

After that they met on the front every day at twelve o'clock, had lunch and dinner together, went for walks, admired the sea. She complained of sleeping badly and of her heart beating uneasily, asked the same questions, alternately worried by feelings of jealousy and by fear that he did not respect her sufficiently. And again and again in the park or in the square, when there was no one in sight, he would draw her to him and kiss her passionately. The complete idleness, these kisses in broad daylight, always having to look round for fear of someone watching them, the heat, the smell of the sea, and the constant looming into sight of idle, well-dressed, and well-fed people seemed to have made a new man of him; he told Anna Sergeyevna that she was beautiful, that she was desirable, made passionate love to her, never left her side, while she was often lost in thought and kept asking him to admit that he did not really respect her, that he was not in the least in love with her and only saw in her a vulgar woman. Almost every night they drove out of town, to Oreanda or to the waterfall; the excursion was always a success, and every time their impressions were invariably grand and beautiful.

They kept expecting her husband to arrive. But a letter came from him in which he wrote that he was having trouble with his eyes and implored his wife to return home as soon as possible. Anna Sergeyevna lost no time in getting ready for her journey home.

'It's a good thing I'm going,' she said to Gurov. 'It's fate.'

She took a carriage to the railway station, and he saw her off. The drive took a whole day. When she got into the express train, after the second bell, she said:

'Let me have another look at you. . . . One last look. So.'

She did not cry, but looked sad, just as if she were ill, and her face quivered.

'I'll be thinking of you, remembering you,' she said. 'Good-bye. You're staying, aren't you? Don't think badly of me. We are parting for ever. Yes, it must be so, for we should never have met. Well, good-bye. . . .'

The train moved rapidly out of the station; its lights soon disappeared, and a minute later it could not even be heard, just as though everything had conspired to put a quick end to this sweet trance, this madness. And standing alone on the platform gazing into the dark distance, Gurov listened to the churring of the grasshoppers and the humming of the telegraph wires with a feeling as though he had just woken up. He told himself that this had been just one more affair in his life, just one more adventure, and that it too was over, leaving nothing but a memory. He was moved and sad, and felt a little penitent that the young woman, whom he would never see again, had not been happy with him; he had been amiable and affectionate with her, but all the same in his behaviour to her, in the tone of his voice and in his caresses, there was a suspicion of light irony, the somewhat coarse arrogance of the successful male, who was, moreover, almost twice her age. All the time she called him good, wonderful, high-minded; evidently she must have taken him to be quite different from what he really was, which meant that he had involuntarily deceived her.

At the railway station there was already a whiff of autumn in the air; the evening was chilly.

'Time I went north too,' thought Gurov, as he walked off the platform. 'High time!'

III

At home in Moscow everything was already like winter: the stoves were heated, and it was still dark in the morning when the children were getting ready to go to school and having breakfast, so that the nurse had to light the lamp for a short time. The frosts had set in. When the first snow falls and the first day one goes out for a ride in a sleigh, one is glad to see the white ground, the white roofs, the air is so soft and wonderful to breathe, and one remembers the days of one's youth. The old lime trees and birches, white with rime, have such a benignant look, they are nearer to one's heart than cypresses and palms, and beside them one no longer wants to think of mountains and the sea.

Gurov had been born and bred in Moscow, and he returned to Moscow on a fine frosty day; and when he put on his fur coat and warm gloves and took a walk down Petrovka Street, and when on Saturday evening he heard the church bells ringing, his recent holiday trip and the places he had visited lost their charm for him. Gradually he became immersed in Moscow life, eagerly reading three newspapers a day and declaring that he never read Moscow papers on principle. Once more he could not resist the attraction of restaurants, clubs, banquets, and anniversary celebrations, and once more he felt flattered that well-known lawyers and actors came to see him and that in the Medical Club he played cards with a professor as his partner. Once again he was capable of eating a whole portion of the Moscow speciality of sour cabbage and meat served in a frying-pan. . . .

Another month and, he thought, nothing but a memory would remain of Anna Sergeyevna; he would remember her as through a haze and only occasionally dream of her with a wistful smile, as he did of the others before her. But over a month passed, winter was at its height, and he remembered her as clearly as though he had only parted from her the day before. His memories haunted him more and more persistently. Every time the voices of his children doing their homework reached him in his study in the stillness of the evening, every time he heard a popular song or some music in a restaurant, every time the wind howled in the chimney—it all came back to him: their walks on the pier, early morning with the mist on the mountains, the Theodosia boat, and the kisses. He kept pacing the room for hours remembering it all and smiling, and then his memories turned into daydreams and the past mingled in his imagination with what was going to happen. He did not dream of Anna Sergeyevna, she accompanied him everywhere like his shadow and followed him wherever he went. Closing his eyes, he saw her as clearly as if she were before him, and she seemed to him lovelier, younger, and tenderer than she had been; and he thought that he too was much better than he had been in Yalta. In the evenings she gazed at him from the bookcase, from the fireplace, from the corner—he heard her breathing, the sweet rustle of her dress. In the street he followed women with his eyes, looking for anyone who resembled her. . . .

He was beginning to be overcome by an overwhelming desire to share his memories with someone. But at home it was impossible to talk of his love, and outside his home there was no one he could talk to. Not the tenants who lived in his house, and certainly not his colleagues in the bank. And what was he to tell them? Had he been in love then? Had there been anything beautiful, poetic, edifying, or even anything interesting about his relations with Anna Sergeyevna? So he had to talk in general terms about love and women, and no one guessed what he was driving at, and his wife merely raised her black eyebrows and said:

'Really, Dimitry, the role of a coxcomb doesn't suit you at all!'

One evening, as he left the Medical Club with his partner, a civil servant, he could not restrain himself, and said:

'If you knew what a fascinating woman I met in Yalta!'

The civil servant got into his sleigh and was about to be driven off, but suddenly he turned round and called out:

'I say!'

'Yes?'

'You were quite right: the sturgeon *was* a bit off.'

These words, so ordinary in themselves, for some reason hurt Gurov's feelings: they seemed to him humiliating and indecent. What savage manners! What faces! What stupid nights! What uninteresting, wasted days!

Crazy gambling at cards, gluttony, drunkenness, endless talk about one and the same thing. Business that was of no use to anyone and talk about one and the same thing absorbed the greater part of one's time and energy, and what was left in the end was a sort of dock-tailed, barren life, a sort of nonsensical existence, and it was impossible to escape from it, just as though you were in a lunatic asylum or a convict chain-gang!

Gurov lay awake all night, fretting and fuming, and had a splitting headache the whole of the next day. The following nights too he slept badly, sitting up in bed thinking, or walking up and down his room. He was tired of his children, tired of the bank, he did not feel like going out anywhere or talking about anything.

In December, during the Christmas holidays, he packed his things, told his wife that he was going to Petersburg to get a job for a young man he knew, and set off for the town of S——. Why? He had no very clear idea himself. He wanted to see Anna Sergeyevna, to talk to her, to arrange a meeting, if possible.

He arrived in S—— in the morning and took the best room in a hotel, with a fitted carpet of military grey cloth and an inkstand grey with dust on the table, surmounted by a horseman with raised hand and no head. The hall porter supplied him with all the necessary information: Von Diederitz lived in a house of his own in Old Potter's Street, not far from the hotel. He lived well, was rich, kept his own carriage horses, the whole town knew him. The hall-porter pronounced the name: Dridiritz.

Gurov took a leisurely walk down Old Potter's Street and found the house. In front of it was a long grey fence studded with upturned nails.

'A fence like that would make anyone wish to run away,' thought Gurov, scanning the windows and the fence.

As it was a holiday, he thought, her husband was probably at home. It did not matter either way, though, for he could not very well embarrass her by calling at the house. If he were to send in a note it might fall into the hands of the husband and ruin everything. The best thing was to rely on chance. And he kept walking up and down the street and along the fence, waiting for his chance. He watched a beggar enter the gate and the dogs attack him; then, an hour later, he heard the faint indistinct sounds of a piano. That must have been Anna Sergeyevna playing. Suddenly the front door opened and an old woman came out, followed by the familiar white pomeranian. Gurov was about to call to the dog, but his heart began to beat violently and in his excitement he could not remember its name.

He went on walking up and down the street, hating the grey fence more and more, and he was already saying to himself that Anna Sergeyevna had forgotten him and had perhaps been having a good time with someone else, which was indeed quite natural for a young woman who had to look at that damned fence from morning till night. He went back to his hotel room and sat on the sofa for a long time, not knowing what to do, then he had dinner and after dinner a long sleep.

'How stupid and disturbing it all is,' he thought, waking up and staring at the dark windows: it was already evening. 'Well, I've had a good sleep, so what now? What am I going to do tonight?'

He sat on a bed covered by a cheap grey blanket looking exactly like a hospital blanket, and taunted himself in vexation:

'A *lady* with a lapdog! Some adventure, I must say! Serves you right!'

At the railway station that morning he had noticed a poster announcing in huge letters the first performance of *The Geisha Girl* at the local theatre. He recalled it now, and decided to go to the theatre.

'Quite possibly she goes to first nights,' he thought.

The theatre was full. As in all provincial theatres, there was a mist over the chandeliers and the people in the gallery kept up a noisy and excited conversation; in the first row of the stalls stood the local dandies with their hands crossed behind their backs; here, too, in the front seat of the Governor's box, sat the Governor's daughter, wearing a feather boa, while the Governor himself hid modestly behind the portière so that only his hands were visible; the curtain stirred, the orchestra took a long time tuning up. Gurov scanned the audience eagerly as they filed in and occupied their seats.

Anna Sergeyevna came in too. She took her seat in the third row, and when Gurov glanced at her his heart missed a beat and he realized clearly that there was no one in the world nearer and dearer or more important to him than that little woman with the stupid lorgnette in her hand, who was in no way remarkable. That woman lost in a provincial crowd now filled his whole life, was his misfortune, his joy, and the only happiness that he wished for himself. Listening to the bad orchestra and the wretched violins played by second-rate musicians, he thought how beautiful she was. He thought and dreamed.

A very tall, round-shouldered young man with small whiskers had come in with Anna Sergeyevna and sat down beside her; he nodded at every step he took and seemed to be continually bowing to someone. This was probably her husband, whom in a fit of bitterness at Yalta she had called a flunkey. And indeed there was something of a lackey's obsequiousness in his lank figure, his whiskers, and the little bald spot on the top of his head. He smiled sweetly, and the gleaming insignia of some scientific society which he wore in his buttonhole looked like the number on a waiter's coat.

In the first interval the husband went out to smoke and she was left in her seat. Gurov, who also had a seat in the stalls, went up to her and said in a trembling voice and with a forced smile:

'Good evening!'

She looked up at him and turned pale, then looked at him again in panic, unable to believe her eyes, clenching her fan and lorgnette in her hand and apparently trying hard not to fall into a dead faint. Both were silent. She sat and he stood, frightened by her embarrassment and not daring to sit down beside her. The violinists and the flautist began tuning their instruments, and they suddenly felt terrified, as though they were being watched from all the boxes. But a moment later she got up and walked rapidly towards one of the exits; he followed her, and both of them walked aimlessly along corridors and up and down stairs. Figures in all sorts of uniforms—lawyers, teachers, civil servants, all wearing badges—flashed by them; ladies, fur coats hanging on pegs, the cold draught bringing with it the odour of cigarette-ends. Gurov, whose heart was beating violently, thought:

'Oh Lord, what are all these people, that orchestra, doing here?'

At that moment he suddenly remembered how after seeing Anna Sergeyevna off he had told himself that evening at the station that all was over and that they would never meet again. But how far they still were from the end!

She stopped on a dark, narrow staircase with a notice over it: 'To the Upper Circle.'

'How you frightened me!' she said, breathing heavily, still looking pale and stunned. 'Oh dear, how you frightened me! I'm scarcely alive. Why did you come? Why?'

'But, please, try to understand, Anna,' he murmured hurriedly. 'I beg you, please, try to understand. . . .'

She looked at him with fear, entreaty, love, looked at him intently, so as to fix his features firmly in her mind.

'I've suffered so much,' she went on, without listening to him. 'I've been thinking of you all the time. The thought of you kept me alive. And yet I tried so hard to forget you—why, oh why did you come?'

On the landing above two schoolboys were smoking and looking down, but Gurov did not care. He drew Anna Sergeyevna towards him and began kissing her face, her lips, her hands.

'What are you doing? What are you doing?' she said in horror, pushing him away. 'We've both gone mad. You must go back tonight, this minute. I implore you, by all that's sacred . . . Somebody's coming!'

Somebody was coming up the stairs.

'You must go back,' continued Anna Sergeyevna in a whisper. 'Do you hear? I'll come to you in Moscow. I've never been happy, I'm unhappy now, and I shall never be happy, never! So please don't make me suffer still more. I swear I'll come to you in Moscow. But now we must part. Oh, my sweet, my darling, we must part!'

She pressed his hand and went quickly down the stairs, looking back at him all the time, and he could see from the expression in her eyes that she really was unhappy. Gurov stood listening for a short time, and when all was quiet he went to look for his coat and left the theatre.

IV

Anna Sergeyevna began going to Moscow to see him. Every two or three months she left the town of S——, telling her husband that she was going to consult a Moscow gynaecologist, and her husband believed and did not believe her. In Moscow she stayed at the Slav Bazaar and immediately sent a porter in a red cap to inform Gurov of her arrival. Gurov went to her hotel, and no one in Moscow knew about it.

One winter morning he went to her hotel as usual (the porter had called with his message at his house the evening before, but he had not been in). He had his daughter with him, and he was glad of the opportunity of taking her to school, which was on the way to the hotel. Snow was falling in thick wet flakes.

'It's three degrees above zero,' Gurov was saying to his daughter, 'and yet it's snowing. But then, you see, it's only warm on the earth's surface, in the upper layers of the atmosphere the temperature's quite different.'

'Why isn't there any thunder in winter, Daddy?'

He explained that, too. As he was speaking, he kept thinking that he was going to meet his mistress and not a living soul knew about it. He led a double life: one for all who were interested to see, full of conventional truth and conventional deception, exactly like the lives of his friends and acquaintances; and another which went on in secret. And by a kind of strange concatenation of circumstances, possibly quite by accident, everything that was important, interesting, essential, everything about which he was sincere and did not deceive himself, everything that made up the quintessence of his life, went on in secret, while everything that was a lie, everything that was merely the husk in which he hid himself to conceal the truth, like his work at the bank, for instance, his discussions at the club, his ideas of the lower breed, his going to anniversary functions with his wife—all that happened in the sight of all. He judged others by himself, did not believe what he saw, and was always of the opinion that every man's real and most interesting life went on in secret, under cover of night. The personal, private life of an individual was kept a secret, and perhaps that was partly the reason why civilized man was so anxious that his personal secrets should be respected.

Having seen his daughter off to her school, Gurov went to the Slav Bazaar. He took off his fur coat in the cloakroom, went upstairs, and knocked softly on the door. Anna Sergeyevna, wearing the grey dress he liked most, tired out by her journey and by the suspense of waiting for him, had been expecting him since the evening before; she was pale, looked at him without smiling, but was in his arms the moment he went into the room. Their kiss was long and lingering, as if they had not seen each other for two years.

'Well,' he asked, 'how are you getting on there? Anything new?'

'Wait, I'll tell you in a moment. . . . I can't . . .'

She could not speak because she was crying. She turned away from him and pressed her handkerchief to her eyes.

'Well, let her have her cry,' he thought, sitting down in an armchair. 'I'll wait.'

Then he rang the bell and ordered tea; while he was having his tea, she was still standing there with her face to the window. She wept because she could not control her emotions, because she was bitterly conscious of the fact that their life was so sad: they could only meet in secret, they had to hide from people, like thieves! Was not their life ruined?

'Please, stop crying!' he said.

It was quite clear to him that their love would not come to an end for a long time, if ever. Anna Sergeyevna was getting attached to him more and more strongly, she worshipped him, and it would have been absurd to tell her that all this would have to come to an end one day. She would not have believed it, anyway.

He went up to her and took her by the shoulders, wishing to be nice to her, to make her smile; and at that moment he caught sight of himself in the looking glass.

His hair was already beginning to turn grey. It struck him as strange that he should have aged so much, that he should have lost his good looks in the last few years. The shoulders on which his hands lay were warm and quivering. He felt so sorry for this life, still so warm and beautiful, but probably soon to fade and wilt like his own. Why did she love him so? To women he always seemed different from what he was, and they loved in him not himself, but the man their imagination conjured up and whom they had eagerly been looking for all their lives; and when they discovered their mistake they still loved him. And not one of them had ever been happy with him. Time had passed, he had met women, made love to them, parted from them, but not once had he been in love; there had been everything between them, but no love.

It was only now, when his hair was beginning to turn grey, that he had fallen in love properly, in good earnest—for the first time in his life.

He and Anna Sergeyevna loved each other as people do who are very dear and near, as man and wife or close friends love each other; they could not help feeling that fate itself had intended them for one another, and they were unable to understand why he should have a wife and she a husband; they were like two migrating birds, male and female, who had been caught and forced to live in separate cages. They had forgiven each other what they had been ashamed of in the past, and forgave each other everything in their present, and felt that this love of theirs had changed them both.

Before, when he felt depressed, he had comforted himself by all sorts of arguments that happened to occur to him on the spur of the moment, but now he had more serious things to think of, he felt profound compassion, he longed to be sincere, tender. . . .

'Don't cry, my sweet,' he said. 'That'll do, you've had your cry. . . . Let's talk now, let's think of something.'

Then they had a long talk. They tried to think how they could get rid of the necessity of hiding, telling lies, living in different towns, not seeing one another for so long. How were they to free themselves from their intolerable chains?

'How? How?' he asked himself, clutching at his head. 'How?'

And it seemed to them that in only a few more minutes a solution would be found and a new, beautiful life would begin; but both of them knew very well that the end was still a long, long way away and that the most complicated and difficult part was only just beginning.

Translated by David Magarshack

QUESTIONS

1. How do we view Gurov and Anna at the time of their first encounter? By what stages does our view change? How do we see them at the end of the story?

2. How does Chekhov use settings and descriptive touches to set mood? Give examples.

3. Compare Chekhov's evocations of Yalta and St. Petersburg. How is it that we see Gurov differently against different backgrounds?

4. How does Chekhov indicate change in Gurov's feelings toward Anna? Is there a moment of transition? Isolate the passage and comment on its significance.

5. Explain how the story depends upon a set of moral constraints (and societal rules). Could it be written today? Compare it to Joyce Carol Oates's "The Lady with the Pet Dog." What are the fundamental differences?

6. How do our responses to Gurov and to Anna change. What does Chekhov want us to feel at the end—empathy, pity, or gratification?

7. Does Gurov believe that their love will survive societal obstacles and the passage of time? What do we believe? Explain your answer.

8. How does Chekhov use well-chosen details to illuminate the largest situation? Pick a scene and show how he lets specific descriptions do the important work of suggestion.

3

THE MODERN AGE

In her essay "Mr. Brown and Mrs. Bennett" Virginia Woolf wrote, "On or about December 1910, human character changed."

The words have been cited frequently, probably because they capture a feeling shared by many of Woolf's contemporaries: simply, that the rhythm of history—indeed, the very *feel* of life—changed suddenly in the early years of the twentieth century.

The outbreak of World War I in 1914 is usually seen as the watershed event. The largest and bloodiest conflict ever known could not but provoke a complete rethinking of societal purpose and of the human capacity for doing injury to our own kind. But it is not enough to point to that one cataclysm as the cause for all that followed. The war itself was caused by a broad array of forces that had been gathering momentum in the preceding decades. The rise of industrialism throughout the Western nations had brought about fierce competition for control over the resource-rich territories of Africa and Asia. At the same time, many of the imperial powers felt the strain of internal unrest. In 1905 there was an unsuccessful revolution against the Russian czar, a challenge to absolute monarchy that would succeed in 1917. Ethnic factions within the great Austro-Hungarian Empire grew increasingly militant about their claims for independence. In fact, it was the assassination of Austria's Archduke Ferdinand by a Serbian nationalist that sparked off the conflagration later known as the Great War.

But there were changes brewing on other fronts as well. At the end of the nineteenth century, the German philosopher Friedrich Nietzsche wrote that "God is dead" and raised a call for the complete reform of all values. He held that we could no longer look to God for solace and a sense of meaning, that we must henceforth accept that we are alone on the earth, and that all value and purpose must be grounded in the human. Nietzsche was, in effect, giving voice to a sense of skepticism that had been growing since the eighteenth-century Enlightenment, a skepticism that had everything to do with the spread of scientific materialism and rationalism.

In 1900 the Viennese psychologist Sigmund Freud published his now-legendary study *The Interpretation of Dreams*. To many, this represented yet another advance of the Godless perspective. In this work and in other studies that followed, Freud established the groundwork for a science of the psyche. Human actions could now be examined and explained in terms of a complex, dynamic internal functioning. Freud gave us our first coherent conception of the unconscious, the field of energies and drives that underlies and often resists rational decision making. Where once we looked outward, to gods and spirits, for clues about our mysterious urges and feelings (for centuries people were felt to be the pawns of godly and evil forces), now we began to look inward.

One could go on at great length trying to account for the myriad changes affecting the public and private spheres. Suffice it to say that a great many shifts of degree converged and brought about a shift of kind. We must take Virginia Woolf's pronouncement on faith: in quite a short time the world was felt to have altered its nature. Things happened more quickly. Surprise and fear were in the air. People could no longer look to the future with confidence, for the ground upon which they had walked unthinkingly began to move under their feet.

This was the climate in which modernity was spawned, not only in Europe. The United States was in the throes of its own industrial expansion; soon enough it would join England and France in the war against the Germans. In the East, Japan was shaking free of long centuries of feudalism and testing itself as an industrial and imperial power. Smaller conflicts—the African Boer War, fought between the Dutch and English in 1899, the Russian-Japanese War, which broke out in 1904—could be read as signs of intensifying global tensions.

As may be expected, it was the artists (often referred to as the "antennae of the race") who picked up and registered the disturbances in the air. In the music of Igor Stravinsky we can hear the first break with traditional harmonic ideals; in painting, revolutionaries like Picasso, Braque, and Duchamp shattered the conventions of representation, producing works with fragmented and disrupted surfaces. Nor did writers continue as before. Indeed, the transformations made by poets, dramatists, novelists, and short story writers gave a whole new definition to literature. Modernism was born.

The modern spirit affected the short story profoundly. Although scholars and literary historians may quibble over the fine points, one can safely venture that the familiar realist tradition of the nineteenth century underwent a threefold alteration.

First, there was a significant change of focus. The narratives of the oral and early written traditions focused, as we know, outward and dramatic events. Heroes had adventures, lovers met with violent and tragic ends, and fantastic and improbable events transpired. The stories of the eighteenth and nineteenth centuries, by contrast, tended to be realistic, taking place in the familiar world and often revolving around daily occurrences; the characters were by and large antiheroic.

In modern stories we still read about ordinary men and women, and the settings and situations are, with certain key exceptions, still familiar ones. But we now encounter a preoccupation with inwardness. Where the realists contented themselves mainly with portraying the outer contours of character and action, the modernists seek to peer inside. They are concerned with inner process, with the mysteries of motivation and memory. Their ambition is, at least in part, to capture the complexity of the inner life. Of course, the progress of literature is not to be measured in tidy categories. There were premodern writers, like Henry James, Nathaniel Hawthorne, Anton Chekhov, and others, who were fascinated by the psychological dimension. And we can point to modernists like Hemingway who make little use of the language of inwardness. All the same, the broad tendency is readily identifiable.

Because Sigmund Freud was doing some of the first pioneering work in psychological science at this time, we should not therefore conclude that modern writers are all good Freudians. To the contrary, many of them proclaim their irritation with the analytic pigeon-holding to which psychologists so often resort. (D. H. Lawrence, whose first novel, *Sons and Lovers*, is a perfect illustration of Freud's theory of the Oedipus complex, himself refused to read Freud.) We could say that Freud sought to probe by scientific means what writers and artists were pursuing intuitively. It would seem that the historical moment for the concerted exploration of the self had finally come. One has only to read works of the period by James Joyce *(Ulysses)*, Marcel Proust *(Remembrance of Things Past)*, Virginia Woolf *(To the Lighthouse)*, and others to appreciate what strenuous efforts were being made to find a language for what we experience inside. Woolf's story "Moments of Being" will shock the reader who is only accustomed to realist modes of presentation. Woolf holds a powerful magnifying glass to a seemingly inconsequential moment in her protagonist's life and transcribes movements and textures of extreme complexity.

A second significant transformation in the short story was thematic. While writers have always given voice to the dark and violent side of human nature—think of Hawthorne, Poe, or even Boccaccio and Apuleius—the eruptions have usually occurred within a framework of a sensible human order. Characters, driven by rage, lust, or ambition, exceed their proper bounds; they are generally punished in some fashion. In the premodern stories we are aware of a coherent moral scheme a universe that makes sense and that is, more often than not, presided over by some deity. But the modernist sensibility is schooled in Nietzsche, in a skepticism that denies any higher anchoring of values. Whereas formerly it was believed that "Man proposes, God disposes," the new variation became "Man proposes, man disposes." The modernists feel that behind our actions lies an unpopulated darkness. This darkness falls like a shadow over a good deal of the art of our age.

In Katherine Mansfield's "The Garden Party," for instance, a young girl is brought face-to-face not only with death but also with the disquieting realization that the worst of tragedies can happen right alongside the grandest moments of gaiety. Franz Kafka's protagonist in "The Hunger Artist" finds that no illusion can stand up against the fact of human indifference to the sufferings of others. While not every selection in this part is quite so dark, most can be said to face up to the harsher human realities with an unflinching gaze.

Finally, the modern short story avails itself of tremendous artistic freedom. Changed circumstances mean changed rules. Writers can make use of whatever approaches they need in order to create the effects they desire. While James Joyce and William Faulkner make use of traditional modes of scene setting, others elect to depart from the norms. Zora Neale Hurston tells a story of a horrible death and retribution in short, carefully controlled scenes, relying almost entirely on dialogue. Eudora Welty gives us the inner life of a blues piano player ("Powerhouse") using the choppy, syncopated rhythms that suggest the pounding of chords. Jorge Luis Borges relates the most fantastical of imaginings in the cool, descriptive tones of a man of science ("The Aleph").

As a whole, these stories make clear the modern pattern. Whether in 1910, as Virginia Woolf affirmed, or later, some enormous change has befallen us. The modernists are our witnesses and interpreters; we read them to find points of reference in the busy chaos surrounding us.

Virginia Woolf

Virginia Woolf (1882–1941) is not known primarily as a short story writer, but her influence upon the tradition of literary modernism is so great that some sample of her work should be included in an anthology of short fiction. She was, to put it simply, one of the leading artistic revolutionaries of her time, and her novels and essays challenged the myth of male supremacy in the realm of letters.

Woolf was the daughter of Sir Leslie Stephen, editor of the enormous *Dictionary of Literary Biography* and one of the leading figures in the intellectual life of late Victorian England. She grew up among books and paintings and the table talk of the best thinkers of her time. She and her husband, the writer and philosopher Leonard Woolf, whom she married in 1912, went on to establish one of the leading intellectual circles of their own day around their home in London's Bloomsbury district. Among their intimates were the novelist E. M. Forster, the biographer Lytton Strachey, the economist John Maynard Keynes, the philosopher Bertrand Russell, and the poet T. S. Eliot.

In 1917 the Woolfs founded the Hogarth Press, which became one of the premier publishing ventures of the century. The press not only printed works by the leading writers and thinkers of the day but also became Virginia Woolf's own channel to publication. Among the novels published under the Hogarth imprint were *Jacob's Room* (1922), *Mrs. Dalloway* (1925), *To the Lighthouse* (1927), and *The Waves* (1931), all works sufficiently experimental to have made publication elsewhere unlikely.

For all her success and cultural influence, Woolf was not a happy woman. She suffered keenly from the exclusions that came with being a woman and vented her thoughts on feminist issues in *A Room of One's Own* (1929) and *Three Guineas* (1938), both of which have in recent years become bibles of the women's movement. But Woolf also fell prey to bouts of melancholic depression that were often so severe as to lead her to the brink of suicide. Her writing, she avowed, was a means for coping with her malady, a valve. Alas, for all its brilliance, it was not enough. In 1941 she committed suicide by drowning.

We need only read a page or two of Woolf's prose to grasp the pitch of her sensitivity. Her sentences, musical and interior, give the impression of having been written with the nerve endings. The prose very nearly quivers—there is not a wasted syllable.

Woolf was not interested in pursuing the traditional aims of fiction. She cared little for devising plot or documenting social clashes. Her entire focus was upon the beauty and mystery of consciousness, and she convoked her words and images with the express intent of reproducing the "feel" of the inner life. Critics, naturally, complained about the absence of the traditional elements in her fiction, but her literary peers and several generations of discriminating readers have found that her work brims over with the rich sap of subjective consciousness.

"Moments of Being" is a fine example of the Woolf approach. She opens up the container of a moment, finding it to be like a system of Chinese boxes. The piece, short as it is, requires several careful readings to appreciate its special magic.

MOMENTS OF BEING

Slater's pins have no points—don't you always find that?" said Miss Craye, turning round as the rose fell out of Fanny Wilmot's dress, and Fanny stooped, with her ears full of the music, to look for the pin on the floor.

The words gave her an extraordinary shock, as Miss Craye struck the last chord of the Bach fugue. Did Miss Craye actually go to Slater's and buy pins then, Fanny Wilmot asked herself, transfixed for a moment. Did she stand at the counter waiting like anybody else, and was she given a bill with coppers wrapped in it, and did she slip them into her purse and then, an hour later, stand by her dressing table and take out the pins? What need had she of pins? For she was not so much dressed as cased, like a beetle compactly in its sheath, blue in winter, green in summer. What need had she of pins—Julia Craye—who lived, it seemed in the cool glassy world of Bach fugues, playing to herself what she liked, and only consenting to take one or two pupils at the Archer Street College of Music (so the Principal, Miss Kingston, said) as a special favor to herself, who had "the greatest admiration for her in every way." Miss Craye was left badly off, Miss Kingston was afraid, at her brother's death. Oh, they used to have such lovely things, when they lived at Salisbury, and her brother Julius was, of course, a very well-known man: a famous archaeologist. It was a great privilege to stay with them, Miss Kingston said ("My family had always known them—they were regular Canterbury people," Miss Kingston said), but a little frightening for a child; one had to be careful not to slam the door or bounce into the room unexpectedly. Miss Kingston, who gave little character sketches like this on the first day of term while she received cheques and wrote out receipts for them, smiled here. Yes, she had been rather a tomboy; she had bounced in and set all those green Roman glasses and things jumping in their case. The Crayes were not used to children. The Crayes were none of them married. They kept cats; the cats, one used to feel, knew as much about the Roman urns and things as anybody.

"Far more than I did!" said Miss Kingston brightly, writing her name across the stamp in her dashing, cheerful, full-bodied hand, for she had always been practical. That was how she made her living, after all.

Perhaps then, Fanny Wilmot thought, looking for the pin, Miss Craye said that about "Slater's pins having no points," at a venture. None of the Crayes had ever married. She knew nothing about pins—nothing whatever. But she wanted to break the spell that had fallen on the house; to break the pane of glass which separated them from other people. When Polly Kingston, that merry little girl, had slammed the door and made the Roman vases jump, Julius, seeing that no harm was done (that would be his first instinct) looked, for the case was stood in the window, at Polly skipping home across the fields; looked with the look his sister often had, that lingering, driving look.

"Stars, sun, moon," it seemed to say, "the daisy in the grass, fires, frost on the window pane, my heart goes out to you. But," it always seemed to add, "you break, you pass, you go." And simultaneously it covered the intensity of both these states of mind with "I can't reach you—I can't get at you," spoken wistfully, frustratedly. And the stars faded, and the child went. That was the kind of spell that was the glassy surface, that Miss Craye wanted to break by showing, when she had played Bach beautifully as a reward to a favorite pupil (Fanny Wilmot knew that she was Miss Craye's favorite pupil), that she, too, knew, like other people, about pins. Slater's pins had no points.

Yes, the "famous archaeologist" had looked like that too. "The famous archaeologist"—as she said that, endorsing cheques, ascertaining the day of the month, speaking so brightly and frankly, there was in Miss Kingston's voice an indescribable tone which hinted at something odd; something queer in Julius Craye; it was the very same thing that was odd perhaps in Julia too. One could have sworn, thought Fanny Wilmot, as she looked for the pin, that at parties, meetings (Miss Kingston's father was a clergyman), she had picked up some piece of gossip, or it might only have been a smile, or a tone when his name was mentioned, which had given her "a feeling" about Julius Craye. Needless to say, she had never spoken about it to anybody. Probably she scarcely knew what she meant by it. But whenever she spoke of Julius, or heard him mentioned, that was the first thing that came to mind; and it was a seductive thought; there was something odd about Julius Craye.

It was so that Julia looked too, as she sat half turned on the music stool, smiling. It's on the field, it's on the pane, it's in the sky—beauty; and I can't get at it; I can't have it—I, she seemed to add, with that little clutch of the hand which was so characteristic, who adore it so passionately, would give the whole world to possess it! And she picked up the carnation which had fallen on the floor, while Fanny searched for the pin. She crushed it, Fanny felt, voluptuously in her smooth veined hands stuck about with water-colored rings set in pearls. The pressure of her fingers seemed to increase all that was most brilliant in the flower; to set it off; to make it more frilled, fresh, immaculate. What was odd in her, and perhaps in her brother, too, was that this crush and grasp of the finger was combined with a perpetual frustration. So it was even now with the carnation. She had her hands on it; she pressed it; but she did not possess it, enjoy it, not entirely and altogether.

None of the Crayes had married, Fanny Wilmot remembered. She had in mind how one evening when the lesson had lasted longer than usual and it was dark, Julia Craye had said "it's the use of men, surely, to protect us," smiling at her that same odd smile, as she stood fastening her cloak, which made her, like the flower, conscious to her finger tips of youth and brilliance, but, like the flower, too, Fanny suspected, made her feel awkward.

"Oh, but I don't want protection," Fanny had laughed, and when Julia Craye, fixing on her that extraordinary look, had said she was not so sure of that, Fanny positively blushed under the admiration in her eyes.

It was the only use of men, she had said. Was it for that reason then, Fanny wondered, with her eyes on the floor, that she had never married? After all, she had not lived all her life in Salisbury. "Much the nicest part of London," she had said once, "(but I'm speaking of fifteen or twenty years ago) is Kensington. One was in the Gardens in ten minutes—it was like the heart of the country. One could dine out in one's slippers without catching cold. Kensington—it was like a village then, you know," she had said.

Here she broke off, to denounce acridly the draughts in the Tubes.

"It was the use of men," she had said, with a queer wry acerbity. Did that throw any light on the problem why she had not married? One could imagine every sort of scene in her youth, when with her good blue eyes, her straight firm nose, her air of cool distinction, her piano playing, her rose flowering with chaste passion in the bosom of her muslin dress, she had attracted first the young men to whom such things, the china tea cups and the silver candlesticks and the inlaid table, for the Crayes had such nice things, were wonderful; young men not sufficiently distinguished; young men of the cathedral town with ambitions. She had attracted them first, and then her brother's friends from Oxford or Cambridge. They would come down in the summer; row her on the river; continue the argument about Browning by letter; and arrange perhaps, on the rare occasions when she stayed in London, to show her—Kensington Gardens?

"Much the nicest part of London—Kensington (I'm speaking of fifteen or twenty years ago)," she had said once. One was in the gardens in ten minutes—in the heart of the country. One could make that yield what one liked, Fanny Wilmot thought, single out, for instance, Mr. Sherman, the painter, an old friend of hers; make him call for her, by appointment, one sunny day in June; take her to have tea under the trees. (They had met, too, at those parties to which one tripped in slippers without fear of catching cold.) The aunt or other elderly relative was to wait there while they looked at the Serpentine. They looked at the Serpentine. He may have rowed her across. They compared it with with the Avon. She would have considered the comparison very furiously. Views of rivers were important to her. She sat hunched a little, a little angular, though she was graceful then, steering. At the critical moment, for he had determined that he must speak now—it was his only chance of getting her alone—he was speaking with his head turned at an absurd angle, in his great nervousness, over his shoulder—at that very moment she interrupted fiercely. He would have them into the Bridge, she cried. It was a moment of horror, of disillusionment, of revelation, for both of them. I can't have it, I can't possess it, she thought. He could not see why she had come then. With a great splash of his oar he pulled the boat round. Merely to snub him? He rowed her back and said good-bye to her.

The setting of that scene could be varied as one chose, Fanny Wilmot reflected. (Where had that pin fallen?) It might be Ravenna; or Edinburgh, where she had kept house for her brother. The scene could be changed; and the young man and the exact manner of it all, but one thing was constant—her refusal, and her frown, and her anger with herself afterwards, and her argument, and her relief—yes, certainly her immense relief. The very next day, perhaps, she would get up at six, put on her cloak, and walk all the way from Kensington to the river. She was so thankful that she had not sacrificed her right to go and look at things when they are at their best—before people are up, that is to say she could have her breakfast in bed if she liked. She had not sacrificed her independence.

Yes, Fanny Wilmot smiled, Julia had not endangered her habits. They remained safe; and her habits would have suffered if she had married. "They're ogres," she had said one evening, half laughing, when another pupil, a girl lately married, suddenly bethinking her that she would miss her husband, had rushed off in haste.

"They're ogres," she had said, laughing grimly. An ogre would have interfered perhaps with breakfast in bed; with walks at dawn down to the river. What would have happened (but one could hardly conceive this) had she had children? She took astonishing precautions against chills, fatigue, rich food, the wrong food, draughts, heated rooms, journeys in the Tube, for she could never determine which of these it was exactly that brought on those terrible headaches that gave her life the semblance of a battlefield. She was always engaged in outwitting the enemy, until it seemed as if the pursuit had its interest; could she have beaten the enemy finally she would have found life a little dull. As it was, the tug-of-war was perpetual—on the one side the nightingale or the view which she loved with passion—yes, for views and birds she felt nothing less than passion; on the other the damp path or the horrid long drag up a steep hill which would certainly make her good for nothing next day and bring on one of her headaches. When, therefore, from time to time, she managed her forces adroitly and brought off a visit to Hampton Court the week the crocuses—those glossy bright flowers were her favorite—were at their best, it was a victory. It was something that lasted; something that mattered forever. She strung the afternoon on the necklace of memorable days, which was not too long for her to be able to recall this one or that one; this view, that city; to finger it, to feel it, to savor, sighing, the quality that made it unique.

"It was so beautiful last Friday," she said, "that I determined I must go there." So she had gone off to Waterloo on her great undertaking—to visit Hampton Court—alone. Naturally, but perhaps foolishly, one pitied her for the thing she never asked pity for (indeed she was reticent habitually, speaking of her health only as a warrior might speak of her foe)—one pitied her for always doing everything alone. Her brother was dead. Her sister was asthmatic. She found the climate of Edinburgh good for her. It was too bleak for Julia. Perhaps, too, she found the associations painful, for her brother, the famous archaeologist, had died there; and she had loved her brother. She lived in a little house off the Brompton Road entirely alone.

Fanny Wilmot saw the pin; she picked it up. She looked at Miss Craye. Was Miss Craye so lonely? No, Miss Craye was steadily, blissfully, if only for that moment, a happy woman. Fanny had surprised her in a moment of ecstasy. She sat there, half turned away from the piano, with her hands clasped in her lap holding the carnation upright, while behind her was the sharp square of the window, uncurtained, purple in the evening, intensely purple after the brilliant electric lights which burnt unshaded in the bare music room. Julia Craye, sitting hunched and compact holding her flower, seemed to emerge out of the London night, seemed to fling it like a cloak behind her, it seemed, in its bareness and intensity, the effluence of her spirit, something she had made which surrounded her. Fanny stared.

All seemed transparent, for a moment, to the gaze of Fanny Wilmot, as if looking through Miss Craye, she saw the very fountain of her being spurting its pure silver drops. She saw back and back into the past behind her. She saw the green Roman vases stood in their case; heard the choristers playing cricket; saw Julia quietly descend the curving steps on to the lawn; then saw her pour out tea beneath the cedar tree; softly enclosed the old man's hand in hers; saw her going round and about the corridors of that ancient Cathedral dwelling place with towels in her hand to mark them; lamenting, as she went, the pettiness of daily life; and slowly aging, and putting away clothes when summer came, because at her age they were too bright to wear; and tending her father's sickness; and cleaving her way ever more definitely as her will stiffened toward her solitary goal; travelling frugally; counting the cost and measuring out of her tight shut purse the sum needed for this journey or for that old mirror; obstinately adhering, what ever people might say, in choosing her pleasures for herself. She saw Julia——

Julia blazed. Julia kindled. Out of the night she burnt like a dead white star. Julia opened her arms. Julia kissed her on the lips. Julia possessed it.

"Slater's pins have no points," Miss Craye said, laughing queerly and relaxing her arms, as Fanny Wilmot pinned the flower to her breast with trembling fingers.

QUESTIONS

1. What is the actual time span of the story? How does Woolf manage to create a narrative within such a limited frame?
2. How does Woolf engineer her transitions? What strategies does she employ to create a sense of expanded time?
3. What is the function of music within the story? Consider its symbolic and structural importance.
4. What are the repeated elements of this story, and how do they function?
5. How are we to see Fanny? What is her role, and how does her character differ from Miss Wilmot's? Characterize the relationship between Fanny and Miss Wilmot.
6. How are men characterized in this story? In what ways might this be considered an early statement of feminist consciousness?
7. How does Woolf create a sense of a vanished culture? What are the values represented by the Wilmots?
8. How does Woolf create the sensations of the flow of consciousness?
9. Are we to see Miss Wilmot as tragic or heroic? Explain.
10. Comment on Woolf's use of images, similes, and metaphors. Use specific examples.

James Joyce

It was said after the publication of James Joyce's *Ulysses* (1922) that if the city of Dublin were to vanish from the face of the earth, it would be possible to restore every brick and nail of it by referring to that novel. Similarly, one could argue that if all evidence of literary modernism were destroyed, the works of Joyce would allow us to reconstruct the full development. For in the course of his restless career Joyce (1882–1941) recapitulated the entire literary tradition.

Born in a suburb of Dublin, Joyce received an excellent but erratic education. He studied first with the Jesuit fathers but after a collapse of the family's fortunes spent some years fending for himself. He took a degree from University College in Dublin in 1902.

Joyce's intellectual independence and brilliance were evident from the start. Discovering his facility for languages, he taught himself a dozen. When he conceived an interest in Henrik Ibsen, he quickly mastered Norwegian so that he could read his works in the original.

After graduating from University College, Joyce flirted briefly with the idea of studying medicine. He moved to Paris to attend the College de Médicine but dropped out after one class. (He made excellent use of his medical background, slight though it may have been, in his creation of the character of Buck Mulligan in *Ulysses.*)

Joyce had begun writing while still an adolescent. During his brief sojourn in Paris he worked at a series of sketches based upon overheard conversations and observed encounters. These he called "Epiphanies," and many were artfully threaded into the stories of *Dubliners* (1914) and the novel *A Portrait of the Artist as a Young Man* (1916).

Returning to Dublin to be with his dying mother, Joyce discovered that despite his Irish heritage he could not work freely in the midst of his people. Like Stephen Dedalus, the protagonist in *Portrait*, he decided that he had to escape the nets of place "to forge in the smithy of my soul the uncreated conscience of my race."

Joyce left Ireland in 1904 and never lived there again. Until his death he supported himself and his family in various European cities—Trieste, Zurich, Paris—on a patchwork of financial arrangements. He translated, taught languages, and accepted generous donations from his brother Stanislaus and from the fundraising activities of his great admirer Ezra Pound.

If Joyce's three novels represent an ever more complex (and for the reader difficult) grappling with inner and outer realities, the short stories of *Dubliners* are still quite conventional. Joyce transferred his interest in "Epiphanies" into a more structured format; the moments of sudden awareness are now orchestrated into the unfolding circumstances of his characters. Without ever relinquishing his concern with internal awareness, he brings to bear a scrupulous sense of external detailing. The Dublin settings are full-dimensional, solid and dense, alive down to the motes of dust dancing in the window light.

"The Dead" is Joyce's longest story. With unerring sureness he brings to life an evening in a crowded room. But then with the most disciplined economy he narrows the focus to the figures of Gabriel and Gretta, tracking their thoughts and movements until he has laid bare the tragic memory that must henceforth shape their life together.

THE DEAD

Lily, the caretaker's daughter, was literally run off her feet. Hardly had she brought one gentleman into the little pantry behind the office on the ground floor and helped him off with his overcoat than the wheezy hall-door bell clanged again and she had to scamper along the bare hallway to let in another guest. It was well for her she had not to attend to the ladies also. But Miss Kate and Miss Julia had thought of that and had converted the bathroom upstairs into a ladies' dressing-room. Miss Kate and Miss Julia were there, gossiping and laughing and fussing, walking after each other to the head of the stairs, peering down over the banisters and calling down to Lily to ask her who had come.

It was always a great affair, the Misses Morkan's annual dance. Everybody who knew them came to it, members of the family, old friends of the family, the members of Julia's choir, any of Kate's pupils that were grown up enough, and even some of Mary Jane's pupils too. Never once had it fallen flat. For years and years it had gone off in splendid style, as long as anyone could remember; ever since Kate and Julia, after the death of their brother Pat, had left the house in Stoney Batter and taken Mary Jane, their only niece, to live with them in the dark, gaunt house on Usher's Island, the upper part of which they had rented from Mr. Fulham, the corn-factor on the ground floor. That was a good thirty years ago if it was a day. Mary Jane, who was then a little girl in short clothes, was now the main prop of the household, for she had the organ in Haddington Road. She had been through the Academy and gave a pupils' concert every year in the upper room of the Antient Concert Rooms. Many of her pupils belonged to the better-class families on the Kingstown and Dalkey line. Old as they were, her aunts also did their share. Julia, though she was quite grey, was still the leading soprano in Adam and Eve's, and Kate, being too feeble to go about much, gave music lessons to beginners on the old square piano in the back room. Lily, the caretaker's daughter, did housemaid's work for them. Though their life was modest, they believed in eating well; the best of everything: diamond-bone sirloins, three-shilling tea and the best bottled stout. But Lily seldom made a mistake in the orders, so that she got on well with her three mistresses. They were fussy, that was all. But the only thing they would not stand was back answers.

Of course, they had good reason to be fussy on such a night. And then it was long after ten o'clock and yet there was no sign of Gabriel and his wife. Besides they were dreadfully afraid that Freddy Malins might turn up screwed. They would not wish for worlds that any of Mary Jane's pupils should see him under the influence; and when he was like that it was sometimes very hard to manage him. Freddy Malins always came late, but they wondered what could be keeping Gabriel: and that was what brought them every two minutes to the banisters to ask Lily had Gabriel or Freddy come.

"O, Mr. Conroy," said Lily to Gabriel when she opened the door for him, "Miss Kate and Miss Julia thought you were never coming. Good-night, Mrs. Conroy."

"I'll engage they did," said Gabriel, "but they forget that my wife here takes three mortal hours to dress herself."

He stood on the mat, scraping the snow from his goloshes, while Lily led his wife to the foot of the stairs and called out:

"Miss Kate, here's Mrs. Conroy."

Kate and Julia came toddling down the dark stairs at once. Both of them kissed Gabriel's wife, said she must be perished alive, and asked was Gabriel with her.

"Here I am as right as the mail, Aunt Kate! Go on up. I'll follow," called out Gabriel from the dark.

He continued scraping his feet vigorously while the three women went upstairs, laughing, to the ladies' dressing-room. A light fringe of snow lay like a cape on the shoulders of his overcoat and like toecaps on the toes of his goloshes; and, as the buttons of his overcoat slipped with a squeaking noise through the snow-stiffened frieze, a cold, fragrant air from out-of-doors escaped from crevices and folds.

"Is it snowing again, Mr. Conroy?" asked Lily.

She had preceded him into the pantry to help him off with his overcoat. Gabriel smiled at the three syllables she had given his surname and glanced at her. She was a slim, growing girl, pale in complexion and with hay-coloured hair. The gas in the pantry made her look still paler. Gabriel had known her when she was a child and used to sit on the lowest step nursing a rag doll.

"Yes, Lily," he answered, "and I think we're in for a night of it."

He looked up at the pantry ceiling, which was shaking with the stamping and shuffling of feet on the floor above, listened for a moment to the piano and then glanced at the girl, who was folding his overcoat carefully at the end of a shelf.

"Tell me, Lily," he said in a friendly tone, "do you still go to school?"

"O no, sir," she answered. "I'm done schooling this year and more."

"O, then," said Gabriel gaily, "I suppose we'll be going to your wedding one of these fine days with your young man, eh?"

The girl glanced back at him over her shoulder and said with great bitterness:

"The men that is now is only all palaver and what they can get out of you."

Gabriel coloured, as if he felt he had made a mistake and, without looking at her, kicked off his goloshes and flicked actively with his muffler at his patent-leather shoes.

He was a stout, tallish young man. The high colour of his cheeks pushed upwards even to his forehead, where it scattered itself in a few formless patches of pale red; and on his hairless face there scintillated restlessly the polished lenses and the bright gilt rims of the glasses which screened his delicate and restless eyes. His glossy black hair was parted in the middle and brushed in a long curve behind his ears where it curled slightly beneath the groove left by his hat.

When he had flicked lustre into his shoes he stood up and pulled his waistcoat down more tightly on his plump body. Then he took a coin rapidly from his pocket.

"O Lily," he said, thrusting it into her hands, "it's Christmas-time, isn't it? Just . . . here's a little. . . ."

He walked rapidly towards the door.

"O no, sir!" cried the girl, following him. "Really, sir, I wouldn't take it."

"Christmas-time! Christmas-time!" said Gabriel, almost trotting to the stairs and waving his hand to her in deprecation.

The girl, seeing that he had gained the stairs, called out after him:

"Well, thank you, sir."

He waited outside the drawing-room door until the waltz should finish, listening to the skirts that swept against it and to the shuffling of feet. He was still discomposed by the girl's bitter and sudden retort. It had cast a gloom over him which he tried to dispel by arranging his cuffs and the bows of his tie. He then took from his waistcoat pocket a little paper and glanced at the headings he had made for his speech. He was undecided about the lines from Robert Browning, for he feared they would be above the heads of his hearers. Some quotation that they would recognise from Shakespeare or from the Melodies would be better. The indelicate clacking of the men's heels and the shuffling of their soles reminded him that their grade of culture differed from his. He would only make himself ridiculous by quoting poetry to them which they could not understand. They would think that he was airing his superior education. He would fail with them just as he had failed with the girl in the pantry. He had taken up a wrong tone. His whole speech was a mistake from first to last, an utter failure.

Just then his aunts and his wife came out of the ladies' dressing-room. His aunts were two small, plainly dressed old women. Aunt Julia was an inch or so the taller. Her hair, drawn low over the tops of her ears, was grey; and grey also, with darker shadows, was her large flaccid face. Though she was stout in build and stood erect, her slow eyes and parted lips gave her the appearance of a woman who did not know where she was or where she was going. Aunt Kate was more vivacious. Her face, healthier than her sister's, was all puckers and creases, like a shrivelled red apple, and her hair, braided in the same old-fashioned way, had not lost its ripe nut colour.

They both kissed Gabriel frankly. He was their favourite nephew, the son of their dead elder sister, Ellen, who had married T. J. Conroy of the Port and Docks.

"Gretta tells me you're not going to take a cab back to Monkstown to-night, Gabriel," said Aunt Kate.

"No," said Gabriel, turning to his wife, "we had quite enough of that last year, hadn't we? Don't you remember, Aunt Kate, what a cold Gretta got out of it? Cab windows rattling all the way, and the east wind blowing in after we passed Merrion. Very jolly it was. Gretta caught a dreadful cold."

Aunt Kate frowned severely and nodded her head at every word.

"Quite right, Gabriel, quite right," she said. "You can't be too careful."

"But as for Gretta there," said Gabriel, "she'd walk home in the snow if she were let."

Mrs. Conroy laughed.

"Don't mind him, Aunt Kate," she said. "He's really an awful bother, what with green shades for Tom's eyes at night and making him do the dumb-bells, and forcing Eva to eat the stirabout. The poor child! And she simply hates the sight of it! . . . O, but you'll never guess what he makes me wear now!"

She broke out into a peal of laughter and glanced at her husband, whose admiring and happy eyes had been wandering from her dress to her face and hair. The two aunts laughed heartily, too, for Gabriel's solicitude was a standing joke with them.

"Goloshes!" said Mrs. Conroy. "That's the latest. Whenever it's wet underfoot I must put on my goloshes. To-night even, he wanted me to put them on, but I wouldn't. The next thing he'll buy me will be a diving suit."

Gabriel laughed nervously and patted his tie reassuringly, while Aunt Kate nearly doubled herself, so heartily did she enjoy the joke. The smile soon faded from Aunt Julia's face and her mirthless eyes were directed towards her nephew's face. After a pause she asked:

"And what are goloshes, Gabriel?"

"Goloshes, Julia!" exclaimed her sister. "Goodness me, don't you know what goloshes are? You wear them over your . . . over your boots, Gretta, isn't it?"

"Yes," said Mrs. Conroy. "Guttapercha things. We both have a pair now. Gabriel says everyone wears them on the continent."

"O, on the continent," murmured Aunt Julia, nodding her head slowly.

Gabriel knitted his brows and said, as if he were slightly angered:

"It's nothing very wonderful, but Gretta thinks it very funny because she says the word reminds her of Christy Minstrels."

"But tell me, Gabriel," said Aunt Kate, with brisk tact. "Of course, you've seen about the room. Gretta was saying . . ."

"O, the room is all right," replied Gabriel. "I've taken one in the Gresham."

"To be sure," said Aunt Kate, "by far the best thing to do. And the children, Gretta, you're not anxious about them?"

"O, for one night," said Mrs. Conroy. "Besides, Bessie will look after them."

"To be sure," said Aunt Kate again. "What a comfort it is to have a girl like that, one you can depend on! There's that Lily, I'm sure I don't know what has come over her lately. She's not the girl she was at all."

Gabriel was about to ask his aunt some questions on this point, but she broke off suddenly to gaze after her sister, who had wandered down the stairs and was craning her neck over the banisters.

"Now, I ask you," she said almost testily, "where is Julia going? Julia! Julia! Where are you going?"

Julia, who had gone half way down one flight, came back and announced blandly:

"Here's Freddy."

At the same moment a clapping of hands and a final flourish of the pianist told that the waltz had ended. The drawing-room door was opened from within and some couples came out. Aunt Kate drew Gabriel aside hurriedly and whispered into his ear:

"Slip down, Gabriel, like a good fellow and see if he's all right, and don't let him up if he's screwed. I'm sure he's screwed. I'm sure he is."

Gabriel went to the stairs and listened over the banisters. He could hear two persons talking in the pantry. Then he recognised Freddy Malins' laugh. He went down the stairs noisily.

"It's such a relief," said Aunt Kate to Mrs. Conroy, "that Gabriel is here. I always feel easier in my mind when he's here. . . . Julia, there's Miss Daly and Miss Power will take some refreshment. Thanks for your beautiful waltz, Miss Daly. It made lovely time."

A tall wizen-faced man, with a stiff grizzled moustache and swarthy skin, who was passing out with his partner, said:

"And may we have some refreshment, too, Miss Morkan?"

"Julia," said Aunt Kate summarily, "and here's Mr. Browne and Miss Furlong. Take them in, Julia, with Miss Daly and Miss Power."

"I'm the man for the ladies," said Mr. Browne, pursing his lips until his moustache bristled and smiling in all his wrinkles. "You know, Miss Morkan, the reason they are so fond of me is——"

He did not finish his sentence, but, seeing that Aunt Kate was out of earshot, at once led the three young ladies into the back room. The middle of the room was occupied by two square tables placed end to end, and on these Aunt Julia and the caretaker were straightening and smoothing a large cloth. On the sideboard were arrayed dishes and plates, and glasses and bundles of knives and forks and spoons. The top of the closed square piano served also as a sideboard for viands and sweets. At a smaller sideboard in one corner two young men were standing, drinking hop-bitters.

Mr. Browne led his charges thither and invited them all, in jest, to some ladies' punch, hot, strong and sweet. As they said they never took anything strong, he opened three bottles of lemonade for them. Then he asked one of the young men to move aside, and, taking hold of the decanter, filled out for himself a goodly measure of whisky. The young men eyed him respectfully while he took a trial sip.

"God help me," he said, smiling, "it's the doctor's orders."

His wizened face broke into a broader smile, and the three young ladies laughed in musical echo to his pleasantry, swaying their bodies to and fro, with nervous jerks of their shoulders. The boldest said:

"O, now, Mr. Browne, I'm sure the doctor never ordered anything of the kind."

Mr. Browne took another sip of his whisky and said, with sidling mimicry:

"Well, you see, I'm like the famous Mrs. Cassidy, who is reported to have said: 'Now, Mary Grimes, if I don't take it, make me take it, for I feel I want it.' "

His hot face had leaned forward a little too confidentially and he had assumed a very low Dublin accent so that the young ladies, with one instinct, received his speech in silence. Miss Furlong, who was one of Mary Jane's pupils, asked Miss Daly what was the name of the pretty waltz she had played; and Mr. Browne, seeing that he was ignored, turned promptly to the two young men who were more appreciative.

A red-faced young woman, dressed in pansy, came into the room, excitedly clapping her hands and crying:

"Quadrilles! Quadrilles!"

Close on her heels came Aunt Kate, crying:

"Two gentlemen and three ladies, Mary Jane!"

"O, here's Mr. Bergin and Mr Kerrigan," said Mary Jane. "Mr. Kerrigan, will you take Miss Power? Miss Furlong, may I get you a partner, Mr. Bergin. O, that'll just do now."

"Three ladies, Mary Jane," said Aunt Kate.

The two young gentlemen asked the ladies if they might have the pleasure, and Mary Jane turned to Miss Daly.

"O, Miss Daly, you're really awfully good, after playing for the last two dances, but really we're so short of ladies to-night."

"I don't mind in the least, Miss Morkan."

"But I've a nice partner for you, Mr. Bartell D'Arcy, the tenor. I'll get him to sing later on. All Dublin is raving about him."

"Lovely voice, lovely voice!" said Aunt Kate.

As the piano had twice begun to prelude to the first figure Mary Jane led her recruits quickly from the room. They had hardly gone when Aunt Julia wandered slowly into the room, looking behind her at something.

"What is the matter, Julia?" asked Aunt Kate anxiously. "Who is it?"

Julia, who was carrying in a column of table-napkins, turned to her sister and said, simply, as if the question had surprised her:

"It's only Freddy, Kate, and Gabriel with him."

In fact right behind her Gabriel could be seen piloting Freddy Malins across the landing. The latter, a young man of about forty, was of Gabriel's size and build, with very round shoulders. His face was fleshy and pallid, touched with colour only at the thick hanging lobes of his ears and at the wide wings of his nose. He had coarse features, a blunt nose, a convex and receding brow, tumid and protruded lips. His heavy-lidded eyes and the disorder of his scanty hair made him look sleepy. He was laughing heartily in a high key at a story which he had been telling Gabriel on the stairs and at the same time rubbing the knuckles of his left fist backwards and forwards into his left eye.

"Good-evening, Freddy," said Aunt Julia.

Freddy Malins bade the Misses Morkan good-evening in what seemed an offhand fashion by reason of the habitual catch in his voice and then, seeing that Mr. Browne was grinning at him from the sideboard, crossed the room on rather shaky legs and began to repeat in an undertone the story he had just told to Gabriel.

"He's not so bad, is he?" said Aunt Kate to Gabriel.

Gabriel's brows were dark but he raised them quickly and answered:

"O, no, hardly noticeable."

"Now, isn't he a terrible fellow!" she said. "And his poor mother made him take the pledge on New Year's Eve. But come on, Gabriel, into the drawing-room."

Before leaving the room with Gabriel she signalled to Mr. Browne by frowning and shaking her forefinger in warning to and fro. Mr. Browne nodded in answer and, when she had gone, said to Freddy Malins:

"Now, then, Teddy, I'm going to fill you out a good glass of lemonade just to buck you up."

Freddy Malins, who was nearing the climax of his story, waved the offer aside impatiently but Mr. Browne, having first called Freddy Malins' attention to a disarray in his dress, filled out and handed him a full glass of lemonade. Freddy Malins' left hand accepted the glass mechanically, his right hand being engaged in the mechanical readjustment of his dress. Mr. Browne, whose face was once more wrinkling with mirth, poured out for himself a glass of whisky while Freddy Malins exploded, before he had well reached the climax of his story, in a kink of high-pitched bronchitic laughter and, setting down his untasted and overflowing glass, began to rub the knuckles of his left fist backwards and forwards into his left eye, repeating words of his last phrase as well as his fit of laughter would allow him.

Gabriel could not listen while Mary Jane was playing her Academy piece, full of runs and difficult passages, to the hushed drawing-room. He liked music but the piece she was playing had no melody for him and he doubted whether it had any melody for the other listeners, though they had begged Mary Jane to play something. Four young men, who had come from the refreshment-room to stand in the doorway at the sound of the piano, had gone away quietly in couples after a few minutes. The only persons who seemed to follow the music were Mary Jane herself, her hands racing along the key-board or lifted from it at the pauses like those of a priestess in momentary imprecation, and Aunt Kate standing at her elbow to turn the page.

Gabriel's eyes, irritated by the floor, which glittered with beeswax under the heavy chandelier, wandered to the wall above the piano. A picture of the balcony scene in *Romeo and Juliet* hung there and beside it was a picture of the two murdered princes in the Tower which Aunt Julia had worked in red, blue and brown wools when she was a girl. Probably in the school they had gone to as girls that kind of work had been taught for one year. His mother had worked for him as a birthday present a waistcoat of purple tabinet, with little foxes' heads upon it, lined with brown satin and having round mulberry buttons. It was strange that his mother had had no musical talent though Aunt Kate used to call her the brains carrier of the Morkan family. Both she and Julia had always seemed a little proud of their serious and matronly sister. Her photograph stood before the pierglass. She held an open book on her knees and was pointing out something in it to Constantine who, dressed in a man-o'-war suit, lay at her feet. It was she who had chosen the names of her sons for she was very sensible of the dignity of family life. Thanks to her, Constantine was now senior curate in Balbriggan and, thanks to her, Gabriel himself had taken his degree in the Royal University. A shadow passed over his face as he remembered her sullen opposition to his marriage. Some slighting phrases she had used still rankled in his memory; she had once spoken of Gretta as being country cute and that was not true of Gretta at all. It was Gretta who had nursed her during all her last long illness in their house at Monkstown.

He knew that Mary Jane must be near the end of her piece for she was playing again the opening melody with runs of scales after every bar and while he waited for the end the resentment died down in his heart. The piece ended with a trill of octaves in the treble and a final deep octave in the bass. Great applause greeted Mary Jane as, blushing and rolling up her music nervously, she escaped from the room. The most vigorous clapping came from the four young men in the doorway who had gone away to the refreshment-room at the beginning of the piece but had come back when the piano had stopped.

Lancers were arranged. Gabriel found himself partnered with Miss Ivors. She was a frank-mannered talkative young lady, with a freckled face and prominent brown eyes. She did not wear a low-cut bodice and the large brooch which was fixed in the front of her collar bore on it an Irish device and motto.

When they had taken their places she said abruptly:

"I have a crow to pluck with you."

"With me?" said Gabriel.

She nodded her head gravely.

"What is it?" asked Gabriel, smiling at her solemn manner.

"Who is G. C.?" answered Miss Ivors, turning her eyes upon him.

Gabriel coloured and was about to knit his brows, as if he did not understand, when she said bluntly:

"O, innocent Amy! I have found out that you write for *The Daily Express*. Now, aren't you ashamed of yourself?"

"Why should I be ashamed of myself?" asked Gabriel, blinking his eyes and trying to smile.

"Well, I'm ashamed of you," said Miss Ivors frankly. "To say you'd write for a paper like that. I didn't think you were a West Briton."

A look of perplexity appeared on Gabriel's face. It was true that he wrote a literary column every Wednesday in *The Daily Express,* for which he was paid fifteen shillings. But that did not make him a West Briton surely. The books he received for review were almost more welcome than the paltry cheque. He loved to feel the covers and turn over the pages of newly printed books. Nearly every day when his teaching in the college was ended he used to wander down the quays to the second-hand booksellers, to Hickey's on Bachelor's Walk, to Webb's or Massey's on Aston's Quay, or to O'Clohissey's in the by-street. He did not know how to meet her charge. He wanted to say that literature was above politics. But they were friends of many years' standing and their careers had been parallel, first at the University and then as teachers: he could not risk a grandiose phrase with her. He continued blinking his eyes and trying to smile and murmured lamely that he saw nothing political in writing reviews of books.

When their turn to cross had come he was still perplexed and inattentive. Miss Ivors promptly took his hand in a warm grasp and said in a soft friendly tone:

"Of course, I was only joking. Come, we cross now."

When they were together again she spoke of the University question and Gabriel felt more at ease. A friend of hers had shown her his review of Browning's poems. That was how she had found out the secret: but she liked the review immensely. Then she said suddenly:

"O, Mr. Conroy, will you come for an excursion to the Aran Isles this summer? We're going to stay there a whole month. It will be splendid out in the Atlantic. You ought to come. Mr. Clancy is coming, and Mr. Kilkelly and Kathleen Kearney. It would be splendid for Gretta too if she'd come. She's from Connacht, isn't she?"

"Her people are," said Gabriel shortly.

"But you will come, won't you?" said Miss Ivors, laying her warm hand eagerly on his arm.

"The fact is," said Gabriel, "I have just arranged to go——"

"Go where?" asked Miss Ivors.

"Well, you know, every year I go for a cycling tour with some fellows and so———"

"But where?" asked Miss Ivors.

"Well, we usually go to France or Belgium or perhaps Germany," said Gabriel awkwardly.

"And why do you go to France and Belgium," said Miss Ivors, "instead of visiting your own land?"

"Well," said Gabriel, "it's partly to keep in touch with the languages and partly for a change."

"And haven't you your own language to keep in touch with—Irish?" asked Miss Ivors.

"Well," said Gabriel, "if it comes to that, you know, Irish is not my language."

Their neighbours had turned to listen to the cross-examination. Gabriel glanced right and left nervously and tried to keep his good humour under the ordeal which was making a blush invade his forehead.

"And haven't you your own land to visit," continued Miss Ivors, "that you know nothing of, your own people, and your own country?"

"O, to tell you the truth," retorted Gabriel suddenly, "I'm sick of my own country, sick of it!"

"Why?" asked Miss Ivors.

Gabriel did not answer for his retort had heated him.

"Why?" repeated Miss Ivors.

They had to go visiting together and, as he had not answered her, Miss Ivors said warmly:

"Of course, you've no answer."

Gabriel tried to cover his agitation by taking part in the dance with great energy. He avoided her eyes for he had seen a sour expression on her face. But when they met in the long chain he was surprised to feel his hand firmly pressed. She looked at him from under her brows for a moment quizzically until he smiled. Then, just as the chain was about to start again, she stood on tiptoe and whispered into his ear:

"West Briton!"

When the lancers were over Gabriel went away to a remote corner of the room where Freddy Malins' mother was sitting. She was a stout feeble old woman with white hair. Her voice had a catch in it like her son's and she stuttered slightly. She had been told that Freddy had come and that he was nearly all right. Gabriel asked her whether she had had a good crossing. She lived with her married daughter in Glasgow and came to Dublin on a visit once a year. She answered placidly that she had had a beautiful crossing and that the captain had been most attentive to her. She spoke also of the beautiful house her daughter kept in Glasgow, and of all the friends they had there. While her tongue rambled on Gabriel tried to banish from his mind all memory of the unpleasant incident with Miss Ivors. Of course the girl or woman, or whatever she was, was an enthusiast but there was a time for all things. Perhaps he ought not to have answered her like that. But she had no right to call him a West Briton before people, even in joke. She had tried to make him ridiculous before people, heckling him and staring at him with her rabbit's eyes.

He saw his wife making her way towards him through the waltzing couples. When she reached him she said into his ear:

"Gabriel, Aunt Kate wants to know won't you carve the goose as usual. Miss Daly will carve the ham and I'll do the pudding."

"All right," said Gabriel.

"She's sending in the younger ones first as soon as this waltz is over so that we'll have the table to ourselves."

"Were you dancing?" asked Gabriel.

"Of course I was. Didn't you see me? What row had you with Molly Ivors?"

"No row. Why? Did she say so?"

"Something like that. I'm trying to get that Mr. D'Arcy to sing. He's full of conceit, I think."

"There was no row," said Gabriel moodily, "only she wanted me to go for a trip to the west of Ireland and I said I wouldn't."

His wife clasped her hands excitedly and gave a little jump.

"O, do go, Gabriel," she cried. "I'd love to see Galway again."

"You can go if you like," said Gabriel coldly.

She looked at him for a moment, then turned to Mrs. Malins and said:

"There's a nice husband for you, Mrs. Malins."

While she was threading her way back across the room Mrs. Malins, without adverting to the interruption, went on to tell Gabriel what beautiful places there were in Scotland and beautiful scenery. Her son-in-law brought them every year to the lakes and they used to go fishing. Her son-in-law was a splendid fisher. One day he caught a beautiful big fish and the man in the hotel cooked it for their dinner.

Gabriel hardly heard what she said. Now that supper was coming near he began to think again about his speech and about the quotation. When he saw Freddy Malins coming across the room to visit his mother Gabriel left the chair free for him and retired into the embrasure of the window.

The room had already cleared and from the back room came the clatter of plates and knives. Those who still remained in the drawing-room seemed tired of dancing and were conversing quietly in little groups. Gabriel's warm trembling fingers tapped the cold pane of the window. How cool it must be outside! How pleasant it would be to walk out alone, first along by the river and then through the park! The snow would be lying on the branches of the trees and forming a bright cap on the top of the Wellington Monument. How much more pleasant it would be there than at the supper-table!

He ran over the headings of his speech: Irish hospitality, sad memories, the Three Graces, Paris, the quotation from Browning. He repeated to himself a phrase he had written in his review: "One feels that one is listening to a thought-tormented music." Miss Ivors had praised the review. Was she sincere? Had she really any life of her own behind all her propagandism? There had never been any ill-feeling between them until that night. It unnerved him to think that she would be at the supper-table, looking up at him while he spoke with her critical quizzing eyes. Perhaps she would not be sorry to see him fail in his speech. An idea came into his mind and gave him courage. He would say, alluding to Aunt Kate and Aunt Julia: "Ladies and Gentlemen, the generation which is now on the wane among us may have had its faults but for my part I think it had certain qualities of hospitality, of humour, of humanity, which the new and very serious and hypereducated generation that is growing up around us seems to me to lack." Very good: that was one for Miss Ivors. What did he care that his aunts were only two ignorant old women?

A murmur in the room attracted his attention. Mr. Browne was advancing from the door, gallantly escorting Aunt Julia, who leaned upon his arm, smiling and hanging her head. An irregular musketry of applause escorted her also as far as the piano and then, as Mary Jane seated herself on the stool, and Aunt Julia, no longer smiling, half turned so as to pitch her voice fairly into the room, gradually ceased. Gabriel recognised the prelude. It was that of an old song of Aunt Julia's—*Arrayed for the Bridal.* Her voice, strong and clear in tone, attacked with great spirit the runs which embellish the air and though she sang very rapidly she did not miss even the smallest of the grace notes. To follow the voice, without looking at the singer's face, was to feel and share the excitement of swift and secure flight. Gabriel applauded loudly with all the others at the close of the song and loud applause was borne in from the invisible supper table. It sounded so genuine that a little colour struggled into Aunt Julia's face as she bent to replace in the music-stand the old leather-bound song-book that had her initials on the cover. Freddy Malins, who had listened with his head perched sideways to hear her better, was still applauding when everyone else had ceased and talking animatedly to his mother who nodded her head gravely and slowly in acquiescence. At last, when he could clap no more, he stood up suddenly and hurried across the room to Aunt Julia whose hand he seized and held in both his hands, shaking it when words failed him or the catch in his voice proved too much for him.

"I was just telling my mother," he said, "I never heard you sing so well, never. No, I never heard your voice so good as it is to-night. Now! Would you believe that now? That's the truth. Upon my word and honour that's the truth. I never heard your voice sound so fresh and so . . . so clear and fresh, never."

Aunt Julia smiled broadly and murmured something about compliments as she released her hand from his grasp. Mr. Browne extended his open hand towards her and said to those who were near him in the manner of a showman introducing a prodigy to an audience:

"Miss Julia Morkan, my latest discovery!"

He was laughing very heartily at this himself when Freddy Malins turned to him and said:

"Well, Browne, if you're serious you might make a worse discovery. All I can say is I never heard her sing half so well as long as I am coming here. And that's the honest truth."

"Neither did I," said Mr. Browne. "I think her voice has greatly improved."

Aunt Julia shrugged her shoulders and said with meek pride:

"Thirty years ago I hadn't a bad voice as voices go."

"I often told Julia," said Aunt Kate emphatically, "that she was simply thrown away in that choir. But she never would be said by me."

She turned as if to appeal to the good sense of the others against a refractory child while Aunt Julia gazed in front of her, a vague smile of reminiscence playing on her face.

"No," continued Aunt Kate, "she wouldn't be said or led by anyone, slaving there in that choir night and day, night and day. Six o'clock on Christmas morning! And all for what?"

"Well, isn't it for the honour of God, Aunt Kate?" asked Mary Jane, twisting round on the piano-stool and smiling.

Aunt Kate turned fiercely on her niece and said:

"I know all about the honour of God. Mary Jane, but I think it's not at all honourable for the pope to turn out the women out of the choirs that have slaved there all their lives and put little whipper-snappers of boys over their heads. I suppose it is for the good of the Church if the pope does it. But it's not just, Mary Jane, and it's not right."

She had worked herself into a passion and would have continued in defence of her sister for it was a sore subject with her but Mary Jane, seeing that all the dancers had come back, intervened pacifically:

"Now, Aunt Kate, you're giving scandal to Mr. Browne who is of the other persuasion."

Aunt Kate turned to Mr. Browne, who was grinning at this allusion to his religion, and said hastily:

"O, I don't question the pope's being right. I'm only a stupid old woman and I wouldn't presume to do such a thing. But there's such a thing as common everyday politeness and gratitude. And if I were in Julia's place I'd tell that Father Healey straight up to his face . . ."

"And besides, Aunt Kate," said Mary Jane, "we really are all hungry and when we are hungry we are all very quarrelsome."

"And when we are thirsty we are also quarrelsome," added Mr. Browne.

"So that we had better go to supper," said Mary Jane, "and finish the discussion afterwards."

On the landing outside the drawing-room Gabriel found his wife and Mary Jane trying to persuade Miss Ivors to stay for supper. But Miss Ivors, who had put on her hat and was buttoning her cloak, would not stay. She did not feel in the least hungry and she had already overstayed her time.

"But only for ten minutes, Molly," said Mrs. Conroy. "That won't delay you."

"To take a pick itself," said Mary Jane, "after all your dancing."

"I really couldn't," said Miss Ivors.

"I am afraid you didn't enjoy yourself at all," said Mary Jane hopelessly.

"Ever so much, I assure you," said Miss Ivors, "but you really must let me run off now."

"But how can you get home?" asked Mrs. Conroy.

"O, it's only two steps up the quay."

Gabriel hesitated a moment and said:

"If you will allow me, Miss Ivors, I'll see you home if you are really obliged to go."

But Miss Ivors broke away from them.

"I won't hear of it," she cried. "For goodness' sake go in to your suppers and don't mind me. I'm quite well able to take care of myself."

"Well, you're the comical girl, Molly," said Mrs. Conroy frankly.

"Beannachl libh," cried Miss Ivors, with a laugh, as she ran down the staircase.

Mary Jane gazed after her, a moody puzzled expression on her face, while Mrs. Conroy leaned over the banisters to listen for the hall-door. Gabriel asked himself was he the cause of her abrupt departure. But she did not seem to be in ill humour: she had gone away laughing. He stared blankly down the staircase.

At the moment Aunt Kate came toddling out of the supper-room, almost wringing her hands in despair.

"Where is Gabriel?" she cried. "Where on earth is Gabriel? There's everyone waiting in there, stage to let, and nobody to carve the goose!"

"Here I am, Aunt Kate!" cried Gabriel, with sudden animation, "ready to carve a flock of geese, if necessary."

A fat brown goose lay at one end of the table and at the other end, on a bed of creased paper strewn with sprigs of parsley, lay a great ham, stripped of its outer skin and peppered over with crust crumbs, a neat paper frill round its ship and beside this was a round of spiced beef.

Between these rival ends ran parallel lines of side-dishes: two little minsters of jelly, red and yellow; a shallow dish full of blocks of blancmange and red jam, a large green leaf-shaped dish with a stalk-shaped handle, on which lay bunches of purple raisins and peeled almonds, a companion dish on which lay a solid rectangle of Smyrna figs, a dish of custard topped with grated nutmeg, a small bowl full of chocolates and sweets wrapped in gold and silver papers and a glass vase in which stood some tall celery stalks. In the centre of the table there stood, as sentries to a fruit-stand which upheld a pyramid of oranges and American apples, two squat old-fashioned decanters of cut glass, one containing port and the other dark sherry. On the closed square piano a pudding in a huge yellow dish lay in waiting and behind it were three squads of bottles of stout and ale and minerals, drawn up according to the colours of their uniforms, the first two black, with brown and red labels, the third and smallest squad white, with transverse green sashes.

Gabriel took his seat boldly at the head of the table and, having looked to the edge of the carver, plunged his fork firmly into the goose. He felt quite at ease now for he was an expert carver and liked nothing better than to find himself at the head of a well-laden table.

"Miss Furlong, what shall I send you?" he asked. "A wing or a slice of the breast?"

"Just a small slice of the breast."

"Miss Higgins, what for you?"

"O, anything at all, Mr. Conroy."

While Gabriel and Miss Daly exchanged plates of goose and plates of ham and spiced beef Lily went from guest to guest with a dish of hot floury potatoes wrapped in a white napkin. This was Mary Jane's idea and she had also suggested apple sauce for the goose but Aunt Kate had said that plain roast goose without any apple sauce had always been good enough for her and she hoped she might never eat worse. Mary Jane waited on her pupils and saw that they got the best slices and Aunt Kate and Aunt Julia opened and carried across from the piano bottles of stout and ale for the gentlemen and bottles of minerals for the ladies. There was a great deal of confusion and laughter and noise, the noise of orders and counter-orders, of knives and forks, of corks and glass-stoppers. Gabriel began to carve second helpings as soon as he had finished the first round without serving himself. Everyone protested loudly so that he compromised by taking a long draught of stout for he had found the carving hot work. Mary Jane settled down quietly to her supper but Aunt Kate and Aunt Julia were still toddling round the table, walking on each other's heels, getting in each other's way and giving each other unheeded orders. Mr. Browne begged of them to sit down and eat their suppers and so did Gabriel but they they said there was time enough, so that, at last, Freddy Malins stood up and, capturing Aunt Kate, plumped her down on her chair amid general laughter.

When everyone had been well served Gabriel said, smiling:

"Now, if anyone wants a little more of what vulgar people call stuffing let him or her speak."

A chorus of voices invited him to begin his own supper and Lily came forward with three potatoes which she had reserved for him.

"Very well," said Gabriel amiably, as he took another preparatory draught, "kindly forget my existence, ladies and gentlemen, for a few minutes."

He set to his supper and took no part in the conversation with which the table covered Lily's removal of the plates. The subject of talk was the opera company which was then at the Theatre Royal. Mr. Bartell D'Arcy, the tenor, a dark-complexioned young man with a smart moustache, praised very highly the leading contralto of the company but Miss Furlong thought she had a rather vulgar style of production. Freddy Malins said there was a negro chieftain singing in the second part of the Gaiety pantomime who had one of the finest tenor voices he had ever heard.

"Have you heard him?" he asked Mr. Bartell D'Arcy across the table.

"No," answered Mr. Bartell D'Arcy carelessly.

"Because," Freddy Malins explained, "now I'd be curious to hear your opinion of him. I think he has a grand voice."

"It takes Teddy to find out the really good things," said Mr. Browne familiarly to the table.

"And why couldn't he have a voice too?" asked Freddy Malins sharply. "Is it because he's only a black?"

Nobody answered this question and Mary Jane led the table back to the legitimate opera. One of her pupils had given her a pass for *Mignon.* Of course it was very fine, she said, but it made her think of poor Georgina Burns. Mr. Browne could go back farther still to the old Italian companies that used to come to Dublin—Tietjens, Ilma de Murzka, Campanini, the great Trebelli Giuglini, Ravelli, Aramburo. Those were the days, he said, when there was something like singing to be heard in Dublin. He told too of how how the top gallery of the old Royal used to be packed night after night, of how one night an Italian tenor had sung five encores to *Let me like a Soldier fall,* introducing a high C every time and of how the gallery boys would sometimes in their enthusiasm unyoke the horses from the carriage of some great *prima donna* and pull her themselves through the streets to her hotel. Why did they never play the grand old operas now, he asked, *Dinorah, Lucrezia Borgia?* Because they could not get the voices to sing them: that was why."

"O, well," said Mr. Bartell D'Arcy, "I presume there are as good singers to-day as there were then."

"Where are they?" asked Mr. Browne defiantly.

"In London, Paris, Milan," said Mr. Bartell D'Arcy warmly. "I suppose Caruso, for example, is quite as good, if not better than any of the men you have mentioned."

"Maybe so," said Mr. Browne. "But I may tell you I doubt it strongly."

"O, I'd give anything to hear Caruso sing," said Mary Jane.

"For me," said Aunt Kate, who had been picking a bone, "there was only one tenor. To please me, I mean. But I suppose none of you ever heard of him."

"Who was he, Miss Morkan?" asked Mr. Bartell D'Arcy politely.

"His name," said Aunt Kate, "was Parkinson. I heard him when he was in his prime and I think he had then the purest tenor voice that was ever put into a man's throat."

"Strange," said Mr. Bartell D'Arcy. "I never even heard of him."

"Yes, yes, Miss Morkan is right," said Mr. Browne. "I remember hearing of old Parkinson but he's too far back for me."

"A beautiful, pure, sweet, mellow English tenor," said Aunt Kate with enthusiasm.

Gabriel having finished, the huge pudding was transferred to the table. The clatter of forks and spoons began again. Gabriel's wife served out spoonfuls of the pudding and passed the plates down the table. Midway down they were held up by Mary Jane, who replenished them with raspberry or orange jelly or with blancmange and jam. The pudding was of Aunt Julia's making and she received praises for it from all quarters. She herself said that it was not quite brown enough.

"Well, I hope, Miss Morkan," said Mr. Browne, "that I'm brown enough for you because, you know, I'm all brown."

All the gentlemen, except Gabriel, ate some of the pudding out of compliment to Aunt Julia. As Gabriel never ate sweets the celery had been left for him. Freddy Malins also took a stalk of celery and ate it with his pudding. He had been told that celery was a capital thing for the blood and he was just then under doctor's care. Mrs. Malins, who had been silent all through the supper, said that her son was going down to Mount Melleray in a week or so. The table then spoke of Mount Melleray, how bracing the air was down there, how hospitable the monks were and how they never asked for a penny-piece from their guests.

"And do you mean to say," asked Mr. Browne incredulously, "that a chap can go down there and put up there as if it were a hotel and live on the fat of the land and then come away without paying anything?"

"O, most people give some donation to the monastery when they leave," said Mary Jane.

"I wish we had an institution like that in our Church," said Mr. Browne candidly.

He was astonished to hear that the monks never spoke, got up at two in the morning and slept in their coffins. He asked what they did it for.

"That's the rule of the order," said Aunt Kate firmly.

"Yes, but why?" asked Mr. Browne.

Aunt Kate repeated that it was the rule, that was all. Mr. Browne still seemed not to understand. Freddy Malins explained to him, as best he could, that the monks were trying to make up for the sins committed by all the sinners in the outside world. The explanation was not very clear for Mr. Browne grinned and said:

"I like that idea very much but wouldn't a comfortable spring bed do them as well as a coffin?"

"The coffin," said Mary Jane, "is to remind them of their last end."

As the subject had grown lugubrious it was buried in a silence of the table during which Mrs. Malins could be heard saying to her neighbour in an indistinct undertone:

"They are very good men, the monks, very pious men."

The raisins and almonds and figs and apples and oranges and chocolates and sweets were now passed about the table and Aunt Julia invited all the guests to have either port or sherry. At first Mr. Bartell D'Arcy refused to take either but one of his neighbours nudged him and whispered something to him upon which he allowed his glass to be filled. Gradually as the last glasses were being filled the conversation ceased. A pause followed, broken only by the noise of the wine and by unsettlings of chairs. The Misses Morkan, all three, looked down at the tablecloth. Someone coughed once or twice and then a few gentlemen patted the table gently as a signal for silence. The silence came and Gabriel pushed back his chair and stood up.

The patting at once grew louder in encouragement and then ceased altogether. Gabriel leaned his ten trembling fingers on the tablecloth and smiled nervously at the company. Meeting a row of upturned faces he raised his eyes to the chandelier. The piano was playing a waltz tune and he could hear the skirts sweeping against the drawing-room door. People, perhaps, were standing in the snow on the quay outside, gazing up at the lighted windows and listening to the waltz music. The air was pure there. In the distance lay the park where the trees were weighted with snow. The Wellington Monument wore a gleaming cap of snow that flashed westward over the white field of Fifteen Acres.

He began:

"Ladies and Gentlemen,

"It has fallen to my lot this evening, as in years past, to perform a very pleasing task but a task for which I am afraid my poor powers as a speaker are all too inadequate."

"No, no!" said Mr. Browne.

"But, however that may be, I can only ask you to-night to take the will for the deed and to lend me your attention for a few moments while I endeavour to express to you in words what my feelings are on this occasion.

"Ladies and Gentlemen, it is not the first time that we have gathered together under this hospitable roof, around this hospitable board. It is not the first time that we have been the recipients—or perhaps, I had better say, the victims—of the hospitality of certain good ladies."

He made a circle in the air with his arm and paused. Everyone laughed or smiled at Aunt Kate and Aunt Julia and Mary Jane who all turned crimson with pleasure. Gabriel went on more boldly:

"I feel more strongly with every recurring year that our country has no tradition which does it so much honour and which it should guard so jealously as that of its hospitality. It is a tradition that is unique as far as my experience goes (and I have visited not a few places abroad) among the modern nations. Some would say, perhaps, that with us it is rather a failing than anything to be boasted of. But granted even that, it is, to my mind, a princely failing, and one that I trust will long be cultivated among us. Of one thing, at least, I am sure. As long as this one roof shelters the good ladies aforesaid—and I wish from my heart it may do so for many and many a long year to come—the tradition of genuine warm-hearted courteous Irish hospitality, which our forefathers have handed down to us and which we in turn must hand down to our descendants, is still alive among us."

A hearty murmur of assent ran round the table. It shot through Gabriel's mind that Miss Ivors was not there and that she had gone away discourteously: and he said with confidence in himself:

"Ladies and Gentlemen,

"A new generation is growing up in our midst, a generation actuated by new ideas and new principles. It is serious and enthusiastic for these new ideas and its enthusiasm, even when it is misdirected, is, I believe, in the main sincere. But we are living in a sceptical and, if I may use the phrase, a thought-tormented age: and sometimes I fear that this new generation, educated or hypereducated as it is, will lack those qualities of humanity, of hospitality, of kindly humour which belonged to an older day. Listening to-night to the names of all those great singers of the past it seemed to me, I must confess, that we were living in a less spacious age. Those days might, without exaggeration, be called spacious days: and if they are gone beyond recall let us hope, at least, that in gatherings such as this we shall still speak of them with pride and affection, still cherish in our hearts the memory of those dead and gone great ones whose fame the world will not willingly let die."

"Hear, hear!" said Mr. Browne loudly.

"But yet," continued Gabriel, his voice falling into a softer inflection, "there are always in gatherings such as this sadder thoughts that will recur to our minds: thoughts of the past, of youth, of changes, of absent faces that we miss here to-night. Our path through life is strewn with many such sad memories: and were we to brood upon them always we could not find the heart to go on bravely with our work among the living. We have all of us living duties and living affections which claim, and rightly claim, our strenuous endeavours.

"Therefore, I will not linger on the past. I will not let any gloomy moralising intrude upon us here to-night. Here we are gathered together for a brief moment from the bustle and rush of our everyday routine. We are met here as friends, in the spirit of good-fellowship, as colleagues, also to a certain extent, in the true spirit of *camaraderie,* and as the guests of—what shall I call them?—the Three Graces of the Dublin musical world."

The table burst into applause and laughter at this allusion. Aunt Julia vainly asked each of her neighbours in turn to tell her what Gabriel had said.

"He says we are the Three Graces, Aunt Julia," said Mary Jane.

Aunt Julia did not understand but she looked up, smiling, at Gabriel, who continued in the same vein:

"Ladies and Gentlemen,

"I will not attempt to play to-night the part that Paris played on another occasion. I will not attempt to choose between them. The task would be an invidious one and one beyond my poor powers. For when I view them in turn, whether it be our chief hostess herself, whose good heart, whose too good heart, has become a byword with all who know her, or her sister, who seems to be gifted with perennial youth and whose singing must have been a surprise and a revelation to us all to-night, or, last but not least when I consider our youngest hostess, talented, cheerful, hard-working and the best of nieces, I confess, Ladies and Gentlemen, that I do not know to which of them I should award the prize."

Gabriel glanced down at his aunts and, seeing the large smile on Aunt Julia's face and the tears which had risen to Aunt Kate's eyes, hastened to his close. He raised his glass of port gallantly, while every member of the company fingered a glass expectantly, and said loudly:

"Let us toast them all three together. Let us drink to their health, wealth, long life, happiness and prosperity and may they long continue to hold the proud and self-won position which they hold in their profession and the position of honour and affection which they hold in our hearts."

All the guests stood up, glass in hand, and turning towards the three seated ladies, sang in unison, with Mr. Browne as leader:

For they are jolly gay fellows,
For they are jolly gay fellows,
For they are jolly gay fellows,
Which nobody can deny.

Aunt Kate was making frank use of her handkerchief and even Aunt Julia seemed moved. Freddy Malins beat time with his pudding-fork and the singers turned towards one another, as if in melodious conference, while they sang with emphasis:

Unless he tells a lie,
Unless he tells a lie,

Then, turning once more towards their hostesses, they sang:

For they are jolly gay fellows,
For they are jolly gay fellows,
For they are jolly gay fellows,
Which nobody can deny.

The acclamation which followed was taken up beyond the door of the supper-room by many of the other guests and renewed time after time, Freddy Malins acting as officer with his fork on high.

The piercing morning air came into the hall where they were standing so that Aunt Kate said:

"Close the door, somebody. Mrs. Malins will get her death of cold."

"Browne is out there, Aunt Kate," said Mary Jane.

"Browne is everywhere," said Aunt Kate, lowering her voice.

Mary Jane laughed at her tone.

"Really," she said archly, "he is very attentive."

"He has been laid on here like the gas," said Aunt Kate in the same tone, "all during the Christmas."

She laughed herself this time good-humouredly and then added quickly:

"But tell him to come in, Mary Jane, and close the door. I hope to goodness he didn't hear me."

At that moment the hall-door was opened and Mr. Browne came in from the doorstep, laughing as if his heart would break. He was dressed in a long green overcoat with mock astrakhan cuffs and collar and wore on his head an oval fur cap. He pointed down the snow-covered quay from where the sound of shrill prolonged whistling was borne in.

"Teddy will have all the cabs in Dublin out," he said.

Gabriel advanced from the little pantry behind the office, struggling into his overcoat and, looking round the hall, said:

"Gretta not down yet?"

"She's getting on her things, Gabriel," said Aunt Kate.

"Who's playing up there?" asked Gabriel.

"Nobody. They're all gone."

"O no, Aunt Kate," said Mary Jane. "Bartell D'Arcy and Miss O'Callaghan aren't gone yet."

"Someone is fooling at the piano anyhow," said Gabriel.

Mary Jane glanced at Gabriel and Mr. Browne and said with a shiver:

"It makes me feel cold to look at you two gentlemen muffled up like that. I wouldn't like to face your journey home at this hour."

"I'd like nothing better this minute," said Mr. Browne stoutly, "than a rattling fine walk in the country or a fast drive with a good spanking goer between the shafts."

"We used to have a very good horse and trap at home," said Aunt Julia sadly.

"The never-to-be-forgotten Johnny," said Mary Jane, laughing.

Aunt Kate and Gabriel laughed too.

"Why, what was wonderful about Johnny?" asked Mr. Browne.

"The late lamented Patrick Morkan, our grandfather, that is," explained Gabriel, "commonly known in his later years as the old gentleman, was a glue-boiler."

"O, now, Gabriel," said Aunt Kate, laughing, "he had a starch mill."

"Well, glue or starch," said Gabriel, "the old gentleman had a horse by the name of Johnny. And Johnny used to work in the old gentleman's mill, walking round and round in order to drive the mill. That was all very well; but now comes the tragic part about Johnny. One fine day the old gentleman thought he'd like to drive out with the quality to a military review in the park."

"The Lord have mercy on his soul," said Aunt Kate compassionately.

"Amen," said Gabriel. "So the old gentleman, as I said, harnessed Johnny and put on his very best tall hat and his very best stock collar and drove out in grand style from his ancestral mansion somewhere near Back Lane, I think."

Everyone laughed, even Mrs. Malins, at Gabriel's manner and Aunt Kate said:

"O, now, Gabriel, he didn't live in Back Lane, really. Only the mill was there."

"Out from the mansion of his forefathers," continued Gabriel, "he drove with Johnny. And everything went on beautifully until Johnny came in sight of King Billy's statue: and whether he fell in love with the horse King Billy sits on or whether he thought he was back again in the mill, anyhow he began to walk round the statue."

Gabriel paced in a circle round the hall in his goloshes amid the laughter of the others.

"Round and round he went," said Gabriel, "and the old gentleman, who was a very pompous old gentleman, was highly indignant. 'Go on, sir! What do you mean, sir? Johnny! Johnny! Most extraordinary conduct! Can't understand the horse!' "

The peals of laughter which followed Gabriel's imitation of the incident was interrupted by a resounding knock at the hall door. Mary Jane ran to open it and let in Freddy Malins. Freddy Malins, with his hat well back on his head and his shoulders humped with cold, was puffing and steaming after his exertions.

"I could only get one cab," he said.

"O, we'll find another along the quay," said Gabriel.

"Yes," said Aunt Kate. "Better not keep Mrs. Malins standing in the draught."

Mrs. Malins was helped down the front steps by her son and Mr. Browne and, after many manoeuvres, hoisted into the cab. Freddy Malins clambered in after her and spent a long time settling her on the seat, Mr. Browne helping him with advice. At last she was settled comfortably and Freddy

Malins invited Mr. Browne into the cab. There was a good deal of confused talk, and then Mr. Browne got into the cab. The cabman settled his rug over his knees, and bent down for the address. The confusion grew greater and the cabman was directed differently by Freddy Malins and Mr. Browne, each of whom had his head out through a window of the cab. The difficulty was to know where to drop Mr. Browne along the route, and Aunt Kate, Aunt Julia and Mary Jane helped the discussion from the doorstep with cross-directions and contradictions and abundance of laughter. As for Freddy Malins he was speechless with laughter. He popped his head in and out of the window every moment to the great danger of his hat, and told his mother how the discussion was progressing, till at last Mr. Browne shouted to the bewildered cabman above the din of everybody's laughter:

"Do you know Trinity College?"

"Yes, sir," said the cabman.

"Well, drive bang up against Trinity College gates," said Mr. Browne, "and then we'll tell you where to go. You understand now?"

"Yes, sir," said the cabman.

"Make like a bird for Trinity College."

"Right, sir," said the cabman.

The horse was whipped up and the cab rattled off along the quay amid a chorus of laughter and adieus.

Gabriel had not gone to the door with the others. He was in a dark part of the hall gazing up the staircase. A woman was standing near the top of the first flight, in the shadow also. He could not see her face but he could see the terracotta and salmon-pink panels of her skirt which the shadow made appear black and white. It was his wife. She was leaning on the banisters, listening to something. Gabriel was surprised at her stillness and strained his ear to listen also. But he could hear little save the noise of laughter and dispute on the front steps, a few chords struck on the piano and a few notes of a man's voice singing.

He stood still in the gloom of the hall, trying to catch the air that the voice was singing and gazing up at his wife. There was grace and mystery in her attitude as if she were a symbol of something. He asked himself what is a woman standing on the stairs in the shadow, listening to distant music, a symbol of. If he were a painter he would paint her in that attitude. Her blue felt hat would show off the bronze of her hair against the darkness and the dark panels of her skirt would show off the light ones. *Distant Music* he would call the picture if he were a painter.

The hall-door was closed; and Aunt Kate, Aunt Julia and Mary Jane came down the hall, still laughing.

"Well, isn't Freddy terrible?" said Mary Jane. "He's really terrible."

Gabriel said nothing but pointed up the stairs towards where his wife was standing. Now that the hall-door was closed the voice and the piano could be heard more clearly. Gabriel held up his hand for them to be silent. The song seemed to be in the old Irish tonality and the singer seemed uncertain both of his words and of his voice. The voice, made plaintive by distance and by the singer's hoarseness, faintly illuminated the cadence of the air with words expressing grief:

O, the rain falls on my heavy locks
And the dew wets my skin,
My babe lies cold . . .

"O," exclaimed Mary Jane. "It's Bartell D'Arcy singing and he wouldn't sing all the night. O, I'll get him to sing a song before he goes."

"O, do, Mary Jane," said Aunt Kate.

Mary Jane brushed past the others and ran to the staircase, but before she reached it the singing stopped and the piano was closed abruptly.

"O, what a pity!" she cried. "Is he coming down, Gretta?"

Gabriel heard his wife answer yes and saw her come down towards them. A few steps behind her were Mr. Bartell D'Arcy and Miss O'Callaghan.

"O, Mr. D'Arcy," cried Mary Jane, "it's downright mean of you to break off like that when we were all in raptures listening to you."

"I have been at him all the evening," said Miss O'Callaghan, "and Mrs. Conroy, too, and he told us he had a dreadful cold and couldn't sing."

"O, Mr. D'Arcy," said Aunt Kate, "now that was a great fib to tell."

"Can't you see that I'm as hoarse as a crow?" said Mr. D'Arcy roughly.

He went into the pantry hastily and put on his overcoat. The others, taken aback by his rude speech, could find nothing to say. Aunt Kate wrinkled her brows and made signs to the others to drop the subject. Mr. D'Arcy stood swathing his neck carefully and frowning.

"It's the weather," said Aunt Julia, after a pause.

"Yes, everybody has colds," said Aunt Kate readily, "everybody."

"They say," said Mary Jane, "we haven't had snow like it for thirty years; and I read this morning in the newspapers that the snow is general all over Ireland."

"I love the look of snow," said Aunt Julia sadly.

"So do I," said Miss O'Callaghan. "I think Christmas is never really Christmas unless we have the snow on the ground."

"But poor Mr. D'Arcy doesn't like the snow," said Aunt Kate, smiling.

Mr. D'Arcy came from the pantry, fully swathed and buttoned, and in a repentant tone told them the history of his cold. Everyone gave him advice and said it was a great pity and urged him to be very careful of his throat in the night air. Gabriel watched his wife, who did not join in the conversation. She was standing right under the dusty fanlight and the flame of the gas lit up the rich bronze of her hair, which he had seen her drying at the fire a few days before. She was in the same attitude and seemed unaware of the talk about her. At last she turned towards them and Gabriel saw that there was colour on her cheeks and that her eyes were shining. A sudden tide of joy went leaping out of his heart.

"Mr. D'Arcy," she said, "what is the name of that song you were singing?"

"It's called *The Lass of Aughrim,*" said Mr. D'Arcy, "but I couldn't remember it properly. Why? Do you know it?"

"The Lass of Aughrim," she repeated. "I couldn't think of the name."

"It's a very nice air," said Mary Jane. "I'm sorry you were not in voice to-night."

"Now, Mary Jane," said Aunt Kate, "don't annoy Mr. D'Arcy. I won't have him annoyed."

Seeing that all were ready to start she shepherded them to the door, where good-night was said:

"Well, good-night, Aunt Kate, and thanks for the pleasant evening."

"Good-night, Gabriel. Good-night, Gretta!"

"Good-night, Aunt Kate, and thanks ever so much. Good-night, Aunt Julia."

"O, good-night, Gretta, I didn't see you."

"Good-night, Mr. D'Arcy. Good-night, Miss O'Callaghan."

"Good-night, Miss Morkan."

"Good-night, again."

"Good-night, all. Safe home."

"Good-night. Good-night."

The morning was still dark. A dull, yellow light brooded over the houses and the river; and the sky seemed to be descending. It was slushy underfoot; and only streaks and patches of snow lay on the roofs, on the parapets of the quay and on the area railings. The lamps were still burning redly in the murky air and, across the river, the palace of the Four Courts stood out menacingly against the heavy sky.

She was walking on before him with Mr. Bartell D'Arcy, her shoes in a brown parcel tucked under one arm and her hands holding her skirt up from the slush. She had no longer any grace of attitude, but Gabriel's eyes were still bright with happiness. The blood went bounding along his veins; and the thoughts went rioting through his brain, proud, joyful, tender, valorous.

She was walking on before him so lightly and so erect that he longed to run after her noiselessly, catch her by the shoulders and say something foolish and affectionate into her ear. She seemed to him so frail that he longed to defend her against something and then to be alone with her. Moments of their secret life together burst like stars upon his memory. A heliotrope envelope was lying beside his breakfast-cup and he was caressing it with his hand. Birds were twittering in the ivy and the sunny web of the curtain was shimmering along the floor: he could not eat for happiness. They were standing on the crowded platform and he was placing a ticket inside the warm palm of her glove. He was standing with her in the cold, looking in through a grated window at a man making bottles in a roaring furnace. It was very cold. Her face, fragrant in the cold air, was quite close to his; and suddenly he called out to the man at the furnace:

"Is the fire hot, sir?"

But the man could not hear with the noise of the furnace. It was just as well. He might have answered rudely.

A wave of yet more tender joy escaped from his heart and went coursing in warm flood along his arteries. Like the tender fire of stars moments of their life together, that no one knew of or would ever know of, broke upon and illumined his memory. He longed to recall to her those moments, to make her forget the years of their dull existence together and remember only their moments of ecstasy. For the years, he felt, had not quenched his soul or hers. Their children, his writing, her household cares had not quenched all their souls' tender fire. In one letter that he had written to her then he had said: "Why is it that words like these seem to me so dull and cold? Is it because there is no word tender enough to be your name?"

Like distant music these words that he had written years before were borne towards him from the past. He longed to be alone with her. When the others had gone away, when he and she were in the room in the hotel, then they would be alone together. He would call her softly:

"Gretta!"

Perhaps she would not hear at once: she would be undressing. Then something in his voice would strike her. She would turn and look at him. . . .

At the corner of Winetavern Street they met a cab. He was glad of its rattling noise as it saved him from conversation. She was looking out of the window and seemed tired. The others spoke only a few words, pointing out some building or street. The horse galloped along wearily under the murky morning sky, dragging his old rattling box after his heels, and Gabriel was again in a cab with her, galloping to catch the boat, galloping to their honeymoon.

As the cab drove across O'Connell Bridge Miss O'Callaghan said:

"They say you never cross O'Connell Bridge without seeing a white horse."

"I see a white man this time," said Gabriel.

"Where?" asked Mr. Bartell D'Arcy.

Gabriel pointed to the statue, on which lay patches of snow. Then he nodded familiarly to it and waved his hand.

"Good-night, Dan," he said gaily.

When the cab drew up before the hotel, Gabriel jumped out and, and in spite of Mr. Bartell D'Arcy's protest, paid the driver. He gave the man a shilling over his fare. The man saluted and said:

"A prosperous New Year to you, sir."

"The same to you," said Gabriel cordially.

She leaned for a moment on his arm in getting out of the cab and while standing at the curbstone, bidding the others good-night. She leaned lightly on his arm, as lightly as when she had danced with him a few hours before. He had felt proud and happy then, happy that she was his, proud of her grace and wifely carriage. But now, after the kindling again of so many memories, the first touch of her body, musical and strange and perfumed, sent through him a keen pang of lust. Under cover of her silence he pressed her arm closely to his side; and, as they stood at the hotel door, he felt that they had escaped from their lives and duties, escaped from home and friends and run away together with wild and radiant hearts to a new adventure.

An old man was dozing in a great hooded chair in the hall. He lit a candle in the office and went before them to the stairs. They followed him in silence, their feet falling in soft thuds on the thickly carpeted stairs. She mounted the stairs behind the porter, her head bowed in the ascent, her frail shoulders curved as with a burden, her skirt girt tightly about her. He could have flung his arms about her hips and held her still, for his arms were trembling with desire to seize her and only the stress of his nails against the palms of his hands held the wild impulse of his body in check. The porter halted on the stairs to settle his guttering candle. They halted, too, on the steps below him. In the silence Gabriel could hear the falling of the molten wax into the tray and the thumping of his own heart against his ribs.

The porter led them along a corridor and opened a door. Then he set his unstable candle down on a toilet-table and asked at what hour they were to be called in the morning.

"Eight," said Gabriel.

The porter pointed to the tap of the electric light and began a muttered apology, but Gabriel cut him short.

"We don't want any light. We have light enough from the street. And I say," he added, pointing to the candle, "you might remove that handsome article, like a good man."

The porter took up his candle again, but slowly, for he was surprised by such a novel idea. Then he mumbled good-night and went out. Gabriel shot the lock to.

A ghastly light from the street lamp lay in a long shaft from one window to the door. Gabriel threw his overcoat and hat on a couch and crossed the room towards the window. He looked down into the street in order that his emotion might calm a little. Then he turned and leaned against a chest of drawers with his back to the light. She had taken off her hat and cloak and was standing before a large swinging mirror, unhooking her waist. Gabriel paused for a few moments, watching her, and then said:

"Gretta!"

She turned away from the mirror slowly and walked along the shaft of light towards him. Her face looked so serious and weary that the words would not pass Gabriel's lips. No, it was not the moment yet.

"You looked tired," he said.

"I am a little," she answered.

"You don't feel ill or weak?"

"No, tired: that's all."

She went on to the window and stood there, looking out. Gabriel waited again and then fearing that diffidence was about to conquer him, he said abruptly:

"By the way, Gretta!"

"What is it?"

"You know that poor fellow Malins?" he said quickly.

"Yes. What about him?"

"Well, poor fellow, he's a decent sort of chap, after all," continued Gabriel in a false voice. "He gave me back that sovereign I lent him, and I didn't expect it, really. It's a pity he wouldn't keep away from that Browne, because he's not a bad fellow, really."

He was trembling now with annoyance. Why did she seem so abstracted? He did not know how he could begin. Was she annoyed, too, about something? If she would only turn to him or come to him of her own accord! To take her as she was would be brutal. No, he must see some ardour in her eyes first. He longed to be master of her strange mood.

"When did you lend him the pound?" she asked, after a pause.

Gabriel strove to restrain himself from breaking out into brutal language about the sottish Malins and his pound. He longed to cry to her from his soul, to crush her body against his, to overmaster her. But he said:

"O, at Christmas, when he opened that little Christmas-card shop in Henry Street."

He was in such a fever of rage and desire that he did not hear her come from the window. She stood before him for an instant, looking at him strangely. Then, suddenly raising herself on tiptoe and resting her hands lightly on his shoulders, she kissed him.

"You are a very generous person, Gabriel," she said.

Gabriel, trembling with delight at her sudden kiss and at the quaintness of her phrase, put his hands on her hair and began smoothing it back, scarcely touching it with his fingers. The washing had made it fine and brilliant. His heart was brimming over with happiness. Just when he was wishing for it she had come to him of her own accord. Perhaps her thoughts had been running with his. Perhaps she had felt the impetuous desire that was in him, and then the yielding mood had come upon her. Now that she had fallen to him so easily, he wondered why he had been so diffident.

He stood, holding her head between his hands. Then, slipping one arm swiftly about her body and drawing her towards him, he said softly:

"Gretta, dear, what are you thinking about?"

She did not answer nor yield wholly to his arm. He said again, softly:

"Tell me what it is, Gretta. I think I know what is the matter. Do I know?"

She did not answer at once. Then she said in an outburst of tears:

"O, I am thinking about that song, *The Lass of Aughrim*."

She broke loose from him and ran to the bed and, throwing her arms across the bed-rail, hid her face. Gabriel stood stock-still for a moment in astonishment and then followed her. As he passed in the way of the cheval-glass he caught sight of himself in full length, his broad, well-filled shirt-front, the face whose expression always puzzled him when he saw it in a mirror, and his glimmering gilt-rimmed eyeglasses. He halted a few paces from her and said:

"What about the song? Why does that make you cry?"

She raised her head from her arms and dried her eyes with the back of her hand like a child. A kinder note than he had intended went into his voice.

"Why, Gretta?" he asked.

"I am thinking about a person long ago who used to sing that song."

"And who was the person long ago?" asked Gabriel, smiling.

"It was a person I used to know in Galway when I was living with my grandmother," she said.

The smile passed away from Gabriel's face. A dull anger began to gather again at the back of his mind and the dull fires of his lust began to glow angrily in his veins.

"Someone you were in love with?" he asked ironically.

"It was a young boy I used to know," she answered, "named Michael Furey. He used to sing that song, *The Lass of Aughrim*. He was very delicate."

Gabriel was silent. He did not wish her to think that he was interested in this delicate boy.

"I can see him so plainly," she said, after a moment. "Such eyes as he had: big, dark eyes! And such an expression in them—an expression!"

"O, then, you are in love with him?" said Gabriel.

"I used to go out walking with him," she said, "when I was in Galway."

A thought flew across Gabriel's mind.

"Perhaps that was why you wanted to go to Galway with that Ivors girl?" he said coldly.

She looked at him and asked in surprise:

"What for?"

Her eyes made Gabriel feel awkward. He shrugged his shoulders and said:

"How do I know? To see him, perhaps."

She looked away from him along the shaft of light towards the window in silence.

"He is dead," she said at length. "He died when he was only seventeen. Isn't it a terrible thing to die so young as that?"

"What was he?" asked Gabriel, still ironically.

"He was in the gasworks," she said.

Gabriel felt humiliated by the failure of his irony and by the evocation of this figure from the dead, a boy in the gasworks. While he had been full of memories of their secret life together, full of tenderness and joy and desire, she had been comparing him in her mind with another. A shameful consciousness of his own person assailed him. He saw himself as a ludicrous figure, acting as a pennyboy for his aunts, a nervous, well-meaning sentimentalist, orating to vulgarians and idealising his own clownish lusts, the pitiable fatuous fellow he had caught a glimpse of in the mirror. Instinctively he turned his back more to the light lest she might see the shame that burned upon his forehead.

He tried to keep up his tone of cold interrogation, but his voice when he spoke was humble and indifferent.

"I suppose you were in love with this Michael Furey, Gretta," he said.

"I was great with him at that time," she said.

Her voice was veiled and sad. Gabriel, feeling now how vain it would be to try to lead her whither he had purposed, caressed one of her hands and said, also sadly:

"And what did he die of so young, Gretta? Consumption, was it?"

"I think he died for me," she answered.

A vague terror seized Gabriel at this answer, as if, at that hour when he had hoped to triumph, some impalpable and vindictive being was coming against him, gathering forces against him in its vague world. But he shook himself free of it with an effort of reason and continued to caress her hand. He did not question her again, for he felt that she would tell him of herself. Her hand was warm and moist: it did not respond to his touch, but he continued to caress it just as he had caressed her first letter to him that spring morning.

"It was in the winter," she said, "about the beginning of the winter when I was going to leave my grandmother's and come up here to the convent. And he was ill at the time in his lodgings in Galway and wouldn't be let out, and his people in Oughterard were written to. He was in decline, they said, or something like that. I never knew rightly."

She paused for a moment and sighed.

"Poor fellow," she said. "He was very fond of me and he was such a gentle boy. We used to go out together, walking, you know, Gabriel, like the way they do in the country. He was going to study singing only for his health. He had a very good voice, poor Michael Furey."

"Well; and then?" asked Gabriel.

"And then when it came to the time for me to leave Galway and come up to the convent he was much worse and I wouldn't be let see him so I wrote him a letter saying I was going up to Dublin and would be back in the summer, and hoping he would be better then."

She paused for a moment to get her voice under control, and then went on:

"Then the night before I left, I was in my grandmother's house in Nuns' Island, packing up, and I heard gravel thrown up against the window. The window was so wet I couldn't see, so I ran downstairs as I was and slipped out the back into the garden and there was the poor fellow at the end of the garden, shivering."

"And did you not tell him to go back?" asked Gabriel.

"I implored of him to go home at once and told him he would get his death in the rain. But he said he did not want to live. I can see his eyes as well! He was standing at the end of the wall where there was a tree."

"And did he go home?" asked Gabriel.

"Yes, he went home. And when I was only a week in the convent he died and he was buried in Oughterard, where his people came from. O, the day I heard that, that he was dead!"

She stopped, choking with sobs, and, overcome by emotion, flung herself face downward on the bed, sobbing in the quilt. Gabriel held her hand for a moment longer, irresolutely, and then, shy of intruding on her grief, let it fall gently and walked quietly to the window.

She was fast asleep.

Gabriel, leaning on his elbow, looked for a few moments unresentfully on her tangled hair and half-open mouth, listening to her deep-drawn breath. So she had had that romance in her life: a man had died for her sake. It hardly pained him now to think how poor a part he, her husband, had played in her life. He watched her while she slept, as though he and she had never lived together as man and wife. His curious eyes rested long upon her face and on her hair: and, as he thought of what she must have been then, in that time of her first girlish beauty, a strange, friendly pity for her entered his soul. He did not like to say even to himself that her face was no longer beautiful, but he knew that it was no longer the face for which Michael Furey had braved death.

Perhaps she had not told him all the story. His eyes moved to the chair over which she had thrown some of her clothes. A petticoat string dangled to the floor. One boot stood upright, its limp upper fallen down: the fellow of it lay upon its side. He wondered at his riot of emotions of an hour before. From what had it proceeded? From his aunt's supper, from his own foolish speech, from the wine and dancing, the merry-making when saying good-night in the hall, the pleasure of the walk along the river in the snow. Poor Aunt Julia! She, too, would soon be a shade with the shade of Patrick Morkan and his horse. He had caught that haggard look upon her face for a moment when she was singing *Arrayed for the Bridal*. Soon, perhaps, he would be sitting in that same drawing-room, dressed in black, his silk hat on his knees. The blinds would be drawn down and Aunt Kate would be sitting beside him, crying and blowing her nose and telling him how Julia had died. He would cast about in his mind for some words that might console her, and would find only lame and useless ones. Yes, yes: that would happen very soon.

The air of the room chilled his shoulders. He stretched himself cautiously along under the sheets and lay down beside his wife. One by one, they were all becoming shades. Better pass boldly into that other world, in the full glory of some passion, than fade and wither dismally with age. He thought of how she who lay beside him had locked in her heart for so many years that image of her lover's eyes when he had told her that he did not wish to live.

Generous tears filled Gabriel's eyes. He had never felt like that himself towards any woman but he knew that such a feeling must be love. The tears gathered more thickly in his eyes and in the partial darkness he imagined he saw the form of a young man standing under a dripping tree. Other forms were near. His soul had approached that region where dwell the vast hosts of the dead. He was conscious of, but could not apprehend, their wayward and flickering existence. His own identity was fading out into a grey impalpable world: the solid world itself, which these dead had one time reared and lived in, was dissolving and dwindling.

A few light taps upon the pane made him turn to the window. It had begun to snow again. He watched sleepily the flakes, silver and dark, falling obliquely against the lamplight. The time had come for him to set out on his journey westward. Yes, the newspapers were right snow was general all over Ireland. It was falling on every part of the dark central plain, on the treeless hills, falling softly upon the Bog of Allen and, farther westward, softly falling into the dark mutinous Shannon waves. It was falling, too, upon every part of the lonely churchyard on the hill where Michael Furey lay buried. It lay thickly drifted on the crooked crosses and headstones, on the spears of the little gate, on the barren thorns. His soul swooned slowly as he heard the snow falling faintly through the universe and faintly falling, like the descent of their last end, upon all the living and the dead.

QUESTIONS

1. What is the reader's first impression of Gabriel? of his relationship with Gretta?
2. Why is Gabriel so bothered by the jibes of Miss Ivors? What is at the root of her friendly mockery?
3. Discuss the cross-section of character types that Joyce brings forward in this story. How do they function as a backdrop to the private drama between Gabriel and Gretta?
4. Gabriel and the others spend a great deal of time reflecting upon past events, customs, and personages. Do these reflections have any bearing upon Gretta's revelation at the end of the story? Discuss.
5. How does Joyce use the words of an old song to foreshadow Gretta's admission? How do we perceive that the song has affected her?
6. How does Joyce's language change from the opening pages to the final section? Speculate on the reasons for the change, and what it signals.
7. How do our feelings about Gabriel change over the course of the story?
8. Discuss Joyce's use of snow imagery. How do earlier glimpses of snow enhance the effect of the final passage?
9. Does Joyce want us to see Gabriel as a fool? Is he ultimately more sympathetic toward Gabriel or Gretta—or is he neutral?
10. Many have called "The Dead" the finest story in the English language. What is the source of its special excellence?

Franz Kafka

If the distinguishing features of modernist literature are a concern with violence, godlessness, and personal and collective anxiety, then Franz Kafka (1883–1924) has to be seen as one of its truest representatives.

Born to a Jewish family in Prague, Kafka suffered many of the ills of the spirit that Sigmund Freud analyzed with such penetration. He strove without success to break free from the tyranny of his authoritarian father. He failed to forge a lasting bond with the various women he knew (his epic correspondence with several has been published), and consequently he never married. Nor could he ever be free of the dull desk he job he held as a claims investigator at a large state insurance corporation. He lived in and for his writing.

But writing was not for Kafka an alternative universe; he did not escape into a better life. The world he portrays in his many stories as well as in his unfinished novels is even darker and more constrained than the world he knew in his daily life. Haunted, anxious, often nameless men are sent wandering down drab corridors; they take on errands that they can never complete; they are victimized by mindless representatives of unseen powers. No one would elect to live in a Kafka story.

Kafka's sense of inadequacy extended to his literary life. Although a few of his works appeared in his short lifetime—including *The Metamorphosis* (1915), *The Judgement* (1916), and *In the Penal Colony* (1919)—he asked his friend Max Brod to destroy his many remaining manuscripts at his death. Brod proved to be a better friend to literature than to Kafka: he disobeyed, with the result that we have the texts of the major novels that Kafka had been working on for years—*Amerika, The Trial,* and *The Castle.* All were published posthumously to great acclaim.

Kafka's gift was for rendering his fears and anxieties with enough allegorical suggestion to make them universal. By looking into himself, he also saw into the core of the malaise that gripped a godless and war-torn Europe. His dread of bureaucracy and impersonal power reflected the collective temper of his times. The rise of Nazism and the facelessness of Eastern European socialism are prefigured in distilled form in his writings.

"A Hunger Artist" is representative of the Kafka approach. Powerful as it is to read, its subtler force is manifested later: the voice of this proud, self-annihilating "artist" will echo in the reader's mind long after the simple turns of the narrative have been forgotten.

A HUNGER ARTIST

During these last decades the interest in professional fasting has markedly diminished. It used to pay very well to stage such great performances under one's own management, but today that is quite impossible. We live in a different world now. At one time the whole town took a lively interest in the hunger artist; from day to day of his fast the excitement mounted; everybody wanted to see him at least once a day; there were people who bought season tickets for the last few days and sat from morning till night in front of his small barred cage; even in the nighttime there were visiting hours, when the whole effect was heightened by torch flares; on fine days the cage was set out in the open air, and then it was the children's special treat to see the hunger artist; for their elders he was often just a joke that happened to be in fashion, but the children stood openmouthed, holding each other's hands for greater security, marveling at him as he sat there pallid in black tights, with his ribs sticking out so prominently, not even on a seat but down among straw on the ground, sometimes giving a courteous nod, answering questions with a constrained smile, or perhaps stretching an arm through the bars so that one might feel how thin it was, and then again withdrawing deep into himself, paying no attention to anyone or anything, not even to the all-important striking of the clock that was the only piece of furniture in his cage, but merely staring into vacancy with half-shut eyes, now and then taking a sip from a tiny glass of water to moisten his lips.

Besides casual onlookers there were also relays of permanent watchers selected by the public, usually butchers, strangely enough, and it was their task to watch the hunger artist day and night, three of them at a time, in case he should have some secret recourse to nourishment. This was nothing but a formality, instituted to reassure the masses, for the initiates knew well enough that during his fast the artist would never in any circumstances, not even under forcible compulsion, swallow the smallest morsel of food; the honor of his profession forbade it. Not every watcher, of course, was capable of understanding this, there were often groups of night watchers who were very lax in carrying out their duties and deliberately huddled together in a retired corner to play cards with great absorption, obviously intending to give the hunger artist the chance of a little refreshment, which they supposed he could draw from some private hoard. Nothing annoyed the artist more than such watchers; they made him miserable; they made his fast seem unendurable; sometimes he mastered his feebleness sufficiently to sing during their watch for as long as he could keep going, to show them how unjust their suspicions were. But that was of little use; they only wondered at his cleverness in being able to fill his mouth even while singing. Much more to his taste were the watchers who sat close up to the bars, who were not content with the dim night lighting of the hall but focused him in the full glare of the electric pocket torch given them by the impresario. The harsh light did not trouble him at all, in any case he could never sleep properly, and he could always drowse a little, whatever the light, at any hour, even when the hall was thronged with noisy onlookers. He was quite happy at the prospect of spending a sleepless night with such watchers; he was ready to exchange jokes with them, to tell them stories out of his nomadic life, anything at all to keep them awake and demonstrate to them again that he had no eatables in his cage and that he was fasting as not one of them could fast. But his happiest moment was when the morning came and an enormous breakfast was brought them, at his expense, on which they flung themselves with the keen appetite of healthy men after a weary night of wakefulness. Of course there were people who argued that this breakfast was an unfair attempt to bribe the watchers, but that was going rather too far, and when they were invited to take on a night's vigil without a breakfast, merely for the sake of the cause, they made themselves scarce, although they stuck stubbornly to their suspicions.

Such suspicions, anyhow, were a necessary accompaniment to the profession of fasting. No one could possibly watch the hunger artist continuously, day and night, and so no one could produce first-hand evidence that the fast had really been rigorous and continuous; only the artist himself could know that, he was therefore bound to be the sole completely satisfied spectator of his own fast. Yet for other reasons he was never satisfied; it was not perhaps mere fasting that had brought him to such skeleton thinness that many people had regretfully to keep away from his exhibitions, because the sight of him was too much for them, perhaps it was dissatisfaction with himself that had worn him down. For he alone knew, what no other initiate knew, how easy it was to fast. It was the easiest thing in the world. He made no secret of this, yet people did not believe him, at the best they set him down as modest, most of them, however, thought he was out for publicity or else was some kind of cheat who found it easy to fast because he had discovered a way of making it easy, and then had the impudence to admit the fact, more or less. He had to put up with all that, and in the course of time had got used to it, but his inner dissatisfaction always rankled, and never yet, after any term of fasting—this must be granted to his credit—had he left the cage of his own free will. The longest period of fasting was fixed by his impresario at forty days, beyond that term he was not allowed to go, not even in great cities, and there was good reason for it, too. Experience had proved that for about forty days the interest of the public could be stimulated by a steadily increasing pressure of advertisement, but after that the town began to lose interest, sympathetic support began notably to fall off; there were of course local variations as between one town and another or one country and another, but as a general rule forty days marked the limit. So on the fortieth day the flower-bedecked cage was opened, enthusiastic spectators filled the hall, a military band played, two doctors entered the cage to measure the results of the fast, which were announced through a megaphone, and finally two young ladies appeared, blissful at having been selected for the honor, to help the hunger artist down the few steps leading to a small table on which was spread a carefully chosen invalid repast. And at this very moment the artist always turned stubborn. True, he would entrust his bony arms to the outstretched helping hands of the ladies bending over him, but stand up he would not. Why stop fasting at this particular moment, after forty days of it? He had held out for a long time, an illimitably long time; why stop now, when he was in his best fasting form, or rather, not yet quite in his best fasting form? Why should he be cheated of the fame he would get for fasting longer, for being not only the record hunger artist of all time, which presumably he was already, but for beating his own record by a performance beyond human imagination, since he felt that there were no limits to his capacity for fasting? His public pretended to admire him so much, why should it have so little patience with him; if he could endure fasting longer, why shouldn't the public endure it? Besides, he was tired, he was comfortable sitting in the straw, and now he was supposed to lift himself to his full height and go down to a meal the very thought of which gave him a nausea that only the presence of the ladies kept him from betraying, and even that with an effort. And he looked up into the eyes of the ladies who were apparently so friendly and in reality so cruel, and shook his head, which felt too heavy on its strengthless neck. But then there happened yet again what always happened. The impresario came forward, without a word—for the band made speech impossible—lifted his arms in the air above the artist, as if inviting Heaven to look down upon its creature here in the straw, this suffering martyr, which indeed he was, although in quite another sense; grasped him around the emaciated waist, with exaggerated caution, so that the frail condition he was in might be appreciated; and committed him to the care of the blenching ladies, not without secretly giving him a shaking so that his legs and body tottered and swayed. The artist now submitted completely; his head lolled on his breast as if it had landed there by chance; his body was hollowed out; his legs in a spasm of self-preservation clung close to each other at the knees, yet scraped on the ground as if it were not really solid ground, as if they were only trying to find solid ground; and the whole weight of his body, a featherweight after all, relapsed onto one of the ladies, who, looking around for help and panting a little—this post of honor was not at all what she had expected it to be—first stretched her neck as far as she could to keep her face at least free from contact with the artist, then finding this impossible, and her more fortunate companion not coming to her aid but merely holding extended in her own trembling hand the little bunch of knucklebones that was the artist's, to the great delight of the spectators burst into tears and had to be replaced by an attendant who had long been stationed in readiness. Then came the food, a little of which the impresario managed to get between the artist's lips, while he sat in a kind of half-fainting trance, to the accompaniment of cheerful patter designed to distract the public's attention from the artist's condition; after that, a toast was drunk to the public, supposedly prompted by a whisper from the artist in the impresario's ear; the band confirmed it with a mighty flourish, the spectators melted away, and no one had any cause to be dissatisfied with the proceedings, no one except the hunger artist himself, he only, as always.

So he lived for many years, with small regular intervals of recuperation, in visible glory, honored by the world, yet in spite of that troubled in spirit, and all the more troubled because no one would take his trouble seriously. What comfort could he possibly need? What more could he possibly wish for? And if some good-natured person, feeling sorry for him, tried to console him by pointing out that his melancholy was probably caused by fasting, it could happen, especially when he had been fasting for some time, that he reacted with an outburst of fury and to the general alarm began to shake the bars of his cage like a wild animal. Yet the impresario had a way of punishing these outbreaks which he rather enjoyed putting into operation. He would apologize publicly for the artist's behavior, which was only to be excused, he admitted, because of the irritability caused by fasting; a condition hardly to be understood by well-fed people; then by natural transition he went on to mention the artist's equally incomprehensible boast that he could fast for much longer than he was doing; he praised the high ambition, the good will, the great self-denial undoubtedly implicit in such a statement; and then quite simply countered it by bringing out photographs, which were also on sale to the public, showing the artist on the fortieth day of a fast lying in bed almost dead from exhaustion. This perversion of the truth, familiar to the artist though it was, always unnerved him afresh and proved too much for him. What was a consequence of the premature ending of his fast was here presented as the cause of it! To fight against this lack of understanding, against a whole world of non-understanding, was impossible. Time and again in good faith he stood by the bars listening to the impresario, but as soon as the photographs appeared he always let go and sank with a groan back onto his straw, and the reassured public could once more come close and gaze at him.

A few years later when the witnesses of such scenes called them to mind, they often failed to understand themselves at all. For meanwhile the aforementioned change in public interest had set in; it seemed to happen almost overnight; there may have been profound causes for it, but who was going to bother about that; at any rate the pampered hunger artist suddenly found himself deserted one fine day by the amusement-seekers, who went streaming past him to other more-favored attractions. For the last time the impresario hurried him over half Europe to discover whether the old interest might still survive here and there; all in vain; everywhere, as if by secret agreement, a positive revulsion from professional fasting was in evidence. Of course it could not really have sprung up so suddenly as all that, and many premonitory symptoms which had not been sufficiently remarked or suppressed during the rush and glitter of success now came retrospectively to mind, but it was now too late to take any countermeasures. Fasting would surely come into fashion again at some future date, yet that was no comfort for those living in the present. What, then, was the hunger artist to do? He had been applauded by thousands in his time and could hardly come down to showing himself in a street booth at village fairs, and as for adopting another profession, he was not only too old for that but too fanatically devoted to fasting. So he took leave of the impresario, his partner in an unparalleled career, and hired himself to a large circus; in order to spare his own feelings he avoided reading the conditions of his contract.

A large circus with its enormous traffic in replacing and recruiting men, animals, and apparatus can always find a use for people at any time, even for a hunger artist, provided of course that he does not ask too much, and in this particular case anyhow it was not only the artist who was taken on but his famous and long-known name as well, indeed considering the peculiar nature of his performance, which was not impaired by advancing age, it could not be objected that here was an artist past his prime, no longer at the height of his professional skill, seeking a refuge in some quiet corner of a circus; on the contrary, the hunger artist averred that he could fast as well as ever, which was entirely credible, he even alleged that if he were allowed to fast as he liked, and this was at once promised him without more ado, he could astound the world by establishing a record never yet achieved, a statement that certainly provoked a smile among the other professionals, since it left out of account the change in public opinion, which the hunger artist in his zeal conveniently forgot.

He had not, however, actually lost his sense of the real situation and took it as a matter of course that he and his cage should be stationed, not in the middle of the ring as a main attraction, but outside, near the animal cages, on a site that was after all easily accessible. Large and gaily painted placards made a frame for the cage and announced what was to be seen inside it. When the public came thronging out in the intervals to see the animals, they could hardly avoid passing the hunger artist's cage and stopping there for a moment, perhaps they might even have stayed longer had not those pressing behind them in the narrow gangway, who did not understand why they should be held up on their way toward the excitements of the menagerie, made it impossible for anyone to stand gazing quietly for any length of time. And that was the reason why the hunger artist, who had of course been looking forward to these visiting hours as the main achievement of his life, began instead to shrink from them. At first he could hardly wait for the intervals; it was exhilarating to watch the crowds come streaming his way, until only too soon—not even the most obstinate self-deception, clung to almost consciously, could hold out against the fact—the conviction was borne in upon him that these people, most of them, to judge from their actions, again and again, without exception, were all on their way to the menagerie. And the first sight of them from the distance remained the best. For when they reached his cage he was at once deafened by the storm of shouting and abuse that arose from the two contending factions, which renewed themselves continuously, of those who wanted to stop and stare at him—he soon began to dislike them more than the others—not out of real interest but only out of obstinate self-assertiveness, and those who wanted to go straight on to the animals. When the first great rush was past, the stragglers came along, and these, whom nothing could have prevented from stopping to look at him as long as they had breath, raced past with long strides, hardly even glancing at him, in their haste to get to the menagerie in time. And all too rarely did it happen that he had a stroke of luck, when some father of a family fetched up before him with his children, pointed a finger at the hunger artist, and explained at length what the phenomenon meant, telling stories of earlier years when he himself had watched similar but much more thrilling performances, and the children, still rather uncomprehending, since neither inside nor outside school had they been sufficiently prepared for this lesson—what did they care about fasting?—yet showed by the brightness of their intent eyes that new and better times might be coming. Perhaps, said the hunger artist to himself many a time, things would be a little better if his cage were set not quite so near the menagerie. That made it too easy for people to make their choice, to say nothing of what he suffered from the stench of the menagerie, the animals' restlessness by night, the carrying past of raw lumps of flesh for the beasts of prey, the roaring at feeding times, which depressed him continually. But he did not dare to lodge a complaint with the management; after all, he had the animals to thank for the troops of people who passed his cage, among whom there might always be one here and there to take an interest in him, and who could tell where they might seclude him if he called attention to his existence and thereby to the fact that, strictly speaking, he was only an impediment on the way to the menagerie.

A small impediment, to be sure, one that grew steadily less. People grew familiar with the strange idea that they could be expected, in times like these, to take an interest in a hunger artist, and with this familiarity the verdict went out against him. He might fast as much as he could, and he did so; but nothing could save him now, people passed him by. Just try to explain to anyone the art of fasting! Anyone who has no feeling for it cannot be made to understand it. The fine placards grew dirty and illegible, they were torn down; the little notice board telling the number of fast days achieved, which at first was changed carefully every day, had long stayed at the same figure, for after the first few weeks even this small task seemed pointless to the staff; and so the artist simply fasted on and on, as he had once dreamed of doing, and it was no trouble to him, just as he had always foretold, but no one counted the days, no one, not even the artist himself, knew what records he was already breaking, and his heart grew heavy. And when once in a while some leisurely passer-by stopped, made merry over the old figure on the board, and spoke of swindling, that was in its way the stupidest lie ever invented by indifference and inborn malice, since it was not the hunger artist who was cheating, he was working honestly, but the world was cheating him of his reward.

Many more days went by, however, and that too came to an end. An overseer's eye fell on the cage one day and he asked the attendants why this perfectly good cage should be left standing there unused with dirty straw inside it; nobody knew, until one man, helped out by the notice board, remembered about the hunger artist. They poked into the straw with sticks and found him in it. "Are you still fasting?" asked the overseer, "when on earth do you mean to stop?" "Forgive me, everybody," whispered the hunger artist; only the overseer, who had his ear to the bars, understood him. "Of course," said the overseer, and tapped his forehead with a finger to let the attendants know what state the man was in, "we forgive you." "I always wanted you to admire my fasting," said the hunger artist. "We do admire it," said the overseer, affably. "But you shouldn't admire it," said the hunger artist. "Well then we don't admire it," said the overseer "but why shouldn't we admire it?" "Because I have to fast, I can't help it," said the hunger artist. "What a fellow you are," said the overseer, "and why can't you help it?" "Because," said the hunger artist, lifting his head a little and speaking, with his lips pursed, as if for a kiss, right into the overseer's ear, so that no syllable might be lost, "because I couldn't find the food I liked. If I had found it, believe me, I should have made no fuss and stuffed myself like you or anyone else." These were his last words, but in his dimming eyes remained the firm though no longer proud persuasion that he was still continuing to fast.

"Well, clear this out now!" said the overseer, and they buried the hunger artist, straw and all. Into the cage they put a young panther. Even the most insensitive felt it refreshing to see this wild creature leaping around the cage that had so long been dreary. The panther was all right. The food he liked was brought him without hesitation by the attendants; he seemed not even to miss his freedom; his noble body, furnished almost to the bursting point with all that it needed, seemed to carry freedom around with it too; somewhere in his jaws it seemed to lurk; and the joy of life streamed with such ardent passion from his throat that for the onlookers it was not easy to stand the shock of it. But they braced themselves, crowded around the cage, and did not want ever to move away.

Translated by Willa and Edwin Muir

QUESTIONS

1. Is there any sense in which this story may be viewed as an allegory about the place of the serious artist in modern society?

2. Find and discuss some instances of what might be called reverse psychology, that is, where the hunger artist's attitudes seem paradoxical, the opposite of what we might expect. How does this side of his nature play a role in the story?

3. Is Kafka writing a story for the intellect alone, or are we to have some feelings for the hunger artist? Explain.

4. Does he die a total failure, or is there some way in which his end is a triumph of vocation?

5. Why does Kafka conclude the story with the image of the panther? How are we to understand the difference between the two spectacles—hunger artist and wild animal?

6. What does the hunger artist mean when he says that he *has* to fast, that he became what he did because he couldn't find the food he liked?

7. Are we to read the physical as a kind of symbol for the unseen, the body as a figure for the soul? If so, then what is the story telling us about the conditions of modern life?

Junichiro Tanizaki

Junichiro Tanizaki (1886–1965) was born into an old Japanese merchant family. At the outset of his long literary career he proclaimed a devotion to the innovative writings of his Western masters, among them Poe, Baudelaire and Oscar Wilde. His early works reveal an obsession with themes of cruelty and sexual power. His critics labeled his prose "satanic," and many professed to be shocked at his frankly sensual depictions of male-female relationships.

In time, Tanizaki modified his approach, turning more and more to reflection upon the Japanese cultural heritage. His celebrated novel *Some Prefer Nettles* (1928) portrayed the deep conflict within the Japanese psyche between the traditional ways and the lure of the West. His massive novel *The Makioka Sisters* (1934–1938) is a faithfully realistic chronicle of family life in prewar Osaka. In later years, however, as in the short novel *The Key* (1958), Tanizaki returned to some of the preoccupations of his younger years. The novel presents the inside story of a marriage with a special view to the sexual interactions of the couple.

"Tattoo" was first published in 1910. It is included here to suggest how the modernist influences of the West interacted with Eastern traditions.

TATTOO

These things happened at a time when the noble virtue of frivolity still flourished, when today's relentless struggle for existence was yet unknown. The faces of the young aristocrats and squires were darkened by no cloud; at court the maids of honor and the great courtesans always wore smiles on their lips; the occupations of clown and professional teahouse wit were held in high esteem; life was peaceful and full of joy. In the theater and in the writings of the time, beauty and power were portrayed as inseparable.

Physical beauty, indeed, was the chief aim of life, and in its pursuit people went so far as to have themselves tattooed. On their bodies, brilliant lines and colors were raveled in a sort of dance. When visiting the gay quarters, they would choose as bearers for their palanquins men whose bodies were skillfully tattooed, and the courtesans of Yoshiwara and Tatsumi gave their love to men whose bodies boasted beautiful tattoos. Frequenters of the gambling dens, firemen, merchants, and even samurai all had recourse to the tattooer's art. Tattoo exhibitions were frequently arranged where the participants, fingering the tattoo marks on each other's bodies, would praise the original design of one and criticize the shortcomings of another.

There was a young tattooer of outstanding talent. He was much in fashion and his reputation rivaled even those of the great masters of old, Charibun of Asakusa, Yakkohei of Matsushimachō, and Konkonjirō. His works were greatly prized at the tattoo exhibitions and most admirers of the art aspired to become his clients. While the artist Darumakin was known for his fine drawings and Karakusa Gonta was the master of the vermilion tattoo, this man Seikichi was famous for the originality of his compositions and for their voluptuous quality.

Previously he had achieved a certain reputation as a painter, belonging to the school of Toyokuni and Kunisada and specializing in genre paintings. In descending to the rank of tattooer, he still preserved the true spirit of an artist and a great sensitivity. He declined to execute his work on people whose skin or general physique did not appeal to him, and such customers as he did accept had to agree implicitly to the design of his choosing and also to his price. Moreover, they had to endure for as long as one or two months the excruciating pain of his needles.

Within this young tattooer's heart lurked unsuspected passions and pleasures. When the pricking of his needles caused the flesh to swell and the crimson blood to flow, his patients, unable to endure the agony, would emit groans of pain. The more they groaned, the greater was the artist's strange pleasure. He took particular delight in vermilion designs, which are known to be the most painful of tattoos. When his clients had received five or six hundred pricks of the needle and then taken a scalding hot bath the more vividly to bring out the colors, they would often collapse half dead at Seikichi's feet. As they lay there unable to move, he would ask with a satisfied smile: "So it really hurts?"

When he had to deal with a fainthearted customer whose teeth would grind or who gave out shrieks of pain, Seikichi would say: "Really, I thought you were a native of Kyoto where people are supposed to be courageous. Please try to be patient. My needles are unusually painful." And glancing from the corner of his eyes at the victim's face, now moist with tears, he would continue his work with utter unconcern. If, on the contrary, his patient bore the agony without flinching, he would say: "Ah, you are much braver than you look. But wait a while. Soon you will be unable to endure it in silence, try as you may." And he would laugh, showing his white teeth.

For many years now, Seikichi's great ambition had been to have under his needle the lustrous skin of some beautiful girl, on which he dreamed of tattooing, as it were, his very soul. This imaginary woman had to meet many conditions as to both physique and character; a lovely face and a fine skin would not in themselves satisfy Seikichi. In vain had he searched among the well-known courtesans for a woman who would measure up to his ideal. Her image was constantly in his mind, and although three years had now elapsed since he started this quest, his desire had only grown with time.

It was on a summer's evening while walking in the Fukagawa district that his attention was caught by a feminine foot of dazzling whiteness disappearing behind the curtains of a palanquin. A foot can convey as many variations of expression as a face, and this white foot seemed to Seikichi like the rarest of jewels. The perfectly shaped toes, the iridescent nails, the rounded heel, the skin, as lustrous as if it had been washed for ages by the limpid waters of some mountain brook—all combined to make a foot of absolute perfection designed to stir the heart of a man and to trample upon his soul. Seikichi knew at once that this was the foot of the woman for whom he had searched these many years. Joyously he hurried after the palanquin, hoping to catch a glimpse of its occupant, but after following it for several streets, he lost sight of it around a corner. From then on what had been a vague yearning was transformed into the most violent of passions.

One morning a year later Seikichi received a visit at his house in the Fukagawa district. It was a young girl sent on an errand by a friend of his, a certain geisha from the Tatsumi quarter.

"Excuse me, sir," the girl said timidly. "My mistress has asked me to deliver this coat to you personally and to request you to be so good as to make a design on the lining."

She handed him a letter and a woman's coat, the latter wrapped in a paper bearing the portrait of the actor Iwai Tojaku. In her letter the geisha informed Seikichi that the young messenger was her newly adopted ward and was soon to make her debut as a geisha in the restaurants of the capital. She asked him to do what he could to launch the girl on her new career.

Seikichi looked closely at the visitor who, though no more than sixteen or seventeen, had in her face something strangely mature. In her eyes were reflected the dreams of all the handsome men and beautiful women who had lived in this city, where the virtues and vices of the whole country converged. Then Seikichi's glance went to her delicate feet, shod in street clogs covered with plaits of straw.

"Could it have been you who left the Hirasei restaurant last June in a palanquin?"

"Yes, sir, it was I," she said, laughing at his strange question. "My father was still alive then and he used to take me occasionally to the Hirasei restaurant."

"I have been waiting for you now for five years," said Seikichi. "This is the first time that I have seen your face but I know you by your feet. . . . There is something that I should like you to see. Please come inside, and do not be afraid."

So saying, he took the hand of the reluctant girl and led her upstairs into a room which looked out on the great river. He fetched two large picture scrolls and spread one of them before her.

It was a painting of Mo Hsi, the favorite princess of the ancient Chinese emperor, Chou the Cruel. Languidly she leaned against a balustrade, and the bottom of her richly brocaded gown rested on the steps of the staircase leading to a garden. Her tiny head seemed almost too delicate to support the weight of her crown, which was encrusted with lapis lazuli and coral. In her right hand she held a cup, slightly tilted, and with an indolent expression she watched a prisoner who was about to be beheaded in the garden below. Secured hand and foot to a stake, he stood there awaiting his last moment; his eyes were closed, his head bent down. Pictures of such scenes tend to vulgarity, but so skillfully had the painter portrayed the expressions of the princess and of the condemned man that this picture scroll was a work of consummate art.

For a while the young girl fixed her gaze on the strange painting. Unconsciously her eyes began to shine and her lips trembled; gradually her face took on a resemblance to that of the young Chinese princess.

"Your spirit is reflected in that painting," said Seikichi, smiling with pleasure as he gazed at her.

"Why have you shown me such a terrible picture?" asked the girl, passing her hand over her pale forehead.

"The woman depicted here is yourself. Her blood flows through your veins."

Seikichi then unrolled the other scroll, which was entitled "The Victims." In the center of the picture a young woman leaned against a cherry tree, gazing at a group of men's corpses which lay about her feet; pride and satisfaction were to be discerned in her pale face. Hopping about among the corpses, a swarm of little birds chirped happily. Impossible to tell whether the picture represented a battlefield or a spring garden!

"This painting symbolizes your future," said Seikichi, indicating the face of the young woman, which again strangely resembled that of his visitor. "The men fallen on the ground are those who will lose their lives because of you."

"Oh, I beg you," she cried, "put that picture away." And as if to escape its terrifying fascination, she turned her back to the scroll and threw herself on the straw matting. There she lay with lips trembling and her whole body shuddering. "Master, I will confess to you. . . . As you have guessed, I have in me the nature of that woman. Take pity on me and hide the picture."

"Do not talk like a coward! On the contrary, you should study the painting more carefully and then you will soon stop being frightened of it."

The girl could not bring herself to raise her head, which remained hidden in the sleeve of her kimono. She lay prostrate on the floor saying over and over: "Master, let me go home. I am frightened to be with you."

"You shall stay for a while," said Seikichi imperiously. "I alone have the power to make of you a beautiful woman."

From among the bottles and needles on his shelf Seikichi selected a vial containing a powerful narcotic.

The sun shone brightly on the river. Its reflected rays threw a pattern like golden waves on the sliding doors and on the face of the young sleeping woman. Seikichi closed the doors and sat down beside her. Now for the first time he was able to relish her strange beauty fully, and he thought that he could have spent years sitting there gazing at that perfect, immobile face.

But the urge to accomplish his design overcame him before many moments. Having fetched his tattooing instruments from the shelf, Seikichi uncovered the girl's body and began to apply to her back the point of his pen, held between the thumb, ring finger, and little finger of his left hand. With the needle, held in his right hand, he pricked along the lines as they were drawn. As the people of Memphis once embellished with sphinxes and pyramids the fine land of Egypt, so Seikichi now adorned the pure skin of this young girl. It was as if the tattooer's very spirit entered into the design, and each injected drop of vermilion was like a drop of his own blood penetrating the girl's body.

He was quite unconscious of the passage of time. Noon came and went, and the quiet spring day moved gradually toward its close. Indefatigably Seikichi's hand pursued its work without ever waking the girl from her slumber. Presently the moon hung in the sky, pouring its dreamy light over the rooftops on the other side of the river. The tattoo was not yet half done. Seikichi interrupted his work to turn up the lamp, then sat down again and reached for his needle.

Now each stroke demanded an effort, and the artist would let out a sigh, as if his own heart had felt the prick. Little by little there began to appear the outline of an enormous spider. As the pale glow of dawn entered the room, this animal of diabolic mien spread its eight legs over the girl's back.

The spring night was almost over. Already one could hear the dip of the oars as the rowboats passed up and down the river; above the sails of the fishing smacks, swollen with the morning breeze, one could see the mists lifting. And at last Seikichi brought himself to put down his needle. Standing aside, he studied the enormous female spider tattooed on the girl's back, and as he gazed at it, he realized that in this work he had expressed the essence of his whole life. Now that it was completed, the artist was aware of a great emptiness.

"To give you beauty I have poured my whole soul into this tattoo," Seikichi murmured. "From now on there is not a woman in Japan to rival you! Never again will you know fear. All men, all men will be your victims. . . ."

Did she hear his words? A moan rose to her lips, her limbs moved. Gradually she began to regain consciousness, and as she lay breathing heavily in and out, the spider's legs moved on her back like those of a living animal.

"You must be suffering," said Seikichi. "That is because the spider is embracing your body so closely."

She half opened her eyes. At first they had a vacant look, then the pupils began to shine with a brightness that matched the moonlight reflected on Seikichi's face.

"Master, let me see the tattoo on my back! If you have given me your soul, I must indeed have become beautiful."

She spoke as in a dream, and yet in her voice there was a new note of confidence, of power.

"First you must take a bath to brighten the colors," Seikichi answered her. And he added with unwonted solicitude: "It will be painful, most painful. Have courage!"

"I will bear anything to become beautiful," said the girl.

She followed Seikichi down some stairs into the bathroom, and as she stepped into the steaming water her eyes glistened with pain.

"Ah, ah, how it burns!" she groaned. "Master, leave me and wait upstairs. I shall join you when I am ready. I do not want any man to see me suffer."

But when she stepped out of the bath, she did not even have strength to dry herself. She pushed aside Seikichi's helping hand and collapsed on the floor. Groaning, she lay with her long hair flowing across the floor. The mirror behind her reflected the soles of two feet, iridescent as mother-of-pearl.

Seikichi went upstairs to wait for her, and when at last she joined him she was dressed with care. Her damp hair had been combed out and hung about her shoulders. Her delicate mouth and curving eyebrows no longer betrayed her ordeal, and as she gazed out at the river there was a cold glint in her eyes. Despite her youth she had the mien of a woman who had spent years in teahouses and acquired the art of mastering men's hearts. Amazed, Seikichi reflected on the change in the timid girl since the day before. Going to the other room, he fetched the two picture scrolls which he had shown her.

"I offer you these paintings," he said. "And also, of course, the tattoo. They are yours to take away."

"Master," she answered, "my heart is now free from all fear. And you . . . you shall be my first victim!"

She threw him a look, piercing as a newly sharpened sword blade. It was the look of the young Chinese princess, and of that other woman who leaned against a cherry tree surrounded by singing birds and dead bodies. A feeling of triumph raced through Seikichi.

"Let me see your tattoo," he said to her. "Show me your tattoo."

Without a word, she inclined her head and unfastened her dress. The rays of the morning sun fell on the young girl's back and its golden gleam seemed to set fire to the spider.

Translated by Ivan Morris

QUESTIONS

1. What details does Tanizaki use to convey impressions of perfection and innocence?
2. What is the tattoo artist's nature? How are we to understand his obsession—*if* we are?
3. Discuss the girl's reaction to the pictures that the artist shows her? What do the images say about the character of the woman depicted? How does Tanizaki convey the deep ambivalence of the girl's response?
4. Are we to see the artist as corrupting the girl, or is he merely bringing her essential character into the light?
5. Why would the artist tattoo a spider on the girl's back? What associations do we have with spiders?
6. What does this story reveal about Tanizaki's vision of the relationships between the sexes?

D. H. Lawrence

David Herbert Lawrence (1885–1930) was a miner's son from the coal-mining district of Nottinghamshire. His psyche was molded at a very young age by the powerful contrast between his rough, unlettered father and his more refined, highly possessive mother. Critics have said that his novel *Sons and Lovers* (1913) presents a classic instance of the Freudian Oedipus complex. The son struggles against the brutal father for his mother's love; in the end that love very nearly chokes him.

Lawrence had studied to be a teacher, but he began to publish prose and poetry very soon after taking a post in South London. His first novel, *The White Peacock,* appeared in 1909. Lawrence was so prolific that he was soon able to devote himself strictly to literature.

For the twenty years of his career, Lawrence was a highly controversial figure because of his strongly worded, emancipated views on love and sexuality—expressed in his novels *The Rainbow* (1915), *Women in Love* (1920), and *Lady Chatterley's Lover* (1928)—not to mention his own scandalous elopement with Frieda Weekley, wife of a well-known scholar. In addition, Lawrence held outspoken views on most social issues. He detested hypocrisy, bureaucracies, church morality, and anything that smacked of constraint. He was drawn to the more sensuous life possible in warmer climates, and he and Frieda traveled from Italy to Australia to Mexico to the American Southwest. (Lawrence, like Chekhov and Katherine Mansfield, suffered from tuberculosis and needed a dry climate for his health.) He wrote memorable descriptions of every locale; indeed, he has been called one of the greatest writers of "place." In his vision the roughest landscapes took on a breathing life.

As a writer of fiction Lawrence might be likened to an insect hurling itself at a bright bulb. He sets upon his subject from every side, drawing forth its deepest essences and contradictions. The prose itself modulates. It can be rough, reflective of the harsh environments he depicts, or it can shine with a sudden lyrical beauty. But his greatest contribution to literature is his frank, complex way of treating the relationships between men and women. Lawrence located the truth of an underlying ambivalence and worked it into a profound assessment of the nature of romantic love. "Odour of Chrysanthemums," written in 1909, is one of his earliest statements of the struggle at the heart of love.

ODOUR OF CHRYSANTHEMUMS

I

The small locomotive engine, Number 4, came clanking, stumbling down from Selston with seven full wagons. It appeared round the corner with loud threats of speed, but the colt that it startled from among the gorse, which still flickered indistinctly in the raw afternoon, out-distanced it at a canter. A woman, walking up the railway line to Underwood, drew back into the hedge, held her basket aside, and watched the footplate[1] of the engine advancing. The trucks thumped heavily past, one by one, with slow inevitable movement, as she stood insignificantly trapped between the jolting black wagons and the hedge; then they curved away towards the coppice where the withered oak leaves dropped noiselessly, while the birds, pulling at the scarlet hips beside the track, made off into the dusk that had already crept into the spinney. In the open, the smoke from the engine sank and cleaved to the rough grass. The fields were dreary and forsaken, and in the marshy strip that led to the whimsey, a reedy pit-pond, the fowls had already abandoned their run among the alders, to roost in the tarred fowlhouse. The pit-bank loomed up beyond the pond, flames like red sores licking its ashy sides, in the afternoon's stagnant light. Just beyond rose the tapering chimneys and the clumsy black headstocks of Brinsley Colliery. The two wheels were spinning fast up against the sky, and the winding engine rapped out its little spasms. The miners were being turned up.

The engine whistled as it came into the wide bay of railway lines beside the colliery, where rows of trucks stood in harbour.

Miners, single, trailing and in groups, passed like shadows diverging home. At the edge of the ribbed level of sidings squat a low cottage, three steps down from the cinder track. A large bony vine clutched at the house, as if to claw down the tiled roof. Round the bricked yard grew a few wintry primroses. Beyond, the long garden sloped down to a bush-covered brook course. There were some twiggy apple trees, winter-crack trees, and ragged cabbages. Beside the path hung dishevelled pink chrysanthemums, like pink cloths hung on bushes. A woman came stooping out of the felt-covered fowl-house, half-way down the garden. She closed and padlocked the door, then drew herself erect, having brushed some bits from her white apron.

She was a tall woman of imperious mien, handsome, with definite black eyebrows. Her smooth black hair was parted exactly. For a few moments

1. Platform on early locomotives for the engineer to stand on.

she stood steadily watching the miners as they passed along the railway: then she turned towards the brook course. Her face was calm and set, her mouth was closed with disillusionment. After a moment she called:

"John!" There was no answer. She waited, and then said distinctly:

"Where are you?"

"Here!" replied a child's sulky voice from among the bushes. The woman looked piercingly through the dusk.

"Are you at that brook?" she asked sternly.

For answer the child showed himself before the raspberry-canes that rose like whips. He was a small, sturdy boy of five. He stood quite still, defiantly.

"Oh!" said the mother, conciliated. "I thought you were down at that wet brook—and you remember what I told you—"

The boy did not move or answer.

"Come, come on in," she said more gently, "it's getting dark. There's your grandfather's engine coming down the line!"

The lad advanced slowly, with resentful, taciturn movement. He was dressed in trousers and waistcoat of cloth that was too thick and hard for the size of the garments. They were evidently cut down from a man's clothes.

As they went slowly towards the house he tore at the ragged wisps of chrysanthemums and dropped the petals in handfuls among the path.

"Don't do that—it does look nasty," said his mother. He refrained, and she, suddenly pitiful, broke off a twig with three or four wan flowers and held them against her face. When mother and son reached the yard her hand hesitated, and instead of laying the flower aside, she pushed it in her apron-band. The mother and son stood at the foot of the three steps looking across the bay of lines at the passing home of the miners. The trundle of the small train was imminent. Suddenly the engine loomed past the house and came to a stop opposite the gate.

The engine-driver, a short man with round grey beard, leaned out of the cab high above the woman.

"Have you got a cup of tea?" he said in a cheery, hearty fashion.

It was her father. She went in, saying she would mash. Directly, she returned.

"I didn't come to see you on Sunday," began the little grey-bearded man.

"I didn't expect you," said his daughter.

The engine-driver winced; then, reassuming his cheery, airy manner, he said:

"Oh, have you heard then? Well, and what do you think—?"

"I think it is soon enough," she replied.

At her brief censure the little man made an impatient gesture, and said coaxingly, yet with dangerous coldness:

"Well, what's a man to do? It's no sort of life for a man of my years, to sit at my own hearth like a stranger. And if I'm going to marry again it may as well be soon as late—what does it matter to anybody?"

The woman did not reply, but turned and went into the house. The man in the engine-cab stood assertive, till she returned with a cup of tea and a piece of bread and butter on a plate. She went up the steps and stood near the footplate of the hissing engine.

"You needn't 'a' brought me bread an' butter," said her father. "But a cup of tea"—he sipped appreciatively—"it's very nice." He sipped for a moment or two, then: "I hear as Walter's got another bout on," he said.

"When hasn't he?" said the woman bitterly.

"I heerd tell of him in the 'Lord Nelson' braggin' as he was going to spend that b——afore he went: half a sovereign that was."

"When?" asked the woman.

"A' Sat'day night—I know that's true."

"Very likely," she laughed bitterly. "He gives me twenty-three shillings."

"Aye, it's a nice thing, when a man can do nothing with his money but make a beast of himself!" said the grey-whiskered man. The woman turned her head away. Her father swallowed the last of his tea and handed her the cup.

"Aye," he sighed, wiping his mouth. "It's a settler, it is——"

He put his hand on the lever. The little engine strained and groaned, and the train rumbled towards the crossing. The woman again looked across the metals. Darkness was settling over the spaces of the railway and trucks: the miners, in grey sombre groups, were still passing home. The winding engine pulsed hurriedly, with brief pauses. Elizabeth Bates looked at the dreary flow of men, then she went indoors. Her husband did not come.

The kitchen was small and full of firelight; red coals piled glowing up the chimney mouth. All the life of the room seemed in the white, warm hearth and the steel fender reflecting the red fire. The cloth was laid for tea; cups glinted in the shadows. At the back, where the lowest stairs protruded into the room, the boy sat struggling with a knife and a piece of white wood. He was almost hidden in the shadow. It was half-past four. They had but to await the father's coming to begin tea. As the mother watched her son's sullen little struggle with the wood, she saw herself in his silence and pertinacity; she saw the father in her child's indifference to all but himself. She seemed to be occupied by her husband. He had probably gone past his home, slunk past his own door, to drink before he came in, while his dinner spoiled and wasted in waiting. She glanced at the clock, then took the potatoes to strain them in the yard. The garden and fields beyond the brook were closed in uncertain darkness. When she rose with the saucepan, leaving the drain steaming into the night behind her, she saw the yellow lamps were lit along the high road that went up the hill away beyond the space of the railway lines and the field.

Then again she watched the men trooping home, fewer now and fewer.

Indoors the fire was sinking and the room was dark red. The woman put her saucepan on the hob, and set a batter-pudding near the mouth of the oven. Then she stood unmoving. Directly, gratefully, came quick young steps to the door. Someone hung on the latch a moment, then a little girl entered and began pulling off her outdoor things, dragging a mass of curls, just ripening from gold to brown, over her eyes with her hat.

Her mother chid her for coming late from school, and said she would have to keep her at home the dark winter days.

"Why, mother, it's hardly a bit dark yet. The lamp's not lighted, and my father's not home."

"No, he isn't. But it's a quarter to five! Did you see anything of him?"

The child became serious. She looked at her mother with large, wistful blue eyes.

"No, mother, I've never seen him. Why? Has he come up an' gone past, to Old Brinsley? He hasn't, mother,'cos I never saw him."

"He'd watch that," said the mother bitterly, "he'd take care as you didn't see him. But you may depend upon it, he's seated in the 'Prince o' Wales.' He wouldn't be this late."

The girl looked at her mother piteously.

"Let's have our teas, mother, should we?" said she.

The mother called John to table. She opened the door once more and looked out across the darkness of the lines. All was deserted: she could not hear the winding-engines.

"Perhaps," she said to herself, "he's stopped to get some ripping done."

They sat down to tea. John, at the end of the table near the door, was almost lost in the darkness. Their faces were hidden from each other. The girl crouched against the fender slowly moving a thick piece of bread before the fire. The lad, his face a dusky mark on the shadow, sat watching her who was transfigured in the red glow.

"I do think it's beautiful to look in the fire," said the child.

"Do you?" said her mother. "Why?"

"It's so red, and full of little caves—and it feels so nice, and you can fair smell it."

"It'll want mending directly," replied her mother, "and then if your father comes he'll carry on and say there never is a fire when a man comes home sweating from the pit. A public house is always warm enough."

There was silence till the boy said complainingly: "Make haste, our Annie."

"Well, I am doing! I can't make the fire do it no faster, can I?"

"She keeps wafflin' it about so's to make 'er slow," grumbled the boy.

"Don't have such an evil imagination, child," replied the mother.

Soon the room was busy in the darkness with the crisp sound of crunching. The mother ate very little. She drank her tea determinedly, and sat thinking. When she rose her anger was evident in the stern unbending of her head. She looked at the pudding in the fender and broke out:

"It is a scandalous thing as a man can't even come home to his dinner! If it's crozzled up to a cinder I don't see why I should care. Past his very door he goes to get to a public-house, and here I sit with his dinner waiting for him—"

She went out. As she dropped piece after piece of coal on the red fire, the shadows fell on the walls, till the room was almost in total darkness.

"I canna see," grumbled the invisible John. In spite of herself, the mother laughed.

"You know the way to your mouth," she said. She set the dust-pan outside the door. When she came again like a shadow on the hearth, the lad repeated, complaining sulkily:

"I canna see."

"Good gracious!" cried the mother irritably, "you're as bad as your father if it's a bit dusk!"

Nevertheless, she took a paper spill from a sheaf on the mantelpiece and proceeded to light the lamp that hung from the ceiling in the middle of the room. As she reached up, her figure displayed itself just rounding with maternity.

"Oh, mother——!" exclaimed the girl.

"What?" said the woman, suspended in the act of putting the lamp-glass over the flame. The copper reflector shone handsomely on her, as she stood with uplifted arm, turning to face her daughter.

"You've got a flower in your apron!" said the child, in a little rapture at this unusual event.

"Goodness me!" exclaimed the woman, relieved. "One would think the house was afire." She replaced the glass and waited a moment before turning up the wick. A pale shadow was seen floating vaguely on the floor.

"Let me smell!" said the child, still rapturously, coming forward and putting her face to her mother's waist.

"Go along, silly!" said the mother, turning up the lamp. The light revealed their suspense so that the woman felt it almost unbearable. Annie was still bending at her waist. Irritably, the mother took the flowers out from her apron-band.

"Oh, mother—don't take them out!" Annie cried, catching her hand and trying to replace the sprig.

"Such nonsense!" said the mother, turning away. The child put the pale chrysanthemums to her lips, murmuring:

"Don't they smell beautiful!"

Her mother gave a short laugh.

"No," she said, "not to me. It was chrysanthemums when I married him, and chrysanthemums when you were born, and the first time they ever brought him home drunk, he'd got brown chrysanthemums in his buttonhole."

She looked at the children. Their eyes and their parted lips were wondering. The mother sat rocking in silence for some time. Then she looked at the clock.

"Twenty minutes to six!" In a tone of fine bitter carelessness she continued: "Eh, he'll not come now till they bring him. There he'll stick! But he needn't come rolling in here in his pit-dirt, for *I* won't wash him. He can lie on the floor——Eh, what a fool I've been, what a fool! And this is what I came here for, to this dirty hole, rats and all, for him to slink past his very door. Twice last week—he's begun now——"

She silenced herself, and rose to clear the table.

While for an hour or more the children played, subduedly intent, fertile of imagination, united in fear of the mother's wrath, and in dread of their father's home-coming, Mrs. Bates sat in her rocking-chair making a "singlet" of thick cream-coloured flannel, which gave a dull wounded sound as she tore off the grey edge. She worked at her sewing with energy, listening to the children, and her anger wearied itself, lay down to rest, opening its eyes from time to time and steadily watching, its ears raised to listen. Sometimes even her anger quailed and shank, and the mother suspended her sewing, tracing the footsteps that thudded along the sleepers outside: she would lift her head sharply to bid the children "hush," but she recovered herself in time, and the footsteps went past the gate, and the children were not flung out of their play-world.

But at last Annie sighed, and gave in. She glanced at her wagon of slippers, and loathed the game. She turned plaintively to her mother.

"Mother!"—but she was inarticulate.

John crept out like a frog from under the sofa. His mother glanced up. "Yes," she said, "just look at those shirt-sleeves!"

The boy held them out to survey them, saying nothing. Then somebody called in a hoarse voice away down the line, and suspense bristled in the room, till two people had gone by outside, talking.

"It is time for bed," said the mother.

"My father hasn't come," wailed Annie plaintively. But her mother was primed with courage.

"Never mind. They'll bring him when he does come—like a log." She meant there would be no scene. "And he may sleep on the floor till he wakes himself. I know he'll not go to work to-morrow after this!"

The children had their hands and faces wiped with a flannel. They were very quiet. When they had put on their night-dresses, they said their prayers, the boy mumbling. The mother looked down at them, at the brown silken bush of intertwining curls in the nape of the girl's neck, at the little black head of the lad, and her heart burst with anger at their father, who caused all three such distress. The children hid their faces in her skirts for comfort.

When Mrs. Bates came down, the room was strangely empty, with a tension of expectancy. She took up her sewing and stitched for some time without raising her head. Meantime her anger was tinged with fear.

II

The clock struck eight and she rose suddenly, dropping her sewing on her chair. She went to the stair-foot door, opened it, listening. Then she went out, locking the door behind her.

Something scuffled in the yard, and she started, though she knew it was only the rats with which the place was over-run. The night was very dark. In the great bay of railway lines, bulked with trucks, there was no trace of light, only away back she could see a few yellow lamps at the pit-top, and the red smear of the burning pit-bank on the night. She hurried along the edge of the track, then, crossing the converging lines, came to the stile by the white gates, whence she emerged on the road. Then the fear which had led her shrank. People were walking up to New Brinsley; she saw the lights in the houses; twenty yards farther on were the broad windows of the "Prince of Wales," very warm and bright, and the loud voices of men could be heard distinctly. What a fool she had been to imagine that anything had happened to him! He was merely drinking over there at the "Prince of Wales." She faltered. She had never yet been to fetch him, and she never would go. So she continued her walk towards the long straggling line of houses, standing back on the highway. She entered a passage between the dwellings.

"Mr. Rigley?—Yes! Did you want him? No, he's not in at this minute."

The raw-boned woman leaned forward from her dark scullery and peered at the other, upon whom fell a dim light through the blind of the kitchen window.

"Is it Mrs. Bates?" she asked in a tone tinged with respect.

"Yes. I wondered if your Master was at home. Mine hasn't come yet."

" 'Asn't 'e! Oh, Jack's been 'ome an' 'ad 'is dinner an' gone out. 'E's just gone for 'alf an hour afore bed-time. Did you call at the 'Prince of Wales'?"

"No——"

"No, you didn't like——! It's not very nice." The other woman was indulgent. There was an awkward pause. "Jack never said nothink about—about your Master," she said.

"No!—I expect he's stuck in there!"

Elizabeth Bates said this bitterly, and with recklessness. She knew that the woman across the yard was standing at her door listening, but she did not care. As she turned:

"Stop a minute! I'll just go an' ask Jack if 'e knows anythink," said Mrs. Rigley.

"Oh no—I wouldn't like to put——!"

"Yes, I will, if you'll just step inside an' see as th' childer doesn't come downstairs and set theirselves afire."

Elizabeth Bates, murmuring a remonstrance, stepped inside. The other woman apologised for the state of the room.

The kitchen needed apology. There were little frocks and trousers and childish undergarments on the squab and on the floor, and a litter of playthings everywhere. On the black American cloth of the table were pieces of bread and cake, crusts, slops, and a teapot with cold tea.

"Eh, ours is just as bad," said Elizabeth Bates, looking at the woman, not at the house. Mrs. Rigley put a shawl over her head and hurried out, saying:

"I shanna be a minute."

The other sat, noting with faint disapproval the general untidiness of the room. Then she fell to counting the shoes of various sizes scattered over the floor. There were twelve. She sighed and said to herself: "No wonder!"—glancing at the litter. There came the scratching of two pairs of feet on the yard, and the Rigleys entered. Elizabeth Bates rose. Rigley was a big man, with very large bones. His head looked particularly bony. Across his temple was a blue scar, caused by a wound got in the pit, a wound in which the coal-dust remained blue like tattooing.

" 'Asna 'e come whoam yit?" asked the man, without any form of greeting, but with deference and sympathy. "I couldna say wheer he is—'e's non ower theer!"—he jerked his head to signify the "Prince of Wales."

" 'E's 'appen gone up to th' 'Yew,' " said Mrs. Rigley.

There was another pause. Rigley had evidently something to get off his mind:

"Ah left 'im finishin' a stint,' he began. "Loose-all' 'ad bin gone about ten minutes when we com'n away, an' I shouted: 'Are ter comin', Walt?' an' 'e said: 'Go on, Ah shanna be but a'ef a minnit,' so we com'n ter th' bottom, me an' Bowers, thinkin' as 'e wor just behint, an' 'ud come up i' th' next bantle——"

He stood perplexed, as if answering a charge of deserting his mate. Elizabeth Bates, now again certain of disaster, hastened to reassure him:

"I expect 'e's gone up to th' 'Yew Tree,' as you say. It' not the first time. I've fretted myself into a fever before now. He'll come home when they carry him."

"Ay, isn't it too bad!" deplored the other woman.

"I'll just step up to Dick's an' see if'e *is* theer," offered the man, afraid of appearing alarmed, afraid of taking liberties.

"Oh, I wouldn't think of bothering you that far," said Elizabeth Bates, with emphasis, but he knew she was glad of his offer.

As they stumbled up the entry, Elizabeth Bates heard Rigley's wife run across the yard and open her neighbour's door. At this, suddenly all the blood in her body seemed to switch away from her heart.

"Mind!" warned Rigley. "Ah've said many a time as Ah'd fill up them ruts in this entry, sumb'dy 'll be breakin' their legs yit."

She recovered herself and walked quickly along with the miner.

"I don't like leaving the children in bed, and nobody in the house," she said.

"No, you dunna!" he replied courteously. They were soon at the gate of the cottage.

"Well, I shanna be many minnits. Dunna you be frettin' now,'e'll be all right," said the butty.[2]

"Thank you very much, Mr. Rigley," she replied.

"You're welcome!" he stammered, moving away. "I shanna be many minnits."

The house was quiet. Elizabeth Bates took off her hat and shawl, and rolled back the rug. When she had finished, she sat down. It was a few minutes past nine. She was startled by the rapid chuff of the winding-engine at the pit, and the sharp whirr of the brakes on the rope as it descended. Again she felt the painful sweep of her blood, and she put her hand to her side, saying aloud: "Good gracious!—it's only the nine o'clock deputy going down," rebuking herself.

She sat still listening. Half an hour of this, and she was wearied out.

"What am I working myself up like this for?" she said pitiably to herself, "I s'll only be doing myself some damage."

She took out her sewing again.

At a quarter to ten there were footsteps. One person! She watched for the door to open. It was an elderly woman, in a black bonnet and a black woollen shawl—his mother. She was about sixty years old, pale, with blue eyes, and her face all wrinkled and lamentable. She shut the door and turned to her daughter-in-law peevishly.

"Eh, Lizzie, whatever shall we do, whatever shall we do!" she cried.

Elizabeth drew back a little, sharply.

"What is it, mother?" she said.

The elder woman seated herself on the sofa. "I don't know, child, I can't tell you!"—she shook her head slowly. Elizabeth sat watching her, anxious and vexed.

"I don't know," replied the grandmother, sighing very deeply. "There's no end to my troubles, there isn't. The things I've gone through, I'm sure it's enough——!" She wept without wiping her eyes, the tears running.

"But, mother," interrupted Elizabeth, "what do you mean? What is it?"

The grandmother slowly wiped her eyes. The fountains of her tears were stopped by Elizabeth's directness. She wiped her eyes slowly.

"Poor child! Eh, you poor thing!" she moaned. "I don't know what we're going to do, I don't—and you as you are—it's a thing, it is indeed!"

Elizabeth waited.

"Is he dead?" she asked, and at the words her heart swung violently, though she felt a slight flush of shame at the ultimate extravagance of the question. Her words sufficiently frightened the old lady, almost brought her to herself.

[2]A fellow workman in a colliery.

"Don't say so, Elizabeth! We'll hope it's not as bad as that; no, may the Lord spare us that, Elizabeth. Jack Rigley came just as I was sittin' down to a glass afore going to bed, an' 'e said: ' 'Appen you'll go down th' line, Mrs. Bates. Walt's had an accident. 'Appen you'll go an' sit wi' 'er till we can get him home.' I hadn't time to ask him a word afore he was gone. An' I put my bonnet on an' come straight down, Lizzie. I thought to myself: 'Eh, that poor blessed child, if anybody should come an' tell her of a sudden, there's no knowing' what'll 'appen to 'er.' You mustn't let it upset you, Lizzie—or you know what to expect. How long is it, six months—or is it five, Lizzie? Ay!"—the old woman shook her head—"time slips on, it slips on! Ay!"

Elizabeth's thoughts were busy elsewhere. If he was killed—would she be able to manage on the little pension and what she could earn?—she counted up rapidly. If he was hurt—they wouldn't take him to the hospital—how tiresome he would be to nurse!—but perhaps she'd be able to get him away from the drink and his hateful ways. She would—while he was ill. The tears offered to come to her eyes at the picture. But what sentimental luxury was this she was beginning? She turned to consider the children. At any rate she was absolutely necessary for them. They were her business.

"Ay!" repeated the old woman, "it seems but a week or two since he brought me his first wages. Ay—he was a good lad, Elizabeth, he was, in his way. I don't know why he got to be such a trouble, I don't. He was a happy lad at home, only full of spirits. But there's no mistake he's been a handful of trouble, he has! I hope the Lord'll spare him to mend his ways. I hope so, I hope so. You've had a sight o' trouble with him, Elizabeth, you have indeed. But he was a jolly enough lad wi' me, he was, I can assure you. I don't know how it is. . . ."

The old woman continued to muse aloud, a monotonous irritating sound, while Elizabeth thought concentratedly, startled once, when she heard the winding-engine chuff quickly, and the brakes skirr with a shriek. Then she heard the engine more slowly, and the brakes made no sound. The old woman did not notice. Elizabeth waited in suspense. The mother-in-law talked, with lapses into silence.

"But he wasn't your son, Lizzie, an' it makes a difference. Whatever he was, I remember him when he was little, an' I learned to understand him and to make allowances. You've got to make allowances for them——"

It was half-past ten, and the old woman was saying: "But it's trouble from beginning to end; you're never too old for trouble, never too old for that——" when the gate banged back, and there were heavy feet on the steps.

"I'll go, Lizzie, let me go," cried the old woman, rising. But Elizabeth was at the door. It was a man in pit-clothes.

"They're bringin' 'im, Missis," he said. Elizabeth's heart halted a moment. Then it surged on again, almost suffocating her.

"Is he—is it bad?" she asked.

The man turned away, looking at the darkness:

"The doctor says 'e'd been dead hours. 'E saw 'im i' th' lamp-cabin."

The old woman, who stood just behind Elizabeth, dropped into a chair, and folded her hands, crying: "Oh, my boy, my boy!"

"Hush!" said Elizabeth, with a sharp twitch of a frown. "Be still, mother, don't waken th' children: I wouldn't have them down for anything!"

The old woman moaned softly, rocking herself. The man was drawing away. Elizabeth took a step forward.

"How was it?" she asked.

"Well, I couldn't say for sure," the man replied, very ill at ease. " 'E wor finishin' a stint an' th' butties 'ad gone, an' a lot o' stuff come down atop 'n 'im."

"And crushed him?" cried the widow, with a shudder.

"No," said the man, "it fell at th' back of 'im. 'E wor under th' face, an' it niver touched 'im. It shut 'im in. It seems 'e wor smothered."

Elizabeth shrank back. She heard the old woman behind her cry:

"What?—what did 'e say it was?"

The man replied, more loudly: " 'E wor smothered!"

Then the old woman wailed aloud, and this relieved Elizabeth.

"Oh, mother," she said, putting her hand on the old woman, "don't waken th' children, don't waken th' children."

She wept a little, unknowing, while the old mother rocked herself and moaned. Elizabeth remembered that they were bringing him home, and she must be ready. "They'll lay him in the parlour," she said to herself, standing a moment pale and perplexed.

Then she lighted a candle and went into the tiny room. The air was cold and damp, but she could not make a fire, there was no fireplace. She set down the candle and looked round. The candlelight glittered on the lustre-glasses, on the two vases that held some of the pink chrysanthemums, and on the dark mahogany. There was a cold, deathly smell of chrysanthemums in the room. Elizabeth stood looking at the flowers. She turned away, and calculated whether there would be room to lay him on the floor, between the couch and the chiffonier. She pushed the chairs aside. There would be room to lay him down and to step round him. Then she fetched the old red tablecloth, and another old cloth, spreading them down to save her bit of carpet. She shivered on leaving the parlour; so, from the dresser drawer she took a clean shirt and put it at the fire to air. All the time her mother-in-law was rocking herself in the chair and moaning.

"You'll have to move from there, mother," said Elizabeth. "They'll be bringing him in. Come in the rocker."

The old mother rose mechanically, and seated herself by the fire, continuing to lament. Elizabeth went into the pantry for another candle, and there, in the little pent-house under the naked tiles, she heard them coming. She stood still in the pantry doorway, listening. She heard them pass the end of the house, and come awkwardly down the three steps, a jumble of shuffling footsteps and muttering voices. The old woman was silent. The men were in the yard.

Then Elizabeth heard Matthews, the manager of the pit, say: "You go in first, Jim. Mind!"

The door came open, and the two women saw a collier backing into the room, holding one end of a stretcher, on which they could see the nailed pit-boots of the dead man. The two carriers halted, the man at the head stooping to the lintel of the door.

"Wheer will you have him?" asked the manager, a short, white-bearded man.

Elizabeth roused herself and came from the pantry carrying the unlighted candle.

"In the parlour," she said.

"In there, Jim!" pointed the manager, and the carriers backed round into the tiny room. The coat with which they had covered the body fell off as they awkwardly turned through the two doorways, and the women saw their man, naked to the waist, lying stripped for work. The old woman began to moan in a low voice of horror.

"Lay th' stretcher at th' side," snapped the manager, "an' put 'im on th' cloths. Mind now, mind! Look you now——!"

One of the men had knocked off a vase of chrysanthemums. He stared awkwardly, then they set down the stretcher. Elizabeth did not look at her husband. As soon as she could get in the room, she went and picked up the broken vase and the flowers.

"Wait a minute!" she said.

The three men waited in silence while she mopped up the water with a duster.

"Eh, what a job, what a job, to be sure!" the manager was saying, rubbing his brow with trouble and perplexity. "Never knew such a thing in my life, never! He'd no business to ha' been left. I never knew such a thing in my life! Fell over him clean as a whistle, an' shut him in. Not four foot of space, there wasn't—yet it scarce bruised him."

He looked down at the dead man, lying prone, half naked, all grimed with coal-dust.

" ' 'Sphyxiated,' the doctor said. It *is* the most terrible job I've ever known. Seems as if it was done o' purpose. Clean over him, an' shut 'im in, like a mouse-trap"—he made a sharp, descending gesture with his hand.

The colliers standing by jerked aside their heads in hopeless comment.

The horror of the thing bristled upon them all.

Then they heard the girl's voice upstairs calling shrilly: "Mother, mother—who is it? Mother, who is it?"

Elizabeth hurried to the foot of the stairs and opened the door:

"Go to sleep!" she commanded sharply. "What are you shouting about? Go to sleep at once—there's nothing——"

Then she began to mount the stairs. They could hear her on the boards, and on the plaster floor of the little bedroom. They could hear her distinctly:

"What's the matter now?—what's the matter with you, silly thing?"—her voice was much agitated, with an unreal gentleness.

"I thought it was some men come," said the plaintive voice of the child. "Has he come?"

"Yes, they've brought him. There's nothing to make a fuss about. Go to sleep now, like a good child."

They could hear her voice in the bedroom, they waited whilst she covered the children under the bedclothes.

"Is he drunk?" asked the girl, timidly, faintly.

"No! No—he's not! He—he's asleep."

"Is he asleep downstairs?"

"Yes—and don't make a noise."

There was silence for a moment, then the men heard the frightened child again:

"What's that noise?"

"It's nothing, I tell you, what are you bothering for?"

The noise was the grandmother moaning. She was oblivious of everything, sitting on her chair rocking and moaning. The manager put his hand on her arm and bade her "Sh—sh!!"

The old woman opened her eyes and looked at him. She was shocked by this interruption, and seemed to wonder.

"What time is it?" the plaintive thin voice of the child, sinking back unhappily into sleep, asked this last question.

"Ten o'clock," answered the mother more softly. Then she must have bent down and kissed the children.

Matthews beckoned to the men to come away. They put on their caps and took up the stretcher. Stepping over the body, they tiptoed out of the house. None of them spoke till they were far from the wakeful children.

When Elizabeth came down she found her mother alone on the parlour floor, leaning over the dead man, the tears dropping on him.

"We must lay him out," the wife said. She put on the kettle, then returning knelt at the feet, and began to unfasten the knotted leather laces. The room was clammy and dim with only one candle, so that she had to bend her face almost to the floor. At last she got off the heavy boots and put them away.

"You must help me now," she whispered to the old woman. Together they stripped the man.

When they arose, saw him lying in the naïve dignity of death, the women stood arrested in fear and respect. For a few moments they remained still, looking down, the old mother whimpering. Elizabeth felt countermanded. She saw him, how utterly inviolable he lay in himself. She had nothing to do with him. She could not accept it. Stooping, she laid her hand on him, in claim. He was still warm, for the mine was hot where he had died. His mother had his face between her hands, and was murmuring incoherently. The old tears fell in succession as drops from wet leaves; the mother was not weeping, merely her tears flowed. Elizabeth embraced the body of her husband, with cheek and lips. She seemed to be listening, inquiring, trying to get some connection. But she could not. She was driven away. He was impregnable.

She rose, went into the kitchen, where she poured warm water into a bowl, brought soap and flannel and a soft towel.

"I must wash him," she said.

Then the old mother rose stiffly, and watched Elizabeth as she carefully washed his face, carefully brushing the big blond moustache from his mouth with the flannel. She was afraid with a bottomless fear, so she ministered to him. The old woman, jealous, said:

"Let me wipe him!"—and she kneeled on the other side drying slowly as Elizabeth washed, her big black bonnet sometimes brushing the dark head of her daughter-in-law. They worked thus in silence for a long time. They never forgot it was death, and the touch of the man's dead body gave them strange emotions, different in each of the women; a great dread possessed them both, the mother felt the lie was given to her womb, she was denied; the wife felt the utter isolation of the human soul, the child within her was a weight apart from her.

At last it was finished. He was a man of handsome body, and his face showed no traces of drink. He was blond, full-fleshed, with fine limbs. But he was dead.

"Bless him," whispered his mother, looking always at his face, and speaking out of sheer terror. "Dear lad—bless him!" She spoke in a faint, sibilant ecstasy of fear and mother love.

Elizabeth sank down again to the floor, and put her face against his neck, and trembled and shuddered. But she had to draw away again. He was dead, and her living flesh had no place against his. A great dread and weariness held her: she was so unavailing. Her life was gone like this.

"White as milk he is, clear as a twelve-month baby, bless him, the darling!" the old mother murmured to herself. "Not a mark on him, clear and clean and white, beautiful as ever a child was made," she murmured with pride. Elizabeth kept her face hidden.

"He went peaceful, Lizzie—peaceful as sleep. Isn't he beautiful, the lamb? Ay—he must ha' made his peace, Lizzie. 'Appen he made it all right, Lizzie, shut in there. He'd have time. He wouldn't look like this if he hadn't made his peace. The lamb, the dear lamb. 'Eh, but he had a hearty laugh. I loved to hear it. He had the heartiest laugh, Lizzie, as a lad——"

Elizabeth looked up. The man's mouth was fallen back, slightly open under the cover of the moustache. The eyes, half shut, did not show glazed in the obscurity. Life with its smoky burning gone from him, had left him apart and utterly alien to her. And she knew what a stranger he was to her. In her womb was ice of fear, because of this separate stranger with whom she had been living as one flesh. Was this what it all meant—utter, intact separateness, obscured by heat of living? In dread she turned her face away. The fact was too deadly. There had been nothing between them, and yet they had come together, exchanging their nakedness repeatedly. Each time he had taken her, they had been two isolated beings, far apart as now. He was no more responsible than she. The child was like ice in her womb. For as she looked at the dead man, her mind, cold and detached, said clearly: "Who am I? What have I been doing? I have been fighting a husband who did not exist. *He* existed all the time. What wrong have I done? What was that I have been living with? There lies the reality, this man." And her soul died in her for fear: she knew she had never seen him, he had never seen her, they had met in the dark and had fought in the dark, not knowing whom they met nor whom they fought. And now she saw, and turned silent in seeing. For she had been wrong. She had said he was something he was not; she had felt familiar with him. Whereas he was apart all the while, living as she never lived, feeling as she never felt.

In fear and shame she looked at his naked body, that she had known falsely. And he was the father of her children. Her soul was torn from her body and stood apart. She looked at his naked body and was ashamed, as if she had denied it. After all, it was itself. It seemed awful to her. She looked at his face, and she turned her own face to the wall. For his look was other than hers, his way was not her way. She had denied him what he was—she saw it now. She had refused him as himself. And this had been her life, and his life. She was grateful to death, which restored the truth. And she knew she was not dead.

And all the while her heart was bursting with grief and pity for him. What had he suffered? What stretch of horror for this helpless man! She was rigid with agony. She had not been able to help him. He had been cruelly injured, this naked man, this other being, and she could make no reparation. There were the children—but the children belonged to life. This dead man had nothing to do with them. He and she were only channels through which life had flowed to issue in the children. She was a mother—but how awful she knew it now to have been a wife. And he, dead now, how awful he must have felt it to be a husband. She felt that in the next world he would be a stranger to her. If they met there, in the beyond, they would only be ashamed of what had been before. The children had come, for some mysterious reason, out of both of them. But the children did not unite them. Now he was dead, she knew how eternally he was apart from her, how eternally he had nothing more to do with her. She saw this episode of her life closed. They had denied each other in life. Now he had withdrawn. An anguish came over her. It was finished then: it had become hopeless between them long before he died. Yet he had been her husband. But how little!

"Have you got his shirt, 'Lizabeth?"

Elizabeth turned without answering, though she strove to weep and behave as her mother-in-law expected. But she could not, she was silenced. She went into the kitchen and returned with the garment.

"It is aired," she said, grasping the cotton shirt here and there to try. She was almost ashamed to handle him; what right had she or anyone to lay hands on him; but her touch was humble on his body. It was hard work to clothe him. He was so heavy and inert. A terrible dread gripped her all the while: that he could be so heavy and utterly inert, unresponsive, apart. The horror of the distance between them was almost too much for her—it was so infinite a gap she must look across.

At last it was finished. They covered him with a sheet and left him lying, with his face bound. And she fastened the door of the little parlour, lest the children should see what was lying there. Then, with peace sunk heavy on her heart, she went about making tidy the kitchen. She knew she submitted to life, which was her immediate master. But from death, her ultimate master, she winced with fear and shame.

QUESTIONS

1. How does Lawrence use physical description at the beginning of the story to evoke the world of the miners ? What is the significance of the train sequence?
2. What is our first impression of the mother? How does her appearance suggest aspects of her character?
3. What do her interactions with her father, her children, her neighbors, and her mother-in-law reveal about her personality?
4. What do the chrysanthemums represent to her? Why does she tuck them into her apron?
5. How does Lawrence use descriptive detail to convey the stark finality of death?
6. Discuss the emotional struggles that underlie the scene where the two women are washing the body?
7. What is the symbolism of the manner in which the husband died?
8. Why is it important that the woman should have believed that her husband was out drinking?
9. Is her recognition in the presence of the body in any sense positive? Explain.
10. What does this story suggest about Lawrence's beliefs about love between men and women? about social class?
11. Compare the ending of this story to the revelation scene in Kate Chopin's "The Story of an Hour."

Katherine Mansfield

Born in New Zealand, Katherine Mansfield (1888–1923) traveled to London in 1903 to pursue what she thought would be a musician's career. While in London, however, she made contact with some of the leading literary figures, including D.H. Lawrence, and decided to direct her energies into writing. She soon revealed a singular aptitude for writing stories that combined shrewd observation with lyrical compression. Her first collection of stories, *In a German Pension,* was published in 1911. *Bliss and Other Stories* (1920) and *The Garden Party* (1922) secured her reputation as a worthy perpetuator of the Chekhov tradition.

Mansfield married literary critic John Middleton Murry in 1918, the same year that she was striken with tuberculosis (the disease that had killed her Russian master, Chekhov). She spent some time at the Gurdjieff Institute in France, seeking a cure; the mystical doctrines of Gurdjieff himself absorbed her increasingly as her health failed. Mansfield was thirty-four when she died.

THE GARDEN PARTY

And after all the weather was ideal. They could not have had a more perfect day for a garden-party if they had ordered it. Windless, warm, the sky without a cloud. Only the blue was veiled with a haze of light gold, as it is sometimes in early summer. The gardener had been up since dawn, mowing the lawns and sweeping them, until the grass and the dark flat rosettes where the daisy plants had been seemed to shine. As for the roses, you could not help feeling they understood that roses are the only flowers that impress people at garden-parties; the only flowers that everybody is certain of knowing. Hundreds, yes, literally hundreds, had come out in a single night; the green bushes bowed down as though they had been visited by archangels.

Breakfast was not yet over before the men came to put up the marquee.

"Where do you want the marquee put, mother?"

"My dear child, it's no use asking me. I'm determined to leave everything to you children this year. Forget I am your mother. Treat me as an honored guest."

But Meg could not possibly go and supervise the men. She had washed her hair before breakfast, and she sat drinking her coffee in a green turban, with a dark wet curl stamped on each cheek. Jose, the butterfly, always came down in a silk petticoat and a kimono jacket.

"You'll have to go, Laura; you're the artistic one."

Away Laura flew, still holding her piece of bread-and-butter. It's so delicious to have an excuse for eating out of doors, and besides, she loved having to arrange things; she always felt she could do it so much better than anybody else.

Four men in their shirt-sleeves stood grouped together on the garden path. They carried staves covered with rolls of canvas, and they had big tool-bats slung on their backs. They looked impressive. Laura wished now that she had not got the bread-and-butter, but there was nowhere to put it, and she couldn't possibly throw it away. She blushed and tried to look severe and even a little bit short-sighted as she came up to them.

"Good morning," she said, copying her mother's voice. But that sounded so fearfully affected that she was ashamed, and stammered like a little girl, "Oh—er—have you come—is it about the marquee?"

"That's right, miss," said the tallest of the men, a lanky, freckled fellow, and he shifted his tool-bag, knocked back his straw hat and smiled down at her. "That's about it."

His smile was so easy, so friendly that Laura recovered. What nice eyes he had, small, but such a dark blue! And now she looked at the others, they were smiling too. "Cheer up, we won't bite," their smile seemed to say. How very nice workmen were! And what a beautiful morning! She mustn't mention the morning; she must be businesslike. The marquee.

"Well, what about the lily-lawn? Would that do?"

And she pointed to the lily-lawn with the hand that didn't hold the bread-and-butter. They turned, they stared in the direction. A little fat chap thrust out his under-lip, and the tall fellow frowned.

"I don't fancy it," said he. "Not conspicuous enough. You see, with a thing like a marquee," and he turned to Laura in his easy way, "you want to put it somewhere where it'll give you a bang slap in the eye, if you follow me."

Laura's upbringing made her wonder for a moment whether it was quite respectful of a workman to talk to her of bangs slap in the eye. But she did quite follow him.

"A corner of the tennis-court," she suggested. "But the band's going to be in one corner."

"H'm, going to have a band, are you?" said another of the workmen. He was pale. He had a haggard look as his dark eyes scanned the tennis-court. What was he thinking?

"Only a very small band," said Laura gently. Perhaps he wouldn't mind so much if the band was quite small. But the tall fellow interrupted.

"Look here, miss, that's the place. Against those trees. Over there. That'll do fine."

Against the karakas. Then the karaka-trees would be hidden. And they were so lovely, with their broad, gleaming leaves, and their clusters of yellow fruit. They were like trees you imagined growing on a desert island, proud, solitary, lifting their leaves and fruits to the sun in a kind of silent splendor. Must they be hidden by a marquee?

They must. Already the men had shouldered their staves and were making for the place. Only the tall fellow was left. He bent down, pinched a sprig of lavender, put his thumb and forefinger to his nose and snuffed up the smell. When Laura saw that gesture she forgot all about the karakas in her wonder at him caring for things like that—caring for the smell of lavender. How many men that she knew would have done such a thing? Oh, how extraordinarily nice workmen were, she thought. Why couldn't she have workmen for friends rather than the silly boys she danced with and who came to Sunday night supper? She would get on much better with men like these.

It's all the fault, she decided, as the tall fellow drew something on the back of an envelope, something that was to be looped up or left to hang, of these absurd class distinctions. Well, for her part, she didn't feel them. Not a bit, not an atom. . . . And now there came the chock-chock of wooden hammers. Some one whistled, some one sang out, "Are you right there, matey?" "Matey!" The friendliness of it, the—the—Just to prove how happy she was, just to show the tall fellow how at home she felt, and how she despised stupid conventions, Laura took a big bite of her bread-and-butter as she stared at the little drawing. She felt just like a work-girl.

"Laura, Laura, where are you? Telephone, Laura!" a voice cried from the house.

"Coming!" Away she skimmed, over the lawn, up the path, up the steps, across the veranda, and into the porch. In the hall her father and Laurie were brushing their hats ready to go to the office.

"I say, Laura," said Laurie very fast, "you might just give a squiz at my coat before this afternoon. See if it wants pressing."

"I will," said she. Suddenly she couldn't stop herself. She ran at Laurie and gave him a small, quick squeeze. "Oh, I do love parties, don't you?" gasped Laura.

"Ra-ther," said Laurie's warm, boyish voice, and he squeezed his sister too, and gave her a gentle push. "Dash off to the telephone, old girl."

The telephone. "Yes, yes; oh yes. Kitty? Good morning, dear. Come to lunch? Do, dear. Delighted of course. It will only be a very scratch meal—just the sandwich crusts and broken meringue-shells and what's left over. Yes, isn't it a perfect morning? Your white? Oh, I certainly should. One moment—hold the line. Mother's calling." And Laura sat back. "What, mother? Can't hear."

Mrs. Sheridan's voice floated down the stairs. "Tell her to wear that sweet hat she had on last Sunday."

"Mother says you're to wear that *sweet* hat you had on last Sunday. Good. One o'clock. Bye-bye."

Laura put back the receiver, flung her arms over her head, took a deep breath, stretched and let them fall. "Huh," she sighed, and the moment after the sigh she sat up quickly. She was still, listening. All the doors in the house seemed to be open. The house was alive with soft, quick steps and running voices. The green baize door that led to the kitchen regions swung open and shut with a muffled thud. And now there came a long, chuckling absurd sound. It was the heavy piano being moved on its stiff castors. But the air! If you stopped to notice, was the air always like this? Little faint winds were playing chase, in at the tops of the windows, out at the doors. And there were two tiny spots of sun, one on the inkpot, one on a silver photograph frame, playing too. Darling little spots. Especially the one on the inkpot lid. It was quite warm. A warm little silver star. She could have kissed it.

The front door bell pealed, and there sounded the rustle of Sadie's print skirt on the stairs. A man's voice murmured; Sadie answered, careless, "I'm sure I don't know. Wait. I'll ask Mrs. Sheridan."

"What is it, Sadie?" Laura came into the hall.

"It's the florist, Miss Laura."

It was, indeed. There, just inside the door, stood a wide, shallow tray full of pots of pink lilies. No other kind. Nothing but lilies—canna lilies, big pink flowers, wide open, radiant, almost frighteningly alive on bright crimson stems.

"O-oh, Sadie!" said Laura, and the sound was like a little moan. She crouched down as if to warm herself at that blaze of lilies; she felt they were in her fingers, on her lips, growing in her breast.

"It's some mistake," she said faintly. "Nobody ever ordered so many. Sadie, go and find mother."

But at that moment Mrs. Sheridan joined them.

"It's quite right," she said calmly. "Yes, I ordered them. Aren't they lovely?" She pressed Laura's arm. "I was passing the shop yesterday, and I saw them in the window. And I suddenly thought for once in my life I shall have enough canna lilies. The garden-party will be a good excuse."

"But I thought you said you didn't mean to interfere," said Laura. Sadie had gone. The florist's man was still outside at his van. She put her arm round her mother's neck and gently, very gently, she bit her mother's ear.

"My darling child, you wouldn't like a logical mother, would you? Don't do that. Here's the man."

He carried more lilies still, another whole tray.

"Bank them up, just inside the door, on both sides of the porch, please," said Mrs. Sheridan. "Don't you agree, Laura?"

"Oh, I *do,* mother."

In the drawing-room Meg, Jose and good little Hans had at last succeeded in moving the piano.

"Now, if we put this chesterfield against the wall and move everything out of the room except the chairs, don't you think?"

"Quite."

"Hans, move these tables into the smoking-room, and bring a sweeper to take these marks off the carpet and—one moment, Hans—" Jose loved giving orders to the servants, and they loved obeying her. She always made them feel they were taking part in some drama. "Tell mother and Miss Laura to come here at once."

"Very good, Miss Jose."

She turned to Meg. "I want to hear what the piano sounds like, just in case I'm asked to sing this afternoon. Let's try over 'This Life is Weary.' "

Pom! Ta-ta-ta *Tee*-ta! The piano burst out so passionately that Jose's face changed. She clasped her hands. She looked mournfully and enigmatically at her mother and Laura as they came in.

This Life is *Wee*-ary,
A Tear—a Sigh.
A Love that *Chan*-ges,
This Life is *Wee*-ary,
A Tear—a Sigh.
A Love that *Chan*-ges,
And then . . . Goodbye!

But at the word "Goodbye," and although the piano sounded more desperate than ever, her face broke into a brilliant, dreadfully unsympathetic smile.

"Aren't I in good voice, mummy?" she beamed.

This Life is *Wee*-ary,
Hope comes to Die.
A Dream—a *Wa*-kening.

But now Sadie interrupted them. "What is it, Sadie?"

"If you please, m'm, cook says have you got the flags for the sandwiches?"

"The flags for the sandwiches, Sadie?" echoed Mrs. Sheridan dreamily. And the children knew by her face that she hadn't got them. "Let me see." And she said to Sadie firmly, "Tell cook I'll let her have them in ten minutes."

Sadie went.

"Now, Laura," said her mother quickly. "Come with me into the smoking-room. I've got the names somewhere on the back of an envelope. You'll have to write them out for me. Meg, go upstairs this minute and take that wet thing off your head. Jose, run and finish dressing this instant. Do you hear me, children, or shall I have to tell your father when he comes home to-night? And—and, Jose, pacify cook if you do go into the kitchen, will you? I'm terrified of her this morning."

The envelope was found at last behind the dining-room clock, though how it had got there Mrs. Sheridan could not imagine.

"One of you children must have stolen it out of my bag, because I remember vividly—cream cheese and lemon-curd. Have you done that?"

"Yes."

"Egg and—" Mrs. Sheridan held the envelope away from her. "It looks like mice. It can't be mice, can it?"

"Olive, pet," said Laura, looking over her shoulder.

"Yes, of course, olive. What a horrible combination it sounds. Egg and olive."

They were finished at last, and Laura took them off to the kitchen. She found Jose there pacifying the cook, who did not look at all terrifying.

"I have never seen such exquisite sandwiches," said Jose's rapturous voice. "How many kinds did you say there were, cook? Fifteen?"

"Fifteen, Miss Jose."

"Well, cook, I congratulate you."

Cook swept up crusts with the long sandwich knife, and smiled broadly.

"Godber's has come," announced Sadie, issuing out of the pantry. She had seen the man pass the window.

That meant the cream puffs had come. Godber's were famous for their cream puffs. Nobody ever thought of making them at home.

"Bring them in and put them on the table, my girl," ordered cook.

Sadie brought them in and went back to the door. Of course Laura and Jose were far too grown-up to really care about such things. All the same, they couldn't help agreeing that the puffs looked very attractive. Very. Cook began arranging them, shaking off the extra icing sugar.

"Don't they carry one back to all one's parties?" said Laura.

"I suppose they do," said practical Jose, who never liked to be carried back. "They look beautifully light and feathery, I must say."

"Have one each, my dears," said cook in her comfortable voice. "Yer ma won't know."

Oh, impossible. Fancy cream puffs so soon after breakfast. The very idea made one shudder. All the same, two minutes later Jose and Laura were licking their fingers with that absorbed inward look that only comes from whipped cream.

"Let's go into the garden, out by the back way," suggested Laura. "I want to see how the men are getting on with the marquee. They're such awfully nice men."

But the back door was blocked by cook, Sadie, Godber's man and Hans.

Something had happened.

"Tuk-tuk-tuk," clucked cook like an agitated hen. Sadie had her hand clapped to her cheek as though she had toothache. Hans's face was screwed up in the effort to understand. Only Godber's man seemed to be enjoying himself; it was his story.

"What's the matter? What's happened?"

"There's been a horrible accident," said Cook. "A man killed."

"A man killed! Where? How? When?"

But Godber's man wasn't going to have his story snatched from under his very nose.

"Know those little cottages just below here, miss?" Know them? Of course, she knew them. "Well, there's a young chap living there, name of Scott, a carter. His horse shied at a traction-engine, corner of Hawke Street this morning, and he was thrown out on the back of his head. Killed."

"Dead!" Laura stared at Godber's man.

"Dead when they picked him up," said Godber's man with relish. "They were taking the body home as I come up here." And he said to the cook, "He's left a wife and five little ones."

"Jose, come here." Laura caught hold of her sister's sleeve and dragged her through the kitchen to the other side of the green baize door. There she paused and leaned against it. "Jose!" she said, horrified, "however are we going to stop everything?"

"Stop everything, Laura!" cried Jose in astonishment. "What do you mean?"

"Stop the garden-party, of course." Why did Jose pretend?

But Jose was still more amazed. "Stop the garden-party? My dear Laura, don't be so absurd. Of course we can't do anything of the kind. Nobody expects us to. Don't be so extravagant."

"But we can't possibly have a garden-party with a man dead just outside the front gate."

That really was extravagant, for the little cottages were in a lane to themselves at the very bottom of a steep rise that led up to the house. A broad road ran between. True, they were far too near. They were the greatest possible eyesore, and they had no right to be in that neighborhood at all. They were little mean dwellings painted a chocolate brown. In the garden patches there was nothing but cabbage stalks, sick hens and tomato cans. The very smoke coming out of their chimneys was poverty-stricken. Little rags and shreds of smoke, so unlike the great silvery plumes that uncurled from the Sheridans' chimneys. Washerwomen lived in the lane and sweeps and a cobbler, and a man whose house-front was studded all over with minute bird-cages. Children swarmed. When the Sheridans were little they were forbidden to set foot there because of the revolting language and of what they might catch. But since they were grown up, Laura and Laurie on their prowls sometimes walked through. It was disgusting and sordid. They came out with a shudder. But still one must go everywhere; one must see everything. So through they went.

"And just think of what the band would sound like to that poor woman," said Laura.

"Oh, Laura!" Jose began to be seriously annoyed. "If you're going to stop a band playing every time some one has an accident, you'll lead a very strenuous life. I'm every bit as sorry about it as you. I feel just as sympathetic." Her eyes hardened. She looked at her sister just as she used to when they were little and fighting together. "You won't bring a drunken workman back to life by being sentimental," she said softly.

"Drunk! Who said he was drunk?" Laura turned furiously on Jose. She said, just as they had used to say on those occasions, "I'm going straight up to tell mother."

"Do, dear," cooed Jose.

"Mother, can I come into your room?" Laura turned the big glass doorknob.

"Of course, child. Why, what's the matter? What's given you such a color?" And Mrs. Sheridan turned round from her dressing-table. She was trying on a new hat.

"Mother, a man's been killed," began Laura.

"*Not* in the garden?" interrupted her mother.

"No, no!"

"Oh, what a fright you gave me!" Mrs. Sheridan sighed with relief, and took off the big hat and held it on her knees.

"But listen, mother," said Laura. Breathless, half-choking, she told the dreadful story. "Of course, we can't have our party, can we?" she pleaded. "The band and everybody arriving. They'd hear us, mother; they're nearly neighbors!"

To Laura's astonishment her mother behaved just like Jose; it was harder to bear because she seemed amused. She refused to take Laura seriously.

"But, my dear child, use your common sense. It's only by accident we've heard of it. If some one had died there normally—and I can't understand how they keep alive in those poky little holes—we should still be having our party, shouldn't we?"

Laura had to say "yes" to that, but she felt it was all wrong. She sat down on her mother's sofa and pinched the cushion frill.

"Mother, isn't it really terribly heartless of us?" she asked.

"Darling!" Mrs. Sheridan got up and came over to her, carrying the hat. Before Laura could stop her she had popped it on. "My child!" said her mother, "the hat is yours. It's made for you. It's much too young for me. I have never seen you look such a picture. Look at yourself!" And she held up her hand-mirror.

"But, mother," Laura began again. She couldn't look at herself; she turned aside.

This time Mrs. Sheridan lost patience just as Jose had done.

"You are being very absurd, Laura," she said coldly. "People like that don't expect sacrifices from us. And it's not very sympathetic to spoil everybody's enjoyment as you're doing now."

"I don't understand," said Laura, and she walked quickly out of the room into her own bedroom. There, quite by chance, the first thing she saw was this charming girl in the mirror, in her black hat trimmed with gold daisies, and a long black velvet ribbon. Never had she imagined she could look like that. Is mother right? she thought. And now she hoped her mother was right. Am I being extravagant? Perhaps it was extravagant. Just for a moment she had another glimpse of that poor woman and those little children, and the body being carried into the house. But it all seemed blurred, unreal, like a picture in the newspaper. I'll remember it again after the party's over, she decided. And somehow that seemed quite the best plan. . . .

Lunch was over by half-past one. By half-past two they were all ready for the fray. The green-coated band had arrived and was established in a corner of the tennis-court.

"My dear!" trilled Kitty Maitland, "aren't they too like frogs for words? You ought to have arranged them round the pond with the conductor in the middle on a leaf."

Laurie arrived and hailed them on his way to dress. At the sight of him Laura remembered the accident again. She wanted to tell him. If Laurie agreed with the others, then it was bound to be all right. And she followed him into the hall.

"Laurie!"

"Hallo!" He was half-way upstairs, but when he turned round and saw Laura he suddenly puffed out his cheeks and goggled his eyes at her. "My word, Laura! You do look stunning," said Laurie, "What an absolutely topping hat!"

Laura said faintly "Is it?" and smiled up at Laurie, and didn't tell him after all.

Soon after that people began coming in streams. The band struck up; the hired waiters ran from the house to the marquee. Wherever you looked there were couples strolling, bending to the flowers, greeting, moving on over the lawn. They were like bright birds that had alighted in the Sheridans' garden for this one afternoon, on their way to—where? Ah, what happiness it is to be with people who all are happy, to press hands, press cheeks, smile into eyes.

"Darling Laura, how well you look!"

"What a becoming hat, child!"

"Laura, you look quite Spanish. I've never seen you look so striking."

And Laura, glowing, answered softly, "Have you had tea? Won't you have an ice? The passion-fruit ices really are rather special." She ran to her father and begged him. "Daddy darling, can't the band have something to drink?"

And the perfect afternoon slowly ripened, slowly faded, slowly its petals closed.

"Never a more delightful garden-party . . ." "The greatest success . . ." "Quite the most . . ."

Laura helped her mother with the good-byes. They stood side by side in the porch till it was all over.

"All over, all over, thank heaven," said Mr. Sheridan. "Round up the others, Laura. Let's go and have some fresh coffee. I'm exhausted. Yes, it's been very successful. But oh, these parties, these parties! Why will you children insist on giving parties!" And they all of them sat down in the deserted marquee.

"Have a sandwich, daddy dear. I wrote the flag."

"Thanks." Mr. Sheridan took a bite and the sandwich was gone. He took another. "I suppose you didn't hear of a beastly accident that happened today?" he said.

"My dear," said Mrs. Sheridan, holding up her hand, "we did. It nearly ruined the party. Laura insisted we should put it off."

"Oh, mother!" Laura didn't want to be teased about it.

"It was a horrible affair all the same," said Mr. Sheridan. "The chap was married too. Lived just below in the lane, and leaves a wife and half a dozen kiddies, so they say."

An awkward little silence fell. Mrs. Sheridan fidgeted with her cup. Really, it was very tactless of father . . .

Suddenly she looked up. There on the table were all those sandwiches, cakes, puffs, all uneaten, all going to be wasted. She had one of her brilliant ideas.

"I know," she said. "Let's make up a basket. Let's send that poor creature some of this perfectly good food. At any rate, it will be the greatest treat for the children. Don't you agree? And she's sure to have neighbors calling in and so on. What a point to have it all ready prepared. Laura!" She jumped up. "Get me the big basket out of the stairs cupboard."

"But, mother, do you really think it's a good idea?" said Laura.

Again, how curious, she seemed to be different from them all. To take scraps from their party. Would the poor woman really like that?

"Of course! What's the matter with you today? An hour or two ago you were insisting on us being sympathetic, and now—"

Oh, well! Laura ran for the basket. It was filled, it was heaped by her mother.

"Take it yourself, darling," said she. "Run down just as you are. No, wait, take the arum lilies too. People of that class are so impressed by arum lilies."

"The stems will ruin her lace frock," said practical Jose.

So they would. Just in time. "Only the basket, then. And, Laura!"—her mother followed her out of the marquee—"don't on any account—"

"What, mother?"

No, better not put such ideas into the child's head! "Nothing! Run along."

It was just growing dusky as Laura shut their garden gates. A big dog ran by like a shadow. The road gleamed white, and down below in the hollow the little cottages were in deep shade. How quiet it seemed after the afternoon. Here she was going down the hill to somewhere where a man lay dead, and she couldn't realize it. Why couldn't she? She stopped a minute. And it seemed to her that kisses, voices, tinkling spoons, laughter, the smell of crushed grass were somehow inside her. She had no room for anything else. How strange! She looked up at the pale sky, and all she thought was, "Yes, it was the most successful party."

Now the broad road was crossed. The lane began, smoky and dark. Women in shawls and men's tweed caps hurried by. Men hung over the palings; the children played in the doorways. A low hum came from the mean little cottages. In some of them there was a flicker of light, and a shadow, crab-like, moved across the window. Laura bent her head and hurried on. She wished now she had put on a coat. How her frock shone! And the big hat with the velvet streamer—if only it was another hat! Were the people looking at her? They must be. It was a mistake to have come; she knew all along it was a mistake. Should she go back even now?

No, too late. This was the house. It must be. A dark knot of people stood outside. Beside the gate an old, old woman with a crutch sat in a chair, watching. She had her feet on a newspaper. The voices stopped as Laura drew near. The group parted. It was as though she was expected, as though they had known she was coming here.

Laura was terribly nervous. Tossing the velvet ribbon over her shoulder, she said to a woman standing by, "Is this Mrs. Scott's house?" and the woman, smiling queerly, said, "It is, my lass."

Oh, to be away from this! She actually said, "Help me, God," as she walked up the tiny path and knocked. To be away from those staring eyes, or to be covered up in anything, one of those women's shawls even. I'll just leave the basket and go, she decided. I shan't even wait for it to be emptied.

Then the door opened. A little woman in black showed in the gloom.

Laura said, "Are you Mrs. Scott?" But to her horror the woman answered, "Walk in please, miss," and she was shut in the passage.

"No," said Laura, "I don't want to come in. I only want to leave this basket. Mother sent—"

The little woman in the gloomy passage seemed not to have heard her. "Step this way, please, miss," she said in an oily voice, and Laura followed her.

She found herself in a wretched little low kitchen, lighted by a smoky lamp. There was a woman sitting before the fire.

"Em," said the little creature who had let her in. "Em! It's a young lady." She turned to Laura. She said meaningly, "I'm 'er sister, Miss. You'll excuse 'er, won't you?"

"Oh, but of course!" said Laura. "Please, please don't disturb her. I—I only want to leave—"

But at that moment the woman at the fire turned round. Her face, puffed up, red, with swollen eyes and swollen lips, looked terrible. She seemed as though she couldn't understand why Laura was there. What did it mean? Why was this stranger standing in the kitchen with a basket? What was it all about? And the poor face puckered up again.

"All right, my dear," said the other. "I'll thank the young lady."

And again she began, "You'll excuse her, miss, I'm sure," and her face, swollen too, tried an oily smile.

Laura only wanted to get out, to get away. She was back in the passage. The door opened. She walked straight through into the bedroom, where the dead man was lying.

"You'd like a look at 'im, wouldn't you?" said Em's sister, and she brushed past Laura over to the bed. "Don't be afraid, my lass—" and now her voice sounded fond and sly, and fondly she drew down the sheet—" 'e looks a picture. There's nothing to show. Come along, my dear."

Laura came.

There lay a young man, fast asleep—sleeping so soundly, so deeply, that he was far, far away from them both. Oh, so remote, so peaceful. He was dreaming. Never wake him up again. His head was sunk in the pillow, his eyes were closed; they were blind under the closed eyelids. He was given up to his dream. What did garden-parties and baskets and lace frocks matter to him? He was far from all those things. He was wonderful, beautiful. While they were laughing and while the band was playing, this marvel had come to the lane. Happy . . . happy. . . . All is well, said that sleeping face. This is just as it should be. I am content.

But all the same you had to cry, and she couldn't go out of the room without saying something to him. Laura gave a loud childish sob.

"Forgive my hat," she said.

And this time she didn't wait for Em's sister. She found her way out of the door, down the path, past all those dark people. At the corner of the lane she met Laurie.

He stepped out of the shadow. "Is that you, Laura?"

"Yes."

"Mother was getting anxious. Was it all right?"

"Yes, quite. Oh, Laurie!" She took his arm, she pressed up against him.

"I say, you're not crying, are you?" asked her brother.

Laura shook her head. She was.

Laurie put his arm round her shoulder. "Don't cry," he said in his warm, loving voice. "Was it awful?"

"No," sobbed Laura. "It was simply marvelous. But, Laurie—" She stopped, she looked at her brother. "Isn't life," she stammered, "isn't life—" But what life was she couldn't explain. No matter. He quite understood.

"*Isn't* it, darling?" said Laurie.

QUESTIONS

1. How does Mansfield manage to convey a wide range of attitudes in her characters? Cite examples, looking at her use of dialogue and physical description.

2. How do the lyrics of "This Life is Weary" reflect upon the development of the story?

3. Find examples of how Mansfield uses sharp contrasts to give her portrayal of the well-to-do an ironic edge.

4. We see how the rich view the poor; what do we see about the ways that the poor regard the rich?

5. Why does Meg say of her experience of seeing the corpse that "It was simply marvelous"? Does her phrasing evoke a still sharper sense of irony?

6. Are we to believe that her experience will change her life?

7. Is Meg's response just an instance of girlish romanticism, or is there some way in which the repose of death could look beautiful?

8. What is the final revelation of this story?

9. Compare Meg's awakening to that experienced by the woman in D. H. Lawrence's "Odour of Chrysanthemums."

William Faulkner

Although William Faulkner (1897–1962) is abundantly represented in anthologies of short fiction, he was not in any real sense a short story writer. His interest was less in the contained dramas that take place in the life of the individual, far more in trying to capture the destinies of families and groups over time. To achieve his aim, Faulkner more or less invented and populated an entire county in his native Mississippi. He called it Yoknapatawpha County, and a substantial portion of his highly productive career was devoted to the chronicling of its citizens and their doings. Many of his short stories—he published four collections in his lifetime—can be seen as threads extracted from the larger fabric of that place. "Wash" is a case in point.

Faulkner began his literary apprenticeship as a newspaperman in New Orleans. He met writer Sherwood Anderson there, and Anderson helped him to publish his first novel, *Soldier's Pay* (1926). Soon after that he conceived the scheme that would become his life's work, and in a period spanning just over a decade he published the novels that made his name famous: *The Sound and the Fury* (1929), *As I Lay Dying* (1930), *Sanctuary* (1931), *Light in August* (1932), *Absalom, Absalom!* (1936), and *The Hamlet* (1940). Ten years later, in 1950, he was awarded the Nobel prize for literature.

In Faulkner's best work we find a potent, often suggestively discordant, blend of subject and approach. His great theme could be said to be the erosion of the culture of the South in the onrush of the modern age, and a great deal of the prose details the rich legacies of place. But this concern is repeatedly subjected to the pressures of the modern. To this end, Faulkner freely adapts modernist stylistic devices to his needs, fracturing narrative, plunging into interior monologues, and distributing point of view among various characters. Reading him, one reaches toward the past, but with the instruments of the present. A world is preserved, but so is the rush of change that eventually destroyed it.

WASH

Sutpen stood above the pallet bed on which the mother and child lay. Between the shrunken planking of the wall the early sunlight fell in long pencil strokes, breaking upon his straddled legs and upon the riding whip in his hand, and lay across the still shape of the mother, who lay looking up at him from still, inscrutable, sullen eyes, the child at her side wrapped in a piece of dingy though clean cloth. Behind them an old Negro woman squatted beside the rough hearth where a meager fire smoldered.

"Well, Milly," Sutpen said, "too bad you're not a mare. Then I could give you a decent stall in the stable."

Still the girl on the pallet did not move. She merely continued to look up at him without expression, with a young, sullen, inscrutable face still pale from recent travail. Sutpen moved, bringing into the splintered pencils of sunlight the face of a man of sixty. He said quietly to the squatting Negress, "Griselda foaled this morning."

"Horse or mare?" the Negress said.

"A horse. A damned fine colt. . . . What's this?" He indicated the pallet with the hand which held the whip.

"That un's a mare, I reckon."

"Hah," Sutpen said. "A damned fine colt. Going to be the spit and image of old Rob Roy when I rode him North in '61. Do you remember?"

"Yes, Master."

"Hah." He glanced back towards the pallet. None could have said if the girl still watched him or not. Again his whip hand indicated the pallet. "Do whatever they need with whatever we've got to do it with." He went out, passing out the crazy doorway and stepping down into the rank weeds (there yet leaned rusting against the corner of the porch the scythe which Wash had borrowed from him three months ago to cut them with) where his horse waited, where Wash stood holding the reins.

When Colonel Sutpen rode away to fight the Yankees, Wash did not go. "I'm looking after the Kernel's place and niggers," he would tell all who asked him and some who had not asked—a gaunt, malaria-ridden man with pale, questioning eyes, who looked about thirty-five, though it was known that he had not only a daughter but an eight-year-old granddaughter as well. This was a lie, as most of them—the few remaining men between eighteen and fifty—to whom he told it, knew, though there were some who believed that he himself really believed it, though even these believed that he had better sense than to put it to the test with Mrs. Sutpen or the Sutpen slaves. Knew better or was just too lazy and shiftless to try it, they said, knowing that his sole connection with the Sutpen plantation lay in the fact that for years now Colonel Sutpen had allowed him to squat in a crazy shack on a slough in the river bottom on the Sutpen place, which Sutpen had built for a fishing lodge in his bachelor days and which had since fallen in dilapidation from disuse, so that now it looked like an aged or sick wild beast crawled terrifically there to drink in the act of dying.

The Sutpen slaves themselves heard of his statement. They laughed. It was not the first time they had laughed at him, calling him white trash behind his back. They began to ask him themselves, in groups, meeting him in the faint road which led up from the slough and the old fish camp, "Why ain't you at de war, white man?"

Pausing, he would look about the ring of black faces and white eyes and teeth behind which derision lurked. "Because I got a daughter and a family to keep," he said. "Git out of my road, niggers."

"Niggers?" they repeated; "niggers?" laughing now. "Who him, calling us niggers?"

"Yes," he said. "I ain't got no niggers to look after my folks if I was gone."

"Nor nothing else but dat shack down yon dat Cunnel wouldn't *let* none of us live in."

Now he cursed them; sometimes he rushed at them, snatching up a stick from the ground while they scattered before him, yet seeming to surround him still with that black laughing, derisive, evasive, inescapable, leaving him panting and impotent and raging. Once it happened in the very back yard of the big house itself. This was after bitter news had come down from the Tennessee mountains and from Vicksburg, and Sherman had passed through the plantation, and most of the Negroes had followed him. Almost everything else had gone with the Federal troops, and Mrs. Sutpen had sent word to Wash that he could have the scuppernongs ripening in the arbor in the back yard. This time it was a house servant, one of the few Negroes who remained; this time the Negress had to retreat up the kitchen steps, where she turned. "Stop right dar, white man. Stop right whar you is. You ain't never crossed dese steps whilst Cunnel here, and you ain't ghy' do hit now."

This was true. But there was this of a kind of pride: he had never tried to enter the big house, even though he believed that if he had, Sutpen would have received him, permitted him. "But I ain't going to give no black nigger the chance to tell me I can't go nowhere," he said to himself. "I ain't even going to give Kernel the chance to have to cuss a nigger on my account." This, though he and Sutpen had spent more than one afternoon together on those rare Sundays when there would be no company in the house. Perhaps his mind knew that it was because Sutpen had nothing else to do, being a man who could not bear his own company. Yet the fact remained that the two of them would spend whole afternoons in the scuppernong arbor, Sutpen in the hammock and Wash squatting against a post, a pail of cistern water between them, taking drink for drink from the same demijohn. Meanwhile on weekdays he would see the fine figure of the man—they were the same age almost to a day, though neither of them (perhaps because Wash had a grandchild while Sutpen's son was a youth in school) ever thought of himself as being so—on the fine figure of the black stallion, galloping about the plantation. For that moment his heart would be quiet and proud. It would seem to him that that world in which Negroes, whom the Bible told him had been created and cursed by God to be brute and vassal to all men of white skin, were better found and housed and even clothed than he and his; that world in which he sensed always about him mocking echoes of black laughter was but a dream and an illusion, and that the actual world was this one across which his own lonely apotheosis seemed to gallop on the black thoroughbred, thinking how the Book said also that all men were created in the image of God and hence all men made the same image in God's eyes at least; so that he could say, as though speaking of himself, "A fine proud man. If God Himself was to come down and ride the natural earth, that's what He would aim to look like."

Sutpen returned in 1865, on the black stallion. He seemed to have aged ten years. His son had vanished the same winter in which his wife had died. He returned with his citation for gallantry from the hand of General Lee to a ruined plantation, where for a year now his daughter had subsisted partially on the meager bounty of the man to whom fifteen years ago he had granted permission to live in that tumbledown fishing camp whose very existence he had at the time forgotten. Wash was there to meet him, unchanged: still gaunt, still ageless, with his pale, questioning gaze, his air diffident, a little servile, a little familiar. "Well, Kernel," Wash said, "they kilt us but they ain't whupped us yit, air they?"

That was the tenor of their conversation for the next five years. It was inferior whiskey which they drank now together from a stoneware jug, and it was not in the scuppernong arbor. It was in the rear of the little store which Sutpen managed to set up on the highroad: a frame shelved room where, with Wash for clerk and porter, he dispensed kerosene and staple foodstuffs and stale gaudy candy and cheap beads and ribbons to Negroes or poor whites of Wash's own kind, who came afoot or on gaunt mules to haggle tediously for dimes and quarters with a man who at one time could gallop (the black stallion was still alive; the stable in which his jealous get lived was in better repair than the house where the master himself lived) for ten miles across his own fertile land and who had led troops gallantly in battle; until Sutpen in fury would empty the store, close and lock the doors from the inside. Then he and Wash would repair to the rear and the jug. But the talk would not be quiet now, as when Sutpen lay in the hammock, delivering an arrogant monologue while Wash squatted guffawing against his post. They both sat now, though Sutpen had the single chair while Wash used whatever box or keg was handy, and even this for just a little while, because soon Sutpen would reach that stage of impotent and furious undefeat in which he would rise, swaying and plunging, and declare again that he would take his pistol and the black stallion and ride single-handed into Washington and kill Lincoln, dead now, and Sherman, now a private citizen. "Kill them!" he would shout. "Shoot them down like the dogs they are—"

"Sho, Kernel; sho, Kernel," Wash would say, catching Sutpen as he fell. Then he would commandeer the first passing wagon or, lacking that, he would walk the mile to the nearest neighbor and borrow one and return and carry Sutpen home. He entered the house now. He had been doing so for a long time, taking Sutpen home in whatever borrowed wagon might be, talking him into locomotion with cajoling murmurs as though he were a horse, a stallion himself. The daughter would meet them and hold open the door without a word. He would carry his burden through the once white formal entrance, surmounted by a fanlight imported piece by piece from Europe and with a board now nailed over a missing pane, across a velvet carpet from which all nap was now gone, and up a formal stairs, now but a fading ghost of bare boards between two strips of fading paint, and into the bedroom. It would be dusk by now, and he would let his burden sprawl onto the bed and undress it and then he would sit quietly in a chair beside. After a time the daughter would come to the door. "We're all right now," he would tell her. "Don't you worry none, Miss Judith."

Then it would become dark, and after a while he would lie down on the floor beside the bed, though not to sleep, because after a time—sometimes before midnight—the man on the bed would stir and groan and then speak. "Wash?"

"Hyer I am, Kernel. You go back to sleep. We ain't whupped yit, air we? Me and you kin do hit."

Even then he had already seen the ribbon about his granddaughter's waist. She was now fifteen, already mature, after the early way of her kind. He knew where the ribbon came from; he had been seeing it and its kind daily for three years, even if she had lied about where she got it, which she did not, at once bold, sullen, and fearful.

"Sho now," he said. "Ef Kernel wants to give hit to you, I hope you minded to thank him."

His heart was quiet, even when he saw the dress, watching her secret, defiant, frightened face when she told him that Miss Judith, the daughter, had helped her to make it. But he was quite grave when he approached Sutpen after they closed the store that afternoon, following the other to the rear.

"Get the jug," Sutpen directed.

"Wait," Wash said. "Not yit for a minute."

Neither did Sutpen deny the dress. "What about it?" he said.

But Wash met his arrogant stare; he spoke quietly. "I've knowed you for going on twenty years. I ain't never yit denied to do what you told me to do. And I'm a man nigh sixty. And she ain't nothing but a fifteen-year-old gal."

"Meaning that I'd harm a girl? I, a man as old as you are?"

"If you was ara other man, I'd say you was as old as me. And old or no old, I wouldn't let her keep that dress nor nothing else that come from your hand. But you are different."

"How different?" But Wash merely looked at him with his pale, questioning, sober eyes. "So that's why you are afraid of me?"

Now Wash's gaze no longer questioned. It was tranquil, serene. "I ain't afraid. Because you air brave. It ain't that you were a brave man at one minute or day of your life and got a paper to show hit from General Lee.

But you air brave, the same as you air alive and breathing. That's where hit's different. Hit don't need no ticket from nobody to tell me that. And I know that whatever you handle or tech, whether hit's a regiment of men or a ignorant gal or just a hound dog, that you will make hit right."

Now it was Sutpen who looked away, turning suddenly, brusquely. "Get the jug," he said sharply.

"Sho, Kernel," Wash said.

So on that Sunday dawn two years later, having watched the Negro midwife, whom he had walked three miles to fetch, enter the crazy door beyond which his granddaughter lay wailing, his heart was still quiet though concerned. He knew what they had been saying—the Negroes in cabins about the land, the white men who loafed all day long about the store, watching quietly the three of them: Sutpen, himself, his granddaughter with her air of brazen and shrinking defiance as her condition became daily more and more obvious, like three actors that came and went upon a stage. "I know what they say to one another," he thought. "I can almost hyear them: *Wash Jones has fixed old Sutpen at last. Hit taken him twenty years, but he has done hit at last.*"

It would be dawn after a while, though not yet. From the house, where the lamp shone dim beyond the warped door frame, his granddaughter's voice came steadily as though run by a clock, while thinking went slowly and terrifically, fumbling, involved somehow with a sound of galloping hooves, until there broke suddenly free in mid-gallop the fine proud figure of the man on the fine proud stallion, galloping; and then that at which thinking fumbled, broke free too and quite clear, not in justification nor even explanation, but as the apotheosis, lonely, explicable, beyond all fouling by human touch: "He is bigger than all them Yankees that kilt his son and his wife and taken his niggers and ruined his land, bigger than this hyer durn country that he fit for and that has denied him into keeping a little country store; bigger than the denial which hit helt to his lips like the bitter cup in the Book. And how could I have lived this nigh to him for twenty years without being teched and changed by him? Maybe I ain't as big as him and maybe I ain't done none of the galloping. But at least I done been drug along. Me and him kin do hit, if so be he will show me what he aims for me to do."

Then it was dawn. Suddenly he could see the house, and the old Negress in the door looking at him. Then he realized that his granddaughter's voice had ceased. "It's a girl," the Negress said. "You can go tell him if you want to." She reëntered the house.

"A girl," he repeated; "a girl"; in astonishment, hearing the galloping hooves, seeing the proud galloping figure emerge again. He seemed to watch it pass, galloping through avatars which marked the accumulation of years, time, to the climax where it galloped beneath a brandished sabre and a shot-torn flag rushing down a sky in color like thunderous sulphur, thinking for the first time in his life that perhaps Sutpen was an old man like himself. "Gittin a gal," he thought in that astonishment; then he thought with the pleased surprise of a child: "Yes, sir. Be dawg if I ain't lived to be a great-grandpaw after all."

He entered the house. He moved clumsily, on tiptoe, as if he no longer lived there, as if the infant which had just drawn breath and cried in light had dispossessed him, be it of his own blood too though it might. But even above the pallet he could see little save the blur of his granddaughter's exhausted face. Then the Negress squatting at the hearth spoke, "You better gawn tell him if you going to. Hit's daylight now."

But this was not necessary. He had no more than turned the corner of the porch where the scythe leaned which he had borrowed three months ago to clear away the weeds through which he walked, when Sutpen himself rode up on the old stallion. He did not wonder how Sutpen had got the word. He took it for granted that this was what had brought the other out at this hour on Sunday morning, and he stood while the other dismounted, and he took the reins from Sutpen's hand, and expression on his gaunt face almost imbecile with a kind of weary triumph, saying, "Hit's a gal, Kernel. I be dawg if you ain't as old as I am—" until Sutpen passed him and entered the house. He stood there with the reins in his hand and heard Sutpen cross the floor to the pallet. He heard what Sutpen said, and something seemed to stop dead in him before going on.

The sun was now up, the swift sun of Mississippi latitudes, and it seemed to him that he stood beneath a strange sky, in a strange scene, familiar only as things are familiar in dream, like the dreams of falling to one who has never climbed. "I kain't have heard what I thought I heard," he thought quietly. "I know I kain't." Yet the voice, the familiar voice which had said the words was still speaking, talking now to the old Negress about a colt foaled that morning. "That's why he was up so early," he thought. "That was hit. Hit ain't me and mine. Hit ain't even hisn that got him outen bed."

Sutpen emerged. He descended into the weeds, moving with that heavy deliberation which would have been haste when he was younger. He had not yet looked full at Wash. He said, "Dicey will stay and tend to her. You better—" Then he seemed to see Wash facing him and paused. "What?" he said.

"You said—" To his own ears Wash's voice sounded flat and ducklike, like a deaf man's. "You said if she was a mare, you could give her a good stall in the stable."

"Well?" Sutpen said. His eyes widened and narrowed, almost like a man's fists flexing and shutting, as Wash began to advance towards him, stooping a little. Very astonishment kept Sutpen still for the moment, watching that man whom in twenty years he had no more known to make any motion save at command than he had the horse which he rode. Again his eyes narrowed and widened; without moving he seemed to rear suddenly upright. "Stand back," he said suddenly and sharply. "Don't you touch me."

"I'm going to tech you, Kernel," Wash said in that flat, quiet, almost soft voice, advancing.

Sutpen raised the hand which held the riding whip; the old Negress peered around the crazy door with her black gargoyle face of a worn gnome. "Stand back, Wash," Sutpen said. Then he struck. The old Negress leaped down into the weeds with the agility of a goat and fled. Sutpen slashed Wash again across the face with the whip, striking him to his knees. When Wash rose and advanced once more he held in his hands the scythe which he had borrowed from Sutpen three months ago and which Sutpen would never need again.

When he reëntered the house his granddaughter stirred on the pallet bed and called his name fretfully. "What was that?" she said.

"What was what, honey?"

"That ere racket out there."

" 'Twarn't nothing," he said gently. He knelt and touched her hot forehead clumsily. "Do you want ara thing?"

"I want a sup of water," she said querulously. "I been laying here wanting a sup of water a long time, but don't nobody care enough to pay me no mind."

"Sho now," he said soothingly. He rose stiffly and fetched the dipper of water and raised her head to drink and laid her back and watched her turn to the child with an absolutely stonelike face. But a moment later he saw that she was crying quietly. "Now, now," he said, "I wouldn't do that. Old Dicey says hit's a right fine gal. Hit's all right now. Hit's all over now. Hit ain't no need to cry now."

But she continued to cry quietly, almost sullenly, and he rose again and stood uncomfortably above the pallet for a time, thinking as he had thought when his own wife lay so and then his daughter in turn: "Women. Hit's a mystry to me. They seem to want em, and yit when they git em they cry about hit. Hit's a mystry to me. To ara man." Then he moved away and drew a chair up to the window and sat down.

Through all that long, bright, sunny forenoon he sat at the window, waiting. Now and then he rose and tiptoed to the pallet. But his granddaughter slept now, her face sullen and calm and weary, the child in the crook of her arm. Then he returned to the chair and sat again, waiting, wondering why it took them so long, until he remembered that it was Sunday. He was sitting there at mid-afternoon when a half-grown white boy came around the corner of the house upon the body and gave a choked cry and looked up and glared for a mesmerized instant at Wash in the window before he turned and fled. Then Wash rose and tiptoed again to the pallet.

The granddaughter was awake now, wakened perhaps by the boy's cry without hearing it. "Milly," he said, "air you hungry?" She didn't answer, turning her face away. He built up the fire on the hearth and cooked the food which he had brought home the day before: fatback it was, and cold corn pone; he poured water into the stale coffee pot and heated it. But she would not eat when he carried the plate to her, so he ate himself, quietly, alone, and left the dishes as they were and returned to the window.

Now he seemed to sense, feel, the men who would be gathering with horses and guns and dogs—the curious, and the vengeful: men of Sutpen's own kind, who had made the company about Sutpen's table in the time when Wash himself had yet to approach nearer to the house than the scuppernong arbor—men who had also shown the lesser ones how to fight in battle, who maybe also had signed papers from the generals saying that they were among the first of the brave; who had also galloped in the old days arrogant and proud on the fine horses across the fine plantations—symbols also of admiration and hope; instruments too of despair and grief.

That was who they would expect him to run from. It seemed to him that he had no more to run from than he had to run to. If he ran, he would merely be fleeing one set of bragging and evil shadows for another just like them, since they were all of a kind throughout all the earth which he knew, and he was old, too old to flee far even if he were to flee. He could never escape them, no matter how much or how far he ran: a man going on sixty could not run that far. Not far enough to escape beyond the boundaries of earth where such men lived, set the order and the rule of living. It seemed to him that he now saw for the first time, after five years, how it was that Yankees or any other living armies had managed to whip them: the gallant, the proud, the brave; the acknowledged and chosen best among them all to carry courage and honor and pride. Maybe if he had gone to the war with them he would have discovered them sooner. But if he had discovered them sooner, what would he have done with his life since? How could he have borne to remember for five years what his life had been before?

Now it was getting toward sunset. The child had been crying; when he went to the pallet he saw his granddaughter nursing it, her face still bemused, sullen, inscrutable. "Air you hungry yit?" he said.

"I don't want nothing."

"You ought to eat."

This time she did not answer at all, looking down at the child. He returned to his chair and found that the sun had set. "Hit kain't be much longer," he thought. He could feel them quite near now, the curious and the vengeful. He could even seem to hear what they were saying about him, the undercurrent of believing beyond the immediate fury: *Old Wash Jones he come a tumble at last. He thought he had Sutpen, but Sutpen fooled him. He thought he had Kernel where he would have to marry the gal or pay up. And Kernel refused.* "But I never expected that, Kernel!" he cried aloud, catching himself at the sound of his own voice, glancing quickly back to find his granddaughter watching him.

"Who you talking to now?" she said.

"Hit ain't nothing. I was just thinking and talked out before I knowed hit."

Her face was becoming indistinct again, again a sullen blur in the twilight. "I reckon so. I reckon you'll have to holler louder than that before he'll hear you, up yonder at that house. And I reckon you'll need to do more than holler before you get him down here too."

"Sho now," he said. "Don't you worry none." But already thinking was going smoothly on: "You know I never. You know how I ain't never expected or asked nothing from ara living man but what I expected from you. And I never asked that. I didn't think hit would need. I said, *I don't need to. What need has a fellow like Wash Jones to question or doubt the man that General Lee himself says in a handwrote ticket that he was brave?* Brave," he thought. "Better if nara one of them had never rid back home in '65"; thinking *Better if his kind and mine too had never drawn the breath of life on this earth. Better that all who remain of us be blasted from the face of the earth than that another Wash Jones should see his whole life shredded from him and shrivel away like a dried shuck thrown onto the fire.*

He ceased, became still. He heard the horses, suddenly and plainly; presently he saw the lantern and the movement of men, the glint of gun barrels, in its moving light. Yet he did not stir. It was quite dark now, and he listened to the voices and the sounds of underbrush as they surrounded the house. The lantern itself came on; its light fell upon the quiet body in the weeds and stopped, the horses tall and shadowy. A man descended and stooped in the lantern light, above the body. He held a pistol; he rose and faced the house. "Jones," he said.

"I'm here," Wash said quietly from the window "That you, Major?"

"Come out."

"Sho," he said quietly. "I just want to see to my granddaughter."

"We'll see to her. Come on out."

"Sho, Major. Just a minute."

"Show a light. Light your lamp."

"Sho. In just a minute." They could hear his voice retreat into the house, though they could not see him as he went swiftly to the crack in the chimney where he kept the butcher knife: the one thing in his slovenly life and house in which he took pride, since it was razor sharp. He approached the pallet, his granddaughter's voice:

"Who is it? Light the lamp, grandpaw."

"Hit won't need no light, honey. Hit won't take but a minute," he said, kneeling, fumbling toward her voice, whispering now. "Where air you?"

"Right here," she said fretfully. "Where would I be? What is. . . ." His hand touched her face. "What is. . . . Grandpaw! Grand. . . ."

"Jones!" the sheriff said. "Come out of there!"

"In just a minute, Major," he said. Now he rose and moved swiftly. He knew where in the dark the can of kerosene was, just as he knew that it was full, since it was not two days ago that he had filled it at the store and held it there until he got a ride home with it, since the five gallons were heavy. There were still coals on the hearth; besides the crazy building itself was like tinder: the coals, the hearth, the walls exploding in a single blue glare. Against it the waiting men saw him in a wild instant springing toward them with the lifted scythe before the horses reared and whirled. They checked the horses and turned them back toward the glare, yet still in wild relief against it the gaunt figure ran toward them with the lifted scythe.

"Jones!" the sheriff shouted. "Stop! Stop, or I'll shoot. Jones! *Jones!*" Yet still the gaunt, furious figure came on against the glare and roar of the flames. With the scythe lifted, it bore down upon them, upon the wild glaring eyes of the horses and the swinging glints of gun barrels, without any cry, any sound.

QUESTIONS

1. How does Faulkner use precise physical details to create an atmosphere at the beginning of the story? What kind of atmosphere is it?
2. What does the opening description suggest about Sutpen's relation to Milly?
3. What is the reader's first impression of Wash's character? What is Wash's image of Sutpen, and how does that relate to his character?
4. What is the nature of the relationship between Wash and Sutpen? What does this relationship tell us about Sutpen's character?
5. How do circumstances change after Sutpen's return from the war?
6. How does Wash respond when he learns that Sutpen has been paying attention to his granddaughter? What is the reader's first signal that there is tension between the two men?
7. How does Faulkner convey the ambivalence of Wash's feelings toward Sutpen?
8. What drives Wash to his breaking point?
9. What is Faulkner's larger message about the tragedy of Southern history?
10. How does Faulkner use images and descriptions to create a final epic effect?

Ernest Hemingway

Ernest Hemingway (1898–1961) has probably done more to shape the course of American fiction than any writer in our time, both in terms of spawning a legion of imitators and in leaving a stylistic imprint on our prose. Needless to say, he has also engendered strong dissenting reaction in other quarters. The Hemingway themes—of finding manhood, of self-testing in the face of danger, of the futility of human relationships—have proved anything but popular with readers attuned to feminist issues. Moreover, his flat, understated declarative style has been imitated almost to the point of parody. But the influence lives on. Macho or no, Hemingway managed to install himself in the myth-making portion of the American psyche. He wrote and lived according to a code that still exerts a strong appeal in part, one might guess, because we live in an age so lacking in such codes.

To the would-be writer concerned with openings, he said: "Write the truest thing you know." The advice sounds simplistic, but Hemingway learned it himself after a long apprenticeship. No simple command could be more difficult to carry out.

Hemingway was born in Oak Park, Illinois. He passed his boyhood summers hunting and fishing in the wooded country of Northern Michigan, a setting that recurs throughout his early stories. After a few months as a reporter at the *Kansas City Star*, Hemingway enlisted in an ambulance unit and was sent to the French front. He was only eighteen. A shrapnel wound cut short his service; he returned home to his family.

But war and travel had infected his soul. After only a short stay with his family, Hemingway sailed for Paris. He was determined to make his way as a writer. And there, in the midst of a great many other expatriates—Gertrude Stein, F. Scott Fitzgerald, Ezra Pound, James Joyce, and others—he honed the style that would make his name.

Hemingway has cited many influences upon his prose, including Ivan Turgenev, Joseph Conrad, Sherwood Anderson, and Gertrude Stein. He has also cited the paintings of Paul Cézanne, and the reader might at some point look for the comparison. Both painter and writer forged an intense, highly focused, but also highly restrained manner. In Cézanne, short, rough-looking strokes are worked with great care to bring out the solidity and depth of the object in question. Hemingway, for his part, professed the now well-known "iceberg technique," arguing that the greater power in a work of art derives from what is below the surface, suggested but not overtly stated.

Hemingway's career was tumultuous in the extreme. Apart from attaining world celebrity as a writer, he was constantly in the public eye for other exploits: he fished, hunted on safari, married and divorced, drank and fought; he served as a correspondent in the Spanish Civil War and World War II, survived spectacular accidents, traveled incessantly. . . . In short, he created a myth for his times. What almost no one realized was that there was a dark, depressive side to this most flamboyant man. His father had died a suicide, and he would, too. Hemingway shot himself at his hunting lodge in Ketchum, Idaho, in 1961 after a lingering period of mental distress.

Hemingway's many books include the story collection *In Our Time* (1925) and the novels *A Farewell to Arms* (1929), *The Sun Also Rises* (1926), and *For Whom the Bell Tolls* (1940).

THE KILLERS

The door of Henry's lunch-room opened and two men came in. They sat down at the counter.

"What's yours?" George asked them.

"I don't know," one of the men said. "What do you want to eat, Al?"

"I don't know," said Al. "I don't know what I want to eat."

Outside it was getting dark. The street-light came on outside the window. The two men at the counter read the menu. From the other end of the counter Nick Adams watched them. He had been talking to George when they came in.

"I'll have a roast pork tenderloin with apple sauce and mashed potatoes," the first man said.

"It isn't ready yet."

"What the hell do you put it on the card for?"

"That's the dinner," George explained. "You can get that at six o'clock."

George looked at the clock on the wall behind the counter.

"It's five o'clock."

"The clock says twenty minutes past five," the second man said.

"It's twenty minutes fast."

"Oh, to hell with the clock," the first man said. "What have you got to eat?"

"I can give you any kind of sandwiches," George said. "You can have ham and eggs, bacon and eggs, liver and bacon, or a steak."

"Give me chicken croquettes with green peas and cream sauce and mashed potatoes."

"That's the dinner."

"Everything we want's the dinner, eh? That's the way you work it."

"I can give you ham and eggs, bacon and eggs, liver——"

"I'll take ham and eggs," the man called Al said. He wore a derby hat and a black overcoat buttoned across the chest. His face was small and white and he had tight lips. He wore a silk muffler and gloves.

"Give me bacon and eggs," said the other man. He was about the same size as Al. Their faces were different, but they were dressed like twins. Both wore overcoats too tight for them. They sat leaning forward, their elbows on the counter.

"Got anything to drink?" Al asked.
"Silver beer, bevo, ginger-ale," George said.
"I mean you got anything to *drink?*"
"Just those I said."
"This is a hot town," said the other. "What do they call it?"
"Summit."
"Ever hear of it?" Al asked his friend.
"No," said the friend.
"What do you do here nights?" Al asked.
"They eat the dinner," his friend said. "They all come here and eat the big dinner."
"That's right," George said.
"So you think that's right?" Al asked George.
"Sure."
"You're a pretty bright boy, aren't you?"
"Sure," said George.
"Well, you're not," said the other little man. "Is he, Al?"
"He's dumb," said Al. He turned to Nick. "What's your name?"
"Adams."
"Another bright boy," Al said. "Ain't he a bright boy, Max?"
"The town's full of bright boys," Max said.
George put the two platters, one of ham and eggs, the other of bacon and eggs, on the counter. He set down two side-dishes of fried potatoes and closed the wicket into the kitchen.
"Which is yours?" he asked Al.
"Don't you remember?"
"Ham and eggs."
"Just a bright boy," Max said. He leaned forward and took the ham and eggs. Both men ate with their gloves on. George watched them eat.
"What are *you* looking at?" Max looked at George.
"Nothing."
"The hell you were. You were looking at me."
"Maybe the boy meant it for a joke, Max," Al said.
George laughed.
"*You* don't have to laugh," Max said to him. "*You* don't have to laugh at all, see?"
"All right," said George.
"So he thinks it's all right." Max turned to Al. "He thinks it's all right. That's a good one."
"Oh, he's a thinker," Al said. They went on eating.
"What's the bright boy's name down the counter?" Al asked Max.
"Hey, bright boy," Max said to Nick. "You go around on the other side of the counter with your boy friend."
"What's the idea?" Nick asked.
"There isn't any idea."

"You better go around, bright boy," Al said. Nick went around behind the counter.

"What's the idea?" George asked.

"None of your damn business," Al said. "Who's out in the kitchen?"

"The nigger."

"What do you mean the nigger?"

"The nigger that cooks."

"Tell him to come in."

"What's the idea?"

"Tell him to come in."

"Where do you think you are?"

"We know damn well where we are," the man called Max said. "Do we look silly?"

"You talk silly," Al said to him. "What the hell do you argue with this kid for? Listen," he said to George, "tell the nigger to come out here."

"What are you going to do to him?"

"Nothing. Use your head, bright boy. What would we do to a nigger?"

George opened the slit that opened back into the kitchen. "Sam," he called. "Come in here a minute."

The door to the kitchen opened and the nigger came in. "What was it?" he asked. The two men at the counter took a look at him.

"All right, nigger. You stand right there," Al said.

Sam, the nigger, standing in his apron, looked at the two men sitting at the counter. "Yes, sir," he said. Al got down from his stool.

"I'm going back to the kitchen with the nigger and bright boy," he said. "Go on back to the kitchen, nigger. You go with him, bright boy." The little man walked after Nick and Sam, the cook, back into the kitchen. The door shut after them. The man called Max sat at the counter opposite George. He didn't look at George but looked in the mirror that ran along back of the counter. Henry's had been made over from a saloon into a lunch-counter.

"Well, bright boy," Max said, looking into the mirror, "why don't you say something?"

"What's it all about?"

"Hey, Al," Max called, "bright boy wants to know what it's all about."

"Why don't you tell him?" Al's voice came from the kitchen.

"What do you think it's all about?"

"I don't know."

"What do you think?"

Max looked into the mirror all the time he was talking.

"I wouldn't say."

"Hey, Al, bright boy says he wouldn't say what he thinks it's all about."

"I can hear you, all right," Al said from the kitchen. He had propped open the slit that dishes passed through into the kitchen with a catsup bottle. "Listen, bright boy," he said from the kitchen to George. "Stand a little further along the bar. You move a little to the left, Max." He was like a photographer arranging for a group picture.

"Talk to me, bright boy," Max said. "What do you think's going to happen?"

George did not say anything.

"I'll tell you," Max said. "We're going to kill a Swede. Do you know a big Swede named Ole Andreson?"

"Yes."

"He comes here to eat every night, don't he?"

"Sometimes he comes here."

"He comes here at six o'clock, don't he?"

"If he comes."

"We know all that, bright boy," Max said. "Talk about something else. Ever go to the movies?"

"Once in a while."

"You ought to go to the movies more. The movies are fine for a bright boy like you."

"What are you going to kill Ole Andreson for? What did he ever do to you?"

"He never had a chance to do anything to us. He never even seen us."

"And he's only going to see us once," Al said from the kitchen.

"What are you going to kill him for, then?" George asked.

"We're killing him for a friend. Just to oblige a friend, bright boy."

"Shut up," said Al from the kitchen. "You talk too goddam much."

"Well, I got to keep bright boy amused. Don't I, bright boy?"

"You talk too damn much," Al said. "The nigger and my bright boy are amused by themselves. I got them tied up like a couple of girl friends in the convent."

"I suppose you were in a convent?"

"You never know."

"You were in a kosher convent. That's where you were."

George looked up at the clock.

"If anybody comes in you tell them the cook is off, and if they keep after it, you tell them you'll go back and cook yourself. Do you get that, bright boy?"

"All right," George said. "What you going to do with us afterward?"

"That'll depend," Max said. "That's one of those things you never know at the time."

George looked up at the clock. It was a quarter past six. The door from the street opened. A street-car motorman came in.

"Hello, George," he said. "Can I get supper?"

"Sam's gone out," George said. "He'll be back in about half an hour."

"I'd better go up the street," the motorman said. George looked at the clock. It was twenty minutes past six.

"That was nice, bright boy," Max said. "You're a regular little gentleman."

"He knew I'd blow his head off," Al said from the kitchen.

"No," said Max. "It ain't that. Bright boy is nice. He's a nice boy. I like him."

At six-fifty-five George said: "He's not coming."

Two other people had been in the lunch-room. Once George had gone out to the kitchen and made a ham-and-egg sandwich "to go" that a man wanted to take with him. Inside the kitchen he saw Al, his derby hat tipped back, sitting on a stool beside the wicket with the muzzle of a sawed-off shotgun resting on the ledge. Nick and the cook were back to back in the corner, a towel tied in each of their mouths. George had cooked the sandwich, wrapped it up in oiled paper, put it in a bag, brought it in, and the man had paid for it and gone out.

"Bright boy can do everything," Max said. "He can cook and everything. You'd make some girl a nice wife, bright boy."

"Yes?" George said. "Your friend, Ole Andreson, isn't going to come."

"We'll give him ten minutes," Max said.

Max watched the mirror and the clock. The hands of the clock marked seven o'clock, and then five minutes past seven.

"Come on, Al," said Max. "We better go. He's not coming."

"Better give him five minutes," Al said from the kitchen.

In the five minutes a man came in, and George explained that the cook was sick.

"Why the hell don't you get another cook?" the man asked. "Aren't you running a lunch-counter?" He went out.

"Come on, Al," Max said.

"What about the two bright boys and the nigger?"

"They're all right."

"You think so?"

"Sure. We're through with it."

"I don't like it," said Al. "It's sloppy. You talk too much."

"Oh, what the hell," said Max. "We got to keep amused, haven't we?"

"You talk too much, all the same," Al said. He came out from the kitchen. The cut-off barrels of the shotgun made a slight bulge under the waist of his too tight-fitting overcoat. He straightened his coat with his gloved hands.

"So long, bright boy," he said to George. "You got a lot of luck."

"That's the truth," Max said. "You ought to play the races, bright boy."

The two of them went out the door. George watched them, through the window, pass under the arc-light and cross the street. In their tight overcoats and derby hats they looked like a vaudeville team. George went back through the swinging-door into the kitchen and untied Nick and the cook.

"I don't want any more of that," said Sam, the cook. "I don't want any more of that."

Nick stood up. He had never had a towel in his mouth before.

"Say," he said. "What the hell?" He was trying to swagger it off.

"They were going to kill Ole Andreson," George said. "They were going to shoot him when he came in to eat."

"Ole Andreson?"

"Sure."

The cook felt the corners of his mouth with his thumbs.

"They all gone?" he asked.

"Yeah," said George. "They're gone now."

"I don't like it," said the cook. "I don't like any of it at all."

"Listen," George said to Nick. "You better go see Ole Andreson."

"All right."

"You better not have anything to do with it at all," Sam, the cook, said. "You better stay way out of it."

"Don't go if you don't want to," George said.

"Mixing up in this ain't going to get you anywhere," the cook said. "You stay out of it."

"I'll go see him," Nick said to George. "Where does he live?"

The cook turned away.

"Little boys always know what they want to do," he said.

"He lives up at Hirsch's rooming-house," George said to Nick.

"I'll go up there."

Outside the arc-light shone through the bare branches of a tree. Nick walked up the street beside the car-tracks and turned at the next arc-light down a side-street. Three houses up the street was Hirsch's rooming-house. Nick walked up the two steps and pushed the bell. A woman came to the door.

"Is Ole Andreson here?"

"Do you want to see him?"

"Yes, if he's in."

Nick followed the woman up a flight of stairs and back to the end of a corridor. She knocked on the door.

"Who is it?"

"It's somebody to see you, Mr. Andreson," the woman said.

"It's Nick Adams."

"Come in."

Nick opened the door and went into the room. Ole Andreson was lying on the bed with all his clothes on. He had been a heavyweight prizefighter and he was too long for the bed. He lay with his head on two pillows. He did not look at Nick.

"What was it?" he asked.

"I was up at Henry's," Nick said, "and two fellows came in and tied up me and the cook, and they said they were going to kill you."

It sounded silly when he said it. Ole Andreson said nothing.

"They put us out in the kitchen," Nick went on. "They were going to shoot you when you came in to supper."

Ole Andreson looked at the wall and did not say anything.

"George thought I better come and tell you about it."

"There isn't anything I can do about it," Ole Andreson said.

"I'll tell you what they were like."

"I don't want to know what they were like," Ole Andreson said. He looked at the wall. "Thanks for coming to tell me about it."

"That's all right."

Nick looked at the big man lying on the bed.

"Don't you want me to go and see the police?"

"No," Ole Andreson said. "That wouldn't do any good."

"Isn't there something I could do?"

"No. There ain't anything to do."

"Maybe it was just a bluff."

"No. It ain't just a bluff."

Ole Andreson rolled over toward the wall.

"The only thing is," he said, talking toward the wall, "I just can't make up my mind to go out. I been in here all day."

"Couldn't you get out of town?"

"No," Ole Andreson said. "I'm through with all that running around." He looked at the wall.

"There ain't anything to do now."

"Couldn't you fix it up some way?"

"No. I got in wrong." He talked in the same flat voice. "There ain't anything to do. After a while I'll make up my mind to go out."

"I better go back and see George," Nick said.

"So long," said Ole Andreson. He did not look toward Nick. "Thanks for coming around."

Nick went out. As he shut the door he saw Ole Andreson with all his clothes on, lying on the bed looking at the wall.

"He's been in his room all day," the landlady said down-stairs. "I guess he don't feel well. I said to him: 'Mr. Andreson, you ought to go out and take a walk on a nice fall day like this,' but he didn't feel like it."

"He doesn't want to go out."

"I'm sorry he don't feel well," the woman said. "He's an awfully nice man. He was in the ring, you know."

"I know it."

"You'd never know it except from the way his face is," the woman said. They stood talking just inside the street door. "He's just as gentle."

"Well, good-night, Mrs. Hirsch," Nick said.

"I'm not Mrs. Hirsch," the woman said. "She owns the place. I just look after it for her. I'm Mrs. Bell."

"Well, good-night, Mrs. Bell," Nick said.

"Good-night," the woman said.

Nick walked up the dark street to the corner under the arclight, and then along the car-tracks to Henry's eating-house. George was inside, back of the counter.

"Did you see Ole?"

"Yes," said Nick. "He's in his room and he won't go out."

The cook opened the door from the kitchen when he heard Nick's voice.

"I don't even listen to it," he said and shut the door.

"Did you tell him about it?" George asked.

"Sure. I told him but he knows what it's all about."

"What's he going to do?"

"Nothing."

"They'll kill him."

"I guess they will."

"He must have got mixed up in something in Chicago."

"I guess so," said Nick.

"It's a hell of a thing."

"It's an awful thing," Nick said.

They did not say anything. George reached down for a towel and wiped the counter.

"I wonder what he did?" Nick said.

"Double-crossed somebody. That's what they kill them for."

"I'm going to get out of this town," Nick said.

"Yes," said George. "That's a good thing to do."

"I can't stand to think about him waiting in the room and knowing he's going to get it. It's too damned awful."

"Well," said George, "you better not think about it."

QUESTIONS

Hemingway is known for his use of the "iceberg technique," which means that he shows the reader only selected portions of the story, trusting that the unstated elements will create a powerful effect.

1. How does "The Killers" exemplify Hemingway's method? What are the unstated elements that contribute to the reader's reaction?
2. How does Hemingway use common dialogue to create a sense of mounting tension? Read a section of dialogue aloud. Can you detect Hemingway's deliberate use of rhythms and repetitions? Comment upon the effect these have on the portrayal of character and drama?
3. How does Hemingway establish a sense of locale? And how do Max and Al reveal that they are intruders?
4. Does it matter that we never know why the two men are after the Swede? Would the story be different if we did? How so?
5. How does Hemingway present the Swede? In what ways does Nick's visit to the rooming house change the story?
6. Why does the Swede avoid Nick's eyes?
7. What emotions does Hemingway finally leave with his reader?

Jorge Luis Borges

Born in Buenos Aires, Argentina, and educated in Europe, Jorge Luis Borges (1899–1986) was most truly a citizen of the imaginary universe of his own creation. Possibly no writer has ever been possessed of so complex and idiosyncratic a sensibility. His father, a professor of psychology, may have planted the original seed—he instilled his son with a love for philosophical puzzles and paradoxes; he left the boy free to roam through his voluminous library. Infirmity certainly played a part, for a progressive blindness left Borges increasingly isolated in the world of memories and fancies. Not so isolated, however, that he could not fulfill his duties in the National Library in Buenos Aires: Borges managed with memory and erudition to rule over an enormous kingdom of books.

Borges began to write while he was still a student in Europe. For a time he was a member of a Spanish avant-garde movement known as Ultraisme, which rejected fictional conventions in favor of expressionistic imagery and elaborate metaphor. The stories he began to publish decades later, as *Ficciones* (1944), *Labyrinths* (1962), and *The Aleph and Other Stories* (1970), show traces of this early apprenticeship, though in fact Borges proved himself a superb, if unusual, maker of plots.

Borges' special genius was to insist upon an order of reality that was hidden to the five senses but accessible to the speculative intelligence. He often alluded to the idea of a once-known universal meaning that had somehow gotten scrambled and was now nearly beyond human recognition. His mazes, mystical references, and carefully calibrated twists of destiny all point back to this first and last mystery.

But we must not forget that Borges was also a great trickster and that one of his fondest tricks was to tread the line between mystical revelation and outright absurdity. The reader can never be sure when Borges is referring to an actual author or work or historical circumstance and when he is inventing the reference out of his fertile imagination. And this confusion, too, is part of his message. For Borges finally believed that reality and meaning were sophisticated fables devised by the mind. What we believe we know of the world is really just a story we tell ourselves. Unusual minds—like the mind of the character named Borges in "The Aleph"—will tell unusual stories. And they will be true.

THE ALEPH

O God! I could be bounded in a nutshell, and count myself a King of infinite space. . . .

HAMLET, II, 2

But they will teach us that Eternity is the Standing still of the Present Time, a Nunc-stans *(as the Schools call it); which neither they, nor any else understand, no more than they would a* Hic-stans *for an Infinite greatness of Place.*

LEVIATHAN, IV, 46

On the burning February morning Beatriz Viterbo died, after braving an agony that never for a single moment gave way to self-pity or fear, I noticed that the sidewalk billboards around Constitution Plaza were advertising some new brand or other of American cigarettes. The fact pained me, for I realized that the wide and ceaseless universe was already slipping away from her and that this slight change was the first of an endless series. The universe may change but not me, I thought with a certain sad vanity. I knew that at times my fruitless devotion had annoyed her; now that she was dead, I could devote myself to her memory, without hope but also without humiliation. I recalled that the thirtieth of April was her birthday; on that day to visit her house on Garay Street and pay my respects to her father and to Carlos Argentino Daneri, her first cousin, would be an irreproachable and perhaps unavoidable act of politeness. Once again I would wait in the twilight of the small, cluttered drawing room, once again I would study the details of her many photographs: Beatriz Viterbo in profile and in full color; Beatriz wearing a mask, during the Carnival of 1921; Beatriz at her First Communion; Beatriz on the day of her wedding to Roberto Alessandri; Beatriz soon after her divorce, at a luncheon at the Turf Club; Beatriz at a seaside resort in Quilmes with Delia San Marco Porcel and Carlos Argentino; Beatriz with the Pekinese lapdog given her by Villegas Haedo; Beatriz, front and three-quarter views, smiling, hand on her chin. . . . I would not be forced, as in the past, to justify my presence with modest offerings of books—books whose pages I finally learned to cut beforehand, so as not to find out, months later, that they lay around unopened.

Beatriz Viterbo died in 1929. From that time on, I never let a thirtieth of April go by without a visit to her house. I used to make my appearance at seven-fifteen sharp and stay on for some twenty-five minutes. Each year, I arrived a little later and stayed a little longer. In 1933, a torrential downpour coming to my aid, they were obliged to ask me to dinner. Naturally,

I took advantage of that lucky precedent. In 1934, I arrived, just after eight, with one of those large Santa Fe sugared cakes, and quite matter-of-factly I stayed to dinner. It was in this way, on these melancholy and vainly erotic anniversaries, that I came into the gradual confidences of Carlos Argentino Daneri.

Beatriz had been tall, frail, slightly stooped; in her walk there was (if the oxymoron may be allowed) a kind of uncertain grace, a hint of expectancy. Carlos Argentino was pink-faced, overweight, gray-haired, fine-featured. He held a minor position in an unreadable library out on the edge of the Southside of Buenos Aires. He was authoritarian but also unimpressive. Until only recently, he took advantage of his nights and holidays to stay at home. At a remove of two generations, the Italian "S" and demonstrative Italian gestures still survived in him. His mental activity was continuous, deeply felt, far-ranging, and—all in all—meaningless. He dealt in pointless analogies and in trivial scruples. He had (as did Beatriz) large, beautiful, finely shaped hands. For several months he seemed to be obsessed with Paul Fort—less with his ballads than with the idea of a towering reputation. "He is the Prince of poets," Daneri would repeat fatuously. "You will belittle him in vain—but no, not even the most venomous of your shafts will graze him."

On the thirtieth of April, 1941, along with the sugared cake I allowed myself to add a bottle of Argentine cognac. Carlos Argentino tasted it, pronounced it "interesting," and, after a few drinks, launched into a glorification of modern man.

"I view him," he said with a certain unaccountable excitement, "in his inner sanctum, as though in his castle tower, supplied with telephones, telegraphs, phonographs, wireless sets, motion-picture screens, slide projectors, glossaries, timetables, handbooks, bulletins. . . ."

He remarked that for a man so equipped, actual travel was superfluous. Our twentieth century had inverted the story of Mohammed and the mountain; nowadays, the mountain came to the modern Mohammed.

So foolish did his ideas seem to me, so pompous and so drawn out his exposition, that I linked them at once to literature and asked him why he didn't write them down. As might be foreseen, he answered that he had already done so—that these ideas, and others no less striking, had found their place in the Proem, or Augural Canto, or, more simply, the Prologue Canto of the poem on which he had been working for many years now, alone, without publicity, without fanfare, supported only by those twin staffs universally known as work and solitude. First, he said, he opened the floodgates of his fancy; then, taking up hand tools, he resorted to the file. The poem was entitled *The Earth*; it consisted of a description of the planet, and, of course, lacked no amount of picturesque digressions and bold apostrophes.

I asked him to read me a passage, if only a short one. He opened a drawer of his writing table, drew out a thick stack of papers—sheets of a large pad imprinted with the letterhead of the Juan Crisóstomo Lafinur Library—and, with ringing satisfaction, declaimed:

> Mine eyes, as did the Greek's, have known men's towns and fame,
> The works, the days in light that fades to amber;
> I do not change a fact or falsify a name—
> The *voyage* I set down is . . . *autour de ma chambre*.

"From any angle, a greatly interesting stanza," he said, giving his verdict. "The opening line wins the applause of the professor, the academician, and the Hellenist—to say nothing of the would-be scholar, a considerable sector of the public. The second flows from Homer to Hesiod (generous homage, at the very outset, to the father of didactic poetry), not without rejuvenating a process whose roots go back to Scripture—enumeration, congeries, conglomeration. The third—baroque? decadent? example of the cult of pure form?—consists of two equal hemistichs. The fourth, frankly bilingual, assures me the unstinted backing of all minds sensitive to the pleasures of sheer fun. I should, in all fairness, speak of the novel rhyme in lines two and four, and of the erudition that allows me—without a hint of pedantry!—to cram into four lines three learned allusions covering thirty centuries packed with literature—first to the *Odyssey*, second to *Works and Days*, and third to the immortal bagatelle bequeathed us by the frolicking pen of the Savoyard, Xavier de Maistre. Once more I've come to realize that modern art demands the balm of laughter, the scherzo. Decidedly, Goldoni holds the stage!"

He read me many other stanzas, each of which also won his own approval and elicited his lengthy explications. There was nothing remarkable about them. I did not even find them any worse than the first one. Application, resignation, and chance had gone into the writing; I saw, however, that Daneri's real work lay not in the poetry but in his invention of reasons why the poetry should be admired. Of course, this second phase of his effort modified the writing in his eyes, though not in the eyes of others. Daneri's style of delivery was extravagant, but the deadly drone of his metric regularity tended to tone down and to dull that extravagance.[1]

Only once in my life have I had occasion to look into the fifteen thousand alexandrines of the *Polyolbion*, that topographical epic in which Michael Drayton recorded the flora, fauna, hydrography, orography, military and monastic history of England. I am sure, however, that this limited but

1. Among my memories are also some lines of a satire in which he lashed out unsparingly at bad poets. After accusing them of dressing their poems in the warlike armor of erudition, and of flapping in vain their unavailing wings, he concluded with this verse:

> But they forget, alas, one foremost fact—BEAUTY!

Only the fear of creating an army of implacable and powerful enemies dissuaded him (he told me) from fearlessly publishing this poem.

bulky production is less boring than Carlos Argentino's similar vast undertaking. Daneri had in mind to set to verse the entire face of the planet, and, by 1941, had already dispatched a number of acres of the State of Queensland, nearly a mile of the course run by the River Ob, a gasworks to the north of Veracruz, the leading shops in the Buenos Aires parish of Concepción, the villa of Mariana Cambaceres de Alvear in the Belgrano section of the Argentine capital, and a Turkish baths establishment not far from the well-known Brighton Aquarium. He read me certain long-winded passages from his Australian section, and at one point praised a word of his own coining, the color "celestewhite," which he felt "actually *suggests* the sky, an element of utmost importance in the landscape of the continent Down Under." But these sprawling, lifeless hexameters lacked even the relative excitement of the so-called Augural Canto. Along about midnight, I left.

Two Sundays later, Daneri rang me up—perhaps for the first time in his life. He suggested we get together at four o'clock "for cocktails in the salon-bar next door, which the forward-looking Zunino and Zungri—my landlords, as you doubtless recall—are throwing open to the public. It's a place you'll really want to get to know."

More in resignation than in pleasure, I accepted. Once there, it was hard to find a table. The "salon-bar," ruthlessly modern, was only barely less ugly than what I had expected; at the nearby tables, the excited customers spoke breathlessly of the sums Zunino and Zungri had invested in furnishings without a second thought to cost. Carlos Argentino pretended to be astonished by some feature or other of the lighting arrangement (with which, I felt, he was already familiar), and he said to me with a certain severity, "Grudgingly, you'll have to admit to the fact that these premises hold their own with many others far more in the public eye."

He then reread me four or five different fragments of the poem. He had revised them following his pet principle of verbal ostentation: where at first "blue" had been good enough, he now wallowed in "azures," "ceruleans," and "ultramarines." The word "milky" was too easy for him; in the course of an impassioned description of a shed where wool was washed, he chose such words as "lacteal," "lactescent," and even made one up—"lactinacious." After that, straight out, he condemned our modern mania for having books prefaced, "a practice already held up to scorn by the Prince of Wits in his own graceful preface to the *Quixote*." He admitted, however, that for the opening of his new work an attention-getting foreword might prove valuable—"an accolade signed by a literary hand of renown." He next went on to say that he considered publishing the initial cantos of his poem. I then began to understand the unexpected telephone call; Daneri was going to ask me to contribute a foreword to his pedantic hodgepodge. My fear turned out unfounded; Carlos Argentino remarked, with admiration and envy, that surely he could not be far wrong in qualifying with the epithet "solid" the prestige enjoyed in every circle by Álvaro

Melián Lafinur, a man of letters, who would, if I insisted on it, be only too glad to dash off some charming opening words to the poem. In order to avoid ignominy and failure, he suggested I make myself spokesman for two of the book's undeniable virtues—formal perfection and scientific rigor—"inasmuch as this wide garden of metaphors, of figures of speech, of elegances, is inhospitable to the least detail not strictly upholding of truth." He added that Beatriz had always been taken with Álvaro.

I agreed—agreed profusely—and explained for the sake of credibility that I would not speak to Álvaro the next day, Monday, but would wait until Thursday, when we got together for the informal dinner that follows every meeting of the Writers' Club. (No such dinners are ever held, but it is an established fact that the meetings do take place on Thursdays, a point which Carlos Argentino Daneri could verify in the daily papers, and which lent a certain reality to my promise.) Half in prophecy, half in cunning, I said that before taking up the question of a preface I would outline the unusual plan of the work. We then said goodbye.

Turning the corner of Bernardo de Irigoyen, I reviewed as impartially as possible the alternatives before me. They were: *a*) to speak to Álvaro, telling him this first cousin of Beatriz' (the explanatory euphemism would allow me to mention her name) had concocted a poem that seemed to draw out into infinity the possibilities of cacophony and chaos; *b*) not to say a word to Álvaro. I clearly foresaw that my indolence would opt for *b*.

But first thing Friday morning, I began worrying about the telephone. It offended me that that device, which had once produced the irrecoverable voice of Beatriz, could now sink so low as to become a mere receptacle for the futile and perhaps angry remonstrances of that deluded Carlos Argentino Daneri. Luckily, nothing happened—except the inevitable spite touched off in me by this man, who had asked me to fulfill a delicate mission for him and then had let me drop.

Gradually, the phone came to lose its terrors, but one day toward the end of October it rang, and Carlos Argentino was on the line. He was deeply disturbed, so much so that at the outset I did not recognize his voice. Sadly but angrily he stammered that the now unrestrainable Zunino and Zungri, under the pretext of enlarging their already outsized "salon-bar," were about to take over and tear down his house.

"My home, my ancestral home, my old and inveterate Garay Street home!" he kept repeating, seeming to forget his woe in the music of his words.

It was not hard for me to share his distress. After the age of fifty, all change becomes a hateful symbol of the passing of time. Besides, the scheme concerned a house that for me would always stand for Beatriz. I tried explaining this delicate scruple of regret, but Daneri seemed not to hear me. He said that if Zunino and Zungri persisted in this outrage, Doctor Zunni, his lawyer, would sue *ipso facto* and make them pay some fifty thousand dollars in damages.

Zunni's name impressed me; his firm, although at the unlikely address of Caseros and Tacuarí, was nonetheless known as an old and reliable one. I asked him whether Zunni had already been hired for the case. Daneri said he would phone him that very afternoon. He hesitated, then with that level, impersonal voice we reserve for confiding something intimate, he said that to finish the poem he could not get along without the house because down in the cellar there was an Aleph. He explained that an Aleph is one of the points in space that contains all other points.

"It's in the cellar under the dining room," he went on, so overcome by his worries now that he forgot to be pompous. "It's mine—mine. I discovered it when I was a child, all by myself. The cellar stairway is so steep that my aunt and uncle forbade my using it, but I'd heard someone say there was a world down there. I found out later they meant an old-fashioned globe of the world, but at the time I thought they were referring to the world itself. One day when no one was home I started down in secret, but I stumbled and fell. When I opened my eyes, I saw the Aleph."

"The Aleph?" I repeated.

"Yes, the only place on earth where all places are—seen from every angle, each standing clear, without any confusion or blending. I kept the discovery to myself and went back every chance I got. As a child, I did not foresee that this privilege was granted me so that later I could write the poem. Zunino and Zungri will not strip me of what's mine—no, and a thousand times no! Legal code in hand, Doctor Zunni will prove that my Aleph is inalienable."

I tried to reason with him. "But isn't the cellar very dark?" I said.

"Truth cannot penetrate a closed mind. If all places in the universe are in the Aleph, then all stars, all lamps, all sources of light are in it, too."

"You wait there. I'll be right over to see it."

I hung up before he could say no. The full knowledge of a fact sometimes enables you to see all at once many supporting but previously unsuspected things. It amazed me not to have suspected until that moment that Carlos Argentino was a madman. As were all the Viterbos, when you came down to it. Beatriz (I myself often say it) was a woman, a child, with almost uncanny powers of clairvoyance, but forgetfulness, distractions, contempt, and a streak of cruelty were also in her, and perhaps these called for a pathological explanation. Carlos Argentino's madness filled me with spiteful elation. Deep down, we had always detested each other.

On Garay Street, the maid asked me kindly to wait. The master was, as usual, in the cellar developing pictures. On the unplayed piano, beside a large vase that held no flowers, smiled (more timeless than belonging to the past) the large photograph of Beatriz, in gaudy colors. Nobody could see us; in a seizure of tenderness, I drew close to the portrait and said to it, "Beatriz, Beatriz Elena, Beatriz Elena Viterbo, darling Beatriz, Beatriz now gone forever, it's me, it's Borges."

Moments later, Carlos came in. He spoke drily. I could see he was thinking of nothing else but the loss of the Aleph.

"First a glass of pseudo-cognac," he ordered, "and then down you dive into the cellar. Let me warn you, you'll have to lie flat on your back. Total darkness, total immobility, and a certain ocular adjustment will also be necessary. From the floor, you must focus your eyes on the nineteenth step. Once I leave you, I'll lower the trapdoor and you'll be quite alone. You needn't fear the rodents very much—though I know you will. In a minute or two, you'll see the Aleph—the microcosm of the alchemists and Kabbalists, our true proverbial friend, the *multum in parvo!*"

Once we were in the dining room, he added, "Of course, if you don't see it, your incapacity will not invalidate what I have experienced. Now, down you go. In a short while you can babble with *all* of Beatriz' images."

Tired of his inane words, I quickly made my way. The cellar, barely wider than the stairway itself, was something of a pit. My eyes searched the dark, looking in vain for the globe Carlos Argentino had spoken of. Some cases of empty bottles and some canvas sacks cluttered one corner. Carlos picked up a sack, folded it in two, and at a fixed spot spread it out.

"As a pillow," he said, "this is quite threadbare, but if it's padded even a half-inch higher, you won't see a thing, and there you'll lie, feeling ashamed and ridiculous. All right now, sprawl that hulk of yours there on the floor and count off nineteen steps."

I went through with his absurd requirements, and at last he went away. The trapdoor was carefully shut. The blackness, in spite of a chink that I later made out, seemed to me absolute. For the first time, I realized the danger I was in: I'd let myself be locked in a cellar by a lunatic, after gulping down a glassful of poison! I knew that back of Carlos' transparent boasting lay a deep fear that I might not see the promised wonder. To keep his madness undetected, to keep from admitting that he was mad, *Carlos had to kill me*. I felt a shock of panic, which I tried to pin to my uncomfortable position and not to the effect of a drug. I shut my eyes—I opened them. Then I saw the Aleph.

I arrive now at the ineffable core of my story. And here begins my despair as a writer. All language is a set of symbols whose use among its speakers assumes a shared past. How, then, can I translate into words the limitless Aleph, which my floundering mind can scarcely encompass? Mystics, faced with the same problem, fall back on symbols: to signify the godhead, one Persian speaks of a bird that somehow is all birds; Alanus de Insulis, of a sphere whose center is everywhere and circumference is nowhere; Ezekiel, of a four-faced angel who at one and the same time moves east and west, north and south. (Not in vain do I recall these inconceivable analogies; they bear some relation to the Aleph.) Perhaps the gods might grant me a similar metaphor, but then this account would become contaminated by literature, by fiction. Really, what I want to do is impossible, for any listing of an endless series is doomed to be infinitesimal. In that single gigantic instant I saw millions of acts both delightful and awful; not one of them amazed me more than the fact that all of them occupied the same point in space, without overlapping or transparency.

What my eyes beheld was simultaneous, but what I shall now write down will be successive, because language is successive. Nonetheless, I'll try to recollect what I can.

On the back part of the step, toward the right, I saw a small iridescent sphere of almost unbearable brilliance. At first I thought it was revolving; then I realized that this movement was an illusion created by the dizzying world it bounded. The Aleph's diameter was probably little more than an inch, but all space was there, actual and undiminished. Each thing (a mirror's face, let us say) was infinite things, since I distinctly saw it from every angle of the universe. I saw the teeming sea; I saw daybreak and nightfall; I saw the multitudes of America; I saw a silvery cobweb in the center of a black pyramid; I saw a splintered labyrinth (it was London); I saw, close up, unending eyes watching themselves in me as in a mirror; I saw all the mirrors on earth and none of them reflected me; I saw in a backyard of Soler Street the same tiles that thirty years before I'd seen in the entrance of a house in Fray Bentos; I saw bunches of grapes, snow, tobacco, lodes of metal, steam; I saw convex equatorial deserts and each one of their grains of sand; I saw a woman in Inverness whom I shall never forget; I saw her tangled hair, her tall figure, I saw the cancer in her breast; I saw a ring of baked mud in a sidewalk, where before there had been a tree; I saw a summer house in Adrogué and a copy of the first English translation of Pliny—Philemon Holland's—and all at the same time saw each letter on each page (as a boy, I used to marvel that the letters in a closed book did not get scrambled and lost overnight); I saw a sunset in Querétaro that seemed to reflect the color of a rose in Bengal; I saw my empty bedroom; I saw in a closet in Alkmaar a terrestrial globe between two mirrors that multiplied it endlessly; I saw horses with flowing manes on a shore of the Caspian Sea at dawn; I saw the delicate bone structure of a hand; I saw the survivors of a battle sending out picture postcards; I saw in a showcase in Mirzapur a pack of Spanish playing cards; I saw the slanting shadows of ferns on a greenhouse floor; I saw tigers, pistons, bison, tides, and armies; I saw all the ants on the planet; I saw a Persian astrolabe; I saw in the drawer of a writing table (and the handwriting made me tremble) unbelievable, obscene, detailed letters, which Beatriz had written to Carlos Argentino; I saw a monument I worshiped in the Chacarita cemetery; I saw the rotted dust and bones that had once deliciously been Beatriz Viterbo; I saw the circulation of my own dark blood; I saw the coupling of love and the modification of death; I saw the Aleph from every point and angle, and in the Aleph I saw the earth and in the earth the Adelph and in the Adelph the earth; I saw my own face and my own bowels; I saw your face; and I felt dizzy and wept, for my eyes had seen that secret and conjectured object whose name is common to all men but which no man has looked upon—the unimaginable universe.

I felt infinite wonder, infinite pity.

"Feeling pretty cockeyed, are you, after so much spying into places where you have no business?" said a hated and jovial voice. "Even if you were to rack your brains, you couldn't pay me back in a hundred years for this revelation. One hell of an observatory, eh, Borges?"

Carlos Argentino's feet were planted on the topmost step. In the sudden dim light, I managed to pick myself up and utter, "One hell of a—yes, one hell of a."

The matter-of-factness of my voice surprised me. Anxiously, Carlos Argentino went on.

"Did you see everything—really clear, in colors?"

At that very moment I found my revenge. Kindly, openly pitying him, distraught, evasive, I thanked Carlos Argentino Daneri for the hospitality of his cellar and urged him to make the most of the demolition to get away from the pernicious metropolis, which spares no one—believe me, I told him, no one! Quietly and forcefully, I refused to discuss the Aleph. On saying goodbye, I embraced him and repeated that the country, that fresh air and quite were the great physicians.

Out on the street, going down the stairways inside Constitution Station, riding the subway, every one of the faces seemed familiar to me. I was afraid that not a single thing on earth would ever again surprise me; I was afraid I would never again be free of all I had seen. Happily, after a few sleepless nights, I was visited once more by oblivion.

Postscript of March first, 1943—Some six months after the pulling down of a certain building on Garay Street, Procrustes & Co., the publishers, not put off by the considerable length of Daneri's poem, brought out a selection of its "Argentine sections." It is redundant now to repeat what happened. Carlos Argentino Daneri won the Second National Prize for Literature.[2] First Prize went to Dr. Aita; Third Prize, to Dr. Mario Bonfanti. Unbelievably, my own book *The Sharper's Cards* did not get a single vote. Once again dullness and envy had their triumph! It's been some time now that I've been trying to see Daneri; the gossip is that a second selection of the poem is about to be published. His felicitous pen (no longer cluttered by the Aleph) has now set itself the task of writing an epic on our national hero, General San Martín.

I want to add two final observations: one, on the nature of the Aleph; the other, on its name. As is well known, the Aleph is the first letter of the Hebrew alphabet. Its use for the strange sphere in my story may not be accidental. For the Kabbala, that letter stands for the *En Soph,* the pure and boundless godhead; it is also said that it takes the shape of a man pointing to both heaven and earth, in order to show that the lower world is the map and mirror of the higher; for Cantor's *Mengenlehre,* it is the

2. "I have received your pained congratulations," he wrote me. "You rage, my poor friend, with envy, but you must confess—even if it chokes you!—that this time I have crowned my cap with the reddest of feathers; my turban with the most *caliph* of rubies."

symbol of transfinite numbers, of which any part is as great as the whole. I would like to know whether Carlos Argentino chose that name or whether he read it—applied to another point where all points converge—in one of the numberless texts that the Aleph in his cellar revealed to him. Incredible as it may seem, I believe that the Aleph of Garay Street was a false Aleph.

Here are my reasons. Around 1867, Captain Burton held the post of British Consul in Brazil. In July, 1942, Pedro Henríquez Ureña came across a manuscript of Burton's, in a library at Santos, dealing with the mirror which the Oriental world attributes to Iskander Zu al-Karnayn, or Alexander Bicornis of Macedonia. In its crystal the whole world was reflected. Burton mentions other similar devices—the sevenfold cup of Kai Kosru; the mirror that Tariq ibn-Ziyad found in a tower (*Thousand and One Nights,* 272); the mirror that Lucian of Samosata examined on the moon (*True History,* I, 26); the mirrorlike spear that the first book of Capella's *Satyricon* attributes to Jupiter; Merlin's universal mirror, which was "round and hollow . . . and seem'd a world of glas" (*The Faerie Queene,* III, 2, 19)—and adds this curious statement: "But the aforesaid objects (besides the disadvantage of not existing) are mere optical instruments. The Faithful who gather at the mosque of Amr, in Cairo, are acquainted with the fact that the entire universe lies inside one of the stone pillars that ring its central court. . . . No one, of course, can actually see it, but those who lay an ear against the surface tell that after some short while they perceive its busy hum. . . . The mosque dates from the seventh century; the pillars come from other temples of pre-Islamic religions, since, as ibn-Khaldun has written: "In nations founded by nomads, the aid of foreigners is essential in all concerning masonry.' "

Does this Aleph exist in the heart of a stone? Did I see it there in the cellar when I saw all things, and have I now forgotten it? Our minds are porous and forgetfulness seeps in; I myself am distorting and losing, under the wearing away of the years, the face of Beatriz.

QUESTIONS

1. What is the effect upon the reader of Borges' elaborate citing of bookish references and obscure lore?
2. Why does Borges write himself into the story? As what kind of person does he portray himself?
3. Is there any purpose to the lengthy setup? Why does it take us so long to get to the Aleph? Do we need to know the story of Beatriz or Borges' visits to Carlos?
4. Why does Borges come to hate Carlos? What does he see while looking at the Aleph that must change his attitude?
5. Do we believe that Borges-the-narrator is telling us the full truth? Do we credit his claims about his fading memory?

Zora Neale Hurston

In recent years, Zora Neale Hurston (1901–1960) has begun to gain the reputation and influence that eluded her throughout much of her difficult life. Her works are now required reading for anyone who would understand the black contribution to American literary culture.

Hurston was born in the all-black town of Eatonville, Florida. Her mother died when she was eleven, and her father sent her to live with various relatives. Although she never finished grade school, she eventually attended Howard University in Washington, D.C. Her writing career began with a story published in a university literary magazine in 1921.

For a period in the 1920s, Hurston lived in New York City and took an active role in what has come to be known as "the Harlem Renaissance"—it was a time of tremendous cultural ferment not only in literary arts but in music and painting. Hurston collaborated with the great black poet and playwright Langston Hughes on a comedy, "Mule Bone."

With the onset of the Great Depression in the 1930s, Hurston devoted herself to writing fiction and to gathering up tales and legends from her Florida community. (She had studied with the noted anthropologist Franz Boas in New York.) Although she had some success in seeing her work published, financial rewards did not follow. She died as she had begun, impoverished, in her home state.

Hurston's works include the stories of *The Eatonville Anthology* (1927), the lore and reportage of *Mules and Men* (1935), and her celebrated novel *Their Eyes Were Watching God* (1937).

SPUNK

I

A giant of a brown-skinned man sauntered up the one street of the village and out into the palmetto thickets with a small pretty woman clinging lovingly to his arm.

"Looka theah, folkses!" cried Elijah Mosley, slapping his leg gleefully. "Theah they go, big as life an' brassy as tacks."

All the loungers in the store tried to walk to the door with an air of nonchalance but with small success.

"Now pee-eople!" Walter Thomas gasped. "Will you look at 'em!"

"But that's one thing Ah likes about Spunk Banks—he ain't skeered of nothin' on God's green footstool—*nothin'!* He rides that log down at saw-mill jus' like he struts 'round wid another man's wife—jus' don't give a kitty. When Tes' Miller got cut to giblets on that circle-saw, Spunk steps right up and starts ridin'. The rest of us was skeered to go near it."

A round-shouldered figure in overalls much too large came nervously in the door and the talking ceased. The men looked at each other and winked.

"Gimme some soda-water. Sass'prilla Ah reckon," the newcomer ordered, and stood far down the counter near the open pickled pig-feet tub to drink it.

Elijah nudged Walter and turned with mock gravity to the new-comer.

"Say, Joe, how's everything up yo' way? How's yo' wife?"

Joe started and all but dropped the bottle he was holding. He swallowed several times painfully and his lips trembled.

"Aw 'Lige, you oughtn't to do nothin' like that," Walter grumbled Elijah ignored him.

"She jus' passed heah a few minutes ago goin' thata way," with a wave of his hand in the direction of the woods.

Now Joe knew his wife had passed that way. He knew that the men lounging in the general store had seen her, moreover, he knew that the men knew *he* knew. He stood there silent for a long moment staring blankly with his Adam's apple twitching nervously up and down and his throat. One could actually *see* the pain he was suffering, his eyes, his face, his hands, and even the dejected slump of his shoulders. He set the bottle down upon the counter. He didn't bang it, just eased it out of his hand silently and fiddled with his suspender buckle.

"Well, Ah'm goin' after her to-day. Ah'm goin' an' fetch her back. Spunk's done gone too fur."

He reached deep down into his trouser pocket and drew out a hollow ground razor, large and shiny, and passed his moistened thumb back and forth over the edge.

"Talkin' like a man, Joe. 'Course that's *yo'* fambly affairs, but Ah like to see grit in anybody."

Joe Kanty laid down a nickel and stumbled out into the street.

Dusk crept in from the woods. Ike Clarke lit the swinging oil lamp that was almost immediately surrounded by candle-flies. The men laughed boisterously behind Joe's back as they watched him shamble woodward.

"You oughtn't to said whut you said to him,'Lige—look how it worked him up," Walter chided.

"And Ah hope it did work him up. Tain't even decent for a man to take and take like he do."

"Spunk will sho' kill him."

"Aw, Ah doan know. You never kin tell. He might turn him up an' spank him fur gettin' in the way, but Spunk wouldn't shoot no unarmed man. Dat razor he carried outa heah ain't gonna run Spunk down an' cut him, an' Joe ain't got the nerve to go to Spunk with it knowing he totes that Army .45. He makes that break outa heah to bluff us. He's gonna hide that razor behind the first palmetto root an' sneak back home to bed. Don't tell me nothin' 'bout that rabbit-foot colored man. Didn't he meet Spunk an' Lena face to face one day las' week an' mumble sumthin' to Spunk 'bout lettin' his wife alone?"

"What did Spunk say?" Walter broke in. "Ah like him fine but tain't right the way he carries on wid Lena Kanty, jus' 'cause Joe's timid 'bout fightin'."

"You wrong theah, Walter. Tain't 'cause Joe's timid at all, it's 'cause Spunk wants Lena. If Joe was a passle of wile cats Spunk would tackle the job just the same. He'd go after *anything* he wanted the same way. As Ah wuz sayin' a minute ago, he tole Joe right to his face that Lena was his. 'Call her and see if she'll come. A woman knows her boss an' she answers when he calls.' 'Lena, ain't I yo' husband?' Joe sorter whines out. Lena looked at him real disgusted but she don't answer and she don't move outa her tracks. Then Spunk reaches out an' takes hold of her arm an' says: 'Lena, youse mine. From now on Ah works for you an' fights for you an' Ah never wants you to look to nobody for a crumb of bread, a stitch of close or a shingle to go over yo' head, but *me* long as Ah live. Ah'll git the lumber foh owah house to-morrow. Go home an' git yo' things together!"

" 'Thass mah house,' Lena speaks up. 'Papa gimme that.'

" 'Well,' says Spunk, 'doan give up whut's yours, but when youse inside doan forgit youse mine, an' let no other man git outa his place wid you!"

"Lena looked up at him with her eyes so full of love that they wuz runnin' over, an' Spunk seen it an' Joe seen it too, and his lip started to tremblin' and his Adam's apple was galloping up and down his neck like a race horse. Ah bet he's wore out half a dozen Adam's apples since Spunk's been on the job with Lena. That's all he'll do. He'll be back heah after while swallowin' an' workin' his lips like he wants to say somethin' an' can't."

"But didn't he do *nothin'* to stop 'em?"

"Nope, not a frazzlin' thing—jus' stood there. Spunk took Lena's arm and walked off jus' like nothin' ain't happened and he stood there gazin' after them till they was outa sight. Now you know a woman don't want no man like that. I'm jus' waitin' to see whut he's goin' to say when he gits back."

II

But Joe Kanty never came back, never. The men in the store heard the sharp report of a pistol somewhere distant in the palmetto thicket and soon Spunk came walking leisurely, with his big black Stetson set at the same rakish angle and Lena clinging to his arm, came walking right into the general store. Lena wept in a frightened manner.

"Well," Spunk announced calmly, "Joe came out there wid a meat axe an' made me kill him."

He sent Lena home and led the men back to Joe—crumpled and limp with his right hand still clutching his razor.

"See mah back? Mah close cut clear through. He sneaked up an' tried to kill me from the back, but Ah got him, an' got him good, first shot," Spunk said.

The men glared at Elijah, accusingly.

"Take him up an' plant him in Stony Lonesome," Spunk said in a careless voice. "Ah didn't wanna shoot him but he made me do it. He's a dirty coward, jumpin' on a man from behind."

Spunk turned on his heel and sauntered away to where he knew his love wept in fear for him and no man stopped him. At the general store later on, they all talked of locking him up until the sheriff should come from Orlando, but no one did anything but talk.

A clear case of self-defense, the trial was a short one, and Spunk walked out of the court house to freedom again. He could work again, ride the dangerous log-carriage that fed the singing, snarling, biting circle-saw; he could stroll the soft dark lanes with his guitar. He was free to roam the woods again; he was free to return to Lena. He did all of these things.

III

"Whut you reckon, Walt?" Elijah asked one night later. "Spunk's gittin' ready to marry Lena!"

"Naw! Why, Joe ain't had time to git cold yit. Nohow Ah didn't figger Spunk was the marryin' kind."

"Well, he is," rejoined Elijah. "He done moved most of Lena's things—and her along wid 'em—over to the Bradley house. He's buying it. Jus' like Ah told yo' all right in heah the night Joe was kilt. Spunk's crazy 'bout Lena. He don't want folks to keep on talkin' 'bout her—thass reason he's rushin' so. Funny thing 'bout that bob-cat, wan't it?"

"What bob-cat,'Lige? Ah ain't heered 'bout none."

"Ain't cher? Well, night befo' las' as they was goin' to bed, a big black bob-cat, black all over, you hear me, *black*, walked round and round that house and howled like forty, an' when Spunk got his gun an' went to the winder to shoot it, he says it stood right still an' looked him in the eye, an' howled right at him. The thing got Spunk so nervoused up he couldn't shoot. But Spunk says twan't no bob-cat nohow. He says it was Joe done sneaked back from Hell!"

"Humph!" sniffed Walter, "he oughter be nervous after what he done. Ah reckon Joe come back to dare him to marry Lena, or to come out an' fight. Ah bet he'll be back time and again, too. Know what Ah think? Joe wuz a braver man than Spunk."

There was a general shout of derision from the group.

"Thass a fact," went on Walter. "Lookit whut he done; took a razor an' went out to fight a man he knowed toted a gun an' wuz a crack shot, too; 'nother thing Joe wuz skeered of Spunk, skeered plumb stiff! But he went jes' the same. It took him a long time to get his nerve up. Tain't nothin' for Spunk to fight when he ain't skeered of nothin'. Now, Joe's done come back to have it out wid the man that's got all he ever had. Y'all know Joe ain't never had nothin' nor wanted nothin' besides Lena. It musta been a h'ant cause ain't nobody never seen no black bob-cat."

" 'Nother thing," cut in one of the men, "Spunk was cussin' a blue streak to-day 'cause he 'lowed dat saw wuz wobblin'—almos' got 'im once. The machinist come, looked it over an said it wuz alright. Spunk musta been leanin' t'wards it some. Den he claimed somebody pushed 'im but twan't nobody close to 'im. Ah wuz glad when knockin' off time came. I'm skeered of dat man when he gits hot. He'd beat you full of button holes as quick as he's look atcher."

IV

The men gathered the next evening in a different mood, no laughter. No badinage this time.

"Look, 'Lige, you goin' to set up wid Spunk?"

"Naw, Ah reckon not, Walter. Tell yuh the truth, Ah'm a li'l bit skittish. Spunk died too wicket—died cussin' he did. You know he thought he was done outa life."

"Good Lawd, who'd he think done it?"

"Joe."

"Joe Kanty? How come?"

"Walter, Ah b'leeve Ah will walk up thata way an' set. Lena would like it Ah reckon."

"But whut did he say,'Lige?"

Elijah did not answer until they had left the lighted store and were strolling down the dark street.

"Ah wuz loadin' a wagon wid scantlin' right near the saw when Spunk fell on the carriage but 'fore Ah could git to him the saw got him in the body—awful sight. Me an' Skint Miller got him off but it was too late. Anybody could see that. The fust thing he said wuz: 'He pushed me,'Lige—the dirty hound pushed me in the back!'—he was spittin' blood at ev'ry breath. We laid him on the sawdust pile with his face to the East so's he could die easy. He helt mah han' till the last, Walter, and said: 'It was Joe, 'Lige . . . the dirty sneak shoved me . . . he didn't dare come to mah face . . . but Ah'll git the son-of-a-wood louse soon's Ah get there an' make hell too hot for him . . . Ah felt him shove me . . . !" Thass how he died."

"If spirits kin fight, there's a powerful tussle goin' on somewhere ovah Jordan 'cause Ah b'leeve Joe's ready for Spunk an' ain't skeered any more—yas, Ah b'leeve Joe pushed 'im mahself."

They had arrived at the house. Lena's lamentations were deep and loud. She had filled the room with magnolia blossoms that gave off a heavy sweet odor. The keepers of the wake tipped about whispering in frightened tones. Everyone in the village was there, even old Jeff Kanty, Joe's father, who a few hours before would have been afraid to come within ten feet of him, stood leering triumphantly down upon the fallen giant as if his fingers had been the teeth of steel that laid him low.

The cooling board consisted of three sixteen-inch boards on saw horses, a dingy sheet was his shroud.

The women ate heartily of the funeral baked meats and wondered who would be Lena's next. The men whispered coarse conjectures between guzzles of whiskey.

QUESTIONS

1. What expectations are created by the first section?
2. How are these met or left unmet as the story unfolds?
3. Is Joe finally a brave man or a coward? Or is the answer more complex? Can he be both? Comment.
4. How are we asked to interpret the mysterious events that lead up to Spunk's death? Do we have to believe in ghosts in order for the story to succeed?
5. Comment upon Hurston's use of colloquial dialogue. What does dialogue contribute to our sense of character? How does it shape our understanding of the circumstances?
6. Why does Hurston structure the story as she does? Can you imagine alternative arrangements? What would be lost or gained by these?
7. What is this story finally about? Does it have anything to teach about human nature?
8. How does the off-stage presentation of scenes influence our responses?

Frank O'Connor

Frank O'Connor (1903–1966) was born Michael O'Donovan in Cork, Ireland. His family's impoverished circumstances prevented him from finishing even his early schooling, but his tremendous love for books stood him in good stead—he achieved a place as one of the greatest short story writers of all time.

During the Irish struggle for independence, O'Connor was a member of the Irish Republican Army. Afterwards, when he supported himself working as a librarian in Cork and Dublin, he began to work at short fiction. His early stories, he claims, were greatly influenced by Isaac Babel, especially the latter's book *Red Cavalry*. That he might write without fear of jeopardizing his post, he adopted the pseudonym by which we know him.

O'Connor's first important publication came in 1931 when the *Atlantic Monthly* printed "Guests of the Nation," which has remained one of his most popular pieces. His first collection saw print that same year, and from that time on he lived by his pen. O'Connor spent many years in the United States, teaching and writing. By the time of his death he had published close to fifty books—including works of translation and several studies of the fiction writer's art—fourteen of them story collections.

O'Connor's study of the short story, *The Lonely Voice* (1963), gave important expression to the idea that the story is the arena of the "little man." Certainly O'Connor's own fiction bears out his claims. Like his heroes, Chekhov and Babel, O'Connor possessed the uncanny ability to wriggle inside the skin of the ordinary, often hard-luck, person. He knew the language of his characters, the phrases and speech rhythms that couched their fears and longings. He knew, too, the sudden swerves that life unfailingly brings, moments when a belly-laugh goes sour with an inkling of the tragic, or when the mourner's sorrow is cut across by an unfathomable sensation of joy. In everything he wrote, O'Connor stayed close to the irrational, erratic contours of the real. The effect he achieves is of absolute naturalness.

MY OEDIPUS COMPLEX

Father was in the army all through the war—the first war, I mean—so, up to the age of five, I never saw much of him, and what I saw did not worry me. Sometimes I woke and there was a big figure in khaki peering down at me in the candlelight. Sometimes in the early morning I heard the slamming of the front door and the clatter of nailed boots down the cobbles of the lane. These were Father's entrances and exits. Like Santa Claus he came and went mysteriously.

In fact, I rather liked his visits, though it was an uncomfortable squeeze between Mother and him when I got into the big bed in the early morning. He smoked, which gave him a pleasant musty smell, and shaved, an operation of astounding interest. Each time he left a trail of souvenirs—model tanks and Gurkha knives with handles made of bullet cases, and German helmets and cap badges and button-sticks, and all sorts of military equipment—carefully stowed away in a long box on top of the wardrobe, in case they ever came in handy. There was a bit of the magpie about Father; he expected everything to come in handy. When his back was turned, Mother let me get a chair and rummage through his treasures. She didn't seem to think so highly of them as he did.

The war was the most peaceful period of my life. The window of my attic faced southeast. My mother had curtained it, but that had small effect. I always woke with the first light and, with all the responsibilities of the previous day melted, feeling myself rather like the sun, ready to illumine and rejoice. Life never seemed so simple and clear and full of possibilities as then. I put my feet out from under the clothes—I called them Mrs. Left and Mrs. Right—and invented dramatic situations for them in which they discussed the problems of the day. At least Mrs. Right did; she was very demonstrative, but I hadn't the same control of Mrs. Left, so she mostly contented herself with nodding agreement.

They discussed what Mother and I should do during the day, what Santa Claus should give a fellow for Christmas, and what steps should be taken to brighten the home. There was that little matter of the baby, for instance. Mother and I could never agree about that. Ours was the only house in the terrace without a new baby, and Mother said we couldn't afford one till Father came back from the war because they cost seventeen and six. That showed how simple she was. The Geneys up the road had a baby, and everyone knew they couldn't afford seventeen and six. It was probably a cheap baby, and Mother wanted something really good, but I felt she was too exclusive. The Geneys' baby would have done us fine.

Having settled my plans for the day, I got up, put a chair under the attic window, and lifted the frame high enough to stick out my head. The window overlooked the front gardens of the terrace behind ours, and beyond these it looked over a deep valley to the tall, red-brick houses terraced up the opposite hillside, which were all still in shadow, while those at our side of the valley were all lit up, though with long strange shadows that made them seem unfamiliar; rigid and painted.

After that I went into Mother's room and climbed into the big bed. She woke and I began to tell her of my schemes. By this time, though I never seem to have noticed it, I was petrified in my nightshirt, and I thawed as I talked until, the last frost melted, I fell asleep beside her and woke again only when I heard her below in the kitchen, making the breakfast.

After breakfast we went into town; heard Mass at St. Augustine's and said a prayer for Father, and did the shopping. If the afternoon was fine we either went for a walk in the country or a visit to Mother's great friend in the convent, Mother St. Dominic. Mother had them all praying for Father, and every night, going to bed, I asked God to send him back safe from the war to us. Little, indeed, did I know what I was praying for!

One morning, I got into the big bed, and there, sure enough, was Father in his usual Santa Claus manner, but later, instead of uniform, he put on his best blue suit, and Mother was as pleased as anything. I saw nothing to be pleased about, because, out of uniform, Father was altogether less interesting, but she only beamed, and explained that our prayers had been answered, and off we went to Mass to thank God for having brought Father safely home.

The irony of it! That very day when he came in to dinner he took off his boots and put on his slippers, donned the dirty old cap he wore about the house to save him from colds, crossed his legs, and began to talk gravely to Mother, who looked anxious. Naturally, I disliked her looking anxious, because it destroyed her good looks, so I interrupted him.

"Just a moment, Larry!" she said gently.

This was only what she said when we had boring visitors, so I attached no importance to it and went on talking.

"Do be quiet, Larry!" she said impatiently. "Don't you hear me talking to Daddy?"

This was the first time I had heard those ominous words, "talking to Daddy," and I couldn't help feeling that if this was how God answered prayers, he couldn't listen to them very attentively.

"Why are you talking to Daddy?" I asked with as great a show of indifference as I could muster.

"Because Daddy and I have business to discuss. Now, don't interrupt again!"

In the afternoon, at Mother's request, Father took me for a walk. This time we went into town instead of out the country, and I thought at first, in my usual optimistic way, that it might be an improvement. It was nothing of the sort. Father and I had quite different notions of a walk in town. He had no proper interest in trams, ships, and horses, and the only thing that seemed to divert him was talking to fellows as old as himself. When I wanted to stop he simply went on, dragging me behind him by the hand; when he wanted to stop I had no alternative but to do the same. I noticed that it seemed to be a sign that he wanted to stop for a long time whenever he leaned against a wall. The second time I saw him do it I got wild. He seemed to be settling himself forever. I pulled him by the coat and trousers, but, unlike Mother who, if you were too persistent, got into a wax and said: "Larry, if you don't behave yourself, I'll give you a good slap," Father had an extraordinary capacity for amiable inattention. I sized him up and wondered would I cry, but he seemed to be too remote to be annoyed even by that. Really, it was like going for a walk with a mountain! He either ignored the wrenching and pummelling entirely, or else glanced down with a grin of amusement from his peak. I had never met anyone so absorbed in himself as he seemed.

At teatime, "talking to Daddy" began again, complicated this time by the fact that he had an evening paper, and every few minutes he put it down and told Mother something new out of it. I felt this was foul play. Man for man, I was prepared to compete with him any time for Mother's attention, but when he had it all made up for him by other people it left me no chance. Several times I tried to change the subject without success.

"You must be quiet while Daddy is reading, Larry," Mother said impatiently.

It was clear that she either genuinely liked talking to Father better than talking to me, or else that he had some terrible hold on her which made her afraid to admit the truth.

"Mummy," I said that night when she was tucking me up, "do you think if I prayed hard God would send Daddy back to the war?"

She seemed to think about that for a moment.

"No, dear," she said with a smile. "I don't think he would."

"Why wouldn't he, Mummy?"

"Because there isn't a war any longer, dear."

"But, Mummy, couldn't God make another war, if He liked?"

"He wouldn't like to, dear. It's not God who makes wars, but bad people."

"Oh!" I said.

I was disappointed about that. I began to think that God wasn't quite what he was cracked up to be.

Next morning I woke at my usual hour, feeling like a bottle of champagne. I put out my feet and invented a long conversation in which Mrs. Right talked of the trouble she had with her own father till she put him in the Home. I didn't quite know what the Home was but it sounded the right place for Father. Then I got my chair and stuck my head out of the attic window. Dawn was just breaking, with a guilty air that made me feel I had caught it in the act. My head bursting with stories and schemes, I stumbled in next door, and in the half-darkness scrambled into the big bed. There was no room at Mother's side so I had to get between her and Father. For the time being I had forgotten about him, and for several minutes I sat bolt upright, racking my brains to know what I could do with him. He was taking up more than his fair share of the bed, and I couldn't get comfortable, so I gave him several kicks that made him grunt and stretch. He made room all right, though. Mother waked and felt for me. I settled back comfortably in the warmth of the bed with my thumb in my mouth.

"Mummy!" I hummed, loudly and contentedly.

"Sssh! dear," she whispered. "Don't wake Daddy!"

This was a new development, which threatened to be even more serious than "talking to Daddy." Life without my early-morning conferences was unthinkable.

"Why?" I asked severely.

"Because poor Daddy is tired."

This seemed to me a quite inadequate reason, and I was sickened by the sentimentality of her "poor Daddy." I never liked that sort of gush; it always struck me as insincere.

"Oh!" I said lightly. Then in my most winning tone: "Do you know where I want to go with you today, Mummy?"

"No, dear," she sighed.

"I want to go down the Glen and fish for thornybacks with my new net, and then I want to go out to the Fox and Hounds, and—"

"Don't-wake-Daddy!" she hissed angrily, clapping her hand across my mouth.

But it was too late. He was awake, or nearly so. He grunted and reached for the matches. Then he stared incredulously at his watch.

"Like a cup of tea, dear?" asked Mother in a meek, hushed voice I had never heard her use before. It sounded almost as though she were afraid.

"Tea?" he exclaimed indignantly. "Do you know what the time is?"

"And after that I want to go up the Rathcooney Road," I said loudly, afraid I'd forget something in all those interruptions.

"Go to sleep at once, Larry!" she said sharply.

I began to snivel. I couldn't concentrate, the way that pair went on, and smothering my early-morning schemes was like burying a family from the cradle.

Father said nothing, but lit his pipe and sucked it, looking out into the shadows without minding Mother or me. I knew he was mad. Every time I made a remark Mother hushed me irritably. I was mortified. I felt it wasn't fair; there was even something sinister in it. Every time I had pointed out to her the waste of making two beds when we could both sleep in one, she had told me it was healthier like that, and now here was this man, this stranger, sleeping with her without the least regard for her health!

He got up early and made tea, but though he brought Mother a cup he brought none for me.

"Mummy," I shouted, "I want a cup of tea, too."

"Yes, dear," she said patiently. "You can drink from Mummy's saucer."

That settled it. Either Father or I would have to leave the house. I didn't want to drink from Mother's saucer; I wanted to be treated as an equal in my own home, so, just to spite her, I drank it all and left none for her. She took that quietly, too.

But that night when she was putting me to bed she said gently:

"Larry, I want you to promise me something."

"What is it?" I asked.

"Not to come in and disturb poor Daddy in the morning. Promise?"

"Poor Daddy" again! I was becoming suspicious of everything involving that quite impossible man.

"Why?" I asked.

"Because poor Daddy is worried and tired and he doesn't sleep well."

"Why doesn't he, Mummy?"

"Well, you know, don't you, that while he was at the war Mummy got the pennies from the Post Office?"

"From Miss MacCarthy?"

"That's right. But now, you see, Miss MacCarthy hasn't any more pennies, so Daddy must go out and find us some. You know what would happen if he couldn't?"

"No," I said, "tell us."

"Well, I think we might have to go out and beg for them like the poor old woman on Fridays. We wouldn't like that, would we?"

"No," I agreed. "We wouldn't."

"So you'll promise not to come in and wake him?"

"Promise."

Mind you, I meant that. I knew pennies were a serious matter, and I was all against having to go out and beg like the old woman on Fridays. Mother laid out all my toys in a complete ring round the bed so that, whatever way I got out, I was bound to fall over one of them.

When I woke I remembered my promise all right. I got up and sat on the floor and played—for hours, it seemed to me. Then I got my chair and looked out the attic window for more hours. I wished it was time for Father to wake; I wished someone would make me a cup of tea. I didn't feel in the least like the sun; instead, I was bored and so very, very cold! I simply longed for the warmth and depth of the big featherbed.

At last I could stand it no longer. I went into the next room. As there was still no room at Mother's side I climbed over her and she woke with a start.

"Larry," she whispered, gripping my arm very tightly, "what did you promise?"

"But I did, Mummy," I wailed, caught in the very act. "I was quiet for ever so long."

"Oh, dear, and you're perished!" she said sadly, feeling me all over. "Now, if I let you stay will you promise not to talk?"

"But I want to talk, Mummy," I wailed.

"That has nothing to do with it," she said with a firmness that was new to me. "Daddy wants to sleep. Now, do you understand that?"

I understood it only too well. I wanted to talk, he wanted to sleep—whose house was it, anyway?

"Mummy," I said with equal firmness, "I think it would be healthier for Daddy to sleep in his own bed."

That seemed to stagger her, because she said nothing for a while.

"Now, once for all," she went on, "you're to be perfectly quiet or go back to your own bed. Which is it to be?"

The injustice of it got me down. I had convicted her out of her own mouth of inconsistency and unreasonableness, and she hadn't even attempted to reply. Full of spite, I gave Father a kick, which she didn't notice but which made him grunt and open his eyes in alarm.

"What time is it?" he asked in a panic-stricken voice, not looking at Mother but at the door, as if he saw someone there.

"It's early yet," she replied soothingly. "It's only the child. Go to sleep again. . . . Now, Larry," she added, getting out of bed, "you've wakened Daddy and you must go back."

This time, for all her quiet air, I knew she meant it, and knew that my principal rights and privileges were as good as lost unless I asserted them at once. As she lifted me, I gave a screech, enough to wake the dead, not to mind Father. He groaned.

"That damn child! Doesn't he ever sleep?"

"It's only a habit, dear," she said quietly, though I could see she was vexed.

"Well, it's time he got out of it," shouted Father, beginning to heave in the bed. He suddenly gathered all the bedclothes about him, turned to the wall, and then looked back over his shoulder with nothing showing only two small, spiteful, dark eyes. The man looked very wicked.

To open the bedroom door, Mother had to let me down, and I broke free and dashed for the farthest corner, screeching. Father sat bolt upright in bed.

"Shut up, you little puppy!" he said in a choking voice.

I was so astonished that I stopped screeching. Never, never had anyone spoken to me in that tone before. I looked at him incredulously and saw his face convulsed with rage. It was only then that I fully realized how God had codded me, listening to my prayers for the safe return of this monster.

"Shut up, you!" I bawled, beside myself.

"What's that you said?" shouted Father, making a wild leap out of the bed.

"Mick, Mick!" cried Mother. "Don't you see the child isn't used to you?"

"I see he's better fed than taught," snarled Father, waving his arms wildly. "He wants his bottom smacked."

All his previous shouting was as nothing to these obscene words referring to my person. They really made my blood boil.

"Smack your own!" I screamed hysterically. "Smack your own! Shut up! Shut up!"

At this he lost his patience and let fly at me. He did it with the lack of conviction you'd expect of a man under Mother's horrified eyes, and it ended up as a mere tap, but the sheer indignity of being struck at all by a stranger, a total stranger who had cajoled his way back from the war into our big bed as a result of my innocent intercession, made me completely dotty. I shrieked and shrieked, and danced in my bare feet, and Father, looking awkward and hairy in nothing but a short gray army shirt, glared down at me like a mountain out for murder. I think it must have been then that I realized he was jealous too. And there stood Mother in her nightdress, looking as if her heart was broken between us. I hoped she felt as she looked. It seemed to me that she deserved it all.

From that morning out my life was a hell. Father and I were enemies, open and avowed. We conducted a series of skirmishes against one another, he trying to steal my time with Mother and I his. When she was sitting on my bed, telling me a story, he took to looking for some pair of old boots which he alleged he had left behind him at the beginning of the war. While he talked to Mother I played loudly with my toys to show my total lack of concern. He created a terrible scene one evening when he came in from work and found me at his box, playing with his regimental badges, Gurkha knives and button-sticks. Mother got up and took the box from me.

"You mustn't play with Daddy's toys unless he lets you, Larry," she said severely. "Daddy doesn't play with yours."

For some reason Father looked at her as if she had struck him and then turned away with a scowl.

"Those are not toys," he growled, taking down the box again to see had I lifted anything. "Some of those curios are very rare and valuable."

But as time went on I saw more and more how he managed to alienate Mother and me. What made it worse was that I couldn't grasp his method or see what attraction he had for Mother. In every possible way he was less winning than I. He had a common accent and made noises at his tea. I thought for a while that it might be the newspapers she was interested in, so I made up bits of news of my own to read to her. Then I thought it might be the smoking, which I personally thought attractive, and took his pipes and went round the house dribbling into them till he caught me. I even made noises at my tea, but Mother only told me I was disgusting. It all seemed to hinge round that unhealthy habit of sleeping together, so I made a point of dropping into their bedroom and nosing round, talking to myself, so that they wouldn't know I was watching them, but they were never up to anything that I could see. In the end it beat me. It seemed to depend on being grown-up and giving people rings, and I realized I'd have to wait.

But at the same time I wanted him to see that I was only waiting, not giving up the fight. One evening when he was being particularly obnoxious, chattering away well above my head, I let him have it.

"Mummy," I said, "do you know what I'm going to do when I grow up?"

"No, dear," she replied. "What?"

"I'm going to marry you," I said quietly.

Father gave a great guffaw out of him, but he didn't take me in. I knew it must only be pretense. And Mother, in spite of everything, was pleased. I felt she was probably relieved to know that one day Father's hold on her would be broken.

"Won't that be nice?" she said with a smile.

"It'll be very nice," I said confidently. "Because we're going to have lots and lots of babies."

"That's right, dear," she said placidly. "I think we'll have one soon, and then you'll have plenty of company."

I was no end pleased about that because it showed that in spite of the way she gave in to Father she still considered my wishes. Besides, it would put the Geneys in their place.

It didn't turn out like that, though. To begin with, she was very preoccupied—I supposed about where she would get the seventeen and six—and though Father took to staying out late in the evenings it did me no particular good. She stopped taking me for walks, became as touchy as blazes, and smacked me for nothing at all. Sometimes I wished I'd never mentioned the confounded baby—I seemed to have genius for bringing calamity on myself.

And calamity it was! Sonny arrived in the most appalling hullabaloo—even that much he couldn't do without a fuss—and from the first moment I disliked him. He was a difficult child—so far as I was concerned he was always difficult—and demanded far too much attention. Mother was simply silly about him, and couldn't see when he was only showing off. As company he was worse than useless. He slept all day, and I had to go round the house on tiptoe to avoid waking him. It wasn't any longer a question of not waking Father. The slogan now was "Don't-wake-Sonny!" I couldn't understand why the child wouldn't sleep at the proper time, so whenever Mother's back was turned I woke him. Sometimes to keep him awake I pinched him as well. Mother caught me at it one day and gave me a most unmerciful flaking.

One evening, when Father was coming in from work, I was playing trains in the front garden. I let on not to notice him; instead, I pretended to be talking to myself, and said in a loud voice: "If another bloody baby comes into this house, I'm going out."

Father stopped dead and looked at me over his shoulder.

"What's that you said?" he asked sternly.

"I was only talking to myself," I replied, trying to conceal my panic. "It's private."

He turned and went in without a word. Mind you, I intended it as a solemn warning, but its effect was quite different. Father started being quite nice to me. I could understand that, of course. Mother was quite sickening about Sonny. Even at mealtimes she'd get up and gawk at him in the cradle with an idiotic smile, and tell Father to do the same. He was always polite about it, but he looked so puzzled you could see he didn't know what she was talking about. He complained of the way Sonny cried at night, but she only got cross and said that Sonny never cried except when there was something up with him—which was a flaming lie, because Sonny never had anything up with him, and only cried for attention. It was really painful to see how simpleminded she was. Father wasn't attractive, but he had a fine intelligence. He saw through Sonny, and now he knew that I saw through him as well.

One night I woke with a start. There was someone beside me in the bed. For one wild moment I felt sure it must be Mother, having come to her senses and left Father for good, but then I heard Sonny in convulsions in the next room, and Mother saying: "There! There! There!" and I knew it wasn't she. It was Father. He was lying beside me, wide awake, breathing hard and apparently as mad as hell.

After a while it came to me what he was mad about. It was his turn now. After turning me out of the big bed, he had been turned out himself. Mother had no consideration now for anyone but that poisonous pup, Sonny. I couldn't help feeling sorry for Father. I had been through it all myself, and even at that age I was magnanimous. I began to stroke him down and say: "There! There!" He wasn't exactly responsive.

"Aren't you asleep either?" he snarled.

"Ah, come on and put your arm around us, can't you?" I said, and he did, in a sort of way. Gingerly, I suppose, is how you'd describe it. He was very bony but better than nothing.

At Christmas he went out of his way to buy me a really nice model railway.

QUESTIONS

1. How does O'Connor contrast the boy's perspective with our own to create humor? Find an instance where his interpretation of events must strike the reader as absurd.
2. How does our view of the father change over the course of the story? How much is it that the father *is* changing? What are the background circumstances that the boy's involvement with his mother must necessarily distort?
3. The story can be said to come full circle. Explain.
4. Find out about the original Oedipus story and about Sigmund Freud's adaptation of that story to his theory of psychic development. How does O'Connor's rendition illustrate Freud's theory?

Eudora Welty

Eudora Welty was born in 1909 in Jackson, Mississippi where she still lives in her family house. She has pursued what might be called the Henry James career path; that is, she has more or less consecrated her life to her art. She has not moved from her place of birth, nor has she married. But whereas James wrote prose attuned to the complex indirections of the social realm, Welty has gone in the opposite direction. Her stories are seen, heard, and known with the fingertips down to the least real-life cobweb. Her settings may be limited, but what she reveals within those settings about human nature is without limit.

One of Welty's great gifts is with voices and speech rhythms. While "Powerhouse" is more exotic and frenzied than most of her stories, it showcases her feeling for dialect as well as colloquial twists and turns.

Welty's books include *A Curtain of Green* (1941), *The Wide Net and Other Stories* (1943), *The Golden Apples* (1949), *The Bride of the Innisfallen and Other Stories* (1955), and the novels *Delta Wedding* (1946) and *The Optimist's Daughter* (1972).

Welty writes of her approach: "What I do in the writing of any character is to try to enter into the mind, heart, and skin of a human being who is not myself. Whether this happens to be a man or a woman, young or old, with skin black or white, the challenge lies in making the jump itself."

POWERHOUSE

Powerhouse is playing!

He's here on tour from the city—"Powerhouse and His Keyboard"—"Powerhouse and His Tasmanians"—think of the things he calls himself! There's no one in the world like him. You can't tell what he is. "Negro man"?—he looks more Asiatic, monkey, Jewish, Babylonian, Peruvian, fanatic, devil. He has pale gray eyes, heavy lids, maybe horny like a lizard's, but big glowing eyes when they're open. He has African feet of the greatest size, stomping, both together, on each side of the pedals. He's not coal black—beverage colored—looks like a preacher when his mouth is shut, but then it opens—vast and obscene. And his mouth is going every minute: like a monkey's when it looks for something. Improvising, coming on a light and childish melody—*smooch*—he loves it with his mouth.

Is it possible that he could be this! When you have him there performing for you, that's what you feel. You know people on a stage—and people of a darker race—so likely to be marvelous, frightening.

This is a white dance. Powerhouse is not a show-off like the Harlem boys, not drunk, not crazy—he's in a trance; he's a person of joy, a fanatic. He listens as much as he performs, a look of hideous, powerful rapture on his face. When he plays he beats down piano and seat and wears them away. He is in motion every moment—what could be more obscene? There he is with his great head, fat stomach, and little round piston legs, and long yellow-sectioned strong big fingers, at rest about the size of bananas. Of course you know how he sounds—you've heard him on records—but still you need to see him. He's going all the time, like skating around the skating rink or rowing a boat. It makes everybody crowd around, here in this shadowless steel-trussed hall with the rose-like posters of Nelson Eddy and the testimonial for the mind-reading horse in handwriting magnified five hundred times. Then all quietly he lays his finger on a key with the promise and serenity of a sibyl touching the book.

Powerhouse is so monstrous he sends everybody into oblivion. When any group, any performers, come to town, don't people always come out and hover near, leaning inward about them, to learn what it is? What is it? Listen. Remember how it was with the acrobats. Watch them carefully, hear the least word, especially what they say to one another, in another language—don't let them escape you; it's the only time for hallucination, the last time. They can't stay. They'll be somewhere else this time tomorrow.

Powerhouse has as much as possible done by signals. Everybody, laughing as if to hide a weakness, will sooner or later hand him up a written request. Powerhouse reads each one, studying with a secret face: that is the face which looks like a mask—anybody's; there is a moment when he makes a decision. Then a light slides under his eyelids, and he says, "92!" or some combination of figures—never a name. Before a number the band is all frantic, misbehaving, pushing, like children in a schoolroom, and he is the teacher getting silence. His hands over the keys, he says sternly, "You-all ready? You-all ready to do some serious walking?"—waits—then, STAMP. Quiet. STAMP, for the second time. This is absolute. Then a set of rhythmic kicks against the floor to communicate the tempo. Then, O Lord! say the distended eyes from beyond the boundary of the trumpets, Hello and good-bye, and they are all down the first note like a waterfall.

This note marks the end of any known discipline. Powerhouse seems to abandon them all—he himself seems lost—down in the song, yelling up like somebody in a whirlpool—not guiding them—hailing them only. But he knows, really. He cries out, but he must know exactly. "Mercy! . . .

What I say! . . . Yeah!" And then drifting, listening—"Where that skin beater?"—wanting drums, and starting up and pouring it out in the greatest delight and brutality. On the sweet pieces such a leer for everybody! He looks down so benevolently upon all our faces and whispers the lyrics to us. And if you could hear him at this moment on "Marie, the Dawn Is Breaking"! He's going up the keyboard with a few fingers in some very derogatory triplet-routine, he gets higher and higher, and then he looks over the end of the piano, as if over a cliff. But not in a show-off way—the song makes him do it.

He loves the way they all play, too-all those next to him. The far section of the band is all studious, wearing glasses, every one—they don't count. Only those playing around Powerhouse are the real ones. He has a bass fiddler from Vicksburg, black as pitch, named Valentine, who plays with his eyes shut and talking to himself, very young: Powerhouse has to keep encouraging him. "Go on, go on, give it up, bring it on out there!" When you heard him like that on records, did you know he was really pleading?

He calls Valentine out to take a solo.

"What you going to play?" Powerhouse looks out kindly from behind the piano; he opens his mouth and shows his tongue, listening.

Valentine looks down, drawing against his instrument, and says without a lip movement, " 'Honeysuckle Rose.' "

He has a clarinet player named Little Brother, and loves to listen to anything he does. He'll smile and say, "Beautiful!" Little Brother takes a step forward when he plays and stands at the very front, with the whites of his eyes like fishes swimming. Once when he played a low note, Powerhouse muttered in dirty praise, "He went clear downstairs to get that one!"

After a long time, he holds up the number of fingers to tell the band how many choruses still to go—usually five. He keeps his directions down to signals.

It's a bad night outside. It's a white dance, and nobody dances, except a few straggling jitterbugs and two elderly couples. Everybody just stands around the band and watches Powerhouse. Sometimes they steal glances at one another, as if to say, Of course, you know how it is with *them*—Negroes—band leaders—they would play the same way, giving all they've got, for an audience of one. . . . When somebody, no matter who, gives everything, it makes people feel ashamed for him.

Late at night they play the one waltz they will ever consent to play—by request, "Pagan Love Song." Powerhouse's head rolls and sinks like a weight between his waving shoulders. He groans, and his fingers drag into the keys heavily, holding on to the notes, retrieving. It is a sad song.

"You know what happened to me?" says Powerhouse.

Valentine hums a response, dreaming at the bass.

"I got a telegram my wife is dead," says Powerhouse, with wandering fingers.

"Uh-huh?"

His mouth gathers and forms a barbarous O while his fingers walk up straight, unwillingly, three octaves.

"Gypsy? Why how come her to die, didn't you just phone her up in the night last night long distance?"

"Telegram say—here the words: Your wife is dead." He puts 4/4 over the 3/4.

"Not but four words?" This is the drummer, an unpopular boy named Scoot, a disbelieving maniac.

Powerhouse is shaking his vast cheeks. "What the hell was she trying to do? What was she up to?"

"What name has it got signed, if you got a telegram?" Scoot is spitting away with those wire brushes.

Little Brother, the clarinet player, who cannot now speak, glares and tilts back.

"Uranus Knockwood is the name signed." Powerhouse lifts his eyes open. "Ever heard of him?" A bubble shoots out on his lip like a plate on a counter.

Valentine is beating slowly on with his palm and scratching the strings with his long blue nails. He is fond of a waltz. Powerhouse interrupts him.

"I don't know him. Don't know who he is." Valentine shakes his head with the closed eyes.

"Say it agin."

"Uranus Knockwood."

"That ain't Lenox Avenue."

"It ain't Broadway."

"Ain't ever seen it wrote out in any print, even for horse racing."

"Hell, that's on a star, boy, ain't it?" Crash of the cymbals.

"What the hell was she up to?" Powerhouse shudders. "Tell me, tell me, tell me." He makes triplets, and begins a new chorus. He holds three fingers up.

"You say you got a telegram." This is Valentine, patient and sleepy, beginning again.

Powerhouse is elaborate. "Yas, the time I go out, go way downstairs along a long cor-ri-dor to where they puts us: coming back along the cor-ri-dor: steps out and hands me a telegram: Your wife is dead."

"Gypsy?" The drummer like a spider over his drums.

"Aaaaaaaaa!" shouts Powerhouse, flinging out both powerful arms for three whole beats to flex his muscles, then kneading a dough of bass notes. His eyes glitter. He plays the piano like a drum sometimes—why not?

"Gypsy? Such a dancer?"

"Why you don't hear it straight from your agent? Why it ain't come from headquarters? What you been doing, getting telegrams in the *corridor,* signed nobody?"

They all laugh. End of that chorus.

"What time is it?" Powerhouse calls. "What the hell place is this? Where is my watch and chain?"

"I hang it on you," whimpers Valentine. "It still there."

There it rides on Powerhouse's great stomach, down where he can never see it.

"Sure did hear some clock striking twelve while ago. Must be *midnight.*"

"It going to be intermission," Powerhouse declares, lifting up his finger with the signet ring.

He draws the chorus to an end. He pulls a big Northern hotel towel out of the deep pocket in his vast, special-cut tux pants and pushes his forehead into it.

"If she went and killed herself!" he says with a hidden face. "If she up and jumped out that window!" He gets to his feet, turning vaguely, wearing the towel on his head.

"Ha, ha!"

"Sheik, sheik!"

"She wouldn't do that." Little Brother sets down his clarinet like a precious vase, and speaks. He still looks like an East Indian queen, implacable, divine, and full of snakes. "You ain't going to expect people doing what they says over long distance."

"Come on!" roars Powerhouse. He is already at the back door, he has pulled it wide open, and with a wild, gathered-up face is smelling the terrible night.

Powerhouse, Valentine, Scoot and Little Brother step outside into the drenching rain.

"Well, they emptying buckets," says Powerhouse in a mollified voice. On the street he holds his hands out and turns up the blanched palms like sieves.

A hundred dark, ragged, silent, delighted Negroes have come around from under the eaves of the hall, and follow wherever they go.

"Watch out Little Brother don't shrink," says Powerhouse. "You just the right size now, clarinet don't suck you in. You got a dry throat, Little Brother, you in the desert?" He reaches into the pocket and pulls out a paper of mints. "Now hold 'em in your mouth—don't chew 'em. I don't carry around nothing without limit."

"Go in that joint and have beer," says Scoot, who walks ahead.

"Beer? Beer? You know what beer is? What do they say is beer? What's beer? Where I been?"

"Down yonder where it say World Café—that do?" They are in Negrotown now.

Valentine patters over and holds open a screen door warped like a sea shell, bitter in the wet, and they walk in, stained darker with the rain and leaving footprints. Inside, sheltered dry smells stand like screens around a table covered with a red-checkered cloth, in the center of which flies hang on to an obelisk-shaped ketchup bottle. The midnight walls are checkered again with admonishing "Not Responsible" signs and black-figured, smoky calendars. It is a waiting, silent, limp room. There is a burned-out-looking nickelodeon and right beside it a long-necked wall instrument labeled "Business Phone, Don't Keep Talking." Circled phone numbers are written up everywhere. There is a worn-out peacock feather hanging by a thread to an old, thin, pink, exposed light bulb, where it slowly turns around and around, whoever breathes.

A waitress watches.

"Come here, living statue, and get all this big order of beer we fixing to give."

"Never seen you before anywhere." The waitress moves and comes forward and slowly shows little gold leaves and tendrils over her teeth. She shoves up her shoulders and breasts. "How I going to know who you might be? Robbers? Coming in out of the black of night right at midnight, setting down so big at my table?"

"Boogers," says Powerhouse, his eyes opening lazily as in a cave.

The girl screams delicately with pleasure. O Lord, she likes talk and scares.

"Where you going to find enough beer to put out on this here table?"

She runs to the kitchen with bent elbows and sliding steps.

"Here's a million nickels," says Powerhouse, pulling his hand out of his pocket and sprinkling coins out, all but the last one, which he makes vanish like a magician.

Valentine and Scoot take the money over to the nickelodeon, which looks as battered as a slot machine, and read all the names of the records out loud.

"Whose 'Tuxedo Junction'?" asks Powerhouse.

"You know whose."

"Nickelodeon, I request you please to play 'Empty Bed Blues' and let Bessie Smith sing."

Silence: they hold it like a measure.

"Bring me all those nickels on back here," says Powerhouse. "Look at that! What you tell me the name of this place?"

"White dance, week night, raining, Alligator, Mississippi, long ways from home."

"Uh-huh."

"Sent for You Yesterday and Here You Come Today" plays.

The waitress, setting the tray of beer down on a back table, comes up taut and apprehensive as a hen. "Says in the kitchen, back there putting their eyes to little hole peeping out, that you is Mr. Powerhouse.". . .

"They seeing right tonight, that is him," says Little Brother.

"You him?"

"That is him in the flesh," says Scoot.

"Does you wish to touch him?" asks Valentine. "Because he don't bite."

"You passing through?"

"Now you got everything right."

She waits like a drop, hands languishing together in front.

"Little-Bit, ain't you going to bring the beer?"

She brings it, and goes behind the cash register and smiles, turning different ways. The little fillet of gold in her mouth is gleaming.

"The Mississippi River's here," she says once.

Now all the watching Negroes press in gently and bright-eyed through the door, as many as can get in. One is a little boy in a straw sombrero which has been coated with aluminum paint all over.

Powerhouse, Valentine, Scoot and Little Brother drink beer, and their eyelids come together like curtains. The wall and the rain and the humble beautiful waitress waiting on them and the other Negroes watching enclose them.

"Listen!" whispers Powerhouse, looking into the ketchup bottle and slowly spreading his performer's hands over the damp, wrinkling cloth with the red squares. "Listen how it is. My wife gets missing me. Gypsy. She goes to the window. She looks out and sees you know what. Street Sign saying Hotel. People walking. Somebody looks up. Old man. She looks down, out the window. Well? . . . *Ssssst! Plooey!* What she do? Jump out and bust her brains all over the world."

He opens his eyes.

"That's it," agrees Valentine. "You gets a telegram."

"Sure she misses you," Little Brother adds.

"No, it's nighttime." How softly he tells them! "Sure, it's the night time. She say, What do I hear? Footsteps walking up the hall? That him? Footsteps go on off. It's not me. I'm in Alligator, Mississippi, she's crazy. Shaking all over. Listens till her ears and all grow out like old music-box horns but still she can't hear a thing. She says, All right I'll jump out the window then. Got on her nightgown. I know that nightgown, and her thinking there. Says, Ho hum, all right, and jumps out the window. Is she mad at me! Is she crazy! She don't leave *nothing* behind her!"

"Ya! Ha!"

"Brains and insides everywhere, Lord, Lord."

All the watching Negroes stir in their delight, and to their higher delight he says affectionately, "Listen! Rats in here."

"That must be the way, boss."

"Only, naw, Powerhouse, that ain't true. That sound too *bad.*"

"Does? I even know who finds her," cries Powerhouse. "That no good pussyfooted crooning creeper, that creeper that follow around after me, coming up like weeds behind me, following around after me everything I do and messing around on the trail I leave. Bets my numbers, sings my songs, gets close to my agent like a Betsy-bug; when I going out he just coming in. I got him now! I got my eye on him."

"Know who he is?"

"Why, it's that old Uranus Knockwood!"

"Ya! Ha!"

"Yeah, and he coming now, he going to find Gypsy. There he is, coming around that corner, and Gypsy kadoodling down, oh-oh, watch out! *Ssssst! Plooey*! See, there she is in her little old nightgown, and her insides and brains all scattered round."

A sigh fills the room.

"Hush about her brains. Hush about her insides."

"Ya! Ha! You talking about her brains and insides—old Uranus Knockwood," says Powerhouse, "look down and say Jesus! He say, Look here what I'm walking round in!"

They all burst into halloos of laughter. Powerhouse's face looks like a big hot iron stove.

"Why, he picks her up and carries her off!" he says.

"Ya! Ha!"

"Carries her *back* around the corner. . . ."

"Oh, Powerhouse!"

"You know him."

"Uranus Knockwood!"

"Yeahhh!"

"He take our wives when we gone!"

"He come in when we goes out!"

"Uh-huh!"

"He go out when we comes in!"

"Yeahhh!"

"He standing behind the door!"

"Old Uranus Knockwood."

"You know him."

"Middle-size man."

"Wears a hat."

"That's him."

Everybody in the room moans with pleasure. The little boy in the fine silver hat opens a paper and divides out a jelly roll among his followers.

And out of the breathless ring somebody moves forward like a slave, leading a great logy Negro with bursting eyes, and says, "This here is Sugar-Stick Thompson, that dove down to the bottom of July Creek and pulled up all those drownded white people fall out of a boat. Last summer, pulled up fourteen."

"Hello," says Powerhouse, turning and looking around at them all with his great daring face until they nearly suffocate.

Sugar-Stick, their instrument, cannot speak; he can only look back at the others.

"Can't even swim. Done it by holding his breath," says the fellow with the hero.

Powerhouse looks at him.

"I his half brother," the fellow puts in.

They step back.

"Gypsy say," Powerhouse rumbles gently again, looking at *them,* " 'What is the use? I'm gonna jump out so far—so far . . . .' *Ssssst—!*"

"Don't, boss, don't do it agin," says Little Brother.

"It's awful," says the waitress. "I hates that Mr. Knockwoods. All that the truth?"

"Want to see the telegram I got from him?" Powerhouse's hand goes to the vast pocket.

"Now wait, now wait, boss." They all watch him.

"It must be the real truth," says the waitress, sucking in her lower lip, her luminous eyes turning sadly, seeking the windows.

"No, babe, it ain't the truth." His eyebrows fly up, and he begins to whisper to her out of his vast oven mouth. His hand stays in his pocket. "Truth is something worse, I ain't said what, yet. It's something hasn't come to me, but I ain't saying it won't. And when it does, then want me to tell you?" He sniffs all at once, his eyes come open and turn up, almost too far. He is dreamily smiling.

"Don't, boss, don't, Powerhouse!"

"Oh!" the waitress screams.

"Go on git out of here!" bellows Powerhouse, taking his hand out of his pocket and clapping after her red dress.

The ring of watchers breaks and falls away.

"*Look* at that! Intermission is up," says Powerhouse.

He folds money under a glass, and after they go out, Valentine leans back in and drops a nickel in the nickelodeon behind them, and it lights up and begins to play "The Goona Goo." The feather dangles still.

"Take a telegram!" Powerhouse shouts suddenly up into the rain over the street. "Take a answer. Now what was that name?"

They get a little tired.

"Uranus Knockwood."

"You ought to know."

"Yas? Spell it to me."

They spell it all the ways it could be spelled. It puts them in a wonderful humor.

"Here's the answer. I got it right here. 'What in the hell you talking about? Don't make any difference: I gotcha.' Name signed: Powerhouse."

"That going to reach him, Powerhouse?" Valentine speaks in a maternal voice.

"Yas, yas."

All hushing, following him up the dark street at a distance, like old rained-on black ghosts, the Negroes are afraid they will die laughing.

Powerhouse throws back his vast head into the steaming rain, and a look of hopeful desire seems to blow somehow like a vapor from his own dilated nostrils over his face and bring a mist to his eyes.

"Reach him and come out the other side."

"That's it, Powerhouse, that's it. You got him now."

Powerhouse lets out a long sigh.

"But ain't you going back there to call up Gypsy long distance, the way you did last night in that other place? I seen a telephone. . . . Just to see if she there at home?"

There is a measure of silence. That is one crazy drummer that's going to get his neck broken some day.

"No," growls Powerhouse. "No! How many thousand times tonight I got to say No?"

He holds up his arm in the rain.

"You sure-enough unroll your voice some night, it about reach up yonder to her," says Little Brother, dismayed.

They go on up the street, shaking the rain off and on them like birds.

Back in the dance hall, they play "San" (99). The jitterbugs start up like windmills stationed over the floor, and in their orbits—one circle, another, a long stretch and a zigzag—dance the elderly couples with old smoothness, undisturbed and stately.

When Powerhouse first came back from intermission, no doubt full of beer, they said, he got the band tuned up again in his own way. He didn't strike the piano keys for pitch—he simply opened his mouth and gave falsetto howls—in A, D and so on—they tuned by him. Then he took hold of the piano, as if he saw it for the first time in his life, and tested it for strength, hit it down in the bass, played an octave with his elbow, lifted the top, looked inside, and leaned against it with all his might. He sat down and played it for a few minutes with outrageous force and got it under his power—a bass deep and coarse as a sea net—then produced something glimmering and fragile, and smiled. And who could ever remember any of the things he says? They are just inspired remarks that roll out of his mouth like smoke.

They've requested "Somebody Loves Me," and he's already done twelve or fourteen choruses, piling them up nobody knows how, and it will be a wonder if he ever gets through. Now and then he calls and shouts, " 'Somebody loves me! Somebody loves me, I wonder who!' " His mouth gets to be nothing but a volcano. "I wonder who!"

"Maybe . . ." He uses all his right hand on a trill.

"Maybe . . ." He pulls back his spread fingers, and looks out upon the place where he is. A vast, impersonal and yet furious grimace transfigures his wet face.

". . . Maybe it's you!"

QUESTIONS

1. Discuss Welty's telling style. How do her sentence rhythms and quick transitions enhance the reader's involvement in the unfolding situation?

2. How do the descriptions of the music relate to the story that begins to emerge?

3. Why is the restaurant scene essential to the development of this story? What kinds of contrasts do we sense between the black and white cultures in the town?

4. Look closely at the exchanges between Powerhouse and the boys in his band. What is communicated by the responses of the musicians to his statements?

5. How does our sense of the story of the death change?

6. Who or what is Uranus Knockwood? Is he a real person, or simply a spirit of evil, an incarnation of bad luck?

7. What do we finally surmise about the relationship between Powerhouse and his wife?

8. Are we to read the ending as a revelation of triumph or tragedy? Explain.

9. Compare the ending of this story with the ending of James Baldwin's story "Sonny's Blues."

4

ADDITIONAL READINGS

Nathaniel Hawthorne

Nathaniel Hawthorne (1804–1864) published "Young Goodman Brown" in 1835, just one year before he published "The Minister's Black Veil" (see Part II, which also includes a full biographical note). Both works give clear expression to Hawthorne's preoccupation with questions about sin, guilt, and the workings of the private conscience. "Young Goodman Brown" was included in Hawthorne's second collection of stories, *Mosses From an Old Manse.*

YOUNG GOODMAN BROWN

Young Goodman Brown came forth at sunset into the street at Salem village; but put his head back, after crossing the threshold, to exchange a parting kiss with his young wife. And Faith, as the wife was aptly named, thrust her own pretty head into the street, letting the wind play with the pink ribbons of her cap while she called to Goodman Brown.

"Dearest heart," whispered she, softly and rather sadly, when her lips were close to his ear, "prithee put off your journey until sunrise and sleep in your own bed to-night. A lone woman is troubled with such dreams and such thoughts that she's afeard of herself sometimes. Pray tarry with me this night, dear husband, of all nights in the year."

"My love and my Faith," replied young Goodman Brown, "of all nights in the year, this one night must I tarry away from thee. My journey, as thou callest it, forth and back again, must needs be done 'twixt now and sunrise. What, my sweet, pretty wife, dost thou doubt me already, and we but three months married?"

"Then God bless you!" said Faith, with the pink ribbons; "and may you find all well when you come back."

"Amen!" cried Goodman Brown. "Say thy prayers, dear Faith, and go to bed at dusk, and no harm will come to thee."

So they parted; and the young man pursued his way until, being about to turn the corner by the meetinghouse, he looked back and saw the head of Faith still peeping after him with a melancholy air, in spite of her pink ribbons.

"Poor little Faith!" thought he, for his heart smote him. "What a wretch am I to leave her on such an errand! She talks of dreams, too. Methought as she spoke there was trouble in her face, as if a dream had warned her what work is to be done to-night. But no, no; 't would kill her to think it. Well, she's a blessed angel on earth; and after this one night I'll cling to her skirts and follow her to heaven."

With this excellent resolve for the future, Goodman Brown felt himself justified in making more haste on his present evil purpose. He had taken a dreary road, darkened by all the gloomiest trees of the forest, which barely stood aside to let the narrow path creep through, and closed immediately behind. It was all as lonely as could be; and there is this peculiarity in such a solitude, that the traveller knows not who may be concealed by the innumerable trunks and the thick boughs overhead; so that with lonely footsteps he may yet be passing through an unseen multitude.

"There may be a devilish Indian behind every tree," said Goodman Brown to himself; and he glanced fearfully behind him as he added, "What if the devil himself should be at my very elbow!"

His head being turned back, he passed a crook of the road, and, looking forward again, beheld the figure of a man, in grave and decent attire, seated at the foot of an old tree. He arose at Goodman Brown's approach and walked onward side by side with him.

"You are late, Goodman Brown," said he. "The clock of the Old South was striking as I came through Boston, and that is full fifteen minutes agone."

"Faith kept me back a while," replied the young man, with a tremor in his voice, caused by the sudden appearance of his companion, though not wholly unexpected.

It was now deep dusk in the forest, and deepest in that part of it where these two were journeying. As nearly as could be discerned, the second traveller was about fifty years old, apparently in the same rank of life as Goodman Brown, and bearing a considerable resemblance to him, though perhaps more in expression than features. Still, they might have been taken for father and son. And yet, though the elder person was as simply clad as the younger, and as simple in manner too, he had an indescribable air of one who knew the world, and who would not have felt abashed at the governor's dinner table or in King William's court, were it possible that his affairs should call him thither. But the only thing about him that could be fixed upon as remarkable was his staff, which bore the likeness of a great black snake, so curiously wrought that it might almost be seen to twist and wriggle itself like a living serpent. This, of course, must have been an ocular deception, assisted by the uncertain light.

"Come, Goodman Brown," cried his fellow-traveller, "this is a dull pace for the beginning of a journey. Take my staff, if you are so soon weary."

"Friend," said the other, exchanging his slow pace for a full stop, "having kept covenant by meeting thee here, it is my purpose now to return whence I came. I have scruples touching the matter thou wot'st of."

"Sayest thou so?" replied he of the serpent, smiling apart. "Let us walk on, nevertheless, reasoning as we go; and if I convince thee not thou shalt turn back. We are but a little way in the forest yet."

"Too far! too far!" exclaimed the goodman, unconsciously resuming his walk. "My father never went into the woods on such an errand, nor his father before him. We have been a race of honest men and good Christians since the days of the martyrs; and shall I be the first of the name of Brown that ever took this path and kept"—

"Such company, thou wouldst say," observed the elder person, interpreting his pause. "Well said, Goodman Brown! I have been as well acquainted with your family as with ever a one among the Puritans; and that's no trifle to say. I helped your grandfather, the constable, when he lashed the Quaker woman so smartly through the streets of Salem; and it was I that brought your father a pitch-pine knot, kindled at my own hearth, to set fire to an Indian village, in King Philip's war. They were my good friends, both; and many a pleasant walk have we had along this path, and returned merrily after midnight. I would fain be friends with you for their sake."

"If it be as thou sayest," replied Goodman Brown, "I marvel they never spoke of these matters; or, verily, I marvel not, seeing that the least rumor of the sort would have driven them from New England. We are a people of prayer, and good works to boot, and abide no such wickedness."

"Wickedness or not," said the traveller with the twisted staff, "I have a very general acquaintance here in New England. The deacons of many a church have drunk the communion wine with me; the selectmen of divers towns make me their chairman; and a majority of the Great and General Court are firm supporters of my interest. The governor and I, too—But these are state secrets."

"Can this be so?" cried Goodman Brown, with a stare of amazement at his undisturbed companion. "Howbeit, I have nothing to do with the governor and council; they have their own ways, and are no rule for a simple husbandman like me. But, were I to go on with thee, how should I meet the eye of that good old man, our minister, at Salem village? Oh, his voice would make me tremble both Sabbath day and lecture day."

Thus far the elder traveller had listened with due gravity; but now burst into a fit of irrepressible mirth, shaking himself so violently that his snake-like staff actually seemed to wriggle in sympathy.

"Ha! ha! ha!" shouted he again and again; then composing himself, "Well, go on, Goodman Brown, go on; but, prithee, don't kill me with laughing."

"Well, then, to end the matter at once," said Goodman Brown, considerably nettled, "there is my wife, Faith. It would break her dear little heart; and I'd rather break my own."

"Nay, if that be the case," answered the other, "e'en go thy ways, Goodman Brown. I would not for twenty old women like the one hobbling before us that Faith should come to any harm."

As he spoke he pointed his staff at a female figure on the path, in whom Goodman Brown recognized a very pious and exemplary dame, who had taught him his catechism in youth, and was still his moral and spiritual adviser, jointly with the minister and Deacon Gookin.

"A marvel, truly, that Goody Cloyse should be so far in the wilderness at nightfall," said he. "But with your leave, friend, I shall take a cut through the woods until we have left this Christian woman behind. Being a stranger to you, she might ask whom I was consorting with and whither I was going."

"Be it so," said his fellow-traveller. "Betake you the woods, and let me keep the path."

Accordingly the young man turned aside, but took care to watch his companion, who advanced softly along the road until he had come within a staff's length of the old dame. She, meanwhile, was making the best of her way, with singular speed for so aged a woman, and mumbling some indistinct words—a prayer, doubtless—as she went. The traveller put forth his staff and touched her withered neck with what seemed the serpent's tail.

"The devil!" screamed the pious old lady.

"Then Goody Cloyse knows her old friend?" observed the traveller, confronting her and leaning on his writhing stick.

"Ah, forsooth, and is it your worship indeed?" cried the good dame. "Yea, truly is it, and in the very image of my old gossip, Goodman Brown, the grandfather of the silly fellow that now is. But—would your worship believe it?—my broomstick hath strangely disappeared, stolen, as I suspect, by that unhanged witch, Goody Cory, and that, too, when I was all anointed with the juice of smallage, and cinquefoil, and wolf's bane"—

"Mingled with fine wheat and the fat of a new-born babe," said the shape of old Goodman Brown.

"Ah, your worship knows the recipe," cried the old lady, cackling aloud. "So, as I was saying, being all ready for the meeting, and no horse to ride on, I made up my mind to foot it; for they tell me there is a nice young man to be taken into communion to-night. But now your good worship will lend me your arm, and we shall be there in a twinkling.

"That can hardly be," answered her friend. "I may not spare you my arm, Goody Cloyse; but here is my staff, if you will."

So saying, he threw it down at her feet, where, perhaps, it assumed life, being one of the rods which its owner had formerly lent to the Egyptian magi. Of this fact, however, Goodman Brown could not take cognizance. He had cast up his eyes in astonishment, and, looking down again, beheld neither Goody Cloyse nor the serpentine staff, but this fellow-traveller alone, who waited for him as calmly as if nothing had happened.

"That old woman taught me my catechism," said the young man; and there was a world of meaning in this simple comment.

They continued to walk onward, while the elder traveller exhorted his companion to make good speed and persevere in the path, discoursing so aptly that his arguments seemed rather to spring up in the bosom of his auditor than to be suggested by himself. As they went, he plucked a branch of maple to serve for a walking stick, and began to strip it of the twigs and little boughs, which were wet with evening dew. The moment his fingers touched them they became strangely withered and dried up as with a week's sunshine. Thus the pair proceeded, at a good free pace, until suddenly, in a gloomy hollow of the road, Goodman Brown sat himself down on the stump of a tree and refused to go any farther.

"Friend," said he, stubbornly, "my mind is made up. Not another step will I budge on this errand. What if a wretched old woman do choose to go to the devil when I thought she was going to heaven: is that any reason why I should quit my dear Faith and go after her?"

"You will think better of this by and by," said his acquaintance, composedly. "Sit here and rest yourself a while; and when you feel like moving again, there is my staff to help you along."

Without more words, he threw his companion the maple stick, and was as speedily out of sight as if he had vanished into the deepening gloom. The young man sat a few moments by the roadside, applauding himself greatly, and thinking with how clear a conscience he should meet the minister in his morning walk, nor shrink from the eye of good old Deacon Gookin. And what calm sleep would be his that very night, which was to have been spent so wickedly, but so purely and sweetly now, in the arms of Faith! Amidst these pleasant and praiseworthy meditations, Goodman Brown heard the tramp of horses along the road, and deemed it advisable to conceal himself within the verge of the forest, conscious of the guilty purpose that had brought him thither, though now so happily turned from it.

On came the hoof tramps and the voices of the riders, two grave old voices, conversing soberly as they drew near. These mingled sounds appeared to pass along the road, within a few yards of the young man's hiding-place; but, owing doubtless to the depth of the gloom at that particular spot, neither the travellers nor their steeds were visible. Though their figures brushed the small boughs by the wayside, it could not be seen that they intercepted, even for a moment, the faint gleam from the strip of bright sky athwart which they must have passed. Goodman Brown alternately crouched and stood on tiptoe, pulling aside the branches and thrusting forth his head as far as he durst without discerning so much as a shadow. It vexed him the more, because he could have sworn, were such a thing possible, that he recognized the voices of the minister and Deacon Gookin, jogging along quietly, as they were wont to do, when bound to some ordination or ecclesiastical council. While yet within hearing, one of the riders stopped to pluck a switch.

"Of the two, reverend sir," said the voice like the deacon's, "I had rather miss an ordination dinner than to-night's meeting. They tell me that some of our community are to be here from Falmouth and beyond, and others from Connecticut and Rhode Island, besides several of the Indian powwows, who, after their fashion, know almost as much deviltry as the best of us. Moreover, there is a goodly young woman to be taken into communion."

"Mighty well, Deacon Gookin!" replied the solemn old tones of the minister. "Spur up, or we shall be late. Nothing can be done, you know, until I get on the ground."

The hoofs clattered again; and the voices, talking so strangely in the empty air, passed on through the forest, where no church had ever been gathered or solitary Christian prayed. Whither, then, could these holy men be journeying so deep into the heathen wilderness? Young Goodman Brown caught hold of a tree for support, being ready to sink down on the ground, faint and overburdened with the heavy sickness of his heart. He looked up to the sky, doubting whether there really was a heaven above him. Yet there was the blue arch, and the stars brightening in it.

"With heaven above and Faith below, I will yet stand firm against the devil!" cried Goodman Brown.

While he still gazed upward into the deep arch of the firmament and had lifted his hands to pray, a cloud, though no wind was stirring, hurried across the zenith and hid the brightening stars. The blue sky was still visible, except directly overhead, where this black mass of cloud was sweeping swiftly northward. Aloft in the air, as if from the depths of the cloud, came a confused and doubtful sound of voices. Once the listener fancied that he could distinguish the accents of towns-people of his own, men and women, both pious and ungodly, many of whom he had met at the communion table, and had seen others rioting at the tavern. The next moment, so indistinct were the sounds, he doubted whether he had heard aught but the murmur of the old forest, whispering without a wind. Then came a stronger swell of those familiar tones, heard daily in the sunshine at Salem village, but never until now from a cloud of night. There was one voice, of a young woman, uttering lamentations, yet with an uncertain sorrow, and entreating for some favor, which, perhaps, it would grieve her to obtain; and all the unseen multitude, both saints and sinners, seemed to encourage her onward.

"Faith!" shouted Goodman Brown, in a voice of agony and desperation; and the echoes of the forest mocked him, crying. "Faith! Faith!" as if bewildered wretches were seeking her all through the wilderness.

The cry of grief, rage, and terror was yet piercing the night, when the unhappy husband held his breath for a response. There was a scream, drowned immediately in a louder murmur of voices, fading into far-off laughter, as the dark cloud swept away, leaving the clear and silent sky above Goodman Brown. But something fluttered lightly down through the air and caught on the branch of a tree. The young man seized it, and beheld a pink ribbon.

"My Faith is gone!" cried he, after one stupefied moment. "There is no good on earth; and sin is but a name. Come, devil; for to thee is this world given."

And, maddened with despair, so that he laughed loud and long, did Goodman Brown grasp his staff and set forth again, at such a rate that he seemed to fly along the forest path rather than to walk or run. The road grew wilder and drearier and more faintly traced, and vanished at length, leaving him in the heart of the dark wilderness, still rushing onward with the instinct that guides mortal man to evil. The whole forest was peopled with frightful sounds—the creaking of the trees, the howling of wild beasts, and the yell of Indians; while sometimes the wind tolled like a distant church bell, and sometimes gave a broad roar around the traveller, as if all Nature were laughing him to scorn. But he was himself the chief horror of the scene, and shrank not from its other horrors.

"Ha! ha! ha!" roared Goodman Brown when the wind laughed at him. "Let us hear which will laugh loudest. Think not to frighten me with your deviltry. Come witch, come wizard, come Indian powwow, come devil himself, and here comes Goodman Brown. You may as well fear him as he fear you."

In truth, all through the haunted forest there could be nothing more frightful than the figure of Goodman Brown. On he flew among the black pines, brandishing his staff with frenzied gestures, now giving vent to an inspiration of horrid blasphemy, and now shouting forth such laughter as set all the echoes of the forest laughing like demons around him. The fiend in his own shape is less hideous than when he rages in the breast of man. Thus sped the demoniac on his course, until, quivering among the trees, he saw a red light before him, as when the felled trunks and branches of a clearing have been set on fire, and throw up their lurid blaze against the sky, at the hour of midnight. He paused, in a lull of the tempest that had driven him onward, and heard the swell of what seemed a hymn, rolling solemnly from a distance with the weight of many voices. He knew the tune; it was a familiar one in the choir of the village meetinghouse. The verse died heavily away, and was lengthened by a chorus, not of human voices, but of all the sounds of the benighted wilderness pealing in awful harmony together. Goodman Brown cried out, and his cry was lost to his own ear by its unison with the cry of the desert.

In the interval of silence he stole forward until the light glared full upon his eyes. At one extremity of an open space, hemmed in by the dark wall of the forest, arose a rock, bearing some rude, natural resemblance either to an altar or a pulpit, and surrounded by four blazing pines, their tops aflame, their stems untouched, like candles at an evening meeting. The mass of foliage that had overgrown the summit of the rock was all on fire, blazing high into the night and fitfully illuminating the whole field.

Each pendent twig and leafy festoon was in a blaze. As the red light arose and fell, a numerous congregation alternately shone forth, then disappeared in shadow, and again grew, as it were, out of the darkness, peopling the heart of the solitary woods at once.

"A grave and dark-clad company," quoth Goodman Brown.

In truth they were such. Among them, quivering to and fro between gloom and splendor, appeared faces that would be seen next day at the council board of the province, and others which, Sabbath after Sabbath, looked devoutly heavenward, and benignantly over the crowded pews, from the holiest pulpits in the land. Some affirm that the lady of the governor was there. At least there were high dames well known to her, and wives of honored husbands, and widows, a great multitude, and ancient maidens, all of excellent repute, and fair young girls, who trembled lest their mothers should espy them. Either the sudden gleams of light flashing over the obscure field bedazzled Goodman Brown, or he recognized a score of the church members of Salem village famous for their especial sanctity. Good old Deacon Gookin had arrived, and waited at the skirts of that venerable saint, his revered pastor. But, irreverently consorting with these grave, reputable, and pious people, these elders of the church, these chaste dames and dewy virgins, there were men of dissolute lives and women of spotted fame, wretches given over to all mean and filthy vice, and suspected even of horrid crimes. It was strange to see that the good shrank not from the wicked, nor were the sinners abashed by the saints. Scattered also among their pale-faced enemies were the Indian priests, or powwows, who had often scared their native forest with more hideous incantations than any known to English witchcraft.

"But where is Faith?" thought Goodman Brown; and as hope came into his heart, he trembled.

Another verse of the hymn arose, a slow and mournful strain, such as the pious love, but joined to words which expressed all that our nature can conceive of sin, and darkly hinted at far more. Unfathomable to mere mortals is the lore of fiends. Verse after verse was sung; and still the chorus of the desert swelled between like the deepest tone of a mighty organ; and with the final peal of that dreadful anthem there came a sound, as if the roaring wind, the rushing streams, the howling beasts, and every other voice of the unconcerted wilderness were mingling and according with the voice of guilty man in homage to the prince of all. The four blazing pines threw up a loftier flame, and obscurely discovered shapes and visages of horror on the smoke wreaths above the impious assembly. At the same moment the fire on the rock shot redly forth and formed a glowing arch above its base, where now appeared a figure. With reverence be it spoken, the figure bore no slight similitude, both in garb and manner, to some grave divine of the New England churches.

"Bring forth the converts!" cried a voice that echoed through the field and rolled into the forest.

At the word, Goodman Brown stepped forth from the shadow of the trees and approached the congregation, with whom he felt a loathful brotherhood by the sympathy of all that was wicked in his heart. He could have well-nigh sworn that the shape of his own dead father beckoned him to advance, looking downward from a smoke wreath, while a woman, with dim features of despair, threw out her hand to warn him back. Was it his mother? But he had no power to retreat one step, nor to resist, even in thought, when the minister and good old Deacon Gookin seized his arms and led him to the blazing rock. Thither came also the slender form of a veiled female, led between Goody Cloyse, that pious teacher of the catechism, and Martha Carrier, who had received the devil's promise to be queen of hell. A rampant hag was she. And there stood the proselytes beneath the canopy of fire.

"Welcome, my children," said the dark figure, "to the communion of your race. Ye have found thus young your nature and your destiny. My children, look behind you!"

They turned; and flashing forth, as it were, in a sheet of flame, the fiend worshippers were seen; the smile of welcome gleamed darkly on every visage.

"There," resumed the sable form, "are all whom ye have reverenced from youth. Ye deemed them holier than yourselves, and shrank from your own sin, contrasting it with their lives of righteousness and prayerful aspirations heavenward. Yet here are they all in my worshipping assembly. This night it shall be granted you to know their secret deeds: how hoary-bearded elders of the church have whispered wanton words to the young maids of their households; how many a woman, eager for widows' weeds, has given her husband a drink at bedtime and let him sleep his last sleep in her bosom; how beardless youths have made haste to inherit their fathers' wealth; and how fair damsels—blush not, sweet ones—have dug little graves in the garden, and bidden me, the sole guest, to an infant's funeral. By the sympathy of your human hearts for sin ye shall scent out all the places—whether in church, bed-chamber, street, field, or forest—where crime has been committed, and shall exult to behold the whole earth one stain of guilt, one mighty blood spot. Far more than this. It shall be yours to penetrate, in every bosom, the deep mystery of sin, the fountain of all wicked arts, and which inexhaustibly supplies more evil impulses than human power—than my power at its utmost—can make manifest in deeds. And now, my children, look upon each other."

They did so; and, by the blaze of the hell-kindled torches, the wretched man beheld his Faith, and the wife her husband, trembling before that unhallowed altar.

"Lo, there ye stand, my children," said the figure, in a deep and solemn tone, almost sad with its despairing awfulness, as if his once angelic nature could yet mourn for our miserable race. "Depending upon one another's hearts, ye had still hoped that virtue were not all a dream. Now are ye undeceived. Evil is the nature of mankind. Evil must be your only happiness. Welcome again, my children, to the communion of your race."

"Welcome," repeated the fiend worshippers, in one cry of despair and triumph.

And there they stood, the only pair, as it seemed, who were yet hesitating on the verge of wickedness in this dark world. A basin was hallowed, naturally, in the rock. Did it contain water, reddened by the lurid light? or was it blood? or, perchance, a liquid flame? Herein did the shape of evil dip his hand and prepare to lay the mark of baptism upon their foreheads, that they might be partakers of the mystery of sin, more conscious of the secret guilt of others, both in deed and thought, than they could now be of their own. The husband cast one look at his pale wife, and Faith at him. What polluted wretches would the next glance show them to each other, shuddering alike at what they disclosed and what they saw.

"Faith! Faith!" cried the husband, "look up to heaven, and resist the wicked one."

Whether Faith obeyed he knew not. Hardly had he spoken when he found himself amid calm night and solitude, listening to a roar of the wind which died heavily away through the forest. He staggered against the rock, and felt it chill and damp; while a hanging twig, that had been all on fire, besprinkled his cheek with the coldest dew.

The next morning young Goodman Brown came slowly into the street of Salem village, staring around him like a bewildered man. The good old minister was taking a walk along the graveyard to get an appetite for breakfast and meditate his sermon, and bestowed a blessing, as he passed, on Goodman Brown. He shrank from the venerable saint as if to avoid an anathema. Old Deacon Gookin was at domestic worship, and the holy words of his prayer were heard through the open window. "What God doth the wizard pray to?" quoth Goodman Brown. Goody Cloyse, that excellent old Christian, stood in the early sunshine at her own lattice, catechizing a little girl who had brought her a pint of morning's milk. Goodman Brown snatched away the child as from the grasp of the fiend himself. Turning the corner by the meetinghouse, he spied the head of Faith, with the pink ribbons, gazing anxiously forth, and bursting into such joy at sight of him that she skipped along the street and almost kissed her husband before the whole village. But Goodman Brown looked sternly and sadly into her face, and passed on without a greeting.

Had Goodman Brown fallen asleep in the forest and only dreamed a wild dream of a witch-meeting?

Be it so if you will; but, alas! it was a dream of evil omen for young Goodman Brown. A stern, a sad, a darkly meditative, a distrustful, if not a desperate man did he become from the night of that fearful dream. On the Sabbath day, when the congregation were singing a holy psalm, he could not listen because an anthem of sin rushed loudly upon his ear and drowned all the blessed strain. When the minister spoke from the pulpit with power and fervid eloquence, and, with his hand on the open Bible, of the sacred truths of our religion, and of saint-like lives and triumphant deaths, and of future bliss or misery unutterable, then did Goodman Brown turn pale, dreading lest the roof should thunder down upon the gray blasphemer and his hearers. Often, awaking suddenly at midnight, he shrank from the bosom of Faith; and at morning or eventide, when the family knelt down at prayer, he scowled and muttered to himself, and gazed sternly at his wife, and turned away. And when he had lived long, and was borne to his grave a hoary corpse, followed by Faith, an aged woman, and children and grandchildren, a goodly procession, besides neighbors not a few, they carved no hopeful verse upon his tombstone, for his dying hour was gloom.

Charlotte Perkins Gilman

Charlotte Perkins Gilman (1860–1935) was born in Hartford, Connecticut. A grand-niece of the author Harriet Beecher Stowe, she attended the Rhode Island School of Design and later worked as a commercial artist. Married in 1884, Gilman left her husband four years later. During this period, Gilman had a severe nervous breakdown, which forms the partial subject of her best-known work, "The Yellow Wallpaper."

Gilman wrote voluminously in various genres, producing poetry, autobiography, and political and feminist tracts, which include *Concerning Children* (1900) and *Human Work* (1904). She also lectured widely and, from 1909 to 1917, published her own journal, the *Forerunner,* to which she contributed many articles exploring the problematic relations between the sexes. In 1935, suffering from cancer, Gilman took her own life.

THE YELLOW WALLPAPER

It is very seldom that mere ordinary people like John and myself secure ancestral halls for the summer.

A colonial mansion, a hereditary estate, I would say a haunted house and reach the height of romantic felicity—but that would be asking too much of fate!

Still I will proudly declare that there is something queer about it.

Else, why should it be let so cheaply? And why have stood so long untenanted?

John laughs at me, of course, but one expects that.

John is practical in the extreme. He has no patience with faith, an intense horror of superstition, and he scoffs openly at any talk of things not to be felt and seen and put down in figures.

John is a physician, and *perhaps*—(I would not say it to a living soul, of course, but this is dead paper and a great relief to my mind)—*perhaps* that is one reason I do not get well faster.

You see, he does not believe I am sick! And what can one do?

If a physician of high standing, and one's own husband, assures friends and relatives that there is really nothing the matter with one but temporary nervous depression—a slight hysterical tendency—what is one to do?

My brother is also a physician, and also of high standing, and he says the same thing.

So I take phosphates or phosphites—whichever it is—and tonics, and air and exercise, and journeys, and am absolutely forbidden to "work" until I am well again.

Personally, I disagree with their ideas.

Personally, I believe that congenial work, with excitement and change, would do me good.

But what is one to do?

I did write for a while in spite of them; but it *does* exhaust me a good deal—having to be so sly about it, or else meet with heavy opposition.

I sometimes fancy that in my condition, if I had less opposition and more society and stimulus—but John says the very worst thing I can do is to think about my condition, and I confess it always makes me feel bad.

So I will let it alone and talk about the house.

The most beautiful place! It is quite alone, standing well back from the road, quite three miles from the village. It makes me think of English places that you read about, for there are hedges and walls and gates that lock, and lots of separate little houses for the gardeners and people.

There is a *delicious* garden! I never saw such a garden—large and shady, full of box-bordered paths, and lined with long grape-covered arbors with seats under them.

There were greenhouses, but they are all broken now.

There was some legal trouble, I believe, something about the heirs and co-heirs; anyhow, the place has been empty for years.

That spoils my ghostliness, I am afraid, but I don't care—there is something strange about the house—I can feel it.

I even said so to John one midnight evening, but he said what I felt was a draught, and shut the window.

I get unreasonably angry with John sometimes. I'm sure I never used to be so sensitive. I think it is due to this nervous condition.

But John says if I feel so I shall neglect proper self-control; so I take pains to control myself—before him, at least, and that makes me very tired.

I don't like our room a bit. I wanted one downstairs that opened onto the piazza and had roses all over the window, and such pretty old-fashioned chintz hangings! But John would not hear of it.

He said there was only one window and not room for two beds, and no near room for him if he took another.

He is very careful and loving, and hardly lets me stir without special direction.

I have a schedule prescription of each hour in the day; he takes all care from me, and so I feel basely ungrateful not to value it more.

He said he came here solely on my account, that I was to have perfect rest and all the air I could get. "Your exercise depends on your strength, my dear," said he, "and your food somewhat on your appetite; but air you can absorb all the time." So we took the nursery at the top of the house.

It is a big, airy room, the whole floor nearly, with windows that look all ways, and air and sunshine galore. It was nursery first, and then playroom and gymnasium, I should judge, for the windows are barred for little children, and there are rings and things in the walls.

The paint and paper look as if a boys' school had used it. It is stripped off—the paper—in great patches all around the head of my bed, about as far as I can reach, and in a great place on the other side of the room low down. I never saw a worse paper in my life. One of those sprawling, flamboyant patterns committing every artistic sin.

It is dull enough to confuse the eye in following, pronounced enough constantly to irritate and provoke study, and when you follow the lame uncertain curves for a little distance they suddenly commit suicide—plunge off at outrageous angles, destroy themselves in unheard-of contradictions.

The color is repellent, almost revolting: a smouldering unclean yellow, strangely faded by the slow-turning sunlight. It is a dull yet lurid orange in some places, a stickly sulphur tint in others.

No wonder the children hated it! I should hate it myself if I had to live in this room long.

There comes John, and I must put this away—he hates to have me write a word.

We have been here two weeks, and I haven't felt like writing before, since that first day.

I am sitting by the window now, up in this atrocious nursery, and there is nothing to hinder my writings as much as I please, save lack of strength.

John is away all day, and even some nights when his cases are serious.

I am glad my case is not serious!

But these nervous troubles are dreadfully depressing.

John does not know how much I really suffer. He knows there is no reason to suffer, and that satisfies him.

Of course it is only nervousness. It does weigh on me so not to do my duty in any way!

I meant to be such a help to John, such a real rest and comfort, and here I am a comparative burden already!

Nobody would believe what an effort it is to do what little I am able—to dress and entertain, and order things.

It is fortunate Mary is so good with the baby. Such a dear baby!

And yet I *cannot* be with him, it makes me so nervous.

I suppose John never was nervous in his life. He laughs at me so about this wallpaper!

At first he meant to repaper the room, but afterward he said that I was letting it get the better of me, and that nothing was worse for a nervous patient than to give way to such fancies.

He said that after the wallpaper was changed it would be the heavy bedstead, and then the barred windows, and then that gate at the head of the stairs, and so on.

"You know the place is doing you good," he said, "and really, dear, I don't care to renovate the house just for a three months' rental."

"Then do let us go downstairs," I said. "There are such pretty rooms there."

Then he took me in his arms and called me a blessed little goose, and said he would go down cellar, if I wished, and have it whitewashed into the bargain.

But he is right enough about the beds and windows and things.

It is as airy and comfortable a room as anyone need wish, and, of course, I would not be so silly as to make him uncomfortable just for a whim.

I'm really getting quite fond of the big room, all but that horrid paper.

Out of one window I can see the garden—those mysterious deep-shaded arbors, the riotous old-fashioned flowers, and bushes and gnarly trees.

Out of another I get a lovely view of the bay and a little private wharf belonging to the estate. There is a beautiful shaded lane that runs down there from the house. I always fancy I see people walking in these numerous paths and arbors, but John has cautioned me not to give way to fancy in the least. He says that with my imaginative power and habit of story-making, a nervous weakness like mine is sure to lead to all manner of excited fancies, and that I ought to use my will and good sense to check the tendency. So I try.

I think sometimes that if I were only well enough to write a little it would relieve the press of ideas and rest me.

But I find I get pretty tired when I try.

It is so discouraging not to have any advice and companionship about my work. When I get really well, John says we will ask Cousin Henry and Julia down for a long visit; but he says he would as soon put fireworks in my pillow-case as to let me have those stimulating people about now.

I wish I could get well faster.

But I must not think about that. This paper looks to me as if it *knew* what a vicious influence it had!

There is a recurrent spot where the pattern lolls like a broken neck and two bulbous eyes stare at you upside down.

I get positively angry with the impertinence of it and the everlastingness. Up and down and sideways they crawl, and those absurd unblinking eyes are everywhere. There is one place where two breadths didn't match, and the eyes go all up and down the line, one a little higher than the other.

I never saw so much expression in an inanimate thing before, and we all know how much expression they have! I used to lie awake as a child and get more entertainment and terror out of blank walls and plain furniture than most children could find in a toy-store.

I remember what a kindly wink the knobs of our big old bureau used to have, and there was one chair that always seemed like a strong friend.

I used to feel that if any of the other things looked too fierce I could always hop into that chair and be safe.

The furniture in this room is no worse than inharmonious, however, for we had to bring it all from downstairs. I suppose when this was used as a playroom they had to take the nursery things out, and no wonder! I never saw such ravages as the children have made here.

The wallpaper, as I said before, is torn off in spots, and it sticketh closer than a brother—they must have had perseverance as well as hatred.

Then the floor is scratched and gouged and splintered, the plaster itself is dug out here and there, and this great heavy bed, which is all we found in the room, looks as if it had been through the wars.

But I don't mind it a bit—only the paper.

There comes John's sister. Such a dear girl as she is, and so careful of me! I must not let her find me writing.

She is a perfect and enthusiastic housekeeper, and hopes for no better profession. I verily believe she thinks it is the writing which makes me sick!

But I can write when she is out, and see her a long way off from these windows.

There is one that commands the road, a lovely shaded winding road, and one that just looks off over the country. A lovely country, too, full of great elms and velvet meadows.

This wallpaper has a kind of subpattern in a different shade, a particularly irritating one, for you can only see it in certain lights, and not clearly then.

But in the places where it isn't faded and where the sun is just so—I can see a strange, provoking, formless sort of figure that seems to skulk about behind that silly and conspicuous front design.

There's sister on the stairs!

Well, the Fourth of July is over! The people are all gone, and I am tired out. John thought it might do me good to see a little company, so we just had Mother and Nellie and the children down for a week.

Of course I didn't do a thing. Jennie sees to everything now.

But it tired me all the same.

John says if I don't pick up faster he shall send me to Weir Mitchell[1] in the fall.

But I don't want to go there at all. I had a friend who was in his hands once, and she says he is just like John and my brother, only more so!

Besides, it is such an undertaking to go so far.

1. Dr. S. Weir Mitchell (1829–1914) was an eminent Philadelphia neurologist who advocated "rest cures" for nervous disorders. He was the author of *Diseases of the Nervous System, Especially of Women* (1881).

I don't feel as if it was worthwhile to turn my hand over for anything, and I'm getting dreadfully fretful and querulous.

I cry at nothing, and cry most of the time.

Of course I don't when John is here, or anybody else, but when I am alone.

And I am alone a good deal just now. John is kept in town very often by serious cases, and Jennie is good and lets me alone when I want her to.

So I walk a little in the garden or down that lovely lane, sit on the porch under the roses, and lie down up here a good deal.

I'm getting really fond of the room in spite of the wallpaper. Perhaps *because* of the wallpaper.

It dwells in my mind so!

I lie here on this great immovable bed—it is nailed down, I believe—and follow that pattern about by the hour. It is as good as gymnastics, I assure you. I start, we'll say, at the bottom, down in the corner over there where it has not been touched, and I determine for the thousandth time that I *will* follow that pointless pattern to some sort of a conclusion.

I know a little of the principle of design, and I know this thing was not arranged on any laws of radiation, or alternation, or repetition, or symmetry, or anything else that I ever heard of.

It is repeated, of course, by the breadths, but not otherwise.

Looked at in one way, each breadth stands alone; the bloated curves and flourishes—a kind of "debased Romanesque" with delirium tremens go waddling up and down in isolated columns of fatuity.

But, on the other hand, they connect diagonally, and the sprawling outlines run off in great slanting waves of optic horror, like a lot of wallowing sea-weeds in full chase.

The whole thing goes horizontally, too, at least it seems so, and I exhaust myself trying to distinguish the order of its going in that direction.

They have used a horizontal breadth for a frieze, and that adds wonderfully to the confusion.

There is one end of the room where it is almost intact, and there, when the crosslights fade and the low sun shines directly upon it, I can almost fancy radiation after all—the interminable grotesque seems to form around a common center and rush off in headlong plunges of equal distraction.

It makes me tired to follow it. I will take a nap, I guess.

I don't know why I should write this.

I don't want to.

I don't feel able.

And I know John would think it absurd. But I *must* say what I feel and think in some way—it is such a relief!

But the effort is getting to be greater than the relief.

Half the time now I am awfully lazy, and lie down ever so much. John says I mustn't lose my strength, and has me take cod liver oil and lots of tonics and things, to say nothing of ale and wines and rare meat.

Dear John! He loves me very dearly, and hates to have me sick. I tried to have a real earnest reasonable talk with him the other day, and tell him how I wish he would let me go and make a visit to Cousin Henry and Julia.

But he said I wasn't able to go, nor able to stand it after I got there; and I did not make out a very good case for myself, for I was crying before I had finished.

It is getting to be a great effort for me to think straight. Just this nervous weakness, I suppose.

And dear John gathered me up in his arms, and just carried me up stairs and laid me on the bed, and sat by me and read to me till it tired my head.

He said I was his darling and his comfort and all he had, and that I must take care of myself for his sake, and keep well.

He says no one but myself can help me out of it, that I must use my will and self-control and not let any silly fancies run away with me.

There's one comfort—the baby is well and happy, and does not have to occupy this nursery with the horrid wallpaper.

If we had not used it, that blessed child would have! What a fortunate escape! Why, I wouldn't have a child of mine, an impressionable little thing, live in such a room for worlds.

I never thought of it before, but it is lucky that John kept me here after all; I can stand it so much easier than a baby, you see.

Of course I never mention it to them anymore—I am too wise—but I keep watch for it all the same.

There are things in the wallpaper that nobody knows about but me, or ever will.

Behind that outside pattern the dim shapes get clearer every day.

It is always the same shape, only very numerous.

And it is like a woman stooping down and creeping about behind that pattern. I don't like it a bit. I wonder—I begin to think—I wish John would take me away from here!

It is so hard to talk with John about my case, because he is so wise, and because he loves me so.

But I tried it last night.

It was moonlight. The moon shines in all around just as the sun does.

I hate to see it sometimes, it creeps so slowly, and always comes in by one window or another.

John was asleep and I hated to waken him, so I kept still and watched the moonlight on that undulating wallpaper till I felt creepy.

The faint figure behind seemed to shake the pattern, just as if she wanted to get out.

I got up softly and went to feel and see if the paper *did* move, and when I came back John was awake.

"What is it, little girl?" he said. "Don't go walking about like that—you'll get cold."

I thought it was a good time to talk, so I told him that I really was not gaining here, and that I wished he would take me away.

"Why, darling!" said he. "Our lease will be up in three weeks, and I can't see how to leave before.

"The repairs are not done at home, and I cannot possibly leave town just now. Of course, if you were in any danger, I could and would, but you really are better, dear, whether you can see it or not. I am a doctor, dear and I know. You are gaining flesh and color, your appetite is better, I feel really much easier about you."

"I don't weigh a bit more," said I, "nor as much; and my appetite may be better in the evening when you are here but it is worse in the morning when you are away!"

"Bless her little heart," said he with a big hug. "She shall be as sick as she pleases! But now let's improve the shining hours by going to sleep, and talk about it in the morning!"

"And you won't go away?" I asked gloomily.

"Why, how can I, dear? It is only three weeks more and then we will take a nice little trip for a few days while Jennie is getting the house ready. Really, dear, you are better!"

"Better in body perhaps—" I began, and stopped short, for he sat up straight and looked at me with such a stern, reproachful look that I could not say another word.

"My darling," said he, "I beg you, for my sake and for our child's sake, as well as for your own, that you will never for one instant let that idea enter your mind! There is nothing so dangerous, so fascinating, to a temperament like yours. It is a false and foolish fancy. Can you trust me as a physician when I tell you so?"

So of course I said no more on that score, and we went to sleep before long. He thought I was asleep first, but I wasn't, and lay there for hours trying to decide whether that front pattern and the back pattern really did move together or separately.

On a pattern like this, by daylight, there is a lack of sequence, a defiance of law, that is a constant irritant to a normal mind.

The color is hideous enough, and unreliable enough, and infuriating enough, but the pattern is torturing.

You think you have mastered it, but just as you get well under way in following, it turns a back-somersault and there you are. It slaps you in the face, knocks you down, and tramples upon you. It is like a bad dream.

The outside pattern is a florid arabesque, reminding one of a fungus. If you can imagine a toadstool in joints, an interminable string of toadstools, budding and sprouting in endless convolutions—why, that is something like it.

That is, sometimes!

There is one marked peculiarity about this paper, a thing nobody seems to notice but myself, and that is that it changes as the light changes.

When the sun shoots in through the east window—I always watch for that first long, straight ray—it changes so quickly that I never can quite believe it.

That is why I watch it always.

By moonlight—the moon shines in all night when there is a moon—I wouldn't know it was the same paper.

At night in any kind of light, in twilight, candlelight, lamplight, and worst of all by moonlight, it becomes bars! The outside pattern, I mean, and the woman behind it is as plain as can be.

I didn't realize for a long time what the thing was that showed behind, that dim subpattern, but now I am quite sure it is a woman.

By daylight she is subdued, quiet. I fancy it is the pattern that keeps her so still. It is so puzzling. It keeps me quiet by the hour.

I lie down ever so much now. John says it is good for me, and to sleep all I can.

Indeed he started the habit by making me lie down for an hour after each meal.

It is a very bad habit, I am convinced, for you see, I don't sleep.

And that cultivates deceit, for I don't tell them I'm awake—oh, no!

The fact is I am getting a little afraid of John.

He seems very queer sometimes, and even Jennie has an inexplicable look.

It strikes me occasionally, just as a scientific hypothesis, that perhaps it is the paper!

I have watched John when he did not know I was looking, and come into the room suddenly on the most innocent excuses, and I've caught him several times *looking at the paper!* And Jennie too. I caught Jennie with her hand on it once.

She didn't know I was in the room, and when I asked her in a quiet, a very quiet voice, with the most restrained manner possible, what she was doing with the paper, she turned around as if she had been caught stealing, and looked quite angry—asked me why I should frighten her so!

Then she said that the paper stained everything it touched, that she had found yellow smooches on all my clothes and John's and she wished we would be more careful!

Did not that sound innocent? But I know she was studying that pattern, and I am determined that nobody shall find it out but myself!

Life is very much more exciting now than it used to be. You see, I have something more to expect, to look forward to, to watch. I really do eat better, and am more quiet than I was.

John is so pleased to see me improve! He laughed a little the other day, and said I seemed to be flourishing in spite of my wallpaper.

I turned it off with a laugh. I had no intention of telling him it was *because* of the wallpaper—he would make fun of me. He might even want to take me away.

I don't want to leave now until I have found it out. There is a week more, and I think that will be enough.

I'm feeling so much better!

I don't sleep much at night, for it is so interesting to watch developments; but I sleep a good deal during the daytime.

In the daytime it is tiresome and perplexing.

There are always new shoots on the fungus, and new shades of yellow all over it. I cannot keep count of them, though I have tried conscientiously.

It is the strangest yellow, that wallpaper! It makes me think of all the yellow things I ever saw—not beautiful ones like buttercups, but old, foul, bad yellow things.

But there is something else about that paper—the smell! I noticed it the moment we came into the room, but with so much air and sun it was not bad. Now we have had a week of fog and rain, and whether the windows are open or not, the smell is here.

It creeps all over the house.

I find it hovering in the dining-room, skulking in the parlor, hiding in the hall, lying in wait for me on the stairs.

It gets into my hair.

Even when I go to ride, if I turn my head suddenly and surprise it—there is that smell!

Such a peculiar odor, too! I have spent hours in trying to analyze it, to find what it smelled like.

It is not bad—at first—and very gentle, but quite the subtlest, most enduring odor I ever met.

In this damp weather it is awful. I wake up in the night and find it hanging over me.

It used to disturb me at first. I thought seriously of burning the house—to reach the smell.

But now I am used to it. The only thing I can think of that it is like is the *color* of the paper! A yellow smell.

There is a very funny mark on this wall, low down, near the mopboard. A streak that runs around the room. It goes behind every piece of furniture, except the bed, a long straight, even *smooch,* as if it had been rubbed over and over.

I wonder how it was done and who did it, and what they did it for. Round and round and round—round and round and round—it makes me dizzy!

I really have discovered something at last.

Through watching so much at night, when it changes so, I have finally found out.

The front pattern *does* move—and no wonder! The woman behind shakes it!

Sometimes I think there are a great many women behind, and sometimes only one, and she crawls around fast, and her crawling shakes it all over.

Then in the very bright spots she keeps still, and in the very shady spots she just takes hold of the bars and shakes them hard.

And she is all the time trying to climb through. But nobody could climb through that pattern—it strangles so; I think that is why it has so many heads.

They get through and then the pattern strangles them off and turns them upside down, and makes their eyes white!

If those heads were covered or taken off it would not be half so bad.

I think that woman gets out in the daytime!

And I'll tell you why—privately—I've seen her!

I can see her out of every one of my windows!

It is the same woman, I know, for she is always creeping, and most women do not creep by daylight.

I see her in that long shaded lane, creeping up and down. I see her in those dark grape arbors, creeping all round the garden.

I see her on that long road under the trees, creeping along, and when a carriage comes she hides under the blackberry vines.

I don't blame her a bit. It must be very humiliating to be caught creeping by daylight!

I always lock the door when I creep by daylight. I can't do it at night, for I know John would suspect something at once.

And John is so queer now that I don't want to irritate him. I wish he would take another room! Besides, I don't want anybody to get that woman out at night but myself.

I often wonder if I could see her out of all the windows at once.

But, turn as fast as I can, I can only see out of one at one time.

And though I always see her, she *may* be able to creep faster than I can turn! I have watched her sometimes away off in the open country, creeping as fast as a cloud shadow in a wind.

If only that top pattern could be gotten off from the under one! I mean to try it, little by little.

I have found out another funny thing, but I shan't tell it this time! It does not do to trust people too much.

There are only two more days to get this paper off, and I believe John is beginning to notice. I don't like the look in his eyes.

And I heard him ask Jennie a lot of professional questions about me. She had a very good report to give.

She said I slept a good deal in the daytime.

John knows I don't sleep very well at night, for all I'm so quiet!

He asked me all sorts of questions too, and pretended to be very loving and kind.

As If I couldn't see through him!

Still, I don't wonder he acts so, sleeping under this paper for three months.

It only interests me, but I feel sure John and Jennie are affected by it.

Hurrah! This is the last day, but it is enough. John is to stay in town over night, and won't be out until this evening.

Jennie wanted to sleep with me—the sly thing; but I told her I should undoubtedly rest better for a night all alone.

That was clever, for really I wasn't alone a bit! As soon as it was moonlight and that poor thing began to crawl and shake the pattern, I got up and ran to help her.

I pulled and she shook. I shook and she pulled, and before morning we had peeled off yards of that paper.

A strip about as high as my head and half around the room.

And then when the sun came and that awful pattern began to laugh at me, I declared I would finish it today!

We go away tomorrow, and they are moving all my furniture down again to leave things as they were before.

Jennie looked at the wall in amazement, but I told her merrily that I did it out of pure spite at the vicious thing.

She laughed and said she wouldn't mind doing it herself, but I must not get tired.

How she betrayed herself that time!

But I am here, and no person touches this paper but Me—not *alive!*

She tried to get me out of the room—it was too patent! But I said it was so quiet and empty and clean now that I believed I would lie down again and sleep all I could, and not to wake me even for dinner—I would call when I woke.

So now she is gone, and the servants are gone, and the things are gone, and there is nothing left but that great bedstead nailed down, with the canvas mattress we found on it.

We shall sleep downstairs tonight, and take the boat home tomorrow.

I quite enjoy the room, now it is bare again.

How those children did tear about here!

This bedstead is fairly gnawed!

But I must get to work.

I have locked the door and thrown the key down into the front path.

I don't want to go out, and I don't want to have anybody come in, till John comes.

I want to astonish him.

I've got a rope up here that even Jennie did not find. If that woman does get out, and tries to get away, I can tie her!

But I forgot I could not reach far without anything to stand on!

This bed will *not* move!

I tried to lift and push it until I was lame, and then I got so angry I bit off a little piece at one corner—but it hurt my teeth.

Then I peeled off all the paper I could reach standing on the floor. It sticks horribly and the pattern just enjoys it! All those strangled heads and bulbous eyes and waddling fungus growths just shriek with derision!

I am getting angry enough to do something desperate. To jump out of the window would be admirable exercise, but the bars are too strong even to try.

Besides I wouldn't do it. Of course not. I know well enough that a step like that is improper and might be misconstrued.

I don't like to *look* out of the windows even—there are so many of those creeping women, and they creep so fast.

I wonder if they all come out of that wallpaper as I did!

But I am securely fastened now by my well-hidden rope—you don't get *me* out in the road there!

I suppose I shall have to get back behind the pattern when it comes night, and that is hard!

It is so pleasant to be out in this great room and creep around as I please!

I don't want to go outside. I won't, even if Jennie asks me to.

For outside you have to creep on the ground, and everything is green instead of yellow.

But here I can creep smoothly on the floor, and my shoulder just fits in that long smooch around the wall, so I cannot lose my way.

Why, there's John at the door!

It is no use, young man, you can't open it!

How he does call and pound!

Now he's crying to Jennie for an axe.

It would be a shame to break down that beautiful door!

"John, dear!" said I in the gentlest voice. "The key is down by the front steps, under a plantain leaf!"

That silenced him for a few moments.

Then he said, very quietly indeed, "Open the door, my darling!"

"I can't," said I. "The key is down by the front door under a plantain leaf!" And then I said it again, several times, very gently and slowly, and said it so often that he had to go and see, and he got it of course, and came in. He stopped short by the door.

"What is the matter?" he cried. "For God's sake, what are you doing!"

I kept on creeping just the same, but I looked at him over my shoulder.

"I've got out at last," said I, "in spite of you and Jane. And I've pulled off most of the paper, so you can't put me back!"

Now why should that man have fainted? But he did, and right across my path by the wall, so that I had to creep over him every time!

Stephen Crane

Stephen Crane (1871–1900) was born in Newark, New Jersey. His father, a Methodist minister, died when the boy was young, leaving his wife to support a family of fourteen children by writing articles for various newspapers. Crane himself became a journalist, gravitating naturally toward situations of oppression and conflict. His novel *Maggie: A Girl of the Streets* (1893) was based upon his documentary research of New York's Bowery. Two years later he completed his best known work, *The Red Badge of Courage,* selling it to a newspaper syndicate for a pittance. Though he only lived to be 29 years old, Crane packed those years with adventure and exploration. In the last five years of his life he moved from the American West to Florida to Greece to England to Cuba, covering wars and revolutions in the process. He died in Germany of tuberculosis.

Crane is a stylist of great vigor and compression. His training in journalism, like Hemingway's, taught him the lesson of rooting prose in the immediacy of the physical. Crane also tried to keep faith with what he perceived to be the true rhythms of events; his prose avoids false drama and is often deliberately anticlimactic. In this respect he has been compared with Anton Chekhov.

THE OPEN BOAT

A Tale Intended to Be after the Fact,
Being the Experience of Four Men from
the Sunk Steamer Commodore

I

None of them knew the color of the sky. Their eyes glanced level, and were fastened upon the waves that swept toward them. These waves were of the hue of slate, save for the tops, which were of foaming white, and all of the men knew the colors of the sea. The horizon narrowed and widened, and dipped and rose, and at all times its edge was jagged with waves that seemed thrust up in points like rocks.

Many a man ought to have a bath-tub larger than the boat which here rode upon the sea. These waves were most wrongfully and barbarously abrupt and tall, and each froth-top was a problem in small boat navigation.

The cook squatted in the bottom and looked with both eyes at the six inches of gunwale which separated him from the ocean. His sleeves were rolled over his fat forearms, and the two flaps of his unbuttoned vest dangled as he bent to bail out the boat. Often he said: "Gawd! That was a narrow clip." As he remarked it he invariably gazed eastward over the broken sea.

The oiler, steering with one of the two oars in the boat, sometimes raised himself suddenly to keep clear of water that swirled in over the stern. It was a thin little oar and it seemed often ready to snap.

The correspondent, pulling at the other oar, watched the waves and wondered why he was there.

The injured captain, lying in the bow, was at this time buried in that profound dejection and indifference which comes, temporarily at least, to even the bravest and most enduring when, willy nilly, the firm fails, the army loses, the ship goes down. The mind of the master of a vessel is rooted deep in the timbers of her, though he command for a day or a decade, and this captain had on him the stern impression of a scene in the grays of dawn of seven turned faces, and later a stump of a top-mast with a white ball on it that slashed to and fro at the waves, went low and lower, and down. Thereafter there was something strange in his voice. Although steady, it was deep with mourning, and of a quality beyond oration or tears.

"Keep 'er a little more south, Billie," said he.

" 'A little more south,' sir," said the oiler in the stern.

A seat in this boat was not unlike a seat upon a bucking broncho, and, by the same token, a broncho is not much smaller. The craft pranced and reared, and plunged like an animal. As each wave came, and she rose for it, she seemed like a horse making at a fence outrageously high. The manner of her scramble over these walls of water is a mystic thing, and, moreover, at the top of them were ordinarily these problems in white water, the foam racing down from the summit of each wave, requiring a new leap, and a leap from the air. Then, after scornfully bumping a crest, she would slide, and race, and splash down a long incline and arrive bobbing and nodding in front of the next menace.

A singular disadvantage of the sea lies in the fact that after successfully surmounting one wave you discover that there is another behind it just as important and just as nervously anxious to do something effective in the way of swamping boats. In a ten-foot dingey one can get an idea of the resources of the sea in the line of waves that is not probable to the average experience, which is never at sea in a dingey. As each slaty wall of water approached, it shut all else from the view of the men in the boat, and it was not difficult to imagine that this particular wave was the final outburst of the ocean, the last effort of the grim water. There was a terrible grace in the move of the waves, and they came in silence, save for the snarling of the crests.

In the wan light, the faces of men must have been gray. Their eyes must have glinted in strange ways as they gazed steadily astern. Viewed from a balcony, the whole thing would doubtlessly have been weirdly picturesque. But the men in the boat had no time to see it, and if they had had leisure there were other things to occupy their minds. The sun swung steadily up the sky, and they knew it was broad day because the color of the sea changed from slate to emerald-green, streaked with amber lights, and the foam was like tumbling snow. The process of the breaking day was unknown to them. They were aware only of this effect upon the color of the waves that rolled toward them.

In disjointed sentences the cook and the correspondent argued as to the difference between a life-saving station and a house of refuge. The cook had said: "There's a house of refuge just north of the Mosquito Inlet Light, and as soon as they see us, they'll come off in their boat and pick us up."

"As soon as who see us?" said the correspondent.

"The crew," said the cook.

"Houses of refuge don't have crews," said the correspondent. "As I understand them, they are only places where clothes and grub are stored for the benefit of shipwrecked people. They don't carry crews."

"Oh, yes, they do," said the cook.

"No, they don't," said the correspondent.

"Well, we're not there yet, anyhow," said the oiler, in the stern.

"Well," said the cook, "perhaps it's not a house of refuge that I'm thinking of as being near Mosquito Inlet Light. Perhaps it's a life-saving station."

"We're not there yet," said the oiler, in the stern.

II

As the boat bounced from the top of each wave, the wind tore through the hair of the hatless men, and as the craft plopped her stern down again the spray slashed past them. The crest of each of these waves was a hill, from the top of which the men surveyed, for a moment, a broad tumultuous expanse, shining and wind-riven. It was probably splendid. It was probably glorious, this play of the free sea, wild with lights of emerald and white and amber.

"Bully good thing it's an on-shore wind," said the cook. "If not where would we be? Wouldn't have a show."

"That's right," said the correspondent.

The busy oiler nodded his assent.

Then the captain, in the bow, chuckled in a way that expressed humor, contempt, tragedy, all in one. "Do you think we've got a show, now, boys?" said he.

Whereupon the three went silent, save for a trifle of hemming and hawing. To express any particular optimism at this time they felt to be childish and stupid, but they all doubtless possessed this sense of the situation in their mind. A young man thinks doggedly at such times. On the other hand, the ethics of their condition was decidedly against any open suggestion of hopelessness. So they were silent.

"Oh, well," said the captain, soothing his children, "we'll get ashore all right."

But there was that in his tone which made them think, so the oiler quoth: "Yes! If this wind holds!"

The cook was bailing. "Yes! If we don't catch hell in the surf."

Canton flannel gulls flew near and far. Sometimes they sat down on the sea, near patches of brown sea-weed that rolled over the waves with a movement like carpets on a line in a gale. The birds sat comfortably in groups, and they were envied by some in the dingey, for the wrath of the sea was no more to them than it was to a covey of prairie chickens a thousand miles inland. Often they came very close and stared at the men with black bead-like eyes. At these times they were uncanny and sinister in their unblinking scrutiny, and the men hooted angrily at them, telling them to be gone. One came, and evidently decided to alight on the top of the captain's head. The bird flew parallel to the boat and did not circle, but made short sidelong jumps in the air in chicken-fashion. His black eyes were wistfully fixed upon the captain's head. "Ugly brute," said the oiler to the bird. "You look as if you were made with a jack-knife." The cook and the correspondent swore darkly at the creature. The captain naturally wished to knock it away with the end of the heavy painter, but he did not dare do it, because anything resembling an emphatic gesture would have capsized this freighted boat, and so with his open hand, the captain gently and carefully waved the gull away. After it had been discouraged from the pursuit the captain breathed easier on account of his hair, and others breathed easier because the bird struck their minds at this time as being somehow gruesome and ominous.

In the meantime the oiler and the correspondent rowed. And also they rowed.

They sat together in the same seat, and each rowed an oar. Then the oiler took both oars; then the correspondent took both oars; then the oiler; then the correspondent. They rowed and they rowed. The very ticklish part of the business was when the time came for the reclining one in the stern to take his turn at the oars. By the very last star of truth, it is easier to steal eggs from under a hen than it was to change seats in the dingey. First the man in the stern slid his hand along the thwart and moved with care, as if he were of Sèvres.[1] Then the man in the rowing seat slid his hand along the other thwart. It was all done with the most extraordinary care. As the two sidled past each other, the whole party kept watchful eyes on the coming wave, and the captain cried: "Look out now! Steady there!"

The brown mats of sea-weed that appeared from time to time were like islands, bits of earth. They were travelling, apparently, neither one

1. A delicate French porcelain.

way nor the other. They were, to all intents, stationary. They informed the men in the boat that it was making progress slowly toward the land.

The captain, rearing cautiously in the bow, after the dingey soared on a great swell, said that he had seen the light-house at Mosquito Inlet. Presently the cook remarked that he had seen it. The correspondent was at the oars, then, and for some reason he too wished to look at the light-house, but his back was toward the far shore and the waves were important, and for some time he could not seize an opportunity to turn his head. But at last there came a wave more gentle than the others, and when at the crest of it he swiftly scoured the western horizon.

"See it?" said the captain.

"No," said the correspondent, slowly. "I didn't see anything."

"Look again," said the captain. He pointed. "It's exactly in that direction."

At the top of another wave, the correspondent did as he was bid, and this time his eyes chanced on a small still thing on the edge of the swaying horizon. It was precisely like the point of a pin. It took an anxious eye to find a light-house so tiny.

"Think we'll make it, Captain?"

"If this wind holds and the boat don't swamp, we can't do much else," said the captain.

The little boat, lifted by each towering sea, and splashed viciously by the crests, made progress that in the absence of sea-weed was not apparent to those in her. She seemed just a wee thing wallowing, miraculously, top-up, at the mercy of five oceans. Occasionally, a great spread of water, like white flames, swarmed into her.

"Bail her, cook," said the captain, serenely.

"All right, Captain," said the cheerful cook.

III

It would be difficult to describe the subtle brotherhood of men that was here established on the seas. No one said that it was so. No one mentioned it. But it dwelt in the boat, and each man felt it warm him. They were a captain, an oiler, a cook, and a correspondent, and they were friends, friends in a more curiously iron-bound degree than may be common. The hurt captain, lying against the water-jar in the bow, spoke always in a low voice and calmly, but he could never command a more ready and swiftly obedient crew than the motley three of the dingey. It was more than a mere recognition of what was best for the common safety. There was surely in it a quality that was personal and heartfelt. And after this devotion to the commander of the boat there was this comradeship that the correspondent, for instance, who had been taught to be cynical of men, knew even at the time was the best experience of his life. But no one said that it was so. No one mentioned it.

"I wish we had a sail," remarked the captain. "We might try my overcoat on the end of an oar and give you two boys a chance to rest." So the cook and the correspondent held the mast and spread wide the overcoat. The oiler steered, and the little boat made good way with her new rig. Sometimes the oiler had to scull sharply to keep a sea from breaking into the boat, but otherwise sailing was a success.

Meanwhile the light-house had been growing slowly larger. It had now almost assumed color, and appeared like a little gray shadow on the sky. The man at the oars could not be prevented from turning his head rather often to try for a glimpse of this little gray shadow.

At last, from the top of each wave the men in the tossing boat could see land. Even as the light-house was an upright shadow on the sky, this land seemed but a long black shadow on the sea. It certainly was thinner than paper. 'We must be about opposite New Smyrna," said the cook, who had coasted this short often in schooners. "Captain, by the way, I believe they abandoned that life-saving station there about a year ago."

"Did they?" said the captain.

The wind slowly died away. The cook and the correspondent were not now obliged to slave in order to hold the oar. But the waves continued their old impetuous swooping at the dingey, and the little craft, no longer under way, struggled woundily over them. The oiler or the correspondent took the oars again.

Shipwrecks are *apropos* of nothing. If men could only train for them and have them occur when the men had reached pink condition, there would be less drowning at sea. Of the four in the dingey none had slept any time worth mentioning for two days and two nights previous to embarking in the dingey, and in the excitement of clambering about the deck of a foundering ship they had also forgotten to eat heartily.

For these reasons, and for others, neither the oiler nor the correspondent was fond of rowing at this time. The correspondent wondered ingenuously how in the name of all that was sane could there be people who thought it amusing to row a boat. It was not an amusement; it was a diabolical punishment, and even a genius of mental aberrations could never conclude that it was anything but a horror to the muscles and a crime against the back. He mentioned to the boat in general how the amusement of rowing struck him, and the weary-faced oiler smiled in full sympathy. Previously to the foundering, by the way, the oiler had worked double-watch in the engine-room of the ship.

"Take her easy, now, boys," said the captain. "Don't spend yourselves. If we have to run a surf you'll need all your strength, because we'll sure have to swim for it. Take your time."

Slowly the land arose from the sea. From a black line it became a line of black and a line of white—trees and sand. Finally, the captain said that he could make out a house on the shore. "That's the house of refuge, sure," said the cook. "They'll see us before long, and come out after us."

The distant light-house reared high. "The keeper ought to be able to make us out now, if he's looking through a glass," said the captain. "He'll notify the life-saving people."

"None of those other boats could have got ashore to give word of the wreck," said the oiler, in a low voice. "Else the life-boat would be out hunting us."

Slowly and beautifully the land loomed out of the sea. The wind came again. It had veered from the northeast to the southeast. Finally, a new sound struck the ears of the men in the boat. It was the low thunder of the surf on the shore. "We'll never be able to make the light-house now," said the captain. "Swing her head a little more north, Billie."

" 'A little more north,' sir," said the oiler.

Whereupon the little boat turned her nose once more down the wind, and all but the oarsman watched the shore grow. Under the influence of this expansion doubt and direful apprehension were leaving the minds of the men. The management of the boat was still most absorbing, but it could not prevent a quiet cheerfulness. In an hour, perhaps, they would be ashore.

Their back-bones had become thoroughly used to balancing in the boat and they now rode this wild colt of a dingey like circus men. The correspondent thought that he had been drenched to the skin, but happening to feel in the top pocket of his coat, he found therein eight cigars. Four of them were soaked with sea-water; four were perfectly scatheless. After a search, somebody produced three dry matches, and thereupon the four waifs rode impudently in their little boat, and with an assurance of an impending rescue shining in their eyes, puffed at the big cigars and judged well and ill of all men. Everybody took a drink of water.

IV

"Cook," remarked the captain, "there don't seem to be any signs of life about your house of refuge."

"No," replied the cook. "Funny they don't see us!"

A broad stretch of lowly coast lay before the eyes of the men. It was of dunes topped with dark vegetation. The roar of the surf was plain, and sometimes they could see the white lip of a wave as it spun up the beach. A tiny house was blocked out black upon the sky. Southward, the slim light house lifted its little gray length.

Tide, wind, and waves were swinging the dingey northward. "Funny they don't see us," said the men.

The surf's roar was here dulled, but its tone was, nevertheless, thunderous and mighty. As the boat swam over the great rollers, the men sat listening to this roar. "We'll swamp sure," said everybody.

It is fair to say here that there was not a life-saving station within twenty miles in either direction, but the men did not know this fact and in consequence they made dark and opprobrious remarks concerning the eyesight of the nation's life-savers. Four scowling men sat in the dingey and surpassed records in the invention of epithets.

"Funny they don't see us."

The light-heartedness of a former time had completely faded. To their sharpened minds it was easy to conjure pictures of all kinds of incompetency and blindness and, indeed, cowardice. There was the shore of the populous land, and it was bitter and bitter to them that from it came no sign.

"Well," said the captain, ultimately, "I suppose we'll have to make a try for ourselves. If we stay out here too long, we'll none of us have strength left to swim after the boat swamps."

And so the oiler, who was at the oars, turned the boat straight for the shore. There was a sudden tightening of muscles. There was some thinking.

"If we don't all get ashore—" said the captain. "If we don't all get ashore, I suppose you fellows know where to send news of my finish?"

They then briefly exchanged some addresses and admonitions. As for the reflections of the men, there was a great deal of rage in them. Perchance they might be formulated thus: "If I am going to be drowned—if I am going to be drowned—if I am going to be drowned, why, in the name of the seven mad gods who rule the sea, was I allowed to come thus far and contemplate sand and trees? Was I brought here merely to have my nose dragged away as I was about to nibble the sacred cheese of life? It is preposterous. If this old ninny-woman, Fate, cannot do better than this, she should be deprived of the management of men's fortunes. She is an old hen who knows not her intention. If she has decided to drown me, why did she not do it in the beginning and save me all this trouble. The whole affair is absurd. . . . But, no, she cannot mean to drown me. She dare not drown me. She cannot drown me. Not after all this work." Afterward the man might have had an impulse to shake his fist at the clouds. "Just you drown me, now, and then hear what I call you!"

The billows that came at this time were more formidable. They seemed always just about to break and roll over the little boat in a turmoil of foam. There was a preparatory and long growl in the speech of them. No mind unused to the sea would have concluded that the dingey could ascend these sheer heights in time. The shore was still afar. The oiler was a wily surfman. "Boys," he said, swiftly, "she won't live three minutes more and we're too far out to swim. Shall I take her to sea again, Captain?"

"Yes! Go ahead!" said the captain.

This oiler, by a series of quick miracles, and fast and steady oarsmanship, turned the boat in the middle of the surf and took her safely to sea again.

There was a considerable silence as the boat bumped over the furrowed sea to deeper water. Then somebody in gloom spoke. "Well, anyhow, they must have seen us from the shore by now."

The gulls went in slanting flight up the wind toward the gray desolate east. A squall, marked by dingy clouds, and clouds brick-red, like smoke from a burning building, appeared from the southeast.

"What do you think of those life-saving people? Ain't they peaches?"

"Funny they haven't seen us."

"Maybe they think we're out here for sport! Maybe they think we're fishin'. Maybe they think we're damned fools."

It was a long afternoon. A changed tide tried to force them southward, but wind and wave said northward. Far ahead, where coast-line, sea, and sky formed their mighty angle, there were little dots which seemed to indicate a city on the shore.

"St. Augustine?"

The captain shook his head. "Too near Mosquito Inlet."

And the oiler rowed, and then the correspondent rowed. Then the oiler rowed. It was a weary business. The human back can become the seat of more aches and pains than are registered in books for the composite anatomy of a regiment. It is a limited area, but it can become the theatre of innumerable muscular conflicts, tangles, wrenches, knots, and other comforts.

"Did you ever like to row, Billie?" asked the correspondent.

"No," said the oiler, "Hang it."

When one exchanged the rowing-seat for a place in the bottom of the boat, he suffered a bodily depression that caused him to be careless of everything save an obligation to wiggle one finger. There was cold sea-water swashing to and fro in the boat, and he lay in it. His head, pillowed on a thwart, was within an inch of the swirl of a wave crest, and sometimes a particularly obstreperous sea came in-board and drenched him once more. But these matters did not annoy him. It is almost certain that if the boat had capsized he would have tumbled comfortably out upon the ocean as if he felt sure that it was a great soft mattress.

"Look! There's a man on the shore!"

"Where?"

"There! See 'im? See 'im?"

"Yes, sure! He's walking along."

"Now he's stopped. Look! He's facing us!"

"He's waving at us!"

"So he is! By thunder!"

"Ah, now, we're all right! There'll be a boat out here for us in half an hour."

"He's going on. He's running. He's going up to that house there."

The remote beach seemed lower than the sea, and it required a searching glance to discern the little black figure. The captain saw a floating stick and they rowed to it. A bath-towel was by some weird chance in the boat, and, tying this on the stick, the captain waved it. The oarsman did not dare turn his head, so he was obliged to ask questions.

"What's he doing now?"

"He's standing still again. He's looking, I think. . . . There he goes again. Toward the house. . . . Now he's stopped again."

"Is he waving at us?"

"No, not now! He was, though."

"Look! There comes another man!"

"He's running."

"Look at him go, would you."

"Why, he's on a bicycle. Now he's met the other man. They're both waving at us. Look!"

"There comes something up the beach."

"What the devil is that thing?"

"Why, it looks like a boat."

"Why, certainly it's a boat."

"No, it's on wheels."

"Yes, so it is. Well, that must be the life-boat. They drag them along shore on a wagon."

"That's the life-boat, sure."

"No, by, it's—it's an omnibus."

"I tell you it's a life-boat."

"It is not! It's an omnibus. I can see it plain. See? One of those big hotel omnibuses."

"By thunder, you're right. It's an omnibus, sure as fate. What do you suppose they are doing with an omnibus? Maybe they are going around collecting the life-crew, hey?"

"That's it, likely. Look! There's a fellow waving a little black flag. He's standing on the steps of the omnibus. There come those other two fellows. Now they're all talking together. Look at the fellow with the flag. Maybe he ain't waving it!"

"That ain't a flag, is it? That's his coat. Why, certainly, that's his coat."

"So it is. It's his coat. He's taken it off and is waving it around his head. But would you look at him swing it!"

"Oh, say, there isn't any life-saving station there. That's just a winter resort hotel omnibus that has brought over some of the boarders to see us drown."

"What's that idiot with the coat mean? What's he signaling, anyhow?"

"It looks as if he were trying to tell us to go north. There must be a life-saving station up there."

"No! He thinks we're fishing. Just giving us a merry hand. See? Ah, there, Willie."

"Well, I wish I could make something out of those signals. What do you suppose he means?"

"He don't mean anything. He's just playing."

"Well, if he'd just signal us to try the surf again, or to go to sea and wait, or go north, or go south, or go to hell—there would be some reason in it. But look at him. He just stands there and keeps his coat revolving like a wheel. The ass!"

"There come more people."

"Now there's quite a mob. Look! Isn't that a boat?"

"Where? Oh, I see where you mean. No, that's no boat."

"That fellow is still waving his coat."

"He must think we like to see him do that. Why don't he quit it. It don't mean anything."

"I don't know. I think he is trying to make us go north. It must be that there's a life-saving station there somewhere."

"Say, he ain't tired yet. Look at 'im wave."

"Wonder how long he can keep that up. He's been revolving his coat ever since he caught sight of us. He's an idiot. Why aren't they getting men to bring a boat out. A fishing boat—one of those big yawls—could come out here all right. Why don't he do something?"

"Oh, it's all right, now."

"They'll have a boat out here for us in less than no time, now that they've seen us."

A faint yellow tone came into the sky over the low land. The shadows on the sea slowly deepened. The wind bore coldness with it, and the men began to shiver.

"Holy smoke!" said one, allowing his voice to express his impious mood, "if we keep on monkeying out here! If we've got to flounder out here all night!"

"Oh, we'll never have to stay here all night! Don't you worry. They've seen us now, and it won't be long before they'll come chasing out after us."

The shore grew dusky. The man waving a coat blended gradually into this gloom, and it swallowed in the same manner the omnibus and the group of people. The spray, when it dashed uproariously over the side, made the voyagers shrink and swear like men who were being branded.

"I'd like to catch the chump who waved the coat. I feel like soaking him one, just for luck."

"Why? What did he do?"

"Oh, nothing, but then he seemed so damned cheerful."

In the meantime the oiler rowed, and then the correspondent rowed, and then the oiler rowed. Gray-faced and bowed forward, they mechanically, turn by turn, plied the leaden oars. The form of the light-house had vanished from the southern horizon, but finally a pale star appeared, just lifting from the sea. The streaked saffron in the west passed before the all merging darkness, and the sea to the east was black. The land had vanished and was expressed only by the low and drear thunder of the surf.

"If I am going to be drowned—if I am going to be drowned—if I am going to be drowned, why, in the name of the seven mad gods who rule the sea, was I allowed to come thus far and contemplate sand and trees? Was I brought here merely to have my nose dragged away as I was about to nibble the sacred cheese of life?"

The patient captain, drooped over the water-jar, was sometimes obliged to speak to the oarsman.

"Keep her head up! Keep her head up!"

" 'Keep her head up,' sir." The voices were weary and low.

This was surely a quiet evening. All save the oarsman lay heavily and listlessly in the boat's bottom. As for him, his eyes were just capable of noting the tall black waves that swept forward in a most sinister silence, save for an occasional subdued growl of a crest.

The cook's head was on a thwart, and he looked without interest at the water under his nose. He was deep in other scenes. Finally he spoke. "Billie," he murmured, dreamfully, "what kind of pie do you like best?"

V

"Pie," said the oiler and the correspondent, agitatedly. "Don't talk about those things, blast you!"

"Well," said the cook, "I was just thinking about ham sandwiches, and—"

A night on the sea in an open boat is a long night. As darkness settled finally, the shine of the light, lifting from the sea in the south, changed to full gold. On the northern horizon a new light appeared, a small bluish gleam on the edge of the waters. These two lights were the furniture of the world. Otherwise there was nothing but waves.

Two men huddled in the stern, and distances were so magnificent in the dingey that the rower was enabled to keep his feet partly warmed by thrusting them under his companions. Their legs indeed extended far under the rowing-seat until they touched the feet of the captain forward. Sometimes, despite the efforts of the tired oarsman, a wave came piling into the boat, an icy wave of the night, and the chilling water soaked them anew. They would twist their bodies for a moment and groan, and sleep the dead sleep once more, while the water in the boat gurgled about them as the craft rocked.

The plan of the oiler and the correspondent was for one to row until he lost the ability, and then arouse the other from his sea-water couch in the bottom of the boat.

The oiler plied the oars until his head drooped forward, and the overpowering sleep blinded him. And he rowed yet afterward. Then he touched a man in the bottom of the boat, and called his name. "Will you spell me for a little while?" he said, meekly.

"Sure, Billie," said the correspondent, awakening and dragging himself to a sitting position. They exchanged places carefully, and the oiler, cuddling down in the sea-water at the cook's side, seemed to go to sleep instantly.

The particular violence of the sea had ceased. The waves came without snarling. The obligation of the man at the oars was to keep the boat headed so that the tilt of the rollers would not capsize her, and to preserve her from filling when the crests rushed past. The black waves were silent and hard to be seen in the darkness. Often one was almost upon the boat before the oarsman was aware.

In a low voice the correspondent addressed the captain. He was not sure that the captain was awake, although this iron man seemed to be always awake. "Captain, shall I keep her making for that light north, sir?"

The same steady voice answered him. "Yes. Keep it about two points off the port bow."

The cook had tied a life-belt around himself in order to get even the warmth which this clumsy cork contrivance could donate, and he seemed almost stove-like when a rower, whose teeth invariably chattered wildly as soon as he ceased his labor, dropped down to sleep.

The correspondent, as he rowed, looked down at the two men sleeping under foot. The cook's arm was around the oiler's shoulders, and, with their fragmentary clothing and haggard faces, they were the babes of the sea, a grotesque rendering of the old babes in the wood.

Later he must have grown stupid at his work, for suddenly there was a growling of water, and a crest with a roar and a swash into the boat, and it was a wonder that it did not set the cook afloat in his life-belt. The cook continued to sleep, but the oiler sat up, blinking his eyes and shaking with the new cold.

"Oh, I'm awful sorry, Billie," said the correspondent, contritely.

"That's all right, old boy," said the oiler, and lay down again and was asleep.

Presently it seemed that even the captain dozed, and the correspondent thought that he was the one man afloat on all the oceans. The wind had a voice as it came over the waves, and it was sadder than the end.

There was a long, loud swishing astern of the boat, and a gleaming trail of phosphorescence, like blue flame, was furrowed on the black waters. It might have been made by a monstrous knife.

Then there came a stillness, while the correspondent breathed with the open mouth and looked at the sea.

Suddenly there was another swish and another long flash of bluish light, and this time it was alongside the boat, and might almost have been reached with an oar. The correspondent saw an enormous fin speed like a shadow through the water, hurling the crystalline spray and leaving the long glowing trail.

The correspondent looked over his shoulder at the captain. His face was hidden, and he seemed to be asleep. He looked at the babes of the sea. They certainly were asleep. So, being bereft of sympathy, he leaned a little way to one side and swore softly into the sea.

But the thing did not then leave the vicinity of the boat. Ahead or astern, on one side or the other, at intervals long or short, fled the long sparkling streak, and there was to be heard the whirroo of the dark fin. The speed and power of the thing were greatly to be admired. It cut the water like a gigantic and keen projectile.

The presence of this biding thing did not affect the man with the same horror that it would if he had been a picnicker. He simply looked at the sea dully and swore in an undertone.

Nevertheless, it is true that he did not wish to be alone with the thing. He wished one of his companions to awaken by chance and keep him company with it. But the captain hung motionless over the water-jar and the oiler and the cook in the bottom of the boat were plunged in slumber.

VI

"If I am going to be drowned—if I am going to be drowned—if I am going to be drowned, why, in the name of the seven mad gods who rule the sea, was I allowed to come thus far and contemplate sand and trees?"

During this dismal night, it may be remarked that a man would conclude that it was really the intention of the seven mad gods to drown him, despite the abominable injustice of it. For it was certainly an abominable injustice to drown a man who had worked so hard, so hard. The man felt it would be a crime most unnatural. Other people had drowned at sea since galleys swarmed with painted sails, but still—

When it occurs to a man that nature does not regard him as important, and that she feels she would not maim the universe by disposing of him, he at first wishes to throw bricks at the temple, and he hates deeply the fact that there are no bricks and no temples. Any visible expression of nature would surely be pelleted with his jeers.

Then, if there be no tangible thing to hoot he feels, perhaps, the desire to confront a personification and indulge in pleas, bowed to one knee, and with hands supplicant, saying: "Yes, but I love myself."

A high cold star on a winter's night is the word he feels that she says to him. Thereafter he knows the pathos of his situation.

The men in the dingey had not discussed these matters, but each had, no doubt, reflected upon them in silence and according to his mind. There was seldom any expression upon their faces save the general one of complete weariness. Speech was devoted to the business of the boat.

To chime the notes of his emotion, a verse mysteriously entered the correspondent's head. He had even forgotten that he had forgotten this verse, but it suddenly was in his mind.

> A soldier of the Legion lay dying in Algiers,
> There was lack of woman's nursing, there was dearth of woman's tears;
> But a comrade stood beside him, and he took that comrade's hand,
> And he said: "I never more shall see my own, my native land."

In his childhood, the correspondent had been made acquainted with the fact that a soldier of the Legion lay dying in Algiers, but he had never regarded it as important. Myriads of his school-fellows had informed him of the soldier's plight, but the dinning had naturally ended by making him perfectly indifferent. He had never considered it his affair that a soldier of the Legion lay dying in Algiers, nor had it appeared to him as a matter for sorrow. It was less to him than the breaking of a pencil's point.

Now, however, it quaintly came to him as a human, living thing. It was no longer merely a picture of a few throes in the breast of a poet, meanwhile drinking tea and warming his feet at the grate; it as an actuality—stern, mournful, and fine.

The correspondent plainly saw the soldier. He lay on the sand with his feet out straight and still. While his pale left hand was upon his chest in an attempt to thwart the going of his life, the blood came between his fingers. In the far Algerian distance, a city of low square forms was set against a sky that was faint with the last sunset hues. The correspondent, plying the oars and dreaming of the slow and slower movements of the lips of the soldier, was moved by a profound and perfectly impersonal comprehension. He was sorry for the soldier of the Legion who lay dying in Algiers.

The thing which had followed the boat and waited had evidently grown bored at the delay. There was no longer to be heard the slash of the cut-water, and there was no longer the flame of the long trail. The light in the north still glimmered, but it was apparently no nearer to the boat. Sometimes the boom of the surf rang in the correspondent's ears, and he turned the craft seaward then and rowed harder. Southward, some one had evidently built a watch-fire on the beach. It was too low and too far to be seen, but it made a shimmering, roseate reflection upon the bluff back of it, and this could be discerned from the boat. The wind came stronger, and sometimes a wave suddenly raged out like a mountain-cat and there was to be seen the sheen and sparkle of a broken crest.

The captain, in the bow, moved on his water-jar and sat erect. "Pretty long night," he observed to the correspondent. He looked at the shore. "Those life-saving people take their time."

"Did you see that shark playing around?"

"Yes, I saw him. He was a big fellow, all right."

"Wish I had known you were awake."

Later the correspondent spoke into the bottom of the boat.

"Billie!" There was a slow and gradual disentanglement. "Billie, will you spell me?"

"Sure," said the oiler.

As soon as the correspondent touched the cold comfortable sea-water in the bottom of the boat, and had huddled close to the cook's life-belt he was deep in sleep, despite the fact that his teeth played all the popular airs. This sleep was so good to him that it was but a moment before he heard a voice call his name in a tone that demonstrated the last stages of exhaustion. "Will you spell me?"

"Sure, Billie."

The light in the north had mysteriously vanished, but the correspondent took his course from the wide-awake captain.

Later in the night they took the boat farther out to sea, and the captain directed the cook to take one oar at the stern and keep the boat facing the seas. He was to call out if he should hear the thunder of the surf. This plan enabled the oiler and the correspondent to get respite together. "We'll give those boys a chance to get into shape again," said the captain. They curled down and, after a few preliminary chatterings and trembles, slept once more the dead sleep. Neither knew they had bequeathed to the cook the company of another shark, or perhaps the same shark.

As the boat caroused on the waves, spray occasionally bumped over the side and gave them a fresh soaking, but this had no power to break their repose. The ominous slash of the wind and the water affected them as it would have affected mummies.

"Boys," said the cook, with the notes of every reluctance in his voice, "she's drifted in pretty close. I guess one of you had better take her to sea again." The correspondent, aroused, heard the crash of the toppled crests.

As he was rowing, the captain gave him some whiskey and water, and this steadied the chills out of him. "If I ever get ashore and anybody shows me even a photograph of an oar—"

At last there was a short conversation.

"Billie. . . . Billie, will you spell me?"

"Sure," said the oiler.

VII

When the correspondent again opened his eyes, the sea and the sky were each of the gray hue of the dawning. Later, carmine and gold was painted upon the waters. The morning appeared finally, in its splendor, with a sky of pure blue, and the sunlight flamed on the tips of the waves.

On the distant dunes were set many little black cottages, and a tall white wind-mill reared above them. No man, nor dog, nor bicycle appeared on the beach. The cottages might have formed a deserted village.

The voyagers scanned the shore. A conference was held in the boat. "Well," said the captain, "if no help is coming, we might better try a run through the surf right away. If we stay out here much longer we will be too weak to do anything for ourselves at all." The others silently acquiesced in this reasoning. The boat was headed for the beach. The correspondent wondered if none ever ascended the tall wind-tower, and if then they never looked seaward. This tower was a giant, standing with its back to the plight of the ants. It represented in a degree, to the correspondent, the serenity of nature amid the struggles of the individual—nature in the wind, and nature in the vision of men. She did not seem cruel to him then, nor beneficent, nor treacherous, nor wise. But she was indifferent, flatly indifferent. It is, perhaps, plausible that a man in this situation, impressed with the unconcern of the universe, should see the innumerable flaws of his life and have them taste wickedly in his mind and wish for another chance. A distinction between right and wrong seems absurdly clear to him, then, in this new ignorance of the grave-edge, and he understands that if he were given another opportunity he would mend his conduct and his words, and be better and brighter during an introduction, or at a tea.

"Now, boys," said the captain, "she is going to swamp sure. All we can do is to work her in as far as possible, and then when she swamps, pile out and scramble for the beach. Keep cool now, and don't jump until she swamps sure."

The oiler took the oars. Over his shoulder he scanned the surf. "Captain," he said, "I think I'd better bring her about, and keep her head-on to the seas and back her in."

"All right, Billie," said the captain. "Back her in." The oiler swung the boat then and, seated in the stern, the cook and the correspondent were obliged to look over their shoulders to contemplate the lonely and indifferent shore.

The monstrous inshore rollers heaved the boat high until the men were again enabled to see the white sheets of water scudding up the slanted beach. "We won't get in very close," said the captain. Each time a man could wrest his attention from the rollers, he turned his glance toward the shore, and in the expression of the eyes during this contemplation there was a singular quality. The correspondent, observing the others, knew that they were not afraid, but the full meaning of their glances was shrouded.

As for himself, he was too tired to grapple fundamentally with the fact. He tried to coerce his mind into thinking of it, but the mind was dominated at this time by the muscles, and the muscles said they did not care. It merely occurred to him that if he should drown it would be a shame.

There were no hurried words, no pallor, no plain agitation. The men simply looked at the shore. "Now, remember to get well clear of the boat when you jump," said the captain.

Seaward the crest of a roller suddenly fell with a thunderous crash, and the long white comber came roaring down upon the boat.

"Steady now," said the captain. The men were silent. They turned their eyes from the shore to the comber and waited. The boat slid up the incline, leaped at the furious top, bounced over it, and swung down the long back of the wave. Some water had been shipped and the cook bailed it out.

But the next crest crashed also. The tumbling boiling flood of white water caught the boat and whirled it almost perpendicular. Water swarmed in from all sides. The correspondent had his hands on the gunwale at this time, and when the water entered at that place he swiftly withdrew his fingers, as if he objected to wetting them.

The little boat, drunken with this weight of water, reeled and snuggled deeper into the sea.

"Bail her out, cook! Bail her out," said the captain.

"All right, Captain," said the cook.

"Now boys, the next one will do for us, sure," said the oiler. "Mind to jump clear of the boat."

The third wave moved forward, huge, furious, implacable. It fairly swallowed the dingey, and almost simultaneously the men tumbled into the sea. A piece of life-belt had lain in the bottom of the boat, and as the correspondent went overboard he held this to his chest with his left hand.

The January water was icy, and he reflected immediately that it was colder than he had expected to find it off the coast of Florida. This appeared to his dazed mind as a fact important enough to be noted at the time. The coldness of the water was sad; it was tragic. This fact was somehow so mixed and confused with his opinion of his own situation that it seemed almost a proper reason for tears. The water was cold.

When he came to the surface he was conscious of little but the noisy water. Afterward he saw his companions in the sea. The oiler was ahead in the race. He was swimming strongly and rapidly. Off to the correspondent's left, the cook's great white and corked back bulged out of the water, and in the rear the captain was hanging with his one good hand to the keel of the overturned dingey.

There is a certain immovable quality to a shore, and the correspondent wondered at it amid the confusion of the sea.

It seemed also very attractive, but the correspondent knew that it was a long journey, and he paddled leisurely. The piece of life-preserver lay under him, and sometimes he whirled down the incline of a wave as if he were on a hand-sled.

But finally he arrived at a place in the sea where travel was beset with difficulty. He did not pause swimming to inquire what manner of current had caught him, but there his progress ceased. The shore was set before him like a bit of scenery on a stage, and he looked at it and understood with his eyes each detail of it.

As the cook passed, much farther to the left, the captain was calling to him, "Turn over on your back, cook! Turn over on your back and use the oar."

"All right, sir." The cook turned on his back, and, paddling with an oar, went ahead as if he were a canoe.

Presently the boat also passed to the left of the correspondent with the captain clinging with one hand to the keel. He would have appeared like a man raising himself to look over a board fence, if it were not for the extraordinary gymnastics of the boat. The correspondent marvelled that the captain could still hold to it.

They passed on, nearer to shore—the oiler, the cook, the captain—and following them went the water-jar, bouncing gayly over the seas.

The correspondent remained in the grip of this strange new enemy—a current. The shore, with its white slope of sand and its green bluff, topped with little silent cottages, was spread like a picture before him. It was very near to him then, but he was impressed as one who in a gallery looks at a scene from Brittany or Holland.

He thought: "I am going to drown? Can it be possible? Can it be possible? Can it be possible?" Perhaps an individual must consider his own death to be the final phenomenon of nature.

But later a wave perhaps whirled him out of his small deadly current, for he found suddenly that he could again make progress toward the shore. Later still, he was aware that the captain, clinging with one hand to the keel of the dingey, had his face turned away from the shore and toward him, and was calling his name. "Come to the boat! Come to the boat!"

In his struggle to reach the captain and the boat, he reflected that when one gets properly wearied, drowning must really be a comfortable arrangement, a cessation of hostilities accompanied by a large degree of relief, and he was glad of it, for the main thing in his mind for some moments had been the horror of the temporary agony. He did not wish to be hurt.

Presently he saw a man running along the shore. He was undressing with most remarkable speed. Coat, trousers, shirt, everything flew magically off him.

"Come to the boat," called the captain.

"All right, Captain." As the correspondent paddled, he saw the captain let himself down to bottom and leave the boat. Then the correspondent performed his one little marvel of the voyage. A large wave caught him and flung him with ease and supreme speed completely over the boat and far beyond it. It struck him even then as an event in gymnastics, and a true miracle of the sea. An overturned boat in the surf is not a plaything to a swimming man.

The correspondent arrived in water that reached only to his waist, but his condition did not enable him to stand for more than a moment. Each wave knocked him into a heap, and the under-tow pulled at him.

Then he saw the man who had been running and undressing, and undressing and running, come bounding into the water. He dragged ashore the cook, and then waded toward the captain, but the captain waved him away, and sent him to the correspondent. He was naked, naked as a tree in winter, but a halo was about his head, and he shone like a saint. He gave a strong pull, and a long drag, and a bully heave at the correspondent's hand. The correspondent, schooled in the minor formulae, said: "Thanks, old man." But suddenly the man cried: "What's that?" He pointed a swift finger. The correspondent said: "Go."

In the shallows, face downward, lay the oiler. His forehead touched sand that was periodically, between each wave, clear of the sea.

The correspondent did not know all that transpired afterward. When he achieved safe ground he fell, striking the sand with each particular part of his body. It was as if he had dropped from a roof, but the thud was grateful to him.

It seems that instantly the beach was populated with men with blankets, clothes, and flasks, and women with coffee-pots and all the remedies sacred to their minds. The welcome of the land to the men from the sea was warm and generous, but a still and dripping shape was carried slowly up the beach, and the land's welcome for it could only be the different and sinister hospitality of the grave.

When it came night, the white waves paced to and fro in the moonlight, and the wind brought the sound of the great sea's voice to the men on shore, and they felt that they could then be interpreters.

Isaac Babel

Isaac Babel (1894–1941) was born in Odessa, Russia, into a Jewish family. His family placed a great premium on education (the title of one of his autobiographical stories is "You Must Know Everything"), and the boy was given rigorous schooling in languages. Inspired by a love of French, Babel tried his hand early at short stories in the mode of Guy de Maupassant. In time, he became a master of conveying vivid impressions through the use of precise, often odd, details.

Babel moved to St. Petersburg in 1915 and tried to build a literary career. When his early attempts at publication failed, he enlisted in the army and served at the Romanian front during World War I and with the Soviet cavalry in the civil war that followed the 1917 Bolshevik revolution. Most of the stories Babel published during the 1920s, including his celebrated collection, *Red Cavalry,* draw upon his war experiences.

During the Stalinist purges of the 1930s, Babel was persecuted for his ideological leanings as well as for his Jewishness. He was arrested in 1939 by Soviet authorities and sent to a concentration camp, where he died. Babel is cherished today for his charged, pointed prose and for his affirmation of individual dignity in the face of suffering.

GUY DE MAUPASSANT

In the winter of 1916 I found myself in St. Petersburg with a forged passport and not a cent to my name. Alexey Kazantsev, a teacher of Russian literature, took me into his house.

He lived on a yellow, frozen, evil-smelling street in the Peski district. The miserable salary he received was padded out a bit by doing translations from the Spanish. Blasco Ibáñez was just becoming famous at that time.

Kazantsev had never so much as passed through Spain, but his love for that country filled his whole being. He knew every castle, every garden, and every river in Spain. There were many other people huddling around Kazantsev, all of them, like myself, flung out of the round of ordinary life. We were half-starved. From time to time the yellow press would publish, in the smallest print, unimportant news-items we had written.

I spent my mornings hanging around the morgues and police stations.

Kazantsev was happier than any of us, for he had a country of his own—Spain.

In November I was given the chance to become a clerk at the Obukhov Mills. It was a rather good position, and would have exempted me from military service.

I refused to become a clerk.

Even in those days, when I was twenty years old, I had told myself: better starve, go to jail, or become a bum than spend ten hours every day behind a desk in an office.

There was nothing particularly laudable in my resolve, but I have never broken it and I never will. The wisdom of my ancestors was firmly lodged in my head: we are born to enjoy our work, our fights, and our love; we are born for that and for nothing else.

Listening to my bragging, Kazantsev ruffled the short yellow fluff on the top of his head. The horror in his stare was mixed with admiration.

At Christmastime we had luck. Bendersky the lawyer, who owned a publishing house called "Halcyon," decided to publish a new edition of Maupassant's works. His wife Raïsa tried her hand at the translation, but nothing came of her lofty ambition.

Kazantsev, who was known as a translator of Spanish, had been asked whether he could recommend someone to assist Raïsa Mikhaylovna. He told them of me.

The next day, in someone else's coat, I made my way to the Benderskys'. They lived at the corner of the Nevsky and the Moyka, in a house of Finland granite adorned with pink columns, crenellations and coats-of-arms worked in stone.

Bankers without a history and catapulted out of nowhere, converted Jews who had grown rich selling materials to the army, they put up these pretentious mansions in St. Petersburg before the war.

There was a red carpet on the stairs. On the landings, upon their hind legs, stood plush bears. Crystal lamps burned in their open mouths.

The Benderskys lived on the second floor. A high-breasted maid with a white cap on her head opened the door. She led me into a drawing-room decorated in the old Slav style. Blue paintings by Roerich depicting prehistoric stones and monsters hung on the walls. On stands in the corners stood ancestral icons.

The high-breasted maid moved smoothly and majestically. She had an excellent figure, was nearsighted and rather haughty. In her open gray eyes one saw a petrified lewdness. She moved slowly. I thought: when she makes love she must move with unheard-of agility. The brocade portiere over the doorway suddenly swayed, and a black-haired woman with pink eyes and a wide bosom entered the room. It was easy to recognize in Raïsa Bendersky one of those charming Jewesses who have come to us from Kiev and Poltava, from the opulent steppe-towns full of chestnut trees and acacias. The money made by their clever husbands is transformed by these women into a pink layer of fat on the belly, the back of the neck, and the well-rounded shoulders. Their subtle sleepy smiles drive officers from the local garrisons crazy.

"Maupassant," Raïsa said to me, "is the only passion of my life."

Trying to keep the swaying of her great hips under control, she left the room and returned with a translation of "Miss Harriet." In her translation not even a trace was left of Maupassant's free-flowing sentences with their fragrance of passion. Raïsa Bendersky took pains to write correctly and precisely, and all that resulted was something loose and lifeless, the way Jews wrote Russian in the old days.

I took the manuscript with me, and in Kazantsev's attic, among my sleeping friends, spent the night cutting my way through the tangled undergrowth of her prose. It was not such dull work as it might seem. A phrase is born into the world both good and bad at the same time. The secret lies in a slight, an almost invisible twist. The lever should rest in your hand, getting warm, and you can only turn it once, not twice.

Next morning I took back the corrected manuscript. Raïsa wasn't lying when she told me that Maupassant was her sole passion. She sat motionless, her hands clasped, as I read it to her. Her satin hands drooped to the floor, her forehead paled, and the lace between her constricted breasts danced and heaved.

"How did you do it?"

I began to speak of style, of the army of words, of the army in which all kinds of weapons may come into play. No iron can stab the heart with such force as a period put just at the right place. She listened with her head down and her painted lips half open. In her hair, pressed smooth, divided by a parting and looking like patent leather, shone a dark gleam. Her legs in tight-fitting stockings, with their strong soft calves, were planted wide apart on the carpet.

The maid, glancing to the side with her petrified wanton eyes, brought in breakfast on a tray.

The glassy rays of the Petersburg sun lay on the pale and uneven carpet. Twenty-nine volumes of Maupassant stood on the shelf above the desk. The sun with its fingers of melting dissolution touched the morocco backs of the books—the magnificent grave of a human heart.

Coffee was served in blue cups, and we started translating "Idyl." Everyone remembers the story of the youthful, hungry carpenter who sucked the breast of the stout nursing-mother to relieve her of the milk with which she was overladen. It happened in a train going from Nice to Marseille, at noon on a very hot day, in the land of roses, the birthplace of roses, where beds of flowers flow down to the seashore.

I left the Benderskys with a twenty-five rouble advance. That night our crowd at Peski got as drunk as a flock of drugged geese. Between drinks we spooned up the best caviar, and then changed over to liver sausage. Half-soused, I began to berate Tolstoy.

"He turned yellow, your Count; he was afraid. His religion was all fear. He was frightened by the cold, by old age, by death; and he made himself a warm coat out of his faith."

"Go on, go on," Kazantsev urged, swaying his birdlike head.

We fell asleep on the floor beside our beds. I dreamed of Katya, a forty-year-old washerwoman who lived a floor below us. We went to her every morning for our hot water. I had never seen her face distinctly, but in my dream we did god-awful things together. We almost destroyed each other with kisses. The very next morning I couldn't restrain myself from going to her for hot water.

I saw a wan woman, a shawl across her chest, with ash-gray hair and labor-worn, withered hands.

From then on I took my breakfast at the Benderskys' every day. A new stove, herrings, and chocolate appeared in our attic. Twice Raïsa took me out in her carriage for drives to the islands. I couldn't prevent myself from telling her all about my childhood. To my amazement the story turned out of to be very sordid. From under her moleskin cowl her gleaming, frightened eyes stared at me. The rusty fringe of her eyelashes quivered with pity.

I met Raïsa's husband, a yellow-faced Jew with a bald skull and a flat, powerful body that seemed always poised obliquely, ready for flight.

There were rumors about his being close to Rasputin. The enormous profits he made from war supplies drove him almost crazy, giving him the expression of a person with a fixed hallucination. His eyes never remained still: it seemed that reality was lost to him for ever. Raïsa was embarrassed whenever she had to introduce him to new acquaintances. Because of my youth I noticed this a full week later than I should have.

After the New Year Raïsa's two sisters arrived from Kiev. One day I took along the manuscript of *"L'Aveu"* and, not finding Raïsa at home, returned that evening. They were at dinner. Silvery, neighing laughter and excited male voices came from the dining-room. In rich houses without tradition dinners are always noisy. It was a Jewish noise, rolling and tripping and ending up on a melodious, singsong note. Raïsa came out to me in evening dress, her back bare. Her feet stepped awkwardly in wavering patent-leather slippers.

"I'm drunk, darling," she said, and held out her arms, loaded with chains of platinum and emerald stars.

Her body swayed like a snake's dancing to music. She tossed her marcelled hair about, and suddenly, with a tinkle of rings, slumped into a chair with ancient Russian carvings. Scars glowed on her powered back.

Women's laughter again came from the dining-room. Raïsa's sisters, with delicate mustaches and as full-bosomed and round-bodied as Raïsa herself, entered the room. Their busts jutted out and their black hair fluttered. Both of them had their own Benderskys for husbands. The room was filled with disjointed, chaotic feminine merriment, the hilarity of ripe women. The husbands wrapped the sisters in their sealskins and Orenburg shawls and shod them in black boots. Beneath the snowy visors of their shawls only painted glowing cheeks, marble noses, and eyes with their myopic Jewish glitter could be seen. After making some more happy noise they left for the theater, where Chaliapin was singing *Judith.*

"I want to work," Raïsa lisped, stretching her bare arms to me, "we've skipped a whole week."

She brought a bottle and two glasses from the dining-room. Her breasts swung free beneath the sacklike gown, the nipples rose beneath the clinging silk.

"It's very valuable," said Raïsa, pouring out the wine. "Muscatel '83. My husband will kill me when he finds out."

I had never drunk Muscatel '83, and tossed off three glasses one after the other without thinking. They carried me swiftly away into alleys where an orange flame danced and sounds of music could be heard.

"I'm drunk, darling. What are we doing today?"

"Today it's '*L'Aveu*'. 'The Confession,' then. The sun is the hero of this story, *le soleil de France.* Molten drops of it pattering on the red-haired Céleste changed into freckles. The sun's direct rays and wine and apple-cider burnished the face of the coachman Polyte. Twice a week Céleste drove into town to sell cream, eggs and chickens. She gave Polyte ten sous for herself and four for her basket. And every time Polyte would wink at the red-haired Céleste and ask: 'When are we going to have some fun, *ma belle*?'—'What do you mean, Monsieur Polyte?' Jogging up and down on the box, the coachman explained: 'To have some fun means . . . why, what the hell, to have some fun! A lad with a lass; no music necessary . . .'

" 'I do not care for such jokes, Monsieur Polyte,' replied Céleste, moving further away the skirts that hung over her mighty calves in red stockings.

"But that devil Polyte kept right on guffawing and coughing: 'Ah, but one day we shall have our bit of fun, *ma belle,*' while tears of delight rolled down a face the color of brick-red wine and blood."

I downed another glass of the rare muscatel. Raïsa touched glasses with me. The maid with the stony eyes crossed the room and disappeared.

"*Ce diable de Polyte* . . . In the course of two years Céleste had paid him forty-eight francs; that is, two francs short of fifty! At the end of the second year, when they were alone in the carriage, Polyte, who had some cider before setting out, asked her his usual question: 'What about having some fun today, Mamselle Céleste?' And she replied, lowering her eyes: 'I am at your disposal, Monsieur Polyte.' "

Raïsa flung herself down on the table, laughing. "*Ce diable de Polyte* . . ."

"A white spavined mare was harnessed to the carriage. The white hack, its lips pink with age, went forward at a walking pace. The gay sun of France poured down on the ancient coach, screened from the world by a weatherbeaten hood. A lad with a lass; no music necessary . . ."

Raïsa held out a glass to me. It was the fifth.

"*Mon vieux,* to Maupassant."

"And what about having some fun today, *ma belle?*"

I reached over to Raïsa and kissed her on the lips. They quivered and swelled.

"You're funny," she mumbled through her teeth, recoiling.

She pressed herself against the wall, stretching out her bare arms. Spots began to glow on her arms and shoulders. Of all the gods ever put on the crucifix, this was the most ravishing.

"Be so kind as to sit down, Monsieur Polyte."

She pointed to an oblique blue armchair done in Slavonic style. Its back was constructed of carved interlacing bands with colorful pendants. I groped my way to it, stumbling as I went.

Night had blocked the path of my famished youth with a bottle of Muscatel '83 and twenty-nine books, twenty-nine bombs stuffed with pity, genius and passion. I sprang up, knocking over the chair and banging against the shelf. The twenty-nine volumes crashed to the floor, their pages flew open, they fell on their edges . . . and the white mare of my fate went on at a walking pace.

"You are funny," growled Raïsa.

I left the granite house on the Moyka between eleven and twelve, before the sisters and the husband returned from the theater. I was sober and could have walked a chalk line, but it was pleasanter to stagger, so I swayed from side to side, singing in a language I had just invented. Through the tunnels of the streets bounded by lines of street lights the steamy fog billowed. Monsters roared behind the boiling walls. The roads amputated the legs of those walking on them.

Kazantsev was asleep when I got home. He slept sitting up, his thin legs extended in their felt boots. The canary fluff rose on his head. He had fallen asleep by the stove bending over a volume of *Don Quixote,* the edition of 1624. On the title-page of the book was a dedication to the Duc de Broglie. I got into bed quietly, so as not to wake Kazantsev; moved the lamp close to me and began to read a book by Edouard Maynial on Guy de Maupassant's life and work.

Kazantsev's lips moved; his head kept keeling over.

That night I learned from Edouard Maynial that Maupassant was born in 1850, the child of a Normandy gentleman and Laure Lepoiteven, Flaubert's cousin. He was twenty-five when he was first attacked by congenital syphilis. His productivity and *joie de vivre* withstood the onsets of the disease. At first he suffered from headaches and fits of hypochondria. Then the specter of blindness arose before him. His sight weakened. He became suspicious of everyone, unsociable and pettily quarrelsome. He struggled furiously, dashed about the Mediterranean in a yacht, fled to Tunis, Morocco, Central Africa . . . and wrote ceaselessly. He attained fame, and at forty years of age cut his throat; lost a great deal of blood, yet lived through it. He was then put away in a madhouse. There he crawled about on his hands and knees, devouring his own excrement. The last line in his hospital report read: *Monsieur de Maupassant va s'animaliser.* He died at the age of forty-two, his mother surviving him.

I read the book to the end and got out of bed. The fog came close to the window, the world was hidden from me. My heart contracted as the foreboding of some essential truth touched me with light fingers.

Yasunari Kawabata

Yasunari Kawabata (1899–1972) was born in Osaka, Japan. He lost his family while he was still a child, a fact that accounts in some part for the loneliness and melancholy that tinge many of his writings. Kawabata graduated from the Tokyo Imperial University in 1924, and the following year published his first novel, *The Izu Dancer.* Many novels and short stories followed, and by the 1940s he was recognized as Japan's leading writer. Readers found much to admire both in his exploration of the deep struggle between the traditional and modern in Japanese society and in his delicate way of suggesting nuance through detail. Some of Kawabata's major novels include *Thousand Cranes, The Sound of the Mountain*, and *The Old Capital.* He was awarded the Nobel prize for literature in 1968, the first Japanese thus honored. He committed suicide four years later.

A SMILE OUTSIDE THE NIGHT STALL

I stopped short. It must have been two hours since the Hakuhin, a building that always closes at the same time in the evening, had tightly shut its doors. My back to those doors on the thoroughfare in Ueno, I had stopped in front of a firecracker stand and an optician's stall. I had been looking at the crowds on the pavement from evening into night, and, to my eyes, the dirt sidewalk, whose breadth was the space between the Hakuhin and the night stalls, seemed curiously wide, so that I felt shy about walking down the middle of it. Each time a belated pedestrian went by, the color of the packed, water-sprinkled dirt sank all the more blackly into itself, and the scraps of wastepaper floated up all the more whitely. It was late at night. The wagon of a vendor who had closed shop moved off. At the firecracker stand, unwrapped firecracker sticks; Azuma Peonies; Flower Wheels; Land Mines wrapped in colored paper bags; Snow, Moon, and Flowers; and Three-Colored Pine Needles in colored paper boxes were lined up in red-ochre rows. At the optician's stall, old-age glasses; glasses for the nearsighted; tinted glasses; glasses for show with frames of gold (probably gilt), silver, gold and copper alloy, steel, or tortoiseshell; binoculars; dust goggles; swimming goggles; magnifying glasses; and the like were ranged in rows. But I wasn't looking at the firecrackers or the eyeglasses.

The firecracker stand and the optician's stall were about three feet apart. Since no one was looking at their goods, the two vendors had come out of their stalls and seemed to be doing something together in that three-foot space. If the glasses vendor had moved two feet into the space and the firecracker vendor one foot, it was only because the firecracker girl had shifted her shop bench, too, while the glasses vendor had left his bench behind his stall. He didn't seem to miss it.

Floating up on his toes, his legs slightly spread, the man pressed down hard on his left knee with the elbow to which he entrusted the weight of his bent-over upper body. With a girl's short bamboo clog, which he dangled between his legs from his right hand, he was busy writing characters in the black dirt.

The girl was intently reading, from the top down, the column of characters being written by the man. The bench on which she sat was low and her clogs had teeth so that her knees were raised and slightly parted. Her shop apron dangling between her legs, she bent over so that her small breasts pressed against her knees; her arms hung down around them, her hands resting lightly, palms upward, on her insteps. Her crudely patterned summer kimono was somewhat sweat-stained, and her "cleft-peach" coiffure had come slightly undone. Because of her breasts pressing against the slightly parted knees, the collar of her kimono clung to her nape and, in front, revealed a little of her bosom.

Observing these two and the ground being written on, I loitered nearby. Although I could take the pair in at a glance, I wasn't able to make out the characters inscribed by the clog. The man, not erasing a character once he had written it but simply writing over it, kept doing one after the other. Even so, the firecracker girl could probably read them. When some meaning had been completed there on the ground, without thinking to or knowing it, the two would suddenly raise their faces and glance at each other. But, before they could smile at each other or say something with their eyes or lips, the girl would drop her eyes to the ground and the man would start to write again. The girl had the slender fingers and waist of a child born to a poor family in old down-town Tokyo, but she seemed to have shot up ahead of her years.

When the man had written three or four new characters, the girl abruptly leaned forward off the bench. Reaching out her left hand that had rested on her instep, she tried to snatch the clog away from the man. The man nimbly withdrew his hand. They exchanged glances. But neither said a word, and neither showed any change of expression. It was strange. The girl docilely brought her hand back to her instep. The man planted himself solidly on his heels, spread his knees farther apart, and began to write another character. This time, before he had finished the character, the girl shot out her left hand like lightning. But the man's hand was even quicker. Giving up, the firecracker girl again drew back her hand docilely. As she was returning her hand to her instep, she suddenly turned her face to the side and met my eye. I wasn't ready for such an encounter. Involuntarily, she flashed me a little smile. I, also involuntarily, gave her a little smile in return.

The firecracker girl's smile passed straight into my heart. As I watched the postures and actions of the couple, the smile that was in my heart was lured to the surface in all its purity by the girl. It was an innocent smile.

The man, drawn by the direction of the girl's gaze, also looked at me. Giving me a sly grin, he then immediately put on a stern face. Suddenly I felt chilled. The girl, blushing slightly, raised her left hand to her cleft-peach hairdo as if to tidy it. Her face was hidden by her sleeve. All of this had taken place in the short space of time after the girl had stretched out her hand to snatch the bamboo clog from the man. Although I lightly parried the ill will of the look he threw at me, I felt ashamed of having stolen other people's secrets. I walked away.

Glasses vendor! Your displeasure is understandable. Probably you did not know it, but the girl's blushing and hiding her face with her sleeve must have been on your account. Because a little smile that bloomed fleetingly outside the night stall was stolen from you by me. Of course, even though you glanced at each other, you were so intent on what you were doing that your faces were almost expressionless. So the girl's smile ought to have been given to you. If only I hadn't been looking, you probably would have given the girl the same smile in return. However, if I stole a glimpse and a moment of that time before the girl's father or older brother came for her, if my innocent smile at that instant mirrored the girl's own smile, didn't you in turn give me a hard look along with your sly smile? If I may use the terms of your trade, the spectacles of your heart are slightly clouded and out of focus. But there is tomorrow evening, and the evening after. Write down thousands, hundreds of thousands of characters in the dirt until you reach the center of the earth!

Firecracker girl! Left-handed girl! For you, it's probably all the same, but I worry that, as you peer down into the well that the glasses dealer, by writing thousands and hundreds of millions of characters, will carve into the earth with the bamboo clog, you may have a dizzy spell and fall down that well. I cannot tell whether it is better to fall down such a well or to guard against falling. Probably it would be best for you to follow behind the wagon that your father or older brother, who has come for you, draws behind him, thinking of the glasses dealer as you walk along the deserted streets of the neighborhood. . . . But how would it be if you were to set off all at once all of the firecrackers lined up in your stall—the Azuma

Peonies, the Flower Wheels, the Land Mines, the Snow, Moon, and Flowers, the Three-Colored Pine Needles—making a flower of fire bloom in the lonely night? If you did that, even the glasses vendor might jump up in absolute astonishment and run away.

Translated by Lane Dunlop and J. Martin Holman

Frank O'Connor

FIRST CONFESSION

All the trouble began when my grandfather died and my grandmother—my father's mother—came to live with us. Relations in the one house are a strain at the best of times, but, to make matters worse, my grandmother was a real old country woman and quite unsuited to the life in town. She had a fat, wrinkled old face, and, to Mother's great indignation, went round the house in bare feet—the boots had her crippled, she said. For dinner she had a jug of porter and a pot of potatoes with—sometimes—a bit of salt fish, and she poured out the potatoes on the table and ate them slowly, with great relish, using her fingers by way of a fork.

Now, girls are supposed to be fastidious, but I was the one who suffered most from this. Nora, my sister, just sucked up to the old woman for the penny she got every Friday out of the old-age pension, a thing I could not do. I was too honest, that was my trouble; and when I was playing with Bill Connell, the sergeant-major's son, and saw my grandmother steering up the path with the jug of porter sticking out from beneath her shawl I was mortified. I made excuses not to let him come into the house, because I could never be sure what she would be up to when we went in.

When Mother was at work and my grandmother made the dinner I wouldn't touch it. Nora once tried to make me, but I hid under the table from her and took the bread-knife with me for protection. Nora let on to be very indignant (she wasn't, of course, but she knew Mother saw through her, so she sided with Gran) and came after me. I lashed out at her with the bread-knife, and after that she left me alone. I stayed there till Mother came in from work and made my dinner, but when Father came in later Nora said in a shocked voice: "Oh, Dadda, do you know what Jackie did at dinnertime?" Then, of course, it all came out; Father gave me a flaking; Mother interfered, and for days after that he didn't speak to me and Mother barely spoke to Nora. And all because of that old woman! God knows, I was heart-scalded.

Then, to crown my misfortunes, I had to make my first confession and Communion. It was an old woman called Ryan who prepared us for these. She was about the one age with Gran; she was well-to-do, lived in a big house on Montenotte, wore a black cloak and bonnet, and came every day to school at three o'clock when we should have been going home, and talked to us of Hell. She may have mentioned the other place as well, but that could only have been by accident, for Hell had the first place in her heart.

She lit a candle, took out a new half-crown, and offered it to the first boy who would hold one finger—only one finger!—in the flame for five minutes by the school clock. Being always very ambitious I was tempted to volunteer, but I thought it might look greedy. Then she asked were we afraid of holding one finger—only one finger!—in a little candle flame for five minutes and not afraid of burning all over in roasting hot furnaces for all eternity. "All eternity! Just think of that! A whole lifetime goes by and it's nothing, not even a drop in the ocean of your sufferings." The woman was really interesting about Hell, but my attention was all fixed on the half-crown. At the end of the lesson she put it back in her purse. It was a great disappointment; a religious woman like that, you wouldn't think she'd bother about a thing like a half-crown.

Another day she said she knew a priest who woke one night to find a fellow he didn't recognize leaning over the end of his bed. The priest was a bit frightened—naturally enough—but he asked the fellow what he wanted, and the fellow said in a deep, husky voice that he wanted to go to Confession. The priest said it was an awkward time and wouldn't it do in the morning, but the fellow said that last time he went to Confession, there was one sin he kept back, being ashamed to mention it, and now it was always on his mind. Then the priest knew it was a bad case, because the fellow was after making a bad confession and committing a mortal sin. He got up to dress, and just then the cock crew in the yard outside, and—lo and behold!—when the priest looked round there was no sign of the fellow, only a smell of burning timber, and when the priest looked at his bed didn't he see the print of two hands burned in it? That was because the fellow had made a bad confession. This story made a shocking impression on me.

But the worst of all was when she showed us how to examine our conscience. Did we take the name of the Lord, our God, in vain? Did we honor our father and our mother? (I asked her did this include grandmothers and she said it did.) Did we love our neighbor as ourselves? Did we covet our neighbor's goods? (I thought of the way I felt about the penny that Nora got every Friday.) I decided that, between one thing and another, I must have broken the whole ten commandments, all on account of that old woman, and so far as I could see, so long as she remained in the house I had no hope of ever doing anything else.

I was scared to death of Confession. The day the whole class went I let on to have a toothache, hoping my absence wouldn't be noticed; but at three o'clock, just as I was feeling safe, along comes a chap with a message from Mrs. Ryan that I was to go to Confession myself on Saturday and be at the chapel for Communion with the rest. To make it worse, Mother couldn't come with me and sent Nora instead.

Now, that girl had ways of tormenting me that Mother never knew of. She held my hand as we went down the hill, smiling sadly and saying how sorry she was for me, as if she were bringing me to the hospital for an operation.

"Oh, God help us!" she moaned. "Isn't it a terrible pity you weren't a good boy? Oh, Jackie, my heart bleeds for you! How will you ever think of all your sins? Don't forget you have to tell him about the time you kicked Gran on the shin."

"Lemme go!" I said, trying to drag myself free of her. "I don't want to go to Confession at all."

"But sure, you'll have to go to Confession, Jackie," she replied in the same regretful tone. "Sure, if you didn't, the parish priest would be up to the house, looking for you. 'Tisn't, God knows, that I'm not sorry for you. Do you remember the time you tried to kill me with the bread-knife under the table? And the language you used to me? I don't know what he'll do with you at all, Jackie. He might have to send you up to the Bishop."

I remember thinking bitterly that she didn't know the half of what I had to tell—if I told it. I knew I couldn't tell it, and understood perfectly why the fellow in Mrs. Ryan's story made a bad confession; it seemed to me a great shame that people wouldn't stop criticizing him. I remember that steep hill down to the church, and the sunlit hillsides beyond the valley of the river, which I saw in the gaps between the houses like Adam's last glimpse of Paradise.

Then, when she had manoeuvred me down the long flight of steps to the chapel yard, Nora suddenly changed her tone. She became the raging malicious devil she really was.

"There you are!" she said with a yelp of triumph, hurling me through the church door. "And I hope he'll give you the penitential psalms, you dirty little caffler."

I knew then I was lost, given up to eternal justice. The door with the colored-glass panels swung shut behind me, the sunlight went out and gave place to deep shadow, and the wind whistled outside so that the silence within seemed to crackle like ice under my feet. Nora sat in front of me by the confession box. There were a couple of old women ahead of her, and then a miserable-looking poor devil came and wedged me in at the other side, so that I couldn't escape even if I had the courage. He joined his hands and rolled his eyes in the direction of the roof, muttering aspirations in an anguished tone, and I wondered had he a grandmother too. Only a grandmother could account for a fellow behaving in that heartbroken way, but he was better off than I, for he at least could go and confess his sins; while I would make a bad confession and then die in the night and be continually coming back and burning people's furniture.

Nora's turn came, and I heard the sound of something slamming, and then her voice as if butter wouldn't melt in her mouth, and then another slam, and out she came. God, the hypocrisy of women! Her eyes were lowered, her head was bowed, and her hands were joined very low down on her stomach, and she walked up the aisle to the side altar looking like a saint. You never saw such an exhibition of devotion; and I remembered the devilish malice with which she had tormented me all the way from our door, and wondered were all religious people like that, really. It was my turn now. With the fear of damnation in my soul I went in, and the confessional door closed of itself behind me.

It was pitch-dark and I couldn't see priest or anything else. Then I really began to be frightened. In the darkness it was a matter between God and me, and He had all the odds. He knew what my intentions were before I even started; I had no chance. All I had ever been told about Confession got mixed up in my mind, and I knelt to one wall and said: "Bless me, father, for I have sinned; this is my first confession." I waited for a few minutes, but nothing happened, so I tried it on the other wall. Nothing happened there either. He had me spotted all right.

It must have been then that I noticed the shelf at about one height with my head. It was really a place for grown-up people to rest their elbows, but in my distracted state I thought it was probably the place you were supposed to kneel. Of course, it was on the high side and not very deep, but I was always good at climbing and managed to get up all right. Staying up was the trouble. There was room only for my knees, and nothing you could get a grip on but a sort of wooden molding a bit above it. I held on to the molding and repeated the words a little louder, and this time something happened all right. A slide was slammed back; a little light entered the box, and a man's voice said: "Who's there?"

" 'Tis me, father," I said for fear he mightn't see me and go away again. I couldn't see him at all. The place the voice came from was under the molding, about level with my knees, so I took a good grip of the molding and swung myself down till I saw the astonished face of a young priest looking up at me. He had to put his head on one side to see me, and I had to put mine on one side to see him, so we were more or less talking to one another upside-down. It struck me as a queer way of hearing confessions, but I didn't feel it my place to criticize.

"Bless me, father, for I have sinned; this is my first confession," I rattled off all in one breath, and swung myself down the least shade more to make it easier for him.

"What are you doing up there?" he shouted in an angry voice, and the strain the politeness was putting on my hold of the molding, and the shock of being addressed in such an uncivil tone, were too much for me. I lost my grip, tumbled, and hit the door an unmerciful wallop before I found myself flat on my back in the middle of the aisle. The people who had been waiting stood up with their mouths open. The priest opened the door of the middle box and came out, pushing his biretta back from his forehead; he looked something terrible. Then Nora came scampering down the aisle.

"Oh, you dirty little caffler!" she said. "I might have known you'd do it. I might have known you'd disgrace me. I can't leave you out of my sight for one minute."

Before I could even get to my feet to defend myself she bent down and gave me a clip across the ear. This reminded me that I was so stunned I had even forgotten to cry, so that people might think I wasn't hurt at all, when in fact I was probably maimed for life. I gave a roar out of me.

"What's all this about?" the priest hissed, getting angrier than ever and pushing Nora off me. "How dare you hit the child like that, you little vixen?"

"But I can't do my penance with him, father," Nora cried, cocking an outraged eye up at him.

"Well, go and do it, or I'll give you some more to do," he said, giving me a hand up. "Was it coming to Confession you were, my poor man?" he asked me.

" 'Twas, father," said I with a sob.

"Oh," he said respectfully, "a big hefty fellow like you must have terrible sins. Is this your first?"

" 'Tis, father," said I.

"Worse and worse," he said gloomily. "The crimes of a lifetime. I don't know will I get rid of you at all today. You'd better wait now till I'm finished with these old ones. You can see by the looks of them they haven't much to tell."

"I will, father," I said with something approaching joy.

The relief of it was really enormous. Nora stuck out her tongue at me from behind his back, but I couldn't even be bothered retorting. I knew from the very moment that man opened his mouth that he was intelligent above the ordinary. When I had time to think, I saw how right I was. It only stood to reason that a fellow confessing after seven years would have more to tell than people that went every week. The crimes of a lifetime, exactly as he said. It was only what he expected, and the rest was the cackle of old women and girls with their talk of Hell, the Bishop, and the penitential psalms. That was all they knew. I started to make my examination of conscience, and barring the one bad business of my grandmother it didn't seem so bad.

The next time, the priest steered me into the confession box himself and left the shutter back the way I could see him get in and sit down at the further side of the grille from me.

"Well, now," he said, "what do they call you?"

"Jackie, father," said I.

"And what's a-trouble to you, Jackie?"

"Father," I said, feeling I might as well get it over while I had him in good humor, "I had it all arranged to kill my grandmother."

He seemed a bit shaken by that, all right, because he said nothing for quite a while.

"My goodness," he said at last, "that'd be a shocking thing to do. What put that into your head?"

"Father," I said, feeling very sorry for myself, "she's an awful woman."

"Is she?" he asked. "What way is she awful?"

"She takes porter, father," I said, knowing well from the way Mother talked of it that this was a mortal sin, and hoping it would make the priest take a more favorable view of my case.

"Oh, my!" he said, and I could see he was impressed.

"And snuff, father," said I.

"That's a bad case, sure enough, Jackie," he said.

"And she goes round in her bare feet, father," I went on in a rush of self-pity, "and she knows I don't like her, and she gives pennies to Nora and none to me, and my da sides with her and flakes me, and one night I was so heart-scalded I made up my mind I'd have to kill her."

"And what would you do with the body?" he asked with great interest.

"I was thinking I could chop that up and carry it away in a barrow I have," I said.

"Begor, Jackie," he said, "do you know you're a terrible child?"

"I know, father," I said, for I was just thinking the same thing myself. "I tried to kill Nora too with a bread-knife under the table, only I missed her."

"Is that the little girl that was beating you just now?" he asked.

" 'Tis, father."

"Someone will go for her with a bread-knife one day, and he won't miss her," he said rather cryptically. "You must have great courage. Between ourselves, there's a lot of people I'd like to do the same to but I'd never have the nerve. Hanging is an awful death."

"Is it, father?" I asked with the deepest interest—I was always very keen on hanging. "Did you ever see a fellow hanged?"

"Dozens of them," he said solemnly. "And they all died roaring."

"Jay!" I said.

"Oh, a horrible death!" he said with great satisfaction. "Lots of the fellows I saw killed their grandmothers too, but they all said 'twas never worth it."

He had me there for a full ten minutes talking, and then walked out the chapel yard with me. I was genuinely sorry to part with him, because he was the most entertaining character I'd ever met in the religious line. Outside, after the shadow of the church, the sunlight was like the roaring of waves on a beach; it dazzled me; and when the frozen silence melted and I heard the screech of trams on the road my heart soared. I knew now

I wouldn't die in the night and come back, leaving marks on my mother's furniture. It would be a great worry to her, and the poor soul had enough.

Nora was sitting on the railing, waiting for me, and she put on a very sour puss when she saw the priest with me. She was mad jealous because a priest had never come out of the church with her.

"Well," she asked coldly, after he left me, "what did he give you?"

"Three Hail Marys," I said.

"Three Hail Marys," she repeated incredulously. "You mustn't have told him anything."

"I told him everything," I said confidently.

"About Gran and all?"

"About Gran and all."

(All she wanted was to be able to go home and say I'd made a bad confession.)

"Did you tell him you went for me with the bread-knife?" she asked with a frown.

"I did to be sure."

"And he only gave you three Hail Marys?"

"That's all."

She slowly got down from the railing with a baffled air. Clearly, this was beyond her. As we mounted the steps back to the main road she looked at me suspiciously.

"What are you sucking?" she asked.

"Bullseyes."

"Was it the priest gave them to you?"

" 'Twas."

"Lord God," she wailed bitterly, "some people have all the luck! 'Tis no advantage to anybody trying to be good. I might just as well be a sinner like you."

GUESTS OF THE NATION

At dusk the big Englishman Belcher would shift his long legs out of the ashes and ask, "Well, chums, what about it?" and Noble or me would say, "As you please, chum" (for we had picked up some of their curious expressions), and the little Englishman 'Awkins would light the lamp and produce the cards. Sometimes Jeremiah Donovan would come up of an evening and supervise the play, and grow excited over 'Awkins's cards (which he always played badly), and shout at him as if he was one of our own, "Ach, you divil you, why didn't you play the tray?" But, ordinarily, Jeremiah was a sober and contented poor devil like the big Englishman Belcher, and was looked up to at all only because he was a fair hand at documents, though slow enough at these, I vow. He wore a small cloth hat and big gaiters over his long pants, and seldom did I perceive his hands outside the pockets of that pants. He reddened when you talked to him, tilting from toe to heel and back and looking down all the while at his big farmer's feet. His uncommon broad accent was a great source of jest to me, I being from the town as you may recognize.

I couldn't at the time see the point of me and Noble being with Belcher and 'Awkins at all, for it was and is my fixed belief you could have planted that pair in any untended spot from this to Claregalway and they'd have stayed put and flourished like a native weed. I never seen in my short experience two men that took to the country as they did.

They were handed on to us by the Second Battalion to keep when the search for them become too hot, and Noble and myself, being young, took charge with a natural feeling of responsibility. But little 'Awkins made us look right fools when he displayed he knew the countryside as well as we did and something more. "You're the bloke they calls Bonaparte?" he said to me. "Well, Bonaparte, Mary Brigid Ho'Connell was arskin abaout you and said 'ow you'd a pair of socks belonging to 'er young brother." For it seemed, as they explained it, that the Second used to have little evenings of their own, and some of the girls of the neighborhood would turn in, and seeing they were such decent fellows, our lads couldn't well ignore the two Englishmen, but invited them in and were hail-fellow-well-met with them. 'Awkins told me he learned to dance "The Walls of Limerick" and "The Siege of Ennis" and "The Waves of Tory" in a night or two, though naturally he could not return the compliment, because our lads at that time did not dance foreign dances on principle.

So whatever privileges and favors Belcher and 'Awkins had with the Second they duly took with us, and after the first evening we gave up all pretense of keeping a close eye on their behavior. Not that they could have got far, for they had a notable accent and wore khaki tunics and overcoats with civilian pants and boots. But it's my belief they never had an idea of escaping and were quite contented with their lot.

Now, it was a treat to see how Belcher got off with the old woman of the house we were staying in. She was a great warrant to scold, and crotchety even with us, but before ever she had a chance of giving our guests, as I may call them, a lick of her tongue, Belcher had made her his friend for life. She was breaking sticks at the time, and Belcher, who hadn't been in the house for more than ten minutes, jumped up out of his seat and went across to her.

"Allow me, madam," he says, smiling his queer little smile; "please allow me," and takes the hatchet from her hand. She was struck too parlatic to speak, and even after Belcher would be at her heels carrying a bucket, or basket, or load of turf, as the case might be. As Noble wittily remarked, he got into looking before she leapt, and hot water or any little thing she wanted Belcher would have it ready for her. For such a huge man (and though I am five foot ten myself I had to look up to him) he had an uncommon shortness—or should I say lack—of speech. It took us some time to get used to him walking in and out like a ghost, without a syllable out of him. Especially because 'Awkins talked enough for a platoon, it was strange to hear big Belcher with his toes in the ashes come out with a solitary "Excuse me, chum," or "That's right, chum." His one and only abiding passion was cards, and I will say for him he was a good card-player. He could have fleeced me and Noble many a time; only if we lost to him,'Awkins lost to us, and 'Awkins played with the money Belcher gave him.

'Awkins lost to us because he talked too much, and I think now we lost to Belcher for the same reason. 'Awkins and Noble would spit at one another about religion into the early hours of the morning; the little Englishman as you could see worrying the soul out of young Noble (whose brother was a priest) with a string of questions that would puzzle a cardinal. And to make it worse, even in treating of these holy subjects,'Awkins had a deplorable tongue; I never in all my career struck across a man who could mix such a variety of cursing and bad language into the simplest topic. Oh, a terrible man was little 'Awkins, and a fright to argue! He never did a stroke of work, and when he had no one else to talk to he fixed his claws into the old woman.

I am glad to say that in her he met his match, for one day when he tried to get her to complain profanely of the drought she gave him a great comedown by blaming the drought upon Jupiter Pluvius (a deity neither 'Awkins nor I had ever even heard of, though Noble said among the pagans he was held to have something to do with rain). And another day the same 'Awkins was swearing at the capitalists for starting the German war, when the old dame laid down her iron, puckered up her little crab's mouth and said, "Mr. 'Awkins, you can say what you please about the war, thinking to deceive me because I'm an ignorant old woman, but I know well what started the war. It was that Italian count that stole the heathen divinity out of the temple in Japan, for believe me, Mr. 'Awkins, nothing but sorrow and want follows them that disturbs the hidden powers!" Oh, a queer old dame, as you remark!

So one evening we had our tea together, and 'Awkins lit the lamp and we all sat in to cards. Jeremiah Donovan came in too, and sat down and watched us for a while. Though he was a shy man and didn't speak much, it was easy to see he had no great love for the two Englishmen, and I was surprised it hadn't struck me so clearly before. Well, like that in the story, a terrible dispute blew up late in the evening between 'Awkins and Noble, about capitalists and priests and love for your own country.

"The capitalists," says 'Awkins, with an angry gulp, "the capitalists pays the priests to tell you all abaout the next world, so's you won't notice what they do in this!"

"Nonsense, man," says Noble, losing his temper, "before ever a capitalist was thought of people believed in the next world."

'Awkins stood up as if he was preaching a sermon. "Oh, they did, did they?" he says with a sneer. "They believed all the things you believe, that's what you mean? And you believe that God created Hadam and Hadam created Shem and Shem created Jehoshophat? You believe all the silly hold fairy-tale abaout Heve and Heden and the happle? Well, listen to me, chum. If you're entitled to 'old to a silly belief like that, I'm entitled to 'old to my own silly belief—which is, that the fust thing your God created was a bleedin' capitalist with mirality and Rolls Royce complete. Am I right, chum?" he says then to Belcher.

"You're right, chum," says Belcher, with his queer smile, and gets up from the table to stretch his long legs into the fire and stroke his mustache. So, seeing that Jeremiah Donovan was going, and there was no knowing when the conversation about religion would be over, I took my hat and went out with him. We strolled down towards the village together, and then he suddenly stopped, and blushing and mumbling, and shifting, as his way was, from toe to heel, he said I ought to be behind keeping guard on the prisoners. And I, having it put to me so suddenly, asked him what the hell he wanted a guard on the prisoners at all for, and said that so far as Noble and me were concerned we had talked it over and would rather be out with a column. "What use is that pair to us?" I asked him.

He looked at me for a spell and said, "I thought you knew we were keeping them as hostages." "Hostages—?" says I, not quite understanding. "The enemy," he says in his heavy way, "have prisoners belong' to us, and now they talk of shooting them. If they shoot our prisoners we'll shoot theirs, and serve them right." "Shoot them?" said I, the possibility just beginning to dawn on me. "Shoot them exactly," said he. "Now," said I, "wasn't it very unforeseen of you not to tell me and Noble that?" "How so?" he asks. "Seeing that we were acting as guards upon them, of course." "And hadn't you reason enough to guess that much?" "We had not, Jeremiah Donovan, we had not. How were we to know when the men were on our hands so long?" "And what difference does it make? The enemy have our prisoners as long or longer, haven't they?" "It makes a great difference," said I. "How so?" said he sharply; but I couldn't tell him the difference it made, for I was struck too silly to speak. "And when may we expect to be released from this anyway?" said I. "You may expect it tonight," says he. "Or tomorrow or the next day at latest. So if it's hanging round here that worries you, you'll be free soon enough."

I cannot explain it even now, how sad I felt, but I went back to the cottage, a miserable man. When I arrived the discussion was still on,'Awkins holding forth to all and sundry that there was no next world at all and Noble answering in his best canonical style that there was. But I saw 'Awkins was after having the best of it. "Do you know what, chum?" he was saying, with his saucy smile. "I think you're jest as big a bleedin' hunbeliever as I am. You say you believe in the next world and you know jest as much abaout the next world as I do, which is sweet damn-all. What's 'Eaven? You dunno. Where's 'Eaven? You dunno. Who's in 'Eaven? You dunno. You know sweet damn-all! I arsk you again, do they wear wings?"

"Very well then," says Noble, "they do; is that enough for you? They do wear wings. Where do they get them then? Who makes them? 'Ave they a fact'ry for wings? 'Ave they a sort of store where you 'ands in your chit and tikes your bleedin' wings? Answer me that."

"Oh, you're an impossible man to argue with," says Noble. "Now listen to me—" And off the pair of them went again.

It was long after midnight when we locked up the Englishmen and went to bed ourselves. As I blew out the candle I told Noble what Jeremiah Donovan had told me. Noble took it very quietly. After we had been in bed about an hour he asked me did I think we ought to tell the Englishmen. I having thought of the same thing myself (among many others) said no, because it was more than likely the English wouldn't shoot our men, and anyhow it wasn't to be supposed the Brigade who were always up and down with the Second Battalion and knew the Englishmen well would be likely to want them bumped off. "I think so," says Noble. "It would be sort of cruelty to put the wind up them now." "It was very unforeseen of Jeremiah Donovan anyhow," says I, and by Noble's silence I realized he took my meaning.

So I lay there half the night, and thought and thought, and picturing myself and young Noble trying to prevent the Brigade from shooting 'Awkins and Belcher sent a cold sweat out through me. Because there were men on the Brigade you daren't let nor hinder without a gun in your hand, and at any rate, in those days disunion between brothers seemed to me an awful crime. I knew better after.

It was next morning we found it so hard to face Belcher and 'Awkins with a smile. We went about the house all day scarcely saying a word. Belcher didn't mind us much; he was stretched into the ashes as usual with his usual look of waiting in quietness for something unforeseen to happen, but little 'Awkins gave us a bad time with his audacious gibing and questioning. He was disgusted at Noble's not answering him back. "Why can't you tike your beating like a man, chum?" he says. "You with your Hadam and Heve! I'm a Communist—or an Anarchist. An Anarchist, that's what I am." And for hours after he went round the house, mumbling when the fit took him "Hadam and Heve! Hadam and Heve!"

I don't know clearly how we got over that day, but get over it we did, and a great relief it was when the tea things were cleared away and Belcher said in his peaceable manner, "Well, chums, what about it?" So we all sat round the table and 'Awkins produced the cards, and at that moment I heard Jeremiah Donovan's footsteps up the path, and a dark presentiment crossed my mind. I rose quietly from the table and laid my hand on him before he reached the door. "What do you want?" I asked him. "I want those two soldier friends of yours," he says reddening. "Is that the way it is, Jeremiah Donovan?" I ask. "That's the way. There were four of our lads went west this morning, one of them a boy of sixteen." "That's bad, Jeremiah," says I.

At that moment Noble came out, and we walked down the path together talking in whispers. Feeney, the local intelligence officer, was standing by the gate. "What are you going to do about it?" I asked Jeremiah Donovan. "I want you and Noble to bring them out: you can tell them they're being shifted again; that'll be the quietest way." "Leave me out of that," says Noble suddenly. Jeremiah Donovan looked at him hard for a minute or two. "All right so," he said peaceably. "You and Feeney collect a few tools from the shed and dig a hole by the far end of the bog. Bonaparte and I'll be after you in about twenty minutes. But whatever else you do, don't let anyone see you with the tools. No one must know but the four of ourselves."

We saw Feeney and Noble go round to the houseen where the tools were kept, and sidled in. Everything if I can so express myself was tottering before my eyes, and I left Jeremiah Donovan to do the explaining as best he could, while I took a seat and said nothing. He told them they were to go back to the Second. 'Awkins let a mouthful of curses out of him at that, and it was plain that Belcher, though he said nothing, was duly perturbed. The old woman was for having them stay in spite of us, and she did not shut her mouth until Jeremiah Donovan lost his temper and said some nasty things to her. Within the house by this time it was pitch dark, but no one thought of lighting the lamp, and in the darkness the two Englishmen fetched their khaki topcoats and said good-bye to the woman of the house. "Just as a man mikes a 'ome of a bleedin' place," mumbles 'Awkins, shaking her by the hand, "some bastard at Headquarters thinks you're too cushy and shunts you off." Belcher shakes her hand very hearty. "A thousand thanks, madam," he says, "a thousand thanks for everything . . ." as though he'd made it all up.

We go round to the back of the house and down towards the fatal bog. Then Jeremiah Donovan comes out with what is in his mind. "There were four of our lads shot by your fellows this morning so now you're to be bumped off." "Cut that stuff out," says 'Awkins, flaring up. "It's bad enough to be mucked about such as we are without you plying at soldiers." "It's true," says Jeremiah Donovan, "I'm sorry,'Awkins, but 'tis true," and comes out with the usual rigmarole about doing our duty and obeying our superiors. "Cut it out," says 'Awkins irritably. "Cut it out!"

Then, when Donovan sees he is not being believed he turns to me, "Ask Bonaparte here," he says. "I don't need to arsk Bonaparte. Me and Bonaparte are chums." "Isn't it true, Bonaparte?" says Jeremiah Donovan solemnly to me. "It is," I say sadly, "it is." 'Awkins stops. "Now, for Christ's sike. . . ." "I mean it, chum," I say. "You daon't saound as if you mean it. You knaow well you don't mean it." "Well, if he don't I do," says Jeremiah Donovan. "Why the 'ell sh'd you want to shoot me, Jeremiah Donovan?" "Why the hell should your people take out four prisoners and shoot them in cold blood upon a barrack square?" I perceive Jeremiah Donovan is trying to encourage himself with hot words.

Anyway, he took little 'Awkins by the arm and dragged him on, but it was impossible to make him understand that we were in earnest. From which you will perceive how difficult it was for me, as I kept feeling my Smith and Wesson and thinking what I would do if they happened to put up a fight or ran for it, and wishing in my heart they would. I knew if only they ran I would never fire on them. "Was Noble in this?" 'Awkins wanted to know, and we said yes. He laughed. But why should Noble want to shoot him? Why should we want to shoot him? What had he done to us? Weren't we chums (the word lingers painfully in my memory)? Weren't we? Didn't we understand him and didn't he understand us? Did either of us imagine for an instant that he'd shoot us for all the so-and-so brigadiers in the so-and-so British Army? By this time I began to perceive in the dusk the desolate edges of the bog that was to be their last earthly bed, and, so great a sadness overtook my mind, I could not answer him. We walked along the edge of it in the darkness, and every now and then 'Awkins would call a halt and begin again, just as if he was wound up, about us being chums, and I was in despair that nothing but the cold and open grave made ready for his presence would convince him that we meant it all. But all the same, if you can understand, I didn't want him to be bumped off.

At last we saw the unsteady glint of a lantern in the distance and made towards it. Noble was carrying it, and Feeney stood somewhere in the darkness behind, and somehow the picture of the two of them so silent in the boglands was like the pain of death in my heart. Belcher, on recognizing Noble, said " 'Allo, chum" in his usual peaceable way, but 'Awkins flew at the poor boy immediately, and the dispute began all over again, only that Noble hadn't a word to say for himself, and stood there with the swaying lantern between his gaitered legs.

It was Jeremiah Donovan who did the answering. 'Awkins asked for the twentieth time (for it seemed to haunt his mind) if anybody thought he'd shoot Noble. "You would," says Jeremiah Donovan shortly. "I wouldn't, damn you!" "You would if you knew you'd be shot for not doing it." "I wouldn't, not if I was to be shot twenty times over; he's my chum. And Belcher wouldn't—isn't that right, Belcher?" "That's right, chum," says Belcher peaceably. "Damned if I would. Anyway, who says Noble'd be shot if I wasn't bumped off? What d'you think I'd do if I was in Noble's place and we were out in the middle of a blasted bog?" "What would you do?" "I'd go with him wherever he was going. I'd share my last bob with him and stick by 'im through thick and thin."

"We've had enough of this," says Jeremiah Donovan, cocking his revolver. "Is there any message you want to send before I fire?" "No, there isn't, but . . ." "Do you want to say your prayers?" 'Awkins came out with a cold-blooded remark that shocked even me and turned to Noble again. "Listen to me, Noble," he said. "You and me are chums. You won't come over to my side, so I'll come over to your side. Is that fair? Just you give me a rifle and I'll go with you wherever you want."

Nobody answered him.

"Do you understand?" he said. "I'm through with it all. I'm a deserter or anything else you like, but from this on I'm one of you. Does that prove to you that I mean what I say?" Noble raised his head, but as Donovan began to speak he lowered it again without answering. "For the last time have you any messages to send?" says Donovan in a cold and excited voice.

"Ah, shut up, you, Donovan; you don't understand me, but these fellows do. They're my chums; they stand by me and I stand by them. We're not the capitalist tools you seem to think us."

I alone of the crowd saw Donovan raise his Webley to the back of 'Awkins's neck, and as he did so I shut my eyes and tried to say a prayer. 'Awkins had begun to say something else when Donovan let fly, and, as I opened my eyes at the bang, I saw him stagger at the knees and lie out flat at Noble's feet, slowly, and as quiet as a child, with the lantern light falling sadly upon his lean legs and bright farmer's boots. We all stood very still for a while watching him settle out in the last agony.

Then Belcher quietly takes out a handkerchief, and begins to tie it about his own eyes (for in our excitement we had forgotten to offer the same to 'Awkins), and, seeing it is not big enough, turns and asks for a loan of mine. I give it to him and as he knots the two together he points with his foot at 'Awkins. " 'E's not quite dead," he says, "better give 'im another." Sure enough 'Awkins's left knee as we see it under the lantern is rising again. I bend down and put my gun to his ear; then, recollecting myself and the company of Belcher, I stand up again with a few hasty words. Belcher understands what is in my mind. "Give 'im 'is first," he says. "I don't mind. Poor bastard, we dunno what's 'appening to 'im now." As by this time I am beyond all feeling I kneel down again and skilfully give 'Awkins the last shot so as to put him forever out of pain.

Belcher who is fumbling a bit awkwardly with the handkerchiefs comes out with a laugh when he hears the shot. It is the first time I have heard him laugh, and it sends a shiver down my spine, coming as it does so inappropriately upon the tragic death of his old friend. "Poor blighter," he says quietly, "and last night he was so curious abaout it all. It's very queer, chums, I always think. Naow,'e knows as much abaout it as they'll ever let 'im know, and last night 'e was all in the dark."

Donovan helps him to tie the handkerchiefs about his eyes. "Thanks, chum," he says. Donovan asks him if there are any messages he would like to send. "Naow, chum," he says, "none for me. If any of you likes to write to 'Awkins's mother you'll find a letter from 'er in 'is pocket. But my missus left me eight years ago. Went away with another fellow and took the kid with her. I likes the feelin' of a 'ome (as you may 'ave noticed) but I couldn't start again after that."

We stand around like fools now that he can no longer see us. Donovan looks at Noble and Noble shakes his head. Then Donovan raises his Webley again and just at that moment Belcher laughs his queer nervous laugh again. He must think we are talking of him; anyway, Donovan lowers his gun. " 'Scuse me, chums," says Belcher, "I feel I'm talking the 'ell of a lot . . . and so silly . . . abaout me being so 'andy abaout a 'ouse. But this thing come on me so sudden. You'll forgive me, I'm sure." "You don't want to say a prayer?" asks Jeremiah Donovan. "No, chum," he replies, "I don't think that'd 'elp. I'm ready if you want to get it over." "You understand," says Jeremiah Donovan, "it's not so much our doing. It's our duty, so to speak." Belcher's head is raised like a real blind man's, so that you can only see his nose and chin in the lamplight. "I never could make out what duty was myself," he said, "but I think you're all good lads, if that's what you mean. I'm not complaining." Noble, with a look of desperation, signals to Donovan, and in a flash Donovan raises his gun and fires. The big man goes over like a sack of meal, and this time there is no need of a second shot.

I don't remember much about the burying, but that it was worse than all the rest, because we had to carry the warm corpses a few yards before we sunk them in the windy bog. It was all mad lonely, with only a bit of lantern between ourselves and the pitch blackness, and birds hooting and screeching all round disturbed by the guns. Noble had to search 'Awkins first to get the letter from his mother. Then having smoothed all signs of the grave away, Noble and I collected our tools, said good-bye to the others, and went back along the desolate edge of the treacherous bog without a word. We put the tools in the houseen and went into the house. The kitchen was pitch black and cold, just as we left it, and the old woman was sitting over the hearth telling her beads. We walked past her into the room, and Noble struck a match to light the lamp. Just then she rose quietly and came to the doorway, being not at all so bold or crabbed as usual.

"What did ye do with them?" she says in a sort of whisper, and Noble took such a mortal start the match quenched in his trembling hand. "What's that?" he asks without turning round. "I heard ye," she said. "What did you hear?" asks Noble, but sure he wouldn't deceive a child the way he said it. "I heard ye. Do you think I wasn't listening to ye putting the things back in the houseen?" Noble struck another match and this time the lamp lit for him. "Was that what ye did with them?" she said, and Noble said nothing—after all what could he say?

So then, by God, she fell on her two knees by the door, and began telling her beads, and after a minute or two Noble went on his knees by the fireplace, so I pushed my way out past her, and stood at the door, watching the stars and listening to the damned shrieking of the birds. It is so strange what you feel at such moments, and not to be written afterwards. Noble says he felt he seen everything ten times as big, perceiving nothing around him but the little patch of black bog with the two Englishmen stiffening into it; but with me it was the other way, as though the patch of bog where the two Englishmen were was a thousand miles away from me, and even Noble mumbling just behind me and the old woman and the birds and the bloody stars were all far away, and I was somehow very small and very lonely. And anything that ever happened [to] me after I never felt the same about again.

Marguerite Yourcenar

Marguerite Yourcenar (1905–1987) was born in France. Her mother died in childbirth, and Yourcenar was raised by her father. She had a bookish childhood and was fascinated from an early age by history and classical cultures. Her fiction reflected these interests. Yourcenar's celebrated novel *Memoirs of Hadrian* is a keenly imagined reconstruction of the life of the Emperor Hadrian, and *The Abyss* recreates the world of sixteenth-century Europe.

After World War II, Yourcenar traveled to the United States. She settled herself in relative isolation at Mount Desert Island, Maine, where she wrote fiction and essays until her death. Near the end of her life, Yourcenar was inducted into the French Academy, becoming the first woman to have been so honored. Her work includes *A Coin in Nine Hands, Alexis,* and *Oriental Tales.*

HOW WANG-FO WAS SAVED

The old painter Wang-Fo and his disciple Ling were wandering along the roads of the Kingdom of Han.

They made slow progress because Wang-Fo would stop at night to watch the stars and during the day to observe the dragonflies. They carried hardly any luggage, because Wang-Fo loved the image of things and not the things themselves, and no object in the world seemed to him worth buying, except brushes, pots of lacquer and China ink, and rolls of silk and rice paper. They were poor, because Wang-Fo would exchange his paintings for a ration of boiled millet, and paid no attention to pieces of silver. Ling, his disciple, bent beneath the weight of a sack full of sketches, bowed his back with respect as if he were carrying the heavens' vault, because for Ling the sack was full of snow-covered mountains, torrents in spring, and the face of the summer moon.

Ling had not been born to trot down the roads, following an old man who seized the dawn and captured the dusk. His father had been a banker who dealt in gold, his mother the only child of a jade merchant who had left her all his worldly possessions, cursing her for not being a son. Ling had grown up in a house where wealth made him shy: he was afraid of insects, of thunder and the face of the dead. When Ling was fifteen, his father chose a bride for him, a very beautiful one because the thought of the happiness he was giving his son consoled him for having reached the age in which the night is meant for sleep. Ling's wife was as frail as a reed, childish as milk, sweet as saliva, salty as tears. After the wedding, Ling's parents became discreet to the point of dying, and their son was left alone in a house painted vermilion, in the company of his young wife who never stopped smiling and a plum tree that blossomed every spring with pale-pink flowers. Ling loved this woman of a crystal-clear heart as one loves a mirror that will never tarnish, or a talisman that will protect one forever. He visited the teahouses to follow the dictates of fashion, and only moderately favored acrobats and dancers.

One night, in the tavern, Wang-Fo shared Ling's table. The old man had been drinking in order to better paint a drunkard, and he cocked his head to one side as if trying to measure the distance between his hand and his bowl. The rice wine undid the tongue of the taciturn craftsman, and that night Wang spoke as if silence were a wall and words the colors with which to cover it. Thanks to him, Ling got to know the beauty of the drunkards' faces blurred by the vapors of hot drink, the brown splendor of the roasts unevenly brushed by tongues of fire, and the exquisite blush of wine stains strewn on the tablecloths like withered petals. A gust of wind broke the window: the downpour entered the room. Wang-Fo leaned out to make Ling admire the livid zebra stripes of lightning, and Ling, spellbound, stopped being afraid of storms.

Ling paid the old painter's bill, and as Wang-Fo was both without money and without lodging, he humbly offered him a resting place. They walked away together; Ling held a lamp whose light projected unexpected fires in the puddles. That evening, Ling discovered with surprise that the walls of his house were not red, as he had always thought, but the color of an almost rotten orange. In the courtyard, Wang-Fo noticed the delicate shape of a bush to which no one had paid any attention until then, and compared it to a young woman letting down her hair to dry. In the passageway, he followed with delight the hesitant trail of an ant along the cracks in the wall, and Ling's horror of these creatures vanished into thin air. Realizing that Wang-Fo had just presented him with the gift of a new soul and a new vision of the world, Ling respectfully offered the old man the room in which his father and mother had died.

For many years now, Wang-Fo had dreamed of painting the portrait of a princess of olden days playing the lute under a willow. No woman was sufficiently unreal to be his model, but Ling would do because he was not a woman. Then Wang-Fo spoke of painting a young prince shooting an arrow at the foot of a large cedar tree. No young man of the present was sufficiently unreal to serve as his model, but Ling got his own wife to pose under the plum tree in the garden. Later on, Wang-Fo painted her in a fairy costume against the clouds of twilight, and the young woman wept because it was an omen of death. As Ling came to prefer the portraits painted by Wang-Fo to the young woman herself, her face began to fade, like a flower exposed to warm winds and summer rains. One morning, they found her hanging from the branches of the pink plum tree: the ends of the scarf that was strangling her floated in the wind, entangled with her hair. She looked even more delicate than usual, and as pure as the beauties celebrated by the poets of days gone by. Wang-Fo painted her one last time, because he loved the green hue that suffuses the face of the dead. His disciple Ling mixed the colors and the task needed such concentration that he forgot to shed tears.

One after the other, Ling sold his slaves, his jades, and the fish in his pond to buy his master pots of purple ink that came from the West. When the house was emptied, they left it, and Ling closed the door of his past behind him. Wang-Fo felt weary of a city where the faces could no longer teach him secrets of ugliness or beauty, and the master and his disciple walked away together down the roads of the Kingdom of Han.

Their reputation preceded them into the villages, to the gateway of fortresses, and into the atrium of temples where restless pilgrims halt at dusk. It was murmured that Wang-Fo had the power to bring his paintings to life by adding a last touch of color to their eyes. Farmers would come and beg him to paint a watchdog, and the lords would ask him for portraits of their best warriors. The priests honored Wang-Fo as a sage; the people feared him as a sorcerer. Wang enjoyed these differences of opinion which gave him the chance to study expressions of gratitude, fear, and veneration.

Ling begged for food, watched over his master's rest, and took advantage of the old man's raptures to massage his feet. With the first rays of the sun, when the old man was still asleep, Ling went in pursuit of timid landscapes hidden behind bunches of reeds. In the evening, when the master, disheartened, threw down his brushes, he would carefully pick them up. When Wang became sad and spoke of his old age, Ling would smile and show him the solid trunk of an old oak; when Wang felt happy and made jokes, Ling would humbly pretend to listen.

One day, at sunset, they reached the outskirts of the Imperial City and Ling sought out and found an inn in which Wang-Fo could spend the night. The old man wrapped himself up in rags, and Ling lay down next to him to keep him warm because spring had only just begun and the floor of beaten earth was still frozen. At dawn, heavy steps echoed in the corridors of the inn; they heard the frightened whispers of the innkeeper and orders shouted in a foreign, barbaric tongue. Ling trembled, remembering that the night before, he had stolen a rice cake for his master's supper. Certain that they would come to take him to prison, he asked himself who would help Wang-Fo ford the next river on the following day.

The soldiers entered carrying lanterns. The flames gleaming through the motley paper cast red and blue lights on their leather helmets. The string of a bow quivered over their shoulders, and the fiercest among them suddenly let out a roar for no reason at all. A heavy hand fell on Wang-Fo's neck, and the painter could not help noticing that the soldiers' sleeves did not match the color of their coats.

Helped by his disciple, Wang-Fo followed the soldiers, stumbling along uneven roads. The passing crowds made fun of these two criminals who were certainly going to be beheaded. The soldiers answered Wang's questions with savage scowls. His bound hands hurt him, and Ling in despair looked smiling at his master, which for him was a gentler way of crying.

They reached the threshold of the Imperial Palace, whose purple walls rose in broad daylight like a sweep of sunset. The soldiers led Wang-Fo through countless square and circular rooms whose shapes symbolized the seasons, the cardinal points, the male and the female, longevity, and the prerogatives of power. The doors swung on their hinges with a musical note, and were placed in such a manner that one followed the entire scale when crossing the palace from east to west. Everything combined to give an impression of superhuman power and subtlety, and one could feel that here the simplest orders were as final and as terrible as the wisdom of the ancients. At last, the air became thin and the silence so deep that not even a man under torture would have dared to scream. A eunuch lifted a tapestry; the soldiers began to tremble like women, and the small troop entered the chamber in which the Son of Heaven sat on a high throne.

It was a room without walls, held up by thick columns of blue stone. A garden spread out on the far side of the marble shafts, and each and every flower blooming in the greenery belonged to a rare species brought here from across the oceans. But none of them had any perfume, so that the Celestial Dragon's meditations would not be troubled by fine smells. Out of respect for the silence in which his thoughts evolved, no bird had been allowed within the enclosure, and even the bees had been driven away. An enormous wall separated the garden from the rest of the world, so that the wind that sweeps over dead dogs and corpses on the battlefield would not dare brush the Emperor's sleeve.

The Celestial Master sat on a throne of jade, and his hands were wrinkled like those of an old man, though he had scarcely reached the age of twenty. His robe was blue to symbolize winter, and green to remind one of spring. His face was beautiful but blank, like a looking glass placed too high, reflecting nothing except the stars and the immutable heavens. To his right stood his Minister of Perfect Pleasures, and to his left his Counselor of Just Torments. Because his courtiers, lined along the base of the columns, always lent a keen ear to the slightest sound from his lips, he had adopted the habit of speaking in a low voice.

"Celestial Dragon," said Wang-Fo, bowing low, "I am old, I am poor, I am weak. You are like summer; I am like winter. You have Ten Thousand Lives; I have but one, and it is near its close. What have I done to you? My hands have been tied, these hands that never harmed you."

"You ask what you have done to me, old Wang-Fo?" said the Emperor.

His voice was so melodious that it made one want to cry. He raised his right hand, to which the reflections from the jade pavement gave a pale sea-green hue like that of an underwater plant, and Wang-Fo marveled at the length of those thin fingers, and hunted among his memories to discover whether he had not at some time painted a mediocre portrait of either the Emperor or one of his ancestors that would now merit a sentence of death. But it seemed unlikely because Wang-Fo had not been an assiduous visitor at the Imperial Court. He preferred the farmers' huts or, in the cities, the courtesans' quarters and the taverns along the harbor where the dockers liked to quarrel.

"You ask me what it is you have done, old Wang-Fo?" repeated the Emperor, inclining his slender neck toward the old man waiting attentively. "I will tell you. But, as another man's poison cannot enter our veins except through our nine openings, in order to show you your offenses I must take you with me down the corridors of my memory and tell you the story of my life. My father had assembled a collection of your work and hidden it in the most secret chamber in the palace, because he judged that the people in your paintings should be concealed from the world since they cannot lower their eyes in the presence of profane viewers. It was in those same rooms that I was brought up, old Wang-Fo, surrounded by solitude. To prevent my innocence from being sullied by other human souls, the restless crowd of my future subjects had been driven away from me, and no one was allowed to pass my threshold, for fear that his or her shadow would stretch out and touch me. The few aged servants that were placed in my service showed themselves as little as possible; the hours turned in circles; the colors of your paintings bloomed in the first hours of the morning and grew pale at dusk. At night, when I was unable to sleep, I gazed at them, and for nearly ten years I gazed at them every night. During the day, sitting on a carpet whose design I knew by heart, I dreamed of the joys the future had in store for me. I imagined the world, with the Kingdom of Han at the center, to be like the flat palm of my hand crossed by the fatal lines of the Five Rivers. Around it lay the sea in which monsters are born, and farther away the mountains that hold up the heavens. And to help me visualize these things I used your paintings. You made me believe that the sea looked like the vast sheet of water spread across your scrolls, so blue that if a stone were to fall into it, it would become a sapphire; that women opened and closed like flowers, like the creatures that come forward, pushed by the wind, along the paths of your painted gardens; and that the young, slim-waisted warriors who mount guard in the fortresses along the frontier were themselves like arrows that could pierce my heart. At sixteen I saw the doors that separated me from the world open once again; I climbed onto the balcony of my palace to look at the clouds, but they were far less beautiful than those in your sunsets. I ordered my litter; bounced along roads on which I had not foreseen either mud or stones, I traveled across the provinces of the Empire without ever finding your gardens full of women like fireflies, or a woman whose body was in itself a garden. The pebbles on the beach spoiled my taste for oceans; the blood of the tortured is less red than the pomegranates in your paintings; the village vermin prevented me from seeing the beauty of the rice fields; the flesh of mortal women disgusted me like the dead meat hanging from the butcher's hook, and the coarse laughter of my soldiers made me sick. You lied, Wang-Fo, you old impostor. The world is nothing but a mass of muddled colors thrown into the void by an insane painter, and smudged by our tears. The Kingdom of Han is not the most beautiful of kingdoms, and I am not the Emperor. The only empire which is worth reigning over is that which you alone can enter, old Wang, by the road of One Thousand Curves and Ten Thousand Colors. You alone reign peacefully over mountains covered in snow that cannot melt, and over fields of daffodils that cannot die. And that is why, Wang-Fo, I have conceived a punishment for you, for you whose enchantment has filled me with disgust at everything I own, and with desire for everything I shall never possess. And in order to lock you up in the only cell from which there is no escape, I have decided to have your eyes burned out, because your eyes, Wang-Fo, are the two magic gates that open onto your kingdom. And as your hands are the two roads of ten forking paths that lead to the heart of your kingdom, I have decided to have your hands cut off. Have you understood, old Wang-Fo?"

Hearing the sentence, Ling, the disciple, tore from his belt an old knife and leaped toward the Emperor. Two guards immediately seized him. The Son of Heaven smiled and added, with a sigh: "And I also hate you, old Wang-Fo, because you have known how to make yourself beloved. Kill that dog."

Ling jumped to one side so that his blood would not stain his master's robe. One of the soldiers lifted his sword and Ling's head fell from his neck like a cut flower. The servants carried away the remains, and Wang-Fo, in despair, admired the beautiful scarlet stain that his disciple's blood made on the green stone floor.

The Emperor made a sign and two eunuchs wiped Wang's eyes.

"Listen, old Wang-Fo," said the Emperor, "and dry your tears, because this is not the time to weep. Your eyes must be clear so that the little light that is left to them is not clouded by your weeping. Because it is not only the grudge I bear you that makes me desire your death; it is not only the cruelty in my heart that makes me want to see you suffer. I have other plans, old Wang-Fo. I possess among your works a remarkable painting in which the mountains, the river estuary, and the sea reflect each other, on a very small scale certainly, but with a clarity that surpasses the real landscapes themselves, like objects reflected on the walls of a metal sphere. But that painting is unfinished, Wang-Fo; your masterpiece is but a sketch. No doubt, when you began your work, sitting in a solitary valley, you noticed a passing bird, or a child running after the bird. And the bird's beak or the child's cheeks made you forget the blue eyelids of the sea. You never finished the frills of the water's cloak, or the seaweed hair of the rocks. Wang-Fo, I want you to use the few hours of light that are left to you to finish this painting, which will thus contain the final secrets amassed during your long life. I know that your hands, about to fall, will not tremble on the silken cloth, and infinity will enter your work through those unhappy cuts. I know that your eyes, about to be put out, will discover bearings far beyond all human senses. This is my plan, old Wang-Fo, and I can force you to fulfill it. If you refuse, before blinding you, I will have all your paintings burned, and you will be like a father whose children are slaughtered and all hopes of posterity extinguished. However, believe, if you wish, that this last order stems from nothing but my kindness, because I know that the silken scroll is the only mistress you ever deigned to touch. And to offer you brushes, paints, and inks to occupy your last hours is like offering the favors of a harlot to a man condemned to death."

Upon a sign from the Emperor's little finger, two eunuchs respectfully brought forward the unfinished scroll on which Wang-Fo had outlined the image of the sea and the sky. Wang-Fo dried his tears and smiled, because that small sketch reminded him of his youth. Everything in it spoke of a fresh new spirit which Wang-Fo could no longer claim as his, and yet something was missing from it, because when Wang had painted it he had not yet looked long enough at the mountains or at the rocks bathing their naked flanks in the sea, and he had not yet penetrated deep enough into the sadness of the evening twilight. Wang-Fo selected one of the brushes which a slave held ready for him and began spreading wide strokes of blue onto the unfinished sea. A eunuch crouched by his feet, mixing the colors; he carried out his task with little skill, and more than ever Wang-Fo lamented the loss of his disciple Ling.

Wang began by adding a touch of pink to the tip of the wing of a cloud perched on a mountain. Then he painted onto the surface of the sea a few small lines that deepened the perfect feeling of calm. The jade floor became increasingly damp, but Wang-Fo, absorbed as he was in his painting, did not seem to notice that he was working with his feet in water.

The fragile rowboat grew under the strokes of the painter's brush and now occupied the entire foreground of the silken scroll. The rhythmic sound of the oars rose suddenly in the distance, quick and eager like the beating of wings. The sound came nearer, gently filling the whole room, then ceased, and a few trembling drops appeared on the boatman's oars. The red iron intended for Wang's eyes lay extinguished on the executioner's coals. The courtiers, motionless as etiquette required, stood in water up to their shoulders, trying to lift themselves onto the tips of their toes. The water finally reached the level of the imperial heart. The silence was so deep one could have heard a tear drop.

It was Ling. He wore his everyday robe, and his right sleeve still had a hole that he had not had time to mend that morning before the soldiers' arrival. But around his neck was tied a strange red scarf.

Wang-Fo said to him softly, while he continued painting, "I thought you were dead."

"You being alive," said Ling respectfully, "how could I have died?"

And he helped his master into the boat. The jade ceiling reflected itself in the water, so that Ling seemed to be inside a cave. The pigtails of submerged courtiers rippled up toward the surface like snakes, and the pale head of the Emperor floated like a lotus.

"Look at them," said Wang-Fo sadly. "These wretches will die, if they are not dead already. I never thought there was enough water in the sea to drown an Emperor. What are we to do?"

"Master, have no fear," murmured the disciple. "They will soon be dry again and will not even remember that their sleeves were ever wet. Only the Emperor will keep in his heart a little of the bitterness of the sea. These people are not the kind to lose themselves inside a painting."

And he added: "The sea is calm, the wind high, the seabirds fly to their nests. Let us leave, Master, and sail to the land beyond the waves."

"Let us leave," said the old painter.

Wang-Fo took hold of the helm, and Ling bent over the oars. The sound of rowing filled the room again, strong and steady like the beating of a heart. The level of the water dropped unnoticed around the large vertical rocks that became columns once more. Soon only a few puddles glistened in the hollows of the jade floor. The courtiers' robes were dry, but a few wisps of foam still clung to the hem of the Emperor's cloak.

The painting finished by Wang-Fo was leaning against a tapestry. A rowboat occupied the entire foreground. It drifted away little by little, leaving behind it a thin wake that smoothed out into the quiet sea. One could no longer make out the faces of the two men sitting in the boat, but one could still see Ling's red scarf and Wang-Fo's beard waving in the breeze.

The beating of the oars grew fainter, then ceased, blotted out by the distance. The Emperor, leaning forward, a hand above his eyes, watched Wang's boat sail away till it was nothing but an imperceptible dot in the paleness of the twilight. A golden mist rose and spread over the water. Finally the boat veered around a rock that stood at the gateway to the ocean; the shadow of a cliff fell across it; its wake disappeared from the deserted surface, and the painter Wang-Fo and his disciple Ling vanished forever on the jade-blue sea that Wang-Fo had just created.

Translated by Alberto Manguel
and Marguerite Yourcenar

R. K. Narayan

R. K. Narayan (b. 1906) was born in India, and he is widely regarded as that country's premier writer. Narayan has published numerous novels, including *Swami and Friends and The Vendor of Sweets,* and story collections, among them the celebrated *Under the Banyan Tree.* His work includes essays and travel books as well as modern prose versions of the great Indian epics, the *Mahabharata* and the *Ramayana.*

HOUSE OPPOSITE

The hermit invariably shuddered when he looked out of his window. The house across the street was occupied by a shameless woman. Late in the evening, men kept coming and knocking on her door—afternoons, too, if there was a festival or holiday. Sometimes they lounged on the pyol of her house, smoking, chewing tobacco, and spitting into the gutter—committing all the sins of the world, according to the hermit who was striving to pursue a life of austerity, forswearing family, possessions, and all the comforts of life. He found this single-room tenement with a couple of coconut trees and a well at the backyard adequate, and the narrow street swarmed with children: sometimes he called in the children, seated them around, and taught them simple moral lessons and sacred verse. On the walls he had nailed a few pictures of gods cut out of old calendars, and made the children prostrate themselves in front of them before sending them away with a piece of sugar candy each.

His daily life followed an unvarying pattern. Birdlike, he retired at dusk, lying on the bare floor with a wooden block under his head for a pillow. He woke up at four, ahead of the rooster at the street corner, bathed at the well, and sat down on a piece of deerskin to meditate. Later he lit the charcoal stove and baked a few chapattis for breakfast and lunch and cooked certain restricted vegetables and greens, avoiding potato, onion, okra, and such as might stimulate the baser impulses.

Even in the deepest state of meditation, he could not help hearing the creaking of the door across the street when a client left after a night of debauchery. He rigorously suppressed all cravings of the palate, and punished his body in a dozen ways. If you asked him why, he would have been at a loss to explain. He was the antithesis of the athlete who flexed his muscles and watched his expanding chest before a mirror. Our hermit, on the contrary, kept a minute check of his emaciation and felt a peculiar thrill out of such an achievement. He was only following without questioning his ancient guru's instructions, and hoped thus to attain spiritual liberation.

One afternoon, opening the window to sweep the dust on the sill, he noticed her standing on her doorstep, watching the street. His temples throbbed with the rush of blood. He studied her person—chiseled features, but sunk in fatty folds. She possessed, however, a seductive outline; her forearms were cushionlike and perhaps the feel of those encircling arms attracted men. His gaze, once it had begun to hover about her body, would not return to its anchor—which should normally be the tip of one's nose, as enjoined by his guru and the yoga shastras.

Her hips were large, thighs stout like banana stalks, on the whole a mattresslike creature on which a patron could loll all night without a scrap of covering—"Awful monster! Personification of evil." He felt suddenly angry. Why on earth should that creature stand there and ruin his tapas: all the merit he had so laboriously acquired was draining away like water through a sieve. Difficult to say whether it was those monstrous arms and breasts or thighs which tempted and ruined men . . . He hissed under his breath, "Get in, you devil, don't stand there!" She abruptly turned round and went in, shutting the door behind her. He felt triumphant, although his command and her compliance were coincidental. He bolted the window tight and retreated to the farthest corner of the room, settled down on the deerskin, and kept repeating, "Om, Om, Rama, Jayarama": the sound "Rama" had a potency all its own—and was reputed to check wandering thoughts and distractions. He had a profound knowledge of mantras and their efficacy. "Sri Rama . . . ," he repeated, but it was like a dilute and weak medicine for high fever. It didn't work. "Sri Rama, Jayarama . . . ," he repeated with a desperate fervor, but the effect lasted not even a second. Unnoticed, his thoughts strayed, questioning: Who was that fellow in a check shirt and silk upper cloth over his shoulder descending the steps last evening when I went out to the market? Seen him somewhere . . . where? when? . . . ah, he was the big tailor on Market Road . . . with fashionable men and women clustering round him! Master-cutter who was a member of two or three clubs . . . Hobnobbed with officers and businessmen—and this was how he spent his evening, lounging on the human mattress! And yet fashionable persons allowed him to touch them with his measuring tape! Contamination, nothing but contamination; sinful life. He cried out in the lonely room, "Rama! Rama!" as if hailing someone hard of hearing. Presently he realized it was a futile exercise. Rama was a perfect incarnation, of course, but he was mild and gentle until provoked beyond limit, when he would storm and annihilate the evildoer without a trace, even if he was a monster like Ravana. Normally, however, he had forbearance, hence the repetition of his name only resulted in calmness and peace, but the present occasion demanded stern measures. God Siva's mantra should help. Did he not open his Third Eye and reduce the God of Love to ashes, when the latter slyly aimed his arrow at him while he was meditating? Our hermit pictured the god of matted locks and fiery eyes and recited aloud: "Om Namasivaya," that lonely hall resounding with his hoarse voice. His rambling, unwholesome thoughts were halted for a while, but presently regained their vigor and raced after the woman. She opened her door at least six times on an evening. Did she sleep with them all together at the same time? He paused to laugh at this notion, and also realized that his meditation on the austere god was gone. He banged his fist on his temples, which pained but improved his concentration. "Om Namasivaya . . ." Part of his mind noted the creaking of the door of the opposite house. She was a serpent in whose coils everyone was caught and destroyed—old and young and the middle-aged, tailors and students (he had noticed a couple of days ago a young B.Sc. student from Albert Mission Hostel at her door), lawyers and magistrates (why not?) . . . No wonder the world was getting overpopulated—with such pressure of the elemental urge within every individual! O God Siva, this woman must be eliminated. He would confront her some day and tell her to get out. He would tell her, "Oh, sinful wretch, who is spreading disease and filth like an open sewer: think of the contamination you have spread around—from middle-aged tailor to B.Sc. student. You are out to destroy mankind. Repent your sins, shave your head, cover your ample loins with sackcloth, sit at the temple gate and beg or drown yourself in sarayu after praying for a cleaner life at least in the next birth . . ."

Thus went his dialogue, the thought of the woman never leaving his mind, during all the wretched, ill-spent night; he lay tossing on the bare floor. He rose before dawn, his mind made up. He would clear out immediately, cross Nallappa's Grove, and reach the other side of the river. He did not need a permanent roof; he would drift and rest in any temple or mantap or in the shade of a banyan tree: he recollected an ancient tale he had heard from his guru long ago . . . A harlot was sent to heaven when she died, while her detractor, a self-righteous reformer, found himself in hell. It was explained that while the harlot sinned only with her body, her detractor was corrupt mentally, as he was obsessed with the harlot and her activities, and could meditate on nothing else.

Our hermit packed his wicker box with his sparse possessions—a god's image in copper, a rosary, the deerskin, and a little brass bowl. Carrying his box in one hand, he stepped out of the house, closing the door gently behind him. In the dim hour of the dusk, shadowy figures were moving—a milkman driving his cow ahead, laborers bearing crowbars and spades, women with baskets on their way to the market. While he paused to take a final look at the shelter he was abandoning, he heard a plaintive cry,

"Swamiji," from the opposite house, and saw the woman approach him with a tray, heaped with fruits and flowers. She placed it at his feet and said in a low reverential whisper: "Please accept my offering. This is a day of remembrance of my mother. On this day I pray and seek a saint's blessing. Forgive me . . ." All the lines he had rehearsed for a confrontation deserted him at this moment; looking at her flabby figure, the dark rings under her eyes, he felt pity. As she bent down to prostrate, he noticed that her hair was indifferently dyed and that the parting in the middle widened into a bald patch over which a string of jasmine dangled loosely. He touched her tray with the tip of his finger as a token of acceptance, and went down the street without a word.

NAGUIB MAHFOUZ

Naguib Mahfouz (b.1911) was born in Cairo, Egypt. He studied philosophy at Cairo University, graduating in 1934. He worked as a civil servant and a university administrator as well as in the government film broadcasting organization, all the while writing the works that have made him the leading Arab novelist. Mahfouz's early work reflects a preoccupation with history, while in recent decades he has sought to capture life in modern-day Egypt. Mahfouz is known to be a recluse, and even receiving the 1988 Nobel prize for literature did not encourage him to step into the public eye.

Mahfouz's best-known works in English are *Midaq Alley* and *Miramar*.

THE CONJURER MADE OFF WITH THE DISH

'The time has come for you to be useful,' said my mother to me, and she slipped her hand into her pocket, saying:

'Take this piastre and go off and buy some beans. Don't play on the way and keep away from the cars.'

I took the dish, put on my clogs and went out, humming a tune. Finding a crowd in front of the bean-seller, I waited until I discovered a way through to the marble table.

'A piastre's worth of beans, mister,' I called out in my shrill voice.

He asked me impatiently:

'Beans alone? With oil? With cooking butter?'

I didn't answer and he said to me roughly:

'Make way for someone else.'

I withdrew, overcome by embarrassment and returned home defeated.

'Returning with an empty dish?' my mother shouted at me. 'What did you do—spill the beans or lose the piastre, you naughty boy?'

'Beans alone? With oil? With cooking butter—? you didn't tell me,' I protested.

'You stupid, what do you eat every morning?'

'I don't know.'

'You good-for-nothing, ask him for beans with oil.'

I went off to the man and said:

'A piastre's worth of beans with oil, mister.'

With a frown of impatience he asked:

'Linseed oil? Nut oil? Olive oil?'

I was taken aback and again made no answer:

'Make way for someone else,' he shouted at me.

I returned in a rage to my mother, who called out in astonishment:

'You've come back empty-handed—no beans and no oil.'

'Linseed oil? Nut oil? Olive oil?—you didn't tell me,' I said angrily.

'Beans with oil means beans with linseed oil.'

'How should I know?'

'You're a good-for-nothing and he's a tiresome man—tell him beans with linseed oil.'

'How should I know?'

I went off quickly and called out to the man while still some yards from his shop:

'Beans with linseed oil, mister.'

'Put the piastre on the counter,' he said, plunging the ladle into the pot.

I put my hand into my pocket but didn't find the piastre. I searched round for it anxiously. I turned my pocket inside out but found no trace of it. The man withdrew the ladle empty, saying with disgust:

'You've lost the piastre—you're not a boy to be depended on.'

'I haven't lost it,' I said, looking under my feet and round about me. 'It's been in my pocket all the time.'

'Make way for someone else and don't make trouble.'

I returned to my mother with an empty dish.

'Good grief, you idiot boy!'

'The piastre. . . .'

'What of it?'

'It wasn't in my pocket.'

'Did you buy sweets with it?'

'I swear I didn't.'

'How did you lose it?'

'I don't know.'

'Do you swear by the Koran you didn't buy anything with it?'

'I swear.'

'There's a hole in your pocket.'

'No there isn't.'

'Maybe you gave it to the man the first time or the second.'

'Maybe.'

'Are you sure of nothing?'

'I'm hungry.'

She clapped her hands together in a gesture of resignation.

'Never mind,' she said. 'I'll give you another piastre but I'll take it out of your money-box, and if you come back with an empty dish I'll break your head.'

I went off at a run, dreaming of a delicious breakfast. At the turning leading to the alleyway where the bean-seller was I saw a crowd of children and heard merry, festive sounds. My feet dragged as my heart was pulled towards them. At least let me have a fleeting glance. I slipped in amongst them and found the conjurer looking straight at me. A stupefying joy overwhelmed me; I was completely taken out of myself. With the whole of my being I became involved in the tricks of the rabbits and the eggs, and the snakes and the ropes. When the man came up to collect money, I drew back mumbling, 'I haven't got any money.'

He rushed at me savagely and I escaped only with difficulty. I ran off, my back almost broken by his blow, and yet I was utterly happy as I made my way to the seller of beans.

'Beans with linseed oil for a piastre, mister,' I said.

He went on looking at me without moving, so I repeated my request.

'Give me the dish,' he demanded angrily.

The dish! Where was the dish? Had I dropped it while running? Had the conjurer made off with it?

'Boy, you're out of your mind.'

I turned back, searching along the way for the lost dish. The place where the conjurer had been I found empty, but the voices of children led me to him in a nearby lane. I moved round the circle; when the conjurer spotted me he shouted out threateningly:

'Pay up or you'd better scram.'

'The dish!' I called out despairingly.

'What dish, you little devil?'

'Give me back the dish.'

'Scram or I'll make you into food for snakes.'

He had stolen the dish, yet fearfully I moved away out of sight and wept. Whenever a passer-by asked me why I was crying I would reply:

'The conjurer made off with the dish.'

Through my misery I became aware of a voice saying:

'Come along and watch.'

I looked behind me and saw a peep-show had been set up. I saw dozens of children hurrying towards it and taking it in turns to stand in front of the peepholes, while the man began making his commentary on the pictures:

'There you've got the gallant knight and the most beautiful of all ladies, Zainat al-Banat.'

Drying my tears, I gazed up in fascination at the box, completely forgetting the conjurer and the dish. Unable to overcome the temptation, I paid over the piastre and stood in front of the peep-hole next to a girl who was standing in front of the other one, and there flowed across our vision enchanting picture stories. When I came back to my own world I realized

I had lost both the piastre and the dish, and there was no sign of the conjurer. However, I gave no thought to the loss, so taken up was I with the pictures of chivalry, love and deeds of daring. I forgot my hunger; I forgot the fear of what threatened me back home. I took a few paces back so as to lean against an ancient wall of what had once been a Treasury and the seat of office of the Cadi, and gave myself up wholly to my reveries. For a long while I dreamt of chivalry, of Zainat al-Banat and the ghoul. In my dream I spoke aloud, giving meaning to my words with gestures. Thrusting home the imaginary lance, I said:

'Take that, O ghoul, right in the heart!'

'And he raised Zainat al-Banat up behind him on his horse,' came back a gentle voice.

I looked to my right and saw the young girl who had been beside me at the performance. She was wearing a dirty dress and coloured clogs and was playing with her long plait of hair; in her other hand were the red and white sweets called 'Lady's fleas,' which she was leisurely sucking. We exchanged glances and I lost my heart to her.

'Let's sit down and rest,' I said to her.

She appeared to be agreeable to my suggestion, so I took her by the arm and we went through the gateway of the ancient wall and sat down on the step of a stairway that went nowhere, a stairway that rose up until it ended in a platform behind which there could be seen a blue sky and minarets. We sat in silence, side by side. I pressed her hand and we sat on in silence, not knowing what to say. I experienced feelings that were new, strange and obscure. Putting my face close to hers, I breathed in the natural smell of her hair, mingled with an odour of earth, and the fragrance of breath mixed with the aroma of sweets. I kissed her lips. I swallowed my saliva which had taken on a sweetness from the dissolved 'Lady's fleas'. I put my arm around her, without her uttering a word, kissing her cheek and lips. Her lips grew still as they received the kiss, then went back to sucking at the sweets. At last she decided we should get up. I seized her arm anxiously.

'Sit down,' I said.

'I'm going,' she said simply.

'Where to?' I asked irritably.

'To the midwife Umm Ali,' and she pointed to a house at the bottom of which was a small ironing shop.

'Why?'

'To tell her to come quickly.'

'Why?'

'My mother's crying in pain at home. She told me to go to the midwife Umm Ali and to take her along quickly.'

'And you'll come back after that?'

She nodded her head in assent. Her mentioning her mother reminded me of my own and my heart missed a beat. Getting up from the ancient stairway, I made my way back home. I wept out loud, a tried method by which I would defend myself. I expected she would come to me but she did not. I wandered from the kitchen to the bedroom but found no trace of her. Where had my mother gone? When would she return? I was bored with being in the empty house. An idea occurred to me: I took a dish from the kitchen and piastre from my savings and went off immediately to the seller of beans. I found him asleep on a bench outside the shop, his face covered over by his arm. The pots of beans had vanished and the long-necked bottles of oil had been put back on the shelf and the marble top washed down.

'Mister,' I whispered, approaching.

Hearing nothing but his snoring, I touched his shoulder. He raised his arm in alarm and looked at me through reddened eyes.

'Mister.'

'What do you want?' he asked roughly, becoming aware of my presence and recognizing me.

'A piastre's worth of beans with linseed oil.'

'Eh?'

'I've got the piastre and I've got the dish.'

'You're crazy, boy,' he shouted at me. 'Get out or I'll bash your brains in.'

When I didn't move he pushed me so violently I went sprawling on to my back. I got up painfully, struggling to hold back the crying that was twisting my lips. My hands were clenched, one on the dish and the other on the piastre. I threw him an angry look. I thought about returning with my hopes dashed, but dreams of heroism and valour altered my plan of action. Resolutely, I made a quick decision and with all my strength threw the dish at him. It flew through the air and struck him on the head, while I took to my heels, heedless of everything. I was convinced I'd killed him, just as the knight had killed the ghoul. I didn't stop running till I was near the ancient wall. Panting, I looked behind me but saw no signs of any pursuit. I stopped to get my breath back, then asked myself what I should do now that the second dish was lost? Something warned me not to return home directly, and soon I had given myself over to a wave of indifference that bore me off where it willed. It meant a beating, neither more nor less, on my return, so let me put it off for a time. Here was the piastre in my hand and I could have some sort of enjoyment with it before being punished. I decided to pretend I had forgotten my having done wrong—but where was the conjurer, where was the peep-show? I looked everywhere for them but to no avail.

Worn out by this fruitless searching, I went off to the ancient stairway to keep my appointment. I sat down to wait, imagining to myself the meeting. I yearned for another kiss redolent with the fragrance of sweets. I admitted to myself that the little girl had given me sensations I had never experienced before. As I waited and dreamed, a whispering sound came to me from faraway behind me. I climbed the stairs cautiously and at the final landing I lay down flat on my face in order to see what was behind it, without anyone being able to spot me. I saw some ruins surrounded by a high wall, the last of what remained of the Treasury and the Chief Cadi's house. Directly under the stairs sat a man and a woman, and it was from them that the whispering came. The man looked like a tramp; the woman like one of those gypsies that tend sheep. An inner voice told me that their meeting was similar to the one I had had. Their lips and eyes revealed this, but they showed astonishing expertise in the extraordinary things they did. My gaze became rooted upon them with curiosity, surprise, pleasure, and a certain amount of disquiet. At last they sat down side by side, neither of them taking any notice of the other. After quite a while the man said:

'The money!'

'You're never satisfied,' she said irritably.

Spitting on the ground, he said: 'You're crazy.'

'You're a thief.'

He slapped her hard with the back of his hand, and she gathered up a handful of earth and threw it in his face. Then he sprang at her, fastening his fingers on her windpipe. In vain she gathered all her strength to escape from his grip. Her voice failed her, her eyes bulged out of their sockets, while her feet struck out at the air. In dumb terror I stared at the scene till I saw a thread of blood trickling down from her nose. A scream escaped from my mouth. Before the man raised his head, I had crawled backwards; descending the stairs at a jump, I raced off like mad to wherever my legs might carry me. I didn't stop running till I was out of breath. Gasping for breath, I was quite unaware of my whereabouts, but when I came to myself I found I was under a raised vault at the middle of a crossroads. I had never set foot there before and had no idea of where I was in relation to our quarter. On both sides sat sightless beggars, and crossing it from all directions were people who paid attention to no one. In terror I realized I had lost my way and that countless difficulties lay in wait for me before I would find my way home. Should I resort to asking one of the passers-by to direct me? What, though, would happen if chance should lead me to a man like the vendor of beans or the tramp of the waste plot? Would a miracle come about whereby I'd see my mother approaching so that I could eagerly hurry towards her? Should I try to make my own way, wandering about till I came across some familiar landmark that would indicate the direction I should take? I told myself that I should be resolute and take a quick decision: the day was passing and soon mysterious darkness would descend.

Translated by Denys Johnson-Davis

John Cheever

John Cheever (1912–1982) is surely one of the best-loved short story writers of the postwar era. Indeed, when *The Short Stories of John Cheever* was published in 1978, it won both the Pulitzer prize and the National Book Critics Circle Award and found a place on the *New York Times* bestseller list.

Cheever was born in Quincy, Massachusetts. The collapse of his family's business after the 1929 stock market crash seems to have planted in him a sharp sense of societal fragility—throughout his fiction his characters search, usually in vain, for stability and meaning in the face of change.

Cheever began his story-writing career early. After he was expelled from Thayer Academy at 17 for rebelliousness, he moved to New York City and started writing fiction. He had the good fortune to sell his first story to the *New Republic* while still in his teens. Soon he was publishing his work in most of the leading magazines of the day, finding an especially hospitable home at the *New Yorker.* His first collection, *The Way Some People Live,* appeared in 1942, while Cheever was in the army. After the war he published several well-received collections and then followed through with two novels, *The Wapshot Chronicle* (1957) and *The Wapshot Scandal* (1964). The first of these drew heavily upon his memories of growing up on the South Shore of Boston. Cheever's later works include the novels *Bullet Park* (1969) and *Falconer* (1977).

Cheever's personal life was marked by a long struggle with alcoholism and an ambivalence about his homosexual inclinations. His daughter, Susan Cheever, has written movingly about her father's private distress.

While Cheever was applauded from the start for his bright precision and his skill at depicting the lives and aspirations of the American upper-middle class, readers were also well aware of a melancholy, brooding quality. The world, rendered so finely, was always shown to be vulnerable to the work of time. Dreams grew tarnished, passions faded, and a sad evening light was seen in the windows of the houses of the well-to-do.

TORCH SONG

After Jack Lorey had known Joan Harris in New York for a few years, he began to think of her as the Widow. She always wore black, and he was always given the feeling, by a curious disorder in her apartment, that the undertakers had just left. This impression did not stem from malice on his part, for he was fond of Joan. They came from the same city in Ohio and had reached New York at about the same time in the middle thirties. They were the same age, and during their first summer in the city they used to meet after work and drink Martinis in places like the Brevoort and Charles', and have dinner and play checkers at the Lafayette.

Joan went to a school for models when she settled in the city, but it turned out that she photographed badly, so after spending six weeks learning how to walk with a book on her head she got a job as a hostess in a Longchamps. For the rest of the summer she stood by the hatrack, bathed in an intense pink light and the string music of heartbreak, swinging her mane of dark hair and her black skirt as she moved forward to greet the customers. She was then a big, handsome girl with a wonderful voice, and her face, her whole presence, always seemed infused with a gentle and healthy pleasure at her surroundings, whatever they were. She was innocently and incorrigibly convivial, and would get out of bed and dress at three in the morning if someone called her and asked her to come out for a drink, as Jack often did. In the fall, she got some kind of freshman executive job in a department store. They saw less and less of each other and then for quite a while stopped seeing each other altogether. Jack was living with a girl he had met at a party, and it never occurred to him to wonder what had become of Joan.

Jack's girl had some friends in Pennsylvania, and in the spring and summer of his second year in town he often went there with her for weekends. All of this—the shared apartment in the Village, the illicit relationship, the Friday-night train to a country house—was what he had imagined life in New York to be, and he was intensely happy. He was returning to New York with his girl one Sunday night on the Lehigh line. It was one of those trains that move slowly across the face of New Jersey, bringing back to the city hundreds of people, like the victims of an immense and strenuous picnic, whose faces are blazing and whose muscles are lame. Jack and his girl, like most of the other passengers, were overburdened with vegetables and flowers. When the train stopped in Pennsylvania Station, they moved with the crowd along the platform, toward the escalator. As they were passing the wide, lighted windows of the diner, Jack turned his head and saw Joan. It was the first time he had seen her since Thanksgiving, or since Christmas. He couldn't remember.

Joan was with a man who had obviously passed out. His head was in his arms on the table, and an overturned highball glass was near one of his elbows. Joan was shaking his shoulders gently and speaking to him. She seemed to be vaguely troubled, vaguely amused. The waiters had cleared off all the other tables and were standing around Joan, waiting for her to resurrect her escort. It troubled Jack to see in these straits a girl who reminded him of the trees and the lawns of his home town, but there was nothing he could do to help. Joan continued to shake the man's shoulders, and the crowd pressed Jack past one after another of the diner's windows, past the malodorous kitchen, and up the escalator.

He saw Joan again, later that summer, when he was having dinner in a Village restaurant. He was with a new girl, a Southerner. There were many Southern girls in the city that year. Jack and his belle had wandered into the restaurant because it was convenient, but the food was terrible and the place was lighted with candles. Halfway through dinner, Jack noticed Joan on the other side of the room, and when he had finished eating, he crossed the room and spoke to her. She was with a tall man who was wearing a monocle. He stood, bowed stiffly from the waist, and said to Jack, "We are very pleased to meet you." Then he excused himself and headed for the toilet. "He's a count, he's a Swedish count," Joan said. "He's on the radio, Friday afternoons at four-fifteen. Isn't it exciting?" She seemed to be delighted with the count and the terrible restaurant.

Sometime the next winter, Jack moved from the Village to an apartment in the East Thirties. He was crossing Park Avenue one cold morning on his way to the office when he noticed, in the crowd, a woman he had met a few times at Joan's apartment. He spoke to her and asked about his friend. "Haven't you heard?" she said. She pulled a long face. "Perhaps I'd better tell you. Perhaps you can help." She and Jack had breakfast in a drugstore on Madison Avenue and she unburdened herself of the story.

The count had a program called "The Song of the Fiords," or something like that, and he sang Swedish folk songs. Everyone suspected him of being a fake, but that didn't bother Joan. He had met her at a party and, sensing a soft touch, had moved in with her the following night. About a week later, he complained of pains in his back and said he must have some morphine. Then he needed morphine all the time. If he didn't get morphine, he was abusive and violent. Joan began to deal with those doctors and druggists who peddle dope, and when they wouldn't supply her, she went down to the bottom of the city. Her friends were afraid she would be found some morning stuffed in a drain. She got pregnant. She had an abortion. The count left her and moved to a flea bag near Times Square, but she was so impressed by then with his helplessness, so afraid that he would die without her, that she followed him there and shared his room and continued to buy his narcotics. He abandoned her again, and Joan waited a week for him to return before she went back to her place and her friends in the Village.

It shocked Jack to think of the innocent girl from Ohio having lived with a brutal dope addict and traded with criminals, and when he got to his office that morning, he telephoned her and made a date for dinner that night. He met her at Charles'. When she came into the bar, she seemed as wholesome and calm as ever. Her voice was sweet, and reminded him of elms, of lawns, of those glass arrangements that used to be hung from porch ceilings to tinkle in the summer wind. She told him about the count. She spoke of him charitably and with no trace of bitterness, as if her voice, her disposition, were incapable of registering anything beyond simple affection and pleasure. Her walk, when she moved ahead of him toward their table, was light and graceful. She ate a large dinner and talked enthusiastically about her job. They went to a movie and said goodbye in front of her apartment house.

That winter, Jack met a girl he decided to marry. Their engagement was announced in January and they planned to marry in July. In the spring, he received, in his office mail, an invitation to cocktails at Joan's. It was for a Saturday when his fiancée was going to Massachusetts to visit her parents, and when the time came and he had nothing better to do, he took a bus to the Village. Joan had the same apartment. It was a walk-up. You rang the bell above the mailbox in the vestibule and were answered with a death rattle in the lock. Joan lived on the third floor. Her calling card was in a slot in the mailbox, and above her name was written the name Hugh Bascomb.

Jack climbed the two flights of carpeted stairs, and when he reached Joan's apartment, she was standing by the open door in a black dress. After she greeted Jack, she took his arm and guided him across the room. "I want you to meet Hugh, Jack," she said.

Hugh was a big man with a red face and pale-blue eyes. His manner was courtly and his eyes were inflamed with drink. Jack talked with him for a little while and then went over to speak to someone he knew, who was standing by the mantelpiece. He noticed then, for the first time, the indescribable disorder of Joan's apartment. The books were in their shelves and the furniture was reasonably good, but the place was all wrong, somehow. It was as if things had been put in place without thought or real interest, and for the first time, too, he had the impression that there had been a death there recently.

As Jack moved around the room, he felt that he had met the ten or twelve guests at other parties. There was a woman executive with a fancy hat, a man who could imitate Roosevelt, a grim couple whose play was in rehearsal, and a newspaperman who kept turning on the radio for news of the Spanish Civil War. Jack drank Martinis and talked with the woman in the fancy hat. He looked out of the window at the back yards and the ailanthus trees and heard, in the distance, thunder exploding off the cliffs of the Hudson.

Hugh Bascomb got very drunk. He began to spill liquor, as if drinking, for him, were a kind of jolly slaughter and he enjoyed the bloodshed and the mess. He spilled whiskey from a bottle. He spilled a drink on his shirt and then tipped over someone else's drink. The party was not quiet, but Hugh's hoarse voice began to dominate the others. He attacked a photographer who was sitting in a corner explaining camera techniques to a homely woman. "What did you come to the party for if all you wanted to do was to sit there and stare at your shoes?" Hugh shouted. "What did you come for? Why don't you stay at home?"

The photographer didn't know what to say. He was not staring at his shoes. Joan moved lightly to Hugh's side. "Please don't get into a fight now, darling," she said. "Not this afternoon."

"Shut up," he said. "Let me alone. Mind your own business." He lost his balance, and in struggling to steady himself he tipped over a lamp.

"Oh, your lovely lamp, Joan," a woman sighed.

"Lamps!" Hugh roared. He threw his arms into the air and worked them around his head as if he were bludgeoning himself. "Lamps. Glasses. Cigarette boxes. Dishes. They're killing me. They're killing me, for Christ's sake. Let's all go up to the mountains and hunt and fish and live like men, for Christ's sake."

People were scattering as if a rain had begun to fall in the room. It had, as a matter of fact, begun to rain outside. Someone offered Jack a ride uptown, and he jumped at the chance. Joan stood at the door, saying goodbye to her routed friends. Her voice remained soft, and her manner, unlike that of those Christian women who in the face of disaster can summon new and formidable sources of composure, seemed genuinely simple. She appeared to be oblivious of the raging drunk at her back, who was pacing up and down, grinding glass into the rug, and haranguing one of the survivors of the party with a story of how he, Hugh, had once gone without food for three weeks.

In July, Jack was married in an orchard in Duxbury, and he and his wife went to West Chop for a few weeks. When they returned to town, their apartment was cluttered with presents, including a dozen after-dinner coffee cups from Joan. His wife sent her the required note, but they did nothing else.

Late in the summer, Joan telephoned Jack at his office and asked if he wouldn't bring his wife to see her; she named an evening the following week. He felt guilty about not having called her, and accepted the invitation. This made his wife angry. She was an ambitious girl who liked a social life that offered rewards, and she went unwillingly to Joan's Village apartment with him.

Written above Joan's name on the mailbox was the name Franz Denzel. Jack and his wife climbed the stairs and were met by Joan at the open door. They went into her apartment and found themselves among a group of people for whom Jack, at least, was unable to find any bearings.

Franz Denzel was a middle-aged German. His face was pinched with bitterness or illness. He greeted Jack and his wife with that elaborate and clever politeness that is intended to make guests feel that they have come too early or too late. He insisted sharply upon Jack's sitting in the chair in which he himself had been sitting, and then went and sat on a radiator.

There were five other Germans sitting around the room, drinking coffee. In a corner was another American couple, who looked uncomfortable. Joan passed Jack and his wife small cups of coffee with whipped cream. "These cups belonged to Franz's mother," she said. "Aren't they lovely? They were the only things he took from Germany when he escaped from the Nazis."

Franz turned to Jack and said, "Perhaps you will give us your opinion on the American educational system. That is what we were discussing when you arrived."

Before Jack could speak, one of the German guests opened an attack on the American educational system. The other Germans joined in, and went on from there to describe every vulgarity that had impressed them in American life and to contrast German and American culture generally. Where, they asked one another passionately, could you find in America anything like the Mitropa dining cars, the Black Forest, the pictures in Munich, the music in Bayreuth? Franz and his friends began speaking in German. Neither Jack nor his wife nor Joan could understand German, and the other American couple had not opened their mouths since they were introduced. Joan went happily around the room, filling everyone's cup with coffee, as if the music of a foreign language were enough to make an evening for her.

Jack drank five cups of coffee. He was desperately uncomfortable. Joan went into the kitchen while the Germans were laughing at their German jokes, and he hoped she would return with some drinks, but when she came back, it was with a tray of ice cream and mulberries.

"Isn't this pleasant?" Franz asked, speaking in English again.

Joan collected the coffee cups, and as she was about to take them back to the kitchen, Franz stopped her.

"Isn't one of those cups chipped?"

"No, darling," Joan said. "I never let the maid touch them. I wash them myself."

"What's that?" he asked, pointing at the rim of one of the cups.

"That's the cup that's always been chipped, darling. It was chipped when you unpacked it. You noticed it then."

"These things were perfect when they arrived in this country," he said.

Joan went into the kitchen and he followed her.

Jack tried to make conversation with the Germans. From the kitchen there was the sound of a blow and a cry. Franz returned and began to eat his mulberries greedily. Joan came back with her dish of ice cream. Her voice was gentle. Her tears, if she had been crying, had dried as quickly as the tears of a child. Jack and his wife finished their ice cream and made their escape. The wasted and unnerving evening enraged Jack's wife, and he supposed that he would never see Joan again.

Jack's wife got pregnant early in the fall, and she seized on all the prerogatives of an expectant mother. She took long naps, ate canned peaches in the middle of the night, and talked about the rudimentary kidney. She chose to see only other couples who were expecting children, and the parties that she and Jack gave were temperate. The baby, a boy, was born in May, and Jack was very proud and happy. The first party he and his wife went to after her convalescence was the wedding of a girl whose family Jack had known in Ohio.

The wedding was at St. James's, and afterward there was a big reception at the River Club. There was an orchestra dressed like Hungarians, and a lot of champagne and Scotch. Toward the end of the afternoon, Jack was walking down a dim corridor when he heard Joan's voice. "Please don't, darling," she was saying. "You'll break my arm. *Please* don't, darling." She was being pressed against the wall by a man who seemed to be twisting her arm. As soon as they saw Jack, the struggle stopped. All three of them were intensely embarrassed. Joan's face was wet and she made an effort to smile through her tears at Jack. He said hello and went on without stopping. When he returned, she and the man had disappeared.

When Jack's son was less than two years old, his wife flew with the baby to Nevada to get a divorce. Jack gave her the apartment and all its furnishings and took a room in a hotel near Grand Central. His wife got her decree in due course, and the story was in the newspapers. Jack had a telephone call from Joan a few days later.

"I'm awfully sorry to hear about your divorce, Jack," she said. "She seemed like *such* a nice girl. But that wasn't what I called you about. I want your help, and I wondered if you could come down to my place tonight around six. It's something I don't want to talk about over the phone."

He went obediently to the Village that night and climbed the stairs. Her apartment was a mess. The pictures and the curtains were down and the books were in boxes. "You moving, Joan?" he asked.

"That's what I wanted to see you about, Jack. First, I'll give you a drink." She made two Old-Fashioneds. "I'm being evicted, Jack," she said. "I'm being evicted because I'm an immoral woman. The couple who have the apartment downstairs—they're charming people, I've always thought—have told the real-estate agent that I'm a drunk and a prostitute and all kinds of things. Isn't that fantastic? This real-estate agent has always been so nice to me that I didn't think he'd believe them, but he's canceled my lease, and if I make any trouble, he's threatened to take the matter up with the store, and I don't want to lose my job. This nice real-estate agent won't even talk with me any more. When I go over to the office, the receptionist leers at me as if I were some kind of dreadful woman. Of course, there have been a lot of men here and we sometimes are noisy, but I can't be expected to go to bed at ten every night. Can I? Well, the agent who manages this building has apparently told all the other agents in the neighborhood that I'm an immoral and drunken woman, and none of them will give me an apartment. I went in to talk with one man—he seemed to be such a nice old gentleman—and he made me an indecent proposal. Isn't it fantastic? I have to be out of here on Thursday and I'm literally being turned out into the street."

Joan seemed as serene and innocent as ever while she described this scourge of agents and neighbors. Jack listened carefully for some sign of indignation or bitterness or even urgency in her recital, but there was none. He was reminded of a torch song, of one of those forlorn and touching ballads that had been sung neither for him nor for her but for their older brothers and sisters by Marion Harris. Joan seemed to be singing her wrongs.

"They've made my life miserable," she went on quietly. "If I keep the radio on after ten o'clock, they telephone the agent in the morning and tell him I had some kind of orgy here. One night when Philip—I don't think you've met Philip; he's in the Royal Air Force; he's gone back to England—one night when Philip and some other people were here, they called the police. The police came bursting in the door and talked to me as if I were I don't know what and then looked in the bedroom. If they think there's a man up here after midnight, they call me on the telephone and say all kinds of disgusting things. Of course, I can put my furniture into storage and go to a hotel, I guess. I guess a hotel will take a woman with my kind of reputation, but I thought perhaps you might know of an apartment. I thought—"

It angered Jack to think of this big, splendid girl's being persecuted by her neighbors, and he said he would do what he could. He asked her to have dinner with him, but she said she was busy.

Having nothing better to do, Jack decided to walk uptown to his hotel. It was a hot night. The sky was overcast. On his way, he saw a parade in a dark side street off Broadway near Madison Square. All the buildings in the neighborhood were dark. It was so dark that he could not see the placards the marchers carried until he came to a street light. Their signs urged the entry of the United States into the war, and each platoon represented a nation that had been subjugated by the Axis powers. They marched up Broadway, as he watched, to no music, to no sound but their own steps on the rough cobbles. It was for the most part an army of elderly men and women—Poles, Norwegians, Danes, Jews, Chinese. A few idle people like himself lined the sidewalks, and the marchers passed between them with all the self-consciousness of enemy prisoners. There were children among them dressed in the costumes in which they had, for the newsreels, presented the Mayor with a package of tea, a petition, a protest, a constitution, a check, or a pair of tickets. They hobbled through the darkness of the loft neighborhood like a mortified and destroyed people, toward Greeley Square.

In the morning, Jack put the problem of finding an apartment for Joan up to his secretary. She started phoning real-estate agents, and by afternoon she had found a couple of available apartments in the West Twenties. Joan called Jack the next day to say that she had taken one of the apartments and to thank him.

Jack didn't see Joan again until the following summer. It was a Sunday evening; he had left a cocktail party in a Washington Square apartment and had decided to walk a few blocks up Fifth Avenue before he took a bus. As he was passing the Brevoort, Joan called to him. She was with a man at one of the tables on the sidewalk. She looked cool and fresh, and the man appeared to be respectable. His name, it turned out, was Pete Bristol. He invited Jack to sit down and join in a celebration. Germany had invaded Russia that weekend, and Joan and Pete were drinking champagne to celebrate Russia's changed position in the war. The three of them drank champagne until it got dark. They had dinner and drank champagne with their dinner. They drank more champagne afterward and then went over to the Lafayette and then to two or three other places. Joan had always been tireless in her gentle way. She hated to see the night end, and it was after three o'clock when Jack stumbled into his apartment. The following morning he woke up haggard and sick, and with no recollection of the last hour or so of the previous evening. His suit was soiled and he had lost his hat. He didn't get to his office until eleven. Joan had already called him twice, and she called him again soon after he got in. There was no hoarseness at all in her voice. She said that she had to see him, and he agreed to meet her for lunch in a seafood restaurant in the Fifties.

He was standing at the bar when she breezed in, looking as though she had taken no part in that calamitous night. The advice she wanted concerned selling her jewelry. Her grandmother had left her some jewelry, and she wanted to raise money on it but didn't know where to go. She took some rings and bracelets out of her purse and showed them to Jack. He said that he didn't know anything about jewelry but that he could lend her some money. "Oh, I couldn't borrow money from you, Jack," she said. "You see, I want to get the money for Pete. I want to help him. He wants to open an advertising agency, and he needs quite a lot to begin with." Jack didn't press her to accept his offer of a loan after that, and the project wasn't mentioned again during lunch.

He next heard about Joan from a young doctor who was a friend of theirs. "Have you seen Joan recently?" the doctor asked Jack one evening when they were having dinner together. He said no. "I gave her a checkup last week," the doctor said, "and while she's been through enough to kill the average mortal—and you'll never know what she's been through—she still has the constitution of a virtuous and healthy woman. Did you hear about the last one? She sold her jewelry to put him into some kind of business, and as soon as he got the money, he left her for another girl, who had a car—a convertible."

Jack was drafted into the Army in the spring of 1942. He was kept at Fort Dix for nearly a month, and during this time he came to New York in the evening whenever he could get permission. Those nights had for him the intense keenness of a reprieve, a sensation that was heightened by the fact that on the train in from Trenton women would often press upon him dog-eared copies of *Life* and half-eaten boxes of candy, as though the brown clothes he wore were surely cerements. He telephoned Joan from Pennsylvania Station one night. "Come right over, Jack," she said. "Come right over. I want you to meet Ralph."

She was living in that place in the West Twenties that Jack had found for her. The neighborhood was a slum. Ash cans stood in front of her house, and an old woman was there picking out bits of refuse and garbage and stuffing them into a perambulator. The house in which Joan's apartment was located was shabby, but the apartment itself seemed familiar. The furniture was the same. Joan was the same big, easygoing girl. "I'm so glad you called me," she said. "It's so good to see you. I'll make you a drink. I was having one myself. Ralph ought to be here by now. He promised to take me to dinner." Jack offered to take her to Cavanagh's, but she said that Ralph might come while she was out. "If he doesn't come by nine, I'm going to make myself a sandwich. I'm not really hungry."

Jack talked about the Army. She talked about the store. She had been working in the same place for—how long was it? He didn't know. He had never seen her at her desk and he couldn't imagine what she did. "I'm terribly sorry Ralph isn't here," she said. "I'm sure you'd like him. He's not a young man. He's a heart specialist who loves to play the viola." She turned on some lights, for the summer sky had got dark. "He has this dreadful wife on Riverside Drive and four ungrateful children. He—"

The noise of an air-raid siren, lugubrious and seeming to spring from pain, as if all the misery and indecision in the city had been given a voice, cut her off. Other sirens, in distant neighborhoods, sounded, until the dark air was full of their noise. "Let me fix you another drink before I have to turn out the lights," Joan said, and took his glass. She brought the drink back to him and snapped off the lights. They went to the windows, and, as children watch a thunderstorm, they watched the city darken. All the lights nearby went out but one. Air-raid wardens had begun to sound their whistles in the street. From a distant yard came a hoarse shriek of anger. "Put out your lights, you Fascists!" a woman screamed. "Put out your lights, you Nazi Fascist Germans. Turn out your lights. Turn out your lights." The last light went off. They went away from the window and sat in the lightless room.

In the darkness, Joan began to talk about her departed lovers, and from what she said Jack gathered that they had all had a hard time. Nils, the suspect count, was dead. Hugh Bascomb, the drunk, had joined the Merchant Marine and was missing in the North Atlantic. Franz, the German, had taken poison the night the Nazis bombed Warsaw. "We listened to the news on the radio," Joan said, "and then he went back to his hotel and took poison. The maid found him dead in the bathroom the next morning." When Jack asked her about the one who was going to open an advertising agency, she seemed at first to have forgotten him. "Oh, Pete," she said after a pause. "Well, he was always very sick, you know. He was supposed to go to Saranac, but he kept putting it off and putting it off and—" She stopped talking when she heard steps on the stairs, hoping, he supposed, that it was Ralph, but whoever it was turned at the landing and continued to the top of the house. "I wish Ralph would come," she said, with a sigh. "I want you to meet him." Jack asked her again to go out, but she refused, and when the all-clear sounded, he said goodbye.

Jack was shipped from Dix to an infantry training camp in the Carolinas and from there to an infantry division stationed in Georgia. He had been in Georgia three months when he married a girl from the Augusta boarding-house aristocracy. A year or so later, he crossed the continent in a day coach and thought sententiously that the last he might see of the country he loved was the desert towns like Barstow, that the last he might hear of it was the ringing of the trolleys on the Bay Bridge. He was sent into the Pacific and returned to the United States twenty months later, uninjured and apparently unchanged. As soon as he received his furlough, he went to Augusta. He presented his wife with the souvenirs he had brought from the islands, quarreled violently with her and all her family, and, after making arrangements for her to get an Arkansas divorce, left for New York.

Jack was discharged from the Army at a camp in the East a few months later. He took a vacation and then went back to the job he had left in 1942. He seemed to have picked up his life at approximately the moment when it had been interrupted by the war. In time, everything came to look and feel the same. He saw most of his old friends. Only two of the men he knew had been killed in the war. He didn't call Joan, but he met her one winter afternoon on a crosstown bus.

Her fresh face, her black clothes, and her soft voice instantly destroyed the sense—if he had ever had such a sense—that anything had changed or intervened since their last meeting, three or four years ago. She asked him up for cocktails and he went to her apartment the next Saturday afternoon. Her room and her guests reminded him of the parties she had given when she had first come to New York. There was a woman with a fancy hat, an elderly doctor, and a man who stayed close to the radio, listening for news from the Balkans. Jack wondered which of the men belonged to Joan and decided on an Englishman who kept coughing into a handkerchief that he pulled out of his sleeve. Jack was right. "Isn't Stephen brilliant?" Joan asked him a little later, when they were alone in a corner. "He knows more about the Polynesians than anyone else in the world."

Jack had returned not only to his old job but to his old salary. Since living costs had doubled and since he was paying alimony to two wives, he had to draw on his savings. He took another job, which promised more money, but it didn't last long and he found himself out of work. This didn't bother him at all. He still had money in the bank, and anyhow it was easy to borrow from friends. His indifference was the consequence not of lassitude or despair but rather of an excess of hope. He had the feeling that he had only recently come to New York from Ohio. The sense that he was very young and that the best years of his life still lay before him was an illusion that he could not seem to escape. There was all the time in the world. He was living in hotels then, moving from one to another every five days.

In the spring, Jack moved to a furnished room in the badlands west of Central Park. He was running out of money. Then, when he began to feel that a job was a desperate necessity, he got sick. At first, he seemed to have only a bad cold, but he was unable to shake it and he began to run a fever and to cough blood. The fever kept him drowsy most of the time, but he roused himself occasionally and went out to a cafeteria for a meal. He felt sure that none of his friends knew where he was, and he was glad of this. He hadn't counted on Joan.

Late one morning, he heard her speaking in the hall with his landlady. A few moments later, she knocked on his door. He was lying on the bed in a pair of pants and a soiled pajama top, and he didn't answer. She knocked again and walked in. "I've been looking everywhere for you, Jack," she said. She spoke softly. "When I found out that you were in a place like this I thought you must be broke or sick. I stopped at the bank and got some money, in case you're broke. I've brought you some Scotch. I thought a little drink wouldn't do you any harm. Want a little drink?"

Joan's dress was black. Her voice was low and serene. She sat in a chair beside his bed as if she had been coming there every day to nurse him. Her features had coarsened, he thought, but there were still very few lines in her face. She was heavier. She was nearly fat. She was wearing black cotton gloves. She got two glasses and poured Scotch into them. He drank his whiskey greedily. "I didn't get to bed until three last night," she said. Her voice had once before reminded him of a gentle and despairing song, but now, perhaps because he was sick, her mildness, the mourning she wore, her stealthy grace, made him uneasy. "It was one of those nights," she said. "We went to the theatre. Afterward, someone asked us up to his place. I don't know who he was. It was one of those places. They're so strange. There were some meat-eating plants and a collection of Chinese snuff bottles. Why do people collect Chinese snuff bottles? We all autographed a lampshade, as I remember, but I can't remember much."

Jack tried to sit up in bed, as if there were some need to defend himself, and then fell back again, against the pillows. "How did you find me, Joan?" he asked.

"It was simple," she said. "I called that hotel. The one you were staying in. They gave me this address. My secretary got the telephone number. Have another little drink."

"You know, you've never come to a place of mine before—never," he said. "Why did you come now?"

"Why did I come, darling?" she asked. "What a question! I've known you for thirty years. You're the oldest friend I have in New York. Remember that night in the Village when it snowed and we stayed up until morning and drank whiskey sours for breakfast? That doesn't seem like twelve years ago. And that night—"

"I don't like to have you see me in a place like this," he said earnestly. He touched his face and felt his beard.

"And all the people who used to imitate Roosevelt," she said, as if she had not heard him, as if she were deaf. "And that place on Staten Island where we all used to go for dinner when Henry had a car. Poor Henry. He bought a place in Connecticut and went out there by himself one weekend. He fell asleep with a lighted cigarette and the house, the barn, everything burned. Ethel took the children out to California." She poured more Scotch into his glass and handed it to him. She lighted a cigarette and put it between his lips. The intimacy of this gesture, which made it seem not only as if he were deathly ill but as if he were her lover, troubled him.

"As soon as I'm better," he said, "I'll take a room at a good hotel. I'll call you then. It was nice of you to come."

"Oh, don't be ashamed of this room, Jack," she said. "Rooms never bother me. It doesn't seem to matter to me where I am. Stanley had a filthy room in Chelsea. At least, other people told me it was filthy. I never noticed it. Rats used to eat the food I brought him. He used to have to hang the food from the ceiling, from the light chain."

"I'll call you as soon as I'm better," Jack said. "I think I can sleep now if I'm left alone. I seem to need a lot of sleep."

"You really *are* sick, darling," she said. "You must have a fever." She sat on the edge of his bed and put a hand on his forehead.

"How is that Englishman, Joan?" he asked. "Do you still see him?"

"What Englishman?" she said.

"You know. I met him at your house. He kept a handkerchief up his sleeve. He coughed all the time. You know the one I mean."

"You must be thinking of someone else," she said. "I haven't had an Englishman at my place since the war. Of course, I can't remember everyone." She turned and, taking one of his hands, linked her fingers in his.

"He's dead, isn't he?" Jack said. "That Englishman's dead." He pushed her off the bed, and got up himself. "Get out," he said.

"You're sick, darling," she said. "I can't leave you alone here."

"Get out," he said again, and when she didn't move, he shouted, "What kind of an obscenity are you that you can smell sickness and death the way you do?"

"You poor darling."

"Does it make you feel young to watch the dying?" he shouted. "Is that the lewdness that keeps you young? Is that why you dress like a crow? Oh, I know there's nothing I can say that will hurt you. I know there's nothing filthy or corrupt or depraved or brutish or base that the others haven't tried, but this time you're wrong. I'm not ready. My life isn't ending. My life's beginning. There are wonderful years ahead of me. There are, there are wonderful, wonderful, wonderful years ahead of me, and when they're over, when it's time, then I'll call you. Then, as an old friend, I'll call you and give you whatever dirty pleasure you take in watching the dying, but until then, you and your ugly and misshapen forms will leave me alone."

She finished her drink and looked at her watch. "I guess I'd better show up at the office," she said. "I'll see you later. I'll come back tonight. You'll feel better then, you poor darling." She closed the door after her, and he heard her light step on the stairs.

Jack emptied the whiskey bottle into the sink. He began to dress. He stuffed his dirty clothes into a bag. He was trembling and crying with sickness and fear. He could see the blue sky from his window, and in his fear it seemed miraculous that the sky should be blue, that the white clouds should remind him of snow, that from the sidewalk he could hear the shrill voices of children shrieking, "I'm the king of the mountain, I'm the king of the mountain, I'm the king of the mountain." He emptied the ashtray containing his nail parings and cigarette butts into the toilet, and swept the floor with a shirt, so that there would be no trace of his life, of his body, when that lewd and searching shape of death came there to find him in the evening.

Patrick White

Patrick White (b.1912-1990) was born in England to Australian parents. White was still an infant when the family returned to Australia, where his father owned a sheep ranch. In his teens White was sent to school in England. He attended King's College, Cambridge, and there devoted himself to the study of languages. After he graduated, White moved to London and began writing. His first novel, *Happy Valley,* was published in 1939.

White spent the war years as an intelligence officer in the Royal Air Force in the Middle East and Greece. When the war ended, he returned to Australia. White was a prolific novelist, and his best-known works include *The Aunt's Story* (1946), *Voss* (1957), *Riders in the Chariot* (1961), *The Eye of the Storm* (1973), and *The Twyborn Affair* (1979). He was awarded the Nobel prize for literature in 1973.

FIVE-TWENTY

Most evenings, weather permitting, the Natwicks sat on the front veranda to watch the traffic. During the day the stream flowed, but towards five it began to thicken, it sometimes jammed solid like: the semi-trailers and refrigeration units, the decent old-style sedans, the mini-cars, the bombs, the Holdens and the Holdens. She didn't know most of the names. Royal did, he was a man, though never ever mechanical himself. She liked him to tell her about the vehicles, or listen to him take part in conversation with anyone who stopped at the fence. He could hold his own, on account of he was more educated, and an invalid has time to think.

They used to sit side by side on the tiled veranda, him in his wheel chair she had got him after the artheritis took over, her in the old cane. The old cane chair wasn't hardly presentable any more; she had torn her winter cardy on a nail and laddered several pair of stockings. You hadn't the heart to get rid of it, though. They brought it with them from Sarsaparilla after they sold the business. And now they could sit in comfort to watch the traffic, the big steel insects of nowadays, which put the wind up at her times.

Royal said, 'I reckon we're a shingle short to'uv ended up on the Parramatta Road.'

'You said we'd still see life,' she reminded, 'even if we lost the use of our legs.

'But look at the traffic! Worse every year. And air. Rot a man's lungs quicker than the cigarettes. You should've headed me off. You who's supposed to be practical!'

'I thought it was what you wanted,' she said, keeping it soft; she had never been one to crow.

'Anyway, I already lost the use of me legs.'

As if she was to blame for that too. She was so shocked the chair sort of jumped. It made her blood run cold to hear the metal feet screak against the little draught-board tiles.

'Well, I'aven't!' she protested. 'I got me legs, and will be able to get from 'ere to anywhere and bring 'ome the shopping. While I got me strength.'

She tried never to upset him by any show of emotion, but now she was so upset herself.

They watched the traffic in the evenings, as the orange light was stacked up in thick slabs, and the neon signs were coming on.

'See that bloke down there in the parti-coloured Holden?'

'Which?' she asked.

'The one level with our own gate.'

'The pink and brown?' She couldn't take all that interest tonight, only you must never stop humouring a sick man.

'Yairs. Pink. Fancy a man in a pink car!'

'Dusty pink is fashionable.' She knew that for sure.

'But a man!'

'Perhaps his wife chose it. Perhaps he's got a domineering wife.'

Royal laughed low. 'Looks the sort of coot who might like to be domineered, and if that's what he wants, it's none of our business, is it?'

She laughed to keep him company. They were such mates, everybody said. And it was true. She didn't know what she would do if Royal passed on first.

That evening the traffic had jammed. Some of the drivers began tooting. Some of them stuck their heads out, and yarned to one another. But the man in the pink-and-brown Holden just sat. He didn't look to either side.

Come to think of it, she had noticed him pass before. Yes. Though he wasn't in no way a noticeable man. Yes. She looked at her watch.

'Five-twenty,' she said. 'I seen that man in the pink-and-brown before. He's pretty regular. Looks like a business executive.'

Royal cleared his throat and spat. It didn't make the edge of the veranda. Better not to notice it, because he'd only create if she did. She'd get out that watering-can after she had pushed him inside.

'Business executives!' she heard. 'They're afraid people are gunner think they're poor class without they *execute*. In our day nobody was ashamed to *do*. Isn't that about right, eh?' She didn't answer because she knew she wasn't meant to. 'Funny sort of head that cove's got. Like it was half squashed. Silly-lookun bloody head!'

'Could have been born with it,' she suggested. 'Can't help what you're born with. Like your religion.'

There was the evening the Chev got crushed, only a young fellow too. Ahhh, it had stuck in her throat, thinking of the wife and kiddies. She ran in, and out again as quick as she could, with a couple of blankets, and the rug that was a present from Hazel. She had grabbed a pillow off their own bed.

She only faintly heard Royal shouting from the wheel-chair.

She arranged the blankets and the pillow on the pavement, under the orange sky. The young fellow was looking pretty sick, kept on turning his head as though he recognized and wanted to tell her something. Then the photographer from the *Mirror* took his picture, said she ought to be in it to add a touch of human interest, but she wouldn't. A priest came, the *Mirror* took his picture, administering what Mrs Dolan said they call Extreme Unkshun. Well, you couldn't poke fun at a person's religion any more than the shape of their head, and Mrs Dolan was a decent neighbour, the whole family, and clean.

When she got back to the veranda, Royal, a big man, had slipped down in his wheel-chair.

He said, or gasped, 'Wotcher wanter do that for, Ella? How are we gunner get the blood off?'

She hadn't thought about the blood, when of course she was all smeared with it, and the blankets, and Hazel's good Onkaparinka. Anyway, it was her who would get the blood off.

'You soak it in milk or something,' she said. 'I'll ask. Don't you worry.'

Then she did something. She bent down and kissed Royal on the forehead in front of the whole Parramatta Road. She regretted it at once, because he looked that powerless in his invalid chair, and his forehead felt cold and sweaty.

But you can't undo things that are done.

It was a blessing they could sit on the front veranda. Royal suffered a lot by now. He had his long-standing hernia, which they couldn't have operated on, on account of he was afraid of his heart. And then the artheritis.

'Arthritis.'

'All right,' she accepted the correction. 'Arth-er-itis.'

It was all very well for men, they could manage more of the hard words.

'What have we got for tea?' he asked.

'Well,' she said, fanning out her hands on the points of her elbows, and smiling, 'it's a surprise.'

She looked at her watch. It was five-twenty.

'It's a coupler nice little bits of fillet Mr Ballard let me have.'

'Wotcher mean let you have? Didn't you pay for them?'

She had to laugh. 'Anything I have I pay for!'

'Well? Think we're in the fillet-eating class?'

'It's only a treat, Royal,' she said. 'I got a chump chop for myself. I like a nice chop.'

He stopped complaining, and she was relieved.

'There's that gentleman,' she said, 'in the Holden.'

They watched him pass, as sober as their own habits.

Royal—he had been his mother's little king. Most of his mates called him 'Roy'. Perhaps only her and Mrs Natwick had stuck to the christened name, they felt it suited.

She often wondered how Royal had ever fancied her: such a big man, with glossy hair, black, and a nose like on someone historical. She would never have said it, but she was proud of Royal's nose. She was proud of the photo he had of the old family home in Kent, the thatch so lovely, and Grannie Natwick sitting in her apron on a rush-bottom chair in front, looking certainly not all that different from Mum, with the aunts gathered round in leggermutton sleeves, all big nosey women like Royal.

She had heard Mum telling Royal's mother, 'Ella's a plain little thing, but what's better than cheerful and willing?' She had always been on the mousey side, she supposed, which didn't mean she couldn't chatter with the right person. She heard Mum telling Mrs Natwick, 'My Ella can wash and bake against any comers. Clever with her needle too.' She had never entered any of the competitions, like they told her she ought to, it would have made her nervous.

It was all the stranger that Royal had ever fancied her.

Once as they sat on the veranda watching the evening traffic, she said, 'Remember how you used to ride out in the old days from "Bugilbar" to Cootramundra?'

'Cootramundra.'

'Yes,' she said. 'Cootramundra.' (That's why they'd called the house 'Coota' when they moved to the Parramatta Road.)

She had been so dazzled on one occasion by his parti-coloured forehead and his black hair, after he had got down from the saddle, after he had taken off his hat, she had run and fetched a duster, and dusted Royal Natwick's boots. The pair of new elastic-sides was white with dust from the long ride. It only occurred to her as she polished she might be doing something shameful, but when she looked up, it seemed as though Royal Natwick saw nothing peculiar in Ella McWhirter dusting his boots. He might even have expected it. She was so glad she could have cried.

Old Mr Natwick had come out from Kent when a youth, and after working at several uncongenial jobs, and studying at night, had been taken on as bookkeeper at 'Bugilbar'. He was much valued in the end by the owners, and always made use of. The father would have liked his son to follow in his footsteps, and taught him how to keep the books, but Royal wasn't going to hang around any family of purse-proud squatters, telling them the things they wanted to hear. He had ideas of his own for becoming rich and important.

So when he married Ella McWhirter, which nobody could ever understand, not even Ella herself, perhaps only Royal, who never bothered to explain (why should he?) they moved to Juggerawa, and took over the general store. It was in a bad way, and soon was in a worse, because Royal's ideas were above those of his customers.

Fulbrook was the next stage. He found employment as book-keeper on a grazing property outside. She felt so humiliated on account of his humiliation. It didn't matter about herself because she always expected less. She took a job in Fulbrook from the start, at the 'Dixie Cafe' in High Street. She worked there several years as waitress, helping out with the scrubbing for the sake of the extra money. She had never hated anything, but got to hate the flies trampling in the sugar and on the necks of the tomato sauce bottles.

At weekends her husband usually came in, and when she wasn't needed in the shop, they lay on the bed in her upstairs room, listening to the corrugated iron and the warping white-washed weatherboard. She would have loved to do something for him, but in distress he complained about 'wet kisses'. It surprised her. She had always been afraid he might find her a bit too dry in her show of affection.

Those years at the 'Dixie Cafe' certainly dried her up. She got those freckly patches and seams in her skin in spite of the lotions used as directed. Not that it matters so much in anyone born plain. Perhaps her plainness helped her save. There was never a day when she didn't study her savings-book, it became her favourite recreation.

Royal, on the other hand, wasn't the type that dries up, being fleshier, and dark. He even put on weight out at the grazing property, where they soon thought the world of him. When the young ladies were short of a man for tennis the book-keeper was often invited, and to a ball once at the homestead. He was earning good money, and he too saved a bit, though his instincts weren't as mean as hers. For instance, he fancied a choice cigar. In his youth Royal was a natty dresser.

Sometimes the young ladies, if they decided to inspect the latest at Ryan's Emporium, or Mr Philup, if he felt like grogging up with the locals, would drive him in, and as he got out they would look funny at the book-keeper's wife they had heard about, they must have, serving out the plates of frizzled steak and limp chips. Royal always waited to see his employers drive off before coming in.

In spite of the savings, this might have gone on much longer than it did if old Mr Natwick hadn't died. It appeared he had been a very prudent man. He left them a nice little legacy. The evening of the news, Royal was driven in by Mr Philup and they had a few at the Imperial. Afterwards the book-keeper was dropped off, because he proposed to spend the night with his wife and catch the early train to attend his father's funeral.

They lay in the hot little room and discussed the future. She had never felt so hectic. Royal got the idea he would like to develop a grocery business in one of the posh outer suburbs of Sydney. 'Interest the monied residents in some of the luxury lines. Appeal to the imagination as well as the stomach.'

She was impressed, of course, but not as much as she should have been. She wasn't sure, but perhaps she was short on imagination. Certainly their prospects had made her downright feverish, but for no distinct, sufficient reason.

'And have a baby.' She heard her own unnatural voice.

'Eh?'

'We could start a baby.' Her voice grew word by word drier.

'There's no reason why we couldn't have a baby. Or two.' He laughed. 'But starting a new life isn't the time to start a baby.' He dug her in the ribs. 'And you the practical one!'

She agreed it would be foolish, and presently Royal fell asleep.

What could she do for him? As he lay there breathing she would have loved to stroke his nose she could see faintly in the light from the window. Again unpractical, she would have liked to kiss it. Or bite it suddenly off.

She was so disgusted with herself she got creaking off the bed and walked flat across the boards to the washstand and swallowed a couple of Aspros to put her solidly to sleep.

All their life together she had to try in some way to make amends to Royal, not only for her foolishness, but for some of the thoughts that got into her head. Because she hadn't the imagination, the thoughts couldn't have been her own. They must have been put into her.

It was easier of course in later life, after he had cracked up, what with his hernia, and heart, and the artheritis taking over. Fortunately she was given the strength to help him into the wheel-chair, and later still, to lift, or drag him up on the pillows and over, to rub the bed-sores, and stick the pan under him. But even during the years at Sarsaparilla she could make amends in many little ways, though with him still in his prime, naturally he mustn't know of them. So all her acts were mostly for her own self-gratification.

The store at Sarsaparilla, if it didn't exactly flourish, gave them a decent living. She had her problems, though. Some of the locals just couldn't accept that Royal was a superior man. Perhaps she had been partly to blame, she hardly dared admit it, for showing one or two 'friends' the photo of the family home in Kent. She couldn't resist telling the story of one of the aunts, Miss Ethel Natwick, who followed her brother to New South Wales. Ethel was persuaded to accept a situation at Government House, but didn't like it and went back, in spite of the Governor's lady insisting she valued Ethel as a close personal friend. When people began to laugh at Royal on account of his auntie and the family home, as you couldn't help finding out in a place like Sarsaparilla, it was her, she knew, it was her to blame. It hurt her deeply.

Of course Royal could be difficult. Said stockbrokers had no palate and less imagination. Royal said no Australian grocer could make a go of it if it wasn't for flour, granulated sugar, and tomato sauce. Some of the customers turned nasty in retaliation. This was where she could help, and did, because Royal was out on delivery more often than not. It embarrassed her only when some of them took it for granted she was on their side. As if he wasn't her husband. Once or twice she had gone out crying afterwards, amongst the wormy wattles and hens' droppings. Anyone across the gully could have heard her blowing her nose behind the store, but she didn't care. Poor Royal.

There was that Mr Ogburn said, 'A selfish swollen-headed slob who'll chew you up and swallow you down.' She wouldn't let herself hear any more of what he had to say. Mr Ogburn had a hare-lip, badly sewn, opening and closing. There was nothing frightened her so much as even a well-disguised hare-lip. She got the palpitations after the scene with Mr Ogburn.

Not that there was anything wrong with her.

She only hadn't had the baby. It was her secret grief on black evenings as she walked slowly looking for the eggs a flighty hen might have hid in the bracken.

Dr Bamforth said, looking at the nib of his fountain pen, 'You know, don't you, it's sometimes the man?'

She didn't even want to hear, let alone think about it. In any case she wouldn't tell Royal, because a man's pride could be so easily hurt.

After they had sold out at Sarsaparilla and come to live at what they called 'Coota' on the Parramatta Road, it was both easier and more difficult, because if they were not exactly elderly they were getting on. Royal used to potter about in the beginning, while taking care, on account of the hernia and his heart. There was the business of the lawn-mowing, not that you could call it lawn, but it was what she had. She loved her garden. In front certainly there was only the two square of rather sooty grass which she would keep in order with the push-mower. The lawn seemed to get on Royal's nerves until the artheritis took hold of him. He had never liked mowing. He would lean against the veranda post, and shout, 'Don't know why we don't do what they've done down the street. Root the stuff out. Put down a green concrete lawn.'

'That would be copying,' she answered back.

She hoped it didn't sound stubborn. As she pushed the mower she bent her head, and smiled, waiting for him to cool off. The scent of grass and a few clippings flew up through the traffic fumes reminding you of summer.

While Royal shuffled along the veranda and leaned against another post. 'Or pebbles. You can buy clean, river pebbles. A few plastic shrubs, and there's the answer.'

He only gave up when his trouble forced him into the chair. You couldn't drive yourself up and down a veranda shouting at someone from a wheel-chair without the passers-by thinking you was a nut. So he quietened.

He watched her, though. From under the peak of his cap. Because she felt he might still resent her mowing the lawn, she would try to reassure him as she pushed. 'What's wrong, *eh*? While I still have me health, me *strength*—I was always what they call *wiry*—why shouldn't I cut the *grass?*'

She would come and sit beside him, to keep him company in watching the traffic, and invent games to amuse her invalid husband.

'Isn't that the feller we expect?' she might ask. 'The one that passes at five-twenty,' looking at her watch, 'in the old pink-and-brown Holden?'

They enjoyed their snort of amusement all the better because no one else knew the reason for it.

Once when the traffic was particularly dense, and that sort of chemical smell from one of the factories was thickening in the evening air, Royal drew her attention. 'Looks like he's got something on his mind.'

Could have too. Or it might have been the traffic block. The way he held his hands curved listlessly around the inactive wheel reminded her of possums and monkeys she had seen in cages. She shifted a bit. Her squeaky old chair. She felt uneasy for ever having found the man, not a joke, but half of one.

Royal's chair moved so smoothly on its rubber-tyred wheels it was easy to push him, specially after her practice with the mower. There were ramps where necessary now, to cover steps, and she would sometimes wheel him out to the back, where she grew hollyhock and sunflower against the palings, and a vegetable or two on raised beds.

Royal would sit not looking at the garden from under the peak of his cap.

She never attempted to take him down the shady side, between them and Dolans, because the path was narrow from plants spilling over, and the shade might have lowered his spirits.

She loved her garden.

The shady side was where she kept her staghorn ferns, and fishbones, and the pots of maidenhair. The water lay sparkling on the maidenhair even in the middle of the day. In the blaze of summer the light at either end of the tunnel was like you were looking through a sheet of yellow cellophane, but as the days shortened, the light deepened to a cold, tingling green, which might have made a person nervous who didn't know the tunnel by heart.

Take Mrs Dolan the evening she came in to ask for the loan of a cupful of sugar. 'You gave me a shock, Mrs Natwick. What ever are you up to?'

'Looking at the plants,' Mrs Natwick answered, whether Mrs Dolan would think it peculiar or not.

It was the season of cinerarias, which she always planted on that side, it was sheltered and cold-green. The wind couldn't bash the big spires and umbrellas of blue and purple. Visiting cats were the only danger, messing and pouncing. She disliked cats for the smell they left, but didn't have the heart to disturb their elastic forms curled at the cineraria roots, exposing their colourless pads, and sometimes pink, swollen teats. Blushing only slightly for it, she would stand and examine the details of the sleeping cats.

If Royal called she could hear his voice through the window. 'Where'uv you got to, Ella?'

After he was forced to take to his bed, his voice began to sort of dry up like his body. There were times when it sounded less like a voice than a breath of drowsiness or pain.

'Ella?' he was calling. 'I dropped the paper. Where are yer all this time? You know I can't pick up the paper.'

She knew. Guilt sent her scuttling to him, deliberately composing her eyes and mouth so as to arrive looking cheerful.

'I was in the garden,' she confessed, 'looking at the cinerarias.'

'The what?' It was a name Royal could never learn.

The room was smelling of sickness and the bottles standing on odd plates.

'It fell,' he complained.

She picked up the paper as quick as she could.

'Want to go la-la first?' she asked, because by now he depended on her to raise him and stick the pan under.

But she couldn't distract him from her shortcomings; he was shaking the paper at her. 'Haven't you lived with me long enough to know how to treat a newspaper?'

He hit it with his set hand, and certainly the paper looked a mess, like an old white battered brolly.

'Mucked up! You gotter keep the pages *aligned*. A paper's not readable otherwise. Of course you wouldn't understand because you don't read it, without it's to see who's died.' He began to cough.

'Like me to bring you some Bovril?' she asked him as tenderly as she knew.

'Bovril's the morning,' he coughed.

She knew that, but wanted to do something for him.

After she had rearranged the paper she walked out so carefully it made her go lopsided, out to the front veranda. Nothing would halt the traffic, not sickness, not death even.

She sat with her arms folded, realizing at last how they were aching.

'He hasn't been,' she had to call after looking at her watch.

'Who?' she heard the voice rustling back.

'The gentleman in the pink Holden.'

She listened to the silence, wondering whether she had done right.

When Royal called back, 'Could'uv had a blow-out.' Then he laughed. 'Could'uv stopped to get grogged up.' She heard the frail rustling of the paper. 'Or taken an axe to somebody like they do nowadays.'

She closed her eyes, whether for Royal, or what she remembered of the man sitting in the Holden.

Although it was cold she continued watching after dark. Might have caught a chill, when she couldn't afford to. She only went inside to make the bread-and-milk Royal fancied of an evening.

She watched most attentively, always at the time, but he didn't pass, and didn't pass.

'Who?'

'The gentleman in the Holden.'

'Gone on holiday.' Royal sighed, and she knew it was the point where a normal person would have turned over, so she went to turn him.

One morning she said on going in, 'Fancy, I had a dream, it was about that man! He was standing on the side path alongside the cinerarias. I know it was him because of his funny-shaped head.'

'What happened in the dream?' Royal hadn't opened his eyes yet; she hadn't helped him in with his teeth.

'I dunno,' she said, 'it was just a dream.'

That wasn't strictly truthful, because the Holden gentleman had looked at her, she had seen his eyes. Nothing was spoken, though.

'It was a sort of red and purple dream. That was the cinerarias,' she said.

'I don't dream. You don't when you don't sleep. Pills aren't sleep.'

She was horrified at her reverberating dream. 'Would you like a nice softboiled egg?'

'Eggs all have a taste.'

'But you gotter eat *something!*'

On another morning she told him—she could have bitten off her tongue—she *was* stupid, *stupid,* 'I had a dream.'

'What sort of dream?'

'Oh,' she said, 'a silly one. Not worth telling. I dreamed I dropped an egg on the side path, and it turned into two. Not two. A double-yolker.'

She never realized Royal was so much like Mrs Natwick. It was as she raised him on his pillows. Or he had got like that in his sickness. Old men and old women were not unlike.

'Wasn't that a silly one?' she coaxed.

Every evening she sat on the front veranda and watched the traffic as though Royal had been beside her. Looked at her watch. And turned her face away from the steady-flowing stream. The way she bunched her small chest she could have had a sour breath mounting in her throat. Sometimes she had, it was nervousness.

When she went inside she announced, 'He didn't pass.'

Royal said—he had taken to speaking from behind his eyelids—'Something muster happened to 'im. He didn't go on holiday. He went and died.'

'Oh, no! He wasn't of an age!'

At once she saw how stupid she was, and went out to get the bread-and-milk.

She would sit at the beside, almost crouching against the edge of the mattress, because she wanted Royal to feel she was close, and he seemed to realize, though he mostly kept his eyelids down.

Then one evening she came running, she felt silly, her calves felt silly, her voice, 'He's come! At five-twenty! In a new cream Holden!'

Royal said without opening his eyes, 'See? I said 'e'd gone on holiday.'

More than ever she saw the look of Mrs Natwick.

Now every evening Royal asked, 'Has he been, Ella?'

Trying not to make it sound irritable or superior, she would answer, 'Not yet. It's only five.'

Every evening she sat watching, and sometimes would turn proud, arching her back, as she looked down from the veranda. The man was so small and ordinary.

She went in on one occasion, into the more than electric light, lowering her eyelids against the dazzle. 'You know, Royal, you could feel prouder of men when they rode horses. As they looked down at yer from under the brim of their hats. Remember that hat you used to wear? Riding in to Cootramundra?'

Royal died quietly that same year before the cinerarias had folded, while the cold westerlies were still blowing; the back page of the *Herald* was full of those who had been carried off. She was left with his hand, already set, in her own. They hadn't spoken, except about whether she had put out the garbage.

Everybody was very kind. She wouldn't have liked to admit it was enjoyable being a widow. She sat around for longer than she had ever sat, and let the dust gather. In the beginning acquaintances and neighbours brought her little presents of food: a billy-can of giblet soup, moulded veal with hard-boiled egg making a pattern in the jelly, cakes so dainty you couldn't taste them. But when she was no longer a novelty they left off coming. She didn't care any more than she cared about the dust. Sometimes she would catch sight of her face in the glass, and was surprised to see herself looking so calm and white.

Of course she was calm. The feeling part of her had been removed. What remained was a slack, discarded eiderdown. Must have been the pills Doctor gave.

Well-meaning people would call to her over the front fence, 'Don't you feel lonely, Mrs Natwick?' They spoke with a restrained horror, as though she had been suffering from an incurable disease.

But she called back proud and slow, 'I'm under sedation.'

'Arrr!' They nodded thoughtfully. 'What's 'e given yer?'

She shook her head. 'Pills,' she called back. 'They say they're the ones the actress died of.'

The people walked on, impressed.

As the evenings grew longer and heavier she sat later on the front veranda watching the traffic of the Parramatta Road, its flow becoming syrupy and almost benign: big bulbous sedate buses, chrysalis cars still without a life of their own, clinging in line to the back of their host-articulator, trucks loaded for distances, empty loose-sounding jolly lorries. Sometimes women, looking out from the cabins of trucks from beside their men, shared her lack of curiosity. The light was so fluid nobody lasted long enough. You would never have thought boys could kick a person to death, seeing their long soft hair floating behind their sports models.

Every evening she watched the cream Holden pass. And looked at her watch. It was like Royal was sitting beside her. Once she heard herself. 'Thought he was gunner look round tonight, in our direction.' How could a person feel lonely?

She was, though. She came face to face with it walking through the wreckage of her garden in the long slow steamy late summer. The Holden didn't pass of course of a Saturday or Sunday. Something, something had tricked her, not the pills, before the pills. She couldn't blame anybody, probably only herself. Everything depended on yourself. Take the garden. It was a shambles. She would have liked to protest, but began to cough from running her head against some powdery mildew. She could only blunder at first, like a cow, or runty starved heifer, on breaking into a garden. She had lost her old wiriness. She shambled, snapping dead stems, uprooting. Along the bleached palings there was a fretwork of hollyhock, the brown fur of rotting sunflower. She rushed at a praying mantis, a big pale one, and deliberately broke its back, and was sorry afterwards for what was done so easy and thoughtless.

As she stood panting in her black, finally yawning, she saw all she had to repair. The thought of the seasons piling up ahead made her feel tired but necessary, and she went in to bathe her face. Royal's denture in a tumbler on top of the medicine cabinet, she ought to move, or give to the Sallies. In the meantime she changed the water. She never forgot it. The teeth looked amazingly alive.

All that autumn, winter, she was continually amazed, at the dust she had let gather in the house, at old photographs, books, clothes. There was a feather she couldn't remember wearing, a scarlet feather, she *can't* have worn, and gloves with little fussy ruffles at the wrists, silver piping, like a snail had laid its trail round the edges. There was, she knew, funny things she had brought at times, and never worn, but she couldn't remember the gloves or the feather. And books. She had collected a few, though never a reader herself. Old people liked to give old books, and you took them so as not to hurt anybody's feelings. *Hubert's Crusade,* for instance. Lovely golden curls. Could have been Royal's father's book. Everybody was a child once. And almost everybody had one. At least if she had had a child she would have known it wasn't a white turnip, more of a praying mantis, which snaps too easy.

In the same box she had put away a coloured picture, *Cities of the Plain*, she couldn't remember seeing it before. The people escaping from the burning cities had committed some sin or other nobody ever thought, let alone talked, about. As they hurried between rocks, through what must have been the 'desert places', their faces looked long and wooden. All they had recently experienced could have shocked the expression out of them. She was fascinated by what made her shiver. And the couples with their arms still around one another. Well, if you were damned, better hang on to your sin. She didn't blame them.

She put the box away. Its inlay as well as its contents made it something secret and precious.

The autumn was still and golden, the winter vicious only in fits. It was what you could call a good winter. The cold floods of air and more concentrated streams of dark-green light poured along the shady side of the house where her cinerarias had massed. She had never seen such cinerarias: some of the spired ones reached almost as high as her chin, the solid heads of others waited in the tunnel of dark light to club you with their colours, of purple and drenching blue, and what they called 'wine'. She couldn't believe wine would have made her drunker.

Just as she would sit every evening watching the traffic, evening was the time she liked best to visit the cinerarias, when the icy cold seemed to make the flowers burn their deepest, purest. So it was again evening when her two objects converged: for some blissfully confident reason she hadn't bothered to ask herself whether she had seen the car pass, till here was this figure coming towards her along the tunnel. She knew at once who it was, although she had never seen him on his feet; she had never seen him full-face, but knew from the funny shape of his head as Royal had been the first to notice. He was not at all an impressive man, not much taller than herself, but broad. His footsteps on the brickwork sounded purposeful.

'Will you let me use your phone, please, madam?' he asked in a prepared voice. 'I'm having trouble with the Holden.'

This was the situation she had always been expecting: somebody asking to use the phone as a way to afterwards murdering you. Now that it might be about to happen she couldn't care.

She said yes. She thought her voice sounded muzzy. Perhaps he would think she was drunk.

She went on looking at him, at his eyes. His nose, like the shape of his head, wasn't up to much, but his eyes, his eyes, she dared to think, were filled with kindness.

'Cold, eh? but clean cold!' He laughed friendly, shuffling on the brick paving because she was keeping him waiting.

Only then she noticed his mouth. He had a hare-lip, there was no mistaking, although it was well sewn. She felt so calm in the circumstances. She would have even liked to touch it.

But said, 'Why, yes—the telephone,' she said, 'it's this way,' she said, 'it's just off the kitchen—because that's where you spend most of your life. Or in bed,' she ended.

She wished she hadn't added that. For the first time since they had been together she felt upset, thinking he might suspect her of wrong intentions.

But he laughed and said, 'That's correct! You got something there!' It sounded manly rather than educated.

She realized he was still waiting, and took him to the telephone.

While he was phoning she didn't listen. She never listened when other people were talking on the phone. The sight of her own kitchen surprised her. While his familiar voice went on. It was the voice she had held conversations with.

But he was ugly, real ugly, *deformed*. If it wasn't for the voice, the eyes. She couldn't remember the eyes, but seemed to know about them.

Then she heard him laying the coins beside the phone, extra loud, to show.

He came back into the kitchen smiling and looking. She could smell him now, and he had the smell of a clean man.

She became embarrassed at herself, and took him quickly out.

'Fair bit of garden you got.' He stood with his calves curved through his trousers. A cockly little chap, but nice.

'Oh,' she said, 'this', she said, angrily almost, 'is nothing. You oughter see it. There's sunflower and hollyhock all along the palings. I'm famous for me hollyhocks!' She had never boasted in her life. 'But not now—it isn't the season. And I let it go. Mr Natwick passed on. You should'uv seen the cassia this autumn. Now it's only sticks, of course. And hibiscus. There's cream, gold, cerise, scarlet—double and single.'

She was dressing in them for him, revolving on high heels and changing frilly skirts.

He said, 'Gardening's not in my line,' turning his head to hide something, perhaps he was ashamed of his hare-lip.

'No,' she agreed. 'Not everybody's a gardener.'

'But like a garden.'

'My husband didn't even like it. He didn't have to tell me,' she added.

As they moved across the wintry grass, past the empty clothes-line, the man looked at his watch, and said, 'I was reckoning on visiting somebody in hospital tonight. Looks like I shan't make it if the N.R.M.A. takes as long as usual.'

'Do they?' she said, clearing her throat. 'It isn't somebody close, I hope? The sick person?'

Yes he said they was close.

'Nothing serious?' she almost bellowed.

He said it was serious.

Oh she nearly burst out laughing at the bandaged figure they were sitting beside particularly at the bandaged face. She would have laughed at a brain tumour.

'I'm sorry,' she said. 'I understand. Mr Natwick was for many years an invalid.'

Those teeth in the tumbler on top of the medicine cabinet. Looking at her. Teeth can look, worse than eyes. But she couldn't help it, she meant everything she said, and thought.

At this moment they were pressing inside the dark-green tunnel, her sleeve rubbing his, as the crimson-to-purple light was dying.

'These are the cinerarias,' she said.

'The what?' He didn't know, any more than Royal.

As she was about to explain she got switched to another language. Her throat became a long palpitating funnel through which the words she expected to use were poured out in a stream of almost formless agonized sound.

'What is it?' he asked, touching her.

If it had happened to herself she would have felt frightened, it occurred to her, but he didn't seem to be.

'What is it?' he kept repeating in his familiar voice, touching, even holding her.

And for answer, in the new language, she was holding him. They were holding each other, his hard body against her eiderdowny one. As the silence closed round them again, inside the tunnel of light, his face, to which she was very close, seemed to be unlocking, the wound of his mouth, which should have been more horrible, struggling to open. She could see he had recognized her.

She kissed above his mouth. She kissed as though she might never succeed in healing all the wounds they had ever suffered.

How long they stood together she wasn't interested in knowing. Outside them the river of traffic continued to flow between its brick and concrete banks. Even if it overflowed it couldn't have drowned them.

When the man said in his gentlest voice, 'Better go out in front. The N.R.M.A. might have come.'

'Yes,' she agreed. 'The N.R.M.A.'

So they shuffled, still holding each other, along the narrow path. She imagined how long and wooden their faces must look. She wouldn't look at him now, though, just as she wouldn't look back at the still faintly smouldering joys they had experienced together in the past.

When they came out, apart, and into the night, there was the N.R.M.A., his pointed ruby of a light burning on top of the cabin.

'When will you come?' she asked.

'Tomorrow.'

'Tomorrow. You'll stay to tea.'

He couldn't stay.

'I'll make you a *pot* of tea?'

But he didn't drink it.

'Coffee, then?'

He said, 'I like a nice cup of coffee.'

Going down the path he didn't look back, or opening the gate. She would not let herself think of reasons or possibilities, she would not think, but stood planted in the path, swayed slightly by the motion of the night.

Mrs Dolan said, 'You bring the saucepan to the boil. You got that?'

'Yeeehs.' Mrs Natwick had never been a dab at coffee.

'Then you throw in some cold water. That's what sends the gravel to the bottom.' This morning Mrs Dolan had to laugh at her own jokes.

'That's the part that frightens me,' Mrs Natwick admitted.

'Well, you just do it, and see,' said Mrs Dolan; she was too busy.

After she had bought the coffee Mrs Natwick stayed in the city to muck around. If she had stayed at home her nerves might have wound themselves tighter, waiting for evening to come. Though mucking around only irritated in the end. She had never been an idle woman. So she stopped at the cosmetics as though she didn't have to decide, this was her purpose, and said to the young lady lounging behind one of the counters, 'I'm thinking of investing in a lipstick, dear. Can you please advise me?'

As a concession to the girl she tried to make it a laughing matter, but the young person was bored, she didn't bat a silver eyelid. 'Elderly ladies,' she said, 'go for the brighter stuff.'

Mrs Natwick ('my little Ella') had never felt so meek. Mum must be turning in her grave.

'This is a favourite.' With a flick of her long fingers the girl exposed the weapon. It looked too slippery-pointed, crimson-purple, out of its golden sheath.

Mrs Natwick's knees were shaking. 'Isn't it a bit noticeable?' she asked, again trying to make it a joke.

But the white-haired girl gave a serious laugh. 'What's wrong with noticeable?'

As Mrs Natwick tried it out on the back of her hand the way she had seen others do, the girl was jogging from foot to foot behind the counter. She was humming between her teeth, behind her white-smeared lips, probably thinking about a lover. Mrs Natwick blushed. What if she couldn't learn to get the tip of her lipstick back inside its sheath?

She might have gone quickly away without another word if the young lady hadn't been so professional and bored. Still humming, she brought out a little pack of rouge.

'Never saw myself with mauve cheeks!' It was at least dry, and easy to handle.

'It's what they wear.'

Mrs Natwick didn't dare refuse. She watched the long fingers with their silver nails doing up the parcel. The fingers looked as though they might resent touching anything but cosmetics; a lover was probably beneath contempt.

The girl gave her the change, and she went away without counting it.

She wasn't quiet, though, not a bit, booming and clanging in front of the toilet mirror. She tried to make a thin line, but her mouth exploded into a purple flower. She dabbed the dry-feeling pad on either cheek, and thick, mauve-scented shadows fell. She could hear and feel her heart behaving like a squeezed, rubber ball as she stood looking. Then she got at the lipstick again, still unsheathed. Her mouth was becoming enormous, so thick with grease she could hardly close her own lips underneath. A visible dew was gathering round the purple shadows on her cheeks.

She began to retch like, but dry, and rub, over the basin, scrubbing with the nailbrush. More than likely some would stay behind in the pores and be seen. Though you didn't have to see, to see.

There were Royal's teeth in the tumbler on top of the medicine cabinet. Ought to hide the teeth. What if somebody wanted to use the toilet? She must move the teeth. But didn't. In the present circumstances she couldn't have raised her arms that high.

Around five she made the coffee, throwing in the cold water at the end with a gesture copied from Mrs Dolan. If the gravel hadn't sunk to the bottom he wouldn't notice the first time, provided the coffee was hot. She could warm up the made coffee in a jiffy.

As she sat on the veranda waiting, the cane chair shifted and squealed under her. If it hadn't been for her weight it might have run away across the tiles, like one of those old planchette boards, writing the answers to questions.

There was an accident this evening down at the intersection. A head-on collision. Bodies were carried out of the crumpled cars, and she remembered a past occasion when she had run with blankets, and Hazel's Onkaparinka, and a pillow from their own bed. She had been so grateful to the victim. She could not give him enough, or receive enough of the warm blood. She had come back, she remembered, sprinkled.

This evening she had to save herself up. Kept on looking at her watch. The old cane chair squealing, ready to write the answers if she let it. Was he hurt? Was he killed, then? Was he—what?

Mrs Dolan it was, sticking her head over the palings. 'Don't like the accidents, Mrs Natwick. It's the blood. The blood turns me up.'

Mrs Natwick averted her face. Though unmoved by present blood. If only the squealing chair would stop trying to buck her off.

'Did your friend enjoy the coffee?' Mrs Dolan shouted; nothing nasty in her: Mrs Dolan was sincere.

'Hasn't been yet,' Mrs Natwick mumbled from glancing at her watch. 'Got held up.'

'It's the traffic. The traffic at this time of evenun.'

'Always on the dot before.'

'Working back. Or made a mistake over the day.'

Could you make a mistake? Mrs Natwick contemplated. Tomorrow had always meant tomorrow.

'Or he could'uv,' Mrs Dolan shouted, but didn't say it. 'I better go inside,' she said instead. 'They'll be wonderun where I am.'

Down at the intersection the bodies were lying wrapped in someone else's blankets, looking like the grey parcels of mice cats sometimes vomit up.

It was long past five-twenty, not all that long really, but drawing in. The sky was heaped with cold fire. Her city was burning.

She got up finally, and the chair escaped with a last squeal, writing its answer on the tiles.

No, it wasn't lust, not if the Royal God Almighty with bared teeth should strike her down. Or yes, though, it was. She was lusting after the expression of eyes she could hardly remember for seeing so briefly.

In the effort to see, she drove her memory wildly, while her body stumbled around and around the paths of the burning city there was now no point in escaping. You would shrivel up in time along with the polyanthers and out-of-season hibiscus. All the randy mouths would be stopped sooner or later with black.

The cinerarias seemed to have grown so luxuriant she had to force her way past them, down the narrow brick path. When she heard the latch click, and saw him coming towards her.

'Why,' she screamed laughing though it sounded angry, she *was*, 'I'd given you up, you know! It's long after five-twenty!'

As she pushed fiercely towards him, past the cinerarias, snapping one or two of those which were most heavily loaded, she realized he couldn't have known that she set her watch, her life, by his constant behaviour. He wouldn't have dawdled so.

'What is it?' she called at last, in exasperation at the distance which continued separating them.

He was far too slow, treading the slippery moss of her too shaded path. While she floundered on. She couldn't reach the expression of his eyes.

He said, and she could hardly recognize the faded voice, 'There's something—I been feeling off colour most of the day.' His mis-shapen head was certainly lolling as he advanced.

'Tell me!' She heard her voice commanding, like that of a man, or a mother, when she had practised to be a lover; she could still smell the smell of rouge. 'Won't you tell me—*dearest?*' It was thin and unconvincing now. (As a girl she had once got a letter from her cousin Kath Salter, who she hardly knew: *Dearest Ella* . . .)

Oh dear. She had reached him. And was given all strength—that of the lover she had aimed at being.

Straddling the path, unequally matched—he couldn't compete against her strength—she spoke with an acquired, a deafening softness, as the inclining cinerarias snapped.

'You will tell me what is wrong—dear, dear.' She breathed with trumpets.

He hung his head. 'It's all right. It's the pain—here—in my arm—no, the shoulder.'

'Ohhhhh!' She ground her face into his shoulder forgetting it wasn't *her* pain.

Then she remembered, and looked into his eyes and said, 'We'll save you. You'll see.'

It was she who needed saving. She knew she was trying to enter by his eyes. To drown in them rather than be left.

Because, in spite of her will to hold him, he was slipping from her, down amongst the cinerarias, which were snapping off one by one around them.

A cat shot out. At one time she had been so poor in spirit she had wished she was a cat.

'It's all right,' either voice was saying.

Lying amongst the smashed plants, he was smiling at her dreadfully, not his mouth, she no longer bothered about that lip, but with his eyes.

'More air!' she cried. 'What you need is air!' hacking at one or two cinerarias which remained erect.

Their sap was stifling, their bristling columns callous.

'Oh! Oh!' she panted. 'Oh God! Dear love!' comforting with hands and hair and words.

Words.

While all he could say was, 'It's all right.'

Or not that at last. He folded his lips into a white seam. His eyes were swimming out of reach.

'Eh? Dear—dearest—darl—darling—darling love—*love*—LOVE?' All the new words still stiff in her mouth, that she had heard so far only from the mouths of actors.

The words were too strong she could see. She was losing him. The traffic was hanging together only by charred silences.

She flung herself and covered his body, trying to force kisses—no, breath, into his mouth, she had heard about it.

She had seen turkeys, feathers sawing against each other's feathers, rising afterwards like new noisy silk.

She knelt up, and the wing-tips of her hair still dabbled limply in his cheeks. 'Eh? Ohh luff!' She could hardly breathe it.

She hadn't had time to ask his name, before she must have killed him by loving too deep, and too adulterously.

Delmore Schwartz

Delmore Schwartz (1913–1966) was one of the saddest of many sad American success stories. Born in New York City to Jewish immigrant parents, Schwartz early revealed his passion for books and writing. He had already styled himself a poet and man of letters when he attended the University of Wisconsin in the early 1930s. In 1938 he made good on his promise, publishing *In Dreams Begin Responsibilities,* a collection of poems that won the praise of the masters of the age, including T. S. Eliot, Ezra Pound, Wallace Stevens, and William Carlos Williams. Soon after, Schwartz was publishing poems, stories, and essays in the most prestigious publications of the day. His ambition was boundless, and he had the talent to match it. And then he crashed. In the last decades of his life, Schwartz suffered ever more debilitating bouts of depressive illness; he felt his inspiration had deserted him. He grew addicted to alcohol and pills, and when he died in a midtown Manhattan hotel, his body lay unclaimed for days. (Saul Bellow has evoked the friend of his younger years most memorably in his novel *Humboldt's Gift*).

Schwartz's reputation has declined somewhat in recent years, but the best of his poems and stories have a secure place in our literature. They crackle with what might be called a first-generation electricity—the passing of years has not diminished this.

IN DREAMS BEGIN RESPONSIBILITIES

I

I think it is the year 1909. I feel as if I were in a motion picture theatre, the long arm of light crossing the darkness and spinning, my eyes fixed on the screen. This is a silent picture as if an old Biograph one, in which the actors are dressed in ridiculously old-fashioned clothes, and one flash succeeds another with sudden jumps. The actors too seem to jump about and walk too fast. The shots themselves are full of dots and rays, as if it were raining when the picture was photographed. The light is bad.

It is Sunday afternoon, June 12th, 1909, and my father is walking down the quiet streets of Brooklyn on his way to visit my mother. His clothes are newly pressed and his tie is too tight in his high collar. He jingles the coins in his pockets, thinking of the witty things he will say. I feel as if I had by now relaxed entirely in the soft darkness of the theatre; the organist peals out the obvious and approximate emotions on which the audience rocks unknowingly. I am anonymous, and I have forgotten myself. It is always so when one goes to the movies, it is, as they say, a drug.

My father walks from street to street of trees, lawns and houses, once in a while coming to an avenue on which a street-car skates and gnaws, slowly progressing. The conductor, who has a handle-bar mustache helps a young lady wearing a hat like a bowl with feathers on to the car. She lifts her long skirts slightly as she mounts the steps. He leisurely makes change and rings his bell. It is obviously Sunday, for everyone is wearing Sunday clothes, and the street-car's noises emphasize the quiet of the holiday. Is not Brooklyn the City of Churches? The shops are closed and their shades drawn, but for an occasional stationery store or drug-store with great green balls in the window.

My father has chosen to take this long walk because he likes to walk and think. He thinks about himself in the future and so arrives at the place he is to visit in a state of mild exaltation. He pays no attention to the houses he is passing, in which the Sunday dinner is being eaten, nor to the many trees which patrol each street, now coming to their full leafage and the time when they will room the whole street in cool shadow. An occasional carriage passes, the horse's hooves falling like stones in the quiet afternoon, and once in a while an automobile, looking like an enormous upholstered sofa, puffs and passes.

My father thinks of my mother, of how nice it will be to introduce her to his family. But he is not yet sure that he wants to marry her, and once in a while he becomes panicky about the bond already established. He reassures himself by thinking of the big men he admires who are married: William Randolph Hearst, and William Howard Taft, who has just become President of the United States.

My father arrives at my mother's house. He has come too early and so is suddenly embarrassed. My aunt, my mother's sister, answers the loud bell with her napkin in her hand, for the family is still at dinner. As my father enters, my grandfather rises from the table and shakes hands with him. My mother has run upstairs to tidy herself. My grandmother asks my father if he has had dinner, and tells him that Rose will be downstairs soon. My grandfather opens the conversation by remarking on the mild June weather. My father sits uncomfortably near the table, holding his hat in his hand. My grandmother tells my aunt to take my father's hat. My uncle, twelve years old, runs into the house, his hair tousled. He shouts a greeting to my father, who has often given him a nickel, and then runs upstairs. It is evident that the respect in which my father is held in this household is tempered by a good deal of mirth. He is impressive, yet he is very awkward.

II

Finally my mother comes downstairs, all dressed up, and my father being engaged in conversation with my grandfather becomes uneasy, not knowing whether to greet my mother or continue the conversation. He gets up from the chair clumsily and says "hello" gruffly. My grandfather watches, examining their congruence, such as it is, with a critical eye, and meanwhile rubbing his bearded cheek roughly, as he always does when he reflects. He is worried; he is afraid that my father will not make a good husband for his oldest daughter. At this point something happens to the film, just as my father is saying something funny to my mother; I am awakened to myself and my unhappiness just as my interest was rising. The audience begins to clap impatiently. Then the trouble is cared for but the film has been returned to a portion just shown, and once more I see my grandfather rubbing his bearded cheek and pondering my father's character. It is difficult to get back into the picture once more and forget myself, but as my mother giggles at my father's words, the darkness drowns me.

My father and mother depart from the house, my father shaking hands with my mother once more, out of some unknown uneasiness. I stir uneasily also, slouched in the hard chair of the theatre. Where is the older uncle, my mother's older brother? He is studying in his bedroom upstairs, studying for his final examination at the College of the City of New York, having been dead of rapid pneumonia for the last twenty-one years. My mother and father walk down the same quiet streets once more. My mother is holding my father's arm and telling him of the novel which she has been reading; and my father utters judgments of the characters as the plot is made clear to him. This is a habit which he very much enjoys, for he feels the utmost superiority and confidence when he approves and condemns the behavior of other people. At times he feels moved to utter a brief "Ugh"—whenever the story becomes what he would call sugary. This tribute is paid to his manliness. My mother feels satisfied by the interest which she has awakened; she is showing my father how intelligent she is, and how interesting.

They reach the avenue, and the street-car leisurely arrives. They are going to Coney Island this afternoon, although my mother considers that such pleasures are inferior. She has made up her mind to indulge only in a walk on the boardwalk and a pleasant dinner, avoiding the riotous amusements as being beneath the dignity of so dignified a couple.

My father tells my mother how much money he has made in the past week, exaggerating an amount which need not have been exaggerated. But my father has always felt that actualities somehow fall short. Suddenly I begin to weep. The determined old lady who sits next to me in the theatre is annoyed and looks at me with an angry face, and being intimidated, I stop. I drag out my handkerchief and dry my face, licking the drop which has fallen near my lips. Meanwhile I have missed something, for here are my mother and father alighting at the last stop, Coney Island.

III

They walk toward the boardwalk, and my father commands my mother to inhale the pungent air from the sea. They both breathe in deeply, both of them laughing as they do so. They have in common a great interest in health, although my father is strong and husky, my mother frail. Their minds are full of theories of what is good to eat and not good to eat, and sometimes they engage in heated discussions of the subject, the whole matter ending in my father's announcement, made with a scornful bluster, that you have to die sooner or later anyway. On the boardwalk's flagpole, the American flag is pulsing in an intermittent wind from the sea.

My father and mother go to the rail of the boardwalk and look down on the beach where a good many bathers are casually walking about. A few are in the surf. A peanut whistle pierces the air with its pleasant and active whine, and my father goes to buy peanuts. My mother remains at the rail and stares at the ocean. The ocean seems merry to her; it pointedly sparkles and again and again the pony waves are released. She notices the children digging in the wet sand, and the bathing costumes of the girls who are her own age. My father returns with the peanuts. Overhead the sun's lightning strikes and strikes, but neither of them are at all aware of it. The boardwalk is full of people dressed in their Sunday clothes and idly strolling. The tide does not reach as far as the boardwalk, and the strollers would feel no danger if it did. My mother and father lean on the rail of the boardwalk and absently stare at the ocean. The ocean is becoming rough; the waves come in slowly, tugging strength from far back. The moment before they somersault, the moment when they arch their backs so beautifully, showing green and white veins amid the black, that moment is intolerable. They finally crack, dashing fiercely upon the sand, actually driving, full force downward, against the sand, bouncing upward and forward, and at last petering out into a small stream which races up the beach and then is recalled. My parents gaze absentmindedly at the ocean, scarcely interested in its harshness. The sun overhead does not disturb them. But I stare at the terrible sun which breaks up sight, and the fatal, merciless, passionate ocean, I forget my parents. I stare fascinated and finally, shocked by the indifference of my father and mother, I burst out weeping once more. The old lady next to me pats me on the shoulder and says "There, there, all of this is only a movie, young man, only a movie," but I look up once more at the terrifying sun and the terrifying ocean, and being unable to control my tears, I get up and go to the men's room, stumbling over the feet of the other people seated in my row.

IV

When I return, feeling as if I had awakened in the morning sick for lack of sleep, several hours have apparently passed and my parents are riding on the merry-go-round. My father is on a black horse, my mother on a white one, and they seem to be making an eternal circuit for the single purpose of snatching the nickel rings which are attached to the arm of one of the posts. A hand-organ is playing; it is one with the ceaseless circling of the merry-go-round.

For a moment it seems that they will never get off the merry-go-round because it will never stop. I feel like one who looks down on the avenue from the 50th story of a building. But at length they do get off; even the music of the hand-organ has ceased for a moment. My father has acquired ten rings, my mother only two, although it was my mother who really wanted them.

They walk on along the boardwalk as the afternoon descends by imperceptible degrees into the incredible violet of dusk. Everything fades into a relaxed glow, even the ceaseless murmuring from the beach, and the revolutions of the merry-go-round. They look for a place to have dinner. My father suggests the best one on the boardwalk and my mother demurs, in accordance with her principles.

However they do go to the best place, asking for a table near the window, so that they can look out on the boardwalk and the mobile ocean. My father feels omnipotent as he places a quarter in the waiter's hand as he asks for a table. The place is crowded and here too there is music, this time from a kind of string trio. My father orders dinner with a fine confidence.

As the dinner is eaten, my father tells of his plans for the future, and my mother shows with expressive face how interested she is, and how impressed. My father becomes exultant. He is lifted up by the waltz that is being played, and his own future begins to intoxicate him. My father tells my mother that he is going to expand his business, for there is a great deal of money to be made. He wants to settle down. After all, he is twenty-nine, he has lived by himself since he was thirteen, he is making more and more money, and he is envious of his married friends when he visits them in the cozy security of their homes, surrounded, it seems, by the calm domestic pleasures, and by delightful children, and then, as the waltz reaches the moment when all the dancers swing madly, then, then with awful daring, then he asks my mother to marry him, although awkwardly enough and puzzled, even in his excitement, at how he had arrived at the proposal, and she, to make the whole business worse, begins to cry, and my father looks nervously about, not knowing at all what to do now, and my mother says: "It's all I've wanted from the moment I saw you," sobbing, and he finds all of this very difficult, scarcely to his taste, scarcely as he had thought it would be, on his long walks over Brooklyn Bridge in the revery of a fine cigar, and it was then that I stood up in the theatre and shouted: "Don't do it. It's not too late to change your minds, both of you. Nothing good will come of it, only remorse, hatred, scandal, and two children whose characters are monstrous." The whole audience turned to look at me, annoyed, the usher came hurrying down the aisle flashing his searchlight, and the old lady next to me tugged me down into my seat, saying: "Be quiet. You'll be put out, and you paid thirty-five cents to come in." And so I shut my eyes because I could not bear to see what was happening. I sat there quietly.

V

But after awhile I begin to take brief glimpses, and at length I watch again with thirsty interest, like a child who wants to maintain his sulk although offered the bribe of candy. My parents are now having their picture taken in a photographer's booth along the boardwalk. The place is shadowed in the mauve light which is apparently necessary. The camera is set to the side on its tripod and looks like a Martian man. The photographer is instructing my parents in how to pose. My father has his arm over my mother's shoulder, and both of them smile emphatically. The photographer brings my mother a bouquet of flowers to hold in her hand but she holds it at the wrong angle. Then the photographer covers himself with the black cloth which drapes the camera and all that one sees of him is one protruding arm and his hand which clutches the rubber ball which he will squeeze when the picture is finally taken. But he is not satisfied with their appearance. He feels with certainty that somehow there is something wrong in their pose. Again and again he issues from his hidden place with new directions. Each suggestion merely makes matters worse. My father is becoming impatient. They try a seated pose. The photographer explains that he has pride, he is not interested in all of this for the money, he wants to make beautiful pictures. My father says: "Hurry up, will you? We haven't got all night." But the photographer only scurries about apologetically, and issues new directions. The photographer charms me. I approve of him with all my heart, for I know just how he feels, and as he criticizes each revised pose according to some unknown idea of rightness, I become quite hopeful. But then my father says angrily: "Come on, you've had enough time, we're not going to wait any longer." And the photographer, sighing unhappily, goes back under his black covering, holds out his hand, says: "One, two, three, Now!", and the picture is taken, with my father's smile turned to a grimace and my mother's bright and false. It takes a few minutes for the picture to be developed and as my parents sit in the curious light they become quite depressed.

VI

They have passed a fortune-teller's booth, and my mother wishes to go in, but my father does not. They begin to argue about it. My mother becomes stubborn, my father once more impatient, and then they begin to quarrel, and what my father would like to do is walk off and leave my mother there, but he knows that that would never do. My mother refuses to budge. She is near to tears, but she feels an uncontrollable desire to hear what the palm-reader will say. My father consents angrily, and they both go into a booth which is in a way like the photographer's, since it is draped in black cloth and its light is shadowed. The place is too warm, and my father keeps saying this is all nonsense, pointing to the crystal ball on the table. The fortune-teller, a fat, short woman, garbed in what is supposed to be Oriental robes, comes into the room from the back and greets them, speaking with an accent. But suddenly my father feels that the whole thing is intolerable; he tugs at my mother's arm, but my mother refuses to budge. And then, in terrible anger, my father lets go of my mother's arm and strides out, leaving my mother stunned. She moves to go after my father, but the fortune-teller holds her arm tightly and begs her not to do so, and I in my seat am shocked more than can ever be said, for I feel as if I were walking a tight-rope a hundred feet over a circus-audience and suddenly the rope is showing signs of breaking, and I get up from my seat and begin to shout once more the first words I can think of to communicate my terrible fear and once more the usher comes hurrying down the aisle flashing his search-light, and the old lady pleads with me, and the shocked audience has turned to stare at me, and I keep shouting: "What are they doing? Don't they know what they are doing? Why doesn't my mother go after my father? If she does not do that, what will she do? Doesn't my father know what he is doing?"—But the usher has seized my arm and is dragging me away, and as he does so, he says: "What are *you* doing? Don't you know that you can't do whatever you want to do? Why should a young man like you, with your whole life before you, get hysterical like this? Why don't you *think* of what you're doing? You can't act like this even if other people aren't around! You will be sorry if you do not do what you should do, you can't carry on like this, it is not right, you will find that out soon enough, everything you do matters too much," and he said that dragging me through the lobby of the theatre into the cold light, and I woke up into the bleak winter morning of my 21st birthday, the windowsill shining with its lip of snow, and the morning already begun.

Julio Cortázar

Julio Cortázar (1914–1984) was born in Brussels, Belgium, to Argentine parents; his family moved to Buenos Aires when he was four years old. The numerology of his life—and Cortázar was very much interested in numbers and coincidences—works out perfectly. He lived for 33 years in Argentina, and 33 in Paris, where he died.

The Argentina period represents Cortázar's long apprenticeship. He spent years reading and honing his craft, working to learn the arts that would allow him to indulge his peculiar imagination in literary form. In 1951, the year of his self-exile to Paris, he published *Bestiario,* the first of his many luminous story collections. Jorge Luis Borges, the presiding master of South American writers, claimed to be enchanted by the book.

Cortázar lived the life of the literary bohemian—at least to some degree—in Paris. He explored his passion for jazz, avant-garde art, and experimental fiction. When his novel *Hopscotch* was published in 1963, it was praised for its innovative intellectuality. The book has since come to be seen as the first great work in a boom in South American writing, and Cortázar is ranked with García-Márquez, Fuentes, Borges, and Carpentier as one of the giants of the movement.

Cortázar's works include the highly experimental *62: A Model Kit* (1972), a novel that the reader must, in effect, assemble, as well as the superb story collections *A Change Of Light* (1980) and *We Love Glenda So Much* (1983).

AXOLOTL

There was a time when I thought a great deal about the axolotls. I went to see them in the aquarium at the Jardin des Plantes and stayed for hours watching them, observing their immobility, their faint movements. Now I am an axolotl.

I got to them by chance one spring morning when Paris was spreading its peacock tail after a wintry Lent. I was heading down the boulevard Port-Royal, then I took Saint-Marcel and L'Hôpital and saw green among all that grey and remembered the lions. I was friend of the lions and panthers, but had never gone into the dark, humid building that was the aquarium. I left my bike against the gratings and went to look at the tulips. The lions were sad and ugly and my panther was asleep. I decided on the aquarium, looked obliquely at banal fish until, unexpectedly, I hit it off with the axolotls. I stayed watching them for an hour and left, unable to think of anything else.

In the library at Sainte-Geneviève, I consulted a dictionary and learned that axolotls are the larval stage (provided with gills) of a species of salamander of the genus Ambystoma. That they were Mexican I knew already by looking at them and their little pink Aztec faces and the placard at the top of the tank. I read that specimens of them had been found in Africa capable of living on dry land during the periods of drought, and continuing their life under water when the rainy season came. I found their Spanish name, *ajolote,* and the mention that they were edible, and that their oil was used (no longer used, it said) like cod-liver oil.

I didn't care to look up any of the specialized works, but the next day I went back to the Jardin des Plantes. I began to go every morning, morning and afternoon some days. The aquarium guard smiled perplexedly taking my ticket. I would lean up against the iron bar in front of the tanks and set to watching them. There's nothing strange in this, because after the first minute I knew that we were linked, that something infinitely lost and distant kept pulling us together. It had been enough to detain me that first morning in front of the sheet of glass where some bubbles rose through the water. The axolotls huddled on the wretched narrow (only I can know how narrow and wretched) floor of moss and stone in the tank. There were nine specimens, and the majority pressed their heads against the glass, looking with their eyes of gold at whoever came near them. Disconcerted, almost ashamed, I felt it a lewdness to be peering at these silent and immobile figures heaped at the bottom of the tank. Mentally I isolated one, situated on the right and somewhat apart from the others, to study it better. I saw a rosy little body, translucent (I thought of those Chinese figurines of milky glass), looking like a small lizard about six inches long, ending in a fish's tail of extraordinary delicacy, the most sensitive part of our body. Along the back ran a transparent fin which joined with the tail, but what obsessed me was the feet, of the slenderest nicety, ending in tiny fingers with minutely human nails. And then I discovered its eyes, its face. Inexpressive features, with no other trait save the eyes, two orifices, like brooches, wholly of transparent gold, lacking any life but looking, letting themselves be penetrated by my look, which seemed to travel past the golden level and lose itself in a diaphanous interior mystery. A very slender black halo ringed the eye and etched it onto the pink flesh, onto the rosy stone of the head, vaguely triangular, but with curved and irregular sides which gave it a total likeness to a statuette corroded by time. The mouth was masked by the triangular plane of the face, its considerable size would be guessed only in profile; in front a delicate crevice barely slit the lifeless stone. On both sides of the head where the ears should have been, there grew three tiny sprigs red as coral, a vegetal outgrowth, the gills, I suppose. And they were the only thing quick about it; every ten or fifteen seconds the sprigs pricked up stiffly and again subsided. Once in a while a foot would barely move, I saw the diminutive toes poise mildly on the moss. It's that we don't enjoy moving a lot, and the tank is so cramped—we barely move in any direction and we're hitting one of the others with our tail or our head—difficulties arise, fights, tiredness. The time feels like it's less if we stay quietly.

It was their quietness that made me lean toward them fascinated the first time I saw the axolotls. Obscurely I seemed to understand their secret will, to abolish space and time with an indifferent immobility. I knew better later; the gill contraction, the tentative reckoning of the delicate feet on the stones, the abrupt swimming (some of them swim with a simple undulation of the body) proved to me that they were capable of escaping that mineral lethargy in which they spent whole hours. Above all else, their eyes obsessed me. In the standing tanks on either side of them, different fishes showed me the simple stupidity of their handsome eyes so similar to our own. The eyes of the axolotls spoke to me of the presence of a different life, of another way of seeing. Glueing my face to the glass (the guard would cough fussily once in a while), I tried to see better those diminutive golden points, that entrance to the infinitely slow and remote world of these rosy creatures. It was useless to tap with one finger on the glass directly in front of their faces; they never gave the least reaction. The golden eyes continued burning with their soft, terrible light; they continued looking at me from an unfathomable depth which made me dizzy.

And nevertheless they were close. I knew it before this, before being an axolotl. I learned it the day I came near them for the first time. The anthropomorphic features of a monkey reveal the reverse of what most people believe, the distance that is traveled from them to us. The absolute lack of similarity between axolotls and human beings proved to me that my recognition was valid, that I was not propping myself up with easy analogies. Only the little hands . . . But an eft, the common newt, has such hands also, and we are not at all alike. I think it was the axolotls' heads, that triangular pink shape with the tiny eyes of gold. That looked and knew. That laid the claim. They were not *animals*.

It would seem easy, almost obvious, to fall into mythology. I began seeing in the axolotls a metamorphosis which did not succeed in revoking a mysterious humanity. I imagined them aware, slaves of their bodies, condemned infinitely to the silence of the abyss, to a hopeless meditation. Their blind gaze, the diminutive gold disc without expression and nonetheless terribly shining, went through me like a message: "Save us, save us." I caught myself mumbling words of advice, conveying childish hopes. They continued to look at me, immobile; from time to time the rosy branches of the gills stiffened. In that instant I felt a muted pain; perhaps they were seeing me, attracting my strength to penetrate into the impenetrable thing of their lives. They were not human beings, but I had found in no animal such a profound relation with myself. The axolotls were like witnesses of something, and at times like horrible judges. I felt ignoble in front of them; there was such a terrifying purity in those transparent eyes. They were larvas, but larva means disguise and also phantom. Behind those Aztec faces, without expression but of an implacable cruelty, what semblance was awaiting its hour?

I was afraid of them. I think that had it not been for feeling the proximity of other visitors and the guard, I would not have been bold enough to remain alone with them. "You eat them alive with your eyes, hey," the guard said, laughing; he likely thought I was a little cracked. What he didn't notice was that it was they devouring me slowly with their eyes, in a cannibalism of gold. At any distance from the aquarium, I had only to think of them, it was as though I were being affected from a distance. It got to the point that I was going every day, and at night I thought of them immobile in the darkness, slowly putting a hand out which immediately encountered another. Perhaps their eyes could see in the dead of night, and for them the day continued indefinitely. The eyes of axolotls have no lids.

I know now that there was nothing strange, that that had to occur. Leaning over in front of the tank each morning, the recognition was greater. They were suffering, every fiber of my body reached toward that stifled pain, that stiff torment at the bottom of the tank. They were lying in wait for something, a remote dominion destroyed, an age of liberty when the world had been that of the axolotls. Not possible that such a terrible expression which was attaining the overthrow of that forced blankness on their stone faces should carry any message other than one of pain, proof of that eternal sentence, of that liquid hell they were undergoing. Hopelessly, I wanted to prove to myself that my own sensibility was projecting a nonexistent consciousness upon the axolotls. They and I knew. So there was nothing strange in what happened. My face was pressed against the glass of the aquarium, my eyes were attempting once more to penetrate the mystery of those eyes of gold without iris, without pupil. I saw from very close up the face of an axolotl immobile next to the glass. No transition and no surprise, I saw my face against the glass, I saw it on the outside of the tank, I saw it on the other side of the glass. Then my face drew back and I understood.

Only one thing was strange: to go on thinking as usual, to know. To realize that was, for the first moment, like the horror of a man buried alive awaking to his fate. Outside, my face came close to the glass again, I saw my mouth, the lips compressed with the effort of understanding the axolotls. I was an axolotl and now I knew instantly that no understanding was possible. He was outside the aquarium, his thinking was a thinking outside the tank. Recognizing him, being him himself, I was an axolotl and in my world. The horror began—I learned in the same moment—of believing myself prisoner in the body of an axolotl, metamorphosed into him with my human mind intact, buried alive in an axolotl, condemned to move lucidly among unconscious creatures. But that stopped when a foot just grazed my face, when I moved just a little to one side and saw an axolotl next to me who was looking at me, and understood that he knew also, no communication possible, but very clearly. Or I was also in him, or all of us were thinking humanlike, incapable of expression, limited to the golden splendor of our eyes looking at the face of the man pressed against the aquarium.

He returned many times, but he comes less often now. Weeks pass without his showing up. I saw him yesterday, he looked at me for a long time and left briskly. It seemed to me that he was not so much interested in us any more, that he was coming out of habit. Since the only thing I do is think, I could think about him a lot. It occurs to me that at the beginning we continued to communicate, that he felt more than ever one with the mystery which was claiming him. But the bridges were broken between him and me, because what was his obsession is now an axolotl, alien to his human life. I think that at the beginning I was capable of returning to him in a certain way—ah, only in a certain way—and of keeping awake his desire to know us better. I am an axolotl for good now, and if I think like a man it's only because every axolotl thinks like a man inside his rosy stone semblance. I believe that all this succeeded in communicating something to him in those first days, when I was still he. And in this final solitude to which he no longer comes, I console myself by thinking that perhaps he is going to write a story about us, that, believing he's making up a story, he's going to write all this about axolotls.

Translated by Paul Blackburn

Natalia Ginzburg

Natalia Ginzburg (b. 1913) was born in Palermo to Jewish parents. She married Leone Ginzburg, an active antifascist, who died in 1944 in prison. After the war, Ginzburg joined the staff of Einaudi, one of Italy's most distinguished publishing houses. Her writing, marked by penetration and restraint, has won a growing audience. Though her tales are often domestic in their focus, readers have recognized that the resonances extend outward into the culture at large. Ginzburg was awarded the Strega Prize in 1963 for her novel *Family Sayings*. Her story collections include *The Road to the City* and *Dead Yesterdays*.

THE MOTHER

Their mother was small and thin, and slightly round-shouldered; she always wore a blue skirt and a red woollen blouse. She had short, curly black hair which she kept oiled to control its bushiness; every day she plucked her eyebrows, making two black fish of them that swam towards her temples; and she used yellow powder on her face. She was very young; how old, they didn't know, but she seemed much younger than the mothers of the boys at school; they were always surprised to see their friends' mothers, how old and fat they were. She smoked a great deal and her fingers were stained with smoke; she even smoked in bed in the evening, before going to sleep. All three of them slept together, in the big double bed with the yellow quilt; their mother was on the side nearest the door, and on the bedside table she had a lamp with its shade wrapped in a red cloth, because at night she read and smoked; sometimes she came in very late, and the boys would wake up and ask her where she had been: she nearly always answered: 'At the cinema', or else 'With a girl friend of mine'; who this friend was they didn't know, because no woman friend had ever been to the house to see their mother. She told them they must turn the other way while she undressed, they heard the quick rustle of her clothes, and shadows danced on the walls; she slipped into bed beside them, her thin body in its cold silk nightdress, and they moved away from her because she always complained that they came too close and kicked while they slept; sometimes she put out the light so that they should go to sleep and smoked in silence in the darkness.

Their mother was not important. Granny, Grandpa, Aunt Clementina who lived in the country and turned up now and then with chestnuts and maize-flour were important; Diomira the maid was important, Giovanni the tubercular porter who made cane chairs was important; all these were very important to the two boys because they were strong people you could trust, strong people in allowing and forbidding, very good at everything they did and always full of wisdom and strength; people who could defend you from storms and robbers. But if they were at home with their mother the boys were frightened, just as if they had been alone; as for allowing or forbidding, she never allowed or forbade anything, at the most she complained in a weary voice: 'Don't make such a row because I've got a headache,' and if they asked permission to do something or other she answered at once: 'Ask Granny', or she said no first and then yes and then no and it was all a muddle. When they went out alone with their mother they felt uncertain and insecure because she always took wrong turnings and had to ask a policeman the way, and then she had such a funny, timid way of going into shops to ask for things to buy, and in the shops she always forgot something, gloves or handbag or scarf, and had to go back to look and the boys were ashamed.

Their mother's drawers were untidy and she left all her things scattered about and Diomira grumbled about her when she did out the room in the morning. She even called Granny in to see and together they picked up stockings and clothes and swept up the ash that was scattered all over the place. In the morning their mother went to do the shopping: she came back and flung the string bag on the marble table in the kitchen and took her bicycle and dashed off to the office where she worked. Diomira looked at all the things in the string bag, touched the oranges one by one and the meat, and grumbled and called Granny to see what poor meat it was. Their mother came home at two o'clock when they had all eaten and ate quickly with the newspaper propped up against her glass and then rushed off again to the office on her bicycle and they saw her for a minute at supper again, but after supper she nearly always dashed off.

The boys did their homework in the bedroom. There was their father's picture, large at the head of the bed, with his square black beard and bald head and tortoiseshell-rimmed spectacles, and then another small portrait on the table, with the younger of the boys in his arms. Their father had died when they were very small, they remembered nothing about him: or rather in the older boy's memory there was the shadow of a very distant afternoon, in the country at Aunt Clementina's: his father was pushing him across the meadow in a green wheelbarrow: afterwards he had found some pieces of this wheelbarrow, a handle and a wheel, in Aunt Clementina's attic; when it was new it was a splendid wheelbarrow and he was glad to have it; his father ran along pushing him and his long beard flapped. They knew nothing about their father but they thought he must be the sort of person who is strong and wise in allowing and forbidding; when Grandpa or Diomira got angry with their mother Granny said that they should be sorry for her because she had been very unfortunate, and she said that if Eugenio, the boys' father, had been there she would have been an entirely different woman, whereas she had had the misfortune to lose her husband when she was still young. For a time there had been their father's mother as well, they never saw her because she lived in France but she used to write and send Christmas presents: then in the end she died because she was very old.

At tea-time they ate chestnuts, or bread with oil and vinegar, and then if they had finished their homework they could go and play in the small piazza or among the ruins of the public baths, which had been blown up in an air raid. In the small piazza there were a great many pigeons and they took them bread or got Diomira to give them a paper bag of left-over rice. There they met all the local boys, boys from school and others they met in the youth clubs on Sundays when they had football matches with Don Vigliani, who hitched up his black cassock and kicked. Sometimes they played football in the small piazza too or else cops and robbers. Their grandmother appeared on the balcony occasionally and called to them not to get hurt: it was nice seeing the lighted windows of their home, up there on the third floor, from the dark piazza, and knowing that they could go back there, warm up at the stove and guard themselves from the night. Granny sat in the kitchen with Diomira and mended the linen; Grandpa was in the dining-room with his cap on, smoking his pipe. Granny was very fat, and wore black, and on her breast a medal with a picture of Uncle Oreste who had died in the war: she was very good at cooking pizzas and things. Sometimes she took them on her knee, even now when they were quite big boys; she was fat, she had a large soft bosom; from under the neck of her black dress you could see the thick white woollen vest with a scolloped edge which she had made herself. She would take them on her knee and say tender and slightly pitiful-sounding words in dialect; then she would take a long iron hair-pin out of her bun and clean their ears, and they would shriek and try to get away and Grandpa would come to the door with his pipe.

Grandpa had taught Greek and Latin at the high school. Now he was pensioned off and was writing a Greek grammar: many of his old pupils used to come and see him now and then. Then Diomira would make coffee; in the lavatory there were exercise book pages with Latin and Greek unseens on them, and his corrections in red and blue. Grandpa had a small white beard, a sort of goatee, and they were not to make a racket because his nerves were tired after all those years at school; he was always rather alarmed because prices kept going up and Granny always had a bit of row with him in the morning because he was always surprised at the money they needed; he would say that perhaps Diomira pinched the sugar and made coffee in secret and Diomira would hear and rush at him and yell that the coffee was for the students who kept coming; but these were small incidents that quietened down at once and the boys were not alarmed, whereas they were alarmed when there was a quarrel between Grandpa and their mother; this happened sometimes if their mother came home very late at night, he would come out of his room with his overcoat over his pyjamas and bare feet, and he and their mother would shout: he said: 'I know where you've been, I know where you've been, I know what you are,' and their mother said: 'What do I care?' and then: 'Look, now you've woken the children,' and he said: 'A fat lot you care what happens to your children. Don't say anything because I know what you are. You're a bitch. You run around at night like the mad bitch you are.' And then Granny and Diomira would come out in their nightdresses and push him into his room and say: 'Shush, shush,' and their mother would get into bed and sob under the bedclothes, her deep sobs echoing in the dark room: the boys thought that Grandpa must be right, they thought their mother was wrong to go to the cinema and to her girl friends at night. They felt very unhappy, frightened and unhappy, and lay huddled close together in the deep, warm, soft bed, and the older boy who was in the middle pushed away so as not to touch his mother's body: there seemed to him something disgusting in his mother's tears, in the wet pillow: he thought: 'It gives a chap the creeps when his mother cries.' They never spoke between themselves of these rows their mother and Grandpa had, they carefully avoided mentioning them: but they loved each other very much and clung close together at night when their mother cried: in the morning they were faintly embarrassed, because they had hugged so tightly as if to protect themselves, and because there was that thing they didn't want to talk about; besides, they soon forgot that they had been unhappy, the day began and they went to school, and met their friends in the street, and played for a moment at the school door.

In the grey light of morning, their mother got up: with her petticoat wound round her waist she soaped her neck and arms standing bent over the basin: she always tried not to let them see her but in the looking glass they could make out her thin brown shoulders and small naked breasts: in the cold the nipples became dark and protruding, she raised her arms and powdered her armpits: in her armpits she had thick curly hair. When she was completely dressed she started plucking her eyebrows, staring at herself in the mirror from close to and biting her lips hard: then she smothered her face with cream and shook the pink swansdown puff hard and powdered herself: then her face became all yellow. Sometimes she was quite gay in the mornings and wanted to talk to the boys, she asked them about school and their friends and told them things about her time at school: she had a teacher called 'Signorina Dirce' and she was an old maid who tried to seem young. Then she put on her coat and picked up her string shopping bag, leant down to kiss the boys and ran out with her scarf wound round her head and her face all perfumed and powdered with yellow powder.

The boys thought it strange to have been born of her. It would have been much less strange to have been born of Granny or Diomira, with their large warm bodies that protected you from fear, that defended you from storms and robbers. It was very strange to think she was their mother, that she had held them for a while in her small womb. Since they learnt that children are in their mother's tummy before being born, they had felt very surprised and also a little ashamed that that womb had once held them. And that she had given them milk from her breasts as well: this was even more unlikely. But now she no longer had small children to feed and cradle, and every day they saw her dash off on her bicycle when the shopping was done, her body jerking away, free and happy. She certainly didn't belong to them: they couldn't count on her. You couldn't ask her anything: there were other mothers, the mothers of their school friends, whom clearly you could ask about all sorts of things; their friends ran to their mothers when school was over and asked them heaps of things, got their noses blown and their overcoats buttoned, showed their homework and their comics: these mothers were pretty old, with hats or veils or fur collars and they came to talk to the master practically every day: they were people like Granny or like Diomira, large soft imperious bodies of people who didn't make mistakes: people who didn't lose things, who didn't leave their drawers untidy, who didn't come home late at night. But their mother ran off free after the shopping; besides, she was bad at shopping, she got cheated by the butcher and was often given wrong change: she went off and it was impossible to join her where she went, deep down they marvelled at her enormously when they saw her go off: who knows what that office of hers was like, she didn't talk about it much; she had to type and write letters in French and English: who knows, maybe she was pretty good at that.

One day when they were out for a walk with Don Vigliani and with other boys from the youth club, on the way back they saw their mother in a suburban café. She was sitting inside the café; they saw her through the window, and a man was sitting with her. Their mother had laid her tartan scarf on the table and the old crocodile handbag they knew well: the man had a loose light overcoat and a brown moustache and was talking to her and smiling: their mother's face was happy, relaxed and happy, as it never was at home. She was looking at the man and they were holding hands and she didn't see the boys: the boys went on walking beside Don Vigliani who told them all to hurry because they must catch the tram: when they were on the tram the younger boy moved over to his brother and said: 'Did you see Mummy?' and his brother said: 'No, I didn't.' The younger one laughed softly and said: 'Oh yes you did, it was Mummy and there was a man with her.' The older boy turned his head away: he was big, nearly thirteen: his younger brother irritated him because he made him feel sorry for him, he couldn't understand why he felt sorry for him but he was sorry for himself as well and he didn't want to think of what he had seen, he wanted to behave as if he had seen nothing.

They said nothing to Granny. In the morning while their mother was dressing the younger boy said: 'Yesterday when we were out for a walk with Don Vigliani we saw you and there was a man with you.' Their mother jerked round, looking nasty: the black fish on her forehead quivered and met. She said: 'But it wasn't me. What an idea. I've got to stay in the office till late in the evening, as you know. Obviously you made a mistake.' The older boy then said, in a tired calm voice: 'No, it wasn't you. It was someone who looked like you.' And both boys realized that the memory must disappear: and they both breathed hard to blow it away.

But the man in the light overcoat once came to the house. He hadn't got his overcoat because it was summer, he wore blue spectacles and a light linen suit, he asked leave to take off his jacket while they had lunch. Granny and Grandpa had gone to Milan to meet some relations and Diomira had gone to her village, so they were alone with their mother. It was then the man came. Lunch was pretty good: their mother had bought nearly everything at the cooked meat shop: there was chicken with chips and this came from the shop: their mother had done the pasta, it was good, only the sauce was a bit burnt. There was wine, too. Their mother was nervous and gay, she wanted to say so much at once: she wanted to talk of the boys to the man and of the man to the boys. The man was called Max and he had been in Africa, he had lots of photographs of Africa and showed them: there was a photograph of a monkey of his, the boys asked him about this monkey a lot; it was so intelligent and so fond of him and had such a funny, pretty way with it when it wanted a sweet. But he had left it in Africa because it was ill and he was afraid it would die on the steamer. The boys became friendly with this Max. He promised to take them to the cinema one day. They showed him their books, they hadn't got many: he asked them if they had read *Saturnino Farandola* and they said no and he said he would give it to them, and *Robinson delle praterie* as well, as it was very fine. After lunch their mother told them to go and play in the recreation ground. They wished they could stay on with Max. They protested a bit but their mother, and Max too, said they must go; then in the evening when they came home Max was no longer there. Their mother hurriedly prepared the supper, coffee with milk and potato salad: they were happy, they wanted to talk about Africa and the monkey, they were extraordinarily happy and couldn't really understand why: and their mother seemed happy too and told them things, about a monkey she had once seen dancing to a little street organ. And then she told them to go to bed and said she was going out for a minute, they mustn't be scared, there was no reason to be; she bent down to kiss them and told them there was no point in telling Granny and Grandpa about Max because they never liked one inviting people home.

So they stayed on their own with their mother for a few days: they ate unusual things because their mother didn't want to cook, ham and jam and coffee with milk and fried things from the cooked meat shop. Then they washed up together. But when Granny and Grandpa came back the boys felt relieved: the tablecloth was on the dining-room table again, and the glasses and everything there should be: Granny was sitting in her rocking chair again, with her soft body and her smell: Grandma couldn't dash off, she was too old and too fat, it was nice having someone who stayed at home and couldn't ever dash away.

The boys said nothing to Granny about Max. They waited for the book *Saturnino Farandola* and waited for Max to take them to the cinema and show them more photographs of the monkey. Once or twice they asked their mother when they'd be going to the cinema with signor Max. But their mother answered harshly that signor Max had left now. The younger boy asked if he'd gone to Africa. Their mother didn't answer. But he thought he must have gone to Africa to fetch the monkey. He imagined that someday or other he would come and fetch them at school, with a black servant and a monkey in his arms. School began again and Aunt Clementina came to stay with them for a while; she had brought a bag of pears and apples which they put in the oven to cook with marsala and sugar. Their mother was in a very bad temper and quarrelled continually with Grandpa. She came home late and stayed awake smoking. She had got very much thinner and ate nothing. Her face became ever smaller and yellower, she now put black on her eyelashes too, she spat into a little box and picked up the black where she had spat with a brush; she put on masses of powder, Granny tried to wipe it off her face with a handkerchief and she turned her face away. She hardly ever spoke and when she did it seemed an effort, her voice was so weak. One day she came home in the afternoon at about six o'clock: it was strange, usually she came home much later; she locked herself in the bedroom. The younger boy came and knocked because he needed an exercise book: their mother answered angrily from inside that she wanted to sleep and that they were to leave her in peace: the boy explained timidly that he needed the exercise book; then she came to open up and her face was all swollen and wet: the boy realized she was crying, he went back to Granny and said: 'Mummy's crying,' and Granny and Aunt Clementina talked quietly together for a long time, they spoke of their mother but you couldn't make out what they were saying.

One night their mother didn't come home. Grandpa kept coming to see, barefoot, with his overcoat over his pyjamas; Granny came too and the boys slept badly, they could hear Granny and Grandpa walking about the house, opening and shutting the windows. The boys were very frightened. Then in the morning, they rang up from the police station: their mother had been found dead in an hotel, she had taken poison, she had left a letter: Grandpa and Aunt Clementina went along, Granny shrieked, the boys were sent to an old lady on the floor below who said continually: 'Heartless, leaving two babes like this.' Their mother was brought home. The boys went to see her when they had her laid out on the bed: Diomira had dressed her in her patent leather shoes and the red silk dress from the time she was married: she was small, a small dead doll.

It was strange to see flowers and candles in the same old room. Diomira and Aunt Clementina and Granny were kneeling and praying: they had said she took the poison by mistake, otherwise the priest wouldn't come and bless her, if he knew she had done it on purpose. Diomira told the boys they must kiss her: they were terribly ashamed and kissed her cold cheek one after the other. Then there was the funeral, it took ages, they crossed the entire town and felt very tired, Don Vigliani was there too and a great many children from school and from the youth club. It was cold, and very windy in the cemetery. When they went home again, Granny started crying and bawling at the sight of the bicycle in the passage: because it was really just like seeing her dashing away, with her free body and her scarf flapping in the wind: Don Vigliani said she was now in heaven, perhaps because he didn't know she had done it on purpose, or he knew and pretended not to: but the boys didn't really know if heaven existed, because Grandpa said no, and Granny said yes, and their mother had once said there was no heaven, with little angels and beautiful music, but that the dead went to a place where they were neither well nor ill, and that where you wish for nothing you rest and are wholly at peace.

The boys went to the country for a time, to Aunt Clementina's. Everyone was very kind to them, and kissed and caressed them, and they were very ashamed. They never spoke together of their mother nor of signor Max either; in the attic at Aunt Clementina's they found the book of *Saturnino Farandola* and they read it over and over and found it very fine. But the older boy often thought of his mother, as he had seen her that day in the café with Max, holding her hands and with such a relaxed, happy face; he thought then that maybe their mother had taken poison because Max had gone back to Africa for good. The boys played with Aunt Clementina's dog, a fine dog called Bubi, and they learnt to climb trees, as they couldn't do before. They went bathing in the river, too, and it was nice going back to Aunt Clementina's in the evening and doing crosswords all together. The boys were very happy at Aunt Clementina's. Then they went back to Granny's and were very happy. Granny sat in the rocking chair, and wanted to clean their ears with her hairpins. On Sunday they went to the cemetery, Diomira came too, they brought flowers and on the way back stopped at a bar to have hot punch. When they were in the cemetery, at the grave, Granny prayed and cried, but it was very hard to think that the grave and the crosses and the cemetery had anything to do with their mother, who had been cheated by the butcher and dashed off on her bicycle, and smoked, and took wrong turnings, and sobbed at night.

The bed was very big for them now and they had a pillow each. They didn't often think of their mother because it hurt them a little and made them ashamed to think of her. Sometimes they tried to remember how she was, each on his own silence: and they found it harder and harder to reassemble her short curly hair and the fish on her forehead and her lips: she put on a lot of yellow powder, this they remembered quite well; little by little there was a yellow dot, it was impossible to get the shape of her cheeks and face. Besides, they now realized that they had never loved her much, perhaps she too hadn't loved them much, if she had loved them she wouldn't have taken poison, they had heard Diomira and the porter and the lady on the floor below and so many other people say so. The years went by and the boys grew and so many things happened and that face which they had never loved very much disappeared for ever.

Translated by Isabel Quigly

Juan Rulfo

Juan Rulfo (b.1918) was born in the state of Jalisco, Mexico. He studied at universities in Guadalajara and Mexico City. His first book, published in 1953, was a collection of stories, *The Valley in Flames,* but he has found his greatest success with his short novel *Pedro Páramo* (1959). Rulfo writes with anguished sympathy about the peasants of Mexico; he is considered one of that country's most important writers.

TALPA

Natalia threw herself into her mother's arms, crying on and on with a quiet sobbing. She'd bottled it up for many days, until we got back to Zenzontla today and she saw her mother and began feeling like she needed consolation.

But during those days when we had so many difficult things to do—when we had to bury Tanilo in a grave at Talpa without anyone to help us, when she and I, just the two of us alone, joined forces and began to dig the grave, pulling out the clods of earth with our hands, hurrying to hide Tanilo in the grave so he wouldn't keep on scaring people with his smell so full of death—then she didn't cry.

Not afterward either, on the way back, when we were traveling at night without getting any rest, groping our way as if asleep and trudging along the steps that seemed like blows on Tanilo's grave. At that time Natalia seemed to have hardened and steeled her heart so she wouldn't feel it boiling inside her. Not a single tear did she shed.

She came here, near her mother, to cry, just to upset her, so she'd know she was suffering, upsetting all the rest of us besides. I felt that weeping of hers inside me too as if she was wringing out the cloth of our sins.

Because what happened is that Natalia and I killed Tanilo Santos between the two of us. We got him to go with us to Talpa so he'd die. And he died. We knew he couldn't stand all that traveling; but just the same, we pushed him along between us, thinking we'd finished him off forever. That's what we did.

The idea of going to Talpa came from my brother Tanilo. It was his idea before anyone else's. For years he'd been asking us to take him. For years. From the day when he woke up with some purple blisters scattered about on his arms and legs. And later on the blisters became wounds that didn't bleed—just a yellow gummy thing like thick distilled water came out of them. From that time I remember very well he told us how afraid he was that there was no cure for him any more. That's why he wanted to go see the Virgin of Talpa, so she'd cure him with her look. Although he knew Talpa was far away and we'd have to walk a lot under the sun in the daytime and in the cold March nights, he wanted to go anyway. The bleeding Virgin would give him the cure to get rid of that stuff that never dried up. She knew how to do that, by washing them, making everything fresh and new like a recently rained-on field. Once he was there before Her, his troubles would be over; nothing would hurt him then or hurt him ever again. That's what he thought.

And that's what Natalia and I latched on to so we could take him. I had to go with Tanilo because he was my brother. Natalia would have to go too, of course, because she was his wife. She had to help him, taking him by the arm, bearing his weight on her shoulders on the trip there and perhaps on the way back, while he dragged along on his hope.

I already knew what Natalia was feeling inside. I knew something about her. I knew, for example, that her round legs, firm and hot like stones in the noonday sun, had been alone for a long time. I knew that. We'd been together many times, but always Tanilo's shadow separated us; we felt that his scabby hands got between us and took Natalia away so she'd go on taking care of him. And that's the way it'd be as long as he was alive.

I know now that Natalia is sorry for what happened. And I am too; but that won't save us from feeling guilty or give us any peace ever again. It won't make us feel any better to know that Tanilo would've died anyway because his time was coming, and that it hadn't done any good to go to Talpa, so far away, for it's almost sure he would've died just as well here as there, maybe a little afterward, because of all he suffered on the road, and the blood he lost besides, and the anger and everything—all those things together were what killed him off quicker. What's bad about it is that Natalia and I pushed him when he didn't want to go on anymore, when he felt it was useless to go on and he asked us to take him back. We jerked him up from the ground so he'd keep on walking, telling him we couldn't go back now.

"Talpa is closer now than Zenzontla." That's what we told him. But Talpa was still far away then, many days away.

We wanted him to die. It's no exaggeration to say that's what we wanted before we left Zenzontla and each night that we spent on the road to Talpa. It's something we can't understand now, but it was what we wanted. I remember very well.

I remember those nights very well. First we had some light from a wood fire. Afterward we'd let the fire die down, then Natalia and I would search out the shadows to hide from the light of the sky, taking shelter in the loneliness of the countryside, away from Tanilo's eyes, and we disappeared into the night. And that loneliness pushed us toward each other, thrusting Natalia's body into my arms, giving her a release. She felt as if she was resting; she forgot many things and then she'd go to sleep with her body feeling a great relief.

It always happened that the ground on which we slept was hot. And Natalia's flesh, the flesh of my brother Tanilo's wife, immediately became hot with the heat of the earth. Then those two heats burned together and made one wake up from one's dreams. Then my hands groped for her; they ran over her red-hot body, first lightly, but then they tightened on her as if they wanted to squeeze her blood out. This happened again and again, night after night, until dawn came and the cold wind put out the fire of our bodies. That's what Natalia and I did along the roadside to Talpa when we took Tanilo so the Virgin would relieve his suffering.

Now it's all over. Even from the pain of living Tanilo found relief. He won't talk any more about how hard it was for him to keep on living, with his body poisoned like it was, full of rotting water inside that came out in each crack of his legs or arms. Wounds this big, that opened up slow, real slow, and then let out bubbles of stinking air that had us all scared.

But now that he's dead things are different. Now Natalia weeps for him, maybe so he'll see, from where he is, how full of remorse her soul is. She says she's seen Tanilo's face these last days. It was the only part of him that she cared about—Tanilo's face, always wet with the sweat which the effort to bear his pain left him in. She felt it approaching her mouth, hiding in her hair, begging her, in a voice she could scarcely hear, to help him. She says he told her that he was finally cured, that he no longer had any pain. "Now I can be with you, Natalia. Help me to be with you," she says he said to her.

We'd just left Talpa, just left him buried there deep down in that ditch we dug to bury him.

Since then Natalia has forgotten about me. I know how her eyes used to shine like pools lit up by the moon. But suddenly they faded, that look of hers was wiped away as if it'd been stamped into the earth. And she didn't seem to see anything any more. All that existed for her was her Tanilo, whom she'd taken care of while he was alive and had buried when his time came to die.

It took us twenty days to get to the main road to Talpa. Up to then the three of us had been alone. At that point people coming from all over began to join us, people like us who turned onto that wide road, like the current of a river, making us fall behind, pushed from all sides as if we were tied to them by threads of dust. Because from the ground a white dust rose up with the swarm of people like corn fuzz that swirled up high and then came down again; all the feet scuffing against it made it rise again, so that dust was above and below us all the time. And above this land was the empty sky, without any clouds, just the dust, and the dust didn't give any shade.

We had to wait until nighttime to rest from the sun and that white light from the road.

Then the days began to get longer. We'd left Zenzontla about the middle of February, and now that we were in the first part of March it got light very early. We hardly got our eyes closed at night when the sun woke us up again, the same sun that'd gone down just a little while ago.

I'd never felt life so slow and violent as when we were trudging along with so many people, just like we were a swarm of worms all balled together under the sun, wriggling through the cloud of dust that closed us all in on the same path and had us corralled. Our eyes followed the dust cloud and struck the dust as if stumbling against something they could not pass through. And the sky was always gray, like a heavy gray spot crushing us all from above. Only at times, when we crossed a river, did the dust clear up a bit. We'd plunge our feverish and blackened heads into the green water, and for a moment a blue smoke, like the steam that comes out of your mouth when it's cold, would come from all of us. But a little while afterward we'd disappear again, mixed in with the dust, sheltering each other from the sun, from that heat of the sun we all had to endure.

Eventually night will come. That's what we thought about. Night will come and we'll get some rest. Now we have to get through the day, get through it somehow to escape from the heat and the sun. Then we'll stop—afterward. What we've got to do now is keep plugging right along behind so many others just like us and in front of many others. That's what we have to do. We'll really only rest well when we're dead.

That's what Natalia and I thought about, and maybe Tanilo too, when we were walking along the main road to Talpa among the procession, wanting to be the first to reach the Virgin, before she ran out of miracles.

But Tanilo began to get worse. The time came when he didn't want to go any farther. The flesh on his feet had burst open and begun to bleed. We took care of him until he got better. But, he'd decided not to go any farther.

"I'll sit here for a day or two and then I'll go back to Zenzontla." That's what he said to us.

But Natalia and I didn't want him to. Something inside us wouldn't let us feel any pity for Tanilo. We wanted to get to Talpa with him, for at that point he still had life left in him. That's why Natalia encouraged him while she rubbed his feet with alcohol so the swelling would go down. She told him that only the Virgin of Talpa would cure him. She was the only one who could make him well forever. She and no one else. There were lots of other Virgins, but none like the Virgin of Talpa. That's what Natalia told him.

Then Tanilo began to cry, and his tears made streaks down his sweaty face, and he cursed himself for having been bad. Natalia wiped away the streaky tears with her shawl, and between us we lifted him off the ground so he'd walk on a little further before night fell.

So, dragging him along was how we got to Talpa with him.

The last few days we started getting tired too. Natalia and I felt that our bodies were being bent double. It was as if something was holding us and placing a heavy load on top of us. Tanilo fell down more often and we had to pick him up and sometimes carry him on our backs. Maybe that's why we felt the way we did, with our bodies slack and with no desire to keep on walking. But the people who were going along by us made us walk faster.

At night that frantic world calmed down. Scattered everywhere the bonfires shone, and around the fire the pilgrims said their rosaries, with their arms crossed, gazing toward the sky in the direction of Talpa. And you could hear how the wind picked up and carried that noise, mixing it together until it was all one roaring sound. A little bit afterward everything would get quiet. About midnight you could hear someone singing far away. Then you closed your eyes and waited for the dawn to come without getting any sleep.

We entered Talpa singing the hymn praising Our Lord.

We'd left around the middle of February and we got to Talpa the last days of March, when a lot of people were already on their way back. All because Tanilo took it into his head to do penance. As soon as he saw himself surrounded by men wearing cactus leaves hanging down like scapularies, he decided to do something like that too. He tied his feet together with his shirt sleeves so his steps became more desperate. Then he wanted to wear a crown of thorns. A little later he bandaged his eyes, and still later, during the last part of the way, he knelt on the ground and shuffled along on his knees with his hands crossed behind him; so that thing that was my brother Tanilo Santos reached Talpa, that thing so covered with plasters and dried streaks of blood that it left in the air a sour smell like a dead animal when he passed by.

When we least expected it we saw him there among the dancers. We hardly realized it and there he was with a long rattle in his hand, stomping hard on the ground with his bare bruised feet. He seemed to be in a fury, as if he was shaking out all the anger he'd been carrying inside him for such a long time, or making a last effort to try to live a little longer.

Maybe when he saw the dances he remembered going every year to Toliman during the novena of Our Lord and dancing all night long until his bones limbered up without getting tired. Maybe that's what he remembered and he wanted to get back the strength he used to have.

Natalia and I saw him like that for a moment. Right afterward we saw him raise his arms and slump to the ground with the rattle still sounding in his bloodspecked hands. We dragged him out so he wouldn't be tromped on by the dancers, away from the fury of those feet that slipped on stones and leaped about stomping the earth without knowing that something had fallen among them.

Holding him up between us as if he was crippled, we went into the church with him. Natalia had him kneel down next to her before that little golden figure of the Virgin of Talpa. And Tanilo started to pray and let a huge tear fall, from way down inside him, snuffing out the candle Natalia had placed in his hands. But he didn't realize this: the light from so many lit candles kept him from realizing what was happening right there. He went on praying with his candle snuffed out. Shouting his prayers so he could hear himself praying.

But it didn't do him any good. He died just the same.

"*. . . from our hearts filled with pain we all send her the same plea. Many laments mixed with hope. Her tenderness is not deaf to laments nor tears, for She suffers with us. She knows how to take away that stain and to leave the heart soft and pure to receive her mercy and charity. Our Virgin, our mother, who wants to know nothing of our sins, who blames herself for our sins, who wanted to bear us in her arms so life wouldn't hurt us, is right here by us, relieving our tiredness and the sicknesses of our souls and our bodies filled with thorns, wounded and supplicant. She knows that each day our faith is greater because it is made up of sacrifices . . .*"

That's what the priest said from up in the pulpit. And after he quit talking the people started praying all at once with a noise just like a lot of wasps frightened by smoke.

But Tanilo no longer heard what the priest was saying. He'd become still, with his head resting on his knees. And when Natalia moved him so he'd get up he was already dead.

Outside you could hear the noise of the dancing, the drums and the hornpipes, the ringing of bells. That's when I got sad. To see so many living things, to see the Virgin there, right in front of us with a smile on her face, and to see Tanilo on the other hand as if he was in the way. It made me sad.

But we took him there so he'd die, and that's what I can't forget.

Now the two of us are in Zenzontla. We've come back without him. And Natalia's mother hasn't asked me anything, what I did with my brother Tanilo, or anything. Natalia started crying on her shoulder and poured out the whole story to her.

I'm beginning to feel as if we hadn't reached any place; that we're only here in passing, just to rest, and that then we'll keep on traveling. I don't know where to, but we'll have to go on, because here we're very close to our guilt and the memory of Tanilo.

Maybe until we begin to be afraid of each other. Not saying anything to each other since we left Talpa may mean that. Maybe Tanilo's body is too close to us, the way it was stretched out on the rolled petate, filled inside and out with a swarm of blue flies that buzzed like a big snore coming from his mouth, that mouth we couldn't shut in spite of everything we did and that seemed to want to go on breathing without finding any breath. That Tanilo, who didn't feel pain any more but who looked like he was still in pain with his hands and feet twisted and his eyes wide open like he was looking at his own death. And here and there all his wounds dripping a yellow water, full of that smell that spread everywhere and that you could taste in your mouth, like it was a thick and bitter honey melting into your blood with each mouthful of air you took.

I guess that's what we remember here most often—that Tanilo we buried in the Talpa graveyard, that Tanilo Natalia and I threw earth and stones on so the wild animals wouldn't come dig him up.

Translated by George D. Schade

Nadine Gordimer

Nadine Gordimer (b. 1923) was born in a small town near Johannesburg, South Africa. Uninspired by her education at a convent school, she turned to books at an early age. Then, following the pattern so common among writers, she sought to create fictional worlds of her own. Gordimer was greatly influenced by the work of D. H. Lawrence, Henry James, and Ernest Hemingway. From their prose, as well as from her own highly developed skills as an observer, she honed a realistic style that has allowed her to fashion psychologically complex assessments of life in her native land. Gordimer has returned repeatedly in novels and stories to the subject of racial relations, exploring not only the conflicts between black and white cultures but also the many strategies of compromise and coexistence. Not content with exploring the situation through fiction, Gordimer has written a great many essays and polemics that reflect her anger at apartheid policies. Her novels include *The Conservationist, Burger's Daughter, A Guest of Honour,* and *July's People,* while her stories have been collected in *Soft Voice of the Serpent, Something Out There, A Soldier's Embrace,* and other volumes.

TOWN AND COUNTRY LOVERS

I

Dr Franz-Josef von Leinsdorf is a geologist absorbed in his work; wrapped up in it, as the saying goes—year after year the experience of this work enfolds him, swaddling him away from the landscapes, the cities and the people, wherever he lives: Peru, New Zealand, the United States. He's always been like that, his mother could confirm from their native Austria. There, even as a handsome small boy he presented only his profile to her: turned away to his bits of rock and stone. His few relaxations have not changed much since then. An occasional skiing trip, listening to music, reading poetry—Rainer Maria Rilke once stayed in his grandmother's hunting lodge in the forests of Styria and the boy was introduced to Rilke's poems while very young.

Layer upon layer, country after country, wherever his work takes him—and now he has been almost seven years in Africa. First the Côte d'Ivoire, and for the past five years, South Africa. The shortage of skilled manpower brought about his recruitment here. He has no interest in the politics of the countries he works in. His private preoccupation-within-the-preoccupation of his work has been research into underground water-courses, but the mining company that employs him in a senior though not executive capacity is interested only in mineral discovery. So he is much out in the field—which is the veld, here—seeking new gold, copper, platinum and uranium deposits. When he is at home—on this particular job, in this particular country, this city—he lives in a two-roomed flat in a suburban block with a landscaped garden, and does his shopping at a supermarket conveniently across the street. He is not married—yet. That is how his colleagues, and the typists and secretaries at the mining company's head office, would define his situation. Both men and women would describe him as a good-looking man, in a foreign way, with the lower half of the face dark and middle-aged (his mouth is thin and curving, and no matter how close-shaven his beard shows like fine shot embedded in the skin round mouth and chin) and the upper half contradictorily young, with deep-set eyes (some would say grey, some black), thick eyelashes and brows. A tangled gaze: through which concentration and gleaming thoughtfulness perhaps appear as fire and languor. It is this that the women in the office mean when they remark he's not unattractive. Although the gaze seems to promise, he has never invited any one of them to go out with him. There is the general assumption he probably has a girl who's been picked for him, he's bespoken by one of his own kind, back home in Europe where he comes from. Many of these well-educated Europeans have no intention of becoming permanent immigrants; neither the remnant of white colonial life nor idealistic involvement with Black Africa appeals to them.

One advantage, at least, of living in underdeveloped or half-developed countries is that flats are serviced. All Dr von Leinsdorf has to do for himself is buy his own supplies and cook an evening meal if he doesn't want to go to a restaurant. It is simply a matter of dropping in to the supermarket on his way from his car to his flat after work in the afternoon. He wheels a trolley up and down the shelves, and his simple needs are presented to him in the form of tins, packages, plastic-wrapped meat, cheeses, fruit and vegetables, tubes, bottles . . . At the cashiers' counters where customers must converge and queue there are racks of small items uncategorized, for last-minute purchase. Here, as the coloured girl cashier punches the adding machine, he picks up cigarettes and perhaps a packet of salted nuts or a bar of nougat. Or razor-blades, when he remembers he's running short. One evening in winter he saw that the cardboard display was empty of the brand of blades he preferred, and he drew the cashier's attention to this. These young coloured girls are usually pretty unhelpful, taking money and punching their machines in a manner that asserts with the time-serving obstinacy of the half-literate the limit of any responsibility towards customers, but this one ran an alert glance over the selection of razor-blades, apologized that she was not allowed to leave her post, and said she would see that the stock was replenished 'next time'. A day or two later she recognized him, gravely, as he took his turn before her counter—'I ahssed them, but it's out of stock. You can't get it. I did ahss about it.' He said this didn't matter. 'When it comes in, I can keep a few packets for you.' He thanked her.

He was away with the prospectors the whole of the next week. He arrived back in town just before nightfall on Friday, and was on his way from car to flat with his arms full of briefcase, suitcase and canvas bags when someone stopped him by standing timidly in his path. He was about to dodge round unseeingly on the crowded pavement but she spoke. 'We got the blades in now. I didn't see you in the shop this week, but I kept some for when you come. So . . .'

He recognized her. He had never seen her standing before, and she was wearing a coat. She was rather small and finely-made, for one of them. The coat was skimpy but no big backside jutted. The cold brought an apricot-graining of warm colour to her cheekbones, beneath which a very small face was quite delicately hollowed, and the skin was smooth, the subdued satiny colour of certain yellow wood. That crêpey hair, but worn drawn back flat and in a little knot pushed into one of the cheap wool chignons that (he recognized also) hung in the miscellany of small goods along with the razor-blades, at the supermarket. He said thanks, he was in a hurry, he'd only just got back from a trip—shifting the burdens he carried, to demonstrate. 'Oh shame.' She acknowledged his load. 'But if you want I can run in and get it for you quickly. If you want.'

He saw at once it was perfectly clear that all the girl meant was that she would go back to the supermarket, buy the blades and bring the packet to him there where he stood, on the pavement. And it seemed that it was this certainty that made him say, in the kindly tone of assumption used for an obliging underling, 'I live just across there—*Atlantis*—that flat building. Could you drop them by, for me—number seven-hundred-and-eighteen, seventh floor—'

She had not before been inside one of these big flat buildings near where she worked. She lived a bus- and train-ride away to the West of the city, but this side of the black townships, in a township for people her tint. There was a pool with ferns, not plastic, and even a little waterfall pumped electrically over rocks, in the entrance of the building *Atlantis;* she didn't wait for the lift marked GOODS but took the one meant for whites and a white woman with one of those sausage-dogs on a lead got in with her but did not pay her any attention. The corridors leading to the flats were nicely glassed-in, not draughty.

He wondered if he should give her a twenty-cent piece for her trouble—ten cents would be right for a black; but she said, 'Oh no—please, here—' standing outside his open door and awkwardly pushing back at his hand the change from the money he'd given her for the razor-blades. She was smiling, for the first time, in the dignity of refusing a tip. It was difficult to know how to treat these people, in this country; to know what they expected. In spite of her embarrassing refusal of the coin, she stood there, completely unassuming, fists thrust down the pockets of her cheap coat against the cold she'd come in from, rather pretty thin legs neatly aligned, knee to knee, ankle to ankle.

'Would you like a cup of coffee or something?'

He couldn't very well take her into his study-cum-living-room and offer her a drink. She followed him to his kitchen, but at the sight of her pulling out the single chair to drink her cup of coffee at the kitchen table, he said, 'No—bring it in here—' and led the way into the big room where, among his books and his papers, his files of scientific correspondence (and the cigar boxes of stamps from the envelopes) his racks of records, his specimens of minerals and rocks, he lived alone.

It was no trouble to her; she saved him the trips to the supermarket and brought him his groceries two or three times a week. All he had to do was to leave a list and the key under the doormat, and she would come up in her lunch-hour to collect them, returning to put his supplies in the flat after work. Sometimes he was home and sometimes not. He bought a box of chocolates and left it, with a note, for her to find; and that was acceptable, apparently, as a gratuity.

Her eyes went over everything in the flat although her body tried to conceal its sense of being out of place by remaining as still as possible, holding its contours in the chair offered her as a stranger's coat is set aside and remains exactly as left until the owner takes it up to go. 'You collect?'

'Well, these are specimens—connected with my work.'

'My brother used to collect. Miniatures. With brandy and whisky and that, in them. From all over. Different countries.'

The second time she watched him grinding coffee for the cup he had offered her she said, 'You always do that? Always when you make coffee?'

'But of course. Is it no good, for you? Do I make it too strong?'

'Oh it's just I'm not used to it. We buy it ready—you know, it's in a bottle, you just add a bit to the milk or water.'

He laughed, instructive: 'That's not coffee, that's a synthetic flavouring. In my country we drink only real coffee, fresh, from the beans—you smell how good it is as it's being ground?'

She was stopped by the caretaker and asked what she wanted in the building? Heavy with the *bona fides* of groceries clutched to her body, she said she was working at number 718, on the seventh floor. The caretaker did not tell her not to use the whites' lift; after all, she was not black; her family was very light-skinned.

There was the item 'grey button for trousers' on one of his shopping lists. She said as she unpacked the supermarket carrier, 'Give me the pants, so long, then,' and sat on his sofa that was always gritty with fragments of pipe tobacco, sewing in and out through the four holes of the button with firm, fluent movements of the right hand, gestures supplying the articulacy missing from her talk. She had a little yokel's, peasant's (he thought of it) gap between her two front teeth when she smiled that he didn't much like, but, face ellipsed to three-quarter angle, eyes cast down in concentration with soft lips almost closed, this didn't matter. He said, watching her sew, 'You're a good girl'; and touched her.

She remade the bed every late afternoon when they left it and she dressed again before she went home. After a week there was a day when late afternoon became evening, and they were still in the bed.

'Can't you stay the night?'

'My mother,' she said.

'Phone her. Make an excuse.' He was a foreigner. He had been in the country five years, but he didn't understand that people don't usually have telephones in their houses, where she lived. She got up to dress. He didn't want that tender body to go out in the night cold and kept hindering her with the interruption of his hands; saying nothing. Before she put on her coat, when the body had already disappeared, he spoke. 'But you must make some arrangement.'

'Oh my mother!' Her face opened to fear and vacancy he could not read.

He was not entirely convinced the woman would think of her daughter as some pure and unsullied virgin . . . 'Why?'

The girl said, 'S'e'll be scared. S'e'll be scared we get caught.'

'Don't tell her anything. Say I'm employing you.' In this country he was working in now there were generally rooms on the roofs of flat buildings for tenants' servants.

She said: 'That's what I told the caretaker.'

She ground fresh coffee beans every time he wanted a cup while he was working at night. She never attempted to cook anything until she had watched in silence while he did it the way he liked, and she learned to reproduce exactly the simple dishes he preferred. She handled his pieces of rock and stone, at first admiring the colours—'It'd make a beautiful ring or a necklace, ay.' Then he showed her the striations, the formation of each piece, and explained what each was, and how, in the long life of the earth, it had been formed. He named the mineral it yielded, and what that was used for. He worked at his papers, writing, writing, every night, so it did not matter that they could not go out together to public places. On Sundays she got into his car in the basement garage and they drove to the country and picnicked away up in the Magaliesberg, where there was no one. He read or poked about among the rocks; they climbed together, to the mountain pools. He taught her to swim. She had never seen the sea. She squealed and shrieked in the water, showing the gap between her teeth, as—it crossed his mind—she must do when among her own people. Occasionally he had to go out to dinner at the houses of colleagues from the mining company; she sewed and listened to the radio in the flat and he found her in the bed, warm and already asleep, by the time he came in. He made his way into her body without speaking; she made him welcome without a word. Once he put on evening dress for a dinner at his country's consulate; watching him brush one or two fallen hairs from the shoulders of the dark jacket that sat so well on him, she saw a huge room, all chandeliers and people dancing some dance from a costume film—stately, hand-to-hand. She supposed he was going to fetch, in her place in the car, a partner for the evening. They never kissed when either left the flat; he said, suddenly, kindly, pausing as he picked up cigarettes and keys, 'Don't be lonely.' And added, 'Wouldn't you like to visit your family sometimes, when I have to go out?'

He had told her he was going home to his mother in the forests and mountains of his country near the Italian border (he showed her on the map) after Christmas. She had not told him how her mother, not knowing there was any other variety, assumed he was a medical doctor, so she had talked to her about the doctor's children and the doctor's wife who was a very kind lady, glad to have someone who could help out in the surgery as well as the flat.

She remarked wonderingly on his ability to work until midnight or later, after a day at work. She was so tired when she came home from her cash register at the supermarket that once dinner was eaten she could scarcely keep awake. He explained in a way she could understand that while the work she did was repetitive, undemanding of any real response from her intelligence, requiring little mental or physical effort and therefore unrewarding, his work was his greatest interest, it taxed his mental capacities to their limit, exercised all his concentration, and rewarded him constantly as much with the excitement of a problem presented as with the satisfaction of a problem solved. He said later, putting away his papers, speaking out of a silence: 'Have you done other kinds of work?' She said, 'I was in a clothing factory before. Sportbeau shirts; you know? But the pay's better in the shop.'

Of course. Being a conscientious newspaper-reader in every country he lived in, he was aware that it was only recently that the retail consumer trade in this one had been allowed to employ coloureds as shop assistants; even punching a cash register represented advancement. With the continuing shortage of semi-skilled whites a girl like this might be able to edge a little farther into the white-collar category. He began to teach her to type.

He was aware that her English was poor, even though, as a foreigner, in his ears her pronunciation did not offend, nor categorize her as it would in those of someone of his education whose mother tongue was English. He corrected her grammatical mistakes but missed the less obvious ones because of his own sometimes exotic English usage—she continued to use the singular pronoun 'it' when what was required was the plural 'they'. Because he was a foreigner (although so clever, as she saw) she was less inhibited than she might have been by the words she knew she misspelled in her typing. While she sat at the typewriter she thought how one day she would type notes for him, as well as making coffee the way he liked it, and taking him inside her body without saying anything, and sitting (even if only through the empty streets of quiet Sundays) beside him in his car, like a wife.

On a summer night near Christmas—he had already bought and hidden a slightly showy but nevertheless good watch he thought she would like—there was a knocking at the door that brought her out of the bathroom and him to his feet, at his work-table. No one ever came to the flat at night; he had no friends intimate enough to drop in without warning. The summons was an imperious banging that did not pause and clearly would not stop until the door was opened.

She stood in the open bathroom doorway gazing at him across the passage into the living-room; her bare feet and shoulders were free of a big bath-towel. She said nothing, did not even whisper. The flat seemed to shake with the strong unhurried blows.

He made as if to go to the door, at last, but now she ran and clutched him by both arms. She shook her head wildly; her lips drew back but her teeth were clenched, she didn't speak. She pulled him into the bedroom, snatched some clothes from the clean laundry laid out on the bed and got into the wall-cupboard, thrusting the key at his hand. Although his arms and calves felt weakly cold he was horrified, distastefully embarrassed at the sight of her pressed back crouching there under his suits and coat; it was horrible and ridiculous. *Come out!* he whispered. *No! Come out!* She hissed: *Where? Where can I go?*

Never mind! Get out of there!

He put out his hand to grasp her. At bay, she said with all the force of her terrible whisper, baring the gap in her teeth: *I'll throw myself out the window.*

She forced the key into his hand like the handle of a knife. He closed the door on her face and drove the key home in the lock, then dropped it among coins in his trouser pocket.

He unslotted the chain that was looped across the flat door. He turned the serrated knob of the Yale lock. The three policemen, two in plain clothes, stood there without impatience although they had been banging on the door for several minutes. The big dark one with an elaborate moustache held out in a hand wearing a plaited gilt ring some sort of identity card.

Dr von Leinsdorf said quietly, the blood coming strangely back to legs and arms, 'What is it?'

The sergeant told him they knew there was a coloured girl in the flat. They had had information; 'I been watching this flat three months, I know.'

'I am alone here.' Dr von Leinsdorf did not raise his voice.

'I know, I know who is here. Come—' And the sergeant and his two assistants went into the living-room, the kitchen, the bathroom (the sergeant picked up a bottle of after-shave cologne, seemed to study the French label) and the bedroom. The assistants removed the clean laundry that was laid upon the bed and then turned back the bedding, carrying the sheets over to be examined by the sergeant under the lamp. They talked to one another in Afrikaans, which the Doctor did not understand. The sergeant himself looked under the bed, and lifted the long curtains at the window. The wall cupboard was of the kind that has no knobs; he saw that it was locked and began to ask in Afrikaans, then politely changed to English, 'Give us the key.'

Dr von Leinsdorf said, 'I'm sorry, I left it at my office—I always lock and take my keys with me in the mornings.'

'It's no good, man, you better give me the key.'

He smiled a little, reasonably. 'It's on my office desk.'

The assistants produced a screwdriver and he watched while they inserted it where the cupboard doors met, gave it quick, firm but not forceful leverage. He heard the lock give.

She had been naked, it was true, when they knocked. But now she was wearing a long-sleeved T-shirt with an appliquéd butterfly motif on one breast, and a pair of jeans. Her feet were still bare; she had managed, by feel, in the dark, to get into some of the clothing she had snatched from the bed, but she had no shoes. She had perhaps been weeping behind the cupboard door (her cheeks looked stained) but now her face was sullen and she was breathing heavily, her diaphragm contracting and expanding exaggeratedly and her breasts pushing against the cloth. It made her appear angry; it might simply have been that she was half-suffocated in the cupboard and needed oxygen. She did not look at Dr von Leinsdorf. She would not reply to the sergeant's questions.

They were taken to the police station where they were at once separated and in turn led for examination by the district surgeon. The man's underwear was taken away and examined, as the sheets had been, for signs of his seed. When the girl was undressed, it was discovered that beneath her jeans she was wearing a pair of men's briefs with his name on the neatly-sewn laundry tag; in her haste, she had taken the wrong garment to her hiding-place.

Now she cried, standing there before the district surgeon in a man's underwear.

He courteously pretended not to notice. He handed briefs, jeans and T-shirt round the door, and motioned her to lie on a white-sheeted high table where he placed her legs apart, resting in stirrups, and put into her where the other had made his way so warmly a cold hard instrument that expanded wider and wider. Her thighs and knees trembled uncontrollably while the doctor looked into her and touched her deep inside with more hard instruments, carrying wafers of gauze.

When she came out of the examining room back to the charge office, Dr von Leinsdorf was not there; they must have taken him somewhere else. She spent what was left of the night in a cell, as he must be doing; but early in the morning she was released and taken home to her mother's house in the coloured township by a white man who explained he was the clerk of the lawyer who had been engaged for her by Dr von Leinsdorf. Dr von Leinsdorf, the clerk said, had also been bailed out that morning. He did not say when, or if she would see him again.

A statement made by the girl to the police was handed in to Court when she and the man appeared to meet charges of contravening the Immorality Act in a Johannesburg flat on the night of—December, 19—. *I lived with the white man in his flat. He had intercourse with me sometimes. He gave me tablets to take to prevent me becoming pregnant.*

Interviewed by the Sunday papers, the girl said, 'I'm sorry for the sadness brought to my mother.' She said she was one of nine children of a female laundry worker. She had left school in Standard Three because there was no money at home for gym clothes or a school blazer. She had worked as a machinist in a factory and a cashier in a supermarket. Dr von Leinsdorf taught her to type his notes.

Dr Franz-Josef von Leinsdorf, described as the grandson of a baroness, a cultured man engaged in international mineralogical research, said he accepted social distinctions between people but didn't think they should be legally imposed. 'Even in my own country it's difficult for a person from a higher class to marry one from a lower class.'

The two accused gave no evidence. They did not greet or speak to each other in Court. The Defence argued that the sergeant's evidence that they had been living together as man and wife was hearsay. (The woman with the dachshund, the caretaker?) The magistrate acquitted them because the State failed to prove carnal intercourse had taken place on the night of—December, 19—.

The girl's mother was quoted, with photograph, in the Sunday papers: 'I won't let my daughter work as a servant for a white man again.'

II

The farm children play together when they are small; but once the white children go away to school they soon don't play together any more, even in the holidays. Although most of the black children get some sort of schooling, they drop every year farther behind the grades passed by the white children; the childish vocabulary, the child's exploration of the adventurous possibilities of dam, koppies, mealie lands and veld—there comes a time when the white children have surpassed these with the vocabulary of boarding-school and the possibilities of inter-school sports matches and the kind of adventures seen at the cinema. This usefully coincides with the age of twelve or thirteen; so that by the time early adolescence is reached, the black children are making, along with the bodily changes common to all, an easy transition to adult forms of address, beginning to call their old playmates *missus* and *baasie*—little master.

The trouble was Paulus Eysendyck did not seem to realize that Thebedi was now simply one of the crowd of farm children down at the kraal, recognizable in his sisters' old clothes. The first Christmas holidays after he had gone to boarding-school he brought home for Thebedi a painted box he had made in his wood-work class. He had to give it to her secretly because he had nothing for the other children at the kraal. And she gave him, before he went back to school, a bracelet she had made of thin brass wire and the grey-and-white beans of the castor-oil crop his father cultivated. (When they used to play together, she was the one who had taught Paulus how to make clay oxen for their toy spans.) There was a craze, even in the *platteland* towns like the one where he was at school, for boys to wear elephant-hair and other bracelets beside their watch-straps; his was admired, friends asked him to get similar ones for them. He said the natives made them on his father's farm and he would try.

When he was fifteen, six feet tall, and tramping round at school dances with the girls from the 'sister' school in the same town; when he had learnt how to tease and flirt and fondle quite intimately these girls who were the daughters of prosperous farmers like his father; when he had even met one who, at a wedding he had attended with his parents on a nearby farm, had let him do with her in a locked storeroom what people did when they made love—when he was as far from his childhood as all this, he still brought home from a shop in town a red plastic belt and gilt hoop earrings for the black girl, Thebedi. She told her father the missus had given these to her as a reward for some work she had done—it was true she sometimes was called to help out in the farmhouse. She told the girls in the kraal that she had a sweetheart nobody knew about, far away, away on another farm, and they giggled, and teased, and admired her. There was a boy in the kraal called Njabulo who said he wished he could have bought her a belt and ear-rings.

When the farmer's son was home for the holidays she wandered far from the kraal and her companions. He went for walks alone. They had not arranged this; it was an urge each followed independently. He knew it was she, from a long way off. She knew that his dog would not bark at her. Down at the dried-up river-bed where five or six years ago the children had caught a leguaan one great day—a creature that combined ideally the size and ferocious aspect of the crocodile with the harmlessness of the lizard—they squatted side by side on the earth bank. He told her traveller's tales: about school, about the punishments at school, particularly, exaggerating both their nature and his indifference to them. He told her about the town of Middleburg, which she had never seen. She had nothing to tell but she prompted with many questions, like any good listener. While he talked he twisted and tugged at the roots of white stinkwood and Cape willow trees that looped out of the eroded earth around them. It had always been a good spot for children's games, down there hidden by the mesh of old, ant-eaten trees held in place by vigorous ones, wild asparagus bushing up between the trunks, and here and there prickly-pear cactus sunken-skinned and bristly, like an old man's face, keeping alive sapless until the next rainy season. She punctured the dry hide of a prickly-pear again and again with a sharp stick while she listened. She laughed a lot at what he told her, sometimes dropping her face on her knees, sharing amusement with the cool shady earth beneath her bare feet. She put on her pair of shoes—white sandals, thickly Blanco-ed against the farm dust—when he was on the farm, but these were taken off and laid aside, at the river-bed.

One summer afternoon when there was water flowing there and it was very hot she waded in as they used to do when they were children, her dress bunched modestly and tucked into the legs of her pants. The schoolgirls he went swimming with at dams or pools on neighbouring farms wore bikinis but the sight of their dazzling bellies and thighs in the sunlight had never made him feel what he felt now, when the girl came up the bank and sat beside him, the drops of water beading off her dark legs the only points of light in the earth-smelling, deep shade. They were not afraid of one another, they had known one another always; he did with her what he had done that time in the storeroom at the wedding, and this time it was so lovely, so lovely, he was surprised . . . and she was surprised by it, too—he could see in her dark face that was part of the shade, with her big dark eyes, shiny as soft water, watching him attentively: as she had when they used to huddle over their teams of mud oxen, as she had when he told her about detention weekends at school.

They went to the river-bed often through those summer holidays. They met just before the light went, as it does quite quickly, and each returned home with the dark—she to her mother's hut, he to the farmhouse—in time for the evening meal. He did not tell her about school or town any more. She did not ask questions any longer. He told her, each time, when they would meet again. Once or twice it was very early in the morning; the lowing of the cows being driven to graze came to them where they lay, dividing them with unspoken recognition of the sound read in their two pairs of eyes, opening so close to each other.

He was a popular boy at school. He was in the second, then the first soccer team. The head girl of the 'sister' school was said to have a crush on him; he didn't particularly like her, but there was a pretty blonde who put up her long hair into a kind of doughnut with a black ribbon round it, whom he took to see films when the schoolboys and girls had a free Saturday afternoon. He had been driving tractors and other farm vehicles since he was ten years old, and as soon as he was eighteen he got a driver's licence and in the holidays, this last year of his school life, he took neighbours' daughters to dances and to the drive-in cinema that had just opened twenty kilometres from the farm. His sisters were married, by then; his parents often left him in charge of the farm over the weekend while they visited the young wives and grandchildren.

When Thebedi saw the farmer and his wife drive away on a Saturday afternoon, the boot of their Mercedes filled with fresh-killed poultry and vegetables from the garden that it was part of her father's work to tend, she knew that she must come not to the river-bed but up to the house. The house was an old one, thick-walled, dark against the heat. The kitchen was its lively thorough-fare, with servants, food supplies, begging cats and dogs, pots boiling over, washing being damped for ironing, and the big deep-freeze the missus had ordered from town, bearing a crocheted mat and a vase of plastic irises. But the dining-room with the bulging-legged heavy table was shut up in its rich, old smell of soup and tomato sauce. The sitting-room curtains were drawn and the T.V. set silent. The door of the parents' bedroom was locked and the empty rooms where the girls had slept had sheets of plastic spread over the beds. It was in one of these that she and the farmer's son stayed together whole nights—almost: she had to get away before the house servants, who knew her, came in at dawn. There was a risk someone would discover her or traces of her presence if he took her to his own bedroom, although she had looked into it many times when she was helping out in the house and knew well, there, the row of silver cups he had won at school.

When she was eighteen and the farmer's son nineteen and working with his father on the farm before entering a veterinary college, the young man Njabulo asked her father for her. Njabulo's parents met with hers and the money he was to pay in place of the cows it is customary to give a prospective bride's parents was settled upon. He had no cows to offer; he was a labourer on the Eysendyck farm, like her father. A bright youngster; old Eysendyck had taught him brick-laying and was using him for odd jobs in construction, around the place. She did not tell the farmer's son that her parents had arranged for her to marry. She did not tell him, either, before he left for his first term at the veterinary college, that she thought she was going to have a baby. Two months after her marriage to Njabulo, she gave birth to a daughter. There was no disgrace in that; among her people it is customary for a young man to make sure, before marriage, that the chosen girl is not barren, and Njabulo had made love to her then. But the infant was very light and did not quickly grow darker as most African babies do. Already at birth there was on its head a quantity of straight, fine floss, like that which carries the seeds of certain weeds in the veld. The unfocused eyes it opened were grey flecked with yellow. Njabulo was the matt, opaque coffee-grounds colour that has always been called the black; the colour of Thebedi's legs on which beaded water looked oyster-shell blue, the same colour as Thebedi's face, where the black eyes, with their interested gaze and clear whites, were so dominant.

Njabulo made no complaint. Out of his farm labourer's earnings he bought from the Indian store a cellophane-windowed pack containing a pink plastic bath, six napkins, a card of safety pins, a knitted jacket, cap and bootees, a dress, and a tin of Johnson's Baby Powder, for Thebedi's baby.

When it was two weeks old Paulus Eysendyck arrived home from the veterinary college for the holidays. He drank a glass of fresh, still-warm milk in the childhood familiarity of his mother's kitchen and heard her discussing with the old house-servant where they could get a reliable substitute to help out now that the girl Thebedi had had a baby. For the first time since he was a small boy he came right into the kraal. It was eleven o'clock in the morning. The men were at work in the lands. He looked about him, urgently; the women turned away, each not wanting to be the one approached to point out where Thebedi lived. Thebedi appeared, coming slowly from the hut Njabulo had built in white man's style, with a tin chimney, and a proper window with glass panes set in straight as walls made of unfired bricks would allow. She greeted him with hands brought together and a token movement representing the respectful bob with which she was accustomed to knowledge she was in the presence of his father or mother. He lowered his head under the doorway of her home and went in. He said, 'I want to see. Show me.'

She had taken the bundle off her back before she came out into the light to face him. She moved between the iron bedstead made up with Njabulo's checked blankets and the small wooden table where the pink plastic bath stood among food and kitchen pots, and picked up the bundle from the snugly-blanketed grocer's box where it lay. The infant was asleep; she revealed the closed, pale, plump tiny face, with a bubble of spit at the corner of the mouth, the spidery pink hands stirring. She took off the woollen cap and the straight fine hair flew up after it in static electricity, showing gilded strands here and there. He said nothing. She was watching him as she had done when they were little, and the gang of children had trodden down a crop in their games or transgressed in some other way for which he, as the farmer's son, the white one among them, must intercede with the farmer. She disturbed the sleeping face by scratching or tickling gently at a cheek with one finger, and slowly the eyes opened, saw nothing, were still asleep, and then, awake, no longer narrowed, looked out at them, grey with yellowish flecks, his own hazel eyes.

He struggled for a moment with a grimace of tears, anger and self-pity. She could not put out her hand to him. He said, 'You haven't been near the house with it?'

She shook her head.

'Never?'

Again she shook her head.

'Don't take it out. Stay inside. Can't you take it away somewhere. You must give it to someone—'

She moved to the door with him.

He said, 'I'll see what I will do. I don't know.' And then he said: 'I feel like killing myself.'

Her eyes began to glow, to thicken with tears. For a moment there was the feeling between them that used to come when they were alone down at the river-bed.

He walked out.

Two days later, when his mother and father had left the farm for the day, he appeared again. The women were away on the lands, weeding, as they were employed to do as casual labour in summer; only the very old remained, propped up on the ground outside the huts in the flies and the sun. Thebedi did not ask him in. The child had not been well; it had diarrhoea. He asked where its food was. She said, 'The milk comes from me.' He went into Njabulo's house, where the child lay; she did not follow but stayed outside the door and watched without seeing an old crone who had lost her mind, talking to herself, talking to the fowls who ignored her.

She thought she heard small grunts from the hut, the kind of infant grunt that indicates a full stomach, a deep sleep. After a time, long or short she did not know, he came out and walked away with plodding stride (his father's gait) out of sight, towards his father's house.

The baby was not fed during the night and although she kept telling Njabulo it was sleeping, he saw for himself in the morning that it was dead. He comforted her with words and caresses. She did not cry but simply sat, staring at the door. Her hands were cold as dead chickens' feet to his touch.

Njabulo buried the little baby where farm workers were buried, in the place in the veld the farmer had given them. Some of the mounds had been left to weather away unmarked, others were covered with stones and a few had fallen wooden crosses. He was going to make a cross but before it was finished the police came and dug up the grave and took away the dead baby: someone—one of the other labourers? their women?—had reported that the baby was almost white, that, strong and healthy, it had died suddenly after a visit by the farmer's son. Pathological tests on the infant corpse showed intestinal damage not always consistent with death by natural causes.

Thebedi went for the first time to the country town where Paulus had been to school, to give evidence at the preparatory examination into the charge of murder brought against him. She cried hysterically in the witness box, saying yes, yes (the gilt hoop ear-rings swung in her ears), she saw the accused pouring liquid into the baby's mouth. She said he had threatened to shoot her if she told anyone.

More than a year went by before, in that same town, the case was brought to trial. She came to Court with a new-born baby on her back. She wore gilt hoop ear-rings; she was calm; she said she had not seen what the white man did in the house.

Paulus Eysendyck said he had visited the hut but had not poisoned the child.

The Defence did not contest that there had been a love relationship between the accused and the girl, or that intercourse had taken place, but submitted there was no proof that the child was the accused's.

The judge told the accused there was strong suspicion against him but not enough proof that he had committed the crime. The Court could not accept the girl's evidence because it was clear she had committed perjury either at this trial or at the preparatory examination. There was the suggestion in the mind of the Court that she might be an accomplice in the crime; but, again, insufficient proof.

The judge commended the honourable behaviour of the husband (sitting in court in a brown-and-yellow-quartered golf cap bought for Sundays) who had not rejected his wife and had 'even provided clothes for the unfortunate infant out of his slender means'.

The verdict on the accused was 'not guilty'.

The young white man refused to accept the congratulations of press and public and left the Court with his mother's raincoat shielding his face from photographers. His father said to the press, 'I will try and carry on as best I can to hold up my head in the district.'

Interviewed by the Sunday papers, who spelled her name in a variety of ways, the black girl, speaking in her own language, was quoted beneath her photograph: 'It was a thing of our childhood, we don't see each other any more.'

Italo Calvino

Italo Calvino (1923–1985) was born in Cuba to Italian parents. He lived in Italy and France most of his life. Over the years his fiction (mainly stories) evolved from the neorealism of the postwar years to a fantastical, often whimsical, metafiction that challenged the assumptions of conventional forms. The narratives in *Cosmicomics* and *t-zero* adopt many of the techniques of science fiction and combine a scientist's exactitude with a daydreamer's relaxed inventiveness. Calvino's novel *If on a Winter's Night a Traveller* beguiles the reader with a series of suspenseful narratives, all of which are broken off before they can conclude. But the reader is cajoled by the promise of a new story—the cycle goes on and on. Calvino also assembled a highly popular collection, *Italian Folktales,* from which the reader learns that the charming profusion of this man's tales grew from an ancient heritage. Calvino's works include *Invisible Cities, Mr. Palomar, The Baron in the Trees*, and *The Castle of Crossed Destinies.*

THE DISTANCE OF THE MOON

At one time, according to Sir George H. Darwin, the Moon was very close to the Earth. Then the tides gradually pushed her far away: the tides that the Moon herself causes in the Earth's waters, where the Earth slowly loses energy.

How well I know!—*old Qfwfq cried,*—the rest of you can't remember, but I can. We had her on top of us all the time, that enormous Moon: when she was full—nights as bright as day, but with a butter-colored light—it looked as if she were going to crush us; when she was new, she rolled around the sky like a black umbrella blown by the wind; and when she was waxing, she came forward with her horns so low she seemed about to stick into the peak of a promontory and get caught there. But the whole business of the Moon's phases worked in a different way then: because the distances from the Sun were different, and the orbits, and the angle of something or other, I forget what; as for eclipses, with Earth and Moon stuck together the way they were, why, we had eclipses every minute: naturally, those two big monsters managed to put each other in the shade constantly, first one, then the other.

Orbit? Oh, elliptical, of course: for a while it would huddle against us and then it would take flight for a while. The tides, when the Moon swung closer, rose so high nobody could hold them back. There were nights when the Moon was full and very, very low, and the tide was so high that the Moon missed a ducking in the sea by a hair's-breadth; well, let's say a few yards anyway. Climb up on the Moon? Of course we did. All you had to do was row out to it in a boat and, when you were underneath, prop a ladder against her and scramble up.

The spot where the Moon was lowest, as she went by, was off the Zinc Cliffs. We used to go out with those little rowboats they had in those days, round and flat, made of cork. They held quite a few of us: me, Captain Vhd Vhd, his wife, my deaf cousin, and sometimes little Xlthlx—she was twelve or so at that time. On those nights the water was very calm, so silvery it looked like mercury, and the fish in it, violet-colored, unable to resist the Moon's attraction, rose to the surface, all of them, and so did the octopuses and the saffron medusas. There was always a flight of tiny creatures—little crabs, squid, and even some weeds, light and filmy, and coral plants—that broke from the sea and ended up on the Moon, hanging down from that lime-white ceiling, or else they stayed in midair, a phosphorescent swarm we had to drive off, waving banana leaves at them.

This is how we did the job: in the boat we had a ladder: one of us held it, another climbed to the top, and a third, at the oars, rowed until we were right under the Moon; that's why there had to be so many of us (I only mentioned the main ones). The man at the top of the ladder, as the boat approached the Moon, would become scared and start shouting: "Stop! Stop! I'm going to bang my head!" That was the impression you had, seeing her on top of you, immense, and all rough with sharp spikes and jagged, saw-tooth edges. It may be different now, but then the Moon, or rather the bottom, the underbelly of the Moon, the part that passed closest to the Earth and almost scraped it, was covered with a crust of sharp scales. It had come to resemble the belly of a fish, and the smell too, as I recall, if not downright fishy, was faintly similar, like smoked salmon.

In reality, from the top of the ladder, standing erect on the last rung, you could just touch the Moon if you held your arms up. We had taken the measurements carefully (we didn't yet suspect that she was moving away from us); the only thing you had to be very careful about was where you put your hands. I always chose a scale that seemed fast (we climbed up in groups of five or six at a time), then I would cling first with one hand, then with both, and immediately I would feel ladder and boat drifting away from below me, and the motion of the Moon would tear me from the Earth's attraction. Yes, the Moon was so strong that she pulled you up; you realized this the moment you passed from one to the other: you had to swing up abruptly, with a kind of somersault, grabbing the scales, throwing your legs over your head, until your feet were on the Moon's surface. Seen from the Earth, you looked as if you were hanging there with your head down, but for you, it was the normal position, and the only odd thing was that when you raised your eyes you saw the sea above you, glistening, with the boat and the others upside down, hanging like a bunch of grapes from the vine.

My cousin, the Deaf One, showed a special talent for making those leaps. His clumsy hands, as soon as they touched the lunar surface (he was always the first to jump up from the ladder), suddenly became deft and sensitive. They found immediately the spot where he could hoist himself up; in fact just the pressure of his palms seemed enough to make him stick to the satellite's crust. Once I even thought I saw the Moon come toward him, as he held out his hands.

He was just as dextrous in coming back down to Earth, an operation still more difficult. For us, it consisted in jumping, as high as we could, our arms upraised (seen from the Moon, that is, because seen from the Earth it looked more like a dive, or like swimming downwards, arms at our sides), like jumping up from the Earth in other words, only now we were without the ladder, because there was nothing to prop it against on the Moon. But instead of jumping with his arms out, my cousin bent toward the Moon's surface, his head down as if for a somersault, then made a leap, pushing with his hands. From the boat we watched him, erect in the air as if he were supporting the Moon's enormous ball and were tossing it, striking it with his palms; then, when his legs came within reach, we managed to grab his ankles and pull him down on board.

Now, you will ask me what in the world we went up on the Moon for; I'll explain it to you. We went to collect the milk, with a big spoon and a bucket. Moon-milk was very thick, like a kind of cream cheese. It formed in the crevices between one scale and the next, through the fermentation of various bodies and substances of terrestrial origin which had flown up from the prairies and forests and lakes, as the Moon sailed over them. It was composed chiefly of vegetal juices, tadpoles, bitumen, lentils, honey, starch crystals, sturgeon eggs, molds, pollens, gelatinous matter, worms, resins, pepper, mineral salts, combustion residue. You had only to dip the spoon under the scales that covered the Moon's scabby terrain, and you brought it out filled with that precious muck. Not in the pure state, obviously; there was a lot of refuse. In the fermentation (which took place as the Moon passed over the expanses of hot air above the deserts) not all the bodies melted; some remained stuck in it: fingernails and cartilage, bolts, sea horses, nuts and peduncles, shards of crockery, fishhooks, at times even a comb. So this paste, after it was collected, had to be refined, filtered. But that wasn't the difficulty: the hard part was transporting it down to the Earth. This is how we did it: we hurled each spoonful into the air with both hands, using the spoon as a catapult. The cheese flew, and if we had thrown it hard enough, it stuck to the ceiling, I mean the surface of the sea. Once there, it floated, and it was easy enough to pull it into the boat. In this operation, too, my deaf cousin displayed a special gift; he had strength and a good aim; with a single, sharp throw, he could send the cheese straight into a bucket we held up to him from the boat. As for me, I occasionally misfired; the contents of the spoon would fail to overcome the Moon's attraction and they would fall back into my eye.

I still haven't told you everything, about the things my cousin was good at. That job of extracting lunar milk from the Moon's scales was child's play to him: instead of the spoon, at times he had only to thrust his bare hand under the scales, or even one finger. He didn't proceed in any orderly way, but went to isolated places, jumping from one to the other, as if he were playing tricks on the Moon, surprising her, or perhaps tickling her. And wherever he put his hand, the milk spurted out as if from a nanny goat's teats. So the rest of us had only to follow him and collect with our spoons the substance that he was pressing out, first here, then there, but always as if by chance, since the Deaf One's movements seemed to have no clear, practical sense. There were places, for example, that he touched merely for the fun of touching them: gaps between two scales, naked and tender folds of lunar flesh. At times my cousin pressed not only his fingers but—in a carefully gauged leap—his big toe (he climbed onto the Moon barefoot) and this seemed to be the height of amusement for him, if we could judge by the chirping sounds that came from his throat as he went on leaping.

The soil of the Moon was not uniformly scaly, but revealed irregular bare patches of pale, slippery clay. These soft areas inspired the Deaf One to turn somersaults or to fly almost like a bird, as if he wanted to impress his whole body into the Moon's pulp. As he ventured farther in this way, we lost sight of him at one point. On the Moon there were vast areas we had never had any reason or curiosity to explore, and that was where my cousin vanished; I had suspected that all those somersaults and nudges he indulged in before our eyes were only a preparation, a prelude to something secret meant to take place in the hidden zones.

We fell into a special mood on those nights off the Zinc Cliffs: gay, but with a touch of suspense, as if inside our skulls, instead of the brain, we felt a fish, floating, attracted by the Moon. And so we navigated, playing and singing. The Captain's wife played the harp; she had very long arms, silvery as eels on those nights, and armpits as dark and mysterious as sea urchins; and the sound of the harp was sweet and piercing, so sweet and piercing it was almost unbearable, and we were forced to let out long cries, not so much to accompany the music as to protect our hearing from it.

Transparent medusas rose to the sea's surface, throbbed there a moment, then flew off, swaying toward the Moon. Little Xlthlx amused herself by catching them in midair, though it wasn't easy. Once, as she stretched her little arms out to catch one, she jumped up slightly and was also set free. Thin as she was, she was an ounce or two short of the weight necessary for the Earth's gravity to overcome the Moon's attraction and bring her back: so she flew up among the medusas, suspended over the sea. She took fright, cried, then laughed and started playing, catching shellfish and minnows as they flew, sticking some into her mouth and chewing them. We rowed hard, to keep up with the child: the Moon ran off in her ellipse, dragging that swarm of marine fauna through the sky, and a train of long, entwined seaweeds, and Xlthlx hanging there in the midst. Her two wispy braids seemed to be flying on their own, outstretched toward the Moon; but all the while she kept wriggling and kicking at the air, as if she wanted to fight that influence, and her socks—she had lost her shoes in the flight—slipped off her feet and swayed, attracted by the Earth's force. On the ladder, we tried to grab them.

The idea of eating the little animals in the air had been a good one; the more weight Xlthlx gained, the more she sank toward the Earth; in fact, since among those hovering bodies hers was the largest, mollusks and seaweeds and plankton began to gravitate about her, and soon the child was covered with siliceous little shells, chitinous carapaces, and fibers of sea plants. And the farther she vanished into that tangle, the more she was freed of the Moon's influence, until she grazed the surface of the water and sank into the sea.

We rowed quickly, to pull her out and save her: her body had remained magnetized, and we had to work hard to scrape off all the things encrusted on her. Tender corals were wound about her head, and every time we ran the comb through her hair there was a shower of crayfish and sardines; her eyes were sealed shut by limpets clinging to the lids with their suckers; squids' tentacles were coiled around her arms and her neck; and her little dress now seemed woven only of weeds and sponges. We got the worst of it off her, but for weeks afterwards she went on pulling out fins and shells, and her skin, dotted with little diatoms, remained affected forever, looking—to someone who didn't observe her carefully—as if it were faintly dusted with freckles.

This should give you an idea of how the influences of Earth and Moon, practically equal, fought over the space between them. I'll tell you something else: a body that descended to the Earth from the satellite was still charged for a while with lunar force and rejected the attraction of our world. Even I, big and heavy as I was: every time I had been up there, I took a while to get used to the Earth's up and its down, and the others would have to grab my arms and hold me, clinging in a bunch in the swaying boat while I still had my head hanging and my legs stretching up toward the sky.

"Hold on! Hold on to us!" they shouted at me, and in all that groping, sometimes I ended up by seizing one of Mrs. Vhd Vhd's breasts, which were round and firm, and the contact was good and secure and had an attraction as strong as the Moon's or even stronger, especially if I managed, as I plunged down, to put my other arm around her hips, and with this I passed back into our world and fell with a thud into the bottom of the boat, where Captain Vhd Vhd brought me around, throwing a bucket of water in my face.

This is how the story of my love for the Captain's wife began, and my suffering. Because it didn't take me long to realize whom the lady kept looking at insistently: when my cousin's hands clasped the satellite, I watched Mrs. Vhd Vhd, and in her eyes I could read the thoughts that the deaf man's familiarity with the Moon were arousing in her; and when he disappeared in his mysterious lunar explorations, I saw her become restless, as if on pins and needles, and then it was all clear to me, how Mrs. Vhd Vhd was becoming jealous of the Moon and I was jealous of my cousin. Her eyes were made of diamonds, Mrs. Vhd Vhd's; they flared when she looked at the Moon, almost challengingly, as if she were saying: "You shan't have him!" And I felt like an outsider.

The one who least understood all of this was my deaf cousin. When we helped him down, pulling him—as I explained to you—by his legs, Mrs. Vhd Vhd lost all her self-control, doing everything she could to take his weight against her own body, folding her long silvery arms around him; I felt a pang in my heart (the times I clung to her, her body was soft and kind, but not thrust forward, the way it was with my cousin), while he was indifferent, still lost in his lunar bliss.

I looked at the Captain, wondering if he also noticed his wife's behavior; but there was never a trace of any expression on that face of his, eaten by brine, marked with tarry wrinkles. Since the Deaf One was always the last to break away from the Moon, his return was the signal for the boats to move off. Then, with an unusually polite gesture, Vhd Vhd picked up the harp from the bottom of the boat and handed it to his wife. She was obliged to take it and play a few notes. Nothing could separate her more from the Deaf One than the sound of the harp. I took to singing in a low voice that sad song that goes: "Every shiny fish is floating, floating; and every dark fish is at the bottom, at the bottom of the sea . . ." and all the others, except my cousin, echoed my words.

Every month, once the satellite had moved on, the Deaf One returned to his solitary detachment from the things of the world; only the approach of the full Moon aroused him again. That time I had arranged things so it wasn't my turn to go up, I could stay in the boat with the Captain's wife. But then, as soon as my cousin had climbed the ladder, Mrs. Vhd Vhd said: "This time I want to go up there, too!"

This had never happened before; the Captain's wife had never gone up on the Moon. But Vhd Vhd made no objection, in fact he almost pushed her up the ladder bodily, exclaiming: "Go ahead then!," and we all started helping her, and I held her from behind, felt her round and soft on my arms, and to hold her up I began to press my face and the palms of my hands against her, and when I felt her rising into the Moon's sphere I was heartsick at that lost contact, so I started to rush after her, saying: "I'm going to go up for a while, too, to help out!"

I was held back as if in a vise. "You stay here; you have work to do later," the Captain commanded, without raising his voice.

At that moment each one's intentions were already clear. And yet I couldn't figure things out; even now I'm not sure I've interpreted it all correctly. Certainly the Captain's wife had for a long time been cherishing the desire to go off privately with my cousin up there (or at least to prevent him from going off alone with the Moon), but probably she had a still more ambitious plan, one that would have to be carried out in agreement with the Deaf One: she wanted the two of them to hide up there together and stay on the Moon for a month. But perhaps my cousin, deaf as he was, hadn't understood anything of what she had tried to explain to him, or perhaps he hadn't even realized that he was the object of the lady's desires. And the Captain? He wanted nothing better than to be rid of his wife; in fact, as soon as she was confined up there, we saw him give free rein to his inclinations and plunge into vice, and then we understood why he had done nothing to hold her back. But had he known from the beginning that the Moon's orbit was widening?

None of us could have suspected it. The Deaf One perhaps, but only he: in the shadowy way he knew things, he may have had a presentiment that he would be forced to bid the Moon farewell that night. This is why he hid in his secret places and reappeared only when it was time to come back down on board. It was no use for the Captain's wife to try to follow him: we saw her cross the scaly zone various times, length and breadth, then suddenly she stopped, looking at us in the boat, as if about to ask us whether we had seen him.

Surely there was something strange about that night. The sea's surface, instead of being taut as it was during the full Moon, or even arched a bit toward the sky, now seemed limp, sagging, as if the lunar magnet no longer exercised its full power. And the light, too, wasn't the same as the light of other full Moons; the night's shadows seemed somehow to have thickened. Our friends up there must have realized what was happening; in fact, they looked up at us with frightened eyes. And from their mouths and ours, at the same moment, came a cry: "The Moon's going away!"

The cry hadn't died out when my cousin appeared on the Moon, running. He didn't seem frightened, or even amazed: he placed his hands on the terrain, flinging himself into his usual somersault, but this time after he had hurled himself into the air he remained suspended, as little Xlthlx had. He hovered a moment between Moon and Earth, upside down, then laboriously moving his arms, like someone swimming against a current, he headed with unusual slowness toward our planet.

From the Moon the other sailors hastened to follow his example. Nobody gave a thought to getting the Moon-milk that had been collected into the boats, nor did the Captain scold them for this. They had already waited too long, the distance was difficult to cross by now; when they tried to imitate my cousin's leap or his swimming, they remained there groping, suspended in midair. "Cling together! Idiots! Cling together!" the Captain yelled. At this command, the sailors tried to form a group, a mass, to push all together until they reached the zone of the Earth's attraction: all of a sudden a cascade of bodies plunged into the sea with a loud splash.

The boats were now rowing to pick them up. "Wait! The Captain's wife is missing!" I shouted. The Captain's wife had also tried to jump, but she was still floating only a few yards from the Moon, slowly moving her long, silvery arms in the air. I climbed up the ladder, and in a vain attempt to give her something to grasp I held the harp out toward her. "I can't reach her! We have to go after her!" and I started to jump up, brandishing the harp. Above me the enormous lunar disk no longer seemed the same as before: it had become much smaller, it kept contracting, as if my gaze were driving it away, and the emptied sky gaped like an abyss where, at the bottom, the stars had begun multiplying, and the night poured a river of emptiness over me, drowned me in dizziness and alarm.

"I'm afraid," I thought. "I'm too afraid to jump. I'm a coward!" and at that moment I jumped. I swam furiously through the sky, and held the harp out to her, and instead of coming toward me she rolled over and over, showing me first her impassive face and then her backside.

"Hold tight to me!" I shouted, and I was already overtaking her, entwining my limbs with hers. "If we cling together we can go down!" and I was concentrating all my strength on uniting myself more closely with her, and I concentrated my sensations as I enjoyed the fullness of that embrace. I was so absorbed I didn't realize at first that I was, indeed, tearing her from her weightless condition, but was making her fall back on the Moon. Didn't I realize it? Or had that been my intention from the very beginning? Before I could think properly, a cry was already bursting from my throat. "I'll be the one to stay with you for a month!" Or rather, "On you!" I shouted, in my excitement: "On you for a month!" and at that moment our embrace was broken by our fall to the Moon's surface, where we rolled away from each other among those cold scales.

I raised my eyes as I did every time I touched the Moon's crust, sure that I would see above me the native sea like an endless ceiling, and I saw it, yes, I saw it this time, too, but much higher, and much more narrow, bound by its borders of coasts and cliffs and promontories, and how small the boats seemed, and how unfamiliar my friends' faces and how weak their cries! A sound reached me from nearby: Mrs. Vhd Vhd had discovered her harp and was caressing it, sketching out a chord as sad as weeping.

A long month began. The Moon turned slowly around the Earth. On the suspended globe we no longer saw our familiar shore, but the passage of oceans as deep as abysses and deserts of glowing lapilli, and continents of ice, and forests writhing with reptiles, and the rocky walls of mountain chains gashed by swift rivers, and swampy cities, and stone graveyards, and empires of clay and mud. The distance spread a uniform color over everything: the alien perspective made every image alien; herds of elephants and swarms of locusts ran over the plains, so evenly vast and dense and thickly grown that there was no difference among them.

I should have been happy: as I had dreamed, I was alone with her, that intimacy with the Moon I had so often envied my cousin and with Mrs. Vhd Vhd was now my exclusive prerogative, a month of days and lunar nights stretched uninterrupted before us, the crust of the satellite nourished us with its milk, whose tart flavor was familiar to us, we raised our eyes up, up to the world where we had been born, finally traversed in all its various expanse, explored landscapes no Earth-being had ever seen, or else we contemplated the stars beyond the Moon, big as pieces of fruit, made of light, ripened on the curved branches of the sky, and everything exceeded my most luminous hopes, and yet, and yet, it was, instead, exile.

I thought only of the Earth. It was the Earth that caused each of us to be that someone he was rather than someone else; up there, wrested from the Earth, it was as if I were no longer that I, nor she that She, for me. I was eager to return to the Earth, and I trembled at the fear of having lost it. The fulfillment of my dream of love had lasted only that instant when we had been united, spinning between Earth and Moon: torn from its earthly soil, my love now knew only the heart-rending nostalgia for what it lacked: a where, a surrounding, a before, an after.

This is what I was feeling. But she? As I asked myself, I was torn by my fears. Because if she also thought only of the Earth, this could be a good sign, a sign that she had finally come to understand me, but it could also mean that everything had been useless, that her longings were directed still and only toward my deaf cousin. Instead, she felt nothing. She never raised her eyes to the old planet, she went off, pale, among those wastelands, mumbling dirges and stroking her harp, as if completely identified with her temporary (as I thought) lunar state. Did this mean I had won out over my rival? No; I had lost: a hopeless defeat. Because she had finally realized that my cousin loved only the Moon, and the only thing she wanted now was to become the Moon, to be assimilated into the object of that extrahuman love.

When the Moon had completed its circling of the planet, there we were again over the Zinc Cliffs. I recognized them with dismay: not even in my darkest previsions had I thought the distance would have made them so tiny. In that mud puddle of the sea, my friends had set forth again, without the now useless ladders; but from the boats rose a kind of forest of long poles; everybody was brandishing one, with a harpoon or a grappling hook at the end, perhaps in the hope of scraping off a last bit of Moon-milk or of lending some kind of help to us wretches up there. But it was soon clear that no pole was long enough to reach the Moon; and they dropped back, ridiculously short, humbled, floating on the sea; and in that confusion some of the boats were thrown off balance and overturned. But just then, from another vessel a longer pole, which till then they had dragged along on the water's surface, began to rise: it must have been made of bamboo, of many, many bamboo poles stuck one into the other, and to raise it they had to go slowly because—thin as it was—if they let it sway too much it might break. Therefore, they had to use it with great strength and skill, so that the wholly vertical weight wouldn't rock the boat.

Suddenly it was clear that the tip of that pole would touch the Moon, and we saw it graze, then press against the scaly terrain, rest there a moment, give a kind of little push, or rather a strong push that made it bounce off again, then come back and strike that same spot as if on the rebound, then move away once more. And I recognized, we both—the Captain's wife and I—recognized my cousin: it couldn't have been anyone else, he was playing his last game with the Moon, one of his tricks, with the Moon on the tip of his pole as if he were juggling with her. And we realized that his virtuosity had no purpose, aimed at no practical result, indeed you would have said he was driving the Moon away, that he was helping her departure, that he wanted to show her to her more distant orbit. And this, too, was just like him: he was unable to conceive desires that went against the Moon's nature, the Moon's course and destiny, and if the Moon now tended to go away from him, then he would take delight in this separation just as, till now, he had delighted in the Moon's nearness.

What could Mrs. Vhd Vhd do, in the face of this? It was only at this moment that she proved her passion for the deaf man hadn't been a frivolous whim but an irrevocable vow. If what my cousin now loved was the distant Moon, then she too would remain distant, on the Moon. I sensed this, seeing that she didn't take a step toward the bamboo pole, but simply turned her harp toward the Earth, high in the sky, and plucked the strings. I say I saw her, but to tell the truth I only caught a glimpse of her out of the corner of my eye, because the minute the pole had touched the lunar crust, I had sprung and grasped it, and now, fast as a snake, I was climbing up the bamboo knots, pushing myself along with jerks of my arms and knees, light in the rarefied space, driven by a natural power that ordered me to return to the Earth, oblivious of the motive that had brought me here, or perhaps more aware of it than ever and of its unfortunate outcome; and already my climb up the swaying pole had reached the point where I no longer had to make any effort but could just allow myself to slide, head-first, attracted by the Earth, until in my haste the pole broke into a thousand pieces and I fell into the sea, among the boats.

My return was sweet, my home refound, but my thoughts were filled only with grief at having lost her, and my eyes gazed at the Moon, forever beyond my reach, as I sought her. And I saw her. She was there where I had left her, lying on a beach directly over our heads, and she said nothing. She was the color of the Moon; she held the harp at her side and moved one hand now and then in slow arpeggios. I could distinguish the shape of her bosom, her arms, her thighs, just as I remember them now, just as now, when the Moon has become that flat, remote circle, I still look for her as soon as the first silver appears in the sky, and the more it waxes, the more clearly I imagine I can see her, her or something of her, but only her, in a hundred, a thousand different vistas, she who makes the Moon the Moon and, whenever she is full, sets the dogs to howling all night long, and me with them.

Translated by Jonathan Cape

James Baldwin

James Baldwin (1924–1987) was born in New York. He grew up on the streets of Harlem and learned at first-hand the oppressions that came with being poor and black. While yet in his teens, Baldwin preached sermons in local churches. He later turned his back on the religious vocation and began to write. Teachers and editors soon recognized his verbal gifts, and before long Baldwin was writing fiction, essays, and plays. His explorations of racial tension in the United States led to his becoming a spokesman for the black cause. Baldwin was, along with Martin Luther King, Malcolm X, and others, a great force for change during the civil rights agitations of the 1960s. But Baldwin, a homosexual, felt doubly isolated from the American mainstream; he spent many of his adult years in Paris. Baldwin's novels include *Go Tell It on the Mountain, Giovanni's Room, Another Country, If Beale Street Could Talk,* and *Just Above My Head.* His essays have been collected in *The Price of a Ticket.*

SONNY'S BLUES

I read about it in the paper, in the subway, on my way to work. I read it, and I couldn't believe it, and I read it again. Then perhaps I just stared at it, at the newsprint spelling out his name, spelling out the story. I stared at it in the swinging lights of the subway car, and in the faces and bodies of the people, and in my own face, trapped in the darkness which roared outside.

It was not to be believed and I kept telling myself that, as I walked from the subway station to the high school. And at the same time I couldn't doubt it. I was scared, scared for Sonny. He became real to me again. A great block of ice got settled in my belly and kept melting there slowly all day long, while I taught my classes algebra. It was a special kind of ice. It kept melting, sending trickles of ice water all up and down my veins, but it never got less. Sometimes it hardened and seemed to expand until I felt my guts were going to come spilling out or that I was going to choke or scream. This would always be at a moment when I was remembering some specific thing Sonny had once said or done.

When he was about as old as the boys in my classes his face had been bright and open, there was a lot of copper in it; and he'd had wonderfully direct brown eyes, and great gentleness and privacy. I wondered what he looked like now. He had been picked up, the evening before, in a raid on an apartment downtown, for peddling and using heroin.

I couldn't believe it: but what I mean by that is that I couldn't find any room for it anywhere inside me. I had kept it outside me for a long time. I hadn't wanted to know. I had had suspicions, but I didn't name them, I kept putting them away. I told myself that Sonny was wild, but he wasn't crazy. And he'd always been a good boy, he hadn't ever turned hard or evil or disrespectful, the way kids can, so quick, so quick, especially in Harlem. I didn't want to believe that I'd ever see my brother going down, coming to nothing, all that light in his face gone out, in the condition I'd already seen so many others. Yet it had happened and here I was, talking about algebra to a lot of boys who might, every one of them for all I knew, be popping off needles every time they went to the head.[1] Maybe it did more for them than algebra could.

I was sure that the first time Sonny had ever had horse,[2] he couldn't have been much older than these boys were now. These boys, now, were living as we'd been living then, they were growing up with a rush and their heads bumped abruptly against the low ceiling of their actual possibilities. They were filled with rage. All they really knew were two darknesses, the darkness of their lives, which was now closing in on them, and the darkness of the movies, which had blinded them to that other darkness, and in which they now, vindictively, dreamed, at once more together than they were at any other time, and more alone.

When the last bell rang, the last class ended, I let out my breath. It seemed I'd been holding it for all that time. My clothes were wet—I may have looked as though I'd been sitting in a steam bath, all dressed up, all afternoon. I sat alone in the classroom a long time. I listened to the boys outside, downstairs, shouting and cursing and laughing. Their laughter struck me for perhaps the first time. It was not the joyous laughter which—God knows why—one associates with children. It was mocking and insular, its intent was to denigrate. It was disenchanted, and in this, also, lay the authority of their curses. Perhaps I was listening to them because I was thinking about my brother and in them I heard my brother. And myself.

One boy was whistling a tune, at once very complicated and very simple, it seemed to be pouring out of him as though he were a bird, and it sounded very cool and moving through all that harsh, bright air, only just holding its own through all those other sounds.

I stood up and walked over to the window and looked down into the courtyard. It was the beginning of the spring and the sap was rising in the boys. A teacher passed through them every now and again, quickly, as though he or she couldn't wait to get out of that courtyard, to get those

1. Toilet. 2. Heroin.

boys out of their sight and off their minds. I started collecting my stuff. I thought I'd better get home and talk to Isabel.

The courtyard was almost deserted by the time I got downstairs. I saw this boy standing in the shadow of a doorway, looking just like Sonny. I almost called his name. Then I saw that it wasn't Sonny, but somebody we used to know, a boy from around our block. He'd been Sonny's friend. He'd never been mine, having been too young for me, and, anyway, I'd never liked him. And now, even though he was a grown-up man, he still hung around that block, still spent hours on the street corners, was always high and raggy. I used to run into him from time to time and he'd often work around to asking me for a quarter or fifty cents. He always had some real good excuse, too, and I always gave it to him. I don't know why.

But now, abruptly, I hated him. I couldn't stand the way he looked at me, partly like a dog, partly like a cunning child. I wanted to ask him what the hell he was doing in the school courtyard.

He sort of shuffled over to me, and he said, "I see you got the papers. So you already know about it."

"You mean about Sonny? Yes, I already know about it. How come they didn't get you?"

He grinned. It made him repulsive and it also brought to mind what he's looked like as a kid. "I wasn't there. I stay away from them people."

"Good for you." I offered him a cigarette and I watched him through the smoke. "You come all the way down here just to tell me about Sonny?"

"That's right." He was sort of shaking his head and his eyes looked strange, as though they were about to cross. The bright sun deadened his damp dark brown skin and it made his eyes look yellow and showed up the dirt in his kinked hair. He smelled funky.[3] I moved a little away from him and I said, "Well, thanks. But I already know about it and I got to get home."

"I'll walk you a little ways," he said. We started walking. There were a couple of kids still loitering in the courtyard and one of them said goodnight to me and looked strangely at the boy beside me.

"What're you going to do?" he asked me. "I mean, about Sonny?"

"Look. I haven't seen Sonny for over a year, I'm not sure I'm going to do anything. Anyway, what the hell *can* I do?"

"That's right," he said quickly, "ain't nothing you can do. Can't much help old Sonny no more, I guess."

It was what I was thinking and so it seemed to me he had no right to say it.

"I'm surprised at Sonny, though," he went on—he had a funny way of talking, he looked straight ahead as though he were talking to himself—"I thought Sonny was a smart boy, I thought he was too smart to get hung."

3. Unwashed.

"I guess he thought so too," I said sharply, "and that's how he got hung. And how about you? You're pretty goddamn smart, I bet."

Then he looked directly at me, just for a minute. "I ain't smart," he said. "If I was smart, I'd have reached for a pistol a long time ago."

"Look. Don't tell *me* your sad story, if it was up to me, I'd give you one." Then I felt guilty—guilty, probably, for never having supposed that the poor bastard *had* a story of his own, much less a sad one, and I asked, quickly, "What's going to happen to him now?"

He didn't answer this. He was off by himself some place.

"Funny thing," he said, and from his tone we might have been discussing the quickest way to get to Brooklyn, "when I saw the papers this morning, the first thing I asked myself was if I had anything to do with it. I felt sort of responsible."

I began to listen more carefully. The subway station was on the corner, just before us, and I stopped. He stopped, too. We were in front of a bar and he ducked slightly, peering in, but whoever he was looking for didn't seem to be there. The juke box was blasting away with something black and bouncy and I half watched the barmaid as she danced her way from the juke box to her place behind the bar. And I watched her face as she laughingly responded to something someone said to her, still keeping time to the music. When she smiled one saw the little girl, one sensed the doomed, still-struggling woman beneath the battered face of the semi-whore.

"I never *give* Sonny nothing," the boy said finally, "but a long time ago I come to school high and Sonny asked me how it felt." He paused, I couldn't bear to watch him, I watched the barmaid, and I listened to the music which seemed to be causing the pavement to shake. "I told him it felt great." The music stopped, the barmaid paused and watched the juke box until the music began again. "It did."

All this was carrying me some place I didn't want to go. I certainly didn't want to know how it felt. It filled everything, the people, the houses, the music, the dark, quicksilver barmaid, with menace; and this menace was their reality.

"What's going to happen to him now?" I asked again.

"They'll send him away some place and they'll try to cure him." He shook his head. "Maybe he'll even think he's kicked the habit. Then they'll let him loose"—he gestured, throwing his cigarette into the gutter. "That's all."

"What do you mean, that's *all?*"

But I knew what he meant.

"I *mean,* that's *all.*" He turned his head and looked at me, pulling down the corners of his mouth. "Don't you know what I mean?" he asked, softly.

"How the hell *would* I know what you mean?" I almost whispered it, I don't know why.

"That's right," he said to the air, "how would *he* know what I mean?" He turned toward me again, patient and calm, and yet I somehow felt him shaking, shaking as though he were going to fall apart. I felt that ice in my guts again, the dread I'd felt all afternoon; and again I watched the barmaid, moving about the bar, washing glasses, and singing. "Listen. They'll let him out and then it'll just start all over again. That's what I mean."

"You mean—they'll let him out. And then he'll just start working his way back in again. You mean he'll never kick the habit. Is that what you mean?"

"That's right," he said, cheerfully. "*You* see what I mean."

"Tell me," I said at last, "why does he want to die? He must want to die, he's killing himself, why does he want to die?"

He looked at me in surprise. He licked his lips. "He don't want to die. He wants to live. Don't nobody want to die, ever."

Then I wanted to ask him—too many things. He could not have answered, or if he had, I could not have borne the answers. I started walking. "Well, I guess it's none of my business."

"It's going to be rough on old Sonny," he said. We reached the subway station. "This is your station?" he asked, I nodded. I took one step down. "Damn!" he said, suddenly. I looked up at him. He grinned again. "Damn it if I didn't leave all my money home. You ain't got a dollar on you, have you? Just for a couple of days, is all."

All at once something inside gave and threatened to come pouring out of me. I didn't hate him any more. I felt that in another moment I'd start crying like a child.

"Sure," I said. "Don't sweat." I looked in my wallet and didn't have a dollar, I only had a five. "Here," I said. "That hold you?"

He didn't look at it—he didn't want to look at it. A terrible, closed look came over his face, as though he were keeping the number on the bill a secret from him and me. "Thanks," he said, and now he was dying to see me go. "Don't worry about Sonny. Maybe I'll write him or something."

"Sure," I said. "You do that. So long."

"Be seeing you," he said. I went on down the steps.

And I didn't write Sonny or send him anything for a long time. When I finally did, it was just after my little girl died, and he wrote me back a letter which made me feel like a bastard.

Here's what he said:

> Dear brother,
>
> You don't know how much I needed to hear from you. I wanted to write you many a time but I dug how much I must have hurt you and so I didn't write. But now I feel like a man who's been trying to climb up out of some deep, real deep and funky hole and just saw the sun up there, outside. I got to get outside.
>
> I can't tell you much about how I got here. I mean I don't know how to tell you. I guess I was afraid of something or I was trying to escape from something and you know I have never been very strong in the head (smile). I'm glad Mama and Daddy are dead and can't see what's happened

to their son and I swear if I'd known what I was doing I would never have hurt you so, you and a lot of other fine people who were nice to me and who believed in me.

I don't want you to think it had anything to do with me being a musician. It's more than that. Or maybe less than that. I can't get anything straight in my head down here and I try not to think about what's going to happen to me when I get outside again. Sometime I think I'm going to flip and *never* get outside and sometime I think I'll come straight back. I tell you one thing, though, I'd rather blow my brains out than go through this again. But that's what they all say, so they tell me. If I tell you when I'm coming to New York and if you could meet me, I sure would appreciate it. Give my love to Isabel and the kids and I was sure sorry to hear about little Gracie. I wish I could be like Mama and say the Lord's will be done, but I don't know it seems to me that trouble is the one thing that never does get stopped and I don't know what good it does to blame it on the Lord. But maybe it does some good if you believe it.

Your brother,
Sonny

Then I kept in constant touch with him and I sent him whatever I could and I went to meet him when he came back to New York. When I saw him many things I thought I had forgotten came flooding back to me. This was because I had begun, finally, to wonder about Sonny, about the life that Sonny lived inside. This life, whatever it was, had made him older and thinner and it had deepened the distant stillness in which he had always moved. He looked very unlike my baby brother. Yet, when he smiled, when we shook hands, the baby brother I'd never known looked out from the depths of his private life, like an animal waiting to be coaxed into the light.

"How you been keeping?" he asked me.

"All right. And you?"

"Just fine." He was smiling all over his face. "It's good to see you again."

"It's good to see you."

The seven years' difference in our ages lay between us like a chasm: I wondered if these years would ever operate between us as a bridge. I was remembering, and it made it hard to catch my breath, that I had been there when he was born; and I had heard the first words he had ever spoken. When he started to walk, he walked from our mother straight to me. I caught him just before he fell when he took the first steps he ever took in this world.

"How's Isabel?"

"Just fine. She's dying to see you."

"And the boys?"

"They're fine, too. They're anxious to see their uncle."

"Oh, come on. You know they don't remember me."

"Are you kidding? Of course they remember you."

He grinned again. We got into a taxi. We had a lot to say to each other, far too much to know how to begin.

As the taxi began to move, I asked, "You still want to go to India?"

He laughed. "You still remember that. Hell, no. This place is Indian enough for me."

"It used to belong to them," I said.

And he laughed again. "They damn sure knew what they were doing when they got rid of it."

Years ago, when he was around fourteen, he'd been all hipped on the idea of going to India. He read books about people sitting on rocks, naked, in all kinds of weather, but mostly bad, naturally, and walking barefoot through hot coals and arriving at wisdom. I used to say that it sounded to me as though they were getting away from wisdom as fast as they could. I think he sort of looked down on me for that.

"Do you mind," he asked, "if we have the driver drive alongside the park? On the west side—I haven't seen the city in so long."

"Of course not," I said. I was afraid that I might sound as though I were humoring him, but I hoped he wouldn't take it that way.

So we drove along, between the green of the park and the stony, lifeless elegance of hotels and apartment buildings, toward the vivid, killing streets of our childhood. These streets hadn't changed, though housing projects jutted up out of them now like rocks in the middle of a boiling sea. Most of the houses in which we had grown up had vanished, as had the stores from which we had stolen, the basements in which we had first tried sex, the rooftops from which we had hurled tin cans and bricks. But houses exactly like the house of our past yet dominated the landscape, boys exactly like the boys we once had been found themselve smothering in these houses, came down into the streets for light and air and found themselves encircled by disaster. Some escaped the trap, most didn't. Those who got out always left something of themselves behind, as some animals amputate a leg and leave it in the trap. It might be said, perhaps, that I had escaped, after all, I was a school teacher; or that Sonny had, he hadn't lived in Harlem for years. Yet, as the cab moved uptown through streets which seemed, with a rush, to darken with dark people, and as I covertly studied Sonny's face, it came to me that what we both were seeking through our separate cab windows was that part of ourselves which had been left behind. It's always at the hour of trouble and confrontation that the missing member aches.

We hit 110th Street and started rolling up Lenox Avenue. And I'd known this avenue all my life, but it seemed to me again, as it had seemed on the day I'd first heard about Sonny's trouble, filled with a hidden menace which was its very breath of life.

"We almost there," said Sonny.

"Almost." We were both too nervous to say anything more.

We live in a housing project. It hasn't been up long. A few days after it was up it seemed uninhabitably new, now, of course, it's already rundown. It looks like a parody of the good, clean, faceless life—God knows the people who live in it do their best to make it a parody. The beat-looking grass lying around isn't enough to make their lives green, the hedges will never hold out the streets, and they know it. The big windows fool no one, they aren't big enough to make space out of no space. They don't bother with the windows, they watch the TV screen instead. The playground is most popular with the children who don't play at jacks, or skip rope, or roller skate, or swing, and they can be found in it after dark. We moved in partly because it's not too far from where I teach, and partly for the kids; but it's really just like the houses in which Sonny and I grew up. The same things happen, they'll have the same things to remember. The moment Sonny and I started into the house I had the feeling that I was simply bringing him back into the danger he had almost died trying to escape.

Sonny has never been talkative. So I don't know why I was sure he'd be dying to talk to me when supper was over the first night. Everything went fine, the oldest boy remembered him, and the youngest boy liked him, and Sonny had remembered to bring something for each of them; and Isabel, who is really much nicer than I am, more open and giving, had gone to a lot of trouble about dinner and was genuinely glad to see him. And she's always been able to tease Sonny in a way that I haven't. It was nice to see her face so vivid again and to hear her laugh and watch her make Sonny laugh. She wasn't, or, anyway, she didn't seem to be, at all uneasy or embarrassed. She chatted as though there were no subject which had to be avoided and she got Sonny past his first, faint stiffness. And thank God she was there, for I was filled with that icy dread again. Everything I did seemed awkward to me, and everything I said sounded freighted with hidden meaning. I was trying to remember everything I'd heard about dope addiction and I couldn't help watching Sonny for signs. I wasn't doing it out of malice. I was trying to find out something about my brother. I was dying to hear him tell me he was safe.

"Safe!" my father grunted, whenever Mama suggested trying to move to a neighborhood which might be safer for children. "Safe, hell! Ain't no place safe for kids, nor nobody."

He always went on like this, but he wasn't, ever, really as bad as he sounded, not even on weekends, when he got drunk. As a matter of fact, he was always on the lookout for "something a little better," but he died before he found it. He died suddenly, during a drunken weekend in the middle of the war, when Sonny was fifteen. He and Sonny hadn't ever got on too well. And this was partly because Sonny was the apple of his father's eye. It was because he loved Sonny so much and was frightened for him, that he was always fighting with him. It doesn't do any good to fight with Sonny. Sonny just moves back, inside himself, where he can't be reached. But the principal reason that they never hit it off is that they were so much alike. Daddy was big and rough and loud-talking, just the opposite of Sonny, but they both had—that same privacy.

Mama tried to tell me something about this, just after Daddy died. I was home on leave from the army.

This was the last time I ever saw my mother alive. Just the same, this picture gets all mixed up in my mind with pictures I had of her when she was younger. The way I always see her is the way she used to be on a Sunday afternoon, say, when the old folks were talking after the big Sunday dinner. I always see her wearing pale blue. She'd be sitting on the sofa. And my father would be sitting in the easy chair, not far from her. And the living room would be full of church folks and relatives. There they sit, in chairs all around the living room, and the night is creeping up outside, but nobody knows it yet. You can see the darkness growing against the windowpanes and you hear the street noises every now and again, or maybe the jangling beat of a tambourine from one of the churches close by, but it's real quiet in the room. For a moment nobody's talking, but every face looks darkening, like the sky outside. And my mother rocks a little from the waist, and my father's eyes are closed. Everyone is looking at something a child can't see. For a minute they've forgotten the children. Maybe a kid is lying on the rug, half asleep. Maybe somebody's got a kid in his lap and is absent-mindedly stroking the kid's head. Maybe there's a kid, quiet and big-eyed, curled up in a big chair in the corner. The silence, the darkness coming, and the darkness in the faces frighten the child obscurely. He hopes that the hand which strokes his forehead will never stop—will never die. He hopes that there will never come a time when the old folks won't be sitting around the living room, talking about where they've come from, and what they've seen, and what's happened to them and their kinfolk.

But something deep and watchful in the child knows that this is bound to end, is already ending. In a moment someone will get up and turn on the light. Then the old folks will remember the children and they won't talk any more that day. And when light fills the room, the child is filled with darkness. He knows that every time this happens he's moved just a little closer to that darkness outside. The darkness outside is what the old folks have been talking about. It's what they've come from. It's what they endure. The child knows that they won't talk any more because if he knows too much about what's happened to *them,* he'll know too much too soon, about what's going to happen to *him.*

The last time I talked to my mother, I remember I was restless. I wanted to get out and see Isabel. We weren't married then and we had a lot to straighten out between us.

There Mama sat, in black, by the window. She was humming an old church song, *Lord, you brought me from a long ways off.* Sonny was out somewhere. Mama kept watching the streets.

"I don't know," she said, "if I'll ever see you again, after you go off from here. But I hope you'll remember the things I tried to teach you."

"Don't talk like that," I said, and smiled. "You'll be here a long time yet."

She smiled, too, but she said nothing. She was quiet for a long time. And I said, "Mama, don't you worry about nothing. I'll be writing all the time, and you be getting the checks. . . ."

"I want to talk to you about your brother," she said, suddenly. "If anything happens to me he ain't going to have nobody to look out for him."

"Mama," I said, "ain't nothing going to happen to you *or* Sonny. Sonny's all right. He's a good boy and he's got good sense."

"It ain't a question of his being a good boy," Mama said, "nor of his having good sense. It ain't only the bad ones, nor yet the dumb ones that gets sucked under." She stopped, looking at me. "Your Daddy once had a brother," she said, and she smiled in a way that made me feel she was in pain. "You didn't never know that, did you?"

"No," I said, "I never knew that," and I watched her face.

"Oh, yes," she said, "your Daddy had a brother." She looked out of the window again. "I know you never saw your Daddy cry. But *I* did—many a time, through all these years."

I asked her, "What happened to his brother? How come nobody's ever talked about him?"

This was the first time I ever saw my mother look old.

"His brother got killed," she said, "when he was just a little younger than you are now. I knew him. He was a fine boy. He was maybe a little full of the devil, but he didn't mean nobody no harm."

Then she stopped and the room was silent, exactly as it had sometimes been on those Sunday afternoons. Mama kept looking out into the streets.

"He used to have a job in the mill," she said, "and, like all young folks, he just liked to perform on Saturday nights. Saturday nights, him and your father would drift around to different places, go to dances and things like that, or just sit around with people they knew, and your father's brother would sing, he had a fine voice, and play along with himself on his guitar. Well, this particular Saturday night, him and your father was coming home from some place, and they were both a little drunk and there was a moon that night, it was bright like day. Your father's brother was feeling kind of good, and he was whistling to himself, and he had his guitar slung over his shoulder. They was coming down a hill and beneath them was a road that turned off from the highway. Well, your father's brother, being always kind of frisky, decided to run down this hill, and he did, with that guitar banging and clanging behind him, and he ran across the road, and he was making water behind a tree. And your father was sort of amused at him and he was still coming down the hill, kind of slow. Then he heard a car motor and that same minute his brother stepped from behind the tree, into the road, in the moonlight. And he started to cross the road. And your father started to run down the hill, he says he don't know why. This car was full of white men. They was all drunk, and when they seen your father's brother they let out a great whoop and holler and they aimed the car straight at him. They was having fun, they just wanted to scare him, the way they do sometimes, you know. But they was drunk. And I guess the boy, being drunk, too, and scared, kind of lost his head. By the time he jumped it was too late. Your father says he heard his brother scream when the car rolled over him, and he heard the wood of that guitar when it give, and he heard them strings go flying, and he heard them white men shouting, and the car kept on a-going and it ain't stopped till this day. And, time your father got down the hill, his brother weren't nothing but blood and pulp."

Tears were gleaming on my mother's face. There wasn't anything I could say.

"He never mentioned it," she said, "because I never let him mention it before you children. Your Daddy was like a crazy man that night and for many a night thereafter. He says he never in his life seen anything as dark as that road after the lights of that car had gone away. Weren't nothing, weren't nobody on that road, just your Daddy and his brother and that busted guitar. Oh, yes. Your Daddy never did really get right again. Till the day he died he weren't sure but that every white man he saw was the man that killed his brother."

She stopped and took out her handkerchief and dried her eyes and looked at me.

"I ain't telling you all this," she said, "to make you scared or bitter or to make you hate nobody. I'm telling you this because you got a brother. And the world ain't changed."

I guess I didn't want to believe this. I guess she saw this in my face. She turned away from me, toward the window again, searching those streets.

"But I praise my Redeemer," she said at last, "that He called your Daddy home before me. I ain't saying it to throw no flowers at myself, but, I declare, it keeps me from feeling too cast down to know I helped your father get safely through this world. Your father always acted like he was the roughest, strongest man on earth. And everybody took him to be like that. But if he hadn't had me there—to see his tears!"

She was crying again. Still, I couldn't move. I said, "Lord, Lord, Mama, I didn't know it was like that."

"Oh, honey," she said, "there's a lot that you don't know. But you are going to find out." She stood up from the window and came over to me. "You got to hold on to your brother," she said, "and don't let him fall, no matter what it looks like is happening to him and no matter how evil you gets with him. You going to be evil with him many a time. But don't you forget what I told you, you hear?"

"I won't forget," I said. "Don't you worry, I won't forget. I won't let nothing happen to Sonny."

My mother smiled as though she was amused at something she saw in my face. Then, "You may not be able to stop nothing from happening. But you got to let him know you's *there*."

Two days later I was married, and then I was gone. And I had a lot of things on my mind and I pretty well forgot my promise to Mama until I got shipped home on a special furlough for her funeral.

And, after the funeral, with just Sonny and me alone in the empty kitchen, I tried to find out something about him.

"What do you want to do?" I asked him.

"I'm going to be a musician," he said.

For he had graduated, in the time I had been away, from dancing to the juke box to finding out who was playing what, and what they were doing with it, and he had bought himself a set of drums.

"You mean, you want to be a drummer?" I somehow had the feeling that being a drummer might be all right for other people but not for my brother Sonny.

"I don't think," he said, looking at me very gravely, "that I'll ever be a good drummer. But I think I can play a piano."

I frowned. I'd never played the role of the oldest brother quite so seriously before, had scarcely ever, in fact, *asked* Sonny a damn thing. I sensed myself in the presence of something I didn't really know how to handle, didn't understand. So I made my frown a little deeper as I asked: "What kind of musician do you want to be?"

He grinned. "How many kinds do you think there are?"

"Be *serious,*" I said.

He laughed, throwing his head back, and then looked at me. "I *am* serious."

"Well, then, for Christ's sake, stop kidding around and answer a serious question. I mean, do you want to be a concert pianist, you want to play classical music and all that, or—or what?" Long before I finished he was laughing again. "For Christ's *sake,* Sonny!"

He sobered, but with difficulty. "I'm sorry. But you sound so—*scared!*" and he was off again.

"Well, you may think it's funny now, baby, but it's not going to be so funny when you have to make your living at it, let me tell you *that.*" I was furious because I knew he was laughing at me and I didn't know why.

"No," he said, very sober now, and afraid, perhaps, that he'd hurt me, "I don't want to be a classical pianist. That isn't what interests me. I mean"—he paused, looking hard at me, as though his eyes would help me to understand, and then gestured helplessly, as though perhaps his hand would help—"I mean, I'll have a lot of studying to do, and I'll have to study *everything,* but, I mean, I want to play *with*—jazz musicians." He stopped. "I want to play jazz," he said.

Well, the word had never before sounded as heavy, as real, as it sounded that afternoon in Sonny's mouth. I just looked at him and I was probably frowning a real frown by this time. I simply couldn't see why on earth he'd want to spend his time hanging around nightclubs, clowning around on bandstands, while people pushed each other around a dance floor. It seemed—beneath him, somehow. I had never thought about it before, had never been forced to, but I suppose I had always put jazz musicians in a class with what Daddy called "good-time people."

"Are you *serious?*"

"Hell, *yes,* I'm serious."

He looked more helpless than ever, and annoyed, and deeply hurt.

I suggested, helpfully: "You mean—like Louis Armstrong?"

His face closed as though I'd struck him. "No. I'm not talking about none of that old-time, down home crap."

"Well, look, Sonny, I'm sorry, don't get mad. I just don't altogether get it, that's all. Name somebody—you know, a jazz musician you admire."

"Bird."

"Who?"

"Bird! Charlie Parker![4] Don't they teach you nothing in the goddamn army?"

I lit a cigarette. I was surprised and then a little amused to discover that I was trembling. "I've been out of touch," I said. "You'll have to be patient with me. Now. Who's this Parker character?"

"He's just one of the greatest jazz musicians alive," said Sonny, sullenly, his hands in his pockets, his back to me. "Maybe *the* greatest," he added, bitterly, "that's probably why *you* never heard of him."

"All right," I said, "I'm ignorant. I'm sorry. I'll go out and buy all the cat's records right away, all right?"

"It don't," said Sonny, with dignity, "make any difference to me. I don't care what you listen to. Don't do me no favors."

I was beginning to realize that I'd never seen him so upset before. With another part of my mind I was thinking that this would probably turn out to be one of those things kids go through and that I shouldn't make it seem important by pushing it too hard. Still, I didn't think it would do any harm to ask: "Doesn't all this take a lot of time? Can you make a living at it?"

He turned back to me and half leaned, half sat, on the kitchen table. "Everything takes time," he said, "and—well, yes, sure, I can make a living at it. But what I don't seem to be able to make you understand is that it's the only thing I want to do."

"Well, Sonny," I said gently, "you know people can't always do exactly what they *want* to do—"

"*No,* I don't know that," said Sonny, surprising me. "I think people *ought* to do what they want to do, what else are they alive for?"

"You getting to be a big boy," I said desperately, "it's time you started thinking about your future."

4. Charlie "Bird" Parker (1920–1955), musician for whom Birdland ballroom in New York was named. A founder of the new jazz that began to flourish in the 1940's.

"I'm thinking about my future," said Sonny, grimly. "I think about it all the time."

I gave up. I decided, if he didn't change his mind, that we could always talk about it later. "In the meantime," I said, "you got to finish school." We had already decided that he'd have to move in with Isabel and her folks. I knew this wasn't the ideal arrangement because Isabel's folks are inclined to be dicty[5] and they hadn't especially wanted Isabel to marry me. But I didn't know what else to do. "And we have to get you fixed up at Isabel's."

There was a long silence. He moved from the kitchen table to the window. "That's a terrible idea. You know it yourself."

"Do you have a *better* idea?"

He just walked up and down the kitchen for a minute. He was as tall as I was. He had started to shave. I suddenly had the feeling that I didn't know him at all.

He stopped at the kitchen table and picked up my cigarettes. Looking at me with a kind of mocking, amused defiance, he put one between his lips. "You mind?"

"You smoking already?"

He lit the cigarette and nodded, watching me through the smoke. "I just wanted to see if I'd have the courage to smoke in front of you." He grinned and blew a great cloud of smoke to the ceiling. "It was easy." He looked at my face. "Come on, now. I bet you was smoking at my age, tell the truth."

I didn't say anything but the truth was on my face, and he laughed. But now there was something very strained in his laugh. "Sure. And I bet that ain't all you was doing."

He was frightening me a little. "Cut the crap," I said. "We already decided that you was going to go and live at Isabel's. Now what's got into you all of a sudden?"

"*You* decided it," he pointed out. "*I* didn't decide nothing." He stopped in front of me, leaning against the stove, arms loosely folded. "Look, brother. I don't want to stay in Harlem no more, I really don't." He was very earnest. He looked at me, then over toward the kitchen window. There was something in his eyes I'd never seen before, some thoughtfulness, some worry all his own. He rubbed the muscle of one arm. "It's time I was getting out of here."

"Where do you want to *go,* Sonny?"

"I want to join the army. Or the navy, I don't care. If I say I'm old enough, they'll believe me."

Then I got mad. It was because I was so scared. "You must be crazy. You goddamn fool, what the hell do you want to go and join the *army* for?"

"I just told you. To get out of Harlem."

5. Dictatorial, overbearing.

"Sonny, you haven't even finished *school*. And if you really want to be a musician, how do you expect to study if you're in the *army?*"

He looked at me, trapped, and in anguish. "There's ways. I might be able to work out some kind of deal. Anyway, I'll have the G.I. Bill when I come out."

"*If* you come out." We stared at each other. "Sonny, please. Be reasonable. I know the setup is far from perfect. But we got to do the best we can."

"I ain't learning nothing in school," he said. "Even when I go." He turned away from me and opened the window and threw his cigarette out into the narrow alley. I watched his back. "At least, I ain't learning nothing you'd want me to learn." He slammed the window so hard I thought the glass would fly out, and turned back to me. "And I'm sick of the stink of these garbage cans!"

"Sonny," I said, "I know how you feel. But if you don't finish school now, you're going to be sorry later that you didn't." I grabbed him by the shoulders. "And you only got another year. It ain't so bad. And I'll come back and I swear I'll help you do *whatever* you want to do. Just try to put up with it till I come back. Will you please do that? For me?"

He didn't answer and he wouldn't look at me.

"Sonny. You hear me?"

He pulled away. "I hear you. But you never hear anything *I* say."

I didn't know what to say to that. He looked out of the window and then back at me. "OK," he said, and sighed. "I'll try."

Then I said, trying to cheer him up a little, "They got a piano at Isabel's. You can practice on it."

And as a matter of fact, it did cheer him up for a minute. "That's right," he said to himself. "I forgot that." His face relaxed a little. But the worry, the thoughtfulness, played on it still, the way shadows play on a face which is staring into the fire.

But I thought I'd never hear the end of that piano. At first, Isabel would write me, saying how nice it was that Sonny was so serious about his music and how, as soon as he came in from school, or wherever he had been when he was supposed to be at school, he went straight to that piano and stayed there until suppertime. And, after supper, he went back to that piano and stayed there until everybody went to bed. He was at the piano all day Saturday and all day Sunday. Then he bought a record player and started playing records. He'd play one record over and over again, all day long sometimes, and he'd improvise along with it on the piano. Or he'd play one section of the record, one chord, one change, one progression, then he'd do it on the piano. Then back to the record. Then back to the piano.

Well, I really don't know how they stood it. Isabel finally confessed that it wasn't like living with a person at all, it was like living with sound.

And the sound didn't make any sense to her, didn't make any sense to any of them—naturally. They began, in a way, to be afflicted by this presence that was living in their home. It was as though Sonny were some sort of god, or monster. He moved in an atmosphere which wasn't like theirs at all. They fed him and he ate, he washed himself, he walked in and out of their door; he certainly wasn't nasty or unpleasant or rude, Sonny isn't any of those things; but it was as though he were all wrapped up in some cloud, some fire, some vision all his own; and there wasn't any way to reach him.

At the same time, he wasn't really a man yet, he was still a child, and they had to watch out for him in all kinds of ways. They certainly couldn't throw him out. Neither did they dare to make a great scene about that piano because even they dimly sensed, as I sensed, from so many thousands of miles away, that Sonny was at that piano playing for his life.

But he hadn't been going to school. One day a letter came from the school board and Isabel's mother got it—there had, apparently, been other letters but Sonny had torn them up. This day, when Sonny came in, Isabel's mother showed him the letter and asked where he'd been spending his time. And she finally got it out of him that he'd been down in Greenwich Village, with musicians and other characters, in a white girl's apartment. And this scared her and she started to scream at him and what came up, once she began—though she denies it to this day—was what sacrifices they were making to give Sonny a decent home and how little he appreciated it.

Sonny didn't play the piano that day. By evening, Isabel's mother had calmed down but then there was the old man to deal with, and Isabel herself. Isabel says she did her best to be calm but she broke down and started crying. She says she just watched Sonny's face. She could tell, by watching him, what was happening with him. And what was happening was that they penetrated his cloud, they had reached him. Even if their fingers had been a thousand times more gentle than human fingers ever are, he could hardly help feeling that they had stripped him naked and were spitting on that nakedness. For he also had to see that his presence, that music, which was life or death to him, had been torture for them and that they had endured it, not at all for his sake, but only for mine. And Sonny couldn't take that. He can take it a little better today than he could then but he's still not very good at it and, frankly, I don't know anybody who is.

The silence of the next few days must have been louder than the sound of all the music ever played since time began. One morning, before she went to work, Isabel was in his room for something and she suddenly realized that all of his records were gone. And she knew for certain that he was gone. And he was. He went as far as the navy would carry him. He finally sent me a postcard from some place in Greece and that was the first I knew that Sonny was still alive. I didn't see him any more until we were both back in New York and the war had long been over.

He was a man by then, of course, but I wasn't willing to see it. He came by the house from time to time, but we fought almost every time we met. I ddn't like the way he carried himself, loose and dreamlike all the time, and I didn't like his friends, and his music seemed to be merely an excuse for the life he led. It sounded just that weird and disordered.

Then we had a fight, a pretty awful fight, and I didn't see him for months. By and by I looked him up, where he was living, in a furnished room in the Village, and I tried to make it up. But there were lots of other people in the room and Sonny just lay on his bed, and he wouldn't come downstairs with me, and he treated these other people as though they were his family and I weren't. So I got mad and then he got mad, and then I told him that he might just as well be dead as live the way he was living. Then he stood up and he told me not to worry about him any more in life, that he *was* dead as far as I was concerned. Then he pushed me to the door and the other people looked on as though nothing were happening, and he slammed the door behind me. I stood in the hallway, staring at the door. I heard somebody laugh in the room and then the tears came to my eyes. I started down the steps, whistling to keep from crying, I kept whistling to myself, *You going to need me, baby, one of these cold, rainy days.*

I read about Sonny's trouble in the spring. Little Grace died in the fall. She was a beautiful little girl. But she only lived a little over two years. She died of polio and she suffered. She had a slight fever for a couple of days, but it didn't seem like anything and we just kept her in bed. And we would certainly have called the doctor, but the fever dropped, she seemed to be all right. So we thought it had just been a cold. Then, one day, she was up, playing, Isabel was in the kitchen fixing lunch for the two boys when they'd come in from school, and she heard Grace fall down in the living room. When you have a lot of children you don't always start running when one of them falls, unless they start screaming or something. And, this time, Gracie was quiet. Yet, Isabel says that when she heard that *thump* and then that silence, something happened to her to make her afraid. And she ran to the living room and there was little Grace on the floor, all twisted up, and the reason she hadn't screamed was that she couldn't get her breath. And when she did scream, it was the worst sound, Isabel says, that she'd ever heard in all her life, and she still hears it sometimes in her dreams. Isabel will sometimes wake me up with a low, moaning, strangling sound and I have to be quick to awaken her and hold her to me and where Isabel is weeping against me seems a mortal wound.

I think I may have written Sonny the very day that little Grace was buried. I was sitting in the living room in the dark, by myself, and I suddenly thought of Sonny. My trouble made his real.

One Saturday afternoon, when Sonny had been living with us, or anyway, been in our house, for nearly two weeks, I found myself wandering aimlessly about the living room, drinking from a can of beer, and trying to work up courage to search Sonny's room. He was out, he was usually out whenever I was home, and Isabel had taken the children to see their grandparents. Suddenly I was standing still in front of the living room window, watching Seventh Avenue. The idea of searching Sonny's room made me still. I scarcely dared to admit to myself what I'd be searching for. I didn't know what I'd do if I found it. Or if I didn't.

On the sidewalk across from me, near the entrance to a barbecue joint, some people were holding an old-fashioned revival meeting. The barbecue cook, wearing a dirty white apron, his conked[6] hair reddish and metallic in the pale sun, and a cigarette between his lips, stood in the doorway, watching them. Kids and older people paused in their errands and stood there, along with some older men and a couple of very tough-looking women who watched everything that happened on the avenue, as though they owned it, or were maybe owned by it. Well, they were watching this, too. The revival was being carried on by three sisters in black, and a brother. All they had were their voices and their Bibles and a tambourine. The brother was testifying[7] and while he testified two of the sisters stood together, seeming to say, amen, and the third sister walked around with the tambourine outstretched and a couple of people dropped coins into it. Then the brother's testimony ended and the sister who had been taking up the collection dumped the coins into her palm and transferred them to the pocket of her long black robe. Then she raised both hands, striking the tambourine against the air, and then against one hand, and she started to sing. And the two other sisters and the brother joined in.

It was strange, suddenly, to watch, though I had been seeing these meetings all my life. So, of course, had everybody else down there. Yet, they paused and watched and listened and I stood still at the window. "*'Tis the old ship of Zion,*" they sang, and the sister with the tambourine kept a steady, jangling beat, "*it has rescued many a thousand!*" Not a soul under the sound of their voices was hearing this song for the first time, not one of them had been rescued. Nor had they seen much in the way of rescue work being done around them. Neither did they especially believe in the holiness of the three sisters and the brother, they knew too much about them, knew where they lived, and how. The woman with the tambourine, whose voice dominated the air, whose face was bright with joy, was divided by very little from the woman who stood watching her, a cigarette between her heavy, chapped lips, her hair a cuckoo's nest, her face scarred and swollen from many beatings, and her black eyes glittering like coal. Perhaps they both knew this, which was why, when, as rarely, they addressed each other, they addressed each other as Sister. As the singing filled the air the watching, listening faces underwent a change, the eyes focusing on something within; the music seemed to soothe a poison out of them; and time seemed, nearly, to fall away from the sullen, belligerent, battered faces, as though they were fleeing back to their first condition, while dreaming of their last. The

6. Straightened and greased. 7. Proclaiming his religious belief.

barbecue cook half shook his head and smiled, and dropped his cigarette and disappeared into his joint. A man fumbled in his pockets for change and stood holding it in his hand impatiently, as though he had just remembered a pressing appointment further up the avenue. He looked furious. Then I saw Sonny, standing on the edge of the crowd. He was carrying a wide, flat notebook with a green cover, and it made him look, from where I was standing, almost like a schoolboy. The coppery sun brought out the copper in his skin, he was very faintly smiling, standing very still. Then the singing stopped, the tambourine turned into a collection plate again. The furious man dropped in his coins and vanished, so did a couple of the women, and Sonny dropped some change in the plate, looking directly at the woman with a little smile. He started across the avenue, toward the house. He has a slow, loping walk, something like the way Harlem hipsters walk, only he's imposed on this his own half-beat. I had never really noticed it before.

I stayed at the window, both relieved and apprehensive. As Sonny disappeared from my sight, they began singing again. And they were still singing when his key turned in the lock.

"Hey," he said.

"Hey, yourself. You want some beer?"

"No. Well, maybe." But he came up to the window and stood beside me, looking out. "What a warm voice," he said.

They were singing *If I could only hear my mother pray again!*

"Yes," I said, "and she can sure beat that tambourine."

"But what a terrible song," he said, and laughed. He dropped his notebook on the sofa and disappeared into the kitchen. "Where's Isabel and the kids?"

"I think they want to see their grandparents. You hungry?"

"No." He came back into the living room with his can of beer. "You want to come some place with me tonight?"

I sensed, I don't know how, that I couldn't possibly say no. "Sure. Where?"

He sat down on the sofa and picked up his notebook and started leafing through it. "I'm going to sit in with some fellows in a joint in the Village."

"You mean, you're going to play, tonight?"

"That's right." He took a swallow of his beer and moved back to the window. He gave me a sidelong look. "If you can stand it."

"I'll try," I said.

He smiled to himself and we both watched as the meeting across the way broke up. The three sisters and the brother, heads bowed, were singing *God be with you till we meet again.* The faces around them were very quiet. Then the song ended. The small crowd dispersed. We watched the three women and the lone man walk slowly up the avenue.

"When she was singing before," said Sonny, abruptly, "her voice reminded me for a minute of what heroin feels like sometimes—when it's in your veins. It makes you feel sort of warm and cool at the same time. And distant. And—and sure." He sipped his beer, very deliberately not looking at me. I watched his face. "It makes you feel—in control. Sometimes you've got to have that feeling."

"Do you?" I sat down slowly in the easy chair.

"Sometimes." He went to the sofa and picked up his notebook again. "Some people do."

"In order," I asked, "to play?" And my voice was very ugly, full of contempt and anger.

"Well"—he looked at me with great, troubled eyes, as though, in fact, he hoped his eyes would tell me things he could never otherwise say—"they *think* so. And *if* they think so—!"

"And what do *you* think?" I asked.

He sat on the sofa and put his can of beer on the floor. "I don't know," he said, and I couldn't be sure if he were answering my question or pursuing his thoughts. His face didn't tell me. "It's not so much to *play*. It's to *stand* it, to be able to make it at all. On any level." He frowned and smiled: "In order to keep from shaking to pieces."

"But these friends of yours," I said, "they seem to shake themselves to pieces pretty goddamn fast."

"Maybe." He played with the notebook. And something told me that I should curb my tongue, that Sonny was doing his best to talk, that I should listen. "But of course you only know the ones that've gone to pieces. Some don't—or at least they haven't *yet* and that's just about all *any* of us can say." He paused. "And then there are some who just live, really, in hell, and they know it and they see what's happening and they go right on. I don't know." He sighed, dropped the notebook, folded his arms. "Some guys, you can tell from the way they play, they on something *all* the time. And you can see that, well, it makes something real for them. But of course," he picked up his beer from the floor and sipped it and put the can down again, "they *want* to, too, you've got to see that. Even some of them that say they don't—*some,* not all."

"And what about you?" I asked—I couldn't help it. "What about you? Do *you* want to?"

He stood up and walked to the window and I remained silent for a long time. Then he sighed. "Me," he said. Then: "While I was downstairs before, on my way here, listening to that woman sing, it struck me all of a sudden how much suffering she must have had to go through—to sing like that. It's *repulsive* to think you have to suffer that much."

I said: "But there's no way not to suffer—is there, Sonny?"

"I believe not," he said and smiled, "but that's never stopped anyone from trying." He looked at me. "Has it?" I realized, with this mocking look, that there stood between us, forever, beyond the power of time or forgiveness, the fact that I had held silence—so long!—when he had needed human speech to help him. He turned back to the window. "No, there's no way not to suffer. But you try all kinds of ways to keep from drowning in it, to keep on top of it, and to make it seem—well, like *you*. Like you did something, all right, and now you're suffering for it. You know?" I said nothing. "Well you know," he said, impatiently, "why *do* people suffer? Maybe it's better to do something to give it a reason, *any* reason."

"But we just agreed," I said, "that there's no way not to suffer. Isn't it better, then, just to—take it?"

"But nobody just takes it," Sonny cried, "that's what I'm telling you! *Everybody* tries not to. You're just hung up on the *way* some people try—it's not *your* way!"

The hair on my face began to itch, my face felt wet. "That's not true," I said, "that's not true. I don't give a damn what other people do, I don't even care how they suffer. I just care how *you* suffer." And he looked at me. "Please believe me," I said, "I don't want to see you—die—trying not to suffer."

"I won't," he said flatly, "die trying not to suffer. At least, not any faster than anybody else."

"But there's no need," I said, trying to laugh, "is there? in killing yourself."

I wanted to say more, but I couldn't. I wanted to talk about will power and how life could be—well, beautiful. I wanted to say that it was all within; but was it? or, rather, wasn't that exactly the trouble? And I wanted to promise that I would never fail him again. But it would all have sounded—empty words and lies.

So I made the promise to myself and prayed that I would keep it.

"It's terrible sometimes, inside," he said, "that's what's the trouble. You walk these streets, black and funky and cold, and there's not really a living ass to talk to, and there's nothing shaking, and there's no way of getting it out—that storm inside. You can't talk it and you can't make love with it, and when you finally try to get with it and play it, you realize *nobody's* listening. So *you've* got to listen. You got to find a way to listen."

And then he walked away from the window and sat on the sofa again, as though all the wind had suddenly been knocked out of him. "Sometimes you'll do *anything* to play, even cut your mother's throat." He laughed and looked at me. "Or your brother's." Then he sobered. "Or your own." Then: "Don't worry. I'm all right now and I think I'll *be* all right. But I can't forget—where I've been. I don't mean just the physical place I've been, I mean where I've *been*. And *what* I've been."

"What have you been, Sonny?" I asked.

He smiled—but sat sideways on the sofa, his elbow resting on the back, his fingers playing with his mouth and chin, not looking at me. "I've been something I didn't recognize, didn't know I could be. Didn't know anybody could be." He stopped, looking inward, looking helplessly young, looking old. "I'm not talking about it now because I feel *guilty* or anything like that—maybe it would be better if I did, I don't know. Anyway, I can't really talk about it. Not to you, not to anybody," and now he turned and faced me. "Sometimes, you know, and it was actually when I was most *out* of the world, I felt that I was in it, that I was *with* it, really, and I could play or I didn't really have to *play,* it just came out of me, it was there. And I don't know how I played, thinking about it now, but I know I did awful things, those times, sometimes, to people. Or it wasn't that I *did* anything to them—it was that they weren't real." He picked up the beer can; it was empty; he rolled it between his palms: "And other times—well, I needed a fix, I needed to find a place to lean, I needed to clear a space to *listen*—and I couldn't find it, and I—went crazy, I did terrible things to *me,* I was terrible *for* me." He began pressing the beer can between his hands, I watched the metal begin to give. It glittered, as he played with it like a knife, and I was afraid he would cut himself, but I said nothing. "Oh well. I can never tell you. I was all by myself at the bottom of something, stinking and sweating and crying and shaking, and I smelled it, you know? *my* stink, and I thought I'd die if I couldn't get away from it and yet, all the same, I knew that everything I was doing was just locking me in with it. And I didn't know," he paused, still flattening the beer can, "I didn't know, I still *don't* know, something kept telling me that maybe it was good to smell your own stink, but I didn't think that *that* was what I'd been trying to do—and—who can stand it?" and he abruptly dropped the ruined beer can, looking at me with a small, still smile, and then rose, walking to the window as though it were the lodestone rock. I watched his face, he watched the avenue. "I couldn't tell you when Mama died—but the reason I wanted to leave Harlem so bad was to get away from drugs. And then, when I ran away, that's what I was running from—really. When I came back, nothing had changed, *I* hadn't changed, I was just—older." And he stopped, drumming with his fingers on the windowpane. The sun had vanished, soon darkness would fall. I watched his face. "It can come again," he said, almost as though speaking to himself. Then he turned to me. "It can come again," he repeated. "I just want you to know that."

"All right," I said, at last. "So it can come again. All right."

He smiled, but the smile was sorrowful. "I had to try to tell you," he said.

"Yes," I said. "I understand that."

"You're my brother," he said, looking straight at me, and not smiling at all.

"Yes," I repeated, "yes. I understand that."

He turned back to the window, looking out. "All that hatred down there," he said, "all that hatred and misery and love. It's a wonder it doesn't blow the avenue apart."

We went to the only nightclub on a short, dark street, downtown. We squeezed through the narrow, chattering, jampacked bar to the entrance of the big room, where the bandstand was. And we stood there for a moment, for the lights were very dim in this room and we couldn't see. Then, "Hello, boy," said the voice and an enormous black man, much older than Sonny or myself, erupted out of all that atmospheric lighting and put an arm around Sonny's shoulder. "I been sitting right here," he said, "waiting for you."

He had a big voice, too, and heads in the darkness turned toward us.

Sonny grinned and pulled a little away, and said, "Creole, this is my brother. I told you about him."

Creole shook my hand. "I'm glad to meet you, son," he said, and it was clear that he was glad to meet me *there,* for Sonny's sake. And he smiled, "You got a real musician in *your* family," and he took his arm from Sonny's shoulder and slapped him, lightly, affectionately, with the back of his hand.

"Well. Now I've heard it all," said a voice behind us. This was another musician, and a friend of Sonny's, a coal-black, cheerful-looking man, built close to the ground. He immediately began confiding to me, at the top of his lungs, the most terrible things about Sonny, his teeth gleaming like a lighthouse and his laugh coming up out of him like the beginning of an earthquake. And it turned out that everyone at the bar knew Sonny, or almost everyone; some were musicians, working there, or nearby, or not working, some were simply hangers-on, and some were there to hear Sonny play. I was introduced to all of them and they were all very polite to me. Yet, it was clear that, for them, I was only Sonny's brother. Here, I was in Sonny's world. Or, rather: his kingdom. Here, it was not even a question that his veins bore royal blood.

They were going to play soon and Creole installed me, by myself, at a table in a dark corner. Then I watched them, Creole, and the little black man, and Sonny, and the others, while they horsed around, standing just below the bandstand. The light from the bandstand spilled just a little short of them and, watching them laughing and gesturing and moving about, I had the feeling that they, nevertheless, were being most careful not to step into that circle of light too suddenly; that if they moved into the light too suddenly, without thinking, they would perish in flame. Then, while I watched, one of them, the small black man, moved into the light and crossed the bandstand and started fooling around with his drums. Then—being funny and being, also, extremely ceremonious—Creole took Sonny by the arm and led him to the piano. A woman's voice called Sonny's name and a few hands started clapping. And Sonny, also being funny and being ceremonious, and so touched, I think, that he could have cried, but neither hiding it nor showing it, riding it like a man, grinned, and put both hands to his heart and bowed from the waist.

Creole then went to the bass fiddle and a lean, very bright-skinned brown man jumped up on the bandstand and picked up his horn. So there they were, and the atmosphere on the bandstand and in the room began to change and tighten. Someone stepped up to the microphone and announced them. Then there were all kinds of murmurs. Some people at the bar shushed others. The waitress ran around, frantically getting in the last orders, guys and chicks got closer to each other, and the lights on the bandstand, on the quartet, turned to a kind of indigo. Then they all looked different there. Creole looked about him for the last time, as though he were making certain that all his chickens were in the coop, and then he—jumped and struck the fiddle. And there they were.

All I know about music is that not many people ever really hear it. And even then, on the rare occasions when something opens within, and the music enters, what we mainly hear, or hear corroborated, are personal, private, vanishing evocations. But the man who creates the music is hearing something else, is dealing with the roar rising from the void and imposing order on it as it hits the air. What is evoked in him, then, is of another order, more terrible because it has no words, and triumphant, too, for that same reason. And his triumph, when he triumphs, is ours. I just watched Sonny's face. His face was troubled, he was working hard, but he wasn't with it. And I had the feeling that, in a way, everyone on the bandstand was waiting for him, both waiting for him and pushing him along. But as I began to watch Creole, I realized that it was Creole who held them all back. He had them on a short rein. Up there, keeping the beat with his whole body, wailing on the fiddle, with his eyes half closed, he was listening to everything, but he was listening to Sonny. He was having a dialogue with Sonny. He wanted Sonny to leave the shoreline and strike out for the deep water. He was Sonny's witness that deep water and drowning were not the same thing—he had been there, and he knew. And he wanted Sonny to know. He was waiting for Sonny to do the things on the keys which would let Creole know that Sonny was in the water.

And, while Creole listened, Sonny moved, deep within, exactly like someone in torment. I had never before thought of how awful the relationship must be between the musician and his instrument. He has to fill it, this instrument, with the breath of life, his own. He has to make it do what he wants it to do. And a piano is just a piano. It's made out of so much wood and wires and little hammers and big ones, and ivory. While there's only so much you can do with it, the only way to find this out is to try; to try and make it do everything.

And Sonny hadn't been near a piano for over a year. And he wasn't on much better terms with his life, not the life that stretched before him now. He and the piano stammered, started one way, got scared, stopped; started another way, panicked, marked time, started again; then seemed to have found a direction, panicked again, got stuck. And the face I saw on Sonny I'd never seen before. Everything had been burned out of it, and at the same time, things usually hidden were being burned in, by the fire and fury of the battle which was occurring in him up there.

Yet, watching Creole's face as they neared the end of the first set, I had the feeling that something had happened, something I hadn't heard. Then they finished, there was scattered applause, and then, without an instant's warning, Creole started into something else, it was almost sardonic, it was *Am I Blue*. And, as though he commanded, Sonny began to play. Something began to happen. And Creole let out the reins. The dry, low, black man said something awful on the drums, Creole answered, and the drums talked back. Then the horn insisted, sweet and high, slightly detached perhaps, and Creole listened, commenting now and then, dry, and driving, beautiful and calm and old. Then they all came together again, and Sonny was part of the family again. I could tell this from his face. He seemed to have found, right there beneath his fingers, a damn brand-new piano. It seemed that he couldn't get over it. Then, for a while, just being happy with Sonny, they seemed to be agreeing with him that brand-new pianos certainly were a gas.

Then Creole stepped forward to remind them that what they were playing was the blues. He hit something in all of them, he hit something in me, myself, and the music tightened and deepened, apprehension began to beat the air. Creole began to tell us what the blues were all about. They were not about anything very new. He and his boys up there were keeping it new, at the risk of ruin, destruction, madness, and death, in order to find new ways to make us listen. For, while the tale of how we suffer, and how we are delighted, and how we may triumph is never new, it always must be heard. There isn't any other tale to tell, it's the only light we've got in all this darkness.

And this tale, according to that face, that body, those strong hands on those strings, has another aspect in every country, and a new depth in every generation. Listen, Creole seemed to be saying, listen. Now these are Sonny's blues. He made the little black man on the drums know it, and the bright, brown man on the horn. Creole wasn't trying any longer to get Sonny in the water. He was wishing him Godspeed. Then he stepped back, very slowly, filling the air with the immense suggestion that Sonny speak for himself.

Then they all gathered around Sonny and Sonny played. Every now and again one of them seemed to say, amen. Sonny's fingers filled the air with life, his life. But that life contained so many others. And Sonny went all the way back, he really began with the spare, flat statement of the opening phrase of the song. Then he began to make it his. It was very beautiful because it wasn't hurried and it was no longer a lament. I seemed to hear with what burning he had made it his, and what burning we had yet to make it ours, how we could cease lamenting. Freedom lurked around us and I understood, at last, that he could help us to be free if we would listen, that he would never be free until we did. Yet, there was no battle in his face now, I heard what he had gone through, and would continue to go through until he came to rest in earth. He had made it his: that long line, of which we knew only Mama and Daddy. And he was giving it back, as everything must be given back, so that, passing through death, it can live forever. I saw my mother's face again, and felt, for the first time, how the stones of the road she had walked on must have bruised her feet. I saw the moonlit road where my father's brother died. And it brought something else back to me, and carried me past it, I saw my little girl again and felt Isabel's tears again, and I felt my own tears begin to rise. And I was yet aware that this was only a moment, that the world waited outside, as hungry as a tiger, and that trouble stretched above us, longer than the sky.

Then it was over. Creole and Sonny let out their breath, both soaking wet, and grinning. There was a lot of applause and some of it was real. In the dark, the girl came by and I asked her to take drinks to the bandstand. There was a long pause, while they talked up there in the indigo light and after awhile I saw the girl put a Scotch and milk on top of the piano for Sonny. He didn't seem to notice it, but just before they started playing again, he sipped from it and looked toward me, and nodded. Then he put it back on top of the piano. For me, then, as they began to play again, it glowed and shook above my brother's head like the very cup of trembling.[8]

8. Isaiah 51:22, ". . . I have taken out of thine hand the cup of trembling . . . thou shalt no more drink it again . . ."

Gabriel García-Márquez

Gabriel García-Márquez (1928–) was born in Aracataca, near the coast of Colombia. He was raised by his maternal grandparents and recalls a childhood filled with stories and legends, many of which later surfaced in his fiction. García-Márquez worked for many years as a reporter, in Colombia and later in Paris. But his real love from the first was storytelling. In 1955 he published his first book, *Leaf Storm and Other Stories,* and three years later a short novel entitled *No One Writes to the Colonel.* But his masterpiece, the book that changed the complexion of Latin American writing, was *One Hundred Years of Solitude* (1967), written while the author lived in Mexico City. Although the stories hinted at his talent and inventiveness, no one, including the author himself, was prepared for this explosion of writing. García-Márquez had managed to retrieve the myriad legends told to him in childhood and to recast them into an epic comic novel. He made use of a narrative mode that has since come to be called magical realism, a fusion of the historical, the sensuous, and the uncanny. The reader is never quite sure where realistic depiction first begins to shade into the fantastic. On the strength of this novel, the author was awarded the 1982 Nobel prize for literature.

García-Márquez's novels include *The Autumn of the Patriarch, Love in a Time of Cholera,* and *The General in His Labyrinth.*

A VERY OLD MAN WITH ENORMOUS WINGS

On the third day of rain they had killed so many crabs inside the house that Pelayo had to cross his drenched courtyard and throw them into the sea, because the newborn child had a temperature all night and they thought it was due to the stench. The world had been sad since Tuesday. Sea and sky were a single ash-gray thing and the sands of the beach, which on March nights glimmered like powdered light, had become a stew of mud and rotten shellfish. The light was so weak at noon that when Pelayo was coming back to the house after throwing away the crabs, it was hard for him to see what it was that was moving and groaning in the rear of the courtyard. He had to go very close to see that it was an old man, a very old man, lying face down in the mud, who, in spite of his tremendous efforts, couldn't get up, impeded by his enormous wings.

Frightened by that nightmare, Pelayo ran to get Elisenda, his wife, who was putting compresses on the sick child, and he took her to the rear of the courtyard. They both looked at the fallen body with mute stupor. He was dressed like a ragpicker. There were only a few faded hairs left on his bald skull and very few teeth in his mouth, and his pitiful condition of a drenched great-grandfather had taken away any sense of grandeur he might have had. His huge buzzard wings, dirty and half-plucked, were forever entangled in the mud. They looked at him so long and so closely that Pelayo and Elisenda very soon overcame their surprise and in the end found him familiar. Then they dared speak to him, and he answered in an incomprehensible dialect with a strong sailor's voice. That was how they skipped over the inconvenience of the wings and quite intelligently concluded that he was a lonely castaway from some foreign ship wrecked by the storm. And yet, they called in a neighbor woman who knew everything about life and death to see him, and all she needed was one look to show them their mistake.

"He's an angel," she told them. "He must have been coming for the child, but the poor fellow is so old that the rain knocked him down."

On the following day everyone knew that a flesh-and-blood angel was held captive in Pelayo's house. Against the judgment of the wise neighbor woman, for whom angels in those times were the fugitive survivors of a celestial conspiracy, they did not have the heart to club him to death. Pelayo watched over him all afternoon from the kitchen, armed with his bailiff's club, and before going to bed he dragged him out of the mud and locked him up with the hens in the wire chicken coop. In the middle of the night, when the rain stopped, Pelayo and Elisenda were still killing crabs. A short time afterward the child woke up without a fever and with a desire to eat. Then they felt magnanimous and decided to put the angel on a raft with fresh water and provisions for three days and leave him to his fate on the high seas. But when they went out into the courtyard with the first light of dawn, they found the whole neighborhood in front of the chicken coop having fun with the angel, without the slightest reverence, tossing him things to eat through the openings in the wire as if he weren't a supernatural creature but a circus animal.

Father Gonzaga arrived before seven o'clock, alarmed at the strange news. By that time onlookers less frivolous than those at dawn had already arrived and they were making all kinds of conjectures concerning the captive's future. The simplest among them thought that he should be named mayor of the world. Others of sterner mind felt that he should be promoted to the rank of five-star general in order to win all wars. Some visionaries hoped that he could be put to stud in order to implant on earth a race of winged wise men who could take charge of the universe. But Father Gonzaga, before becoming a priest, had been a robust woodcutter. Standing by the wire, he reviewed his catechism in an instant and asked them to open the door so that he could take a close look at that pitiful man who looked more like a huge decrepit hen among the fascinated chickens. He was lying in a corner drying his open wings in the sunlight among the fruit peels and breakfast leftovers that the early risers had thrown him. Alien to the impertinences of the world, he only lifted his antiquarian eyes and murmured something in his dialect when Father Gonzaga went into the chicken coop and said good morning to him in Latin. The parish priest had his first suspicion of an imposter when he saw that he did not understand the language of God or know how to greet His ministers. Then he noticed that seen close up he was much too human: he had an unbearable smell of the outdoors, the back side of his wings was strewn with parasites and his main feathers had been mistreated by terrestrial winds, and nothing about him measured up to the proud dignity of angels. Then he came out of the chicken coop and in a brief sermon warned the curious against the risks of being ingenuous. He reminded them that the devil had the bad habit of making use of carnival tricks in order to confuse the unwary. He argued that if wings were not the essential element in determining the difference between a hawk and an airplane, they were even less so in the recognition of angels. Nevertheless, he promised to write a letter to his bishop so that the latter would write to his primate so that the latter would write to the Supreme Pontiff in order to get the final verdict from the highest courts.

His prudence fell on sterile hearts. The news of the captive angel spread with such rapidity that after a few hours the courtyard had the bustle of a marketplace and they had to call in troops with fixed bayonets to disperse the mob that was about to knock the house down. Elisenda, her spine all twisted from sweeping up so much marketplace trash, then got the idea of fencing in the yard and charging five cents admission to see the angel.

The curious came from far away. A traveling carnival arrived with a flying acrobat who buzzed over the crowd several times, but no one paid any attention to him because his wings were not those of an angel but, rather, those of a sidereal bat. The most unfortunate invalids on earth came in search of health: a poor woman who since childhood had been counting her heartbeats and had run out of numbers; a Portuguese man who couldn't sleep because the noise of the stars disturbed him; a sleepwalker who got up at night to undo the things he had done while awake; and many others with less serious ailments. In the midst of that shipwreck disorder that made the earth tremble, Pelayo and Elisenda were happy with fatigue, for in less than a week they had crammed their rooms with money and the line of pilgrims waiting their turn to enter still reached beyond the horizon.

The angel was the only one who took no part in his own act. He spent his time trying to get comfortable in his borrowed nest, befuddled by the hellish heat of the oil lamps and sacramental candles that had been placed along the wire. At first they tried to make him eat some mothballs, which, according to the wisdom of the wise neighbor woman, were the food prescribed for angels. But he turned them down, just as he turned down the papal lunches that the penitents brought him, and they never found out whether it was because he was an angel or because he was an old man that in the end he ate nothing but eggplant mush. His only supernatural virtue seemed to be patience. Especially during the first days, when the hens pecked at him, searching for the stellar parasites that proliferated in his wings, and the cripples pulled out feathers to touch their defective parts with, and even the most merciful threw stones at him, trying to get him to rise so they could see him standing. The only time they succeeded in arousing him was when they burned his side with an iron for branding steers, for he had been motionless for so many hours that they thought he was dead. He awoke with a start, ranting in his hermetic language and with tears in his eyes, and he flapped his wings a couple of times, which brought on a whirlwind of chicken dung and lunar dust and a gale of panic that did not seem to be of this world. Although many thought that his reaction had been one not of rage but of pain, from then on they were careful not to annoy him, because the majority understood that his passivity was not that of a hero taking his ease but that of a cataclysm in repose.

Father Gonzaga held back the crowd's frivolity with formulas of maidservant inspiration while awaiting the arrival of a final judgment on the nature of the captive. But the mail from Rome showed no sense of urgency. They spent their time finding out if the prisoner had a navel, if his dialect had any connection with Aramaic, how many times he could fit on the head of a pin, or whether he wasn't just a Norwegian with wings. Those meager letters might have come and gone until the end of time if a providential event had not put an end to the priest's tribulations.

It so happened that during those days, among so many other carnival attractions, there arrived in town the traveling show of the woman who had been changed into a spider for having disobeyed her parents. The admission to see her was not only less than the admission to see the angel, but people were permitted to ask her all manner of questions about her absurd state and to examine her up and down so that no one would ever doubt the truth of her horror. She was a frightful tarantula the size of a ram and with the head of a sad maiden. What was most heart-rending, however, was not her outlandish shape but the sincere affliction with which she recounted the details of her misfortune. While still practically a child she had sneaked out of her parents' house to go to a dance, and while she was coming back through the woods after having danced all night without permission, a fearful thunderclap rent the sky in two and through the crack came the lightning bolt of brimstone that changed her into a spider. Her only nourishment came from the meatballs that charitable souls chose to toss into her mouth. A spectacle like that, full of so much human truth and with such a fearful lesson, was bound to defeat without even trying that of a haughty angel who scarcely deigned to look at mortals. Besides, the few miracles attributed to the angel showed a certain mental disorder, like the blind man who didn't recover his sight but grew three new teeth, or the paralytic who didn't get to walk but almost won the lottery, and the leper whose sores sprouted sunflowers. Those consolation miracles, which were more like mocking fun, had already ruined the angel's reputation when the woman who had been changed into a spider finally crushed him completely. That was how Father Gonzaga was cured forever of his insomnia and Pelayo's courtyard went back to being as empty as during the time it had rained for three days and crabs walked through the bedrooms.

The owners of the house had no reason to lament. With the money they saved they built a two-story mansion with balconies and gardens and high netting so that crabs wouldn't get in during the winter, and with iron bars on the windows so that angels wouldn't get in. Pelayo also set up a rabbit warren close to town and gave up his job as bailiff for good, and Elisenda bought some satin pumps with high heels and many dresses of iridescent silk, the kind worn on Sunday by the most desirable women in those times. The chicken coop was the only thing that didn't receive any attention. If they washed it down with creolin and burned tears of myrrh inside it every so often, it was not in homage to the angel but to drive away the dungheap stench that still hung everywhere like a ghost and was turning the new house into an old one. At first, when the child learned to walk, they were careful that he not get too close to the chicken coop. But then they began to lose their fears and got used to the smell, and before the child got his second teeth he'd gone inside the chicken coop to play, where the wires were falling apart. The angel was no less standoffish with him than with other mortals, but he tolerated the most ingenious infamies with the patience of a dog who had no illusions. They both came down with chicken pox at the same time. The doctor who took care of the child couldn't resist the temptation to listen to the angel's heart, and he found so much whistling in the heart and so many sounds in his kidneys that it seemed impossible for him to be alive. What surprised him most, however, was the logic of his wings. They seemed so natural on that completely human organism that he couldn't understand why other men didn't have them too.

When the child began school it had been some time since the sun and rain had caused the collapse of the chicken coop. The angel went dragging himself about here and there like a stray dying man. They would drive him out of the bedroom with a broom and a moment later find him in the kitchen. He seemed to be in so many places at the same time that they grew to think that he'd been duplicated, that he was reproducing himself all through the house, and the exasperated and unhinged Elisenda shouted that it was awful living in that hell full of angels. He could scarcely eat and his antiquarian eyes had also become so foggy that he went about bumping into posts. All he had left were the bare cannulae of his last feathers. Pelayo threw a blanket over him and extended him the charity of letting him sleep in the shed, and only then did they notice that he had a temperature at night, and was delirious with the tongue twisters of an old Norwegian. That was one of the few times they became alarmed, for they thought he was going to die and not even the wise neighbor woman had been able to tell them what to do with dead angels.

And yet he not only survived his worst winter, but seemed improved with the first sunny days. He remained motionless for several days in the farthest corner of the courtyard, where no one would see him, and at the beginning of December some large, stiff feathers began to grow on his wings, the feathers of a scarecrow, which looked more like another misfortune of decrepitude. But he must have known the reason for those changes, for he was quite careful that no one should notice them, that no one should hear the sea chanteys that he sometimes sang under the stars. One morning Elisenda was cutting some bunches of onions for lunch when a wind that seemed to come from the high seas blew into the kitchen. Then she went to the window and caught the angel in his first attempts at flight. They were so clumsy that his fingernails opened a furrow in the vegetable patch and he was on the point of knocking the shed down with the ungainly flapping that slipped on the light and couldn't get a grip on the air. But he did manage to gain altitude. Elisenda let out a sigh of relief, for herself and for him, when she saw him pass over the last houses, holding himself up in some way with the risky flapping of a senile vulture. She kept watching him even when she was through cutting the onions and she kept on watching until it was no longer possible for her to see him, because then he was no longer an annoyance in her life but an imaginary dot on the horizon of the sea.

Translated by Gregory Rabassa

William Trevor

William Trevor (b.1928) was born in County Cork, Ireland, but now resides in Devonshire, England. His novels and stories have brought him a major reputation in Europe and the United States. Trevor navigates with great skill among the tensions and conflicts brought on by decaying class structures and by ancient national and cultural grievances between the English and Irish. His collections of stories include *Angels at the Ritz, Lovers of Their Time,* and *Beyond the Pale.*

BEYOND THE PALE

We always went to Ireland in June.

Ever since the four of us began to go on holidays together, in 1965 it must have been, we had spent the first fortnight of the month at Glencorn Lodge in Co. Antrim. Perfection, as Dekko put it once, and none of us disagreed. It's a Georgian house by the sea, not far from the village of Ardbeag. It's quite majestic in its rather elegant way, a garden running to the very edge of a cliff, its long rhododendron drive—or avenue, as they say in Ireland. The English couple who bought the house in the early sixties, the Malseed's, have had to build on quite a bit but it's all been discreetly done, the Georgian style preserved throughout. Figs grow in the sheltered gardens, and apricots, and peaches in the greenhouses which old Mr Saxton presides over. He's Mrs Malseed's father actually. They brought him with them from Surrey, and their Dalmatians, Charger and Snooze.

It was Strafe who found Glencorn for us. He'd come across an advertisement in the *Lady* in the days when the Malseeds still felt the need to advertise. 'How about this?' he said one evening at the end of the second rubber, and then read out the details. We had gone away together the summer before, to a hotel that had been recommended on the Costa del Sol, but it hadn't been a success because the food was so appalling. 'We could try this Irish one,' Dekko suggested cautiously, which is what eventually we did.

The four of us have been playing bridge together for ages, Dekko, Strafe, Cynthia and myself. They call me Milly, though strictly speaking my name is Dorothy Milson. Dekko picked up his nickname at school,

Dekko Deakin sounding rather good, I dare say. He and Strafe were in fact at school together, which must be why we all call Strafe by his surname: Major R. B. Strafe he is, the initials standing for Robert Buchanan. We're of an age, the four of us, all in the early fifties: the prime of life, so Dekko insists. We live quite close to Leatherhead, where the Malseeds were before they decided to make the change from Surrey to Co. Antrim. Quite a coincidence, we always think.

'How *very* nice,' Mrs Malseed said, smiling her welcome again this year. Some instinct seems to tell her when guests are about to arrive, for she's rarely not waiting in the large low-ceilinged hall that always smells of flowers. She dresses beautifully, differently every day, and changing of course in the evening. Her blouse on this occasion was scarlet and silver, in stripes, her skirt black. This choice gave her a brisk look, which was fitting because being so busy she often has to be a little on the brisk side. She has smooth grey hair which she once told me she entirely looks after herself, and she almost always wears a black velvet band in it. Her face is well made up, and for one who arranges so many vases of flowers and otherwise has to use her hands she manages to keep them marvelously in condition. Her fingernails are varnished a soft pink, and a small gold bangle always adorns her right wrist, a wedding present from her husband.

'Arthur, take the party's luggage,' she commanded the old porter, who doubles as odd-job man. 'Rose, Geranium, Hydrangea, Fuchsia.' She referred to the titles of the rooms reserved for us: in winter, when no one much comes to Glencorn Lodge, pleasant little details like that are seen to. Mrs Malseed herself painted the flower-plaques that are attached to the doors of the hotel instead of numbers; her husband sees to redecoration and repairs.

'Well, well, well,' Mr Malseed said now, entering the hall through the door that leads to the kitchen regions. 'A hundred thousand welcomes,' he greeted us in the Irish manner. He's rather shorter than Mrs Malseed, who's handsomely tall. He wears Donegal tweed suits and is brown as a berry, including his head, which is bald. His dark brown eyes twinkle at you, making you feel rather more than just another hotel guest. They run the place like a country house, really.

'Good trip?' Mr Malseed enquired.

'Super,' Dekko said. 'Not a worry all the way.'

'Splendid.'

'The wretched boat sailed an hour early one day last week,' Mrs Malseed said. 'Quite a little band were left stranded at Stranraer.'

Strafe laughed. Typical of that steamship company, he said. 'Catching the tide, I dare say?'

'They caught a rocket from me,' Mrs Malseed replied good-humouredly. 'A couple of old dears were due with us on Tuesday and had to spend the night in some awful Scottish lodging-house. It nearly finished them.'

Everyone laughed, and I could feel the others thinking that our holiday had truly begun. Nothing had changed at Glencorn Lodge, all was well with its Irish world. Kitty from the dining-room came out to greet us, spotless in her uniform. 'Ach, you're looking younger,' she said, paying the compliment to all four of us, causing everyone in the hall to laugh again. Kitty's a bit of a card.

Arthur led the way to the rooms called Rose, Geranium, Hydrangea and Fuchsia, carrying as much of our luggage as he could manage and returning for the remainder. Arthur has a beaten, fisherman's face and short grey hair. He wears a green baize apron, and a white shirt with an imitation-silk scarf tucked into it at the neck. The scarf, in different swirling greens which blend nicely with the green of his apron, is an idea of Mrs Malseed's and one appreciates the effort, if not at a uniform, at least at tidiness.

'Thank you very much,' I said to Arthur in my room, smiling and finding him a coin.

We played a couple of rubbers after dinner as usual, but not of course going on for as long as we might have because we were still quite tired after the journey. In the lounge there was a French family, two girls and their parents, and a honeymoon couple—or so we had speculated during dinner—and a man on his own. There had been other people at dinner of course, because in June Glencorn Lodge is always full: from where we sat in the window we could see some of them strolling about the lawns, a few taking the cliff path down to the seashore. In the morning we'd do the same: we'd walk along the sands to Ardbeag and have coffee in the hotel there, back in time for lunch. In the afternoon we'd drive somewhere.

I knew all that because over the years this kind of pattern had developed. We had our walks and our drives, tweed to buy in Cushendall, Strafe's and Dekko's fishing day when Cynthia and I just sat on the beach, our visit to the Giant's Causeway and one to Donegal perhaps, though that meant an early start and taking pot-luck for dinner somewhere. We'd come to adore Co. Antrim, its glens and coastline, Rathlin Island and Tievebulliagh. Since first we got to know it, in 1965, we'd all four fallen hopelessly in love with every variation of this remarkable landscape. People in England thought us mad of course: they see so much of the troubles on television that it's naturally difficult for them to realize that most places are just as they've always been. Yet coming as we did, taking the road along the coast, dawdling through Ballygally, it was impossible to believe that somewhere else the unpleasantness was going on. We'd never seen a thing, nor even heard people talking about incidents that might have taken place. It's true that after a particularly nasty carry-on a few winters ago we did consider finding somewhere else, in Scotland perhaps, or Wales. But as Strafe put it at the time, we felt we owed a certain loyalty to the Malseeds and indeed to everyone we'd come to know round about, people who'd always been glad to welcome us back. It seemed silly to lose our heads, and when we returned the following summer we knew immediately we'd been right. Dekko said that nothing could be further away from all the violence than Glencorn Lodge, and though his remark could hardly be taken literally I think we all knew what he meant.

'Cynthia's tired,' I said because she'd been stifling yawns. 'I think we should call it a day.'

'Oh, not at all,' Cynthia protested. 'No, please.'

But Dekko agreed with me that she was tired, and Strafe said he didn't mind stopping now. He suggested a nightcap, as he always does, and as we always do also, Cynthia and I declined. Dekko said he'd like a Cointreau.

The conversation drifted about. Dekko told us an Irish joke about a drunk who couldn't find his way out of a telephone box, and then Strafe remembered an incident at school concerning his and Dekko's housemaster, A. D. Cowley-Stubbs, and the house wag, Thrive Major. A. D. Cowley-Stubbs had been known as Cows and often featured in our after-bridge reminiscing. So did Thrive Major.

'Perhaps I *am* sleepy,' Cynthia said. 'I don't think I closed my eyes once last night.'

She never does on a sea crossing. Personally I'm out like a light the moment my head touches the pillow; I often think it must be the salt in the air because normally I'm an uneasy sleeper at the best of times.

'You run along, old girl,' Strafe advised.

'Brekky at nine,' Dekko said.

Cynthia said good-night and went, and we didn't remark on her tiredness because as a kind of unwritten rule we never comment on one another. We're four people who play bridge. The companionship it offers, and the holidays we have together, are all part of that. We share everything: the cost of petrol, the cups of coffee or drinks we have; we even each make a contribution towards the use of Strafe's car because it's always his we go on holiday in, a Rover it was on this occasion.

'Funny, being here on your own,' Strafe said, glancing across what the Malseeds call the After-Dinner Lounge at the man who didn't have a companion. He was a red-haired man of about thirty, not wearing a tie, his collar open at the neck and folded back over the jacket of his blue serge suit. He was uncouth-looking, though it's a hard thing to say, not at all the kind of person one usually sees at Glencorn Lodge. He sat in the After-Dinner Lounge as he had in the dining-room, lost in some concentration of his own, as if calculating sums in his mind. There had been a folded newspaper on his table in the dining-room. It now reposed tidily on the arm of his chair, still unopened.

'Commercial gent,' Dekko said. 'Fertilizers.'

'Good heavens, never. You wouldn't get a rep in here.'

I took no part in the argument. The lone man didn't much interest me, but I felt that Strafe was probably right: if there was anything dubious about the man's credentials he might have found it difficult to secure a room. In the hall of Glencorn Lodge there's a notice which reads: *We prefer not to feature in hotel guides, and we would be grateful to our guests if they did not seek to include Glencorn Lodge in the Good Food Guide, the Good Hotel Guide, the Michelin, Egon Ronay or any others. We have not advertised Glencorn since our early days, and prefer our recommendations to be by word of mouth.*

'Ah, thank you,' Strafe said when Kitty brought his whisky and Dekko's Cointreau. 'Sure you won't have something?' he said to me, although he knew I never did.

Strafe is on the stout side, I suppose you could say, with a gingery moustache and gingery hair, hardly touched at all by grey. He left the Army years ago, I suppose because of me in a sense, because he didn't want to be posted abroad again. He's in the Ministry of Defense now.

I'm still quite pretty in my way, though nothing like as striking as Mrs Malseed, for I've never been that kind of woman. I've put on weight, and wouldn't have allowed myself to do so if Strafe hadn't kept saying he can't stand a bag of bones. I'm careful about my hair and, unlike Mrs Malseed, I have it very regularly seen to because if I don't it gets a salt and pepper look, which I hate. My husband, Ralph, who died of food-poisoning when we were still quite young, used to say I wouldn't lose a single look in middle age, and to some extent that's true. We were still putting off having children when he died, which is why I haven't any. Then I met Strafe, which meant I didn't marry again.

Strafe is married himself, to Cynthia. She's small and ineffectual, I suppose you'd say without being untruthful or unkind. Not that Cynthia and I don't get on or anything like that, in fact we get on extremely well. It's Strafe and Cynthia who don't seem quite to hit it off, and I often think how much happier all round it would have been if Cynthia had married someone completely different, someone like Dekko in a way, except that that mightn't quite have worked out either. The Strafes have two sons, both very like their father, both of them in the Army. And the very sad thing is they think nothing of poor Cynthia.

'Who's that chap?' Dekko asked Mr Malseed, who'd come over to wish us good-night.

'Awfully sorry about that, Mr Deakin. My fault entirely, a booking that came over the phone.'

'Good heavens, not at all,' Strafe protested, and Dekko looked horrified in case it should be thought he was objecting to the locals. 'Splendid-looking fellow,' he said, overdoing it.

Mr Malseed murmured that the man had only booked in for a single night, and I smiled the whole thing away, reassuring him with a nod. It's one of the pleasantest of the traditions at Glencorn Lodge that every evening Mr Malseed makes the rounds of his guests just to say good-night. It's because of little touches like that that I, too, wished Dekko hadn't questioned Mr Malseed about the man because it's the kind of thing one doesn't do at Glencorn Lodge. But Dekko is a law unto himself, very tall and gangling, always immaculately suited, a beaky face beneath mousy hair in which flecks of grey add a certain distinction. Dekko has money of his own and though he takes out girls who are half his age he has never managed to get around to marriage. The uncharitable might say he has a rather gormless laugh; certainly it's sometimes on the loud side.

We watched while Mr Malseed bade the lone man good-night. The man didn't respond, but just sat gazing. It was ill-mannered, but this lack of courtesy didn't appear to be intentional: the man was clearly in a mood of some kind, miles away.

'Well, I'll go up,' I said. 'Good-night, you two.'

'Cheery-bye, Milly,' Dekko said. 'Brekky at nine, remember.'

'Good-night, Milly,' Strafe said.

The Strafes always occupy different rooms on holidays, and at home also. This time he was in Geranium and she in Fuchsia. I was in Rose, and in a little while Strafe would come to see me. He stays with her out of kindness, because he fears for her on her own. He's a sentimental, good-hearted man, easily moved to tears: he simply cannot bear the thought of Cynthia with no one to talk to in the evenings, with no one to make her life around. 'And besides,' he often says when he's being jocular, 'it would break up our bridge four.' Naturally we never discuss her shortcomings or in any way analyse the marriage. The unwritten rule that exists among the four of us seems to extend as far as that.

He slipped into my room after he'd had another drink or two, and I was waiting for him as he likes me to wait, in bed but not quite undressed. He has never said so, but I know that that is something Cynthia would not understand in him, or ever attempt to comply with. Ralph, of course, would not have understood either; poor old Ralph would have been shocked. Actually it's all rather sweet, Strafe and his little ways.

'I love you dear,' I whispered to him in the darkness, but just then he didn't wish to speak of love and referred instead to my body.

If Cynthia hadn't decided to remain in the hotel the next morning instead of accompanying us on our walk to Ardbeag everything might have been different. As it happened, when she said at breakfast she thought she'd just potter about the garden and sit with her book out of the wind somewhere, I can't say I was displeased. For a moment I hoped Dekko might say he'd stay with her, allowing Strafe and myself to go off on our own, but Dekko—who doesn't go in for saying what you want him to say—didn't. 'Poor old sausage,' he said instead, examining Cynthia with a solicitude that suggested she was close to the grave, rather than just a little lowered by the change of life or whatever it was.

'I'll be perfectly all right,' Cynthia assured him. 'Honestly.'

'Cynthia likes to mooch, you know,' Strafe pointed out, which of course is only the truth. She reads too much, I always think. You often see her putting down a book with the most melancholy look in her eyes, which can't be good for her. She's an imaginative woman, I suppose you would say, and of course her habit of reading so much is often useful on our holidays: over the years she has read her way through dozens of Irish guide-books. 'That's where the garrison pushed the natives over the cliffs,' she once remarked on a drive. 'Those rocks are known as the Maidens,' she remarked on another occasion. She has led us to places of interest which we had no idea existed: Garron Tower on Garron Point, the mausoleum at Bonamargy, the Devil's Backbone. As well as which, Cynthia is extremely knowledgeable about all matters relating to Irish history. Again she has read endlessly: biographies and autobiographies, long accounts of the centuries of battling and politics there've been. There's hardly a town or village we ever pass through that hasn't some significance for Cynthia, although I'm afraid her impressive fund of information doesn't always receive the attention it deserves. Not that Cynthia ever minds; it doesn't seem to worry her when no one listens. My own opinion is that she'd have made a much better job of her relationship with Strafe and her sons if she could have somehow developed a bit more character.

We left her in the garden and proceeded down the cliff path to the shingle beneath. I was wearing slacks and a blouse, with the arms of a cardigan looped round my neck in case it turned chilly: the outfit was new, specially bought for the holiday, in shades of tangerine. Strafe never cares how he dresses and of course she doesn't keep him up to the mark: that morning, as far as I remember, he wore rather shapeless corduroy trousers, the kind men sometimes garden in, and a navy-blue fisherman's jersey. Dekko as usual was a fashion plate: a pale green linen suit with pleated jacket pockets, a maroon shirt open at the neck, revealing a medallion on a fine gold chain. We didn't converse as we crossed the rather difficult shingle, but when we reached the sand Dekko began to talk about some girl or other, someone called Juliet who had apparently proposed marriage to him just before we'd left Surrey. He'd told her, so he said, that he'd think about it while on holiday and he wondered now about dispatching a telegram from Ardbeag saying, *Still thinking*. Strafe, who has a simple sense of humour, considered this hugely funny and spent most of the walk persuading Dekko that the telegram must certainly be sent, and other telegrams later on, all with the same message. Dekko kept laughing, throwing his head back in a way that always reminds me of an Australian bird I once saw in a nature film on television. I could see this was going to become one of those jokes that would accompany us all through the holiday, a man's thing really, but of course I didn't mind. The girl called Juliet was nearly thirty years younger than Dekko. I supposed she knew what she was doing.

Since the subject of telegrams had come up, Strafe recalled the occasion when Thrive Major had sent one to A. D. Cowley-Stubbs: *Darling regret three months gone love Rowena*. Carefully timed, it had arrived during one of Cows' Thursday evening coffee sessions. Rowena was a maid, known as the Bicycle, who had been sacked the previous term, and old Cows had something of a reputation as a misogynist. When he read the message he apparently went white and collapsed into an armchair. Warrington P. J. managed to read it too, and after that the fat was in the fire. The consequences went on rather, but I never minded listening when Strafe and Dekko drifted back to their schooldays. I just wish I'd known Strafe then, before either of us had gone and got married.

We had our coffee at Ardbeag, the telegram was sent off, and then Strafe and Dekko wanted to see a man called Henry O'Reilly whom we'd met on previous holidays, who organizes mackerel-fishing trips. I waited on my own, picking out postcards in the village shop that sells almost everything, and then I wandered down towards the shore. I knew that they would be having a drink with the boatman because a year had passed since they'd seen him last. They joined me after about twenty minutes, Dekko apologizing but Strafe not seeming to be aware that I'd had to wait because Strafe is not a man who notices little things. It was almost one o'clock when we reached Glencorn Lodge and were told by Mr Malseed that Cynthia needed looking after.

The hotel, in fact, was in a turmoil. I have never seen anyone as ashen-faced as Mr Malseed; his wife, in a forget-me-not dress, was limp. It wasn't explained to us immediately what had happened, because in the middle of telling us that Cynthia needed looking after Mr Malseed was summoned to the telephone. I could see through the half-open door of their little office a glass of whisky or brandy on the desk and Mrs Malseed's bangled arm reaching out for it. Not for ages did we realize that it all had to do with the lone man whom we'd speculated about the night before.

'He just wanted to talk to me,' Cynthia kept repeating hysterically in the hall. 'He sat with me by the magnolias.'

I made her lie down. Strafe and I stood on either side of her bed as she lay there with her shoes off, her rather unattractively cut plain pink dress crumpled and actually damp from her tears. I wanted to make her take it off and to slip under the bed-clothes in her petticoat but somehow it seemed all wrong, in the circumstances, for Strafe's wife to do anything so intimate in my presence.

'I couldn't stop him,' Cynthia said, the rims of her eyes crimson by now, her nose beginning to run again. 'From half past ten till well after twelve. He had to talk to someone, he said.'

I could sense that Strafe was thinking precisely the same as I was: that the red-haired man had insinuated himself into Cynthia's company by talking about himself and had then put a hand on her knee. Instead of simply standing up and going away Cynthia would have stayed where she was, embarrassed or tongue-tied, at any rate unable to cope. And when the moment came she would have turned hysterical. I could picture her screaming in the garden, running across the lawn to the hotel, and then the pandemonium in the hall. I could sense Strafe picturing that also.

'My God, it's terrible,' Cynthia said.

'I think she should sleep,' I said quietly to Strafe. 'Try to sleep, dear,' I said to her, but she shook her head, tossing her jumble of hair about on the pillow.

'Milly's right,' Strafe urged. 'You'll feel much better after a little rest. We'll bring you a cup of tea later on.'

'My God!' she cried again. 'My God, how could I sleep?'

I went away to borrow a couple of mild sleeping pills from Dekko, who is never without them, relying on the things too much in my opinion. He was tidying himself in his room, but found the pills immediately. Strangely enough, Dekko's always sound in a crisis.

I gave them to her with water and she took them without asking what they were. She was in a kind of daze, one moment making a fuss and weeping, the next just peering ahead of her, as if frightened. In a way she was like someone who'd just had a bad nightmare and hadn't yet completely returned to reality. I remarked as much to Strafe while we made our way down to lunch, and he said he quite agreed.

'Poor old Cynth!' Dekko said when we'd all ordered lobster bisque and entrecôte béarnaise. 'Poor old sausage.'

You could see that the little waitress, a new girl this year, was bubbling over with excitement; but Kitty, serving the other half of the dining-room, was grim, which was most unusual. Everyone was talking in hushed tones and when Dekko said, 'Poor old Cynth!' a couple of heads were turned in our direction because he can never keep his voice down. The little vases of roses with which Mrs Malseed must have decorated each table before the fracas had occurred seemed strangely out of place in the atmosphere which had developed.

The waitress had just taken away our soup-plates when Mr Malseed hurried into the dining-room and came straight to our table. The lobster bisque surprisingly hadn't been quite up to scratch, and in passing I couldn't help wondering if the fuss had caused the kitchen to go to pieces also.

'I wonder if I might have a word, Major Strafe,' Mr Malseed said, and Strafe rose at once and accompanied him from the dining-room. A total silence had fallen, everyone in the dining-room pretending to be intent on eating. I had an odd feeling that we had perhaps got it all wrong, that because we'd been out for our walk when it had happened all the other guests knew more of the details than Strafe and Dekko and I did. I began to wonder if poor Cynthia had been raped.

Afterwards Strafe told us what occurred in the Malseeds' office, how Mrs Malseed had been sitting there, slumped, as he put it, and how two policemen had questioned him. 'Look, what on earth's all this about?' he had demanded rather sharply.

'It concerns this incident that's taken place, sir,' one of the policemen explained in an unhurried voice. 'On account of your wife—'

'My wife's lying down. She must not be questioned or in any way disturbed.'

'Ach, we'd never do that, sir.'

Strafe does a good Co. Antrim brogue and in relating all this to us he couldn't resist making full use of it. The two policemen were in uniform and their natural slowness of intellect was rendered more noticeable by the lugubrious air the tragedy had inspired in the hotel. For tragedy was what it was; after talking to Cynthia for nearly two hours the lone man had walked down to the rocks and been drowned.

When Strafe finished speaking I placed my knife and fork together on my plate, unable to eat another mouthful. The facts appeared to be that the man, having left Cynthia by the magnolias, had clambered down the cliff to a place no one ever went to, on the other side of the hotel from the sands we had walked along to Ardbeag. No one had seen him except Cynthia, who from the cliff-top had apparently witnessed his battering by the treacherous waves. The tide had been coming in, but by the time old Arthur and Mr Malseed reached the rocks it had begun to turn, leaving behind it the fully dressed corpse. Mr Malseed's impression was that the man had lost his footing on the seaweed and accidentally stumbled into the depths, for the rocks were so slippery it was difficult to carry the corpse more than a matter of yards. But at least it had been placed out of view, while Mr Malseed hurried back to the hotel to telephone for assistance. He told Strafe that Cynthia had been most confused, insisting that the man had walked out among the rocks and then into the sea, knowing what he was doing.

Listening to it all, I no longer felt sorry for Cynthia. It was typical of her that she should so sillily have involved us in all this. Why on earth had she sat in the garden with a man of that kind instead of standing up and making a fuss the moment he'd begun to paw her? If she'd acted intelligently the whole unfortunate episode could clearly have been avoided. Since it hadn't, there was no point whatsoever in insisting that the man had committed suicide when at that distance no one could possibly be sure.

'It really does astonish me,' I said at the lunch table, unable to prevent myself from breaking our unwritten rule. 'Whatever came over her?'

'It can't be good for the hotel,' Dekko commented, and I was glad to see Strafe giving him a little glance of irritation.

'It's hardly the point,' I said coolly.

'What I meant was, hotels occasionally hush things like this up.'

'Well, they haven't this time.' It seemed an age since I had waited for them in Ardbeag, since we had been so happily laughing over the effect of Dekko's telegram. He'd included his address in it so that the girl could send a message back, and as we'd returned to the hotel along the seashore there'd been much speculation between the two men about the form this would take.

'I suppose what Cynthia's thinking,' Strafe said, 'is that after he'd tried something on with her he became depressed.'

'Oh, but he could just as easily have lost his footing. He'd have been on edge anyway, worried in case she reported him.'

'Dreadful kind of death,' Dekko said. His tone suggested that that was that, that the subject should now be closed, and so it was.

After lunch we went to our rooms, as we always do at Glencorn Lodge, to rest for an hour. I took my slacks and blouse off, hoping that Strafe would knock on my door, but he didn't and of course that was understandable. Oddly enough I found myself thinking of Dekko, picturing his long form stretched out in the room called Hydrangea, his beaky face in profile on his pillow. The precise nature of Dekko's relationship with these girls he picks up has always privately intrigued me: was it really possible that somewhere in London there was a girl called Juliet who was prepared to marry him for his not inconsiderable money?

I slept and briefly dreamed. Thrive Major and Warrington P. J. were running the post office in Ardbeag, sending telegrams to everyone they could think of, including Dekko's friend Juliet. Cynthia had been found dead beside the magnolias and people were waiting for Hercule Poirot to arrive. 'Promise me you didn't do it,' I whispered to Strafe, but when Strafe replied it was to say that Cynthia's body reminded him of a bag of old chicken bones.

Strafe and Dekko and I met for tea in the tea-lounge. Strafe had looked in to see if Cynthia had woken, but apparently she hadn't. The police officers had left the hotel, Dekko said, because he'd noticed their car wasn't parked at the front any more. None of the three of us said, but I think we presumed, that the man's body had been removed from the rocks during the quietness of the afternoon. From where we sat I caught a glimpse of Mrs Malseed passing quite briskly through the hall, seeming almost herself again. Certainly our holiday would be affected, but it might not be totally ruined. All that remained to hope for was Cynthia's recovery, and then everyone could set about forgetting the unpleasantness. The nicest thing would be if a jolly young couple turned up and occupied the man's room, exorcising the incident, as newcomers would.

The family from France—the two little girls and their parents—were chattering away in the tea-lounge, and an elderly trio who'd arrived that morning were speaking in American accents. The honeymoon couple appeared, looking rather shy, and began to whisper and giggle in a corner. People who occupied the table next to ours in the dining-room, a Wing-Commander Orfell and his wife, from Guildford, nodded and smiled as they passed. Everyone was making an effort, and I knew it would help matters further if Cynthia felt up to a rubber or two before dinner. That life should continue as normally as possible was essential for Glencorn Lodge, the example already set by Mrs Malseed.

Because of our interrupted lunch I felt quite hungry, and the Malseeds pride themselves on their teas. The chef, Mr McBride, whom of course we've met, has the lightest touch I know with sponge cakes and little curranty scones. I was, in fact, buttering a scone when Strafe said:

'Here she is.'

And there indeed she was. By the look of her she had simply pushed herself off her bed and come straight down. Her pink dress was even more crumpled than it had been. She hadn't so much as run a comb through her hair, her face was puffy and unpowdered. For a moment I really thought she was walking in her sleep.

Strafe and Dekko stood up. 'Feeling better, dear?' Strafe said, but she didn't answer.

'Sit down, Cynth,' Dekko urged, pushing back a chair to make room for her.

'He told me a story I can never forget. I've dreamed about it all over again.' Cynthia swayed in front of us, not even attempting to sit down. To tell the truth, she sounded inane.

'Story, dear?' Strafe enquired, humouring her.

She said it was the story of two children who had apparently ridden bicycles through the streets of Belfast, out into Co. Antrim. The bicycles were dilapidated, she said; she didn't know if they were stolen or not. She didn't know about the children's homes because the man hadn't spoken of them, but she claimed to know instinctively that they had ridden away from poverty and unhappiness. 'From the clatter and the quarrelling,' Cynthia said. 'Two children who later fell in love.'

'Horrid old dream,' Strafe said. 'Horrid for you, dear.'

She shook her head, and then sat down. I poured another cup of tea. 'I had the oddest dream myself,' I said. 'Thrive Major was running the post office in Ardbeag.'

Strafe smiled and Dekko gave his laugh, but Cynthia didn't in any way acknowledge what I'd said.

'A fragile thing the girl was, with depths of mystery in her wide brown eyes. Red-haired of course he was himself, thin as a rake in those days. Glencorn Lodge was derelict then.'

'You've had a bit of a shock, old thing,' Dekko said.

Strafe agreed, kindly adding, 'Look, dear, if the chap actually interfered with you—'

'Why on earth should he do that?' Her voice was shrill in the tea-lounge, edged with a note of hysteria. I glanced at Strafe, who was frowning into his teacup. Dekko began to say something, but broke off before his meaning emerged. Rather more calmly Cynthia said:

'It was summer when they came here. Honeysuckle he described. And mother of thyme. He didn't know the name of either.'

No one attempted any kind of reply, not that it was necessary, for Cynthia just continued.

'At school there were the facts of geography and arithmetic. And the legends of scholars and of heroes, of Queen Maeve and Finn MacCool. There was the coming of St. Patrick to a heathen people. History was full of kings and high-kings, and Silken Thomas and Wolfe Tone, the Flight of the Earls, the Siege of Limerick.'

When Cynthia said that, it was impossible not to believe that the unfortunate events of the morning had touched her with some kind of madness. It seemed astonishing that she had walked into the tea-lounge without having combed her hair, and that she'd stood there swaying before sitting down, that out of the blue she had started on about two children. None of it made an iota of sense, and surely she could see that the nasty experience she'd suffered should not be dwelt upon? I offered her the plate of scones, hoping that if she began to eat she would stop talking, but she took no notice of my gesture.

'Look, dear,' Strafe said, 'there's not one of us who knows what you're talking about.'

'I'm talking about a children's story, I'm talking about a girl and a boy who visited this place we visit also. He hadn't been here for years, but he returned last night, making one final effort to understand. And then he walked out into the sea.'

She had taken a piece of her dress and was agitatedly crumpling it between the finger and thumb of her left hand. It was dreadful really, having her so grubby-looking. For some odd reason I suddenly thought of her cooking, how she wasn't in the least interested in it or in anything about the house. She certainly hadn't succeeded in making a home for Strafe.

'They rode those worn-out bicycles through a hot afternoon. Can you feel all that? A newly surfaced road, the snap of chippings beneath their tyres, the smell of tar? Dust from a passing car, the city they left behind?'

'Cynthia dear,' I said, 'drink your tea, and why not have a scone?'

'They swam and sunbathed on the beach you walked along today. They went to a spring for water. There were no magnolias then. There was no garden, no neat little cliff paths to the beach. Surely you can see it clearly?'

'No,' Strafe said. 'No, we really cannot, dear.'

'This place that is an idyll for us was an idyll for them too: the trees, the ferns, the wild roses near the water spring, the very sea and sun they shared. There was a cottage lost in the middle of the woods: they sometimes looked for that. They played a game, a kind of hide and seek. People in a white farmhouse gave them milk.'

For the second time I offered Cynthia the plate of scones and for the second time she pointedly ignored me. Her cup of tea hadn't been touched. Dekko took a scone and cheerfully said:

'All's well that's over.'

But Cynthia appeared to have drifted back into a daze, and I wondered again if it could really be possible that the experience had unhinged her. Unable to help myself, I saw her being led away from the hotel, helped into the back of a blue van, something like an ambulance. She was talking about the children again, how they had planned to marry and keep a sweetshop.

'Take it easy, dear,' Strafe said, which I followed up by suggesting for the second time that she should make an effort to drink her tea.

'Has it to do with the streets they came from? Or the history they learnt, he from his Christian Brothers, she from her nuns? History is unfinished in this island; long since it has come to a stop in Surrey.'

Dekko said, and I really had to hand it to him:

'Cynth, we have to put it behind us.'

It didn't do any good. Cynthia just went rambling on, speaking again of the girl being taught by nuns, and the boy by Christian Brothers. She began to recite the history they might have learnt, the way she sometimes did when we were driving through an area that had historical connections. 'Can you imagine,' she embarrassingly asked, 'our very favourite places bitter with disaffection, with plotting and revenge? Can you imagine the treacherous murder of Shane O'Neill the Proud?'

Dekko made a little sideways gesture of his head, politely marvelling. Strafe seemed about to say something, but changed his mind. Confusion ran through Irish history, Cynthia said, like convolvulus in a hedgerow. On May 24th, 1487, a boy of ten called Lambert Simnel, brought to Dublin by a priest from Oxford, was declared Edward VI of all England and Ireland, crowned with a golden circlet taken from a statue of the Virgin Mary. On May 24th, 1798, here in Antrim, Presbyterian farmers fought for a common cause with their Catholic labourers. She paused and looked at Strafe. Chaos and contradiction, she informed him, were hidden everywhere beneath nice-sounding names. 'The Battle of the Yellow Ford,' she suddenly chanted in a singsong way that sounded thoroughly peculiar, 'the Statutes of Kilkenny. The Battle of Glenmama, the Convention of Drumceat. The Act of Settlement, the Renunciation Act. The Act of Union, the Toleration Act. Just so much history it sounds like now, yet people starved or died while other people watched. A language was lost, a faith forbidden. Famine followed revolt, plantation followed that. But it was people who were struck into the soil of other people's land, not forests of new trees; and it was greed and treachery that spread as a disease among them all. No wonder unease clings to these shreds of history and shots ring out in answer to the mockery of drums. No wonder the air is nervy with suspicion.'

There was an extremely awkward silence when she ceased to speak. Dekko nodded, doing his best to be companionable. Strafe nodded also. I simply examined the pattern of roses on our tea-time china, not knowing what else to do. Eventually Dekko said:

'What an awful lot you know, Cynth!'

'Cynthia's always been interested,' Strafe said. 'Always had a first-rate memory.'

'Those children of the streets are part of the battles and the Acts,' she went on, seeming quite unaware that her talk was literally almost crazy. 'They're part of the blood that flowed around those nice-sounding names.' She paused, and for a moment seemed disinclined to continue. Then she said:

'The second time they came here the house was being rebuilt. There were concrete-mixers, and lorries drawn up on the grass, noise and scaffolding everywhere. They watched all through another afternoon and then they went their different ways: their childhood was over, lost with their idyll. He became a dockyard clerk. She went to London, to work in a betting shop.'

'My dear,' Strafe said very gently, 'it's interesting, everything you say, but it really hardly concerns us.'

'No, of course not.' Quite emphatically Cynthia shook her head, appearing wholly to agree. 'They were degenerate, awful creatures. They must have been.'

'No one's saying that, my dear.'

'Their story should have ended there, he in the docklands of Belfast, she recording bets. Their complicated childhood love should just have dissipated, as such love often does. But somehow nothing was as neat as that.'

Dekko, in an effort to lighten the conversation, mentioned a boy called Gollsol who'd been at school with Strafe and himself, who'd formed a romantic attachment for the daughter of one of the groundsmen and had later actually married her. There was a silence for a moment, then Cynthia, without emotion, said:

'You none of you care. You sit there not caring that two people are dead.'

'Two people, Cynthia?' I said.

'For God's sake, I'm telling you!' she cried. 'That girl was murdered in a room in Maida Vale.'

Although there is something between Strafe and myself, I do try my best to be at peace about it. I go to church and take communion, and I know Strafe occasionally does too, though not as often as perhaps he might. Cynthia has no interest in that side of life, and it rankled with me now to hear her blaspheming so casually, and so casually speaking about death in Maida Vale on top of all this stuff about history and children. Strafe was shaking his head, clearly believing that Cynthia didn't know what she was talking about.

'Cynthia dear,' I began, 'are you sure you're not muddling something up here? You've been upset, you've had a nightmare: don't you think your imagination, or something you've been reading—'

'Bombs don't go off on their own. Death doesn't just happen to occur in Derry and Belfast, in London and Amsterdam and Dublin, in Berlin and Jerusalem. There are people who are murderers: that is what this children's story is about.'

A silence fell, no one knowing what to say. It didn't matter of course because without any prompting Cynthia continued.

'We drink our gin with Angostura bitters, there's lamb or chicken Kiev. Old Kitty's kind to us in the dining-room and old Arthur in the hall. Flowers are everywhere, we have our special table.'

'Please let us take you to your room now,' Strafe begged, and as he spoke I reached out a hand in friendship and placed it on her arm. 'Come on, old thing,' Dekko said.

'The limbless are left on the streets, blood spatters the car-parks. *Brits Out* it says on a rockface, but we know it doesn't mean us.'

I spoke quietly then, measuring my words, measuring the pause between each so that its effect might be registered. I felt the statement had to be made, whether it was my place to make it or not. I said:

'You are very confused, Cynthia.'

The French family left the tea-lounge. The two Dalmatians, Charger and Snooze, ambled in and sniffed and went away again. Kitty came to clear the French family's tea things. I could hear her speaking to the honeymoon couple, saying the weather forecast was good.

'Cynthia,' Strafe said, standing up, 'we've been very patient with you but this is now becoming silly.'

I nodded just a little. 'I really think,' I softly said, but Cynthia didn't permit me to go on.

'Someone told him about her. Someone mentioned her name, and he couldn't believe it. She sat alone in Maida Vale, putting together the mechanisms of her bombs: this girl who had laughed on the seashore, whom he had loved.'

'Cynthia,' Strafe began, but he wasn't permitted to continue either. Hopelessly, he just sat down again.

'Whenever he heard of bombs exploding he thought of her, and couldn't understand. He wept when he said that; her violence haunted him, he said. He couldn't work, he couldn't sleep at night. His mind filled up with images of her, their awkward childhood kisses, her fingers working neatly now. He saw her with a carrier-bag, hurrying it through a crowd, leaving it where it could cause most death. In front of the mouldering old house that had once been Glencorn Lodge they'd made a fire and cooked their food. They'd lain for ages on the grass. They'd cycled home to their city streets.'

It suddenly dawned on me that Cynthia was knitting this whole fantasy out of nothing. It all worked backwards from the moment when she'd had the misfortune to witness the man's death in the sea. A few minutes before he'd been chatting quite normally to her, he'd probably even mentioned a holiday in his childhood and some girl there'd been: all of it would have been natural in the circumstances, possibly even the holiday had taken place at Glencorn. He'd said good-bye and then unfortunately he'd had his accident. As she watched from the cliff edge, something had cracked in poor Cynthia's brain, she having always been a prey to melancholy. I suppose it must be hard having two sons who don't think much of you, and a marriage not offering you a great deal, bridge and holidays probably the best part of it. For some odd reason of her own she'd created her fantasy about a child turning into a terrorist. The violence of the man's death had clearly filled her imagination with Irish violence, so regularly seen on television. If we'd been on holiday in Suffolk I wondered how it would have seemed to the poor creature.

I could feel Strafe and Dekko beginning to put all that together also, beginning to realize that the whole story of the red-haired man and the girl was clearly Cynthia's invention. 'Poor creature,' I wanted to say, but did not do so.

'For months he searched for her, pushing his way among the people of London, the people who were her victims. When he found her she just looked at him, as if the past hadn't even existed. She didn't smile, as if incapable of smiling. He wanted to take her away, back to where they came from, but she didn't reply when he suggested that. Bitterness was like a disease in her, and when he left her he felt the bitterness in himself.'

Again Strafe and Dekko nodded, and I could feel Strafe thinking that there really was no point in protesting further. All we could hope for was that the end of the saga was in sight.

'He remained in London, working on the railways. But in the same way as before he was haunted by the person she'd become, and the haunting was more awful now. He bought a gun from a man he'd been told about and kept it hidden in a shoe-box in his rented room. Now and again he took it out and looked at it, then put it back. He hated the violence that possessed her, yet he was full of it himself: he knew he couldn't betray her with anything but death. Humanity had left both of them when he visited her again in Maida Vale.'

To my enormous relief and, I could feel, to Strafe's and Dekko's too, Mr and Mrs Malseed appeared beside us. Like his wife, Mr Malseed had considerably recovered. He spoke in an even voice, clearly wishing to dispose of the matter. It was just the diversion we needed.

'I must apologize, Mrs Strafe,' he said. 'I cannot say how sorry we are that you were bothered by that man.'

'My wife is still a little dicky,' Strafe explained, 'but after a decent night's rest I think we can say she'll be as right as rain again.'

'I only wish, Mrs Strafe, you had made contact with my wife or myself when he first approached you.' There was a spark of irritation in Mr Malseed's eyes, but his voice was still controlled. 'I mean, the unpleasantness you suffered might just have been averted.'

'Nothing would have been averted, Mr Malseed, and certainly not the horror we are left with. Can you see her as the girl she became, seated at a chipped white table, her wires and fuses spread around her? What were her thoughts in that room, Mr Malseed? What happens in the mind of anyone who wishes to destroy? In a back street he bought his gun for too much money. When did it first occur to him to kill her?'

'We really are a bit at sea,' Mr Malseed replied without the slightest hesitation. He humoured Cynthia by displaying no surprise, by speaking very quietly.

'All I am saying, Mr Malseed, is that we should root our heads out of the sand and wonder about two people who are beyond the pale.'

'My dear,' Strafe said, 'Mr Malseed is a busy man.'

Still quietly, still perfectly in control of every intonation, without a single glance around the tea-lounge to ascertain where his guests' attention was, Mr Malseed said:

'There is unrest here, Mrs Strafe, but we do our best to live with it.'

'All I am saying is that perhaps there can be regret when two children end like this.'

Mr Malseed did not reply. His wife did her best to smile away the awkwardness. Strafe murmured privately to Cynthia, no doubt beseeching her to come to her senses. Again I imagined a blue van drawn up in front of Glencorn Lodge, for it was quite understandable now that an imaginative woman should go mad, affected by the ugliness of death. The garbled speculation about the man and the girl, the jumble in the poor thing's mind—a children's story as she called it—all somehow hung together when you realized they didn't have to make any sense whatsoever.

'Murderers are beyond the pale, Mr Malseed, and England has always had its pales. The one in Ireland began in 1395.'

'Dear,' I said, 'what has happened has nothing whatsoever to do with calling people murderers and placing them beyond some pale or other. You witnessed a most unpleasant accident, dear, and it's only to be expected that you've become just a little lost. The man had a chat with you when you were sitting by the magnolias and then the shock of seeing him slip on the seaweed—'

'He didn't slip on the seaweed,' she suddenly screamed. 'My God, he didn't slip on the seaweed.'

Strafe closed his eyes. The other guests in the tea-lounge had fallen silent ages ago, openly listening. Arthur was standing near the door and was listening also. Kitty was waiting to clear away our tea things, but didn't like to because of what was happening.

'I must request you to take Mrs Strafe to her room, Major,' Mr Malseed said. 'And I must make it clear that we cannot tolerate further upset in Glencorn Lodge.'

Strafe reached for her arm, but Cynthia took no notice.

'An Irish joke,' she said, and then she stared at Mr and Mrs Malseed, her eyes passing over each feature of their faces. She stared at Dekko and Strafe, and last of all at me. She said eventually:

'An Irish joke, an unbecoming tale: of course it can't be true. Ridiculous, that a man returned here. Ridiculous, that he walked again by the seashore and through the woods, hoping to understand where a woman's cruelty had come from.'

'This talk is most offensive,' Mr Malseed protested, his calmness slipping just a little. The ashen look that had earlier been in his face returned. I could see he was beside himself with rage. 'You are trying to bring something to our doorstep which most certainly does not belong there.'

'On your doorstep they talked about a sweetshop: Cadbury's bars and different-flavoured creams, nut-milk toffee, Aero and Crunchie.'

'For God's sake pull yourself together,' I clearly heard Strafe whispering, and Mrs Malseed attempted to smile. 'Come along now, Mrs Strafe,' she said, making a gesture. 'Just to please us, dear. Kitty wants to clear away the dishes. Kitty!' she called out, endeavouring to bring matters down to earth.

Kitty crossed the lounge with her tray and gathered up the cups and saucers. The Malseeds, naturally still anxious, hovered. No one was surprised when Cynthia began all over again, by crazily asking Kitty what she thought of us.

'I think, dear,' Mrs Malseed began, 'Kitty's quite busy really.'

'Stop this at once,' Strafe quietly ordered.

'For fourteen years, Kitty, you've served us with food and cleared away the tea-cups we've drunk from. For fourteen years we've played our bridge and walked about the garden. We've gone for drives, we've bought our tweed, we've bathed as those children did.'

'Stop it,' Strafe said again, a little louder. Bewildered and getting red in the face, Kitty hastily bundled china on to her tray. I made a sign at Strafe because for some reason I felt that the end was really in sight. I wanted him to retain his patience, but what Cynthia said next was almost unbelievable.

'In Surrey we while away the time, we clip our hedges. On a bridge night there's coffee at nine o'clock, with macaroons or *petits fours*. Last thing of all we watch the late-night News, packing away our cards and scoring-pads, our sharpened pencils. There's been an incident in Armagh, one soldier's had his head shot off, another's run amok. Our lovely Glens of Antrim, we all four think, our coastal drives: we hope that nothing disturbs the peace. We think of Mr Malseed, still busy in Glencorn Lodge, and Mrs Malseed finishing her flower-plaques for the rooms of the completed annexe.'

'Will you for God's sake shut up?' Strafe suddenly shouted. I could see him struggling with himself, but it didn't do any good. He called Cynthia a bloody spectacle, sitting there talking rubbish. I don't believe she even heard him.

'Through honey-tinted glasses we love you and we love your island, Kitty. We love the lilt of your racy history, we love your earls and heroes. Yet we made a sensible pale here once, as civilized people create a garden, pretty as a picture.'

Strafe's outburst had been quite noisy and I could sense him being ashamed of it. He muttered that he was sorry, but Cynthia simply took advantage of his generosity, continuing about a pale.

'Beyond it lie the bleak untouchables, best kept as dots on the horizon, too terrible to contemplate. How can we be blamed if we make neither head nor tail of anything, Kitty, your past and your present, those battles and Acts of Parliament? We people of Surrey: how can we know? Yet I stupidly thought, you see, that the tragedy of two children could at least be understood. He didn't discover where her cruelty had come from because perhaps you never can: evil breeds evil in a mysterious way. That's the story the red-haired stranger passed on to me, the story you huddle away from.'

Poor Strafe was pulling at Cynthia, pleading with her, still saying he was sorry.

'Mrs Strafe,' Mr Malseed tried to say, but got no further. To my horror Cynthia abruptly pointed at me.

'That woman,' she said, 'is my husband's mistress, a fact I am supposed to be unaware of, Kitty.'

'My God!' Strafe said.

'My husband is perverted in his sexual desires. His friend, who shared his schooldays, has never quite recovered from that time. I myself am a pathetic creature who has closed her eyes to a husband's infidelity and his mistress's viciousness. I am dragged into the days of Thrive Major and A. D. Cowley-Stubbs: mechanically I smile. I hardly exist, Kitty.'

There was a most unpleasant silence, and then Strafe said:

'None of that's true. For God's sake, Cynthia,' he suddenly shouted, 'go and rest yourself.'

Cynthia shook her head and continued to address the waitress. She'd had a rest, she told her. 'But it didn't do any good, Kitty, because hell has invaded the paradise of Glencorn, as so often it has invaded your island. And we, who have so often brought it, pretend it isn't there. Who cares about children made into murderers?'

Strafe shouted again. 'You fleshless ugly bitch!' he cried. 'You bloody old fool!' He was on his feet, trying to get her to hers. The blood was thumping in his bronzed face, his eyes had a fury in them I'd never seen before. 'Fleshless!' he shouted at her, not caring that so many people were listening. He closed his eyes in misery and in shame again, and I wanted to reach out and take his hand but of course I could not. You could see the Malseeds didn't blame him, you could see them thinking that everything was ruined for us. I wanted to shout at Cynthia too, to batter the silliness out of her, but of course I could not do that. I could feel the tears behind my eyes, and I couldn't help noticing that Dekko's hands were shaking. He's quite sensitive behind his joky manner, and had quite obviously taken to heart her statement that he had never recovered from his schooldays. Nor had it been pleasant, hearing myself described as vicious.

'No one cares,' Cynthia said in the same unbalanced way, as if she hadn't just been called ugly and a bitch. 'No one cares, and on our journey home we shall all four be silent. Yet is the truth about ourselves at least a beginning? Will we wonder in the end about the hell that frightens us?'

Strafe still looked wretched, his face deliberately turned away from us. Mrs Malseed gave a little sigh and raised the fingers of her left hand to her cheek, as if something tickled it. Her husband breathed heavily. Dekko seemed on the point of tears.

Cynthia stumbled off, leaving a silence behind her. Before it was broken I knew she was right when she said we would just go home, away from this country we had come to love. And I knew as well that neither here nor at home would she be led to a blue van that was not quite an ambulance. Strafe would stay with her because Strafe is made like that, honourable in his own particular way. I felt a pain where perhaps my heart is, and again I wanted to cry. Why couldn't it have been she who had gone down to the rocks and slipped on the seaweed or just walked into the sea, it didn't matter which? Her awful rigmarole hung about us as the last of the tea things were gathered up—the earls who'd fled, the famine and the people planted. The children were there too, grown up into murdering riff-raff.

Milan Kundera

Milan Kundera (b.1929) was born in Brno, Czechoslovakia. In 1948, after a long apprenticeship in music, Kundera decided to pursue a career in film. He studied at the Prague Academy of Music and Dramatic Arts and later joined the faculty there. But it was finally writing that proved to be his path to self-expression. Though he had written poetry since his early teens, Kundera tried his hand at short stories in the late 1950s. His first collection, *Laughable Loves,* won him great notoriety.

Kundera came into collision with the government authorities after the 1968 invasion of Czechoslovakia by the Soviets. His calls for freedom of artistic expression branded him a troublemaker. In 1975 Kundera traveled to France to accept a teaching post at the University of Rennes. He has remained in France, although he has not given up his Czech citizenship.

Kundera has attained great success in Europe and the United States with his novels, which include *The Joke, Life Is Elsewhere, The Farewell Party, The Book of Laughter and Forgetting,* and *The Unbearable Lightness of Being*. This last novel was made into an acclaimed film.

Kundera achieves an uncanny blend of humor, philosophical inquiry, and situational ominousness in his work, much of which deals with the conflict between the demands of private life and the abstract demands and regulations imposed by repressive government systems.

THE HITCHHIKING GAME

1

The needle on the gas gauge suddenly dipped toward empty and the young driver of the sports car declared that it was maddening how much gas the car ate up. "See that we don't run out of gas again," protested the girl (about twenty-two), and reminded the driver of several places where this had already happened to them. The young man replied that he wasn't worried, because whatever he went through with her had the charm of adventure for him. The girl objected; whenever they had run out of gas on the highway it had, she said, always been an adventure only for her. The young man had hidden and she had had to make ill use of her charms by thumbing a ride and letting herself be driven to the nearest gas station, then thumbing a ride back with a can of gas. The young man asked the girl whether the drivers who had given her a ride had been unpleasant, since she spoke as if her task had been a hardship. She replied (with awkward flirtatiousness) that sometimes they had been *very* pleasant but that it hadn't done her any good as she had been burdened with the can and had had to leave them before she could get anything going. "Pig," said the young man. The girl protested that she wasn't a pig, but that he really was. God knows how many girls stopped him on the highway, when he was driving the car alone! Still driving, the young man put his arm around the girl's shoulders and kissed her gently on the forehead. He knew that she loved him and that she was jealous. Jealousy isn't a pleasant quality, but if it isn't overdone (and if it's combined with modesty), apart from its inconvenience there's even something touching about it. At least that's what the young man thought. Because he was only twenty-eight, it seemed to him that he was old and knew everything that a man could know about women. In the girl sitting beside him he valued precisely what, until now, he had met with least in women: purity.

The needle was already on empty, when to the right the young man caught sight of a sign, announcing that the station was a quarter of a mile ahead. The girl hardly had time to say how relieved she was before the young man was signaling left and driving into a space in front of the pumps. However, he had to stop a little way off, because beside the pumps was a huge gasoline truck with a large metal tank and a bulky hose, which was refilling the pumps. "We'll have to wait," said the young man to the girl and got out of the car. "How long will it take?" he shouted to the man in overalls. "Only a moment," replied the attendant, and the young man said: "I've heard that one before." He wanted to go back and sit in the car, but he saw that the girl had gotten out the other side. "I'll take a little walk in the meantime," she said. "Where to?" the young man asked on purpose, wanting to see the girl's embarrassment. He had known her for a year now but she would still get shy in front of him. He enjoyed her moments of shyness, partly because they distinguished her from the women he'd met before, partly because he was aware of the law of universal transience, which made even his girl's shyness a precious thing to him.

2

The girl really didn't like it when during the trip (the young man would drive for several hours without stopping) she had to ask him to stop for a moment somewhere near a clump of trees. She always got angry when, with feigned surprise, he asked her why he should stop. She knew that her shyness was ridiculous and old-fashioned. Many times at work she had noticed that they laughed at her on account of it and deliberately provoked her. She always got shy in advance at the thought of how she was going to get shy. She often longed to feel free and easy about her body, the way most of the women around her did. She had even invented a special course in self-persuasion: she would repeat to herself that at birth every human being received one out of the millions of available bodies, as one would receive an allotted room out of the millions of rooms in an enormous hotel. Consequently, the body was fortuitous and impersonal, it was only a ready-made, borrowed thing. She would repeat this to herself in different ways, but she could never manage to feel it. This mind-body dualism was alien to her. She was too much one with her body; that is why she always felt such anxiety about it.

She experienced this same anxiety even in her relations with the young man, whom she had known for a year and with whom she was happy, perhaps because he never separated her body from her soul and she could live with him *wholly*. In this unity there was happiness, but right behind the happiness lurked suspicion, and the girl was full of that. For instance, it often occurred to her that the other women (those who weren't anxious) were more attractive and more seductive and that the young man, who did not conceal the fact that he knew this kind of woman well, would someday leave her for a woman like that. (True, the young man declared that he'd had enough of them to last his whole life, but she knew that he was still much younger than he thought.) She wanted him to be completely hers and she to be completely his, but it often seemed to her that the more she tried to give him everything, the more she denied him something: the very thing that a light and superficial love or a flirtation gives to a person. It worried her that she was not able to combine seriousness with lightheartedness.

But now she wasn't worrying and any such thoughts were far from her mind. She felt good. It was the first day of their vacation (of their two-week vacation, about which she had been dreaming for a whole year), the sky was blue (the whole year she had been worrying about whether the sky would really be blue), and he was beside her. At his, "Where to?" she blushed, and left the car without a word. She walked around the gas station, which was situated beside the highway in total isolation, surrounded by fields. About a hundred yards away (in the direction in which they were traveling), a wood began. She set off for it, vanished behind a little bush, and gave herself up to her good mood. (In solitude it was possible for her to get the greatest enjoyment from the presence of the man she loved. If his presence had been continuous, it would have kept on disappearing. Only when alone was she able to *hold on* to it.)

When she came out of the wood onto the highway, the gas station was visible. The large gasoline truck was already pulling out and the sports car moved forward toward the red turret of the pump. The girl walked on along the highway and only at times looked back to see if the sports car was coming. At last she caught sight of it. She stopped and began to wave at it like a hitchhiker waving at a stranger's car. The sports car slowed down and stopped close to the girl. The young man leaned toward the window, rolled it down, smiled, and asked, "Where are you headed, miss?"

"Are you going to Bystritsa?" asked the girl, smiling flirtatiously at him. "Yes, please get in," said the young man, opening the door. The girl got in and the car took off.

3

The young man was always glad when his girl friend was gay. This didn't happen too often; she had a quite tiresome job in an unpleasant environment, many hours of overtime without compensatory leisure and, at home, a sick mother. So she often felt tired. She didn't have either particularly good nerves or self-confidence and easily fell into a state of anxiety and fear. For this reason he welcomed every manifestation of her gaiety with the tender solicitude of a foster parent. He smiled at her and said: "I'm lucky today. I've been driving for five years, but I've never given a ride to such a pretty hitchhiker."

The girl was grateful to the young man for every bit of flattery; she wanted to linger for a moment in its warmth and so she said, "You're very good at lying."

"Do I look like a liar?"

"You look like you enjoy lying to women," said the girl, and into her words there crept unawares a touch of the old anxiety, because she really did believe that her young man enjoyed lying to women.

The girl's jealousy often irritated the young man, but this time he could easily overlook it for, after all, her words didn't apply to him but to the unknown driver. And so he just casually inquired, "Does it bother you?"

"If I were going with you, then it would bother me," said the girl and her words contained a subtle, instructive message for the young man; but the end of her sentence applied only to the unknown driver, "but I don't know you, so it doesn't bother me."

"Things about her own man always bother a woman more than things about a stranger" (this was now the young man's subtle, instructive message to the girl), "so seeing that we are strangers, we could get on well together."

The girl purposely didn't want to understand the implied meaning of his message, and so she now addressed the unknown driver exclusively:

"What does it matter, since we'll part company in a little while?"

"Why?" asked the young man.

"Well, I'm getting out at Bystritsa."

"And what if I get out with you?"

At these words the girl looked up at him and found that he looked exactly as she imagined him in her most agonizing hours of jealousy. She was alarmed at how he was flattering her and flirting with her (an unknown hitchhiker), and *how becoming it was to him.* Therefore she responded with defiant provocativeness, "What would *you* do with me, I wonder?"

"I wouldn't have to think too hard about what to do with such a beautiful woman," said the young man gallantly and at this moment he was once again speaking far more to his own girl than to the figure of the hitchhiker.

But this flattering sentence made the girl feel as if she had caught him at something, as if she had wheedled a confession out of him with a fraudulent trick. She felt toward him a brief flash of intense hatred and said, "Aren't you rather too sure of yourself?"

The young man looked at the girl. Her defiant face appeared to him to be completely convulsed. He felt sorry for her and longed for her usual, familiar expression (which he used to call childish and simple). He leaned toward her, put his arm around her shoulders, and softly spoke the name with which he usually addressed her and with which he now wanted to stop the game.

But the girl released herself and said: "You're going a bit too fast!"

At this rebuff the young man said: "Excuse me, miss," and looked silently in front of him at the highway.

4

The girl's pitiful jealousy, however, left her as quickly as it had come over her. After all, she was sensible and knew perfectly well that all this was merely a game. Now it even struck her as a little ridiculous that she had repulsed her man out of jealous rage. It wouldn't be pleasant for her if he found out why she had done it. Fortunately women have the miraculous ability to change the meaning of their actions after the event. Using this ability, she decided that she had repulsed him not out of anger but so that she could go on with the game, which, with its whimsicality, so well suited the first day of their vacation.

So again she was the hitchhiker, who had just repulsed the overenterprising driver, but only so as to slow down his conquest and make it more exciting. She half turned toward the young man and said caressingly:

"I didn't mean to offend you, mister!"

"Excuse me, I won't touch you again," said the young man.

He was furious with the girl for not listening to him and refusing to be herself when that was what he wanted. And since the girl insisted on continuing in her role, he transferred his anger to the unknown hitchhiker whom she was portraying. And all at once he discovered the character of his own part: he stopped making the gallant remarks with which he had wanted to flatter his girl in a roundabout way, and began to play the tough guy who treats women to the coarser aspects of his masculinity: willfulness, sarcasm, self-assurance.

This role was a complete contradiction of the young man's habitually solicitous approach to the girl. True, before he had met her, he had in fact behaved roughly rather than gently toward women. But he had never resembled a heartless tough guy, because he had never demonstrated either a particularly strong will or ruthlessness. However, if he did not resemble such a man, nonetheless he had *longed* to at one time. Of course it was a quite naive desire, but there it was. Childish desires withstand all the snares of the adult mind and often survive into ripe old age. And this childish desire quickly took advantage of the opportunity to embody itself in the proffered role.

The young man's sarcastic reserve suited the girl very well—it freed her from herself. For she herself was, above all, the epitome of jealousy. The moment she stopped seeing the gallantly seductive young man beside her and saw only his inaccessible face, her jealousy subsided. The girl could forget herself and give herself up to her role.

Her role? What was her role? It was a role out of trashy literature. The hitchhiker stopped the car not to get a ride, but to seduce the man who was driving the car. She was an artful seductress, cleverly knowing how to use her charms. The girl slipped into this silly, romantic part with an ease that astonished her and held her spellbound.

5

There was nothing the young man missed in his life more than lightheartedness. The main road of his life was drawn with implacable precision. His job didn't use up merely eight hours a day, it also infiltrated the remaining time with the compulsory boredom of meetings and home study, and, by means of the attentiveness of his countless male and female colleagues, it infiltrated the wretchedly little time he had left for his private life as well. This private life never remained secret and sometimes even became the subject of gossip and public discussion. Even two weeks' vacation didn't give him a feeling of liberation and adventure; the gray shadow of precise planning lay even here. The scarcity of summer accommodations in our country compelled him to book a room in the Tatras six months in advance, and since for that he needed a recommendation from his office, its omnipresent brain thus did not cease knowing about him even for an instant.

He had become reconciled to all this, yet all the same from time to time the terrible thought of the straight road would overcome him—a road along which he was being pursued, where he was visible to everyone, and from which he could not turn aside. At this moment that thought returned to him. Through an odd and brief conjunction of ideas the figurative road became identified with the real highway along which he was driving—and this led him suddenly to do a crazy thing.

"Where did you say you wanted to go?" he asked the girl.

"To Banska Bystritsa," she replied.

"And what are you going to do there?"

"I have a date there."

"Who with?"

"With a certain gentleman."

The car was just coming to a large crossroads. The driver slowed down so he could read the road signs, then turned off to the right.

"What will happen if you don't arrive for that date?"

"It would be your fault and you would have to take care of me."

"You obviously didn't notice that I turned off in the direction of Nove Zamky."

"Is that true? You've gone crazy!"

"Don't be afraid, I'll take care of you," said the young man.

So they drove and chatted thus—the driver and the hitchhiker who did not know each other.

The game all at once went into a higher gear. The sports car was moving away not only from the imaginary goal of Banska Bystritsa, but also from the real goal, toward which it had been heading in the morning: the Tatras and the room that had been booked. Fiction was suddenly making an assault upon real life. The young man was moving away from himself and from the implacable straight road, from which he had never strayed until now.

"But you said you were going to the Low Tatras!" The girl was surprised.

"I am going, miss, wherever I feel like going. I'm a free man and I do what I want and what it pleases me to do."

6

When they drove into Nove Zamky it was already getting dark.

The young man had never been here before and it took him a while to orient himself. Several times he stopped the car and asked the passersby directions to the hotel. Several streets had been dug up, so that the drive to the hotel, even though it was quite close by (as all those who had been asked asserted), necessitated so many detours and roundabout routes that it was almost a quarter of an hour before they finally stopped in front of it. The hotel looked unprepossessing, but it was the only one in town and the young man didn't feel like driving on. So he said to the girl, "Wait here," and got out of the car.

Out of the car he was, of course, himself again. And it was upsetting for him to find himself in the evening somewhere completely different from his intended destination—the more so because no one had forced him to do it and as a matter of fact he hadn't even really wanted to. He blamed himself for this piece of folly, but then became reconciled to it. The room in the Tatras could wait until tomorrow and it wouldn't do any harm if they celebrated the first day of their vacation with something unexpected.

He walked through the restaurant—smoky, noisy, and crowded—and asked for the reception desk. They sent him to the back of the lobby near the staircase, where behind a glass panel a superannuated blonde was sitting beneath a board full of keys. With difficulty, he obtained the key to the only room left.

The girl, when she found herself alone, also threw off her role. She didn't feel ill-humored, though, at finding herself in an unexpected town.

She was so devoted to the young man that she never had doubts about anything he did, and confidently entrusted every moment of her life to him. On the other hand the idea once again popped into her mind that perhaps—just as she was now doing—other women had waited for her man in his car, those women whom he met on business trips. But surprisingly enough this idea didn't upset her at all now. In fact, she smiled at the thought of how nice it was that today she was this other woman, this irresponsible, indecent other woman, one of those women of whom she was so jealous. It seemed to her that she was cutting them all out, that she had learned how to use their weapons; how to give the young man what until now she had not known how to give him: lightheartedness, shamelessness, and dissoluteness. A curious feeling of satisfaction filled her, because she alone had the ability to be all women and in this way (she alone) could completely captivate her lover and hold his interest.

The young man opened the car door and led the girl into the restaurant. Amid the din, the dirt, and the smoke he found a single, unoccupied table in a corner.

7

"So how are you going to take care of me now?" asked the girl provocatively.

"What would you like for an aperitif?"

The girl wasn't too fond of alcohol, still she drank a little wine and liked vermouth fairly well. Now, however, she purposely said: "Vodka."

"Fine," said the young man. "I hope you won't get drunk on me."

"And if I do?" said the girl.

The young man did not reply but called over a waiter and ordered two vodkas and two steak dinners. In a moment the waiter brought a tray with two small glasses and placed it in front of them.

The man raised his glass, "To you!"

"Can't you think of a wittier toast?"

Something was beginning to irritate him about the girl's game. Now sitting face to face with her, he realized that it wasn't just the *words* which were turning her into a stranger, but that her *whole persona* had changed, the movements of her body and her facial expression, and that she unpalatably and faithfully resembled that type of woman whom he knew so well and for whom he felt some aversion.

And so (holding his glass in his raised hand), he corrected his toast: "O.K., then I won't drink to you, but to your kind, in which are combined so successfully the better qualities of the animal and the worse aspects of the human being."

"By 'kind' do you mean all women?" asked the girl.

"No, I mean only those who are like you."

"Anyway it doesn't seem very witty to me to compare a woman with an animal."

"O.K.," the young man was still holding his glass aloft, "then I won't drink to your kind, but to your soul. Agreed? To your soul, which lights up when it descends from your head into your belly, and which goes out when it rises back up to your head."

The girl raised her glass. "O.K., to my soul, which descends into my belly."

"I'll correct myself once more," said the young man. "To your belly, into which your soul descends."

"To my belly," said the girl, and her belly (now that they had named it specifically), as it were, responded to the call; she felt every inch of it.

Then the waiter brought their steaks and the young man ordered them another vodka and some soda water (this time they drank to the girl's breasts), and the conversation continued in this peculiar, frivolous tone. It irritated the young man more and more how *well able* the girl was to become the lascivious miss. If she was able to do it so well, he thought, it meant that she really *was* like that. After all, no alien soul had entered into her from somewhere in space. What she was acting now was she herself; perhaps it was that part of her being which had formerly been locked up and which the pretext of the game had let out of its cage. Perhaps the girl supposed that by means of the game she was *disowning* herself, but wasn't it the other way around? Wasn't she becoming herself only through the game? Wasn't she freeing herself through the game? No, opposite him was not sitting a strange woman in his girl's body; it was his girl, herself, no one else. He looked at her and felt growing aversion toward her.

However, it was not only aversion. The more the girl withdrew from him *psychically,* the more he longed for her *physically*. The alien quality of her soul drew attention to her body, yes, as a matter of fact it turned her body into a body for *him* as if until now it had existed for the young man hidden within clouds of compassion, tenderness, concern, love, and emotion, as if it had been lost in these clouds (yes, as if this body had been lost!). It seemed to the young man that today he was seeing his girl's body for the first time.

After her third vodka and soda the girl got up and said flirtatiously, "Excuse me."

The young man said, "May I ask you where you are going, miss?"

"To piss, if you'll permit me," said the girl and walked off between the tables back toward the plush screen.

8

She was pleased with the way she had astounded the young man with this word, which—in spite of all its innocence—he had never heard from her. Nothing seemed to her truer to the character of the woman she was playing than this flirtatious emphasis placed on the word in question. Yes, she was pleased, she was in the best of moods. The game captivated her. It allowed her to feel what she had not felt till now: a *feeling of happy-go-lucky irresponsibility*.

She, who was always uneasy in advance about her every next step, suddenly felt completely relaxed. The alien life in which she had become involved was a life without shame, without biographical specifications, without past or future, without obligations. It was a life that was extraordinarily free. The girl, as a hitchhiker, could do anything, *everything was permitted her*. She could say, do, and feel whatever she liked.

She walked through the room and was aware that people were watching her from all the tables. It was a new sensation, one she didn't recognize: *indecent joy caused by her body*. Until now she had never been able to get rid of the fourteen-year-old girl within herself who was ashamed of her breasts and had the disagreeable feeling that she was indecent, because they stuck out from her body and were visible. Even though she was proud of being pretty and having a good figure, this feeling of pride was always immediately curtailed by shame. She rightly suspected that feminine beauty functioned above all as sexual provocation and she found this distasteful. She longed for her body to relate only to the man she loved. When men stared at her breasts in the street it seemed to her that they were invading a piece of her most secret privacy which should belong only to herself and her lover. But now she was the hitchhiker, the woman without a destiny. In this role she was relieved of the tender bonds of her love and began to be intensely aware of her body. And her body became more aroused the more alien the eyes watching it.

She was walking past the last table when an intoxicated man, wanting to show off his worldliness, addressed her in French: "*Combien, mademoiselle?*"

The girl understood. She thrust out her breasts and fully experienced every movement of her hips, then disappeared behind the screen.

9

It was a curious game. This curiousness was evidenced, for example, in the fact that the young man, even though he himself was playing the unknown driver remarkably well, did not for a moment stop seeing his girl in the hitchhiker. And it was precisely this that was tormenting. He saw his girl seducing a strange man, and had the bitter privilege of being present, of seeing at close quarters how she looked and of hearing what she said when she was cheating on him (when she had cheated on him, when she would cheat on him). He had the paradoxical honor of being himself the pretext for her unfaithfulness.

This was all the worse because he worshipped rather than loved her. It had always seemed to him that her inward nature was *real* only within the bounds of fidelity and purity, and that beyond these bounds it simply didn't exist. Beyond these bounds she would cease to be herself, as water ceases to be water beyond the boiling point. When he now saw her crossing this horrifying boundary with nonchalant elegance, he was filled with anger.

The girl came back from the rest room and complained: "A guy over there asked me: *Combien, mademoiselle?*"

"You shouldn't be surprised," said the young man, "after all, you look like a whore."

"Do you know that it doesn't bother me in the least?"

"Then you should go with the gentleman!"

"But I have you."

"You can go with him after me. Go and work out something with him."

"I don't find him attractive."

"But in principle you have nothing against it, having several men in one night."

"Why not, if they're good-looking."

"Do you prefer them one after the other or at the same time?"

"Either way," said the girl.

The conversation was proceeding to still greater extremes of rudeness; it shocked the girl slightly but she couldn't protest. Even in a game there lurks a lack of freedom; even a game is a trap for the players. If this had not been a game and they had really been two strangers, the hitchhiker could long ago have taken offense and left. But there's no escape from a game. A team cannot flee from the playing field before the end of the match, chess pieces cannot desert the chessboard: the boundaries of the playing field are fixed. The girl knew that she had to accept whatever form the game might take, just because it was a game. She knew that the more extreme the game became, the more it would be a game and the more obediently she would have to play it. And it was futile to evoke good sense and warn her dazed soul that she must keep her distance from the game and not take it seriously. Just because it was only a game her soul was not afraid, did not oppose the game, and narcotically sank deeper into it.

The young man called the waiter and paid. Then he got up and said to the girl, "We're going."

"Where to?" The girl feigned surprise.

"Don't ask, just come on," said the young man.

"What sort of way is that to talk to me?"

"The way I talk to whores," said the young man.

10

They went up the badly lit staircase. On the landing below the second floor a group of intoxicated men was standing near the rest room. The young man caught hold of the girl from behind so that he was holding her breast with his hand. The men by the rest room saw this and began to call out. The girl wanted to break away, but the young man yelled at her: "Keep still!" The men greeted this with general ribaldry and addressed several dirty remarks to the girl. The young man and the girl reached the second floor. He opened the door of their room and switched on the light.

It was a narrow room with two beds, a small table, a chair, and a washbasin. The young man locked the door and turned to the girl. She was standing facing him in a defiant pose with insolent sensuality in her eyes. He looked at her and tried to discover behind her lascivious expression the familiar features which he loved tenderly. It was as if he were looking at two images through the same lens, at two images superimposed one upon the other with the one showing through the other. These two images showing through each other were telling him that *everything* was in the girl, that her soul was terrifyingly amorphous, that it held faithfulness and unfaithfulness, treachery and innocence, flirtatiousness and chastity. This disorderly jumble seemed disgusting to him, like the variety to be found in a pile of garbage. Both images continued to show through each other and the young man understood that the girl differed only on the surface from other women, but deep down was the same as they: full of all possible thoughts, feelings, and vices, which justified all his secret misgivings and fits of jealousy. The impression that certain outlines delineated her as an individual was only a delusion to which the other person, the one who was looking, was subject—namely himself. It seemed to him that the girl he loved was a creation of his desire, his thoughts, and his faith and that the *real* girl now standing in front of him was hopelessly alien, hopelessly *ambiguous*. He hated her.

"What are you waiting for? Strip," he said.

The girl flirtatiously bent her head and said, "Is it necessary?"

The tone in which she said this seemed to him very familiar; it seemed to him that once long ago some other woman had said this to him, only he no longer knew which one. He longed to humiliate her. Not the hitchhiker, but his own girl. The game merged with life. The game of humiliating the hitchhiker became only a pretext for humiliating his girl. The young man had forgotten that he was playing a game. He simply hated the woman standing in front of him. He stared at her and took a fifty-crown bill from his wallet. He offered it to the girl. "Is that enough?"

The girl took the fifty crowns and said: "You don't think I'm worth much."

The young man said: "You aren't worth more."

The girl nestled up against the young man. "You can't get around me like that! You must try a different approach, you must work a little!"

She put her arms around him and moved her mouth toward his. He put his fingers on her mouth and gently pushed her away. He said: "I only kiss women I love."

"And you don't love me?"

"No."

"Whom do you love?"

"What's that got to do with you? Strip!"

11

She had never undressed like this before. The shyness, the feeling of inner panic, the dizziness, all that she had always felt when undressing in front of the young man (and she couldn't hide in the darkness), all this was gone. She was standing in front of him self-confident, insolent, bathed in light, and astonished at where she had all of a sudden discovered the gestures, heretofore unknown to her, of a slow, provocative striptease. She took in his glances, slipping off each piece of clothing with a caressing movement and enjoying each individual stage of this exposure.

But then suddenly she was standing in front of him completely naked and at this moment it flashed through her head that now the whole game would end, that, since she had stripped off her clothes, she had also stripped away her dissimulation, and that being naked meant that she was now herself and the young man ought to come up to her now and make a gesture with which he would wipe out everything and after which would follow only their most intimate love-making. So she stood naked in front of the young man and at this moment stopped playing the game. She felt embarrassed and on her face appeared the smile, which really belonged to her—a shy and confused smile.

But the young man didn't come to her and didn't end the game. He didn't notice the familiar smile. He saw before him only the beautiful, alien body of his own girl, whom he hated. Hatred cleansed his sensuality of any sentimental coating. She wanted to come to him, but he said: "Stay where you are, I want to have a good look at you." Now he longed only to treat her as a whore. But the young man had never had a whore and the ideas he had about them came from literature and hearsay. So he turned to these ideas and the first thing he recalled was the image of a woman in black underwear (and black stockings) dancing on the shiny top of a piano. In the little hotel room there was no piano, there was only a small table covered with a linen cloth leaning against the wall. He ordered the girl to climb up on it. The girl made a pleading gesture, but the young man said, "You've been paid."

When she saw the look of unshakable obsession in the young man's eyes, she tried to go on with the game, even though she no longer could and no longer knew how. With tears in her eyes she climbed onto the table. The top was scarcely three feet square and one leg was a little bit shorter than the others so that standing on it the girl felt unsteady.

But the young man was pleased with the naked figure, now towering above him, and the girl's shy insecurity merely inflamed his imperiousness. He wanted to see her body in all positions and from all sides, as he imagined other men had seen it and would see it. He was vulgar and lascivious. He used words that she had never heard from him in her life. She wanted to refuse, she wanted to be released from the game. She called him by his first name, but he immediately yelled at her that she had no right to address him so intimately. And so eventually in confusion and on the verge of tears, she obeyed, she bent forward and squatted according to the young man's wishes, saluted, and then wiggled her hips as she did the Twist for him. During a slightly more violent movement, when the cloth slipped beneath her feet and she nearly fell, the young man caught her and dragged her to the bed.

He had intercourse with her. She was glad that at least now finally the unfortunate game would end and they would again be the two people they had been before and would love each other. She wanted to press her mouth against his. But the young man pushed her head away and repeated that he only kissed women he loved. She burst into loud sobs. But she wasn't even allowed to cry, because the young man's furious passion gradually won over her body, which then silenced the complaint of her soul. On the bed there were soon two bodies in perfect harmony, two sensual bodies, alien to each other. This was exactly what the girl had most dreaded all her life and had scrupulously avoided till now: love-making without emotion or love. She knew that she had crossed the forbidden boundary, but she proceeded across it without objections and as a full participant—only somewhere, far off in a corner of her consciousness, did she feel horror at the thought that she had never known such pleasure, never so much pleasure as at this moment—beyond that boundary.

12

Then it was all over. The young man got up off the girl and, reaching out for the long cord hanging over the bed, switched off the light. He didn't want to see the girl's face. He knew that the game was over, but didn't feel like returning to their customary relationship. He feared this return. He lay beside the girl in the dark in such a way that their bodies would not touch.

After a moment he heard her sobbing quietly. The girl's hand diffidently, childishly touched his. It touched, withdrew, then touched again, and then a pleading, sobbing voice broke the silence, calling him by his name and saying, "I am me, I am me . . ."

The young man was silent, he didn't move, and he was aware of the sad emptiness of the girl's assertion, in which the unknown was defined in terms of the same unknown quantity.

And the girl soon passed from sobbing to loud crying and went on endlessly repeating this pitiful tautology: "I am me, I am me, I am me . . ."

The young man began to call compassion to his aid (he had to call it from afar, because it was nowhere near at hand), so as to be able to calm the girl. There were still thirteen days' vacation before them.

Translated by Suzanne Rappaport

Amos Oz

Amos Oz (b.1929) was born in Jerusalem. He studied at Hebrew University and took an M.A. degree from Oxford University. Oz served with an Israeli tank force in the Golan Heights in 1973. At present, he lives on a kibbutz. His books, written in Hebrew, include *The Hill of Evil Counsel* and *Where the Jackels Howl.*

IF THERE IS JUSTICE

Rami Rimon came home for the weekend on leave.

His face was thinner. His skin had shrunk a little. His jaws seemed more prominent. The lines on his face were sharper. His mother's face struggling to get out. Fine creases ringed his mouth. The sun had etched wrinkles round his eyes. Twin furrows ran from his nose to the corners of his mouth.

He was wearing an impeccable greenish uniform, with his beret tucked in his pocket. His stout boots were shod with steel at toe and heel. His sleeves were rolled up to reveal hairy forearms, and his hands were covered with little scars. He was conscious of his manly appearance as he strode slowly across the yard with an air of studied indifference. The men and women he met greeted him warmly. He responded with an offhand nod. There were traces of gun grease under his fingernails, and his left elbow was dressed with a grubby bandage.

When the first tumult of hugs and kisses, received by Rami with a wavering smile, had died down, Fruma said:

"Well, you won't believe it, but I was just thinking of you the moment before you turned up. Mother's intuition."

Rami thought there was nothing strange in that. He had said in his letter that he would come on Friday afternoon, and she knew perfectly well what time the bus came. As he spoke, he put down his shabby kit bag, pulled his shirt outside his trousers, lit a cigarette, and laid a heavy hand on Fruma's shoulder.

"It's good to see you, Mom. I wanted to tell you that I'm really glad to see you again."

Fruma glanced at his dusty boots and said:

"You've lost so much weight."

Rami drew on his cigarette and asked about her health.

"Come inside and have a shower before dinner. You're all sweaty. Would you like a cold drink first? No. A warm drink would be better for you. Wait, though, the first thing is to take you along to the surgery. I want the nurse to have a look at your elbow."

Rami started to explain about the wound. It happened during a bayonet practice; the clumsy oaf of a section commander . . . but Fruma did not let him finish the story.

"There you go dropping your ash on the floor. I've just washed it in your honor. There are four ash trays in the house, and you . . ."

Rami sat down in his filthy clothes on the clean white bedspread and kicked off his boots. Fruma rushed to fetch her husband's old slippers. Her eyes were dry, but she tried to turn her face away from her son to hide the look he disliked so much. Rami, however, pretended not to have seen that strained look, as of a dam about to burst. He lay back on the bed, looked up at the ceiling, drew the ash tray that Fruma had put in his hand closer to him and blew out a puff of smoke.

"The day before yesterday we crossed a river on a rope bridge. Two ropes stretched one above the other, one to walk on and the other to hold. With all our stuff on our backs, spade, blankets, gun, ammunition, the lot. Now, who do you suppose it was who lost his balance and fell in the water? The section commander! We all . . ."

Fruma eyed her son and exclaimed:

"You've lost at least ten pounds. Have you had any lunch? Where? No, you haven't. I'll dash across to the hall and get you something to eat. Just a snack—I'll make you a proper meal when you've had a rest. How about some raw carrot? It's very good for you. Are you sure? I can't force you. All right, then, have a shower and go to sleep. You can eat when you wake up. But perhaps I'd better take you to the surgery right away. Wait a minute. Here's a nice glass of orange juice. Don't argue, drink it."

"I jumped in the water and fished him out," Rami continued. "Then I had to dive in again to look for his rifle. Poor wretch! It was hilarious. It wasn't his first accident, though. Once, on an exercise . . ."

"You need some new socks. They're all falling apart," Fruma remarked as she pulled his dirty laundry out of the kit bag.

"Once, on an exercise, he fired his submachine gun by accident. Nearly killed the battalion commander. He's the clumsiest fool you can imagine. You can tell what he's like from his name. He's called Zalman Zulman. I've written a song about him, and we sing it all day long. Listen."

"But they don't feed you there. And you didn't write every other day, as you promised. But I saw in the letter box that you wrote to Noga Harish. That's life. Your mother works her fingers to the bone, and some child comes and collects the honey. It doesn't matter now. There's something I must know: Did she answer your letter? No? Just as I thought. You don't know what she's like. It was just as well you ditched her. Everybody knows what she is. The mistress of a man who's old enough to be her grandfather. It's disgusting. Disgusting. Have you got enough razor blades? It's disgusting, I tell you."

"Is it true they're starting to work the Camel's Field? That's going to cause a flare-up, all right. Provided, of course, the powers that be don't get cold feet. You know, Jewish sentimentality and all that. My buddies say . . ."

"Go and have a shower. The water's just right now. No, I heard every word. Test me. 'Jewish sentimentality.' There aren't many boys of your age with such an independent way of thinking. After your shower you can have a nap. Meanwhile, I'll ask the nurse to come here. That wound looks very nasty. You've got to have it seen to."

"By the way, Mom, did you just say that she . . ."

"Yes, son?"

"All right. Never mind. It doesn't matter now."

"Tell me, tell me what you need. I'm not tired. I can do anything you want me to."

"No, thanks, I don't need anything. I just wanted to say something, but it's not important. It's irrelevant. I've forgotten. Stop running around. I can't bear it. We'll talk this evening. Meanwhile, you must have a rest, too."

"Me! I'll rest in my grave. I don't need to rest. I'm not tired. When you were a baby, you had something wrong with your ears. A chronic infection. There weren't any antibiotics then. You cried all night, night after night. You were in pain. And you've always been a sensitive boy. I rocked your cradle all night, night after night, and sang you songs. One does everything for children, without counting the cost. You won't repay me. You'll repay it to your own children. I won't be here any more, but you'll be a good father, because you're so sensitive. You don't think about rest when you're doing something for your children. How old were you then? You've forgotten all about it. It was the time when Yoash started going to school, so it must have been when you were eighteen months old. You were always a delicate child. Here am I rambling on, and you need to sleep. Go to sleep now."

"By the way, Mom, if you're going to the surgery could you bring me some corn ointment. You won't forget, will you?"

At five o'clock Rami woke up, put on a clean white shirt and gray trousers, quietly helped himself to a snack, and then went to the basketball field. On the way he met Einav, limping awkwardly. She asked how he was. He said he was fine. She asked if it was a hard life. He said he was ready to face any hardship. She asked if his mother was pleased with him and answered her own question:

"Of course Fruma's pleased with you. You're so bronzed and handsome."

The field was floodlit, but the light was not noticeable in the bright twilight. The only living souls there were Oren's gang. Rami put his hands in his pockets and stood for a while without doing or saying anything. The Sabbath will go by. Empty. Without anything happening. With mother. Sticky. What do I need? A cigarette. That thin boy playing by himself over there in the corner is called Ido Zohar. Once I caught him sitting in the common room at night writing a poem. What was I saying? A cigarette.

Rami put the cigarette to his mouth and two planes roared by, shattering the Sabbatical calm, hidden in the twilight glow. The dying sun struck sparks off their fuselage. The metal shone back dazzlingly. In a flash Rami realized that they were not our planes. They had the enemy's markings on their wings. An excited shout burst from his throat.

"Theirs!"

Instinctively he looked down, just long enough to hear Oren's confused cry, but by the time he looked up again the drama was almost over. The enemy planes had turned tail and were fleeing from other planes that were approaching powerfully from the southwest, evidently trying to block their escape. Instantly, dark shapes fell through the air toward the orchards to the north. Both planes had jettisoned the spare fuel tanks fixed to their wings to speed their flight. Rami clenched his fists and growled through his teeth, "Let them have it." Before he had finished there was an answering burst of gunfire. Lightning flashed. After what seemed a long interval, there came a dull roll of thunder. The fate of the raid was settled in an instant. The enemy planes disappeared over the mountains, one of them trailing a cloud of white smoke mixed with gray. Their pursuers paused, circled the valley twice like angry hounds, then vanished into the darkening sky.

Oren shouted jubilantly:

"We hit one! We smashed one! We brought one down!"

And Rami Rimon, like a child, not like a soldier, hugged Oren Geva and exclaimed:

"I hope they burn! I hope they burn to death!"

He pounded Oren's ribs exultantly with his fists until Oren drew away groaning with pain. Rami was seized by demented joy.

His joy accompanied him to the dining hall, where a spirit of noisy excitement reigned. He made his way among the tables to where Noga Harish stood in her best dress, looking at the notice board. He put his hands on her shoulders and whispered in her ear:

"Well, silly girl, did you see or didn't you?"

Noga turned to face him with a condescending smile.

"Good Sabbath, Rami. You're very brown. It suits you. You look happy."

"I . . . I saw it all. From beginning to end. I was up at the basketball field. Suddenly I heard a noise to the east, and I realized at once that . . ."

"You're like my little brother. You're cute. You're happy."

These remarks encouraged Rami. He spoke up boldly:

"Shall we go outside? Will you come outside with me?"

Noga thought for a moment. Then she smiled inwardly, with her eyes, not with her mouth.

"Why not?" she said.

"Come on then," said Rami, and took hold of her arm. Almost at once he let it go.

When they were outside the dining hall, Noga said:

"Where shall we go?"

Strangely enough, at that moment Noga remembered something she had forgotten: Rami's full name was Avraham. Avraham Rominov.

"Anywhere," Rami said. "Let's go."

Noga suggested they sit down on the yellow bench, facing the door of the dining hall. Rami was embarrassed. People would see them there, he said. And stare at them. And talk.

Noga smiled again, and again she asked calmly, "Why not?"

Rami could find no answer to her question. He crossed his legs, took a cigarette out of his shirt pocket, tapped it three times on his matchbox, stuck it in the corner of his mouth, struck a match, shielded the flame with both hands even though there was no wind, inhaled deeply with half-closed eyes, blew out a long stream of smoke, and when all this was done, lowered his eyes to the ground once more. Finally, he gave her a sidelong glance and began:

"Well? What have you got to say for yourself?"

Noga replied that she hadn't been going to say anything. On the contrary, she thought it was he who was going to do the talking.

"Oh, nothing special. Just . . . What do you expect me to do?" he suddenly burst out violently. "Spend the whole evening, the whole Sabbath, my whole leave with my mother, like some mother's darling?"

"Why not? She's missed you badly."

"Why not? Because . . . All right. I can see I bore you. Don't think I can't live without you. I can get on quite well without you. Do you think I can't?"

Noga said she was sure he could manage perfectly well without her.

They fell silent.

Hasia Ramigolski and Esther Klieger-Isarov came toward them, chatting in Yiddish and laughing. When they caught sight of Noga and Rami their conversation stopped dead. As they walked past, Hasia said:

"Good evening. Shabbat Shalom." She dwelt suggestively on the stressed syllables.

Rami grunted, but Noga smiled and said gently:

"A very good evening to you both."

Rami said nothing for a while. Then he murmured:

"Well?"

"I'm listening."

"I hear they're going to start working on the hill," Rami said. "There's going to be trouble."

"It's so pointless."

Rami quickly changed the subject. He told the story of his section commander who had fallen in the water while trying to demonstrate how to cross a river on a rope bridge. He went on to say that it wasn't the poor fool's first accident. "Once, on an exercise, he accidentally fired his submachine gun and nearly killed the battalion commander. You can tell what he's like from his name. He's called Zalman Zulman, of all things. I've written a rhyme about him:

Zalman Zulman's full of fun,
Always letting off his gun.
Zalman Zulman lost his grip,
Took an unexpected dip.
Zalman Zulman . . .

"Just a minute. Does he play an instrument?"

"Who?"

"Zalman. The man you were talking about. What's the matter with your elbow?"

"What's that got to do with it?" Rami asked indignantly.

"With what?"

"With what we were talking about."

"You were telling me about someone called Zalman. I asked if he played an instrument. You haven't answered my question."

"But I don't see what . . ."

"You're very brown. It suits you."

"It's hardly surprising. We train all day in the sun. Of course we get brown. Listen: we went on a fifty-mile route march, with all the kit, gun, pack, spade, and all at the trot. Eight of the people in my squad . . ."

"Chilly, don't you think?"

". . . collapsed on the way. And we had to carry them on stretchers. I . . ."

"I'm cold. Couldn't you finish the story tomorrow? If you don't mind terribly."

"What's the matter?" Rami considered, and then asked thickly, "What's up? Is somebody waiting for you? Are you rushing off to . . . to keep an appointment?"

"Yes. I've got to take my father his dinner. He isn't well."

"What, again?" Rami asked absently. Noga explained that he had a pain in his chest and the doctor had ordered him to go to bed.

"Next week he's got to go and have an examination. That's all. Shall we meet here again tomorrow afternoon?"

Rami did not answer. He lit another cigarette and threw the lighted match away behind the bench. Noga said good night and started to go. Then she stopped, turned, and said:

"Don't smoke too much."

At that moment five steps separated them. Rami asked irritably why she should care whether he smoked a lot or a little. Noga ignored his question and said:

"You're very brown. It suits you. Good night."

Rami said nothing. He sat alone on the bench until the dancing started in the square, as it did every Friday night at a quarter past nine.

When it was over, shortly before midnight, he set off for his mother's room. He changed his course, however, because he met Dafna Isarov, who asked him if he was going home to bed already, and Rami thought he detected a sneer in her voice. So he turned off the path. His feet guided him toward the cow shed, where he had worked before he was called up. And as he walked he talked to himself.

This could never have happened to Yoash. It's happened to me, though. Women understand only one language, brute force. But, as mother said, I was always a delicate child. Hell. Now they're laughing. Everybody wants something bad to happen to someone else so as to make life more interesting. It's like that everywhere; it's like that on the kibbutz and it's even like that in the army. You're a child you're a child you're a child. You're like my little brother. Maybe being brown does suit me, but it hasn't got me anywhere. She didn't insult me for once. She didn't even call me a horse. What did she do to me tonight, how did she make fun of me? My Rami is a delicate, sensitive boy. I wish I could die. That'd show them. I can bend this sprinkler with my bare hands. That'll drive Theodor Herzl Goldring mad. I've got stronger hands than Yoash. If only he weren't dead, I'd show him. Where am I going? Walking around like some Jack looking for his Jill. Leaping on the mountains, skipping in the hills, as that filthy old lecher would say. People like that ought to be put down. Like Arabs. Punch him in the face, he raises his hands to protect himself, you hit him in the stomach and give him a kick for good measure. All over. Here we are at the cow shed. Hey, Titan, good bull. Are you awake? Bulls sleep standing up because they can't lie down because of the iron ring. If they come to slaughter you, Titan, don't let them. Don't give in. Show your mettle. Don't be a ghetto bull. Give them a *corrida*. We mustn't give in without a struggle. We must be strong and quick and light and violent like a jet fighter. Swoop and dart and turn and soar like a knife flashing through the sky like a fighter. A fighter is such a powerful thing. I could have been a pilot, but Mother.

Strange that the moon is shining. The moon does strange things. Changes things strangely. Changes the colors of things. Silver. My Rami is a delicate sensitive child Rami writes poems like Izo Zohar he loves nature hell he loves plants and animals hope they burn to death. Her father has a pain in his chest. It's because of old Berger. Dirty old man. Her father taught us a poem by Bialik once, called "The Slaughter," where it says that there is no justice in this world. It's true. It's a ghetto poem, but it's true. He's lived his life, he's got grown-up children, he's found his niche. Why did he steal her from me? What have I done to him? And she said I was brown and handsome. If I'm brown and handsome, and he's old and fat, then why.

When I die, she'll know. It'll shatter her. The moon colors everything white. Silver. Listen, Noga, listen. I've also got a pain in my chest, I'm also in pain, so why don't you. I make fun of Zalman Zulman, she makes fun of me, they all make fun of me. It shows there isn't any justice in the world, only slaughter, Titan, worse than anything the Devil could invent. That's from the same poem. The man who's being slaughtered starts thinking about justice. The man who's slaughtering him thinks only about violence. My mistake was not to use force on her. Why, Titan, why didn't I use force, do you know why? I'll tell you. Because my Rami is a delicate boy curse them he loves nature hope they burn he loves plants and animals filthy whores. That sounds like planes overhead. It's after midnight. I love these planes, roaring along without lights. There's going to be a big war. I'll die. Then they'll know.

The fish ponds. A light in Grisha's hut. A pressure lamp. I can hear Grisha's voice. In the boat. Shouting to his fishermen. He's been in three wars and he's come out alive.

Maybe Dafna, his daughter. Ridiculous. They'd laugh. What's in this filthy shed? Barrels. Sacks of fish food. The fishermen's supper. If they find me here. Grisha's belt. A pistol. It's a revolver. Fancy leaving a revolver in an empty shed. They'll be coming back to eat soon. They'll laugh, they'll laugh. They'll say I went for a walk to look for inspiration. I know how it works. It has a revolving drum with six chambers. You put a bullet in each chamber. After each shot the drum revolves and brings another bullet in line with the barrel. That's how the revolver works. Now let's see how Rami Rimon works. A trial. Without a judge. I'm the judge. Now let's begin.

Rami takes a bullet out of the leather holster, a yellow metal case containing a little brown metal projectile. First of all, he puts the bullet in his mouth. A sharp, metallic taste. Then he puts the bullet in one of the chambers. He spins the drum without looking, because luck must be blind. He puts the gun to his temple. The chances are five to one. He squeezes the trigger. A dry thud. Rami inserts a second bullet. Spins the blind drum. Four to two. Gun to temple. Squeezes. Dry thud. Maybe I'm being silly. We'll soon know, Judge. I'm not trying to kill myself. It's only an experiment. Up to five. A delicate sensitive child couldn't do this. A third bullet. Blind spin. Cold damp hand. I've touched something damp. If I can do this, I'm not a delicate sensitive child. Up to five. Gun to temple. Squeeze the trigger. Dry thud. I'm past halfway. Two more tries. Fourth bullet. Now the odds are against me. Now comes the test. Watch carefully, Judge.

Spin. Slowly. The drum, slowly. Without looking. Slowly. Temple. You're crazy. But you're no coward. Slowly squeeze. It's cold here.

Now the fifth. Last one. Like an injection. Delicate sensitive child's trembling. Why? Nothing will happen because nothing's happened so far, even though according to the odds I should have died with the fourth bullet. Don't tremble, dear little delicate child who cried all night with earache, don't tremble, think of Grisha Isarov who's come out of three wars alive. Yoash wouldn't have trembled, because he was Yoash. Little ghetto boy, with a little cap and a gray coat and side curls. I want to know how many I. Not to kill myself. Four. That's enough. Madness to go on. No, we said five—five let it be. Don't change your mind, coward, don't lie, you said five, not four. Five let it be. Put the gun to your temple. Now squeeze, horse, squeeze, you're a ghetto child, you're a little boy, you're my little brother, squeeze. Wait a moment. I'm allowed to think first. Suppose I die here. She'll know. She'll know I wasn't joking. But they'll say "broken heart" they'll say "unrequited love" they'll say "emotional crisis." Sticky, very sticky. Hell. Squeeze. You won't feel a thing. A bullet in the brain is instant death. No time for pain. And afterward? Like plunging through the sky. An invisible fighter. It doesn't hurt. Perhaps I've already pressed the trigger and died perhaps when you die nothing changes. Other people see a corpse blood bones and you carry on as usual. I can try again. If I press the trigger, it's a sign I'm still alive. Afterward everything will be black and warm. When you die it's warm even though the body gets cold. Warm and safe like under a blanket in winter. And quiet. Squeeze. You've got a chance. Like when we used to play dice when I was little and sometimes I wanted very badly to throw a six and I threw a six. Now I want very badly to press the trigger but my finger won't press. Trembling. Careful you don't press it accidentally. Everything is different when the moon shines yellow. Can hear Grisha cursing next week we're going to the firing range that'll be interesting I'll be top of the class I'm an excellent shot now count up to three and shoot. Eyes open. No. Eyes closed. No. One, two, th- no. Up to ten. One, two, three, four, five, six, seven, eight, nine, t-.

But Rami Rimon did not try his luck the fifth time. He put down the revolver and went out into the fields and wandered about till his feet guided him back to the cow shed. Grisha won't notice. And if he does, he'll have a shock. I forgot to check the most important thing. I didn't look inside the gun to see what would have happened if I'd pressed the fifth time. Better not to know. Some things are better left undone.

A new thought occurred to Rami. It soothed him like a gentle caress. Not all men are born to be heroes. Maybe I wasn't born to be a hero. But in every man there's something special, something that isn't in the other men. In my nature, for instance, there's a certain sensitivity. A capacity to suffer and feel pain. Perhaps I was born to be an artist, or even a doctor. Some women go for doctors and others go for artists. Men aren't all cast in the same mold. It's true, I'm not Yoash. But Yoash wasn't me. I've got some things he didn't have. A painter, perhaps.

It'll be morning soon. Planes in the sky. Sad Zalman Zulman's full of fun, always letting off his gun. Zalman Zulman lost his grip, took an unexpected dip. Zalman Zulman, whore like me, looking for justice in the w.c. Zalman Zulman go to bed, time to rest your weary head.

I composed the poem. I can abolish it. It's an abolished poem.

Translated by Nicholas de Lange, assisted by the author

Taieb Saleh

Taieb Saleh (b.1929) was born in the northern province of the Sudan. He studied at Khartoum as well as at London University. While living in England, he worked for the B.B.C. Arabic Service, and he has been more recently employed by the Sudan Broadcasting Corporation. His books include a story collection, *The Wedding of Zion,* and the acclaimed novel *Season of Migration to the North.*

A HANDFUL OF DATES

I must have been very young at the time. While I don't remember exactly how old I was, I do remember that when people saw me with my grandfather they would pat me on the head and give my cheek a pinch—things they didn't do to my grandfather. The strange thing was that I never used to go out with my father, rather it was my grandfather who would take me with him wherever he went, except for the mornings when I would go to the mosque to learn the Koran. The mosque, the river and the fields—these were the landmarks in our life. While most of the children of my age grumbled at having to go to the mosque to learn the Koran, I used to love it. The reason was, no doubt, that I was quick at learning by heart and the Sheikh always asked me to stand up and recite the *Chapter of the Merciful* whenever we had visitors, who would pat me on my head and cheek just as people did when they saw me with my grandfather.

Yes, I used to love the mosque, and I loved the river too.

Directly we finished our Koran reading in the morning I would throw down my wooden slate and dart off, quick as a genie, to my mother, hurriedly swallow down my breakfast, and run off for a plunge in the river. When tired of swimming about I would sit on the bank and gaze at the strip of water that wound away eastwards and hid behind a thick wood of acacia trees. I loved to give rein to my imagination and picture to myself a tribe of giants living behind that wood, a people tall and thin with white beards and sharp noses, like my grandfather. Before my grandfather ever replied to my many questions he would rub the tip of his nose with his forefinger; as for his beard, it was soft and luxuriant and as white as cotton-wool—never in my life have I seen anything of a purer whiteness or greater beauty. My grandfather must also have been extremely tall, for I never saw anyone in the whole area address him without having to look up at him, nor did I see him enter a house without having to bend so low that I was put in mind of the way the river would round behind the wood of acacia trees. I loved him and would imagine myself, when I grew to be a man, tall and slender like him, walking along with great strides.

I believed I was his favorite grandchild: no wonder, for my cousins were a stupid bunch and I—so they say—was an intelligent child. I used to know when my grandfather wanted me to laugh, when to be silent; also I would remember the times for his prayers and would bring him his prayer-rug and fill the ewer for his ablutions without his having to ask me. When he had nothing else to do he enjoyed listening to me reciting to him from the Koran in a lilting voice, and I could tell from his face that he was moved.

One day I asked him about our neighbour Masood. I said to my grandfather: 'I fancy you don't like our neighbour Masood?'

To which he answered, having rubbed the tip of his nose: 'He's an indolent man and I don't like such people.'

I said to him: 'What's an indolent man?'

My grandfather lowered his head for a moment, then looking across at the wide expanse of field, he said: 'Do you see it stretching out from the edge of the desert up to the Nile bank? A hundred feddans. Do you see all those date palms? And those trees—*sant,* acacia, and *sayal?* All this fell into Masood's lap, was inherited by him from his father.'

Taking advantage of the silence that had descended upon my grandfather, I turned my gaze from him to the vast area defined by his words. 'I don't care,' I told myself, 'who owns those date palms, those trees or this black, cracked earth—all I know is that it's the arena for my dreams and my playground.'

My grandfather then continued: 'Yes, my boy, forty years ago all this belonged to Masood—two-thirds of it is now mine.'

This was news to me, for I had imagined that the land had belonged to my grandfather ever since God's Creation.

'I didn't own a single feddan when I first set foot in this village. Masood was then the owner of all these riches. The position has changed now, though, and I think that before Allah calls me to Him I shall have bought the remaining third as well.'

I do not know why it was I felt fear at my grandfather's words—and pity for our neighbour Masood. How I wished my grandfather wouldn't do what he'd said! I remembered Masood's singing, his beautiful voice and powerful laugh that resembled the gurgling of water. My grandfather never used to laugh.

I asked my grandfather why Masood had sold his land.

'Women,' and from the way my grandfather pronounced the word I felt that 'women' was something terrible. 'Masood, my boy, was a much-married man. Each time he married he sold me a feddan or two.' I made the quick calculation that Masood must have married some ninety women. Then I remembered his three wives, his shabby appearance, his lame donkey and its dilapidated saddle, his *galabia* with the torn sleeves. I had all but rid my mind of the thoughts that jostled in it when I saw the man approaching us, and my grandfather and I exchanged glances.

'We'll be harvesting the dates today,' said Masood. 'Don't you want to be there?'

I felt, though, that he did not really want my grandfather to attend. My grandfather, however, jumped to his feet and I saw that his eyes sparkled momentarily with an intense brightness. He pulled me by the hand and we went off to the harvesting of Masood's dates.

Someone brought my grandfather a stool covered with an ox-hide, while I remained standing. There was a vast number of people there, but though I knew them all, I found myself for some reason watching Masood: aloof from that great gathering of people he stood as though it were no concern of his, despite the fact that the date palms to be harvested were his own. Sometimes his attention would be caught by the sound of a huge clump of dates crashing down from on high. Once he shouted up at the boy perched on the very summit of the date palm who had begun hacking at a clump with his long, sharp sickle: 'Be careful you don't cut the heart of the palm.'

No one paid any attention to what he said and the boy seated at the very summit of the date palm continued, quickly and energetically, to work away at the branch with his sickle till the clump of dates began to drop like something descending from the heavens.

I, however, had begun to think about Masood's phrase 'the heart of the palm.' I pictured the palm tree as something with feeling, something possessed of a heart that throbbed. I remembered Masood's remark to me when he had once seen me playing about with the branch of a young palm tree: 'Palm trees, my boy, like humans, experience joy and suffering.' And I had felt an inward and unreasoned embarrassment.

When I again looked at the expanse of ground stretching before me I saw my young companions swarming like ants around the trunks of the palm trees, gathering up dates and eating most of them. The dates were collected into high mounds. I saw people coming along and weighing them into measuring bins and pouring them into sacks, of which I counted thirty. The crowd of people broke up, except for Hussein the merchant, Mousa the owner of the field next to ours on the east, and two men I'd never seen before.

I heard a low whistling sound and saw that my grandfather had fallen asleep. Then I noticed that Masood had not changed his stance, except that he had placed a stalk in his mouth and was munching at it like someone surfeited with food who doesn't know what to do with the mouthful he still has.

Suddenly my grandfather woke up, jumped to his feet and walked towards the sacks of dates. He was followed by Hussein the merchant, Mousa the owner of the field next to ours, and the two strangers. I glanced at Masood and saw that he was making his way towards us with extreme slowness, like a man who wants to retreat but whose feet insist on going forward. They formed a circle round the sacks of dates and began examining them, some taking a date or two to eat. My grandfather gave me a fistful, which I began munching. I saw Masood filling the palms of both hands with dates and bringing them up close to his nose, then returning them.

Then I saw them dividing up the sacks between them. Hussein the merchant took ten; each of the strangers took five. Mousa the owner of the field next to ours on the eastern side took five, and my grandfather took five. Understanding nothing, I looked at Masood and saw that his eyes were darting about to left and right like two mice that have lost their way home.

'You're still fifty pounds in debt to me,' said my grandfather to Masood. 'We'll talk about it later.'

Hussein called his assistants and they brought along donkeys, the two strangers produced camels, and the sacks of dates were loaded on to them. One of the donkeys let out a braying which set the camels frothing at the mouth and complaining noisily. I felt myself drawing close to Masood, felt my hand stretch out towards him as though I wanted to touch the hem of his garment. I heard him make a noise in his throat like the rasping of a lamb being slaughtered. For some unknown reason, I experienced a sharp sensation of pain in my chest.

I ran off into the distance. Hearing my grandfather call after me, I hesitated a little, then continued on my way. I felt at that moment that I hated him. Quickening my pace, it was as though I carried within me a secret I wanted to rid myself of. I reached the river bank near the bend it made behind the wood of acacia trees. Then, without knowing why, I put my finger into my throat and spewed up the dates I'd eaten.

Translated by Denys Johnson-Davies

Donald Barthelme

Donald Barthelme (1931–1989) was born in Philadelphia and grew up in Houston, where he attended the University of Houston. He took up writing early, winning high school awards and later working as a reporter. Barthelme's quirky, intelligent, and darkly humorous short stories, many of them published in the *New Yorker,* established his reputation as an original contemporary stylist. He had a flair for composing striking narrative collages, mixing and matching materials from all parts of the cultural spectrum. The stories range from the dark and brooding to the brightly celebratory. Barthelme's collections include *Come Back, Dr. Caligari; Unspeakable Practices, Unnameable Acts;* and *Great Days.*

ME AND MISS MANDIBLE

13 September

Miss Mandible wants to make love to me but she hesitates because I am officially a child; I am, according to the records, according to the gradebook on her desk, according to the card index in the principal's office, eleven years old. There is a misconception here, one that I haven't quite managed to get cleared up yet. I am in fact thirty-five, I've been in the Army, I am six feet one, I have hair in the appropriate places, my voice is a baritone, I know very well what to do with Miss Mandible if she ever makes up her mind.

In the meantime we are studying common fractions. I could, of course, answer all the questions, or at least most of them (there are things I don't remember). But I prefer to sit in this too-small seat with the desktop cramping my thighs and examine the life around me. There are thirty-two in the class, which is launched every morning with the pledge of allegiance to the flag. My own allegiance, at the moment, is divided between Miss Mandible and Sue Ann Brownly, who sits across the aisle from me all day long and is, like Miss Mandible, a fool for love. Of the two I prefer, today, Sue Ann; although between eleven and eleven and a half (she refuses to reveal her exact age) she is clearly a woman, with a woman's disguised aggression and a woman's peculiar contradictions.

15 September

Happily our geography text, which contains maps of all the principal land-masses of the world, is large enough to conceal my clandestine journal-keeping, accomplished in an ordinary black composition book. Every day I must wait until Geography to put down such thoughts as I may have had during the morning about my situation and my fellows. I have tried writing at other times and it does not work. Either the teacher is walking up and down the aisles (during this period, luckily, she sticks close to the map rack in the front of the room) or Bobby Vanderbilt, who sits behind me, is punching me in the kidneys and wanting to know what I am doing. Vanderbilt, I have found out from certain desultory conversations on the playground, is hung up on sports cars, a veteran consumer of *Road & Track*. This explains the continual roaring sounds which seem to emanate from his desk; he is reproducing a record album called *Sounds of Sebring*.

19 September

Only I, at times (only at times), understand that somehow a mistake has been made, that I am in a place where I don't belong. It may be that Miss Mandible also knows this, at some level, but for reasons not fully understood by me she is going along with the game. When I was first assigned to this room I wanted to protest, the error seemed obvious, the stupidest principal could have seen it; but I have come to believe it was deliberate, that I have been betrayed again.

Now it seems to make little difference. This life-role is as interesting as my former life-role, which was that of a claims adjuster for the Great Northern Insurance Company, a position which compelled me to spend my time amid the debris of our civilization: rumpled fenders, roofless sheds, gutted warehouses, smashed arms and legs. After ten years of this one has a tendency to see the world as a vast junkyard, looking at a man and seeing only his (potentially) mangled parts, entering a house only to trace the path of the inevitable fire. Therefore when I was installed here, although I knew an error had been made, I countenanced it, I was shrewd; I was aware that there might well be some kind of advantage to be gained from what seemed a disaster. The role of The Adjuster teaches one much.

22 September

I am being solicited for the volleyball team. I decline, refusing to take unfair profit from my height.

23 September

Every morning the roll is called: Bestvina, Bokenfohr, Broan, Brownly, Cone, Coyle, Crecelius, Darin, Durbin, Geiger, Guiswite, Heckler, Jacobs,

Kleinschmidt, Lay, Logan, Masei, Mitgang, Pfeilsticker. It is like the litany chanted in the dim miserable dawns of Texas by the cadre sergeant of our basic training company.

In the Army, too, I was ever so slightly awry. It took me a fantastically long time to realize what the others grasped almost at once: that much of what we were doing was absolutely pointless, to no purpose. I kept wondering why. Then something happened that proposed a new question. One day we were commanded to whitewash, from the ground to the topmost leaves, all of the trees in our training area. The corporal who relayed the order was nervous and apologetic. Later an off-duty captain sauntered by and watched us, white-splashed and totally weary, strung out among the freakish shapes we had created. He walked away swearing. I understood the principle (orders are orders), but I wondered: Who decides?

29 September

Sue Ann is a wonder. Yesterday she viciously kicked my ankle for not paying attention when she was attempting to pass me a note during History. It is swollen still. But Miss Mandible was watching me, there was nothing I could do. Oddly enough Sue Ann reminds me of the wife I had in my former role, while Miss Mandible seems to be a child. She watches me constantly, trying to keep sexual significance out of her look; I am afraid the other children have noticed. I have already heard, on that ghostly frequency that is the medium of classroom communication, the words "*Teacher's pet!*"

2 October

Sometimes I speculate on the exact nature of the conspiracy which brought me here. At times I believe it was instigated by my wife of former days, whose name was . . . I am only pretending to forget. I know her name very well, as well as I know the name of my former motor oil (Quaker State) or my old Army serial number (US 54109268). Her name was Brenda.

7 October

Today I tiptoed up to Miss Mandible's desk (when there was no one else in the room) and examined its surface. Miss Mandible is a clean-desk teacher, I discovered. There was nothing except her gradebook (the one in which I exist as a sixth-grader) and a text, which was open at a page headed *Making the Processes Meaningful.* I read: "Many pupils enjoy working fractions when they understand what they are doing. They have confidence in their ability to take the right steps and to obtain correct answers. However, to give the subject full social significance, it is necessary that many realistic situations requiring the processes be found. Many interesting and lifelike problems involving the use of fractions should be solved . . ."

8 October

I am not irritated by the feeling of having been through all this before. Things are done differently now. The children, moreover, are in some ways different from those who accompanied me on my first voyage through the elementary schools: "*They have confidence in their ability to take the right steps and to obtain correct answers.*" This is surely true. When Bobby Vanderbilt, who sits behind me and has the great tactical advantage of being able to maneuver in my disproportionate shadow, wishes to bust a classmate in the mouth he first asks Miss Mandible to lower the blind, saying that the sun hurts his eyes. When she does so, *bip!* My generation would never have been able to con authority so easily.

13 October

I misread a clue. Do not misunderstand me: it was a tragedy only from the point of view of the authorities. I conceived that it was my duty to obtain satisfaction for the injured, for an elderly lady (not even one of our policyholders, but a claimant against Big Ben Transfer & Storage, Inc.) from the company. The settlement was $165,000; the claim, I still believe, was just. But without my encouragement Mrs. Bichek would never have had the self-love to prize her injury so highly. The company paid, but its faith in me, in my efficacy in the role, was broken. Henry Goodykind, the district manager, expressed this thought in a few not altogether unsympathetic words, and told me at the same time that I was to have a new role. The next thing I knew I was here, at Horace Greeley Elementary, under the lubricious eye of Miss Mandible.

17 October

Today we are to have a fire drill. I know this because I am a Fire Marshal, not only for our room but for the entire right wing of the second floor. This distinction, which was awarded shortly after my arrival, is interpreted by some as another mark of my somewhat dubious relations with our teacher. My armband, which is red and decorated with white felt letters reading FIRE, sits on the little shelf under my desk, next to the brown paper bag containing the lunch I carefully make for myself each morning. One of the advantages of packing my own lunch (I have no one to pack it for me) is that I am able to fill it with things I enjoy. The peanut butter sandwiches that my mother made in my former existence, many years ago, have been banished in favor of ham and cheese. I have found that my diet has mysteriously adjusted to my new situation; I no longer drink, for instance, and when I smoke, it is in the boys' john, like everybody else. When school is out I hardly smoke at all. It is only in the matter of sex that I feel my own true age; this is apparently something that, once learned, can never be forgotten. I live in fear that Miss Mandible will one day keep me after school, and when we are alone, create a compromising situation. To avoid this I have become a model pupil: another reason for the pronounced dislike I have encountered in certain quarters. But I cannot deny that I am singed by those long glances from the vicinity of the chalkboard; Miss Mandible is in many ways; notably about the bust, a very tasty piece.

24 October

There are isolated challenges to my largeness, to my dimly realized position in the class as Gulliver. Most of my classmates are polite about this matter, as they would be if I had only one eye, or wasted, metal-wrapped legs. I am viewed as a mutation of some sort but essentially a peer. However Harry Broan, whose father has made himself rich manufacturing the Broan Bathroom Vent (with which Harry is frequently reproached; he is always being asked how things are in Ventsville), today inquired if I wanted to fight. An interested group of his followers had gathered to observe this suicidal undertaking. I replied that I didn't feel quite up to it, for which he was obviously grateful. We are now friends forever. He has given me to understand privately that he can get me all the bathroom vents I will ever need, at a ridiculously modest figure.

25 October

"*Many interesting and lifelike problems involving the use of fractions should be solved . . .*" The theorists fail to realize that everything that is either interesting or lifelike in the classroom proceeds from what they would probably call interpersonal relations: Sue Ann Brownly kicking me in the ankle. How lifelike, how womanlike, is her tender solicitude after the deed! Her pride in my newly acquired limp is transparent; everyone knows that she has set her mark upon me, that it is a victory in her unequal struggle with Miss Mandible for my great, overgrown heart. Even Miss Mandible knows, and counters in perhaps the only way she can, with sarcasm. "Are you wounded, Joseph?" Conflagrations smolder behind her eyelids, yearning for the Fire Marshal clouds her eyes. I mumble that I have bumped my leg.

30 October

I return again and again to the problem of my future.

4 November

The underground circulating library has brought me a copy of *Movie-TV Secrets,* the multicolor cover blazoned with the headline "Debbie's Date Insults Liz!" It is a gift from Frankie Randolph, a rather plain girl who until today has had not one word for me, passed on via Bobby Vanderbilt. I nod and smile over my shoulder in acknowledgment; Frankie hides her head under her desk. I have seen these magazines being passed around among the girls (sometimes one of the boys will condescend to inspect a particularly lurid cover). Miss Mandible confiscates them whenever she finds one. I leaf through *Movie-TV Secrets* and get an eyeful. "The exclusive picture on these pages isn't what it seems. We know how it looks and we know what the gossipers will do. So in the interests of a nice guy, we're publishing the facts first. Here's what really happened!" The picture shows a rising young movie idol in bed, pajama-ed and bleary-eyed, while an equally blowzy young woman looks startled beside him. I am happy to know that the picture is not really what it seems; it seems to be nothing less than divorce evidence.

What do these hipless eleven-year-olds think when they come across, in the same magazine, the full-page ad for Maurice de Paree, which features "Hip Helpers" or what appear to be padded rumps? ("A real undercover agent that adds appeal to those hips and derriere, both!") If they cannot decipher the language the illustrations leave nothing to the imagination. "Drive him frantic . . ." the copy continues. Perhaps this explains Bobby Vanderbilt's preoccupation with Lancias and Maseratis; it is a defense against being driven frantic.

Sue Ann has observed Frankie Randolph's overture, and catching my eye, she pulls from her satchel no less than seventeen of these magazines, thrusting them at me as if to prove that anything any of her rivals has to offer, she can top. I shuffle through them quickly, noting the broad editorial perspective:

"Debbie's Kids Are Crying"
"Eddie Asks Debbie: Will You . . . ?"
"The Nightmares Liz Has About Eddie!"
"The Things Debbie Can Tell About Eddie"
"The Private Life of Eddie and Liz"
"Debbie Gets Her Man Back?"
"A New Life for Liz"
"Love Is a Tricky Affair"
"Eddie's Taylor-Made Love Nest"
"How Liz Made a Man of Eddie"
"Are They Planning to Live Together?"
"Isn't It Time to Stop Kicking Debbie Around?"
"Debbie's Dilemma"
"Eddie Becomes a Father Again"
"Is Debbie Planning to Re-wed?"
"Can Liz Fulfill Herself?"
"Why Debbie Is Sick of Hollywood"

Who are these people, Debbie, Eddie, Liz, and how did they get themselves in such a terrible predicament? Sue Ann knows, I am sure; it is obvious that she has been studying their history as a guide to what she may expect when she is suddenly freed from this drab, flat classroom.

I am angry and I shove the magazines back at her with not even a whisper of thanks.

5 November

The sixth grade at Horace Greeley Elementary is a furnace of love, love, love. Today it is raining, but inside the air is heavy and tense with passion. Sue Ann is absent; I suspect that yesterday's exchange has driven her to her bed. Guilt hangs about me. She is not responsible, I know, for what she reads, for the models proposed to her by a venal publishing industry; I should not have been so harsh. Perhaps it is only the flu.

Nowhere have I encountered an atmosphere as charged with aborted sexuality as this. Miss Mandible is helpless; nothing goes right today. Amos Darin has been found drawing a dirty picture in the cloakroom. Sad and inaccurate, it was offered not as a sign of something else but as an act of love in itself. It has excited even those who have not seen it, even those who saw but understood only that it was dirty. The room buzzes with imperfectly comprehended titillation. Amos stands by the door, waiting to be taken to the principal's office. He wavers between fear and enjoyment of his temporary celebrity. From time to time Miss Mandible looks at me reproachfully, as if blaming me for the uproar. But I did not create this atmosphere, I am caught in it like all the others.

8 November

Everything is promised my classmates and me, most of all the future. We accept the outrageous assurances without blinking.

9 November

I have finally found the nerve to petition for a larger desk. At recess I can hardly walk; my legs do not wish to uncoil themselves. Miss Mandible says she will take it up with the custodian. She is worried about the excellence of my themes. Have I, she asks, been receiving help? For an instant I am on the brink of telling her my story. Something, however, warns me not to attempt it. Here I am safe, I have a place; I do not wish to entrust myself once more to the whimsy of authority. I resolve to make my themes less excellent in the future.

11 November

A ruined marriage, a ruined adjusting career, a grim interlude in the Army when I was almost not a person. This is the sum of my existence to date, a dismal total. Small wonder that re-education seemed my only hope.

It is clear even to me that I need reworking in some fundamental way. How efficient is the society that provides thus for the salvage of its clinkers!

14 November

The distinction between children and adults, while probably useful for some purposes, is at bottom a specious one, I feel. There are only individual egos, crazy for love.

15 November

The custodian has informed Miss Mandible that our desks are all the correct size for sixth-graders, as specified by the Board of Estimate and furnished the schools by the Nu-Art Educational Supply Corporation of Englewood, California. He has pointed out that if the desk size is correct, then the pupil size must be incorrect. Miss Mandible, who has already arrived at this conclusion, refuses to press the matter further. I think I know why. An appeal to the administration might result in my removal from the class, in a transfer to some sort of setup for "exceptional children." This would be a disaster of the first magnitude. To sit in a room with child geniuses (or, more likely, children who are "retarded") would shrivel me in a week. Let my experience here be that of the common run, I say; let me be, please God, typical.

20 November

We read signs as promises. Miss Mandible understands by my great height, by my resonant vowels, that I will one day carry her off to bed. Sue Ann interprets these same signs to mean that I am unique among her male acquaintances, therefore most desirable, therefore her special property as is everything that is Most Desirable. If neither of these propositions works out then life has broken faith with them.

I myself, in my former existence, read the company motto ("Here to Help in Time of Need") as a description of the duty of the adjuster, drastically mislocating the company's deepest concerns. I believed that because I had obtained a wife who was made up of wife-signs (beauty, charm, softness, perfume, cookery) I had found love. Brenda, reading the same signs that have now misled Miss Mandible and Sue Ann Brownly, felt she had been promised that she would never be bored again. All of us, Miss Mandible, Sue Ann, myself, Brenda, Mr. Goodykind, still believe that the American flag betokens a kind of general righteousness.

But I say, looking about me in this incubator of future citizens, that signs are signs, and some of them are lies.

23 November

It may be that my experience as a child will save me after all. If only I can remain quietly in this classroom, making my notes while Napoleon plods through Russia in the droning voice of Harry Broan, reading aloud from our History text. All of the mysteries that perplexed me as an adult have their origins here. But Miss Mandible will not permit me to remain ungrown. Her hands rest on my shoulders too warmly, and for too long.

7 December

It is the pledges that this place makes to me, pledges that cannot be redeemed, that will confuse me later and make me feel I am not *getting anywhere*. Everything is presented as the result of some knowable process; if I wish to arrive at four I get there by way of two and two. If I wish to burn Moscow the route I must travel has already been marked out by another visitor. If, like Bobby Vanderbilt, I yearn for the wheel of the Lancia 2.4-liter coupé, I have only to go through the appropriate process, that is, get the money. And if it is money itself that I desire, I have only to *make* it. All of these goals are equally beautiful in the sight of the Board of Estimate; the proof is all around us, in the no-nonsense ugliness of this steel and glass building, in the straightline matter-of-factness with which Miss Mandible handles some of our less reputable wars. Who points out that arrangements sometimes slip, that errors are made, that signs are misread? "*They have confidence in their ability to take the right steps and to obtain correct answers*."

8 December

My enlightenment is proceeding wonderfully.

9 December

Disaster once again. Tomorrow I am to be sent to a doctor, for observation. Sue Ann Brownly caught Miss Mandible and me in the cloakroom, during recess, Miss Mandible's naked legs in a scissors around my waist. For a moment I thought Sue Ann was going to choke. She ran out of the room weeping, straight for the principal's office, certain now which of us was Debbie, which Eddie, which Liz. I am sorry to be the cause of her disillusionment, but I know that she will recover. Miss Mandible is ruined but fulfilled. Although she will be charged with contributing to the delinquency of a minor, she seems at peace, *her* promise has been kept. She knows now that everything she has been told about life, about America, is true.

I have tried to convince the school authorities that I am a minor only in a very special sense, that I am in fact mostly to blame—but it does no good. They are as dense as ever. My contemporaries are astounded that I present myself as anything other than an innocent victim. Like the Old Guard marching through the Russian drifts, the class marches to the conclusion that truth is punishment.

Bobby Vanderbilt has given me his copy of *Sounds of Sebring,* in farewell.

Alice Munro

Alice Munro (b.1931) was born in rural Ontario, Canada. She discovered her ambition to write fiction early, but it would be many years—after college, and years of raising children—before her first collection of stories, *Dance of the Happy Shades,* would be published. The book won a prestigious Canadian award and established her as one of her country's most talented story writers. (Although Munro has written one novel, *Lives of Girls and Women*, she feels that her talents favor the short story form.)

Munro writes with great sensuality and vigor about the country of her youth, and captures the turmoil and poignancy of growing up. Few contemporary writers can evoke so convincingly the specific density of place.

ROYAL BEATINGS

R*oyal Beating*. That was Flo's promise. You are going to get one Royal Beating.

The word Royal lolled on Flo's tongue, took on trappings. Rose had a need to picture things, to pursue absurdities, that was stronger than the need to stay out of trouble, and instead of taking this threat to heart she pondered: how is a beating royal? She came up with a tree-lined avenue, a crowd of formal spectators, some white horses and black slaves. Someone knelt, and the blood came leaping out like banners. An occasion both savage and splendid. In real life they didn't approach such dignity, and it was only Flo who tried to supply the event with some high air of necessity and regret. Rose and her father soon got beyond anything presentable.

Her father was king of the royal beatings. Those Flo gave never amounted to much; they were quick cuffs and slaps dashed off while her attention remained elsewhere. You get out of my road, she would say. You mind your own business. You take that look off your face.

They lived behind a store in Hanratty, Ontario. There were four of them: Rose, her father, Flo, Rose's young half brother Brian. The store was really a house, bought by Rose's father and mother when they married and set up here in the furniture and upholstery repair business. Her mother could do upholstery. From both parents Rose should have inherited clever hands, a quick sympathy with materials, an eye for the nicest turns of mending, but she hadn't. She was clumsy, and when something broke she couldn't wait to sweep it up and throw it away.

Her mother had died. She said to Rose's father during the afternoon, "I have a feeling that is so hard to describe. It's like a boiled egg in my chest, with the shell left on." She died before night, she had a blood clot on her lung. Rose was a baby in a basket at the time, so of course could not remember any of this. She heard it from Flo, who must have heard it from her father. Flo came along soon afterward, to take over Rose in the basket, marry her father, open up the front room to make a grocery store. Rose, who had known the house only as a store, who had known only Flo for a mother, looked back on the sixteen or so months her parents spent here as an orderly, far gentler and more ceremonious time, with little touches of affluence. She had nothing to go on but some egg cups her mother had bought, with a pattern of vines and birds on them, delicately drawn as if with red ink; the pattern was beginning to wear away. No books or clothes or pictures of her mother remained. Her father must have got rid of them, or else Flo would. Flo's only story about her mother, the one about her death, was oddly grudging. Flo liked the details of a death: the things people said, the way they protested or tried to get out of bed or swore or laughed (some did those things), but when she said that Rose's mother mentioned a hard-boiled egg in her chest she made the comparison sound slightly foolish, as if her mother really was the kind of person who might think you could swallow an egg whole.

Her father had a shed out behind the store, where he worked at this furniture repairing and restoring. He caned chair seats and backs, mended wickerwork, filled cracks, put legs back on, all most admirably and skillfully and cheaply. That was his pride: to startle people with such fine work, such moderate, even ridiculous charges. During the Depression people could not afford to pay more, perhaps, but he continued the practice through the war, through the years of prosperity after the war, until he died. He never discussed with Flo what he charged or what was owing. After he died she had to go out and unlock the shed and take all sorts of scraps of paper and torn envelopes from the big wicked-looking hooks that were his files. Many of these she found were not accounts or receipts at all but records of the weather, bits of information about the garden, things he had been moved to write down.

> Ate new potatoes 25th June. Record.
> Dark Day, 1880's nothing supernatural. Clouds of ash from forest fires.
> Aug 16, 1938. Giant thunderstorm in evng. Lightning str. Pres. Church, Turberry Twp. Will of God?
> Scald strawberries to remove acid.
> All things are alive. Spinoza.

Flo thought Spinoza must be some new vegetable he planned to grow, like broccoli or eggplant. He would often try some new thing. She showed the scrap of paper to Rose and asked, did she know what Spinoza was? Rose did know, or had an idea—she was in her teens by that time—but she replied that she did not. She had reached an age where she thought she could not stand to know any more, about her father, or about Flo; she pushed any discovery aside with embarrassment and dread.

There was a stove in the shed, and many rough shelves covered with cans of paint and varnish, shellac and turpentine, jars of soaking brushes and also some dark sticky bottles of cough medicine. Why should a man who coughed constantly, whose lungs took in a whiff of gas in the War (called, in Rose's earliest childhood, not the First, but the Last, War) spend all his days breathing fumes of paint and turpentine? At the time, such questions were not asked as often as they are now. On the bench outside Flo's store several old men from the neighborhood sat gossiping, drowsing, in the warm weather, and some of these old men coughed all the time too. The fact is they were dying, slowly and discreetly, of what was called, without any particular sense of grievance, "the foundry disease." They had worked all their lived at the foundry in town, and now they sat still, with their wasted yellow faces, coughing, chuckling, drifting into aimless obscenity on the subject of women walking by, or any young girl on a bicycle.

From the shed came not only coughing, but speech, a continual muttering, reproachful or encouraging, usually just below the level at which separate words could be made out. Slowing down when her father was at a tricky piece of work, taking on a cheerful speed when he was doing something less demanding, sandpapering or painting. Now and then some words would break through and hang clear and nonsensical on the air. When he realized they were out, there would be a quick bit of cover-up coughing, a swallowing, an alert, unusual silence.

"Macaroni, pepperoni, Botticelli, beans—"

What could that mean? Rose used to repeat such things to herself. She could never ask him. The person who spoke these words and the person who spoke to her as her father were not the same, though they seemed to occupy the same space. It would be the worst sort of taste to acknowledge the person who was not supposed to be there; it would not be forgiven. Just the same, she loitered and listened.

The cloud-capped towers, she heard him say once.

"The cloud-capped towers, the gorgeous palaces."

That was like a hand clapped against Rose's chest, not to hurt, but astonish her, to take her breath away. She had to run then, she had to get away. She knew that was enough to hear, and besides, what if he caught her? It would be terrible.

This was something the same as bathroom noises. Flo had saved up, and had a bathroom put in, but there was no place to put it except in a corner of the kitchen. The door did not fit, the walls were only beaverboard. The result was that even the tearing of a piece of toilet paper, the shifting of a haunch, was audible to those working or talking or eating in the kitchen.

They were all familiar with each other's nether voices, not only in their more explosive moments but in their intimate sighs and growls and pleas and statements. And they were all most prudish people. So on one ever seemed to hear, or be listening, and no reference was made. The person creating the noises in the bathroom was not connected with the person who walked out.

They lived in a poor part of town. There was Hanratty and West Hanratty, with the river flowing between them. This was West Hanratty. In Hanratty the social structure ran from doctors and dentist and lawyers down to foundry workers and factory workers and draymen; in West Hanratty it ran from factory workers and foundry workers down to large improvident families of casual bootleggers and prostitutes and unsuccessful thieves. Rose thought of her own family as straddling the river, belonging nowhere, but that was not true. West Hanratty was where the store was and they were, on the straggling tail end of the main street. Across the road from them was a blacksmith shop, boarded up about the time the war started, and a house that had been another store at one time. The Salada Tea sign had never been taken out of the front window; it remained as a proud and interesting decoration though there was no Salada Tea for sale inside. There was just a bit of sidewalk, too cracked and tilted for roller-skating, though Rose longed for roller skates and often pictured herself whizzing along in a plaid skirt, agile and fashionable. There was one street light, a tin flower; then the amenities gave up and there were dirt roads and boggy places, front-yard dumps and strange-looking houses. What made the houses strange-looking were the attempts to keep them from going completely to ruin. With some the attempts had never been made. These were gray and rotted and leaning over, falling into a landscape of scrub hollows, frog ponds, cattails and nettles. Most houses, however, had been patched up with tarpaper, a few fresh shingles, sheets of tin, hammered-out stovepipes, even cardboard. This was, of course, in the days before the war, days of what would later be legendary poverty, from which Rose would remember mostly lowdown things—serious-looking anthills and wooden steps, and a cloudy, interesting, problematical light on the world.

There was a long truce between Flo and Rose in the beginning. Rose's nature was growing like a prickly pineapple, but slowly, and secretly, hard pride and skepticism overlapping, to make something surprising even to herself. Before she was old enough to go to school, and while Brian was still in the baby carriage, Rose stayed in the store with both of them—Flo sitting on the high stool behind the counter, Brian asleep by the window; Rose knelt or lay on the wide creaky floorboards working with crayons on pieces of brown paper too torn or irregular to be used for wrapping.

People who came to the store were mostly from the houses around. Some country people came too, on their way home from town, and a few people from Hanratty, who walked across the bridge. Some people were always on the main street, in and out of stores, as if it was their duty to be always on display and their right to be welcomed. For instance, Becky Tyde.

Becky Tyde climbed up on Flo's counter, made room for herself beside an open tin of crumbly jam-filled cookies.

"Are these any good?" she said to Flo, and boldly began to eat one.

"When are you going to give us a job, Flo?"

"You could go and work in the butcher shop," said Flo innocently. "You could go and work for your brother."

"Roberta?" said Becky with a stagey sort of contempt. "You think I'd work for him?" Her brother who ran the butcher shop was named Robert but often called Roberta, because of his meek and nervous ways. Becky Tyde laughed. Her laugh was loud and noisy like an engine bearing down on you.

She was a big-headed loud-voiced dwarf, with a mascot's sexless swagger, a red velvet tam, a twisted neck that forced her to hold her head on one side, always looking up and sideways. She wore little polished high-heeled shoes, real lady's shoes. Rose watched her shoes, being scared of the rest of her, of her laugh and her neck. She knew from Flo that Becky Tyde had been sick with polio as a child, that was why her neck was twisted and why she had not grown any taller. It was hard to believe that she had started out differently, that she had ever been normal. Flo said she was not cracked, she had as much brains as anybody, but she knew she could get away with anything.

"You know I used to live out here?" Becky said, noticing Rose. "Hey! What's-your-name! Didn't I used to live out here, Flo?"

"If you did it was before my time," said Flo, as if she didn't know anything.

"That was before the neighborhood got so downhill. Excuse me saying so. My father built his house out here and he built his slaughterhouse and we had half an acre of orchard."

"Is that so?" said Flo, using her humoring voice, full of false geniality, humility even. "Then why did you ever move away?"

"I told you, it got to be such a downhill neighborhood," said Becky. She would put a whole cookie in her mouth if she felt like it, let her cheeks puff out like a frog's. She never told any more.

Flo knew anyway, and who didn't. Everyone knew the house, red brick with the veranda pulled off and the orchard, what was left of it, full of the usual outflow—car seats and washing machines and bedsprings and junk. The house would never look sinister, in spite of what had happened in it, because there was so much wreckage and confusion all around.

Becky's old father was a different kind of butcher from her brother according to Flo. A bad-tempered Englishman. And different from Becky in the matter of mouthiness. His was never open. A skinflint, a family tyrant. After Becky had polio he wouldn't let her go back to school. She was seldom seen outside the house, never outside the yard. He didn't want people gloating. That was what Becky said, at the trial. Her mother was dead by that time and her sisters married. Just Becky and Robert at home. People would stop Robert on the road and ask him, "How about your sister, Robert? Is she altogether better now?"

"Yes."

"Does she do the housework? Does she get your supper?"

"Yes."

"And is your father good to her, Robert?"

The story being that the father beat them, had beaten all his children and beaten his wife as well, beat Becky more now because of her deformity, which some people believed he had caused (they did not understand about polio). The stories persisted and got added to. The reason that Becky was kept out of sight was now supposed to be her pregnancy, and the father of the child was supposed to be her own father. Then people said it had been born, and disposed of.

"What?"

"Disposed of," Flo said. "They used to say go and get your lamb chops at Tyde's, get them nice and tender! It was all lies in all probability," she said regretfully.

Rose could be drawn back—from watching the wind shiver along the old torn awning, catch in the tear—by this tone of regret, caution, in Flo's voice. Flo telling a story—and this was not the only one, or even the most lurid one, she knew—would incline her head and let her face go soft and thoughtful, tantalizing, warning.

"I shouldn't even be telling you this stuff."

More was to follow.

Three useless young men, who hung around the livery stable, got together—or were got together, by more influential and respectable men in town—and prepared to give old man Tyde a horsewhipping, in the interests of public morality. They blacked their faces. They were provided with whips and a quart of whiskey apiece, for courage. They were: Jelly Smith, a horse-racer and a drinker; Bob Temple, a ball-player and strong-man; and Hat Nettleton, who worked on the town dray, and had his nick-name from a bowler hat he wore, out of vanity as much as for the comic effect. He still worked on the dray, in fact; he had kept the name if not the hat, and could often be seen in public—almost as often as Becky Tyde—delivering sacks of coal, which blackened his face and arms. That should have brought to mind his story, but didn't. Present time and past, the shady melodramatic past of Flo's stories, were quite separate, at least for Rose. Present people could not be fitted into the past. Becky herself, town oddity and public pet, harmless and malicious, could never match the butcher's prisoner, the cripple daughter, a white streak at the window: mute, beaten, impregnated. As with the house, only a formal connection could be made.

The young men primed to do the horsewhipping showed up late, outside Tyde's house, after everybody had gone to bed. They had a gun, but they used up their ammunition firing it off in the yard. They yelled for the butcher and beat on the door; finally they broke it down. Tyde concluded they were after his money, so he put some bills in a handkerchief and sent Becky down with them, maybe thinking those men would be touched or scared by the sight of a little wry-necked girl, a dwarf. But that didn't content them. They came upstairs and dragged the butcher out from under his bed, in his nightgown. They dragged him outside and stood him in the snow. The temperature was four below zero, a fact noted later in court. They meant to hold a mock trail but they could not remember how it was done. So they began to beat him and kept beating him until he fell. They yelled at him, *Butcher's meat!* and continued beating him while his nightgown and the snow he was lying in turned red. His son Robert said in court that he had not watched the beating. Becky said that Robert had watched at first but had run away and hid. She herself had watched all the way through. She watched the men leave at last and her father make his delayed bloody progress through the snow and up the steps of the veranda. She did not go out to help him, or open the door until he got to it. Why not? she was asked in court, and she said she did not go out because she just had her nightgown on, and she did not open the door because she did not want to let the cold into the house.

Old man Tyde then appeared to have recovered his strength. He sent Robert to harness the horse, and made Becky heat water so that he could wash. He dressed and took all the money and with no explanation to his children got into the cutter and drove to Belgrave where he left the horse tied in the cold and took the early morning train to Toronto. On the train he behaved oddly, groaning and cursing as if he was drunk. He was picked up on the streets of Toronto a day later, out of his mind with fever, and was taken to a hospital, where he died. He still had all the money. The cause of death was given as pneumonia.

But the authorities got wind, Flo said. The case came to trial. The three men who did it all received long prison sentences. A farce, said Flo. Within a year they were all free, had all been pardoned, had jobs waiting for them. And why was that? It was because too many higher-ups were in on it. And it seemed as if Becky and Robert had no interest in seeing justice done. They were left well-off. They bought a house in Hanratty. Robert went into the store. Becky after her long seclusion started on a career of public sociability and display.

That was all. Flo put the lid down on the story as if she was sick of it. It reflected no good on anybody.

"Imagine," Flo said.

Flo at this time must have been in her early thirties. A young woman. She wore exactly the same clothes that a woman of fifty, or sixty, or seventy, might wear: print housedresses loose at the neck and sleeves as well as the waist; bib aprons, also of print, which she took off when she came from the kitchen into the store. This was a common costume at the time, for a poor though not absolutely poverty-stricken woman; it was also, in a way, a scornful deliberate choice. Flo scorned slacks, she scorned the outfits of people trying to be in style, she scorned lipstick and permanents. She wore her own black hair cut straight across, just long enough to push behind her ears. She was tall but fine-boned, with narrow wrists and shoulders, a small head, a pale, freckled, mobile, monkeyish face. If she had thought it worthwhile, and had the resources, she might have had a black-and-pale, fragile, nurtured sort of prettiness; Rose realized that later. But she would have to have been a different person altogether; she would have to have learned to resist making faces, at herself and others.

Rose's earliest memories of Flo were of extraordinary softness and hardness. The soft hair, the long, soft, pale cheeks, soft almost invisible fuzz in front of her ears and above her mouth. The sharpness of her knees, hardness of her lap, flatness of her front.

When Flo sang:

> Oh the buzzin' of the bees in the cigarette trees
> And the soda-*water* fountain . . .

Rose thought of Flo's old life before she married her father, when she worked as a waitress in the coffee shop in Union Station, and went with her girl friends Mavis and Irene to Centre Island, and was followed by men on dark streets and knew how pay phones and elevators worked. Rose heard in her voice the reckless dangerous life of cities, the gum-chewing sharp answers.

And when she sang:

> Then slowly, slowly, she got up
> And slowly she came nigh him
> And all she said, that she ever did say,
> Was young man I think, you're dyin'!

Rose thought of a life Flo seemed to have had beyond that, earlier than that, crowded and legendary, with Barbara Allen and Becky Tyde's father and all kinds of outrages and sorrows jumbled up together in it.

The royal beatings. What got them started?

Suppose a Saturday, in spring. Leaves not out yet but the doors open to the sunlight. Crows. Ditches full of running water. Hopeful weather. Often on Saturdays Flo left Rose in charge of the store—it's a few years now, these are the years when Rose was nine, ten, eleven, twelve—while she herself went across the bridge to Hanratty (going uptown they called it) to shop and see people, and listen to them. Among the people she listened to were Mrs. Lawyer Davies, Mrs. Anglican Rector Henley-Smith, and Mrs. Horse-Doctor McKay. She came home and imitated their flibberty voices.

Monsters, she made them seem; of foolishness, and showiness, and self-approbation.

When she finished shopping she went into the coffee shop of the Queen's Hotel and had a sundae. What kind? Rose and Brian wanted to know when she got home, and they would be disappointed if it was only pineapple or butterscotch, pleased if it was a Tin Roof, or Black and White. Then she smoked a cigarette. She had some ready-rolled, that she carried with her, so that she wouldn't have to roll one in public. Smoking was the one thing she did that she would have called showing off in anybody else. It was a habit left over from her working days, from Toronto. She knew it was asking for trouble. Once the Catholic priest came over to her right in the Queen's Hotel, and flashed his lighter at her before she could get her matches out. She thanked him but did not enter into conversation, lest he should try to convert her.

Another time, on the way home, she saw at the town end of the bridge a boy in a blue jacket, apparently looking at the water. Eighteen, nineteen years old. Nobody she knew. Skinny, weakly looking, something the matter with him, she saw at once. Was he thinking of jumping? Just as she came up even with him, what does he do but turn and display himself, holding his jacket open, also his pants. What he must have suffered from the cold, on a day that had Flo holding her coat collar tight around her throat.

When she first saw what he had in his hand, Flo said, all she could think of was, what is he doing out here with a baloney sausage?

She could say that. It was offered as truth; no joke. She maintained that she despised dirty talk. She would go out and yell at the old men sitting in front of her store.

"If you want to stay where you are you better clean your mouths out!"

Saturday, then. For some reason Flo is not going uptown, has decided to stay home and scrub the kitchen floor. Perhaps this has put her in a bad mood. Perhaps she was in a bad mood anyway, due to people not paying their bills, or the stirring-up of feelings in spring. The wrangle with Rose has already commenced, has been going on forever, like a dream that goes back and back into other dreams, over hills and through doorways, maddeningly dim and populous and familiar and elusive. They are carting all the chairs out of the kitchen preparatory to the scrubbing, and they have also got to move some extra provisions for the store, some cartons of canned goods, tins of maple syrup, coal-oil cans, jars of vinegar. They take these things out to the woodshed. Brian who is five or six by this time is helping drag the tins.

"Yes," says Flo, carrying on from our lost starting point. "Yes, and that filth you taught to Brian."

"What filth?"

"And he doesn't know any better."

There is one step down from the kitchen to the woodshed, a bit of carpet on it so worn Rose can't ever remember seeing the pattern. Brian loosens it, dragging a tin.

"Two Vancouvers," she says softly.

Flo is back in the kitchen. Brain looks from Flo to Rose and Rose says again in a slightly louder voice, an encouraging sing-song, "Two Vancouvers—"

"Fried in snot!" finishes Brain, not able to control himself any longer.

"Two pickled arseholes—"

"—tied in a knot!"

There it is. The filth.

Two Vancouvers fried in snot!
Two pickled arseholes tied in a knot!

Rose has known that for years, learned it when she first went to school. She came home and asked Flo, what is a Vancouver?

"It's a city. It's a long ways away."

"What else besides a city?"

Flo said, what did she mean, what else? How could it be fried, Rose said, approaching the dangerous moment, the delightful moment, when she would have to come out with the whole thing.

"Two Vancouvers fried in snot!/Two pickled arseholes tied in a knot!"

"You're going to get it!" cried Flo in a predictable rage. "Say that again and you'll get a good clout!"

Rose couldn't stop herself. She hummed it tenderly, tried saying the innocent words aloud, humming through the others. It was not just the words snot and arsehole that gave her pleasure, though of course they did. It was the pickling and tying and the unimaginable Vancouvers. She saw them in her mind shaped rather like octopuses, twitching in the pan. The tumble of reason; the spark and spit of craziness.

Lately she has remembered it again and taught it to Brian, to see if it has the same effect on him, and of course it has.

"Oh, I heard you!" says Flo. "I heard that! And I'm warning you!"

So she is. Brian takes the warning. He runs away, out the woodshed door, to do as he likes. Being a boy, free to help or not, involve himself or not. Not committed to the household struggle. They don't need him anyway, except to use against each other, they hardly notice his going. They continue, can't help continuing, can't leave each other alone. When they seem to have given up they really are just waiting and building up steam.

Flo gets out the scrub pail and the brush and the rag and the pad for her knees, a dirty red rubber pad. She starts to work on the floor. Rose sits on the kitchen table, the only place left to sit, swinging her legs. She can feel the cool oilcloth, because she is wearing shorts, last summer's tight faded shorts dug out of the summer-clothes bag. They smell a bit moldy from winter storage.

Flo crawls underneath, scrubbing with the brush, wiping with the rag. Her legs are long, white and muscular, marked all over with blue veins as if somebody had been drawing rivers on them with an indelible pencil. An abnormal energy, a violent disgust, is expressed in the chewing of the brush at the linoleum, the swish of the rag.

What do they have to say to each other? It doesn't really matter. Flo speaks of Rose's smart-aleck behavior, rudeness and sloppiness and conceit. Her willingness to make work for others, her lack of gratitude. She mentions Brian's innocence, Rose's corruption. Oh, don't you think you're somebody, says Flo, and a moment later, Who do you think you are? Rose contradicts and objects with such poisonous reasonableness and mildness, displays theatrical unconcern. Flo goes beyond her ordinary scorn and self-possession and becomes amazingly theatrical herself, saying it was for Rose that she sacrificed her life. She saw her father saddled with a baby daughter and she thought, what is that man going to do? So she married him, and here she is, on her knees.

At that moment the bell rings, to announce a customer in the store. Because the fight is on, Rose is not permitted to go into the store and wait on whoever it is. Flo gets up and throws off her apron, groaning—but not communicatively, it is not a groan whose exasperation Rose is allowed to share—and goes in and serves. Rose hears her using her normal voice.

"About time! Sure is!"

She comes back and ties on her apron and is ready to resume.

"You never have a thought for anybody but your ownself! You never have a thought for what I'm doing."

"I never asked you to do anything. I wish you never had. I would have been a lot better off."

Rose says this smiling directly at Flo, who has not yet gone down on her knees. Flo sees the smile, grabs the scrub rag that is hanging on the side of the pail, and throws it at her. It may be meant to hit her in the face but instead it falls against Rose's leg and she raises her foot and catches it, swinging it negligently against her ankle.

"All right," says Flo. "You've done it this time. All right."

Rose watches her go to the woodshed door, hears her tramp through the woodshed, pause in the doorway, where the screen door hasn't yet been hung, and the storm door is standing open, propped with a brick. She calls Rose's father. She calls him in a warning, summoning voice, as if against her will preparing him for bad news. He will know what this is about.

The kitchen floor has five or six different patterns of linoleum on it. Ends, which Flo got for nothing and ingeniously trimmed and fitted together, bordering them with tin strips and tacks. While Rose sits on the table waiting, she looks at the floor, at this satisfying arrangement of rectangles, triangles, some other shape whose name she is trying to remember. She hears Flo coming back through the woodshed, on the creaky plank walk laid over the dirt floor. She is loitering, waiting, too. She and Rose can carry this no further, by themselves.

Rose hears her father come in. She stiffens, a tremor runs through her legs, she feels them shiver on the oilcloth. Called away from some peaceful, absorbing task, away from the words running in his head, called out of himself, her father has to say something. He says, "Well? What's wrong?"

Now comes another voice of Flo's. Enriched, hurt, apologetic, it seems to have been manufactured on the spot. She is sorry to have called him from his work. Would never have done it, if Rose was not driving her to distraction. How to distraction? With her back talk and impudence and her terrible tongue. The things Rose has said to Flo are such that, if Flo had said them to her mother, she knows her father would have thrashed her into the ground.

Rose tries to butt in, to say this isn't true.

What isn't true?

Her father raises a hand, doesn't look at her, says, "Be quiet."

When she says it isn't true, Rose means that she herself didn't start this, only responded, that she was goaded by Flo, who is now, she believes, telling the grossest sort of lies, twisting everything to suit herself. Rose puts aside her other knowledge that whatever Flo has said or done, whatever she herself has said or done, does not really matter at all. It is the struggle itself that counts, and that can't be stopped, can never be stopped, short of where it has got to, now.

Flo's knees are dirty, in spite of the pad. The scrub rag is still hanging over Rose's foot.

Her father wipes his hands, listening to Flo. He takes his time. He is slow at getting into the spirit of things, tired in advance, maybe, on the verge of rejecting the role he has to play. He won't look at Rose, but at any sound or stirring from Rose, he holds up his hand.

"Well we don't need the public in on this, that's for sure," Flo says, and she goes to lock the door of the store, putting in the store window the sign that says BACK SOON, a sign Rose made for her with a great deal of fancy curving and shading of letters in black and red crayon. When she comes back she shuts the door to the store, then the door to the stairs, then the door to the woodshed.

Her shoes have left marks on the clean wet part of the floor.

"Oh, I don't know," she says now, in a voice worn down from its emotional peak. "I don't know what to do about her." She looks down and sees her dirty knees (following Rose's eyes) and rubs at them viciously with her bare hands, smearing the dirt around.

"She humiliates me," she says, straightening up. There it is, the explanation. "She humiliates me," she repeats with satisfaction. "She has no respect."

"I do not!"

"Quiet, you!" says her father.

"If I hadn't called your father you'd still be sitting there with that grin on your face! What other way is there to manage you?"

Rose detects in her father some objections to Flo's rhetoric, some embarrassment and reluctance. She is wrong, and ought to know she is wrong, in thinking that she can count on this. The fact that she knows about it, and he knows she knows, will not make things any better. He is beginning to warm up. He gives her a look. This look is at first cold and challenging. It informs her of his judgment, of the hopelessness of her position. Then it clears, it begins to fill up with something else, the way a spring fills up when you clear the leaves away. It fills with hatred and pleasure. Rose sees that and knows it. Is that just a description of anger, should she see his eyes filling up with anger? No. Hatred is right. Pleasure is right. His face loosens and changes and grows younger, and he holds up his hand this time to silence Flo.

"All right," he says, meaning that's enough, more than enough, this part is over, things can proceed. He starts to loosen his belt.

Flo has stopped anyway. She has the same difficulty Rose does, a difficulty in believing that what you know must happen really will happen, that there comes a time when you can't draw back.

"Oh, I don't know, don't be too hard on her." She is moving around nervously as if she has thoughts of opening some escape route. "Oh, you don't have to use the belt on her. Do you have to use the belt?"

He doesn't answer. The belt is coming off, not hastily. It is being grasped at the necessary point. *All right you.* He is coming over to Rose. He pushes her off the table. His face, like his voice, is quite out of character. He is like a bad actor, who turns a part grotesque. As if he must savor and insist on just what is shameful and terrible about this. That is not to say he is pretending, that he is acting, and does not mean it. He is acting, and he means it. Rose knows that, she knows everything about him.

She has since wondered about murders, and murderers. Does the thing have to be carried through, in the end, partly for the effect, to prove to the audience of one—who won't be able to report, only register, the lesson—that such a thing can happen, that there is nothing that can't happen, that the most dreadful antic is justified, feelings can be found to match it?

She tries again looking at the kitchen floor, that clever and comforting geometrical arrangement, instead of looking at him or his belt. How can this go on in front of such daily witnesses—the linoleum, the calendar with the mill and creek and autumn trees, the old accommodating pots and pans?

Hold out your hand!

Those things aren't going to help her, none of them can rescue her. They turn bland and useless, even unfriendly. Pots can show malice, the patterns of linoleum can leer up at you, treachery is the other side of dailiness.

At the first, or maybe the second, crack of pain, she draws back. She will not accept it. She runs around the room, she tries to get to the doors. Her father blocks her off. Not an ounce of courage or of stoicism in her, it would seem. She runs, she screams, she implores. Her father is after her, cracking the belt at her when he can, then abandoning it and using his hands. Bang over the ear, then bang over the other ear. Back and forth, her head ringing. Bang in the face. Up against the wall and bang in the face again. He shakes her and hits her against the wall, he kicks her legs. She is incoherent, insane, shrieking. *Forgive me! Oh please, forgive me!*

Flo is shrieking too. *Stop, stop!*

Not yet. He throws Rose down. Or perhaps she throws herself down. He kicks her legs again. She has given up on words but is letting out a noise, the sort of noise that makes Flo cry, *Oh, what if people can hear her?* The very last-ditch willing sound of humiliation and defeat it is, for it seems Rose must play her part in this with the same grossness, the same exaggeration, that her father displays, playing his. She plays his victim with a self-indulgence that arouses, and maybe hopes to arouse, his final, sickened contempt.

They will give this anything that is necessary, it seems, they will go to any lengths.

Not quite. He has never managed really to injure her, though there are times, of course, when she prays that he will. He hits her with an open hand, there is some restraint in his kicks.

Now he stops, he is out of breath. He allows Flo to move in, he grabs Rose up and gives her a push in Flo's direction, making a sound of disgust. Flo retrieves her, opens the stair door, shoves her up the stairs.

"Go on up to your room now! Hurry!"

Rose goes up the stairs, stumbling, letting herself stumble, letting herself fall against the steps. She doesn't bang her door because a gesture like that could still bring him after her, and anyway, she is weak. She lies on the bed. She can hear through the stovepipe hole Flo snuffling and remonstrating, her father saying angrily that Flo should have kept quiet then, if she did not want Rose punished she should not have recommended it. Flo says she never recommended a hiding like that.

They argue back and forth on this. Flo's frightened voice is growing stronger, getting its confidence back. By stages, by arguing, they are being drawn back into themselves. Soon it's only Flo talking; he will not talk anymore. Rose has had to fight down her noisy sobbing, so as to listen to them, and when she loses interest in listening, and wants to sob some more, she finds she can't work herself up to it. She has passed into a state of calm, in which outrage is perceived as complete and final. In this state events and possibilities take on a lovely simplicity. Choices are mercifully clear.

The words that come to mind are not the quibbling, seldom the conditional. Never is a word to which the right is suddenly established. She will never speak to them, she will never look at them with anything but loathing, she will never forgive them. She will punish them; she will finish them. Encased in these finalities, and in her bodily pain, she floats in curious comfort, beyond herself, beyond responsibility.

Suppose she dies now? Suppose she commits suicide? Suppose she runs away? Any of these things would be appropriate. It is only a matter of choosing, of figuring out the way. She floats in her pure superior state as if kindly drugged.

And just as there is a moment, when you are drugged, in which you feel perfectly safe, sure, unreachable, and then without warning and right next to it a moment in which you know the whole protection has fatally cracked, though it is still pretending to hold soundly together, so there is a moment now—the moment, in fact, when Rose hears Flo step on the stairs—that contains for her both present peace and freedom and a sure knowledge of the whole down-spiraling course of events from now on.

Flo comes into the room without knocking, but with a hesitation that shows it might have occurred to her. She brings a jar of cold cream. Rose is hanging on to advantage as long as she can, lying face down on the bed, refusing to acknowledge or answer.

"Oh come on," Flo says uneasily. "You aren't so bad off, are you? You put some of this on and you'll feel better."

She is bluffing. She doesn't know for sure what damage has been done. She has the lid off the cold cream. Rose can smell it. The intimate, babyish, humiliating smell. She won't allow it near her. But in order to avoid it, the big ready clot of it in Flo's hand, she has to move. She scuffles, resists, loses dignity, and lets Flo see there is not really much the matter.

"All right," Flo says. "You win. I'll leave it here and you can put it on when you like."

Later still a tray will appear. Flo will put it down without a word and go away. A large glass of chocolate milk on it, made with Vita-Malt from the store. Some rich streaks of Vita-Malt around the bottom of the glass. Little sandwiches, neat and appetizing. Canned salmon of the first quality and reddest color, plenty of mayonnaise. A couple of butter tarts from a bakery package, chocolate biscuits with a peppermint filling. Rose's favorites, in the sandwich, tart and cookie line. She will turn away, refuse to look, but left alone with these eatables will be miserably tempted, roused and troubled and drawn back from thoughts of suicide or flight by the smell of salmon, the anticipation of crisp chocolate, she will reach out a finger, just to run it around the edge of one of the sandwiches (crusts cut off!) to get the overflow, get a taste. Then she will decide to eat one, for strength to refuse the rest. One will not be noticed. Soon, in helpless corruption, she will eat them all. She will drink the chocolate milk, eat the tarts, eat the cookies. She will get the malty syrup out of the bottom of the glass with her finger, though she sniffles with shame. Too late.

Flo will come up and get the tray. She may say, "I see you got your appetite still," or, "Did you like the chocolate milk, was it enough syrup in it?" depending on how chastened she is feeling, herself. At any rate, all advantage will be lost. Rose will understand that life has started up again, that they will all sit around the table eating again, listening to the radio news. Tomorrow morning, maybe even tonight. Unseemly and unlikely as that may be. They will be embarrassed, but rather less than you might expect considering how they have behaved. They will feel a queer lassitude, a convalescent indolence, not far off satisfaction.

One night after a scene like this they were all in the kitchen. It must have been summer, or at least warm weather, because her father spoke of the old men who sat on the bench in front of the store.

"Do you know what they're talking about now?" he said, and nodded his head toward the store to show who he meant, though of course they were not there now, they went home at dark.

"Those old coots," said Flo. "What?"

There was about them both a geniality not exactly false but a bit more emphatic than was normal, without company.

Rose's father told them then that the old men had picked up the idea somewhere that what looked like a star in the western sky, the first star that came out after sunset, the evening star, was in reality an airship hovering over Bay City, Michigan, on the other side of Lake Huron. An American invention, sent up to rival the heavenly bodies. They were all in agreement about this, the idea was congenial to them. They believed it to be lit by ten thousand electric light bulbs. Her father had ruthlessly disagreed with them, pointing out that it was the planet Venus they saw, which had appeared in the sky long before the invention of an electric light bulb. They had never heard of the planet Venus.

"Ignoramuses," said Flo. At which Rose knew, and knew her father knew, that Flo had never heard of the planet Venus either. To distract them from this, or even apologize for it, Flo put down her teacup, stretched out with her head resting on the chair she had been sitting on and her feet on another chair (somehow she managed to tuck her dress modestly between her legs at the same time), and lay stiff as a board, so that Brian cried out in delight, "Do that! Do that!"

Flo was double-jointed and very strong. In moments of celebration or emergency she would do tricks.

They were silent while she turned herself around, not using her arms at all but just her strong legs and feet. Then they all cried out in triumph, though they had seen it before.

Just as Flo turned herself Rose got a picture in her mind of that airship, an elongated transparent bubble, with its strings of diamond lights, floating in the miraculous American sky.

"The planet Venus!" her father said, applauding Flo. "Ten thousand electric lights!"

There was a feeling of permission, relaxation, even a current of happiness, in the room.

Years later, many years later, on a Sunday morning, Rose turned on the radio. This was when she was living by herself in Toronto.

Well sir.

It was a different kind of place in our day. Yes it was.

It was all horses then. Horses and buggies. Buggy races up and down the main street on the Saturday nights.

"Just like the chariot races," says the announcer's, or interviewer's, smooth encouraging voice.

I never seen a one of them.

"No sir, that was the old Roman chariot races I was referring to. That was before your time."

Musta been before my time. I'm a hunerd and two years old.

"That's a wonderful age, sir."

It is so.

She left it on, as she went around the apartment kitchen, making coffee for herself. It seemed to her that this must be a staged interview, a scene from some play, and she wanted to find out what it was. The old man's voice was so vain and belligerent, the interviewer's quite hopeless and alarmed, under its practiced gentleness and ease. You were surely meant to see him holding the microphone up to some toothless, reckless, preening centenarian, wondering what in God's name he was doing here, and what would he say next?

"They must have been fairly dangerous."

What was dangerous?

"Those buggy races."

They was. Dangerous. Used to be the runaway horses. Used to be a-plenty of accidents. Fellows was dragged along on the gravel and cut their face open. Wouldna matter so much if they were dead. Heh.

Some of them horses was the high-steppers. Some, they had to have the mustard under their tail. Some wouldn step out for nothin. That's the thing it is with the horses. Some'll work and pull till they drop down dead and some wouldn pull your cock out of a pail of lard. Hehe.

It must be a real interview after all. Otherwise they wouldn't have put that in, wouldn't have risked it. It's all right if the old man says it. Local color. Anything rendered harmless and delightful by his hundred years.

Accidents all the time then. In the mill. Foundry. Wasn't the precautions.

"You didn't have so many strikes then, I don't suppose? You didn't have so many unions?"

Everybody taking it easy nowadays. We worked and we was glad to get it. Worked and was glad to get it.

"You didn't have television."

Didn't have no TV. Didn't have no radio. No picture show.

"You made your own entertainment."

That's the way we did.

"You had a lot of experiences young men growing up today will never have."

Experiences.

"Can you recall any of them for us?"

I eaten groundhog meat one time. One winter. You wouldna cared for it. Heh.

There was a pause, of appreciation, it would seem, then the announcer's voice saying that the foregoing had been an interview with Mr. Wilfred Nettleton of Hanratty, Ontario, made on his hundred and second birthday, two weeks before his death, last spring. A living link with our past. Mr. Nettleton had been interviewed in the Wawanash County Home for the Aged.

Hat Nettleton.

Horsewhipper into centenarian. Photographed on his birthday, fussed over by nurses, kissed no doubt by a girl reporter. Flash bulbs popping at him. Tape recorder drinking in the sound of his voice. Oldest resident. Oldest horsewhipper. Living link with our past.

Looking out from her kitchen window at the cold lake, Rose was longing to tell somebody. It was Flo who would enjoy hearing. She thought of her saying *Imagine!* in a way that meant she was having her worst suspicions gorgeously confirmed. But Flo was in the same place Hat Nettleton had died in, and there wasn't any way Rose could reach her. She had been there even when that interview was recorded, though she would not have heard it, would not have known about it. After Rose put her in the Home, a couple of years earlier, she had stopped talking. She had removed herself, and spent most of her time sitting in a corner of her crib, looking crafty and disagreeable, not answering anybody, though she occasionally showed her feelings by biting a nurse.

John Updike

John Updike (b. 1932) was born in Shillington, Pennsylvania. Although he originally aspired to a career as a visual artist, Updike early decided to make use of his literary gifts instead. Over the past three decades he has emerged as one of our most prolific and versatile men of letters, writing essays, stories and novels, poetry, art criticism, and speeches and addresses (which he views not as chores but further opportunities for literary expression). Updike's fiction holds up a mirror to our changing society, exploring the manners and morals of the upper-middle class. His work includes the novels *Of the Farm* and *The Centaur* and the four volumes of his Rabbit tetralogy: *Rabbit, Run, Rabbit Redux, Rabbit Is Rich,* and *Rabbit at Rest.*

SEPARATING

The day was fair. Brilliant. All that June the weather had mocked the Maples' internal misery with solid sunlight—golden shafts and cascades of green in which their conversations had wormed unseeing, their sad murmuring selves the only stain in Nature. Usually by this time of the year they had acquired tans; but when they met their elder daughter's plane on her return from a year in England they were almost as pale as she, though Judith was too dazzled by the sunny opulent jumble of her native land to notice. They did not spoil her homecoming by telling her immediately. Wait a few days, let her recover from jet lag, had been one of their formulations, in that string of gray dialogues—over coffee, over cocktails, over Cointreau—that had shaped the strategy of their dissolution, while the earth performed its annual stunt of renewal unnoticed beyond their closed windows. Richard had thought to leave at Easter; Joan had insisted they wait until the four children were at last assembled, with all exams passed and ceremonies attended, and the bauble of summer to console them. So he had drudged away, in love, in dread, repairing screens, getting the mowers sharpened, rolling and patching their new tennis court.

The court, clay, had come through its first winter pitted and windswept bare of redcoat. Years ago the Maples had observed how often, among their friends, divorce followed a dramatic home improvement, as if the marriage were making one last effort to live; their own worst crisis had come amid the plaster dust and exposed plumbing of a kitchen renovation.

Yet, a summer ago, as canary-yellow bulldozers gaily churned a grassy, daisy-dotted knoll into a muddy plateau, and a crew of pigtailed young men raked and tamped clay into a plane, this transformation did not strike them as ominous, but festive in its impudence; their marriage could rend the earth for fun. The next spring, waking each day at dawn to a sliding sensation as if the bed were being tipped, Richard found the barren tennis court—its net and tapes still rolled in the barn—an environment congruous with his mood of purposeful desolation, and the crumbling of handfuls of clay into cracks and holes (dogs had frolicked on the court in a thaw; rivulets had eroded trenches) an activity suitably elemental and interminable. In his sealed heart he hoped the day would never come.

Now it was here. A Friday. Judith was re-acclimated; all four children were assembled, before jobs and camps and visits again scattered them. Joan thought they should be told one by one. Richard was for making an announcement at the table. She said, "I think just making an announcement is a cop-out. They'll start quarrelling and playing to each other instead of focusing. They're each individuals, you know, not just some corporate obstacle to your freedom."

"O.K., O.K. I agree." Joan's plan was exact. That evening, they were giving Judith a belated welcome-home dinner, of lobster and champagne. Then, the party over, they, the two of them, who nineteen years before would push her in a baby carriage along Fifth Avenue to Washington Square, were to walk her out of the house, to the bridge across the salt creek, and tell her, swearing her to secrecy. Then Richard Jr., who was going directly from work to a rock concert in Boston, would be told, either late when he returned on the train or early Saturday morning before he went off to his job; he was seventeen and employed as one of a golf-course maintenance crew. Then the two younger children, John and Margaret, could, as the morning wore on, be informed.

"Mopped up, as it were," Richard said.

"Do you have any better plan? That leaves you the rest of Saturday to answer any questions, pack, and make your wonderful departure."

"No," he said, meaning he had no better plan, and agreed to hers, though to him it showed an edge of false order, a hidden plea for control, like Joan's long chore lists and financial accountings and, in the days when he first knew her, her too-copious lecture notes. Her plan turned one hurdle for him into four—four knife-sharp walls, each with a sheer blind drop on the other side.

All spring he had moved through a world of insides and outsides, of barriers and partitions. He and Joan stood as a thin barrier between the children and the truth. Each moment was a partition, with the past on one side and the future on the other, a future containing this unthinkable *now*. Beyond four knifelike walls a new life for him waited vaguely. His skull cupped a secret, a white face, a face both frightened and soothing, both strange and known, that he wanted to shield from tears, which he felt all about him, solid as the sunlight. So haunted, he had become obsessed with battening down the house against his absence, replacing screens and sash cords, hinges and latches—a Houdini making things snug before his escape.

The lock. He had still to replace a lock on one of the doors of the screened porch. The task, like most such, proved more difficult than he had imagined. The old lock, aluminum frozen by corrosion, had been deliberately rendered obsolete by manufacturers. Three hardware stores had nothing that even approximately matched the mortised hole its removal (surprisingly easy) left. Another hole had to be gouged, with bits too small and saws too big, and the old hole fitted with a block of wood—the chisels dull, the saw rusty, his fingers thick with lack of sleep. The sun poured down, beyond the porch, on a world of neglect. The bushes already needed pruning, the windward side of the house was shedding flakes of paint, rain would get in when he was gone, insects, rot, death. His family, all those he would lose, filtered through the edges of his awareness as he struggled with screw holes, splinters, opaque instructions, minutiae of metal.

Judith sat on the porch, a princess returned from exile. She regaled them with stories of fuel shortages, of bomb scares in the Underground, of Pakistani workmen loudly lusting after her as she walked past on her way to dance school. Joan came and went, in and out of the house, calmer than she should have been, praising his struggles with the lock as if this were one more and not the last of their long succession of shared chores. The younger of his sons for a few minutes held the rickety screen door while his father clumsily hammered and chiseled, each blow a kind of sob in Richard's ears. His younger daughter, having been at a slumber party, slept on the porch hammock through all the noise—heavy and pink, trusting and forsaken. Time, like the sunlight, continued relentlessly; the sunlight slowly slanted. Today was one of the longest days. The lock clicked, worked. He was through. He had a drink; he drank it on the porch, listening to his daughter. "It was so sweet," she was saying, "during the worst of it, how all the butchers and bakery shops kept open by candlelight. They're all so plucky and cute. From the papers, things sounded so much worse here—people shooting people in gas lines, and everybody freezing."

Richard asked her, "Do you still want to live in England forever?" *Forever:* the concept, now a reality upon him, pressed and scratched at the back of his throat.

"No," Judith confessed, turning her oval face to him, its eyes still childishly far apart, but the lips set as over something succulent and satisfactory. "I was anxious to come home. I'm an American." She was a woman. They had raised her; he and Joan had endured together to raise her, alone of the four. The others had still some raising left in them. Yet it was the thought of telling Judith—the image of her, their first baby, walking between them arm in arm to the bridge—that broke him. The partition between his face and the tears broke. Richard sat down to the celebratory meal with the back of his throat aching; the champagne, the lobster seemed phases of sunshine; he saw them and tasted them through tears. He blinked, swallowed, croakily joked about hay fever. The tears would not stop leaking through; they came not through a hole that could be plugged but through a permeable spot in a membrane, steadily, purely, endlessly, fruitfully. They became, his tears, a shield for himself against these others—their faces, the fact of their assembly, a last time as innocents, at a table where he sat the last time as head. Tears dropped from his nose as he broke the lobster's back; salt flavored his champagne as he sipped it; the raw clench at the back of his throat was delicious. He could not help himself.

His children tried to ignore his tears. Judith, on his right, lit a cigarette, gazed upward in the direction of her too energetic, too sophisticated exhalation; on her other side, John earnestly bent his face to the extraction of the last morsels—legs, tail segments—from the scarlet corpse. Joan, at the opposite end of the table, glanced at him surprised, her reproach displaced by a quick grimace, of forgiveness, or of salute to his superior gift of strategy. Between them, Margaret, no longer called Bean, thirteen and large for her age, gazed from the other side of his pane of tears as if into a shopwindow at something she coveted—at her father, a crystalline heap of splinters and memories. It was not she, however, but John who, in the kitchen, as they cleared the plates and carapaces away, asked Joan the question: *"Why is Daddy crying?"*

Richard heard the question but not the murmured answer. Then he heard Bean cry, "Oh, no-oh!"—the faintly dramatized exclamation of one who had long expected it.

John returned to the table carrying a bowl of salad. He nodded tersely at his father and his lips shaped the conspiratorial words "She told."

"Told what?" Richard asked aloud, insanely.

The boy sat down as if to rebuke his father's distraction with the example of his own good manners. He said quietly, "The separation."

Joan and Margaret returned; the child, in Richard's twisted vision, seemed diminished in size, and relieved, relieved to have had the bogieman at last proved real. He called out to her—the distances at the table had grown immense—"You knew, you always knew," but the clenching at the back of his throat prevented him from making sense of it. From afar he heard Joan talking, levelly, sensibly, reciting what they had prepared: it was a separation for the summer, an experiment. She and Daddy both agreed it would be good for them; they needed space and time to think; they liked each other but did not make each other happy enough, somehow.

Judith, imitating her mother's factual tone, but in her youth off-key, too cool, said, "I think it's silly. You should either live together or get divorced."

Richard's crying, like a wave that has crested and crashed, had become tumultuous; but it was overtopped by another tumult, for John, who had been so reserved, now grew larger and larger at the table. Perhaps his younger sister's being credited with knowing set him off. "Why didn't you *tell* us?" he asked, in a large round voice quite unlike his own. "You should have *told* us you weren't getting along."

Richard was startled into attempting to force words through his tears. "We *do* get along, that's the trouble, so it doesn't show even to us—" *That we do not love each other* was the rest of the sentence; he couldn't finish it.

Joan finished for him, in her style. "And we've always, *especially,* loved our children."

John was not mollified. "What do you care about *us?*" he boomed. "We're just little things you *had.*" His sisters' laughing forced a laugh from him, which he turned hard and parodistic: "Ha ha *ha.*" Richard and Joan realized simultaneously that the child was drunk, on Judith's homecoming champagne. Feeling bound to keep the center of the stage, John took a cigarette from Judith's pack, poked it into his mouth, let it hang from his lower lip, and squinted like a gangster.

"You're not little things we had," Richard called to him. "You're the whole point. But you're grown. Or almost."

The boy was lighting matches. Instead of holding them to his cigarette (for they had never seen him smoke; being "good" had been his way of setting himself apart), he held them to his mother's face, closer and closer, for her to blow out. Then he lit the whole folder—a hiss and then a torch, held against his mother's face. Prismed by tears, the flame filled Richard's vision; he didn't know how it was extinguished. He heard Margaret say, "Oh stop showing off," and saw John, in response, break the cigarette in two and put the halves entirely into his mouth and chew, sticking out his tongue to display the shreds to his sister.

Joan talked to him, reasoning—a fountain of reason, unintelligible. "Talked about it for years . . . our children must help us . . . Daddy and I both want . . ." As the boy listened, he carefully wadded a paper napkin into the leaves of his salad, fashioned a ball of paper and lettuce, and popped it into his mouth, looking around the table for the expected laughter. None came. Judith said, "Be mature," and dismissed a plume of smoke.

Richard got up from this stifling table and led the boy outside. Though the house was in twilight, the outdoors still brimmed with light, the lovely waste light of high summer. Both laughing, he supervised John's spitting out the lettuce and paper and tobacco into the pachysandra. He took him by the hand—a square gritty hand, but for its softness a man's. Yet, it held on. They ran together up into the field, past the tennis court. The raw banking left by the bulldozers was dotted with daisies. Past the court and a flat stretch where they used to play family baseball stood a soft green rise glorious in the sun, each weed and species of grass distinct as illumination on parchment. "I'm sorry, so sorry," Richard cried. "You were the only one who ever tried to help me with all the goddam jobs around this place."

Sobbing, safe within his tears and the champagne, John explained, "It's not just the separation, it's the whole crummy year, I *hate* that school, you can't make any friends, the history teacher's a scud."

They sat on the crest of the rise, shaking and warm from their tears but easier in their voices, and Richard tried to focus on the child's sad year—the weekdays long with homework, the weekends spent in his room with model airplanes, while his parents murmured down below, nursing their separation. How selfish, how blind, Richard thought; his eyes felt scoured. He told his son, "We'll think about getting you transferred. Life's too short to be miserable."

They had said what they could, but did not want the moment to heal, and talked on, about the school, about the tennis court, whether it would ever again be as good as it had been that first summer. They walked to inspect it and pressed a few more tapes more firmly down. A little stiltedly, perhaps trying now to make too much of the moment, Richard led the boy to the spot in the field where the view was best, of the metallic blue river, the emerald marsh, the scattered islands velvety with shadow in the low light, the white bits of beach far away. "See," he said. "It goes on being beautiful. It'll be here tomorrow."

"I know," John answered, impatiently. The moment had closed.

Back in the house, the others had opened some white wine, the champagne being drunk, and still sat at the table, the three females, gossiping. Where Joan sat had become the head. She turned, showing him a tearless face, and asked, "All right?"

"We're fine," he said, resenting it, though relieved, that the party went on without him.

In bed she explained, "I couldn't cry I guess because I cried so much all spring. It really wasn't fair. It's your idea, and you made it look as though I was kicking you out."

"I'm sorry," he said. "I couldn't stop. I wanted to but couldn't."

"You *didn't* want to. You loved it. You were having your way, making a general announcement."

"I love having it over," he admitted. "God, those kids were great. So brave and funny." John, returned to the house, had settled to a model airplane in his room, and kept shouting down to them, "I'm O.K. No sweat." "And the way," Richard went on, cozy in his relief, "they never questioned the reasons we gave. No thought of a third person. Not even Judith."

"That *was* touching," Joan said.

He gave her a hug. "You were great too. Very reassuring to everybody. Thank you." Guiltily, he realized he did not feel separated.

"You still have Dickie to do," she told him. These words set before him a black mountain in the darkness; its cold breath, its near weight affected his chest. Of the four children, his elder son was most nearly his conscience. Joan did not need to add, "That's one piece of your dirty work I won't do for you."

"I know. I'll do it. You go to sleep."

Within minutes, her breathing slowed, became oblivious and deep. It was quarter to midnight. Dickie's train from the concert would come in at one-fourteen. Richard set the alarm for one. He had slept atrociously for weeks. But whenever he closed his lids some glimpse of the last hours scorched them—Judith exhaling toward the ceiling in a kind of aversion, Bean's mute staring, the sunstruck growth in the field where he and John had rested. The mountain before him moved closer, moved within him; he was huge, momentous. The ache at the back of his throat felt stale. His wife slept as if slain beside him. When, exasperated by his hot lids, his crowded heart, he rose from bed and dressed, she awoke enough to turn over. He told her then, "Joan, if I could undo it all, I would."

"Where would you begin?" she asked. There was no place. Giving him courage, she was always giving him courage. He put on shoes without socks in the dark. The children were breathing in their rooms, the downstairs was hollow. In their confusion they had left lights burning. He turned off all but one, the kitchen overhead. The car started. He had hoped it wouldn't. He met only moonlight on the road; it seemed a diaphanous companion, flickering in the leaves along the roadside, haunting his rearview mirror like a pursuer, melting under his headlights. The center of town, not quite deserted, was eerie at this hour. A young cop in uniform kept company with a gang of T-shirted kids on the steps of the bank. Across from the railroad station, several bars kept open. Customers, mostly young, passed in and out of the warm night, savoring summer's novelty. Voices shouted from cars as they passed; an immense conversation seemed in progress. Richard parked and in his weariness put his head on the passenger seat, out of the commotion and wheeling lights. It was as when, in the movies, an assassin grimly carries his mission through the jostle of a carnival—except the movies cannot show the precipitous, palpable slope you cling to within. You cannot climb back down; you can only fall. The synthetic fabric of the car seat, warmed by his cheek, confided to him an ancient, distant scent of vanilla.

A train whistle caused him to lift his head. It was on time; he had hoped it would be late. The slender draw-gates descended. The bell of approach tingled happily. The great metal body, horizontally fluted, rocked to a stop, and sleepy teen-agers disembarked, his son among them. Dickie did not show surprise that his father was meeting him at this terrible hour. He sauntered to the car with two friends, both taller than he. He said "Hi" to his father and took the passenger's seat with an exhausted promptness that expressed gratitude. The friends got in the back, and Richard was grateful; a few more minutes' postponement would be won by driving them home.

He asked, "How was the concert?"

"Groovy," one boy said from the back seat.

"It bit," the other said.

"It was O.K.," Dickie said, moderate by nature, so reasonable that in his childhood the unreason of the world had given him headaches, stomach aches, nausea. When the second friend had been dropped off at his dark house, the boy blurted, "Dad, my eyes are killing me with hay fever! I'm out there cutting that mothering grass all day!"

"Do we still have those drops?"

"They didn't do any good last summer."

"They might this." Richard swung a U-turn on the empty street. The drive home took a few minutes. The mountain was here, in his throat. "Richard," he said, and felt the boy, slumped and rubbing his eyes, go tense at his tone, "I didn't come to meet you just to make your life easier. I came because your mother and I have some news for you, and you're a hard man to get ahold of these days. It's sad news."

"That's O.K." The reassurance came out soft, but quick, as if released from the tip of a spring.

Richard had feared that his tears would return and choke him, but the boy's manliness set an example, and his voice issued forth steady and dry. "It's sad news, but it needn't be tragic news, at least for you. It should have no practical effect on your life, though it's bound to have an emotional effect. You'll work at your job, and go back to school in September. Your mother and I are really proud of what you're making of your life; we don't want that to change at all."

"Yeah," the boy said lightly, on the intake of his breath, holding himself up. They turned the corner; the church they went to loomed like a gutted fort. The home of the woman Richard hoped to marry stood across the green. Her bedroom light burned.

"Your mother and I," he said, "have decided to separate. For the summer. Nothing legal, no divorce yet. We want to see how it feels. For some years now, we haven't been doing enough for each other, making each other as happy as we should be. Have you sensed that?"

"No," the boy said. It was an honest, unemotional answer: true or false in a quiz.

Glad for the factual basis, Richard pursued, even garrulously, the details. His apartment across town, his utter accessibility, the split vacation arrangements, the advantages to the children, the added mobility and variety of the summer. Dickie listened, absorbing. "Do the others know?"

"Yes."

"How did they take it?"

"The girls pretty calmly. John flipped out; he shouted and ate a cigarette and made a salad out of his napkin and told us how much he hated school."

His brother chuckled. "He did?"

"Yeah. The school issue was more upsetting for him than Mom and me. He seemed to feel better for having exploded."

"He did?" The repetition was the first sign that he was stunned.

"Yes. Dickie, I want to tell you something. This last hour, waiting for your train to get in, has been about the worst of my life. I hate this. *Hate* it. My father would have died before doing it to me." He felt immensely lighter, saying this. He had dumped the mountain on the boy. They were home. Moving swiftly as a shadow, Dickie was out of the car, through the bright kitchen. Richard called after him, "Want a glass of milk or anything?"

"No thanks."

"Want us to call the course tomorrow and say you're too sick to work?"

"No, that's all right." The answer was faint, delivered at the door to his room; Richard listened for the slam that went with a tantrum. The door closed normally, gently. The sound was sickening.

Joan had sunk into that first deep trough of sleep and was slow to awake. Richard had to repeat, "I told him."

"What did he say?"

"Nothing much. Could you go say goodnight to him? Please."

She left their room, without putting on a bathrobe. He sluggishly changed back into his pajamas and walked down the hall. Dickie was already in bed, Joan was sitting beside him, and the boy's bedside clock radio was murmuring music. When she stood, an inexplicable light—the moon?—outlined her body through the nightie. Richard sat on the warm place she had indented on the child's narrow mattress. He asked him, "Do you want the radio on like that?"

"It always is."

"Doesn't it keep you awake? It would me."

"No."

"Are you sleepy?"

"Yeah."

"Good. Sure you want to get up and go to work? You've had a big night."

"I want to."

Away at school this winter he had learned for the first time that you can go short of sleep and live. As an infant he had slept with an immobile, sweating intensity that had alarmed his babysitters. In adolescence he had often been the first of the four children to go to bed. Even now, he would go slack in the middle of a television show, his sprawled legs hairy and brown. "O.K. Good boy. Dickie, listen. I love you so much, I never knew how much until now. No matter how this works out, I'll always be with you. Really."

Richard bent to kiss an averted face but his son, sinewy, turned and with wet cheeks embraced him and gave him a kiss, on the lips, passionate as a woman's. In his father's ear he moaned one word, the crucial, intelligent word: "*Why*?"

Why. It was a whistle of wind in a crack, a knife thrust, a window thrown open on emptiness. The white face was gone, the darkness was featureless. Richard had forgotten why.

Susan Sontag

Susan Sontag (b.1933) was born in New York and raised in Tucson and Los Angeles. She realized early that books and writers mattered to her more than anything else. Though she studied philosophy at the University of Chicago and has taught and lectured widely, she often adopts a decidedly nonacademic stance. She has established herself as a leading intellectual, publishing criticism, screenplays, and fiction. Sontag's fiction, which includes the novels *Death Kit* and *The Benefactor* as well as the stories collected in *I, Etcetera,* reflects a sensibility attuned to the fragmenting forces of our culture but pledged to the possibilities of private integrity.

THE WAY WE LIVE NOW

At first he was just losing weight, he felt only a little ill, Max said to Ellen, and he didn't call for an appointment with his doctor, according to Greg, because he was managing to keep on working at more or less the same rhythm, but he did stop smoking, Tanya pointed out, which suggests he was frightened, but also that he wanted, even more than he knew, to be healthy, or healthier, or maybe just to gain back a few pounds, said Orson, for he told her, Tanya went on, that he expected to be climbing the walls (isn't that what people say?) and found, to his surprise, that he didn't miss cigarettes at all and reveled in the sensation of his lungs' being ache-free for the first time in years. But did he have a good doctor, Stephen wanted to know, since it would have been crazy not to go for a checkup after the pressure was off and he was back from the conference in Helsinki, even if by then he was feeling better. And he said, to Frank, that he would go, even though he was indeed frightened, as he admitted to Jan, but who wouldn't be frightened now, though, odd as that might seem, he hadn't been worrying until recently, he avowed to Quentin, it was only in the last six months that he had the metallic taste of panic in his mouth, because becoming seriously ill was something that happened to other people, a normal delusion, he observed to Paolo, if one was thirty-eight and had never had a serious illness; he wasn't, as Jan confirmed, a hypochondriac. Of course, it was hard not to worry, everyone was worried, but it wouldn't do to panic, because, as Max pointed out to Quentin, there wasn't anything one could do except wait and hope, wait and start being careful, be careful, and hope. And even if one did prove to be ill, one shouldn't give up, they had new treatments that promised an arrest of the disease's inexorable course, research was progressing. It seemed that everyone was in touch with everyone else several times a week, checking in, I've never spent so many hours at a time on the phone, Stephen said to Kate, and when I'm exhausted after the two or three calls made to me, giving me the latest, instead of switching off the phone to give myself a respite I tap out the number of another friend or acquaintance, to pass on the news. I'm not sure I can afford to think so much about it, Ellen said, and I suspect my own motives, there's something morbid I'm getting used to, getting excited by, this must be like what people felt in London during the Blitz. As far as I know, I'm not at risk, but you never know, said Aileen. This thing is totally unprecedented, said Frank. But don't you think he ought to see a doctor, Stephen insisted. Listen, said Orson, you can't force people to take care of themselves, and what makes you think the worst, he could be just run down, people still do get ordinary illnesses, awful ones, why are you assuming it has to be *that*. But all I want to be sure, said Stephen, is that he understands the options, because most people don't, that's why they won't see a doctor or have the test, they think there's nothing one can do. But is there anything one can do, he said to Tanya (according to Greg), I mean what do I gain if I go to the doctor; if I'm really ill, he's reported to have said, I'll find out soon enough.

And when he was in the hospital, his spirits seemed to lighten, according to Donny. He seemed more cheerful than he had been in the last months, Ursula said, and the bad news seemed to come almost as a relief, according to Ira, as a truly unexpected blow, according to Quentin, but you'd hardly expect him to have said the same thing to all his friends, because his relation to Ira was so different from his relation to Quentin (this according to Quentin, who was proud of their friendship), and perhaps he thought Quentin wouldn't be undone by seeing him weep, but Ira insisted that couldn't be the reason he behaved so differently with each, and that maybe he was feeling less shocked, mobilizing his strength to fight for his life, at the moment he saw Ira but overcome by feelings of hopelessness when Quentin arrived with flowers, because anyway the flowers threw him into a bad mood, as Quentin told Kate, since the hospital room was choked with flowers, you couldn't have crammed another flower into that room, but surely you're exaggerating, Kate said, smiling, everybody likes flowers. Well, who wouldn't exaggerate at a time like this, Quentin said sharply. Don't you think *this* is an exaggeration. Of course I do, said Kate gently, I was only teasing, I mean I didn't mean to tease. I know that, Quentin said, with tears in his eyes, and Kate hugged him and said well, when I go this evening I guess I won't bring flowers, what does he want, and Quentin said, according to Max, what he likes best is chocolate. Is there anything else, asked Kate, I mean like chocolate but not chocolate. Licorice, said Quentin, blowing his nose. And besides that. Aren't *you* exaggerating now, Quentin said, smiling. Right, said Kate, so if I want to bring him a whole raft of stuff, besides chocolate and licorice, what else. Jelly beans, Quentin said.

He didn't want to be alone, according to Paolo, and lots of people came in the first week, and the Jamaican nurse said there were other patients on the floor who would be glad to have the surplus flowers, and people weren't afraid to visit, it wasn't like the old days, as Kate pointed out to Aileen, they're not even segregated in the hospital anymore, as Hilda observed, there's nothing on the door of his room warning visitors of the possibility of contagion, as there was a few years ago; in fact, he's in a double room and, as he told Orson, the old guy on the far side of the curtain (who's clearly on the way out, said Stephen) doesn't even have the disease, so, as Kate went on, you really should go and see him, he'd be happy to see you, he likes having people visit, you aren't not going because you're afraid, are you. Of course not, Aileen said, but I don't know what to say, I think I'll feel awkward, which he's bound to notice, and that will make him feel worse, so I won't be doing him any good, will I. But he won't notice anything, Kate said, patting Aileen's hand, it's not like that, it's not the way you imagine, he's not judging people or wondering about their motives, he's just happy to see his friends. But I never was really a friend of his, Aileen said, you're a friend, he's always liked you, you told me he talks about Nora with you, I know he likes me, he's even attracted to me, but he respects you. But, according to Wesley, the reason Aileen was so stingy with her visits was that she could never have him to herself, there were always others there already and by the time they left still others had arrived, she'd been in love with him for years, and I can understand, said Donny, that Aileen should feel bitter that if there could have been a woman friend he did more than occasionally bed, a woman he really loved, and my God, Victor said, who had known him in those years, he was crazy about Nora, what a heart-rending couple they were, two surly angels, then it couldn't have been she.

And when some of the friends, the ones who came every day, waylaid the doctor in the corridor, Stephen was the one who asked the most informed questions, who'd been keeping up not just with the stories that appeared several times a week in the *Times* (which Greg confessed to have stopped reading, unable to stand it anymore) but with articles in the medical journals published here and in England and France, and who knew socially one of the principal doctors in Paris who was doing some much-publicized research on the disease, but his doctor said little more than that the pneumonia was not life-threatening, the fever was subsiding, of course he was still weak but he was responding well to the antibiotics, that he'd have to complete his stay in the hospital, which entailed a minimum of twenty-one days on the IV, before she could start him on the new drug, for she was optimistic about the possibility of getting him into the protocol; and when Victor said that if he had so much trouble eating (he'd say to everyone when they coaxed him to eat some of the hospital meals, that food didn't taste right, that he had a funny metallic taste in his mouth) it couldn't be good that friends were bringing him all that chocolate, the doctor just smiled and said that in these cases the patient's morale was also an important factor, and if chocolate made him feel better she saw no harm in it, which worried Stephen, as Stephen said later to Donny, because they wanted to believe in the promises and taboos of today's high-tech medicine but here this reassuringly curt and silver-haired specialist in the disease, someone quoted frequently in the papers, was talking like some oldfangled country GP who tells the family that tea with honey or chicken soup may do as much for the patient as penicillin, which might mean, as Max said, that they were just going through the motions of treating him, that they were not sure about what to do, or rather, as Xavier interjected, that they didn't know what the hell they were doing, that the truth, the real truth, as Hilda said, upping the ante, was that they didn't, the doctors, really have any hope.

Oh, no, said Lewis, I can't stand it, wait a minute, I can't believe it, are you sure, I mean are they sure, have they done all the tests, it's getting so when the phone rings I'm scared to answer because I think it will be someone telling me someone else is ill; but did Lewis really not know until yesterday, Robert said testily, I find that hard to believe, everybody is talking about it, it seems impossible that someone wouldn't have called Lewis; and perhaps Lewis did know, was for some reason pretending not to know already, because, Jan recalled, didn't Lewis say something months ago to Greg, and not only to Greg, about his not looking well, losing weight, and being worried about him and wishing he'd see a doctor, so it couldn't come as a total surprise. Well, everybody is worried about everybody now, said Betsy, that seems to be the way we live, the way we live now. And, after all, they were once very close, doesn't Lewis still have the keys to his apartment, you know the way you let someone keep the keys after you've broken up, only a little because you hope the person might just saunter in, drunk or high, late some evening, but mainly because it's wise to have a few sets of keys strewn around town, if you live alone, at the top of a former commercial building that, pretentious as it is, will never acquire a doorman or even a resident superintendent, someone whom you can call on for the keys late one night if you find you've lost yours or have locked yourself out. Who else has keys, Tanya inquired, I was thinking somebody might drop by tomorrow before coming to the hospital and bring some treasures, because the other day, Ira said, he was complaining about how dreary the hospital room was, and how it was like being locked up in a motel room, which got everybody started telling funny stories about motel rooms they'd known, and at Ursula's story, about the Luxury Budget Inn in Schenectady, there was an uproar of laughter around his bed, while he watched them in silence, eyes bright with fever, all the while, as Victor recalled, gobbling that damned chocolate. But, according to Jan, whom Lewis's keys enabled to tour the swank of his bachelor lair with an eye to bringing over some art consolation to brighten up the hospital room, the Byzantine icon wasn't on the wall over his bed, and that was a puzzle until Orson remembered that he'd recounted without seeming upset (this disputed by Greg) that the boy he'd recently gotten rid of had stolen it, along with four of the *maki-e* lacquer boxes, as if these were objects as easy to sell on the street as a TV or a stereo. But he's always been very generous, Kate said quietly, and though he loves beautiful things isn't really attached to them, to things, as Orson said, which is unusual in a collector, as Frank commented, and when Kate shuddered and tears sprang to her eyes and Orson inquired anxiously if he, Orson, had said something wrong, she pointed out that they'd begun talking about him in a retrospective mode, summing up what he was like, what made them fond of him, as if he were finished, completed, already a part of the past.

Perhaps he was getting tired of having so many visitors, said Robert, who was, as Ellen couldn't help mentioning, someone who had come only twice and was probably looking for a reason not to be in regular attendance, but there could be no doubt, according to Ursula, that his spirits had dipped, not that there was any discouraging news from the doctors, and he seemed now to prefer being alone a few hours of the day; and he told Donny that he'd begun keeping a diary for the first time in his life, because he wanted to record the course of his mental reactions to this astonishing turn of events, to do something parallel to what the doctors were doing, who came every morning and conferred at his bedside about his body, and that perhaps it wasn't so important what he wrote in it, which amounted, as he said wryly to Quentin, to little more than the usual banalities about terror and amazement that this was happening to him, to him also, plus the usual remorseful assessments of his past life, his pardonable superficialities, capped by resolves to live better, more deeply, more in touch with his work and his friends, and not to care so passionately about what people thought of him, interspersed with admonitions to himself that in this situation his will to live counted more than anything else and that if he really wanted to live, and trusted life, and liked himself well enough (down, ol' debbil Thanatos!), he *would* live, he would be an exception; but perhaps all this, as Quentin ruminated, talking on the phone to Kate, wasn't the point, the point was that by the very keeping of the diary he was accumulating something to reread one day, slyly staking out his claim to a future time, in which the diary would be an object, a relic, in which he might not actually reread it, because he would want to have put this ordeal behind him, but the diary would be there in the drawer of his stupendous Majorelle desk, and he could already, he did actually say to Quentin one late sunny afternoon, propped up in the hospital bed, with the stain of chocolate framing one corner of a heartbreaking smile, see himself in the penthouse, the October sun streaming through those clear windows instead of this streaked one, and the diary, the pathetic diary, safe inside the drawer.

It doesn't matter about the treatment's side effects, Stephen said (when talking to Max), I don't know why you're so worried about that, every strong treatment has some dangerous side effects, it's inevitable, you mean otherwise the treatment wouldn't be effective, Hilda interjected, and anyway, Stephen went on doggedly, just because there *are* side effects it doesn't mean he has to get them, or all of them, each one, or even some of them. That's just a list of all the possible things that could go wrong, because the doctors have to cover themselves, so they make up a worst-case scenario, but isn't what's happening to him, and to so many other people, Tanya interrupted, a worst-case scenario, a catastrophe no one could have imagined, it's too cruel, and isn't everything a side effect, quipped Ira, even *we* are all side effects, but we're not bad side effects, Frank said, he likes having his friends around, and we're helping each other, too; because his illness sticks us all in the same glue, mused Xavier, and, whatever the jealousies and grievances from the past that have made us wary and cranky with each other, when something like this happens (the sky is falling, the sky is falling!) you understand what's really important. I agree, Chicken Little, he is reported to have said. But don't you think, Quentin observed to Max, that being as close to him as we are, making time to drop by the hospital every day, is a way of our trying to define ourselves more firmly and irrevocably as the well, those who aren't ill, who aren't going to fall ill, as if what's happened to him couldn't happen to us, when in fact the chances are that before long one of us will end up where he is, which is probably what he felt when he was one of the cohort visiting Zack in the spring (you never knew Zack, did you?), and, according to Clarice, Zack's widow, he didn't come very often, he said he hated hospitals, and didn't feel he was doing Zack any good, that Zack would see on his face how uncomfortable he was. Oh, he was one of those, Aileen said. A coward. Like me.

And after he was sent home from the hospital, and Quentin had volunteered to move in and was cooking meals and taking telephone messages and keeping the mother in Mississippi informed, well, mainly keeping her from flying to New York and heaping her grief on her son and confusing the household routine with her oppressive ministrations, he was able to work an hour or two in his study, on days he didn't insist on going out, for a meal or a movie, which tired him. He seemed optimistic, Kate thought, his appetite was good, and what he said, Orson reported, was that he agreed when Stephen advised him that the main thing was to keep in shape, he was a fighter, right, he wouldn't be who he was if he weren't, and was he ready for the big fight, Stephen asked rhetorically (as Max told it to Donny), and he said you bet, and Stephen added it could be a lot worse, you could have gotten the disease two years ago, but now so many scientists are working on it, the American team and the French team, everyone bucking for that Nobel Prize a few years down the road, that all you have to do is stay healthy for another year or two and then there will be good treatment, real treatment. Yes, he said, Stephen said, my timing is good. And Betsy, who had been climbing on and rolling off macrobiotic diets for a decade, came up with a Japanese specialist she wanted him to see but thank God, Donny reported, he'd had the sense to refuse, but he did agree to see Victor's visualization therapist, although what could one possibly visualize, said Hilda, when the point of visualizing disease was to see it as an entity with contours, borders, here rather than there, something limited, something you were the host of, in the sense that you could disinvite the disease, while this was so total; or would be, Max said. But the main thing, said Greg, was to see that he didn't go the macrobiotic route, which might be harmless for plump Betsy but could only be devastating for him, lean as he'd always been, with all the cigarettes and other appetite-suppressing chemicals he'd been welcoming into his body for years; and now was hardly the time, as Stephen pointed out, to be worried about cleaning up his act, and eliminating the chemical additives and other pollutants that we're all blithely or not so blithely feasting on, blithely since we're healthy, healthy as we can be; so far, Ira said. Meat and potatoes is what I'd be happy to see him eating, Ursula said wistfully. And spaghetti and clam sauce, Greg added. And thick cholesterol-rich omelets with smoked mozzarella, suggested Yvonne, who had flown from London for the weekend to see him. Chocolate cake, said Frank. Maybe not chocolate cake, Ursula said, he's already eating so much chocolate.

And when, not right away but still only three weeks later, he was accepted into the protocol for the new drug, which took considerable behind-the-scenes lobbying with the doctors, he talked less about being ill, according to Donny, which seemed like a good sign, Kate felt, a sign that he was not feeling like a victim, feeling not that he *had* a disease but, rather, was living *with* a disease (that was the right cliché, wasn't it?), a more hospitable arrangement, said Jan, a kind of cohabitation which implied that it was something temporary, that it could be terminated, but terminated how, said Hilda, and when you say hospitable, Jan, I hear hospital. And it was encouraging, Stephen insisted, that from the start, at least from the time he was finally persuaded to make the telephone call to his doctor, he was willing to say the name of the disease, pronounce it often and easily, as if it were just another word, like boy or gallery or cigarette or money or deal, as in no big deal, Paolo interjected, because, as Stephen continued, to utter the name is a sign of health, a sign that one has accepted being who one is, mortal, vulnerable, not exempt, not an exception after all, it's a sign that one is willing, truly willing, to fight for one's life. And we must say the name, too, and often, Tanya added, we mustn't lag behind him in honesty, or let him feel that, the effort of honesty having been made, it's something done with and he can go on to other things. One is so much better prepared to help him, Wesley replied. In a way he's fortunate, said Yvonne, who had taken care of a problem at the New York store and was flying back to London this evening, sure, fortunate, said Wesley, no one is shunning him, Yvonne went on, no one's afraid to hug him or kiss him lightly on the mouth, in London we are, as usual, a few years behind you, people I know, people who would seem to be not even remotely at risk, are just terrified, but I'm impressed by how cool and rational you all are; you find us cool, asked Quentin. But I have to say, he's reported to have said, I'm terrified, I find it very hard to read (and you know how he loves to read, said Greg; yes, reading is his television, said Paolo) or to think, but I don't feel hysterical. I feel quite hysterical, Lewis said to Yvonne. But you're able to *do* something for him, that's wonderful, how I wish I could stay longer, Yvonne answered, it's rather beautiful, I can't help thinking, this utopia of friendship you've assembled around him (this pathetic utopia, said Kate), so that the disease, Yvonne concluded, is not, anymore, out there. Yes, don't you think we're more at home here, with him, with the disease, said Tanya, because the imagined disease is so much worse than the reality of him, whom we all love, each in our fashion, having it. I know for me his getting it has quite demystified the disease, said Jan, I don't feel afraid, spooked, as I did before he became ill, when it was only news about remote acquaintances, whom I never saw again after they became ill. But you know you're not going to come down with the disease, Quentin said, to which Ellen replied, on her behalf, that's not the point, and possibly untrue, my gynecologist says that everyone is at risk, everyone who has a sexual life, because sexuality is a chain that links each of us to many others, unknown others, and now the great chain of being has become a chain of death as well. It's not the same for you, Quentin insisted, it's not the same for you as it is for me or Lewis or Frank or Paolo or Max, I'm more and more frightened, and I have every reason to be. I don't think about whether I'm at risk or not, said Hilda, I know that I was afraid to know someone with the disease, afraid of what I'd see, what I'd feel, and after the first day I came to the hospital I felt so relieved. I'll never feel that way, that fear, again; he doesn't seem different from me. He's not, Quentin said.

According to Lewis, he talked more often about those who visited more often, which is natural, said Betsy, I think he's even keeping a tally. And among those who came or checked in by phone every day, the inner circle as it were, those who were getting more points, there was still a further competition, which was what was getting on Betsy's nerves, she confessed to Jan; there's always that vulgar jockeying for position around the bedside of the gravely ill, and though we all feel suffused with virtue at our loyalty to him (speak for yourself, said Jan), to the extent that we're carving time out of every day, or almost every day, though some of us are dropping out, as Xavier pointed out, aren't we getting at least as much out of this as he is. Are we, said Jan. We're rivals for a sign from him of special pleasure over a visit, each stretching for the brass ring of his favor, wanting to feel the most wanted, the true nearest and dearest, which is inevitable with someone who doesn't have a spouse and children or an official in-house lover, hierarchies that no one would dare contest, Betsy went on, so we are the family he's founded, without meaning to, without official titles and ranks (we, we, snarled Quentin); and is it so clear, though some of us, Lewis and Quentin and Tanya and Paolo, among others, are ex-lovers and all of us more or less than friends, which one of us he prefers, Victor said (now it's us, raged Quentin), because sometimes I think he looks forward more to seeing Aileen, who has visited only three times, twice at the hospital and once since he's been home, than he does you or me; but, according to Tanya, after being very disappointed that Aileen hadn't come, now he was angry, while, according to Xavier, he was not really hurt but touchingly passive, accepting Aileen's absence as something he somehow deserved. But he's happy to have people around, said Lewis; he says when he doesn't have company he gets very sleepy, he sleeps (according to Quentin), and then perks up when someone arrives, it's important that he not feel ever alone. But, said Victor, there's one person he hasn't heard from, whom he'd probably like to hear from more than most of us; but she didn't just vanish, even right after she broke away from him, and he knows exactly where she lives now, said Kate, he told me he put in a call to her last Christmas Eve, and she said it's nice to hear from you and Merry Christmas, and he was shattered, according to Orson, and furious and disdainful, according to Ellen (what do you expect of her, said Wesley, she was burned out), but Kate wondered if maybe he hadn't phoned Nora in the middle of a sleepless night, what's the time difference, and Quentin said no, I don't think so, I think he wouldn't want her to know.

And when he was feeling even better and had regained the pounds he'd shed right away in the hospital, though the refrigerator started to fill up with organic wheat germ and grapefruit and skimmed milk (he's worried about his cholesterol count, Stephen lamented), and told Quentin he could manage by himself now, and did, he started asking everyone who visited how he looked, and everyone said he looked great, so much better than a few weeks ago, which didn't jibe with what anyone had told him at that time; but then it was getting harder and harder to know how he looked, to answer such a question honestly when among themselves they wanted to be honest, both for honesty's sake and (as Donny thought) to prepare for the worst, because he'd been looking like *this* for so long, at least it seemed so long, that it was as if he'd always been like this, how did he look before, but it was only a few months, and those words, pale and wan looking and fragile, hadn't they always applied? And one Thursday Ellen, meeting Lewis at the door of the building, said, as they rode up together in the elevator, how is he *really?* But you see how he is, Lewis said tartly, he's fine, he's perfectly healthy, and Ellen understood that of course Lewis didn't think he was perfectly healthy but that he wasn't worse, and that was true, but wasn't it, well, almost heartless to talk like that. Seems inoffensive to me, Quentin said, but I know what you mean, I remember once talking to Frank, somebody, after all, who has volunteered to do five hours a week of office work at the Crisis Center (I know, said Ellen), and Frank was going on about this guy, diagnosed almost a year ago, and so much further along, who'd been complaining to Frank on the phone about the indifference of some doctor, and had gotten quite abusive about the doctor, and Frank was saying there was no reason to be so upset, the implication being that *he,* Frank, wouldn't behave so irrationally, and I said, barely able to control my scorn, but Frank, Frank, he has every reason to be upset, he's dying, and Frank said, said according to Quentin, oh, I don't like to think about it that way.

And it was while he was still home, recuperating, getting his weekly treatment, still not able to do much work, he complained, but, according to Quentin, up and about most of the time and turning up at the office several days a week, that bad news came about two remote acquaintances, one in Houston and one in Paris, news that was intercepted by Quentin on the ground that it could only depress him, but Stephen contended that it was wrong to lie to him, it was so important for him to live in the truth; that had been one of his first victories, that he was candid, that he was even willing to crack jokes about the disease, but Ellen said it wasn't good to give him this end-of-the-world feeling, too many people were getting ill, it was becoming such a common destiny that maybe some of the will to fight for his life would be drained out of him if it seemed to be as natural as, well, death. Oh, Hilda said, who didn't know personally either the one in Houston or the one in Paris, but knew *of* the one in Paris, a pianist who specialized in twentieth-century Czech and Polish music, I have his records, he's such a valuable person, and, when Kate glared at her, continued defensively, I know every life is equally sacred, but that *is* a thought, another thought, I mean, all these valuable people who aren't going to have their normal four score as it is now, these people aren't going to be replaced, and it's such a loss to the culture. But this isn't going to go on forever, Wesley said, it can't, they're bound to come up with something (they, they, muttered Stephen), but did you ever think, Greg said, that if some people don't die, I mean even if they can keep them alive (they, they, muttered Kate), they continue to be carriers, and that means, if you have a conscience, that you can never make love, make love fully, as you'd been wont—wantonly, Ira said—to do. But it's better than dying, said Frank. And in all his talk about the future, when he allowed himself to be hopeful, according to Quentin, he never mentioned the prospect that even if he didn't die, if he were so fortunate as to be among the first generation of the disease's survivors, never mentioned, Kate confirmed, that whatever happened it was over, the way he had lived until now, but, according to Ira, he did think about it, the end of bravado, the end of folly, the end of trusting life, the end of taking life for granted, and of treating life as something that, samurai-like, he thought himself ready to throw away lightly, impudently; and Kate recalled, sighing, a brief exchange she'd insisted on having as long as two years ago, huddling on a banquette covered with steel-gray industrial carpet on an upper level of The Prophet and toking up for their next foray onto the dance floor: she'd said hesitantly, for it felt foolish asking a prince of debauchery to, well, take it easy, and she wasn't keen on playing big sister, a role, as Hilda confirmed, he inspired in many women, are you being careful, honey, you know what I mean. And he replied, Kate went on, no, I'm not, listen, I can't, I just can't, sex is too important to me, always has been (he started talking like that, according to Victor, after Nora left him), and if I get it, well, I get it. But he wouldn't talk like that now, would he, said Greg; he must feel awfully foolish now, said Betsy, like someone who went on smoking, saying I can't give up cigarettes, but when the bad X-ray is taken even the most besotted nicotine addict can stop on a dime. But sex isn't like cigarettes, is it, said Frank, and, besides, what good does it do to remember that he was reckless, said Lewis angrily, the appalling thing is that you just have to be unlucky once, and wouldn't he feel even worse if he'd stopped three years ago and had come down with it anyway, since one of the most terrifying features of the disease is that you don't know when you contracted it, it could have been ten years ago, because surely this disease has existed for years and years, long before it was recognized; that is, named. Who knows how long (I think a lot about that, said Max) and who knows (I know what you're going to say, Stephen interrupted) how many are going to get it.

I'm feeling fine, he's reported to have said whenever someone asked him how he was, which was almost always the first question anyone asked. Or: I'm feeling better, how are you? But he said other things, too. I'm playing leapfrog with myself, he is reported to have said, according to Victor. And: There must be a way to get something positive out of this situation, he's reported to have said to Kate. How American of him, said Paolo. Well, said Betsy, you know the old American adage: When you've got a lemon, make lemonade. The one thing I'm sure I couldn't take, Jan said he said to her, is becoming disfigured, but Stephen hastened to point out the disease doesn't take that form very often anymore, its profile is mutating, and, in conversation with Ellen, wheeled up words like blood-brain barrier; I never thought there was a barrier *there,* said Jan. But he mustn't know about Max, Ellen said, that would really depress him, please don't tell him, he'll have to know, Quentin said grimly, and he'll be furious not to have been told. But there's time for that, when they take Max off the respirator, said Ellen; but isn't it incredible, Frank said, Max was fine, not feeling ill at all, and then to wake up with a fever of a hundred and five, unable to breathe, but that's the way it often starts, with absolutely no warning, Stephen said, the disease has so many forms. And when, after another week had gone by, he asked Quentin where Max was, he didn't question Quentin's account of a spree in the Bahamas, but then the number of people who visited regularly was thinning out, partly because the old feuds that had been put aside through the first hospitalization and the return home had resurfaced, and the flickering enmity between Lewis and Frank exploded, even though Kate did her best to mediate between them, and also because he himself had done something to loosen the bonds of love that united the friends around him, by seeming to take them all for granted, as if it were perfectly normal for so many people to carve out so much time and attention for him, visit him every few days, talk about him incessantly on the phone with each other; but, according to Paolo, it wasn't that he was less grateful, it was just something he was getting used to, the visits. It had become, with time, a more ordinary kind of situation, a kind of ongoing party, first at the hospital and now since he was home, barely on his feet again, it being clear, said Robert, that I'm on the B list; but Kate said, that's absurd, there's no list; and Victor said, but there is, only it's not he, it's Quentin who's drawing it up. He wants to see us, we're helping him, we have to do it the way he wants, he fell down yesterday on the way to the bathroom, he mustn't be told about Max (but he already knew, according to Donny), it's getting worse.

When I was home, he is reported to have said, I was afraid to sleep, as I was dropping off each night it felt like just that, as if I were falling down a black hole, to sleep felt like giving in to death, I slept every night with the light on; but here, in the hospital, I'm less afraid. And to Quentin he said, one morning, the fear rips through me, it tears me open; and, to Ira, it presses me together, squeezes me toward myself. Fear gives everything its hue, its high. I feel so, I don't know how to say it, exalted, he said to Quentin. Calamity is an amazing high, too. Sometimes I feel *so* well, so powerful, it's as if I could jump out of my skin. Am I going crazy, or what? Is it all this attention and coddling I'm getting from everybody, like a child's dream of being loved? Is it the drugs? I know it sounds crazy but sometimes I think this is a *fantastic* experience, he said shyly; but there was also the bad taste in the mouth, the pressure in the head and at the back of the neck, the red, bleeding gums, the painful, if pink-lobed, breathing, and his ivory pallor, color of white chocolate. Among those who wept when told over the phone that he was back in the hospital were Kate and Stephen (who'd been called by Quentin), and Ellen, Victor, Aileen, and Lewis (who were called by Kate), and Xavier and Ursula (who were called by Stephen). Among those who didn't weep were Hilda, who said that she'd just learned that her seventy-five-year-old aunt was dying of the disease, which she'd contracted from a transfusion given during her successful double bypass of five years ago, and Frank and Donny and Betsy, but this didn't mean, according to Tanya, that they weren't moved and appalled, and Quentin thought they might not be coming soon to the hospital but would send presents; the room, he was in a private room this time, was filling up with flowers, and plants, and books, and tapes. The high tide of barely suppressed acrimony of the last weeks at home subsided into the routines of hospital visiting, though more than a few resented Quentin's having charge of the visiting book (but it was Quentin who had the idea, Lewis pointed out); now, to insure a steady stream of visitors, preferably no more than two at a time (this, the rule in all hospitals, wasn't enforced here, at least on this floor; whether out of kindness or inefficiency, no one could decide), Quentin had to be called first, to get one's time slot, there was no more casual dropping by. And his mother could no longer be prevented from taking a plane and installing herself in a hotel near the hospital; but he seemed to mind her daily presence less than expected, Quentin said; said Ellen it's we who mind, do you suppose she'll stay long. It was easier to be generous with each other visiting him here in the hospital, as Donny pointed out, than at home, where one minded never being alone with him; coming here, in our twos and twos, there's no doubt about what our role is, how we should be, collective, funny, distracting, undemanding, light, it's important to be light, for in all this dread there is gaiety, too, as the poet said, said Kate. (His eyes, his glittering eyes, said Lewis.) His eyes looked dull, extinguished, Wesley said to Xavier, but Betsy said his face, not just his eyes, looked soulful, warm; whatever is there, said Kate, I've never been so aware of his eyes; and Stephen said, I'm afraid of what my eyes show, the way I watch him, with too much intensity, or a phony kind of casualness, said Victor. And, unlike at home, he was clean-shaven each morning, at whatever hour they visited him; his curly hair was always combed; but he complained that the nurses had changed since he was here the last time, and that he didn't like the change, he wanted everyone to be the same. The room was furnished now with some of his personal effects (odd word for one's things, said Ellen), and Tanya brought drawings and a letter from her nine-year-old dyslexic son, who was writing now, since she'd purchased a computer; and Donny brought champagne and some helium balloons, which were anchored to the foot of his bed; tell me about something that's going on, he said, waking up from a nap to find Donny and Kate at the side of his bed, beaming at him; tell me a story, he said wistfully, said Donny, who couldn't think of anything to say; *you're* the story, Kate said. And Xavier brought an eighteenth-century Guatemalan wooden statue of Saint Sebastian with upcast eyes and open mouth, and when Tanya said what's that, a tribute to eros past, Xavier said where I come from Sebastian is venerated as a protector against pestilence. Pestilence symbolized by arrows? Symbolized by arrows. All people remember is the body of a beautiful youth bound to a tree, pierced by arrows (of which he always seems oblivious, Tanya interjected), people forget that the story continues, Xavier continued, that when the Christian women came to bury the martyr they found him still alive and nursed him back to health. And he said, according to Stephen, I didn't know Saint Sebastian didn't die. It's undeniable, isn't it, said Kate on the phone to Stephen, the fascination of the dying. It makes me ashamed. We're learning how to die, said Hilda, I'm not ready to learn, said Aileen; and Lewis, who was coming straight from the other hospital, the hospital where Max was still being kept in ICU, met Tanya getting out of the elevator on the tenth floor, and as they walked together down the shiny corridor past the open doors, averting their eyes from the other patients sunk in their beds, with tubes in their noses, irradiated by the bluish light from the television sets, the thing I can't bear to think about, Tanya said to Lewis, is someone dying with the TV on.

He has that strange, unnerving detachment now, said Ellen, that's what upsets me, even though it makes it easier to be with him. Sometimes he was querulous. I can't stand them coming in here taking my blood every morning, what are they doing with all that blood, he is reported to have said; but where was his anger, Jan wondered. Mostly he was lovely to be with, always saying how are *you*, how are you feeling. He's so sweet now, said Aileen. He's so nice, said Tanya. (Nice, nice, groaned Paolo.) At first he was very ill, but he was rallying, according to Stephen's best information, there was no fear of his not recovering this time, and the doctor spoke of his being discharged from the hospital in another ten days if all went well, and the mother was persuaded to fly back to Mississippi, and Quentin was readying the penthouse for his return. And he was still writing his diary, not showing it to anyone, though Tanya, first to arrive one late-winter morning, and finding him dozing, peeked, and was horrified, according to Greg, not by anything she read but by a progressive change in his handwriting: in the recent pages, it was becoming spidery, less legible, and some lines of script wandered and tilted about the page. I was thinking, Ursula said to Quentin, that the difference between a story and a painting or photograph is that in a story you can write, He's still alive. But in a painting or a photo you can't show "still." You can just show him being alive. He's still alive, Stephen said.

Jack Pulaski

Jack Pulaski (b. 1935) was born in the Williamsburg section of Brooklyn. He served in the U.S. army and has held a number of jobs, working in textile plants and bookstores as well as teaching in colleges and prison writing programs. Pulaski's stories have won high praise for their rare combination of lyricism and toughness. The situations he depicts are often harsh, his characters are generally hard-luck working people, but Pulaski renders their circumstances with a poet's ear for language and a beguiling, tender humor. His stories have been collected in *The St. Veronica Gig Stories* (1986).

THE MERRY-GO-ROUND

The merry-go-round truck came down the street, the calliope piping the overture to the *Barber of Seville*. Children leapt from their mothers' laps and shrieked for nickels. Hoodlums in their gaberdine suits, removed their hands from their testicles—the stance, dignified, stoic, their hands modestly cupped their balls; they contemplated the daily double and fished in their pockets, showering a largesse of nickels, as windows five stories up showered a consolation of apples. Below, the children snatched at the coins parachuted in knotted handkerchiefs, apples exploding on the sidewalk, a hubbub of knees and fists contesting nickels and apples.

The merry-go-round truck stopped in front of our building. From stoops, milk boxes, and folding chairs, acres of mommas, their laps suddenly bereft, turned from one to another, a presentiment of separation, as the children lined up under Paddy the Merry-Go-Round man's third stomach. Marching single file we handed over the sweaty coins which Paddy slipped into the pocket of a huge green apron that hung below his stomach like a veil; marching beneath that concave awning of flesh touching the top of our heads in benediction as it breathed, it counted us as well, tap, tap, on the top of the head, one to a dozen, and we climbed aboard and mounted the iron horses.

The merry-go-round sat in the flat bed of the truck, enclosed in a circular wire mesh fence. My horse was black with one terrified cracked eye that stared at the roof. Up on his hind legs, poised to charge, the one cracked frightened eye begged the ceiling for deliverance. I would have changed horses, but it was too late; all the horses had riders. Opposite me Blossom Lipshitz sat daintily side saddle on a spotted pony, her huge knees glistening like moons, whispering encouragement into her horse's ear. I looked around to see if anyone wanted to trade. The face of one boy, eager to barter, found mine, but the thing he sat on looked like a peeling radiator. Stroking my horse's mane, I checked the other riders—they were all eager to ride, kicking the iron haunches, screaming "Giddyap"—the only possibility was "Izzy the Mongolian Idiot." He wore a Roy Rogers cowboy suit. A ten gallon hat propped on his ears, his nose running, his tongue lolling on his chin, he sat on a stallion the color of lightning. Although I wanted to negotiate I didn't know how to talk to him.

Below Blossom Lipshitz's knees, through the wire mesh, Paddy's face grew red and huge as he cranked the crank, and we began to move. A prairie of steaming sewers and asphalt began to rotate around us. Picking up speed, the innards of the machine began to scream. The street whirled around us, Paddy's red face contracting and expanding. I raised an invisible saber above my head, charging into a wind that reeked of the feather factory on the corner, and the Love Nest candy-bar factory across the street. Squinting beyond the circle of mothers ringing the merry-go-round, and the fathers behind them (it was either the Fourth of July or Labor Day, not as big a holiday as Passover or Good Friday in our neighborhood), I leaned forward in my saddle, squinting in the wind and stink toward the Greek's luncheonette, where the Filipino book-makers hung out. They were my Comanches.

The calliope lost its song to the howling guts of the machine which began to spit parts all over the street. We had hardly begun our ride and the merry-go-round, turning slower and slower, stopped. Blossom kicked at the haunches of her spotted pony, knocking bits of color from his hide. Izzy, drooling and wide-eyed, tore the mane from the stallion's neck. The boy sitting on the horse that looked like a radiator put his face to the wire mesh fence and asked for a refund of his nickel. Paddy climbed under the truck; we could hear clanging and wrenching of steel parts, and Paddy singing "Casey would waltz with the strawberry blonde" into the innards of the machine. He emerged from under the truck and conferred with the circle of men. Beyond them the circle of mothers clamored for their children. At the center, ringed around by the iron horses, we waited, despondent, several of the younger children crying. Paddy left the circle of men, walked toward us, scooping nickels from his apron—the palms of his hands proffering refunds like bird seed. Blossom's uncle, Willie Brodsky, came up behind Paddy, reached for Paddy's arm, and said, "Colleague . . ." (any creature over two hundred and fifty pounds was a colleague) enveloped his colleague in flesh and whispered into his ear. Oceans of wind filled Paddy's head, his eyes rattling like a doll's. "Kitts," said Willie, "get on horses and gyddy-yap." Willie, Paddy, and two other men spaced themselves evenly around the merry-go-round, their fingers locked around the thick wire mesh of the fence, and they pushed. We began to move. Something in the mechanism of the machine held and dragged, and we went round at a slow walking pace. Willie went round and round at my side, his huge fists closed around the wire mesh at the level of my ankle. Sweat shingled the hollows of his eyes. We went round slowly, and the calliope, singing on the insufficient breath furnished from the merry-go-round's turning, moaned an imbecilic *Barber of Seville*. No matter how hard the men pushed we went at the same slow walking pace. The older children booed and hissed, some of the younger ones cried. "Nothin' doin'," said Willie; Paddy nodded his head in agreement, and we rolled to a complete stop.

"No!" I heard my mother's voice screaming, "No!" Father came walking toward the merry-go-round, wearing his truss and girdle, laughing over some joke that kept repeating itself over and over inside his head. "Abe," my mother said, pointing to his hernia, "your killer will come out. Don't show off." "Killer's tied up," he said, patting the laces of his truss, tied in opulent bows just above his hernia. Mother repeated that "charity begins at home," and that one's obligation was first to one's family. "That's right," Father agreed and moved on to the merry-go-round. His left shoulder a full two inches lower than his right, the girdle bending his torso forward, he looked like an ape that had fallen out of a tree. Small in stature, he appeared a midget between Paddy and Willie. They stood there, the Three Graces, trussed, hirsute, and radiant, grunting "yes." "He's here," said Mr. Willie Brodsky. Paddy sucked on his straw, the almost empty bottle gurgling.

"Impossible," said Willie. "Don't nobody touch it," said Father. "O.K. *bullvon,* be mine guest, bust a gut, collapse a lung, enjoy yourself." "Always I enjoy myself, Brodsky," said Father, pinching Brodsky's cheek into a purple jowl, "Always and always I enjoy myself."

Again the world went round, the steaming sewers, a gallery of windows, potted aspidistras, old faces, firescapes with mattresses raining lice, and the lordly hoodlums rotating, statuesque, eternal, their hands modestly and forever cupping their balls. Slowly it all went round and round. The machine protested, screaming hammer and tongs, making a bedlam of the *Barber of Seville*. The twin branches of vein on Father's forehead swelled into a pair of horns, his eyes livid and blind with the effort, my eyes resembling, I knew, my horse's cracked terrified eye, expecting at any moment that Father would explode into a geyser of blood. Willie and Paddy were now begging him to stop; their voices worried, solicitous, they did not touch him but followed behind, travelling the circle he walked, talking at his back. I couldn't look at his face anymore.

Suddenly, there was an enormous twanging, as if a pair of giant suspenders had snapped. My horse jumped in the air, carrying the steel plates affixed to its hooves. I landed, still in the saddle, my horse on its hind legs, poised as always to charge, and we went round faster. Izzy's stallion had leapt in the air too, and he rode it with the calm of a wizard on a flying carpet, rocking with his eyes closed and blowing spit bubbles. The windows whirled around: for an instant something in the machine held and then snapped, we lurched in our saddles, the whirling gallery of windows collided like boxcars, people and potted plants trembled and tossed in their window frames, and we went round even faster. Blossom no longer rode side saddle; she was bent low like a jockey, except for her arms, which were locked around her horse's neck. Father neither walked nor trotted the merry-go-round; now he stood, legs braced, his arms perpetual motion, twirling the merry-go-round like a giant top. Several children began to cry. I felt a little queasy in the stomach. The boy on the radiator horse fell and bloodied his nose. Father was singing to us, breath pumped to the song on the rhythm of his movement, " 'Appy Birdsday to you . . .'Appy Birdsday to you,'appy birdsday dear kiddies . . ." Speed endowed me with the sight of the blind, Father a silhouette of boiling vapor—two mothers who had come to rescue their children flew from his arms like pennants. The hoodlums flew round us, so many sentinels on a conveyor belt. I caught a glimpse of an old woman in a window; she appeared to be wearing her neighbor's potted plants for earrings, and a mattress floated by under her chin. Screams inside the merry-go-round like the end of the world. Blossom rolled around the floor in a fetal position, bouncing off the legs of the horses, trying to lick her scraped knee. Only Izzy and I were still in the saddle, and I was close to being sick.

The circle of mothers broke and charged: from stoops, milk boxes, and folding chairs they charged. Paddy and Willie disappeared. "It's a holiday. It's a holiday," Father explained to the woman who clawed his face as she climbed into the wrecked merry-go-round. Shrieks, whimpers, wails, bloody noses, scraped knees, puke, toppled horses—children rescued from all this, wiped clean, bellies caressed, and wounds tended to. Father now proffered the explanation to himself: "Holiday, holiday," he said. Mother went by him, wiping my face, as though she didn't know who he was. Somebody's mother spit in his face. Years later, when I read in the Old Testament of a woman taken in adultery and stoned at the city gates, at once I saw Father's face, spit dripping from his cheek, blood running, explaining, "It's a holiday. It's a holiday."

Lars Gustafsson

Lars Gustafsson (b.1936) was born in Sweden, where he took his degree from the University of Uppsala in 1962. Gustafsson is known throughout Europe for his fiction and poetry as well as for his more scholarly writings in mathematics, history, philosophy, and social criticism. Recently he has divided his time between his native Sweden and various teaching posts at U.S. universities. His translated works include the novels *The Death of a Beekeeper* and *Sigismund* and the story collection *Stories for Happy People.*

A WATER STORY

One afternoon during the cold, rainy, summer of 1977, I left Lake Åmänningen with my son Joen in a white-painted but by that time rather leaky motorboat. We went by Flodhäll, through Virsbo Lock, where the trailer trucks rumble across the bridge and the children swim happily by the sluice basin, then through Lake Virsbo, which is long and shallow, into the swampy delta country between Virsbo and Seglingsberg, where twelve wild geese flew up in front of our bow and a wonderful pair of cranes crossed our route, passed Bo Rocks, where fishermen sat so close to one another that they obscured the red paint spot which is a landmark on the starboard side of the Canal; they've been sitting like that for hundreds of years with their fishing rods, where the channel is narrowest and the current runs deep, and the skippers of oreboats and barges have cursed them as we did when, at the last second, we realized that we were on our way into what lies between the two outer rocks; but all went well, and we continued through the Seglingsberg and Fårmansbo locks, noticing that Fårmansbo has acquired a fat, handsome woman lock keeper with a Finnish accent and a huge cat and a small child playing by the water, carefully protected from falling into the deep changing element by a wooden playpen; through the last bends of the river, we arrived at dusk on North Nadden, my childhood lake.

"It's so small," said Joen, who has always heard it described as large, and I, who had started to feel chilly in the dusk and was just struck by the thought that we had a long way back, about eighteen miles, or sixty feet up to the surface of Lake Åmänningen (and that during a summer when the lock keeper in Virsbo closed for the night at seven),

I, poor confused daddy in faded jeans and bare feet, who got cold from hours in the tea-brown humus water that continually leaked in from somewhere in the stern,

I suddenly discovered how right he was. How closed in, how melancholy was my childhood lake, with its slowly deteriorating sawmill to the north, its deforested area, barely concealed by so-called shore trees to the west, where the new road was put in quite some time ago, with the little idyllic summer houses in Brattheden to the east. The only thing that has stayed the same, relatively speaking, is the swampland to the north, the watery labyrinths of reeds and red water lilies, where you can still hear cranes occasionally.

It was that small, that closed in. Almost like a childhood in a washtub!

And while we filled up with gas from the five-liter gas can through the old blue funnel that disappeared in the spring storms in '74 and was found again among the nettles in Kyrkviken in June of '77, a faithful-retainer funnel, an honorable funnel, it occurred to me to start telling him:

"You only see a small, melancholy lake that's getting over-grown. You see a sawmill that's falling into ruin, and you see some silly little summer houses on a ridge. Most of it grown over.

"You have to understand that I see something different. In my childhood, there were lots of people here. College students in white suits and white caps gingerly rowing young girls among the reeds, conversing with them shyly. The trains come into the station, puffing coal smoke, dropping off swarms of passengers from Stockholm, my eccentric uncles and aunts among them—"

"A good half of them only exist in your novels," says Joen, who has just entered puberty and is starting to talk back.

"—I see old workingmen sitting on their porches at dusk," I continue easily, "scratching out their pipes with a nail and telling stories of fathers and forefathers, stories so old that they go back to the eighteenth century, stories about coal burners' huts and foundry owners who are so evil that the Devil himself comes to get them on Christmas Eve, and stories of the big, mysterious fish, the Giant Catfish in Bo Basin, the Great Fish, the Primordial Fish who hides in the depths where the sunlight only penetrates like a star among all the others, the Inexorable Fish who cuts off all the lead-lines with one snap of his giant teeth, so that rope and chain come up to the surface neatly cut . . ."

"—Why," said Joen, who is a modern young man who does not approve of long stories; he's in a hurry to get to the end, as if the end would be something remarkable in itself,

"—Why," said Joen, "what's he hiding, anyway?"

"—There's gold down there in the depths; far down something unbelievably rich is glistening; the darkness possesses something, and the

Catfish is the Monster who protects it and hides it. Never, never will any living creature bring the gold to the surface. The monster would rather die than give up his gold. Rather die than show himself.

"As distinct from those vulgar lake monsters we read about in the papers, the Loch Ness Monster, the Great Sea Beast, and whatever they are called, the Giant Catfish in Bo Basin is a lake monster whose whole existence consists of never showing himself."

We'd hardly finished filling up before we turned north again among darkening reeds.

We rushed a bit, since we were about to miss the closing time at the locks. Joen steered through the increasingly abstract landscape while I bailed.

Frightened ducks flew by the bow; a hawk stood almost still over the forest's edge, but no cranes this time. The lock house at Fårmansbo shone yellow, friendly, inviting. Exercising all our charm, we managed to borrow the lock key. It was already so dark that the white water down there looked luminous; agitated bats whirred across the sluice basin.

It was the beginning of August; the summer light was beating a retreat.

"I often ran around here as a child, or boy, along the edge, fishing," I said. "There's some species of morels that you don't find anywhere else around here, small black ones. They're only edible after you parboil them. They grow in the old slag piles. Once there was a hut there."

We got out on Lake Åmänningen again at the last moment. The canal in back of us started getting dark, but in front of us we had the large lake which reflected the evening light. Everything was very still. Our wake spread out like a theorem in a perfect geometry, an occasional grebe dived in front of us, abruptly, as if it had had second thoughts.

Outside Dentist's Point—a desolate wooded spot which got that name because the man who once built a summer house there was a dentist—with the islet called Gärholmen closest to it, we noticed something peculiar, which made Joen slow the engine to idle.

A canoe was leaving Gärholmen, evidently with a single person in it. It passed between the hazardous, sharp rocks at Enträ as if they didn't even exist and made a swift turn toward Kyrkviken.

It was so far away that it was impossible to see who was paddling it, but the way he was paddling was somehow upsetting: hectic.

"Who on earth could that be," I said.

"That's odd," Joen said. "Let's go in to Gärholmen and have a look. I have a feeling that something strange may have happened."

"It's so dark," I said.

"But I still want to put in at Gärholmen. Anyway, I hid some one-kroner pieces under a rock in the middle of the island when we were out doing long distance skating in February of '76."

He still had the small boy's mania for hiding things under rocks, especially on islands, perhaps to make himself invulnerable, perhaps to leave something invulnerable behind, perhaps just to create a secret for himself.

We approached the island at half throttle. It's quite small, a narrow islet. There are such a number of sharp, wicked rocks in the water around it that I hardly ever put in there by boat. On the other hand, it makes an excellent stopping place in the winter, the first few days after Christmas when the ice is safe and lies there blue-black because no snow has fallen yet.

By now it was almost dark. Just as we started getting in among the really dangerous shoals, simultaneously we caught sight of something that had to be a swimming animal, perhaps an elk, on its way from the island in the direction of Kyrkviken. The same direction the canoe had taken.

I made a careful ninety-degree turn. While Joen kept a lookout for the dark brown boulders that might rise to the surface at any moment, unreal, only becoming tangible the moment they touch the bow, I stood up and scouted ahead.

It was too small to be an elk, it was too large to be a swimming snake.

Thirty yards off, we realized that it was a man. He had darkish hair with a few gray strands; the hair was plastered across a rather small head, determinedly but rather slowly making its way toward shore. He seemed to be completely naked.

Were we disturbing him?

He was rather low in the water. It seemed he was swimming more and more slowly, in a determined way.

He should have seen us by now.

I made up my mind. We had hardly reached him before I realized that the man was exhausted.

We pulled him on board as well as we could. Everyone who has done this sort of thing knows that it isn't an easy matter.

A man you pull up over the stern of a motorboat and who hardly makes any effort himself easily gets his chest scraped.

We put him in the bottom of the boat, toward the bow, and pulled my wool sweater over him.

"How are you doing?" I asked.

He seemed too exhausted to be able to reply.

"What are we going to do with him?" Joen asked.

"We'll bring him back home with us," I said.

"He's very cold," Joen said. "Let's take him to Gärholmen and make a fire."

Sure enough, on Gärholmen we found a tent, an LPG stove in front of the tent, some clothes hung to dry across a low fir branch.

We put as many clothes as we could on him and made a fire with the dry sticks heaped far in under the spruces next to the tent.

The first thing he said when he could speak again was something rather surprising to us.

"Not to worry. She'll come back. She always comes back."

"O.K.," I said. "But then it might have been overdoing it a bit trying to swim after her all the way to Kyrkviken. The water turns cold faster than you like to think, here in Västmanland. And if you aren't an experienced long-distance swimmer, it makes sense to take it easy."

He didn't seem to be listening. He might have been between thirty-five and forty, a rather attractive face, commonplace as well. You might guess at some intellectual occupation, but in that case not one that would confer status. A line across his nose indicated that he normally wore glasses; I guess the thin-rimmed variety. He was still shivering and crept closer to the fire.

Actually, there was nothing to indicate that he was particularly mad or even desperate. He didn't even seem unhappy, just cold.

Consequently, I went down to the shore to see how we had disposed the boat in our haste; I had a strong feeling that the wind had changed.

It had, too: the boat was knocking against the rocks, and I took the opportunity to pull it over into the shelter of a large boulder at the edge of the shore. Now it was so dark that the closest trees were illuminated by the fire in front of the tent.

I could see some feminine underwear on a clothesline. The two figures, my son and the strange man, now had bent closer to the fire.

When I got closer, I realized that they had started to heat water.

"I thought I might make you some coffee by way of thanking you for your help," the man said. "Just instant, of course."

There was a short silence. Nobody had anything to say right then. In the silence, I felt that I was out of breath: everything had happened so fast. Also I was damn cold and hungry.

"You wouldn't have some bread and butter," I said. "You see, we've been going up and down the canal all afternoon."

"Sure thing," the swimmer said. "I even think I might have some excellent Finnish juniper-smoked sausage from Arvid Nordquist."

Bread and sausage appeared. I have to admit that we helped ourselves without restraint.

"So you're from Stockholm," I said.

"I was born around here," he said. "A bit further down the canal, that is, just above Kolbäck. My father had a farm there. I went to school in Västerås. What year did you graduate?"

"Fifty-five," I said.

"I was a bit earlier," he said. "I graduated in 1950. Then I taught for a while, but that was no good. It was the worst years in the beginning of the '60s; there wasn't a chance of maintaining discipline. Since then, I've been in the travel business. I was assigned to Athens quite a while, as the local representative of charter agency. I've been back in Stockholm seven years now."

He paused again. I tried in vain to get my wet matches to light.

"It's amazing how you can get tangled up in your life," he said.

"What do you mean?" I said.

"This girl I met for the first time in Stockholm toward the end of the '50s," he said. "It must have been 1959, something like that. I remember that the National Museum had just started their series of summer night concerts; right after we met, we went to one of those concerts. The summer of 1959 was very warm and dry, if I remember correctly. There were still quite a few streetcar lines in the city.

"We came out from the summer night concert and the city was warm, abandoned, empty in some surprising way. There were just the two of us.

"We took a streetcar to Söder; we walked along Söder Mälarstrand for a long time. I remember the wonderful elder in Skinnarvik Park, above Heleneborgsgatan. It was in bloom and had a very strong scent.

"We must have been terribly happy."

"Where did you meet originally?"

"That's not important," he said, almost offended by my interruption. "I think it was in a seminar at the university. I really can't remember any longer. I have the feeling that I've known her forever. She was a rather shy, slender little girl in those days. Intelligent, but shy. She was rather afraid of speaking up in the seminar. I was shy, too. I'd gone to bed with girls before her, I guess, but she was the first one I had the feeling that I *possessed;* she belonged to me, I could do what I wanted with her. Do you know what I mean?"

I nodded.

"There was something strange between us; a kind of fire, poison perhaps, like toadstool poison, muscarine, like the bog myrtle on the big bogs around Märrsjön. When we were together it was like entering a different world.

"I had a room on Hornsgatan that summer. I was supposed to study for one of the big history comprehensive exams. I didn't do that much studying. We'd often lock ourselves in for days on end, we nestled in each other like creatures on the bottom of a deep lake. What I mean to say is that reality above was no more than the glimmer of light that creatures in a lake like that would see above them, a glimmer of light through dark brown, humus-rich water.

"Like I said, both of us were shy to start with. I don't think I knew much about how to satisfy a woman in those days. I remember wondering why she had such a hard time getting to sleep now and then. Of course it didn't take very long for the shyness to wear off. She had marvelous orgasms; they would go up to her shoulders, practically. A kind of cramp that shook her whole body."

"Think of the young man," I said.

"Not to worry. He's gone to sleep. I'll get another sweater to put over him. You don't have to leave yet, do you? He could stand to get some rest after a long trip like that, right? You see—it feels a little lonely right now. And strictly speaking, you're my only connection with the mainland."

"O.K.," I said. "The boy gets to sleep for a while."

"We shared depressions, too. A kind of strange, white melancholy, the two of us. I think it has to be that way in such circumstances. I might go out into the city around eleven, walk carefully down Hornsgatan; I say carefully, because in our condition we often had the feeling that we were walking on glass all the way. It's a bit difficult to explain—well, we'd walk down Hornsgatan with the firm intention of buying food for lunch and come back with some flatbread and cheese.

"It was a terribly odd state. Like some great, metaphysical absent-mindedness, a feeling that the whole world was completely meaningless really, and that we were the only ones to have discovered it.

"Do you understand? Not the usual feeling that what you're *doing* is meaningless, but a much larger feeling: existence as a whole had lost its meaning; you had passed through all the stages that it was possible to pass through. *And there was nothing there, either.*

"Our friends started wondering what had become of us. I suspect that at the university they'd given up on us. All of this was a short time, just a few months, and quite mad. And at bottom, we always had the feeling that this wasn't going to last very long.

"We made some attempt to work together. It wasn't that easy. I only had one room and a kitchen, and between the room and kitchen such bizarre tensions developed that the walls creaked when we tried to keep away from each other so that we could at least read a book for three or four hours.

"By fall, we both realized it was dangerous. You couldn't intensify it further. There was no real road back, I mean back to the level where you have ordinary conversations with each other.

"I remember the morning she left quite well. I had packed up her things for her; she couldn't do it. The breakup paralyzed her: it was as if she'd realized something important at the last minute, something quite different, that remained to be done.

"For some reason, God knows why, perhaps she had a lot to carry—some luggage had accumulated during two and a half months—we had ordered a cab, and I was standing in the window waiting for it to drive up.

"Why didn't I stand down there, why didn't I say goodbye to her down in the street? You know, that's the kind of thing that's impossible to remember after so many years. One reason might be that we'd had a stupendous fight, but that doesn't have to be it. It might have been some kind of agreement.

"I must have gone into my room for a moment, I remember that. Anyway, I discovered that she had left something there, her umbrella, her little red umbrella. I remember shouting through the window, 'Do you want me to bring it down?' And she answered, 'Just throw it down.'

"There are goodbyes like that, believe it or not."

"I believe it," I said.

"Have you ever noticed an oddity about the topographical map of Västmanland," he said, and I wasn't actually surprised any longer.

"No, what do you mean?"

He went into the tent and fetched a small map, Västeråas NV, as it's called, scale 1:50,000.

"Well, almost every one of those small lakes has an insignificant twin that is a bog: just look here, Acktjärn, and then Acktjärn Bog right next to it; Big Grillsjön, and then Grillsjön Bog like a shadow of the lake to the north. All over the place, you find a humble shadow of the lake, a bog. If you like, it's the lake that was once upon a time, a bigger lake that was there.

"But the bog is still there. Under the bog-myrtle and the meadowsweet, the cottongrass and the tussocks of cloudberries, there is still water, although it no longer reflects the sky as the lake does.

"It's still there. And then? What happens under the surface? What does a lake turned bog reflect?"

"Itself?"

"Or a different sky. A sky of peat? Have you thought about the mushrooms, how different they are from the phanerogams. Much closer to the earth, much more—how shall I put it—dramatic in their whole demeanor, with all those strange poisons, their way of growing, lightning-fast in the space of a few nights. And their way of dying, a kind of dissolution from inside. They look quite whole long after they've died."

"Don't forget that they leave filaments in the earth that go on making new mushroom bodies. Mycelium. We hardly ever see the most interesting thing about mushrooms. The underground filaments."

"I have thought about it."

"And how about you? Are you living or dead?"

"She disappeared over the horizon. I'd see her now and then, sometimes with somebody, sometimes alone. Then she married an expert of some kind, God knows what kind, and went to the U.S.

"I think we exchanged a few letters, and I remember them as rather unimportant.

"I got myself back to the point at which I'd been interrupted, so to speak. I think it was damn smart of me, that time.

"I married, a nice girl, had kids. By the way, now she's married to a forestry agent around here. It was more that she lost interest in me than the other way around. It was about the same time, by the way, that I left teaching.

"Well, then came the time in Athens. That was rather fun.

"You know, a branch office like that is the right place to get to know the country, and, I'd like to add, the right place to learn business dealings with Greeks. Their game rules are a bit different from ours; it costs you something to learn their system, and when you know both systems, it's possible to do some entertaining things.

"The risk of a situation like that, of course, is that you live rather too well. You drink a fair amount. You have a good time. You get flabby in different ways.

"You get like the steamship agents on the little islands out in the Aegean, little kings who rule the district from some café or other, standing behind some modest counter, letting the workers polish the brass while they ponder freights and real-estate prices and cement transports.

"Suddenly it can get all empty. You see, the worst thing I know is emptiness.

"You know, suddenly a dry paper will rustle along the street in the stubborn August wind, an old newspaper that someone has dropped or thrown away. In southern countries where everything is dry, where everything stays put, it's somehow more obvious than in northern countries. The summer wind rustles in the plane trees. You look up for a moment and get all scared by your own emptiness; you ask yourself what you're doing, actually.

"You know what I mean?"

He asked this last question with such eagerness, almost obstinacy, that I became uneasy. Even the boy started in his sleep. I started thinking seriously about waking him up and going home.

Then it struck me how childish this impulse to flee was, how strongly dictated by my own weaknesses, and I said:

"Of course I know what you mean. Sometimes I tell myself that it's in those moments that we look truth in the face."

"What do you mean?"

"Suppose it's that kind of emptiness that's the truth about this world? Take this lake, for instance. Certain days when I feel sad, I walk down to the shore. The rocks are out there, huge, heavy, each one a statement that cannot be refuted. Times like that, I see that the lake has always been sad. The natural world is like that. We're the only ones who try to create meaning."

There was silence for a while. Then he suddenly continued his story.

"I don't think I'd given her a thought for the last ten years. Then one day she comes into my office in Athens. She wanted to change her ticket. I was in the back room and heard one of my assistants having a bit of an argument with her out there; he tried to explain that if you're on a charter trip, you can't just change your ticket.

"I was on the phone, I think I was talking to Stockholm, and all of a sudden I hear her voice out there. It's rather a husky voice, always a bit drawling. It's hard to mistake that voice.

"I went out like a sleepwalker, and there she was. She was obviously married—at least she was wearing a wedding ring—and obviously she was there with some guy other than the one she was married to. I changed their tickets right away. They wanted to stay another week. They wanted to go to Poros. I told them it isn't easy to find a hotel on Poros right in the middle of the Greek Easter. I asked for their hotel in Athens so that I could call them. The guy seemed totally negligible to me, just a nice-looking clod.

"I had time to ask her how she was. 'Fine,' she said, 'as you can see.'

" 'That's good,' I said. 'Too bad we won't have time for a drink. We could walk down to Syntagma and have some coffee.'

" 'We won't have time,' she said. 'We've promised to meet some friends at four.'

" 'Too bad, after all these years,' I said.

"I was the last one to leave the office, as usual, going through a few things I'd always go through. Telexes, lists of things to do, orders. I had promised to play tennis with a guy who used to play on the courts up by the university. I remember thinking that I'd just get a sandwich first and that I might as well wait until the worst traffic was over.

"Then there's a knock on the door. I go over and open up. It's the doorkeeper in the building.

" 'There's a lady here looking for you who's very insistent,' he said. 'I've told her that you close at four and that she should come back tomorrow. But nothing helps. She just pushes in. Do you know her?'

" 'Not really,' I said.

"I heard the clock ticking. I looked at the teletype, still and silent under its dust cover. I looked at the typewriters. Oh yes, I remember thinking: So there are moments that can decide your whole life."

"And then?"

"And then I went and opened up. It was like opening a sluice gate.

"We went to her hotel and got her stuff. It was a little awkward to move her into my apartment, since I had a Greek girlfriend living there. We borrowed an apartment from a friend for a couple of days.

"Well," he said, "if she didn't take the train she should be here pretty soon."

"Does she often take off like that?" I asked.

"Sometimes she feels she can't stand it. Me, too. Quite honestly, it's rather trying to be as terribly dependent on each other as we are. Sometimes she runs off, sometimes I do."

"There is a desire for solitude," I said, rather stupidly. "I mean" (and I think I increased my stupidity by that remark) "there is even a desire for unhappiness."

"I still don't think you've quite grasped it," he said.

"In a way, I think we're living in different worlds," I said.

I thought that was a polite way of getting away from it.

When the boy woke up, he stretched his arms in the air and yawned loudly. It took a while for him to grasp where he was. He went behind some bushes to take a leak, and he was gone longer than expected.

At the same time, a canoe came into the inlet, just beside my boat. It appeared almost ghostlike out of the August darkness.

I was already down by the shore.

I said a polite hello. She was shorter than I'd imagined. Not really beautiful, actually. She treated me with polite indifference.

Then the boy came at last. We said goodbye and pushed the boat out.

It took us quite a while to get the old Archimedes E 4 going.

In the intervals, while I pulled on the starter cord, Joen sat jingling something in his right hand.

"What's that you're jingling?" I asked.

"The coins of course. The one-kroner pieces I hid under the rock last winter, when we took a break when we were out skating. I've got them now."

I often wonder in how many places on the lake he hides such coins.

Translated by Yvonne L. Sandstroem and John Weinstock

Bessie Head

Bessie Head (1937–1986) was born in South Africa. She spent many years working as an educator in her adopted country of Botswana. She worked for a time as a journalist in Johannesburg. She published three novels and a collection of stories, *The Collector of Treasures,* before her death from hepatitis.

LOOKING FOR A RAIN GOD

It is lonely at the lands where the people go to plough. These lands are vast clearings in the bush, and the wild bush is lonely too. Nearly all the lands are within walking distance from the village. In some parts of the bush where the underground water is very near the surface, people made little rest camps for themselves and dug shallow wells to quench their thirst while on their journey to their own lands. They experienced all kinds of things once they left the village. They could rest at shady watering places full of lush, tangled trees with delicate pale-gold and purple wildflowers springing up between soft green moss and the children could hunt around for wild figs and any berries that might be in season. But from 1958, a seven-year drought fell upon the land and even the watering places began to look as dismal as the dry open thornbush country; the leaves of the trees curled up and withered; the moss became dry and hard and, under the shade of the tangled trees, the ground turned a powdery black and white, because there was no rain. People said rather humorously that if you tried to catch the rain in a cup it would only fill a teaspoon. Toward the beginning of the seventh year of drought, the summer had become an anguish to live through. The air was so dry and moisture-free that it burned the skin. No one knew what to do to escape the heat and tragedy was in the air. At the beginning of that summer, a number of men just went out of their homes and hung themselves to death from trees. The majority of the people had lived off crops, but for two years past they had all returned from the lands with only their rolled-up skin blankets and cooking utensils. Only the charlatans, incanters, and witch doctors made a pile of money during this time because people were always turning to them in desperation for little talismans and herbs to rub on the plough for the crops to grow and the rain to fall.

The rains were late that year. They came in early November, with a promise of good rain. It wasn't the full, steady downpour of the years of good rain but thin, scanty, misty rain. It softened the earth and a rich growth of green things sprang up everywhere for the animals to eat. People were called to the center of the village to hear the proclamation of the beginning of the ploughing season; they stirred themselves and whole families began to move off to the lands to plough.

The family of the old man, Mokgobja, were among those who left early for the lands. They had a donkey cart and piled everything onto it, Mokgobja—who was over seventy years old; two girls, Neo and Boseyong; their mother Tiro and an unmarried sister, Nesta; and the father and supporter of the family, Ramadi, who drove the donkey cart. In the rush of the first hope of rain, the man, Ramadi, and the two women, cleared the land of thornbush and then hedged their vast ploughing area with this same thornbush to protect the future crop from the goats they had brought along for milk. They cleared out and deepened the old well with its pool of muddy water and still in this light, misty rain, Ramadi inspanned two oxen and turned the earth over with a hand plough.

The land was ready and ploughed, waiting for the crops. At night, the earth was alive with insects singing and rustling about in search of food. But suddenly, by mid-November, the rain flew away; the rain clouds fled away and left the sky bare. The sun danced dizzily in the sky, with a strange cruelty. Each day the land was covered in a haze of mist as the sun sucked up the last drop of moisture out of the earth. The family sat down in despair, waiting and waiting. Their hopes had run so high; the goats had started producing milk, which they had eagerly poured on their porridge, now they ate plain porridge with no milk. It was impossible to plant the corn, maize, pumpkin, and watermelon seeds in the dry earth. They sat the whole day in the shadow of the huts and even stopped thinking, for the rain had fled away. Only the children, Neo and Boseyong, were quite happy in their little-girl world. They carried on with their game of making house like their mother and chattered to each other in light, soft tones. They made children from sticks around which they tied rags, and scolded them severely in an exact imitation of their own mother. Their voices could be heard scolding the day long: "You stupid thing, when I send you to draw water, why do you spill half of it out of the bucket!" "You stupid thing! Can't you mind the porridge pot without letting the porridge burn!" And then they would beat the rag dolls on their bottoms with severe expressions.

The adults paid no attention to this; they did not even hear the funny chatter; they sat waiting for rain; their nerves were stretched to breaking-point willing the rain to fall out of the sky. Nothing was important, beyond that. All their animals had been sold during the bad years to purchase food, and of all their herd only two goats were left. It was the women of the family who finally broke down under the strain of waiting for rain. It was really the two women who caused the death of the little girls. Each night they started a weird, high-pitched wailing that began on a low, mournful note and whipped up to a frenzy. Then they would stamp their feet and shout as though they had lost their heads. The men sat quiet and self-controlled; it was important for men to maintain their self control at all times but their nerve was breaking too. They knew the women were haunted by the starvation of the coming year.

Finally, an ancient memory stirred in the old man, Mokgobja. When he was very young and the customs of the ancestors still ruled the land, he had been witness to a rain-making ceremony. And he came alive a little, struggling to recall the details which had been buried by years and years of prayer in a Christian church. As soon as the mists cleared a little, he began consulting in whispers with his youngest son, Ramadi. There was, he said, a certain rain god who accepted only the sacrifice of the bodies of children. Then the rain would fall; then the crops would grow, he said. He explained the ritual and as he talked, his memory became a conviction and he began to talk with unshakable authority. Ramadi's nerves were smashed by the nightly wailing of the women and soon the two men began whispering with the two women. The children continued their game: "You stupid thing! How could you have lost the money on the way to the shop! You must have been playing again!"

After it was all over and the bodies of the two little girls had been spread across the land, the rain did not fall. Instead, there was a deathly silence at night and the devouring heat of the sun by day. A terror, extreme and deep, overwhelmed the whole family. They packed, rolling up their skin blankets and pots, and fled back to the village.

People in the village soon noted the absence of the two little girls. They had died at the lands and were buried there, the family said. But people noted their ashen, terror-stricken faces and a murmur arose. What had killed the children, they wanted to know? And the family replied that they had just died. And people said amongst themselves that it was strange that the two deaths had occurred at the same time. And there was a feeling of great unease at the unnatural looks of the family. Soon the police came around. The family told them the same story of death and burial at the lands. They did not know what the children had died of. So the police asked to see the graves. At this, the mother of the children broke down and told everything.

Throughout that terrible summer the story of the children hung like a dark cloud of sorrow over the village, and the sorrow was not assuaged when the old man and Ramadi were sentenced to death for ritual murder. All they had on the statute books was that ritual murder was against the law and must be stamped out with the death penalty. The subtle story of strain and starvation and breakdown was inadmissible evidence at court;

but all the people who lived off crops knew in their hearts that only a hair's breadth had saved them from sharing a fate similar to that of the Mokgobja family. They could have killed something to make the rain fall.

Luisa Valenzuela

Luisa Valenzuela (b. 1938) was born in Buenos Aires, Argentina. She has lived for many years in New York City, working as a journalist. Her translated works include *Clara, Strange Things Happen Here,* and *Other Weapons*.

I'M YOUR HORSE IN THE NIGHT

The doorbell rang: three short rings and one long one. That was the signal, and I got up, annoyed and a little frightened; it could be them, and then again, maybe not; at these ungodly hours of the night it could be a trap. I opened the door expecting anything except him, face to face, at last.

He came in quickly and locked the door behind him before embracing me. So much in character, so cautious, first and foremost checking his—our—rear guard. Then he took me in his arms without saying a word, not even holding me too tight but letting all the emotions of our new encounter overflow, telling me so much by merely holding me in his arms and kissing me slowly. I think he never had much faith in words, and there he was, as silent as ever, sending me messages in the form of caresses.

We finally stepped back to look at one another from head to foot, not eye to eye, out of focus. And I was able to say Hello showing scarcely any surprise despite all those months when I had no idea where he could have been, and I was able to say

> I thought you were fighting up north
> I thought you'd been caught
> I thought you were in hiding
> I thought you'd been tortured and killed
> I thought you were theorizing about the revolution in another country

Just one of many ways to tell him I'd been thinking of him, I hadn't stopped thinking of him or felt as if I'd been betrayed. And there he was, always so god-damn cautious, so much the master of his actions.

"Quiet, Chiquita. You're much better off not knowing what I've been up to."

Then he pulled out his treasures, potential clues that at the time eluded me: a bottle of cachaça and a Gal Costa record. What had he been up to in Brazil? What was he planning to do next? What had brought him back, risking his life, knowing they were after him? Then I stopped asking myself questions (quiet, Chiquita, he'd say). Come here, Chiquita, he was saying, and I chose to let myself sink into the joy of having him back again, trying not to worry. What would happen to us tomorrow, and the days that followed?

Cachça's a good drink. It goes down and up and down all the right tracks, and then stops to warm up the corners that need it most. Gal Costa's voice is hot, she envelops us in its sound and half-dancing, half-floating, we reach the bed. We lie down and keep on staring deep into each other's eyes, continue caressing each other without allowing ourselves to give into the pure senses just yet. We continue recognizing, rediscovering each other.

Beto, I say, looking at him. I know that isn't his real name, but it's the only one I can call him out loud. He replies:

"We'll make it someday, Chiquita. but let's not talk now."

It's better that way. Better if he doesn't start talking about how we'll make it someday and ruin the wonder of what we're about to attain right now, the two of us, all alone.

"A noite eu so teu cavalo," Gal Costa suddenly sings from the record player.

"I'm your horse in the night," I translate slowly. And so as to bind him in a spell and stop him from thinking about other things:

"It's a saint's song, like in the *macumba.* Someone who's in a trance says she's the horse of the spirit who's riding her, she's his mount."

"Chiquita, you're always getting carried away with esoteric meanings and witchcraft. You know perfectly well that she isn't talking about spirits. If you're my horse in the night it's because I ride you, like this, see? . . . Like this . . . That's all."

It was so long, so deep and so insistent, so charged with affection that we ended up exhausted. I fell asleep with him still on top of me.

I'm your horse in the night.

The goddamn phone pulled me out in waves from a deep well. Making an enormous effort to wake up, I walked over to the receiver, thinking it could be Beto, sure, who was no longer by my side, sure, following his inveterate habit of running away while I'm asleep without a word about where he's gone. To protect me, he says.

From the other end of the line, a voice I thought belonged to Andrés—the one we call Andrés—began to tell me:

"They found Beto dead, floating down the river near the other bank. It looks as if they threw him alive out of a chopper. He's all bloated and decomposed after six days' in the water, but I'm almost sure it's him."

"No, it can't be Beto," I shouted carelessly. Suddenly the voice no longer sounded like Andrés: it felt foreign, impersonal.

"You think so?"

"Who is this?" Only then did I think to ask. But that very moment they hung up.

Ten, fifteen minutes? How long must I have stayed there staring at the phone like an idiot until the police arrived? I didn't expect them. But, then again, how could I not? Their hands feeling me, their voices insulting and threatening, the house searched, turned inside out. But I already knew. So what did I care if they broke every breakable object and tore apart my dresser?

They wouldn't find a thing. My only real possession was a dream and they can't deprive me of my dreams just like that. My dream the night before, when Beto was there with me and we loved each other. I'd dreamed it, dreamed every bit of it, I was deeply convinced that I'd dreamed it all in the richest detail, even in full color. And dreams are none of the cops' business.

They want reality, tangible facts, the kind I couldn't even begin to give them.

Where is he, you saw him, he was here with you, where did he go? Speak up, or you'll be sorry. Let's hear you sing, bitch, we know he came to see you, where is he, where is he holed up? He's in the city, come on, spill it, we know he came to get you.

I haven't heard a word from him in months. He abandoned me, I haven't heard from him in months. He ran away, went underground. What do I know, he ran off with someone else, he's in another country. What do I know, he abandoned me, I hate him, I know nothing.

(Go ahead, burn me with your cigarettes, kick me all you wish, threaten, go ahead, stick a mouse in me so it'll eat my insides out, pull my nails out, do as you please. Would I make something up for that? Would I tell you he was here when a thousand years ago he left me forever?)

I'm not about to tell them my dreams. Why should they care? I haven't seen that so-called Beto in more than six months, and I loved him. The man simply vanished. I only run into him in my dreams, and they're bad dreams that often become nightmares.

Beto, you know now, if it's true that they killed you, or wherever you may be, Beto, I'm your horse in the night and you can inhabit me whenever you wish, even if I'm behind bars. Beto, now that I'm in jail I know that I dreamed you that night; it was just a dream. And if by some wild chance there's a Gal Costa record and a half-empty bottle of cachaça in my house, I hope they'll forgive me: I will them out of existence.

Translated by Deborah Bonner

Joyce Carol Oates

Joyce Carol Oates (b.1938) was born in Lockport, New York. From earliest childhood she manifested a desire to get words onto paper. Indeed, she has been writing continually since she was fourteen. To date, she has published over fifty books, including novels, story collections, essays, mysteries, and poetry. Oates's concern is with the tensions in the societal fabric and the way those tensions erupt within family systems. She has a ready perception of how individuals move in crises; her gift is for setting these characters in credible dramatic situations and bringing them to moments of self-recognition. Oates has won many awards and honors for her work. Her novels include *With Shuddering Fall, Them, Do With Me What You Will, Bellefleur,* and *You Must Remember This,* and among her story collections are *By the North Gate, Upon the Sweeping Flood,* and *Raven's Wing.* Oates currently teaches at Princeton University.

THE LADY WITH THE PET DOG

I

Strangers parted as if to make way for him.

There he stood. He was there in the aisle, a few yards away, watching her.

She leaned forward at once in her seat, her hand jerked up to her face as if to ward off a blow—but then the crowd in the aisle hid him, he was gone. She pressed both hands against her cheeks. He was not there, she had imagined him.

"My God," she whispered.

She was alone. Her husband had gone out to the foyer to make a telephone call; it was intermission at the concert, a Thursday evening.

Now she saw him again, clearly. He was standing there. He was staring at her. Her blood rocked in her body, draining out of her head . . . she was going to faint. . . . They stared at each other. They gave no sign of recognition. Only when he took a step forward did she shake her head *no—no—keep away*. It was not possible.

When her husband returned, she was staring at the place in the aisle where her lover had been standing. Her husband leaned forward to interrupt that stare.

"What's wrong?" he said. "Are you sick?"

Panic rose in her in long shuddering waves. She tried to get to her feet, panicked at the thought of fainting here, and her husband took hold of her. She stood like an aged woman, clutching the seat before her.

At home he helped her up the stairs and she lay down. Her head was like a large piece of crockery that had to be held still, it was so heavy. She was still panicked. She felt it in the shallows of her face, behind her knees, in the pit of her stomach. It sickened her, it made her think of mucus, of something thick and gray congested inside her, stuck to her, that was herself and yet not herself—a poison.

She lay with her knees drawn up toward her chest, her eyes hotly open, while her husband spoke to her. She imagined that other man saying, *Why did you run away from me?* Her husband was saying other words. She tried to listen to them. He was going to call the doctor, he said, and she tried to sit up. "No, I'm all right now," she said quickly. The panic was like lead inside her, so thickly congested. How slow love was to drain out of her, how fluid and sticky it was inside her head!

Her husband believed her. No doctor. No threat. Grateful, she drew her husband down to her. They embraced, not comfortably. For years now they had not been comfortable together, in their intimacy and at a distance, and now they struggled gently as if the paces of this dance were too rigorous for them. It was something they might have known once, but had now outgrown. The panic in her thickened at this double betrayal: she drew her husband to her, she caressed him wildly, she shut her eyes to think about that other man.

A crowd of men and women parting, unexpectedly, and there he stood—there he stood—she kept seeing him, and yet her vision blotched at the memory. It had been finished between them, six months before, but he had come out here . . . and she had escaped him, now she was lying in her husband's arms, in his embrace, her face pressed against his. It was a kind of sleep, this love-making. She felt herself falling asleep, her body falling from her. Her eyes shut.

"I love you," her husband said fiercely, angrily.

She shut her eyes and thought of that other man, as if betraying him would give her life a center.

"Did I hurt you? Are you—?" her husband whispered.

Always this hot flashing of shame between them, the shame of her husband's near failure, the clumsiness of his love—

"You didn't hurt me," she said.

II

They had said good-by six months before. He drove her from Nantucket, where they had met, to Albany, New York, where she visited her sister.

The hours of intimacy in the car had sealed something between them, a vow of silence and impersonality: she recalled the movement of the highways, the passing of other cars, the natural rhythms of the day hypnotizing her toward sleep while he drove. She trusted him, she could sleep in his presence. Yet she could not really fall asleep in spite of her exhaustion, and she kept jerking awake, frightened, to discover that nothing had changed—still the stranger who was driving her to Albany, still the highway, the sky, the antiseptic odor of the rented car, the sense of a rhythm behind the rhythm of the air that might unleash itself at any second. Everywhere on this highway, at this moment, there were men and women driving together, bonded together—what did that mean, to be together? What did it mean to enter into a bond with another person?

No, she did not really trust him; she did not really trust men. He would glance at her with his small cautious smile and she felt a declaration of shame between them.

Shame.

In her head she rehearsed conversations. She said bitterly, "You'll be relieved when we get to Albany. Relieved to get rid of me." They had spent so many days talking, confessing too much, driven to a pitch of childish excitement, laughing together on the beach, breaking into that pose of laughter that seems to eradicate the soul, so many days of this that the silence of the trip was like the silence of a hospital—all these surface noises, these rattles and hums, but an interior silence, a befuddlement. She said to him in her imagination, "One of us should die." Then she leaned over to touch him. She caressed the back of his neck. She said, aloud, "Would you like me to drive for a while?"

They stopped at a picnic area where other cars were stopped—couples, families—and walked together, smiling at their good luck. He put his arm around her shoulders and she sensed how they were in a posture together, a man and a woman forming a posture, a figure, that someone might sketch and show to them. She said slowly, "I don't want to go back. . . ."

Silence. She looked up at him. His face was heavy with her words, as if she had pulled at his skin with her fingers. Children ran nearby and distracted him—yes, he was a father too, his children ran like that, they tugged at his skin with their light, busy fingers.

"Are you so unhappy?" he said.

"I'm not unhappy, back there. I'm nothing. There's nothing to me," she said.

They stared at each other. The sensation between them was intense, exhausting. She thought that this man was her savior, that he had come to her at a time in her life when her life demanded completion, an end, a permanent fixing of all that was troubled and shifting and deadly. And yet it was absurd to think this. No person could save another. So she drew back from him and released him.

A few hours later they stopped at a gas station in a small city. She went to the women's rest room, having to ask the attendant for a key, and when she came back her eye jumped nervously onto the rented car—why? did she think he might have driven off without her?—onto the man, her friend, standing in conversation with the young attendant. Her friend was as old as her husband, over forty, with lanky, sloping shoulders, a full body, his hair thick, a dark, burnished brown, a festive color that made her eye twitch a little—and his hands were always moving, always those rapid conversational circles, going nowhere, gestures that were at once a little aggressive and apologetic.

She put her hand on his arm, a claim. He turned to her and smiled and she felt that she loved him, that everything in her life had forced her to this moment and that she had no choice about it.

They sat in the car for two hours, in Albany, in the parking lot of a Howard Johnson's restaurant, talking, trying to figure out their past. There was no future. They concentrated on the past, the several days behind them, lit up with a hot, dazzling August sun, like explosions that already belonged to other people, to strangers. Her face was faintly reflected in the green-tinted curve of the windshield, but she could not have recognized that face. She began to cry; she told herself: *I am not here, this will pass, this is nothing.* Still, she could not stop crying. The muscles of her face were springy, like a child's unpredictable muscles. He stroked her arms, her shoulders, trying to comfort her. "This is so hard . . . this is impossible . . ." he said. She felt panic for the world outside this car, all that was not herself and this man, and at the same time she understood that she was free of him, as people are free of other people, she would leave him soon, safely, and within a few days he would have fallen into the past, the impersonal past. . . .

"I'm so ashamed of myself!" she said finally.

She returned to her husband and saw that another woman, a shadow-woman, had taken her place—noiseless and convincing, like a dancer performing certain difficult steps. Her husband folded her in his arms and talked to her of his own loneliness, his worries about his business, his health, his mother, kept tranquillized and mute in a nursing home, and her spirit detached itself from her and drifted about the rooms of the large house she lived in with her husband, a shadow-woman delicate and imprecise. There was no boundary to her, no edge. Alone, she took hot baths and sat exhausted in the steaming water, wondering at her perpetual exhaustion. All that winter she noticed the limp, languid weight of her arms, her veins bulging slightly with the pressure of her extreme weariness. *This is fate,* she thought, to be here and not there, to be one person and not another, a certain man's wife and not the wife of another man. The long, slow pain of this certainty rose in her, but it never became clear, it was baffling and imprecise. She could not be serious about it; she kept congratulating herself on her own good luck, to have escaped so easily, to have freed herself. So much love had gone into the first several years of her marriage that there wasn't much left, now, for another man. . . . She was certain of that. But the bath water made her dizzy, all that perpetual heat, and one day in January she drew a razor blade lightly across the inside of her arm, near the elbow, to see what would happen.

Afterward she wrapped a small towel around it, to stop the bleeding. The towel soaked through. She wrapped a bath towel around that and walked through the empty rooms of her home, lightheaded, hardly aware of the stubborn seeping of blood. There was no boundary to her in this house, no precise limit. She could flow out like her own blood and come to no end.

She sat for a while on a blue love seat, her mind empty. Her husband telephoned her when he would be staying late at the plant. He talked to her always about his plans, his problems, his business friends, his future. It was obvious that he had a future. As he spoke she nodded to encourage him, and her heartbeat quickened with the memory of her own, personal shame, the shame of this man's particular, private wife. One evening at dinner he leaned forward and put his head in his arms and fell asleep, like a child. She sat at the table with him for a while watching him. His hair had gone gray, almost white, at the temples—no one would guess that he was so quick, so careful a man, still fairly young about the eyes. She put her hand on his head, lightly, as if to prove to herself that he was real. He slept, exhausted.

One evening they went to a concert and she looked up to see her lover there, in the crowded aisle, in this city, watching her. He was standing there, with his overcoat on, watching her. She went cold. That morning the telephone had rung while her husband was still home, and she had heard him answer it, heard him hang up—it must have been a wrong number—and when the telephone rang again, at 9:30, she had been afraid to answer it. She had left home to be out of the range of that ringing, but now, in this public place, in this busy auditorium, she found herself staring at that man, unable to make any sign to him, any gesture of recognition. . . .

He would have come to her but she shook her head. *No. Stay away.*

Her husband helped her out of the row of seats, saying, "Excuse us, please. Excuse us," so that strangers got to their feet, quickly, alarmed, to let them pass. Was that woman about to faint? What was wrong?

At home she felt the blood drain slowly back into her head. Her husband embraced her hips, pressing his face against her, in that silence that belonged to the earliest days of their marriage. She thought, *He will drive it out of me.* He made love to her and she was back in the auditorium again, sitting alone, now that the concert was over. The stage was empty; the heavy velvet curtains had not been drawn; the musicians' chairs were empty, everything was silent and expectant; in the aisle her lover stood and smiled at her—Her husband was impatient. He was apart from her, working on her, operating on her; and then, stricken, he whispered, "Did I hurt you?"

The telephone rang the next morning. Dully, sluggishly, she answered it. She recognized his voice at once—that "Anna?" with its lifting of the second syllable, questioning and apologetic and making its claim—"Yes, what do you want?" she said.

"Just to see you. Please—"

"I can't."

"Anna, I'm sorry, I didn't mean to upset you—"

"I can't see you."

"Just for a few minutes—I have to talk to you—"

"But why, why now? Why now?" she said.

She heard her voice rising, but she could not stop it. He began to talk again, drowning her out. She remembered his rapid conversation. She remembered his gestures, the witty energetic circling of his hands.

"Please don't hang up!" he cried.

"I can't—I don't want to go through it again—"

"I'm not going to hurt you. Just tell me how you are."

"Everything is the same."

"Everything is the same with me."

She looked up at the ceiling, shyly. "Your wife? Your children?"

"The same."

"Your son?"

"He's fine—"

"I'm glad to hear that. I—"

"Is it still the same with you, your marriage? Tell me what you feel. What are you thinking?"

"I don't know. . . ."

She remembered his intense, eager words, the movement of his hands, that impatient precise fixing of the air by his hands, the jabbing of his fingers.

"Do you love me?" he said.

She could not answer.

"I'll come over to see you," he said.

"No," she said.

What will come next, what will happen?

Flesh hardening on his body, aging. Shrinking. He will grow old, but not soft like her husband. They are two different types: he is nervous, lean, energetic, wise. She will grow thinner, as the tension radiates out from her backbone, wearing down her flesh. Her collarbones will jut out of her skin. Her husband, caressing her in their bed, will discover that she is another woman—she is not there with him—instead she is rising in an elevator in a downtown hotel, carrying a book as a prop, or walking quickly away from that hotel, her head bent and filled with secrets. Love, what to do with it? . . . Useless as moths' wings, as moths' fluttering. . . . She feels the flutterings of silky, crazy wings in her chest.

He flew out to visit her every several weeks, staying at a different hotel each time. He telephoned her, and she drove down to park in an underground garage at the very center of the city.

She lay in his arms while her husband talked to her, miles away, one body fading into another. He will grow old, his body will change, she thought, pressing her cheek against the back of one of these men. If it was her lover, they were in a hotel room: always the propped-up little booklet describing the hotel's many services, with color photographs of its cocktail lounge and dining room and coffee shop. Grow old, leave me, die, go back to your neurotic wife and your sad, ordinary children, she thought, but still her eyes closed gratefully against his skin and she felt how complete their silence was, how they had come to rest in each other.

"Tell me about your life here. The people who love you," he said, as he always did.

One afternoon they lay together for four hours. It was her birthday and she was intoxicated with her good fortune, this prize of the afternoon, this man in her arms! She was a little giddy, she talked too much. She told him about her parents, about her husband. . . . "They were all people I believed in, but it turned out wrong. Now, I believe in you. . . ." He laughed as if shocked by her words. She did not understand. Then she understood. "But I believe truly in you. I can't think of myself without you," she said. . . . He spoke of his wife, her ambitions, her intelligence, her use of the children against him, her use of his younger son's blindness, all of his words gentle and hypnotic and convincing in the late afternoon peace of this hotel room . . . and she felt the terror of laughter, threatening laughter. Their words, like their bodies, were aging.

She dressed quickly in the bathroom, drawing her long hair up around the back of her head, fixing it as always, anxious that everything be the same. Her face was slightly raw, from his face. The rubbing of his skin. Her eyes were too bright, wearily bright. Her hair was blond but not so blond as it had been that summer in the white Nantucket air.

She ran water and splashed it on her face. She blinked at the water. Blind. Drowning. She thought with satisfaction that soon, soon, he would be back home, in that house on Long Island she had never seen, with that woman she had never seen, sitting on the edge of another bed, putting on his shoes. She wanted nothing except to be free of him. Why not be free? *Oh,* she thought suddenly, *I will follow you back and kill you. You and her and the little boy. What is there to stop me?*

She left him. Everyone on the street pitied her, that look of absolute zero.

III

A man and a child, approaching her. The sharp acrid smell of fish. The crashing of waves. Anna pretended not to notice the father with his son—there was something strange about them. That frank, silent intimacy, too gentle, the man's bare feet in the water and the boy a few feet away, leaning away from his father. He was about nine years old and still his father held his hand.

A small yipping dog, a golden dog, bounded near them.

Anna turned shyly back to her reading; she did not want to have to speak to these neighbors. She saw the man's shadow falling over her legs, then over the pages of her book, and she had the idea that he wanted to see what she was reading. The dog nuzzled her; the man called him away.

She watched them walk down the beach. She was relieved that the man had not spoken to her.

She saw them in town later that day, the two of them brown-haired and patient, now wearing sandals, walking with that same look of care. The man's white shorts were soiled and a little baggy. His pullover shirt was a faded green. His face was broad, the cheekbones wide, spaced widely apart, the eyes stark in their sockets, as if they fastened onto objects for no reason, ponderous and edgy. The little boy's face was pale and sharp; his lips were perpetually parted.

Anna realized that the child was blind.

The next morning, early, she caught sight of them again. For some reason she went to the back door of her cottage. She faced the sea breeze eagerly. Her heart hammered. . . . She had been here, in her family's old house, for three days, alone, bitterly satisfied at being alone, and now it was a puzzle to her how her soul strained to fly outward, to meet with another person. She watched the man with his son, his cautious, rather stooped shoulders above the child's small shoulders.

The man was carrying something, it looked like a notebook. He sat on the sand, not far from Anna's spot of the day before, and the dog rushed up to them. The child approached the edge of the ocean, timidly. He moved in short jerky steps, his legs stiff. The dog ran around him. Anna heard the child crying out a word that sounded like "Ty"—it must have been the dog's name—and then the man joined in, his voice heavy and firm.

"Ty—"

Anna tied her hair back with a yellow scarf and went down to the beach.

The man glanced around at her. He smiled. She stared past him at the waves. To talk to him or not to talk—she had the freedom of that choice. For a moment she felt that she had made a mistake, that the child and the dog would not protect her, that behind this man's ordinary, friendly face there was a certain arrogant maleness—then she relented, she smiled shyly.

"A nice house you've got there," the man said.

She nodded her thanks.

The man pushed his sunglasses up on his forehead. Yes, she recognized the eyes of the day before—intelligent and nervous, the sockets pale, untanned.

"Is that your telephone ringing?" he said.

She did not bother to listen. "It's a wrong number," she said.

Her husband calling: she had left home for a few days, to be alone.

But the man, setting himself on the sand, seemed to misinterpret this.

He smiled in surprise, one corner of his mouth higher than the other. He said nothing. Anna wondered: *What is he thinking?* The dog was leaping about her, panting against her legs, and she laughed in embarrassment. She bent to pet it, grateful for its busyness. "Don't let him jump up on you," the man said. "He's a nuisance."

The dog was a small golden retriever, a young dog. The blind child, standing now in the water, turned to call the dog to him. His voice was shrill and impatient.

"Our house is the third one down—the white one," the man said.

She turned, startled. "Oh, did you buy it from Dr. Patrick? Did he die?"

"Yes, finally. . . ."

Her eyes wandered nervously over the child and the dog. She felt the nervous beat of her heart out to the very tips of her fingers, the fleshy tips of her fingers: little hearts were there, pulsing. *What is he thinking*? The man had opened his notebook. He had a piece of charcoal and he began to sketch something.

Anna looked down at him. She saw the top of his head, his thick brown hair, the freckles on his shoulders, the quick, deft movement of his hand. Upside down, Anna herself being drawn. She smiled in surprise.

"Let me draw you. Sit down," he said.

She knelt awkwardly a few yards away. He turned the page of the sketch pad. The dog ran to her and she sat, straightening out her skirt beneath her, flinching from the dog's tongue. "Ty!" cried the child. Anna sat, and slowly the pleasure of the moment began to glow in her; her skin flushed with gratitude.

She sat there for nearly an hour. The man did not talk much. Back and forth the dog bounded, shaking itself. The child came to sit near them, in silence. Anna felt that she was drifting into a kind of trance while the man sketched her, half a dozen rapid sketches, the surface of her face given up to him. "Where are you from?" the man asked.

"Ohio. My husband lives in Ohio."

She wore no wedding band.

"Your wife—" Anna began.

"Yes?"

"Is she here?"

"Not right now."

She was silent, ashamed. She had asked an improper question. But the man did not seem to notice. He continued drawing her, bent over the sketch pad. When Anna said she had to go, he showed her the drawings—one after another of her, Anna, recognizably Anna, a woman in her early thirties, her hair smooth and flat across the top of her head, tied behind by a scarf. "Take the one you like best," he said, and she picked one of her with the dog in her lap, sitting very straight, her brows and eyes clearly defined, her lips girlishly pursed, the dog and her dress suggested by a few quick irregular lines.

"Lady with pet dog," the man said.

She spent the rest of the day reading, nearer her cottage. It was not really a cottage—it was a two-story house, large and ungainly and weathered. It was mixed up in her mind with her family, her own childhood, and she glanced up from her book, perplexed, as if waiting for one of her parents or her sister to come up to her. Then she thought of the man, the man with the blind child, the man with the dog, and she could not concentrate on her reading. Someone—probably her father—had marked a passage that must be important, but she kept reading and rereading it: *We try to discover in things, endeared to us on that account, the spiritual glamour which we ourselves have cast upon them; we are disillusioned, and learn that they are in themselves barren and devoid of the charm that they owed, in our minds, to the association of certain ideas. . . .*

She thought again of the man on the beach. She lay the book aside and thought of him: his eyes, his aloneness, his drawings of her.

They began seeing each other after that. He came to her front door in the evening, without the child; he drove her into town for dinner. She was shy and extremely pleased. The darkness of the expensive restaurant released her; she heard herself chatter; she leaned forward and seemed to be offering her face up to him, listening to him. He talked about his work on a Long Island newspaper and she seemed to be listening to him, as she stared at his face, arranging her own face into the expression she had seen in that charcoal drawing. Did he see her like that, then?—girlish and withdrawn and patrician? She felt the weight of his interest in her, a force that fell upon her like a blow. A repeated blow. Of course he was married, he had children—of course she was married, permanently married. This flight from her husband was not important. She had left him before, to be alone, it was not important. Everything in her was slender and delicate and not important.

They walked for hours after dinner, looking at the other strollers, the weekend visitors, the tourists, the couples like themselves. Surely they were mistaken for a couple, a married couple. *This is the hour in which everything is decided,* Anna thought. They had both had several drinks and they talked a great deal. Anna found herself saying too much, stopping and starting giddily. She put her hand to her forehead, feeling faint.

"It's from the sun—you've had too much sun—" he said.

At the door to her cottage, on the front porch, she heard herself asking him if he would like to come in. She allowed him to lead her inside, to close the door. *This is not important,* she thought clearly, *he doesn't mean it, he doesn't love me, nothing will come of it.* She was frightened, yet it seemed to her necessary to give in; she had to leave Nantucket with that act completed, an act of adultery, an accomplishment she would take back to Ohio and to her marriage.

Later, incredibly, she heard herself asking: "Do you . . . do you love me?"

"You're so beautiful!" he said, amazed.

She felt this beauty, shy and glowing and centered in her eyes. He stared at her. In this large, drafty house, alone together, they were like accomplices, conspirators. She could not think: how old was she? which year was this? They had done something unforgivable together, and the knowledge of it was tugging at their faces. A cloud seemed to pass over her. She felt herself smiling shrilly.

Afterward, a peculiar raspiness, a dryness of breath. He was silent. She felt a strange, idle fear, a sense of the danger outside this room and this old, comfortable bed—a danger that would not recognize her as the lady in that drawing, the lady with the pet dog. There was nothing to say to this man, this stranger. She felt the beauty draining out of her face, her eyes fading.

"I've got to be alone," she told him.

He left, and she understood that she would not see him again. She stood by the window of the room, watching the ocean. A sense of shame overpowered her: it was smeared everywhere on her body, the smell of it, the richness of it. She tried to recall him, and his face was confused in her memory: she would have to shout to him across a jumbled space, she would have to wave her arms wildly. *You love me! You must love me!* But she knew he did not love her, and she did not love him; he was a man who drew everything up into himself, like all men, walking away, free to walk away, free to have his own thoughts, free to envision her body, all the secrets of her body. . . . And she lay down again in the bed, feeling how heavy this body had become, her insides heavy with shame, the very backs of her eyelids coated with shame.

"This is the end of one part of my life," she thought.

But in the morning the telephone rang. She answered it. It was her lover: they talked brightly and happily. She could hear the eagerness in his voice, the love in his voice, that same still, sad amazement—she understood how simple life was, there were no problems.

They spent most of their time on the beach, with the child and the dog. He joked and was serious at the same time. He said, once, "You have defined my soul for me," and she laughed to hide her alarm. In a few days it was time for her to leave. He got a sitter for the boy and took the ferry with her to the mainland, then rented a car to drive her up to Albany. She kept thinking: *Now something will happen. It will come to an end.* But most of the drive was silent and hypnotic. She wanted him to joke with her, to say again that she had defined his soul for him, but he drove fast, he was serious, she distrusted the hawkish look of his profile—she did not know him at all. At a gas station she splashed her face with cold water. Alone in the grubby little rest room, shaky and very much alone. In such places are women totally alone with their bodies. The body grows heavier, more evil, in such silence. . . . On the beach everything had been noisy with sunlight and gulls and waves; here, as if run to earth, everything was cramped and silent and dead.

She went outside, squinting. There he was, talking with the station attendant. She could not think as she returned to him whether she wanted to live or not.

She stayed in Albany for a few days, then flew home to her husband. He met her at the airport, near the luggage counter, where her three pieces of pale-brown luggage were brought to him on a conveyer belt, to be claimed by him. He kissed her on the cheek. They shook hands, a little embarrassed. She had come home again.

"How will I live out the rest of my life?" she wondered.

In January her lover spied on her: she glanced up and saw him, in a public place, in the DeRoy Symphony Hall. She was paralyzed with fear. She nearly fainted. In this faint she felt her husband's body, loving her, working its love upon her, and she shut her eyes harder to keep out the certainty of his love—sometimes he failed at loving her, sometimes he succeeded, it had nothing to do with her or her pity or her ten years of love for him, it had nothing to do with a woman at all. It was a private act accomplished by a man, a husband or a lover, in communion with his own soul, his manhood.

Her husband was forty-two years old now, growing slowly into middle age, getting heavier, softer. Her lover was about the same age, narrower in the shoulders, with a full, solid chest, yet lean, nervous. She thought, in her paralysis, of men and how they love freely and eagerly so long as their bodies are capable of love, love for a woman; and then, as love fades in their bodies, it fades from their souls and they become immune and immortal and ready to die.

Her husband was a little rough with her, as if impatient with himself. "I love you," he said fiercely, angrily. And then, ashamed, he said, "Did I hurt you? . . ."

"You didn't hurt me," she said.

Her voice was too shrill for their embrace.

While he was in the bathroom she went to her closet and took out that drawing of the summer before. There she was, on the beach at Nantucket, a lady with a pet dog, her eyes large and defined, the dog in her lap hardly more than a few snarls, a few coarse soft lines of charcoal . . . her dress smeared, her arms oddly limp . . . her hands not well drawn at all. . . . She tried to think: did she love the man who had drawn this? did he love her? The fever in her husband's body had touched her and driven her temperature up, and now she stared at the drawing with a kind of lust, fearful of seeing an ugly soul in that woman's face, fearful of seeing the face suddenly through her lover's eyes. She breathed quickly and harshly, staring at the drawing.

And so, the next day, she went to him at his hotel. She wept, pressing against him, demanding of him, "What do you want? Why are you here? Why don't you let me alone?" He told her that he wanted nothing. He expected nothing. He would not cause trouble.

"I want to talk about last August," he said.

"Don't—" she said.

She was hypnotized by his gesturing hands, his nervousness, his obvious agitation. He kept saying, "I understand. I'm making no claims upon you."

They became lovers again.

He called room service for something to drink and they sat side by side on his bed, looking through a copy of *The New Yorker*, laughing at the cartoons. It was so peaceful in this room, so complete. They were on a holiday. It was a secret holiday. Four-thirty in the afternoon, on a Friday, an ordinary Friday: a secret holiday.

"I won't bother you again," he said.

He flew back to see her again in March, and in late April. He telephoned her from his hotel—a different hotel each time—and she came down to him at once. She rose to him in various elevators, she knocked on the doors of various rooms, she stepped into his embrace, breathless and guilty and already angry with him, pleading with him. One morning in May, when he telephoned, she pressed her forehead against the doorframe and could not speak. He kept saying, "What's wrong? Can't you talk? Aren't you alone?" She felt that she was going insane. Her head would burst. Why, why did he love her, why did he pursue her? Why did he want her to die?

She went to him in the hotel room. A familiar room: had they been here before? "Everything is repeating itself. Everything is stuck," she said. He framed her face in his hands and said that she looked thinner—was she sick?—what was wrong? She shook herself free. He, her lover, looked about the same. There was a small, angry pimple on his neck. He stared at her, eagerly and suspiciously. Did she bring bad news?

"So you love me? You love me?" she asked.

"Why are you so angry?"

"I want to be free of you. The two of us free of each other."

"That isn't true—you don't want that—"

He embraced her. She was wild with that old, familiar passion for him, her body clinging to his, her arms not strong enough to hold him. Ah, what despair!—what bitter hatred she felt!—she needed this man for her salvation, he was all she had to live for, and yet she could not believe in him. He embraced her thighs, her hips, kissing her, pressing his warm face against her, and yet she could not believe in him, not really. She needed him in order to live, but he was not worth her love, he was not worth her dying. . . . She promised herself this: when she got back home, when she was alone, she would draw the razor more deeply across her arm.

The telephone rang and he answered it: a wrong number.

"Jesus," he said.

They lay together, still. She imagined their posture like this, the two of them one figure, one substance; and outside this room and this bed there was a universe of disjointed, separate things, blank things, that had nothing to do with them. She would not be Anna out there, the lady in the drawing. He would not be her lover.

"I love you so much. . . ." she whispered.

"Please don't cry! We have only a few hours, please. . . ."

It was absurd, their clinging together like this. She saw them as a single figure in a drawing, their arms and legs entwined, their heads pressing mutely together. Helpless substance, so heavy and warm and doomed. It was absurd that any human being should be so important to another human being. She wanted to laugh: a laugh might free them both.

She could not laugh.

Sometime later he said, as if they had been arguing, "Look. It's you. You're the one who doesn't want to get married. You lie to me—"

"Lie to you?"

"You love me but you won't marry me, because you want something left over—Something not finished—All your life you can attribute your misery to me, to our not being married—you are using me—"

"Stop it! You'll make me hate you!" she cried.

"You can say to yourself that you're miserable because of *me*. We will never be married, you will never be happy, neither one of us will ever be happy—"

"I don't want to hear this!" she said.

She pressed her hands flatly against her face.

She went to the bathroom to get dressed. She washed her face and part of her body, quickly. The fever was in her, in the pit of her belly. She would rush home and strike a razor across the inside of her arm and free the pressure, that fever.

The impatient bulging of the veins: an ordeal over.

The demand of the telephone's ringing: that ordeal over.

The nuisance of getting the car and driving home in all that five o'clock traffic: an ordeal too much for a woman.

The movement of this stranger's body in hers: over, finished.

Now, dressed, a little calmer, they held hands and talked. They had to talk swiftly, to get all their news in: he did not trust the people who worked for him, he had faith in no one, his wife had moved to a textbook publishing company and was doing well, she had inherited a Ben Shahn painting from her father and wanted to "touch it up a little"—she was crazy!—his blind son was at another school, doing fairly well, in fact his children were all doing fairly well in spite of the stupid mistake of their parents' marriage—and what about her? what about her life? She told him in a rush the one thing he wanted to hear: that she lived with her husband lovelessly, the two of them polite strangers, sharing a bed, lying side by side in the night in that bed, bodies out of which souls had fled. There was no longer even any shame between them.

"And what about me? Do you feel shame with me still?" he asked.

She did not answer. She moved away from him and prepared to leave.

Then, a minute later, she happened to catch sight of his reflection in the bureau mirror—he was glancing down at himself, checking himself mechanically, impersonally, preparing also to leave. He too would leave this room: he too was headed somewhere else.

She stared at him. It seemed to her that in this instant he was breaking from her, the image of her lover fell free of her, breaking from her . . . and she realized that he existed in a dimension quite apart from her, a mysterious being. And suddenly, joyfully, she felt a miraculous calm. This man was her husband, truly—they were truly married, here in this room—they had been married haphazardly and accidentally for a long time. In another part of the city she had another husband, a "husband," but she had not betrayed that man, not really. This man, whom she loved above any other person in the world, above even her own self-pitying sorrow and her own life, was her truest lover, her destiny. And she did not hate him, she did not hate herself any longer; she did not wish to die; she was flooded with a strange certainty, a sense of gratitude, of pure selfless energy. It was obvious to her that she had, all along, been behaving correctly; out of instinct.

What triumph, to love like this in any room, anywhere, risking even the craziest of accidents!

"Why are you so happy? What's wrong?" he asked, startled. He stared at her. She felt the abrupt concentration in him, the focusing of his vision on her, almost a bitterness in his face, as if he feared her. What, was it beginning all over again? Their love beginning again, in spite of them? "How can you look so happy?" he asked. "We don't have any right to it. Is it because. . . ?"

"Yes," she said.

NAIROBI

Early Saturday afternoon the man who had introduced himself as Oliver took Ginny to several shops on Madison Avenue above 70th Street to buy her what he called an appropriate outfit. For an hour and forty-five minutes she modeled clothes, watching with critical interest her image in the three-way mirrors, unable to decide if this was one of her really good days or only a mediocre day. Judging by Oliver's expression she looked all right, but it was difficult to tell. The salesclerks saw too many beautiful young women to be impressed, though one told Ginny she envied her her hair—not just that shade of chestnut red but the thickness too. In the changing room she told Ginny that her own hair was "coming out in handfuls" but Ginny told her it didn't show. It will begin to show one of these days, the salesgirl said.

Ginny modeled a green velvet jumpsuit with a brass zipper and oversized buckles, and an Italian knit dress with bunchy sleeves in a zigzag pattern of beige, brown, and cream, and a ruffled organdy "tea dress" in pale orange, and a navy-blue blazer made of Irish linen, with a pleated white linen skirt and a pale blue silk blouse. Assuming she could only have one costume, which seemed to be the case, she would have preferred the jumpsuit, not just because it was the most expensive outfit (the price tag read $475) but because the green velvet reflected in her eyes. Oliver decided on the Irish linen blazer and the skirt and blouse, however, and told the salesclerk to remove the tags and to pack up Ginny's own clothes, since she intended to wear the new outfit.

Strolling uptown, he told her that with her hair down like that, and her bangs combed low on her forehead, she looked like a "convent schoolgirl." In theory, that was. Tangentially.

It was a balmy, windy day in early April. Everyone was out. Ginny kept seeing people she almost knew, Oliver waved hello to several acquaintances. There were baby buggies, dogs being walked, sports cars with their tops down. In shop windows—particularly in the broad windows of galleries—Ginny's reflection in the navy-blue blazer struck her as unfamiliar and quirky but not bad: the blazer with its built-up shoulders and wide lapels was more stylish than she'd thought at first. Oliver too was pleased. He had slipped on steel-frame tinted glasses. He said they had plenty of time. A pair of good shoes—really good shoes—might be an idea.

But first they went into a jewelry boutique at 76th Street, where Oliver bought her four narrow silver bracelets, engraved in bird and animal heads, and a pair of conch-shaped silver earrings from Mexico. Ginny slipped her gold studs out and put on the new earrings as Oliver watched. Doesn't it hurt to force those wires through your flesh? He was standing rather close.

No, Ginny said. My earlobes are numb, I don't feel a thing. It's easy.

When did you get your ears pierced? Oliver asked.

Ginny felt her cheeks color slightly—as if he were asking a favor of her and her instinct wasn't clear enough, whether to acquiesce or draw away just perceptibly. She drew away, still adjusting the earrings, but said: I don't have any idea, maybe I was thirteen, maybe twelve, it was a long time ago. We all went out and had our ears pierced.

In a salon called Michel's she exchanged her chunky-heeled red shoes for a pair of kidskin sandals that might have been the most beautiful shoes she'd ever seen. Oliver laughed quizzically over them: they were hardly anything but a few straps and a price tag, he told the salesman, but they looked like the real thing, they were what he wanted. The salesman told Oliver that his taste was "unerring."

Do you want to keep your old shoes? Oliver asked Ginny.

Of course, Ginny said, slightly hurt, but as the salesman was packing them she changed her mind. No, the hell with them, she said. They're too much trouble to take along.—Which she might regret afterward: but it was the right thing to say at that particular moment.

In the cab headed west and then north along the park, Oliver gave her instructions in a low, casual voice. The main thing was that she should say very little. She shouldn't smile unless it was absolutely necessary. While he and his friends spoke—if they spoke at any length, he couldn't predict Marguerite's attitude—Ginny might even drift away, pick up a magazine and leaf through it if something appropriate was available, not nervously, just idly, for something to do, as if she were bored; better yet, she might look out the window or even step out on the terrace, since the afternoon was so warm. Don't even look at me, Oliver said. Don't give the impression that anything I say—anything the three of us say—matters very much to you.

Yes, said Ginny.

The important thing, Oliver said, squeezing her hand and releasing it, is that you're basically not concerned. I mean with the three of us. With Marguerite. With anyone. Do you understand?

Yes, said Ginny. She was studying her new shoes. Kidskin in a shade called "vanilla," eight straps on each shoe, certainly the most beautiful shoes she'd ever owned. The price had taken her breath away too. She hadn't any questions to ask Oliver.

When Ginny had been much younger—which is to say, a few years ago, when she was new to the city—she might have had some questions to ask. In fact she had had a number of questions to ask, then. But the answers had invariably disappointed. The answers had contained so much less substance than her own questions, she had learned, by degrees, not to ask.

So she told Oliver a second time, to assure *him:* Of course I understand.

The apartment building they entered at Fifth and 88th was older than Ginny might have guessed from the outside—the mosaic murals in the lobby were in a quaint ethereal style unknown to her. Perhaps they were meant to be amusing, but she didn't think so. It was impressive that the uniformed doorman knew Oliver, whom he called "Mr. Leahy," and that he was so gracious about keeping their package for them while they visited upstairs; it was impressive that the black elevator operator nodded and murmured hello in a certain tone. Smiles were measured and respectful all around, but Ginny didn't trouble to smile; she knew it wasn't expected of her.

In the elevator—which was almost uncomfortably small—Oliver looked at Ginny critically, standing back to examine her from her toes upward and finding nothing wrong except a strand of hair or two out of place. The Irish linen blazer was an excellent choice, he said. The earrings too. The bracelets. The shoes. He spoke with assurance though Ginny had the idea he was nervous, or excited. He turned to study his own reflection in the bronze-frosted mirror on the elevator wall, facing it with a queer childlike squint. This was his "mirror face," Ginny supposed, the way he had of confronting himself in the mirror so that it wasn't *really* himself but a certain habitual expression that protected him. Ginny hadn't any mirror face herself. She had gone beyond that, she knew better, those childish frowns and half-smiles and narrowed eyes and heads turned coyly or hopefully to one side—ways of protecting her from seeing "Ginny" when the truth of "Ginny" was that she required being seen head-on. But it would have been difficult to explain to another person.

Oliver adjusted his handsome blue-striped cotton tie and ran his fingers deftly through his hair. It was pale, fine, airily colorless hair, blond perhaps, shading into premature silver, rather thin, Ginny thought, for a man his age. (She estimated his age at thirty-four, which seemed "old" to her in certain respects, but she knew it was reasonably "young" in others.) Oliver's skin was slightly coarse; his nose wide at the bridge, and the nostrils disfigured by a few dark hairs that should have been snipped off; his lower jaw was somewhat heavy. But he was a handsome man. In his steel-rimmed blue-tinted glasses he was a handsome man, and Ginny saw for the first time that they made an attractive couple.

Don't trouble to answer any questions they might ask, Oliver said. In any case the questions won't be serious—just conversation.

I understand, Ginny said.

A Hispanic maid answered the door. The elevator and the corridor had been so dimly lit, Ginny wasn't prepared for the flood of sunlight in the apartment. They were on the eighteenth floor overlooking the park and the day was still cloudless.

Oliver introduced Ginny to his friends Marguerite and Herbert—the last name sounded like Crews—and Ginny shook hands with them unhesitatingly, as if it were a customary gesture with her. The first exchanges were about the weather. Marguerite was vehement in her gratitude since the past winter, January in particular, had been uncommonly long and dark and depressing. Ginny assented without actually agreeing. For the first minute or two she felt thrown off balance, she couldn't have said why, by the fact that Marguerite Crews was so tall a woman—taller even than Ginny. And she was, or had been, a very beautiful woman as well, with a pale olive-dark complexion and severely black hair parted in the center of her head and fixed in a careless knot at the nape of her neck.

Oliver was explaining apologetically that they couldn't stay. Not even for a drink, really: they were in fact already late for another engagement in the Village. Both the Crewses expressed disappointment. And Oliver's plans for the weekend had been altered as well, unavoidably. At this announcement the disappointment was keener, and Ginny looked away before Marguerite's eyes could lock with hers.

But Oliver was working too hard, Marguerite protested.

But he *must* come out to the Point as they'd planned, Herbert said, and bring his friend along.

Ginny eased discreetly away. She was aloof, indifferent, just slightly bored, but unfailingly courteous: a mark of good breeding. And the Irish linen blazer and skirt were just right.

After a brief while Herbert Crews came over to comment on the view and Ginny thought it wouldn't be an error to agree: the view of Central Park was, after all, something quite real. He told her they'd lived here for eleven years "off and on." They traveled a good deal, he was required to travel almost more than he liked, being associated with an organization Ginny might have heard of—the Zieboldt Foundation. He had just returned from Nairobi, he said. Two days ago. And still feeling the strain—the fatigue. Ginny thought that his affable talkative "social" manner showed not the least hint of fatigue but did not make this observation to Herbert Crews.

She felt a small pinprick of pity for the way Marguerite Crews's collarbones showed through her filmy muslin Indian blouse, and for the extreme thinness of her waist (cinched tight with a belt of silver coins or medallions), and for the faint scolding voice—so conspicuously a "voice"—with which she was speaking to Oliver. She saw that Oliver, though smiling nervously, and standing in a self-conscious pose with the thumb of his right hand hooked in his sports coat pocket, was enjoying the episode very much—she noted for the first time something vehement and cruel though at the same time unmistakably boyish in his face. Herbert Crews was telling her about Nairobi but she couldn't concentrate on his words. She was wondering if it might be proper to ask where Nairobi was—she assumed it was a country somewhere in Africa—but Herbert Crews continued, speaking now with zest of the wild animals, including great herds of "the most exquisitely beautiful gazelles," in the Kenya preserves. Had she ever been there, he asked. No, Ginny said. Well, said Herbert, nodding vigorously, it really *is* worth it. Next time Marguerite promised to come along.

Ginny heard Oliver explain again that they were already late for an appointment in the Village, unfortunately they couldn't stay for a drink, yes it was a pity but he hoped they might do it another time: with which Marguerite warmly agreed. Though it was clearly all right for Oliver and Ginny to leave now, Herbert Crews was telling her about the various animals he'd seen—elands, giraffes, gnus, hippopotami, crocodiles, zebras, "feathered monkeys," impalas—he had actually eaten impala and found it fairly good. But the trip was fatiguing and his business in Nairobi disagreeable. He'd discovered—as in fact the Foundation had known from certain clumsily fudged reports—that the microbiological research being subsidized there had not only come to virtually nothing, but that vast sums of money had "disappeared" into nowhere. Ginny professed to feel some sympathy though at the same time, as she said, she wasn't surprised. Well, she said, easing away from Herbert Crews's side, that seems to be human nature, doesn't it. All around the world.

Americans and Swedes this time, Herbert Crews said—equally taken in.

It couldn't be avoided that Herbert tell Oliver what he'd been saying—Oliver in fact seemed to be interested, he might have had some indirect connection with the Foundation himself—but unfortunately they were late for their engagement downtown, and within five minutes they were out of the apartment and back in the elevator going down.

Oliver withdrew a handkerchief from his breast pocket, unfolded it, and carefully wiped his forehead. Ginny was studying her reflection in the mirror and felt a pinprick of disappointment—her eyes looked shadowed and tired, and her hair wasn't really all that wonderful, falling straight to her shoulders. Though she'd shampooed it only that morning, it was already getting dirty—the wind had been so strong on their walk up Madison.

On Fifth Avenue, in the gusty sunlight, they walked together for several blocks. Ginny slid her arm through Oliver's as if they were being watched, but at an intersection they were forced to walk at different paces and her arm slipped free. It was time in any case to say good-bye: she sensed that he wasn't going to ask her, even out of courtesy, to have a drink with him: and she had made up her mind not to feel even tangentially insulted. After all, she hadn't been insulted.

He signaled a cab for her. He handed over the pink cardboard box with her denim jumper and sweater in it and shook her hand vigorously. You were lovely up there, Oliver said—just perfect. Look, I'll call you, all right?

She felt the weight, the subtle dizzying blow, of the "were." But she thanked him just the same. And got into the cab. And wasn't so stricken by a sudden fleeting sense of loss—of loss tinged with a queer cold sickish knowledge—that, as the cab pulled away into the traffic stream, she couldn't give him a final languid wave of her hand, and even shape her mouth into a puckish kiss. All she had really lost, in a sense, was her own pair of shoes.

THE TRYST

She was laughing. At first he thought she might be crying, but she was laughing.

Raggedy Ann, she said. You asked about nicknames—I've forgotten about it for years—but Raggedy Ann it was, for a while. They called me Raggedy Ann.

She lay sprawled on her stomach, her face pressed into the damp pillow, one arm loose and gangly, falling over the edge of the bed. Her hair was red-orange and since it had the texture of straw he had thought it was probably dyed. The bed jiggled, she was laughing silently. Her arms and shoulders were freckled and pale, her long legs were unevenly tanned, the flesh of her young body not so soft as it appeared but rather tough, ungiving. She was in an exuberant mood; her laughter was childlike, bright, brittle.

What were you called?—when you were a boy? she asked. Her voice was muffled by the pillow. She did not turn to look at him.

John, he said.

What! John! Never a nickname, never Johnny or Jack or Jackie?

I don't think so, he said.

She found that very funny. She laughed and kicked her legs and gave off an air, an odor, of intense fleshy heat. I won't survive this one, she giggled.

He was one of the adults of the world now. He was in charge of the world.

Sometimes he stood at the bedroom window and surveyed the handsome sloping lawn, the houses of his neighbors and their handsome lawns, his eye moving slowly along the memorized street. He knew it. The Tilsons . . . the Dwyers . . . the Pitkers . . . the Reddingers . . . the Schells. Like beads on a string were the houses, solid and baronial, each inhabited, each protected. Day or night he knew them and the knowledge made him pleasurably intoxicated.

He was Reddinger. Reddinger, John.

Last Saturday night, late, his wife asked: Why are you standing there, why aren't you undressing? It's after two.

He was not thinking of Annie. That long restless rangy body, that rather angular, bony face, her fingers stained with ink, her fingernails never very clean, the throaty mocking voice: he had pushed her out of his mind. He was breathing the night air and the sharp autumnal odor of pine needles stirred him, moved him deeply. He was in charge of the world but why should he not shiver with delight of the world? For he did love it. He loved it.

I loved it—this—all of you—

He spoke impulsively. She did not hear. Advancing upon him, her elbows raised as she labored to unfasten a hook at the back of her neck, she did not look at him; she spoke with a sleepy absentmindedness, as if they had had this conversation before. Were you drunk, when you were laughing so much? she asked. It wasn't like you. Then, at dinner, you were practically mute. Poor Frances Mason, trying to talk to you! That wasn't like you either, John.

There must have been a party at the Buhls', across the way. Voices lifted. Car doors were slammed. John Reddinger felt his spirit stirred by the acrid smell of the pines and the chilly bright-starred night and his wife's warm, perfumed, familiar closeness. His senses leaped, his eyes blinked rapidly as if he might burst into tears. In the autumn of the year he dwelt upon boyhood and death and pleasures of a harsh, sensual nature, the kind that are torn out of human beings, like cries; he dwelt upon the mystery of his own existence, that teasing riddle. The world itself was an intoxicant to him.

Wasn't it like me? he asked seriously. What am I like, then?

I don't ask you about your family, the girl pointed out. Why should you ask me about other men?

He admired her brusque, comic manner, the tomboyish wag of her foot.

Natural curiosity, he said.

Your wife! Your children!—I don't ask, do I?

They were silent and he had the idea she was waiting for him to speak, to volunteer information. But he was disingenuous. Her frankness made him uncharacteristically passive; for once he was letting a woman take the lead, never quite prepared for what happened. It was a novelty, a delight. It was sometimes unnerving.

You think I'm too proud to ask for money, I mean for a loan—for my rent, Annie said. I'm not, though. I'm not too proud.

Are you asking for it, then?

No. But not because I'm proud or because I'm afraid of altering our relationship. You understand? Because I want you to know I could have asked and I didn't—you understand?

I think so, John said, though in fact he did not.

At Christmas, somehow, they lost contact with each other. Days passed. Twelve days. Fifteen. His widowed mother came to visit them in the big red-brick colonial in Lathrup Park, and his wife's sister and her husband and two young children, and his oldest boy, a freshman at Swarthmore, brought his Japanese roommate home with him; life grew dense, robustly complicated. He telephoned her at the apartment but no one answered. He telephoned the gallery where she worked but the other girl answered and when he said softly and hopefully, Annie? Is that Annie?, the girl told him that it was *not* Annie; and the gallery owner, Mr. Helnutt, disapproved strongly of personal calls. She was certain Annie knew about this policy and surprised that Annie had not told him about it.

He hung up guiltily, like a boy.

A previous autumn, years ago, he had made a terrible mistake. What a blunder!

The worst blunder of my life, he said.

What was it? Annie asked at once.

But his mood changed. A fly was buzzing somewhere in her small, untidy apartment, which smelled of cats. His mood changed. His spirit changed.

He did not reply. After a while Annie yawned. I've never made any really bad mistakes, she said. Unless I've forgotten.

You're perfect, he said.

She laughed, irritated.

. . . Perfect. So beautiful, so confident. . . . So much at home in your body. . . .

He caressed her and forced himself to think of her, only of her. It was not true that she was beautiful but she was striking—red hair, brown eyes, a quick tense dancer's body—and he saw how other people looked at her, women as well as men. It was a fact. He loved her, he was silly and dizzy and sickened with love for her, and he did not wish to think of his reckless mistake of that other autumn. It had had its comic aspects, but it had been humiliating. And dangerous. While on a business trip to Atlanta he had strolled downtown and in a dimly lit bar had drifted into a conversation with a girl, a beautiful blonde in her twenties, soft-spoken and sweet and very shy. She agreed to come back with him to his hotel room for a nightcap, but partway back, on the street, John sensed something wrong, something terribly wrong, he heard his voice rattling on about the marvelous view from his room on the twentieth floor of the hotel and about how fine an impression Atlanta was making on him—then in midsentence he stopped, staring at the girl's heavily made-up face and at the blond hair which was certainly a wig—he stammered that he had made a mistake, he would have to say good night now; he couldn't bring her back to the room after all. She stared at him belligerently. She asked what was wrong, just what in hell was wrong?—her voice cracking slightly so that he knew she wasn't a girl, a woman, at all. It was a boy of about twenty-five. He backed away and the creature asked why he had changed his mind, wasn't she good enough for him, who did he think he was? Bastard! Shouting after John as he hurried away: *who did he think he was?*

I never think about the past, Annie said lazily. She was smoking in bed, her long bare legs crossed at the knee. I mean what the hell?—it's all over with.

He had not loved any of the others as he loved Annie. He was sure of that.

He thought of her, raking leaves. A lawn crew serviced the Reddingers' immense lawn but he sometimes raked leaves on the weekend, for the pleasure of it. He worked until his arm and shoulder muscles ached. Remarkable, he thought. Life, living. In this body. Now.

She crowded out older memories. Ah, she was ruthless! An Amazon, a Valkyrie maiden. Beautiful. Unpredictable. She obliterated other women, other sweetly painful memories of women. That was her power.

Remarkable, he murmured.

Daddy!

He looked around. His eleven-year-old daughter, Sally, was screaming at him.

Daddy, I've been calling and calling you from the porch, couldn't you hear me?—Momma wants you for something! A big grin. Amused, she was, at her father's absentmindedness; and she had a certain sly, knowing look as well, as if she could read his thoughts.

But of course that was only his imagination.

He's just a friend of mine, an old friend, Annie said vaguely. He doesn't count.

A friend from where?

From around town.

Meaning—?

From around town.

A girl in a raw, unfinished painting. Like the crude canvases on exhibit at the gallery, that day he had drifted by: something vulgar and exciting about the mere droop of a shoulder, the indifference of a strand of hair blown into her eyes. And the dirt-edged fingernails. And the shoes with the run-over heels. She was raw, unfinished, lazy, slangy, vulgar, crude, mouthing in her cheerful insouciant voice certain words and phrases John Reddinger would never have said aloud, in the presence of a member of the opposite sex; but at the same time it excited him to know that she was highly intelligent, and really well-educated, with a master's degree in art history and a studied, if rather flippant, familiarity with the monstrousness of contemporary art. He could not determine whether she was as impoverished as she appeared or whether it was a pose, an act. Certain items of clothing, he knew, were expensive. A suede leather coat, a pair of knee-high boots, a long skirt of black soft wool. And one of her rings might have been genuine. But much of the time she looked shabby—ratty. She nearly fainted once, at the airport; she had confessed she hadn't eaten for a while, had run out of money that week. In San Francisco, where she spent three days with him, she had eaten hungrily enough and it had pleased him to feed her, to nourish her on so elementary a level.

Who bought you this? he asked, fingering the sleeve of her coat.

What? This? I bought it myself.

Who paid for it?

It's a year old, I bought it myself.

It's very beautiful.

Yes?

He supposed, beforehand, that they would lose contact with each other when Christmas approached. The routine of life was upset, schedules were radically altered, obligations increased. He disliked holidays; yet in a way he liked them, craved them. Something wonderful must happen! Something wonderful must happen soon.

He was going to miss her, he knew.

She chattered about something he wasn't following. A sculptor she knew, his odd relationship with his wife. A friend. A former friend. She paused and he realized it was a conversation and he must reply, must take his turn. What was she talking about? Why did these girls talk so, when he wanted nothing so much as to stare at them, in silence, in pained awe? I don't really have friends any longer, he said slowly. It was a topic he and his wife had discussed recently. She had read an article on the subject in a woman's magazine: American men of middle age, especially in the higher income brackets, tended to have very few close friends, very few indeed. It was sad. It was unfortunate. I had friends in high school and college, he said, but I've lost touch . . . we've lost touch. It doesn't seem to happen afterward, after you grow up. Friendship, I mean.

God, that's sad. That's really sad. She shivered, staring at him. Her eyes were darkly brown and lustrous, at times almost too lustrous. They reminded him of a puppy's eyes.

Yes, I suppose it is, he said absently.

On New Year's Eve, driving from a party in Lathrup Park to another party in Wausau Heights, he happened to see a young woman who resembled Annie—in mink to midcalf, her red hair fastened in a bun, being helped out of a sports car by a young man. That girl! Annie! His senses leaped, though he knew it wasn't Annie.

For some reason the connection between them had broken. He didn't know why. He had had to fly to London; and then it was mid-December and the holiday season; then it was early January. He had tried to telephone two or three times, without success. His feeling for her ebbed. It was curious—other faces got in the way of hers, distracting him. Over the holidays there were innumerable parties: brunches and luncheons and cocktail parties and open houses and formal dinner parties and informal evening parties, a press of people, friends and acquaintances and strangers, all demanding his attention. He meant to telephone her, meant to send a small gift, but time passed quickly and he forgot.

After seeing the girl on New Year's Eve, however, he found himself thinking again of Annie. He lay in bed, sleepless, a little feverish, thinking of her. They had done certain things together and now he tried to picture them, from a distance. How he had adored her! Bold, silly, gawky, beautiful, not afraid to sit slumped in a kitchen chair, naked, pale, her uncombed hair in her eyes, drinking coffee with him as he prepared to leave. Not afraid of him—not afraid of anyone. That had been her power.

His imagination dwelt upon her. The close, stale, half-pleasant odor of her apartment, the messy bed, the lipstick-and mascara-smeared pillows, the ghostly presence of other men, strangers to him, and yet brothers of a kind: brothers. He wondered if any of them knew about *him.* (And what would she say?—what might her words be, describing him?) It excited him to imagine her haphazard, promiscuous life; he knew she was entirely without guilt or shame or self-consciousness, as if, born of a different generation, she were of a different species as well.

At the same time, however, he was slightly jealous. When he thought at length about the situation he was slightly jealous. Perhaps, if he returned to her, he would ask her not to see any of the others.

What have you been doing? What is your life, now?

Why do you want to know?

I miss you—missed you.

Did you really?

In early March he saw her again, but only for lunch. She insisted he return to the gallery to see their current show—ugly, frantic, oversized hunks of sheet metal and aluminum, seemingly thrown at will onto the floor. She was strident, talkative from the several glasses of wine she had had at lunch, a lovely girl, really, whose nearness seemed to constrict his chest, so that he breathed with difficulty. And so tall—five feet ten, at least. With her long red hair and her dark, intense eyes and her habit of raising her chin, as if in a gesture of hostility, she was wonderfully attractive; and she knew it. But she would not allow him to touch her.

I think this is just something you're doing, she said. I mean—something you're watching yourself do.

When can I see you?

I don't know. I don't want to.

What?

I'm afraid.

They talked for a while, pointlessly. He felt his face redden. She was backing away, with that pose of self-confidence, and he could not stop her. But I love you! I love you! Had he said these words aloud? She looked so frightened, he could not be certain.

Afraid! he laughed. Don't be ridiculous.

One day in early summer he came to her, in a new summer suit of pale blue, a lover, his spirit young and gay and light as dandelion seed. She was waiting for him in a downtown square. She rose from the park bench as he appeared, the sun gleaming in her hair, her legs long and elegant in a pair of cream-colored trousers. They smiled. They touched hands. Was it reckless, to meet the girl here, where people might see him?—at midday? He found that he did not care.

We can't go to my apartment.

We can go somewhere else.

He led her to his car. They were both smiling.

Where are we going? she asked.

For the past several weeks a girl cousin of hers had been staying with her in the apartment, so they had been going to motels; the motels around the airport were the most convenient. But today he drove to the expressway and out of the city, out along the lake, through the suburban villages north of the city: Elmwood Farms, Spring Arbor, Wausau Heights, Lathrup Park. He exited at Lathrup Park.

Where are we going? she asked.

He watched her face as he drove along Washburn Lane, which was graveled and tranquil and hilly. Is this—? Do you live—? she asked. He brought her to the big red-brick colonial he had bought nearly fifteen years ago; it seemed to him that the house had never looked more handsome, and the surrounding trees and blossoming shrubs had never looked more beautiful.

Do you like it? he asked.

He watched her face. He was very excited.

But—Where is—Aren't you afraid—?

There's no one home, he said.

He led her through the foyer, into the living room with its thick wine-colored rug, its gleaming furniture, its many windows. He led her through the formal dining room and into the walnut-paneled recreation room where his wife had hung lithographs and had arranged innumerable plants, some of them hanging from the ceiling in clay pots, spidery-leafed, lovely. He saw the girl's eyes dart from place to place.

You live here, she said softly.

In an alcove he kissed her and made them each a drink. He kissed her again. She shook her hair from her eyes and pressed her forehead against his face and made a small convulsive movement—a shudder, or perhaps it was suppressed laughter. He could not tell.

You live here, she said.

What do you mean by that? he asked.

She shrugged her shoulders and moved away. Outside, birds were calling to one another excitedly. It was early summer. It was summer again. The world renewed itself and was beautiful. Annie wore the cream-colored trousers and a red jersey blouse that fitted her tightly and a number of bracelets that jingled as she walked. Her ears were pierced: she wore tiny loop earrings. On her feet, however, were shoes that pleased him less—scruffy sandals, once black, now faded to no color at all.

Give me a little more of this, she said, holding out the glass.

My beauty, he said. My beautiful girl.

She asked him why he had brought her here and he said he didn't know. Why had he taken the risk?—why was he taking it at this moment, still? He said he didn't know, really; he didn't usually analyze his own motives.

Maybe because it's here in this room, in this bed, that I think about you so much, he said.

She was silent for a while. Then she kicked about, and laughed, and chattered. He was sleepy, pleasantly sleepy. He did not mind her chatter, her high spirits. While she spoke of one thing or another—of childhood memories, of nicknames—Raggedy Ann they had called her, and it fitted her, he thought, bright red hair like straw and a certain ungainly but charming manner—what had been the boy's name, the companion to Raggedy Ann?—Andy?—he watched through half-closed eyes the play of shadows on the ceiling, imagining that he could smell the pines, the sunshine, the rich thick grass, remembering himself at the windows of this room not long ago, staring out into the night, moved almost to tears by an emotion he could not have named. You're beautiful, he told Annie, there's no one like you. No one. He heard his mother's voice: Arthritis, you don't know what it's like—you don't *know!* A woman approached him, both hands held out, palms up, appealing to him, the expanse of bare pale flesh troubling to him because he did not know what it meant. You don't know, don't *know.* He tried to protest but no words came to him. Don't know, don't know. Don't *know.* His snoring disturbed him. For an instant he woke, then sank again into a warm grayish ether. His wife was weeping. The sound of her weeping was angry. You brought that creature here—that filthy sick thing—you brought her to our bed to soil it, to soil me—to kill me—Again he wanted to protest. He raised his hands in a gesture of innocence and helplessness. But instead of speaking he began to laugh. His torso and belly shook with laughter. The bed shook. It was mixed suddenly with a gigantic fly that hovered over the bed, a few inches from his face; then his snoring woke him again and he sat up.

Annie?

Her things were still lying on the floor. The red blouse lay draped across a chintz-covered easy chair whose bright red and orange flowers, glazed, dramatic, seemed to be throbbing with energy. Annie? Are you in the bathroom?

The bathroom door was ajar, the light was not on. He got up. He saw that it was after two. A mild sensation of panic rose in his chest, for no reason. He was safe. They were safe here. No one would be home for hours—the first person to come home, at about three-thirty, would be Sally. His wife had driven with several other women to a bridge luncheon halfway across the state and would not be home, probably, until after six. The house was silent. It was empty.

He thought: What if she steals something?

But that was ridiculous and cruel. Annie would never do anything like that.

No one was in this bathroom, which was his wife's. He went to a closet and got a robe and put it on, and went out into the the hallway, calling Annie?—Honey?—and knew, before he turned the knob to his own bathroom, that she was in there and that she would not respond. Annie? What's wrong?

The light switch to the bathroom operated a fan; the fan was on; he pressed his ear against the door and listened. Had she taken a shower? He didn't think so. Had not heard any noises. Annie, he said, rattling the knob, are you in there, is anything wrong? He waited. He heard the fan whirring. Annie? His voice was edged with impatience. Annie, will you unlock the door? Is anything wrong?

She said something—the words were sharp and unintelligible.

Annie? What? What did you say?

He rattled the knob again, angrily.

What did you say? I couldn't—

Again her high, sharp voice. It sounded like an animal's shriek. But the words were unintelligible.

Annie? Honey? Is something wrong?

He tried to fight his panic. He knew, he knew. Must get the bitch out of there. Out of the house. He knew. But if he smashed the paneling on the door?—how could he explain it? He began to plead with her, in the voice he used on Sally, asking her to please be good, be good, don't make trouble, don't make a fuss, why did she want to ruin everything? Why did she want to worry him?

He heard the lock being turned, suddenly.

He opened the door.

She must have taken the razor blade out of his razor, which she had found in the medicine cabinet. Must have leaned over the sink and made one quick, deft, hard slash with it—cutting the fingers of her right hand also. The razor blade slipped from her then and fell into the sink. There was blood on the powder-blue porcelain of the sink and the toilet, and on the fluffy black rug, and on the mirror, and on the blue-and-white tiled walls. When he opened the door and saw her, she screamed, made a move as if to strike him with her bleeding arm, and for an instant he could not think: could not think: what had happened, what was happening, what had this girl done to him? Her face was wet and distorted. Ugly. She was sobbing, whimpering. There was blood, bright blood, smeared on her breasts and belly and thighs: he had never seen anything so repulsive in his life.

My God—

He was paralyzed. Yet, in the next instant, a part of him came to life. He grabbed a towel and wrapped it around her arm, struggling with her. Stop! Stand still! For God's sake! He held her; she went limp; her head fell forward. He wrapped the towel tight around her arm. Tight, tight. They were both panting.

Why did you do it? Why? Why? You're crazy! You're sick! This is a—this is a terrible, terrible—a terrible thing, a crazy thing—

Her teeth were chattering. She had begun to shiver convulsively.

Did you think you could get away with it? With this? he cried.

I hate you—

Stop, be still! I hate you—I don't want to live—

She pushed past him, she staggered into the bedroom. The towel came loose. He ran after her and grabbed her and held the towel against the wound again, wrapping it tight, so tight she flinched. His brain reeled. He saw blood, splotches of blood, starlike splashes on the carpet, on the yellow satin bedspread that had been pulled onto the floor. Stop. Don't fight. Annie, stop. Goddamn you, stop!

I don't want to live—

You're crazy, you're sick! Shut up!

The towel was soaked. He stooped to get something else—his shirt—he wrapped that around the outside of the towel, trembling so badly himself that he could hardly hold it in place. The girl's teeth were chattering. His own teeth were chattering.

Why did you do it! Oh, you bitch, you bitch!

After some time the bleeding was under control. He got another towel, from his wife's bathroom, and wrapped it around her arm again. It stained, but not so quickly. The bleeding was under control; she was not going to die.

He had forced her to sit down. He crouched over her, breathing hard, holding her in place. What if she sprang up, what if she ran away?—through the house? He held her still. She was spiritless, weak. Her eyes were closed. In a softer voice he said, as if speaking to a child: Poor Annie, poor sweet girl, why did you do it, why, why did you want to hurt yourself, why did you do something so ugly . . . ? It was an ugly, ugly thing to do. . . .

Her head slumped against his arm.

He walked her to the cab, holding her steady. She was white-faced, haggard, subdued. Beneath the sleeve of her blouse, wound tightly and expertly, were strips of gauze and adhesive tape. The bleeding had stopped. The wound was probably not too deep—had probably not severed an important vein.

Seeing her, the taxi driver got out and offered to help. But there was no need. John waved him away.

Slide in, he told Annie. Can you make it? Watch out for your head.

He told the driver her address in the city. He gave the man a fifty-dollar bill, folded.

Thanks, the man said gravely.

It was 2:55.

From the living room, behind one of the windows, he watched the cab descend the drive—watched it turn right on Washburn Lane—watched its careful progress along the narrow street. He was still trembling. He watched the blue-and-yellow cab wind its way along Washburn Lane until it was out of sight. Then there was nothing more to see: grass, trees, foliage, blossoms, his neighbors' homes.

Tilsons . . . Dwyers . . . Pitkers . . . Reddingers . . . Schells.

He must have spoken aloud; he heard his own slow dazed voice. But what he had said, what words those were, he did not know.

Raymond Carver

Raymond Carver (1938–1988) was born in Clatskanie, Oregon. His early years were, he often wrote, filled with struggle. Married at nineteen, Carver lived for years among the working poor, drifting from job to job. In 1958 he enrolled at a state college in California and took a writing class from John Gardner. Although he was inspired to try his hand at story writing, many years would pass before he found his subject and his voice. Carver, like so many other writers, fell prey to alcoholism; only decades later did he fight clear of his addiction.

Carver's hard living found its way into his fiction. His first collection of stories, *Will You Please Be Quiet, Please* was nominated for a National Book Award in 1976. Readers and critics recognized the power of his hard but compassionate narrative style and his extraordinary empathy for the working people about whom he wrote.

Carver discovered that he had lung cancer while still in his mid-forties. He died just as his greatness was being recognized by the larger reading public.

CHEF'S HOUSE

That summer Wes rented a furnished house north of Eureka from a recovered alcoholic named Chef. Then he called to ask me to forget what I had going and to move up there and live with him. He said he was on the wagon. I knew about that wagon. But he wouldn't take no for an answer. He called again and said, Edna, you can see the ocean from the front window. You can smell salt in the air. I listened to him talk. He didn't slur his words. I said, I'll think about it. And I did. A week later he called again and said, Are you coming? I said I was still thinking. He said, We'll start over. I said, If I come up there, I want you to do something for me. Name it, Wes said. I said, I want you to try and be the Wes I used to know. The old Wes. The Wes I married. Wes began to cry, but I took it as a sign of his good intentions. So I said, All right, I'll come up.

Wes had quit his girlfriend, or she'd quit him—I didn't know, didn't care. When I made up my mind to go with Wes, I had to say goodbye to my friend. My friend said, You're making a mistake. He said, Don't do this to me. What about us? he said. I said, I have to do it for Wes's sake. He's trying to stay sober. You remember what that's like. I remember, my friend said, but I don't want you to go. I said, I'll go for the summer. Then I'll see. I'll come back, I said. He said, What about me? What about *my* sake? Don't come back, he said.

We drank coffee, pop, and all kinds of fruit juice that summer. The whole summer, that's what we had to drink. I found myself wishing the summer wouldn't end. I knew better, but after a month of being with Wes in Chef's house, I put my wedding ring back on. I hadn't worn the ring in two years. Not since the night Wes was drunk and threw his ring into a peach orchard.

Wes had a little money, so I didn't have to work. And it turned out Chef was letting us have the house for almost nothing. We didn't have a telephone. We paid the gas and light and shopped for specials at the Safeway. One Sunday afternoon Wes went out to get a sprinkler and came back with something for me. He came back with a nice bunch of daisies and a straw hat. Tuesday evenings we'd go to a movie. Other nights Wes would go to what he called his Don't Drink meetings. Chef would pick him up in his car at the door and drive him home again afterward. Some days Wes and I would go fishing for trout in one of the freshwater lagoons nearby. We'd fish off the bank and take all day to catch a few little ones. They'll do fine, I'd say, and that night I'd fry them for supper.

Sometimes I'd take off my hat and fall asleep on a blanket next to my fishing pole. The last thing I'd remember would be clouds passing overhead toward the central valley. At night, Wes would take me in his arms and ask me if I was still his girl.

Our kids kept their distance. Cheryl lived with some people on a farm in Oregon. She looked after a herd of goats and sold the milk. She kept bees and put up jars of honey. She had her own life, and I didn't blame her. She didn't care one way or the other about what her dad and I did so long as we didn't get her into it. Bobby was in Washington working in the hay. After the haying season, he planned to work in the apples. He had a girl and was saving his money. I wrote letters and signed them, "Love always."

One afternoon Wes was in the yard pulling weeds when Chef drove up in front of the house. I was working at the sink. I looked and saw Chef's big car pull in. I could see his car, the access road and the freeway, and, behind the freeway, the dunes and the ocean. Clouds hung over the water. Chef got out of his car and hitched his pants. I knew there was something. Wes stopped what he was doing and stood up. He was wearing his gloves and a canvas hat. He took off the hat and wiped his face with the back of his hand. Chef walked over and put his arm around Wes's shoulders. Wes took off one of his gloves. I went to the door. I heard Chef say to Wes God knows he was sorry but he was going to have to ask us to leave at the end of the month. Wes pulled off his other glove. Why's that, Chef? Chef said his daughter, Linda, the woman Wes used to call Fat Linda from the time of his drinking days, needed a place to live and this place was it. Chef told Wes that Linda's husband had taken his fishing boat out a few weeks back and nobody had heard from him since. She's my own blood, Chef said to Wes. She's lost her husband. She's lost her baby's father. I can help. I'm glad I'm in a position to help, Chef said. I'm sorry, Wes, but you'll have to look for another house. Then Chef hugged Wes again, hitched his pants, and got in his big car and drove away.

Wes came inside the house. He dropped his hat and gloves on the carpet and sat down in the big chair. Chef's chair, it occurred to me. Chef's carpet, even. Wes looked pale. I poured two cups of coffee and gave one to him.

It's all right, I said. Wes, don't worry about it, I said. I sat down on Chef's sofa with my coffee.

Fat Linda's going to live here now instead of us, Wes said. He held his cup, but he didn't drink from it.

Wes, don't get stirred up, I said.

Her man will turn up in Ketchikan, Wes said. Fat Linda's husband has simply pulled out on them. And who could blame him? Wes said. Wes said if it came to that, he'd go down with his ship, too, rather than live the rest of his days with Fat Linda and her kid. Then Wes put his cup down next to his gloves. This has been a happy house up to now, he said.

We'll get another house, I said.

Not like this one, Wes said. It wouldn't be the same, anyway. This house has been a good house for us. This house has good memories to it. Now Fat Linda and her kid will be in here, Wes said. He picked up his cup and tasted from it.

It's Chef's house, I said. He has to do what he has to do.

I know that, Wes said. But I don't have to like it.

Wes had this look about him. I knew that look. He kept touching his lips with his tongue. He kept thumbing his shirt under his waistband. He got up from the chair and went to the window. He stood looking out at the ocean and at the clouds, which were building up. He patted his chin with his fingers like he was thinking about something. And he *was* thinking.

Go easy, Wes, I said.

She wants me to go easy, Wes said. He kept standing there.

But in a minute he came over and sat next to me on the sofa. He crossed one leg over the other and began fooling with the buttons on his shirt. I took his hand. I started to talk. I talked about the summer. But I caught myself talking like it was something that had happened in the past. Maybe years back. At any rate, like something that was over. Then I started talking about the kids. Wes said he wished he could do it over again and do it right this time.

They love you, I said.

No, they don't, he said.

I said, Someday, they'll understand things.

Maybe, Wes said. But it won't matter then.

You don't know, I said.

I know a few things, Wes said, and looked at me. I know I'm glad you came up here. I won't forget you did it, Wes said.

I'm glad, too, I said. I'm glad you found this house, I said.

Wes snorted. Then he laughed. We both laughed. That Chef, Wes said, and shook his head. He threw us a knuckle-ball, that son of a bitch. But I'm glad you wore your ring. I'm glad we had us this time together, Wes said.

Then I said something. I said, Suppose, just suppose, nothing had ever happened. Suppose this was for the first time. Just suppose. It doesn't hurt to suppose. Say none of the other had ever happened. You know what I mean? Then what? I said.

Wes fixed his eyes on me. He said, Then I suppose we'd have to be somebody else if that was the case. Somebody we're not. I don't have that kind of supposing left in me. We were born who we are. Don't you see what I'm saying?

I said I hadn't thrown away a good thing and come six hundred miles to hear him talk like this.

He said, I'm sorry, but I can't talk like somebody I'm not. I'm not somebody else. If I was somebody else, I sure as hell wouldn't be here. If I was somebody else, I wouldn't be me. But I'm who I am. Don't you see?

Wes, it's all right, I said. I brought his hand to my cheek. Then, I don't know, I remembered how he was when he was nineteen, the way he looked running across this field to where his dad sat on a tractor, hand over his eyes, watching Wes run toward him. We'd just driven up from California. I got out with Cheryl and Bobby and said, There's Grandpa. But they were just babies.

Wes sat next to me patting his chin, like he was trying to figure out the next thing. Wes's dad was gone and our kids were grown up. I looked at Wes and then I looked around Chef's living room at Chef's things, and I thought, We have to do something now and do it quick.

Hon, I said. Wes, listen to me.

What do you want? he said. But that's all he said. He seemed to have made up his mind. But, having made up his mind, he was in no hurry. He leaned back on the sofa, folded his hands in his lap, and closed his eyes. He didn't say anything else. He didn't have to.

I said his name to myself. It was an easy name to say, and I'd been used to saying it for a long time. Then I said it once more. This time I said it out loud. Wes, I said.

He opened his eyes. But he didn't look at me. He just sat where he was and looked toward the window. Fat Linda, he said. But I knew it wasn't her. She was nothing. Just a name. Wes got up and pulled the drapes and the ocean was gone just like that. I went in to start supper. We still had some fish in the icebox. There wasn't much else. We'll clean it up tonight, I thought, and that will be the end of it.

INTIMACY

I have some business out west anyway, so I stop off in this little town where my former wife lives. We haven't seen each other in four years. But from time to time, when something of mine appeared, or was written about me in the magazines or papers—a profile or an interview—I sent her these things. I don't know what I had in mind except I thought she might be interested. In any case, she never responded.

It is nine in the morning, I haven't called, and it's true I don't know what I am going to find.

But she lets me in. She doesn't seem surprised. We don't shake hands, much less kiss each other. She takes me into the living room. As soon as I sit down she brings me some coffee. Then she comes out with what's on her mind. She says I've caused her anguish, made her feel exposed and humiliated.

Make no mistake, I feel I'm home.

She says, But then you were into betrayal early. You always felt comfortable with betrayal. No, she says, that's not true. Not in the beginning, at any rate. You were different then. But I guess I was different too. Everything was different, she says. No, it was after you turned thirty-five, or thirty-six, whenever it was, around in there anyway, your mid-thirties somewhere, then you started in. You really started in. You turned on me. You did it up pretty then. You must be proud of yourself.

She says, Sometimes I could scream.

She says she wishes I'd forget about the hard times, the bad times, when I talk about back then. Spend some time on the good times, she says. Weren't there some good times? She wishes I'd get off that other subject. She's bored with it. Sick of hearing about it. Your private hobby horse, she says. What's done is done and water under the bridge, she says. A tragedy, yes. God knows it was a tragedy and then some. But why keep it going? Don't you ever get tired of dredging up that old business?

She says, Let go of the past, for Christ's sake. Those old hurts. You must have some other arrows in your quiver, she says.

She says, You know something? I think you're sick. I think you're crazy as a bedbug. Hey, you don't believe the things they're saying about you, do you? Don't believe them for a minute, she says. Listen, I could tell them a thing or two. Let them talk to me about it, if they want to hear a story.

She says, Are you listening to me?

I'm listening, I say. I'm all ears, I say.

She says, I've really had a bellyful of it, buster! Who asked you here today anyway? I sure as hell didn't. You just show up and walk in. What the hell do you want from me? Blood? You want more blood? I thought you had your fill by now.

She says, Think of me as dead. I want to be left in peace now. That's all I want anymore is to be left in peace and forgotten about. Hey, I'm forty-five years old, she says. Forty-five going on fifty-five, or sixty-five. Lay off, will you.

She says, Why don't you wipe the blackboard clean and see what you have left after that? Why don't you start with a clean slate? See how far that gets you, she says.

She has to laugh at this. I laugh too, but it's nerves.

She says, You know something? I had my chance once, but I let it go. I just let it go. I don't guess I ever told you. But now look at me. Look! Take a good look while you're at it. You threw me away, you son of a bitch.

She says, I was younger then and a better person. Maybe you were too, she says. A better person, I mean. You had to be. You were better then or I wouldn't have had anything to do with you.

She says, I loved you so much once. I loved you to the point of distraction. I did. More than anything in the whole wide world. Imagine that. What a laugh that is now. Can you imagine it? We were so *intimate* once upon a time I can't believe it now. I think that's the strangest thing of all now. The memory of being that intimate with somebody. We were so intimate I could puke. I can't imagine ever being that intimate with somebody else. I haven't been.

She says, Frankly, and I mean this, I want to be kept out of it from here on out. Who do you think you are anyway? You think you're God or somebody? You're not fit to lick God's boots, or anybody else's for that matter. Mister, you've been hanging out with the wrong people. But what do I know? I don't even know what I know any longer. I know I don't like what you've been dishing out. I know that much. You know what I'm talking about, don't you? Am I right?

Right, I say. Right as rain.

She says, You'll agree to anything, won't you? You give in too easy. You always did. You don't have any principles, not one. Anything to avoid a fuss. But that's neither here nor there.

She says, You remember that time I pulled the knife on you?

She says this as if in passing, as if it's not important.

Vaguely, I say. I must have deserved it, but I don't remember much about it. Go ahead, why don't you, and tell me about it.

She says, I'm beginning to understand something now. I think I know why you're here. Yes. I know why you're here, even if you don't. But you're a slyboots. You know why you're here. You're on a fishing expedition. You're hunting for *material*. Am I getting warm? Am I right?

Tell me about the knife, I say.

She says, If you want to know, I'm real sorry I didn't use that knife. I am. I really and truly am. I've thought and thought about it, and I'm sorry I didn't use it. I had the chance. But I hesitated. I hesitated and was lost, as somebody or other said. But I should have used it, the hell with everything and everybody. I should have nicked your arm with it at least. At least that.

Well, you didn't, I say. I thought you were going to cut me with it, but you didn't. I took it away from you.

She says, You were always lucky. You took it away and then you slapped me. Still, I regret I didn't use that knife just a little bit. Even a little would have been something to remember me by.

I remember a lot, I say. I say that, then wish I hadn't.

She says, Amen, brother. That's the bone of contention here, if you hadn't noticed. That's the whole problem. But like I said, in my opinion you remember the wrong things. You remember the low, shameful things. That's why you got interested when I brought up the knife.

She says, I wonder if you ever have any regret. For whatever that's worth on the market these days. Not much, I guess. But you ought to be a specialist in it by now.

Regret, I say. It doesn't interest me much, to tell the truth. Regret is not a word I use very often. I guess I mainly don't have it. I admit I hold to the dark view of things. Sometimes, anyway. But regret? I don't think so.

She says, You're a real son of a bitch, did you know that? A ruthless, coldhearted son of a bitch. Did anybody ever tell you that?

You did, I say. Plenty of times.

She says, I always speak the truth. Even when it hurts. You'll never catch me in a lie.

She says, My eyes were opened a long time ago, but by then it was too late. I had my chance but I let it slide through my fingers. I even thought for a while you'd come back. Why'd I think that anyway? I must have been out of my mind. I could cry my eyes out now, but I wouldn't give you that satisfaction.

She says, You know what? I think if you were on fire right now, if you suddenly burst into flame this minute, I wouldn't throw a bucket of water on you.

She laughs at this. Then her face closes down again.

She says, Why in hell *are* you here? You want to hear some more? I could go on for days. I think I know why you turned up, but I want to hear it from you.

When I don't answer, when I just keep sitting there, she goes on.

She says, After that time, when you went away, nothing much mattered after that. Not the kids, not God, not anything. It was like I didn't know what hit me. It was like I had *stopped living*. My life had been going along, going along, and then it just stopped. It didn't just come to a stop, it screeched to a stop. I thought, If I'm not worth anything to him, well, I'm not worth anything to myself or anybody else either. That was the worst thing I felt. I thought my heart would break. What am I saying? It did break. Of course it broke. It broke, just like that. It's still broke, if you want to know. And so there you have it in a nutshell. My eggs in one basket, she says. A tisket, a tasket. All my rotten eggs in one basket.

She says, You found somebody else for yourself, didn't you? It didn't take long. And you're happy now. That's what they say about you anyway: "He's happy now." Hey, I read everything you send! You think I don't? Listen, I know your heart, mister. I always did. I knew it back then, and I know it now. I know your heart inside and out, and don't you ever forget it. Your heart is a jungle, a dark forest, it's a garbage pail, if you want to know. Let them talk to me if they want to ask somebody something. I know how you operate. Just let them come around here, and I'll give them an earful. I was there. I served, buddy boy. Then you held me up for display and ridicule in your so-called work. For any Tom or Harry to pity or pass judgment on. Ask me if I cared. Ask me if it embarrassed me. Go ahead, ask.

No, I say, I won't ask that. I don't want to get into that, I say.

Damn straight you don't! she says. And you know *why,* too!

She says, Honey, no offense, but sometimes I think I could shoot you and watch you kick.

She says, You can't look me in the eyes, can you?

She says, and this is exactly what she says, You can't even look me in the eyes when I'm talking to you.

So, okay, I look her in the eyes.

She says, Right. Okay, she says. Now we're getting someplace, maybe. That's better. You can tell a lot about the person you're talking to from his eyes. Everybody knows that. But you know something else? There's nobody in this whole world who would tell you this, but I can tell you. I have the right. I *earned* that right, sonny. You have yourself confused with somebody else. And that's the pure truth of it. But what do I know? they'll say in a hundred years. They'll say, Who was she anyway?

She says, In any case, you sure as hell have *me* confused with somebody else. Hey, I don't even have the same name anymore! Not the name I was born with, not the name I lived with you with, not even the name I had two years ago. What is this? What is this in hell all about anyway? Let me say something. I want to be left alone now. Please. That's not a crime.

She says, Don't you have someplace else you should be? Some plane to catch? Shouldn't you be somewhere far from here at this very minute?

No, I say. I say it again: No. No place, I say. I don't have anyplace I have to be.

And then I do something. I reach over and take the sleeve of her blouse between my thumb and forefinger. That's all. I just touch it that way, and then I just bring my hand back. She doesn't draw away. She doesn't move.

Then here's the thing I do next. I get down on my knees, a big guy like me, and I take the hem of her dress. What am I doing on the floor? I wish I could say. But I know it's where I ought to be, and I'm there on my knees holding on to the hem of her dress.

She is still for a minute. But in a minute she says, Hey, it's all right, stupid. You're so dumb, sometimes. Get up now. I'm telling you to get up. Listen, it's okay. I'm over it now. It look me a while to get over it. What do you think? Did you think it wouldn't? Then you walk in here and suddenly the whole cruddy business is back. I felt a need to ventilate. But you know, and I know, it's over and done with now.

She says, For the longest while, honey, I was inconsolable. *Inconsolable,* she says. Put that word in your little notebook. I can tell you from experience that's the saddest word in the English language. Anyway, I got over it finally. Time is a gentleman, a wise man said. Or else maybe a worn-out old woman, one or the other anyway.

She says, I have a life now. It's a different kind of life than yours, but I guess we don't need to compare. It's my life, and that's the important thing I have to realize as I get older. Don't feel *too* bad, anyway, she says. I mean, it's all right to feel a *little* bad, maybe. That won't hurt you, that's only to be expected after all. Even if you can't move yourself to regret.

She says, Now you have to get up and get out of here. My husband will be along pretty soon for his lunch. How would I explain this kind of thing?

It's crazy, but I'm still on my knees holding the hem of her dress. I won't let it go. I'm like a terrier, and it's like I'm stuck to the floor. It's like I can't move.

She says, Get up now. What is it? You still want something from me. What do you want? Want me to forgive you? Is that why you're doing this? That's it, isn't it? That's the reason you came all this way. The knife thing kind of perked you up, too. I think you'd forgotten about that. But you needed me to remind you. Okay, I'll say something if you'll just go.

She says, I forgive you.

She says, Are you satisfied now? Is that better? Are you happy? He's happy now, she says.

But I'm still there, knees to the floor.

She says, Did you hear what I said? You have to go now. Hey, stupid. Honey, I said I forgive you. And I even reminded you about the knife thing. I can't think what else I can do now. You got it made in the shade, baby. Come *on* now, you have to get out of here. Get up. That's right. You're still a big guy, aren't you. Here's your hat, don't forget your hat.

You never used to wear a hat. I never in my life saw you in a hat before.

She says, Listen to me now. Look at me. Listen carefully to what I'm going to tell you.

She moves closer. She's about three inches from my face. We haven't been this close in a long time. I take these little breaths that she can't hear, and I wait. I think my heart slows way down, I think.

She says, You just tell it like you have to, I guess, and forget the rest. Like always. You been doing that for so long now anyway it shouldn't be hard for you.

She says, There, I've done it. You're free, aren't you? At least you think you are anyway. Free at last. That's a joke, but don't laugh. Anyway, you feel better, don't you?

She walks with me down the hall.

She says, I can't imagine how I'd explain this if my husband was to walk in this very minute. But who really cares anymore, right? In the final analysis, nobody gives a damn anymore. Besides which, I think everything that can happen that way has already happened. His name is Fred, by the way. He's a decent guy and works hard for his living. He cares for me.

So she walks me to the front door, which has been standing open all this while. The door that was letting in light and fresh air this morning, and sounds off the street, all of which we had ignored. I looked outside and, Jesus, there's this white moon hanging in the morning sky. I can't think when I've ever seen anything so remarkable. But I'm afraid to comment on it. I am. I don't know what might happen. I might break into tears even. I might not understand a word I'd say.

She says, Maybe you'll be back sometime, and maybe you won't. This'll wear off, you know. Pretty soon you'll start feeling bad again. Maybe it'll make a good story, she says. But I don't want to know about it if it does.

I say good-bye. She doesn't say anything more. She looks at her hands, and then she puts them into the pockets of her dress. She shakes her head. She goes back inside, and this time she closes the door.

I move off down the sidewalk. Some kids are tossing a football at the end of the street. But they aren't my kids, and they aren't her kids either. There are these leaves everywhere, even in the gutters. Piles of leaves wherever I look. They're falling off the limbs as I walk. I can't take a step without putting my shoe into leaves. Somebody ought to make an effort here. Somebody ought to get a rake and take care of this.

CAREFUL

After a lot of talking—what his wife, Inez, called *assessment*—Lloyd moved out of the house and into his own place. He had two rooms and a bath on the top floor of a three-story house. Inside the rooms, the roof slanted down sharply. If he walked around, he had to duck his head. He had to stoop to look from his windows and be careful getting in and out of bed. There were two keys. One key let him into the house itself. Then he climbed some stairs that passed through the house to a landing. He went up another flight of stairs to the door of his room and used the other key on that lock.

Once, when he was coming back to his place in the afternoon, carrying a sack with three bottles of André champagne and some lunch meat, he stopped on the landing and looked into his landlady's living room. He saw the old woman lying on her back on the carpet. She seemed to be asleep. Then it occurred to him she might be dead. But the TV was going, so he chose to think she was asleep. He didn't know what to make of it. He moved the sack from one arm to the other. It was then that the woman gave a little cough, brought her hand to her side, and went back to being quiet and still again. Lloyd continued on up the stairs and unlocked his door. Later that day, toward evening, as he looked from his kitchen window, he saw the old woman down in the yard, wearing a straw hat and holding her hand against her side. She was using a little watering can on some pansies.

In his kitchen, he had a combination refrigerator and stove. The refrigerator and stove was a tiny affair wedged into a space between the sink and the wall. He had to bend over, almost get down on his knees, to get anything out of the refrigerator. But it was all right because he didn't keep much in there, anyway—except fruit juice, lunch meat, and champagne. The stove had two burners. Now and then he heated water in a saucepan and made instant coffee. But some days he didn't drink any coffee. He forgot, or else he just didn't feel like coffee. One morning he woke up and promptly fell to eating crumb doughnuts and drinking champagne. There'd been a time, some years back, when he would have laughed at having a breakfast like this. Now, there didn't seem to be anything very unusual about it. In fact, he hadn't thought anything about it until he was in bed and trying to recall the things he'd done that day, starting with when he'd gotten up that morning. At first, he couldn't remember anything noteworthy. Then he remembered eating those doughnuts and drinking champagne. Time was when he would have considered this a mildly crazy thing to do, something to tell friends about. Then, the more he thought about it, the more he could see it didn't matter much one way or the other. He'd had doughnuts and champagne for breakfast. So what?

In his furnished rooms, he also had a dinette set, a little sofa, an old easy chair, and a TV set that stood on a coffee table. He wasn't paying the electricity here, it wasn't even his TV, so sometimes he left the set on all day and all night. But he kept the volume down unless he saw there was something he wanted to watch. He did not have a telephone, which was fine with him. He didn't want a telephone. There was a bedroom with a double bed, a nightstand, a chest of drawers, a bathroom.

The one time Inez came to visit, it was eleven o'clock in the morning. He'd been in his new place for two weeks, and he'd been wondering if she were going to drop by. But he was trying to do something about his drinking, too, so he was glad to be alone. He'd made that much clear—being alone was the thing he needed most. The day she came, he was on the sofa, in his pajamas, hitting his fist against the right side of his head. Just before he could hit himself again, he heard voices downstairs on the landing. He could make out his wife's voice. The sound was like the murmur of voices from a faraway crowd, but he knew it was Inez and somehow knew the visit was an important one. He gave his head another jolt with his fist, then got to his feet.

He'd awakened that morning and found that his ear had stopped up with wax. He couldn't hear anything clearly, and he seemed to have lost his sense of balance, his equilibrium, in the process. For the last hour, he'd been on the sofa, working frustratedly on his ear, now and again slamming his head with his fist. Once in a while he'd massage the gristly underpart of his ear, or else tug at his lobe. Then he'd dig furiously in his ear with his little finger and open his mouth, simulating yawns. But he'd tried everything he could think of, and he was nearing the end of his rope. He could hear the voices below break off their murmuring. He pounded his head a good one and finished the glass of champagne. He turned off the TV and carried the glass to the sink. He picked up the open bottle of champagne from the drainboard and took it into the bathroom, where he put it behind the stool. Then he went to answer the door.

"Hi, Lloyd," Inez said. She didn't smile. She stood in the doorway in a bright spring outfit. He hadn't seen these clothes before. She was holding a canvas handbag that had sunflowers stitched onto its sides. He hadn't seen the handbag before, either.

"I didn't think you heard me," she said. "I thought you might be gone or something. But the woman downstairs—what's her name? Mrs. Matthews—she thought you were up here."

"I heard you," Lloyd said. "But just barely." He hitched his pajamas and ran a hand through his hair. "Actually, I'm in one hell of a shape. Come on in."

"It's eleven o'clock," she said. She came inside and shut the door behind her. She acted as if she hadn't heard him. Maybe she hadn't.

"I know what time it is," he said. "I've been up for a long time. I've been up since eight. I watched part of the *Today* show. But just now I'm about to go crazy with something. My ear's plugged up. You remember that other time it happened? We were living in that place near the Chinese takeout joint. Where the kids found that bulldog dragging its chain? I had to go to the doctor then and have my ears flushed out. I know you remember. You drove me and we had to wait a long time. Well, it's like that now. I mean it's that bad. Only I can't go to a doctor this morning. I don't have a doctor for one thing. I'm about to go nuts, Inez. I feel like I want to cut my head off or something."

He sat down at one end of the sofa, and she sat down at the other end. But it was a small sofa, and they were still sitting close to each other. They were so close he could have put out his hand and touched her knee. But he didn't. She glanced around the room and then fixed her eyes on him again. He knew he hadn't shaved and that his hair stood up. But she was his wife, and she knew everything there was to know about him.

"What have you tried?" she said. She looked in her purse and brought up a cigarette. "I mean, what have you done for it so far?"

"What'd you say?" He turned the left side of his head to her. "Inez, I swear, I'm not exaggerating. This thing is driving me crazy. When I talk, I feel like I'm talking inside a barrel. My head rumbles. And I can't hear good, either. When *you* talk, it sounds like you're talking through a lead pipe."

"Do you have any Q-tips, or else Wesson oil?" Inez said.

"Honey, this is serious," he said. "I don't have any Q-tips or Wesson oil. Are you kidding?"

"If we had some Wesson oil, I could heat it and put some of that in your ear. My mother used to do that," she said. "It might soften things up in there."

He shook his head. His head felt full and like it was awash with fluid. It felt like it had when he used to swim near the bottom of the municipal pool and come up with his ears filled with water. But back then it'd been easy to clear the water out. All he had to do was fill his lungs with air, close his mouth, and clamp down on his nose. Then he'd blow out his cheeks and force air into his head. His ears would pop, and for a few seconds he'd have the pleasant sensation of water running out of his head and dripping onto his shoulders. Then he'd heave himself out of the pool.

Inez finished her cigarette and put it out. "Lloyd, we have things to talk about. But I guess we'll have to take things one at a time. Go sit in the chair. Not *that* chair, the chair in the kitchen! So we can have some light on the situation."

He whacked his head once more. Then he went over to sit on a dinette chair. She moved over and stood behind him. She touched his hair with her fingers. Then she moved the hair away from his ears. He reached for her hand, but she drew it away.

"Which ear did you say it was?" she said.

"The right ear," he said. "The right one."

"First," she said, "you have to sit here and not move. I'll find a hairpin and some tissue paper. I'll try to get in there with that. Maybe it'll do the trick."

He was alarmed at the prospect of her putting a hairpin inside his ear. He said something to that effect.

"What?" she said. "Christ, I can't hear you, either. Maybe this is catching."

"When I was a kid, in school," Lloyd said, "we had this health teacher. She was like a nurse, too. She said we should never put anything smaller than an elbow into our ear." He vaguely remembered a wall chart showing a massive diagram of the ear, along with an intricate system of canals, passageways, and walls.

"Well, your nurse was never faced with this exact problem," Inez said. "Anyway, we need to try *something*. We'll try this first. If it doesn't work, we'll try something else. That's life, isn't it?"

"Does that have a hidden meaning or something?" Lloyd said.

"It means just what I said. But you're free to think as you please. I mean, it's a free country," she said. "Now, let me get fixed up with what I need. You just sit there."

She went through her purse, but she didn't find what she was looking for. Finally, she emptied the purse out onto the sofa. "No hairpins," she said. "Damn." But it was as if she were saying the words from another room. In a way, it was almost as if he'd imagined her saying them. There'd been a time, long ago, when they used to feel they had ESP when it came to what the other one was thinking. They could finish sentences that the other had started.

She picked up some nail clippers, worked for a minute, and then he saw the device separate in her fingers and part of it swing away from the other part. A nail file protruded from the clippers. It looked to him as if she were holding a small dagger.

"You're going to put that in my ear?" he said.

"Maybe you have a better idea," she said. "It's this, or else I don't know what. Maybe you have a pencil? You want me to use that? Or maybe you have a screwdriver around," she said and laughed. "Don't worry. Listen, Lloyd, I won't hurt you. I said I'd be careful. I'll wrap some tissue around the end of this. It'll be all right. I'll be careful, like I said. You just stay where you are, and I'll get some tissue for this. I'll make a swab."

She went into the bathroom. She was gone for a time. He stayed where he was on the dinette chair. He began thinking of things he ought to say to her. He wanted to tell her he was limiting himself to champagne and champagne only. He wanted to tell her he was tapering off the champagne, too. It was only a matter of time now. But when she came back into the room, he couldn't say anything. He didn't know where to start. But she didn't look at him, anyway. She fished a cigarette from the heap of things she'd emptied onto the sofa cushion. She lit the cigarette with her lighter and went to stand by the window that faced onto the street. She said something, but he couldn't make out the words. When she stopped talking, he didn't ask her what it was she'd said. Whatever it was, he knew he didn't want her to say it again. She put out the cigarette. But she went on standing at the window, leaning forward, the slope of the roof just inches from her head.

"Inez," he said.

She turned and came over to him. He could see tissue on the point of the nail file.

"Turn your head to the side and keep it that way," she said. "That's right. Sit still now and don't move. Don't move," she said again.

"Be careful," he said. "For Christ's sake."

She didn't answer him.

"Please, please," he said. Then he didn't say any more. He was afraid. He closed his eyes and held his breath as he felt the nail file turn past the inner part of his ear and begin its probe. He was sure his heart would stop beating. Then she went a little farther and began turning the blade back and forth, working at whatever it was in there. Inside his ear, he heard a squeaking sound.

"Ouch!" he said.

"Did I hurt you?" She took the nail file out of his ear and moved back a step. "Does anything feel different, Lloyd?"

He brought his hands up to his ears and lowered his head.

"It's just the same," he said.

She looked at him and bit her lips.

"Let me go to the bathroom," he said. "Before we go any farther, I have to go to the bathroom."

"Go ahead," Inez said. "I think I'll go downstairs and see if your landlady has any Wesson oil, or anything like that. She might even have some Q-tips. I don't know why I didn't think of that before. Of asking her."

"That's a good idea," he said. "I'll go to the bathroom."

She stopped at the door and looked at him, and then she opened the door and went out. He crossed the living room, went into his bedroom, and opened the bathroom door. He reached down behind the stool and brought up the bottle of champagne. He took a long drink. It was warm but it went right down. He took some more. In the beginning, he'd really thought he could continue drinking if he limited himself to champagne. But in no time he found he was drinking three or four bottles a day. He knew he'd have to deal with this pretty soon. But first, he'd have to get his hearing back. One thing at a time, just like she'd said. He finished off the rest of the champagne and put the empty bottle in its place behind the stool. Then he ran water and brushed his teeth. After he'd used the towel, he went back into the other room.

Inez had returned and was at the stove heating something in a little pan. She glanced in his direction, but didn't say anything at first. He looked past her shoulder and out the window. A bird flew from one tree to another and preened its feathers. But if it made any kind of bird noise, he didn't hear it.

She said something that he didn't catch.

"Say again," he said.

She shook her head and turned back to the stove. But then she turned again and said, loud enough and slow enough so he could hear it: "I found your stash in the bathroom."

"I'm trying to cut back," he said.

She said something else. "What?" he said. "What'd you say?" He really hadn't heard her.

"We'll talk later," she said. "We have things to discuss, Lloyd. Money is one thing. But there are other things, too. First we have to see about this ear." She put her finger into the pan and then took the pan off the stove. "I'll let it cool for a minute," she said. "It's too hot right now. Sit down. Put this towel around your shoulders."

He did as he was told. He sat on a chair and put the towel around his neck and shoulders. Then he hit the side of his head with his fist.

"Goddamn it," he said.

She didn't look up. She put her finger into the pan once more, testing. Then she poured the liquid from the pan into his plastic glass. She picked up the glass and came over to him.

"Don't be scared," she said. "It's just some of your landlady's baby oil, that's all it is. I told her what was wrong, and she thought this might help. No guarantees," Inez said. "But maybe this'll loosen things up in there. She said it used to happen to her husband. She said this one time she saw a piece of wax fall out of his ear, and it was like a big plug of something. It was ear wax, was what it was. She said try this. And she didn't have any Q-tips. I can't understand that, her not having any Q-tips. That part really surprises me."

"Okay," he said. "All right. I'm willing to try anything. Inez, if I had to go on like this, I think I'd rather be dead. You know? I mean it, Inez."

"Tilt your head all the way to the side now," she said. "Don't move. I'll pour this in until your ear fills up, then I'll stopper it with this dishrag. And you just sit there for ten minutes, say. Then we'll see. If this doesn't do it, well, I don't have any other suggestions. I just don't know what to do then."

"This'll work," he said. "If this doesn't work, I'll find a gun and shoot myself. I'm serious. That's what I feel like doing, anyway."

He turned his head to the side and let it hang down. He looked at the things in the room from this new perspective. But it wasn't any different from the old way of looking, except that everything was on its side.

"Farther," she said. He held on to the chair for balance and lowered his head even more. All of the objects in his vision, all of the objects in his life, it seemed, were at the far end of this room. He could feel the warm liquid pour into his ear. Then she brought the dishrag up and held it there. In a little while, she began to massage the area around his ear. She pressed into the soft part of the flesh between his jaw and skull. She moved her fingers to the area over his ear and began to work the tips of her fingers back and forth. After a while, he didn't know how long he'd been sitting there. It could have been ten minutes. It could have been longer. He was still holding on to the chair. Now and then, as her fingers pressed the side of his head, he could feel the warm oil she'd poured in there wash back and forth in the canals inside his ear. When she pressed a certain way, he imagined he could hear, inside his head, a soft, swishing sound.

"Sit up straight," Inez said. He sat up and pressed the heel of his hand against his head while the liquid poured out of his ear. She caught it in the towel. Then she wiped the outside of his ear.

Inez was breathing through her nose. Lloyd heard the sound her breath made as it came and went. He heard a car pass on the street outside the house and, at the back of the house, down below his kitchen window, the clear *snick-snick* of pruning shears.

"Well?" Inez said. She waited with her hands on her hips, frowning.

"I can hear you," he said. "I'm all right! I mean, I can *hear*. It doesn't sound like you're talking underwater anymore. It's fine now. It's okay. God, I thought for a while I was going to go crazy. But I feel fine now. I can hear everything. Listen, honey, I'll make coffee. There's some juice, too."

"I have to go," she said. "I'm late for something. But I'll come back. We'll go out for lunch sometime. We need to talk."

"I just can't sleep on this side of my head, is all," he went on. He followed her into the living room. She lit a cigarette. "That's what happened. I slept all night on this side of my head, and my ear plugged up. I think I'll be all right as long as I don't forget and sleep on this side of my head. If I'm careful. You know what I'm saying? If I can just sleep on my back, or else on my left side."

She didn't look at him.

"Not forever, of course not, I know that. I couldn't do that. I couldn't do it the rest of my life. But for a while, anyway. Just my left side, or else flat on my back."

But even as he said this, he began to feel afraid of the night that was coming. He began to fear the moment he would begin to make his preparations for bed and what might happen afterward. That time was hours away, but already he was afraid. What if, in the middle of the night, he accidentally turned onto his right side, and the weight of his head pressing into the pillow were to seal the wax again into the dark canals of his ear? What if he woke up then, unable to hear, the ceiling inches from his head?

"Good God," he said. "Jesus, this is awful. Inez, I just had something like a terrible nightmare. Inez, where do you have to go?"

"I told you," she said, as she put everything back into her purse and made ready to leave. She looked at her watch. "I'm late for something." She went to the door. But at the door she turned and said something else to him. He didn't listen. He didn't want to. He watched her lips move until she'd said what she had to say. When she'd finished, she said, "Goodbye." Then she opened the door and closed it behind her.

He went into the bedroom to dress. But in a minute he hurried out, wearing only his trousers, and went to the door. He opened it and stood there, listening. On the landing below, he heard Inez thank Mrs. Matthews for the oil. He heard the old woman say, "You're welcome." And then he heard her draw a connection between her late husband and himself. He heard her say, "Leave me your number. I'll call if something happens. You never know."

"I hope you don't have to," Inez said. "But I'll give it to you, anyway. Do you have something to write it down with?"

Lloyd heard Mrs. Matthews open a drawer and rummage through it. Then her old woman's voice said, "Okay."

Inez gave her their telephone number at home. "Thanks," she said.

"It was nice meeting you," Mrs. Matthews said.

He listened as Inez went on down the stairs and opened the front door. Then he heard it close. He waited until he heard her start their car and drive away. Then he shut the door and went back into the bedroom to finish dressing.

After he'd put on his shoes and tied the laces, he lay down on the bed and pulled the covers up to his chin. He let his arms rest under the covers at his sides. He closed his eyes and pretended it was night and pretended he was going to fall asleep. Then he brought his arms up and crossed them over his chest to see how this position would suit him. He kept his eyes closed, trying it out. All right, he thought. Okay. If he didn't want that ear to plug up again, he'd have to sleep on his back, that was all. He knew he could do it. He just couldn't forget, even in his sleep, and turn onto the wrong side. Four or five hours' sleep a night was all he needed, anyway. He'd manage. Worse things could happen to a man. In a way, it was a challenge. But he was up to it. He knew he was. In a minute, he threw back the covers and got up.

He still had the better part of the day ahead of him. He went into the kitchen, bent down in front of the little refrigerator, and took out a fresh bottle of champagne. He worked the plastic cork out of the bottle as carefully as he could, but there was still the festive *pop* of champagne being opened. He rinsed the baby oil out of his glass, then poured it full of champagne. He took the glass over to the sofa and sat down. He put the glass on the coffee table. Up went his feet onto the coffee table, next to the champagne. He leaned back. But after a time he began to worry some more about the night that was coming on. What if, despite all his efforts, the wax decided to plug his other ear? He closed his eyes and shook his head. Pretty soon he got up and went into the bedroom. He undressed and put his pajamas back on. Then he moved back into the living room. He sat down on the sofa once more, and once more put his feet up. He reached over and turned the TV on. He adjusted the volume. He knew he couldn't keep from worrying about what might happen when he went to bed. It was just something he'd have to learn to live with. In a way, this whole business reminded him of the thing with the doughnuts and champagne. It was not that remarkable at all, if you thought about it. He took some champagne. But it didn't taste right. He ran his tongue over his lips, then wiped his mouth on his sleeve. He looked and saw a film of oil on the champagne.

He got up and carried the glass to the sink, where he poured it into the drain. He took the bottle of champagne into the living room and made himself comfortable on the sofa. He held the bottle by its neck as he drank. He wasn't in the habit of drinking from the bottle, but it didn't seem that much out of the ordinary. He decided that even if he were to fall asleep sitting up on the sofa in the middle of the afternoon, it wouldn't be any more strange than somebody having to lie on his back for hours at a time. He lowered his head to peer out the window. Judging from the angle of sunlight, and the shadows that had entered the room, he guessed it was about three o'clock.

Toni Cade Bambara

Toni Cade Bambara (b.1939) was born in New York City and grew up in Harlem. She discovered her passion for writing at an early age and began to publish her stories while in her early twenties. She was greatly influenced by a trip to Cuba in 1973. Writing, she discovered, was a vital form of political participation. Bambara has been active ever since on behalf of black causes. Her stories were collected in *Gorilla, My Love* in 1972. Her 1980 novel *The Salt Eaters* was given the American Book Award.

Bambara writes an expressive prose incorporating poetic elements as well as colloquial street dialect. She stands, along with Alice Walker and Toni Morrison, as one of the leading voices in what might be called the renaissance of African American women's writing.

THE HAMMER MAN

I was glad to hear that Manny had fallen off the roof. I had put out the tale that I was down with yellow fever, but nobody paid me no mind, least of all Dirty Red who stomped right in to announce that Manny had fallen off the roof and that I could come out of hiding now. My mother dropped what she was doing, which was the laundry, and got the whole story out of Red. "Bad enough you gots to hang around with boys," she said. "But fight with them too. And you would pick the craziest one at that."

Manny was supposed to be crazy. That was his story. To say you were bad put some people off. But to say you were crazy, well, you were officially not to be messed with. So that was his story. On the other hand, after I called him what I called him and said a few choice things about his mother, his face did go through some piercing changes. And I did kind of wonder if maybe he sure was nuts. I didn't wait to find out. I got in the wind. And then he waited for me on my stoop all day and all night, not hardly speaking to the people going in and out. And he was there all day Saturday, with his sister bringing him peanut-butter sandwiches and cream sodas. He must've gone to the bathroom right there cause every time I looked out the kitchen window, there he was. And Sunday, too. I got to thinking the boy was mad.

"You got no sense of humor, that's your trouble," I told him. He looked up, but he didn't say nothing. All at once I was real sorry about the whole thing. I should've settled for hitting off the little girls in the school yard, or waiting for Frankie to come in so we could raise some kind of hell. This way I had to play sick when my mother was around cause my father had already taken away my BB gun and hid it.

I don't know how they got Manny on the roof finally. Maybe the Wakefield kids, the ones who keep the pigeons, called him up. Manny was a sucker for sick animals and things like that. Or maybe Frankie got some nasty girls to go up on the roof with him and got Manny to join him. I don't know. Anyway, the catwalk had lost all its cement and the roof always did kind of slant downward. So Manny fell off the roof. I got over my yellow fever right quick, needless to say, and ventured outside. But by this time I had already told Miss Rose that Crazy Manny was after me. And Miss Rose, being who she was, quite naturally went over to Manny's house and said a few harsh words to his mother, who, being who she was, chased Miss Rose out into the street and they commenced to get with it, snatching bottles out of the garbage cans and breaking them on the johnny pumps and stuff like that.

Dirty Red didn't have to tell us about this. Everybody could see and hear all. I never figured the garbage cans for an arsenal, but Miss Rose came up with sticks and table legs and things, and Manny's mother had her share of scissor blades and bicycle chains. They got to rolling in the streets and all you could see was pink drawers and fat legs. It was something else. Miss Rose is nutty but Manny's mother's crazier than Manny. They were at it a couple of times during my sick spell. Everyone would congregate on the window sills or the fire escape, commenting that it was still much too cold for this kind of nonsense. But they watched anyway. And then Manny fell off the roof. And that was that. Miss Rose went back to her dream books and Manny's mother went back to her tumbled-down kitchen of dirty clothes and bundles and bundles of rags and children.

My father got in on it too, cause he happened to ask Manny one night why he was sitting on the stoop like that every night. Manny told him right off that he was going to kill me first chance he got. Quite naturally this made my father a little warm, me being his only daughter and planning to become a doctor and take care of him in his old age. So he had a few words with Manny first, and then he got hold of the older brother, Bernard, who was more his size. Bernard didn't see how any of it was his business or my father's business, so my father got mad and jammed Bernard's head into the mailbox. Then my father started getting messages from Bernard's uncle about where to meet him for a showdown and all. My father didn't say a word to my mother all this time; just sat around mumbling and picking up the phone and putting it down, or grabbing my stickball bat and putting it back. He carried on like this for days till I thought I would scream if the yellow fever didn't have me so weak. And then Manny fell off the roof, and my father went back to his beer-drinking buddies.

I was in the school yard, pitching pennies with the little boys from the elementary school, when my friend Violet hits my brand-new Spaudeen over the wall. She came running back to tell me that Manny was coming down the block. I peeked beyond the fence and there he was all right. He had his head all wound up like a mummy and his arm in a sling and his leg in a cast. It looked phony to me, especially that walking cane. I figured Dirty Red had told me a tale just to get me out there so Manny could stomp me, and Manny was playing it up with costume and all till he could get me.

"What happened to him?" Violet's sisters whispered. But I was too busy trying to figure out how this act was supposed to work. Then Manny passed real close to the fence and gave me a look.

"You had enough, Hammer Head," I yelled. "Just bring your crummy self in this yard and I'll pick up where I left off." Violet was knocked out and the other kids went into a huddle. I didn't have to say anything else. And when they all pressed me later, I just said, "You know that hammer he always carries in his fatigues?" And they'd all nod waiting for the rest of a long story. "Well, I took it away from him." And I walked off nonchalantly.

Manny stayed indoors for a long time. I almost forgot about him. New kids moved into the block and I got all caught up with that. And then Miss Rose finally hit the numbers and started ordering a whole lot of stuff through the mail and we would sit on the curb and watch these weird-looking packages being carried in, trying to figure out what simpleminded thing she had thrown her money away on when she might just as well wait for the warm weather and throw a block party for all her godchildren.

After a while a center opened up and my mother said she'd increase my allowance if I went and joined because I'd have to get out of my pants and stay in skirts, on account of that's the way things were at the center. So I joined and got to thinking about everything else but old Hammer Head. It was a rough place to get along in, the center, but my mother said that I needed to be be'd with and she needed to not be with me, so I went. And that time I sneaked into the office, that's when I really got turned on. I looked into one of those not-quite-white folders and saw that I was from a deviant family in a deviant neighborhood. I showed my mother the word in the dictionary, but she didn't pay me no mind. It was my favorite word after that. I ran it in the ground till one day my father got the strap just to show how deviant he could get. So I gave up trying to improve my vocabulary. And I almost gave up my dungarees.

Then one night I'm walking past the Douglas Street park cause I got thrown out of the center for playing pool when I should've been sewing, even though I had already decided that this was going to be my last fling with boy things, and starting tomorrow I was going to fix my hair right and wear skirts all the time just so my mother would stop talking about her gray hairs, and Miss Rose would stop calling me by my brother's name by mistake. So I'm walking past the park and there's ole Manny on the basketball court, perfecting his lay-ups and talking with himself. Being me, I quite naturally walk right up and ask what the hell he's doing playing in the dark, and he looks up and all around like the dark had crept up on him when he wasn't looking. So I knew right away that he'd been out there for a long time with his eyes just going along with the program.

"There was two seconds to go and we were one point behind," he said, shaking his head and staring at his sneakers like they was somebody. "And I was in the clear. I'd left the man in the backcourt and there I was, smiling, you dig, cause it was in the bag. They passed the ball and I slid the ball up nice and easy cause there was nothing to worry about. And . . ." He shook his head. "I muffed the goddamn shot. Ball bounced off the rim . . ." He stared at his hands. "The game of the season. Last game." And then he ignored me altogether, though he wasn't talking to me in the first place. He went back to the lay-ups, always from the same spot with his arms crooked in the same way, over and over. I must've gotten hypnotized cause I probably stood there for at least an hour watching like a fool till I couldn't even see the damn ball, much less the basket. But I stood there anyway for no reason I know of. He never missed. But he cursed himself away. It was torture. And then a squad car pulled up and a short cop with hair like one of the Marx Brothers came out hitching up his pants. He looked real hard at me and then at Manny.

"What are you two doing?"

"He's doing a lay-up. I'm watching." I said with my smart self. Then the cop just stood there and finally turned to the other one who was just getting out of the car.

"Who unlocked the gate?" the big one said.

"It's always unlocked," I said. Then we three just stood there like a bunch of penguins watching Manny go at it.

"This on the level?" the big guy asked, tilting his hat back with the thumb the way big guys do in hot weather. "Hey you," he said, walking over to Manny. "I'm talking to you." He finally grabbed the ball to get Manny's attention. But that didn't work. Manny just stood there with his arms out waiting for the pass so he could save the game. He wasn't paying no mind to the cop. So, quite naturally, when the cop slapped him upside his head it was a surprise. And when the cop started counting three to go, Manny had already recovered from the slap and was just ticking off the seconds before the buzzer sounded and all was lost.

"Gimme the ball, man." Manny's face was all tightened up and ready to pop.

"Did you hear what I said, black boy?"

Now, when somebody says that word like that, I gets warm. And crazy or no crazy, Manny was my brother at that moment and the cop was the enemy.

"You better give him back his ball," I said. "Manny don't take no mess from no cops. He ain't bothering nobody. He's gonna be Mister Basketball when he grows up. Just trying to get a little practice in before the softball season starts."

"Look here, sister, we'll run you in too," Harpo said.

"I damn sure can't be your sister seeing how I'm a black girl. Boy, I sure will be glad when you run me in so I can tell everybody about that. You must think you're in the South, mister."

The big guy screwed his mouth up and let one of them hard-day sighs. "The park's closed, little girl, so why don't you and your boyfriend go on home."

That really got me. The "little girl" was bad enough but that "boyfriend" was too much. But I kept cool, mostly because Manny looked so pitiful waiting there with his hands in a time-out and there being no one to stop the clock. But I kept my cool mostly cause of that hammer in Manny's pocket and no telling how frantic things can get what with a big-mouth like me, a couple of wise cops, and a crazy boy too.

"The gates are open," I said real quiet-like, "and this here's a free country. So why don't you give him back his ball?"

The big cop did another one of those sighs, his specialty I guess, and then he bounced the ball to Manny who went right into his gliding thing clear up to the backboard, damn near like he was some kind of very beautiful bird. And then he swooshed that ball in, even if there was no net, and you couldn't really hear the swoosh. Something happened to the bones in my chest. It was something.

"Crazy kids anyhow," the one with the wig said and turned to go. But the big guy watched Manny for a while and I guess something must've snapped in his head, cause all of a sudden he was hot for taking Manny to jail or court or somewhere and started yelling at him and everything, which is a bad thing to do to Manny, I can tell you. And I'm standing there thinking that none of my teachers, from kindergarten right on up, none of them knew what they were talking about. I'll be damned if I ever knew one of them rosy-cheeked cops that smiled and helped you get to school without neither you or your little raggedy dog getting hit by a truck that had a smile on its face, too. Not that I ever believed it. I knew Dick and Jane was full of crap from the get-go, especially them cops. Like this dude, for example, pulling on Manny's clothes like that when obviously he had just done about the most beautiful thing a man can do and not be a fag. No cop could swoosh without a net.

"Look out, man," was all Manny said, but it was the way he pushed the cop that started the real yelling and threats. And I thought to myself, Oh God here I am trying to change my ways, and not talk back in school, and do like my mother wants, but just have this last fling, and now this—getting shot in the stomach and bleeding to death in Douglas Street park and poor Manny getting pistol-whipped by those bastards and whatnot. I could see it all, practically crying too. And it just wasn't no kind of thing to happen to a small child like me with my confirmation picture in the paper next to my weeping parents and schoolmates. I could feel the blood sticking to my shirt and my eyeballs slipping away, and then that confirmation picture again; and my mother and her gray hair; and Miss Rose heading for the precinct with a shotgun; and my father getting old and feeble with no one to doctor him up and all.

And I wished Manny had fallen off the damn roof and died right then and there and saved me all this aggravation of being killed with him by these cops who surely didn't come out of no fifth-grade reader. But it didn't happen. They just took the ball and Manny followed them real quiet-like right out of the park into the dark, then into the squad car with his head drooping and his arms in a crook. And I went on home cause what the hell am I going to do on a basketball court, and it getting to be nearly midnight?

I didn't see Manny no more after he got into that squad car. But they didn't kill him after all cause Miss Rose heard he was in some kind of big house for people who lose their marbles. And then it was spring finally, and me and Violet was in this very boss fashion show at the center. And Miss Rose bought me my first corsage—yellow roses to match my shoes.

Stuart Dybek

Stuart Dybek (b. 1942) was born in Chicago. He attended Loyola University and the University of Iowa. His stories, first collected in *Childhood and Other Neighborhoods,* have won him a small but devoted following among readers of fiction. Dybek has a superb feeling for the gritty neighborhoods of his youth and a strong identification with his working-class characters. The stories combine a stern naturalism with an unexpected, always surprising, sense of the fantastic. His is a world where the light of dreams can suddenly flash across the drabness of the daily routine.

DEATH OF THE RIGHT FIELDER

After too many balls went out and never came back we went out to check. It was a long walk—he always played deep. Finally we saw him, from the distance resembling the towel we sometimes threw down for second base.

It was hard to tell how long he'd been lying there, sprawled on his face. Had he been playing infield his presence, or lack of it, would, of course, have been noticed immediately. The infield demands communication—the constant, reassuring chatter of team play. But he was remote, clearly an outfielder (the temptation is to say out*sider*). The infield is for wisecrackers, pepperpots, gum-poppers: the outfield is for loners, onlookers, brooders who would rather study clover and swat gnats than holler. People could pretty much be divided between infielders and outfielders. Not that one always has a choice. He didn't necessarily choose right field so much as accept it.

There were several theories as to what killed him. From the start the most popular was that he'd been shot. Perhaps from a passing car, possibly by that gang calling themselves the Jokers who played 16 inch softball on the concrete diamond with painted bases in the center of the housing project, or by the Latin Lords who didn't play sports period. Or maybe some pervert with a telescopic sight from a bedroom window, or a mad sniper from a water tower, or a terrorist with a silencer from the expressway overpass, or maybe it was an accident, a stray slug from a robbery, or shootout, or assassination attempt miles away.

No matter who pulled the trigger it seemed more plausible to ascribe his death to a bullet than to natural causes like, say, a heart attack. Young deaths are never natural; they're all violent. Not that kids don't die of heart attacks. But he never seemed the type. Sure, he was quiet, but not the quiet of someone always listening to the heart murmur his family has repeatedly warned him about since he was old enough to play. Nor could it have been leukemia. He wasn't a talented enough athlete to die of that. He'd have been playing center, not right, if leukemia was going to get him.

The shooting theory was better, even though there wasn't a mark on him. Couldn't it have been, as some argued, a high-powered bullet traveling with such velocity that its hole fuses behind it? Still, not everyone was satisfied. Other theories were formulated, rumors became legends over the years: he'd had an allergic reaction to a bee sting, been struck by a single bolt of lightning from a freak, instantaneous electric storm, ingested too strong a dose of insecticide from the grass blades he chewed on, sonic waves, radiation, pollution, etc. And a few of us liked to think it was simply that chasing a sinking liner, diving to make a shoestring catch, he broke his neck.

There *was* a ball in the webbing of his mitt when we turned him over. His mitt had been pinned under his body and was coated with an almost luminescent gray film. There was the same gray on his black, hightop gym shoes, as if he'd been running through lime, and along the bill of his baseball cap—the blue felt one with the red C which he always denied stood for the Chicago Cubs. He may have been a loner, but he didn't want to be identified with a loser. He lacked the sense of humor for that, lacked the perverse pride that sticking up for losers season after season breeds, and the love. He was just an ordinary guy, .250 at the plate, and we stood above him not knowing what to do next. By then the guys from the other outfield positions had trotted over. Someone, the shortstop probably, suggested team prayer. But no one could think of a team prayer. So we all just stood there silently bowing our heads, pretending to pray while the shadows moved darkly across the outfield grass. After awhile the entire diamond was swallowed and the field lights came on.

In the bluish squint of those lights he didn't look like someone we'd once known—nothing looked quite right—and we hurriedly scratched a shallow grave, covered him over, and stamped it down as much as possible so that the next right fielder, whoever he'd be, wouldn't trip. It could be just such a juvenile, seemingly trivial stumble that would ruin a great career before it had begun, or hamper it years later the way Mantle's was hampered by bum knees. One can never be sure the kid beside him isn't another Roberto Clemente; and who can ever know how many potential Great Ones have gone down in the obscurity of their neighborhoods? And so, in the catcher's phrase, we "buried the grave" rather than contribute to any further tragedy. In all likelihood the next right fielder, whoever he'd be, would be clumsy too, and if there was a mound to trip over he'd find it and break *his* neck, and soon right field would get the reputation as haunted, a kind of sandlot Bermuda Triangle, inhabited by phantoms calling for ghostly fly balls, where no one but the most desperate outcasts, already on the verge of suicide, would be willing to play.

Still, despite our efforts, we couldn't totally disguise it. A fresh grave is stubborn. Its outline remained visible—a scuffed bald spot that might have been confused for an aberrant pitcher's mound except for the bat jammed in earth with the mitt and blue cap fit over it. Perhaps we didn't want to eradicate it completely—a part of us was resting there. Perhaps we wanted the new right fielder, whoever he'd be, to notice and wonder about who played there before him, realizing he was now the only link between past and future that mattered. A monument, epitaph, flowers wouldn't be necessary.

As for us, we walked back, but by then it was too late—getting on to supper, getting on to the end of summer vacation, time for other things, college, careers, settling down and raising a family. Past thirty-five the talk starts about being over the hill, about a graying Phil Niekro in his forties still fanning them with the knuckler as if it's some kind of miracle, about Pete Rose still going in head-first at forty-two, beating the odds. And maybe the talk is right. One remembers Mays, forty and a Met, dropping that can-of-corn fly in the '71 Series, all that grace stripped away and with it the conviction, leaving a man confused and apologetic about the boy in him. It's sad to admit it ends so soon, but everyone knows those are the lucky ones. Most guys are washed up by seventeen.

James Alan McPherson

James Alan McPherson (b. 1943) was born in Savannah, Georgia. He attended Harvard University and the University of Iowa, where he later taught writing. McPherson's stories, collected in *Hue and Cry* (1969) and *Elbow Room* (1977), have marked him as a black writer intent upon exploring a terrain beyond the immediately racial. He does not turn his eye from the issues that have divided American life so deeply, but he does not focus upon the struggle between black and white cultures. McPherson writes with great compassion and insight about ordinary people confronting the problems we all confront. The fact that most of his characters are black ensures that the circumstances and pressures will be different from those facing most whites, but what interests McPherson—what *compels* him—is the human being, the life beneath the skin.

McPherson has won both the Pulitzer prize and a MacArthur Fellowship.

WHY I LIKE COUNTRY MUSIC

No one will believe that I like country music. Even my wife scoffs when told such a possibility exists. "Go on!" Gloria tells me. "I can see blues, bebop, maybe even a little buckdancing. But not bluegrass." Gloria says, "Hillbilly stuff is not just music. It's like the New York Stock Exchange. The minute you see a sharp rise in it, you better watch out."

I tend to argue the point, but quietly, and mostly to myself. Gloria was born and raised in New York; she has come to believe in the stock exchange as the only index of economic health. My perceptions were shaped in South Carolina; and long ago I learned there, as a waiter in private clubs, to gauge economic flux by the tips people gave. We tend to disagree on other matters too, but the thing that gives me most frustration is trying to make her understand why I like country music. Perhaps it is because she hates the South and has capitulated emotionally to the horror stories told by refugees from down home. Perhaps it is because Gloria is third generation Northern-born. I do not know. What I do know is that, while the two of us are black, the distance between us is sometimes as great as that between Ibo and Yoruba. And I do know that, despite her protestations, I like country music.

"You are crazy," Gloria tells me.

I tend to argue the point, but quietly, and mostly to myself.

Of course I do not like all country stuff; just pieces that make the right connections. I like banjo because sometimes I hear ancestors in the strumming. I like the fiddle-like refrain in "Dixie" for the very same reason. But most of all I like square dancing—the interplay between fiddle and caller, the stomping, the swishing of dresses, the strutting, the proud turnings, the laughter. Most of all I like the laughter. In recent months I have wondered why I like this music and this dance. I have drawn no general conclusions, but from time to time I suspect it is because the square dance is the only dance form I ever mastered.

"I wouldn't say that in public," Gloria warns me.

I agree with her, but still affirm the truth of it, although quietly, and mostly to myself.

Dear Gloria: This is the truth of how it was:

In my youth in that distant country, while others learned to strut, I grew stiff as a winter cornstalk. When my playmates harmonized their rhythms, I stood on the sidelines in atonic detachment. While they shimmied, I merely jerked in lackluster imitation. I relate these facts here, not in remorse or self-castigation, but as a true confession of my circumstances. In those days, down in our small corner of South Carolina, proficiency in dance was a form of storytelling. A boy could say, "I traveled here and there, saw this and fought that, conquered him and made love to her, lied to them, told a few others the truth, just so I could come back here and let you know what things out there are really like." He could communicate all this with smooth, graceful jiggles of his round bottom, synchronized with intricately coordinated sweeps of his arms and small, unexcited movements of his legs. Little girls could communicate much more.

But sadly, I could do none of it. Development of these skills depended on the ministrations of family and neighbors. My family did not dance; our closest neighbor was a true-believing Seventh Day Adventist. Moreover, most new dances came from up North, brought to town usually by people returning to riff on the good life said to exist in those far Northern places. They prowled our dirt streets in rented Cadillacs; paraded our brick sidewalks exhibiting styles abstracted from the fullness of life in Harlem, South Philadelphia, Roxbury, Baltimore and the South Side of Chicago. They confronted our provincial clothes merchants with the arrogant reminder, "But people ain't wearin' this in New Yo*kkk!*" Each of their movements, as well as their world-weary smoothness, told us locals meaningful tales of what was missing in our lives. Unfortunately, those of us under strict parental supervision, or those of us without Northern connections, could only stand at a distance and worship these envoys of culture. We stood on the sidelines—styleless, gestureless, danceless, doing nothing more than an improvised one-butt shuffle—hoping for one of them to touch our lives. It was my good fortune, during my tenth year on the sidelines, to have one of these Northerners introduce me to the square dance.

My dear, dear Gloria, her name was Gweneth Lawson:

She was a pretty, chocolate-brown little girl with dark brown eyes and two long black braids. After all these years, the image of these two braids evokes in me all there is to remember about Gweneth Lawson. They were plaited across the top of her head and hung to a point just above the back of her Peter Pan collar. Sometimes she wore two bows, one red and one blue, and these tended to sway lazily near the place on her neck where the smooth brown of her skin and the white of her collar met the ink-bottle black of her hair. Even when I cannot remember her face, I remember the rainbow of deep, rich colors in which she lived. This is so because I watched them, every weekday, from my desk directly behind hers in our fourth-grade class. And she wore the most magical perfume, or lotion, smelling just slightly of fresh-cut lemons, that wafted back to me whenever she made the slightest movement at her desk. Now I must tell you this much more, dear Gloria: whenever I smell fresh lemons, whether in the market or at home, I look around me—not for Gweneth Lawson, but for some quiet corner where I can revive in private certain memories of her. And in pursuing these memories across such lemony bridges, I rediscover that I loved her.

Gweneth was from the South Carolina section of Brooklyn. Her parents had sent her south to live with her uncle, Mr. Richard Lawson, the brick mason, for an unspecified period of time. Just why they did this I do not know, unless it was their plan to have her absorb more of South Carolina folkways than conditions in Brooklyn would allow. She was a gentle, soft-spoken girl; I recall no condescension in her manner. This was all the more admirable because our unrestrained awe of a Northern-born black person usually induced in him some grand sense of his own importance. You must know that in those days older folks would point to someone and say, "He's from the North," and the statement would be sufficient in itself. Mothers made their children behave by advising that, if they led exemplary lives and attended church regularly, when they died they would go to New York. Only someone who understands what London meant to Dick Whittington, or how California and the suburbs function in the national mind, could appreciate the mythical dimensions of this Northlore.

But Gweneth Lawson was above regional idealization. Though I might have loved her partly because she was a Northerner, I loved her more because of the world of colors that seemed to be suspended above her head. I loved her glowing forehead and I loved her bright, dark brown eyes; I loved the black braids, the red and blue and sometimes yellow and pink ribbons; I loved the way the deep, rich brown of her neck melted into the pink or white cloth of her Peter Pan collar; I loved the lemony vapor on which she floated and from which, on occasion, she seemed to be inviting me to be buoyed up, up, up into her happy world; I loved the way she caused my heart to tumble whenever, during a restless moment, she seemed about to turn her head in my direction; I loved her more, though torturously, on the many occasions when she did not turn. Because I was a shy boy, I loved the way I could love her silently, at least six hours a day, without ever having to disclose my love.

My platonic state of mind might have stretched onward into a blissful infinity had not Mrs. Esther Clay Boswell, our teacher, made it her business to pry into the affair. Although she prided herself on being a strict disciplinarian, Mrs. Boswell was not without a sense of humor. A round, full-breasted woman in her early forties, she liked to amuse herself, and sometimes the class as well, by calling the attention of all eyes to whomever of us violated the structure she imposed on classroom activities. She was particularly hard on people like me who could not contain an impulse to daydream, or those who allowed their eyes to wander too far away from lessons printed on the blackboard. A black and white sign posted under the electric clock next to the door summed up her attitude toward this kind of truancy: NOTICE TO ALL CLOCK WATCHERS, it read, TIME PASSES, WILL YOU? Nor did she abide timidity in her students. Her voice booming, "Speak up, boy!" was more than enough to cause the more emotional among us, including me, to break into convenient flows of warm tears. But by doing this we violated yet another rule, one on which depended our very survival in Mrs. Esther Clay Boswell's class. She would spell out this rule for us as she paced before her desk, slapping a thick, homemade ruler against the flat of her brown palm. "There ain't no *babies* in here," she would recite. *Thaap!* "Anybody thinks he's still a *baby* . . ." *Thaap!* ". . . should crawl back home to his mama's *titty*." *Thaap!* "You little bunnies shed your *last water* . . ." *Thaap!*". . . the minute you left home to come in here." *Thaap!* "From now on, you g'on do all your *cryin'* . . ." *Thaap!* ". . . in *church!*" *Thaap!* Whenever one of us compelled her to make this speech it would seem to me that her eyes paused overlong on my face. She would seem to be daring me, as if suspicious that, in addition to my secret passion for Gweneth Lawson, which she might excuse, I was also in the habit of throwing fits of temper.

She had read me right. I was the product of too much attention from my father. He favored me, paraded me around on his shoulder, inflated my ego constantly with what, among us at least, was a high compliment: "You my nigger if you don't get no bigger." This statement, along with my father's generous attentions, made me selfish and used to having my own way. I *expected* to have my own way in most things, and when I could not, I tended to throw tantrums calculated to break through any barrier raised against me.

Mrs. Boswell was also perceptive in assessing the extent of my infatuation with Gweneth Lawson. Despite my stealth in telegraphing emissions of affection into the back part of Gweneth's brain, I could not help but observe, occasionally, Mrs. Boswell's cool glance pausing on the two of us. But she never said a word. Instead, she would settle her eyes momentarily on Gweneth's face and then pass quickly to mine. But in that instant she seemed to be saying, "Don't look back now, girl, but I *know* that bald-headed boy behind you has you on his mind." She seemed to watch me daily, with a combination of amusement and absolute detachment in her brown eyes. And when she stared, it was not at me but at the normal focus of my attention: the end of Gweneth Lawson's black braids. Whenever I sensed Mrs. Boswell watching I would look away quickly, either down at my brown desk top or across the room to the blackboard. But her eyes could not be eluded this easily. Without looking at anyone in particular, she could make a specific point to one person in a manner so general that only long afterward did the real object of her attention realize it had been intended for him.

"Now you little brown bunnies," she might say, "and you black buck rabbits and you few cottontails mixed in, some of you starting to smell yourselves under the arms without knowing what it's all about." And here, it sometimes seemed to me, she allowed her eyes to pause casually on me before resuming their sweep of the entire room. "Now I know your mamas already made you think life is a bed of roses, but in *my* classroom you got to know the footpaths through the *sticky* parts of the rose bed." It was her custom during this ritual of prod and goad those of us who were developing reputations for meekness and indecision; yet her method was Socratic in that she compelled us, indirectly, to supply our own answers by exploiting one person as the walking symbol of the error she intended to correct. Clarence Buford, for example, an oversized but good-natured boy from a very poor family, served often as the helpmeet in this exercise.

"Buford," she might begin, slapping the ruler against her palm, "how does a tongue-tied country boy like you expect to get a wife?"

"I don't want no wife," Buford might grumble softly.

Of course the class would laugh.

"Oh yes you do," Mrs. Boswell would respond. "All you buck rabbits want wives." *Thaap!* "So how do you let a girl know you're not just a bump on a log?"

"I know! I know!" a high voice might call from a seat across from mine. This, of course, would be Leon Pugh. A peanut-brown boy with curly hair, he seemed to know everything. Moreover, he seemed to take pride in being the only one who knew answers to life questions and would wave his arms excitedly whenever our attentions were focused on such matters. It seemed to me his voice would be extra loud and his arms waved more strenuously whenever he was certain that Gweneth Lawson, seated across from him, was interested in an answer to Mrs. Esther Clay Boswell's question. His eager arms, it seemed to me, would be reaching out to grasp Gweneth instead of the question asked.

"Buford, you twisted-tongue, bunion-toed country boy," Mrs. Boswell might say, ignoring Leon Pugh's hysterical arm waving, "you gonna let a cottontail like Leon get a girlfriend before you?"

"I don't want no girlfriend," Clarence Buford would almost sob. "I don't like no girls."

The class would laugh again while Leon Pugh manipulated his arms like a flight navigator under battle conditions. "I know! I know! I swear to *God* I know!"

When at last Mrs. Boswell would turn in his direction, I might sense that she was tempted momentarily to ask me for an answer. But as in most such exercises, it was the worldly-wise Leon Pugh who supplied this. "What do *you* think, Leon?" she would ask inevitably, but with a rather lifeless slap of the ruler against her palm.

"My daddy told me . . ." Leon would shout, turning slyly to beam at Gweneth, ". . . my daddy and my big brother from the Bronx New York told me that to git *anythin'* in this world you gotta learn how to blow your own horn."

"Why, Leon?" Mrs. Boswell might ask in a bored voice.

"Because," the little boy would recite, puffing out his chest, "because if you don't blow your own horn ain't nobody else g'on blow it for you. That's what my daddy said."

"What do you think about that, Buford?" Mrs. Boswell would ask.

"I don't want no girlfriend anyhow," the puzzled Clarence Buford might say.

And then the cryptic lesson would suddenly be dropped.

This was Mrs. Esther Clay Boswell's method of teaching. More than anything written on the blackboard, her questions were calculated to make us turn around in our chairs and inquire in guarded whispers of each other, and especially of the wise and confident Leon Pugh, "What does she mean?" But none of us, besides Pugh, seemed able to comprehend what it was we ought to know but did not know. And Mrs. Boswell, plump brown fox that she was, never volunteered any more in the way of confirmation than was necessary to keep us interested. Instead, she paraded around us, methodically slapping the homemade ruler against her palm, suggesting by her silence more depth to her question, indeed, more implications in Leon's answer, than we were then able to perceive. And during such moments, whether inspired by selfishness or by the peculiar way Mrs. Boswell looked at me, I felt that finding answers to such questions was a task she had set for me, of all the members of the class.

Of course Leon Pugh, among other lesser lights, was my chief rival for the affections of Gweneth Lawson. All during the school year, from September through the winter rains, he bested me in my attempts to look directly into her eyes and say a simple, heartfelt "hey." This was my ambition, but I never seemed able to get close enough to get her attention. At Thanksgiving I helped draw a bounteous yellow cornucopia on the blackboard, with fruits and flowers matching the colors that floated around Gweneth's head; Leon Pugh made one by himself, a masterwork of silver paper and multicolored crepe, which he hung on the door. Its silver tail curled upward to a point just below the face of Mrs. Boswell's clock. At Christmas, when we drew names out of a hat for the exchange of gifts, I drew the name of Queen Rose Phipps, a fairly unattractive squash-yellow girl of absolutely no interest to me. Pugh, whether through collusion with the boy who handled the lottery or through pure luck, pulled forth from the hat the magic name of Gweneth Lawson. He gave her a set of deep purple bows for her braids and a basket of pecans from his father's tree. Uninterested now in the spirit of the occasion, I delivered to Queen Rose Phipps a pair of white socks. Each time Gweneth wore the purple bows she would glance over at Leon and smile. Each time Queen Rose wore my white socks I would turn away in embarrassment, lest I should see them pulling down into her shoes and exposing her skinny ankles.

After class, on wet winter days, I would trail along behind Gweneth to the bus stop, pause near the steps while she entered, and follow her down the aisle until she chose a seat. Usually, however, in clear violation of the code of conduct to which all gentlemen were expected to adhere, Leon Pugh would already be on the bus and shouting to passersby, "Move off! Get away! This here seat by me is reserved for the girl from Brooklyn New York." Discouraged but not defeated, I would swing into the seat next nearest her and cast calf-eyed glances of wounded affection at the back of her head or at the brown, rainbow profile of her face. And at her stop, some eight or nine blocks from mine, I would disembark behind her along with a crowd of other love-struck boys. There would then follow a well-rehearsed scene in which all of us, save Leon Pugh, pretended to have gotten off the bus either too late or too soon to wend our proper paths homeward. And at slight cost to ourselves we enjoyed the advantage of being able to walk close by her as she glided toward her uncle's green-frame house. There, after pausing on the wooden steps and smiling radiantly around the crowd like a spring sun in that cold winter rain, she would sing, "Bye, y'all," and disappear into the structure with the mystery of a goddess. Afterward I would walk away, but slowly, much slower than the other boys, warmed by the music and light in her voice against the sharp, wet winds of the February afternoon.

I loved her, dear Gloria, and I danced with her and smelled the lemony youth of her and told her that I loved her, all this in a way you would never believe:

You would not know or remember, as I do, that in those days, in our area of the country, we enjoyed a pleasingly ironic mixture of Yankee and Confederate folkways. Our meals and manners, our speech, our attitudes toward certain ambiguous areas of history, even our acceptance of tragedy as the normal course of life—these things and more defined us as Southern. Yet the stern morality of our parents, their toughness and penny-pinching and attitudes toward work, their covert allegiance toward certain ideals, even the directions toward which they turned our faces, made us more Yankee than Cavalier. Moreover, some of our schools were named for Confederate men of distinction, but others were named for the stern-faced believers who had swept down from the North to save a people back, back long ago, in those long-forgotten days of once upon a time. Still, our schoolbooks, our required classrooms songs, our flags, our very relation to the statues and monuments in public parks, negated the story that these dreamers from the North had ever come. We sang the state song, memorized the verses of homegrown poets, honored in our books the names and dates of historical events both before and after that Historical Event which, in our region, supplanted even the division of the millennia introduced by the followers of Jesus Christ. Given the silent circumstances of our cultural environment, it was ironic, and perhaps just, that we maintained a synthesis of two traditions no longer supportive of each other. Thus it became traditional at our school to celebrate the arrival of spring on May first by both the ritual plaiting of the Maypole and square dancing.

On that day, as on a few others, the Superintendent of Schools and several officials were likely to visit our schoolyard and stand next to the rusty metal swings, watching the fourth, fifth, and sixth graders bob up and down and behind and before each other, around the gaily painted Maypoles. These happy children would pull and twist long runs of billowy crepe paper into wondrous, multicolored plaits. Afterward, on the edges of thunderous applause from teachers, parents and visiting dignitaries, a wave of elaborately costumed children would rush out onto the grounds in groups of eight and proceed with the square dance. "Dog*gone!*" the Superintendent of Schools was heard to exclaim on one occasion. "Y'all do it so good it just makes your *bones* set up and take notice."

Such was the schedule two weeks prior to May first, when Mrs. Boswell announced to our class that as fourth graders we were now eligible to participate in the festivities. The class was divided into two general sections of sixteen each, one group preparing to plait the pole and a second group, containing an equal number of boys and girls, practicing turns for our part in the square dance. I was chosen to square dance; so was Leon Pugh. Gweneth Lawson was placed with the pole plaiters. I was depressed until I remembered, happily, that I could not dance a lick. I reported this fact to Mrs. Boswell just after drawing, during recess, saying that my lack of skill would only result in our class making a poor showing. I asked to be reassigned to the group of Maypole plaiters. Mrs. B. looked me over with considerable amusement tugging at the corners of her mouth. "Oh, you don't have to *dance* to do the square dance," she said. "That's a dance that was made up to mock folks that couldn't dance." She paused a second before adding thoughtfully: "The worse you are at dancing, the better you can square dance. It's just about the best dance in the world for a stiff little bunny like you."

"I want to plait the Maypole," I said.

"You'll square dance or I'll grease your little butt," Mrs. Esther Clay Boswell said.

"I ain't gonna do *nothin'!*" I muttered. But I said this quietly, and mostly to myself, while walking away from her desk. For the rest of the day she watched me closely, as if she knew what I was thinking.

The next morning I brought a note from my father. "Dear Mrs. Boswell:" I had watched him write earlier that morning, "My boy does not square dance. Please excuse him as I am afraid he will break down and cry and mess up the show. Yours truly . . ."

Mrs. Boswell said nothing after she had read the note. She merely waved me to my seat. But in the early afternoon, when she read aloud the lists of those assigned to dancing and Maypole plaiting, she paused as my name rolled off her tongue. "You don't have to stay on the square dance team," she called to me. "You go on out in the yard with the Maypole team."

I was ecstatic. I hurried to my place in line some three warm bodies behind Gweneth Lawson. We prepared to march out.

"Wait a minute," Mrs. Boswell called. "Now it looks like we got seventeen bunnies on the Maypole team and fifteen on the square dance. We have to even things up." She made a thorough examination of both lists, scratching her head. Then she looked carefully up and down the line of stomping Maypoleites. "Miss Gweneth Lawson, you cute little cottontail you, it looks like you gonna have to go over to the square dance team. That'll give us eight sets of partners for the square dance . . . but now we have another problem." She made a great display of counting the members of the two squads of square dancers. "Now there's sixteen square dancers all right, but when we pair them off we got a problem of higher mathematics. With nine girls and only seven *boys,* looks like we gotta switch a girl from square dancing to Maypole and a boy from Maypole to square dancing."

I waited hopefully for Gweneth Lawson to volunteer. But just at that moment the clever Leon Pugh grabbed her hand and began jitterbugging as though he could hardly wait for the record player to be turned on and the dancing to begin.

"What a cute couple," Mrs. Boswell observed absently. "Now which one of you other girls wants to join up with the Maypole team?"

Following Pugh's example, the seven remaining boys grabbed the girls they wanted as partners. Only skinny Queen Rose Phipps and shy Beverly Hankins remained unclaimed. Queen Rose giggled nervously.

"Queen Rose," Mrs. B. called, "I know you don't mind plaiting the Maypole." She waved her ruler in a gesture of casual dismissal. Queen Rose raced across the room and squeezed into line.

"*Now,*" Mrs. Boswell said, "I need a boy to come across to the square dancers."

I was not unmindful of the free interchange of partners involved in square dancing, even though Leon Pugh had beat me in claiming the partner of my choice. All I really wanted was one moment swinging Gweneth Lawson in my arms. I raised my hand slowly.

"Oh, not *you,* little bunny," Mrs. Boswell said. "You and your daddy claim you don't like to square dance." She slapped her ruler against her palm. *Thaap! Thaap!* Then she said, "Clarence Buford, I *know* a big-footed country boy like you can square dance better than anybody. Come on over here and kiss cute little Miss Beverly Hankins."

"I don't like no girls *noway,*" Buford mumbled. But he went over and stood next to the giggling Beverly Hankins.

"Now!" said Mrs. B. "March on out in that yard and give that pole a good plaiting!"

We started to march out. Over my shoulder, as I reached the door, I glimpsed the overjoyed Leon Pugh whirling lightly on his toes. He sang in a confident tone:

> I saw the Lord give Moses a pocketful of roses.
> I skid Ezekiel's wheel on a ripe banana peel.
> I rowed the Nile, flew over a stile,
> Saw Jack Johnson pick his teeth
> With toenails from Jim Jeffries' feets . . .

"Grab your partners!" Mrs. Esther Clay Boswell was saying as the oak door slammed behind us.

I had been undone. For almost two weeks I was obliged to stand on the sidelines and watch Leon Pugh allemande left and do-si-do my beloved Gweneth. Worse, she seemed to be enjoying it. But I must give Leon proper credit: he was a dancing fool. In a matter of days he had mastered, and then improved on, the various turns and bows and gestures of the square dance. He leaped while the others plodded, whirled each girl through his arms with lightness and finesse, chattered playfully at the other boys when they tumbled over their own feet. Mrs. Boswell stood by the record player calling. "Put some *strut* in it, Buford, you big potato sack. Watch Leon and see how *he* does it." I leaned against the classroom wall and watched the dancers, my own group having already exhausted the limited variations possible in matters of Maypole plaiting.

At home each night I begged my father to send another note to Mrs. Boswell, this time stating that I had no interest in the Maypole. But he resisted my entreaties and even threatened me with a whipping if I did not participate and make him proud of me. The real cause of his irritation was the considerable investment he had already made in purchasing an outfit for me. Mrs. Boswell had required all her students, square dancers and Maypole plaiters alike, to report on May first in outfits suitable for square dancing. My father had bought a new pair of dungarees, a blue shirt, a red and white polka-dot bandanna and a cowboy hat. He was in no mood to bend under the emotional weight of my new demands. As a matter of fact, early in the morning of May first he stood beside my bed with the bandanna in his left hand and his leather belt in his right hand, just in case I developed a sudden fever.

I dragged myself heavily through the warm, blue spring morning toward school, dressed like a carnival cowboy. When I entered the classroom I sulked against the wall, being content to watch the other children. And what happy buzzings and jumping and excitement they made as they compared costumes. Clarence Buford wore a Tom Mix hat and a brown vest over a green shirt with red six-shooter patterns embossed on its collar. Another boy, Paul Carter, was dressed entirely in black, with a fluffy white handkerchief puffing from his neck. But Leon Pugh caught the attention of all our eyes. He wore a red and white checkered shirt, a loose green bandanna clasped at his throat by a shining silver buffalo head, brown chaps sewed onto his dungarees, and shiny brown cowboy boots with silver spurs that clanked each time he moved. In his hand he carried a carefully creased brown cowboy hat. He announced his fear that it would lose its shape and planned to put it on only when the dancing started. He would allow no one to touch it. Instead, he stood around clanking his feet and smoothing the crease in his fabulous hat and saying loudly, "My daddy says it pays to look good no matter what you put on."

The girls seemed prettier and much older than their ages. Even Queen Rose Phipps wore rouge on her cheeks that complemented her pale color. Shy Beverly Hankins had come dressed in a blue and white checkered bonnet and a crisp blue apron; she looked like a frontier mother. But Gweneth Lawson, my Gweneth Lawson, dominated the group of girls. She wore a long red dress with sheaves and sheaves of sparkling white crinoline belling it outward so it seemed she was floating. On her honey-brown wrists golden bracelets sparkled. A deep blue bandanna enclosed her head with the wonder of a summer sky. Black patent leather shoes glistened like half-hidden stars beneath the red and white of her hemline. She stood smiling before us and we marveled. At that moment I would have given the world to have been able to lead her about on my arm.

Mrs. Boswell watched us approvingly from behind her desk. Finally, at noon, she called, "Let's go on out!" Thirty-two living rainbows cascaded toward the door. Pole plaiters formed one line. Square dancers formed another. Mrs. Boswell strolled officiously past us in review. It seemed to me she almost paused while passing the spot where I stood on line. But she brushed past me, straightening an apron here, applying spittle and a rub to a rouged cheek there, waving a wary finger at an over-anxious boy. Then she whacked her ruler against her palm and led us out into the yard. The fifth and sixth graders had already assembled. On one end of the playground were a dozen or so tall painted poles with long, thin wisps of green and blue and yellow and rust-brown crepe floating lazily on the sweet spring breezes.

"Maypole teams *up!*" called Mr. Henry Lucas, our principal, from his platform by the swings. Beside him stood the white Superintendent of Schools (who said later of the square dance, it was reported to all the classes, "Lord y'all square dance so *good* it makes me plumb *ashamed* us white folks ain't takin' better care of our art stuff.") "Maypole teams up!" Mr. Henry Lucas shouted again. Some fifty of us, screaming shrilly, rushed to grasp our favorite color crepe. Then, to the music of "Sing Praise for All the Brightness and the Joy of Spring," we pulled and plaited in teams of six or seven until every pole was twisted as tight and as colorfully as the braids on Gweneth Lawson's head. Then, to the applause of proud teachers and parents and the whistles of the Superintendent of Schools, we scattered happily back under the wings of our respective teachers. I stood next to Mrs. Boswell, winded and trembling but confident I had done my best. She glanced down at me and said in a quiet voice, "I do believe you are learning the rhythm of the thing."

I did not respond.

"Let's *go!*" Leon Pugh shouted to the other kids, grabbing Gweneth Lawson's arm and taking a few clanking steps forward.

"Wait a minute, Leon," Mrs. Boswell hissed. "Mr. Lucas has to change the record."

Leon sighed. "But if we don't git out there first, all them other teams will take the best spots."

"Wait!" Mrs. Boswell ordered.

Leon sulked. He inched closer to Gweneth. I watched him swing her hand impatiently. He stamped his feet and his silver spurs jangled.

Mrs. Boswell looked down at his feet. "Why, Leon," she said, "you can't go out there with razors on your shoes."

"These ain't razors," Leon muttered. "These here are spurs my brother in Bronx New York sent me just for this here dance."

"You have to take them off," Mrs. Boswell said.

Leon growled. But he reached down quickly and attempted to jerk the silver spurs from the heels of his boots. They did not come off. "No time!" he called, standing suddenly. "Mr. Lucas done put the record on."

"Leon, you might *cut* somebody with those things," Mrs. Boswell said. "Miss Gweneth Lawson's pretty red dress could get caught in those things and then she'll fall as surely as I'm standin' here."

"I'll just go out with my boots off," Leon replied.

But Mrs. Boswell shook her head firmly. "You just run on to the lunchroom and ask Cook for some butter or mayo. That'll help 'em slip off." She paused, looking out over the black dirt playground. "And if you miss the first dance, why, there'll be a second and maybe even a third. We'll get a Maypole plaiter to sub for you."

My heart leaped. Leon sensed it and stared at me. His hand tightened on Gweneth's as she stood radiant and smiling in the loving spring sunlight. Leon let her hand drop and bent quickly, pulling at the spurs with the fury of a Samson.

"Square dancers *up!*" Mr. Henry Lucas called.

"Sonofa*bitch!*" Leon grunted.

"Square dancers *up!*" called Mr. Lucas.

The fifth and sixth graders were screaming and rushing toward the center of the yard. Already the record was scratching out the high, slick voice of the caller. "*Sonofabitch!*" Leon moaned.

Mrs. Boswell looked directly at Gweneth, standing alone and abandoned next to Leon. "Miss Gweneth Lawson," Mrs. Boswell said in a cool voice, "it's a cryin' shame there ain't no prince to take you to that ball out there."

I do not remember moving, but I know I stood with Gweneth at the center of the yard. What I did there I do not know, but I remember watching the movements of others and doing what they did just after they had done it. Still, I cannot remember just when I looked into my partner's face or what I saw there. The scratchy voice of the caller bellowed directions and I obeyed:

> Allemande left with your left hand
> Right to your partner with a right and left grand . . .

Although I was told later that I made an allemande right instead of left, I have no memory of the mistake.

> When you get to your partner pass her by
> And pick up the next girl on the sly . . .

Nor can I remember picking up any other girl. I only remember that during many turns and do-si-dos I found myself looking into the warm brown eyes of Gweneth Lawson. I recall that she smiled at me. I recall that she laughed on another turn. I recall that I laughed with her an eternity later.

> . . . promenade that dear old thing
> Throw your head right back and sing *be*-cause, just
> *be*-cause . . .

I do remember quite well that during the final promenade before the record ended, Gweneth stood beside me and I said to her in a voice much louder than that of the caller, "When I get up to Brooklyn I hope I see you." But I do not remember what she said in response. I want to remember that she smiled.

I know I smiled, dear Gloria. I smiled with the lemonness of her and the loving of her pressed deep into those saving places of my private self. It was my plan to savor these, and I did savor them. But when I reached New York, many years later, I did not think of Brooklyn. I followed the old, beaten, steady paths into uptown Manhattan. By then I had learned to dance to many other kinds of music. And I had forgotten the savory smell of lemon. But I think sometimes of Gweneth now when I hear country music. And although it is difficult to explain to you, I still maintain that I am no mere arithmetician in the art of the square dance. I am into the calculus of it.

"Go on!" you will tell me, backing into your Northern mythology. "I can see the hustle, the hump, maybe even the Ibo highlife. But no hillbilly."

These days I am firm about arguing the point, but, as always, quietly, and mostly to myself.

Alice Walker

Alice Walker (b.1944) was born in Eatonton, Georgia, to a sharecropper family. She attended Spelman College in Atlanta and later studied at Sarah Lawrence College in New York. Walker's literary career has been both energetic and politically engaged. Through her poetry, fiction, and essays she has explored the ongoing legacies of racism and sexism in our society. Her Pulitzer prize-winning novel *The Color Purple,* which was made into a movie by Steven Spielberg, aroused considerable controversy in the literary community. Feminist critics hailed Walker's bold and sympathetic treatment of black women; others protested that Walker was stigmatizing the black man, portraying him in stereotyped terms as brutal and sexist. Walker herself does not deny that the focus of her attention is upon the black woman and that her struggle is on behalf of what she calls "womanism."

Critic Melissa Walker has drawn attention to Walker's use of a quotation from Albert Camus as an epigraph to her first book of poetry, finding the words especially relevant to Walker's vision. "Poverty," wrote Camus, "was not a calamity for me. It was always balanced by the richness of light . . . circumstances helped me. To correct a natural indifference I was placed half-way between misery and the sun. Misery kept me from believing that all was well under the sun, and the sun taught me that history wasn't everything."

Walker's works include the story collections *In Love and Trouble* and *You Can't Keep a Good Woman Down,* and the novels *The Third Life of Grange Copeland, Meridian,* and *The Temple of My Familiar.*

THE ABORTION

They had discussed it, but not deeply, whether they wanted the baby she was now carrying. "I don't *know* if I want it," she said, eyes filling with tears. She cried at anything now and was often nauseous. That pregnant women cried easily and were nauseous seemed banal to her, and she resented banality.

"Well, think about it," he said, with his smooth reassuring voice (but with an edge of impatience she now felt) that used to soothe her.

It was all she *did* think about, all she apparently *could;* that he could dream otherwise enraged her. But she always lost when they argued. Her temper would flare up, he would become instantly reasonable, mature, responsible, if not responsive precisely, to her mood, and she would swallow down her tears and hate herself. It was because she believed him "good." The best human being she had ever met.

"It isn't as if we don't already have a child," she said in a calmer tone, carelessly wiping at the tear that slid from one eye.

"We have a perfect child," he said with relish, "thank the good Lord!"

Had she ever dreamed she'd marry someone humble enough to go around thanking the good Lord? She had not.

Now they left the bedroom, where she had been lying down on their massive king-size bed with the forbidding ridge in the middle, and went down the hall—hung with bright prints—to the cheerful, spotlessly clean kitchen. He put water on for tea in a bright yellow pot.

She wanted him to want the baby so much he would try to save its life. On the other hand, she did not permit such presumptuousness. As he praised the child they already had, a daughter of sunny disposition and winning smile, Imani sensed subterfuge, and hardened her heart.

"What am I talking about?" she said, as if she'd been talking about it. "Another child would kill me. I can't imagine life with two children. Having a child is a good experience *to have had,* like graduate school. But if you've had one, you've had the experience and that's enough."

He placed the tea before her and rested a heavy hand on her hair. She felt the heat and pressure of his hand as she touched the cup and felt the odor and steam rise up from it. Her throat contracted.

"I can't drink that," she said through gritted teeth. "Take it away."

There were days of this.

Clarice, their daughter, was barely two years old. A miscarriage brought on by grief (Imani had lost her fervidly environmentalist mother to lung cancer shortly after Clarice's birth; the asbestos ceiling in the classroom where she taught first graders had leaked for twenty years) separated Clarice's birth from the new pregnancy. Imani felt her body had been assaulted by these events and was, in fact, considerably weakened, and was also, in any case, chronically anemic and run-down. Still, if she had wanted the baby more than she did not want it, she would not have planned to abort it.

They lived in a small town in the South. Her husband, Clarence, was, among other things, legal adviser and defender of the new black mayor of the town. The mayor was much in their lives because of the difficulties being the first black mayor of a small town assured, and because, next to the major leaders of black struggles in the South, Clarence respected and admired him most.

Imani reserved absolute judgment, but she did point out that Mayor Carswell would never look at her directly when she made a comment or posed a question, even sitting at her own dinner table, and would instead talk to Clarence as if she were not there. He assumed that as a woman she would not be interested in, or even understand, politics. (He would comment occasionally on her cooking or her clothes. He noticed when she cut her hair.) But Imani understood every shade and variation of politics: she understood, for example, why she fed the mouth that did not speak to her, because for the present she must believe in Mayor Carswell, even as he could not believe in her. Even understanding this, however, she found dinners with Carswell hard to swallow.

But Clarence was dedicated to the mayor, and believed his success would ultimately mean security and advancement for them all.

On the morning she left to have the abortion, the mayor and Clarence were to have a working lunch, and they drove her to the airport deep in conversation about municipal funds, racist cops, and the facilities for teaching at the chaotic, newly integrated schools. Clarence had time for the briefest kiss and hug at the airport ramp.

"Take care of yourself," he whispered lovingly as she walked away. He was needed, while she was gone, to draft the city's new charter. She had agreed this was important; the mayor was already being called incompetent by local businessmen and the chamber of commerce, and one inferred from television that no black person alive even knew what a city charter was.

"Take care of myself." Yes, she thought. I see that is what I have to do. But she thought this self-pityingly, which invalidated it. She had expected *him* to take care of her, and she blamed him for not doing so now.

Well, she was a fraud, anyway. She had known after a year of marriage that it bored her. "The Experience of Having a Child" was to distract her from this fact. Still, she expected him to "take care of her." She was lucky he didn't pack up and leave. But he seemed to know, as she did, that if anyone packed and left, it would be her. Precisely *because* she was a fraud and because in the end he would settle for fraud and she could not.

On the plane to New York her teeth ached and she vomited bile—bitter, yellowish stuff she hadn't even been aware her body produced. She resented and appreciated the crisp help of the stewardess, who asked if she needed anything, then stood chatting with the cigarette-smoking white man next to her, whose fat hairy wrist, like a large worm, was all Imani could bear to see out of the corner of her eye.

Her first abortion, when she was still in college, she frequently remembered as wonderful, bearing as it had all the marks of a supreme coming of age and a seizing of the direction of her own life, as well as a comprehension of existence that never left her: that life—what one saw about one and called Life—was not a facade. There was nothing behind it which used "Life" as its manifestation. Life was itself. Period. At the time, and afterward, and even now, this seemed a marvelous thing to know.

The abortionist had been a delightful Italian doctor on the Upper East Side in New York, and before he put her under he told her about his own daughter who was just her age, and a junior at Vassar. He babbled on and on until she was out, but not before Imani had thought how her thousand dollars, for which she would be in debt for years, would go to keep her there.

When she woke up it was all over. She lay on a brown Naugahyde sofa in the doctor's outer office. And she heard, over her somewhere in the air, the sound of a woman's voice. It was a Saturday, no nurses in attendance, and she presumed it was the doctor's wife. She was pulled gently to her feet by this voice and encouraged to walk.

"And when you leave, be sure to walk as if nothing is wrong," the voice said.

Imani did not feel any pain. This surprised her. Perhaps he didn't do anything, she thought. Perhaps he took my thousand dollars and put me to sleep with two dollars' worth of ether. Perhaps this is a racket.

But he was so kind, and he was smiling benignly, almost fatherly, at her (and Imani realized how desperately she needed this "fatherly" look, this "fatherly" smile). "Thank you," she murmured sincerely: she was thanking him for her life.

Some of Italy was still in his voice. "It's nothing, nothing," he said. "A nice, pretty girl like you; in school like my own daughter, you didn't need this trouble."

"He's nice," she said to herself, walking to the subway on her way back to school. She lay down gingerly across a vacant seat and passed out.

She hemorrhaged steadily for six weeks, and was not well again for a year.

But this was seven years later. An abortion law now made it possible to make an appointment at a clinic, and for seventy-five dollars a safe, quick, painless abortion was yours.

Imani had once lived in New York, in the Village, not five blocks from where the abortion clinic was. It was also near the Margaret Sanger clinic, where she had received her very first diaphragm, with utter gratitude and amazement that someone apparently understood and actually cared about young women as alone and ignorant as she. In fact, as she walked up the block, with its modern office buildings side by side with older, more elegant brownstones, she felt how close she was still to that earlier self. Still not in control of her sensuality, and only through violence and with money (for the flight, for the operation itself) in control of her body.

She found that abortion had entered the age of the assembly line. Grateful for the lack of distinction between herself and the other women—all colors, ages, states of misery or nervousness—she was less happy to notice, once the doctor started to insert the catheter, that the anesthesia she had been given was insufficient. But assembly lines don't stop because the product on them has a complaint. Her doctor whistled, and assured her she was all right, and carried the procedure through to the horrific end. Imani fainted some seconds before that.

They laid her out in a peaceful room full of cheerful colors. Primary colors: yellow, red, blue. When she revived, she had the feeling of being in a nursery. She had a pressing need to urinate.

A nurse, kindly, white-haired, and with firm hands, helped her to the toilet. Imani saw herself in the mirror over the sink and was alarmed. She was literally gray, as if all her blood had leaked out.

"Don't worry about how you look," said the nurse. "Rest a bit here and take it easy when you get back home. You'll be fine in a week or so."

She could not imagine being fine again. Somewhere her child—she never dodged into the language of "fetuses" and "amorphous growths"—was being flushed down a sewer. Gone all her or his chances to see the sunlight, savor a fig.

"Well," she said to this child, "it was you or me, kiddo, and I chose me."

There were people who thought she had no right to choose herself, but Imani knew better than to think of those people now.

It was a bright, hot Saturday when she returned.

Clarence and Clarice picked her up at the airport. They had brought flowers from Imani's garden, and Clarice presented them with a stout-hearted hug. Once in her mother's lap she rested content all the way home, sucking her thumb, stroking her nose with the forefinger of the same hand, and kneading a corner of her blanket with the three fingers that were left.

"How did it go?" asked Clarence.

"It went," said Imani.

There was no way to explain abortion to a man. She thought castration might be an apt analogy, but most men, perhaps all, would insist this could not possibly be true.

"The anesthesia failed," she said. "I thought I'd never faint in time to keep from screaming and leaping off the table."

Clarence paled. He hated the thought of pain, any kind of violence. He could not endure it; it made him physically ill. This was one of the reasons he was a pacifist, another reason she admired him.

She knew he wanted her to stop talking. But she continued in a flat, deliberate voice.

"All the blood seemed to run out of me. The tendons in my legs felt cut. I was gray."

He reached for her hand. Held it. Squeezed.

"But," she said, "at least I know what I don't want. And I intend never to go through any of this again."

They were in the living room of their peaceful, quiet, and colorful house. Imani was in her rocker, Clarice dozing on her lap. Clarence sank to the floor and rested his head against her knees. She felt he was asking for nurture when she needed it herself. She felt the two of them, Clarence and Clarice, clinging to her, using her. And that the only way she could claim herself, feel herself distinct from them, was by doing something painful, self-defining, but self-destructive.

She suffered the pressure of his head as long as she could.

"Have a vasectomy," she said, "or stay in the guest room. Nothing is going to touch me anymore that isn't harmless."

He smoothed her thick hair with his hand. "We'll talk about it," he said, as if that was not what they were doing. "We'll see. Don't worry. We'll take care of things."

She had forgotten that the third Sunday in June, the following day, was the fifth memorial observance for Holly Monroe, who had been shot down on her way home from her high school graduation ceremony five years before. Imani *always* went to these memorials. She liked the reassurance that her people had long memories, and that those people who fell in struggle or innocence were not forgotten. She was, of course, too weak to go. She was dizzy and still losing blood. The white lawgivers attempted to get around assassination—which Imani considered extreme abortion—by saying the victim provoked it (there had been some difficulty saying this about Holly Monroe, but they had tried) but were antiabortionist to a man. Imani thought of this as she resolutely showered and washed her hair.

Clarence had installed central air-conditioning their second year in the house. Imani had at first objected. "I want to smell the trees, the flowers, the natural air!" she cried. But the first summer of 110-degree heat had cured her of giving a damn about any of that. Now she wanted to be cool. As much as she loved trees, on a hot day she would have sawed through a forest to get to an air conditioner.

In fairness to him, she had to admit he asked her if she thought she was well enough to go. But even to be asked annoyed her. She was not one to let her own troubles prevent her from showing proper respect and remembrance toward the dead, although she understood perfectly well that once dead, the dead do not exist. So respect, remembrance was for herself, and today herself needed rest. There was something mad about her refusal to rest, and she felt it as she tottered about getting Clarice dressed. But she did not stop. She ran a bath, plopped the child in it, scrubbed her plump body on her knees, arms straining over the tub awkwardly in a way that made her stomach hurt—but not yet her uterus—dried her hair, lifted her out and dried the rest of her on the kitchen table.

"You are going to remember as long as you live what kind of people they are," she said to the child, who, gurgling and cooing, looked into her mother's stern face with lighthearted fixation.

"You are going to hear the music," Imani said. "The music they've tried to kill. The music they try to steal." She felt feverish and was aware she was muttering. She didn't care.

"They think they can kill a continent—people, trees, buffalo—and then fly off to the moon and just forget about it. But you and me, we're going to remember the people, the trees, and the fucking buffalo. Goddammit."

"Buffwoe," said the child, hitting at her mother's face with a spoon.

She placed the baby on a blanket in the living room and turned to see her husband's eyes, full of pity, on her. She wore pert green velvet slippers and a lovely sea-green robe. Her body was bent within it. A reluctant tear formed beneath his gaze.

"Sometimes I look at you and I wonder 'What is this man doing in my house?' "

This had started as a joke between them. Her aim had been never to marry, but to take in lovers who could be sent home at dawn, freeing her to work and ramble.

"I'm here because you love me," was the traditional answer. But Clarence faltered, meeting her eyes, and Imani turned away.

It was a hundred degrees by ten o'clock. By eleven, when the memorial service began, it would be ten degrees hotter. Imani staggered from the heat. When she sat in the car she had to clench her teeth against the dizziness until the motor prodded the air-conditioning to envelop them in coolness. A dull ache started in her uterus.

The church was not, of course, air conditioned. It was authentic Primitive Baptist in every sense.

Like the four previous memorials, this one was designed by Holly Monroe's classmates. All twenty-five of whom—fat and thin—managed to look like the dead girl. Imani had never seen Holly Monroe, though there were always photographs of her dominating the pulpit of this church where she had been baptized and where she had sung in the choir—and to her, every black girl of a certain vulnerable age *was* Holly Monroe. And an even deeper truth was that Holly Monroe was herself. Herself shot down, aborted on the eve of becoming herself.

She was prepared to cry and to do so with abandon. But she did not. She clenched her teeth against the steadily increasing pain, and her tears were instantly blotted by the heat.

Mayor Carswell had been waiting for Clarence in the vestibule of the church, mopping his plumply jowled face with a voluminous handkerchief and holding court among half a dozen young men and women who listened to him with awe. Imani exchanged greetings with the mayor, he ritualistically kissed her on the cheek, and kissed Clarice on the cheek, but his rather heat-glazed eye was already fastened on her husband. The two men huddled in a corner away from the awed young group. Away from Imani and Clarice, who passed hesitantly, waiting to be joined or to be called back, into the church.

There was a quarter hour's worth of music.

"Holly Monroe was five feet, three inches tall, and weighed one hundred and eleven pounds," her best friend said, not reading from notes, but talking to each person in the audience. "She was a stubborn, loyal Aries, the best kind of friend to have. She had black kinky hair that she experimented with a lot. She was exactly the color of this oak church pew in the summer; in the winter she was the color [pointing up] of this heart pine ceiling. She loved green. She did not like lavender because she said she also didn't like pink. She had brown eyes and wore glasses, except when she was meeting someone for the first time. She had a sort of rounded nose. She had beautiful large teeth, but her lips were always chapped so she didn't smile as much as she might have if she'd ever gotten used to carrying Chap Stick. She had elegant feet.

"Her favorite church song was 'Leaning on the Everlasting Arms.' Her favorite other kind of song was 'I Can't Help Myself—I Love You and Nobody Else.' She was often late for choir rehearsal though she loved to sing. She made the dress she wore to her graduation in Home Ec. She *hated* Home Ec. . . ."

Imani was aware that the sound of low, murmurous voices had been the background for this statement all along. Everything was quiet around her, even Clarice sat up straight, absorbed by the simple friendliness of the young woman's voice. All of Holly Monroe's classmates and friends in the choir wore vivid green. Imani imagined Clarice entranced by the brilliant, swaying color as by a field of swaying corn.

Lifting the child, her uterus burning, and perspiration already a stream down her back, Imani tiptoed to the door, Clarence and the mayor were still deep in conversation. She heard "board meeting . . . aldermen . . . city council." She beckoned to Clarence.

"Your voices are carrying!" she hissed.

She meant: How dare you not come inside.

They did not. Clarence raised his head, looked at her, and shrugged his shoulders helplessly. Then, turning, with the abstracted air of priests, the two men moved slowly toward the outer door, and into the churchyard, coming to stand some distance from the church beneath a large oak tree. There they remained throughout the service.

Two years later, Clarence was furious with her: What is the matter with you? he asked. You never want me to touch you. You told me to sleep in the guest room and I did. You told me to have a vasectomy I didn't want and I *did*. (Here, there was a sob of hatred for her somewhere in the anger, the humiliation: he thought of himself as a eunuch, and blamed her.)

She was not merely frigid, she was remote.

She had been amazed after they left the church that the anger she'd felt watching Clarence and the mayor turn away from the Holly Monroe memorial did not prevent her accepting a ride home with him. A month later it did not prevent her smiling on him fondly. Did not prevent a trip to Bermuda, a few blissful days of very good sex on a deserted beach screened by trees. Did not prevent her listening to his mother's stories of Clarence's youth as though she would treasure them forever.

And yet. From that moment in the heat at the church door, she had uncoupled herself from him, in a separation that made him, except occasionally, little more than a stranger.

And he had not felt it, had not known.

"What have I done?" he asked, all the tenderness in his voice breaking over her. She smiled a nervous smile at him, which he interpreted as derision—so far apart had they drifted.

They had discussed the episode at the church many times. Mayor Carswell—whom they never saw anymore—was now a model mayor, with wide biracial support in his campaign for the legislature. Neither could easily recall him, though television frequently brought him into the house.

"It was so important that I help the mayor!" said Clarence. "He was our *first!*"

Imani understood this perfectly well, but it sounded humorous to her. When she smiled, he was offended.

She had known the moment she left the marriage, the exact second. But apparently that moment had left no perceptible mark.

They argued, she smiled, they scowled, blamed and cried—as she packed.

Each of them almost recalled out loud that about this time of the year their aborted child would have been a troublesome, "terrible" two-year-old, a great burden on its mother, whose health was by now in excellent shape, each wanted to think aloud that the marriage would have deteriorated anyway, because of that.

Richard Ford

Richard Ford (b. 1944) was born in Jackson, Mississippi. His father was a traveling salesman, and his family was in the hotel business, and Ford early got a taste of transience. He tried his hand at many occupations before he turned to writing. He explained his decision thus in an interview: "One day, my mother asked me what I was going to do and I said, 'I'm going to try to be a writer.' I could as easily have said I wanted to be a chiropractor, but, at that moment, something about being a writer felt like 'turning towards some kind of light,' as my friend Donald Hall wrote not long ago in an essay about James Wright. As soon as I said it, I could feel a door open, and there was a light behind the door, and I walked through."

Ford has written four novels, including *The Sportswriter,* and a collection of stories, *Rock Springs*. He writes with sensitivity and uneasy restraint about males, often in late adolescence, working their way through significant emotional recognitions. His feeling for American settings, especially rough and rural places, is exceptionally keen.

COMMUNIST

My mother once had a boyfriend named Glen Baxter. This was in 1961. We—my mother and I—were living in the little house my father had left her up the Sun River, near Victory, Montana, west of Great Falls. My mother was thirty-one at the time. I was sixteen. Glen Baxter was somewhere in the middle, between us, though I cannot be exact about it.

We were living then off the proceeds of my father's life insurance policies, with my mother doing some part-time waitressing work up in Great Falls and going to the bars in the evenings, which I know is where she met Glen Baxter. Sometimes he would come back with her and stay in her room at night, or she would call up from town and explain that she was staying with him in his little place on Lewis Street by the GN yards. She gave me his number every time, but I never called it. I think she probably thought that what she was doing was terrible, but simply couldn't help herself. I thought it was all right, though. Regular life it seemed and still does. She was young, and I knew that even then.

Glen Baxter was a Communist and liked hunting, which he talked about a lot. Pheasants. Ducks. Deer. He killed all of them, he said. He had been to Vietnam as far back as then, and when he was in our house he often talked about shooting the animals over there—monkeys and beautiful parrots—using military guns just for sport. We did not know what Vietnam was then, and Glen, when he talked about that, referred to it only as "the far east." I think now he must've been in the CIA and been disillusioned by something he saw or found out about and had been thrown out, but that kind of thing did not matter to us. He was a tall, dark-eyed man with thick black hair, and was usually in a good humor. He had gone halfway through college in Peoria, Illinois, he said, where he grew up. But when he was around our life he worked wheat farms as a ditcher, and stayed out of work winters and in the bars drinking with women like my mother, who had work and some money. It is not an uncommon life to lead in Montana.

What I want to explain happened in November. We had not been seeing Glen Baxter for some time. Two months had gone by. My mother knew other men, but she came home most days from work and stayed inside watching television in her bedroom and drinking beers. I asked about Glen once, and she said only that she didn't know where he was, and I assumed they had had a fight and that he was gone off on a flyer back to Illinois or Massachusetts, where he said he had relatives. I'll admit that I liked him. He had something on his mind always. He was a labor man as well as a Communist, and liked to say that the country was poisoned by the rich, and strong men would need to bring it to life again, and I liked that because my father had been a labor man, which was why we had a house to live in and money coming through. It was also true that I'd had a few boxing bouts by then—just with town boys and one with an Indian from Choteau—and there were some girlfriends I knew from that. I did not like my mother being around the house so much at night, and I wished Glen Baxter would come back, or that another man would come along and entertain her somewhere else.

At two o'clock on a Saturday, Glen drove up into our yard in a car. He had had a big brown Harley-Davidson that he rode most of the year, in his black-and-red irrigators and a baseball cap turned backwards. But this time he had a car, a blue Nash Ambassador. My mother and I went out on the porch when he stopped inside the olive trees my father had planted as a shelter belt, and my mother had a look on her face of not much pleasure. It was starting to be cold in earnest by then. Snow was down already onto the Fairfield Bench, though on this day a chinook was blowing, and it could as easily have been spring, though the sky above the Divide was turning over in silver and blue clouds of winter.

"We haven't seen you in a long time, I guess," my mother said coldly.

"My little retarded sister died," Glen said, standing at the door of his old car. He was wearing his orange VFW jacket and canvas shoes we called wino shoes, something I had never seen him wear before. He seemed to be in a good humor. "We buried her in Florida near the home."

"That's a good place," my mother said in a voice that meant she was a wronged party in something.

"I want to take this boy hunting today, Aileen," Glen said. "There's snow geese down now. But we have to go right away or they'll be gone to Idaho by tomorrow."

"He doesn't care to go," my mother said.

"Yes I do," I said and looked at her.

My mother frowned at me. "Why do you?"

"Why does he need a reason?" Glen Baxter said and grinned.

"I want him to have one, that's why." She looked at me oddly. "I think Glen's drunk, Les."

"No, I'm not drinking," Glen said, which was hardly ever true. He looked at both of us, and my mother bit down on the side of her lower lip and stared at me in a way to make you think she thought something was being put over on her and she didn't like you for it. She was very pretty, though when she was mad her features were sharpened and less pretty by a long way. "All right then, I don't care," she said to no one in particular. "Hunt, kill, maim. Your father did that too." She turned to go back inside.

"Why don't you come with us, Aileen?" Glen was smiling still, pleased.

"To do what?" my mother said. She stopped and pulled a package of cigarettes out of her dress pocket and put one in her mouth.

"It's worth seeing."

"See dead animals?" my mother said.

"These geese are from Siberia, Aileen," Glen said. "They're not like a lot of geese. Maybe I'll buy us dinner later. What do you say?"

"Buy what with?" my mother said. To tell the truth, I didn't know why she was so mad at him. I would've thought she'd be glad to see him. But she just suddenly seemed to hate everything about him.

"I've got some money," Glen said. "Let me spend it on a pretty girl tonight."

"Find one of those and you're lucky," my mother said, turning away toward the front door.

"I already found one," Glen Baxter said. But the door slammed behind her, and he looked at me then with a look I think now was helplessness, though I could not see a way to change anything.

My mother sat in the back seat of Glen's Nash and looked out the window while we drove. My double gun was in the seat between us beside Glen's Belgian pump, which he kept loaded with five shells in case, he said, he saw something beside the road he wanted to shoot. I had hunted rabbits before, and had ground-sluiced pheasants and other birds, but I had never been on an actual hunt before, one where you drove out to some special place and did it formally. And I was excited. I had a feeling that something important was about to happen to me and that this would be a day I would always remember.

My mother did not say anything for a long time, and neither did I. We drove up through Great Falls and out the other side toward Fort Benton, which was on the benchland where wheat was grown.

"Geese mate for life," my mother said, just out of the blue, as we were driving. "I hope you know that. They're special birds."

"I know that," Glen said in the front seat. "I have every respect for them."

"So where were you for three months?" she said. "I'm only curious."

"I was in the Big Hole for a while," Glen said, "and after that I went over to Douglas, Wyoming."

"What were you planning to do there?" my mother asked.

"I wanted to find a job, but it didn't work out."

"I'm going to college," she said suddenly, and this was something I had never heard about before. I turned to look at her, but she was staring out her window and wouldn't see me.

"I knew French once," Glen said. "Rose's pink. Rouge's red." He glanced at me and smiled. "I think that's a wise idea, Aileen. When are you going to start?"

"I don't want Les to think he was raised by crazy people all his life," my mother said.

"Les ought to go himself," Glen said.

"After I go, he will."

"What do you say about that, Les?" Glen said, grinning.

"He says it's just fine," my mother said.

"It's just fine," I said.

Where Glen Baxter took us was out onto the high flat prairie that was disked for wheat and had high, high mountains out to the east, with lower heartbreak hills in between. It was, I remember, a day for blues in the sky, and down in the distance we could see the small town of Floweree and the state highway running past it toward Fort Benton and the high line. We drove out on top of the prairie on a muddy dirt road fenced on both sides, until we had gone about three miles, which is where Glen stopped.

"All right," he said, looking up in the rearview mirror at my mother. "You wouldn't think there was anything here, would you?"

"*We're* here," my mother said. "You brought us here."

"You'll be glad though," Glen said, and seemed confident to me. I had looked around myself but could not see anything. No water or trees, nothing that seemed like a good place to hunt anything. Just wasted land. "There's a big lake out there, Les," Glen said. "You can't see it now from here because it's low. But the geese are there. You'll see."

"It's like the moon out here, I recognize that," my mother said, "only it's worse." She was staring out at the flat, disked wheatland as if she could actually see something in particular and wanted to know more about it. "How'd you find this place?"

"I came once on the wheat push," Glen said.

"And I'm sure the owner told you just to come back and hunt any time you like and bring anybody you wanted. Come one, come all. Is that it?"

"People shouldn't own land anyway," Glen said. "Anybody should be able to use it."

"Les, Glen's going to poach here," my mother said. "I just want you to know that, because that's a crime and the law will get you for it. If you're a man now, you're going to have to face the consequences."

"That's not true," Glen Baxter said, and looked gloomily out over the steering wheel down the muddy road toward the mountains. Though for myself I believed it was true, and didn't care. I didn't care about anything at that moment except seeing geese fly over me and shooting them down.

"Well, I'm certainly not going out there," my mother said. "I like towns better, and I already have enough trouble."

"That's okay," Glen said. "When the geese lift up you'll get to see them. That's all I wanted. Les and me'll go shoot them, won't we, Les?"

"Yes," I said, and I put my hand on my shotgun, which had been my father's and was heavy as rocks.

"Then we should go on," Glen said, "or we'll waste our light."

We got out of the car with our guns. Glen took off his canvas shoes and put on his pair of black irrigators out of the trunk. Then we crossed the barbed-wire fence and walked out into the high, tilled field toward nothing. I looked back at my mother when we were still not so far away, but I could only see the small, dark top of her head, low in the back seat of the Nash, staring out and thinking what I could not then begin to say.

On the walk toward the lake, Glen began talking to me. I had never been alone with him and knew little about him except what my mother said—that he drank too much, or other times that he was the nicest man she had ever known in the world and that some day a woman would marry him, though she didn't think it would be her. Glen told me as we walked that he wished he had finished college, but that it was too late now, that his mind was too old. He said he had liked "the far east" very much, and that people there knew how to treat each other, and that he would go back some day but couldn't go now. He said also that he would like to live in Russia for a while and mentioned the names of people who had gone there, names I didn't know. He said it would be hard at first, because it was so different, but that pretty soon anyone would learn to like it and wouldn't want to live anywhere else, and that Russians treated Americans who came to live there like kings. There were Communists everywhere now, he said. You didn't know them, but they were there. Montana had a large number, and he was in touch with all of them. He said that Communists were always in danger and that he had to protect himself all the time. And when he said that he pulled back his VFW jacket and showed me the butt of a pistol he had stuck under his shirt against his bare skin. "There are people who want to kill me right now," he said, "and I would kill a man myself if I thought I had to." And we kept walking. Though in a while he said, "I don't think I know much about you, Les. But I'd like to. What do you like to do?"

"I like to box," I said. "My father did it. It's a good thing to know."

"I suppose you have to protect yourself too," Glen said.

"I know how to," I said.

"Do you like to watch TV?" Glen said, and smiled.

"Not much."

"I love to," Glen said. "I could watch it instead of eating if I had one."

I looked out straight ahead over the green tops of sage that grew at the edge of the disked field, hoping to see the lake Glen said was there. There was an airishness and a sweet smell that I thought might be the place we were going, but I couldn't see it. "How will we hunt these geese?" I said.

"It won't be hard," Glen said. "Most hunting isn't even hunting. It's only shooting. And that's what this will be. In Illinois you would dig holes in the ground to hide in and set out your decoys. Then the geese come to you, over and over again. But we don't have time for that here." He glanced at me. "You have to be sure the first time here."

"How do you know they're here now?" I asked. And I looked toward the Highwood Mountains twenty miles away, half in snow and half dark blue at the bottom. I could see the little town of Floweree then, looking shabby and dimly lighted in the distance. A red bar sign shone. A car moved slowly away from the scattered buildings.

"They always come November first," Glen said.

"Are we going to poach them?"

"Does it make any difference to you?" Glen asked.

"No, it doesn't."

"Well then we aren't," he said.

We walked then for a while without talking. I looked back once to see the Nash far and small in the flat distance. I couldn't see my mother, and I thought that she must've turned on the radio and gone to sleep, which she always did, letting it play all night in her bedroom. Behind the car the sun was nearing the rounded mountains southwest of us, and I knew that when the sun was gone it would be cold. I wished my mother had decided to come along with us, and I thought for a moment of how little I really knew her at all.

Glen walked with me another quarter mile, crossed another barbed-wire fence where sage was growing, then went a hundred yards through wheatgrass and spurge until the ground went up and formed a kind of long hillock bunker built by a farmer against the wind. And I realized the lake was just beyond us. I could hear the sound of a car horn blowing and a dog barking all the way down in the town, then the wind seemed to move and all I could hear then and after then were geese. So many geese, from the sound of them, though I still could not see even one. I stood and listened to the high-pitched shouting sound, a sound I had never heard so close, a sound with size to it—though it was not loud. A sound that meant great numbers and that made your chest rise and your shoulders tighten with expectancy. It was a sound to make you feel separate from it and everything else, as if you were of no importance in the grand scheme of things.

"Do you hear them singing?" Glen asked. He held his hand up to make me stand still. And we both listened. "How many do you think, Les, just hearing?"

"A hundred," I said. "More than a hundred."

"Five thousand," Glen said. "More than you can believe when you see them. Go see."

I put down my gun and on my hands and knees crawled up the earthwork through the wheatgrass and thistle until I could see down to the lake and see the geese. And they were there, like a white bandage laid on the water, wide and long and continuous, a white expanse of snow geese, seventy yards from me, on the bank, but stretching onto the lake, which was large itself—a half mile across, with thick tules on the far side and wild plums farther and the blue mountain behind them.

"Do you see the big raft?" Glen said from below me, in a whisper.

"I see it," I said, still looking. It was such a thing to see, a view I had never seen and have not since.

"Are any on the land?" he said.

"Some are in the wheatgrass," I said, "but most are swimming."

"Good," Glen said. "They'll have to fly. But we can't wait for that now."

And I crawled backwards down the heel of land to where Glen was, and my gun. We were losing our light, and the air was purplish and cooling. I looked toward the car but couldn't see it, and I was no longer sure where it was below the lighted sky.

"Where do they fly to?" I said in a whisper, since I did not want anything to be ruined because of what I did or said. It was important to Glen to shoot the geese, and it was important to me.

"To the wheat," he said. "Or else they leave for good. I wish your mother had come, Les. Now she'll be sorry."

I could hear the geese quarreling and shouting on the lake surface. And I wondered if they knew we were here now. "She might be," I said with my heart pounding, but I didn't think she would be much.

It was a simple plan he had. I would stay behind the bunker, and he would crawl on his belly with his gun through the wheatgrass as near to the geese as he could. Then he would simply stand up and shoot all the ones he could close up, both in the air and on the ground. And when all the others flew up, with luck some would turn toward me as they came into the wind, and then I could shoot them and turn them back to him, and he would shoot them again. He could kill ten, he said, if he was lucky, and I might kill four. It didn't seem hard.

"Don't show them your face," Glen said. "Wait till you think you can touch them, then stand up and shoot. To hesitate is lost in this."

"All right," I said. "I'll try it."

"Shoot one in the head, and then shoot another one," Glen said. "It won't be hard." He patted me on the arm and smiled. Then he took off his VFW jacket and put it on the ground, climbed up the side of the bunker, cradling his shotgun in his arms, and slid on his belly into the dry stalks of yellow grass out of my sight.

Then for the first time in that entire day I was alone. And I didn't mind it. I sat squat down in the grass, loaded my double gun, and took my other two shells out of my pocket to hold. I pushed the safety off and on to see that it was right. The wind rose a little then, scuffed the grass and made me shiver. It was not the warm chinook now, but a wind out of the north, the one geese flew away from if they could.

Then I thought about my mother in the car alone, and how much longer I would stay with her, and what it might mean to her for me to leave. And I wondered when Glen Baxter would die and if someone would kill him, or whether my mother would marry him and how I would feel about it. And though I didn't know why, it occurred to me then that Glen Baxter and I would not be friends when all was said and done, since I didn't care if he ever married my mother or didn't.

Then I thought about boxing and what my father had taught me about it. To tighten your fists hard. To strike out straight from the shoulder and never punch backing up. How to cut a punch by snapping your fist inwards, how to carry your chin low, and to step toward a man when he is falling so you can hit him again. And most important, to keep your eyes open when you are hitting in the face and causing damage, because you need to see what you're doing to encourage yourself, and because it is when you close your eyes that you stop hitting and get hurt badly. "Fly all over your man, Les," my father said. "When you see your chance, fly on him and hit him till he falls." That, I thought, would always be my attitude in things.

And then I heard the geese again, their voices in unison, louder and shouting, as if the wind had changed and put all new sounds in the cold air. And then a *boom*. And I knew Glen was in among them and had stood up to shoot. The noise of geese rose and grew worse, and my fingers burned where I held my gun too tight to the metal, and I put it down and opened my fist to make the burning stop so I could feel the trigger when the moment came. *Boom*, Glen shot again, and I heard him shuck a shell, and all the sounds out beyond the bunker seemed to be rising—the geese, the shots, the air itself going up. *Boom*, Glen shot another time, and I knew he was taking his careful time to make his shots good. And I held my gun and started to crawl up the bunker so as not to be surprised when the geese came over me and I could shoot.

From the top I saw Glen Baxter alone in the wheatgrass field, shooting at a white goose with black tips of wings that was on the ground not far from him, but trying to run and pull into the air. He shot it once more, and it fell over dead with its wings flapping.

Glen looked back at me and his face was distorted and strange. The air around him was full of white rising geese and he seemed to want them all. "Behind you, Les," he yelled at me and pointed. "They're all behind you now." I looked behind me, and there were geese in the air as far as I could see, more than I knew how many, moving so slowly, their wings wide out and working calmly and filling the air with noise, though their voices were not as loud or as shrill as I had thought they would be. And they were so close! Forty feet, some of them. The air around me vibrated and I could feel the wind from their wings and it seemed to me I could kill as many as the times I could shoot—a hundred or a thousand—and I raised my gun, put the muzzle on the head of a white goose and fired. It shuddered in the air, its wide feet sank below its belly, its wings cradled out to hold back air, and it fell straight down and landed with an awful sound, a noise a human would make, a thick, soft, *hump* noise. I looked up again and shot another goose, could hear the pellets hit its chest, but it didn't fall or even break its pattern for flying. *Boom*, Glen shot again. And then again. "Hey," I heard him shout. "Hey, hey." And there were geese flying over me, flying in line after line. I broke my gun and reloaded, and thought to myself as I did: I need confidence here, I need to be sure with this. I pointed at another goose and shot it in the head, and it fell the way the first one had, wings out, its belly down, and with the same thick noise of hitting. Then I sat down in the grass on the bunker and let geese fly over me.

By now the whole raft was in the air, all of it moving in a slow swirl above me and the lake and everywhere, finding the wind and heading out south in long wavering lines that caught the last sun and turned to silver as they gained a distance. It was a thing to see, I will tell you now. Five thousand white geese all in the air around you, making a noise like you have never heard before. And I thought to myself then: This is something I will never see again. I will never forget this. And I was right.

Glen Baxter shot twice more. One shot missed, but with the other he hit a goose flying away from him and knocked it half-falling and flying into the empty lake not far from shore, where it began to swim as though it was fine and make its noise.

Glen stood in the stubbly grass, looking out at the goose, his gun lowered. "I didn't need to shoot that, did I, Les?"

"I don't know," I said, sitting on the little knoll of land, looking at the goose swimming in the water.

"I don't know why I shoot 'em. They're so beautiful." He looked at me.

"I don't know either," I said.

"Maybe there's nothing else to do with them." Glen stared at the goose again and shook his head. "Maybe this is exactly what they're put on earth for."

I did not know what to say because I did not know what he could mean by that, though what I felt was embarrassment at the great number of geese there were, and a dulled feeling like a hunger because the shooting had stopped and it was over for me now.

Glen began to pick up his geese, and I walked down to my two that had fallen close together and were dead. One had hit with such an impact that its stomach had split and some of its inward parts were knocked out. Though the other looked unhurt, its soft white belly turned up like a pillow, its head and jagged bill-teeth and its tiny black eyes looking as if it were alive.

"What's happened to the hunters out here?" I heard a voice speak. It was my mother, standing in her pink dress on the knoll above us, hugging her arms. She was smiling though she was cold. And I realized that I had lost all thought of her in the shooting. "Who did all this shooting? Is this your work, Les?"

"No," I said.

"Les is a hunter, though, Aileen," Glen said. "He takes his time." He was holding two white geese by their necks, one in each hand, and he was smiling. He and my mother seemed pleased.

"I see you didn't miss too many," my mother said and smiled. I could tell she admired Glen for his geese, and that she had done some thinking in the car alone. "It *was* wonderful, Glen," she said. "I've never seen anything like that.They were like snow."

"It's worth seeing once, isn't it?" Glen said. "I should've killed more, but I got excited."

My mother looked at me then. "Where's yours, Les?"

"Here," I said and pointed to my two geese on the ground beside me.

My mother nodded in a nice way, and I think she liked everything then and wanted the day to turn out right and for all of us to be happy. "Six, then. You've got six in all."

"One's still out there," I said and motioned where the one goose was swimming in circles on the water.

"Okay," my mother said and put her hand over her eyes to look. "Where is it?"

Glen Baxter looked at me then with a strange smile, a smile that said he wished I had never mentioned anything about the other goose. And I wished I hadn't either. I looked up in the sky and could see the lines of geese by the thousands shining silver in the light, and I wished we could just leave and go home.

"That one's my mistake there," Glen Baxter said and grinned. "I shouldn't have shot that one, Aileen. I got too excited."

My mother looked out on the lake for a minute, then looked at Glen and back again. "Poor goose." She shook her head. "How will you get it, Glen?"

"I can't get that one now," Glen said.

My mother looked at him. "What do you mean?" she said.

"I'm going to leave that one," Glen said.

"Well, no. You can't leave one," my mother said. "You shot it. You have to get it. Isn't that a rule?"

"No," Glen said.

And my mother looked from Glen to me. "Wade out and get it, Glen," she said, in a sweet way, and my mother looked young then for some reason, like a young girl, in her flimsy short-sleeved waitress dress, and her skinny, bare legs in the wheatgrass.

"No." Glen Baxter looked down at his gun and shook his head. And I didn't know why he wouldn't go, because it would've been easy. The lake was shallow. And you could tell that anyone could've walked out a long way before it got deep, and Glen had on his boots.

My mother looked at the white goose, which was not more than thirty yards from the shore, its head up, moving in slow circles, its wings settled and relaxed so you could see the black tips. "Wade out and get it, Glenny, won't you please?" she said. "They're special things."

"You don't understand the world, Aileen," Glen said. "This can happen. It doesn't matter."

"But that's so cruel, Glen," she said, and a sweet smile came on her lips.

"Raise up your own arms, Leeny," Glen said. "I can't see any angel's wings, can you Les?" He looked at me, but I looked away.

"Then you go on and get it, Les," my mother said. "You weren't raised by crazy people." I started to go, but Glen Baxter suddenly grabbed me by my shoulder and pulled me back hard, so hard his fingers made bruises in my skin that I saw later.

"Nobody's going," he said. "This is over with now."

And my mother gave Glen a cold look then. "You don't have a heart, Glen," she said. "There's nothing to love in you. You're just a son of a bitch, that's all."

And Glen Baxter nodded at my mother as if he understood something that he had not understood before, but something that he was willing to know. "Fine," he said, "that's fine." And he took his big pistol out from against his belly, the big blue revolver I had only seen part of before and that he said protected him, and he pointed it out at the goose on the water, his arm straight away from him, and shot and missed. And then he shot and missed again. The goose made its noise once. And then he hit it dead, because there was no splash. And then he shot it three times more until the gun was empty and the goose's head was down and it was floating toward the middle of the lake where it was empty and dark blue. "Now who has a heart?" Glen said. But my mother was not there when he turned around. She had already started back to the car and was almost lost from sight in the darkness. And Glen smiled at me then and his face had a wild look on it. "Okay, Les?" he said.

"Okay," I said.

"There're limits to everything, right?"

"I guess so," I said.

"Your mother's a beautiful woman, but she's not the only beautiful woman in Montana." I did not say anything. And Glen Baxter suddenly said, "Here," and he held the pistol out at me. "Don't you want this? Don't you want to shoot me? Nobody thinks they'll die. But I'm ready for it right now." And I did not know what to do then. Though it is true that what I wanted to do was to hit him, hit him as hard in the face as I could, and see him on the ground bleeding and crying and pleading for me to stop. Only at that moment he looked scared to me, and I had never seen a grown man scared before—though I have seen one since—and I felt sorry for him, as though he was already a dead man. And I did not end up hitting him at all.

A light can go out in the heart. All of this went on years ago, but I still can feel now how sad and remote the world was to me. Glen Baxter, I think now, was not a bad man, only a man scared of something he'd never seen before—something soft in himself—his life going a way he didn't like. A woman with a son. Who could blame him there? I don't know what makes people do what they do or call themselves what they call themselves, only that you have to live someone's life to be the expert.

My mother had tried to see the good side of things, tried to be hopeful in the situation she was handed, tried to look out for us both, and it hadn't worked. It was a strange time in her life then and after that, a time when she had to adjust to being an adult just when she was on the thin edge of things. Too much awareness too early in life was her problem, I think.

And what I felt was only that I had somehow been pushed out into the world, into the real life then, the one I hadn't lived yet. In a year I was gone to hardrock mining and no-paycheck jobs and not to college. And I have thought more than once about my mother saying that I had not been raised by crazy people, and I don't know what that could mean or what difference it could make, unless it means that love is a reliable commodity, and even that is not always true, as I have found out.

Late on the night that all this took place I was in bed when I heard my mother say, "Come outside, Les. Come and hear this." And I went out onto the front porch barefoot and in my underwear, where it was warm like spring, and there was a spring mist in the air. I could see the lights of the Fairfield Coach in the distance on its way up to Great Falls.

And I could hear geese, white birds in the sky, flying. They made their high-pitched sound like angry yells, and though I couldn't see them high up, it seemed to me they were everywhere. And my mother looked up and said, "Hear them?" I could smell her hair wet from the shower. "They leave with the moon," she said. "It's still half wild out here."

And I said, "I hear them," and I felt a chill come over my bare chest, and the hair stood up on my arms the way it does before a storm. And for a while we listened.

"When I first married your father, you know, we lived on a street called Bluebird Canyon, in California. And I thought that was the prettiest street and the prettiest name. I suppose no one brings you up like your first love. You don't mind if I say that, do you?" She looked at me hopefully.

"No," I said.

"We have to keep civilization alive somehow." And she pulled her little housecoat together because there was a cold vein in the air, a part of the cold that would be on us the next day. "I don't feel part of things tonight, I guess."

"It's all right," I said.

"Do you know where I'd like to go?" she said.

"No," I said. And I suppose I knew she was angry then, angry with life but did not want to show me that.

"To the Straits of Juan de Fuca. Wouldn't that be something? Would you like that?"

"I'd like it," I said. And my mother looked off for a minute, as if she could see the Straits of Juan de Fuca out against the line of mountains, see the lights of things alive and a whole new world.

"I know you liked him," she said after a moment. "You and I both suffer fools too well."

"I didn't like him too much," I said. "I didn't really care."

"He'll fall on his face. I'm sure of that," she said. And I didn't say anything because I didn't care about Glen Baxter anymore, and was happy not to talk about him. "Would you tell me something if I asked you? Would you tell me the truth?"

"Yes," I said.

And my mother did not look at me. "Just tell the truth," she said.

"All right," I said.

"Do you think I'm still very feminine? I'm thirty-two years old now. You don't know what that means. But do you think I am?"

And I stood at the edge of the porch, with the olive trees before me, looking straight up into the mist where I could not see geese but could still hear them flying, could almost feel the air move below their white wings. And I felt the way you feel when you are on a trestle all alone and the train is coming, and you know you have to decide. And I said, "Yes, I do." Because that was the truth. And I tried to think of something else then and did not hear what my mother said after that.

And how old was I then? Sixteen. Sixteen is young, but it can also be a grown man. I am forty-one years old now, and I think about that time without regret, though my mother and I never talked in that way again, and I have not heard her voice now in a long, long time.

Tim O'Brien

Tim O'Brien (b.1946) was born in Austin, Minnesota. He served as a sergeant in Vietnam, an experience that significantly affected his career as a writer. *If I Die in a Combat Zone,* a collection of anecdotes drawn from his period of service, was published in 1973 and earned him great acclaim. His novel *Going After Cacciato* (1978) established his place as the premier fictional chronicler of the Vietnam War. While comparisons to Ernest Hemingway and Joseph Heller are inevitable—O'Brien has been influenced by both—he has invested his stories and novels with an imaginative sensibility that is entirely his own. O'Brien's works include *The Nuclear Age,* a novel, and *The Things They Carried,* a Vietnam memoir.

THE THINGS THEY CARRIED

First Lieutenant Jimmy Cross carried letters from a girl named Martha, a junior at Mount Sebastian College in New Jersey. They were not love letters, but Lieutenant Cross was hoping, so he kept them folded in plastic at the bottom of his rucksack. In the late afternoon, after a day's march, he would dig his foxhole, wash his hands under a canteen, unwrap the letters, hold them with the tips of his fingers, and spend the last hour of light pretending. He would imagine romantic camping trips into the White Mountains in New Hampshire. He would sometimes taste the envelope flaps, knowing her tongue had been there. More than anything, he wanted Martha to love him as he loved her, but the letters were mostly chatty, elusive on the matter of love. She was a virgin, he was almost sure. She was an English major at Mount Sebastian, and she wrote beautifully about her professors and roommates and midterm exams, about her respect for Chaucer and her great affection for Virginia Woolf. She often quoted lines of poetry; she never mentioned the war, except to say, Jimmy, take care of yourself. The letters weighed 10 ounces. They were signed Love, Martha, but Lieutenant Cross understood that Love was only a way of signing and did not mean what he sometimes pretended it meant. At dusk, he would carefully return the letters to his rucksack. Slowly, a bit distracted, he would get up and move among his men, checking the perimeter, then at full dark he would return to his hole and watch the night and wonder if Martha was a virgin.

The things they carried were largely determined by necessity. Among the necessities or near-necessities were P-38 can openers, pocket knives, heat tabs, wristwatches, dog tags, mosquito repellent, chewing gum, candy, cigarettes, salt tablets, packets of Kool-Aid, lighters, matches, sewing kits, Military Payment Certificates, C rations, and two or three canteens of water. Together, these items weighed between 15 and 20 pounds, depending upon a man's habits or rate of metabolism. Henry Dobbins, who was a big man, carried extra rations; he was especially fond of canned peaches in heavy syrup over pound cake. Dave Jensen, who practiced field hygiene, carried a toothbrush, dental floss, and several hotel-sized bars of soap he'd stolen on R&R in Sydney, Australia. Ted Lavender, who was scared, carried tranquilizers until he was shot in the head outside the village of Than Khe in mid-April. By necessity, and because it was SOP, they all carried steel helmets that weighed 5 pounds including the liner and camouflage cover. They carried the standard fatigue jackets and trousers. Very few carried underwear. On their feet they carried jungle boots—2.1 pounds—and Dave Jensen carried three pairs of socks and a can of Dr. Scholl's foot powder as a precaution against trench foot. Until he was shot, Ted Lavender carried six or seven ounces of premium dope, which for him was a necessity. Mitchell Sanders, the RTO, carried condoms. Norman Bowker carried a diary. Rat Kiley carried comic books. Kiowa, a devout Baptist, carried an illustrated New Testament that had been presented to him by his father, who taught Sunday school in Oklahoma City, Oklahoma. As a hedge against bad times, however, Kiowa also carried his grandmother's distrust of the white man, his grandfather's old hunting hatchet. Necessity dictated. Because the land was mined and booby-trapped, it was SOP for each man to carry a steel-centered, nylon-covered flak jacket, which weighed 6.7 pounds, but which on hot days seemed much heavier. Because you could die so quickly, each man carried at least one large compress bandage, usually in the helmet band for easy access. Because the nights were cold, and because the monsoons were wet, each carried a green plastic poncho that could be used as a raincoat or groundsheet or makeshift tent. With its quilted liner, the poncho weighed almost two pounds, but it was worth every ounce. In April, for instance, when Ted Lavender was shot, they used his poncho to wrap him up, then to carry him across the paddy, then to lift him into the chopper that took him away.

They were called legs or grunts.

To carry something was to hump it, as when Lieutenant Jimmy Cross humped his love for Martha up the hills and through the swamps. In its intransitive form, to hump meant to walk, or to march, but it implied burdens far beyond the intransitive.

Almost everyone humped photographs. In his wallet, Lieutenant Cross carried two photographs of Martha. The first was a Kodacolor snapshot signed Love, though he knew better. She stood against a brick wall. Her eyes were gray and neutral, her lips slightly open as she stared straight-on at the camera. At night, sometimes, Lieutenant Cross wondered who had taken the picture, because he knew she had boyfriends, because he loved her so much, and because he could see the shadow of the picture-taker spreading out against the brick wall. The second photograph had been clipped from the 1968 Mount Sebastian yearbook. It was an action shot—women's volleyball—and Martha was bent horizontal to the floor, reaching, the palms of her hands in sharp focus, the tongue taut, the expression frank and competitive There was no visible sweat. She wore white gym shorts. Her legs, he thought, were almost certainly the legs of a virgin, dry and without hair, the left knee cocked and carrying her entire weight, which was just over one hundred pounds. Lieutenant Cross remembered touching that left knee. A dark theater, he remembered, and the movie was *Bonnie and Clyde*, and Martha wore a tweed skirt, and during the final scene, when he touched her knee, she turned and looked at him in a sad, sober way that made him pull his hand back, but he would always remember the feel of the tweed skirt and the knee beneath it and the sound of the gunfire that killed Bonnie and Clyde, how embarrassing it was, how slow and oppressive. He remembered kissing her good night at the dorm door. Right then, he thought, he should've done something brave. He should've carried her up the stairs to her room and tied her to the bed and touched that left knee all night long. He should've risked it. Whenever he looked at the photographs, he thought of new things he should've done.

What they carried was partly a function of rank, partly of field specialty.

As a first lieutenant and platoon leader, Jimmy Cross carried a compass, maps, code books, binoculars, and a .45-caliber pistol that weighed 2.9 pounds full loaded. He carried a strobe light and the responsibility for the lives of his men.

As an RTO, Mitchell Sanders carried the PRC-25 radio, a killer, 26 pounds with its battery.

As a medic, Rat Kiley carried a canvas satchel filled with morphine and plasma and malaria tablets and surgical tape and comic books and all the things a medic must carry, including M&M's for especially bad wounds, for a total weight of nearly 20 pounds.

As a big man, therefore a machine gunner, Henry Dobbins carried the M-60, which weighed 23 pounds unloaded, but which was almost always loaded. In addition, Dobbins carried between 10 and 15 pounds of ammunition draped in belts across his chest and shoulders.

As PFCs or Spec 4s, most of them were common grunts and carried the standard M-16 gas-operated assault rifle. The weapon weighed 7.5 pounds unloaded, 8.2 pounds with its full 20-round magazine. Depending on numerous factors, such as topography and psychology, the riflemen carried anywhere from 12 to 20 magazines, usually in cloth bandoliers, adding on another 8.4 pounds at minimum, 14 pounds at maximum. When it was available, they also carried M-16 maintenance gear—rods and steel brushes and swabs and tubes of LSA oil—all of which weighed about a pound. Among the grunts, some carried the M-79 grenade launcher, 5.9 pounds unloaded, a reasonably light weapon except for the ammunition, which was heavy. A single round weighed 10 ounces. The typical load was 25 rounds. But Ted Lavender, who was scared, carried 34 rounds when he was shot and killed outside Than Khe, and he went down under an exceptional burden, more than 20 pounds of ammunition, plus the flak jacket and helmet and rations and water and toilet paper and tranquilizers and all the rest, plus the unweighed fear. He was dead weight. There was no twitching or flopping. Kiowa, who saw it happen, said it was like watching a rock fall, or a big sandbag or something—just boom, then down—not like the movies where the dead guy rolls around and does fancy spins and goes ass over teakettle—not like that, Kiowa said, the poor bastard just flat-fuck fell. Boom. Down. Nothing else. It was a bright morning in mid-April. Lieutenant Cross felt the pain. He blamed himself. They stripped off Lavender's canteens and ammo, all the heavy things, and Rat Kiley said the obvious, the guy's dead, and Mitchell Sanders used his radio to report one U.S. KIA and to request a chopper. Then they wrapped Lavender in his poncho. They carried him out to a dry paddy, established security, and and sat smoking the dead man's dope until the chopper came. Lieutenant Cross kept to himself. He pictured Martha's smooth young face, thinking he loved her more than anything, more than his men, and now Ted Lavender was dead because he loved her so much and could not stop thinking about her. When the dustoff arrived, they carried Lavender aboard. Afterward they burned Than Khe. They marched until dusk, then dug their holes, and that night Kiowa kept explaining how you had to be there, how fast it was, how the poor guy just dropped like so much concrete. Boom-down, he said. Like cement.

In addition to the three standard weapons—the M-60, M-16, and M-79—they carried whatever presented itself, or whatever seemed appropriate as a means of killing or staying alive. They carried catch-as-catch-can. At various times, in various situations, they carried M-14s and CAR-15S and Swedish Ks and grease guns and captured AK-47S and Chi-Coms and RPGs and Simonov carbines and black market Uzis and .38-caliber Smith & Wesson handguns and 66 mm LAWs and shotguns and silencers and blackjacks and bayonets and C-4 plastic explosives. Lee Strunk carried a slingshot; a weapon of last resort, he called it. Mitchell Sanders carried brass knuckles. Kiowa carried his grandfather's feathered hatchet. Every third or fourth man carried a Claymore antipersonnel mine—3.5 pounds with its firing device. They all carried fragmentation grenades—14 ounces each. They all carried at least one M-18 colored smoke grenade—24 ounces. Some carried CS or tear gas grenades. Some carried white phosphorus grenades. They carried all they could bear, and then some, including a silent awe for the terrible power of the things they carried.

In the first week of April, before Lavender died, Lieutenant Jimmy Cross received a good-luck charm from Martha. It was a simple pebble, an ounce at most. Smooth to the touch, it was a milky white color with flecks of orange and violet, oval-shaped, like a miniature egg. In the accompanying letter, Martha wrote that she had found the pebble on the Jersey shoreline, precisely where the land touched water at high tide, where things came together but also separated. It was this separate-but-together quality, she wrote, that had inspired her to pick up the pebble and to carry it in her breast pocket for several days, where it seemed weightless, and then to send it through the mail, by air, as a token of her truest feelings for him. Lieutenant Cross found this romantic. But he wondered what her truest feelings were, exactly, and what she meant by separate-but-together. He wondered how the tides and waves had come into play on that afternoon along the Jersey shoreline when Martha saw the pebble and bent down to rescue it from geology. He imagined bare feet. Martha was a poet, with the poet's sensibilities, and her feet would be brown and bare, the toenails unpainted, the eyes chilly and somber like the ocean in March, and though it was painful, he wondered who had been with her that afternoon. He imagined a pair of shadows moving along the strip of sand where things came together but also separated. It was phantom jealousy, he knew, but he couldn't help himself. He loved her so much. On the march, through the hot days of early April, he carried the pebble in his mouth, turning it with his tongue, tasting sea salt and moisture. His mind wandered. He had difficulty keeping his attention on the war. On occasion he would yell at his men to spread out the column, to keep their eyes open, but then he would slip away into daydreams, just pretending, walking barefoot along the Jersey shore, with Martha, carrying nothing. He would feel himself rising. Sun and waves and gentle winds, all love and lightness.

What they carried varied by mission.

When a mission took them to the mountains, they carried mosquito netting, machetes, canvas tarps, and extra bug juice.

If a mission seemed especially hazardous, or if it involved a place they knew to be bad, they carried everything they could. In certain heavily mined AOs, where the land was dense with Toe Poppers and Bouncing Betties, they took turns humping a 28-pound mine detector. With its headphones and big sensing plate, the equipment was a stress on the lower back and shoulders, awkward to handle, often useless because of the shrapnel in the earth, but they carried it anyway, partly for safety, partly for the illusion of safety.

On ambush, or other night missions, they carried peculiar little odds and ends. Kiowa always took along his New Testament and a pair of moccasins for silence. Dave Jensen carried night-sight vitamins high in carotene. Lee Strunk carried his slingshot; ammo, he claimed, would never be a problem. Rat Kiley carried brandy and M&M's candy. Until he was shot, Ted Lavender carried the starlight scope, which weighed 6.3 pounds with its aluminum carrying case. Henry Dobbins carried his girlfriend's pantyhose wrapped around his neck as a comforter. They all carried ghosts. When dark came, they would move out single file across the meadows and paddies to their ambush coordinates, where they would quietly set up the Claymores and lie down and spend the night waiting.

Other missions were more complicated and required special equipment. In mid-April, it was their mission to search out and destroy the elaborate tunnel complexes in the Than Khe area south of Chu Lai. To blow the tunnels, they carried one-pound blocks of pentrite high explosives, four blocks to a man, 68 pounds in all. They carried wiring, detonators, and battery-powered clackers. Dave Jensen carried ear-plugs. Most often, before blowing the tunnels, they were ordered by higher command to search them, which was considered bad news, but by and large they just shrugged and carried out orders. Because he was a big man, Henry Dobbins was excused from tunnel duty. The others would draw numbers. Before Lavender died there were 17 men in the platoon, and whoever drew the number 17 would strip off his gear and crawl in headfirst with a flashlight and Lieutenant Cross's .45-caliber pistol. The rest of them would fan out as security. They would sit down or kneel, not facing the hole, listening to the ground beneath them, imagining cobwebs and ghosts, whatever was down there—the tunnel walls squeezing in—how the flashlight seemed impossibly heavy in the hand and how it was tunnel vision in the very strictest sense, compression in all ways, even time, and how you had to wiggle in—ass and elbows—a swallowed-up feeling—and how you found yourself worrying about odd things: Will your flashlight go dead? Do rats carry rabies? If you screamed, how far would the sound carry? Would your buddies hear it? Would they have the courage to drag you out? In some respects, though not many, the waiting was worse than the tunnel itself. Imagination was a killer.

On April 16, when Lee Strunk drew the number 17, he laughed and muttered something and went down quickly. The morning was hot and very still. Not good, Kiowa said. He looked at the tunnel opening, then out across a dry paddy toward the village of Than Khe. Nothing moved. No clouds or birds or people. As they waited, the men smoked and drank Kool-Aid, not talking much, feeling sympathy for Lee Strunk but also feeling the luck of the draw. You win some, you lose some, said Mitchell Sanders, and sometimes you settle for a rain check. It was a tired line and no one laughed.

Henry Dobbins ate a tropical chocolate bar. Ted Lavender popped a tranquilizer and went off to pee.

After five minutes, Lieutenant Jimmy Cross moved to the tunnel, leaned down, and examined the darkness. Trouble, he thought—a cave-in maybe. And then suddenly, without willing it, he was thinking about Martha. The stresses and fractures, the quick collapse, the two of them buried alive under all that weight. Dense, crushing love. Kneeling, watching the hole, he tried to concentrate on Lee Strunk and the war, all the dangers, but his love was too much for him, he felt paralyzed, he wanted to sleep inside her lungs and breathe her blood and be smothered. He wanted her to be a virgin and not a virgin, all at once. He wanted to know her. Intimate secrets: Why poetry? Why so sad? Why that grayness in her eyes? Why so alone? Not lonely, just alone—riding her bike across campus or sitting off by herself in the cafeteria—even dancing, she danced alone—and it was the aloneness that filled him with love. He remembered telling her that one evening. How she nodded and looked away. And how, later, when he kissed her, she received the kiss without returning it, her eyes wide open, not afraid, not a virgin's eyes, just flat and uninvolved.

Lieutenant Cross gazed at the tunnel. But he was not there. He was buried with Martha under the white sand at the Jersey shore. They were pressed together, and the pebble in his mouth was her tongue. He was smiling. Vaguely, he was aware of how quiet the day was, the sullen paddies, yet he could not bring himself to worry about matters of security. He was beyond that. He was just a kid at war, in love. He was twenty-four years old. He couldn't help it.

A few moments later Lee Strunk crawled out of the tunnel. He came up grinning, filthy but alive. Lieutenant Cross nodded and closed his eyes while the others clapped Strunk on the back and made jokes about rising from the dead.

Worms, Rat Kiley said. Right out of the grave. Fuckin' zombie.

The men laughed. They all felt great relief.

Spook city, said Mitchell Sanders.

Lee Strunk made a funny ghost sound, a kind of moaning, yet very happy, and right then, when Strunk made that high happy moaning sound, when he went *Ahhooooo*, right then Ted Lavender was shot in the head on his way back from peeing. He lay with his mouth open. The teeth were broken. There was a swollen black bruise under his left eye. The cheekbone was gone. Oh shit, Rat Kiley said, the guy's dead. The guy's dead, he kept saying, which seemed profound—the guy's dead. I mean really.

The things they carried were determined to some extent by superstition. Lieutenant Cross carried his good-luck pebble. Dave Jensen carried a rabbit's foot. Norman Bowker, otherwise a very gentle person, carried a thumb that had been presented to him as a gift by Mitchell Sanders. The thumb was dark brown, rubbery to the touch, and weighed four ounces at most. It had been cut from a VC corpse, a boy of fifteen or sixteen. They'd found him at the bottom of an irrigation ditch, badly burned, flies in his mouth and eyes. The boy wore black shorts and sandals. At the time of his death he had been carrying a pouch of rice, a rifle, and three magazines of ammunition.

You want my opinion, Mitchell Sanders said, there's a definite moral here.

He put his hand on the dead boy's wrist. He was quiet for a time, as if counting a pulse, then he patted the stomach, almost affectionately, and used Kiowa's hunting hatchet to remove the thumb.

Henry Dobbins asked what the moral was.

Moral?

You know. *Moral.*

Sanders wrapped the thumb in toilet paper and handed it across to Norman Bowker. There was no blood. Smiling, he kicked the boy's head, watched the flies scatter, and said, It's like with that old TV show—Paladin. Have gun, will travel.

Henry Dobbins thought about it.

Yeah, well, he finally said. I don't see no moral.

There it *is*, man.

Fuck off.

They carried USO stationery and pencils and pens. They carried Sterno, safety pins, trip flares, signal flares, spools of wire, razor blades, chewing tobacco, liberated joss sticks and statuettes of the smiling Buddha, candles, grease pencils, *The Stars and Stripes,* fingernail clippers, Psy Ops leaflets, bush hats, bolos, and much more. Twice a week, when the resupply choppers came in, they carried hot chow in green mermite cans and large canvas bags filled with iced beer and soda pop. They carried plastic water containers, each with a two-gallon capacity. Mitchell Sanders carried a set of starched tiger fatigues for special occasions. Henry Dobbins carried Black Flag insecticide. Dave Jensen carried empty sandbags that could be filled at night for added protection. Lee Strunk carried tanning lotion. Some things they carried in common. Taking turns, they carried the big PRC-77 scrambler radio, which weighed 30 pounds with its battery. They shared the weight of memory. They took up what others could no longer bear. Often, they carried each other, the wounded or weak. They carried infections. They carried chess sets, basketballs, Vietnamese-English dictionaries, insignia of rank, Bronze Stars and Purple Hearts, plastic cards imprinted with the Code of Conduct. They carried diseases, among them malaria and dysentery. They carried lice and ringworm and leeches and paddy algae and various rots and molds. They carried the land itself—Vietnam, the place, the soil—a powdery orange-red dust that covered their boots and fatigues and faces. They carried the sky. The whole atmosphere, they carried it, the humidity, the monsoons, the stink of fungus and decay, all of it, they carried gravity. They moved like mules. By daylight they took sniper fire, at night they were mortared, but it was not battle, it was just the endless march, village to village, without purpose, nothing won or lost.

They marched for the sake of the march. They plodded along slowly, dumbly, leaning forward against the heat, unthinking, all blood and bone, simple grunts, soldiering with their legs, toiling up the hills and down into the paddies and across the rivers and up again and down, just humping, one step and then the next and then another, but no volition, no will, because it was automatic, it was anatomy, and the war was entirely a matter of posture and carriage, the hump was everything, a kind of inertia, a kind of emptiness, a dullness of desire and intellect and conscience and hope and human sensibility. Their principles were in their feet. Their calculations were biological. They had no sense of strategy or mission. They searched the villages without knowing what to look for, not caring, kicking over jars of rice, frisking children and old men, blowing tunnels, sometimes setting fires and sometimes not, then forming up and moving on to the next village, then other villages, where it would always be the same. They carried their own lives. The pressures were enormous. In the heat of early afternoon, they would remove their helmets and flak jackets, walking bare, which was dangerous but which helped ease the strain. They would often discard things along the route of march. Purely for comfort, they would throw away rations, blow their Claymores and grenades, no matter, because by nightfall the resupply choppers would arrive with more of the same, then a day or two later still more, fresh watermelons and crates of ammunition and sunglasses and woolen sweaters—the resources were stunning—sparklers for the Fourth of July, colored eggs for Easter—it was the great American war chest—the fruits of science, the smokestacks, the canneries, the arsenals at Hartford, the Minnesota forests, the machine shops, the vast fields of corn and wheat—they carried like freight trains; they carried it on their backs and shoulders—and for all the ambiguities of Vietnam, all the mysteries and unknowns, there was at least the single abiding certainty that they would never be at a loss for things to carry.

After the chopper took Lavender away, Lieutenant Jimmy Cross led his men into the village of Than Khe. They burned everything. They shot chickens and dogs, they trashed the village well, they called in artillery and watched the wreckage, then they marched for several hours through the hot afternoon, and then at dusk, while Kiowa explained how Lavender died, Lieutenant Cross found himself trembling.

He tried not to cry. With his entrenching tool, which weighed five pounds, he began digging a hole in the earth.

He felt shame. He hated himself. He had loved Martha more than his men, and as a consequence Lavender was now dead, and this was something he would have to carry like a stone in his stomach for the rest of the war.

All he could do was dig. He used his entrenching tool like an ax, slashing, feeling both love and hate, and then later, when it was full dark, he sat at the bottom of his foxhole and wept. It went on for a long while. In part, he was grieving for Ted Lavender, but mostly it was for Martha, and for himself, because she belonged to another world, which was not quite real, and because she was a junior at Mount Sebastian College in New Jersey, a poet and a virgin and uninvolved, and because he realized she did not love him and never would.

Like cement, Kiowa whispered in the dark. I swear to God—boom, down. Not a word.

I've heard this, said Norman Bowker.

A pisser, you know? Still zipping himself up. Zapped while zipping.

All right, fine. That's enough.

Yeah, but you had to see it, the guy just—

I *heard*, man. Cement. So why not shut the fuck *up?*

Kiowa shook his head sadly and glanced over at the hole where Lieutenant Jimmy Cross sat watching the night. The air was thick and wet. A warm dense fog had settled over the paddies and there was the stillness that precedes rain.

After a time Kiowa sighed.

One thing for sure, he said. The lieutenant's in some deep hurt. I mean that crying jag—the way he was carrying on—it wasn't fake or anything, it was real heavy-duty hurt. The man cares.

Sure, Norman Bowker said.

Say what you want, the man does care.

We all got problems.

Not Lavender.

No, I guess not, Bowker said. Do me a favor, though.

Shut up?

That's a smart Indian. Shut up.

Shrugging, Kiowa pulled off his boots. He wanted to say more, just to lighten up his sleep, but instead he opened his New Testament and arranged it beneath his head as a pillow. The fog made things seem hollow and unattached. He tried not to think about Ted Lavender, but then he was thinking how fast it was, no drama, down and dead, and how it was hard to feel anything except surprise. It seemed unchristian. He wished he could find some great sadness, or even anger, but the emotion wasn't there and he couldn't make it happen. Mostly he felt pleased to be alive. He liked the smell of the New Testament under his cheek, the leather and ink and paper and glue, whatever the chemicals were. He liked hearing the sounds of night. Even his fatigue, it felt fine, the stiff muscles and the prickly awareness of his own body, a floating feeling. He enjoyed not being dead. Lying there, Kiowa admired Lieutenant Jimmy Cross's capacity for grief. He wanted to share the man's pain, he wanted to care as Jimmy Cross cared. And yet when he closed his eyes, all he could think was Boom-down, and all he could feel was the pleasure of having his boots off and the fog curling in around him and the damp soil and the Bible smells and the plush comfort of night.

After a moment Norman Bowker sat up in the dark.

What the hell, he said. You want to talk, *talk*. Tell it to me.

Forget it.

No, man, go on. One thing I hate, it's a silent Indian.

For the most part they carried themselves with poise, a kind of dignity. Now and then, however, there were times of panic, when they squealed or wanted to squeal but couldn't, when they twitched and made moaning sounds and covered their heads and said Dear Jesus and flopped around on the earth and fired their weapons blindly and cringed and sobbed and begged for the noise to stop and went wild and made stupid promises to themselves and to God and to their mothers and fathers, hoping not to die. In different ways, it happened to all of them. Afterward, when the firing ended, they would blink and peek up. They would touch their bodies, feeling shame, then quickly hiding it. They would force themselves to stand. As if in slow motion, frame by frame, the world would take on the old logic—absolute silence, then the wind, then sunlight, then voices. It was the burden of being alive. Awkwardly, the men would reassemble themselves, first in private, then in groups, becoming soldiers again. They would repair the leaks in their eyes. They would check for casualties, call in dustoffs, light cigarettes, try to smile, clear their throats and spit and begin cleaning their weapons. After a time someone would shake his head and say, No lie, I almost shit my pants, and someone else would laugh, which meant it was bad, yes, but the guy had obviously not shit his pants, it wasn't that bad, and in any case nobody would ever do such a thing and then go ahead and talk about it. They would squint into the dense, oppressive sunlight. For a few moments, perhaps, they would fall silent, lighting a joint and tracking its passage from man to man, inhaling, holding in the humiliation. Scary stuff, one of them might say. But then someone else would grin or flick his eyebrows and say, Roger-dodger, almost cut me a new asshole, *almost*.

There were numerous such poses. Some carried themselves with a sort of wistful resignation, others with pride or stiff soldierly discipline or good humor or macho zeal. They were afraid of dying but they were even more afraid to show it.

They found jokes to tell.

They used a hard vocabulary to contain the terrible softness. *Greased* they'd say. *Offed, lit up, zapped while zipping*. It wasn't cruelty, just stage presence. They were actors. When someone died, it wasn't quite dying, because in a curious way it seemed scripted, and because they had their lines mostly memorized, irony mixed with tragedy, and because they called it by other names, as if to encyst and destroy the reality of death itself. They kicked corpses. They cut off thumbs. They talked grunt lingo. They told stories about Ted Lavender's supply of tranquilizers, how the poor guy didn't feel a thing, how incredibly tranquil he was.

There's a moral here, said Mitchell Sanders.

They were waiting for Lavender's chopper, smoking the dead man's dope.

The moral's pretty obvious, Sanders said, and winked. Stay away from drugs. No joke, they'll ruin your day every time.

Cute, said Henry Dobbins.

Mind blower, get it? Talk about wiggy. Nothing left, just blood and brains.

They made themselves laugh.

There it is, they'd say. Over and over—there it is, my friend, there it is—as if the repetition itself were an act of poise, a balance between crazy and almost crazy, knowing without going, there it is, which meant be cool, let it ride, because Oh yeah, man, you can't change what can't be changed, there it is, there it absolutely and positively and fucking well *is*.

They were tough.

They carried all the emotional baggage of men who might die. Grief, terror, love, longing—these were intangibles, but the intangibles had their own mass and specific gravity, they had tangible weight. They carried shameful memories. They carried the common secret of cowardice barely restrained, the instinct to run or freeze or hide, and in many respects this was the heaviest burden of all, for it could never be put down, it required perfect balance and perfect posture. They carried their reputations. They carried the soldier's greatest fear, which was the fear of blushing. Men killed, and died, because they were embarrassed not to. It was what had brought them to the war in the first place, nothing positive, no dreams of glory or honor, just to avoid the blush of dishonor. They died so as not to die of embarrassment. They crawled into tunnels and walked point and advanced under fire. Each morning, despite the unknowns, they made their legs move. They endured. They kept humping. They did not submit to the obvious alternative, which was simply to close the eyes and fall. So easy, really. Go limp and tumble to the ground and let the muscles unwind and not speak and not budge until your buddies picked you up and lifted you into the chopper that would roar and dip its nose and carry you off to the world. A mere matter of falling, yet no one ever fell. It was not courage, exactly; the object was not valor. Rather, they were too frightened to be cowards.

By and large they carried these things inside, maintaining the masks of composure. They sneered at sick call. They spoke bitterly about guys who had found release by shooting off their own toes or fingers. Pussies, they'd say. Candy-asses. It was fierce, mocking talk, with only a trace of envy or awe, but even so the image played itself out behind their eyes.

They imagined the muzzle against flesh. So easy: squeeze the trigger and blow away a toe. They imagined it. They imagined the quick, sweet pain, then the evacuation to Japan, then a hospital with warm beds and cute geisha nurses.

And they dreamed of freedom birds.

At night, on guard, staring into the dark, they were carried away by jumbo jets. They felt the rush of takeoff. *Gone!* they yelled. And then velocity—wings and engines—a smiling stewardess—but it was more than a plane, it was a real bird, a big sleek silver bird with feathers and talons and high screeching. They were flying. The weights fell off; there was nothing to bear. They laughed and held on tight, feeling the cold slap of wind and altitude, soaring, thinking *It's over, I'm gone!*—they were naked, they were light and free—it was all lightness, bright and fast and buoyant, light as light, a helium buzz in the brain, a giddy bubbling in the lungs as they were taken up over the clouds and the war, beyond duty, beyond gravity and mortification and global entanglements—*Sin loi!* they yelled. *I'm sorry, mother-fuckers, but I'm out of it, I'm goofed, I'm on a space cruise, I'm gone!*—and it was a restful, unencumbered sensation, just riding the light waves, sailing that big silver freedom bird over the mountains and oceans, over America, over the farms and great sleeping cities and cemeteries and highways and the golden arches of McDonald's, it was flight, a kind of fleeing, a kind of falling, falling higher and higher, spinning off the edge of the earth and beyond the sun and through the vast, silent vacuum where there were no burdens and where everything weighed exactly nothing—*Gone!* they screamed. *I'm sorry but I'm gone!*—and so at night, not quite dreaming, they gave themselves over to lightness, they were carried, they were purely borne.

On the morning after Ted Lavender died, First Lieutenant Jimmy Cross crouched at the bottom of his foxhole and burned Martha's letters. Then he burned the two photographs. There was a steady rain falling, which made it difficult, but he used heat tabs and Sterno to build a small fire, screening it with his body, holding the photographs over the tight blue flame with the tips of his fingers.

He realized it was only a gesture. Stupid, he thought. Sentimental, too, but mostly just stupid.

Lavender was dead. You couldn't burn the blame.

Besides, the letters were in his head. And even now, without photographs, Lieutenant Cross could see Martha playing volleyball in her white gym shorts and yellow T-shirt. He could see her moving in the rain.

When the fire died out, Lieutenant Cross pulled his poncho over his shoulders and ate breakfast from a can.

There was no great mystery, he decided.

In those burned letters Martha had never mentioned the war, except to say, Jimmy, take care of yourself. She wasn't involved. She signed the letters Love, but it wasn't love, and all the fine lines and technicalities did not matter. Virginity was no longer an issue. He hated her. Yes, he did. He hated her. Love, too, but it was a hard, hating kind of love.

The morning came up wet and blurry. Everything seemed part of everything else, the fog and Martha and the deepening rain.

He was a soldier, after all.

Half smiling, Lieutenant Jimmy Cross took out his maps. He shook his head hard, as if to clear it, then bent forward and began planning the day's march. In ten minutes, or maybe twenty, he would rouse the men and they would pack up and head west, where the maps showed the country to be green and inviting. They would do what they had always done. The rain might add some weight, but otherwise it would be one more day layered upon all the other days.

He was realistic about it. There was that new hardness in his stomach. He loved her but he hated her.

No more fantasies, he told himself.

Henceforth, when he thought about Martha, it would be only to think that she belonged elsewhere. He would shut down the daydreams. This was not Mount Sebastian, it was another world, where there were no pretty poems or mid-term exams, a place where men died because of carelessness and gross stupidity. Kiowa was right. Boom-down, and you were dead, never partly dead.

Briefly, in the rain, Lieutenant Cross saw Martha's gray eyes gazing back at him.

He understood.

It was very sad, he thought. The things men carried inside. The things men did or felt they had to do.

He almost nodded at her, but didn't.

Instead he went back to his maps. He was now determined to perform his duties firmly and without negligence. It wouldn't help Lavender, he knew that, but from this point on he would comfort himself as an officer. He would dispose of his good-luck pebble. Swallow it, maybe, or use Lee Strunk's slingshot, or just drop it along the trail. On the march he would impose strict field discipline. He would be careful to send out flank security, to prevent straggling or bunching up, to keep his troops moving at the proper pace and at the proper interval. He would insist on clean weapons. He would confiscate the remainder of Lavender's dope. Later in the day, perhaps, he would call the men together and speak to them plainly. He would accept the blame for what had happened to Ted Lavender. He would be a man about it. He would look them in the eyes, keeping his chin level, and he would issue the new SOPs in a calm, impersonal tone of voice, a lieutenant's voice, leaving no room for argument or discussion. Commencing immediately, he'd tell them, they would no longer abandon equipment along the route of march. They would police up their acts. They would get their shit together, and keep it together, and maintain it neatly and in good working order.

He would not tolerate laxity. He would show strength, distancing himself.

Among the men there would be grumbling, of course, and maybe worse, because their days would seem longer and their loads heavier, but Lieutenant Jimmy Cross reminded himself that his obligation was not to be loved but to lead. He would dispense with love; it was not now a factor. And if anyone quarreled or complained, he would simply tighten his lips and arrange his shoulders in the correct command posture. He might give a curt little nod. Or he might not. He might just shrug and say, Carry on, then they would saddle up and form into a column and move out toward the villages west of Than Khe.

Amy Hempel

Amy Hempel (b. 1951) was born in Chicago. She lived for a time on the West Coast, where many of the stories in her collection *Reasons To Live* are set. She now makes her home in New York.

Hempel's stories are aggressively contemporary. She favors sketchy plot lines and builds her narratives around snapshots of characters interacting. These features, combined with her penchant for details incorporated from the brand-name present, make her a good representative of the so-called minimalist camp. Her humor and keen ear for speech habits are some of Hempel's distinguishing features as a writer.

IN THE CEMETERY WHERE AL JOLSON IS BURIED

"Tell me things I won't mind forgetting," she said. "Make it useless stuff or skip it."

I began. I told her insects fly through rain, missing every drop, never getting wet. I told her no one in America owned a tape recorder before Bing Crosby did. I told her the shape of the moon is like a banana—you see it looking full, you're seeing it end-on.

The camera made me self-conscious and I stopped. It was trained on us from a ceiling mount—the kind of camera banks use to photograph robbers. It played us to the nurses down the hall in Intensive Care.

"Go on, girl," she said. "You get used to it."

I had my audience. I went on. Did she know that Tammy Wynette had changed her tune? Really. That now she sings "Stand by Your *Friends*"? That Paul Anka did it too, I said. Does "You're Having *Our* Baby." That he got sick of all that feminist bitching.

"What else?" she said. "Have you got something else?"

Oh, yes.

For her I would always have something else.

"Did you know that when they taught the first chimp to talk, it lied? That when they asked her who did it on the desk, she signed back the name of the janitor. And that when they pressed her, she said she was sorry, that it was really the project director. But she was a mother, so I guess she had her reasons."

"Oh, that's good," she said. "A parable."

"There's more about the chimp," I said. "But it will break your heart."

"No, thanks," she says, and scratches at her mask.

We look like good-guy outlaws. Good or bad, I am not used to the mask yet. I keep touching the warm spot where my breath, thank God, comes out. She is used to hers. She only ties the strings on top. The other ones—a pro by now—she lets hang loose.

We call this place the Marcus Welby Hospital. It's the white one with the palm trees under the opening credits of all those shows. A Hollywood hospital, though in fact it is several miles west. Off camera, there is a beach across the street.

She introduces me to a nurse as the Best Friend. The impersonal article is more intimate. It tells me that *they* are intimate, the nurse and my friend.

"I was telling her we used to drink Canada Dry ginger ale and pretend we were in Canada."

"That's how dumb we were," I say.

"You could be sisters," the nurse says.

So how come, I'll bet they are wondering, it took me so long to get to such a glamorous place? But do they ask?

They do not ask.

Two months, and how long is the drive?

The best I can explain it is this—I have a friend who worked one summer in a mortuary. He used to tell me stories. The one that really got to me was not the grisliest, but it's the one that did. A man wrecked his car on 101 going south. He did not lose consciousness. But his arm was taken down to the wet bone—and when he looked at it—it scared him to death.

I mean, he died.

So I hadn't dared to look any closer. But now I'm doing it—and hoping that I will live through it.

She shakes out a summer-weight blanket, showing a leg you did not want to see. Except for that, you look at her and understand the law that requires *two* people to be with the body at all times.

"I thought of something," she says. "I thought of it last night. I think there is a real and present need here. You know," she says, "like for someone to do it for you when you can't do it yourself. You call them up whenever you want—like when push comes to shove."

She grabs the bedside phone and loops the cord around her neck.

"Hey," she says, "the end o' the line."

She keeps on, giddy with something. But I don't know with what.

"I can't remember," she says. "What does Kübler-Ross say comes after Denial?"

It seems to me Anger must be next. Then Bargaining, Depression, and so on and so forth. But I keep my guesses to myself.

"The only thing is," she says, "is where's Resurrection? God knows, I want to do it by the book. But she left out Resurrection."

She laughs, and I cling to the sound the way someone dangling above a ravine holds fast to the thrown rope.

"Tell me," she says, "about that chimp with the talking hands. What do they do when the thing ends and the chimp says, 'I don't want to go back to the zoo'?"

When I don't say anything, she says, "Okay—then tell me another animal story. I like animal stories. But not a sick one—I don't want to know about all the seeing-eye dogs going blind."

No, I would not tell her a sick one.

"How about the hearing-ear dogs?" I say. "They're not going deaf, but they are getting very judgmental. For instance, there's this golden retriever in New Jersey, he wakes up the deaf mother and drags her into the daughter's room because the kid has got a flashlight and is reading under the covers."

"Oh, you're killing me," she says. "Yes, you're definitely killing me."

"They say the smart dog obeys, but the smarter dog knows when to disobey."

"Yes," she says, "the smarter anything knows when to disobey. Now, for example."

She is flirting with the Good Doctor, who has just appeared. Unlike the Bad Doctor, who checks the IV drip before saying good morning, the Good Doctor says things like "God didn't give epileptics a fair shake." The Good Doctor awards himself points for the cripples he could have hit in the parking lot. Because the Good Doctor is a little in love with her, he says maybe a year. He pulls a chair up to her bed and suggests I might like to spend an hour on the beach.

"Bring me something back," she says. "Anything from the beach. Or the gift shop. Taste is no object."

He draws the curtain around her bed.

"Wait!" she cries.

I look in at her.

"Anything," she says, "except a magazine subscription."

The doctor turns away.

I watch her mouth laugh.

What seems dangerous often is not—black snakes, for example, or clear-air turbulence. While things that just lie there, like this beach, are loaded with jeopardy. A yellow dust rising from the ground, the heat that ripens melons overnight—this is earthquake weather. You can sit here braiding the fringe on your towel and the sand will all of a sudden suck down like an hourglass. The air roars. In the cheap apartments on-shore, bathtubs fill themselves and gardens roll up and over like green waves. If nothing happens, the dust will drift and the heat deepen till fear turns to desire. Nerves like that are only bought off by catastrophe.

"It never happens when you're thinking about it," she once observed. "Earthquake, earthquake, earthquake," she said.

"Earthquake, earthquake, earthquake," I said.

Like the aviaphobe who keeps the plane aloft with prayer, we kept it up until an aftershock cracked the ceiling.

That was after the big one in seventy-two. We were in college; our dormitory was five miles from the epi-center. When the ride was over and my jabbering pulse began to slow, she served five parts champagne to one part orange juice, and joked about living in Ocean View, Kansas. I offered to drive her to Hawaii on the new world psychics predicted would surface the next time, or the next.

I could not say that now—next.

Whose next? she could ask.

Was I the only one who noticed that the experts had stopped saying *if* and now spoke of *when*? Of course not; the fearful ran to thousands. We watched the traffic of Japanese beetles for deviation. Deviation might mean more natural violence.

I wanted her to be afraid with me. But she said, "I don't know. I'm just not."

She was afraid of nothing, not even of flying.

I have this dream before a flight where we buckle in and the plane moves down the runway. It takes off at thirty-five miles an hour, and then we're airborne, skimming the tree tops. Still, we arrive in New York on time.

It is so pleasant.

One night I flew to Moscow this way.

She flew with me once. That time she flew with me she ate macadamia nuts while the wings bounced. She knows the wing tips can bend thirty feet up and thirty feet down without coming off. She believes it. She trusts the law of aerodynamics. My mind stampedes. I can almost accept that a battleship floats when everybody knows steel sinks.

I see fear in her now, and am not going to try to talk her out of it. She is right to be afraid.

After a quake, the six o'clock news airs a film clip of first-graders yelling at the broken playground per their teacher's instructions.

"*Bad* earth!" they shout, because anger is stronger than fear.

But the beach is standing still today. Everyone on it is tranquilized, numb, or asleep. Teenaged girls rub coconut oil on each other's hard-to-reach places. They smell like macaroons. They pry open compacts like clam-shells; mirrors catch the sun and throw a spray of white rays across glazed shoulders. The girls arrange their wet hair with silk flowers the way they learned in *Seventeen*. They pose.

A formation of low-riders pulls over to watch with a six-pack. They get vocal when the girls check their tan lines. When the beer is gone, so are they—flexing their cars on up the boulevard.

Above this aggressive health are the twin wrought-iron terraces, painted flamingo pink, of the Palm Royale. Someone dies there every time the sheets are changed. There's an ambulance in the driveway, so the remaining residents line the balconies, rocking and not talking, one-upped.

The ocean they stare at is dangerous, and not just the undertow. You can almost see the slapping tails of sand sharks keeping cruising bodies alive.

If she looked, she could see this, some of it, from her window. She would be the first to say how little it takes to make a thing all wrong.

There was a second bed in the room when I got back to it!

For two beats I didn't get it. Then it hit me like an open coffin.

She wants every minute, I thought. She wants my life.

"You missed Gussie," she said.

Gussie is her parents' three-hundred-pound narcoleptic maid. Her attacks often come at the ironing board. The pillowcases in that family are all bordered with scorch.

"It's a hard trip for her," I said. "How is she?"

"Well, she didn't fall asleep, if that's what you mean. Gussie's great—you know what she said? She said, 'Darlin', stop this worriation. Just keep prayin', down on your knees'—me, who can't even get out of bed."

She shrugged. "What am I missing?"

"It's earthquake weather," I told her.

"The best thing to do about earthquakes," she said, "is not to live in California."

"That's useful," I said. "You sound like Reverend Ike—'The best thing to do for the poor is not to be one of them.' "

We're crazy about Reverend Ike.

I noticed her face was bloated.

"You know," she said, "I feel like hell. I'm about to stop having fun."

"The ancients have a saying," I said. " 'There are times when the wolves are silent; there are times when the moon howls.' "

"What's that, Navaho?"

"Palm Royale lobby graffiti," I said. "I bought a paper there. I'll read you something."

"Even though I care about nothing?"

I turned to the page with the trivia column. I said, "Did you know the more shrimp flamingo birds eat, the pinker their feathers get?" I said, "Did you know that Eskimos need refrigerators? Do you know *why* Eskimos need refrigerators? Did you know that Eskimos need refrigerators because how else would they keep their food from freezing?"

I turned to page three, to a UPI filler datelined Mexico City. I read her MAN ROBS BANK WITH CHICKEN, about a man who bought a barbecued chicken at a stand down the block from a bank. Passing the bank, he got the idea. He walked in and approached a teller. He pointed the brown paper bag at her and she handed over the day's receipts. It was the smell of barbecue sauce that eventually led to his capture.

The story had made her hungry, she said—so I took the elevator down six floors to the cafeteria, and brought back all the ice cream she wanted. We lay side by side, adjustable beds cranked up for optimal TV-viewing, littering the sheets with Good Humor wrappers, picking toasted almonds out of the gauze. We were Lucy and Ethel, Mary and Rhoda in extremis. The blinds were closed to keep light off the screen.

We watched a movie starring men we used to think we wanted to sleep with. Hers was a tough cop out to stop mine, a vicious rapist who went after cocktail waitresses.

"This is a good movie," she said when snipers felled them both.

I missed her already.

A Filipino nurse tiptoed in and gave her an injection. The nurse removed the pile of popsicle sticks from the nightstand—enough to splint a small animal.

The injection made us both sleepy. We slept.

I dreamed she was a decorator, come to furnish my house. She worked in secret, singing to herself. When she finished, she guided me proudly to the door. "How do you like it?" she asked, easing me inside.

Every beam and sill and shelf and knob was draped in gay bunting, with streamers of pastel crepe looped around bright mirrors.

"I have to go home," I said when she woke up.

She thought I meant home to her house in the Canyon, and I had to say No, *home* home. I twisted my hands in the time-honored fashion of people in pain. I was supposed to offer something. The Best Friend. I could not even offer to come back.

I felt weak and small and failed.

Also exhilarated.

I had a convertible in the parking lot. Once out of that room, I would drive it too fast down the Coast high-way through the crab-smelling air. A stop in Malibu for sangria. The music in the place would be sexy and loud. They'd serve papaya and shrimp and watermelon ice. After dinner I would shimmer with lust, buzz with heat, vibrate with life, and stay up all night.

Without a word, she yanked off her mask and threw it on the floor. She kicked at the blankets and moved to the door. She must have hated having to pause for breath and balance before slamming out of Isolation, and out of the second room, the one where you scrub and tie on the white masks.

A voice shouted her name in alarm, and people ran down the corridor. The Good Doctor was paged over the intercom. I opened the door and the nurses at the station stared hard, as if this flight had been my idea.

"Where is she?" I asked, and they nodded to the supply closet.

I looked in. Two nurses were kneeling beside her on the floor, talking to her in low voices. One held a mask over her nose and mouth, the other rubbed her back in slow circles. The nurses glanced up to see if I was the doctor—and when I wasn't, they went back to what they were doing.

"There, there, honey," they cooed.

On the morning she was moved to the cemetery, the one where Al Jolson is buried, I enrolled in a "Fear of Flying" class. "What is your worst fear?" the instructor asked, and I answered, "That I will finish this course and still be afraid."

I sleep with a glass of water on the nightstand so I can see by its level if the coastal earth is trembling or if the shaking is still me.

What do I remember?

I remember only the useless things I hear—that Bob Dylan's mother invented Wite-Out, that twenty-three people must be in a room before there is a fifty-fifty chance two will have the same birthday. Who cares whether or not it's true? In my head there are bath towels swaddling this stuff. Nothing else seeps through.

I review those things that will figure in the retelling: a kiss through surgical gauze, the pale hand correcting the position of the wig. I noted these gestures as they happened, not in any retrospect—though I don't know why looking back should show us more than looking *at*.

It is just possible I will say I stayed the night.

And who is there that can say that I did not?

I think of the chimp, the one with the talking hands.

In the course of the experiment, that chimp had a baby. Imagine how her trainers must have thrilled when the mother, without prompting, began to sign to her newborn.

Baby, drink milk.

Baby, play ball.

And when the baby died, the mother stood over the body, her wrinkled hands moving with animal grace, forming again and again the words: Baby, come hug, Baby, come hug, fluent now in the language of grief.

Han Shaogong

Han Shaogong (b.1952) was born in China's Hunan province. During the period of the Cultural Revolution he lived on a commune in rural Hunan. He later moved to Changsha, the provincial capital, and studied at Hunan Teachers' College. He has since worked as an editor at a literary magazine. Since becoming a professional writer he has published several collections of stories and novellas in China.

THE HOMECOMING

Many people have said that once in a while, when they visit some place for the first time, they experience a feeling of familiarity they cannot explain. Now I too know this feeling.

I am walking. The mud path, scoured and eroded by water running down the hillsides, stretches before me in an array of narrow ridges and clumps of pebbles, like bones and dried-out entrails after skin and flesh have been stripped away. In the gully are a few sticks of rotting bamboo and a length of tattered rope, portents that a village is close at hand. Some dark shapes stand motionless in the ditchwater. Only when you look carefully do you discover that they are not rocks at all but water buffalo, their heads barely breaking the surface, their eyes fixed on me in a furtive gaze. Mere calves, these, yet already wrinkled, bearded, already senile at birth, senility running in their blood. Rising above the banana grove ahead is a squat blockhouse, its portholes like cheerless eyes staring out of smoke-darkened walls, walls black from the countless nights congealed within them. I have heard this area used to be infested with bandits, and that every so often there had been pitched battles between hill folk and outlaws. No wonder there is a blockhouse in every village. And the dwellings, in spite of their thick walls and beady-eyed windows set way up high, look fearful as they huddle in a tight circle.

All this seems familiar, yet strange too, like a word you've been staring at for too long—now it looks right, now it doesn't. Damn it, have I been here before or not? Let me take a guess: Down that flagstone path, past the banana grove, left at the oil mill, and just behind the blockhouse I should find an old tree—a gingko or a camphor—long dead from a bolt of lightning.

Moments later I find I am correct—down to the last detail, including the hollow in the tree and the two youngsters in the foreground playing with a small bonfire.

Nervously I try again: Behind the old tree there should be a low barn with piles of dung in front and a rusty plow or rake leaning against the side.

And there they all are, clear as day, seeming to come toward me in greeting as I approach. Even the large stone pestle in its lopsided mortar, with the leaves and muck at the bottom—even these look familiar to me.

Actually, the mortar in my mind's eye is clean and dry. But wait—it stopped raining only a short while ago, and water running off the eaves would have been dripping right into the mortar. So once again a chill rises from my heels all the way to the back of my neck.

No, this is impossible, I cannot have come here before. I have never had meningitis, no mental illness, I still have my wits about me. Maybe I saw this in a movie once, or maybe it was in a dream that . . . Anxiously I rack my brains.

Stranger still, the hill folk all seem to know me. Just now as I was rolling up my pant legs to cross the creek, a fellow came down the slope carrying a couple of logs lashed together at one end. He watched awhile as I teetered along reaching uncertainly for the stepping stones. Then he went over to the melon stand by the side of the road, pulled out a dried branch and tossed it over to me. On his face was an odd, yellow-toothed grin.

"Back, eh?"

"Yeah, I'm back . . ."

"It's been about, what, ten years?"

"Ten years . . ."

"Let's go sit in the house. Sangui is plowing the field up yonder."

Where is his house? And who is Sangui? I am completely baffled.

As I climb up a little hill, tiled roofs and courtyards begin to rise into view. Out in the clearing several figures are swinging at something, their flails cracking away unevenly. All of them have bare feet and closely cropped hair; their faces are covered by a coat of sweat that looks like a brown glaze with ragged edges, little slick patches on their cheekbones catching the light and glistening as they move back and forth under the sun. Short floppy jackets and pants that hang loosely from the hips leave their soft bellies and navels uncovered. Not until I see one of them going over to a cradle and undoing her shirt to breast feed the baby, and notice the earrings on every one of them, do I realize that they are—well, women.

One of them looks at me wide-eyed.

"Is this not Ma . . ."

"Ma Four Eyes." Someone reminds her. The name amuses them, and they all burst out laughing.

"My name is not Ma, it is Huang . . ."

"Changed your name, have you?"

"No I haven't."

"For sure, you still love to jest. Whence have you come?"

"The county seat, of course."

" 'Truth, a rare visitor. How is Missy Liang?"

"Which Missy Liang?"

"Your missus, is not Liang her maiden name?"

"Mine is surnamed Yang."

"Sakes alive, did I remember amiss? No, that cannot be, I know she once told me we were distantly related. My husband's family is the Liang clan, from Liang's Knoll, over at Three Rivers. You know that."

What is it I know? And whatever it is, what does it have to do with me? How did I end up here when it seems I was . . . was I looking for her?

The woman throws down her flail and takes me into her house. The doorsill is very high, very heavyset, and over the years legions of young and old have stepped on it, sat on it, until a gentle depression has been worn into the middle. Yellowish rings in its wood grain spill over the sill like widening circles of moonlight forever petrified. Toddlers have to crawl across on all fours while grownups must crook their legs high in order to clamber over the threshold, their bodies leaning forward awkwardly. Indoors it is very dark. The room smells of swill and chicken droppings, but I cannot see anything except for a thin ray of light that trickles in through a high narrow window, slitting open the dank blackness. When my eyes finally adjust to the dim light I am able to make out some soot-covered beams and an equally grimy basket hanging on the wall. I sit down on a block of wood—for some reason there are no chairs in this place, only wood blocks and benches. Women old and young are crowded around the doorway chattering. The one who is breast-feeding flashes an easy smile at me while she unabashedly pulls out one long tit, still dripping with milk, and presses the other nipple between the baby's lips. They are all saying odd things: "Xiao Qin . . ." "No, not Xiao Qin." "Then who—?" "Her name's Xiao Ling." "Oh yes, Xiao Ling—is she still teaching?" "Why didn't she come for a visit too?" "Have you both gone back to Changsha?" "Do you live in the city or the township?" "Got any youngsters yet?" "One, or two?" "Does Chen Zhihua have any youngsters?" "One, or two?" "How about Bearhead? Has he found himself a wife yet?" "Does he have any youngsters also? One, or two?" . . .

Before long I realize they have all mistaken me for a certain "Ma Four Eyes" who knows these people named Xiao Ling and Bearhead and so forth. That fellow probably looks a lot like me, maybe he also peers out at the world from behind his glasses.

Who is he? Do I need to think about him? From the women's smiling faces I presume that getting food and lodging for the night will be no problem, thank goodness. It's not so bad to be this Ma So-and-so, after all. It's not so hard to answer questions about "one, or two," to surprise or sadden the women as the case may be.

The missus from Liang's Knoll brings over a tray with four large bowls of steaming *youcha*, a sweet gruel made from fried sesame seeds and rice flour. Only later do I learn that the four bowls signify a wish for peace and prosperity all year long—one bowl for each season. At the time I am rather put off by the grubby-looking bowls, though the youcha itself smells delicious. She sets the tray down before me, then scoops some dirty baby clothes off the floor into a wooden tub and carries it all into the inner room, her words coming to me in snatches: "Long have we not had news of you, then Master Shuigen told us . . . (a long pause, after which she returns to the outer room) as soon as you went back they put you in prison."

I am so startled I almost scald my hand with the youcha.

"No, never! What prison?"

"A pox on that Shuigen, always running on at the mouth! My poor father-in-law was so afeared he burned plenty of incense for your sake." She covers her mouth and begins to giggle. "Aiyo! I'll be darned."

The women are all laughing. The one with a mouthful of yellow teeth adds: "He even went to pray to the buddha at Daigongling."

Nuts, now it's buddhas and incense too! What if this Ma Whatsis-name is really under a jinx, really rotting away in a jail somewhere? And here I sit in his place, drinking youcha and grinning stupidly.

Mistress Liang brings me another bowl. As before, one hand is clasped over the wrist of the other, as if in some kind of ritual. I am still working on my first bowl—the sesame-and-rice mush has settled onto the bottom and I don't know how to get at it politely. "He was forever fretting about you, always telling us what a kind and upstanding person you were. That coat of yours—he wore it for many winters, and after he departed I turned it into a pair of trousers. Now little Manzai is wearing it. . . ."

I try to talk about the weather.

Suddenly the room darkens. I turn around to see a black figure almost blocking the entire doorway. From the shape I can tell it belongs to a man, his upper body bare, his bulging muscles angular and hard-edged like rocks. In his hand he is carrying something—an oxhead probably, to judge from its contour. The silhouette closes in on me before I get a good look at his face. Then, dropping his load with a thud, he reaches out both of his paws and starts pumping my hand. "Aiyoyo! If it isn't Comrade Ma, hiyaya!"

I am not some hideous maggot. Why on earth is he carrying on like this?

It is not until he turns toward the fireplace and his profile is etched in light that I see the smile on his face, as well as his gaping black hole of a mouth and the tattoos on both arms.

"Comrade Ma, when did you get here?"

I want to say my name is not Ma at all, it is Huang—Huang Zhixian, as a matter of fact—and that I have not come in search of a once-familiar place in some kind of heartfelt and heroic gesture.

"Still wist (know? recognize?) me? The year you left we were working together on the Spiral Hill highway. I am Ai Ba."

"Ai Ba, sure I remember you," I reply shamelessly. "You were the crew leader then."

"No, I only recorded the workpoints. Wist you my wife?"

"Of course, she's famous for her youcha."

"You and I, we used to chase prey together, remember? (Is that the same as hunting?) That time when I wanted to make an offering to the mountain god, you said I was just being superstitious, but then you ended up with terrible sores all over your body from the poisonous *muma* weed. And then you ran right into a muntjac, but it slipped through your legs before you could spear it and—"

"Uh, yeah . . . I just missed it . . . my eyes are bad . . ."

The cavernous mouth starts to guffaw. Slowly the women get up and leave the room, swaying their ample hips as they walk away. The man who calls himself Ai Ba brings out a gourd. From this he pours me bowl after bowl of a cloudy brew that tastes sweet and fiery and bitter all at the same time—a drink made from steeping herbs and tiger bones in alcohol, I am told. Turning down the cigarettes I offer him, he shakes some tobacco onto a strip of newspaper and rolls it up into a little cone, which he lights. The paper begins to burn, brightly, and I watch with increasing apprehension while he calmly takes a drag without so much as a glance at the flame. But at last he blows it out with a casual puff, and the cigarette looks none the worse.

"Nowadays there's as much wine and meat as you want, every family's slaughtered plenty of cattle for the New Year." Wiping his mouth he adds: "That year when we were learning from Dazhai[1] we all had to tighten our belts instead. Remember?"

"Sure I do." I think I will talk about the excellent situation today.

"Have you beheld Delong? He's now the village chief. Yesterday he went over to Zhuomeiqiao to plant some saplings, so mayhap he'll come, mayhap not, but mayhap he will." He goes on to talk about other people and events that leave me more confused than ever: So-and-so built a new house sixteen feet high; So-and-so also built a new house, eighteen feet high; So-and-so is about to build one sixteen feet high; So-and-so is just breaking ground for his, it may be sixteen feet high or it may be eighteen. I listen intently, trying hard to catch his train of thought behind the jumble of words, but all I notice is the occasional odd usage of "wist" for "know," "behold" for "see," and so on.

1. Dazhai was known as model commune during the years of the Cultural Revolution, and the entire country was exhorted to learn from its example.

My head begins to reel, and I find myself cheering just as heartily for sixteen feet as for eighteen, and just as witlessly.

"You're a good fellow, coming back to regard your old friends and all." Once more he lights his cigarette and lets it blaze for a couple of seconds—enough to set me on edge again. "I've still got those books you gave out when you were the local schoolteacher." He clomps up the stairs, and at length reappears, cobwebs in his hair, clutching in his hand a sheaf of dusty yellow papers smelling of mildew and tung oil. It turns out to be a mimeographed pamphlet, crudely printed, with splotches of ink all over the pages. The cover has been torn off, but I gather it is a reading primer: One page is devoted to the night school anthem, others contain things like basic agricultural terms, the story of the 1911 Revolution, passages from Marx's writings on peasant movements, and maps and so forth—all copied in a large, ordinary hand. It is something I could well have produced, but so what?

"Poor devil, you had a hard time too, so thin only the eyes were left in your face, but you never missed a class."

"It was nothing really."

"It snowed a lot that December, damned cold too."

"Yeah, so cold our noses almost fell off."

"And still we had to till the fields. We'd hoist our pine torches and go to work."

"Uh-huh, pine torches."

All of a sudden he turns mysterious. The glint on his cheekbone and the blackheads underneath press close to me. "I want to know something. Was it you who slew Yang the Runt?"

What Yang the Runt? Instantly my scalp constricts, my lips freeze—all I can do is shake my head repeatedly. For heaven's sake, my name is not even Ma, I have never set eyes on this Yang the Runt or whatever, so why is someone trying to incriminate me?

"They all say it was you. That guy was a snake in the grass, he had it coming to him!" Ai Ba rages. When he sees my denial, he looks as much disappointed as disbelieving.

"Any more wine?" I change the subject.

"Sure, sure, as much as you want."

"Lots of mosquitoes around here."

"They always pick on newcomers. Shall I put some rushes on the fire for you?"

The rushes begin to burn. More people come to see me, filing through the door in droves. Invariably they would ask about my health and inquire after my family. The men would smilingly accept the cigarettes I offer them and suck noisily on one end as they sit by the door or against the wall, silent for the most part. Once in a while someone would make a remark, telling me I look fatter, thinner, older, or "young faced" as ever—must be from all that easy living in the city, they would add. Then, their cigarettes finished, they would smile again and say they have to go cut a tree or lay some manure. Several little kids run over to examine my eyeglasses, only to scamper away pellmell a few moments later, screaming excitedly in a mixture of delight and fear: "Goblins! goblins! in his glasses!" Then there is the girl who hovers by the doorway chewing on a stalk of grass. She keeps staring at me almost as if possessed, and her luminous eyes seem to be swimming in tears. I have no idea what it means but it makes me very uncomfortable, so I put on an earnest look and keep my eyes fixed on Ai Ba.

In fact this kind of thing has happened to me more than once. Just now, for instance, while I was on my way to see their poppy fields I ran across a middle-aged woman. She seemed horror stricken at the sight of me and her face darkened like a lamp that had been suddenly snuffed out. Then she lowered her head and hurried away on tiptoe. I have no idea what that was all about either.

Ai Ba says I should go and see Grandpa San as well. Actually Grandpa is not around anymore—died from a snakebite not long ago, they say—only his name still crops up in people's conversations. Over by the brick kiln is the solitary little hut where he used to live, already tilting so badly it may keel over at any minute. But the two large tung trees are still standing. And beneath them the weeds are flourishing. Standing waist high, they have closed in from all sides and sidled up the steps, their undulating blades like sharp tongues waiting to devour the little shack, waiting to devour the last bones of a clan. The wooden door is padlocked, but termites have riddled it with little black holes. Would the house have fallen into such disrepair if its owner were still around, I wonder. Can it be that the soul of a house is its human inhabitant, and when the soul is fled the carcass decomposes oh so rapidly? A rusty lantern stands upended in the undergrowth, its top and sides spattered with chalky bird droppings. Close by is a cracked earthen jug from which clouds of buzzing mosquitoes would pour forth at the drop of a hat. Ai Ba says this is the pot that Grandpa San always used for pickling. He also says I used to visit Grandpa a lot just so I could have some of his pickled cucumbers. (Really?) Big pieces of plaster have fallen off the walls, but some writing can still be seen in faded outline: "Have the whole world in view." Ai Ba tells me I painted those words on the wall. (Really?) He has plucked a handful of herbs and is now checking some birds' nests for eggs. I glance inside the window. Standing in one corner is a basket half filled with lime, and next to it is a big round disc that on closer inspection turns out to be a metal barbell, so rusted it is almost unrecognizable. I am amazed: What is this unusual piece of athletic equipment doing here? How was it brought into these remote mountains?

Perhaps I already know the answer: I gave it to Grandpa San, right? I gave it to him to beat into a hoe or a plow, but in the end he left it untouched. Right?

Up on the slope someone is calling the cows: "Ooo-mah . . . ooh-mah

. . ." and from the woods across the way comes the faint tinkling of cowbells. These cattle calls are rather unusual: They sound like someone crying for mother, plaintive cries. Perhaps it was their keening that had blackened the walls of the blockhouse.

An old woman comes down the hill carrying a small bundle of twigs. Her back is bent almost double, and her thrust-out chin punches downward like a hoe with every step she takes. When she looks up to stare at me (or is she merely looking straight through to the tung tree behind me?) her murky pupils push right up against her eyelids. What startles me, though, are the deep lines in her otherwise expressionless face. She takes one look at Grandpa's dilapidated shack, turns around to look at the old tree near the blockhouse, and mutters enigmatically: "Tree is dead too." Then she continues onward in her oddly plodding way, the breeze flattening the few limp white hairs bobbing up and down, up and down on her head.

I am now absolutely sure. I have never been here before. As for the old woman's statement, I have no idea what it means either—an unfathomable pool.

Dinner is a grand affair: fist-sized hunks of beef and pork, all somewhat gamy and undercooked but full of pomp and swagger. They arrive in mounds piled high above the edges of the bowls, held together by loops of straw and stacked layer upon layer like bricks in a kiln—no doubt a custom dating back to the beginning of time. Only men are allowed at the table. One person does not show up, so in front of the empty seat the host places a sheet of straw paper onto which he would plunk down a piece of meat from time to time, for the enjoyment of the absent guest. During the meal I ask about their premium white rice, but they refuse to even discuss prices, they seem ready to give it to me for nothing. As for opium—well, there is a good crop of it this year, but the state pharmacy has a monopoly on the entire supply. I can say no more.

"The Runt got what he deserved." Ai Ba slurps some hot soup from a ladle, returns it to its gluey spot on the table, then glares at a bowl of meat as he taps it with his chopsticks. "Him and his fat ass and soft hands, a real good-for-nothing, but he had money enough to build himself a new house. If you ask me, I think he was up to no good."

"That's right! And how he used to torture us at those mass criticism meetings, tying us up like animals. Not a single one of us managed to escape that! I've still got two scars on my wrists to show for it. Damn that motherfucker!"

"How did he really die? Did he really run into a vampire and fall off a cliff?"

"No matter how mean you are, you still can't fight your stars. Don't be wanting a bushel when a peck is all you're meant to have. Hongsheng from Xia's Cove was the same way."

"Rats, he even ate rats. How mean can you get?"

"That sure is mean. Unheard of."

"Poor Bearface really got smacked around by him. I saw those little cylinders—tubes of dye, no question about it. Hardly enough to paint a few dolls, let alone to dye cloth. And he claimed they were bullets."

"But Bearface also had his own class background to blame."

I muster up all my courage to butt in: "About Yang the Runt, didn't the authorities send anyone to investigate?"

Ai Ba munches noisily on a piece of fatty meat. "Sure they did. What a load of shit! When they tried to talk to me I went looking for my chickens. Hey, Comrade Ma, you haven't even touched your wine! Come, come, have some more to eat. Here."

He presses another slab of meat into my bowl. I begin to gag and leave the table pretending to get some more rice, but as soon as I reach a dark corner I toss the meat to a dog scampering underfoot.

After dinner they insist on preparing a bath for me. I suspect this may be another local custom, and I try to appear well acquainted with the routine. The bathtub is actually a very large barrel standing in one corner of the cookhouse. It is filled with steaming hot water that seems to have been boiled with some herbs, maybe *qinghao*. Women walk about freely in front of it, the missus from Liang's Knoll even bringing me more hot water in a gourd dipper from time to time. I am embarrassed but all I can do is crouch lower in the barrel. When she finally steps outside with a pail of slop I let out a long sigh of relief.

By now I am sweating from the heat of the bathwater, but the herbs seem to have taken the itch out of all those mosquito bites. I rub my fingers over an inch-long scar on my calf, the result of a spiking on the soccer field. But maybe that's not it, maybe it's from . . . being bitten by some guy named The Runt. Maybe it was on that morning dripping with fog, along that narrow path up the hill. He was coming toward me under his umbrella, but when he caught the look in my eyes he began to tremble. And falling to his knees he cried out that he would never do it again, never ever, that he'd had nothing to do with Er Sao's death, that he knew nothing about Grandpa San's buffalo. In the end he put up a fight, his eyes bulging till they seemed ready to pop out and his jaws clamped around my leg. Then his hands began to clutch at a lariat around his throat. But all of a sudden they flew apart, and like two crabs began to crawl and squirm and gouge the dirt. Later, who knows when, the crabs gradually calmed down and became still. . . .

I dare not think on. I am even afraid to look at my hands—would I find on them the stench of blood, and rope marks from a lariat?

I now decide with all my might: I have never been to this place, nor do I know this fellow The Runt. No. Never.

I dress quickly and return to the main room. It is alive with people and activity. An old man comes in and stamps out his glowing pine brand, says he once asked me to buy him a little dye, he still owes me two dollars for it, now he's come to pay his debt, and also to invite me to his house tomorrow for dinner and to sleep over. At this Ai Ba gets into the act, protesting that it is his turn to play host to me, he has already invited the traveling tailor to his house tomorrow, he's got plenty of meat butchered anyway, no question about it but I am going to his house tomorrow. . . .

While they are arguing I slip out the door and, stumbling a little, set out to take a look at the house "I" used to live in. According to Ai Ba it's that shack right behind the old tree, and it wasn't until year before last that they turned it into a cowshed.

Again I pass beneath the tung trees, again I see the encroaching weeds and their prey, Grandpa San's sagging grass shack. And its shadow. It is watching me silently. It coughs in the raven's cries, talks to me in the rustling of the leaves. I think I even sniff an elusive aroma of alcohol in the air.

Child, have you come back? Pull up a chair and sit down. I told you to get away, far, far away, never to come back here.

But, I miss your pickled cucumbers. I tried making them myself, but they never taste the same.

What's so good about those wretched things? I only made them back then because I felt so sorry for all of you, poor devils. You were always hungry, always scrounging around for something to eat, and while you were plowing the fields if you found some broad beans on the ridges, you'd even eat them raw.

I know, you were always looking out for us.

Sooner or later we all find ourselves far from home. I did no more than I ought.

That time when we had to gather firewood, we only brought in nine loads. You were keeping tally, and you told them we brought in ten.

I don't remember anymore.

And you were always after us to shave our heads. You would tell us that hair and whiskers are both blood-eaters, if we let them grow they'd sap the life force right out of us.

Is that so? I don't remember.

I should have come back earlier to see you. I had no idea things would be so different, that you would be gone so soon.

It was time to go. Otherwise I would have turned into an immortal. My only fondness was for a drink or two, and now I've had my fill, I will sleep soundly.

Grandpa, would you like a cigarette.

Go and make yourself some tea, Xiao Ma.

I leave that aura of wine and head for home, holding aloft the almost extinguished pine brand and thinking about the morrow's chores. From time to time I would hear the splash of a frog jumping into the ditch. But I have no pine brand in my hand now, and my home has become a cowshed that feels so unfamiliar, so unfriendly. I can barely see a thing, though the sounds of cattle chewing cud and the warm musty smell of compost gush out of the barn door. Thinking their master has come, the cattle jostle each other trying to poke their heads outside and bump against the railing in a huge clatter. As I walk away, the sounds of my footsteps echo from the mud walls of the barn, almost as if there were someone walking on the other side, perhaps even within the wall itself—someone who knows my secrets.

The hills across the valley are pitch black. In the dark they appear taller and closer, stiflingly so. Looking up at the uneven strip of starry sky far above me, I suddenly feel so close, too close to the ground, as though I have been seized by an unnamed force and am about to be pulled inexorably down, down through this crack in the earth into the depths.

Just then an enormous moon appears, and the dogs in the village bay as if in fright. I turn toward the creek, treading on the flecks of moonlight that have been sifted through the trees and now dapple the ground like the floating leaves of some aquatic plant. There may be someone sitting on the bank, I think—probably a young woman, a leaf whistle between her lips.

There is no one by the creek. But when I walk back I see the shadow of a person underneath the old tree.

A silhouette—the perfect touch for such a beautiful night.

"Is that you, Xiao Ma?"

"Yes, it's me." How calm and confident comes the answer.

"Did you just come from the creek?"

"Who . . . who are you?"

"Simeizi."

"How you've grown! I wouldn't recognize you at all if I'd run into you somewhere else."

"You've seen the outside world, now everything seems different to you."

"How is everyone at home?"

Suddenly she falls silent. Looking at the mill, she finally answers in a rather strange voice: "My older sister, how she hated you. . . ."

"Hated . . ." I am so unnerved I glance at the path leading to the clearing and some lights, thinking of escape. "I . . . many things are hard for me to say. I told her once that . . ."

"Why did you put those ears of corn in her basket that day? Did you not know you cannot just up and put something in a maiden's basket? And she gave you one of her hairs, did you not understand that either?"

"I . . . I didn't, I didn't know any of the customs around here then. I needed some help that day, so I asked her to carry the corn for me."

My answer seems to pass muster.

"Everyone was talking about it, were you deaf too? I beheld it with my own eyes, you were teaching her acupuncture."

"She wanted to learn, she wanted to be a doctor. Actually, back then I didn't really know much about it myself. We were just fiddling around."

"You city folk are all heartless."

"Don't be like this. . . ."

"It's true! It's true!"

"I know . . . your sister was a good girl, I know that. She could really sing, and her needlework was so fine. Once we went eel fishing, and she caught one right after another. When I got sick she cried her eyes out. . . . I know all of that. But, some things you don't understand, and I can't explain. My way of life will never be easy, I will always be on the go, I . . . I've got my lifework to do."

I finally settle on the term "lifework," even though it sticks a little in my throat.

She covers her face and begins to sob. "That fellow Hu, he was so nasty."

I seem to know what this means, though I continue to answer tentatively: "I heard about that. I'm going to make him pay for it."

"What's the use? What's the use?" She stamps her feet as she sobs even more bitterly. "If only you had said something back then, none of this would have happened. Now my sister has turned into a bird, she sits here day after day calling, calling for you. Can you not hear it?"

Her slender shoulders heave with each sob. I can see them clearly in the moonlight, as well as her smooth neck, even her creamy-white scalp showing through the center parting of her hair. I want so much to wipe away her tears, I yearn to hold her by the shoulders and kiss that thin line of scalp, just as I would kiss my own little sister, I want to let her tears—salty ones—cling to my lips, and I will drink them in.

But I dare not. This is a strange story, and I dare not prick it.

There really is a bird singing in the tree: "Do not go-go-go, do not go-go-go . . ."—a lonesome cry that shoots high into the heavens like an arrow before it flutters down amid hills and forests, down into those black clouds and noiseless flashes of lightning in the distance. I smoke a cigarette as I gaze at the silent thunderbolts.

Do not go, go, go.

I leave. Before going I ask the missus from Liang's Knoll to give Simeizi a letter from me. In it I talk about her sister's wish—unfulfilled in the end—to become a doctor, and how I hope she would be able to realize her sister's ambition. Where there is a will there is a way. Would she like to take the entrance exams for medical training? I will send her all kinds of study materials. I promise. I also tell her I will never forget her sister. Ai Ba caught that partridge in the tree, and I am going to take it home with me where it will sing in my window every day and be my constant companion.

I steal away like a fugitive, without saying goodbye to the people in the village, and without taking care of the premium white rice. Anyway, what do I want with rice or with opium? It seems they are not what I came for originally. I feel suffocated by it all—the whole village, the entire enigma that is me. I must escape. But I turn around for another look, and once more I see the old tree that lightning killed, still standing at the entrance to the village, its withered limbs outstretched like trembling fingers. The master of that hand fell in a battle long ago and turned into a mountain, but he struggles to keep his hand raised above the earth, where even now it is grasping for something.

I go to the inn in the county seat and fall asleep to the twittering of the partridge by my bed. A dream comes to me. In it I am still walking on and on along a rutted path, its skin and muscles of mud long since stripped away by runoffs from the hills, only bones and bowels left now to bear the trample of the hill folk's straw shoes. The road is endless. The calendar watch on my wrist tells me I have been walking for an hour, a day, a week . . . but still the road runs beneath my feet. Later I am to have the same dream over and over, no matter where I go.

I awake in terror, I get a drink of water, then another, and another, I go to the bathroom, once, twice—finally I make a long-distance call to a friend. I mean to ask him whether he has managed to "waste" Mangyhead Cao at cards yet, but instead I blurt out a question about how to study for entrance exams on your own.

My friend addresses me as "Huang Zhixian."

"What?"

"What do you mean 'what'?"

"What did you call me?"

"Aren't you called Huang Zhixian?"

"Did you call me Huang Zhixian?"

"Didn't I call you Huang Zhixian?"

I am stunned. My mind is blank. It is true, I am at the inn, in the corridor is a dim light swarming with bugs, underneath it a row of makeshift cots. Right beneath the telephone there is even a big round face snoring away. But . . . is there still someone in the world named Huang Zhixian? And this Huang Zhixian—is that me?

I will never be able to walk out of the enormity that is me. I am tired.

Translated by Jeanne Tai

Appendices

APPENDIX A

ELEMENTS OF FICTION

A work of fiction is generally an organic whole, with all its parts, or elements, united into a total artistic effect. The actions of characters make up plot, the narration of the plot is determined by point of view, and so on. When we read for pleasure alone, we usually don't think of the elements in isolation.

But as students of literature we are required to look at stories differently. We are to see them as works of art written with deliberate intent. We recognize that they are made up of certain components and that these can be isolated and examined. These elements give us a kind of language for talking about fiction; they are the terms that we agree to agree upon. Moreover, they are useful. Taken together, they account for all the aspects of a work. Indeed, in this respect, they are very much like the news reporter's six basic questions: who (character), what (plot), when, where (setting), why (theme), and how (point of view, tone, symbolism). The correlation should not be surprising—fiction reveals no less about life than the news story does, although its vantages and insights are sometimes more startling.

CHARACTER

Character is indispensable. Without character there is no work of fiction. And while it is not essential that the central figure, or *protagonist* (Greek, "first actor"), be human—Kafka's story "The Metamorphosis" is narrated by a man who has become a giant beetle—it is vital that our basic human impulses be engaged.

"Character is destiny," said the Greek philosopher Heraclitus. The story, with all its turns and complications, emerges in some significant way from the personality of the protagonist. Character in combination with circumstance creates and moves the events that make up the plot. Consider, for example, Guy de Maupassant's story "The String." The frugal Hauchecorne, on his way to market, picks up and pockets a piece of string. His long-time adversary, who sees him bend over, passes the word that he has found another man's wallet. The confusion is eventually cleared up, and Hauchecorne is exonerated. But his character being what it is, the episode obsesses him for the rest of his days. Any other person would have acted differently, but Hauchecorne is driven to his destiny. He dies in a delirium, crying out, "A piece of string—look—here it is." We are who we are, suggests Maupassant, and everything flows from that.

Characters in fiction can be of several kinds. *Rounded* and *dynamic* characters are lifelike. They exhibit complexity in behavior and motivation; they emerge from the background and give the impression of three-dimensionality. The dynamic (usually rounded) character undergoes some significant change during the course of the story's events. However, not every rounded character is necessarily dynamic. Anton Chekhov's Gurov in "Lady with Lapdog" is both. When we meet him at the beginning of the story, he is an unhappily married playboy. Through his infatuation, which later becomes love, with a young married woman, he deepens into a reflective individual capable of expressing genuine emotion.

Writers also make use of *flat* and *static* characters. This is not because they lack the energy or inclination to develop individual figures fully. Usually it is a matter of artistic need. A short story writer wants to create an impression of believability. For this to happen there must be a foreground and a background. A rounded character will appear all the more rounded if she or he is set against a flat character, or a type. Or very possibly the writer is using a character for a limited function. In Sarah Orne Jewett's "A White Heron," for example, the heroine is a young girl named Sylvia, but the balance of the story and the sequence of events require that she have a guardian. Mrs. Tilley is both flat and static, but the story could not move forward naturally without her. Note, however, that not all flat characters are *stereotypes*. A stereotyped character generally exhibits standardized attributes, often for comic effect. Literature abounds with greedy landlords, dashing officers, and the like. Jewett's Mrs. Tilley is undeveloped as a character, but she is not a type.

A different kind of character, but one well worth mentioning, is the *antagonist*. This figure, flat or round, is a foil to the protagonist. Hauchecorne's adversary in "The String," the man who falsely accuses him of picking up a wallet, is an antagonist of sorts. For more obvious antagonist figures we might look to the folk tale tradition. Cinderella's wicked stepmother is the perfect instance; she is as evil as the young girl is good, and the full resolution of the story comes only when she has been defeated.

Fictional characters are as diverse as people themselves, and there can be no neat categorization of types, especially from the nineteenth century on. What is fascinating to note is the growing psychological complexity as we move forward in time, until in the twentieth century character finally takes precedence over plot in much so-called serious literature.

PLOT

People often use *plot* and *narrative* as if they were interchangeable terms, but actually there is a crucial distinction. This was stated most concisely by the writer E. M. Forster, who observed that if we write "The king died, and the queen died," we have a narrative—a simple relating of events in sequence—but if we write instead "The king died, and the queen died of grief," then we have a plot. In the second instance, we have established a connection of cause between the two events. And this, the making of connections, is the very essence of the storyteller's art. For narrative to become plot it must reveal meaning in human terms. Events themselves just happen; events become interesting and relevant when we see their effects upon people or, in the case of fiction, upon characters.

This is not to say, however, that the writer always explains the causal connection. This task is very often left to the reader; it is the puzzle that we solve as we read and that draws us more deeply into the world of the story. The writer may present the narrative in such a way that the reader assembles it into a plot. In a story by Olive Schreiner, "The Woman's Rose," we are told by the narrator that she has for many years kept a rose in her box of mementos. Later she reveals how it happened that one night long ago another woman presented her with the flower. Schreiner leaves it to the reader to determine that the rose was bestowed as a beautiful woman's tribute to a rival's beauty and that the woman who received it kept it because it had taught her something about human generosity. The plot, in other words, depends on our willingness as readers to draw the necessary inferences. If we read the story without thinking about the connection between the elements, then we have only absorbed its narrative component.

Plot is the basic material of any work of fiction. How it is handled determines the shape of the work and, to a large extent, its effect upon us as readers. In longer works like novels an author can generate complexity by introducing additional plots (called *subplots*). When we read a novel by Charles Dickens, for instance, we often find ourselves holding several plot lines in mind at any one time. The short story, by contrast, tends to work toward what Edgar Allan Poe called "the single effect," a culmination that pulls together and resolves the tensions created by the characters and their circumstances. There are, of course, exceptions. A number of modern story writers have experimented with techniques of breaking up the traditional form. They have introduced fractured plot lines and, in some instances, multiple narrators. But, by and large, the short story remains what it has been for centuries—a straightforward account of one or more human beings changed by the events in their lives.

The survival of the classic short story form despite all the changes proposed by experimentalists is remarkable. It would seem that there is a certain deep logic to engaging and holding a reader, which an author disregards at great risk. So even in our day, after decades of artistic upheaval, the great majority of short stories are still constructed around the classic pattern of beginning, middle, and end. There is a set-up, or *exposition,* wherein the characters and their situations are introduced. This is followed by the *rising action,* which poses and then intensifies the complications, building toward a *climax.* Finally there comes a *resolution,* also called the *falling action,* which shows the consequences. The resolution tells us how things turned out; it answers the inevitable reader's question, "What finally happened?" Sometimes an author will attach a further explanation so that the reader does not mistake the meaning of the outcome. This is the *denouement,* originally a French term for "unraveling." Most authors, though, especially modern authors, prefer to leave the meanings and implications for the reader. They proceed by *indirection,* suggesting rather than telling.

Washington Irving's "The Legend of Sleepy Hollow" is a perfect example of a classic short story. The exposition introduces the protagonist, Ichabod Crane, showing his character and hinting at his particular weaknesses (Ichabod is presented as a foolish, self-satisfied bookworm who imagines himself—wrongly—to be attractive to the ladies). The rising action brings on the young lady who is the object of his interest *and* her other suitor, the rough and rowdy Brom Bones (the antagonist). The rising action brings all the main characters together at a party. Irving builds tension and expectation in the reader, who knows that Ichabod will have to ride home along the lonely, supposedly haunted, road. The climax comes when Ichabod, riding, is attacked by what he believes to be the legendary Headless Horseman (it is Brom in disguise). The resolution then tells us what the villagers found the next morning and gives us a good idea about what they surmised as to the fate of their schoolmaster, Ichabod.

Stories like Irving's hold our attention by creating an atmosphere of *suspense* around the characters and events. We turn the pages because we want to know what will happen next. Suspense is the writer's way of keeping us expectant. Information is held back; there is a promise of revelation. Sometimes the promise is implicit in the situation: two rivals fight a duel, and we read on to see who will win. In other cases, the author may subtly prepare the ground for us through *foreshadowing,* passing cues and hints to the reader. Thus, in "The Legend of Sleepy Hollow," Irving devotes several long passages early to descriptions of the spooky countryside and to the retelling of legends of ghosts and headless riders. When Ichabod finally sets out on his homeward ride, our memory of this lore adds to the atmosphere.

Of course, not every story is structured according to the classic pattern. Some proceed through *flashback,* showing what finally happened and then tracking backward to disclose the chain of events up to the present. Still others may begin in the middle of the climactic action and step backward to fill in information as the reader needs it. The variations are the same ones we find in films. What remains constant is that the reader needs to be drawn in, informed, and, finally, affected. The rest is up to the taste and ingenuity of the writer.

SETTING

Setting, which for our purposes includes both time and place, is a fundamental component of any work of fiction. How the author makes use of setting depends entirely on the desired effects. One of the first things we as readers do is attempt to situate the events, to place them within a framework. Thus, setting affects our reading even when it appears to be irrelevant. Old legends and folk tales often begin in the haziest manner: "Once upon a time in a faraway place . . ." The dreamy and universal impression they create arises, at least in part, from our inability to fix the particulars of when and where.

Setting fulfills two obvious functions. First, it gives the reader the impression that *this really happened*. The Russian storyteller Nikolai Gogol begins his story "The Nose" as follows: "A most extraordinary thing happened in Petersburg on the twenty-fifth of March." We immediately situate ourselves in the realm of the specific, and we extend our trust, preparing to hear of documented happenings. As it turns out, Gogol tells the story of a man who wakes up to find that his nose is missing. A clever strategy on Gogol's part: he has used the concrete setting to create in the reader a tension between the desire to believe and the utter improbability of what he then reads. Our response to the story would be very different if Gogol had written: "Once, long ago, in a city in Russia . . ." We would then be inclined to read the work more as a fairy tale than as an unsettling excursion into the absurd.

The second function, obvious but worth spelling out, is to situate us in space and time so that we can understand the events of the story as shaped by specific factors. To put it simply, people behave differently—and in some ways *are* different—in different places and at different times. Historical contexts often define the meanings of actions and statements. Maupassant's story about Hauchecorne, "The String," asks that we believe certain things about the character of the French peasant—namely, that he is frugal and shrewd. There are certainly frugal and shrewd individuals everywhere and in all eras, but some part of the story's power depends upon the activation of an ancient stereotype.

The placing of events in time functions in the same way. It is essential that we know when reading Nathaniel Hawthorne's stories that they are set in New England villages in the seventeenth and early eighteenth centuries. His investigations of human morality only take on full meaning when we understand the intense religiosity of the early Puritans. The same situations—that is, the same moral tensions—could not be created in present-day Salem.

Setting, especially locale, is often treated with great specificity. The author may be lavish in describing in order to draw the reader more deeply into the events: the better we can *see* a situation, the more involved we are likely to become. Consider just how much a few atmospheric touches compel our involvement in the opening paragraph of Sarah Orne Jewett's "A White Heron":

> The woods were already filled with shadows one June evening, just before eight o'clock, though a bright sunset still glimmered faintly among the trunks of the trees. A little girl was driving home her cow, a plodding, dilatory, provoking creature in her behavior, but a valued companion for all that. They were going away from the western light, and striking deep into the dark woods, but their feet were familiar with the path, and it was no matter whether their eyes could see it or not.

Jewett's description not only gives the reader the details needed for a mental picture but also starts up—as so much fictional description does—thematic suggestions. Jewett depicts the natural world as great and mysterious, dwarfing the little girl and her cow. She sketches in lightly the opposition between the familiar and the unknown. Events to come will only confirm and deepen these impressions. No less important, Jewett weaves together images of light and dark that will, by story's end, hold powerful symbolic value.

One could continue to cite the ways in which different writers make use of settings and descriptions to bring depth into their work. But the point would remain the same: as readers we cannot afford to regard these elements as merely decorative or incidental. The setting is the soil out of which all fictional surprises must flower.

THEME

Of the various elements of fiction, theme is probably the most difficult to discuss. This is paradoxical for, in a sense, theme, or meaning, is very often what we seek in literature. We all want to find out truths about human nature and to enrich our understanding of the psychological and moral bases of our lives. And, indeed, the expression of themes and meanings is what drives an author to write. Fiction, however fanciful or entertaining it may be, arises from the writer's desire to communicate some insight about life.

The difficulty of discussing themes and meanings has to do with the fact that they are very often complex and ambiguous. In many cases, they are woven deeply into the fabric of the whole work and cannot be plucked clear with a single motion. And this is their value. There is a great difference between reading a story that explores the theme of the difficulty of love and reading the message LOVE IS DIFFICULT in a fortune cookie. The difference is that the mere message does not allow us to experience its truth—we either accept it or we don't. The same truth, expressed in a story, has everything to do with the specific characters and situations.

In other words, the thematic elements in a short story do not always take a form that lends itself to simple statement. Often they nudge us to probe and to raise questions. A writer like D. H. Lawrence, for example, has many complex stories that explore the relationships between men and women. But unless we are willing to strip away the subtleties and ambiguities, we can never reduce his work to simple formulation: that men are like this and women like that, or that the nature of love is such and such. Lawrence's intent is to guide us toward new ways of considering the meaning of human encounters. We finish reading his stories and novels with a strong sense of forces in collision. We recognize many things at once: the needs of the body and the needs of the emotional self are very different; or affection and aggression can live side by side. These are Lawrence's themes, and we can discuss them. But it would be a mistake to think that the value of his fiction lies in a series of readily extractable statements.

This tendency for literary meanings to be diffuse and multiple should not stop our search for important themes when we discuss stories or write essays. If anything, it opens the gates to inquiry and interpretation.

A theme is, briefly, the understanding that the author seeks to communicate through the work. It gives the work its purpose and has a great deal to do with the way the whole is structured. We can—and often we need to—generalize, to say, "Kafka's stories depict the alienation that results when the foundations of faith have been destroyed," or "D. H. Lawrence views human relationships as a struggle between the desire for freedom and the desire for surrender." But we cannot pretend that we have thereby said all that needs to be said. The thematic generalization is but a beginning, a way of giving our own thoughts focus. We must then be willing to show just how these truths apply to the works in question. Theme is at once the beginning and end of our search. The search itself is what gives value to our engagement with literature.

POINT OF VIEW

The story writer has a great many options to consider when deciding how to present events. The final effect of the story is achieved through specific manipulations of character and plot. In this regard, the writer's most important technical decision is what *point of view* to use. To decide this, he or she needs to ask certain questions: "How involved do I want the reader to be in the thoughts and actions of my characters?" "How much should be revealed?" "What vantage will allow the strongest climax and the most effective resolution of tensions?"

The basic possibilities are as follows:

First-person. This means that the story is told from the point of view—seen through the eyes—of a participant. The *narrator,* or teller, uses the first-person "I", and the access to information is limited by the role of the narrator. That is, the reader will only know what "I" reports. However, the writer can exercise a good deal of control by deciding how to place that "I". The speaking voice can belong to a minor character who sees the key events from a distance, thus giving a greater appearance of objectivity. Or, at the other extreme, the viewer can be positioned at—or even *be*—the center of interest. Frank O'Connor's story "My Oedipus Complex," for instance, is told strictly in the voice of a young boy. It is, as the title indicates, *his* story. The humorous effect results from the tension between what the boy reports as his truth and our interpretation, as older and wiser readers, of his words.

Second-person. We rarely encounter fiction written in the second-person voice, or "you", but it does exist. The Mexican writer Carlos Fuentes has written a powerful short story, "Aura," and an ambitious novel, *The Change of Skin,* using "you". More recently, Jay McInerney adopted the tactic for his highly popular novel *Bright Lights, Big City.* But there are not many other instances, and this is for a good reason. The use of "you" creates an immediate problem: "you" is not a subject but an object of address; its use implies that there is an unidentified other. The sentence, "You wake up and get dressed," suggests either an all-seeing on-looker or else a personality capable of commenting upon its every movement with a self-conscious detachment. Either possibility raises huge problems for the writer with a story to tell, which is why we encounter the second-person address so rarely.

Third person. This is the most widely used vantage, probably because it is the most adaptable. Third-person narration assumes a neutral, or objective, presentation. The narrator is the author, standing outside the narration. The possible variations are manifold, for the author can choose the degree of involvement as well as the extent of knowledge. He or she can have full *omniscience,* with access to every thought and emotion of all characters, or *limited omniscience,* with insight into only certain characters. Or the author can be restricted to the position of pure observer, noting external actions and conversations but having no access to characters' inner thoughts.

In his long story "The Dead," James Joyce shows how a writer can shift from one vantage to another, achieving, in this case, a texture of great complexity and mounting psychological force. Joyce begins the story with a straightforward objective use of the third-person voice:

> Lily, the caretaker's daughter, was literally run off her feet. Hardly had she brought one gentleman into the little pantry behind the office on the ground floor and helped him off with his overcoat than the wheezy doorbell clanged again and she had to scamper along the bare hallway to let in another guest.

And when he introduces his protagonist, Gabriel, the treatment is similarly objective.

Very soon, though, we are let in on what might be called Gabriel's uppermost thoughts and emotions. Joyce describes his reaction to a remark made by Lily:

> He was still discomposed by the girl's bitter and sudden retort. It had cast a gloom over him which he tried to dispel by arranging his cuffs and the bows of his tie.

By the end of the story, however, we have been brought into the deepest reaches of Gabriel's self. Joyce skillfully slides us over the barrier between objective and subjective until we feel that we have come to inhabit Gabriel's mind:

> He stretched himself cautiously along under the sheets and lay down beside his wife. One by one they were all becoming shades. Better pass boldly into that other world, in the full glory of some passion, than fade and wither dismally with age.

Some part of the story's power surely has to do with the distance we have traveled from that first mention of Lily.

In the last passage quoted, Joyce switches from the third-person objective to the omniscient mode. In giving us Gabriel's thoughts (notice that he dispenses with the customary "he thought"), he makes use of the *interior monologue*. The thoughts are composed into orderly sentences; they give a stylized transcription of Gabriel's inner life. Interior monologue is in this way distinct from *stream of consciousness*. Stream of consciousness, used by Joyce in his novel *Ulysses,* attempts to express the inner process directly, including all incidental thoughts and stray observations. Here is Joyce's protagonist from *Ulysses,* Leopold Bloom:

> Where is my hat, by the way? Must have put it back on the peg. Or hanging up on the floor. Funny, I don't remember that. Hallstand too full. Four umbrellas, her raincloak.

Not only do writers use different vantages to tell their stories but they may also grant their narrators varying degrees of intelligence and reliability. The story is filtered through the voice that tells it. That voice may belong to a liar, a fool, or a person so taken up with appearances that he misses the real point of what he is reporting. The reader should always be alert for clues about the narrator's own personality and strive to measure the truth of what is told accordingly. As the old adage has it, "Trust the tale, not the teller."

TONE

Tone is directly related to point of view. How the story is told is a direct consequence of who is telling it, and this bears on the question of reliability just mentioned.

Third-person narration, usually selected because it allows for a pretense of objectivity, is generally given in an appropriately neutral tone. Indeed, any deviation from matter-of-factness tends to call attention to the teller, and this inevitably undermines the effectiveness of the third-person vantage.

When a story is told in the first-person voice, however, the speaker's personality and involvement are intimately bound up with the final effect. The writer must therefore be very careful to ensure that *what* and *how* are in the right relation. The whole point of a story like Mark Twain's "The Notorious Jumping Frog of Calaveras Country" is that the leaping contest between two frogs is told by a braggart—if one changed the manner of telling, the humor might disappear.

Every story has its own specific tone, which is used for specific effect. There is always some intended relation between what is being told and the way in which the telling is orchestrated. In some cases, we find a perfect obviousness—the narrator provides a clear window on the situation. In other instances, there is tension, and the effect is often ironic. Irony naturally arises wherever there is an imbalance between what is presented and what is felt. It can be *situational irony,* as in "My Oedipus Complex," where a boy tells about adult things he does not understand, or *tonal irony,* resulting from a discrepancy between the speaker's reaction and what would be expected. A speaker might recount a traumatic situation in casual words or carry on with great excitement about an event that everyone else would regard as trivial.

SYMBOLISM AND ALLEGORY

Symbols, like themes, are hard to describe in cut-and-dried.terms, and for similar reasons. Many readers mistakenly believe that symbols are in a work like raisins in dough and that one simply finds them and plucks them out. Every so often, it's true, we do encounter an old-fashioned, unambiguous symbol—a character cast as a Christ figure, a flying bird meant to signify freedom—but the matter is seldom so simple.

A symbol is an element in a work of art that represents something else; it carries a powerfully condensed meaning. In a certain context, a gun may symbolize a character's destructive nature, or a specific illness of the body may point to a corresponding ailment of the soul. But even where this seems obvious, we must be careful to keep the lines clearly drawn. That is, a gun is also itself—a common weapon—and an illness is primarily physical. The larger relevance requires an appropriate context. We need some reason for thinking that the author intended A to represent B. As Freud said, "Sometimes a cigar is just a cigar."

Symbols function in different ways in a work of fiction. In some instances, a character is aware of the symbolic nature of a given thing. The protagonist of "The Woman's Rose" preserved the rose that had been given to her because she knew that the flower had been presented as a symbolic token. In Hawthorne's story "The Minister's Black Veil," on the other hand, the protagonist, the Reverend Mr. Hooper, one day dons a sinister-looking black veil. Certainly it has some special significance for him, but for his fellow townspeople as well as for the reader it remains a mystery—any number of interpretations can be made.

In other cases, a symbol is only apparent to the reader, for only the reader can see enough of the situation to attribute significance. Young Sylvia, in Sarah Orne Jewett's "A White Heron" knows the beauty and rarity of the lone white heron, but she does not draw the connection that is so obvious to the reader: the bird is a symbol of her own youthful innocence. A certain ambiguity with respect to symbols is inevitable in most cases. An object can be charged with significance, but sometimes the significance points in several directions at once. Nearly always, though, the symbol deepens the resonance of the work, involving the reader more fully in the process of discovering meanings.

Allegory is a kind of symbolic system in which each element possesses a secondary, usually abstract, reference. Allegory was a favored mode for conveying elaborate religious messages, as in John Bunyan's well-known tale of his hero Christian's journey to the Heavenly City in *Pilgrim's Progress*. Every action in the work is part of a larger code: one man's physical journey stands for the spiritual voyage that every Christian must undergo. While many contemporary writers make some use of symbolic elements in their work, few attempt to devise a complete and self-consistent allegorical structure. Possibly the last well-known instance was George Orwell's novel *Animal Farm,* which portrays postwar political alignments by using a group of barnyard animals. The allegorist must be careful, as Orwell was, that the equivalences be clear to the reader.

All the elements of fiction are, in a sense, tools adapted by the writer to serve a desired end. Artists working in other media make use of different elements. To become trained in appreciation, whether of fiction, painting, film, or any of the other arts, we must learn the trick of "double vision." That is, we must be able to launch ourselves into the work in order to experience it and yet be able to step back in order to see how its effects were created. A student of film sees at least two different movies—the one we all get immersed in, and the other one, with all its cuts and camera angles. The same is true of the student of literature and the work of fiction. At times, the twin focus will seem difficult, but in the end it enriches the experience of reading immeasurably.

APPENDIX B

WRITING ABOUT LITERATURE

Anyone who would pass along useful advice on writing about literature faces an enormous obstacle. Simply, there is no one right, or best, way to do it. Different teachers have different requirements, based upon their own notions and expectations of their students. The works themselves—the stories, novels, poems, and plays, that are to be written *about*—are so diverse that no tidy pattern or set of patterns can be applied. Finally, you, as students, each have your own aptitudes, interests, and favored ways of working. Who can really lay down the law that *this* is the way to do it?

The observations that follow, therefore, are not in any sense meant as prescriptions. They are rather suggestions, things you might think about when you undertake to write about a work of literature. But they are not entirely arbitrary, either. They are useful and represent something of a consensus view. A great many practicing writers—of fiction, essays, biographies, and nonfiction prose—have set down their reflections on the writing process. The shelves sag with "how I do it" accounts. And from these accounts a certain representative picture emerges, a picture that suggests that the human brain digests, processes, and spins out information and ideas in basic sequences. Some knowledge of these sequences will likely help you with your own writing.

There are always exceptions, of course. We have all heard of writers who have but to pick up a pen to generate perfect prose as fast as they can write it down. These reflections are meant for those who are not quite so fortunate, those who have to sweat and groan before producing anything fit for a reader's eyes.

WHY WRITE ABOUT LITERATURE?

There are several things to be said for writing about literature (in this case, the short story) aside from the obvious fact that you sometimes have no choice. First, it puts you into a new and demanding relation to a work of art. Writing is, in one sense, a highly intensified form of reading; it is an active, rather than passive, engagement. Writing about a literary work requires a kind of attentiveness that goes far beyond the usual ways of reading. And this attentiveness is a virtue in itself. It brings you to a new level of response, allowing you to grapple with the deeper messages of the work. To write about a story—to write *well*—you have to approach it as though it truly matters. Address a serious work seriously, and it will pay off. You will find not only ideas to write about but also ideas that can change the way you think about your life. Writing is one of the best ways to establish the connection between literature and the realm of actual experience.

The process of writing, distilling and expressing ideas, is nearly always difficult. But then so is running five miles or working with weights. And just as you don't always lace up your running shoes for the sheer fun of it, but do it because you like the results—the feeling, the *gain*—so you don't always wrestle with words and ideas because it brings pleasure. You do it, rather, because the act of writing, whatever the subject, is the most useful discipline imaginable for the nonphysical self. Language is the very stuff of consciousness; it is a tool for knowing the self as well as for making contact with others. It stands to reason that the more pressure and articulation you can bring to your use of language, the more decisively you will know yourself. The act of writing, painful as it sometimes is, can bring a larger clarity into your life. You may be writing and struggling with an essay on Chekhov or Hemingway, but when your thoughts finally find their way, you have illuminated something more than just the topic at hand.

Then there is the undeniable joy of internal combustion. It does not always come. You will write essays and papers that lack it—this is inevitable. But sometimes, in mid-sentence, as you are looking off toward the window and pondering the significance of a particular passage, you will suddenly find an idea that is unexpected and new. And as you start to note it on a scrap of paper, it may open up into another new idea. Something unforeseen is happening: combustion. At such moments, the importance of the assignment diminishes; the ideas themselves take over. Runners talk about the body's release of endorphins as the payoff for pain. The mind rewards you with a different—but no less pleasurable—excitement.

WRITING BEGINS WITH READING

No matter who the writer or how short the interval between assignment and submission date, the process of writing a literary essay or paper can be broken down into distinct stages. Hardly anyone just sits down and produces, with no reflection or revision, a finished work. Beginners and professionals alike go through the same basic process, only at different rates and with differing degrees of success. While not everyone who takes up a pen will win the Pulitzer prize, anyone who is willing to make the effort can learn to write skillful and effective prose. Needless to say, what you learn in the course of writing about literature can be applied, with some slight retooling, to other disciplines. This is one of the main reasons why law schools look at the applications of English majors with special interest. Admissions officers know that the ability to marshal one's thoughts clearly and persuasively is essential to future success.

The literary essay is by definition about a literary work. It may be an *analysis,* breaking the whole work down into its constituent parts and focusing upon some particular aspect. Or it may zoom in to explicate in great detail a key passage, showing how the part functions within the whole (*explication* derives from the Latin, "unfolding"). Or the essay may *compare and contrast* elements from separate works. It may, further, seize the opportunity for thematic exploration, using the story as a way of reflecting upon some larger issue. (You might, for instance, build on an analysis of Kate Chopin's "The Story of an Hour" to discuss the changing social role of women.) But whatever the essay is finally about, it will nearly always have its roots in a reading of one or more works. The writing process, then, begins with reading.

There are obviously many kinds of reading. Whatever it is that you do with the Sunday paper is not to be compared with the sustained attentiveness that you bring to a work of literature. But even with this more serious kind of reading there are levels and degrees of focus. If you are reading a book of stories purely for pleasure, you approach the words on the page with different attitudes and expectations than if you were reading in order to write. This is not to say that you should reject the pleasure you take in reading, but the fact is that an engagement with literature does not always begin and end in pleasure. When you read in order to write, you fix your sights upon larger matters of intent and significance. You absorb the *what* of the story, but you also consider the *how* and the *why*.

Switching from one mode of reading to another is not always easy. You can't just put on your "serious" glasses and get to work. If you are going to write about an author's work, no matter what the context of the assignment, you should be willing to read it several times. The first reading, however careful, is preliminary. You need to get through the story once just in order to find out how to approach it best a second time. And even though you have probably not picked up a pencil to make a single note, the writing process has begun. For as soon as you adjust your expectations to make a second approach, you have started the sifting and sorting process that will ultimately lead to words on paper.

This matter of adjusting expectations is fairly automatic—you don't really need to do anything special. Your first reading gives you a sense of the terrain; you know who does what to whom, and how. You may even feel that you understand the work quite well. Nevertheless, the second time through it will be a different story. Once you know how things develop, the mainspring of suspense slackens. You are free to slow down, to look at other features, to inspect details. And you know, in the most basic sense, where you need to look. Your first reading has given you a set of cues:

this is about a man's crisis of faith, about a woman's suppressed love; the author expends great energy—or none—in describing the surroundings; there is an obvious use of water imagery; and so on. You have strewn the work with your own private markers, and now you return to them for a closer look.

The first reading naturally yields the more obvious kinds of information, but an essay will be more interesting, and will stand a better chance of holding a reader, if it departs from the obvious. Who wants to read or write another essay that simply announces that Hemingway was concerned with issues of manhood in his fiction or that D. H. Lawrence built a given story around a struggle between the sexes? These are observations, necessary but obvious, that anyone can derive from a first reading. The second reading will likely lead to a more specific set of responses. Knowing about the struggle between the sexes, say, you would pick up a more powerful lens. You would look for subtleties of motivation, hints of ambivalence, and significant turning points in the narration. You would be ready to start planning your essay.

PLANNING AND PONDERING

Much about the writing process is, frankly, mysterious. Despite all our research in psychology and cognitive science, we do not yet have a reliable explanation of what ideas are or how they are generated. And, indeed, of all the internal steps you will go through in producing an essay, none is quite as hard to account for as the passage from reading to the first notation of ideas. Still, a few observations can be made.

To begin with, in preparing to write you are not faced, as some might suppose, with moving from no thought to thought. The fact is that you are thinking with greater or lesser intensity all the time. You may try to suppress your thought process while reading so as to be better able to concentrate, but success is only partial. As you move from sentence to sentence, following the trail of the story, you are constantly reacting, sending out feelers, making connections. The thoughts are often fairly basic, taking the form of response or surmise: "She is going to have to leave him" "A life like that would be depressing," "He acts just like John," and so on. In the course of the first reading especially, it is hard to discriminate between more and less relevant reactions, for until you know how things turn out, nearly everything has potential application.

The second reading is crucial because it allows the responses to take on sharper relief. Scattered impressions come together into clusters, and thematic outlines begin to emerge. It is time to start generating ideas.

Assuming that you have some choice in the matter—that is, your teacher has not assigned you an analysis of the snow imagery in James Joyce's "The Dead"—you begin by interrogating your own reading. "Was I affected by what I read? How so?" "What caused my reaction?" "Was there a scene, a character, a description, or an image that most struck me? What *about* it struck me?" The more securely you can ground yourself in your own reading experience, the better will be your chance for finding a subject that seems worth doing. The best possible point of departure is the discovery of a puzzle or question, for the sincere attempt to answer it can bring a powerful momentum to an essay.

The most common mistake that unpracticed writers make is to go rushing from the first inklings of insight right to the typewriter or word processor. Resist hurry if you can. For ideas have a life of their own and cannot be hurried. That insight of yours may not be ready to be deepened or extended yet, and there is every chance that a hasty assault will kill it altogether. Before it can be fixed into paragraph form, the idea needs to percolate in the back of your mind.

Again, this sounds mysterious. But most writers who would agree that a period of gestation has to come before the work of development. This does not mean that you just walk around twiddling your thumbs—though that might do the trick for some—but it does mean that you should refrain from trying to crystallize the idea in final form at this stage. If you lock an idea into the mold of concrete expression too soon, you seal it off from the possibility of transformation. At this stage, you want to leave yourself open to all kinds of surprises and discoveries. One of the most useful things you can do at this point is to make use of associative freewriting.

FREEWRITING

Freewriting is not to be confused with "sprinting," in which a writer puts down words as quickly as possible with the hope that the preconscious mind will release some unexpected and useful strand of association. Freewriting is more like the process of doodling. The writer notes down ideas and responses as they naturally occur, exercising no restraint or discipline. There is no attempt at this stage to devise a sequence; outlining will come later. Freewriting ought to be relaxed, even playful. The purpose, as with sprinting, is to trigger connections. The natural tendency—a few trial attempts will probably bear this out—is for ideas to get sharper, more specific; the general gives way to the more particular. Thus, a phrase like "tension in marriage" may fairly quickly lead to refinements like "woman frustrated by lack of emotional contact" and "man feels misunderstood, has violent outbursts." The mind keeps circling, making further discriminations.

So far, the notations are more or less descriptive—they register what seems true. As yet there is no idea. But suppose you now noted another aspect of the relationship in this hypothetical story: "the woman fears her husband's rage, but also seems to welcome it." This, too, is mainly descriptive. But it has brought you into the vicinity of an idea. There is a paradox here that might be useful for building a thesis, or central argument. The idea might be something like this: there is a cycle in this relationship; at the point of greatest frustration, the husband expresses his rage, and this brings the couple closer together by allowing for emotional contact.

Though you are a long way from the writing stage, the germ of an idea has developed. You have discovered that the tension in the marriage cuts two ways: it makes for distance, on the one hand, and it also creates the explosions that break that distance down. When you begin to trace the specific workings of this pattern in the story, you will begin to find a way to shape the material.

THESIS

One of the main functions of the freewriting process is to lead you to a workable thesis. The thesis can be defined as the major point of your essay or paper. It gives you, the writer, a purpose, and it gives your reader a goal. Although you may begin writing before you know all the fine points of your presentation, you should never set out to write before your thesis is clear to you. So clear, in fact, that you could write it out on a 3 × 5 index card. The thesis of your essay on the preceding hypothetical story might be, "The tensions in the marriage between X and Y are part of a larger cycle: emotional distance creates the conditions for confrontation, which allows for contact." You might then go on to write an essay that shows, with examples and discussion, how the cycle works itself out in the course of the story. You could then take up the larger question of whether such a relationship falsifies the ideals of marriage or whether it simply illustrates the pitfalls common to all human relationships. Any number of variations are possible.

The main thing about a thesis is that it should be specific enough to be interesting and at the same time general enough to allow for exploration. To say "relationships often have problems" is to say very little, and the reader is likely to yawn. But you can go too far the other way, asserting, for example, "In the course of her marriage to Y, X often found that Y would start to show anger after he'd been drinking and that he would then start to criticize her actions." A statement like this is really part of the discussion of a thesis—by itself it does not have the breadth or interest to support an essay. In deciding on whether a thesis is right or not, you need judgment. You also need to be able to picture how you might build an argument. And you need to ask yourself whether you, as a reader, would have any desire to read a paper on the chosen idea.

Usually (though not always) the thesis is presented early in the essay. It gives the writer a way to organize the material and the reader a frame within which to understand it. Once the thesis has been determined, you can move from the more casual associations of freewriting to the more structured notations of the outline.

OUTLINING

Not all writers use outlines—at least, formal outlines—and those who do have generally adapted the traditional format to their own needs. An outline is really nothing more than a map of logical procedures. Most of you were probably taught the standard form in high school. The odds are, however, that few of you set about making a plan with numbers and letters of the alphabet. The procedure has an air of formality about it; moreover, it requires that you know what you are going to say from start to finish. Many writers prefer some element of surprise and trust that they will find the right arguments and examples as they go along. But very few begin work without notations of one sort or another. A basic grasp of the structure is essential.

Even if you refuse the rigors of the formal outline, you will need to develop some sort of intelligible visual shorthand. You should never just begin at the beginning and trust that your native intelligence will get you where you need to go. It very well may, but you will find that in the process you have expended a great deal of energy in checking and rechecking what you've written in order to make sure that it hangs together. Even the sketchiest outline can help you to avoid this. A few key words and arrows may be enough. Use whatever will serve your memory best. The idea is that you be able to hold the whole of your essay in mind at once. The step-by-step development of an idea is much easier to sustain if you can take in the trajectory of the essay at a glance.

As important as it is to reach the right level of readiness before writing, it will not do to wait too long. The writer never knows everything about the subject or approach. Indeed, too detailed a map can take the pleasure out of the journey. While you will not want to be as vague as the novelist E. M. Forster, who once stated that he wrote in order to find out what he was thinking, you should probably be ready to plunge in while there are still a few blanks in your conception. But study your outline closely to make sure that you can account for the major steps of the argument and to assure yourself that they make logical sense.

A good thing to do while you are working through the outline phase is to gather up the specific quotations you plan to use in your essay. Nothing so effectively disrupts the actual process of writing as having to pause for long periods while you hunt around in the text for the best passage to cite. Gathering the material in advance has the additional advantage of sharpening the focus before you write. If you know that you will be quoting a specific passage, you stand a much better chance of preparing the way for it in your discussion. If, on the other hand, you find yourself thinking, "How do I know which quote to use if I don't know what I'm going to be arguing?" the chances are that you are not yet ready to launch your essay. By the same token, once you have a clear sense of what examples you will use, you are probably ready to start writing your draft.

A draft is a trial run, a full presentation that is yet open to modifications and fine-tuning. No matter how accomplished you are as a writer, it is folly to think that you will get your thoughts and prose into final form right away. Assuming this only sets you up for disappointment and inhibits the entire writing process. A draft is a pencil sketch that gives you the freedom an eraser provides. In the lucky event that your first venture is near-perfect, you have only to follow over the contours with ink.

Before the advent of the word processor, a rewrite meant complete retyping. Most writers now have the option of making selective changes. This brings ease but also certain dangers. You can make changes and additions in the body of a paragraph without rewriting the whole. But don't forget that language is always in context. Make sure that you read over closely what precedes and follows the alteration so that you do not upset the balance of the presentation.

There is something to be said for the more painstaking process of typing and retyping. Mainly, a full retyping encourages secondary—or stylistic—revision. In going over what you thought was a perfectly satisfactory sentence, you often can find a better, more evocative way to phrase the idea. If you use a word processor, you should at least give yourself that option. When you have written your first draft, print out a clean copy and read it through slowly, first word to last, with a pencil in your hand. Make changes and incorporate them. Don't succumb to the temptation to leave well enough alone.

SAMPLE ESSAYS

What follows now is a more specific account of the essay-writing process. Here, as a sample text, is Isak Dinesen's very short story, "The Blue Jar." You will see how one student worked through the stages of outlining, drafting, and writing.

THE BLUE JAR

There was once an immensely rich old Englishman who had been a courtier and a councillor to the Queen and who now, in his old age, cared for nothing but collecting ancient blue china. To that end he travelled to Persia, Japan and China, and he was everywhere accompanied by his daughter, the Lady Helena. It happened, as they sailed in the Chinese Sea, that the ship caught fire on a still night, and everybody went into the lifeboats and left her. In the dark and the confusion the old peer was separated from his daughter. Lady Helena got up on deck late, and found the ship quite deserted. In the last moment a young English sailor carried her down into a lifeboat that had been forgotten. To the two fugitives it seemed as if fire was following them from all sides, for the phosphorescence played in the dark sea, and, as they looked up, a falling star ran across the sky, as if it was going to drop into the boat. They sailed for nine days, till they were picked up by a Dutch merchantman, and came home to England.

The old lord had believed his daughter to be dead. He now wept with joy, and at once took her off to a fashionable watering-place so that she might recover from the hardships she had gone through. And as he thought it must be unpleasant to her that a young sailor, who made his bread in the merchant service, should tell the world that he had sailed for nine days alone with a peer's daughter, he paid the boy a fine sum, and made him promise to go shipping in the other hemisphere and never come back. "For what," said the old nobleman, "would be the good of that?"

When Lady Helena recovered, and they gave her the news of the Court and of her family, and in the end also told her how the young sailor had been sent away never to come back, they found that her mind had suffered from her trials, and that she cared for nothing in all the world. She would not go back to her father's castle in its park, nor go to Court, nor travel to any gay town of the continent. The only thing which she now wanted to do was to go, like her father before her, to collect rare blue china. So she began to sail, from one country to the other, and her father went with her.

In her search she told the people, with whom she dealt, that she was looking for a particular blue color, and would pay any price for it. But although she bought many hundred blue jars and bowls, she would always after a time put them aside and say: "Alas, alas, it is not the right blue." Her father, when they had sailed for many years, suggested to her that perhaps the color which she sought did not exist. "O God, Papa," said she, "how can you speak so wickedly? Surely there must be some of it left from the time when all the world was blue."

Her two old aunts in England implored her to come back, still to make a great match. But she answered them: "Nay, I have got to sail. For you must know, dear aunts, that it is all nonsense when learned people tell you that the seas have got a bottom to them. On the contrary, the water, which is the noblest of the elements, does, of course, go all through the earth, so that our planet really floats in the ether, like a soap bubble. And there, on the other hemisphere, a ship sails, with which I have got to keep pace. We two are like the reflection of one another, in the deep sea, and the ship of which I speak is always exactly beneath my own ship, upon the opposite side of the globe. You have never seen a big fish swimming underneath a boat, following it like a dark-blue shade in the water. But in that way this ship goes, like the shadow of my ship, and I draw it to and fro wherever I go, as the moon draws the tides, all through the bulk of the earth. If I stopped sailing, what would those poor sailors who made their bread in the merchant service do? But I shall tell you a secret," she said. "In the end my ship will go down, to the centre of the globe, and at the very same hour the other ship will sink as well—for people call it sinking, although I can assure you that there is no up and down in the sea—and there, in the midst of the world, we two shall meet."

Many years passed, the old lord died and Lady Helena became old and deaf, but she still sailed. Then it happened, after the plunder of the summer palace of the Emperor of China, that a merchant brought her a very old blue jar. The moment she set eyes on it she gave a terrible shriek. "There it is!" she cried. "I have found it at last. This is the true blue. Oh, how light it makes one. Oh, it is as fresh as a breeze, as deep as a deep secret, as full as I say not what." With trembling hands she held the jar to her bosom, and sat for six hours sunk in contemplation of it. Then she said to her doctor and her lady-companion: "Now I can die. And when I am dead you will cut out my heart and lay it in the blue jar. For then everything will be as it was then. All shall be blue round me, and in the midst of the blue world my heart will be innocent and free, and will beat gently, like a wake that sings, like the drops that fall from an oar blade." A little later she asked them: "Is it not a sweet thing to think that, if only you have patience, all that has ever been, will come back to you?" Shortly afterwards the old lady died.

The assignment given in this writing class asked the students to pick one short story from the anthology and to write either an explication of one passage or an analysis of one of the central elements. *Explication,* as the teacher explained, is a highly magnified inspection of one crucial portion of the work, a portion usually no longer than two paragraphs. The point of the explication is to isolate specific components—turns of phrase, images, even single words—in order to show how they contribute to the effect of the whole. The process, the teacher said, is like taking a tissue culture: by looking closely enough at an isolated group of cells, a doctor is very often able to make discoveries about the functions of the whole organism.

The second option, *analysis,* allows for a larger perspective. An analysis singles out one of several elements of the story—the author's presentation of character, the function of setting or point of view, the use of symbols—in order to explore its function. Unlike explication, analysis can range freely through the work, focusing in on relevant materials. Each approach has its own advantages, of course. Nor are the differences between them absolute. A paper explicating part of a story may use some analysis, separating out aspects of the passage and studying their contribution. In the same way, an analysis, of setting or character, say, might focus on a particular description, subjecting it to explication.

One student chose Dinesen's "The Blue Jar" and decided that she would write an essay analyzing the significance of the artifact that gives the story its name. Having read the story several times, she knew that there were a few scenes crucial to her purpose and that she would probably have to perform some explication.

The student did not make a formal outline before starting on her first draft, but she did write down a simple list, trusting that her sequence would give the paper its basic shape. With a longer story she might have copied out passages to use in her presentation, but in this case she did not feel that to be necessary. Here is her list:

1. Introduction—say how it is like a fairy tale
2. General plot summary—keep it simple
3. General discussion of blue color and search for jar
4. Closer look at final scene
5. Conclusion—What is Dinesen saying?

Soon after sketching out her plan, the student began to write her first draft. She knew enough about her writing habits to know that a rough version, however clumsy and incomplete, would give her something concrete to work with. She wrote as follows (the annotations in the margin have been added):

"The Blue Jar"--A Search for True Love

In "The Blue Jar," Danish story writer Isak Dinesen has created a mysterious fairy tale (parable?) to explore the meaning of true love. Her characters are simple and never really come to life, but that does not matter to the reader. We are, like Dinesen, more interested in the search itself, for it is common to all.

Check dictionary meanings

Too general to serve as a thesis

A young woman, Lady Helena, is stranded in a lifeboat with an English sailor. They are together for a long time. When they are saved, the girl's father, "a rich old Englishman," sends the sailor away to the other side of the world so that there won't be talk.

Misquoted—no reason for quoting brief identification

Lady Helena is ill for a time. When she recovers she is changed. She has no interest in romance or courtship. Instead, she joins her father in his search for rare blue china, sailing the world to find the perfect shade of blue. When he suggests that there might not even be such a color, she says, "Surely there must be some of it left from the time when all the world was blue." This is our first clue that blue has a symbolic value.

Avoid strings of short sentences; vary structure

Comment further on this suggestive quotation

Lady Helena also imagines that there is a ship on the other side of the world following hers and that one day the two ships will

Weak transition; avoid "also" as a linking word

sink and meet at the middle of the world. She grows old, still sailing.

One day a merchant brings her a blue jar, the very one she has been looking for. "There it is!" she cries. She tells her doctor that when she dies her heart should be placed in that jar. "For then everything will be as it was then," she explains. Before she dies, she asks: "Is it not a sweet thing to think that, if only you have patience, all that has ever been, will come back to you?"

Mysterious quotation needs commentary

Dinesen is obviously using blue as a symbol. When Lady Helena speaks of the time "when all the world was blue," we associate the color with original innocence, a Garden of Eden kind of thing. Her idea that there is another ship on the other side of the world following hers suggests that she has not stopped thinking of the sailor. Though we are not told what happened while Lady Helena and the sailor were in the boat together, we assume that they fell in love. This would explain why she never married.

"Kind of thing" is too casual

When the perfect jar is found, Lady Helena knows that her death is near. But she is not afraid. She believes that she has recovered her long-ago happiness and that if her heart is placed in the jar she will experience a kind of eternal bliss. She dies happily--or so we are to think.

In the final scene, Dinesen clarifies her use of the symbol. Thinking of her heart in the jar, Lady Helena says, "All shall be blue around me, and in the midst of the blue world my heart will be innocent and free, and will beat gently, like a wake that sings, like the drops that fall from an oar blade." These two similes, about the wake and the drops, make it clear that her fantasy is connected to a memory--that the wake and the drops are from her days with the sailor.

Good use of specific evidence

Lady Helena never meets her sailor again, and yet when she dies it is as if she has fulfilled her love. Dinesen says a great deal here about the power of love. That it can be as real in memory as in the present. "The Blue Jar" shows how belief affects a life. Some people may say that Lady Helena is crazy, but what is crazy and who is to say? If she believes that she has fulfilled her life, then maybe she has.

Not a sentence

Too general, needs elaboration

Reading over her draft, the student was not completely satisfied. She felt that she had gotten the main points down, but that she had not really explored the implications with any depth. The story seemed to her more profound and interesting than her treatment revealed. She also thought that she had spent too much time simply retelling the plot. She decided that when she rewrote the draft she would try to compress the summary and to devote correspondingly more space to a discussion of Dinesen's use of symbols to convey a philosophy about love.

The longer she thought about it, the more the writer knew that her essay lacked a strong thesis. Too many of her observations struck her as obvious. As she stared at her own sentences (she had printed out her draft), she had an inkling. The part at the end about love and madness seemed interesting and worthy of some expansion. But she was not yet sure what to say or how to fit in any further ideas. Later, while she was away from the paper, an idea came to her. She remembered studying Shakespeare's *Romeo and Juliet* in high school, and that brought to mind a class discussion about lovers driven beyond all bounds of accepted behavior. She dug out her notebooks from the Shakespeare class, and there she found a passage copied out from another Shakespeare play, *A Midsummer Night's Dream*. It was just what she needed:

> Lovers and madmen have such seething brains,
> Such shaping fantasies, that apprehend
> More than cool reason ever comprehends.

Writers speak reverently of what have sometimes been called "gift" moments—unexpected discoveries or realizations that solve a problem. This writer felt as though she had made a lucky find, although in fact she had been pursuing a trail. Thinking about the connection between love and madness, which she had already found in the story, she recalled her Shakespeare class, then her notebook. The stroke of fortune was finding the very quote she needed. Not only would Shakespeare's words embellish the paper but also the discovery gave her the idea about how to rewrite. She knew right away that if she led off with the quote and the idea of the love-madness connection, she would have a strong controlling idea, a thesis. The rest would follow, and much of it could be adapted from what she had already written in her draft.

Here is the student's final version. She spent quite a long time hunched before her screen, trying to get the sentences to flow smoothly and making sure that her transitions were logical. The final essay was, as she had expected, longer than the draft.

"The Blue Jar"--Love's Shaping Fantasies

Good incorporation of part of Shakespeare's quote into title

The idea that love and madness are somehow linked is as old as literature. "Lovers and madmen have such seething brains," wrote Shakespeare in *A Midsummer Night's Dream*. "Such shaping fantasies, that apprehend/More than cool reason ever comprehends." There are no rules for lovers. True passion will throw True passion will throw itself at every

Quotation introduces theme elegantly

behavior is very much like madness, we insist on thinking that love makes it noble. We think of the suicides of Romeo and Juliet as tragic, not crazy.

Useful comparison

The Danish writer Isak Dinesen (1885–1962) has another variation on the theme of doomed love. Though her story "The Blue Jar" is full of romantic assumptions about perfect love, lovers meeting up after death, and so on, it differs from the usual pattern. There are no love scenes, no violent climaxes (unless putting a heart in a jar counts), and the ending is happy. But in spite of this, Dinesen makes her reader think about the meaning of true love.

Author's dates help reader place the story

A smart procedure—characterizing the story by how it differs from romantic pattern

"The Blue Jar" is as simple as a fairy tale. The main characters--a rich old councillor and his daughter--are two-dimensional. The plot is written like a summary. But the story works, because against this flatness the mysterious symbol of blue stands out and works on the imagination.

Clear statement of key idea

The plot, like the characters, is simple. A rich man's daughter is rescued from a burning ship by a young English sailor. The two spend nine days together in a small boat. When Lady Helena returns to her father, he finds the sailor a post in the other hemisphere. We never learn what took place between Lady Helena and the sailor.

Repetitious—avoid restating points

Lady Helena's family, writes Dinesen, "found that her mind had suffered from her trials, and that she cared for nothing at all in the world." The young woman refuses all suitors. Like her father, she devotes herself to searching for rare blue china.

It is permissible to speak of a dead author in present tense when discussing a work

One day, when she is old, she finds what she has been searching for: the perfect blue jar. She knows that her mysterious mission has been accomplished and that she will soon die. She then gives instructions to her doctor and traveling companion that after her death her heart is to be removed and placed in the jar. She dies soon after.

Passage lacking emphasis, does not convey the extraordinary quality of this plot development

Dinesen is not interested in plot or character but in showing how strong the power of love can be. After her father sends the sailor away, Lady Helena is obviously depressed. But she does not go against his wishes as Shakespeare's Juliet did. Instead, she creates a world of her own--a world of true love where the limits of reality have no place. She hunts for her blue jar, the color symbolic of innocence. Some of it must be left over, she tells her father, "from the time when all the world was blue." She also believes that there is another ship following hers on the opposite side of the world.

Needs smoother paragraph transition

A good way to re-establish opening comparison

Writer assumes symbolic value of blue without giving reason

Better to quote full sentence

Comment on quotation

The image of the two ships is also a kind of symbol. Lady Helena believes that the

Avoid "also" constructions

sailor shares her love and that they are together in their love even though they are a world apart. "In the end," she tells her aunts, "my ship will go down, to the center of the globe, and at the very same hour the other ship will sink as well . . . and there, in the midst of the world, we two shall meet."

Comma missing from quotation

Use of ellipses to avoid quoting unnecessary material

Just as Lady Helena goes against all scientific knowledge when she insists that the oceans are joined in the middle of the earth, so she rejects common sense in her final fantasy.

A strong transitional idea, but needs to be expressed more fully to make a paragraph

In the last scene, Dinesen clarifies her use of the symbolic blue color. Thinking of her heart inside that jar, Lady Helena visualizes innocence and freedom. Her heart, she says, "will beat gently, like a wake that sings, like the drops that fall from an oar blade." These two similes, about the wake and the drops, make it clear that her lifelong fantasy is connected to a specific memory. Those are the images that she remembers from her days with the sailor, and the perfect shade of blue must be the one that lives in her memory.

Writer wisely retained strong passage from rough draft

Overstated—writer does not know this for certain; phrase it as a surmise

The reader of "The Blue Jar" is finally left to hover between Lady Helena's absolute conviction and the more common-sense view that lovers are not reunited after death and that hearts do not go on beating after they are removed from the body. This strain is probably what Dinesen wanted us to feel. She plays on the fact that death is a mystery and that we don't really know what comes after. For Lady Helena, believing may have made it so. People can argue that she is just crazy, but who will say for sure? There is a small chance that her happiness was complete, that true love *did* conquer all. That small chance is just what Dinesen needed to bring her puzzling story to a close.

Nicely suggestive ending—captures the mysteriousness of the story

---

The discovery of a thesis allowed this student to rewrite her paper with a broader scope for her discussion. When she reread the final draft, however, she was still not completely satisfied. She felt that she had not succeeded in compressing the plot as she had hoped. She also noted that her explication of the final scene was anything but thorough. In trying to get her basic points across, she had not left herself room for more focused questioning. She would have liked to pick apart the images with more care. And she had other ideas that she could have worked in, especially the idea that the heart in the blue jar was in some way a symbol for the two lovers together in their boat. But time had run out. She was happy enough with her work, especially her opening, to hand in the paper.

COMPARISON AND CONTRAST

One of the most effective ways to engage a work of literature is to set it alongside another and to search out comparisons and contrasts (it is possible, but difficult, to do one without doing the other). The options are various. You can look at two works by a single author, checking for similarities and differences in approach, treatment of character, and so on. Or you can pick works by two authors who are contemporaries, or authors from different periods. The selections can be made on the basis of general similarity or obvious divergence, or anything in between. Strictly speaking, anything can be compared with anything else. Write a paper comparing a grapefruit and a tractor—it's possible. But the point, at least when talking about works of fiction, is to compare and contrast in order to gain specific insights. If you look at Hemingway's treatment of women in his fiction in isolation, you get one picture. A larger, more suggestive, picture emerges when you compare his treatment with Virginia Woolf's (the two were more or less contemporaries). Both approaches have their uses. One of the main uses of comparison and contrast is to create a wider context for the works in question. But the process also underlines the tremendous differences between one artistic vision and another.

There is a general procedure for writing this kind of essay. To begin with, you will almost never find yourself comparing or contrasting one complete work with another. Most stories are just too complex to permit point-by-point comparisons. Each has its own characters, plot designs, settings, points of view, and so on. The first step is to determine *what* is to be considered. Do you want to explore similarities and differences between Virginia Woolf's and James Joyce's use of interior monologue? Or D. H. Lawrence's and Katherine Mansfield's portrayals of death? Or do you want to look at two stories by Raymond Carver to compare the depictions of male-female relationships? There is no dearth of rich topics.

You may want to begin by isolating some particular element from the stories you have chosen. The basic elements of fiction, as discussed in the previous appendix section, are character, plot, setting, theme, point of view, symbols (or figurative language in general), and tone. Almost every story makes some use of each, and once you have determined which seems most fruitful, you can get to work. With your two stories before you, you can start charting an approach.

How you build your essay will depend upon several things. As with the analytic essay, a comparison and contrast essay needs to be organized around some thesis, some main point. Your key to finding this lies in the basic nature of your approach. If you have picked two stories that exhibit a certain strong similarity—in theme, say—then you must ask yourself what is the strongest assertion you can make. For example: "Though their stories are vastly different in plot, setting, and point of view, Sarah Orne Jewett's "A White Heron" and Kate Chopin's "The Story of an Hour" both depict their protagonists finding self-recognition in solitary struggles." Having made such an assertion early in your essay, you might then explain how those struggles came about and inquire into their specific similarities and differences.

The same basic tactic holds true for approaches stressing contrast, although here you might take a common attribute as your pivot: "While James Joyce's "The Dead" and D. H. Lawrence's "Odour of Chrysanthemums" both dissect the failures of communication in marriages, the stories use very different approaches to achieve their end." Of course, not every thesis needs to be set up in such a fashion—how boring it would be if they were!—but you might try out such a formulation simply to clarify your topic for yourself.

As you set about writing the main part of your essay, you might keep several suggestions in mind. First, it is much easier to feature one story and to use the other as an examining tool. Although your democratic instinct might favor giving each work equal time, the practical result is a loss of focus. It becomes very hard to avoid the "on the one hand . . . on the other hand" effect. By putting one story in the foreground, you automatically create a focus. Thus: "Of the two stories, Joyce's makes subtler use of characterization, and while his approach is not nearly as dramatic as Lawrence's, his conclusion reflects a deeper despair." You would then set the stage with a preliminary discussion of "The Dead," clarifying Joyce's approach, before bringing Lawrence forward.

This brings up the question of how to structure a comparison and contrast paper. There is no one right answer. Some writers favor the two-part approach, in which, say, Joyce's story would be examined in its entirety and Lawrence's would then be introduced and discussed with reference to points made about "The Dead." Others might be more comfortable switching back and forth several times, comparing Joyce's and Lawrence's presentation of husband and wife, then looking at their treatment of the climactic scene, and then assessing the darkness of their respective visions. What you should avoid is an uncentered fidgeting from one work to the other: "Lawrence uses obvious symbols; Joyce does not. But Joyce's way of setting nearly all his scenes in rooms and corridors makes for an atmosphere every bit as constricting as Lawrence's. Lawrence, though . . . ." If you go on like this for more than a paragraph, you will very likely lose the goodwill of your reader, not to mention the main thread of your argument.

As suggested earlier, analysis, explication, and comparison and contrast are the main ways to discuss literary works. Each has something to teach; they are worth practicing independently. But, in fact, the best literary writing makes use of all three modes. Analysis is often most effective when it builds upon the careful sifting that is explication; and the strongest insights are often found when one thing is related to another. The final version of the student paper showed this clearly. While the essay was written as an analysis of the thematic use of symbol, it scored points early by making a comparison with Shakespeare's lovers. And though space did not permit, the student could have strengthened her final paragraphs by explicating Lady Helena's last words.

Every writer refines his or her approach over years of writing, mastering different tools, learning what works best in any given situation, and learning the quirks of the process. Some find that they need to be painstaking about making outlines; others trust themselves to inspiration and then revise innumerable times. The formula? Whatever works. An interviewer once asked the writer Susan Sontag how many times she generally revised a given essay. "Seventeen or eighteen, usually," she answered. This is not meant to intimidate you as an essayist but to suggest the lengths to which a writer will go to get a work right. The fact is, the reward must finally outweigh the struggle. Otherwise Sontag, or any other writer, would not persist.

APPENDIX C

GLOSSARY

Allegory: A narrative—George Orwell's *Animal Farm* is a good example—in which characters and events represent larger ideas. The isolated elements function very much like symbols, enabling the reader to make direct correspondences from particular to general.

Allusion: An author's indirect reference to something outside the work, often to another work with which the reader may be acquainted. Poets and fiction writers often allude to episodes in the Bible, or Shakespeare, or other writings they expect may be familiar to many.

Ambiguity: The quality in any situation or expression that allows for several possible interpretations. Since human actions themselves are often ambiguous, stemming from mixed motives, it is only natural that interactions of characters should follow suit. Authors often use ambiguity to bring complexity to their portrayals and to deepen the thematic resonance of their work.

Analysis: The act of separating a work into its constituent elements. Analysis is often a preliminary step in finding a topic to write about.

Antagonist: The character in a literary work who in some way opposes the **Protagonist,** or hero. In the Cinderella story, for example, the wicked stepmother is an antagonist—she attempts to foil the heroine's every initiative. The interactions between protagonist and antagonist usually contribute to the **Climax,** after which one or the other is defeated.

Anticlimax: A thwarting of the reader's expectations. Instead of the expected resolution of tensions, there is another, often less dramatic outcome. Realist and modernist storytellers often favor the anticlimax because it conforms more to the way things happen in the real world. The reader may wish the two lovers to marry and live happily ever after, but it is more likely that they squabble over bills and visits from in-laws.

Antihero: Not to be confused with the **Antagonist,** the antihero is a **Protagonist** who lacks heroic attributes. Fiction from the nineteenth century on is increasingly concerned with the ordinary, or antiheroic, character.

Atmosphere: The mood evoked in a work of fiction by the author's descriptions of setting and character interactions.

Character: Any individual depicted in a work of fiction, from the **Protagonist** to a minor functionary. Characters are often described as "round" (developed, with some complexity and independent stature) or "flat" (simple, one-dimensional, introduced mainly to serve a scene). Characters may also be referred to as dynamic (changing over the course of the story) or static (unchanging). A **Stereotype,** or stock character, is a deliberately simple figure who reflects popular assumptions—the dashing officer, the greedy landlord, the sassy barmaid, and so on.

Climax: The moment of highest tension in a story, very often resulting from conflicts between the **Protagonist** and other characters. The action that builds toward the climax, or moment of truth, is often called the **Rising Action.** The events that follow including the **Resolution,** are part of the **Falling Action.**

Complication: The element of tension or conflict that underlies the plot development. The complication is usually essential to the creation of narrative **Suspense;** it creates in the reader the desire to find out what happens next. The complication is part of the **Rising Action,** and reaches culmination in the **Climax.**

Connotation: The suggestion or implication of a particular expression. Words have specific denotative meanings, but they also carry strong associative charges; these are used by the author to bring subtlety and depth to a scene. See also **Denotation.**

Crisis: The situation, often a confrontation, that brings the work to its **Climax.**

Denotation: The explicit meaning of a word. See also **Connotation.**

Denouement: From the French, literally 'untying of a knot'. It is the outcome, the answer to the question, "So what finally happened?" The denouement, which follows the **Climax,** is part of the **Falling Action.**

Description: The use of language to create a picture or impression in the mind's eye. Descriptions usually set before us the particulars of a setting, a character's appearance, or an object.

Dialogue: Conversational exchange between characters, customarily set out between quotation marks. Though 'dia' means *two,* we use the word to refer to multiple exchanges as well. If a character talks to himself or herself aloud or in thought, we call it a monologue, or an interior monologue.

Dramatic Irony: The tension that arises between the reader's perception of a situation and that of the characters. Authors very often enable the reader to hold a larger view than that available to any character; the discrepancy contributes to the **Suspense** of the work.

Dynamic Character: See **Character.**

Epigraph: A quotation, usually from another author's work, placed at the beginning of a story. The purpose is to alert the reader to a particular theme or facet of the story.

Epiphany: Literally 'showing forth', a sudden revelation brought on by some specific action or event. It is an insight delivered in a flash. A character in a story can also experience an epiphanic moment—indeed, many of James Joyce's stories are built around just such a possibility.

Episode: A self-contained incident that is part of the larger **Plot** structure. In novels and more complex stories we often find several episodes in sequence, although a single episode—an event depicted from start to finish—is often suggestive enough to carry a narrative.

Explication: The careful untangling and explaining of a work, or, more commonly, of a crucial passage of a work. Although the explication is a kind of essay in itself, it is also a useful tool in any analysis or thematic assessment of a literary work.

Exposition: Literally 'setting forth' in a work of fiction the presentation of necessary background information. Although some stories begin *in medias res* (the phrase comes from Aristotle), 'in the middle of the action', many others begin with some explanation of past events and characters' histories.

Fable: A short narrative, often fantastic in character, which presents the reader or listener (fables were popular in preliterate cultures) with a **Moral,** or message. The best-known fables are those invented by the Greek slave Aesop, who poked fun at human foibles indirectly, using animals to represent different human attributes.

Fairy Tale: A simple narrative that tells of improbable, generally magical, events. Characters are usually **Stereotypes,** beautiful princesses, wicked witches, heroic princes, and so on. The good and the beautiful unfailingly triumph over evil, and resolutions are always happy.

Falling Action: The events of the story that follow the **Climax,** including the **Resolution** or **Denouement.**

Figurative Language: An expression in which one group of words, generally in the form of metaphor or simile, represents a concept by way of comparison. "Her hair was black like a raven's wing" is a simile, using *like* to make the connection explicit. "Her hair was a raven's wing," is a metaphoric expression, or "figure," making an outright equivalence.

First-Person: Possessing the narrative **Point of View** of "I." The point of view of the story is thereby limited to what the speaker could have seen or learned about.

Flashback: The incorporation of earlier incidents within a narrative sequence, often in the form of a memory.

Flat Character: See **Character.**

Folk Tale: A narrative, often with no known author or creator, which has, or once had, currency in an oral culture. Folk tales often embody that culture's beliefs and traditions; hence they are of great interest to ethnographers as well as to students of early literatures.

Foreshadowing: A narrative device of planting hints and suggestions that anticipate significant upcoming developments.

Hero/Heroine: The **Protagonist** in a work of fiction, usually endowed with certain admirable attributes. While one could call any protagonist the hero or heroine, the term **Antihero** is often used for ordinary protagonists. An antihero is not the same as an **Antagonist.**

Image: An expression meant to appeal directly to the senses, most commonly found in descriptions.

Irony: The tension that arises from discrepancy, either between what one says and what one means (verbal irony) or between what a character perceives/believes and what a reader knows (**Dramatic Irony**).

Limited Omniscience: Narrative access to the inner processes of only a few characters; the thoughts and motives of the others are presumed to be unknowable. See also **Omniscience.**

Metaphor: See **Figurative Language.**

Monologue: See **Dialogue.**

Moral: The specific wisdom that an author or teller intends the audience to get from the story. The well-known **Fables** of the Greek slave Aesop were generally intended to express some edifying moral.

Motivation: The force or forces that compel a character to action. Motivation can be internal, stemming from a belief or a desire, or it can be external, the result of some specific pressure, like economic need.

Myth: A narrative from the oral tradition, distinguished from the **Folk Tale** and **Fairy Tale** in that it generally gives expression to the deepest beliefs of a culture. Myths are very often accounts of origins—how things and places came to be—and commonly invoke heroic figures or gods.

Narrative: A sequence of events, often told as a story.

Narrator: The person who tells the events. This can be a character who is involved, speaking in the **First-Person** "I," or a detached, presumably more neutral voice narrating in the **Third-Person,** using *he, she,* and *they*. In many novels and stories the narrator is assumed to be the omniscient or partially omniscient author. See also **Unreliable Narrator.**

Naturalism: A way of presenting situations and characters that strives for a scrupulously accurate rendering of settings and actions. The naturalist believes that careful observation and accurate depiction are the closest we can get to the *truth,* that the rest belongs to the domain of guesswork. The realist, by contrast, is more willing to search out the psychological motives of characters and to make assertions about the inner life. See also **Realism.**

Objectivity: An ideal of impartiality, of letting the actions of characters and the events speak for themselves; the author's attempt to avoid bias or judgment.

Omniscience: Literally, 'all knowing'. Narrative access to the thoughts and feelings of all the characters. It is through omniscience that the reader is made privy to what any given character is like behind his or her outward appearance. See also **Limited Omniscience.**

Pace: The author's determination of how fast or slow to move a given scene. Pace is determined not only by the amount of information (or description) given but also by the author's style, whether it consists of long, complex sentences or brisk dialogue exchanges.

Parable: A short narrative meant to convey a **Moral,** or lesson, and intended to have a larger, often symbolic, resonance. Parables are often used in religious instruction to clarify elusive concepts. See also **Allegory.**

Parody: An imitation of a work, often for satiric purposes. The parodist singles out and highlights distinctive stylistic and thematic traits, achieving an effect of exaggeration.

Persona: A mask, or character voice, through which the author speaks.

Plot: The shaping of events into a story. See the discussion of plot and narrative in Appendix A, "Elements of Fiction."

Point of View: The vantage from which the story is told—whether by a character or by an author with omniscient or limited omniscient perspective. Character vantages include, most commonly, **First-Person** and **Third-Person.** Second-person narration is rare. See also **Character.** See the discussion of point of view in Appendix A, "Elements of Fiction."

Protagonist: The main character and center of the story's psychological complications. The protagonist is sometimes called the hero or heroine, although the attributes of the character need not be heroic. See also **Antagonist, Antihero.**

Realism: A way of presenting situations and characters that seeks to create the impression of real life. Realism steers clear of the miraculous and the fantastic. The larger movement of Realism in the arts followed on the heels of Romanticism and is often seen as a reaction to it. See also **Naturalism.**

Resolution: The part of the story that follows the **Climax.** Also called **Falling Action.**

Rising Action: The events that lead up to and bring about the **Climax,** or key turning point. The rising action generally involves the building up of the **Complication,** or major conflict.

Round Character: See **Character.**

Satire: A work that makes use of ridicule in order to expose some human folly or vice. While often humorous, the final intent of the satiric work is serious.

Sentimentality: False or exaggerated emotion. A sentimental expression manipulates the reader's feelings by relying on scenes of an overtly sorrowful or tragic nature.

Setting: The time and place in which the story's events unfold.

Simile: See **Figurative Language.**

Static Character: See **Character.**

Stereotype: A flat character who is simplified into a common type, often for comic effect. See also **Character.**

Stock Character: See **Character.**

Stream of Consciousness: A technique that seeks to render the flow of inner thought and sensation. Stream of consciousness is distinguished from interior monologue in that the author does not attempt to shape or heighten the thoughts, striving instead to present the impression of chaotic movement.

Subplot: A story within the story. Subplots unfold alongside the main plot and often involve minor, or secondary, characters. They can serve to counterpoint the central events. The introduction of a subplot allows the author to control suspense by diverting the reader's attention.

Style: The author's manner of expression; *how* the story is told. Important components of style are diction, or word choice; imagery; and **Pace.** A writer's style, like a painter's, is a kind of signature, reflecting sensibility, artistic beliefs, and habitual ways of seeing the world.

Suspense: The holding over of actions and consequences by an author in order to arouse curiosity in the reader. The deliberate manipulation of the reader's natural desire to find out what happens next in a chain of events.

Symbol: An isolated thing, person, or situation that is used to represent a larger thematic concern. A white bird may be a symbol of peace or innocence, but it may just be a white bird. The reader needs to make a judgment about whether the context allows for a symbolic interpretation.

Tale: An earlier form of the story that was passed along by word-of-mouth. Often used as a synonym for *story*. See also **Fairy Tale, Folk Tale.**

Theme: The central meaning, or idea, in a short story. A theme is a generalized or abstract assertion of the story's message.

Thesis Sentence: The statement, usually in the first or second paragraph of an essay, of the key **Theme** to be explored.

Third-Person: Possessing detached narrative vantage that allows the narrator to refer to characters as *he, she,* or *they*. The narrator may be, in effect, the author, claiming full or **Limited Omniscience**. See also **Character.**

Tone: The attitude expressed by the style and overall presentation, reflected mainly through diction, or word choice. An author or narrator may adopt a bemused, urgent, sober, or any one of a number of other tones. See the discussion of tone in Appendix A, "Elements of Fiction."

Unreliable Narrator: A narrator who is deliberately shown to be ignorant, biased, or otherwise flawed in character. The reader must then interpret the narrated events, making allowance for the narrator's limitations. The effect produced is very often ironic.

Verbal Irony: See **Irony.**

CREDITS

Anonymous, "The Third Mendicant's Story of King Ajeeb" from *The Arabian Nights' Entertainments, or The Thousand and One Nights*. Translation by Edward William Lane. Copyright © 1927 by Tudor Publishing Company.

Apuleius, "The Story of Thelyphron" from *The Golden Ass* by Apuleius, translated by Robert Graves. Translation copyright © 1951 by Robert Graves. Renewal copyright © 1978 by Robert Graves. Reprinted by permission of Farrar, Straus and Giroux, Inc.

Isaac Babel, "Guy de Maupassant." Reprinted by permission of S. G. Phillips, Inc. from *The Collected Stories of Isaac Babel*. Copyright © 1955 by S.G. Phillips, Inc.

James Baldwin, "Sonny's Blues." Copyright © 1957 by James Baldwin. From *Going to Meet the Man* by James Baldwin. Used by permission of Doubleday, a Bantam Doubleday Dell Publishing Group, Inc.

Toni Cade Bambara, "The Hammer Man." From *Gorilla, My Love* by Toni Cade Bambara. Copyright © 1960, 1963, 1964, 1965, 1968, 1970, 1971, 1972 by Toni Cade Bambara. Reprinted by permission of Random House, Inc.

Donald Barthelme, "Me and Miss Mandible." From *Sixty Stories* by Donald Barthelme. Copyright © 1981 and 1982 by Donald Barthelme. Reprinted by permission of Wylie, Aitken & Stone.

New English Bible, excerpt from *Genesis*. *New English Bible* © 1970 by permission of Oxford and Cambridge University Presses.

Giovanni Boccaccio, "Fourth Day, First Story" from *The Decameron* by Giovanni Boccaccio, translated by G. H. McWilliam (Penguin Classics, 1972), copyright © G. H. McWilliam, 1972. Reproduced by permission of Penguin Books Ltd.

Jorge Luis Borges, "The Aleph," from *The Aleph and Other Stories* by Jorge Luis Borges, translated by Norman Thomas di Giovanni. Translation copyright © 1968, 1969, 1970 by Emece Editores, S.A. and Norman Thomas di Giovanni. Used by permission of the publisher, Dutton, an imprint of New American Library, a division of Penguin Books USA Inc.

Italo Calvino, "The Distance of the Moon" from *Cosmicomics* by Italo Calvino, copyright © 1965 by Giulio Einaudi editore s.p.a., Torino. English translation © 1968 by Harcourt Brace Jovanovich, Inc. and Jonathan Cape Ltd. Reprinted by permission of Harcourt Brace Jovanovich, Inc.

Raymond Carver, "Careful" and "Chef's House" from *Cathedral* by Raymond Carver. Copyright © 1983 by Raymond Carver. Reprinted by permission of Alfred A. Knopf, Inc. "Intimacy" from *Where I'm Calling From* by Raymond Carver, copyright © 1986, 1987, 1988 by Raymond Carver. Reprinted by permission of Atlantic Monthly Press.

John Cheever, "Torch Song." From *The Stories of John Cheever* by John Cheever. Copyright © 1947 by John Cheever. Reprinted by permission of Alfred A. Knopf, Inc.

Anton Chekhov, "Lady with Lapdog" from *Lady with Lapdog and Other Stories* by Anton Chekhov, translated by David Magarshack (Penguin Classics, 1964), copyright © David Magarshack, 1964. Reproduced by permission of Penguin Books Ltd.

Julio Cortazar, "Axolotl." From *End of the Game and Other Stories* by Julio Cortazar, translated by P. Blackburn. Copyright © 1967, 1963 by Random House, Inc. Reprinted by permission of Pantheon Books, a Division of Random House, Inc.

Stuart Dybek, "The Death of the Right Fielder." From *The Coast of Chicago* by Stuart Dybek. Copyright © 1990 by Stuart Dybek. Reprinted by permission of Alfred A. Knopf, Inc.

William Faulkner, "Wash." From *The Collected Stories of William Faulkner* by William Faulkner. Copyright © 1934 and renewed 1962 by William Faulkner. Reprinted by permission of Random House, Inc.

Richard Ford, "Communist." From the book *Rock Springs*, copyright © 1987 by Richard Ford. Used by permission of Atlantic Monthly Press.

Gabriel García-Márquez, "A Very Old Man with Enormous Wings" from *Leaf Storm and Other Stories* by Gabriel Garcia Marquez. Copyright © (English translation) © 1971 by Gabriel Garcia Marquez. Reprinted by permission of HarperCollins Publishers.

Natalia Ginzburg, "The Mother," translated by Isabel Quigly, from *Italian Short Stories* (Penguin Books, 1965), copyright © Penguin Books, 1965. Reproduced by permission of Penguin Books Ltd.

Nikolai Gogol, "The Nose." From *Tales of Good and Evil* by Nikolai Gogol. Copyright © 1956 by David Magarshack. Used by permission of Doubleday, a division of Bantam Doubleday Dell Publishing Group, Inc.

Nadine Gordimer, "Town and Country Lovers," copyright © 1975 by Nadine Gordimer, from *A Soldier's Embrace* by Nadine Gordimer. Used by permission of Viking Penguin, a division of Penguin Books USA Inc.

Ludwig Karl Grimm and Wilhelm Karl Grimm, "Cinderella." From *The Complete Grimm's Fairy Tales*, translated by Margaret Hunt and James Stern and illustrated by Josef Scharl. Copyright © 1944 by Pantheon Books, Inc. Copyright renewed 1972 by Random House, Inc. Reprinted by permission of Pantheon Books, a division of Random House, Inc.

Lars Gustafsson, "A Water Story." From Lars Gustafsson: *Stories of Happy People*. Copyright © 1981 by Lars Gustafsson. Reprinted by permission of New Directions Publishing Corporation.

Hao Shaogong, "The Homecoming." From *Spring Bamboo* by Jeanne Tai. Compilation and Translation copyright © 1989 by Jeanne Tai. Reprinted by permission of Random House, Inc.

Bessie Head, "Looking for a Rain God" from *A Collector of Treasures* by Bessie Head. Copyright © 1977 by Bessie Head. Reprinted by permission of Heinemann Publishers (Oxford) Ltd.

Ernest Hemingway, "The Killers." Reprinted by permission of Charles Scribner's Sons, an imprint of Macmillan Publishing Company, from *Men Without Women* by Ernest Hemingway. Copyright © 1927 by Charles Scribner's Sons, renewed 1955 by Ernest Hemingway.

Amy Hempel, "In the Cemetery Where Al Jolson Is Buried." From *Reasons to Live* by Amy Hempel. Copyright © 1985 by Amy Hempel. Reprinted by permission of Alfred A. Knopf, Inc.

Homer, "Cyclops." From *The Odyssey* by Homer, translated by E. V. Rieu (Penguin Classics, 1946), copyright © the Estate of E. V. Rieu. Reproduced by permission of Penguin Books Ltd

Zora Neale Hurston, "Spunk." From *Spunk: Selected Short Stories of Zora Neale Hurston*. Copyright © 1985 by Turtle Island Foundation. Reprinted by permission.

Jippensha Ikku, "Hizakurige," translated by Thomas Satchell in *Anthology of Japanese Literature from the Earliest Era to the Mid-Nineteenth Century* edited by Donald Keene. Copyright © 1955 by Grove Press, Inc. Used by permission of Grove Press, Inc.

James Joyce, "The Dead" from *Dubliners* by James Joyce. Copyright © 1916 by B. W. Heubsch.

Franz Kafka, "A Hunger Artist." From *The Metamorphasis, The Penal Colony, and Other Stories* by Franz Kafka, translated by Willa and Edwin Muir. Copyright © 1948 and renewed 1975 by Schocken Books Inc. Reprinted by permission of Schocken Books, published by Pantheon Books, a division of Random House, Inc.

Yasunari Kawabata, "A Smile Outside the Night Stall." Excerpted from *Palm-of-the-Hand Stories* by Yasunari Kawabata, translation copyright © 1988 by Lane Dunlop and J. Martin Holman. Published by North Point Press and reprinted by permission.

Milan Kundera, "The Hitchhiking Game." From *Laughable Loves* by Milan Kundera, translated by Suzanne Rappaport. Copyright © 1984 by Alfred A. Knopf, Inc. Reprinted by permission of the publisher.

D. H. Lawrence, "Odour of Chrysanthemums," from *Complete Short Stories of D. H. Lawrence* by D. H. Lawrence. Copyright © 1933 by the Estate of D. H. Lawrence, renewed © 1961 by Angelo Ravagli and C. M. Weekley, Executors of the Estate of Frieda Lawrence. Used by permission of Viking Penguin, a division of Penguin Books USA Inc.

James Alan McPherson, "Why I Like Country Music." From *Elbow Room* by James Alan McPherson. Copyright © 1974 by James Alan McPherson. First appeared in *The Harvard Advocate*. By permission of Little, Brown and Company.

Naguib Mahfouz, "The Conjurer Made Off with the Dish," from *The Time and the Place and Other Stories* by Naguib Mahfouz. Translation copyright © 1978 by Denys Johnson-Davis. Used by permission of Doubleday, a division of Bantam Doubleday Dell Publishing Group, Inc.

Katherine Mansfield, "The Garden Party." From *The Short Stories of Katherine Mansfield* by Katherine Mansfield. Copyright © 1922 by Alfred A. Knopf, Inc. and renewed 1950 by John Middleton Murry. Reprinted by permission of Alfred A. Knopf, Inc.

Guy de Maupassant, "The String." From *The Collected Novels and Stories of Guy de Maupassant* by Guy de Maupassant, translated by E. Boyd. Copyright © 1923 and renewed 1951 by Alfred A. Knopf, Inc. Reprinted by permission of the publisher.

Alice Munro, "Royal Beatings." From *The Beggar Maid* by Alice Munro. Copyright © 1977, 1978 by Alice Munro. Reprinted by permission of Alfred A. Knopf, Inc.

R. K. Narayan, "House Opposite," from *Under the Banyan Tree* by R. K. Narayan. Copyright © 1985 by R. K. Narayan. Used by permission of Viking Penguin, a division of Penguin Books USA Inc.

Joyce Carol Oates, "Nairobi," from *Raven's Wing* by Joyce Carol Oates. Copyright © 1986 by The Ontario Review. Used by permission of the publisher, Dutton, an imprint of New American Library, a division of Penguin Books USA Inc. "The Lady with the Pet Dog," from *Marriages and Infidelities* by Joyce Carol Oates. Copyright © 1972 by Joyce Carol Oates. Reprinted by permission of John Hawkins & Associates, Inc. "The Tryst," from *Sentimental Education* by Joyce Carol Oates. Copyright © 1981 by Joyce Carol Oates, Inc. Used by permission of the publisher, Dutton, an imprint of New American Library, a division of Penguin Books USA Inc.

Tim O'Brien, "The Things They Carried" from *The Things They Carried* by Tim O'Brien. Copyright © 1990 by Tim O'Brien. Reprinted by permission of Houghton Mifflin Company/Seymour Lawrence.

Frank O'Connor, "My Oedipus Complex" (copyright © 1950 by Frank O'Connor), "First Confession" (copyright © 1951 by Frank O'Connor), and "Guests of the Nation" (copyright © 1981 by Harriet O'Donovan Sheehy, Executrix of the Estate of Frank O'Connor). From *Collected Stories* by Frank O'Connor. Reprinted by permission of Alfred A. Knopf, Inc.

Amos Oz, "If There Is Justice" from *Elsewhere, Perhaps* by Amos Oz, copyright © 1963 by Figriat Poalim. English translation copyright © 1973 by Harcourt Brace Jovanovich, Inc. Reprinted by permission of Harcourt Brace Jovanovich, Inc.

Jack Pulaski, "The Merry-Go-Round" is reprinted from *The St. Veronica Gig Stories* (Zephyr Press, 1986), by permission of Zephyr Press. Copyright © 1986 by Murray Jack Pulaski. All rights reserved.

Francois Rabelais, "Pantagruel's Nativity." From *The Histories of Gargantua and Pantagruel* by Francois Rabelais, translated by J. M. Cohen (Penguin Classics, 1955), copyright © J. M. Cohen, 1955. Reproduced by permission of Penguin Books Ltd.

Juan Rulfo, "Talpa." From *The Burning Plain and Other Stories* by Juan Rulfo, translated by George D. Schade. Copyright © 1967. Reprinted by permission of the University of Texas Press.

Taieb Saleh, "A Handful of Dates" from *The Wedding of Zein* by Talieb Saleh, translated by Denys Johnson-Davies. Copyright © 1968 by Denys Johnson Davis. Reprinted by permission of Heinemann Publishers (Oxford) Ltd.

Delmore Schwartz, from *In Dreams Begin Responsibilities*. Copyright © 1978 by New Directions Publishing Corporation. Reprinted by permission of New Directions Publishing Corporation.

Susan Sontag, "The Way We Live Now." Copyright © 1986 by Susan Sontag. Reprinted by permission of Farrar, Straus and Giroux, Inc.

Junichiro Tanzizaki, "Tattoo," translated by Ivan Morris. From *Modern Japanese Stories: An Anthology*, edited by Ivan Morris. Copyright in Japan, 1962, by Charles E. Tuttle Co., Inc. All rights reserved. Reprinted by permission of Charles E. Tuttle Co., Inc., 77 Central Street, Boston, MA.

William Trevor, "Beyond the Pale," from *Beyond the Pale and Other Stories* by William Trevor. Copyright © 1981 by William Trevor. Used by permission of Viking Penguin, a division of Penguin Books USA Inc.

John Updike, "Separating." From *Problems and Other Stories* by John Updike. Copyright © 1975 by John Updike. Reprinted by permission of Alfred A. Knopf, Inc.

Luisa Valenzuela, "I'm Your Horse in the Night" from *Cambio de Armas* (*Other Weapons*, translated by Deborah Bonner). Copyright © 1985 by Ediciones del Norte. Reprinted by permission of Ediciones del Norte, Hanover, NH 03755.

Eudora Welty, "Powerhouse" from *A Curtain of Green and Other Stories,* copyright © 1941 and renewed 1969 by Eudora Welty. Reprinted by permission of Harcourt Brace Jovanovich, Inc.

Patrick White, "Five-Twenty" from *The Cockatoos*. Copyright © 1966, 1968, 1974 by The Patrick White Estate. Reprinted by permission of Barbara Mobbs, literary executor of the estate.

Virginia Woolf, "Moments of Being" from *A Haunted House and Other Short Stories* by Virginia Woolf, copyright © 1944 and renewed 1972 by Harcourt Brace Jovanovich, Inc. Reprinted by permission of the publisher.

Marguerite Yourcenar, "How Wang-Fo Was Saved" from *Oriental Tales* by Marguerite Yourcenar, translated by Alberto Manguel. Translation copyright © 1983, 1985 by Alberto Manguel. Reprinted by permission of Farrar, Straus and Giroux, Inc.

Alice Walker, "The Abortion" from *You Can't Keep a Good Woman Down,* copyright © 1980 by Alice Walker. Reprinted by permission of Harcourt Brace Jovanovich, Inc.